THE CATHEDRAL TRILOGY

In THE CATHEDRAL TRILOGY Elizabeth Goudge has drawn upon her warm and deep-felt sense of place and on memories of an Edwardian childhood in Wells, Ely and Oxford, where, fifty years ago, 'you could bicycle down the High Street on the wrong side and come to no harm'.

Here are three stories whose characters are bound together by the shared experience of life in a provincial cathedral town:

In Torminster Jocelyn recovers his love of life in the invigorating company of Hugh Anthony, Grandfather the Canon and enchanting little Henrietta.

TOWERS IN THE MIST tells the story of a family living at Christ Church, Oxford, in the days of Queen Elizabeth.

And THE DEAN'S WATCH relates the rich friendship which develops in the 1870s between the awe-inspiring Dean and little Isaac Peabody, a genius of a clockmaker.

Critical acclaim for Elizabeth Goudge

'She goes straight to the heart. Every word must find an echo in some reader'
Irish Times

'Miss Goudge has the art of presenting men and women, not to mention children, as genuinely convincing persons, too human to be either wholly good or wholly bad'
The Scotsman

'Genuine discernment and poignancy'
Sunday Times

'About the novels of Elizabeth Goudge there is always something of a fairy-tale, and THE DEAN'S WATCH is full of the enchantment and goodness – it has that timelessness which marks the author's best work'
The Scotsman

'The author knows and loves the loveliest of cities'
John o'London

'Miss Goudge has worked in some of the most attractive of the rich store of Oxford legends. TOWERS IN THE MIST has that indescribable quality, charm'
Methodist Recorder

About the Author

Elizabeth de Beauchamp Goudge was born on April 24th, 1900, in Wells, Somerset, where her father was Principal of Wells Theological College. She was educated in Hampshire and at Reading University School of Arts. Although she had privately intended writing as a career, her parents insisted she taught handicrafts in Oxford. She began writing in her spare time and her first novel, ISLAND MAGIC, set in Guernsey, was a great success here and in America. GREEN DOLPHIN COUNTRY (1944) projected her to fame, netting a Literary Guild Award and a special prize of £30,000 from Louis B. Mayer of M.G.M. before being filmed.

Miss Goudge also wrote the well-loved novels of the Eliots of Damerosehay, THE BIRD IN THE TREE, THE HERB OF GRACE and THE HEART OF THE FAMILY, as well as several historical novels and books for children.

In her later years Elizabeth Goudge settled in Henley-on-Thames. She died on 1st April, 1984.

The Cathedral Trilogy

A CITY OF BELLS
TOWERS IN THE MIST
THE DEAN'S WATCH

Elizabeth Goudge

CORONET BOOKS
Hodder and Stoughton

First published as three separate volumes:

A CITY OF BELLS © 1936 by Elizabeth Goudge
First published in Great Britain 1936 by
Gerald Duckworth Limited
Coronet edition 1957

TOWERS IN THE MIST © 1938 by Elizabeth Goudge
First published in Great Britain 1938 by
Gerald Duckworth Limited

THE DEAN'S WATCH © 1960 by Elizabeth Goudge
Illustrations © 1960 by Hodder and Stoughton Limited
First published in Great Britain 1960 by
Hodder and Stoughton Limited
Coronet edition 1964

Drawings by A. R. Whitear

This edition 1986

British Library C.I.P.
Goudge, Elizabeth
   The cathedral trilogy.
   I. Title   II. Goudge, Elizabeth. A city
   of bells   III. Goudge, Elizabeth. Towers
   in the mist   IV. Goudge, Elizabeth. The
   dean's watch
   823'.912[F]   PR6013.A74
   ISBN 0–340–39673–3

*The characters and situations in this book are
entirely imaginary and bear no relation to any real
person or actual happening*

This book is sold subject to the condition that
it shall not, by way of trade or otherwise, be
lent, re-sold, hired out or otherwise circulated
without the publisher's prior consent in any
form of binding or cover other than that in
which this is published and without a similar
condition including this condition being
imposed on the subsequent purchaser.

Printed and bound in Great Britain for
Hodder and Stoughton Paperbacks, a
division of Hodder and Stoughton Ltd.,
Mill Road, Dunton Green, Sevenoaks,
Kent (Editorial Office: 47 Bedford
Square, London, WC1B 3DP) by
Cox & Wyman Ltd., Reading.

Book One

A CITY OF BELLS

For
M.L.O.C.

CHAPTER I

I

JOCELYN IRVIN, sitting in a corner seat in a third-class railway-carriage and watching the green and gold of England in the spring slip past the windows, meditated gloomily upon Life with a capital L. A funny business, he came to the conclusion, consisting in climbing painfully to the tops of ladders and falling even more painfully to the bottom of them again.

Looking back over his past career of slow ascents and sudden descents he remembered with amusement the years of hectic scrambling in ink and mud that had finally raised him to the exalted position of captain of the school. . . . Never again would he be so glorious, never again so revered. . . . But the eminence had not lasted and as an undergraduate in his first term his glory had caused no one to blink.

At the end of three years his good sense and good looks and good temper had made their mark, but then had come the Boer War and no one took any notice, except unfavourably and with strong language, of a junior subaltern who did not as yet know his job.

In time he knew it and, as the urgency of war sent him up his third ladder at headlong speed, the army knew his worth. So well did it know it that the final humiliation of death might have seized upon a portly general so armoured with clinking medals, and richly coloured by red tape, that it would have been hard to distinguish him from a boiled lobster.

But the fate that controls our destinies had thought otherwise, and a bursting shell had sent Jocelyn home to

England again with an incurably lamed leg and a future that consisted of nothing but an immense question mark.

What to do with him his large and impecunious family couldn't imagine. It was the beginning of the twentieth century, a moment in the history of the English upper middle class when the things that a gentleman couldn't do far outnumbered the things that he could do. When Jocelyn suggested humbly that he thought he might be a commercial traveller his father blew down his nose contemptuously, and when he said gently that he'd always thought it would be great fun to be a bookie his brother Hubert implored him not to be more of a fool than he could help. His proposal that he should keep an hotel was received in chilly silence and the attractive idea of going round the country with a barrel-organ he dared not even express.

His family's own idea for him, such as shutting him up in somebody's office in Whitehall, or planting him out as somebody else's secretary in the House of Commons, seemed to him detestable. He loathed London, and in any case he was in that state of fatigue of mind and body when all well-meant suggestions immediately make the sufferer want to do the opposite. He was being difficult, and knew it. So difficult did he know he was being that in pity for his family he decided to go and stay with his grandfather, Canon Fordyce of Torminster, and relieve them of his presence.

The family did not think it was a good idea. Torminster was a small Cathedral town in the depths of the country, so far away from everywhere and so difficult to get at that it could hardly be said to belong to the contemporary world at all, and it surely did not hold out much hope of advancement to a young man in search of a profession. Grandfather, too, was hardly likely to be helpful. To begin with he was seventy-eight years old and to go on with he was one of the saints of God, and as such tragically lacking in sound financial judgment and that taking of thought for the morrow that produces a fat balance at the bank and the ability to assist impecunious relations.

"Anyhow Grandfather is restful," said Jocelyn to his protesting family, "and a Cathedral town is at least quiet. . . . Not all this beastly traffic thundering by outside the window so that you can't even hear yourself curse. . . . No, I tell you that I do not want help in packing my bag. Hang it all, I'm not blind, lunatic and incapable because I have a game leg."

His temper, always so sunny in the past, was now distinctly overcast, and when he had taken it and himself and his bag off in a cab to the station his exhausted family heaved sighs of relief and took tickets for the theatre to celebrate his departure.

II

And now, after a railway journey of unbelievable slowness and intricacy, Jocelyn was nearly at Torminster. He had never been there before, for Grandfather's working life had been spent in the slums of a North Country town, and the thought of seeing old friends in a new place, like a prized jewel in a fresh setting, was sufficiently exciting to pierce like a shaft of light into his dark mind.

There would be Grandfather himself, and Grandmother, a forcible old lady who had spent a busy and exhausting life trying to counteract the effect upon the family finances of Grandfather's saintliness, and the orphaned grandson who lived with them, Jocelyn's cousin Hugh Anthony whom he had seen last as a baby, and the little girl they had adopted to keep him company. . . . Just like the lovable stupidity of Grandfather to adopt yet another child in his old age. . . . And there would be the elderly servants, Ellen and Sarah, who had spoilt him so when he was a boy, suffering his booby-traps with admirable patience and letting him lick the jam-spoons after breakfast.

And these beloved people would be living not in the middle of smoke and noise and poverty, but in peace and beauty, in a setting that matched the personalities they had created through their years of hard work. That was as it should be, Jocelyn thought, for who should dare to live in the middle of peace and beauty who has not earned it?

As though to prepare him for the city that lay at its heart the country was becoming more and more beautiful. It was that moment of spring when the world is pink and blue in the distance and yellow and white close at hand. Blue hills were piled against the sky in shapes more lovely than a man can build and the woods that lay at their feet or crept up their sides had all flushed rosily at the kiss of the spring. The gorse was in riotous bloom and each green field broke at its edge into a froth of blossoming blackthorn. The primroses were in flower and the larks were singing. It was a still, warm day after rain, and delicious smells came to Jocelyn through the window, the smell of the gorse and the wallflowers in the cottage gardens, the smell of wood smoke and freshly turned earth and rain-washed grass and fresh beginnings. A pity to be tired of life in such a world, thought Jocelyn. If the old earth could wash herself and begin again so often and so humbly, why could not a man do the same?

The train swung round a bend, the blue hills parted like a curtain and the city of Torminster was visible. Seen from a little distance it had a curiously unsubstantial air, as though it were something real yet intangible, a thing you could see but not touch. It lay in a hollow of the hills like a child in its mother's lap and it seemed that as it lay there it slept. It looked so quiet that it was hard to believe the ordinary life of men and women went on in its streets. Rather it seemed a buried city sunk at the bottom of the sea, where no life stirred and no sound was heard but the ringing of the bells as the tide surged through forgotten towers and steeples. Jocelyn could see a confused mass of roofs and chimneys and church-spires, some high and some low, weather-stained and twisted by age into fantastic shapes. The smoke from the chimneys went straight up into the windless air and then seemed to dissolve into a mist that lay over the city like the waves of the sea that had drowned it, and out of this sea rose a grey rock with three towers. . . . The Cathedral. . . . It stood there gloriously, its majesty softened by the warm day but not diminished, its towers a little withdrawn in the sky yet no less watchful.

III

Jocelyn realized with something of a shock that the train was standing still in a perfectly ordinary station. Machines holding matches and chocolates faced him, and a beery porter was obligingly withdrawing his bag from beneath his legs. He had for a moment seen the real Torminster, the spiritual thing that the love of man for a certain spot of earth had created through long centuries, but now he was back again in the outward seeming of the place. Torminster, he supposed, would have dust-bins like other towns, and a horrible network of drains beneath it, and tax collectors and public-houses. It might even look ugly in a March east wind and smell abominably stuffy on an August night, but these unpleasant things would now never matter much to him, for he would feel towards Torminster as one feels towards a human being when one has, if only once, seen the soul flickering in the eyes.

"Take the bus," Grandfather had said and Jocelyn accordingly took it. The Torminster bus, once experienced, was never forgotten. In shape and colour it was like a pumpkin and its designer had apparently derived inspiration from the immortal conveyance that took Cinderella to the ball. It was pulled by two stout bay horses and driven by Mr. Gotobed, a corpulent gentleman clothed in bottle-green with a wonderful top-hat poised adroitly on the back of the head. His face was red, his whiskers pronounced and his language rich. ... He and the Dean together were the outstanding figures of Torminster.

"Get in, sir," he said genially to Jocelyn. "I was ordered for you by the reverend gentleman. Fine day. Come on with that luggage, 'Erb. One gentleman for the Close and four buff orpingtons for The Green Dragon."

Jocelyn was established on one of the two wooden seats that ran the length of the bus, with the buff orpingtons complaining of their lot and straining agitated necks through the slats of the crate on the seat opposite him.

"All aboard?" continued Mr. Gotobed, as though they were bound for the North Pole. "'Eave up the gentleman's bag, 'Erb; we can't sit 'ere all night while you calculate 'ow many drinks you've 'ad since Christmas."

'Erb heaved up the bag and slammed the door while Mr. Gotobed climbed to the box, flourished his whip, laid it across the backs of the horses, told 'Erb what he thought of his ancestry and set the pumpkin in violent motion.

The outcry of the buff orpingtons was now drowned, for the wheels of the bus were solid and the streets of Torminster in many places cobbled. Jolting through it, and shut away from the subdued hum of its life by the walls of the bus, Torminster once more seemed to Jocelyn to lack everyday reality. The soft, moist air was the atmosphere of dreams and the old houses that lined the streets seemed to be leaning forward a little, as though drowsily nodding. The bus made such a noise that the few vehicles that passed them went by unheard and the handful of passers-by, though their lips moved and their feet trod the quiet pavements, were silent as the dead. Down the side of the sloping High Street, as they climbed up it, a little stream came hurrying down to meet them and Jocelyn gazed at it enchanted. Its water was clear and sparkling as crystal and it must have come down from the hills that surrounded Torminster. The bus stopped for a brief, respectful moment, to let the Archdeacon's plum-pudding dog cross the street, and he could hear the stream's ripple and gurgle. . . . What bliss, he thought, to keep a shop in Torminster and do business to the sound of running water and the chiming of bells.

The High Street ended abruptly and they were in the Market Place, a wide, open square surrounded by tall old houses with shops below them. There was no one in the Market Place, except one old gentleman and two cats, and the peace of this centre of industrial life was complete. In the centre was a holy well that had been there before either the city or the Cathedral had come into being. A high parapet had been built round it, with a canopy overhead, and if you wanted to look inside the well you had to mount a flight of steps. The water, that welled up no one knew how far down in the earth, was always inky black and when you leaned over to look in you could see your own face looking back at you. Sometimes it stirred with a mysterious movement and then the sunlight that pierced through the carved canopy touched it with shifting, broken points of light like stars. There were always pigeons wheeling round the holy well, the reflection of their wings passing over it like light. There were pigeons there now, and it seemed to Jocelyn that their wings splintered the veiled sunshine into falling showers.

The bus clattered round the Market Place and stopped with a flourish in front of The Green Dragon. It was a small hotel and public-house combined, its old woodwork glistening with new paint and its windows shining with prosperity. The dragon, his scales painted emerald green, and scarlet fire belching from his nostrils, pranced upon an azure ground over the porch. Here it seemed that they would wait a long time, for Mr. Gotobed, after the exhaustion of carrying in the buff orpingtons, stopped inside to refresh himself.

Jocelyn got out and strolled a little way up the pavement, and then stopped stock still and stared. The most important moments of a lifetime seem always to arrive out of the blue and it was here that Jocelyn, his thoughts objectively busy with this Hans Andersen city, experienced a subjective moment that startled him like a thunderclap.

Between the tall Green Dragon and the equally tall bakery two doors off was wedged a little house only two stories high. Its walls were plastered and pale pink in colour and its gabled roof was tiled with wavy tiles and ornamented with cushions of green moss. There were two gables, with a small window in each, and under them was a green door with two white, worn steps leading up to it. A large bow-window was to the right of the door and a smaller one to the left. There was something particularly attractive about the bow-window. It reflected the light in every pane, so that it looked alive and dancing, and it bulged in a way that suggested that the room behind was crammed so full of treasures that they were trying to press their way out. But yet it was in reality quite empty, for Jocelyn could see the bare floor and the walls papered with a pattern of rose-sprigs. Behind the house he thought that there must be a garden, for the top of a tall apple-tree was just visible behind the wavy roof.

The house affected him oddly. He was first vividly conscious of it and then overwhelmingly conscious of himself. His own personality seemed enriched by it and he felt less painfully aware of his own shortcomings, less afraid of the business of living that lay in front of him. He had felt like this once before, at the beginning of an important friendship.

"Why is that house empty?" he asked Mr. Gotobed, when that worthy returned to his duties wiping his mouth with the back of his hand.

"Because the gentleman what 'ad it 'as gone away and no one else ain't taken it, sir," explained Mr. Gotobed patiently.

"But why has no one taken it?"

"No drains," said Mr. Gotobed briefly, and climbed to his box.

Jocelyn was now the only passenger left in the bus and they completed the circuit of the Market Place and turned to their right up a steep street at a smart pace. Then they turned to their right a second time and passed under a stone archway into the Close.

Instantly it seemed that they had come to the very centre of peace. In the town beyond the archway there had been the peacefulness of laziness, but here there was the peace of an ordered life that had continued for so long in exactly the same way that its activity had become effortless. Outside in the town new methods of buying and selling might conceivably be drowsily adopted, or some slight modernization of the lighting system might take place after a year's slow discussion of the same, but inside in the Close the word "new" was unknown. Modernity had not so far touched it and even to admit the fear that it might do so seemed sacrilege.

Jocelyn, as the bus rolled along, looked across a space of green grass, elm-bordered, to the grey mass of the Cathedral. Its towers rose four-square against the sky and the wide expanse of the west front, rising like a precipice, was crowded with sculptured figures. They stood in their ranks, rising higher and higher, kings and queens and saints and angels, remote and still. About them the rooks were beating slowly and over their heads the bells were ringing for five o'clock evensong. Behind the Cathedral rose a wooded hill, brilliantly green now with its spring leaves, the Tor from which the city took its name.

"What a place!" ejaculated Jocelyn, and held on to the seat in delighted excitement. To his left, on the opposite side of the road to the Cathedral, was another, smaller mass of grey masonry, the Deanery, and in front of him was a second archway.

Once through it they were in a discreet road bordered on each side with gracious old houses standing back in walled gardens. Here dwelt the Canons of the Cathedral with their respective wives and families, and the few elderly ladies of respectable antecedents, blameless life and orthodox belief who were considered worthy to be on intimate terms with them.

The bus stopped with a jolt at Number Two the Close and Jocelyn got out in front of a blue door in a wall so high that only a grey roof and the tops of some trees could be seen above the wallflowers that grew on top of it. He felt the thrill of excitement inseparable from a walled house and garden; for a house behind railings has no secrets, but a home behind walls holds one knows not what. He opened the door and went in, and Mr. Gotobed, following him with his bag, banged it shut. There was something irrevocable in its clanging and Jocelyn felt that the old life was now dead indeed. Something new was beginning for him and this lovely garden was its starting point.

IV

He stood on a flagged path bordered with pink and white hyacinths and all round him spread a glory of colour and scent. The Torminster gardens had been tended and loved for generations and they all had an amazing luxuriance. Red wallflowers, red and yellow primulas, forget-me-nots, squat apple-trees studded with coral buds, flowering cherry-trees, lilacs and laburnums and syringa bushes were all jumbled together in glorious confusion. On a little patch of lawn to the right grew a mulberry-tree as old as time, its heavy, weary limbs propped up by stakes, and behind the house, where the kitchen-garden was, a cedar-tree towered up against the sky like a blue-black mountain.

The house faced Jocelyn as he walked up the path. It was old and grey and solid, its walls half hidden by creepers and its small, diamond-paned windows so withdrawn among them that nothing could be seen of the rooms inside. It would have looked like a farmhouse but for the extraordinary apparition of a tall grey tower that shot up at one side of it.

It was an astonishing house. When Jocelyn had walked up the flagged path between the flower-beds, and stooped beneath the branches of an apple-tree, he found himself under the porch in front of the open door looking down a flight of steps into what seemed a dark cellar. The walls of the house, he noticed, were three feet thick and the smell of damp was overpowering. He rang the bell and, as his eyes grew accustomed to the darkness, he saw that the cellar was a large, stone-paved, vaulted hall, with no light in it except what filtered through the curtain of wistaria that hung down over the porch. Pots of flowers stood in the corners, their scent unsuccessfully fighting the smell of damp, and a row of candles stood on an oak chest.

"What a place!" murmured Jocelyn again. "Like a chapel."

"The 'ouse is Norman in parts, they say," said Mr. Gotobed. "Full of 'istoric interest if damp. I wouldn't live 'ere meself if you paid me for it, dammit, no. But the gentry are different. They don't object to the rheumatics if caused by 'istory."

A door opened at the farther end of the hall and Sarah appeared, her purple silk apron a glorious splash of colour in the shadows. Sarah was tall and gaunt, with grey hair strained back from a grim, determined countenance. She had a heart of gold, though she kept it hidden, and her preference was for the gloomy side of life rather than the sunny one.

"Mr. Jocelyn," she exclaimed sepulchrally, but there was a gleam of affection behind her glasses.

"How well you look, Sarah," said Jocelyn cheerfully, shaking hands. "Years younger than when I saw you last." The temptation to annoy Sarah by taking an optimistic view was one he had never been able to resist.

"I'm far from well, sir," said Sarah, "the damp of this 'ouse being something cruel, but I keep up for the sake of others. . . . You can take that bag the 'ole way up the back stairs, Gotobed, and not 'alf-way up, as you did last time we 'ad a visitor. . . . Come this way, sir, tea's ready. You'll find the master and mistress much aged, but you must expect that."

She unlatched a door on the left that opened on a flight of uncarpeted stairs and led him up, stumbling in the half-dark, until they reached a landing and the door to the drawing-room.

It was a small, square room panelled in dark wood, with windows looking on the garden. It was Grandmother's room and held the battered treasures that had accompanied her through her arduous working life; her Victorian chairs with their scratched legs and cross-stitch seats worked by herself when young, her miniatures and books and faded antimacassars, her few bits of old china and the two shells that sounded like the sea when you held them to your ears. Not a very beautiful collection, perhaps, but part of Grandmother and therefore priceless.

She sat bolt upright in her arm-chair on one side of the wood fire that was burning in the grate, knitting woollen stockings for the heathen, with Grandfather opposite her in his arm-chair with his hands folded across his stomach, and at sight of them the love that Jocelyn had for them both, compounded of gratitude and amusement and reverence, burnt up as freshly as though he had seen them last only yesterday.

Grandmother was small and withered and gave the impression of having shed everything in her passage through life except the essence of herself, and that a sharp, decided, wholesome essence. Her twinkling black eyes were like a bird's, and as sharp as needles, and her little parchment-coloured face was wrinkled into a thousand lines of humour and decision and commonsensible strong-mindedness. Her iron-grey hair was arranged in corkscrew curls, the fashion of a past age, and on her head was a cap with purple bows. Her grey dress was of great age and made of alpaca so stiff that it could surely stand by itself, and her hands were mittened. She was eighty years old, but neither age nor bereavement nor hard work had in the least dimmed her vitality or stemmed the flow of her fluent, emphatic talk.

Grandfather, who was only seventy-eight and the youngest of the Canons, was quite different. He, too, was very short, but he was the reverse of withered. He was very round indeed. Yet the curves of his person did not suggest either indolence or laziness, they suggested rather a tolerant mind and a large heart, and his round, rosy face bore the unmistakable stamp of personal control and austerity, a stamp that is like clarity in the atmosphere, a thing that you cannot describe but only rejoice in. The eyes behind his powerful, double-lensed glasses were pale blue and slightly astonished, as though he had never ceased to be surprised at the beauty of the world. . . . He was as bald as an egg, but had a little white jutting beard of the type that is usually seen upon the chins of gnomes.

Yet there were a few people in Torminster who did not like him, for he had developed the habit of unconsciously speaking his thoughts aloud, a trait which endeared him to none but those rare lovers of sincerity who really enjoy hearing the truth about themselves. His life in the slums had implanted in him a slight tendency to think that the well-to-do exaggerated the trials of their existence, and also a tendency to get a little impatient if the Cathedral Chapter at its Chapter meetings talked for more than one hour on the subject of Canon Roderick's right of way through Canon Elphinstone's seakale bed, which Canon Roderick said existed and Canon Elphinstone said did not. "Bless my soul!" he would say suddenly in the middle of a Chapter meeting, "what a fuss about nothing! Send 'em all down a coal-mine, dear God, send 'em all down a coal-mine." And then he would smile sweetly at the sudden silence that fell, blissfully unaware that he had given tongue. And it was the same at tea-parties, when he might remark *sotto voce* on the poorness of the tea, and sometimes it was the same in the middle of the Sunday morning anthem at the Cathedral, when he would ejaculate loudly, "Is this what they call modern music? Dreadful! Dreadful!"

V

"Mr. Jocelyn," said Sarah, and left them together.

The welcome that the two old people gave to their grandson was typical of them. Grandfather bounced to his feet and hurried forward delightedly, his hand out and his whole face beaming. Here, his manner implied, was the one person whom of all others he was most anxious to see and in whose welfare he was most interested. And there was no insincerity in his welcome. His interest in his fellow-creatures was so deep that whoever was with him at the moment seemed to him to be the very best of God's creatures. . . . And Jocelyn was his favourite grandson.

Grandmother, meanwhile, sat in her chair very stiffly, her hands folded on her knitting, and waited to see how Jocelyn had developed before committing herself. Her bright eyes darted critically over him, noting his fair, close-cut hair and moustache, his trim figure, well-brushed clothes and slight air of fatigue.

"Humph," she said, "you're improved. More like your dear mother and less like your father, thank God. I never could take to your father, good man of business though he is."

"Dear Jane," murmured Grandfather, "there is good in all."

"I didn't say there wasn't," said Grandmother, "I merely said that I don't take to the good in Thomas. . . . You dress better than you did, Jocelyn. When you were at Oxford you were a radical, I remember, and dressed accordingly. I told your mother what I thought about it at the time, but she said she had no influence. I will say for the Army that it teaches the compatibility of a sense of duty with a crease in the trousers. . . . You may kiss me, Jocelyn."

His kiss produced one of her rare moments of softening and she touched his cheek gently with one of her dainty, mittened hands. "You look tired, dear boy," she said. "You'd better be fed up. I'm sorry about your leg, but, as I said to your grandfather, it's a mercy it wasn't your stomach or your brain. Given belief in God, a good digestion and a mind in working order life's still a thing to be grateful for."

She abruptly stopped talking and became engrossed in the ritual of tea-making, her little hands hovering over the old silver and Worcester cups and saucers. A hush fell, the steam from the tea-kettle rose into the air like incense and the fragrance of china tea mingled with the scent of flowers. Jocelyn leant back restfully in his chair, feeling life halt a little and its grip on him relax. It seemed no longer a river in spate, whirling him along without time for thought or feeling, but a calm backwater where the opening of a flower and the song of a bird would be important and significant.

"Does time ever pass in Torminster?" he asked Grandfather.

"Dear me, no, dear boy, nothing ever passes here. The past steps into the background, of course, but it never seems to disappear. . . . I think, dear Jane, that you are putting too much milk in Jocelyn's tea."

"It's a sleepy place," pronounced Grandmother. "I've

started two working parties for Missions to wake them up a bit, but I never saw women make flannel petticoats so slowly in all my life. . . . Thank you, Theobald, but I am quite capable, at my age, of making a drinkable cup of tea. . . . Help yourself to bread and dripping, Jocelyn."

It was not perhaps usual to eat bread and dripping at afternoon tea, but Grandfather liked bread and dripping and insisted upon having it, in spite of Grandmother's repeated assurances that it "was not done." It was his habit to do what he liked, whether it was "done" or not, provided that what he liked was compatible with his religion. . . . He did not eat dripping in Lent.

"Where's Hugh Anthony?" asked Jocelyn.

"Having his tea downstairs," said Grandfather. "We find that best. He's eight years old and exhausting, though a dear boy. We've adopted a little girl to keep him company, thinking female influence might quiet him down, but there's little improvement noticeable as yet."

"Your grandfather's latest," said Grandmother in resigned tones. "He saw the child at that orphanage he's on the board of, liked her eyes and brought her straight home with nothing to her name but a Bible, three pinafores and a couple of vests. Did you ever hear anything so ridiculous?"

"I was guided to do it," said Grandfather.

"Well, all I can say is I hope someone will be guided to care for the poor children after our death," said Grandmother forcibly, and sighed. She had been married to a saint for fifty years, but still found it as difficult to adjust herself as she had done in the first month of her marriage, when he had given away their bed to a woman whose need, he felt, was greater than theirs.

"When that dear child's eyes met mine," said Grandfather, "I knew that her welfare was my responsibility . . . I have sometimes thought, dear Jane, that, should Jocelyn marry, he might, after our death, feel guided to take upon him the fatherhood of both those dear children."

"Well," said Jocelyn doubtfully, "you never know."

"Not until the time comes," said Grandfather happily. "So, as I say to your dear grandmother, why worry beforehand?"

The atmosphere felt a little tense and to lighten it Jocelyn asked them about the house in the Market Place.

"Who lived there?" he asked. "It's a jolly little house. It's a crime it should be empty."

All the happiness drained away from Grandfather's face, leaving him looking stricken and old, and it was Grandmother who answered.

"A young man called Gabriel Ferranti lived there," she said. "He looked like an organ-grinder and wrote books that nobody could make head or tail of, and was considered to be clever for those reasons, though why untidy hair and an inability to make oneself understood should be the hall-mark of genius I have never been able to understand. Your grandfather took a great fancy to him; what for I don't know."

"There was great good in him," murmured Grandfather sadly.

"What happened to him?" asked Jocelyn.

"He got into the financial difficulties that were only to be expected of a young man with a name like that," said Grandmother, "and disappeared just as your poor grandfather was trying to bring out the good in him. Your grandfather naturally took it all very much to heart, for goodness only knows what has become of the young man now, or of the good that your poor grandfather thought he was bringing out."

"If he had only told me about his difficulties," mourned Grandfather, "I could have relieved them."

"What with?" asked Grandmother a little sharply. "I'm thankful the young person had the good taste to disappear before you'd given him our last halfpenny. . . . If Jocelyn's finished his tea take him to his room while I get on with my knitting."

The two men went out together while Grandmother's voice drifted after them in its habitual chant of, "Knit one, purl one, knit two together."

VI

Jocelyn followed Grandfather's squat black figure and bald head up to the final stairs to the spare-room. It was a perfect panelled room with three windows looking out on the garden. Old oak beams crossed the whitewashed ceiling and in each of the four corners of the room was a carved wooden seraph with two wings covering his feet, two folded across his breast and two outspread behind him. There was no carpet on the oak floor that rose and fell like the waves of the sea, and no pictures on the walls, and the furniture was limited to the barest necessities.

"This is perhaps more of a monk's room than a soldier's," said Grandfather, "but you must remember that Torminster was once a monastery and the Close is the coffin that holds its bones. Some people find this house frightening. The bones of the skeleton show through too clearly, they say, and the damp smell makes them think of death."

"How old is this house?" asked Jocelyn.

"It belongs to all time. The hall and kitchen and larder are Norman, the tower is fifteenth century and this room has an eighteenth-century powdering closet. . . . But my greenhouse is pure Victorian. . . . Have you everything you want?"

"Everything but peace of mind," said Jocelyn unexpectedly and blushed crimson.

He remembered of old that Grandfather's effect upon him was always to make him say exactly what was in his mind. . . . An embarrassing effect. . . . Such people as Grandfather, possessed of a sincerity as catching as measles, shouldn't be allowed about loose in a world where the wearing of a mask was good form.

Grandfather sat down at the foot of the bed and folded his hands across his stomach, always a sign that he was giving a subject his serious consideration. The expression of his face changed from one of trouble to one of deep attention, as Ferranti's disappearance passed from his mind and Jocelyn's mental condition took its place.

"Peace is as essential to mental health, dear boy, as light to human life. What has happened to yours?"

"Mislaid it in South Africa," said Jocelyn bitterly. "My work's gone and I don't know what to do. How can a man be peaceful when he has no future?"

"Don't talk nonsense," said Grandfather almost sharply. "We've all a future. You don't know in what direction yours lies, that's all, and you've not the patience to wait and see which way the wind blows."

"The wind?" asked Jocelyn.

"Our destiny is like a wind blowing," said Grandfather. "It carries us along. But now and again the wind seems to drop. We don't know what to do next. Then it may be that a blade of grass growing in the road beside us bends slightly. It is a tiny movement, slight as a whim, but enough to show us which way to take."

Jocelyn smiled at Grandfather affectionately. "If we were all to yield to our whims," he said, "we'd do some pretty crazy things. I, for instance, would start a shop in Torminster."

"Would you like to start a shop in Torminster?"

"It's an idea that occurred to me as I drove up the High Street."

"Then start it."

Jocelyn laughed. "I was only joking, Grandfather. How could I start a shop with no capital and no experience and no business capacity?"

Grandfather unclasped his hands and rose sighing to his feet. He feared that Jocelyn was in a difficult frame of mind, depressed and restless, and this was hardly the moment to induce him to see reason.

"Stay here and do nothing," he advised him. "Stay a year if you like. What does it matter? It's often necessary in life to do nothing, but so few people do it nicely. And as for peace, there's plenty of it in this house and in this town. They are so weighted with age that they have, as it were, fallen below the surface of time, like a buried city below the sea.... Fall with them.... Dear me, I must go and say evensong or I shall be late for dinner, and that distresses your dear grandmother."

Left alone Jocelyn unpacked slowly, discovering the powdering closet, hardly bigger than a cupboard, where long ago some hooped and panniered lady had silvered her hair with powder, put a round black patch on her chin, rouge on her cheeks and rings on her fingers.... What a fuss about nothing her toilet must have been! ... But perhaps she was one of those people who do nothing so nicely that it becomes something. As he arranged his books on the shelf in the closet he pictured her to himself, slim and golden-haired, clothed in silk that rustled like autumn leaves, tremendously absorbed, as she powdered and patched and laced, in the creation of beauty.

And longer ago still his room was part of the monastery. Some monk sat here, perhaps, making a missal, painting into it purple pansies and ivory roses and queer little animals with long legs and scarlet tongues, the great-grandfathers of the dragon who pranced on the signboard in the Market Place. And the monk, as he painted a blue sky behind his ivory roses and put golden scrolls round the animals' legs, would have been as absorbed in the making of a beautiful thing as the lady with her rouge-pot and her jewel-case.... And on them both the winged seraphim would have looked down, and for them both the time that in Torminster did not pass away but only stepped into the background would have been measured into golden lengths by the chiming of bells.

Jocelyn realized that for him too bells were ringing, for the Cathedral clock was striking seven and he must change for dinner. On the last stroke Sarah knocked at his door and entered with hot water. She did everything by the Cathedral clock. When it chimed half-past six she put the kettle on. When it chimed a quarter-to-seven she slowly filled the cans and toiled up the stairs to the room where Grandfather and Grandmother slept, where she laid out their evening things on their fourposter and dumped their hot water into the basins with resounding bangs, just as the first stroke of seven rang out. ... On the last stroke of seven she knocked at the spare-room door.... It was all a very serious ritual and she stumped across the room to Jocelyn's washstand with the solemnity of a priest approaching the shrine of the oracle.

"You've laid out your own things," she said severely. "I do that."

"I'm sorry, Sarah," said Jocelyn meekly. "But you see I was unpacking and I thought it would save you trouble."

"Trouble!" snorted Sarah. "That's what I'm here for. Life's made up of trouble. You must expect that.... I expect you find the master and mistress sadly changed?"

"I don't see the slightest difference in them, Sarah," said Jocelyn. "They never change."

"Ah," said Sarah, "you don't live with them as I do and see them going down 'ill steady. I 'ope the dinner will be eatable, but Ellen's very 'eavy-'anded with the pastry owing to 'aving been thrown over by the butcher which, as I tell 'er, it's not to be expected that a man should keep faithful to a woman of 'er age, but it takes a light 'eart to make light pastry and it's we that are the sufferers, as is only to be expected when you remember that in this world the innocent suffer for the guilty. ... Dinner's at a quarter-to-eight, sir."

She stalked away again and Jocelyn was left to embark upon the second shave of the day. It was quite unnecessary, but he was fastidious, one of those people whose private as well as whose public moments are controlled and decorous. Without consciously realizing it he liked to make each trivial act of life a thing of individual perfection, and in this he was linked to the monk and the lady.

He was immersed in white lather when there was a sudden pattering of bare feet outside his door, which burst open with no preliminary knock to admit a small boy with freckles and flaming red hair. He cast one glance at Jocelyn and dashed out again, leaving the door open and shouting at the full force of his lungs, " Come on, Henrietta, he's shaving! "

Before Jocelyn had time to draw breath Hugh Anthony was back again with Henrietta. They had evidently arisen from their beds, for they were clothed in white nightgown and nightshirt and were barefooted. They leapt on to his bed with the agility of young rabbits and leant over its foot as though it were the front rail of the dress circle, their eyes bulging and their mouths ajar. Jocelyn realized that, for the first time in his life, he was an exciting entertainment. The parental toilet was, he had heard, as good as a circus to the Edwardian young, but these children, fatherless and with a bearded grandfather, had up till now missed one of the chief thrills in life. He flourished his razor and prepared to do his best. While he did it there was no sound but deep, ecstatic breathing, and when he had finished there was a long-drawn sigh of satisfaction.

" There! He's done! " said Hugh Anthony. " Did you think it would be like that, Henrietta? "

" I thought it would make more noise," said Henrietta, " like when Bates cuts the grass."

" I expect he hadn't got enough beard," said Hugh Anthony. " Now if Grandfather started shaving I dare say it would be more noisy."

Jocelyn put on his coat and turned round to survey the couple.

Hugh Anthony at eight years old was compact and rounded like his grandfather. His blue, astonished eyes were also like his grandfather's, but his circular face, dusted all over with golden freckles, his turned-up nose and flaming red hair were all his own. Quite his own too was his look of perpetual inquiry. His whole body seemed at times to be curved into the shape of a question-mark and the word "why?" was seldom off his lips. The house rang with it from the moment he woke up in the morning until the moment when he fell asleep with his final question still vibrating in the air of the silent, unanswering night.

"Why don't you grow a beard?" he asked Jocelyn.

"I've been a soldier," said Jocelyn, "and in the Army it is the fashion to have a moustache only."

"Why?"

"To distinguish soldiers from sailors, who are either clean-shaven or have beards."

"Why?"

"It's just the fashion."

"Why?"

"I don't know."

"Why don't you know?"

Henrietta pushed Hugh Anthony face downward on the bed and seated herself upon the small of his back where, enthroned in grace, she smiled sweetly at Jocelyn. She was a child of few words, but all her actions were quick, decisive and to the point.

She was an astonishing creature, not conventionally beautiful, but with a grace and certain luminous quality that were far more arresting than the usual nine-year-old female chubbiness. She was small and thin with long-fingered hands and slender feet. Her brown eyes were curiously changeable with her moods, sometimes blazing with light and sometimes opaquely dark, as though the spirit behind them were a newly lit flame so sensitive that a breath of joy or sorrow could fan it into a blaze or extinguish it altogether. Her face, small and pointed, rising from the toby frill of her nightgown like a flower from its calyx and very pale against her straight dark hair, made Jocelyn think of white jasmine.

"I hope we are not intruding," she said politely to Jocelyn. Her voice was curiously deep for a child, with a ringing note in it that was very beautiful.

"Not at all," said Jocelyn. "I am honoured."

"Grandfather says Hugh Anthony is to call you uncle," she said. "Do I call you uncle too even though I'm only adopted?"

"Please," said Jocelyn. "Until now I have had no niece. It's a dreadful thing, you know, to have no niece."

He came close to the bed and smiled down at her, and instantly, with her answering smile, her whole being seemed to come flooding into her face. She was giving him her friendship with the lovely abandonment of childhood that has not learned yet to hold back for fear the love given should be scorned. Jocelyn, in this his first close contact with a child, felt not so much touched as stabbed. This trustfulness and fragility were almost terrifying, for how in the world, as children grew from childhood to maturity and the bloom was rubbed off them, did the sensitive spirit itself escape destruction? ... Well, sometimes it did but sometimes it did not .... And the man who destroyed it? "It were better for him that a millstone were hanged about his neck, and that he were drowned in the depth of the sea." Heaven above, what an alarming thing it must be to be a parent!

But at this moment Hugh Anthony, whose ordinary temperament was always a relief after Henrietta's emotional one, became tired of lying on his face with his mouth full of eiderdown and abruptly heaved up his posterior. Henrietta rolled off the bed to the floor on one side and Hugh Anthony on the other.

"Did you bring your sword?" he asked, while still in a recumbent position.

"No," said Jocelyn.

"Why not?"

"I didn't think I should have any use for it."

"But we could have played at St. George and the Dragon with it, you being the Dragon and me George."

"I'm sorry," said Jocelyn. "I never thought of that."

"Then you should have," said Hugh Anthony severely. "You should have remembered when you packed that I should have wanted to see your sword. Grandfather says that every morning in one's cold bath one should say to oneself, 'Now what can I do for others to-day?'"

The gong rang.

"Hadn't you two kids better go to bed?" inquired Jocelyn.

"We don't go properly to bed till it's dark," said Henrietta, sitting up on the floor and re-plaiting her hair. "We're put there and then we get out again. Come on, Hugh Anthony, we'll go up to the top of the tower and see the stars come out. We'll take Uncle Jocelyn's eiderdown."

They departed as suddenly as they had come, trailing the eiderdown after them like clouds of glory.

VII

Dinner was eaten placidly in the dim old dining-room downstairs. Grandfather wore his dinner-jacket, which had been new twenty years ago and had had to be let out considerably since with new material that did not match the old, so that Grandfather had a very odd striped appearance. Grandmother wore her black silk, which had been recently turned by Sarah so that it looked as good as new, the lace fichu that had belonged to her grandmother and her gold locket containing a lock of the golden hair that Grandfather had, astonishingly, once had.

They ate boiled fowl, a rhubarb tart that was all that could be expected of Ellen in her jilted state, water-biscuits and bananas.

After dinner Grandfather and Grandmother slept in their arm-chairs, waking up now and again to ask Jocelyn if his poor mother had found a cook yet. Jocelyn read a Punch that was several months old, said no, his mother hadn't got a cook yet and the kitchen-maid was leaving, and wondered if the time would come when he might find the peace of Torminster a little monotonous. . . . It might, but it had not done so yet.

When ten o'clock struck Grandfather and Grandmother woke up abruptly, said to each other, "Was that ten, dear?" and got up. Jocelyn lit the bedroom candles that stood on a table outside the drawing-room door and gave his arm to Grandmother, who was a little tottery with sleep. She would, if the truth were told, have liked to go to bed every night at nine, but she never had gone to bed before ten and felt that, unless she was unwell, it would be self-indulgent to indulge the wish. The notes of the clock rang out one by one into the silence as the procession mounted the stairs, Grandfather bringing up the rear with the best silver teapot in a green baize bag. . . . Grandmother kept it by day beside her in her work-basket in the drawing-room, and by night under her bed. . . . The last note was sounding as Jocelyn kissed her good night.

"Good night, dear," she murmured sleepily. "See that the lamp in the drawing-room is properly out. Your poor grandfather is not to be trusted."

Grandfather was oblivious of either of them. Though the teapot was dangling from one hand and his lighted candle, held askew and dropping grease on the floor, was in the other, he was already saying the last office of the day. "Turn Thou us, oh God our Saviour," he murmured, "and let Thine anger cease from us. Oh God, make speed to save us; oh Lord, make haste to help us."

Jocelyn, having piloted him in and shut the door on him, stood outside on the stairs listening.

"Hear me when I call, oh God of my righteousness;

Thou hast set me at liberty when I was in trouble; have mercy upon me and hearken unto my prayer."

It pleased him to imagine that the voice was no longer the voice of Grandfather but that of the painting monk of his fancy. Then it seemed to him that the sound swelled and became not one voice but many. Not far away, perhaps in the chapel-like hall, the light of tapers gleamed on brown habits and tonsured heads and a carved crucifix that hung in the shadows.

"I will lay me down in peace and take my rest, for it is Thou, Lord, only, that makest me dwell in safety."

He strolled happily to his room, but on beholding his bed his peaceful mood turned to rage, for the children had come back in his absence and denuded it of everything except the sheets and the mattress. There was nothing for it but to sally forth with his candle into the dark and find the young demons.

And finding anything in this house was not easy, for it seemed to have no geographical plan. Odd flights of steps ended at locked doors, twisting passages with wavy floors led apparently nowhere, and it was not until he had been barking his shins on sharp corners for ten minutes that Jocelyn opened a door leading into a spiral stone staircase that evidently wound up from the kitchen regions to the top of the tower.

He toiled up, cursing the fate that made a lame man go for a ten-mile walk to find his bedclothes, until a gleam of light through an open door told him that he was at the top and he stepped out on to a flat, leaded space surrounded by a stone parapet.

And there, lying on his blankets and pillows and covered with his eiderdown, were Henrietta and Hugh Anthony, sleeping the sleep of an easy conscience.

They looked so delicious, with dark lashes lying on starlit faces and parted lips a little appealing in their relaxation, that Jocelyn postponed waking them to hear his avuncular remarks. Instead he sat down on the edge of the parapet, lit his pipe and drifted away again into the dreams that seemed to be a necessary part of existence in Torminster.

It was such a night as the gods in their niggardliness do not give often, so still that the sound of his own breathing seemed to him a desecration. The bowl of the sky was a deep blue, golden at its rim where the lights of the city stained it and hung across with a silver cord of stars. The towers of the Cathedral were black against it, like the crags of a mountain, and down in the dark garden the white hyacinths were stars in a reflected sky. The beauty was so unearthly that the thought of its passing was a pain. "Or ever the silver cord be loosed or the golden bowl be broken," muttered Jocelyn, and wished it were possible to draw beauty into oneself and preserve it unfadingly for ever.

If only, he thought, one could preserve as part of oneself the scenes and the events that were beautiful and get rid of all the others. His own memory now was a thing that he did not much care to look into. The horror of war, its futility and bestial cruelty, had injured his mind as a bursting shell had injured his body, leaving it sickened and vaguely aching. He wished he could forget South Africa. Looking back on his life in the Army it seemed to him now nothing but a wilderness of heat and bewilderment, and but for the emptiness and uncertainty of the future he thought that he would not have been sorry that it had ended. He had not, he thought, in spite of his wartime success, been a particularly good soldier. His bent of mind was a scholarly one and his outlook on life that of an artist. Regulations had irked him, and red tape, and that life of routine that so often stifles imagination.

Yet what was he to do with himself? His sense of beauty, though deep, was not sufficiently strong to make an artist of him. It was not a sword driving him on to express it in poetry or music or painting, lest he die, it was rather that faculty of critical appreciation that can separate gold from dross. He had it in him to be a valuable friend both to creators blinded by the sweat of their own effort and to the wistful multitude who need an interpreter in the courts of the spirit. But he knew this only vaguely and the half-knowledge offered no solution to the problem of his future.

"I must be the worst sort of idiot," he said to himself bitterly. "A parasite and a drifter."

He watched the curls of smoke from his pipe wreathing aimlessly away and thought how like they were to his own life, drifting out into the night as he had drifted to this quiet town, and to that empty house and Henrietta.

His figure grew tense. Why had he thought of the house and Henrietta like that? Vividly, and connecting them together in his mind? He felt as though two threads that he must follow had been put into his hands. He was reminded of a game that they had played when they were children, a game they called "treasure hunt." They stood in the lighted hall and the end of a long coloured ribbon was given to each of them. They followed their ribbon all over the house, winding it into a ball as they went, up creaking stairs, through ghostly rooms and down terrifying passages, until at last the persevering and the courageous reached the end of their ribbon and found their treasure, a ball or a box of soldiers or a sugar pig.

Smiling to himself, suddenly hopeful and lighthearted, he knocked out his pipe and tweaked the eiderdown off Hugh Anthony.

CHAPTER II

I

REAL life had begun for Henrietta on the day that she came to Torminster. She had, of course, existed at the orphanage, she had slept and eaten and learnt her tables up to twelve times nine, but it had all seemed dark and queer and now, a year later, she could remember very little of it all except a lot of noise and hurry, the smell of boiled cod and windsor soap and the wart on Matron's chin. She had not been unhappy but she had not been alive. She had been like a jack-in-the-box inside his prison, with the lid smacked down on top, and it was not until Grandfather had lifted the lid that she had shot up into life and power and thought.

Never would she forget the first time that she saw Grandfather. She was sitting with the other children learning about the capes of England, where they stuck out far into the sea and where they did not stick out so far, what towns sat upon them and what towns did not, what counties they stuck out of and what seas they stuck out into, and Henrietta, like Galileo, cared for none of these things. . . . She was bored and though she did not know it she was starved. . . . And then the door had opened and Matron had come in, followed by Grandfather engaged in a tour of inspection. He sat on the board, they told her later, though what the board was and why he sat on it they omitted to explain. Henrietta for ever after had a mental vision of a see-saw and Grandfather sitting on one end of it with the Mayor, who was also on the board, on the other, and soaring to heaven and sinking again to earth with delighted chuckles.

When he and Matron came in Henrietta had been at first completely absorbed by the wart on Matron's chin, which always fascinated her, and then, suddenly, she was aware of Grandfather and her inside turned upside down.

The children had risen to their feet at a word from Matron and stood behind their desks with their hands at their sides, clothed all alike in hideous black overalls, with their hair tightly plaited in plaits that stuck out in horizontal lines at the sides of their heads. Henrietta was at the back of the room and so she was able to gaze at Grandfather as he walked between the lines of children, saying what Matron called "a kind word" to each. She gazed at his rounded form, his bald head, his white beard like a gnome's, his astonished blue eyes behind their powerful glasses, and she loved him.

Henrietta had a startling capacity for falling in love at first sight but, though she was at this time eight years old, it had never before been used. Love was now flaming in her for the first time, a volcano in eruption. Would he, when he got to her desk, speak to her? What would he say? With her soul in her eye she watched his every movement, his every fleeting expression and, as he came nearer to her, though he smiled and nodded and pinched the rosy cheeks of the orphans with every appearance of joviality, she had a feeling that he was unhappy.

Henrietta's instinct was, all her life, unerring, and it was not at fault now, for the orphanage always reduced Grandfather to complete misery. The dear little girls were happy, of course, well fed and well cared for and well educated, and later on they were planted out in situations of the utmost respectability, but yet.... All those black pinafores.... And the unbecoming style of hairdressing.... Every child the same.... Flowers needed individual care, some wanting one sort of soil, some another, some wanting sun, some shade. Was it perhaps the same with children? If you treated them like so many ninepins in a row, what happened to their individuality?

Mechanically pinching and smiling and saying kind words, but inwardly entirely wretched, he arrived at Henrietta and neither pinched nor smiled nor spoke, for Henrietta, her face luminous, was presenting him with her friendship. The effect upon him was much the same as it had been on Jocelyn and he felt not so much touched as stabbed. Then he pulled himself together, located the position of her desk and went on down the line pinching and smiling, and finally followed Matron out of the room, leaving Henrietta in a world where the sun had gone in and no birds sang.

But at the end of the lesson she was sent for to Matron's room and told that she must put on her hat at once and accompany Grandfather to the station, for he had adopted her.

Matron was in a frightful state, and no wonder. People had often told her that Canon Fordyce was "original," "eccentric," "a little touched in the upper story," "saintly," and so on, but this was the first time that she and his practical Christianity had come to a head-on crash.

"Most of Henrietta's clothes are at the wash," she said despairingly.

"I want the child, not her clothes."

"The case ought to go before the whole board for consideration."

"I'll deal with the board."

"I've never had such a thing happen before."

"Then it's high time it did. Routine will be the ruin of you good people," and Grandfather produced his watch and mentioned the time of his train, for the orphanage, though it was in the nearest big town to Torminster, was yet a long way from it, and the last train missed meant a night in the horrible place.

Though undoubtedly a saint Grandfather had the devil's own obstinacy, and Matron was annihilated. A cab was hastily fetched and Henrietta hurled in after him, together with her Bible, three pinafores and a couple of vests, the only bits of her portable property that Matron could seem to lay her hand on in the hurry of the moment.

Henrietta was perfectly serene about the whole business, too serene, Matron thought. Though she kissed Matron very politely on parting from her she showed no sorrow at leaving the institution that had sheltered her infancy. On the contrary, as the cab moved off, she was seen by Matron to be giving one of the ecstatic wriggles with which she always greeted the major joys of life, such as sausages for breakfast or the appearance of the first butterfly of the season.

But the wriggle over she gave no further sign of emotion and sat very still beside Grandfather as the cab rolled off to the station, so still that he was afraid she might be unhappy and looked anxiously down at her. She still wore her black overall, with black stockings and black button boots, her horizontal plaits stuck out on each side of her head, the hard black sailor hat which was at that time the fashionable headgear for orphans was tilted forward over her nose, and her hands were folded placidly on the Bible and underclothes that lay in her lap. . . . He was dreadfully afraid she was unhappy, but he could not see if her eyes were wet because of her hideous hat. . . . He took it off, flinging it contemptuously on to the opposite seat, and then with his rheumaticky old hands he unplaited those detestable plaits. She looked up at him, waves of delight rippling over her face, and he saw that she was silent only from excess of joy.

The railway journey to Torminster was a delight to both of them, though their fellow-passengers thought they had never seen such a peculiar couple in all their lives.

II

No words can describe what Henrietta felt about

Torminster. She arrived, as a year later Jocelyn arrived, in the spring, and if this was not Paradise she would have liked to be told what was. The dreaming city, the west front of the Cathedral with the rows of kings and queens and saints, the wooded Tor, the gardens full of flowers, the singing birds and chiming bells, the old house with its carved angels, the humming High Street and the holy well, these things did not belong to the world as Henrietta had hitherto known it, the world of a cod-and-windsor-soap-smelling orphanage in a big town, and she felt like one born anew on a different planet.

And the people, too, she loved. When she and Grandfather presented themselves before Grandmother, on that amazing day of the adoption, she was not in the least upset by Grandmother's rather sharp greeting of, "And what in the name of goodness have you got hold of this time, Theobald?" Grandmother's bark, she saw at once, was a great deal worse than her bite, and she very soon discovered the intensely grandmotherly heart that operated within Grandmother.

Sarah and Ellen were nice also, though rosy Ellen, who made her dough babies with currant eyes and let her wipe out the mixing basin with her finger after a cake had been made, was perhaps nicer than gaunt, gloomy Sarah.

Then there was Bates the gardener, who sometimes allowed her to assist him in his labours, and Gotobed who brought them their visitors in a yellow pumpkin and used rich-sounding words such as "damn" and "blast" whose meaning she did not know but whose solid sound gave her a great deal of pleasure, and gentle Miss Lavender who taught her and Hugh Anthony in the mornings, and the Dean with his beautiful whiskers, and lots of others.

But Hugh Anthony was the best of all. She had up till now had nothing to do with the male young, for at the orphanage the sexes had been kept in watertight compartments, so that friendship with a little boy was a new experience for her and she found in it something that her friendships with little girls had never given her. She found his questioning mind, so different from her own, very stimulating, and his instinctively protecting attitude towards her was new and sweet. His rare kisses, too, were different from the kisses of little girls, more exciting and more worth while. He was her mate, her fairy lover, her perfect complement. She could not analyse her feelings, but she knew that she loved him with her whole heart and soul and would until she died.

And then there were her lovely clothes. Those she had arrived in, the black hat and black pinafore, the button boots, the black serge bloomers, the thick woollen scratchy combinations that buttoned up under her chin and descended—having become distressingly elongated in the wash—half-way down her legs beneath the black woollen stockings, together with the three pinafores and two vests—the Bible was retained—were returned to Matron with Grandmother's compliments and in their place came clothes that seemed to Henrietta fit for a princess.

Smocks of periwinkle blue and rose-pink for everyday, with white muslin for Sundays, a soft white sailor hat, white socks and little brown sandals, petticoats with scalloped borders and combinations that were soft to the skin and descended no farther than the knee. Grandfather did not allow her to plait her hair, except at night; it hung loose, confined only by snoods of ribbon of the style affected by Alice in Wonderland.

And then there was her bedroom. It was a tiny room over the porch, as monastically furnished as Jocelyn's but with a population of six carved angels instead of four. They were, however, baby angels, not stately seraphim. They had two wings only apiece and no bodies, poor little dears. Henrietta wondered what the originals up in heaven did about their food, stomachless as they were, but supposed God fed them somehow since these prototypes on earth, who had presumably been copied from

the originals, were very fat in the face and jolly-looking.
... Sometimes at night Henrietta would hear a rustling
of wings in the dark and think they were flying round
and round her head, giggling and trying to catch each
other. ... It was probably only a bat.

But this little room, though it was meagrely supplied
with the luxuries of life, always excepting angels, was
rich in good smells. Wistaria covered the wall outside the
window, and in the summer great bunches of blossoms,
heavy and pendulous as grapes, filled the world with
scent. But even when the wistaria was not in bloom the
smells were delicious. In spring there were the hyacinths
and all the summer through there were roses, in autumn
came the sharp smell of chrysanthemums and the pungent
scent of wood smoke and fallen leaves, and in winter
there were perhaps the best smells of all, the faint scent
of the very earth itself and that delicate perfume of the
frost that is hardly a perfume at all, but rather a distillation
of crystal cleanliness.

Just at first Henrietta had been frightened of sleeping
by herself. At the orphanage she had slept in a dormitory
with other little girls and worked and played and eaten
in a seething horde, never knowing a moment's privacy
day or night, and that had seemed so natural to her that
loneliness, when it came, was terrifying. When Sarah
took away her candle and left her to the dark she had
hardly known how to bear it. She had lain awake hour
after hour, shaking with fear, her round black head turned
sideways on the pillow towards the place where she knew
the window was and her eyes straining through the dark
for the first glimpse of the dawn.

But quite soon her fear had left her and she knew that
the most precious possession she had was her room and
the privacy it gave her. She was immensely proud of it.
She dusted it herself every day and Grandmother allowed
her, under the supervision of Bates the gardener, to pick
flowers for the blue pot on the window-sill.

In it she dreamed dreams and saw visions. While she slept it seemed to her that strong arms were carrying her from place to place, showing her ivory palaces where the wind whispered through the pillars like violins playing very softly, and crystal mountains full of musical streams, and green lawns where rose-petals fell with a sound like rain, and she enjoyed it all immensely. And when she woke up she tried, by the exercise of her own will and imagination, to create other lovely things. She built white towers beside gold sands and blue sea and tipped the crest of each wave with curling snow, making them very tall so that as they curved and broke on the sand they made a sound like the organ in the Cathedral. And she planted gardens full of roses and hollyhocks and set singing birds in every bush, and she built caverns under the sea of emerald and mother-of-pearl and put mermaids singing sad songs in them.

For in every dream that Henrietta dreamed music had its place. She even thought that colours and scents had their sounds. Red was a trumpet blast and green was the sound of fairy flutes, and the scent of the wistaria was a tune played by the violins that made one want to sit down on a cushion and never do any work any more.

It was important, because the only memory that Henrietta had of the days before she went to the orphanage was a memory of music. A woman in a blue dress had sat at the piano singing and Henrietta had danced as she sang, her bare feet going pitter-patter on a shiny floor. The woman had sung faster and faster, her voice gay like a blackbird's, and the baby Henrietta had danced and danced, her toes getting pinker and pinker with the effort, until at last her legs had got entangled with each other and she had fallen over with a bump. The woman had run to her and picked her up and they had sat on the floor and laughed. Henrietta could not remember what the woman had looked like, she could only remember the sound of her, her singing and her laughter and her deep, ringing voice. The memory of this woman and her music had become almost submerged at the orphanage, but in the quiet of Henrietta's bedroom at Torminster it came back to her very vividly.

All these things and people combined acted upon her like sunshine on a folded flower. She expanded and the essence of her, the flower's scent, that had been too tightly bottled up to live, came out into the open.

And the essence of Henrietta was a dreamer of dreams. Her mind was not inquiring, like Hugh Anthony's, but it was intensely appreciative. She noticed that certain things were lovely and she stored them in her memory, taking them out later and fastening them together to make a dream, as a woman will embroider a posy of flowers with coloured silks. Later on in her life, when she grew up, she realized that dreams cannot be hoarded selfishly in the mind, lying piled one upon the other, getting dog-eared and faded, but must be generously spilt out into the world, and she learnt how to paint her dreams with a brush on canvas so that other people saw them too. . . . But Henrietta the famous artist was still far in the future, her powers guessed at by no one except Gabriel Ferranti, the man who had lived in the house with the green door.

III

It was Henrietta who had discovered him in the first place, and all because of the stuffed owl in the parlour at The Green Dragon. . . . Afterwards it was extraordinary to think of the effect that owl had had upon the lives of them all, and pathetic to think that the poor thing was dead all the time and could take no pleasure in the fuss and to-do it created.

The discovery of Ferranti by Henrietta was in this wise. When she first came to Torminster it was ordained by Grandfather and Grandmother that in the mornings she should share Hugh Anthony's lessons with Miss Lavender, but that in the afternoons, when Hugh Anthony was playing cricket with the boys at the choir-school, she and Sarah should take a short walk for the good of the health.

But Sarah was not keen on walking. It made her corns jump, she said, and, though corns were only to be expected at her age, she saw no sense in making them jump unnecessarily. So instead of patrolling the lanes where the white violets grew, as Grandmother thought they were doing, Sarah and Henrietta went to The Green Dragon and sat in the parlour and talked to Mrs. Wilks, the proprietress of The Green Dragon, who was a great friend of Sarah's, being in fact Sarah's brother-in-law's second cousin on his mother's side.

Mrs. Wilks was very beautiful, with wonderful golden hair, a bulging figure and a blinding magenta blouse, but Henrietta did not like her. She did not like her loud laugh, nor her well-meant but smacking kisses, nor her jet ear-rings, nor the way she asked questions. Still less did Henrietta like her parlour, which was hot and smelt of lamp-oil and last Sunday's dinner, and least of all did she like the stuffed owl.

It was rather moth-eaten and it had glass eyes that glared and in one of its claws it held a very realistic dead mouse. Henrietta, sitting one day on the edge of a hard chair with her legs dangling, gazed at that mouse and wondered if it had cried when the owl caught it. . . . And if owls eat mice. . . . And who had killed the owl. . . . And whether it had cried. . . . And suddenly she could not bear it any more and slipped off her chair.

"Could I go out in the garden, please?" she asked Mrs. Wilks.

Mrs. Wilks, who had a kind heart in spite of her blouse, said, "To be sure, lovey, you hop along out." So Henrietta hopped.

The garden was at the back of The Green Dragon and

was not particularly interesting, for there was nothing in it but a water butt, a cinder path and Mr. Wilks's nightshirts hanging out to dry on the line, but there was no terrible moth-eaten owl gazing at you out of baleful eyes, so Henrietta preferred it to the parlour.

The only source of amusement available was kicking cinders up and down the path, so for a solid ten minutes Henrietta kicked and then, quite suddenly, she became aware of the next door garden over the wall.

Someone was gardening there, for she could hear the soft thud of a spade being driven into earth. Henrietta loved to watch people digging, for the disinterred worms fascinated her. She liked watching them clinging to the earth with their heads and their tails while they heaved their middle parts up into the air like a railway-arch. She thought it was wonderful of them to be able to move along like that, without legs or wings, and wonderful of God to have invented so many different ways of progression for His creatures. The wall between the two gardens was low and Henrietta, hoping for worms, put her hands on the top of it, gave a little jump, dug in her toes and heaved herself up so that her chin just came above the level of the wall.

She saw a wild, tangled strip of garden, a confused jumble of apple-trees, currant-bushes, weeds, rose-bushes, cabbages and long grass. A tall, thin man was gardening quite close to her. He had untidy black hair and a white face and a torn blue shirt and Henrietta liked him, though he was not in the least like any of the people who came to Grandmother's.

"Hullo," she said.

Gabriel Ferranti started and looked up. He saw the face of a child framed in a sailor hat which had slipped backwards and encircled the back of her head like a halo. Ten finger-tips were gripping the top of the wall, but he could see no more of her. She looked like one of the bodiless little angels in her own room, or like their Italian cousins who float about in pictures of the Madonna. Her dark eyes had the same gravity and her lips the same sweet earnestness.

He stared at her for a moment and then came over to her, smiling at her and pulling down his shirt sleeves. She saw when he came close to her that he had deep lines scored across his forehead and round his mouth and somehow, for a brief moment, they made her feel sad. She did not know that the man in front of her was living through that difficult moment when the scarred and dying beauty of youth is putting up its last fight before the approach of age, and so she did not know why she felt sad.

The sight of her saddened him too, but he knew why. He was a natural pessimist and the sight of the young always depressed him. . . . They seemed to expect so much of life that life would never give them and so soon their smooth flesh would be wrinkled and ugly.

"Hullo," he said. "Are you bodiless, or are you just hung up on the other side like a bat?"

"I've my toes in cracks," said Henrietta.

He reached a long arm over the wall and gripped her blue linen smock in the small of the back. Henrietta on her side scrambled with her toes and in a minute she was on top of the wall and he had lifted her down.

"So you *have* got a body," he said. "I'm sorry."

"Why?" asked Henrietta.

"I had hoped you were a celestial apparition, and so exempt from the troubles of this world."

Henrietta did not know what he was talking about and asked if he had dug up any worms. He said he had and they looked at them together and marvelled at the way they got about. Hugh Anthony, had he been present, would have wanted to know why God made them without legs, and if Ferranti had admitted to ignorance of the divine purpose regarding worms Hugh Anthony would have wanted to know why Ferranti didn't know why God didn't say in the Bible why it was that worms hadn't got legs? But on this occasion Hugh Anthony was not present and Ferranti and Henrietta just marvelled quietly together, storing up a wriggly memory in their very similar minds.... That night he wrote a strange poem called "Convolutions" that was afterwards famous, and years later she painted a picture full of queer spirals that created a great sensation in artistic circles but was never completely understood.

When they had exhausted the charms of worms they sat on the grass and Henrietta made daisy chains, while Ferranti told her a story of how he had sailed in a golden gondola in a city where the streets were not paved with noisy cobbles but with silent, silver water, and where the sun was so hot that it could melt the ice out of your heart and the pain out of your mind. No one ever grew old in that city, he told her, and love never died, and Henrietta, gazing at him spellbound, believed every word he said. It was years since anyone had believed anything he said and he found her faith entrancing.... Here at last, after years wasted in writing books and poetry that no one would read, was an appreciative audience.... They were both completely happy, Ferranti for the first time in years. Two of Nature's oddities as they were they fitted each other like hand and glove.

And then, just as Ferranti was describing the meal of pomegranates and red wine that he had partaken of in the watery city, eating off a blue glass plate and drinking out of a crystal cup, Sarah came out into The Green Dragon garden calling for Henrietta. They could see her gaunt head and shoulders as she stalked up the cinder path, looking for Henrietta behind the water-butt and amongst Mr. Wilks's nightshirts.

"Sssh!" said Henrietta to Ferranti, but he, with that heartless loyalty to each other's discipline that seems to afflict even the best of grown-ups, immediately got up and handed her back over the wall.

"Well, I never," said Sarah, "I didn't expect *that*!"

Henrietta, usually a moderately good child, behaved abominably. She yelled and stamped her foot on the cinder path and wrenched at her hat elastic so that it snapped and her halo fell off. "I won't go home!" she stormed. "I won't! I won't!"

"I never saw such an exhibition in all my life," said Sarah.

"Stop that row!" said Ferranti sternly, from the other side of the wall. "With your face screwed up like that you are no longer beautiful."

Henrietta seemed to know without being told that he cared for nothing that was not beautiful. She choked back her yells and composure came back to her white, starry face. "Please may I come again?" she asked.

"Don't choke like that," said Ferranti, "it spoils the timbre of your voice." And then to Sarah he said, humbly and pleadingly, "May she come again? I will take good care of her.

But Sarah, murmuring something vague about "not knowing, she was sure," hurried Henrietta away, employing the homeward journey in telling her what she thought of her. Henrietta was a naughty girl, she said, to get over walls and talk to strange men like that, strange men who wrote poetry and were erratic about their meals, so Mrs. Wilks said, and though pleasant-spoken enough were probably no better than they should be, as Mrs. Wilks said and should know, living next door and baking him an apple-pie once a week as she did, and Sarah never had trusted men with long hair and never would, and Henrietta must not tell her grandfather what she had done or he would be very angry, and this sort of thing was only to be expected when an old couple as should know better took to adopting children with one foot in the grave, and she'd said the same to Ellen only last Wednesday.

But Henrietta, who always lost her way in Sarah's remarks and hardly ever emerged at the other end with any clear idea of what she was to do or not to do, failed to grasp the fact that she was not to tell Grandfather, and told him all about it that evening while they watered the tulips.

Grandfather, far from being angry, was highly interested. He had heard that some unknown young man who wrote books had come to live in the house with the green door, but had also heard that the young man did not wish to be called upon and so had not called, for Grandfather in his humility was always careful not to push himself in where he might not be wanted.

But Henrietta's story made him feel quite differently. She made Ferranti appear as a fairy-tale man, a teller of tales, tall and thin, with a blue shirt and black hair and a white face with lines upon it, a person of such attraction that it seemed little children would follow him to the world's end.

"Dear me," said Grandfather. "The Pied Piper of Hamelin."

And it was this thought of the Pied Piper that made him decide that he would go and see Ferranti that night, for Grandfather had always felt sorry for the Pied Piper. ... A bitter man. ... A disillusioned man. ... A man whose faith in human nature had been so shaken that he had disappeared inside a mountain and been no more seen. ... Poor fellow. ... Grandfather would go and see him, he told Henrietta, and if he turned out satisfactory of course Henrietta should continue her friendship with him.

So after dinner, disregarding Grandmother's wishes that he should let well alone lest the person turn out peculiar, Grandfather placed his round clerical hat on his bald head, clasped his plump hands behind his back and strolled off under the stars to the house with the green door. ... Returning home again, to the intense annoyance of Grandmother, at the—for him, at his age, as she pointed out for three-quarters of an hour before they slept—disgraceful hour of midnight.

All through that summer the three-cornered friendship between Grandfather, Ferranti and Henrietta flourished like a green bay-tree. Grandmother, though she once met Ferranti at the butcher's and was introduced by Henrietta, thought little of him. The person was, as she had expected, peculiar, and though she asked him to tea from a sense of duty, and bestowed upon him the rather frigid smile that she kept for those unfortunates whom as a Christian she must love but as a human being intensely disliked, she found herself incapable of going farther. Hugh Anthony, too, did not much like Ferranti; his knowledge of cricket was negligible and he always lost his temper if asked more than one question per minute. . . . But Grandfather and Henrietta loved him.

He would hardly ever go to see them at the Close, being afflicted with the misanthrope's "house bound" attachment to the sorrows of his own roof tree in a very acute form, but they went to see him. To Henrietta he revealed one side of the Pied Piper character, the piping side, that opened to her a new world of fairy-tale enchantment, but with Grandmother he ceased to pipe and became just pied, a poor parti-coloured creature whose original bright hues of romance and idealism had been dimmed by failure and disillusionment. He was, as Grandfather had suspected, a bitter man, a man whose faith in human nature had been so shaken that he had elected to disappear from the world as he knew it. The house with the green door was his Pied Piper's mountain, whither he had withdrawn with his unwanted dreams.

Grandfather, though he loved him, could do nothing with him. Their arguments usually ended with Ferranti's parrot cry of, "Religion. . . . Bosh. . . . I've seen through all that." Grandfather, scratching his bald head in perplexity, seemed to remember that George Eliot had once remarked that when people said they had seen through a thing they usually meant they hadn't seen it at all, but this remark, though shrewd, did not help Grandfather in the difficult task of trying to make a man see what to him is invisible. . . . Grandfather knew of nothing harder, except trying to bring home to a wasp or butterfly the existence of a pane of glass in a window.

And then Ferranti disappeared.

IV

It had been Henrietta who had discovered he was there and it was Henrietta who discovered he was not there.

It was a windy Saturday in early November, when the red and yellow leaves were drifting through the streets of the city and torn wisps of grey cloud sailed across the stormy sky behind the Cathedral towers. Every now and then a scurry of rain swept by on the wind and the cry of the bells as they rang for matins, now loud and now faint as the gusts carried the sound and then dropped it again, was inexpressibly sad.

She felt restless and depressed. It was Saturday, and a whole holiday, but Hugh Anthony was in one of his tiresome moods and wouldn't play with her. Instead he lay flat on his stomach on the dining-room floor and studied football, a pursuit from which nothing roused him but the periodical need of going to the kitchen and refreshing the inner man, which seemed to become very empty when lain upon. She decided that she would go and see Ferranti. He never lay on his stomach and studied football, a game he heartily detested, and could always be relied upon to leave his writing, or gardening, or whatever he was engaged upon at the moment, and come into the garden and tell her stories.

Like a flash she ran out of the house, down the garden and out into the Close, just as she was, in her red serge dress and white pinafore, with the rain stinging her cheeks and her hair flying out behind her in the wind.

When she got to the Cathedral she turned to her left

on to the Green by the west front, for it was possible for pedestrians to get from the Green to the Market Place through a little tunnel that bored through one of the houses. Hardly anything was still on the Green and it was wildly beautiful. The elm-trees were swaying and creaking and their leaves were falling and drifting and bowling over the grass in golden battalions. The few people who were about were clutching their hats and billowing skirts and breaking every now and then into absurd little runs when the wind caught them. The rooks, storm buffeted, were cawing angrily and flapping protesting wings. Only the carved figures on the west front were still, those kings and queens and saints and angels who had faced a thousand such days and would face a thousand more. The clock struck as Henrietta went by, booming out over her head, but she was in too much of a hurry to look up at the carved baby over the west door, as she usually did, always hoping that he would jump and crow in his mother's arms at the sound of the bell.

She ran across the Market Place to the house with the green door, but she saw at once that it had a very shut-up appearance, and she thought that Ferranti must be in his garden, so she went in through The Green Dragon, pushing past the astonished Mrs. Wilks and running down the passage to the cinder path. She scaled the wall and clung on with fingers and toes, but there was nobody in the other garden and the roses were gone and the cabbage-stalks looked limp and desolate. She ran back through The Green Dragon and out into the Market Place again and round to the front door of the house. She mounted the two worn steps and beat on the door with her hands. She went on beating, a wild tattoo of brown fists on hard wood, but no footsteps came down the passage inside to answer her, and the windows, shut and clouded with raindrops, were like closed eyes with tears trickling out under the lids.

So he had gone. The Pied Piper had disappeared and

would perhaps never be seen again. She had no doubt that he had gone for good and a terrible feeling of desolation overwhelmed her. She ran back across the Market Place and the Green, so blinded by her tears that it was not until she had actually bumped into him that she saw Grandfather, bobbing along to matins with his hands clasped in the small of his back and the wind bulging out his surplice so that he looked like a white balloon.

"Henrietta, dear child!" he exclaimed in horror.

The relief of finding him was so great that Henrietta's tears, which until now had been a mere sprinkling, became a positive niagara, and Grandfather had to pat and soothe her and mop up her face with his handkerchief before he could make head or tail of her story. But when he did understand he was, though grave, by no means despairing.

"He's just out," he comforted her. "I expect he's gone to the bank."

"He hardly ever goes to the bank," sobbed Henrietta. "He hates the bank because there's never anything in it. And you can see that he's left the house because it's crying."

"Now, dear child, don't be fanciful," said Grandfather, but her distress was so great that he decided to leave matins, which was his responsibility this morning, to the tender mercies of the Dean and the Precentor, risking what the Dean would have to say about it afterwards, and look into this disappearance of Ferranti's at once. . . . He could not bear Henrietta to suffer and her capacity for doing so seemed to him alarming.

So they went together to the Market Place and looking at Ferranti's house Grandfather saw that Henrietta was quite right, for it had that indefinable air of desolation that an abandoned house always wears.

They stood together in the gutter and looked at it sadly and at that moment out came Mrs. Wilks, followed by Mr. Wilks, a large person with a ginger moustache whose waxed ends stood out further than one would have believed possible.

"Do you know where Mr. Ferranti is?" asked Grandfather politely.

"Flitted," said Mr. Wilks, and he said it with such grimness that Henrietta's heart sank.

"How do you mean, Mr. Wilks?" said Grandfather. . . . He said it a little sharply, for he did not like Mr. Wilks.

"Gorn," said Mr. Wilks. "In the night. And owes me a bill for beer as long as your arm."

"And that not the only bill owing," said Mrs. Wilks. "It's no wonder he's taken himself off. He'd better. He's done away with himself, you may be sure."

"That's enough, Mrs. Wilks," said Grandfather with, for him, extraordinary sharpness, and turning round he marched abruptly away across the Market Place with Henrietta pattering after him. He was very angry, she saw to her surprise, and talking to himself. "Saying a thing like that before the child!" he muttered. "Pray God she didn't understand!" She did not, so it was all right.

But at the west door of the Cathedral his rage seemed to evaporate. "We'd better go inside, Henrietta," he said, "and ask God about it."

"Yes, Grandfather," said Henrietta forlornly. Her ideas about God were at this time extremely hazy but correct as far as they went. He lived in the Cathedral, she imagined, much as Grandfather lived in Number Two the Close, and was kind and good like Grandfather, only more so. He had made her, so she understood, and provided her with her dinner daily so as to perpetuate His work, and He must be great and beautiful because His house was like that.

Grandfather pushed open the heavy swing-door and they were inside and in spite of her grief she thrilled a little, as she always did, to its grandeur and loveliness.

From where they stood at the west door it stretched

from their feet away into the shadows in the distance so that they could not see where it ended. Great pillars stood in ordered ranks all the way up the nave, so tall that it gave one a crick in the neck to look up to the place where their straightness curved into lovely dim arching shapes that went up and up into the roof and criss-crossed high over your head like the branches of trees in a forest.

It always seemed to Henrietta that there were flowers growing in the forest, for on sunshiny days the sun shone through the stained-glass windows and spread patches of colour over the floor of the Cathedral, and on wet days the candles lit in the shadows shone like daffodils.

The nave and the choir were separated by a carved screen where angels and saints stood in their ranks as they did on the west front, and when the choirboys were hidden behind it and singing, as they were now, it seemed to listeners in the nave that the angels themselves were singing.

Grandfather and Henrietta walked up the nave towards the first row of chairs, but when they got there they remembered suddenly that St. Paul had very strong feelings about little girls who went into church without their hats, and Grandfather made Henrietta fasten his handkerchief round her head with a safety-pin that she fished up out of her underclothes for the purpose.

This little matter attended to they knelt down side by side and Grandfather in his absentmindedness began to join in with the choir. "I will sing and give praise," he sang in his cracked old voice. "Awake up, my glory, awake, lute and harp, I myself will awake right early."

Henrietta, who could see nothing at all to awake a lute and harp about in their present situation, prodded him gently. "We're going to tell God about Mr. Ferranti," she reminded him.

"Dear me, yes, so we are," said Grandfather, and began to ask God if He would be so kind as to look after Mr. Ferranti and see that no harm came to him.

Henrietta prodded Grandfather again. "But God

doesn't know what's happened," she said. "Couldn't you explain it all from the beginning?"

"God knows everything," said Grandfather gravely.

"But He might have been looking the other way when Mr. Ferranti went off," said Henrietta desperately. "I want God to know about the house crying, and what Mr. Wilks said, and everything."

Grandfather, scratching his head in perplexity and wondering if this was, or was not, the time to try to explain the omnipotence of God to Henrietta, decided it was not, and going back to the beginning again explained the situation to God down to the smallest detail. Henrietta, leaning against Grandfather and gazing up into the soaring arches above her head, was comforted. God, she felt, was now in possession of all the facts and, if He was anything like this wonderful house of His, was quite capable of dealing with them adequately.

Then they walked home together and Grandfather told Henrietta that she must try not to be unhappy because Mr. Ferranti had gone away. She had prayed and must continue to pray, and Grandfather would make inquiries of the police as well as pray, and that was all they could do. . . . In this beautiful world that God had made joy was a duty.

So Henrietta tried very hard to be happy again, and succeeded, but she did not forget Ferranti and the thought of his disappearance was a wound in her mind that never quite healed.

As the months went by and he was not found in spite of all Grandfather's efforts, the past of which he was a part stepped into the background. Henrietta found it quite hard to remember exactly what he had looked like, but she never forgot the stories that he had told her. The pictures that they had created in her imagination linked themselves to the music that a woman in a blue dress had once sung to her and became one with it in her memory.

CHAPTER III

I

THE morning after Jocelyn's arrival dawned blue and lovely.

Grandfather and Grandmother were the only ones who talked during the early stages of breakfast. Jocelyn, who came down a little late, was silent from fatigue and the necessity of catching up, and the tongues of Hugh Anthony and Henrietta were fully employed in dealing with porridge, bacon and egg, milk and water, toast and marmalade.

What, asked Grandfather of Grandmother as the meal drew to an end, was to be done with the dear children this afternoon? The choirboys were on holiday, it was Sarah's afternoon out and Grandfather had a Chapter meeting. . . . In the suggestive pause that followed Jocelyn said nothing. . . . Though in search of a profession he did not feel much drawn to that of nursery governess.

Henrietta bolted a mouthful and, following a rule of life implanted in her by Matron, wiped her mouth before she spoke. "I should like," she said, "to go with Uncle Jocelyn to the house with the green door."

"Why?" asked Hugh Anthony with unwiped mouth.

"Because I dreamed I did. I dreamed that I couldn't get the door open, but Uncle Jocelyn opened it with a big golden key."

"What did you do inside the house?" asked Hugh Anthony.

"I didn't do anything," said Henrietta, "because I woke up before I got inside. But I dreamed all sorts of other things first. There was a tall, thin man who piped, and who looked like Mr. Ferranti, and dancing children in coloured cloaks and houses with red roofs."

"What do these children have for supper, dear?" said Grandfather to Grandmother.

"Milk and biscuits, dear," said Grandmother rather sharply, for she disliked interference with her domestic arrangements.

"Before we go to the house we'll show Uncle Jocelyn the sweet-shop," said Hugh Anthony.

Jocelyn, yielding to fate, squared his shoulders and accepted the responsibilities of resident nursery governess. At half-past two that afternoon, he declared bravely, he would be ready.

Their breakfast finished, Henrietta and Hugh Anthony asked to get down and raced upstairs to get ready for morning school with Miss Lavender. They put on their brown strap shoes, attached the immense sailor hats that were then fashionable for the young to the backs of their heads with the help of elastic under the chin, and slung their satchels over their shoulders. Their grandparents, watching through the dining-room window, saw them go jauntily down the garden path and smiled affectionately. Hugh Anthony wore a dark blue sailor suit and Henrietta a rose-pink smock and they looked very nice if perhaps not as studious as could be wished.

The garden door slammed behind them and they were out in the Close. A blossoming tree that leaned over the garden wall dropped petals on their heads, the sun shone and they were happy. They walked along the pavement hand in hand, being careful to put their feet down in the centre of each paving-stone and not on the cracks, and at every sixth step they gave a little jump. This not walking on the cracks of the paving-stones was part of the ritual of the walk to school and was always observed with great solemnity.

Then they passed under the archway that separated the Close from the Cathedral Green and planted themselves in front of the clock on the north wall of the Cathedral to watch it strike nine. This also was part of the ritual.

It was a wonderful clock. A great bell hung between the life-size figures of two gentlemen sitting down. They had bushy hair and square caps on their heads, and held sticks in their hands, and for most of the day they sat perfectly still gazing at each other with every appearance of acute boredom. But at each hour they suddenly came to agitated life and made savage onslaughts on the bell. They struck it with their sticks and kicked it with their feet and made a great deal of noise indeed. Henrietta and Hugh Anthony adored these two gentlemen and it was one of the griefs of their life that owing to other engagements they could not be present every time they came to life. When they were grown up, they had decided, they would always be present, for to watch that clock was a life's work in itself.

But nine o'clock was good and lasted a long time. Nine kicks and nine blows and a glorious great boom at each. They stood perfectly still, their mouths ajar and their heads thrown back, listening and watching as though they had never seen the thing before.

When it was over they sighed, walked on a little way and descended the steps to the Cathedral Green, where they stopped again to look up at the west front. It did not look to-day as though it were built of stone. The blue air and golden sunlight of the misty spring day seemed to have soaked into it and dissolved its hardness of colour and outline, so that it seemed an apparition that might at any moment vanish. The rows of sculptured figures were not statues to-day, they were ghosts, an army of spirits stepping silently through the veil of mist hanging between earth and heaven.

"I do wish He'd laugh," said Henrietta, looking up at the Christ Child. "If I could reach I'd pinch His toes and then I'm sure He'd laugh."

"Don't be so silly," said Hugh Anthony. "He's only stone. Come on. Run."

Having taken as long as they possibly could to get from home to the west front they then took to their heels and raced each other across the Green to Miss Lavender's house, arriving in a most impressive state of perspiring eagerness for learning that Miss Lavender found very touching.

A half-circle of old houses stood round the Green, back to back with the houses in the Market Place, and Miss Lavender had lodgings in one of them. She was very poor, so poor that she could never tell anyone just how poor she was, and it had been Grandfather's idea that she should eke out her tiny income by teaching Henrietta and Hugh Anthony. She had never done any teaching before, except Sunday-school teaching, and she had no idea how much she ought to be paid for it, so Grandfather was able to pay her too much without her knowing.

Her parlour was on the first floor, a little room looking straight out into the branches of the elm-trees that pressed close up to the window. There were two wooden desks for her pupils, a table with a globe on it, behind which Miss Lavender sat, a bookcase full of books, one shabby armchair, photos of Miss Lavender's relations on the mantelpiece and a picture of "The Soul's Awakening" over the tiny sideboard. That was all there was, except the canary and the cat.

Miss Lavender herself was tall and thin, with grey hair and a kind, meek face. She always wore grey alpaca, and steel-rimmed glasses, and her beautiful voice was never raised either in reproof or anger.

Her method of education was very much ahead of her time, for she employed the modern method of self-government and allowed her pupils to study whatever subject they felt most drawn to at the moment. But in employing this method she was not actuated by a study of child psychology but by a desire for peace and quiet. As she suffered from headaches, and it was quite impossible to induce Hugh Anthony to do what he did not want to do without a frightful row, she was obliged to let him do what he did want to do, and the same in a lesser degree with Henrietta.

The result was not too unsatisfactory, for they were neither of them lazy and, let loose in the field of learning, Hugh Anthony with his inquiring mind and Henrietta with her contemplative one, they made each of them for the food that suited them best and munched away like a couple of young heifers, one devouring buttercups and the other daisies.

"I shall do geography," announced Hugh Anthony that morning, when they had hung their sailor hats on the pegs in the hall and clattered up the stairs to Miss Lavender's room. He loved geography, for the questions that could be asked about it were endless. Why were some people black in the face, for instance, and others yellow and others white, and why was there snow at the North Pole, and was it hotter in India than it was in England, and if so why? Miss Lavender, when asked, never had the slightest idea, but she had a very good geography book provided by Grandfather and Hugh Anthony was able to find these things out for himself to his entire satisfaction.

"I shall do literature," said Henrietta. She did not like geography, for she had had enough of the capes of England at the orphanage to last her a lifetime, and her explorations were all made in that realm of knowledge rather vaguely described by Miss Lavender as "English literature." This included reading, writing, dictation, learning by heart "Be good, sweet maid, and let who will be clever," and looking out of the window.

Henrietta loved words, both the shape and the sound of them. She had not yet discovered her own powers as a picture-maker—for Miss Lavender did not attempt to teach painting—but she had discovered through words the symbolism of sound and shape and their relationship, just as in her dreams she had learnt to link colour and movement with music. "Silver" was a word that she especially loved. She thought it was the loveliest of words because it was so cool. If it gave her pleasure to hear Mr. Gotobed say "damn," as though the word were a fine, strong fist crashed down on a hard table, it gave her even more pleasure to hear Miss Lavender say "silver," for she immediately thought of fountains playing and a long, cool drink on a hot day. It was a satisfactory word to write too, with its capital S flowing like a river, its l tall as a silver spear and the v like an arrow-head upside down. Yellow was another good word because of that glorious capital Y that was like a man standing on a mountain-top at dawn praying to God, with his arms stretched out, his figure black against a sky the colour of buttercups. . . . All her life yellow was her favourite colour and the one that symbolized the divine to her.

From the delight of forming letters into words Henrietta went on to the intoxication of forming words into sentences and here her instinct was unerring. She seemed to know just what words to choose and how to arrange them so that they sounded like a bar of music and not like the tea-things falling downstairs. Miss Lavender, unaware how early a feeling for poetry awakes in children, was astonished at Henrietta's sensitive ear. She had, a few days ago, read them Shelley's "To a Skylark." She had thought it far above their heads, but the larks were just in the middle of their spring ecstasy and Henrietta had demanded "something about larks," and Miss Lavender had not at the moment been able to lay her hand upon any literary lark except Shelley's. She was astonished, as she read, at the hush that fell upon her schoolroom. Henrietta never moved and even Hugh Anthony, who was carving a portrait of the Dean on his desk with a penknife, neglected his activities to listen, leaving the Dean whiskered on one side and not on the other.

"That's nice," said Henrietta when the poem was finished. "That's lots nicer than 'Be good, sweet maid,' or 'How doth the little.'"

"But you didn't understand it, dear, did you?" asked Miss Lavender.

Hugh Anthony, who had gone back to the Dean's

whiskers, did not reply, but Henrietta said, "It sounded good. It jumped up and up like the lark and it sang all the time."

"Well!" said Miss Lavender. "Dear me!"

And now, this spring morning, Hugh Anthony being provided with a chapter on coal and why it behaved in such a peculiar way when set alight to, Henrietta was presented by Miss Lavender with Verses for the Little Ones.

She flung it into the corner of the room.

"Henrietta!" exclaimed Miss Lavender in horror.

"I don't like it," said Henrietta. "I'm not little and I want that lark man."

"Not if you behave like that," said Miss Lavender, and began to shake nervously, for occasionally, mercifully very occasionally, Henrietta could be extremely naughty.

Henrietta saw Miss Lavender shaking and she was sorry, for she was not one of those demon children who enjoy tormenting. . . . She liked power as much as anyone else, but Grandfather had already taught her that in this world you may lay violent hands upon no personality but your own; other people's, if you dare to touch them at all, must be handled with a touch as light as a butterfly's. . . . So she picked up Verses for the Little Ones and apologized for her disgraceful conduct. "Though I'm not going to read it," she ended firmly.

Miss Lavender gave in and produced Shelley.

There was silence in the schoolroom, Hugh Anthony engrossed in coal, Henrietta in turning the pages of Shelley and Miss Lavender in the knitting that she was able to take up when the dear children were good.

The light in the room was a green light, for outside the windows the elm-trees were covered with new leaves and the sunlight had to filter through a green mist before it reached them. . . . Leaves. . . . The thought of them was in the minds of both children, for Hugh Anthony was discovering to his astonishment that buried forests turn into coal and Henrietta was thinking that the pages

of Shelley as she turned them rustled like autumn leaves.
"Leaves." The words suddenly danced up at her from the page and caught her eye.

> "O wild west wind, thou breath of Autumn's being,
> Thou from whose unseen presence the leaves dead
> Are driven like ghosts from an enchanter fleeing,
> Yellow, and black, and pale, and hectic red,
> Pestilence stricken multitudes!"

Suddenly she remembered that autumn day when she had run across the Green to look for Ferranti and the leaves were falling and drifting and bowling over the grass in golden battalions.

> "Thou on whose stream, 'mid the steep sky's commotion,
> Loose clouds like earth's decaying leaves are shed,
> Shook from the tangled boughs of heaven and ocean."

She did not quite understand that, but she had a vision of the sky as it had been that day, with torn wisps of cloud sailing along behind the Cathedral towers, leaf-shaped clouds that blew before the wind just as the leaves did. She read on eagerly, uncomprehending but pouncing eagerly on beautiful individual sentences. "And saw in sleep old palaces and towers" ... "And flowers so sweet the sense faints picturing them." ... Yes, she too could dream of beautiful things and picture them to herself when she woke up.... And here were the leaves again.

> "Drive my dead thoughts over the universe,
> Like withered leaves, to quicken a new birth;
> And, by the incantation of this verse,
> Scatter, as from an unextinguished hearth,
> Ashes and sparks, my words among mankind."

"Miss Lavender," said Hugh Anthony suddenly. "Is it really true that the flame that comes out of coal is the sunshine that got shut up in the leaves of the forests that were buried?"

"If it says so in that book," said Miss Lavender guardedly.

"It does say so."

"Then it's true," said Miss Lavender, "because your dear Grandfather bought that book and he would never buy a book that made incorrect statements."

Hugh Anthony thought hard, and his thinking powers were considerable. "Then when the flames come out of the coal the sunlight that was buried comes alive again."

"Yes," said Miss Lavender, and remembering that Easter was only just past hastened to improve the occasion. "A new birth," she said slowly and reverently, her knitting in mid-air with the heel half turned, "a resurrection."

Henrietta puzzled over the last verse of the poem with knitted brows, saying it over and over so that she had it by heart. "Do all things that have gone away come back again?" she asked.

"Yes," said Miss Lavender.

"Why?" asked Hugh Anthony.

"Because it's a law of life."

"Why?"

"Because God ordained that it should be."

"Why?"

"It is not for us to question the will of God."

"Why not?"

"Hugh Anthony, I don't know."

"Why don't you know?"

Henrietta arose and fell upon him. They rolled over and over together on the floor. They upset an inkpot and frightened the cat and gave the canary, who was elderly, a heart attack. By the time Miss Lavender had quieted the cat and the canary and got the ink out of the carpet with milk and lemon it was, to her great relief, time for the dear children to go home.

When they had gone she wondered for the hundredth

time if teaching the young was really her vocation and what, if anything, the dear children had learnt that morning.

They had, as it happened, learnt a good deal. The fact of resurrection had been brought home to them, some facts about coal were now a part of their mental equipment and Henrietta had memorized some words of a great poem. . . . It was the latter attainment that later turned out of great importance to them all.

II

Henrietta, during lunch, had to be reproved three times by Grandmother for bolting her food. The fact was that she was in a tearing hurry to get Jocelyn to the house with the green door. Things always came back, she had learnt that morning, the spring, the sunshine that had been buried under the earth and, as she had been given to understand at Easter, dead people too. And if dead people, then why not live people? Why should not Ferranti come back? Couldn't Uncle Jocelyn make him come back? In her dream, when she could not get inside his house, it had been Jocelyn who had opened it with a golden key.

"Oh, hurry up, Uncle Jocelyn," she cried impatiently. The meditative way in which he was spreading butter on his biscuit was almost unbearable to watch.

Jocelyn ate a bit of biscuit very slowly and remarked sweetly that it was now a quarter to two and he did not propose leaving the house until two-thirty, as had been stated clearly at breakfast.

After lunch Grandfather went to his Chapter meeting, which had been arranged by the Dean to take place at the sleepiest hour of the day so that all the Canons should go to sleep and he should get his own way in a matter of some dispute, Grandmother to her room to rest and the rest of them to the lawn. Jocelyn and Hugh Anthony established themselves under the mulberry-tree and shared *The Times* between them, Hugh Anthony lying flat on his front with the cricket and Jocelyn sitting upon a deck-chair with the state of Europe. Henrietta sat on the wheelbarrow at a little distance from them, swinging her legs and suggesting at short intervals that it must be nearly half-past two now, of which remarks they took no notice whatsoever. . . . There were times when Henrietta almost disliked men. Their capacity for silently refusing to do what you wanted them to do could be very irritating, far more so than the voluble reasons invented by a woman to account for the fact that she just did not happen to want to do it. . . . Henrietta was of too tender an age to analyse her annoyance, she just knew she was annoyed.

But the Cathedral clock struck two-thirty at last and Jocelyn, who was at least a man of his word, rose to his feet and put his hat on.

"But I've not finished this cricket," objected Hugh Anthony.

"Come along, old chap," said Jocelyn. "You must never break your word to a lady."

"Why not?" asked Hugh Anthony.

No one seemed to know why not and they sallied forth, Jocelyn holding the garden door open for Henrietta with as much courtesy as though she had been the Queen of England. She was at once mollified and slipped her hand into his as she walked along beside him, being careful not to tread on the cracks of the paving-stones.

"We're going to the sweet-shop first, remember," said Hugh Anthony.

They crossed the Green and went through the tunnel into the Market Place. The sweet-shop was on the opposite side of the Market Place from The Green Dragon and was twin sister to the one that Miss Matty kept at Cranford. Its window was as gay as a flower-bed with glass jars of coloured sweets, striped sticks of peppermint rock and families of white sugar mice and pigs with pink noses and string tails. It was kept by Martha and Mary Carroway and their niece 'Arriet Kate.

Martha was in the shop when they went in, a charming little old lady made out of Dresden china, with bright eyes that darted over Jocelyn with burning curiosity.

"Relative of Canon Fordyce?" she murmured audibly and with a worried look.

"My name is Irvin," said Jocelyn obligingly.

"Ah! The Canon's daughter's son from London," said Martha, and was happy. Torminster was one of those small cities where it is a torment to the inhabitants not to know every detail of each other's goings-on and ancestry. It was small enough to make this knowledge possible yet big enough to make it difficult to come by, so there was great ardour in the chase.

"Now then," said Jocelyn, "what shall we buy?"

Hugh Anthony believing in striking while the iron was hot. Uncles, he had discovered, were always filled with avuncular ardour at the beginning of their visit, but as time went on they were apt to cool a little. It might be that Jocelyn would not want to visit the sweet-shop a second time, so he felt it would be as well to lay in a stock of necessities now. He would like two pigs, he said, two mice, an ounce of bullseyes, a stick of rock and some liquorice.

"And you, Henrietta?" asked Jocelyn.

She asked modestly for some hundreds-and-thousands, which she adored. They were coloured sugar-balls the size of pins' heads and were delicious eaten between slices of bread and butter. First you bit through the soft sponginess of the bread and then your teeth crunched gloriously into the sweet grittiness of the rainbow-coloured balls. The contrast was curiously exhilarating, adding a very special savour to life.

"Nothing else, Henrietta?" asked Jocelyn.

Henrietta shook her head. She disliked excess. Things were much more enjoyable, she thought, if you took them singly and in small quantities. Hugh Anthony could never see eye to eye with her in this.

Martha weighed out the sweets in her shiny scales, added an extra one or two in the tradition of Miss Matty, and put them into cone-shaped pink paper bags which were placed in Jocelyn's pockets.

"Good afternoon," he said politely and limped to the door.

Martha, in the excitement of his entry, had not noticed his limp, but now she adjusted her glasses and had a good look at it.

"The step of that bus is very treacherous," she murmured.

Although she seemed to be making a statement there was a world of pleading in her tone and Jocelyn paused before closing the shop door to say, " I injured my leg in Africa. Good day."

Martha gathered up her skirts and fled out of the shop to the back room beyond, where dwelt her elder sister, aged eighty-nine, with the cat and a constant supply of its offspring.

"Mary! " she cried, tripping over a basket of kittens in her excitement, " who do you think I've had in the shop? Canon Fordyce's daughter's son from London. Been telling me all about himself, he has, Mary. Turned out of the army, poor young gentleman, because of having his leg bitten by a tiger. . . . What'll he do now? "

"I couldn't say, Martha, I'm sure," said Mary in her faint, piping treble. "Was it a large tiger? "

She was a beautiful, saintly old person, with white hair curtained on either side of a transparent face. She was so thin and fragile that she could hardly be said to be there, but her figure was given solidity by the fact that she wore, one over the other, out of affection for the dead, every single one of the petticoats once owned by her deceased mother and aunts.

"As to the tiger, Mary, I couldn't say, but could he

go into the Church?" asked Martha, looking worried again.

"Where did he go when he left here?" piped Mary. "If he turned towards the Palace he'd have been going to ask the Bishop if his lordship considered him suitable."

"There! I never thought to look!" cried Martha, clacking her tongue in annoyance, and gathering up her skirts she ran back to the shop again.

On her reappearance she was able to report that Jocelyn and the children were standing on the pavement outside Gabriel Ferranti's house and staring in through the window.

"Ah," said Mary, "he'll be taking the house and setting up for himself in business."

"Go on with you, Mary!" expostulated Martha. "Young gentlemen don't go into trade."

"He's maybe not such a gentleman as he looks," said Mary. "Canon Fordyce's daughter in London married beneath her, so I've heard. It'll be books. Books are very genteel."

By nine o'clock that night it was all over Torminster that Canon Fordyce's grandson from London had taken Gabriel Ferranti's house and was turning it into a bookshop.

III

As though drawn by a magnet Jocelyn and the children had crossed the Market Place to the house with the green door. The paint was cracked now and the two worn steps very dirty because no one had washed them for so long. There were cobwebs in the corners of the window-panes and a few of the wavy tiles had slipped out of place.

But nothing could dim the beauty of the little house, it was no more ugly than a lovely child is ugly because it has smuts on its nose and mud on its pinafore. Yet the house cried out, as the child would not have done, to be washed and tidied. It seemed to Jocelyn to be holding out hands to him, beseeching him to help it.

"How imaginative being with children makes one," he thought, and bent a little nearer to peer through the window at the empty room and the rose-sprig wall-paper. In places it had come away from the wall and hung in strips, and the sight vexed him.

Hugh Anthony was eating a sugar mouse, beginning at its pink nose and working backwards, and so was not much interested in the house, but Henrietta was leaning so close to the window that her nose was flattened out into a white button against the panes and her breath, that came rather pantingly, dimmed the glass and obscured her vision.

"It's all empty," she mourned. "He's not come back yet."

"No," said Jocelyn absently, and stepped back a few paces to see just where the tiles had slipped.

"It's not empty!" cried Henrietta suddenly, her voice rising sharply. "Quick! Look! Someone's come in!"

Her excitement communicated itself to Jocelyn. He stepped quickly forward and bent to look, then exclaimed under his breath and pulled out his handkerchief to polish up the panes that Henrietta had obscured with her breathing.

"No, it's not him," said Henrietta, and let out her breath with a deep sigh.

"It's only that lady who comes to stay in the Close," said Hugh Anthony contemptuously. Everyone was making a lot of fuss about a woman, he thought. It was often done and he could see no sense in it.

Jocelyn did not even hear him, he was too much occupied in gazing at the most enchanting back view he had ever seen. It was that of a slim girl with an aureole of short, curly golden hair that stuck out all round like the petals of a sunflower. She wore a childish cotton frock of delphinium blue, with short sleeves and no collar, that showed the warm, creamy colour of her skin and the lovely moulding of her arms and slender neck. At the beginning of the twentieth century unadorned clothes and short hair were not the fashion for the grown-up and the deliberate simplicity of this girl was somehow arresting, as arresting as her attitude.

She stood with her back to the window and her head thrown back, quite still, poised and attentive, as though she were listening and watching. . . . Listening apparently only to the silence and watching the sunlight on the patterned wall-paper.

"Let us in! Let us in!" cried Henrietta imperatively, and drummed with her finger-tips on the window-panes.

The girl swung round and Jocelyn, entirely forgetting his usually excellent manners, rubbed almost feverishly at the window with his handkerchief, so as to see her face perfectly. It was the most alive face he had ever seen. Her eyes were tawny and full of light and her heart-shaped face, with its delicate yet determined features, had a transparency that made it seem like a window through which she herself could be seen with a delicious clearness. Jocelyn felt that he was looking through two windows at the most courageous, generous person he had ever encountered. She was pale, but not with the moonlight paleness that was Henrietta's, for she looked sun-kissed and warmly loving, and somehow she was familiar. Somewhere else, Jocelyn felt, he had encountered that vivid personality.

"Let us in! Let us in!" cried Henrietta again, and the girl nodded and smiled and ran out of the room.

In a moment the green door creaked and squeaked and then slowly opened.

"The bolt sticks," said a clear voice. "I got in through the scullery window myself."

"Did you go through The Green Dragon and then over the wall into the garden?" asked Henrietta.

"Yes, I did. I was paying a bill to The Dragon and I told them I must get into this house or die, so they showed me the way over the wall and through the window."

Jocelyn had shut the door behind him and they were standing in a dark passage that smelt of damp and rotting wood. Two doors were on their right and one on their left and in front of them narrow stairs crept away into darkness.

"Come into the back room," said the girl. "If we go into the front one they can see us from the Market Place."

She opened the second door on the right and they were in a small, panelled room. It had a beautiful old fireplace and a window with a window-seat looking into the garden.

"It's a bigger house than you'd think," said the girl. "There's another small room downstairs, with a kitchen and scullery behind it, and there are four bedrooms upstairs, all of them old and crooked, the kind of rooms that Hans Andersen's people lived in."

"Don't you think the whole of this city is Hans Andersenish?" asked Jocelyn.

"Yes, I do," she said. "That's why I love it. To come on a visit here is like walking into a fairy story."

"So you're on a visit here too?"

"Yes. My name is Felicity Summers and I'm staying with my godmother, Mrs. Jameson."

"She lives next door to us," explained Hugh Anthony thickly, through mouse. "Sarah says she's wanting in the upper story."

"Hush!" reproved Henrietta. "Grandfather says she is not like other people because her husband was a very noble missionary and was killed by cannibals."

"Hold your tongues, both of you," said Jocelyn embarrassed. "How about running out into the garden?"

He opened the window and they willingly ran. Henrietta wanted nothing better than to go out into the garden of her dreams and Hugh Anthony had got to the mouse's tail and wanted to spit out the string.

"I beg your pardon," said Jocelyn to Felicity.

She laughed. "Aunt Adelaide isn't really mad," she explained. "She's just a little fantastic. . . . I suppose you're yet another of Canon Fordyce's grandsons?"

Jocelyn pleaded guilty and they sat down together on the window-seat.

"What were you doing staring in through the window like that?" she asked.

"What were you doing breaking in through the scullery?"

"Is there anything in this world so attractive as an empty house? Does any normal human being ever pass one without wanting to go all over it?"

"Then let's go all over it. I've not been yet, remember."

They went. The little box of a room on the other side of the front door was not very exciting, but the kitchen behind, with its oak beams and its red-brick floor, was beautiful, and the bedrooms were, as she had said, crooked and enchanted. Two looked out across the dreaming Market Place to the towers of the Cathedral and two looked over the garden to the hills and woods beyond. They explored them in a fascinated silence and then came back to the panelled room and sat down in its window-seat. They both felt thoughtful, and a little sad.

"Why is an empty house so attractive?" asked Felicity.

Jocelyn pondered, looking out into the beautiful garden where the untrimmed flowers and grass and blossoming apple-trees had run riot to such an extent that they were woven tightly together like a tapestry.

"How can we help loving houses when they stand to us for so much," he said. "Warmth and protection and a means of expressing ourselves. You love a new house because it stands there waiting to be good to human beings and an old one because it has been."

"And an old house is a sort of history book," said Felicity. "All that people thought and did in it must be written in it somewhere. . . . Only the ink's invisible."

"Were you trying to read the invisible writing when

I looked at you through the window?" asked Jocelyn. "You looked as though you were listening and watching."

"I was wishing that I knew the story of the man who used to live here and then disappeared. Gabriel Ferranti."

"Why? Did you know him?"

"Only by sight, but a man who looked so odd and had such a fantastic name must have had an interesting story."

"Not necessarily. Some people are obliged to be fantastic because their lives are so dull that otherwise no one would notice them."

"Well, I think he had, and it's written in this house. If I were free to do what I liked I think I should come and live here and learn how to read the invisible writing."

"What did you say your name was?" asked Jocelyn suddenly.

"Felicity Summers."

The name had a familiar ring and at once Jocelyn knew where he had seen this girl before. A picture rose in his mind of a crowded theatre gone mad with enthusiasm, of men and women cheering and clapping and waving their programmes while a slim figure came through the parted curtains again and again to take her calls. He could see her now, clothed in elaborate white and silver and with the eager vivacity of her face heightened by rouge and powder, curtseying and smiling enchantingly at stalls and pit and gallery.

"Now I know you," he said.

"No, you don't, because in Torminster I'm not Felicity Summers the actress, I'm only Felicity."

"You're right about being a different person divorced from one's profession," said Jocelyn. "One's work is what binds one to the world, isn't it? Without it one shrinks, as though one had no point of contact.... A cat without whiskers."

"Have you lost your whiskers?" she asked sympathetically.

"Yes, I was a soldier till I caught a lame leg in South Africa."

"Then for the moment we're both workless. That means that we're left with our essential, untrimmed selves. No make-up on me, no spurs on you. That ought to make it easier to make friends, and I'd like to be friends. Will you bring the children to tea on Wednesday?"

Jocelyn, who as a rule loathed tea-parties, accepted with alacrity.

IV

After dinner that night he found himself unable to keep quiet and look at *Punch* while his grandparents slept. He kept waking them up to talk about Felicity.

"I saw Felicity Summers at Ferranti's house, Grandmother," he announced.

"Oh," said Grandmother. "An actress. She stays with that peculiar woman, Mrs. Jameson, who very frequently has very odd people staying there."

"Have you met her, Grandmother?"

"No, dear, I haven't. I make a point of not going there when Mrs. Jameson has her odd people staying. I may be old-fashioned, I dare say I am, but to see that girl, with no chaperon and no hat, riding through the Close on that old grey pony of Mrs. Jameson's, the one that pulls the mowing-machine, with everything in trousers for miles round following after, sets my teeth on edge."

"Oh come, Grandmother, I don't suppose she can help what follows after," said Jocelyn, grinning. "Beautiful actresses are like a street accident; it's not their fault if crowds collect."

"They need not smile backwards over their shoulders."

"But that's much nicer than frowning frontwards."

Grandmother said it was very warm to-night and went to sleep again, leaving Jocelyn to continue the conversation with Grandfather.

"Is Mrs. Jameson really very odd, Grandfather?"

Grandfather sighed and woke up. "Yes, dear boy, very odd, but there is great good in her. She has money and uses it well. I don't know why, but a small cathedral town always seems to attract peculiar elderly ladies. . . . Of course, no doubt we are all of us much more peculiar than we have any idea of. . . . It may be that I am considered odd myself." And he went to sleep again.

"You've not met Felicity, Grandfather?" said Jocelyn presently. There was a note of interest in his voice that this time woke Grandfather right up.

"No, dear boy, but I should much like to do so. Dear me, yes. A very beautiful young woman."

"She's asked me to take the children to tea there on Wednesday."

"Dear me, I envy you. I should like to see Felicity and Henrietta together. . . . Sunshine and moonlight."

Grandfather looked at Jocelyn attentively and with satisfaction. He noticed that he was looking different; younger, more alive, with a warmth in him that communicated itself to Grandfather and made him, too, feel different. Perhaps this warmth came from yet another love story set burning in the old city. . . . Yet another added to all the hundreds that must have . . . must have. . . . . When ten o'clock struck Grandfather found he had been dozing again.

V

As Jocelyn passed the door of Henrietta's room, always kept ajar in case she should want to yell for Grandfather in the night, he heard her voice. She wanted assurances that there was nothing under the bed, he supposed, and he went in to give them.

But Henrietta was only talking in her sleep, a habit of hers when over-excited.

"Leaves," she said. " Yellow and black and pale and hectic red."

Then there were confused mutterings and then she came out suddenly and clearly with a whole consecutive verse.

> "Drive my dead thoughts over the universe,
>   Like withered leaves, to quicken a new birth;
>   And, by the incantation of this verse,
>   Scatter, as from an unextinguished hearth,
>   Ashes and sparks, my words among mankind."

As he undressed and got into bed the words haunted Jocelyn, and when he drifted towards sleep he thought again of Felicity and of the house in the Market Place. The story of a man's life was written in it, she had said, and she thought it would be possible to learn how to read the invisible writing.

Thoughts became deep sleep, and sleep the dream that comes before waking, and he was standing in one of the bedrooms at the little house, the big one that looked out over the hills and woods, and staring at the blank wall opposite the window. Words were written on the wall and he was reading them. He read on and on and when he got to the end he knew the story of Ferranti's life. Then a sudden beam of light swept across the wall, wiping the words away, and he woke up to find Sarah pulling his curtains.

"Wet to-day," she said. "But we must expect that after all the fine weather we've 'ad."

Jocelyn, sitting up in bed and pouring out his early tea, found that the story he had read in his dream had gone from him. He could not even remember what it had been about. The words of it had been swept away like dead leaves before a wind.

CHAPTER IV

I

WEDNESDAY came and Jocelyn and the children once more sallied forth watched from the front door by Grandfather and Grandmother and from an upper window by Sarah and Ellen. In the placid life of Torminster tea-parties were of importance. They lay on the surface of existence like the markings of the hours on a clock face, measuring the slow movement of time. Events were remembered in relation to tea-parties. "It was the day I went to the Archdeacon's in my blue silk," a Torminster lady would say if asked when her cook gave notice. Or, "We made twelve pounds of crab-apple jelly that year. I counted the pots when I came back from Canon Roderick's. . . . I wore my puce."

So it was important that Jocelyn and the children should go to tea with Mrs. Jameson. Sarah gave Jocelyn's suit an extra pressing and Ellen sewed new elastic in the children's sailor hats, put a white collar on Henrietta's smock and bought her a new pair of strap shoes.

Jocelyn, apart from the fact that he wanted to see Felicity again, felt that the event was epoch-making. He put the feeling down to the fact that the Torminster houses stood in walled gardens, so that when you want to tea next door you seemed to be going a journey into a foreign country.

In Torminster there was no looking over a low fence to see what the butcher was taking next door for dinner, and no watching the road outside through railings to see who attended next door's tea-party to which you had not been invited. No. High walls enclosed you as in a moated fortress and you could know nothing at all of the goings-on of next door except by a system of espionage carried on through the agency of whichever of the tradesmen happened at the moment to be walking out with cook.

From this followed the feeling that next door was a long way off. You went out through the door in your wall and banged it shut behind you. You were now separated from your own citadel. Your hollyhocks and your roses were hidden from you and if you could see anything of your house it was only the top of a crinkled roof; the eyes of the house, the windows, could no longer meet yours and you felt as thought the house had turned its back on you. Abandoned, you turned to your right, advanced a few paces and found yourself opposite another closed door in a high wall.... Next door.... You could see nothing of it and for all you knew anything might have happened beyond that wall since you were there last. The house might have been painted magenta, or peacocks might have been introduced in the kitchen-garden and mock-turtles in the front garden, they might have a new lawn-mower or a bird-bath, or simply anything. You laid your hand upon the door handle with an expectant heart, like a sailor who has sailed from across the seas and lets down his anchor in a foreign harbour.

Savouring this feeling Jocelyn paused for a moment at Mrs. Jameson's door. It was scarlet, with a brass handle, and over the top of the wall looked white lilac-trees already in blossom. The green and white and red made him think of a Chinese plate picturing that enchanting world of bridges and pagodas and lovers who never grow tired.

"Hurry! Hurry!" whispered Henrietta, alternately raising herself on her toes and swinging back on to her heels again, to get the stiffness out of her new, squeaking strap shoes.

The promise of something fantastic contained in Mrs. Jameson's scarlet garden door was fulfilled when one got inside, for her garden was like the palette of a child's paintbox, a confused jumble of all the brightest colours on earth. It was too early for the geraniums and calceolarias that she loved, but there were red tulips, golden marigolds and blue irises in profusion. There were also a sundial, a pond with goldfish in it and a hammock of striped red and green, all of them looking rather odd against the formal dignity of the Queen Anne house behind them.

It was one of the charms of Torminster that though the houses were all of them old they were of different periods, so that Queen Anne jostled William the Conqueror and Queen Elizabeth patronized the Georges. They all had different atmospheres, too, Grandfather's being monastic and Mrs. Jameson's mad Chinese.

Jocelyn and the children mounted the steps to the front door and rang the bell. It was answered by Felicity, who wore her simple blue frock and looked extremely out of place against the assortment of bric-à-brac that the hall contained. Tiger skins lay on the floor, bamboo tables stood about loaded with every kind of silver ornament and the shields and spears of savages covered every space on the walls not already occupied by sticky oil-paintings and photographs of Mrs. Jameson's relations.

There was a twinkle in Felicity's eye as she ushered them in. "I thought I'd better let you in myself," she said, "so as to explain things. Come upstairs and mind the thistles."

Jocelyn saw to his astonishment that the banisters had bunches of thistles tied on to them.

"There are no back-stairs for the maids to use," explained Felicity, "and so Aunt Adelaide ties thistles to the banisters so that the maids shan't put their hands on them."

She walked prancingly up a few stairs, Jocelyn toiling after, and then stopped again. "I'd better explain Aunt Adelaide's clothes. She always dresses in the colours of the Church's seasons, stockings and all. She wears purple in Lent, red at Whitsun, white during festivals and green the rest of the year." She pranced on a little farther, stopping again to give her final instructions. "Whatever you do don't contradict Aunt Adelaide, because that upsets her. And if you don't like parrots, pretend you do."

"Why?" asked Hugh Anthony.

"Don't ask questions, Hugh Anthony," Jocelyn whispered hoarsely.

The drawing-room was a lovely room, curtained, carpeted and furnished in scarlet. There were so many chairs and tables and china ornaments and photographs that it was almost impossible to move, and in each of the four corners of the room was a green parrot in a cage.

Mrs. Jameson rose at their entry and came graciously to meet them. She was a tall and very dignified old woman clothed from head to foot in snow white, it being still the season of Easter, and scintillating with jewels. Her fingers were covered with them, and her wrists, and the bodice of her silk dress, and a string of pearls was even twisted in her white hair. She looked like some superb, barbaric princess until one looked at her face, which was that of a bewildered child.

"Good afternoon," she said in her deep tones. "Sit down. And are these the dear children? I have seen them in the Cathedral at divine service, but I have never yet had the pleasure of receiving them in my house."

She shook hands graciously with Jocelyn and the children, who were mercifully struck dumb with astonishment, while the parrots yelled, "Good-bye, dear," in chorus. Then they all sat down before a silver tea-tray and quantities of plates containing every kind of sugar cake.

When she had poured out the tea, and asked them if they liked milk and sugar, Mrs. Jameson seemed to drift off into a dream and became silent. Felicity and Jocelyn chatted with some constraint about London and the weather, and the children, still overwhelmed, just ate. Only the four parrots were really voluble. "Give us a kiss," said one. "Scratch Poll," said another. "Good-bye," said the third firmly, while the fourth hinted over and over again, "Must you really go now?"

Half-way through tea Mrs. Jameson came to life. "I am sure you are interested in missions," she said to Jocelyn.

Remembering that she must not be contradicted he said that he was.

"Then you will like to hear," she said, "that on the spot where my dear husband was killed there is now a Christian church and school; so you see his death was not wasted."

"No, indeed," said Jocelyn gently.

"There's nothing I hate more than waste," went on Mrs. Jameson, her mind swinging off to another topic. "But for me there'd have been a great deal of waste when that young man who lived in the Market Place ran away. What was his name? Ferranti."

"How do you mean, Aunt?" inquired Felicity with interest.

"His effects were sold, dear, to pay his bills, and I was the first arrival at the sale. I always go to sales. I always say it's wonderful what one can pick up at them. . . . Well, yes. . . . When I arrived there were piles of papers, newspapers and magazines and so on, lying stacked on the floor in a corner of the room. 'What are you going to do with those, Mr. Jones?' I said to the auctioneer. 'Burn them, ma'am,' he said, 'they're no use to no one.' 'What waste, Mr. Jones!' I said. 'I'll buy them to light my fires with.' And I did. I hate waste."

"And are they all used up?" asked Jocelyn.

"Not yet," said Mrs. Jameson, "for I had a good deal of paper of my own laid by, but I'm getting through them gradually."

"I think it was very foreseeing of you to buy those papers," said Jocelyn gravely.

Felicity beamed at him. He was being sweet to Mrs. Jameson and she liked him more than ever for it, for she loved her godmother. She was no more mad, Felicity always maintained, than Felicity herself. She had suffered a great grief and the effect of it upon her had been to make her a child again. Womanhood with its sorrows had been too much for her and subconsciously refusing to face it she had turned backwards into her childhood. But she was always perfectly rational, she never told lies, she never had delusions. She was amazingly generous, giving of herself and her money to every good cause that came along, she was loving and deeply religious and pathetically trusting.

"I should like to play spillikins with the children," she said to Felicity when tea was over. "You can take Captain Irvin into the garden."

Behind the house there was a walled vegetable-garden and down the middle of it ran a wide, moss-grown path arched over by nut-trees, and here Felicity and Jocelyn strolled up and down. The thick moss deadened the sound of their footsteps and the interlaced bright green leaves made Jocelyn think of carved, lacquered Chinese screens obligingly put up by Nature to ensure privacy while his friendship with Felicity put out its first timid leaves.

But only Jocelyn was conscious of timidity, for Felicity did not know the meaning of the word. She had been given the happy gift of a spirit that faced outward and she bothered about herself and her feelings as little as it is possible for a human being to do. Artist though she was the thought of self-expression was hardly ever in her mind except as a gift that was hers to give. When she acted it was of the waiting audience in the dark auditorium that she thought, not of herself. They wanted something of her and her response was as fresh and natural as the reply of the trees to spring sunshine.

And so now it was Jocelyn of whom she thought. He had given her a moment of rather strange experience that had seemed to bring him very close to her. When he had stood in the Market Place and looked at her through the window of Ferranti's house he had seemed to see her herself, the essential untrimmed person whom she had told him was not Felicity Summers but only Felicity, and his look had thrilled her and comforted the lonely place that cries out for help deep inside every human being. Until that moment she had hardly realized that the place existed, but the sudden touch of healing applied to the ache and then withdrawn again had woken her up to awareness. Conscious now of this empty room at the centre of her being, it had been with almost a fellow-feeling that she had learnt from the cook that Jocelyn had taken that house in the Market Place. . . . The poor thing would not be forlorn any more, and neither would Jocelyn.

"I'm so glad about your house," she said impulsively.

"What house?" said Jocelyn.

"That house of Ferranti's that you are turning into a bookshop."

"But I didn't know I was," said the bewildered Jocelyn.

"What?"

"Whoever told you I was?"

"Aunt Adelaide's cook. Everyone in Torminster knows about your bookshop and we're all so pleased."

"But how can everyone in Torminster know about it when I don't know about it myself?"

Felicity began to laugh. "In Torminster everyone knows much more about one than one does oneself, you'll find."

"But I haven't said a word about it to a soul!"

"But perhaps you've thought a thought about it to yourself?"

"Well, it did just cross my mind that it would be fun to keep a shop in Torminster, but it was only an idea——"

"That's enough for Torminster. It's one of those places where thoughts blow from one mind to another and then sprout. It's the quiet, you know. Quiet is to thoughts what air is to seeds. It's wonderful what receptive minds Torminster people have. Now Keziah, the cook, only has to walk past a person's house and she knows all their family history, especially the parts they wouldn't want her to know. It just blows out of their minds and sprouts in her." A note of anxiety crept into her voice. "You don't mean to tell me that you aren't going to open that shop?"

"But of course not. Why should I?"

All the happiness went out of Felicity's face and she looked like a lovely child whose toy has been snatched away. "Oh, I am so disappointed!"

"But why?" said Jocelyn gently.

"Because Torminster needs a good bookshop so badly. What with the relaxing climate and the soporific effect of the bells Torminster people have minds like Tennyson's lotus-eaters."

"But a bookshop wouldn't alter the climate or stop the bells."

"No, but it might counteract their mental effect. . . . And I hate that darling house to be empty. I love it as though it were a person and I want it to be lived in."

"Someone else will take it if I don't."

"No, they won't, because of there being no drains."

"I don't see why it should be me to suffer a drainless existence for the sake of the minds of Torminster."

"Oh, please! Please!" begged Felicity, and Jocelyn saw to his astonishment that she was near tears. He had yet to discover the passionate energy which she bestowed on any new idea.

"But I've no capital," he pleaded.

"You must have your pension, and your Grandfather would help."

"But who would buy the books?"

"The Dean and Chapter. And you could have a circulating library. And we'd have a special department for the children and it would all be perfectly lovely."

"I couldn't let Grandfather lend me money," said Jocelyn firmly.

"If that isn't just like a man!" said Felicity with a sudden flash of the temper that was a part of her temperament. "I thought you had more sense than most, but you're just like all the rest, as proud as Lucifer. You'll disappoint us all and leave that house to its loneliness and prevent the Dean and Chapter learning a little something rather than stoop to a bit of humility!"

Jocelyn tried to change the topic of conversation, not knowing yet that Felicity could never be got to talk of something else until she had said the last word on the first subject, but was entirely unsuccessful.... In sheer self-defence he found himself discussing the books that should be bought and the style of furniture best suited to the house with the green door.

II

When he wanted to go home the children would not come. Their awe had evaporated under the influence of spillikins and they had discovered that the house was an enchanted Chinese palace and that Mrs. Jameson was a child like themselves. When Jocelyn went upstairs to fetch them he found Henrietta telling Mrs. Jameson one of Ferranti's fairy stories. She was listening in open-mouthed delight while the parrots, whom Hugh Anthony was feeding with sugar, said, "Oh, my!" at intervals. When requested by Jocelyn to come home they refused point-blank and with regrettable rudeness.

"Leave them," whispered Felicity. "It's so lovely for Aunt Adelaide to have someone of her own sort to talk to.... I'll see they get home in time for their baths.... I'm so glad you've given in about that shop."

"But I don't think I have, have I?" said Jocelyn, and went downstairs in such a whirl of bewilderment that he put his hand on the banisters and pricked himself severely.

And when he got home things were no better.

Grandfather and Grandmother were both out on the lawn, Grandfather walking up and down and saying evensong and Grandmother sitting under the mulberry-tree and knitting for the heathen.

"Well, Jocelyn!" she said in tones of severe reproach, "I don't think you should have left me to hear of your arrangements from my own parlour-maid. I may be old-fashioned, I dare say I am, but in my young days elders were not so treated by the young."

Grandfather paused in the middle of the psalms to beam. "What does it matter whom we hear it from, dear Jane? I think the course Jocelyn has decided on is most sensible. Dear me, yes. . . . Thou visitest the earth and blessest it, Thou makest it very plenteous. The river of God is full of water. Thou preparest their corn, for so Thou providest for the earth. . . . We all need to have our minds broadened, especially the Dean."

"What exactly has Sarah told you, Grandmother?" inquired Jocelyn.

"I have never heard anything so ridiculous in all my life," said Grandmother. "I can't imagine what your poor mother will say. Or your father either, for that matter. I will say for Thomas that he knows what employment is suited to a gentleman and what not."

"All employment that is compatible with his religion is suited to a gentleman," announced Grandfather. "Do not forget, dear Jane, that the Apostles themselves were in trade. . . . Fish."

"What's that got to do with it?" asked Grandmother. "The Apostles were not my grandsons."

"Thou waterest her furrows," said Grandfather, continuing his perambulations. "Thou sendest rain into the little valleys thereof, Thou makest it soft with the drops of rain, and blessest the increase of it. . . . My dear Jane, just as God sends corn to feed our bodies so He sends books to feed our minds, and the farmer and the bookseller who act as intermediaries are the most blessed among men."

"We've never yet had a shopkeeper in the family," said Grandmother to Jocelyn. "And there are no drains in that house. And who's to provide the capital? Your poor Grandfather, I suppose."

"Who told Sarah I was going to open a shop?" demanded Jocelyn.

"The grocer, who had it from Martha Carroway at the sweet-shop."

"And how did she know?"

"That's neither here nor there, Jocelyn. The point is that you did not inform your Grandmother of your intentions, as you should have done, before informing the whole town."

"But, Grandmother, I haven't the slightest intention of keeping a bookshop. The whole thing is a canard. They abound in Torminster, Felicity Summers tells me."

"What's that?" said Grandmother.

Jocelyn said it again.

"I never heard of such a thing in all my life," said Grandmother when she understood the situation. "And who, I should like to know, is responsible for spreading these lies about my grandson? I'm going in now, Theobald, to talk to Sarah. This is not the first time I have had to reprimand her for listening to idle gossip."

Jocelyn gave Grandmother his arm across the lawn and then came back to Grandfather.

"Thou crownest the year with Thy goodness and the clouds drop fatness," said Grandfather, but he said it very sadly.

"Grandfather!" exclaimed Jocelyn. "Did you want me to open that bookshop?"

"Yes, Jocelyn, I did. Nothing could have given me greater pleasure. Dear me, yes. Just the thing."

"But why, Grandfather?"

"I thought you so suited to the vocation of a bookseller, Jocelyn. You have sympathy and tact. You would have understood the individual needs of your customers. ... And then I should have liked you to live in Ferranti's house."

"But why?"

"You might have been able to discover what has happened to him."

"But how?"

"A man always leaves the print of his personality on his dwelling-place. I thought that living there you might have got to understand what manner of man he was and then, aided by your knowledge, you might have been able to think what we ought to do to find out what has become of him."

"Grandfather, aren't you being rather fantastic?"

"I dare say," said Grandfather forlornly. "I'm old."

"I'm so sorry to disappoint you," murmured Jocelyn.

"Yes, it's a disappointment," said Grandfather. "The moment I heard about it I felt you had been guided. It would have been a joy to me to find the little capital that would have been needed to start you." He sneezed sadly. "It's getting chilly. I think I'll go indoors. Have you any idea, dear boy, where I had got to in evensong?"

"You were somewhere in the psalms."

"Thank you. I shall have to go back to the beginning again now for fear I missed any out."

He walked sadly away, his shoulders a little bowed. His attitude seemed to beseech Jocelyn like Felicity's, "Please! Please!"

"I'll think about it, Grandfather," he said suddenly.

Grandfather swung round, beaming. "That's right, dear boy, that's right. But mind you *do* think. Don't just take out your feelings and look at them, which is what passes for thought with most of us pitiful, self-centred creatures. Look at the question from everyone's point of view, not forgetting that of this illiterate city."

He went indoors, leaving Jocelyn to pace backwards

and forwards on the lawn. He was under the impression that he was thinking things out, but in reality he was only reiterating the one idea that was uppermost in his mind. ... His pride would not allow Grandfather to finance him.... The old man was not wealthy. He would have to take up capital that would be needed later on for Henrietta and Hugh Anthony. The whole idea was preposterous.

The garden door flew open and Henrietta burst in. Her hat had as usual slipped off backwards and dangled by its elastic, her face was flushed and her eyes shining. She looked so lovely that Jocelyn stopped dead with astonishment and allowed his one idea to evaporate.

She careered straight through Grandmother's best flower-bed and flung herself upon him. "I'm so glad! I'm so glad!" she panted.

"What about, Henrietta?" he asked, holding her by her thin elbows and looking down at her transfigured face.

"That you are to live in that little house."

"Who told you I was to live in that little house?"

"Felicity. ... Now it won't be lonely any more and I shall help you sell in the shop."

Jocelyn let go of her elbows and thrust his hands ruefully into his pockets. "*Et tu, Brute!*" he remarked.

His tone chilled Henrietta and fright seized her. "But you are? You are?" she asked wildly.

"But why should you care so much, Henrietta?"

"I do! You must! I want to sell in the shop!" she cried, and began hammering him with her fists. All the joy had left her face and she looked like one of the furies in infancy.

"You will? You will?" she demanded.

He could not endure to see that look on her face and he took hold of her pummelling fists reassuringly.

"Yes, Henrietta, I will," he said.

CHAPTER V

I

IN the difficult weeks that followed Jocelyn consoled himself by thinking that none of it was his responsibility. Torminster had decided that the empty house in the Market Place must be turned into a bookshop and that he must keep it, and he had no choice but to obey.

But it was all very difficult. Grandmother and Jocelyn's family detested the idea. They had never yet had a shopkeeper in the family and it had been their earnest hope that they never would. . . . It was not gentlemanly. . . . Jocelyn reminded them that the family fortunes had been laid by an Irvin who kept a tannery in the reign of Queen Anne and lost by an Irvin in the reign of George the Fourth who thought that tanning was too smelly to be gentlemanly and exchanged it for card-playing in good society.

"Playing games in good society doesn't pay," said Jocelyn, " so I'd better go back to the leather."

But his family snorted and pished and produced for his inspection just what he had been afraid they would produce, a job in an office in Whitehall or a secretaryship to someone who sat about in the House of Commons when he felt like it and dictated his autobiography to his secretary when he did not. The promise of both these positions had been procured for Jocelyn by his family by much hard work, and the giving of several little dinners that they couldn't afford, and they were rightly incensed when he refused them.

"I'd die in an office," said Jocelyn, "and if that old idiot Enderby-Wetherby started dictating his past life to

me I should start telling him what I thought of it. . . .
No. . . . I shall keep that bookshop."

His father once more blew down his nose contemptuously and his brother Hubert for the thousandth time implored him not to be more of a fool than he could help, further remarking that if he liked to behave like a lunatic he could not expect financial assistance from the family along the road to Broadmoor.

"I don't," said Jocelyn. "Torminster wants me, so Torminster shall lend me a hand."

But it was Grandmother who was perhaps more outraged than anyone else. The rest of the family would have Jocelyn making a fool of himself at a comfortable distance, but she would have him doing it at her very door. Every time she bought a leg of mutton from Mr. Atkins the butcher she would be obliged to remember that her own grandson was a colleague of Mr. Atkins, and Mr. Atkins would remember it too and the mutton would probably be tough in consequence. And every time she bought a reel of cotton from Mr. Bell the draper she would remember that just behind her, across the Market Place, Jocelyn was selling *Eric, or Little by Little* to Canon Elphinstone for Canon Elphinstone's grandson's birthday present. . . . The same wooden counter that separated her from Mr. Bell, emphasizing the gulf between them, would be separating Canon Elphinstone from her own grandson. . . . And Canon Elphinstone, whose blood, people said, was not nearly so blue as he gave one to understand, would be very patronizing about it.

But though Grandmother was outraged she was bountiful. There was a strain of generosity in her that shot up every now and then like a volcano. It had erupted when she acquiesced in the adoption of Henrietta and it erupted now when she announced, in the middle of telling Jocelyn what she thought of him, that though Grandfather was paying for the books she, out of her own money, intended to pay the first month's rent.

"Grandmother!" gasped Jocelyn, overwhelmed.

"You may be an idiot, Jocelyn," she snapped, "but at least you shall not be a starving idiot.... Not while I live, that is.... I'm fond of you, Jocelyn," she finished suddenly.

Jocelyn kissed her and thanked her and apologized a little desperately for the burden that he was to everybody who had anything to do with him.

For Jocelyn was not enjoying himself. Grandfather and Grandmother seemed pouring out a mint of money on top of him and he felt suffocated beneath it. And he felt humiliated, for who knew if the shop would pay, and if it did not how could he ever hold up his head again?

Yet he persevered, for he did not seem able to help himself. When he tried to think how it had all come about he found that he had not the slightest idea; but one thing he did know: he had been carried to the place where he found himself by something other than his own will.... It was almost as though the wind of destiny that Grandfather had spoken of had suddenly arisen and lifted him off his feet.

II

But if Jocelyn was not altogether enjoying himself, Felicity was. She was taking several months' rest from the stage and had meant to pay a round of visits to adoring friends, but the shop fascinated her so much that she threw over the adoring friends and remained on the spot to help with the books.

Hugh Anthony was enjoying himself too, asking questions about shopkeeping, and Henrietta and Grandfather, and old Martha of the sweet-shop, who had taken such a fancy to Jocelyn that she announced she would come every morning and "do" for him, leaving the sweets to the care of old Mary and their niece 'Arriet Kate, who though a little wanting in the top story could always manage the change if the kind customers told her what to give. . . . In fact they were all enjoying themselves, except Jocelyn.

Yet even he felt happy sometimes, for he already had for the house with the green door an almost passionate love, and in preparing it for its duties he imagined he felt as a mother must do who dresses her daughter for her bridal.

The front room with the bow-window made a perfect shop. Mr. Loveday, the carpenter and undertaker, very kindly gave them a lot of coffin wood for the shelves quite cheaply. Something about the misty atmosphere of Torminster made everyone live till a hundred and ten, and poor Mr. Loveday, who had only come to the city recently and had been unaware of the preservative quality of its atmosphere, found the coffin trade not what he had expected and was only too thankful for the work of erecting the shelves. There were curved tiers of them in the window, taking the curve of the bow in a most artistic way but not high, so as not to obscure the charming view of Jocelyn inside behind the counter. The walls of the room, and of the little room on the other side of the passage that was to house the library books, were lined from floor to ceiling with shelves, and the floorboards were varnished and polished till they shone like ebony.

The green door was given a coat of new emerald paint and the doors and window-frames inside the front rooms were painted scarlet. It was Henrietta's taste. Jocelyn thought it too bright, but was not listened to.

Felicity was enchanted by the beautiful old kitchen with its beams and rose-red tiles, which had been scrubbed till they took on an almost velvety softness. She bought copper pots and rose-sprigged china, and Grandmother, with another outburst of generosity, unearthed some lovely old silver that she did not use and gave it to Jocelyn for a present.

Jocelyn's mother who, though she dared not say so to

Thomas her husband and Hubert her son, was thrilled by the whole thing, bought lengths of Liberty material out of money she ought to have been buying new blankets with and sent them to Jocelyn for curtains and cushion-covers. Sarah cut them out and Felicity and Henrietta made them, sitting on Grandmother's drawing-room floor and stitching away under her sharp eye.

Felicity was an expert sewer. Her seams were straight as the high road and her neat stitches marched along them at regular intervals like well-drilled soldiers. She never pricked her finger, she kept her cotton clean and she sang as she worked. . . . Henrietta watched her sew in marvelling adoration.

For with Henrietta it was otherwise. Her stitches progressed along her seams like poor little hunchbacks crawling up twisted country lanes. Somehow her cotton, though it might start life blue or pink or green, was always jet black by the time she had been sewing with it for five minutes, and the progress of its journey was marked by dots of blood. But she would not give in. Felicity, Grandmother, Miss Lavender, Ellen and Sarah all offered to relieve her of her pair of curtains, but she would not hear of it. She sewed on and on, hour after hour, breathing heavily, and now and then, when no one saw her, crying a little because her pricked finger was so sore. When at last the labour of love was completed Felicity hung the curtains in the post of honour, the window of Jocelyn's sitting-room looking on the garden. And she did not wash out Henrietta's bloodstains, instead she pointed them out to Jocelyn. "Not every man," she said to him severely, "can say that a woman has literally bled for him."

This sitting-room was the only room in which Jocelyn did not allow himself to be dominated by feminine taste. He sent to London for his few personal treasures and locked the door on the inside while he arranged them. He hung school and regimental groups and a few etchings against the old panelling of the room and spread a shabby but beautiful Persian rug on the floor. He stacked his pipes on the mantelpiece and bought a table and bookcases for his books and two comfortable but modern armchairs from Mr. Bell across the way, who furnished as well as draped. He heaped his walking-sticks in one corner and his fishing tackle in another and put hooks in a third to hang his mackintosh and gardening hat on.

"It won't do, Jocelyn," said Felicity, when admitted. "It simply won't do. The rug is lovely, but it clashes with the curtains, and the chairs are too modern. You want period pieces in a house like this. Look how lovely your bedroom looks, with the little four-poster and the old chest of drawers. . . . You oughtn't to mix etchings with dreadful groups of moustached soldiers, and schoolboys don't look right on panelling."

"They are my friends," Jocelyn told her gently, "and it's my panelling. You know, Felicity, I care about beautiful things as much as you do, but everyone needs one room where they can heap up their past regardless of beauty. Every picture and stick and pipe in this room reminds me a bit of the past that I liked. One can relax in one's past. One hasn't got to do anything about it any more. . . . And it's companionable, too."

Felicity looked up at him anxiously. "Will you be lonely here? Will you regret coming here and hate me for helping to make you come?"

The June sunshine lay in patches on the floor, outside in the garden the roses were in bud and Felicity in her blue frock looked entrancing. . . . Jocelyn laughed, for loneliness seemed as far away as last night's dreams.

"I don't think I shall ever regret coming," he said. "I haven't enjoyed humbling myself to do it, and perhaps I shall go through times in this house that I shan't enjoy either, but I promise you that I'll never regret."

His last word seemed to fall into the stillness of the room like a stone flung into a well. It seemed to Felicity that its falling sent ripples outwards to the walls that broke in echo. "Regret." She could hear the sound of the spoken word fading away into silence yet living on in every room of the house. She walked to the door and then came suddenly back to Jocelyn, seizing his hands impetuously. "Don't regret!" she implored him. "Don't! There's been too much of it here. Regret for the past must be awful to bear. . . . One can't do anything about it any more. . . . You said that yourself."

"Felicity, what's the matter with you?" Jocelyn rallied her. "Come into the shop and see the till for the filthy lucre."

They went out and the room was left with only the word regret alive in it.

III

But the greatest excitement of all was the arrival of the books. Second-hand books for the library and glossy new volumes for the shop, red and blue and green and purple and black, with golden lettering and sometimes leaves edged with gold, so that when the books were closed it seemed as though wise words were enclosed in golden caskets.

Jocelyn, Felicity, Grandfather and the two children unpacked and arranged them. Jocelyn and Felicity did the unpacking and sorting and Henrietta and Hugh Anthony ran backwards and forwards from the counter to the shelves putting the books in their places. Grandfather did the same, arranging one book per half-hour because he always had to stop and read some of it before he put it away.

Half-way through the afternoon he stopped stock-still in the middle of the floor, *Pride and Prejudice* in one hand and *Wuthering Heights* in the other, to deliver a homily on the profession of a bookseller.

"It is the most friendly vocation in the world," he announced.

"Why?" asked Jocelyn. "Leave a hole just there, Henrietta, for Jane when Grandfather has finished holding her."

"A bookseller," said Grandfather, "is the link between mind and mind, the feeder of the hungry, very often the binder up of wounds. There he sits, your bookseller, surrounded by a thousand minds all done up neatly in cardboard cases; beautiful minds, courageous minds, strong minds, wise minds, all sorts and conditions. And there come into him other minds, hungry for beauty, for knowledge, for truth, for love, and to the best of his ability he satisfies them all. . . . Yes. . . . It's a great vocation."

"Greater than a writer's?" asked Felicity. "Yes, Hugh Anthony, leave a space for poor Emily on the third shelf."

"Immeasurably," said Grandfather. "A writer has to spin his work out of himself and the effect upon the character is often disastrous. It inflates the ego. Now your bookseller sinks his own ego in the thousand different egos that he introduces one to the other. . . . Yes. . . . Moreover his life is one of wide horizons. He deals in the stuff of eternity and there's no death in a bookseller's shop. Plato and Jane Austen and Keats sit side by side behind his back, Shakespeare is on his right hand and Shelley on his left." He paused for a moment while Felicity took *Pride and Prejudice* and *Wuthering Heights* gently away from him. "Yes. Writers, from what I've seen of them, are a very queer lot, but booksellers are the salt of the earth."

"Mr. Ferranti was a writer," said Henrietta.

"He was," said Grandfather sadly. "Poor fellow. The ego was terribly inflated. . . . Dear me, where did I put Jane and Emily?"

IV

It was the evening of the day before the shop was to open. The last book had been put in its place and the shop blind had been lowered to hide the glories within from the inquisitive gaze of Torminster. All his helpers had gone home and Jocelyn was alone in his house for the first time. He ate the supper that old Martha had left for him, cold ham and pickles and blancmange so hard that it needed a hatchet, in the kitchen with the rose-red floor. The copper pans that Felicity had arranged on the mantelpiece winked in such a charming way and reflected the red tiles with such a warm glow that they seemed alive, and such good company that he did not notice his loneliness.

But when he went into his sitting-room, the back room that had also been Ferranti's sitting-room, he did not feel so companioned. He was tired and the peculiar feelings that lie in wait to pounce upon those who are both tired and alone proceeded to pounce. The bits of his own past that surrounded him seemed to have receded very far away. His friends hanging on the walls seemed to be looking at him through a veil, and that veil, he felt, was another man's past. It was hanging all round him, obscuring his own, and like a mist it was closing in on him.

He had sat down in an arm-chair with a book, but suddenly he felt that he could not sit still. . . . And he was so cold. . . . The sunny June had given place to a wet July and outside his window the garden was wrapped in a cloak of soft, steady rain that never ceased for an instant. There was no wind and all day long there had not been one rent visible in the muffling pall that shrouded the world. The damp was awful. It penetrated every cranny and it seemed to Jocelyn that the atmosphere inside the house was as saturated with it as the atmosphere outside. It was the sort of weather that Torminster specialized in and its inhabitants were quite used to it, but to Jocelyn, on this his first introduction to its clamminess, it seemed unspeakably depressing.

He put on his mackintosh and went out to the shed

in the garden where he had stored the chopped-up wood of a dead apple-tree. He carried the logs into his sitting-room, fetched paper and matches and lit a fire. The lovely yellow flames burst into flower in the grate and the exquisite smell of burning apple-wood filled the room, as though it were the fragrance of the flame petals.

Jocelyn lit a pipe and drew thankfully nearer to the golden comfort. The damp of the room seemed conquered and the mist that had been closing in on him drew back. . . . He was reminded of a man who lights a fire in a jungle to keep the wild beasts at bay.

He was deep in his book when a knock at the front door startled him. He went down the dark, damp little passage and opened the door almost apprehensively, but outside in the dripping Market Place was no one more alarming than Grandfather, muffled in his voluminous cloak and with his immense old green umbrella erected over his round hat.

"Come in," cried Jocelyn. "Whatever made you come out again in all this wet?"

"I thought you might be lonely," said Grandfather. "Yes. Depressing sort of evening for your first night. I'm lonely myself. Your dear Grandmother has gone to bed early with a cold and Felicity is up in London. Coming back by the late train. Thank you, my dear boy, if you could manage to put the umbrella down."

In the passage Grandfather tenderly uncovered a parcel of books that he was carrying under his cloak. "Ferranti's books," he said. "After his disappearance there was a sale and I bought these—all he had left, poor fellow, that he had not already sold. I did not want them to fall into unsympathetic hands. . . . Yes. . . They are yours now."

"Do you want to give them to me?" asked Jocelyn.

"Yes. They belong here."

Jocelyn hung up Grandfather's cloak in the passage and led the way into the fire-lit sitting-room. He pulled up a second chair to the fire and then went to the kitchen to get hot coffee. Only when two cups of it were steaming on the table between them did he look at the books. There were only three of them, Shakespeare, Byron and Shelley.

"Did he only have these three left at the time of his disappearance?" he asked, holding the shabby volumes between his hands.

"That's all. He had parted with nearly all his possessions. . . . What excellent coffee. Did Martha make it?"

"Yes," said Jocelyn. "But I think that old saint Mary must have made the blancmange I had for supper. It was the kind of blancmange," he added vindictively, "that only a spiritually minded woman would make."

"Mary," said Grandfather, "was once the Archdeacon's cook, but though her influence on the household was very great her beef-and-kidney pudding did not agree with the Archdeacon and he pensioned her off."

Jocelyn carried Ferranti's books to the bookcase and put them with his own. He did not question the gift of them, he did not even say thank you, for it seemed to him quite right that the only tangible things left from Ferranti's past should live here with his. Coming back to the fire he piled on more logs and settled himself in front of Grandfather.

"Tell me about Ferranti," he said.

"There's so little to tell," sighed Grandfather. "That was the trouble with Ferranti, he could tell one nothing. He was an egoist who could not let himself loose in words. The poison of self-absorption had no outlet, if you understand me, and I am afraid that it may have drowned him."

"He lived to himself?" asked Jocelyn.

"Entirely. He was here for two years and as far as I know made no single intimate friend."

"Not even yourself?"

"I tried," said the old man humbly, "but I failed. I

was a friend, but not intimate. I came to see him often, and he came to see me, and we talked of books and music and the fair beauties of this world, but of intimate things he would never speak. I could never get near him. It is difficult to take the citadel of another man's being by storm, dear me, yes, but my failure there I count the worst of the sins I have committed against my God."

He stretched out his hands to the fire and Jocelyn saw to his astonishment that they were trembling. "Sin?" he questioned smiling. "Do you call it a sin that you could not force the confidence of a reserved egoist?"

The old man raised troubled eyes. "When a life is shipwrecked," he said, "one asks oneself, what were those near at hand doing that they did not prevent it?"

"Some ships," said Jocelyn gently, "sail so far away by themselves that no one can get to them when they sink. In a case like that the only man to blame is the man who owns the ship and sets the course."

"I cannot accept your comfort without adding the sin of self-deception to the sin of my failure," said Grandfather. "I know quite well that if after seventy-eight years of the enjoyment of God's goodness I cannot at the end of it kindle a spark of belief in a fellow-creature then I am not worthy of the bounty I have received."

Grandfather's self-scourging was pitiful to see and Jocelyn tried hard to comfort him. "You attempted the impossible," he said. "Some of us are lucky enough to find a causeway for our feet across the slough of this world; belief in God, belief in love, belief in a sound core at the heart of seeming rottenness; something or other. But we find it for ourselves. It's the tragedy of life that we can't communicate it."

"It is to our shame if we cannot."

"Not always. For what can we do? We can cry aloud and hold out a hand to another man, but even though he may take our hand and come nearer to us we have no way of forcing his feet to find rock. That he must do for himself. If he's too lazy or too paralysed by self-absorption or misery to make the effort we can't help that."

"You're wrong there," sighed Grandfather. "A life, such as mine, that has known God's goodness, should act like a magnet. Yes. I can claim no such triumph of personality and therefore I have failed."

"We can't agree," smiled Jocelyn. "Tell me more of Ferranti. Where he came from, what he wrote, why he failed."

"Dear me, yes," said Grandfather. "I came to talk of Ferranti and stay to talk of myself. How typical that is of human nature. How typical of my own gross selfishness. . . . Dear me, now I'm starting on my own gross selfishness. . . . Yes. Ferranti. Where was I?"

"Where did he come from?" asked Jocelyn.

"He had lived for years abroad, he told me, chiefly in Italy, for he was partly Italian, but that was all I could find out. He had that fanatical, dangerous love of beauty, that 'desire of the moth for the star,' that can be content with nothing but perfection. . . . Yes. . . . He could not be content, as we must be in this world, to worship beauty amid imperfection. If he had seen a lovely picture in an ugly frame he would, I think, have destroyed picture and frame together in his rage. From his complete loneliness I gathered that he must have turned aside from every human relationship the moment that it failed to satisfy his ideal."

"And his verse?" asked Jocelyn.

"That was his passion. Dear me, yes. It was the way in which he had elected to serve beauty and nothing would turn him aside from it. He had that fatal gift of identifying his whole being with one object only. . . . Yes. . . . There's a touch of greatness there, but it's dangerous."

"And as a poet he was a failure?"

"How could he be anything else? He wrote the sort of verse that only supersensitives such as himself could have appreciated. You know what I mean. It dealt with problems that are not problems to normal folk, and tortures they would never be likely to feel, and pleasures too delicate for their apprehension. It was verse that needed interpretation and he had no interpreter."

"Did he want a public or did he not care?"

"Of course he cared. He said to me once, 'At rock bottom living is merely a giving of personality in one form or another. If no one wants what you have to give you might as well hang yourself and have done with it.'"

"That sounds bad," said Jocelyn. "The sort of temperament that would turn melancholic under strain."

"Yes. Yes. And he suffered great strain. He told me one day that he had all the money he needed. Private means, he said. Yet, as I told you, when he disappeared we found that he had run through every penny of it. Pride, you see. Life is an appalling strain for those who are both proud and poor together.... The fear that he may have made away with himself haunts me night and day."

"In all that you have told me there are certainly the ingredients for a first-class tragedy," Jocelyn agreed. "But, if it happened, I can't see that it's any fault of yours. And I don't see either," he added gently, "what we can do about it now."

"If he still lives," said Grandfather, "he is not beyond our help. Dear me, no. As I said before, I think that you, living in this house, may yet be able to do something about it."

"Good heavens, what?" asked poor Jocelyn.

"That is for you to find out. You will say that I am shifting my burden on to you. Perhaps I am. But your shoulders are younger than mine.... Dear me, it's late.... I must get home or your dear Grandmother will be seriously displeased."

Jocelyn put his cloak about him, took him to the door, erected his umbrella and bade him good night. "I'll do all I can," he said to the troubled old man, but he spoke as one speaks to a child who has broken a toy beyond hope of repair. . . . For what could he do?

"Well, of all the fantastic nonsense," he said to himself when he was alone in his sitting-room again. "But what a dear old boy Grandfather is!"

He lit a pipe and settled down again, thinking. Grandfather had quoted Shelley and now scraps of Shelley's verse floated through his mind.

> "The desire of the moth for the star,
> Of the night for the morrow,
> The devotion to something afar
> From the sphere of our sorrow."

Yes, that was all right. That was the quest for beauty upon which every soul is engaged; but Ferranti, it seemed, had pursued the spirit of transcendent beauty only, and that way madness lay. Immanent beauty he had missed.

> "Spirit of beauty . . . where art thou gone?
> Why dost thou pass away and leave our state,
> This dim vast vale of tears, vacant and desolate?"

Had beauty always been for Ferranti an elusive, flying thing? Had it never, in this lovely city, sat beside him at his own hearth and brought him peace?

V

It grew dark and the world was still. Outside the silent rain muffled every sound and in Jocelyn's room the flames had ceased whispering and lay dead, still glowing rose-pink and in their winding-sheets of grey ash. It was so quiet that surely peace should have sat enthroned with Jocelyn, yet he had no sense of peace. Frustration, regret and sadness seemed to be written in the house. Although there was no sound and no movement anywhere Jocelyn felt that the stillness was that of impotence rather than of quiescence. . . . If the house could have spoken aloud it would have done so.

He got up and moved about the room, putting things away. He did not want to stay in this lonely room by himself and yet neither did he want to go upstairs to bed in the room above, where it would be horribly cold and even lonelier. Unused to loneliness as he was he felt decidedly queer. He was ashamed of himself, but he did. . . . He almost wished he had not come to live here. . . . It was a creepy place.

Then he resolutely lit his candle with his last match. He had told Felicity he would regret nothing. He might go through bad times here, but they should not drive him either to turn back or to regret the step that he had taken.

Carrying his candle he went out into the passage. The flame guttered in the draught and the chill damp was overpowering. "Spirit of beauty, where art thou gone?" The words said themselves over in his mind so insistently that he felt the question had been asked before in this house. "Spirit of beauty, where art thou?" As if in answer there was another knock at the front door. Jocelyn, stumbling up the stairs, started and dropped the candlestick, plunging himself in darkness. "Fool!" he said to himself, deeply ashamed of his own jarred nerves.

He groped his way to the door and opened it. The street lamp outside The Green Dragon faintly illumined a slim figure in a mackintosh with a dripping hat jammed down on golden hair.

"Felicity!" gasped Jocelyn. "You're beauty! You ought to have come knocking at this door when poor Ferranti lived here."

"I don't know what you're talking about," said Felicity. "I'm looking a perfect sight. . . . But I've brought you this."

She dumped something soft and nondescript into Jocelyn's arms and stretched her own in relief. "What a weight!" she groaned. "I've carried him all the way from the station. He wouldn't walk."

A cold, wet nose suddenly shot up into Jocelyn's face and a warm tongue was passed interrogatively over his chin. "Great scot!" said Jocelyn. "A dog!"

"Black," said Felicity. "Front elevation collie, rear elevation pomeranian. The man I bought him from said he was a spaniel, but I think myself that there's a dash of dachshund about the legs. If I were you I should call him Mixed Biscuits."

"Come in, Felicity," implored Jocelyn.

"I should think not, at this time of night. As it is it'll be all over Torminster by nine o'clock to-morrow that I carried a dead body to your house under cover of the darkness.... I've been thinking about you all day and wondering if you'd be lonely here, and then I saw him sitting in a cage in a shop window, all by himself, crying, and my course seemed clear. He bit the guard. Good night."

"You're an angel, Felicity," cried Jocelyn into the darkness, but she was gone, the rain and the night taking her. He stumbled along to the kitchen, found some matches, lit the lamp and looked at Mixed Biscuits. The creature had lived only a few months in this world and was apprehensive as to what it might do to him. Fearing the worst he rolled over on his back on the kitchen floor, holding up four bandy legs to heaven and exposing all his tenderest parts, thinking perhaps that an attitude of utter defencelessness was his best policy. He thudded his tail on the floor with a pathetically propitiatory action, rolled pleading dewy eyes and panted, exposing all his baby teeth and hanging out his tongue like a yard of pink ribbon.

"Good fellow!" said Jocelyn encouragingly, and placed the remains of the cold ham on a plate on the floor, with the blancmange on top as a relish.

There was a wild confusion of flying legs as Mixed Biscuits leapt right way up and attacked his food. With feet planted far apart, tail extended and quivering with ecstasy, body taut, jaws champing and tongue whirling round the plate with a circular motion that made the onlooker dizzy, he was an example of concentration to all. ... But he was not a tidy eater. ... Bits of blancmange flew into the air and portions of ham skidded along the floor in all directions. Jocelyn, in the intervals of pursuing them with a kitchen fork, gazed at Mixed Biscuits in astonishment.

He was, as Felicity had said, black. He was also woolly. His nose was long and his mouth large, but Jocelyn thought that viewed from the side he was more like a crocodile than a collie. His ears were immense, and flapped, and his tail was like a housemaid's brush. His poor body was weak and thin, as though good food had not come his way too often, and his legs were a great deal too large for the rest of him.

"Good lord!" said Jocelyn.

Mixed Biscuits polished up his empty plate with sweeping movements of his long pink tongue, sighed, panted, had a drink, sat down and looked at Jocelyn. His limpid eyes were exquisite and a character of unusual loveliness had already set its mark upon his countenance. Jocelyn fondled his silky ears with growing enthusiasm and Mixed Biscuits again flung himself on his back and erected his legs. But this time there was nothing cringing in his attitude. With a slight motion of his right forepaw he invited Jocelyn to scratch his chest. Jocelyn scratched, while Mixed Biscuits closed his eyes and simpered, and mutual affection grew every moment stronger.

"What about bed, old man?" asked Jocelyn at last. Mixed Biscuits had no objection and they went upstairs together. It was cold, and the candle sent queer shadows leaping over the walls, but Jocelyn was too absorbed in Mixed Biscuits to notice and climbed into bed with a sense of companionship warm about his heart and grateful thoughts of Felicity flocking like birds in his mind, ready to turn into dreams of beauty as soon as sleep gave them wings.

CHAPTER VI

I

JOCELYN'S fears that the shop would be a failure proved groundless. Torminster, rather to its own astonishment, took a pride and pleasure in Jocelyn and his books. There was something flattering in the fact that an intelligent young man from London should think it worth his while to settle down among them and minister to their intellectual needs. It implied that he had the highest opinion of their mental powers and was grieved that residence so far from the Metropolis should debar them from the full exercise of the same.

Everyone, from the Bishop and the Dean downwards, patronized the bookshop. They bought each other presents at it, they borrowed the library books, they discussed what they read with Jocelyn and they started a literary society. Even the tea-parties took on a mental flavour, the people who had read the latest books being careful to bring the conversation round to them and the people who had not saying, "Ah!" in a very profound way, and implying by their wrinkled brows that they were silent only from excess of thought. Grandmother, instead of finding herself looked down upon for having a grandson in trade, was astonished to find herself on a pinnacle as the relative of a literary character. People even asked her advice on books, and she said, "Don't ask me, I've no time for such rubbish," but was very pleased all the same.

"It can't last," said Jocelyn to Grandfather. "I'm a new turn, like a performing bear."

"I think it will last," said Grandfather. "In my experience when people once begin to read they go on.

They begin because they think they ought to and they go on because they must. Yes. They find it widens life. We're all greedy for life, you know, and our short span of existence can't give us all that we hunger for, the time is too short and our capacity not large enough. But in books we experience all life vicariously."

But Jocelyn became gradually a good deal more to Torminster than just its bookseller, he became its interpreter. He had the gift, born of sympathy and personal humility, of banishing restraint by giving people a good conceit of themselves, and so it happened that people like Mr. Bell the draper and his son Bert summoned courage to drop in in the evenings when the shops were shut and talk books with Jocelyn. In the end so many of them came, and so often, and stayed so long and talked so hard that he began to feel himself the host of a Parisian salon.

He was astonished at his success, both social and financial. He seemed popular as a man and secure as a tradesman, with friends in his back room and a balance, if microscopic, at the bank. He had found his niche and it gave him a glorious feeling of security. His feet seemed set firmly on the causeway of which he had spoken to Grandfather and the slough of the world all round him seemed less black.

But it was there. Side by side with his new happiness there lived with him in the house that sadness that had weighed him down on his first night. How could he rejoice whole-heartedly in his own firm footing when another had not found it here? He felt as though the thread of his own life was woven with that of another, a light thread with a dark, and until both of them were light he could not feel at peace.

II

A certain Wednesday in September dawned mellow

and still. It was the time of year when Torminster was at its loveliest, a moment when it seemed that the streets of the city were paved with gold. The sky above the town was a stainless blue, but below it the faint mist of autumn hung over roofs and towers, a mist that seemed to be of gold dust, as though the sun that burned all day in a glory of raying flame had let fall a distillation of itself that warmed as dew refreshes.

Everywhere there seemed a suggestion of fires burning, orange and red and gold. In the gardens of the Close were scarlet dahlias and yellow chrysanthemums, while the trees on the Tor and the elms on the Cathedral Green were pure gold.

In the utter peace and stillness the world seemed holding its breath, a little apprehensively, drawing near to the fire to warm itself. There was none of that sense of urgeful, pushing life that robs even a calm spring day of the sense of silence; life was over and the year was just waiting, harbouring its strength for the final storms and turmoil of its death. The warmth and the colour of maturity were there, exultant and burning, visible to the eyes, but the prophecy of decay was felt in a faint shiver of cold at morning and evening and a tiny sigh of the elms at midnight when a wandering ghost of a wind plucked a little of their gold away from them.

Jocelyn got up on that Wednesday morning in the best of spirits, for it was early-closing day. This afternoon the shop would be shut and he would be a free man. He loved his new life, but its airlessness irked him sometimes and the exercising of Mixed Biscuits was a problem that at times seemed to fill the whole world; especially at night when Mixed Biscuits, suffering from insomnia for lack of walks, alternately howled at the moon, chased mice and slaked his thirst at the water jug.

As he dressed and shaved Jocelyn looked out of the window. In his tangled garden, as in all the gardens of Torminster, there was a riot of flaming flowers. The red-hot pokers were looking especially proud that morning, spearing up from among their lesser brethren with the arrogance of the Cathedral towers themselves. Beyond them the woods and hills were shrouded in mist and beyond those again the eastern sky was still a gold-barred lattice window that the sun looked through.

Jocelyn went downstairs, unlocked the front door, sent Mixed Biscuits into the garden to bark at the blackbirds and set about getting his breakfast. He did not allow Martha to come to his assistance until later in the morning, when old Mary had been arrayed in her petticoats and the sweet-shop started for the day.

He hummed a tune as he fried his bacon over the oil-stove, wondering who would come to the shop this morning. The coming and going of customers was a continual amusement and interest, for unconsciously they revealed so much of themselves to him that he felt at times as though he was the audience in a theatre and each ring of his shop-bell was the ring that sent up the curtain on a human drama. . . . It was absurd how people showed their character while shopping. . . . Their decision or their lack of it; their attitude towards the weather; their taste in books and bindings; the way in which they treated Jocelyn himself, some of them being aware of his humanity, grateful for it and courteous towards it, and others regarding him merely as the Man in the Shop, an automaton whose feelings need not in any way be considered; their reaction to the fact that an ordered book had not come yet; the way they behaved if Mixed Biscuits tripped them up on the doorstep; all these things were straws which showed which way the wind blew, and sometimes Jocelyn felt that what he did not know about the character of every reading man, woman and child in Torminster was not worth knowing.

He had just finished his breakfast when Martha arrived, cheery as ever, with her little black bonnet perched delicately on top of her head and her jet-trimmed mantle hiding the working print dress that she wore beneath it from the gaze of Torminster. . . . For when Martha crossed the Market Place from her house to Jocelyn's she always dressed up as though she were bound for America. . . . Besides the bonnet and mantle she wore gloves, and on windy days a veil, and she carried her apron in a brown paper parcel fastened with safety-pins.

When Jocelyn had greeted her he went out into the Market Place to take down his shutters. This daily opening of the shop was a continual delight to him. As he came out into the sunlight, where the pigeons were whirling softly through the golden air and the sleepy cats were stretching themselves in the sun, he glanced round him to see who else had come out to take their shutters down. . . . Yes, they were all there. . . . The landlord of The Green Dragon, Mr. Bell, Mr. Jones, Mr. Atkins, Mr. Loveday, 'Arriet Kate of the sweet-shop and several others. They glanced at each other across the Market Place and nodded and smiled, for this was their hour of fellowship and in the absence of those whom they served they were conscious of each other as a brotherhood of servers, and then, with a creaking and grinding, the shutters came down and the eyes of the shops were open. Nine o'clock rang out from the Cathedral, mellow and lovely, and the work of the day had begun.

Jocelyn took a duster from his pocket and began polishing his bow-window from the outside. As he smoothed its face lovingly, going carefully into all the corners, he remembered how, when he had first seen this window, even though the shop behind had been empty, he had thought of it as being bulged outwards by the wealth behind. . . . Well, the wealth was there now, rows and rows of it, the greatest treasures of mankind.

He went into the shop, accompanied by Mixed

Biscuits, and began dusting and rearranging and reading the books, a job that kept him endlessly happy between the visits of customers. His desultory reading during the daytime was giving him a nodding acquaintance with nearly every author in the shop and during the long evenings when the shop was closed he picked out a few of them and let the acquaintance deepen into friendship.

III

But to-day he did not get farther than a few nods and bows, for the shop-bell tinkled and the curtain rang up on the drama of the Dean of Torminster. He was a character. He had a commanding figure, bushy white side-whiskers and legs especially moulded by Nature to wear gaiters. Like Mr. Gotobed he always wore a top-hat, but whereas Mr. Gotobed's hat was always poised on the back of the head the Dean's was always tipped forward over the nose, which was in this case aquiline. The Dean's blood was very blue indeed and his balance at the bank heavy. These things, he thought, were to his credit, and the knowledge tinged his bearing and his high-pitched, nasal, fluting voice with a slight pomposity. As a Father in God he had his limitations, but as a figurehead he was perfect, and as such Torminster was proud to wear him on the prow of its ship.

"Fine day, fine day," piped the Dean, as though patronizing it, and tripped over Mixed Biscuits. "Must this animal take upon himself the duties of a doormat?" he continued in icy and falsetto annoyance, though the catastrophe was just as much his fault as Mixed Biscuits', for why should Mixed Biscuits look out for him any more than he for Mixed Biscuits? But the Dean was one of those who are far more aware of the obligations of others to them than of theirs to others. . . . Mixed Biscuits, unapologized to for a nasty kick on the hind parts, growled and went under the counter. . . . "And might one ask what kind of a dog he is?" went on the Dean, implying that Mixed Biscuits' lack of breeding should prevent him from sunning himself on a respectable doormat.

"I've decided to call him a Rumanian mousehound," said Jocelyn a little coldly.

"Ah!" commented the Dean, "another of these Balkan problems," and became quite sunny again, for no one appreciated his occasional gleams of humour more than he did himself.

"What can I do for you?" asked Jocelyn.

The Dean sat down, readjusted his top-hat and folded his hands on top of his silver-headed stick.

"This annual difficulty of the choir-school prize-giving," he proclaimed through his nose, "will be upon us in a couple of months and I should like to consult with you upon the choice of books for that purpose."

Jocelyn bowed with great solemnity to hide the twinkle in his eyes. He always enjoyed the Dean immensely.

"For the dear boys these are the formative years," continued the Dean, "and I realize the importance of the personal touch. I write each boy's name in his book with my own hand and I trust that the book with its inscription will recall to him throughout life the few words that I may have occasion to speak at the moment of presentation. But I naturally cannot set my seal to any work but that of the highest quality."

Jocelyn quite saw that.

"The books should be instructive but not heavy," fluted the Dean, "suitable to their tender years yet sufficiently advanced in thought to act as counsellors through life, and of course of irreproachable purity.... Difficult.... Difficult."

Jocelyn agreed that it was.

"And what would you suggest?"

"Verse," said Jocelyn promptly.

"Eh?" piped the Dean, surprised. "Personally I distrust verse. There is a luxuriance about it that appears to me slightly sensual."

"Why should luxuriance be sensual?" asked Jocelyn. "Look at the seraphim.... All that wing."

The Dean thought this remark flippant and waved it aside with the well-kept left hand that wore a diamond ring. "May I inquire your reasons for advising verse?" he asked.

"Children love good poetry," said Jocelyn. "It appeals to their sense of rhythm, I think.... You know how a baby loves to watch anything swinging.... And grown people love it because its very luxuriance recaptures their youth for them. Therefore verse fulfils one of your requirements and provides something that will appeal throughout life."

"H'm. Yes," said the Dean. "Possibly, possibly."

"And then as regards instruction without heaviness," said Jocelyn. "I have heard it said that real poetry is always the expression of very intense perception. The jog-trot of prose is sufficient for the mere observer to record his observations in, but the man who has seen behind an appearance to its significance employs winged verse. He must, like a lark, leap up above the material plane if he is to convey any impression of the significance to which he has penetrated."

"I doubt if I follow you," said the Dean shortly.... There were times when he had a very slight suspicion that Jocelyn led him on.

"When an artist, be he poet or painter, has expressed the significance of a thing he has said the inevitable word on that subject and by doing so has created a masterpiece. And surely a masterpiece is instructive? And it is certainly never heavy or, as Anatole France tells us, it could not fly over the ages in the way it does."

"Possibly, possibly," said the Dean. "But we are still left with the need for literature of irreproachable purity.

The lives of the poets do not always show that. Shelley, for instance.... Regrettable.... Regrettable."

"That's got nothing to do with it."

"Eh?"

"You've got no business to inquire into an artist's private life."

The Dean snorted. He enjoyed his talks with Jocelyn, but there were times when the young man presumed.

"It's got nothing to do with you unless you happen to be attending his soul in a professional capacity," continued the intrepid Jocelyn. "What matters to you is what he gives you, not the flaws in a personality that has perhaps been cracked and strained by the effort of giving."

"Possibly, possibly," said the Dean, and then, with a sudden change of tone, "Ah! Spring roses and June sunshine!"

He was gazing out of the window, preening himself slightly and inserting his eyeglass as he did so, for outside in the Market Place was Felicity.

The Dean had an eye for a pretty woman. Never did he allow it to lead him beyond the bounds of propriety, but still, he had it. "Ah!" he said again. "Exquisite! Exquisite!"

Both men gazed, the Dean with the appraising yet detached eye of the connoisseur, Jocelyn with the hunger of the lover.

Felicity was standing by the holy well among the pigeons, feeding them and watching them, engrossed in them, her body taut in its habitual attitude of poised attentiveness, as though she had sent her mind up into the air with the pigeons and her body were just going to take wing to join it. She wore yellow to-day, instead of her usual blue, and looked as though she were spun out of the warm air and the golden light of autumn. The pigeons were strutting round her feet and circling round her head and shoulders, obscuring her gold with the silvery colour of their wings. Jocelyn had not noticed that they flocked round other people as they did round Felicity, but then all birds and animals loved her. Like all happy people she always seemed to be very close to the earth and to all growing, living things. Perhaps her joy in life gave her a special unity with all forms of life, and entry into that state of awareness where self's forgotten and the horizon of love creeps out and out until it embraces all that can be seen and known while the body still hems in the spirit.

"Charming, charming," said the Dean. "A little too thin, perhaps, but very nearly perfection. Do you know the lady?"

"She is Mrs. Jameson's goddaughter."

"I should be honoured by an introduction."

Jocelyn could have cheerfully slain him, for it was a crime to disturb that picture of golden stillness and silvery movement. . . . What was more he was not going to. . . . He strolled to the front door and stood watching, letting the picture of Felicity grave itself so deeply on his mind that when with the passing of time it would seem to other people that she had grown old and lost her beauty it would not seem so to him.

But his attention was too burning not to affect her. She felt it as a warmth in her secret spot of loneliness and she swung round towards him as one turns unconsciously towards a fire. "The Dean," said Jocelyn, strolling towards her, "wishes to be introduced. You're a little too thin, perhaps, but charming."

Felicity, her eyes twinkling, returned with him to the shop, where the Dean had risen to his feet and removed his hat.

The introduction took place, the Dean and Felicity seated themselves on Jocelyn's two hard shop chairs and exchanged beautiful Victorian compliments, Felicity rising to the occasion with amazing histrionic skill.

"Will you convey my compliments to your admirable

godmother," summed up the Dean at the end of a quarter of an hour, "and my wife and I will be delighted if you will both drink tea with us on Thursday next."

"I am unfortunately obliged to leave Torminster this afternoon," said Felicity sweetly, "but I am sure that my godmother will be most happy to accept your invitation."

The Dean was perturbed. His wife could not stand Mrs. Jameson, and if she were to turn up on Thursday next undiluted by Felicity he feared that there would be domestic trouble later. . . . But his courtesy was not only on the surface. . . . "Delighted, delighted," he murmured distractedly. "My wife will write. Good day. Good day."

He shook hands, bowed, re-poised his top-hat over his aquiline nose and issued out into the Market Place in some distress of mind, entirely forgetting the choirboys' books.

"Now that was really wrong of me," said Felicity with contrition. "But it hurts Aunt Adelaide that they never ask her to the Deanery, and now they'll have to."

But Jocelyn was not interested in Aunt Adelaide's feelings. "Are you really going to-day?" he asked.

"Yes. I was coming to say good-bye when you saw me. I've been offered a part in a new play."

Jocelyn felt stricken, the more so that he had not realized until this moment what it would mean if Felicity went away. There was suddenly no warmth in the sunshine and no brightness in the fires of autumn. The chill of it, that sighed at midnight and touched the morning and the evening with icy fingers, struck at him like a sword. . . . These warm lovers of life, born under dancing stars, how without them was life tolerable for those, such as himself, whose bias was towards sadness, their stars cloud-hidden when their spirits woke to life. . . . In this world, surely, there should always be a mating between the lovers of life and the endurers of it, in couples they should find a causeway for their feet and walk it together, the star-shine of the one comforting the darkness of the other.

"When will you be back?" he asked tonelessly.

"If the play is a failure, and it's so clever and beautiful that it's sure to be, I shall be back for Christmas."

"You'll be glad to get back to your work?"

"Yes. I love it."

"Is it so wonderful?" He spoke carelessly, trying to hide his burning eagerness to know just how much her stage life meant to her.

"Of course it's wonderful. It's the only form of art in which you actually feel what you are giving accepted. It gives you a glorious feeling of power."

"And fills every corner of your life?"

"Of course it doesn't. How silly you're being, Jocelyn! It wouldn't fill every corner of me unless I were a genius, and I'm not, I'm only a perfectly ordinary woman gifted with a personality that happens to give pleasure on the stage. And that life has not got the whole of me; there seems to be something of me, the kernel perhaps, that I can't give to it however much I try. I couldn't give up my work, but I want something besides, something deeper that will satisfy deep things in me."

Their eyes met and she hoped she had made herself understood, but feared not, men were so obtuse. . . .

"I wonder what sort of financial condition the shop will be in when you come back," said Jocelyn lightly. Their eyes met again and he hoped he had made her see what he was driving at, but was afraid not—women being sometimes rather slow at the uptake.

Further mutual enlightenment was impossible, for the Dean reappeared, slightly breathless. Half-way home it had occurred to his subconscious mind that if he did not go back and have another good look at Felicity he would not get the chance again for some while to come. This idea, slightly altered in transit, appeared in his conscious mind as a conviction that it was his plain duty to go back to the bookshop and settle the matter of the choirboys' prizes.

"Ah, Miss Felicity!" he proclaimed, hat in hand. "Still here?"

"I'm just going home."

"Then I can have the happiness of offering my escort. Permit me."

He offered his arm with an air, Felicity accepting it with an even greater air.

"I'll see you off at the station," whispered Jocelyn.

"Two-forty-five," whispered Felicity.

"Send up a selection of the poets to the Deanery, Captain Irvin," piped the Dean. Then he and Felicity bowed to Jocelyn, swept from the shop, sailed across the Market Place and glided superbly towards the Close, exchanging mutual compliments as they went.

Only in Torminster, thought Jocelyn as he watched them, was the world sufficiently leisured for such a display of *la politesse*.

IV

The rest of the day was exhausting. When the Dean and Felicity had disappeared there was a constant stream of ladies to change their library books before the shop shut for the day. Ladies with library books could be very irritating, Jocelyn found. They wanted the perfect book without knowing what it was called or who it was by, and when nothing in the library seemed to be just right they blamed Jocelyn. On the rare occasions when they did know what they wanted it was always out and they again blamed Jocelyn.

"I want a *nice* book," they would say to him.

"What kind?" he would say.

"Oh, just nice. . . . By the way, I didn't like the second book by that man, I can't remember his name, but you know who I mean; it was quite different from his first."

"But he couldn't write the same one over again, could he?"

"Well, anyway, I didn't like it, and I don't know why you gave it to me. Can't you find me a really nice book?"

Or they would say, "I want a book for my husband to read over the week-end."

"What sort of book?" he would say with a little sigh, for week-end husbands were the worst problem of all.

"Something he hasn't read before."

"What has he read before?"

"Really, he reads so many I can't keep pace. You choose. You're a man and you ought to know what men like."

"What did he say about the last one I sent him?"

"He said he wasn't senile yet."

After lunch there was Felicity to be seen off at the station. They travelled down in the bus, accompanied by Henrietta and Hugh Anthony, so that conversation was impossible. The only really private remark that Felicity managed to murmur in a moment's quiet was, "Read that story of Ferranti's before I come back."

"You're as bad as Grandfather," sighed Jocelyn. "I'm a jaded bookseller, not a magician."

Then, when Felicity had gone, Mixed Biscuits had to be exercised. Jocelyn and the children took him round by the Palace, his favourite walk, because he could bark at the swans on the moat. At the far end of the Market Place yet another of the archways in which Torminster abounded led to the great trees and green grass that surrounded the moated Bishop's Palace. If the houses in the Close, hidden behind their high walls, could be seen with the eyes of imagination as fortresses, the Palace was one in actual fact. Grey, battlemented walls, with loopholes for arrows, surrounded it and its gardens, completely hiding them from sight, and a wide moat, brimful of water, surrounded the walls. The portcullis was still there, and the drawbridge that linked this warlike island to the peace of Torminster.

As they stood watching, the swans obligingly rounded the curve of the moat and sailed royally towards the drawbridge, their necks curving and sinister, their snowy wings graciously folded. Mixed Biscuits barked ecstatically, but Henrietta did not like them. "They're like snakes," she said.

The foremost swan turned gracefully towards her and reared his head almost as though he meant to shoot out a fanged, poisoned tongue, but thinking better of it he fixed upon her for a moment the swan's cold, inhuman stare, and then turning from her with beautiful contempt he pulled with his beak the bell-rope that hung from the Palace wall. He rang it once, imperiously, his concubines falling into place behind him, and instantly a human menial showered bread from a window. This ringing of the bell was the superb accomplishment of the swans of Torminster, an accomplishment that had made them world-famous. . . . Indolent black beaks were lowered to the bread and the crescents of curved necks met other, reflected crescents, and formed together flawless circles. . . . Billowy white feathers, lying on blue water, had the snowy softness of cumulus clouds on a summer day.

"They may be lovely," said Jocelyn, "but they're certainly rude birds. Let's look for the kingfisher."

They walked on under the trees until a sudden meteor flash of blue shot over the water and was gone. They stood and blinked, but there was nothing there except the unchanging grey walls and their mirrored reflection.

"It's like a falling star," said Henrietta.
"Why?" said Hugh Anthony.
"Well, it's there and then it isn't there."
"Too lovely to be permanent," said Jocelyn gloomily,

and wondered if it was true that Felicity had ever been in Torminster.

"We're coming back to tea with you so as to cheer you up," said Henrietta.

"Oh, are you?" said Jocelyn. "Thank you."

"We'll play hide-and-seek all over your house," said Hugh Anthony.

"Oh, will we?" said Jocelyn. "Thank you."

V

Alone in his sitting-room that evening he found that once again he had to light a fire of apple-wood to banish gloom. He had walked and hidden-and-sought more than his lame leg liked, and he was filled with the restlessness and depression of fatigue. He wanted to read, so as to stop himself thinking about Felicity, but he found himself as difficult to please as his library-book ladies. Every book he took up seemed the wrong book and every time he sat down in his chair a spring seemed broken in a different place.

Resolutely he lit a pipe and opened a new novel. These depressed fits submerged him very often in Torminster and his inability to get the better of them infuriated him, for though he was not naturally joyous he was no pessimist. . . . Sometimes he thought that unhappiness was alive in the house as an actual personality, sometimes seeming a part of the house as on his first night, and sometimes, as to-night, entering into him.

His left foot went to sleep and the novel seemed the stupidest ever written. Getting up for the eighth time he went to his bookcase, envying the unsusceptibility to atmosphere of Mixed Biscuits, who snored in front of the fire in utter content. What was he to read? He would have a shot at something he knew almost by heart already. That at least would be no effort. . . . When in doubt choose Shakespeare. . . . His own was upstairs, but Ferranti's, that he had never yet opened, was here on the shelf. He carried it to the fire and settled down to read *Hamlet*.

And almost at once his unhappy mood slipped from him and he felt instead dreamy and contented. As his eyes slid over the words the poetry of the opening scene sang itself in his mind, as though his eyes on the printed page were fingers gliding over a piano.

"But look, the morn, in russet mantle clad,
Walks o'er the dew of yon high eastward hill."

He turned the pages and with the entrance of Hamlet himself his new mood of lulled peacefulness turned to one of tingling interest, for it seemed that Ferranti was one of those criminals who mark their books. Passage after passage was pencilled in the margin with strokes that in places had cut like a knife. Jocelyn had always declared that if you want insight into a man's state of mind you have but to look at the marked passages in his books, and now, as he read, he felt that he was getting to know Ferranti.

"Or that the Everlasting had not fix'd
His canon 'gainst self-slaughter! O God! God!
To die: to sleep;
No more; and by a sleep to say we end
The heart ache.
By the o'ergrowth of some complexion,
Oft breaking down the pales and forts of reason.
What is he whose grief
Bears such an emphasis? Whose phase of sorrow
Conjures the wandering stars and makes them stand
Like wonder-wounded heroes? This is I."

These and many others seemed to come to him in the

tones of an actual voice. He read on and on, pity and a sense of friendship deepening in him, until he came to the last marked passage of all, where the pencil had scored the margin twice over.

> "O good Horatio, what a wounded name,
> Things standing thus unknown, shall live behind me!
> If thou didst ever hold me in thy heart,
> Absent thee from felicity awhile,
> And in this harsh world draw thy breath in pain
> To tell my story."

The book still open on his knees Jocelyn leant back in his chair and stared at the fire. He felt normal and alert, both depression and a too painful interest lifted off his mind so that he could think clearly. He turned back to the earlier marked passages and read them through again, although they told him nothing except that Ferranti had been a tormented man, now in all probability dead by his own act, who had perhaps found comfort in communing with someone equally tormented yet able to give him the vicarious relief of self-expression. But why had he marked the last passage? "And draw thy breath in pain to tell my story." Who was his Horatio? Who was the ordinary, normal man who stood beside him as the foil of his twisted genius and the interpreter of it? . . . Jocelyn had the feeling that it was himself. . . . But he knew next to nothing about Ferranti's history, and how could he tell a story he did not know?

"To tell my story," he murmured to himself, and then, the one line bringing another to his mind, "Drive my dead thoughts over the universe." Now where in the world did that come from? He sat bolt upright, thinking, and then remembered that Henrietta had murmured it in her sleep one night and that it came from Shelley's "Ode to the West Wind."

He shot out of his chair, went to the bookcase and pulled out Ferranti's Shelley, turning the pages feverishly.

> "Drive my dead thoughts over the universe,
> Like withered leaves, to quicken a new birth;
> And, by the incantation of this verse,
> Scatter, as from an unextinguished hearth,
> Ashes and sparks, my words among mankind."

It was marked, like the speech in Hamlet, twice over.

Ten o'clock had struck and the fire was dying. Jocelyn went upstairs to his bedroom, sat on the bed and stared at the blank wall opposite his window. Had he seen the Hamlet only he would have thought no more about it, but the passage at the end of Hamlet, backed by the one in Shelley, had taken on the character of a direct command.

"And yet the whole thing's fantastic," he murmured, and suddenly remembered the fantastic dream in which he had read Ferranti's story written on this very wall. Well, it was not written there now. There was nothing on the wall but shadows and a spider. Could Ferranti have left any of his manuscripts behind in the house? No, it had been cleaned and repainted from top to toe, and each cupboard had been revealed bare as Mother Hubbard's. What had happened to them all? "I hate waste. I'll buy them to light my fires with." Now who had said that? Good heavens! The crazy Mrs. Jameson!

Jocelyn could not possibly wait till the morning, for goodness only knew with what Mrs. James's housemaid might not have lit the fire by that time. He dashed downstairs as fast as his lame leg would allow, seized his hat and let himself out into the Market Place. There was no moon to-night and as he crossed the Green the Cathedral and the Tor were visible only as dark shapes that blotted out the stars.

"But I think Mrs. Jameson is just going to bed, sir," said the astonished maid who opened the door.

"Then I must catch her before she gets there," said Jocelyn, and hurried upstairs past the thistles without waiting to be announced.

Mrs. Jameson was still in her drawing-room. She had just given the parrots a lump of sugar each to avert night starvation and was covering them over with embroidered Chinese shawls. It was the season of Trinity and she was dressed in superb green velvet, with green shoes and stockings and emeralds in her lovely hair.

"'Ullo, dearie," remarked the only uncovered parrot, and Mrs. Jameson swung round.

"Captain Irvin," she said calmly. She was not at all startled, for like a child she took everything that happened quite for granted. "How nice. Let's have tea."

The astonished maid, appearing at the door at this moment, was sent for tea. "And cakes," said Mrs. Jameson, "and I think I'd like a banana."

They sat down and Jocelyn explained himself slowly and clearly, and found to his relief that Mrs. Jameson had quite understood the essentials. Gabriel Ferranti had been a poet and his poems were lost and it was important that they should be found, and were there any poems among the papers she had bought?

"How am I to know," she asked sweetly, "now that they are burnt?"

"Are you sure they're all burnt?"

"There might be some in the housemaid's cupboard. Shall we go and see? Have you any matches?"

Jocelyn lit two candles in tall silver candlesticks and taking one each they set out, eleven o'clock striking as they went. The cupboard was at the end of a dark passage and in it, beneath brooms and dustpans, was a small pile of very dirty papers. Jocelyn pulled it out with fingers that trembled and saw newspapers and, here and there among them, some pages of manuscript.

"This is all?" he asked huskily.

"That's all. There was a great deal more, of course, before we burnt it. . . . And now shall we have tea?"

At sight of the silver tea-tray and the cakes and bananas Mrs. Jameson lost interest in Ferranti and began to tell Jocelyn some fantastic tale about parrots building nests in banana-trees, and then she asked him to tell her a story, and out of pity and gratitude he did his best, relating another of Ferranti's that had come to him via Henrietta. . . . And all the time, perhaps, the story lay on his knee.

When he let himself into his own house again it was striking midnight. He went into his sitting-room, rekindled the lamp and the nearly extinguished fire, and set to work to sort out the papers on the floor. The pages of manuscript, when gleaned from the newspapers, seemed for the most part to be only jotted notes or unfinished poems, and Jocelyn's heart sank as he wondered what had already gone to feed Mrs. Jameson's flames.

But at last, folded between a two-year-old copy of *The Times*, he found a bundle of pages roughly fastened together with a piece of string. He laid them on the table, pulled the lamp towards him and unfastened them, wildly excited, for they seemed to be a long dramatic poem.

And then excitement turned to despair for the thing was almost illegible and in wild confusion. It was written in pencil in a tiny, crabbed handwriting, with gaps and erasions, evidently dashed down in a hurry and never re-read or corrected. And Jocelyn was bitterly disappointed as well as despairing, for it seemed to be some queer symbolic tragedy that had no connection with reality and therefore could not be Ferranti's relation of his own story. . . . That, if the marked passages in the books were more than chance and it had ever existed, must have been destroyed. . . . For a mad moment, tired and discouraged, he was on the point of throwing the whole thing into the fire, but then, ashamed of himself, he turned to it once more and began puzzling over it again.

And now, as he grew more accustomed to the writing, he found himself deciphering whole consecutive phrases, and found that they were good. If this was not Ferranti's own story it was at any rate fine poetry, with here and there a ring of genius.

"Have I got to make all this out and rewrite it?" Jocelyn's weary mind inquired of his spirit. "God! It'll take me months!"

But Jocelyn's real self, that seemed now to be standing a little apart from the aching body and tired mind that it used, assured him that he had. Was he not a bookseller, a link between mind and mind? Had he not discovered that he had it in him to interpret genius? He must try to explain this Ferranti to a world eager for beauty just as he tried to explain the minds in his front shop to Mr. Bell and Bert.

One o'clock struck and he put the pages together again and stretched himself. "The bell then striking one," he murmured, his mind going back to Hamlet. "This is the point where the ghost should enter. Are you alive, Ferranti, or are you dead?"

He put everything away and went upstairs to bed, lying awake until the bird of dawning awoke the god of day.

"If you're a ghost, Ferranti," he thought, "you must go away now and let me sleep. At the cock's warning the extravagant and erring spirit flies to his confine. Rest, rest, perturbed spirit! Remember thee? Ay, thou poor ghost, while memory holds a seat in this distracted globe. Remember thee!"

CHAPTER VII

I

In November Torminster Cathedral commemorated its patron saint and benefactors. The Cathedral was great at festivals, each Christmas and Easter and Whitsun marching by in the procession of the days in flower-decked pomp, but in after years it seemed to Henrietta and Hugh Anthony that this particular festival surpassed all the others. It of course lacked the secular excitement of Christmas and Easter, for no one hung up stockings on it or ate pink boiled eggs for breakfast on it, but it had a peaceful and rather wistful beauty that was unforgettable.

It had been led up to by a season of remembrance. In September they had commemorated St. Michael and all the angels. In the Cathedral a great brass pot of michaelmas daisies had been placed under the window in the Lady Chapel that showed the good angels, looking very strong-minded and muscular, heaving the bad angels out of heaven on the end of pitchforks, and at home they had an iced cake for tea and while they ate it Grandfather told them how busy the angels were kept looking after little children. Henrietta felt that what with one thing and another the poor angels were very overworked, and she felt so grateful for their exertions that she made garlands of autumn flowers and hung them round the necks of the cherubs in her bedroom and the seraphim in the spare room.

And then had come All Saints' Day, a lovely, wonderful day when the choir at evensong sang, "Who are these like stars appearing?" and the figures on the west front surely swelled a little to find themselves so appreciated. At bedtime that night Grandfather told them stories about the saints. They heard about St. Francis who loved birds and animals, St. Martin who shared his cloak with the beggar, St. Cecilia who loved music, St. Elizabeth who told such a shocking lie about the roses in her apron but was forgiven because she meant well, and St. Joan whom Grandfather loved best of all because when people laughed at her for saying she had been guided she took no notice whatever but just went straight on and did it.

Henrietta listened in a dreaming silence to these stories, utterly satisfied by their beauty, but Hugh Anthony was much exercised by the various points that they raised in his mind.

"When the saints die," he asked Grandfather, "how long does it take their souls to get to heaven?"

"Ten minutes," said Grandfather.

"How do they get there?"

"In the arms of their angels."

"What do the angels do with the saints when they get them there?"

"Give them a thorough cleaning. It is, I believe, painful but very necessary. Dear me, yes. Not even the saints are perfect."

"Are you a saint, Grandfather?"

"Dear me, no!"

"Why not?"

Grandfather replied in the words of Falstaff, "I have more flesh than another man and therefore more frailty."

"What does that mean?"

"It means that I am stout and therefore inclined to be lazy. I can't help being stout, but I ought to help being lazy and I fear I do not always do so. I go to sleep in the psalms."

"Do saints never go to sleep in the psalms?"

"Dear me, no!"

Hugh Anthony returned to the point that was really worrying him more than he cared to admit. "Are you quite sure that it takes exactly ten minutes to get from earth to heaven?"

"I am absolutely certain," replied Grandfather, meeting Hugh Anthony's searching eyes with a keen, steady glance that brought conviction.

"Really, Theobald!" protested Grandmother, who was sitting by knitting and clicking her tongue in annoyance at Grandfather's flights of fancy. "The things you say! One plain. One purl."

But Grandfather was not penitent, for he believed with St. Elizabeth that there are times when a little inaccuracy is not only advisable but right. He was convinced that if a child with a naturally sceptical mind is ever to have faith there must never be any uncertainty about the answers given to his questions. He never said, "I don't know," or "I'm not sure," to his grandson, though very occasionally, when completely floored, he replied to a question in the words used by the Angel Uriel when coping with the insatiable curiosity of the prophet Esdras. "Go thy way, weigh me the weight of the fire, or measure me the blast of the wind, or call me again the day that is past. . . . Thou canst give me no answer. . . . Thine own things, and such as are grown up with thee, canst thou not know; how should thy vessel then be able to comprehend the way of the most Highest?"

II

And so, by way of the archangels and the angels and the saints, they came to the humble benefactors, remembering them in the very middle of St. Martin's summer. . . . And St. Martin played up. . . . But then, Henrietta thought, he would be sure to. That splendid young man who came dashing out of the town on a frosty winter's night, with his scarlet cloak gleaming in the torchlight like a great dahlia and his horse's hoofs striking sparks from the stones, was bound to be lavish in the way of weather. Just as he flung the rich folds of his cloak over the beggar who cowered by the roadside so, year after year, did he fling warm sunshine and a final largesse of autumn flowers over Torminster on its great day.... A nice man.

And this year it was lovelier than ever. As soon as she woke up Henrietta scurried to the window to inspect the day. A sky of pale milky blue was tenderly arched over a world misted with silvery dew, and so frail and still and shining that it seemed like a blown soap bubble. Henrietta, leaning out of her window, was almost afraid to breathe lest it should break in spray against her face.

And after breakfast, as she helped Grandfather pick flowers in the garden for the Cathedral decorations, she was still afraid, for the flowers they picked were fragile as rainbows. There had been no cold weather yet and there were actually a few pink roses left, their petals transparent and faintly brown at the edges. The Japanese anemones, folded and hanging their heads after a touch of frost, were fairy lanterns of pearl and lilac that might at any moment vanish, and the scarlet leaves of the virginia-creeper fell at a touch like dead butterflies.

"They'll all come to pieces when we put them on the graves," mourned Henrietta, laying her spoils tenderly in the basket.

"Never mind," said Grandfather, "the fallen petals are as precious in God's sight as the dust of His dead." He spoke sadly, for he was always depressed by the disintegration of autumn.

"Now, don't be morbid, Theobald," said Grandmother, issuing out of the front door in her goloshes. "And don't stand about on that wet grass in those shoes. You've no more sense than a child of two.... Here's Bates with the chrysanthemums.... Give them to Mrs. Elphinstone with my compliments, Theobald, and if she wants any more she can have them, but you must fetch them, mind. I won't have her running about in my garden without a with-your-leave or a by-your-leave, wife of the senior Canon though she may be."

Bates came out from behind the mulberry-tree with a huge bunch of yellow and red chrysanthemums and their colour and sturdiness, together with Grandmother's strong-minded remarks, were somehow exhilarating in this dreamlike, vanishing autumn world.

They set off for the Cathedral, Grandfather and Henrietta and Hugh Anthony and Bates and the flowers. Grandmother did not come. She had been decorating churches for festivals for fifty years and had now come to the conclusion that she had had enough of it. ... Let other women take their turn at keeping the jam-pots from showing and mopping up the water that the clergy kicked over.

Grandfather and Henrietta walked on ahead, talking softly about the angels, and Hugh Anthony and Bates followed behind discussing horticulture.

"Bates, if I was to pour all the water over one plant in a flower-bed would it run along underneath the ground and make the others wet too?" asked Hugh Anthony.

"No, sir, it wouldn't. If you was to 'ave a drink of beer it wouldn't do me no good."

"Bates, if you planted all the bulbs upside down would they come up in Australia?"

"I couldn't say, sir. I ain't never done such a thing."

"Bates, why do peas grow in pods?"

"I couldn't say, sir, I'm sure. Maybe they're fond of a bit of company."

"Bates, do you like radishes for tea?"

"I'm more partial to a kipper, sir. More tasty."

"Bates, do you believe in God?"

"Yes, sir. I took religion when I started gardening.

Wot I say is, 'oo put them peas in them pods and made them flowers so pretty and all?"

III

The Cathedral presented a scene of frantic activity, with all the canons' female dependants scurrying about in overalls with scissors hanging from their waists. Not only had the lectern and the pulpit and the high altar to be flower-decked, as at other festivals, but every single tomb and memorial tablet in the Cathedral, no matter how humble and obscure, must have what Peppercue, the head verger, called its " floral tribute " before three o'clock that afternoon.

There was always a little difficulty as to who should decorate what, all the ladies having the lowest opinion of each other's decorative powers. There was especial difficulty over the side chapel vases. . . . If there is one thing in the world that every woman is quite sure no other woman but herself can do it is vases. . . . The vases on the high altar were of course, as always, the duty of the wife or daughter of the Canon in residence (though goodness knew that poor Nell Roderick could no more make a dahlia stick upright than fly), but the side chapel vases were only filled on benefactors' day and there was no real precedent as to who did them. Mrs. Elphinstone, as wife of the senior Canon, naturally thought she should, and Miss Roderick thought she should because she was doing the high altar vases and might as well do the lot together, and Mrs. Allenby thought she should because she had once been to the Scilly Isles and therefore must know more about flowers than anyone else, and no one knew why Mrs. Phillips, who was only the organist's wife, thought she should. . . . The Archdeacon had no female dependants.

It was at moments such as these that Grandfather came in useful. As he came smilingly up the aisle with his arms full of Japanese anemones it suddenly did not seem to matter very much who did what. For one thing his serene presence smoothed away all disagreement and for another thing he would be quite likely, with his fatal habit of thinking aloud, to repeat later at the Deanery tea-party, saying it over slowly and sadly to himself, any little remark that he had overheard and not liked. . . . They all fell to on something or other and the side chapel vases were left to Mrs. Phillips.

Behind the high altar was the tomb of the patron saint of the Cathedral, a glorious canopy raised over a sculptured figure lying peacefully in his monk's habit with his hands crossed on his breast and his eyes closed. It was a lovely piece of work, the luxuriant carving that had been hewn out of stone and raised over his bones for love of him contrasting touchingly with the simple figure. . . . But alas, heavy doubts were entertained as to whether his bones were really there at all.

For he had lived in the Torminster valley as long ago as the age of miracles. He had been swineherd to a king whose name no one remembered but whose behaviour had been most distressing. So bad had he been that the whole land had groaned beneath his wickedness, the blue hills hiding their heads beneath the clouds for very shame, and the waters of the streams that ran down to the Torminster valley turning blood-red in horror. And the swineherd, who was a good man, was much upset. It was terrible, he thought, that this lovely valley, lying in the lap of these fair hills, should be so polluted, and one day while he sat beside the well where he watered his herd he earnestly prayed to God, as Grandfather would have done under similar circumstances, that he might be guided. And God in reply sent the Angel Gabriel down to the swineherd to talk the matter over and Gabriel said he thought the best thing to do would be to found a monastery, so that the radiance of the holy lives led by the monks might spread over the valley and conquer the darkness of its wickedness. That's all very well, replied the swineherd, but where am I to find the holy monks? Gabriel made no verbal reply to this, but he picked up the stick that the swineherd carried and waved it over the backs of the pigs and over the well, and lo and behold, each pig became on the spot a holy monk while the well, that until now had been rather piggy and secular, became clear and holy, and the swineherd became the first Abbot of Torminster.

Helped by the holy angels, whose images are found carved everywhere in Torminster, he ruled long and wisely, living until the age of one hundred and ten and becoming holier and holier and sterner and sterner, for he was fully determined that never again should there be wickedness in the beautiful Torminster valley. . . . And there never has been. . . . To this day the inhabitants of Torminster are, on the whole and taking everything into consideration, exceptionally well-behaved, so well-behaved indeed that the disciplinary measure practised by the first Abbot, that of walling up alive indiscreet members of the community, has been discontinued.

But no one could ever be quite sure about the Abbot's bones. After his death they took on extraordinary powers. Once a year his tomb was opened and they were displayed and people with whooping-cough who prayed beside them and touched them whooped no more, and other diseases were similarly benefited. This brought great credit upon the monastery and another monastery near by whose Abbot's bones stayed put and did simply nothing at all was exceedingly jealous, and when there was a terrible fire at the Torminster monastery and vigilance was relaxed the miraculous bones mysteriously disappeared. . . . And plague fell upon the neighbouring monastery. . . . And a parcel of bones was mysteriously returned but, alas, they never cured the whooping-cough again, so were they the same bones?

The twentieth-century ladies of the Close did not know, but they gave them the benefit of the doubt and the Deanery hothouse plants.

Lady Lavinia Umphreville, the Dean's wife, did not take any active part in the good work, for decorating tombs is a dusty business and she bought her clothes in Paris and knew what was due to them, but she always put in an appearance, walking very slowly and beautifully up the north choir aisle and down the south choir aisle and then out, bowing and smiling to the ladies of the Close as she went.

She arrived soon after Grandfather and the children, looking very exquisite in grey silk, with a pink ostrich feather in her hat and her grey hair beautifully done with the curling-tongs. . . . She had a ladies' maid and paid her, so Mrs. Allenby said, a fabulous sum, so no wonder she looked as she did. Mrs. Allenby would have looked the same, so she said, had Canon Allenby seen his way to providing her with a ladies' maid too. . . . Lady Lavinia had the willowy grace and dignity that so often go with aristocratic birth and her voice was low and gentle . . . though Henrietta had heard it said that the Dean was henpecked, but then Grandfather said one should not listen to gossip.

In Lady Lavinia's wake followed the Deanery undergardeners and the footman carrying the hothouse flowers, exotic things that seemed out of keeping with the memory of the simple man who had once kept swine in the valley.

Mrs. Elphinstone was not quite sure whether Grandfather and the children could be entrusted with any really important decorating, so she handed over to them an obscure chantry whose interior decorations could not be seen from outside. Its floor was covered with six flat tombstones whose lettering had been so worn away by the passing feet of the generations that it was impossible to make out the names of the dead whose dust lay under one's feet. Though aware that he was being poked into a corner Grandfather was not in the least resentful, for he liked to feel that his flowers were honouring the unknown and this chantry was one of his favourite spots in the Cathedral.

The children loved it too, for it was like a fairy house

carved out of an iceberg. You went up two steps, opened a door and there you were inside it. The walls and the ceiling were built of very white stone fretted into a hundred intricate shapes of flower and leaf and bird and demon, and so passionately had the sculptor enjoyed himself that he had taken as much trouble with the parts that did not show as the parts that did; you could put your finger round behind a grinning imp and find he had an unseen tail lashing away in the dark. And once upon a time the carving had all been coloured, for its whiteness was still stained here and there with patches of rose-pink and azure and lilac, as though the iceberg reflected a rainbow overhead.

The east end was entirely filled up by the huge tomb of the founder of the family in whose honour this chantry had been built. His sculptured likeness lay upon it, a colossal figure in armour with a huge plumed helmet on his head and a hound of no recognizable breed lying at his feet. His legs were crossed in token that he had been to the Crusades and his mailed hands were joined finger-tip to finger-tip as though in prayer.... And looked a little awkward like that, as though it were a position not frequently adopted in life.

"Shall we give some flowers to Sir Despard Murgatroyd?" asked Henrietta. This was not really his name, but the children had once been taken to see a performance of *Ruddigore* and had been struck with the strong family likeness between the Bad Baronet and the gentleman in the chantry, whose grim face could just be seen below his raised vizor.

"Not too many," said Grandfather. "I don't think he's the kind of man to appreciate flowers on his chest. But we'll make wreaths to lay on the graves of these unknown descendants of his."

"I bet you they're his six wives," said Hugh Anthony, "and I bet you he beat them. If he did a crime every day, like the Murgatroyds, I bet you he beat one every weekday and the dog on Sunday."

"I don't think they're his wives," said Henrietta, standing astride one of the tombs, "I think they're six Saracens that he killed at the Crusades, and he had them pickled and brought them home to show that he'd really done it."

"Then if they're Saracens they're not benefactors," said Hugh Anthony, "and it's waste of time decorating them."

"That will do," reproved Grandfather. "Put the flowers down there, please, Bates, and fetch us some jam-pots and water and then you can go home and see about those potatoes."

Mrs. Elphinstone was quite wrong in thinking that Grandfather and the children could not decorate. Grandfather, of course, could not get down on the floor and actually do it because of his rheumatics, but he sat on one of the praying-chairs that stood in a row at the back of the chantry and was full of bright ideas which Henrietta and Hugh Anthony carried out with deft fingers.

The chantry looked lovely when they had done. Each wife, or Saracen, had a wreath of virginia-creeper and Japanese anemones, Sir Despard had a rose in his helmet and in all the niches in the walls they put pots of chrysanthemums. It was sad to think that both the rose and the wreaths on the floor would be dead by night, but the people in the tombs were dead too, and Grandfather assured them that death did not really matter at all, what mattered was that life while it lasted should be beautiful.

When they had finished decorating, and had cleared up the mess, Grandfather announced that they would now say a prayer for the repose of the souls of Sir Despard Murgatroyd and his relations. So they knelt in a row on the praying-chairs and Grandfather pleaded for Sir Despard, making use of the word Murgatroyd in his prayer in all innocence, for he had entirely forgotten how Sir Despard had originally come by it. . . . "Give rest, O Christ, to Thy servants with Thy saints, where sorrow and pain are no more, neither sighing, but life everlasting," he finished, and the children said "Amen."

"And now we'll go home to dinner," said Grandfather, getting up from his rheumatic knees with a grimace of pain that was hastily repressed lest the children should see it.

"Roast beef," said Hugh Anthony.

"I'll stop a minute," said Henrietta.

Grandfather nodded and left her, taking Hugh Anthony with him. There was something in Henrietta that he loved and respected, a power that she had of attuning herself to the things that are not seen. And it was because of this that he let her do things alone and go about by herself far more than Grandmother thought proper. He knew that she must discover by solitary experiment the way in which she herself could most easily learn to listen to the ditties of no tone that are piped to the spirit. She must learn to say, "Therefore, ye soft pipes, play on," and know that they would obey her.

Left alone Henrietta dived about in the basket and found a long spray of virginia-creeper and three anemones. She twisted them together to form a collar and then, kneeling down in front of the dog who propped Sir Despard's feet up, she slipped it round his neck.

She loved that dog, mongrel though he might be, and ugly into the bargain. The sculptor must have loved him too, for he had been carved so realistically that it was hard to realize his tail did not wag. Henrietta stroked his back, where the ribs stuck out under the skin as badly as Mixed Biscuits' had before Jocelyn fed him up, and rubbed him behind the ears in the place where Mixed Biscuits liked to be rubbed and scratched his chest in the place where Mixed Biscuits liked to be scratched, and then she very gently kissed his nose.

Did dogs have immortal souls, she wondered? She had once asked Grandfather, but he had been distressingly vague about it. They might, he thought, or they might not. If it was a nice dog one could but hope.

Henrietta was sure this one had been a nice dog. After she had kissed his nose she knelt on with her eyes shut, thinking about him and his master. She doubted if Sir Despard had gone straight up to heaven to play a harp when he died.... He did not look like that.... He looked like one of those who went to a place called "the realms of darkness" and had a good deal done to them before they were suitable for harp playing. One of Grandfather's prayers for the dead went like this—"King of majesty, deliver the souls of the departed from the pit of destruction that the grave devour them not; that they go not down to the realms of darkness: but let Michael, the holy standard bearer, make speed to restore them to the brightness of glory." It was a prayer that suited Sir Despard very well, Henrietta thought. She could see him behind her closed lids, a dead man striding down long, black corridors, with his armour clanking and his feet kicking up a lot of dust, down and down into deepening darkness, with his dog at his heels.... The dog was frightened by the dark and the dust and the silence of death and had his tail tucked in and his ears back, but he did not dream of leaving his master.... And they tramped for hundreds of years until they came out into a great vaulted place like the crypt of the Cathedral and there Michael was waiting for them, with a sword in his hand and looking very grim, and he had a great deal to say to Sir Despard about his behaviour to the wives, or Saracens, before he could make him sorry for it, and a good deal to do to him before he could make him fit for heavenly society.... And the poor dog had to sit in the corner and watch, trembling all over and whining, but not dreaming of running away.... And then at last they went on again, Michael leading and Sir Despard following, feeling properly ashamed of himself, but this time they went up and up into deepening light, on and on for hundreds of years, so that the poor dog got terribly exhausted and his tongue hung out and his legs dragged. And so they came to the door of Paradise and Michael knocked on it with his sword and cried out, "Open! Bring the prisoner out of his prison house and he that sitteth in darkness out of the shadow of death!" And Saint Peter opened the door and Michael and Sir Despard went in. . . . But the little dog, because he had no soul, was left crying outside and scratching at the door. . . . Perhaps he was still there at this moment, after all these centuries, still trying to get in. . . . Desperately Henrietta began to pray for him. "Give rest, O Christ, to Thy servant with Thy saints, where sorrow and pain are no more; neither sighing, but life everlasting." And behind her closed eyelids she saw the door open a crack and heard Saint Peter say, "Come along in and don't make that noise," and the little dog ran in, his tail wagging, and disappeared in a blaze of light.

Henrietta opened her eyes and discovered that tears were running out of the far corners of them and making stiff wet tracks down her face in front of her ears. She wiped them away with the backs of her hands and giggled at herself, for during the last five minutes she had been living with that dog as intensely as it is possible to live. . . . She had thought it was all real. . . . It was odd, she thought, how that faculty that Grandfather said was called imagination could make one actually see and hear what was not really happening at all.

Yet surely that story she had imagined was a real thing? If you created a story with your mind surely it was just as much there as a piece of needlework that you created with your fingers? You could not see it with your bodily eyes, that was all. As she got up and dusted her knees Henrietta realized how the invisible world must be saturated with the stories that men tell both in their minds and by their lives. They must be everywhere, these stories, twisting together, penetrating existence like air breathed into the lungs, and how terrible, how awful, thought Henrietta, if the air breathed should be foul.

How dare men live, how dare they think or imagine, when every action and every thought is a tiny thread to mar or enrich that tremendous tapestried story that man weaves on the loom that God has set up, a loom that stretches from heaven above to hell below and from side to side of the universe. . . . It was all rather terrifying and Henrietta was glad to hurry home to lunch.

IV

At ten minutes to three Grandmother was sitting in her pew in the choir with the children one on each side of her. She wore her Sunday clothes and carried her best umbrella, that she never used unless it was sure not to rain. She had three umbrellas; one for rain, one for uncertain weather and one for fine weather. Henrietta wore her new red winter coat trimmed with beaver, with a round beaver cap on her head and a little muff hung round her neck on a chain. She was much too hot, but she did not mind because she knew she looked very sweet. Hugh Anthony, in his new nautical overcoat with brass buttons, neither knew nor cared what he looked like, but was comforted in his heated state by a whistle on a white cord. For years he had been telling his grandparents that a whistle should always accompany marine attire and now at last, just in time for the festival, this remark had sunk in. With his lovely eyes fixed on the altar and an expression of great spiritual beauty on his face he was wondering just when to blow the whistle. Should he accompany the last hymn on it or should be blow one shrill blast in the middle of the Dean's sermon? It was difficult to decide. He must, as Grandfather said one should, wait and be guided.

The ladies of the Close had their pews near the altar and these were always reserved for them. Lady Lavinia had the front pew on the right with the Palace pew opposite her across the aisle. Behind these were ranged the pews of the Canons' ladies in order of seniority.

Barleycorn, the second verger, attired in his black gown and carrying his wand of office, was in charge of these pews, and it was his business to see that no presuming stranger dared to sit itself down in the seats of the mighty. It sometimes seemed to Henrietta that Barleycorn thoroughly enjoyed the ejection of a stranger. He would wait until the poor wretch had lowered itself, very tentatively, on to the square of wood sacred to Lady Lavinia and then he would glide swiftly forward with an expression of horror on his face, his gown floating behind him and his wand outstretched like the neck of a hissing swan. There would be a whispered colloquy, and the poor stranger would get up and creep away as though detected in the act of shoplifting, leaving its umbrella behind. . . . On these occasions Henrietta detested Barleycorn, for she hated to see people made to feel ashamed.

But to-day no one sat down where they should not and very soon Barleycorn hurried away, a bell tinkled, they all rose to their feet and far away the choir were heard singing a hymn, "Ye holy angels bright," as they came in procession from the vestry.

And now they had reached the entrance to the choir and were passing under the carved angels of the screen, the sound of their singing swelling gloriously.

Henrietta, her muff swinging and her hands holding her prayer-book upside down, forgot all distractions in her excitement as the procession came up the choir. First came one of the masters of the choir-school holding the great golden cross and after him came the choirboys singing fit to burst themselves, and then the choirmen singing more moderately but yet with extreme heartiness:

> "Ye blessed souls at rest,
>   Who ran this earthly race,
>   And now, from sin released,
>   Behold the Saviour's face,

His praises sound,
As in His light
With sweet delight
Ye do abound."

After them came another choir-school master carrying the patron saint's banner, a needlework picture embroidered in blues and greens and pinks and purples. It showed the saint, attired in his swineherd's get-up, sitting beside the holy well and brooding sadly over the sins of the Torminster valley. At his feet flowers grew—pansies and violets and cowslips—and behind him were the blue hills, and up in the sky the Angel Gabriel was sitting comfortably on a cloud and holding an architect's model of the Cathedral on his left palm. It was a beautiful picture, but by some extraordinary oversight the pigs had been omitted.

Behind the banner came Peppercue and Barleycorn, the vergers, followed by the Dean and Canons and the Archdeacon.

The combined ages of the Dean, the four Canons and the Archdeacon at this time came to four hundred and eighty-four, but it was marvellous how they got about. First came the two juniors, Grandfather and the Archdeacon, aged seventy-eight and eighty, who walked quite easily without sticks, then came Canon Allenby aged eighty-two, who used one stick, and Canon Roderick aged eighty-six, who used two sticks, and behind them came Canon Elphinstone aged eighty-eight in his bathchair, pushed by his gardener.

The Dean, who was only seventy, came behind the bathchair and was apt to complain to his wife that shepherding his Chapter in a procession made him feel exactly like a—er—nursemaid. . . . The Dean never used strong language, but in conversation he quite unconsciously left expressive pauses where he would have used it had he not been a clergyman.

Behind the Dean came the Bishop's chaplain carrying the Bishop's pastoral staff and behind him came the Bishop's cope with the Bishop just visible inside it, limping a little because his sciatica was bad that day. Spiritually the Bishop was a very great man, but physically he was not, being small and thin and lacking that autocratic bearing that made the Dean such a fine figure of a man at dinner-parties. The Dean and Lady Lavinia always patronized the Bishop a little. The man lacked private means and as a result the soles at his dinner parties were lemon, not Dover. . . . But it was noticeable that people in difficulties always went to the Bishop for help rather than to the Dean.

> "My soul, bear thou thy part,
>   Triumph in God Above,
> And with a well-tuned heart
>   Sing thou the songs of love:
> Let all thy days
> Till life shall end,
> Whate'er He send,
> Be filled with praise."

They all filed singing into their seats and knelt down to pray and Henrietta found to her delight that she was feeling good, a feeling she adored. Tears of happy emotion pricked behind her eyelids, her throat swelled and she was certain that she was never going to be naughty any more. God and His angels were near and one only had to be absolutely good and everything would be perfect. . . . It was all quite easy.

"Shall I blow it now?" whispered Hugh Anthony, nudging her behind Grandmother's back.

"Blow what now?" demanded Henrietta, opening her eyes.

"My whistle."

"You dare blow your beastly whistle! You dare!"

she whispered savagely. She was in an ugly rage that tore at her. She stretched across Grandmother, dragged the lanyard roughly over his head and buried it and the whistle in the depths of her muff. "You beast! You beast!" she panted.

"Here, give me that back," said Hugh Anthony loudly. "It's my whistle."

Lady Lavinia, Mrs. Elphinstone, Miss Roderick, Mrs. Allenby and all the ladies of the Close raised their bowed heads and gazed at the couple more in sorrow than in anger.... Really, if Mrs. Fordyce must adopt children at her age she could at least make some attempt to keep them in order during divine service.

Grandmother made it, for she was very angry. Her eyes were shining quite dangerously and her mouth, until she opened it, was a thin line. "Be quiet, children! Henrietta, give me that whistle. One more word from either of you and you go straight home. I never saw such an exhibition in all my life!"

The whistle was placed in Grandmother's bag, which was snapped to with a resounding click, and everybody's heads were lowered again. But Henrietta no longer felt good and the tears that trickled down behind her fingers were those of rage instead of sweet piety.... How dared Hugh Anthony! . . . Little beast! . . . Just let him wait till they got outside and she would show him!

Hugh Anthony was not at all angry, for he was a firm believer in destiny. Things happened because they were ordained to happen. It was interesting to find out by what sequence of cause and effect they did happen, but useless to try to avert them. His whistle was gone and he was unlikely to see it again, but never mind; he would now be able to use on Henrietta, in punishment for her theft, a new booby-trap that he had recently invented but lacked opportunity to put into action. During the prayers and psalms he employed himself in working out a few minor touches that would perfect its mechanism.... By the time they got to the first lesson he had decided that when he grew up he was going to be an inventor.

The Dean's high, nasal voice piped out from the lectern. "Let us now praise famous men, and our fathers that begat us. . . . Such as found out musical tunes and recited verses in writing. . . . All these were honoured in their generations, and were the glory of their times. . . . And some there be, that have no memorial; who are perished, as though they had never been; and are become as though they had never been born. . . . But these were merciful men, whose righteousness hath not been forgotten. . . . Their bodies are buried in peace; but their name liveth for evermore."

That penetrated Henrietta's rage and she began to feel less wicked. She whispered the words to herself and they were so calming that by the time the final hymn was reached she had quite forgotten what it was she was going to do to Hugh Anthony when she got him outside.

This hymn was the climax of the service and lifted her up into the seventh heaven. The choir, followed by the whole congregation, sang it in procession, going all round the Cathedral and passing by all the decorated graves, leaving none of them out, so that everyone who had loved Torminster, alive or dead, was gathered together in one company.

"For all the saints who from their labours rest,
Who Thee by faith before the world confessed,
Thy name, O Jesu, be for ever blessed.
Alleluia! "

They were singing that verse as they passed Sir Despard Murgatroyd's chantry, though he hardly deserved it, and Henrietta stood on tiptoe trying to see the dog with his wreath round his neck, but she could not.

"The golden evening brightens in the west:
Soon, soon to faithful warriors comes their rest;
Sweet is the calm of paradise the blest.
Alleluia! "

She did so hope her little dog was in Paradise, lying curled round in a ball in a bed of lilies, sleeping off the fatigue of following Sir Despard through purgatory.

They sang the end of the hymn standing in a group by the west door.

"From earth's wide bounds, from ocean's farthest coast,
Through gates of pearl streams in the countless host,
Singing to Father, Son and Holy Ghost.
                Alleluia!"

Then they bowed their heads and the Bishop blessed them. "The peace of God which passeth all understanding keep your hearts and minds in the knowledge and love of God." Then for a few moments there was silence, a deep, cool silence like the inside of a well. . . . Peace. . . . Henrietta was not quite sure what it was, but she knew it was very important. If one wanted it, Grandfather had told her once, one must not hit back when fate hit hard but must allow the hammer-strokes to batter out a hollow place inside one into which peace, like cool water, could flow.

The festival was over for another year and they drifted out through the west door on to the Green. It was dusk now, a smoky orange dusk that made the universe look like a lighted Chinese lantern swinging in space.

"I think I should like to go and help Uncle Jocelyn sell in the shop," whispered Henrietta to Grandmother.

"Aren't you coming to the Deanery tea-party?" whispered Hugh Anthony in astonishment. "There'll be iced cakes, and cream in the tea."

"I want to show Uncle Jocelyn my muff," said Henrietta.

"Very well, dear," said Grandmother, slightly relieved. . . . One child alone at the Deanery party would probably behave itself, but with two together you never knew.

V

Henrietta ran across the Green and into the Market Place. She did not really want to show Jocelyn her muff, but she did not want to face all those people at the party; it would have been an anticlimax. She could not have explained why she ran away, but she knew instinctively that she must let herself down lightly.

It was nice in the Market Place. The chimneys and roofs were sharp and black against the orange sky, but below them purple veils had been drawn over unsightly things like dustbins and paper in the gutter, so that the Market Place looked mysteriously beautiful. Here and there a light had been lit in a window, orange to match the sky, and overhead a few stars were like pinholes pricked in the swinging Chinese lantern.

The gas was lit in the bookshop, but it was empty, so Henrietta went on to Jocelyn's sitting-room. He was sitting writing, his table strewn with manuscript and a large black pot of tea and a plate of ginger biscuits beside him.

"You ought to be in the shop, Uncle Jocelyn," said Henrietta severely. She herself, on the occasions when Jocelyn allowed her to help sell, was frightfully serious about it.

"No one will come," said Jocelyn. "The laws of commerce command that I shall keep this establishment open till six, but with all this to-do over the dead going on I can't expect customers."

"The service was glorious," said Henrietta. "It was dreadful that you couldn't come."

"Tragic," agreed Jocelyn, but he did not seem overwhelmed. "Fetch yourself a cup from the kitchen. And there are chocolate biscuits in that tin with Windsor Castle on it."

Henrietta always enjoyed Jocelyn's haphazard teas. Very strong tea out of a black pot, with heaps of sugar, was much nicer than the milk and water with a dash of tea only that she had at home, and nothing is nicer than a chocolate biscuit held in one hand and a ginger one in the other, with alternate bites taken of each.

"Have you any bullseyes?" she asked, pulling up a chair to sit beside Jocelyn at his table.

"No. Why?"

They're lovely after ginger biscuits. They cool them down."

"I'll have them next time you come," Jocelyn promised.

Henrietta put her half-eaten biscuits down on his manuscript and had a long pull at her tea, leaving off in the middle of that to show Jocelyn her new clothes.

"Exquisite," said Jocelyn, as she turned slowly round.

She took off her coat so that he could see her dress, green silk smocked by Grandmother, and lifted the skirt a little to show him her new petticoat and frilly knickers. Then she got back into her chair again and finished her biscuits.

She was always very happy with Jocelyn, though his presence gave her a tiny ache somewhere. So much love was showered on her by Grandfather, Grandmother and Hugh Anthony that she did not usually remember that she was an orphan, but when she was with Jocelyn she did remember it. She thought that if she had had a father he might have been rather like Jocelyn; nice and teasing and young enough to feel nearer to her in time than Grandmother did. She finished her tea down to the dregs, scooped up what was left of the sugar in her spoon and ate it, and leant her head against Jocelyn's shoulder.

"I'd like you to be my father," she said. "And Hugh Anthony's father too."

Jocelyn started slightly. This idea had already occurred to Grandfather and, fond as he was of both children, he was not altogether sure that he relished it.

"You funny little scrap," he said. "If I were your father I'd whack you every day."

Henrietta giggled and then, the pangs of hunger being now satisfied, was at leisure to have her eye caught by the manuscript in front of her.

"It's verses in writing," she said. "Did you write all that, Uncle Jocelyn?"

"Most of it was written by a friend of mine," said Jocelyn, "but he didn't quite finish what he wrote and so I am finishing it for him."

"Is it a story?"

"Yes, it's a sort of fairy story. I'll read it to you on Christmas Day."

"Felicity will be here for Christmas," said Henrietta.

"What?" said Jocelyn, and upset the tin of chocolate biscuits.

"She wrote and told Grandmother. She said we were to tell you, but we forgot."

"Brutes!" said Jocelyn, with quite unnecessary fierceness.

"Will you read the story to all of us on Christmas Day?"

"Yes, if I get it finished in time."

"Verses in writing," repeated Henrietta. "That's what the Dean said in church. 'Such as found out musical tunes and recited verses in writing. Their bodies are buried in peace but their name liveth for evermore.' Is it because you want your friend's name to live that you are finishing his verses for him?"

"That's the idea," said Jocelyn.

"Is he dead?" asked Henrietta.

Jocelyn hesitated a moment and then said, "I think so."

"That's a pity," said Henrietta, "but it can't be helped. Shall we go and sell in the shop?"

No one arrived to buy anything in the shop, but that did not worry Henrietta; the mere fact of sitting up behind the counter in the capacity of shop assistant was sufficient for her joy.

And as she perched beside Jocelyn she repeated to him all she could remember of the words of Ecclesiasticus that the Dean had read.

"What a memory you've got!" said Jocelyn in admiration.

"I remember things that I like," said Henrietta. "They go in at my eyes or my ears and down inside and stay there."

Jocelyn got up and went to one of the bookshelves. "There are some rather similar remarks by a gentleman called Pericles that you might like," he said, and bringing the book back with him to the counter he read them to her.

"They received, each for his own memory, praise that will never die, and with it the grandest of all sepulchres, not that in which their mortal bones are laid, but a home in the minds of men, where their glory remains fresh to stir to speech or action as the occasion comes by. For the whole earth is the sepulchre of famous men; and their story is not graven only on stone over their native earth, but lives on far away, without visible symbol, woven into the stuff of other men's lives."

When he had finished Henrietta seized the book and read the last words of the passage to herself several times over. "That's what I thought this morning," she said. "All the stories that people tell and live get so mixed up with other people's stories that they never come to an end. Now if you finish that story for your friend his life will be woven with yours, won't it?"

Jocelyn stared at her, remembering how he had felt himself that the thread of his own life was woven with that of another, a light thread with a dark. "Henrietta," he said, "for a little 'un you're too perspicacious to live."

CHAPTER VIII

I

As soon as the festival was over St. Martin withdrew his summer and the rain came down in the way peculiar to Torminster, day after day of steady, penetrating downpour that made everybody and everything feel like a saturated sponge. It was very cold in the old, damp bedrooms of the Close. Grandfather got rheumatics very badly in his knees and Grandmother in her hands, and Henrietta sneezed incessantly. Hugh Anthony's health remained unaffected, though he felt the chill of his little bedroom to such an extent that his nightly query was, " Grandmother, need I wash? "

Jocelyn, now that winter was upon them in good earnest, found the discomfort of a house without modern conveniences acute. His morning's cold bath lacked thrill, but to boil enough water in his two little kettles for a hot one took a good hour. A large and loathsome fungus appeared in the corner of his bedroom and the paper in the hall peeled off with the damp. Very few customers came to the shop and he found a dead rat in the bread-bin. Martha Carroway went down with bronchitis and Mixed Biscuits with distemper. Jocelyn himself caught a bad cough through sitting up with Mixed Biscuits at night, and his balance at the bank mysteriously disappeared.

But the worst of all his trials was the mess he was getting into over Ferranti's dramatic poem. The more he worked at it the more convinced he became that it was amazingly beautiful poetry, but though the plot of the story was mapped out to the end the actual writing was only a little more than half finished, and Jocelyn found himself obliged to fill up the gaps with his own verse.

And though, like everyone else, he had written passable poetry in his youthful days he did not find it so easy now that life and its disillusionment had a little dulled his perception of beauty and his response to it. "How is it that artists keep their powers of perception even in the days when life darkens?" he asked himself. Thinking about it and taking as his model Grandfather, an artist in religion who had given to its study the devotion and the hours of discipline that a violinist devotes to his instrument, he thought that their perception was born of the faculty of wonder, deepening to meditation and to penetrating sight and so strong that it could last out a lifetime. Grandfather wondered, all day and every day, at the wisdom of God and the beauty of the world, and Ferranti had wondered at the waste and pain and frustration of life.

In him, judging from the scraps of poems that had been rescued from Mrs. Jameson, wonder had become a sense of outrage, but it had had its fruits of meditation and a rather terrible penetration. The verse that expressed it was vivid as lightning and cruel as a microscope in its power of enlarging horror.

So Jocelyn too tried to acquire the perceptive outlook, the outlook of Hamlet when he cried, "This most excellent canopy the air, look you, this brave o'erhanging firmament, this majestical roof fretted with golden fire." Even the bitter words that followed, "it appears to me no other than a foul and pestilent congregation of vapours," were the words of an artist, Jocelyn thought, stabbing like a sword in their quick flash from joy to despair. Night after night and during every spare moment of the day he steeped himself in Ferranti's poetry, and in all poetry that seemed to him akin to it, and he tried to feel every trivial happening of the day acutely and see every beauty and sorrow trebly intensified. And, though he reduced himself to a nervous wreck, he had his reward, for his verse became more and more like Ferranti's, lighter and clearer and with a winged quality that Henrietta would have told him, had she heard it, made it jump up like a lark.

Not that Jocelyn thought so. Domestic trials and the weather and his own nervous exhaustion had reduced him to depths of depression as yet unplumbed by him. When at midnight on Christmas Eve he wrote the last word, completely unsatisfied yet knowing that he could not get the thing better, he felt that he had failed Ferranti utterly. . . . This man Ferranti whom he had never seen and yet who, alive or dead, had mysteriously become his friend.

II

Yet when next morning he set out to spend Christmas Day at the Close he had the manuscript under his arm. He had promised Henrietta to read it to them and he would keep his word, even though his additions to Ferranti's original work had, in his opinion, ruined the whole thing. . . . One could not disappoint Henrietta and see the light in her eyes flicker and die out. . . . For Henrietta was very excited about this story. She had told the others that Uncle Jocelyn was finishing a fairy story begun by a friend of his and that he would read it to them on Christmas Day. He should do so, she had ordained, between tea and bed, and Mrs. Jameson and Felicity, who was to arrive at Torminster on Christmas Eve, were to come to tea and listen too.

It had seemed to Jocelyn in anticipation that the hours until tea, Felicity and the story would be a howling wilderness of impatience, but it proved not to be so, for on this first Christmas Day since his own childhood that he had spent with children he found himself recapturing a glamour that he thought had vanished completely.

For years Christmas Day had been for him a day when one ate too much so as not to disappoint cook, stifled a great many yawns and made a lot of silly jokes to hide an inner sadness that was both a lament for romance and belief that had faded and a vague sense of unsatisfied expectation.

But to-day, in company with Henrietta and Hugh Anthony, romance and belief and satisfaction were vicariously his again. He stood in the Cathedral during morning service with the children one on each side of him and sang, "Hark, the herald angels sing," aware that Henrietta, whose eyes were beaming with joy and whose muff was swinging from side to side like a pendulum as her figure swayed in time to the music, was seeing a starlit sky full of wings and a manger with a baby in it, and seeing them with her. Hugh Anthony on his other side was singing the tune a semitone flat with the full force of his lungs, but he looked happily distrait and his left hand was plunged deep in his pocket; it clutched, Jocelyn knew, the knife with two blades, a corkscrew and a thing for getting stones out of one's horse's hoofs (if one happened to have a horse that got into this predicament) that had been in his stocking. . . . Jocelyn seemed to feel the delightful outside roughness of the knife against the fingers of his own left hand and knew the sensation of satisfaction that it brought.

Beyond Henrietta was Grandmother. She was sitting down with her eyes shut because she was tired with the Christmas preparations, but her mind was thankfully fixed upon the fact of God made man. She was too practical, of necessity too concerned with the details of daily living, to be romantic in her religion like Henrietta, or quixotic like Grandfather, but her faith was the strength of her strong-minded life.

As she sat there she was in that state of detachment and tranquil concentration that brings one mind very near to another, and Jocelyn could distinctly feel her sober certainty reaching him through Henrietta's stars and wings, as though what she and her like believed was the thread strung through the lovely bead of things that Henrietta and her like imagined, giving them form and value.

During the Dean's sermon Jocelyn's thoughts wandered, for the Dean's remarks never brought conviction to sceptical minds. . . . Yet to-day he was almost persuaded by the silence of others, Grandfather, Grandmother, Henrietta and the small, thin Bishop who sat opposite him on his throne. It struck him as he meditated that if these four, whom he held to be his superiors, were believers, then their belief was more likely to be true than his own unbelief. The Bishop, a distinguished scholar with a mind far more able to test and probe than his, Grandfather with his artist's perceptiveness, Grandmother with her everyday common sense and Henrietta, sensitive and romantic, playing so happily with the toys of religion and finding reality through them, had arrived through their different avenues of approach at the same place and who was he, in the face of their evidence, to say that the place did not exist?

III

The Christmas dinner, too, seemed because of the children to take on a new value. The turkey was a noble bird, brought overnight by Father Christmas in his sledge, and the flaming plum-pudding, that they had stirred laboriously in its earlier stages, was alight with the wishes they had wished as the spoon went round.

And then came the ecstasy of present giving, and then a short walk to assist the processes of digestion, and then, at last, it was tea-time and they were sitting in the drawing-room waiting for Mrs. Jameson and Felicity.

"I'll go down and meet them," said Jocelyn with

extreme casualness, as soon as the garden door was heard to click.

"Me too!" yelled the children, but Grandfather quite unaccountably seized one by the slack of his jersey and the other by her sash and seemed not to want to be left.

Jocelyn went downstairs and out into the garden. It was quite dark, with stars burning frostily, and the lantern that Felicity carried swung very gently on its chain, backwards and forwards, as Henrietta's muff had swayed in church, accompanying her singing, as the pendulum of the clock moves, measuring time, as the tides swing in time to the measured movement of the moon. . . . And love too has its rhythm, its partings and its reunions, its times of waiting and its times of movement. . . . And love to-night was on the move. Jocelyn standing still, and Felicity coming a little nearer with every swing of her lantern, both seemed to themselves to be drawing together without any volition of their own.

They were suddenly together in the lighted hall without any very clear idea as to how they had got there. As Jocelyn sat her down on the oak chest and took off her fur coat and goloshes Felicity chattered as a bird sings, joy being with her a thing that must be instantly expressed lest she burst, but Jocelyn did not speak, it being with him a thing that silenced. He took as long as possible over the removal of each golosh so that he could quietly verify all Felicity's high-lights. . . . Her sunflower hair and tawny eyes, her laugh and her gaiety were mercifully unchanged. . . . The velvet frock that reached to her ankles was a warm brown and she was not so unaware of her own charms as to forget to lift it a little now and then so that her orange satin petticoat could be enjoyed by an admiring world.

"I can't undo this safety-pin," complained Mrs. Jameson from the shadows.

Their joy had been like four walls that shut out all remembrance of an outside world, but at the sound of her voice they jumped up in compunction and hurried to help her, unwrapping the five white shawls that hid the glory of her festival snow-white velvet dress and icy, sparkling diamonds.

The two women made a strange contrast as they followed Jocelyn and his lighted candle up the dark stairs, the one looking as though she were carved out of the same wintry grief that had paralysed her mind and the other in her brown and orange as palpitant with life as the crocuses when they spear their way through spring earth.

"Henrietta says you're going to tell us a story," said Mrs. Jameson.

"A story?" said Felicity. "What story?"

Jocelyn on the top stair turned to face her and their eyes met. Between them the candle-flame danced like a live thing, reflected in two pin-points of excitement in Felicity's eyes.

IV

Henrietta never forgot that Christmas tea-party. Grandmother had lit twelve wax candles all round the drawing-room and there were twenty tiny candles on the small Christmas-tree that stood in the centre of the tea-table. The room seemed full of stars and all the stars were singing, like those that sang to the young-eyed cherubim when Lorenzo and Jessica sat on the bank where the moonlight slept. . . . At least Henrietta thought they sang, but perhaps what she heard were the bells ringing for the evensong that no one had time to go to on Christmas Day because of the cake having to be cut.

Hugh Anthony cut it, with Jocelyn applying a little pressure in the background, and it was all that it should be, white icing and fruity inside and all, though the latter was a little plainer than was customary because of Henrietta's weak digestion.

It struck Henrietta as she ate, biting it all up very carefully as Grandmother bade her, that they were all looking extraordinarily beautiful. Grandmother in her lace cap, Mrs. Jameson in her diamonds, Felicity with her lovely petticoat, Hugh Anthony with his flaming hair and Jocelyn smiling with his eyes in the way that she liked. Even Grandfather looked beautiful, with his snowy beard, and his bald head reflecting the candlelight so merrily. . . . How safe they were, she thought. In this warm, cosy place nothing could hurt them. . . . Outside it was cold and frosty, but the cold could not get in to them.

v

And then it did.

Tea was finished and cleared away, they pulled their chairs round the fire, the children sitting on the floor at Grandfather's feet with their Sunday playthings, the shells that sounded like the sea when you held them against your ears, ready to hand in case they should be bored, and Jocelyn read them his story.

It began all right and like the nicest kind of fairy story, with a wandering Minstrel playing his flute in the forest, and it went on all right, with the Minstrel engaged on a quest, as all the best fairy-tale heroes should be, but after that it went all wrong and a cold air blew through the room. For this hero was not a homely Dick Whittington, whom you felt at the start was bound to end up as a well-fed mayor, he was someone fine and strange and likely, Henrietta felt, to be a tragic figure just because he was different. And his quest, too, was peculiar, because instead of searching for a sleeping beauty, a tangible person who could be relied on to stay put till found, he was searching for what he called the spirit of perfect beauty, an elusive thing like the will-o'-the-wisp.

Jocelyn related this hero's adventures in verse that

sang like Lorenzo's stars, but its beauty did not comfort Henrietta, for that unhappy wind was blowing through it all the time. . . . And yet, though she did not altogether understand, she found that she had to listen. . . . She could not do as Hugh Anthony did, close her ears to Jocelyn's story and open them to the song the sea was singing inside the shells, she was obliged to follow the Minstrel on his journey.

At first he tried to find this beauty in his forest, among the trees and the flowers and the nymphs who danced to the music of his flute, but he found that there were snakes coiled on the branches of the trees, and worms and dead bodies under the roots of the flowers, and as the nymphs twisted and turned in the measure of their dance he saw to his horror that there was a satyr prancing about in the middle of them. So he took off the garland of roses that the nymphs had given him and trampled on it, and he turned his back on the woods and the fields and tramped over the mountains until he came to a lovely city set on a hill and here, in the world of man's art, he tried again to find his beauty.

There were lovely things in this city, cathedrals and shrines and pictures and books and statues, but they were none of them quite perfect, sharing as they did the imperfection of the men who had made them, and they did not satisfy the hunger for the absolute that was destroying the Minstrel. Yet he stayed in the city, searching everywhere, until one day he did a dreadful thing. A certain sculptor had just completed a new statue and he invited all the chief artists of his city to come to see it, and among them he invited the Minstrel, who was full of excitement and hope, thinking that perhaps here at last he would find perfection. The party dragged on until at last the great moment came and the veil was taken from the statue. The Minstrel caught his breath and tears of delight came into his eyes as he looked at the figure of a peasant woman. His eyes travelled from the perfectly poised head and the eager face to the arms stretched out in supplication and the figure swaying a little forward as though in a passion of self-giving. . . . And then he saw the feet. . . . The sculptor's inspiration must have flagged when he got to the feet, he must have been bored or drunk or tired, for they were all wrong. The woman should have been poised on tiptoe, as though she were just going to take flight in her eagerness, but these feet were heavy as lead, ugly and shapeless, and planted on the pedestal as though fixed in mud. A sick rage took hold of the Minstrel, he rushed to the statue and flung it on the floor, smashing it into a thousand pieces. All the artists rushed at him like wild beasts and hounded him out of the city.

So he went off on his wanderings again and as he tramped along the road, weary and very sore from the beating he had had, he found that his memory was haunted by the tenderness in the face of the statue he had smashed and he wondered if perhaps he might find perfection in love. The figure he had broken had been a peasant, a woman of the people, and so he looked for the living woman in all the villages along the way. As soon as he came to a village he would go to the cross at its centre and stand there playing on his flute and all the women and children would come running out of the cottages to listen to his tunes. And at last one day he saw her, golden-haired and mysteriously beautiful, standing on the outskirts of the crowd that had collected, with a little black-haired child clinging to her skirts, her figure swaying a little to his music and her hands outstretched in her eagerness. He did not stop his playing, but over the heads of the people his eyes met hers and said to her, "Wait."

When he had finished his tune and the crowd had gone she was still there, with the child clinging to her skirts, and he went to her and took her hands and asked her to go with him.

"To the world's end," she said, "I and the child."

"I don't want the child," he said.

She looked at him steadily out of eyes that were much wiser than his. "Love is a child," she said, "and after him as he runs along with his bow and arrows come the pattering feet of little children."

So he gave in and the three of them took the road together. They earned their bread quite easily, for the woman had a lovely voice and sang to the music of his flute, so that in the towns and villages they passed through people flocked to hear them and flung silver and gold into the hat that the black-haired child carried round.

For a little while the Minstrel thought that his quest was ended, for his love made the world such a paradise that he thought he had found his perfect beauty; until one day he realized that the woman was not all that he had thought her. She had a quick temper and could say stinging things when she was tired, and she did not always give him the perfect response of sympathy that he demanded. And though her voice remained unchanged her loveliness became tarnished by her hard life, and as her mysterious beauty faded his love faded too. This third failure, far more bitter than the others because he had been nearer to attainment, made him so wretched that it robbed him of the power of clear judgment; he thought his misery was the woman's fault and he was no longer kind to her and the child.

So one day as they played and sang at a village cross another man noticed the figures of the woman and the child. He was a careless, thoughtless man, but he thought that the woman looked tired and her faded beauty touched him so much that he went to her and said, "Bring the child and come with me," and because she was proud and hated to stay with the Minstrel when he no longer loved her she obeyed.

Then it seemed to the Minstrel that nothing was left to him but himself. The natural world had failed him and the world of man's art and the world of human relationships, yet perhaps out of himself he could still spin perfection. So the music that had been to him merely a pleasure or a means of livelihood became a passion, the one thing that he lived for. He composed tune after tune for his flute, trying always to achieve perfection, always feeling it elude him by a hair's breadth yet always trying again.... But he could no longer earn his living, for these new tunes of his, into which he had poured all his longing and passion, did not please people as had the light, gay tunes of the old days, they were too intricate and too sad, and they would not listen to them or put money into the Minstrel's hat.... And so one day, as he stumbled along the road faint with hunger, he swooned and fell, and when he came to himself again he found that his flute had been broken by his fall. He picked himself up and went into a green meadow through which a river ran and here he lay down and went to sleep and in a little while he was dreaming.

He dreamed that he was looking at a pattern woven from earth to heaven, a pattern composed of shape and colour and scent and music, and the pattern was perfect beauty.... So what he had been searching for was a pattern.... For what seemed an eternity he gazed on its satisfying loveliness and then, closing the dazzled eyes that could not look any longer, he tried with his mind to separate the pattern into its component parts. They were a scent of roses, the shapely head and figure of a statue, a woman's voice, the black hair and white face of a child and a few notes from his own music.... And suddenly he was awake again and the pattern had vanished.

It was dark now and sitting near the rushing river, and talking to it as though it were a spirit, he tried to think how it was that these random memories of his life could so have combined together as to form perfection.

Out of the night there came to him the realization that man while still in the body cannot look upon pure spirit, for the white circle of transcendent beauty would strike him blind, he can apprehend it only when its light is split into coloured fragments by the prism of his own senses. And if it is his senses that apprehend these coloured fragments it is his mind that must pluck them out of the mud that he has strewn about his dwelling-place and form them into a pattern, perfect in its degree, that shall satisfy him by shadowing faintly the perfection of pattern that he cannot see.

Despair seized the Minstrel. The fragments had been there for his taking and what had he done with them? The roses he had trampled underfoot, the statue he had destroyed, the beauty that was in the woman and the child he had driven from him and the stupidity that had caused his bodily weakness had smashed his flute into a hundred pieces. He had destroyed beauty. Beauty was dead and he must follow it, for without it his life was useless to him. His feet carried him through the darkness to the water's edge and the river of death closed over his head.

VI

Jocelyn's voice ceased and Grandmother, who had become bored with the Minstrel at the end of Scene II and had gone to sleep, woke up for a moment to send the children to bed and then dozed off again. Mrs. Jameson had slept throughout and was still sleeping. When the children had been kissed and blessed and dispatched upstairs Grandfather, Felicity and Jocelyn looked at each other strangely and then at the sleeping old ladies.

"Better come downstairs," whispered Grandfather.

They lit a candle and stole down to his study, where they lit the green-shaded oil-lamp, poked up the log fire and pulled their chairs close to it. Books lined the walls and were piled in pyramids on the table. More books lay on the floor and the window-sills and, owing to the difficulty of housework in the study when Grandfather would not allow anything to be touched, a light coating of dust gave to the whole room a rather pleasant neutral tint, like the silvering of dew in early morning. The mingled scent of old leather, damp and burning wood was a singularly studious smell, suggesting the treasures of the past and the torch of learning. . . . The room had the indescribable fascination of all studies, the atmosphere of a room where the life of the mind only is carried on and the fret and business of practical living are shut out.

"When did you find that poem, and how and where?" whispered Felicity.

Jocelyn told her the whole history, and when he had finished Grandfather, who had been leaning back in his chair with his hands folded across his stomach, suddenly leant forward. "My dear boy, do you mean to tell me that you wrote only a little less than half of that exquisite poetry yourself?"

"Weren't the joins and patches obvious?" asked Jocelyn.

"No," said Grandfather, and could say no more. There had been times in the past when his children had given him severe shocks by suddenly displaying unguessed-at powers, but none of their shocks had been equal to the earthquake with which his grandson had just shot him skywards. . . . He needed to get his breath.

"Well, Horatio," said Felicity, "you've told that story very well."

"Why do you call me Horatio?" asked Jocelyn, smiling.

"'And in this harsh world draw thy breath in pain to tell my story.' Heavens, how you must have worked! No wonder you look like a dug-up corpse."

"This is only a fairy tale. What makes you think it is Ferranti's own story?" queried Jocelyn.

"Because every word of it digs into you. You know yourself the difference between the poetry of experience and the poetry of imagination. Take the Elizabethan love poetry, it affects you just like a dance tune, tickling awake one's surface pleasure, and compare that with a poem like Emily Brontë's, 'If grief for grief can touch thee.' When I first read that I didn't know a thing about Emily, who she was or why she wrote as she did, but it gave me such a wound that I stayed awake at night. ... This poetry affects one in the same way."

"I can't judge of it from the outside like that because I've identified myself with Ferranti so closely that I feel the whole thing is my own work."

"Yet you think it is his own story?"

"Yes. I didn't at first, but I do now."

"Why?"

"You'll laugh," said Jocelyn, "but you told me that Ferranti's story must be written in the house, and Grandfather told me that the print of his personality must be there, and after all they are the same thing, for a man's history is just the shadow thrown by his personality, isn't it?"

"Yes. Well?"

"And I've felt that personality, read the story if you like to put it like that, in several ways. I've felt it internally, weaving itself into my own life as though two threads were twisted together, and externally, as though it were part of the house, and it's a frustrated, remorseful thing, the very same person as the Minstrel in that story."

"What do you think?" Felicity asked Grandfather.

"That Minstrel," said Grandfather, "is Ferranti as I knew him."

"Is Ferranti alive or dead?" asked Felicity.

"Dead," said Jocelyn. "The Minstrel followed the beauty he had killed beyond death and at the beginning of his poem Ferranti wrote these words from Shelley's

'Adonais,' 'Die, if thou wouldst be with that which thou dost seek, follow where all is fled.'"

Grandfather made a restless, unhappy movement. Suicide was to him a confession of failure more humiliating to the spirit of man than any other, and the thought that his friend had stooped to it hurt him intolerably.

"Alive or dead it doesn't make any difference," said Felicity. "The play must be put on. If he's alive it will bring him back and if he's dead it will also bring him back."

"How?" asked Jocelyn.

"Ferranti once said to me," said Grandfather, "that at rock-bottom living is merely a giving of personality. Therefore if you and Felicity give his personality to the world he lives whether he be alive or dead. Is that right, Felicity?"

Felicity nodded, her face eager and her eyes bright as her mind grappled delightedly with ways and means, an activity it adored.

"No manager in his senses would put on a tragic dramatic poem," said Jocelyn firmly. "We must try and get it published."

"But the public won't read him," objected Felicity, "they've refused to already. . . . No, it must be acted."

"But I tell you——" began Jocelyn.

Felicity stamped her foot. "Now don't begin to be sensible and defeatist or we'll get nowhere. No one ever does anything in this world until they go a little mad."

"But are there any insane managers in London now? You ought to know."

"Not loose, but there's plenty about this play to appeal to the sane ones," declared Felicity. "The scenes would be an effective spectacle; the dancing nymphs and the satyr, the smashing of the statue and the finding of the woman and the child at the village cross. Then there's a chance for lovely music. . . . I know a composer who would help us there. . . . And there's the poetry; that's not just good, it's great, and spoken rightly it can't fail of its effect; for the public does care for what's great, you know, it's only the just plain good that's not sharp enough to get through its thick skin. And, best of all for commercial purposes, we can advertise Ferranti as dead."

"I never knew that death was commercial before."

"Oh, very. You see it is always the people who are furthest away from us who seem most worth while, and death is a great distancer. And then producers love a dead author because he can't come and interfere."

"What if Ferranti is alive after all and turns up in the middle of rehearsals?"

"Well, we must take the risk."

"What shall we do if no one will put on this play unless we provide a little capital?"

"I shall borrow money from everyone I know, including the Dean."

"But the Dean didn't like Ferranti."

"No, but he likes me."

Grandfather roused himself from the silence that had wrapped him round while they talked. "Go on," he said, "and God guide you, but go carefully. Go mad with circumspection."

VII

Jocelyn and Felicity stood in the dark porch while behind them in the hall Mrs. Jameson was saying goodbye to Grandfather and Grandmother. They were about to embark together on an adventure and they felt taut and excited and very close together.

With a sudden unthinking movement he flung his arms round her and kissed her on the highlights that he loved, her hair and her eyes and her pointed chin, and then as suddenly let go again.

Felicity, smiling and unflurried, returned his kiss

gently, aware that the instinctive fling of his arms round her was what his heart knew about his love, while his considered withdrawal was what his mind knew about his bank balance. She was used to being fallen in love with, she had in fact reduced the business of saying no to a fine art, but the art of saying yes she had yet to master and she felt a little afraid. She was capable of earning enough for both of them, but if she humiliated him in any way she would upset the balance of their relationship, put the weight of dependence on the wrong side of the scales and strain their love with the drag of it. She would have to go slowly, as Grandfather said, and yield to the madness of love with circumspection.

"Good night, Horatio," she said lightly. "You and I and Ferranti, we're together in this, but Ferranti comes first. Happy people can always wait."

Instantly their positions seemed to Jocelyn rightly adjusted. They stood one on each side of Ferranti, for the moment separated by him. It would be time enough for their positions to change when he no longer needed them.

VIII

A quarter-past ten o'clock and Grandfather was alone in his study, having actually let Grandmother go to bed without him, though of course he had carried up the teapot as usual.

He felt too tired for sleep to be possible. He said compline, but even that failed to soothe him. "I will lay me down in peace and take my rest." He was at the end of his life as well as at the end of the day, but his over-active conscience caused him to doubt if he deserved rest.

It was the weight of his responsibility for other lives that troubled him most; the children and the grandchildren whose lives derived from his and, in a lesser sense, all those other lives that had touched his at any point and been glad or sorry because of their contact.

They seemed to pass him by in a terrible procession. The men, such as Ferranti, in whom he had not kindled faith, the little children whose sorrows he had not comforted, the animals to whom he had not given the full measure of affection.

And his own children.... They passed by him in the shadows, grown men and women whose faces were marked by their sorrows and whose eyes were reproachful because they need not have suffered had they not been conceived by his act.... And his grandchildren.... How would they fare in life? Jocelyn with that streak of sadness in him, Hugh Anthony with his questioning mind, and the other boys and girls each with a seed of danger in their natures that growing crookedly might wreck their lives.

And yet the terrible law of life must be obeyed, that law of which we know nothing but that life must go on, at whatever cost, through whatever darkness, to whatever goal. Our responsibility, thought Grandfather, is not for life but for living, and on that may God, Who only knows the end and the beginning, have mercy.

The door opened and closed and Grandfather started up. Henrietta was standing by his chair in her nightgown, her feet bare and her face very white against her black hair. He was reminded for an instant of the child who had flickered across the stage in Ferranti's story.

"Dear me!" he said, and lifting her on to his knee he adjusted his spectacles to have a look at her. Her eyes seemed without light, a sure sign that she was unhappy, and her toes were very cold. He rubbed them, repeating the time-honoured formula, so soothing to cold toes, about the little pigs who went to market, wrapped her up in his old cassock and inquired what the matter was.

"I can't go to sleep because I have a pain here," said Henrietta, laying her hand upon her front.

"That's the cake," said Grandfather, who had suffered similarly, and administered a peppermint lozenge.

"And I have a pain in my mind," she said.

"That's the Minstrel," said Grandfather, who had a pain in his from the same cause.

"I didn't understand," she sighed. . . . She had been terribly out of sorts all the evening, quite unable to enter whole-heartedly into the nightly game with Hugh Anthony, that of seeing who could spit farthest into the fire the skin that they removed with their tongues from the top of their supper glass of hot milk, and crying when she was alone in bed, as though she and the Minstrel were in some way connected. . . . "I didn't understand why the Minstrel was so unhappy."

Grandfather told her the story all over again, explaining it as well as he could, and with clear understanding Henrietta was comforted. Few things upset her when she understood them, she was only disturbed, like every human creature on this earth, by the unexplainable.

"Poor Minstrel," she said sleepily, "I'd like to tell him how silly he was."

"It's only a fairy story," said Grandfather. "How does your inside feel now?"

"Nice and hot," said Henrietta.

He took her upstairs to bed, tucked her up and sat by her till she fell asleep. Just as she was drowsing off she made a rather startling announcement.

"They are both here to-night," she murmured.

"Who?" asked Grandfather.

"The monk who sits in the spare room and paints and the lady with the lovely petticoat who goes tap-tap up and down the stairs."

She was asleep already, her lashes lying on her cheeks and her lids lowered like blinds between her dreaming mind and the created figures of her fancy who moved about the old house. She needed her sleep more than most children, Grandfather thought, needed it to draw

the curtain now and again between reality and illusion.
... When she woke up in the morning she would see
only the creatures of flesh and blood who move upon
the material plane.

And yet he felt it was right that she, with her sensitive
imagination, should grow to womanhood in such a place
as Torminster, for imagination, like the honey-sucking
bee, creates from what it feeds upon. Surrounded with
flowering beauty it creates sweetness, surrounded with
harshness and ugliness the fruits of its toil are bitter.

A mood of humble thankfulness descended upon
Grandfather, banishing his former sadness. His failures
were many, but Henrietta was quite certainly a success.
In planting this life in the right soil he felt he had done
at least one good bit of gardening before the shadows
lengthened and his work was done.

CHAPTER IX

I

JOCELYN and Felicity spent the next few days after Christmas feverishly discussing the play. How exactly should it be presented? Was it a tragedy or a romantic fairy tale? Should it be produced with the simplicity suitable to the one or the fantastic splendour demanded by the other? Above all what was the central idea that must link music, scenery, movement and poetry into one unity? They argued with some heat until Torminster itself, that was already so deeply concerned in Ferranti's play, became even more so by providing the answer at the choirboys' annual Christmas party.

This always took place on Holy Innocents' Day and was a great event, for the entire Close, as well as the choirboys, came to it. It took place at the Palace and not at the Deanery, because the Bishop liked giving parties for small boys and Lady Lavinia did not. It was regarded by all as an act of reparation made to the choirboys by Torminster. Other small boys tasted the joys of leisure at Christmas time, but these sweet innocents were obliged by the exigency of their profession to work harder than ever. Christmas Eve, Christmas Day, Saint Stephen's Day, Saint John the Evangelist's and Innocents' Day followed close upon each other's heels with that singular lack of proportion in the matter of festivals displayed by Mother Church, who might surely have spaced them out a bit, and on all of them the poor children had to attend at the Cathedral twice daily and shout themselves hoarse in anthems, carols, hymns and special psalms. . . . It was hard.

But the party, a gargantuan one, made up for it, and how fitting it was, said those who never came into close contact with the choirboys, that it should take place on Holy Innocents' Day. . . . All those sweet little boys with their round cherubic faces, guileless eyes and clean white collars. . . . It was noticeable that those, such as the organist and the headmaster of the choir-school, who did come into contact with the cherubs, never expressed an opinion on the matter.

The party began soon after three o'clock and lasted for five hours.

Henrietta and Hugh Anthony began dressing for it at twelve o'clock. They wrestled with underclothes from twelve till one, when they had lunch with overalls over the underclothes, and from two onwards, with the assistance of the entire household, they coped with the parts that show.

The underclothes of the young at that period were no light matter. The amazing amount of heat that is stored within the bodies of little children was not perhaps realized, and it was considered that they must be kept warm. Henrietta wore immensely thick woollen combinations, a woollen liberty-bodice, a woollen vest, a flannel petticoat, a silk petticoat and finally her winter party frock of blue velvet trimmed with fur. Hugh Anthony was not quite so overburdened with clothes, though his pants were tremendous, because Grandmother did not consider the bodies of the male young to be so tender as those of the female of the species, but his brown velvet suit with its frilly collar drove him nearly mad.

"I look a fool," he growled at Henrietta. "Why can't I wear Etons?"

"Grandmother says you can when you've worn out that," said Henrietta. "And I think you look sweet. . . . Like Bubbles."

Hugh Anthony made a rude noise in his throat and hurled his shoes across the floor.

Yet when it was time to go his philosophic temperament had come to his rescue. What cannot be helped must be endured and he was not without hope that some untoward accident at the party might ruin his detested suit for ever.

Grandfather, Grandmother and the children started off together, the children carrying their party shoes in brown holland bags and all of them swathed to the eyes in coats and shawls and mufflers.

For it had turned very cold. The stars that had shone so brightly on the evening of Christmas Day had been the first torchbearers in a procession of sparkling days and nights. Every morning the sun rose out of a glowing bed of fire and slowly climbed a sky of cold, brilliant blue. There was not much warmth in the sun, though he was so bright and gay, and he seemed a little aloof from the earth that loved him, but at midday he unbent a little and graciously touched the frosted trees with his fingers so that each grey twig was strung with diamonds. Then he withdrew again, flinging as final largesse an orange glow like a veil over the roofs of the city and painting the shadows of the elm-trees deep blue across the snow. Close at his heels the stars came marching and the moon blazed over the Cathedral towers like a round shield carried on the arm of a giant.

As the four of them crossed the Green the world was at that moment of pause between day and night. Henrietta had already noticed that there was always a haunting, unearthly beauty about this time of transition and that it was very varied. On grey, stormy days it was a gradual strange darkening that blotted out familiar shapes and divorced sound from its cause in a way that terrified. On sunshiny summer days it was a gradual intensification of colour and scent that came near to ecstasy. On other days it was a sudden blaze as of fire, on others a hard, bright flatness as though the earth was a painted picture.

It was this last to-day. The bare branches of the

elm-trees were strokes of paint laid on sharply against the primrose wash of the sky. The Cathedral towers stood out hard and black against the sheeted gold of the west and the snow-covered grass stretched smooth and pure. Here and there a sudden speck of colour burned as the painter's brush touched the flat surfaces; an orange square of lamplight leaping out in a dark house, a flash of colour on the snow as a robin hopped across it, a gleam of blue and green as a child in a gay muffler ran home from school. As always on these days when the earth is a painted picture it was very still; the cawing of a rook and the chime of a bell fell sharply as pebbles dropped in a deep well.

They crossed the Green and came to the Market Place, then turned to their left under the great archway that led to the Palace. Here they were overtaken by Mrs. Jameson and Felicity, accompanied by Jocelyn, who had found someone to take charge of the shop till closing time. . . . Grandfather had noticed before that when Felicity was in Torminster Jocelyn found it perfectly easy to leave the shop, but when she was not it was sheer impossibility.

They crossed the drawbridge and passed under the portcullis into the courtyard beyond. In front of them the old walls of the Palace rose majestically, quiet and withdrawn in the evening light, only the windows lighted. They paused to look at it for a moment, for it was very lovely, then scurried hastily to one side as the Dean's carriage and pair swept by them bearing Lady Lavinia in grey velvet, with a purple boa, and the Dean in a new top-hat.

"Do they want to run over us?" inquired Jocelyn with irritation.

"We're not carriage folk," explained Felicity.

II

There was no need to ring at the front door, for it

stood hospitably wide open, and Peppercue and Barleycorn, who always assisted the Bishop's decrepit old butler Baggersley on festive occasions, were hovering about to help them off with their coats. The huge stone-floored, vaulted hall was very cold and they parted with their wraps reluctantly. "There are two fires lit in the gallery," whispered Baggersley, with intent to cheer, and totteringly led the way up the lovely carved staircase.

Baggersley was very old, looked like a tortoise and was not of the slightest use. His dress clothes, green with age, hung loosely upon his withered old body and he could not now remember anyone's name, but suggestions that he should be pensioned off were not favourably received by him, so the Bishop kept him on.... "A disgrace to the place," the Dean said. "A—er—disgrace."

"Archdeacon Jones and family," quavered Baggersley at the gallery door and the Fordyces, Mrs. Jameson, Felicity and Jocelyn trooped smilingly in.

The Bishop, whose sight was poor, had a moment of confusion until Grandfather whispered hoarsely, "'Smee, Bishop," when he identified them with relief. The shortness of Baggersley's memory, together with the shortness of his own sight, made the arrival of guests something of a strain.

Few lovelier rooms were to be met with at this time in England than the gallery of the Bishop's Palace at Torminster. It stretched the whole length of one wing of the Palace and was perfectly proportioned for its length. The polished floor shone like dark water and the linen-fold panelling on the walls roused the students of these things to ecstasy. At each end of the gallery a log-fire was blazing, its glow reflected on floor and walls, and in the centre was a Christmas-tree, its top reaching to the ceiling and its branches laden with twinkling candles and presents done up in coloured paper. The choirboys stood in an excited group near the tree, looking terribly clean in their Etons, their faces shining with soaps and their eyes with expectation, while near them stood the dignitaries of the Close with their dependents, smiling with the urbanity of those who feel themselves to be in the position of benefactors but yet have had no bother with the preparations. It was certainly a great occasion, and from the walls of the gallery the former bishops of Torminster looked down upon it from their portraits, the flickering firelight playing queer tricks with their painted faces so that some of them seemed to smile at the happiness, and some to frown at the frivolity, while one gentleman at the far end of the room was distinctly seen by Henrietta to raise a hand in blessing.

The choirboys' presents were given first. Peppercue and Barleycorn mounted two rickety step-ladders and cut them off the tree, calling out the boys' names in stentorian voices, while Baggersley trotted round in circles calling out instructions to Peppercue and Barleycorn, after the manner of those who while doing no work themselves see all the more clearly how it should be done. Paper and string strewed the floor and happy squeals greeted the appearance of knives, watches, whistles, blood-curdling books about Red Indians and boxes of those explosives which, when placed beneath the chairs of corpulent relations, go off with loud and satisfying reports. . . . The Bishop always insisted upon this type of present, disregarding the complaints of the Dean and Lady Lavinia who maintained that they were in no way calculated to improve the morals of the dear boys. " No one," said the Bishop, "wants to be bothered with morals at Christmas"; which the Dean and Lady Lavinia considered such an outrageous remark that they were careful not to repeat it. . . . Delight mounted higher and higher, reaching the peak of ecstasy when the tree caught fire and Barleycorn fell off his step-ladder, Baggersley remarking with acid pleasure that he had said so all along.

Grandfather took advantage of the confusion and

howls of joy that ensued to press little packets into the hands of his young grandchildren. He remembered from his own childhood how difficult it is to watch other children receiving presents when you do not get any yourself. You may have a toy-cupboard at home stocked with good things, you may be going to a party every day for a fortnight, but it does not make any difference, for in childhood there is no past and no future, but only the joy or desolation of the moment. The tight, polite smiles that Henrietta and Hugh Anthony were maintaining with difficulty changed in the twinkling of an eye into happy grins as knobbly parcels were slipped into their hot palms from behind. . . . Surreptitiously they opened them. . . . A tiny china teapot and a box of pink pistol-caps numerous enough to turn every day of the next fortnight into a fifth of November.

Looking over their shoulders they saw Grandfather standing with his back to them, gazing with an appearance of great innocence at a portrait of an eighteenth-century bishop with a white wig and sleeves like balloons. . . . They chuckled.

The fire put out and Barleycorn smoothed down, they all went downstairs to the banqueting hall for tea.

The original banqueting hall, where kings and queens had feasted, was now a ruin standing out in the Palace grounds in the moonlight, but its name had been transferred to the sombre great room below the gallery, where damp stains disfigured the walls and where the wind always howled in the chimney.

Not that this worried the choirboys, for the Bishop's cook had surpassed herself. They sat themselves down round the groaning table and they did not speak again.

But at the buffet at the far end of the room, where the grown-ups balanced delicate sandwiches and little iced cakes in their saucers, there was a polite hum of conversation. Extraordinary, thought Hugh Anthony and

Henrietta, who had to-day to be perforce counted among them, how grown-ups talk when they eat. Don't they want to taste their food? Don't they want to follow it in imagination as it travels down that fascinating pink-lined lane to the larder below? Sometimes Henrietta tried to picture that larder. It had shelves, she thought, and a lot of gnomes called "digestive juices" ran about putting things to rights. . . . Or sometimes, unfortunately, forgetting to.

"Please," said Henrietta plaintively to Felicity, "could you hold my cup while I eat my cake? It's so dreadfully difficult not sitting down."

Felicity, who had finished her own tea, was most helpful. She held Henrietta's cup in one hand and with the other she held the saucer below the cake so that Henrietta should not drop crumbs on the carpet.

"Shall I hold yours, Hugh Anthony?" asked Jocelyn, for Hugh Anthony's cup of milk was slopping over into the saucer in the most perilous way.

"No, thank you," said Hugh Anthony, and his eyes were very bright because he had just had a brilliant idea.

Putting it into immediate practice he placed himself and his cup behind the Archdeacon, who was holding forth to Mrs. Elphinstone about total abstinence. Now when the Archdeacon held forth he had a curious habit of stepping suddenly backwards when he reached his peroration. He did it in the pulpit, frightening everyone into fits lest he should fall over the edge and kill himself, and he did it on his own hearthrug so that in winter his visitors had to keep a sharp look-out and make a dash for it when his coat-tails caught the flames, and he did it now. "Temperance, my dear lady," he said to Mrs. Elphinstone, "is the foundation stone of national welfare," and stepped backwards on top of Hugh Anthony.

Everyone rushed to pick the poor child up. He was patted, soothed, kissed, and the milk that had spilled all over him was mopped up, though it was distressingly evident that his velvet suit was ruined.

The courage with which Hugh Anthony bore the pain of his trampled feet was much admired by everyone but Henrietta, for Henrietta, standing grave-eyed and aloof, knew quite well that he had done it on purpose.

III

"And now," said the Bishop, when the boys could eat no more, "I'm afraid we must go to evensong."

This was not the end of the party but only an interruption to it, and it was not even necessary to go out of doors, for a covered way led from the Palace to the Cloisters and the Cloisters led directly into the Cathedral.

A silence fell upon them all as they entered the Cloisters, for the Cloisters always imposed silence. They were built round three sides of a square, the fourth side being occupied by the Cathedral itself, and in the square the dead were buried; those very same bishops whose pictured faces had smiled and frowned upon the Christmas party, together with deans and canons whose names on the headstones had been washed out by wind and rain. It was bright moonlight now, with a blaze of stars, and the headstones showed up black and sharp against the snow. The feet of the living clanked harshly as they passed and all unconsciously they tried to go on tiptoe. Mr. Phillips, the organist, had gone on ahead with Peppercue and Barleycorn so that when the others came into the Cathedral the candles were already flowering in the darkness and the organ playing softly.

They began with a hymn, "Once in royal David's city," after which evensong pursued its accustomed course until they got to the anthem, and it was here that Felicity and Jocelyn, who had never before attended evensong on the party day, had a shock, for it was

Steggall's anthem, "Remember now thy Creator in the days of thy youth."

It was always sung on the party day and Grandfather considered it a most depressing choice, and had said so more than once at Chapter meetings, but was not listened to because what always had been done at Torminster always was done, suitable or not, and would be till the Day of Judgment, but Felicity and Jocelyn were not concerned with its suitability so much as with its beauty.

Felicity had always considered the twelfth chapter of Ecclesiastes the most haunting poem ever written. She found in it the same beauty, tinged with a feeling of eeriness, that years later she was to find in the poetry of Mr. Walter de la Mare. "Remember now thy Creator in the days of thy youth, while the evil days come not, nor the years draw nigh, when thou shalt say, I have no pleasure in them; while the sun, or the light, or the moon, or the stars, be not darkened, nor the clouds return after the rain." A boy's clear treble rang out in the great Cathedral, where the candlelight fitfully shone on shadowed faces and carved stone and wood dark with age, while above them the pillars soared into darkness and all around them the night pressed in. A strange mutter of voices, quiet but very ominous, took up the next verse. "In the days when the keepers of the house shall tremble, and the strong men shall bow themselves, and the grinders cease because they are few, and those that look out of the windows shall be darkened." This lament for the fate of man, for the passing of his youth and joy and the coming of old age and death, was very queer and frightening, all the more so because one was not quite certain what it was all about. "Vanity of vanities, saith the preacher, all is vanity. . . . The mourners go about the streets. . . . The wheel broken at the cistern." Was that the end of the matter? "The spirit shall return unto God Who gave it." In that word "return" Felicity suddenly found comfort. The fate of man in this world was certainly a thing to be lamented over, a thing of uncertainty and loss and pain, and no amount of easy optimism could alter the facts of the case, yet in death he "returned" to his starting point of sun and moon and stars that are not darkened. Her mind wandering, she thought that the writer of this poem, when he chose sun and moon and stars as the supreme givers of joy, must have felt as Ferranti had done that man can best understand the meaning of perfection when he takes as its symbol a circle of white light. They were very akin, Ferranti and this writer whose name she did not know. . . . Suddenly she started and touched Jocelyn's arm as he sat beside her. The mist of sorrow that was in his eyes cleared away as he looked at her and whispered the thought that was in both their minds. "The answer. . . . Our play must be presented as a great lament."

The anthem ended and they knelt down to pray, their lowered eyelids shutting out even the faint candlelight so that each of them was alone in darkness. To Jocelyn, even more deeply depressed than Felicity because depression came more naturally to him, it seemed that the darkness of human life was too great to be endured. The words of the prayers flowed on unheard by him as he sank deeper and deeper into desolation. It seemed that he had touched rock-bottom when Felicity, wise through that knowledge of his thoughts that had come to her through love, put out a hand and gently touched his side. Instantly his spirits rose a little and opening his eyes he saw the candlelight. So often in his experience the minor miseries of life had been eased by the touch of humanity; would the great miseries, when they came, be eased by God's touch? One would have to be old to know and the old, he had noticed, and not the young, were more often the men of faith.

They sang a last hymn and filed silently out of the dark Cathedral and through the moonlit Cloisters. Safely back in the Palace any eerie feelings that might remain were dispelled by Mrs. Phillips. "How those boys can sing like that after all that tea," she said, "beats me."

IV

After this pious interruption the party became secular again. There was snapdragon in the darkened banqueting hall and races in the gallery, followed by the giving of prizes to the winners of the races and a few speeches. It was one of the habits of Torminster, a habit to be deplored, that upon every possible occasion it spoke. There were speeches at the choir-school prize-giving, speeches at the annual missionary sale of work, speeches at drawing-room meetings, speeches at concerts in aid of charity and, as if that was not enough, speeches at the party. Why there should be speeches at the party no one knew, but there always had been speeches at the party and so there always must be.

When the races had all been run, the orange-and-teaspoon race, the three-legged race, the wheel-barrow race, the hopping race and all the others, they sat down, the boys on the floor and the grown-ups on chairs, and the Bishop said a few words.

He made them as brief as possible, hoping that others might follow his example. He merely told his guests what a delight it was to entertain them at the Palace —at this point Baggersley, who sometimes, like Grandfather, spoke his thoughts aloud, began to say something forcible to the contrary, but his remarks were drowned by a very loud fit of coughing on the part of Barleycorn— hoped the boys had enjoyed themselves and congratulated Binks Major and Minor, Hopkins Minor and Jenkins upon carrying off the prizes. Then he sat down and the Dean got up, clearing his throat and grasping the lapels of his coat in his beautiful hands.

With the light shining on his silver-white hair and whiskers he looked magnificent. His coat was without a crease and on his gaiters every button was done up. His diamond ring sparkled and the toes of his boots, just showing below his gaiters, shone like glass. . . . Torminster glowed with pride. Not every Cathedral city, it thought, had a dean like theirs. You could have put him down anywhere and within two minutes he would have looked as though he owned the place.

"Dear friends and dear boys," fluted the Dean. This party, he felt, always had too worldly a tone—out of the tail of his eye he could see that the prizes the Bishop would soon bestow on Jenkins, Binks Major and Minor and Hopkins Minor were boxes of fireworks and waterpistols—and he always did his best, in this speech, to raise things to a higher level. He did so now for a full quarter of an hour. He told the boys how grave and noble a calling was that of a choirboy. He likened them all to the infant Samuel serving in the Temple. He went on a long time about the infant Samuel. Then he warned them very seriously, with a sidelong glance at the fireworks, of the pernicious effects upon the character of frivolity. In the midst of life, he said, we are in death, and we should not allow pleasures to lull us to forgetfulness of our sins. Then he sat down amid loud and prolonged applause, for really, the boys thought, the old boy had looked splendid while he gassed, and dear old Canon Roderick, the senior canon present—for it was impossible to get Canon Elphinstone's bathchair up the Palace stairs—tottered to his feet. Everyone loved Canon Roderick, for he had a face like a rosy apple and he never saw a child but he gave it sixpence. Moreover he always made exactly the same speech, both at the prize-giving and at the party, so that you knew exactly where you were and could applaud automatically in the right place without having to listen too hard. He always related the histories of his own sons—now elderly men —for he found, he said, that young people always like to hear about other young people. They began with Tom and followed his career through Eton and Sandhurst and into the army, went with him to India where he won distinction in a frontier skirmish, scurried at his heels to South Africa, where he won the V.C.—terrific cheers— and finally settled down with him in Hampshire where he was now, would you believe it, a retired general. Loud cheering, and they passed on to James, a sailor, following with deep interest and for the twentieth time as he climbed from midshipman to admiral and greeting his final elevation with a storm of cheering that nearly brought the roof off. Charles, a doctor, was a rugger blue—loud cheers—and Thomas, a schoolmaster, was a double first—rather subdued cheers. Henry was a leading barrister and last of all Edward, the baby, was actually a bishop. At this point, the company being what it was, the applause became deafening. Cheers, claps and even stamping greeted the achievement of Edward. Canon Roderick was helped to his seat, with his rosy face beaming with pride, and the Archdeacon rose to take his place with one of those speeches without which no prize-giving, not even a tiny one, is complete.

He began by saying that people who make long speeches are a great nuisance. Then for ten minutes or longer he explained why it is that they are a nuisance. Then he spoke a few words of congratulation to the boys who were to receive prizes, then a few words of consolation to the boys who would not receive prizes— conveying the impression that on the whole it is better not to receive prizes—followed by a few words to the grown-ups, followed by a peroration during which he suddenly stepped backwards on top of some potted plants and sent them flying.

The choir-school headmaster seized this opportunity to get up and begin his speech, which was always the last to be made at the party, hoping by this ruse to prevent anybody else from saying anything, for time was getting on and the longer they were over the speeches the longer it would be before his wife could get the boys to bed and there would be a little peace. On behalf of the choir he thanked everyone for their kindness and sat down.

It then seemed that Canon Allenby was going to make a speech, for he began to pant and grunt and heave his large person forward in his chair, and the headmaster cast a glance of anguished entreaty at the Bishop, for there was no reason whatever why Canon Allenby should make a speech, and once he started he never stopped. . . . The Bishop got up hastily, while Canon Allenby was still heaving and grunting, and called upon Binks Major and Minor, Hopkins Minor and Jenkins to come and receive their prizes. . . . Henrietta felt unhappy, and she could see that Grandfather felt unhappy too, for it was obvious that Canon Allenby was put out, and the old ought not to be put out. Let the young be put out, thought Grandfather fiercely, for the self-adjustment necessary to getting in again is so good for them. Then both he and Henrietta felt happy once more, for they saw the Dean give Canon Allenby a glance of commiseration behind the Bishop's back and Canon Allenby, who adored the Dean and felt exactly as he did about the Bishop, was comforted.

The four boys received their prizes amid renewed applause and it was time for hide-and-seek all over the house.

The ardour of the grown-ups now began to cool a little and those of them who only liked children within reason gradually melted away, leaving behind those who after four hours of a party still liked children; on this occasion Mr. Phillips, Felicity, Jocelyn—though perhaps he only stayed because he liked Felicity—Hugh Anthony, Henrietta, Grandfather and the Bishop. The two latter, when hide-and-seek was well started, sank into chairs before one of the fires in the gallery, stretched their feet to the blaze, folded tired hands and meditated silently upon the amazing vitality of the young.

At eight o'clock the dishevelled children, their heated faces smeared with dirt and their Etons ornamented with cobwebs, were assembled in the banqueting hall and again fed, after which they all went home. . . . It had been a grand party. The Bishop and Baggersley, as they saw their guests off at the hall door, could scarcely stand, while Grandfather did not refuse Jocelyn's offer of an arm home.

Felicity walked behind with the children.

"I've milked my front," said Hugh Anthony triumphantly, "and torn the seat of my trousers."

"You're a wicked boy," said Henrietta, "and your suit will have to be given to the poor. . . . I'm not milked or torn," she continued with pride, and opened her coat for Felicity to see.

It was quite true. She was one of those fortunate people who are never untidy. Whatever Henrietta might do, and to-day she had fished raisins out of the snapdragon, slid down the banisters and hidden in corners that the Palace housemaid, having no mistress, consistently overlooked as a matter of principle, she always emerged at the end of it with unruffled hair and spotless dress. At this moment, in her blue frock in the moonlight, with her opened coat held out like wings and her eyes stars in her tilted face, she looked as much like a little angel as makes no difference.

"Oh, but I love you!" cried Felicity, and the garden door of Number Two the Close being now reached she gave way to that extravagance of action which so annoyed those who did not like her, went down on her knees in the snow and flung her arms round both children. "Don't ever go away from me," she implored them. "Never. Never." Hugh Anthony, kissing her chin politely, wriggled and went away but Henrietta remained, pressing closer.

V

The day after the party was the day chosen by Grandfather for the children's annual lesson on the connection between Faith and Works, and it was a black day. Faith, as understood by Henrietta and Hugh Anthony, was saying your prayers and going to church and this they had no objection to, but Works was giving away your toys to the poor and that was another thing altogether. What connection was there, they demanded indignantly of each other, between kneeling in your nightgown at the side of your bed at night and saying "Our-Father-witchard-in-heaven," followed by "Now-I-lay-me," and parting next day from the dolls' perambulator and the tin helmet? ... There seemed none.

The giving away of the toys always took place in the afternoon, and in the morning, as soon as breakfast was over, Grandfather and the children withdrew to the little room half-way up the tower where the toy-cupboards were kept. They toiled up the stone stairs, carrying two large baskets and the oil-stove that was to warm them during their melancholy employment, in a depressing silence.

The little room had been given to the children because it was like a room in a fairy tale. It was nearly at the top of the tower and its mullioned window, set in the thickness of the wall, had a lovely view of the Cathedral towers, the Tor and the jumbled roofs of the city. It was quite empty, except for the children's treasures, and in it they were never required to tidy up.

They had a cupboard each whose state, Grandfather thought, was typical of their owners. In Henrietta's cupboard her dolls, together with their garments, furniture, crockery and cooking utensils, were laid out in neat rows on the top shelf. Her books were on the second shelf and treasures such as ribbons, tinsel off the Christmas-tree and boxes of beads were on the third shelf. You could see at once where everything was, and what it was, and when you opened the cupboard door nothing fell out.

With Hugh Anthony's cupboard it was not so, for as soon as the door was opened an avalanche descended. Jumbled up among engines with their wheels off, cricket bats cracked in the middle, headless soldiers and a moth-eaten golliwog who had seen better days, were chestnuts, bits of silver-paper, birds' feathers, the skin of a defunct snake, a mangel-wurzel and, most horrible of all, a baby chicken with two heads which had been preserved in a bottle of spirits and given to Hugh Anthony by Bates two Christmases ago. . . . Hugh Anthony with his scientific mind adored this chicken and could never understand why everyone else averted their eyes when it was produced.

Having lit the oil-stove Grandfather sat himself down on the old rocking-horse and proceeded to superintend. Each child was required to fill a basket, but they were not required to give away anything they had received this Christmas. They chose themselves what they should give away and Grandfather only interfered when he considered the choice unsuitable.

The cupboards were opened, the avalanche fell and work began.

Hugh Anthony always started by picking out the things that he really did not want, the heads of the soldiers, for instance, and the moth-eaten golliwog, but Grandfather's voice would thunder out behind him, " No, Hugh Anthony! Rubbish must not be given to God's poor! " Then Hugh Anthony, after getting no answer to his " Why not? " which Grandfather considered a rhetorical question unworthy of answer, would be obliged to choose instead the soldiers that were very nearly intact and the least beloved of his engines, pistols and bricks. The things that he cared for most deeply, such as the two-headed chicken and the skin of the snake, Grandfather mercifully considered unsuitable.

Henrietta was the stuff of which martyrs are made, for when she had to give away she always gave what she loved best. Grandfather, as he watched her dark head bent sadly over the basket and her dainty fingers slowly placing her treasures side by side inside it, understood her and suffered agonies. Yet he never interfered with the suggestion that Gladys Hildegarde, the least-loved of Henrietta's dolls, would do just as well to give away as Irene Emily Jane the worshipped and adored. . . . No. . . . For who knew what spiritual strength and beauty might not pass from Henrietta to the sawdust bosom of Irene Emily Jane, and from thence to the little girl to whom she would be given?

But the sacrifice of this lady had taken place a year ago and she was now forgotten, for time heals even the worst of wounds. Henrietta had this year, so her conscience said, to part from the snowstorm that Miss Lavender had given her on her birthday. It was an incomparable toy. It consisted of a glass globe inside which a red man in a yellow hat stood on a green field. His cottage stood in the middle distance while to the right was a fir-tree and to the left a dog. This in itself was amazing, for how in the world did the red man, his cottage, his dog and the fir-tree get inside the globe? But there was a greater marvel yet to come, for when the globe was held upside down it began to snow. First a few flakes fell, then a few more, then they fell so thick and fast that the man and his house and his dog and the fir-tree were hidden from sight. Then you turned the globe right way up again and the storm ceased. . . . It was amazing. . . . Henrietta took it out of the cupboard and held it in her hands, her head bent. Then for the last time she held it upside down and watched the snow fall. Then she placed it in the basket and turned her back on it.

Grandfather watched her with painful attention and her action seemed to him to take on a mystic meaning. The globe was the world itself, containing all creation, trees, animals, man and his works, the earth and the sky, and Henrietta, it seemed, was one of those rare beings who, like Catherine Earnshaw, are prepared for love's sake to see "the universe turn to a mighty stranger."

After she had parted with the snowstorm it seemed to Henrietta quite easy to part with other things; with her necklace of blue beads, her set of drawing-room furniture made by herself out of chestnuts, with pins for legs and pink wool twisted round more pins for the backs of the chairs, her toy sewing-machine and her Dolly Dimple, a cardboard person with twelve sets of cardboard underclothes, and ten hats.

When the baskets were packed they went downstairs and Grandfather read to them to cheer them up, and after that there was a rather penitential dinner of boiled cod and rice pudding at which Hugh Anthony did not behave well.

"Will you have skin, Hugh Anthony?" asked Grandmother, for she did not make the children eat milk-pudding-skin if they did not want to.

"No," said Hugh Anthony shortly.

"No, what?" asked Grandmother, who was punctilious about "thank you" being inserted in the proper place.

"No skin," said Hugh Anthony.

VI

After dinner they started out, carrying the baskets and watched with disapproval by Grandmother. It was not that she disapproved of self-sacrifice, in fact she approved of it within limits set by herself, but in this case she feared its after results. At the worst visiting the poor led to whooping-cough and at the best it resulted in the bringing home of insect life.

It had been snowing and the children insisted upon walking behind Grandfather so as to tread in his footsteps, for he was good King Wenceslas and they were the page who, they decided, was really a twin.

"Couldn't you walk with me?" asked Grandfather, who felt a bit lonely by himself.

"No," they said, but they did not explain why such a thing was totally out of the question so he went on feeling lonely. They looked very odd, going up the street treading in each other's footsteps, but then Torminster was used to Grandfather and the children looking odd, and took no notice.

Beyond the Close a steep street wound uphill and here lived those people referred to by the Dean as the Lower Orders and by Grandfather as God's Poor. The part of the city where they lived had a fascination for the children because in its own way it was beautiful. The street knew, as the streams knew, that it looks ugly to come down a hill in a straight line, and it wound about with stream-like windings so that you never knew what was coming round the corner. The cottages on each side were old, with weather-stained walls and flights of steps leading up to their front doors, and their crinkled roofs made a lovely pattern against the sky. No street that climbs a hill can be unattractive, Henrietta used to say in after years, the irregular line of the climbing roofs sees to that, but an old street on a hillside is one of the loveliest things on earth.

To-day the curious white light of snow was over the world and a stinging cleanliness was in the air. The sky, emptied now of its snowflakes, was a pale grey with jagged rents torn in it through which one saw the blue behind; aquamarine just over the hills, turquoise higher up and sapphire overhead. To their right the trees that covered the Tor showed to perfection the softness of their winter dress. The bare twigs seemed by their interlacing to create colour, the brown of them melting into blue and red and purple. The Tor looked like the breast of a bird, Henrietta thought. It was hard to realize that if you came close to the trees their softness would melt into hardness and their colour into stark black and brown.

Firelight shone ruddily from windows and open doors and in spite of the cold the elder children were sitting on the steps that led to them, while the babies peered over the wooden boards put across the doors to keep them from hurtling down the steps. Inside the rooms busy mothers could be seen moving backwards and forwards, their figures dark against bright-patterned wallpaper and shining pots and pans.

It was of course difficult to know which cottages they ought to go to, for they could not go everywhere. The only thing to do, Grandfather had said when he first started the annual lesson on Works, was to begin at the bottom of the street and stop whenever they saw children, and next year to begin where they had left off the previous year. There were bound to be complaints, of course, in the cottages where they did not go, but he was primarily concerned with the characters of his own grandchildren so he tried not to think about them.

"Last year," said Henrietta from the rear, "we stopped at the cottage half-way up on the left hand side where the wicked little boy showed Hugh Anthony how to make a long nose."

Grandfather remembered the regrettable incident, as indeed he might, for Hugh Anthony had been making long noses ever since, no amount of spanking curing him of the habit. That was the worst of Hugh Anthony. The wrong things seemed always to make an indelible impression on him while sweet and good influences ran off him like water off a duck's back. . . . Or so it seemed. . . . Grandfather could only hope and pray that future years might prove it otherwise.

"We'll go and see that little boy again," said Hugh Anthony.

"We will not," said Grandfather firmly. "We will go to the first house beyond him that has respectable-looking children."

The wicked little boy seemed out and they passed the

danger point in safety. Beyond were several cottages where there were no children, but after that things began to happen.

They began well.

Three little tow-haired girls sat on a flight of steps one behind the other. They wore stout boots and mufflers crossed over their chests and tied in bows behind. The dirt on their faces was only surface dirt, for their necks in contrast with their black faces were white as snow, and they had the eyes of children who have been loved from the beginning. Large handkerchiefs were attached to their persons with safety-pins and they were eating bread and jam. . . . A delightful family. . . . A family after Grandfather's own heart. . . . He smiled at them and they stopped eating bread and jam, wiped their mouths with the backs of their hands—the handkerchiefs being apparently intended for nasal use only—and smiled back at him. Then shyness seized them; they cast down their eyes and squirmed.

But Grandfather had seen behind them a clean, fire-lit kitchen, a cheerful mother and two tow-haired boys, and he led the way in, patting the heads of the girls as he climbed over them.

Inside, in an atmosphere of welcome, he was utterly happy. He sat himself down in a windsor chair, placed his hat on the floor and talked to the cheerful mother as though he had known her all his life. He felt as though the hard, happy days of his parish work were back with him again, those days when he had not felt conscious, as he was always conscious in the Close, of living a segregated life. He hated segregation, inevitable though he knew it to be. He hated the barriers of time and age and class and language. He longed for the time when all the different lights carried by man in the pageantry of life should glow into one.

But his ease was as yet impossible to Henrietta and Hugh Anthony. They stood side by side, stiff and miserable, subjected to the unwinking stare of five pairs of eyes; for the tow-headed little girls had now joined the little boys in a group as far removed as possible from their visitors. The whole width of the kitchen separated the well-dressed from the ill-dressed and it was the well-dressed, weighed down by numbers, who felt themselves at a disadvantage. What makes one feel uncomfortable, they discovered suddenly, is not what one has got or has not got, but being different.

But gradually the situation eased itself. First Henrietta took a step forward, then one of the little girls, and then before they knew where they were the chestnut chairs with the wool backs had been set out on the stone floor, becoming in a flash mahogany upon a marble pavement.

After that the giving of gifts was easy. Hugh Anthony parted almost willingly from an engine with three wheels and a box of soldiers, and Henrietta added to the chestnut chairs her blue bead necklace and Dolly Dimple.

"Isn't 'Arold goin' to 'ave nothink?" asked the eldest little girl.

"Who's Harold?" asked Grandfather with benign interest.

"My eldest," said the woman. "Upstairs with the measles." She sighed, glancing at the youngest little girl, who was sniffling. "They'll all 'ave it now. There's Rosie sneezing already."

Grandfather's eyes popped a little behind his glasses, but he was careful to go quietly on with the conversation until the end, when he rose and thought they ought to be going. A picture-book was found for Harold, mutual good-byes were said and they departed.

"I think," said Grandfather, when they were out in the street again, "that it would be better not to mention the measles to your dear Grandmother."

"Why not?" asked Hugh Anthony.

"It would distress her," said Grandfather, "to think of the poor little boy being ill."

"Oh no, it wouldn't," said Hugh Anthony.

Henrietta privately agreed with him, for he had noticed that Grandmother and Sarah enjoyed hearing about other people's ups and downs. Whenever anybody's chimney caught on fire, or cook gave notice, or appendix had to come out, Sarah would come running to tell Grandmother and Grandmother would say, " Dear me, Sarah, you don't say so! " and look most bright and interested.

They went on up the street, giving toys to the children whom they saw and sometimes going inside their homes, and all went well until they turned a corner and came upon a dingy-looking house from which no firelight shone. The broken window-panes were stuffed with rag, a most unusual sight in Torminster, and over the board across the door there peeped a dirty baby with a cold in its head, and no handkerchief. Grandfather, seeing the cold, would have passed on, but as the children were still in single file behind him, treading in the footsteps of Good King Wenceslas, he had no control over them and before he could stop her Henrietta had darted across the pavement to the baby.

She had never seen such a pitiful baby and the sight of it made her feel dreadful. It was dirty all over, from its matted hair to its bare toes, and its poor little upper lip was terribly sore because no one had ever blown its dribbling nose. In a flash Henrietta climbed over the board and blew the nose on her own clean handkerchief, then picking up the scrap in her arms she staggered with it into the gloom beyond.

Inside were dirt and evil smells and dead ashes in the grate. A horrible-looking old woman, the grandmother perhaps, with greasy strands of grey hair escaping from a man's cap, was peeling potatoes and shouting raucously at the children who seemed swarming all over the place. Henrietta, unseen, stood still and stared, for the children had not got faces like the children she was accustomed to. They had old faces and their eyes did not seem to look at anything steadily. When the old woman hit out at two of the little ones they ducked cleverly, and without fear, but their cunning was somehow horrible. Then they saw Henrietta and came boldly crowding up to her, shouting out things that she did not understand, though she knew they were mocking things. She recoiled a little and found to her relief that Grandfather was just behind her.

"Give them some toys," he said quietly, "and then come away."

But before she had time to do anything a door burst open and a drink-sodden brute of a man was upon them, a man as repellent as it is possible for a human creature to become upon this earth. It was lucky for Henrietta that in her fright she did not see him very clearly, or understand anything of the torrent of abuse that he hurled at Grandfather, except his last shout of, "I'll have none of your damned charity."

"I have no wish to inflict it on you at the moment," said Grandfather sternly, and he moved to the door, pushing Henrietta and Hugh Anthony in front of him and quite unmoved, apparently, by the flung boot that missed his head by inches. . . . This was not the first time in the course of his ministry that boots had been hurled at his head and he supposed it would not be the last, for with the vicar's permission he intended to visit this gentleman again.

Out in the street Henrietta suddenly dived under Grandfather's arm and ran back. When that terrible man had come in she had seen the children all cowering back, as they had not shrunk from the grandmother, and the sight had awakened in her some queer agony of understanding, for these were children who were not wanted. Deep down in Henrietta's mind was a half-formed memory of a time when she herself had not been wanted. It was not a real memory, like the memory of her singing mother, it was only a shadow that spread itself behind the figure of her mother, not emanating from her but from someone else, and faintly darkening those days at the orphanage when she discovered that her mother was dead and that no one would tell her anything about her father. . . . Someone, at some time, had not wanted her, that was all she knew. . . . The horrible man had disappeared again, but the children were still cowering in their corner. She pushed fiercely in among them and took the snowstorm from her basket. "Look!" she cried, and held it upside down. "Look at the snow falling."

Suddenly they were crowding round her, kicking and scuffling, fear and hatred forgotten and their eyes and mouths "ohs" of amazement. One of the boys seized the globe rudely from her and hit out indiscriminately at all the others so that he could have this treasure for himself. His hard fist caught Henrietta in the chest and nearly winded her, but she did not mind. Backing out from among them she ran back to Grandfather at the door, momentarily happy again.

But the swift changes of mood possible to childhood were not possible to Grandfather and he was by no means happy. He had had no idea that Torminster possessed such a family and he was terribly sorry that the children should have seen it. . . . Henrietta, he knew, would never forget. . . . And he was grieved, too, that she should have parted with her snowstorm when she did, for he had not the slightest doubt that within two hours it would be at the pawnbroker's. Well, for two hours, for the first time and probably the last, those wretched children would possess for their own the world and its beauty, earth and sky, a tree, a cottage, a dog and a red man in a yellow hat.

They visited no more houses that afternoon, for there was no more spirit left in them. They trailed rather sadly home, giving away the few toys that were left to the children they met.

When they got to their own garden door the light was fading and the shadows were long across the snow. The Tor woods had lost their colour and the bright patches of blue sky were swallowed up in the grey.

Henrietta and Hugh Anthony ran straight upstairs to Grandmother in the drawing-room, where the warm fire gleamed on dark panelling and coloured china and where the smell of the fresh chrysanthemums was clean and pungent. Grandfather went to his study, shut the door, fell upon his knees and prayed that the dear children might not catch the measles. . . . They did not.

CHAPTER X

I

GRASS might grow in many places, but it never grew under Felicity's feet. She threw herself into a fury of activity over Ferranti's play, dragging Grandfather and Jocelyn down with her into the whirlpool. Most of her time was spent in London, interviewing managers, composers, producers, designers of scenery, editors, journalists and gentlemen with money. She made shameless use of her attractions, proving an adorable companion to those whose services she required and smiling over her shoulder in a devastating way at the gentlemen with money.

Jocelyn, constantly summoned to her aid by a stream of telegrams whose number and volubility was at her time a great source of revenue to the Government, was obliged to leave the shop to the care of Grandfather, the children and Miss Lavender on at least three days a week.... Grandmother was outraged.... That she should live to see her own husband on the wrong side of a counter was really the last straw in a married life strewn with straws. "A Canon of the Cathedral serving in a shop," she said indignantly to Jocelyn. "I never heard of such a thing in all my life. What the Dean thinks I don't know and don't want to know. And what your poor Grandfather, who has never, let me tell you, been able to subtract a penny from three-halfpence since the day he was born, gives in the way of change I'm sure I don't know."

"Perhaps you could give him arithmetical help in the shop, Grandmother?" suggested Jocelyn mischievously.

"I help in a shop?" exclaimed Grandmother in horror. "Thank you, Jocelyn. You and your poor Grandfather may have lost the sense you were born with, but I thank God that I still retain mine."

II

On a certain February evening Jocelyn waited for the London train at Torminster station. . . . That is to say it was known as the London train because people who had left London in the dim past occupied it during the last lap of their journey to the city of dreams, but of what agonies of changes and waits and missing of connections they had passed through before they reached its shelter they were generally too exhausted to give a coherent account. . . . It was quite dark and a soft wind was blowing, a friendly buffeting wind that slapped you on the back in a cheery way, assuring you that winter was over and spring was on the way at last. Jocelyn could almost fancy that the smell of flowers was in the wind, and standing out in the darkness at the far end of the platform, looking at a round green light in the distance, he could think he was walking down the tunnel of winter and coming nearer and nearer to the green light of spring beyond.

Through the wind he could hear the grinding of wheels and see a threaded line of lights winding its way through the valley, that prosaic thing a train transformed by the alchemy of darkness into a jewelled snake. His heart beat a little faster, for one of those dots of lights represented Felicity.

The train blew its whistle and 'Erb, the beery porter, appeared upon the platform and spat upon his hands in case manual labour of any sort should be required of him.

"Blowy night, sir," he confided.

"Feeling of spring in it," said Jocelyn.

"Ah," said 'Erb profoundly, and then, yelling with the full force of his lungs as the line of lights rounded the last bend and slid into the station, "Tor-min-ster! Tor-min-ster!"

To hear him you would have thought the train was full to bursting with strangers from the Antipodes with no idea where they were, yet nothing got out but Felicity and her suitcase and Mr. Wilks and a case of stout.

Felicity looked tired, and in her grey fur coat that had been rained on during the day she seemed a depressed squirrel recently fished up out of a pond. She sighed with relief when she saw Jocelyn, feeling as she always did when she was with him that the burden of two lives fused into one, with the weight shared equally between them.

"You look dead beat," said Jocelyn. "Gotobed's here with the bus. Shall we go up in it?"

"No. Mr. Wilks and his stout are going up in the bus, and Mr. Wilks is a bit cheery. . . . He's been to a licensed victuallers' luncheon. . . . 'Erb shall put in my suitcase and we'll walk."

Mr. Wilks, with his bowler hat on the side of his head and a song on his lips and the stout, a present for Mrs. Wilks, beside him on the seat, was driven off in Cinderella's pumpkin, with Mr. Gotobed joyously cracking his whip on the box to indicate to Torminster the state of mind that Mr. Wilks was in. When they had gone, with the bus creaking from side to side and the lamps swinging, the peace of the windy night seemed intensified to Jocelyn and Felicity, strolling along in the dark.

"What a lovely wind!" murmured Felicity, slipping her arm through Jocelyn's. "It sounds like a big giant laughing up in the hills."

"What luck?" asked Jocelyn.

"Everything is practically settled and we hope to open this spring. Rehearsals begin next week and that friend of mine I told you of, Nigel Compton, is composing the loveliest music, with one tune especially that will haunt everyone till their dying day. The scenery and the ballet will be heavenly, I think, and those articles you are writing about Ferranti in the *Evening Journal* are making people quite excited. You're a splendid journalist, Jocelyn. That suggestion of yours that he's probably killed himself for lack of appreciation was first-rate propaganda."

"Who's to play the lead?" asked Jocelyn, slithering modestly away from the subject of his own journalistic efforts, of which, as a matter of fact, he was inordinately proud.

"Oliver Standish. He has a lovely singing voice, and though he has the largest appetite of any man I ever met he's slim with it and looks wonderfully ethereal and sad on the stage. That's what we want in the Minstrel; we must give the impression of a lost spirit; something in the wrong place, out of tune with its environment. . . . Man himself. . . . If this play is not a lament for the spirit of man astray in the world it is nothing at all."

"Do they understand that?"

"I've tried to rub it in and the scenery and the music and the dancing are all being designed to that end. . . . It will be a great lament."

"And who," asked Jocelyn, "is to play the golden-haired woman?"

"Felicity Summers."

"I'm glad. I wanted that," said Jocelyn, though his jealousy of Oliver Standish suddenly painted the hitherto blue night a hideous green.

"My singing is not first class but it's adequate, and they say I'm a draw."

Her voice suddenly dragged a little and Jocelyn sensed in her weariness and fear. "Are you afraid, Felicity?"

"For the first time in my life," she whispered. "You see I'm responsible for all this. It's I who've made men risk their money and their reputations over this play.

They think it's their own doing, but I know it's mine, for they've seen the play through a rosy flame and the flame was my own thoughts about it, burning before their eyes. It's terrible, Jocelyn, to be the sort of person who lights fires. I wish I wasn't."

"It will be all right," Jocelyn comforted her. "I know it will be all right."

But Felicity was still afraid. For the first time she had been realizing the heavy burden to herself that her own strength could be. That her personality could attract her stage experience had proved to her, but she had not known before that her vitality was a dynamic force to inspire others, to guide and control them, and often without their knowledge. In a sudden moment of rather dreadful clarity she saw herself going through life paying the penalty of her vitality. . . . Galvanizing other people into action, making their decisions for them, bearing their burdens, enduring their reproaches when her advice proved wrong, while all the while her ceaselessly tapped strength ebbed from her and her weariness grew. . . . Yet life, said Ferranti, was a giving of personality.

"The human race," said Jocelyn, answering her unspoken thought with that uncanny insight into her mind that was growing on him with his knowledge of her, "is divided into the proppers and the propped. The propped have an easier time, of course, but they do not live so deeply or so excitingly and they get very bored."

Felicity drew gratefully closer to him in the dark street. If their two lives ran together, as she wanted them to, and this man beside her became her husband she knew just how the propping would be divided. On the surface it would be all hers, he would rely on her to charm away his depression, to light his imagination, to reassure his self-distrust and to lighten his fears and she would sometimes perhaps, as life went on, get rather weary of doing it, yet deep down he had something that

she had not got, some sober quality of level-headedness
and caution, together with an unchangeable endurance in
love and work upon which in her bad times she would
be able to rest her whole weight.

The shops were shut and the hum of life stilled. The
High Street, as they made their way up it, with the wind
pushing jovially behind, was lit only by the sparse
street-lamps that shed pools of light here and there in
the darkness. The stream that came down from the hills
slid from darkness into light and then back into darkness
again, talking to itself all the while. As a companion it
was unobtrusive and the whole of the dreaming city
seemed theirs alone.

III

It had not been only the London gentlemen who had
provided the backing for the play, what they alone were
willing to give would not have been enough. *The Minstrel* had been written in Torminster by Ferranti and
Jocelyn and it seemed to Felicity that the beauty of the
city was enshrined in it and that in its verse she could
hear the ringing of the bells. Therefore, she argued, the
worst financial risk must be taken by Torminster for its
own child. Mrs. Jameson gave what she could afford,
Grandfather gave what he could not afford, Felicity herself gave all she could, pawning all her jewels except her
mother's pearls, and the Dean and the Bishop between
them gave quite a substantial sum.

The evening when she abstracted this from them, just
a week earlier than the night when Jocelyn met her at
the station, was the only really light-hearted evening that
Felicity enjoyed in all that difficult time. She chose to call
upon the Dean after dinner in the evening because, like
all women, she was quite sure that she looked her best
in evening dress by artificial light. She dressed with
extreme care, putting on a green silk frock that was

girdled at the waist with gold and fell to her golden
shoes in long folds that shimmered like water when she
moved. It had an Elizabethan collar that rolled softly
back from her face and stood up high behind her yellow
head, so that she looked like one of those wild arum
lilies that children call lords-and-ladies. . . . Very lordly
she looked, very ladylike. . . . She did not usually wear
jewels, and in any case most of hers were pawned now,
but to-night she hung her mother's pearls in her ears and
put a string of them round her neck because the Dean,
she felt sure, liked a woman to be discreetly jewelled.
When she was ready she sat in front of her mirror and
studied the finished work of art very seriously, as she
was wont to do before her stage appearances.

Wax candlelight, that most flattering of all light to a
woman, lit up her beauty with a mysterious softness, but
left the far corners of her bedroom dark, so that she
saw her own reflection in the mirror bright against the
darkness of night. Her gift of unselfconsciousness had
given her a curious sense of detachment regarding her
own beauty. She made use of it in her art, and she
employed it to gain the ends that she wanted, but it
always seemed to her a thing external to herself, a thing
that she picked up and used as she would have used a
sword or a rose. But to-night, seeing it so lit against
darkness, she felt for the first time the fear that haunts
beautiful women. When it left her would she find that
it had been more valuable than she knew? Would it
leave her with only the darkness? "Shall I miss you?"
she asked it. "Will Jocelyn miss you?" It was love,
she discovered suddenly, that had brought this fear to
birth within her. Jocelyn, she had been so sure, would
be a constant lover, but how could she know? How
could he know himself? Was there anything in this
world of which one could be certain, of which one could
take hold and say "This will never forsake me"? The
lovely face in the mirror, that was herself and beauty too,

suddenly smiled at her. "We will be with you always," it seemed to say, "we two." Herself, she would always have herself, that tiny spark that illness or madness or death might hide or distort or torture but would never obliterate because, paradoxically, it was not herself but God. And beauty, she would always have that because, as the Minstrel had discovered, it was not a rose that could fade or a statue that could be broken or a love that could die, but the immanent something in all these things that threaded them together into a pattern that would last as long as human life, would last until at death the pattern gave way to the blinding circle of white light and the spark of oneself was absorbed into eternity.

Well, she could not stay meditating here for ever or the mellowing effect of the Dean's nightly glass of port would have worn off. She folded a cloak that was black like the night outside and pink like the dawn inside over her green lordliness and went downstairs and out into the starlight.

IV

The Close, flooded by the moon, was quite deserted and her high-heeled gold shoes went clack-clack along the stone pavement, echoing strangely in the stillness. She held up her skirts carefully on each side and she was careful to step in the centre of each paving-stone and not on the cracks, a habit that she had caught from Henrietta. Why, she asked herself, do children never step on the cracks? Is it because it would do violence to their sense of pattern? Those beautiful paving-stones, shaped like the squares in that game called noughts and crosses, simply cried out for something planted plumb in the middle. She had heard it said that man is a pattern-making animal. For ever, in sound or sight or movement, he must be making patterns. . . . Perhaps, like the Minstrel, he has discovered that in it lies his salvation.

She turned under the great stone archway into the Deanery courtyard.

The Deanery, built of grey stone, old and frowning, took up two sides of a square, the third side being the wall of the stables and the fourth the great wall that held the gateway. At night, with the windows shuttered and the moon behind a cloud, the Deanery was alarmingly like the Bastille.

Felicity crossed the courtyard to a smaller archway in the wall opposite her where, as in some French châteaux, a flight of stone steps led up to a front door that was set right back in the heart of the building. A lamp shone over the door and a great iron bell hung down at one side. Felicity, guessing its unrelenting character, hung on to it with both hands and lifted her feet from the ground for a brief second. The result was a clanging that seemed to be ringing the knell of all the demons in the nether regions.

Wotherspoon, the Deanery butler, was so prompt and outraged in his opening of the door that Felicity retreated a few steps downwards, the black and white curves of his enormous figure looming over her like the prow of a ship intent on bearing her down. What the devil, inquired Wotherspoon's beetling brows and arched nose, did she mean by ringing the bell like that?

"Is the Dean in?" she quavered from below him.

"Have you an appointment, madam?" inquired Wotherspoon with contemptuous dignity. He always asked this question of callers of whom he did not approve; shabby callers who might beg, hungry-looking callers who arrived near lunch-time, timid callers whom it gratified his love of power to frighten out of their wits and impudent callers like Felicity who dared to ring the bell in this outrageous manner.

But Felicity had only been scared for the moment by the suddenness of Wotherspoon's eruption and his tone roused all her fighting spirit. Like a meteor she flashed by him into the lighted hall, the great man unconsciously giving ground, swept off her velvet cloak with a superb gesture of her right arm and held it out to him.

"Miss Summers," she informed him through her nose.

Wotherspoon looked from her proud golden head, rising superbly from the winged, leaf-green collar, to the silken folds of her dress and there was no more spirit left in him. Carefully he laid her cloak on a chair, reverently noting that it must have cost a pretty penny, and signified with a gracious inclination of the head that she might follow him.

It was a long way to the Dean's study and they walked slowly, as befitted the dignity of them both, Wotherspoon going first, the curves of his person protruding well in front of him, his shoulders well back and his arms held rigidly at his sides, and Felicity following, her chin in the air and her skirts whispering over the thick pile carpets. Very luxurious the Deanery was, oppressively warm with blazing fires, scented with hothouse plants and rich with all the lovely things that strew a house owned by wealth and taste. Yet Felicity thought defiantly that she did not like it as much as Grandfather's cold, monastic house. There were too many things in it. The distilled loveliness of so many centuries lay here that one felt as in a picture gallery, confused and tired, one's attention pulled into small pieces instead of braced into that one act of concentration that is like a knock flinging open a door into Paradise.

Wotherspoon opened the door of the study and anounced her. She had chosen the moment well, for the Dean had just left the ladies in the drawing-room but was not yet absorbed in whatever work it was, if any, that he did till bedtime, and so felt no sense of irritation in interruption. . . . Not that he would have minded at any time being interrupted by such a vision.

"Charming! Charming!" he murmured, fixing his eyeglass more firmly in his eye with one hand and slipping the novel he was reading under a pile of sermons with the other. Then he rose to his feet with alacrity, came to her where she stood radiantly under the hanging-lamp and kissed her hand gallantly, retaining it in his as he led her to his best arm-chair.

"This is indeed an honour," he piped, and seated himself where he could see her to the best advantage, the firelight painting roses on her green dress and the whole of his lovely room disposed around her like the setting of a jewel. Could she, he wondered, have come to him for spiritual advice? He was touched, for so few people came to him for spiritual advice, a fact that saddened him. He shot out his snowy white cuffs a little further, a habit of his when bracing himself for any activity and an action performed as unconsciously as 'Erb the porter's when he spat upon his hands.

"I want help," said Felicity, her voice vibrating with the pathos that with her theatrical training she was able to pump into it at will.

"Dear child, tell me," said the Dean, and a richness had come into his voice, as though cream had been poured into skim milk. "You can tell me anything you like with perfect certainty that I shall not abuse your confidence, and I will give you all the help that an old man has in his power to give."

Felicity realized at once that she was going to disappoint him terribly. Here he was waiting to give advice on a matter of conduct and pleased as punch because she had come to ask it of him, while she, mercenary minx that she was, had simply come to ask for money. Suddenly she was conscious of an element of pathos in him. Did he sometimes feel, during that wakeful hour of the night between one and two when sorrows loom too large and the taste of failure is at its most bitter, that as a priest he was not the shining light he had meant to be? Very quickly she rearranged in her mind the appeal that she had to make, so as to give him what he wanted while at the same time getting what she wanted without his knowing it.

"I have done something," she said, "and I don't know if I was right to do it.... I'm so worried.... I thought that perhaps you, with all your wisdom and experience, would be able to advise me. It's not too late to turn back and I will be guided by what you say."

The Dean purred.

Pleating her dress between her fingers in an adorable assumed shyness she told him the whole story. Had she done right, she asked pathetically, to make so many people risk their money and their reputations in a crazy effort to win appreciation for a man in all probability dead? With a childlike trustfulness she flung her burden upon him.

"H'm," said the Dean, and joined finger-tip to finger-tip, considering, while into his silence she dropped little remarks calculated to make him give the judgment she wanted. Surely one should be willing to take any risk, however great, to help another? She had heard him say that in a sermon once. She could not help feeling that the trend of modern literature was becoming distressingly materialistic and immoral. Did he think so? Didn't he think that artists, such as herself, should put up a fight for good and pure literature such as this play of Ferranti's undoubtedly was? She had heard him say once, in another sermon, that the battle-front of morality must fling itself out through every department of thought and action before the victory could be won. "The battle-front of morality." She had thought that such a stirring phrase of his.

Her little remarks, dropped so unobtrusively that they were hardly noticed, yet built themselves up as banks to guide the stream of the Dean's thoughts. After a long pause he told her that she had done right. "Quite right, dear child," he said. "That is my considered and unbiased judgment, given you for what it is worth."

Felicity rose to her feet with a sigh of relief. "Thank

you," she murmured tremulously. "Thank you so very much. You don't know how much you have helped me."

"This fight of yours to keep your art pure, dear child," he said, "is a noble fight, and it is a delight to an old man to see nobility and beauty so allied."

Felicity drooped her lovely head and again her fingers pleated her shining skirt in that pathetically childish action.

"If only," she whispered, "I had not got to carry on the fight with other people's money." She flung up her head in a challenging way. "If only I could back the play myself. Those horrible men I have had to beg from! If you could see them!"

Was there a suspicion of tears in her tawny eyes that they shone so brilliantly? The Dean was not sure, but the mere idea was enough to turn his mind into a veritable battle-ground.... Though he had so much money he found it, as he grew older, increasingly difficult to part with it.... He seated himself at his exquisite, inlaid writing-desk and began to make jerky remarks about the weather while his plump left hand, with its gleaming diamond ring, groped uncertainly over its drawers.

Felicity watched in an agony of uncertainty.... His fingers touched the first drawer.... His keys would be in that.... They touched the second drawer.... Unanswered letters would be there.... They touched the third drawer, that sacred third drawer where methodical people always keep their cheque-books, and she made a swift movement as though to go. "I know!" she exclaimed in sudden delight, "I'll sell my pearls! And now I really must go. Thank you so very much for all the help you have given me."

If there is one thing that an admirer of beautiful ladies dislikes more than another it is the idea of a woman selling her pearls. Like a flash that third drawer flew open and the Dean extracted his cheque-book.

"Wait!" he cried triumphantly, "Wait!" and he wrote feverishly.

Felicity gasped at the amount. He would not miss it, but even so his generosity amazed her and made her feel ashamed of her deceitful ways. . . . And yet if she had not behaved so badly he would never have won that sharp, miser's battle. . . . Was one perhaps justified in doing evil that good might come? In any case she was so overwhelmed between gratitude and shame that her thanks were a display of female sensibility that nearly stirred the Dean, deeply moved as he already was by his own generosity, to tears.

"The Bishop of Torminster," announced Wotherspoon.

The Bishop limped in, looking very small and insignificant. "About a living for that poor fellow Brown," he began at once, being a man who never wasted time or words.

"You know Miss Felicity Summers?" piped the Dean. "But of course you do, she was at the Christmas party. She is one of our leading actresses and frequently honours Torminster with her presence."

"Intensely grateful to you for your labours at the party," said the Bishop, and gave Felicity a kind smile and a grip of the hand, but seemed not really to want to notice her. He rather fought shy of women, as indeed a man who has succeeded through sheer strength of will in being both a bachelor and a clergyman for forty-five years is bound to do. "He can't support six children on a curate's stipend and he's perfectly suitable for that living in the Chapter gift," he went on, and subsided into a chair.

But the Dean was still absorbed by his recent magnificent behaviour and could not be side-tracked.

"Bishop," he proclaimed, "under the guidance of this dear young lady I have this moment become a dabbler in theatrical affairs."

"Rather you than me," said the Bishop. "Now about Brown——"

"We are to produce a play of Ferranti's," went on the Dean inexorably. "You remember Ferranti? That crazy fellow who lived in the Market Place."

"Ferranti?" said the Bishop quickly, and putting Brown on the shelf for the moment he turned to Felicity. "Tell me about it," he demanded.

Felicity told him, quickly and accurately, employing a method of narration so different from that used with the Dean that had he not been sunk in his arm-chair in that happy, dreamy state that comes after a well-fought battle he would surely not have recognized it for the same story.

"Good luck to you," said the Bishop, and felt in his pocket.

"Did you know Ferranti?" asked Felicity.

"Met him once up in the Tor woods, talked to him and liked him. Wouldn't come and see me. Funny fellow. He haunted one. A reflection on us all that he apparently made away with himself." He took something crumpled out of his pocket and began writing.

"I'm backing the play," proclaimed the Dean.

"No more than you ought to do," said the Bishop. "So am I," and he handed a cheque to Felicity.

"Thank you," said Felicity quietly.

The Dean passed behind Felicity's chair ostensibly to adjust the lamp, and so was able by sheer chance to see how much the cheque was made out for. . . . Twice as much as his.

"Bishop!" he exclaimed, outraged and reproachful, "you can't afford it."

Only last week he had again dined with the Bishop and the soles had still been lemon, not Dover.

"That's my affair," said the Bishop.

"But how do you know," smiled Felicity, "that the play is a suitable one for a bishop to back?"

"Take Canon Fordyce's word for it. Finest man I know. . . . Good night, Miss Summers, and good luck. . . Now, Dean, about that living."

The Dean was obliged to ring for Wotherspoon to show Felicity out, feeling, as he often did, that at times the Bishop was rather a thorn in the flesh.

V

Out in the moonlit Close again Felicity's shoes went clack-clack along the deserted pavement, stepping this time on the cracks and not in the centres of the paving-stones, so as to make a change. Her cloak, lined with the dawn, floated out behind her because she could not hold it, both hands being occupied with cheques.

She looked from one to the other, the Dean's so sleek and shining, the Bishop's crumpled and smelling of cheap tobacco, and smiled wickedly.

"Where will your influence stop, Ferranti?" she asked. "You were a stone thrown into Torminster as though into a pond and the ripples go out and out."

High over her head the two gentlemen with bushy hair and square caps stirred out of their habitual torpor and struck the bell ten times.

VI

One of the big days of Henrietta's life came only a few weeks later. It was the occasion of her and Hugh Anthony's annual visit to the dentist, which was a great occasion, for they patronized a London dentist and were obliged also, owing to the peculiarities of the Torminster train service, to spend a night either with Jocelyn's mother or at a respectable hotel opposite the British Museum. . . . A very respectable hotel indeed, temperance, patronized by clergymen and their wives and daughters from country parishes and Cathedral towns who were always a little disappointed, at dinner in the evening, when they hoped and expected to see a little life, at seeing only each other.

"Perfect nonsense," Grandmother said, "spending all this money going to London when there's an adequate dentist at your very door."

But Grandfather thought otherwise. Mr. Algernon Royde, who had his torture-chamber over Mr. Loveday the undertaker's, had an excellent moral character and there was doubtless great good in him professionally as well as morally, though Grandfather had not personally been able to test his capabilities because of having no teeth, but only the best dentist in England, Grandfather considered, was fit to touch the precious pearls upon which his beloved grandchildren relied for mastication. ... So to London the three of them went annually, the visit to the dentist washed down, so to speak, by a visit to the zoo. They enjoyed it all immensely, except the dentist, but that did not last long and by concentrating their minds upon the monkey-house they were able to forget about it beforehand.

The excitement of it all was much increased by the fact that they arose at dawn so as to catch the milk-train. Grandmother did not get up, of course, but she woke up, and with a lace cap tied over her curl papers and a pink woolly shawl round her shoulders and her bedroom door open she issued directions about the children's clothes and food to Sarah and Ellen, who had scarcely slept all night with all the anxiety of early breakfast and one thing and another.

They wore their best clothes of course. Henrietta had on her red coat and green silk dress and beaver cap and muff, Hugh Anthony wore naval attire and Grandfather had on the least green of his overcoats and his best round clerical hat, which was only six years old, rather than his everyday one that he could not remember how long he had had.

Mr. Gotobed, with a bunch of the first snowdrops in his buttonhole, fetched them in the bus. Very extravagant to have the bus, Grandmother said, but Grandfather did not want the dear children's legs to ache. Their legs, and his too for that matter, must be kept for the zoo.

In the train the three of them sat very still because they were so excited. The children sat one on each side of Grandfather, holding his hands, facing the way they were going, with the carpet-bag containing their night things on the seat opposite them. It was wonderful to see the Torminster hills just showing like opals against the pale blue sky, and the cows standing knee-deep in mist. The early morning was very nice, Henrietta thought, and it was lovely to see the world all misted over with the dreams of the night. The dreams that people dreamed were not visible when they came down to breakfast, except sometimes as a shadow in their eyes, but the dreams of the earth clung about her till the sun was up, soft and filmy and rainbow-tinted. . . . What did she dream of? . . . Perhaps of the days to come when men would have eyes to see her beauty and minds that would not pollute it.

The changes were enjoyable because Grandfather gave them a penny each to spend at the slot-machines, and chocolate out of a slot-machine tastes so much nicer than chocolate bought at a shop because of the risk that you run in procuring it. . . . For how are you to know, when you poke your penny into the slot, that something will not go wrong with the machinery and the chocolate never appear at all? . . . You cast your bread upon the waters and it returneth after many seconds, terrible seconds during which you listen agonizedly to those curious clicking sounds inside the machine, your eyes glued to the place where the chocolate will, perhaps, appear, and your mouth ajar and watering.

VII

They reached London at one o'clock and to Grandfather the journey had seemed to take a long time, because travelling always made his head ache and did not do his rheumatism any good, but to the children it had passed like a few seconds. They had lunch at the station in a great room packed full of people and gleaming with glass and silver that they thought must be as wonderful as Buckingham Palace, and were waited on by a real live waiter. Grandfather said they might choose what they liked to eat and they chose pork and ices. He was a little nervous about their choice and the waiter, who had children at home, said tentatively that the mutton and semolina pudding were both particularly good that day. But Henrietta and Hugh Anthony had minds of their own and knew them and Grandfather consoled himself by remembering that there is something in the atmosphere of a festive occasion which acts as a digestive. He himself could at the Deanery dinner-parties eat without any unfortunate after-effects food which if partaken of at home would have put him to bed for a week.

When they could not eat any more Grandfather unfastened the carpet-bag and took out a tooth mug, two toothbrushes and a tube of toothpaste and the children went to the cloakroom and cleaned their teeth, because Grandfather did not think it would be polite to Mr. Arbuthnot, their kind dentist, to give him teeth to look at that had pork in the corners. And anyhow, Grandfather said, one must always be as clean in the parts of one that are not seen, such as one's soul and one's back teeth, as one is in the parts that are seen, such as face and hands.

Then they took a hansome-cab to Mr. Arbuthnot's.

Twenty years later, when they were grown up, Henrietta and Hugh Anthony used to try to recapture in imagination the London of their childhood, that London of hansom-cabs and horse buses, with barrel-organs and monkeys in every square, and flower-girls and crossing-sweepers at every corner. . . . In memory it seemed a very magical city. . . . It seemed to be always spring there, with a yellow sun shining in a blue sky and a river of colour flowing before one's enchanted eyes; scarlet coats of little brown monkeys, bunches of yellow daffodils, bales of coloured silk and baskets of tomatoes in shop windows, gleaming chestnut coats of trotting horses and here and there flashes of silver and gold where the sun caught the metal on their harness. And in retrospect the smell of London had been good in those days, the mingled smell of horses and flowers and that delicious smell a dusty street has just after a water-cart has passed along it. . . . And the noise of London in those days. . . . At the time people used to complain about it, but twenty years later the alchemy of time had transformed it into a symphony. The clip-clop of the horses' hoofs, the rattle of the hansom-cabs, the cracking of the whips wielded by the jovial bus-drivers, the cries of the paper-boys, the soft swish of the crossing-sweepers' brooms, and sounding through it all, weaving the sounds together into one piece of music, a melody from Verdi's *Il Trovatore* played on the barrel-organ.

And to-day it was all at its best and the children's hearts beat high in their hansom-cab. . . . Surely a chariot of the gods, this hansom-cab. . . . The glorious thrill of it, bowling along at a great pace driven by someone you could not even see; the genius shown in the design of the thing, two wheels only, so that you swayed as in a rocking-chair, the graceful curve of the hood over your head, the slanting shutters that were slapped down over your knees, shutting you as firmly in as though you were about to turn a somersault, the trap-door through which you could if you wished hold converse with the god in the sky who drove you. And this god! Always his eyes were blue and twinkling and his nose was red and his hair was ginger; he wore a bowler hat on the side of his head and a flower in his buttonhole and when you peeped at him through the trap-door he winked one eye.

With a final breath-taking swirl round a corner they clattered to a standstill, swaying frantically, and the joyous drive was over. It had lasted, it seemed, for one second only, but in it they had flown over the moon and girdled the earth in forty minutes. They got out, too depressed now even to smile at the jovial god in the sky, and suddenly the world was darkened and all the colour and gallantry of London dwindled to a flight of ominous stone steps, and a huge expanse of shining front door with a brass plate on it inscribed with the name of Mr. Arbuthnot.

Grandfather rang the bell that pealed far away, funereally, like the bell that rings up the curtain on a tragedy. . . . Silence.

"Perhaps he's gone out," whispered Henrietta hoarsely.

"Perhaps he's dead," said Hugh Anthony with sudden hope.

But his hope was a tiny flower, nipped in the bud as soon as born, for the door was flung open by a bright young man smiling that excessively large-hearted smile that is only to be met with on the faces of dentists' assistants. . . . They went in.

Henrietta and Hugh Anthony were on the whole good children, trained to courage. To see them sitting motionless on two chairs in the dentist's waiting-room, holding copies of the *Illustrated London News* stiffly before their unseeing eyes, you would never have guessed how bad they felt. It was only Grandfather who showed traces of emotion. His hands trembled and his old head wobbled nervously. . . . These dear children and their teeth. . . . What would they not suffer before they reached that haven that he had now reached, that harbour of a top and bottom plate? He felt at that moment in his own heart every pang of dentistry that they would suffer throughout the whole course of their lives. To steady himself he pulled out his office-book and began to say evensong, though it was only two o'clock. "O Lord, open Thou our lips and our mouth shall show forth Thy praise." Surely, he thought, God Who created our mouths that they should praise Him did not intend that we should so suffer in them? Surely toothache is of the devil?

The bright young man reappeared, grinning like the Cheshire cat. "Master and Miss Fordyce," he said.

They went upstairs, the bright young man going first and Grandfather following sadly in the rear with the carpet-bag, and it was astonishing how quickly they got there.

Mr. Arbuthnot, very black and tall and slim, with grey hair and glasses and a jovial smile that showed all his flashing white teeth, was washing his hands in a high, light room where everything was very bright and shining, especially the rows of instruments set out on trays. A black chair that could move magically up and down, and should have proved attractive but did not, stood in the window and beside it was a round white basin with a fountain splashing into it that ought to have been fascinating but somehow was not.

Mr. Arbuthnot, as he dried his hands, chatted charmingly about this and that but met with very little response.

"What about a ride in the chair?" he asked. "Or do you prefer that afterwards?"

"I think," said Grandfather, "that they prefer it afterwards."

"Right," said Mr. Arbuthnot. "Ladies first?"

Without a word, and with the calm dignity of Mary Stuart on the scaffold, Henrietta removed her cap and muff and coat, climbed into the chair and opened her mouth. Mr. Arbuthnot tucked a white napkin round her neck in case she should dribble over her best frock, that he admired very much, and it began.

"Shan't hurt you," said Mr. Arbuthnot—though how could he possibly know? "A little wider please."

But he did hurt. He hurt very much indeed. Three teeth did he fill and scraped off a lot of tartar, but Henrietta never moved or made a sound, though she felt pain more than most children, and felt, too, the awful indignity that it is to a woman to have a member of the opposite sex who is in no way related to her poking about in the inside of her mouth.

"Teeth decay very easily," said Mr. Arbuthnot in an undertone to Grandfather. "She'll have trouble later."

"Dear me!" sighed Grandfather and looked dreadfully unhappy.

"Good girl," said Mr. Arbuthnot when he had done. "Now, sir, your turn."

Hugh Anthony felt these things less than Henrietta, indeed after the first minutes were over he almost enjoyed it because of his interest in seeing how things were done. Every time an instrument was removed from his mouth he asked a question. "Why is that one curved like that? Why do you have that flame burning? What's stopping made of? Must one be clever to be a dentist? Could I be a dentist? Why do you have that fountain playing into that basin?"

"Now look here, young man," said Mr. Arbuthnot. "If you don't hold your tongue I'll put stopping into it."

Hugh Anthony said no more and his tartar was removed in silence.

"This fellow will never have much trouble," said Mr. Arbuthnot in an undertone to Grandfather. "Sound teeth. No nerves."

It was over and they had rides in the chair, that had suddenly become a thing of fascination, while the fountain was a fountain playing in a fairy tale.

VIII

Out in the street, to their astonishment, they found Jocelyn waiting for them. He had come up to London the night before, leaving Miss Lavender in charge of the shop, and was to have travelled back to Torminster with them in the morning, but they had not expected to see him that afternoon.

"Are you coming to the zoo with us?" asked Hugh Anthony.

"If you don't mind," said Jocelyn, "Felicity wants you to give up the zoo and come to a rehearsal at the theatre instead."

They did not mind, indeed they were delighted, for they thought that actors and actresses rehearsing would probably be even funnier than the monkey-house and would, too, be something quite new in the way of an entertainment.

As there was not room for four in a hansom they went to the Firebird Theatre on top of a horse bus. It lacked the excitement of a hansom-cab, but had an enchantment all its own, for one felt one was riding over the turbulent sea of London in a golden galleon. It was thrilling to hang over the edge and watch the figures below sway backwards and forwards like weeds under the water.

"We get down here," said Jocelyn.

They turned up a dark alley like a cave and went through a narrow opening marked "Stage Door." It was very dark and rather mysterious to the children.

"They're rehearsing in the studio," said Jocelyn. "It's a long way up, I'm afraid."

They seemed to climb for ever, up long stone staircases and along stone passages. Grandfather got very puffed and thought the zoo preferable, but Henrietta's lively imagination transformed the ugly place into the inside of an enchanted mountain where the gnomes with their pickaxes had hollowed out a city, the sort of mountain to which the Pied Piper had taken the children. ... With a sudden leaping up of her heart she wondered if she would find the Pied Piper inside this mountain, the Pied Piper with Ferranti's face. ... As if in answer a thin thread of music came creeping through the passages to meet them, a lilting tune played on the flute.

"The Pied Piper! The Pied Piper!" she cried, and pummelled Jocelyn in the back.

"What?" said Jocelyn. "Oh, that's only Oliver Standish. Listen. Grandfather, you can hear Felicity now."

A clear voice that sang as effortlessly as a blackbird had taken up the tune. It was a wonderful tune, beautiful with the beckoning beauty of woods in the spring yet sad as a man's heart when the clouded years are upon him and he stands between birth and death with empty hands.

Grandfather stopped on the steps so suddenly that his following grandchildren nearly toppled over backwards. There had come to him one of those moments of quiet despair that lie in wait for even the happiest. Stealthy-footed they leap upon us, as we walk along the street, as we sit at evening with fruit and wine upon the table and laughter on our lips, as we wake suddenly from sleep in the hour before dawn; neither at our work nor our play nor our prayers are we safe, those moments can leap at any time out of the blackness around human life and suddenly the colours that we have nailed to our mast are there no longer and all that we have grasped is dust.

For a moment it was so with Grandfather, then he reaffirmed his faith in the existence of God by an ejaculatory prayer and blew his nose. "That tune," he murmured to Jocelyn, "that tune."

"Isn't it amazing?" said Jocelyn. "He's a genius, that fellow Compton. If that tune alone doesn't take London by storm I don't know what will."

"But so sad," said Grandfather.

"This play is a lament, remember. A lament for the spirit of man astray in the world."

"But have we any right," asked Grandfather, "to let such sadness loose?"

"I don't think it saddens people to have their heartache expressed for them in art," said Jocelyn. "It relieves them as a burst of tears would."

"Please are we going to stay here all the afternoon?" asked Hugh Anthony plaintively, and they went on.

The blackbird's voice came to them clearer and louder as they climbed, strengthening and deepening as though bird after bird were joining in the dawn chorus, until at last they found themselves in the doorway of a barn of a room under the roof. At one end of it steps led up to a platform, and here Felicity stood singing, accompanied on a cracked piano by a stout man who swore under his breath whenever he struck a faulty note. Near her, with a flute in his hand, stood a dark young man with his back to them, and at sight of him, with his height and his grace and his black hair, Henrietta's heart gave another leap. . . . It was the Pied Paper. It was Ferranti. . . . But then a short-tempered man who was standing below the platform with pages of typescript in his hand shouted out disagreeably, "Oliver, must you stand like a lamppost? If you have a waist, man, turn this way and use it," and the dark young man, turning and using it, revealed himself as a quite ordinary stranger.

Henrietta's heart ceased pounding and she was able to notice the other ladies and gentlemen who sat about on chairs near her, the men either yawning or reading books and the women knitting or sewing. They all looked dreadfully bored and the room was very dusty and bare. . . . The zoo would have been much nicer, Hugh Anthony thought, and Grandfather thought how incredible it seemed that a beautiful play could ever flower out of these dusty beginnings.

Then they came right into the room and the ladies and gentlemen stopped looking bored and looked intensely amused instead. Grandfather and the children were never in the least put out when their appearance together caused twinkles to leap into the eyes of strangers. They did not know why they were funny, but if they were, and it gave pleasure, no one was more delighted than they. They would have agreed with Herman Melville that " a good laugh is a mighty good thing and if any one man in his own proper person afford stuff for a good joke to anybody, let him not be backward, but let him cheerfully allow himself to spend and be spent in that way." Grandfather, his round clerical hat in one hand and his carpet-bag in the other and his bald head shining, beamed on the company as though they were all his own dear children. Hugh Anthony, his hair like a flame in the general dinginess, grinned, and Henrietta hurled her muff madly from hand to hand, a habit of hers when excited. " Darlings! " cried Felicity, and leaped from the stage like a kangaroo. . . . The rehearsal came to an abrupt stop and they were all introduced.

The short-tempered man was Miles Harpenden the producer, the stout man who swore was, incredibly, Nigel Compton the composer of that glorious tune. . . . Though how a man who looked like that could have written a tune that sounded like that it was impossible to say. . . . The dark young man who looked so romantic from behind but was a little disappointing from the front was the Minstrel and all the other ladies and gentlemen would one day be nymphs, artists, villagers and a satyr, though it was difficult to believe it. The satyr was the nicest of them and told Henrietta he had two little girls just her age at home. " Twins," he said, " and they go to St. Paul's day school for girls."

" You see, Grandfather," Felicity was explaining, " Flossie has chickenpox and we can't find any other child who would look the part as Henrietta does."

Henrietta, talking to the satyr about his little girls, suddenly realized that something of great importance to her was being discussed. Felicity was looking eager and Grandfather distressed.

"Her dear Grandmother wouldn't like it," he said. "She disapproves of the theatre in any case, and if a grandchild of her own——"

"It would only be for a little while," pleaded Felicity. "Just still Flossie is well again. And Henrietta is perfect for the part, she's so luminous, just the sort of child to represent an idea rather than a person. Look, Miles," and she pulled Henrietta towards Miles Harpenden and took off her beaver cap.

Miles, his habitual short temper by no means lengthened by the sight of Henrietta, grunted. "Can she act?" he asked disagreeably.

"My good man, she doesn't need to. It's the tiniest part. And she has—oh, I don't know how to say it—a grace and a swiftness that are a part of beauty. . . . Henrietta, take off your coat and go and walk across that platform."

Henrietta did not quite understand what it was all about, and she was very frightened, but she was a disciplined child and she did what she was told. Half-way across the platform, when she was feeling at her worst, the satyr made a sudden funny face at her and she smiled, her own particular brand of smile that was like a light lit behind alabaster.

"H'm," said Miles Harpenden when he saw it. "Can she be relied on to smile like that to order?"

"It's the smile she always uses," said Felicity. "Now dance, Henrietta. Just anything."

This was worse, but Nigel Compton bounced to the piano and played such a glorious jigging tune that her feet had to run after it, like two kittens after a coloured ball. And after the first few minutes she was not really frightened, for these watching people below her seemed to call out from her a power that she did not know she had. She realized afterwards that achievement is born of circumstances, a certain response that would never be called out but for a certain challenge.

The tune stopped and her feet stopped too and she found that she wanted to cry. " Darling! " cried Felicity, and ran to her and lifted her down. " What did I say? " she cried to the others over Henrietta's head.

"Good," said Miles Harpenden. "Good. Done."

" I don't think I can allow it," said Grandfather miserably. " It might be bad for her character."

" Why? " asked Felicity. " Is it bad for people to develop the talent that's in them? Can't you see that she has talent? And it will only be for a very little while and she shall live with me. Have you no trust in me? "

" Yes, dear," said Grandfather. " But what would her Grandmother say? "

No one knew.

" Let her choose for herself," suggested the satyr.

" Yes," said Grandfather, brightening. " The dear child will know what is right for herself to do."

So the situation was explained to Henrietta and when she understood what she might do if she wished she jigged for joy. She too was to become a part of this lovely thing that her friend Mr. Ferranti had made. She was not to be shut out of this stone mountain, as the boy in the story of the Pied Piper had been shut out, she too was one of the company who had followed the lilting of a tune inside its fastnesses. . . . Yet where was he himself, the Pied Piper who had brought them here? . . . Perhaps if they sang the song that he had taught them he would come back, following them as they now were following him.

CHAPTER XI

I

JOCELYN opened the door of the box and ushered them in, Grandfather and Grandmother, Mrs. Jameson, Miss Lavender and Hugh Anthony. They had come up that day from Torminster to attend the first night of *The Minstrel* and, Jocelyn's mother being away, were spending the night at the respectable temperance hotel opposite the British Museum. Jocelyn regarded them with an affectionate twinkle, wondering if quite such an extraordinary party had ever before occupied a box at the Firebird Theatre on a first night. Grandfather in his dinner-jacket, the one that had been let out with fresh material so that it looked stripy, Grandmother in her black silk, lace fichu, locket and corkscrew curls, Miss Lavender in grey silk and black mittens, Hugh Anthony in his sailor suit, and Mrs. Jameson, it being the season of Lent, in purple velvet with a tiara of amethysts.

Grandmother, though she highly disapproved of the whole thing and had only come to keep an eye on Grandfather, was nevertheless enjoying herself very much. She seated herself well to the front of the box, bolt upright, severe, bright-eyed and alert. She polished and adjusted her glasses, and Jocelyn put a cushion behind her back and saw that her smelling-salts were ready to her hand, so that she could disapprove in comfort of the fashionable crowd already filing into the stalls below her. Miss Lavender, frightened by this unusual excitement, shrank into the shadows, but Mrs. Jameson, childishly eager to show her lovely clothes, seated herself superbly beside Grandmother and raised the lorgnette that hung round her neck by a purple ribbon. Hugh Anthony, dropping on to his hands and knees, crawled through the old ladies' skirts and popped up in front of them, his blazing red head appearing like a jack-in-the-box over the edge of the box.

Grandfather sat in the shadows beside Miss Lavender. He was miserable and kept nervously clasping and unclasping his hands. He had said evensong in the train and compline in the cab, but nothing seemed to do him any good. For one thing he was attending a theatrical performance on a Friday in Lent, a crime that he had never in his wildest moments dreamed of committing, and for another thing he was so anxious about the play itself. He could not imagine how it had all come about, though he felt sure that he had had something to do with it, though he could not now remember what, and it seemed to him a very desperate undertaking. . . . What if it failed? . . . All this money and trouble wasted. . . . All these dear children, Jocelyn, Felicity, Henrietta and Gabriel Ferranti, the success or otherwise of this evening might make the whole difference to their lives. . . . Terrible to think what little things could affect the fate of men and women. . . . Terrible. . . . Yet he could not but think that they had been guided and his lips moved silently as he clasped and unclasped his hands for the hundredth time.

"I don't know if your poor Grandfather expects a blessing on this ridiculous performance," said Grandmother to Jocelyn. "What the Bishop would say if he knew we were all sitting like this in a devil's playhouse on a Friday in Lent I'm sure I don't know."

"The Bishop is in the stalls, dear," said Grandfather mildly.

"You don't say so, Theobald!" cried Grandmother, and polished her spectacles frantically.

"Why, so he is!" cried Mrs. Jameson loudly. "Bishop! Bishop! Hi!" and she leaned right out of the box and waved her lorgnette. The Bishop waved his programme jovially back and the stalls were all agog with amusement.

"You and the Bishop, Theobald," said Grandmother severely, "should be ashamed of yourselves. I can only hope the Dean won't come to hear of it."

"The Dean and Lady Lavinia," said Miss Lavender gently, "are in the dress-circle."

"I don't know," said Grandmother in despair, "what the Church is coming to."

"Look, dear Mrs. Fordyce," cried Mrs. Jameson, "that woman below us. Her lips are painted and I am quite sure that her hair is dyed."

"Where?" exclaimed Grandmother eagerly. "Where? Oh, I see. Disgraceful!"

"Let me see too," whispered Miss Lavender, creeping forward.

They were all quite happy now, except Grandfather, who would not be till the thing was safely over, and Jocelyn left them and went round behind to Felicity's dressing-room.

It was a warm, glowing room curtained in pink, its air heavy with the scent of cosmetics and the bouquets of flowers that filled its every corner. Felicity in a silk dressing-gown, with her dresser Mrs. Baker hovering behind her, was sitting in front of her looking-glass intent on her face. She smiled at him in the glass, but she did not speak, and he sat down in one of her arm-chairs to wait until she was free. Somehow he felt a little strange with this new Felicity. She looked so different in this luxurious setting, with her altered face and her strained smile, that he had that feeling, intolerable to love, of being shut out.

"Uncle Jocelyn," said a voice, and there, standing beside him, was Henrietta. She was dressed in a little green frock, the dress of a peasant girl, and her dark hair lay over her shoulders in two plaits. Mrs. Baker had not made up her face yet and her jasmine whiteness was just the same.

"You do look grand," she whispered, regarding his

brand-new dress-clothes from Savile Row and the carnation in his buttonhole. "Does it make you feel better inside to look grand outside?"

"Much better," said Jocelyn. "It's a great thing to have an outside that one must live up to, don't you think?"

Henrietta nodded gravely. "I was afraid last week," she said in her calm, deep voice, "that I was going to have a pimple on my nose. But it's all right, I haven't."

"Are you frightened?" he asked her.

"Only a little," she said. "You see, nothing can really go wrong because this is the inside of an enchanted mountain. And I mustn't be frightened, Felicity says, or I shall hurt Mr. Ferranti's play.... And it's your play, too."

"Hush!" said Jocelyn, one eye on Mrs. Baker. His own share in this play was a secret that he had kept from the world at large. It was being given to London as the work of Gabriel Ferranti only.... That poet whom this very same London had hounded to death by its neglect.... So he had told London.

"That will do for the moment, Mrs. Baker," said Felicity, and Mrs. Baker tactfully withdrew.

Felicity stood up and slipped off her dressing-gown. Under it she wore a peasant's blue dress, cornflower colour, and her feet and her arms were bare. Her hair, freshly washed and burnished, seemed a blaze of light, and she had used a make-up that made her look sunburnt. She was the beauty of the earth incarnate, Jocelyn thought extravagantly.

"You look perfect," he told her.

"I dare say," said Felicity peevishly, "but I can't find my gargle."

His sense of being shut out vanished as he hunted through the bottles on her dressing-table, and when he knocked something over and she snapped, "Idiot!" at him he felt positively comforted... When one is sufficiently intimate with the beloved to be snapped at one is intimate indeed

He found it and she gargled, pausing at intervals to be sorry because she had been so cross.

"I feel awful, Jocelyn," she said in excuse. "I've never felt so awful on a first night before. . . . What if we fail?"

"We won't fail," he rallied her. "Buck up, Felicity. You told Henrietta she mustn't be frightened and now you're frightened yourself."

She looked at him, a little surprised at his cheerfulness, a little surprised at finding him the stronger and the more courageous of the two of them. In his new clothes he looked amazingly handsome and trim and erect. His habitual shyness and self-distrust seemed to have vanished, he was laughing and confident, the hidden strength in him called out by strain. She laughed back at him, her courage leaping to meet his so that a taut wire caught and held between them, her delight in him lifting her up like a wave.

"I didn't know you were so good in danger," she said, holding out her hands. "Do you realize that this is our first adventure together?"

"It won't be our last," he laughed, "and you so wildly impulsive as you are."

The shrill voice of the call-boy echoed down the corridors. "Beginners in ten minutes, please!"

"Good-bye! Good luck!" they cried to each other.

Henrietta, watching like a mouse in her corner, thought they must have hurt themselves, they gripped each other's hands so hard.

Jocelyn tore along the passage and knocked at Oliver's door.

"Come in, damn you."

Oliver stood in the middle of his dressing-room glowering. He was dressed, at the suggestion originally of Henrietta, though the designer of the scenery and dresses thought it was his own idea, like the Pied Piper, in parti-coloured tights, with a cloak that was half of yellow and half of red. He looked very tall and thin, very charming and romantic and unearthly, and appallingly bad-tempered. Jocelyn, in spite of his confidence, felt a stab of apprehension. This man was the Minstrel himself and everything depended on him. He carried the weight of the whole thing on his shoulders. . . . And he was being exceedingly temperamental.

"Good luck," said Jocelyn cheerfully.

"Rotten bad play," growled Oliver.

Jocelyn fought down his rage. "Only you could make a success of it," he agreed. "Without you there'd be no hope."

The voice of the call-boy was heard again. "Beginners for the first act, please!"

His cry was like the pistol-shot that transforms the crouching athlete into a creature of fire and grace, a swiftly moving spirit that is hardly a human being. "Get out of the way," snapped Oliver, and pushed Jocelyn away from the door. Gone was the disagreeable, glowering young man of a moment ago and in his place there swept past Jocelyn the spirit of all young men; eager, adventurous, a little wild, foredoomed to tragedy by the very greatness of his hope. His feet made no sound as he ran down the steps, his cloak floating behind him, yellow and red like poppies in the corn.

Jocelyn went slowly back to the box, dimly aware of the subdued stir going on behind the stage. Harpenden in his shirt-sleeves swearing softly, looming shapes of scenery, moving figures of silent men and women, that behind-world packed with activity and vibrating with it like a great hive. The orchestra was playing the overture and in and out of it there ran the haunting tune that Grandfather had heard Felicity singing. It came louder and clearer as Jocelyn drew nearer to the unseen orchestra and it seemed curiously one with the yellow and red figure that had just vanished.

Back in the box he gave a little gasp as he realized the

change that had come over the auditorium since he left it. From floor to ceiling it was packed with silent figures. The lights had been lowered and one saw them only as phantom shapes filling a great cavern of darkness (what had Henrietta said about this being the inside of a mountain?) all the more ominous because of their ghostliness. ... That army of witnesses.... All that activity behind the stage, all those strained nerves, all the weeks of hard work and travail of creation that lay behind them, all Ferranti's tortured thoughts, all his own wakeful nights had been directed to one end, the pleasing of this unseen, critical multitude....

"Full house," whispered Grandfather, by whom he unexpectedly found himself sitting. "Curtain's going up."

II

Never had Nigel Compton's genius been shown more clearly than in the way in which, as the curtain rose, the overture melted into the play. Imperceptibly, with the sobbing of wind in the branches of a forest, the music died away. One hardly realized it had ceased, or that the curtain was up, before one was in the heart of that wood, soundless now except for the haunting tune that had slipped from the first violin to the flute that the Minstrel was playing under an oak-tree, an enchanted oak-tree that shone faintly silver against a dim green background.

Then the tune passed from the flute to the Minstrel himself and the voice that had already made Oliver Standish famous rang out into the dark cavern full of listening phantoms, singing words of inimitable poetry that were Ferranti's own, and the best he could do. In and out among the phantoms crept that song, now ringing out like a bell, now whispering like wind among the grasses, weaving that curious spell that destroys the sense of distance in a theatre, as though the stage itself moved forward and stood in the very heart of the audience.

Jocelyn leant back in his chair with a sigh of relief. . . . They had begun well. . . . Acutely sensitive as he was to every sensation that swept the audience, he could feel, as though balm were laid on a wound, that they were touched, interested, aroused, those twin ogres of boredom and censoriousness banished at the very outset.

The orchestra was playing again, a dance tune with an undercurrent of fear in it that grew in volume as one after the other the nymphs danced through the trees, reaching its full loveliness as they came together, swaying, parting, converging, yet always keeping visible to the audience, but hidden from the Minstrel, that hideous prancing satyr in their midst.

Jocelyn began to be able to notice things; the dim loveliness of that mysterious wood, the rainbow colouring of the nymphs' dresses, very soft and faint so that the brilliant red and yellow of the Minstrel's cloak flamed out like reality against illusion, that stark reality that man seems to himself to be against the background whose very existence apart from himself he cannot even prove.

The scene moved on to its horrible conclusion, the satyr made visible to the Minstrel and the skeletons hidden under the fair earth rising again to pollute it. The undercurrent of fear that had been in the dance tune swelled until it seemed that the figures in the dance were moving in time to the chanting of death. Oliver could act, it seemed, as well as sing, for his horror and despair caused even Jocelyn, who had written the words in which he expressed it, to shiver a little. . . . The curtain came down, the lights went up and there was a silence, the confused silence of a dreamer waking suddenly to daylight, before the thunder of applause rang out.

"That's all right," said Jocelyn to Grandfather.

"Dear me. Is it?" murmured Grandfather distractedly. "How is it that that young man is now so like Ferranti? His looks, his voice, everything. . . . He wasn't like him on the day of the rehearsal. . . . It's uncanny."

"The character he is acting has taken possession of him, that's all."

"I think it's a dreadful play," said Miss Lavender. "Those horrible skeletons! It's too terrible to think we shall all look like that one day!"

"We shan't know it, my dear," Grandmother consoled sharply. "We aren't put into our coffins with a looking-glass."

Mrs. Jameson was weeping softly into a white handkerchief with a purple border. The theme had upset her, the skeletons had upset her, everything had upset her, reminding her as it all did of the late Mr. Jameson and his end.

"I liked that satyr," said Hugh Anthony. "I liked his legs. Could I be a satyr?"

"The next act will cheer you up quite a lot," Jocelyn informed them.

And it did. The adventures of the Minstrel in the city that man had made were comic rather than tragic. The artists, attired in outrageous overalls stiff with smears of oil-paint and all of them in their make-up caricatures of famous artists and musicians of the day, including Nigel Compton who appeared in person as a caricature of himself, were amusingly grotesque against the background of beauty that they had themselves created; and the scene of the sculptor's party, where everyone reached that stage of intoxication which, like the amateur Hamlet, is funny without being vulgar, sent ripples of laughter over the audience. How comic a creature is man, cried the whisper of music that was all this scene was allowed, an ant of a creature who can yet create cathedrals and pictures and music that may live a thousand years after he is dust. How pitiful a thing he is, with his squabbles and his meanness and his cruelty, and yet how great is the vitality that raises him to life again and again when the blows of his fate strike him down.

Jocelyn was rather proud of this scene for he had written most of it. The verse had the same superb rhythm as the poetry of the rest of the play, but the matter of it was comic, an echo of the motif of the scene, the contrast between man and his works.

But the end of the act, the smashing of the statue, the cruel rage of the artists and the hounding of the Minstrel out of the city, was Ferranti's own and terrible. Ferranti seemed to say that in man, grotesque, creative, mean and courageous, there lives still the cruelty of the jungle, and who should know better than Ferranti who had felt himself to be hounded out of the life of men?

"Will it be Felicity and Henrietta now?" asked Hugh Anthony in the next interval.

"It's them next," said Jocelyn, and the expectation of the little party in the box was roused to fever pitch.

The orchestra played a country dance, the lights dimmed, the curtain rose on a village green and Jocelyn entered upon one of the most curious experiences of his life, an experience for which at the time he could find no practical explanation.

During the last few months he had thought ceaselessly about Ferranti, while he had been re-writing *The Minstrel* he had identified himself with him, while he had watched the first two acts of the play he had felt increasingly conscious of the fact that he was sitting where Ferranti ought to have been sitting, feeling probably as Ferranti would have felt had he been here, and now, during the third act, he lost all consciousness of being himself and became his friend. . . . He was Ferranti. . . . And he was watching not a scene in a play but a scene of his own life, and watching it in an anguish of love and remorse that was harder to bear than almost anything he had endured yet.

The act was the central one of the play, and the longest, and through its several scenes was traced the tragic course of human love. Its glorious birth, with the woman the incarnation of the mystery of beauty to the man, and the man a god to the woman, and each of them to the other the fulfilment of all longing. And then the gradual realization that human longing is too vast a thing to be satisfied by anything that the earth holds, human love like natural beauty can comfort but it cannot satisfy. Gradually the beauty of the woman ceased to have any mystery for the man and the end of the mystery was the end of love. With the woman it was not so. To find her god only a man roused in her not disgust but a passionate maternity. Over his faults she mourned as over the bruises of a little child, but such mourning was wearisome to him, striking at the very roots of his pride and turning the remnants of his love to hatred. Her fault, he cried, if he was but a bruised creature after all, her fault for tricking him to his fall by the lure of a mystery that was no mystery and a promise of satisfaction that was unfulfilled.

With a terrible sense of helplessness Jocelyn watched his own cruelty to the woman he had once loved; watched the growth of his bitter pride that would not humble itself to woo her again, watched her go with the careless, thoughtless man who was her second lover and who, he knew, would give her no happiness; felt anew, when she and the child had gone, the terrible sense of loss and loneliness that had nearly overwhelmed him before.... Fool that he had been.... Fools that they both had been.... Unable to take human love for what it is, man's chief support in his search for the unattainable but not its satisfaction, and so losing that inimitable comfort.... Jocelyn clenched his hands together.... It was terrible to see it happen all over again and, because it was the past, be unable to alter the march of events.

And the child! She was so delicious with her swift, graceful movements and her white face like a jasmine flower against her dark hair. Why had he not realized how lovable she was? Her hurt look when she realized he did not want her stabbed him. She had a luminous quality that was like moonlight and in her way she was as beautiful as that incomparable woman with her golden voice and her aureole of burnished hair. Together they were sunshine and moonlight and without them his life was a pitch-black night. He looked at himself in his desolation, crouching alone on the steps of a village cross, wrapped in his torn and tarnished cloak; that cloak that once had been half of yellow and half of red, the colours of divinity and humanity, yellow for the sunshine of God in man's soul that he calls idealism, red for the marching song of a young man's blood in his veins that he calls romance. He looked at himself and no hatred that he had ever felt was like his hatred of that crouching, contemptible figure.

The stage darkened round that desolate man, a lament of music was born in the shadows, grew into a tumult of despair and died. The curtain fell slowly and from far away Jocelyn heard Grandfather's voice, speaking in the drawing-room at Torminster. "I should like to see Felicity and Henrietta together. . . . Sunshine and moonlight."

Felicity and Henrietta? But that woman and child had not been Felicity and Henrietta! Or had they? The lights were up in the auditorium, a hum of conversation was rising from its crowded seats and in the box the three old ladies were chattering like starlings. "How lovely Felicity looked! And how beautifully she sang. Dear little Henrietta! She was so sweet and calm. If she was frightened no one knew it. The two of them together were quite perfect."

While the old ladies were admiring Henrietta Grandfather was painfully puzzling over her. How could she, with her inexperience, portray so poignantly the sorrow of an unwanted child? "That house where she gave away her snowstorm," he muttered. "She has remembered it and the wretched children. I should not have taken her there."

He raised his voice and spoke aloud to Jocelyn. "I did not know Felicity could act like that. . . . I did not know. . . . That was a painful scene, that last one. Dear me. Very painful."

Jocelyn blinked like an owl and found he was as cold

as ice, but yet had perspiration on his forehead as though it were eighty in the shade. He felt for his handkerchief and tried to readjust himself to reality. He, Jocelyn Irvin, had been sitting in a box at a London theatre and watching Oliver Standish and Felicity Summers, the popular actor and actress whose countenances were well known to the *Daily Mail*, acting very superbly in a play partly written by himself. His own little adopted niece, Henrietta Fordyce, had also had a tiny part to play and very taking she had been in it. . . . But it had all been nothing to do with him. . . . He was neither Ferranti nor the Minstrel, he was Jocelyn Irvin who loved Felicity Summers and would do till he died. . . . Had he had a fit, or what?

The lact act was a difficult one and its production had taxed every ounce of ingenuity possessed by Miles Harpenden, Nigel Compton, Oliver and Jocelyn. The first scenes showed the Minstrel striving to spin perfection out of his own music and for the second time rejected by men. The tunes that Nigel Compton had composed as the Minstrel's own were very haunting, expressing his longing and despair and as different from the tunes that he had played in his hey-day as the songs of nightingale and robin. The last scene was played in the semi-dark beside the river of death. Behind the Minstrel as he slept moved the figures of his dream, the beauty he had rejected; the nymphs and their flowers, the statue of the peasant that he had smashed and the woman and the child, their figures forming into a pattern as they moved. The figure of the Minstrel was very dim now, his torn cloak a dull grey in colour. At the beginning of the play he had been bright reality against a dim background, utterly sure of himself in his arrogant youth, but now it was the background that stood out gloriously as his figure faded. "We are such stuff as dreams are made on," sobbed the music, "and our little life is rounded with a sleep."

The dream faded, the dark-winged spirit of death was present with the Minstrel and the music died as they spoke together of the circle of transcendent beauty, of the pattern of immanent beauty, of the murder of beauty by man and the despair of the murderer. It was a curious dialogue, Ferranti at his most obscure and only partially illumined by Jocelyn, but it was great poetry and the audience, though with minds completely baffled, were yet lifted by it into that clear air where we lose consciousness of ourselves. Like the Minstrel they lost their sense of their own reality, and the things that in broad daylight are shadowy and dim became in that enchanted cavern where they sat the things that mattered.

As the voices ceased the orchestra began softly lamenting and as the Minstrel's feet carried him over the grass to the water's edge and darkness blotted out the scene it broke into a dirge as wild as the Highland coronach. Played in the pitch-dark it was a strange and fearful ending to what the critics afterwards described as "the most peculiar play ever produced in London."

III

But it was a success. Within three minutes the anxious ears of the actors heard a ripple of cheering breaking through the storm of clapping that had broken out as soon as the lights were up. When the curtains parted to show the whole company grouped together the roar that met them was like a great wave breaking in their faces. For a moment they were breathless with astonished relief and then, on the faces of Miles Harpenden, Nigel Compton and Oliver, there dawned the sleek expression, seen so often upon the countenance of a cat absorbing cream, of a man who is taking to himself the entire credit.... But Felicity did not look sleek. She shot a swift glance to the right, towards the nearest box, and her eyes met Jocelyn's. Humility was in their look, for between them stood a ghost.

Then followed what seemed to Jocelyn, overwrought as he was, the intolerable absurdity of a first-night finale.

Cheers. Excitement. Speeches. Felicity and Oliver taking call after call as though no one had ever seen them before or was ever likely to see them again. Then more excitement behind the stage. Mutual congratulations. Felicity snowed under by flowers. Henrietta kissed until she was quite sure the surface of her face must be worn away. Inability to find a cab for the Torminster party. Cab found. Inability to find Torminster party. Torminster party found and despatched to the respectable hotel opposite the British Museum. A party on the stage at which everyone got noisier and noisier and Oliver was quite intolerable. Inability to find a cab to take Felicity home in. Oliver's offer of his own brougham in which he himself, by himself, would take Felicity home rejected by Jocelyn with the utmost rudeness. Finding of a cab by the satyr in which Jocelyn and Felicity departed together, Felicity crying the whole way and extremely cross because she was so dreadfully tired. . . . And, at last, Jocelyn alone on the embankment with the dark river running by him and the stars over his head.

One o'clock struck from all the churches in London. . . . One o'clock. . . . Jocelyn remembered how it had struck from Torminster Cathedral on that wakeful night when he had first agonized over the manuscript of *The Minstrel*. How incredible it seemed that the great work of art that had just come to full-grown life in the city of London, the combined work of poet, artist, composer and actors, had flowered from the seed of a few dirty pages of manuscript found in a housemaid's cupboard in a small cathedral town.

"The bell then striking one," he murmured, as he had murmured on that other night. "This is the point where the ghost should enter. Are you alive, Ferranti, or are you dead?"

There was no answer; only a whisper of wind that swept little bits of paper along the dry pavement and ruffled the surface of the dark river.

CHAPTER XII

I

"The Minstrel" and Felicity remained in London as the successes of the season while Jocelyn and Henrietta, Flossie recovering from the chickenpox in due course, went back to Torminster and took up again the quiet lives that had been so strangely interrupted. It was typical of them both that they did this without difficulty. Henrietta, at heart a contemplative person, enjoyed alarums and excursions for a short while only. For her a background of quiet was essential to happiness. It had been fun to stay with Felicity, to be petted and spoiled by all her friends, to be applauded by big audiences in a crowded theatre, to have lovely things to eat and go to the zoo whenever she liked, but it had completely upset her equilibrium and she had felt as though she had been turned upside down so that everything that was worth while in her mind fell out. She, like everyone else, had to find out by experience in what mode of life she could best adjust herself to the twin facts of her own personality and the moment of time in which destiny had planted it, and she was lucky perhaps that she found out so early.

The day when she returned to Torminster was another of her great days.

Felicity's Mrs. Baker took her as far as the last change before Torminster, but from there home she travelled alone in the care of the guard, Mr. Ebenezer Wilbraham, a cousin of Mr. Bates, a nice man with a grey beard and thirteen grandchildren.

This in itself was epoch-making, for she had never

before been alone in a railway-carriage. It was true that at every stop Mr. Wilbraham came along, poked his head in, gave her a peppermint lozenge and inquired, "All serene? Eh?" but as he immediately went away again upon perceiving her still intact he did not really disturb her lovely loneliness.

There was no one in the carriage with her, so she was able to taste to the full that delicious feeling of moving through space by oneself. Why it should be so delicious it is hard to say, but the pilot alone in his 'plane, the motorist solitary at the wheel of his car and the lark mounting towards the sun will all tell you that it is.

Henrietta thought there was no adventure like it. Here she was, being flung from the world of London to the world of Torminster, belonging at the moment to neither of them and so untrammelled by their cares and worries. It was lovely until she began to wonder what would happen if she never arrived.... What if she fell between one world and the other and went down into space.... She was just beginning to feel a bit frightened when the train swung round a bend, the blue hills parted like a curtain and the city of Torminster was visible.

With a squeal of delight she jumped to her feet and leaned out of the window, which she had faithfully promised Felicity she would not do, many disobedient little girls having met their end in that way, according to Felicity. It was her first return home after her first long absence from all that she loved and the joy of it was like nothing that she had ever felt before or ever would feel again.

There it was, Torminster, her home, the place that she loved as she would love no other place all her life long. There were the old roofs and chimneys and the church spires, the smoke lying over them like a mist, and there, towering up above the smoke, was the grey rock of the Cathedral with its three towers. Her heart seemed to turn right over and she found that she was laughing and crying at the same time.

Who would meet her, she wondered; would the entire family come? She hung out of the window at the most perilous angle, only the tips of her toes touching the floor, until she could see the platform and a small dark blue figure with a flaming red head, his hands in his pockets and his legs wide apart.... Hugh Anthony had come to meet her by himself.

Instantly she knew that this was just as it should be. No one was nearer to her than Hugh Anthony and what she felt for Torminster only he in the years to come would understand; because he was a child when she was a child and had lived with her, within it, in the same enchanted land.

"Hugh Anthony!" she screamed, and falling headlong out of the carriage as soon as 'Erb had got the door open she flung her arms round his neck.

"Hullo," said Hugh Anthony, "I've got a guinea pig," and he gave her a wet kiss.

Henrietta was enchanted. That he should kiss her like that in front of 'Erb and the station-master and Mr. Gotobed was an overwhelming proof of his affection. "I do love you, Hugh Anthony," she cried.

"If you hold it up by its tail its eyes fall out," said Hugh Anthony. "Your luggage is to go up in the bus, but we can walk if we want to."

"Did you ask if you could come alone to meet me?" asked Henrietta.

"Mm."

"Why?" she asked, in trembling eagerness to hear him express his love for her.

"I thought it would be nice for Solomon to have a walk."

"Who's Solomon?"

"The guinea-pig, silly."

"Is he here?"

"Mm. In the ticket-office."

Mr. Gotobed took charge of the luggage while they

hurried to the ticket-office, where Solomon was awaiting them in a perforated cardboard hat-box tied up with string.

"He's lovely," breathed Henrietta, squinting at him through the perforations.

"I haven't held him up by his tail yet," said Hugh Anthony magnanimously. "I waited till you came back."

"Oh, but you mustn't," wailed Henrietta. "It would be awful if his eyes fell out."

"But how are we to know if it's true that his eyes will fall out unless we hold him up by his tail to see?" asked Hugh Anthony.

Henrietta sighed, for this was not the first time that this type of problem had confronted her. How, for instance, could one prove that there was life after death unless one died to see? And it would be such a pity to be dead, just as it would be such a pity for poor Solomon to lose his eyes.

"What does Grandfather say?" she asked.

"Grandfather says that the situation is an opportunity for the exercise of simple faith.... I don't know what he means."

"Not to hold up the guinea-pig," said Henrietta firmly. "Come on."

Carrying Solomon between them they slowly traversed the enchanted streets of the city. It did not look to them as it did to the grown-ups hurrying by. To them the houses seemed very tall, reaching nearly to heaven, so that the angels could pace along the tops of the curly old roofs if they wished; and very mysterious because of the unknown things that happened inside them. The little stream that ran down the side of the High Street seemed very wide to them, almost a river. It had waves in it, with jewelled fish in the curves of them, and its waters were crystal-clear. The pigeons in the Market Place all had human voices and they cried, "We are glad you are back, Henrietta, we are glad you are back," and on the Cathedral Green the birds in the elm-trees were singing like mad.

They stopped under the west front and Henrietta looked up at the ranks of kings and queens and saints. They were gazing out over her head towards the hills, as they had gazed for hundreds of years, and they did not seem to notice that she had come home. They looked very superior and they made her feel small and insignificant, human beings like herself though they were, and she turned from them to the Christ Child over the west door. His eyes met hers and suddenly He laughed, leaning His head back against His mother's shoulder and clapping His hands.

"Look, look, Hugh Anthony!" cried Henrietta, "the Baby is laughing!"

Hugh Anthony looked from the grave, unsmiling statue to Henrietta's rapt face and hoped, not for the first or the last time in his life, that his Henrietta wasn't going funny in the head. "Duffer!" he said. "He isn't!"

"No more He is," said Henrietta, looking again. "But it's funny," she continued, following Hugh Anthony homewards, "that human people can make one feel mean and small when God, Who is so much greater, doesn't."

At home there was a joyous reunion with Grandfather and Grandmother, Sarah, Ellen and Bates, and then there was high tea, followed by unpacking, and then at last she was alone in her scented bedroom with the carved angels, standing on the bare floor in her nightgown and listening to a spring shower pattering down on the garden path outside her window.... And mingling with the shower was the sound of footsteps coming clack-clack up the stairs and along the passage.

Henrietta smiled, for she knew who it was. It was the lovely lady with the powdered hair and the great billowing rosy skirt and the green petticoat, who had rings on her fingers and a black patch on her chin and pattered up and down the stairs in the evening when the house was quiet. Henrietta opened her door very softly and peeped out, but she could not see anything, or hear anything now but a mouse. It was funny how she could never see that lady with her bodily eyes but only with the eyes of her mind, and that so clearly that she could describe her appearance down to the smallest detail.

She tiptoed down the passage and opened the door of the spare-room. No one was sleeping there now and the furniture was shrouded with dust-sheets and the curtains drawn. The light was so dim that it must have been difficult for the man who sat there painting to see what he was doing. She could hardly see him herself though she knew so well what he looked like. . . . He had a kind, lined face and a circular bald patch on the top of his head, and he wore a long brown robe that reached to his toes and a rope round his middle. . . . He was painting a book, ornamenting its pages with purple pansies and ivory roses and queer little animals with long legs and scarlet tongues. . . . It was strange that she knew all about that book though she only saw it in the dark.

She went back to her room, happy and unafraid in her sense of companionship, and stood listening again. The shower had stopped and she found herself listening only to the lovely silence and it seemed to her that in it she came right way up again and her dreams, that had deserted her in London, came flocking back, so that with joy she flung open the doors of her mind and welcomed them in. Never again, she vowed, would she live a noisy life that killed her dreams. They were her reason for living, the only thing that she had to give to the world, and she must live in the way that suited them best.

II

Next day she and Hugh Anthony went to tea with

Martha and Mary of the sweet-shop on the occasion of the latter's ninetieth birthday.

It was suggested by Henrietta at breakfast that it would be a good idea if lessons that morning took the form of Nature study, so that they could go up to the Tor woods and pick wild flowers as a present for old Mary. Incidentally she was not feeling like staying indoors that morning, not even to do English literature, for after weeks of London the Tor woods were pulling at her feet and whispering in her ears. As she sat at breakfast she could almost hear the sounds that soft, furry beasts make as they slip through the undergrowth, and the tap-tap of a tree-creeper's beak on dry bark and the whisper of the wind in the branches that met one at the top of the hill.

Grandfather, reading her thoughts in her eyes, was amenable. Producing his writing-pad he wrote a note to Miss Lavender in his beautiful spidery handwriting. "Dear Miss Lavender, I find that Nature study commends itself to the young as a branch of learning to be studied on this May morning. Henrietta is certainly a little pale after London and fresh air will do her good. Yours, my dear Miss Lavender, in gratitude, Hilary Theobald Fordyce."

He handed this epistle to Grandmother to see if it met with her approval. He always asked her opinion about what he did or wrote, though if it did not coincide with what he felt to be right he was careful not to let it influence him in any way.

"H'm," said Grandmother, handing it back. "The children will never learn anything."

"Nature study is lessons, Grandmother," explained Henrietta.

"H'm," said Grandmother. "Poking about in the mud," and she went to the kitchen to tell Ellen what she thought of the consistency of last night's cutlets.

Miss Lavender, on receiving the note, was delighted, for she loved a country walk with the dear children. She had no clear idea what Nature study was, or how it should be pursued, but she thought they were doing their duty if they took with them a volume called *Wild Life Shown to the Children*, and then when they found any queer-looking fauna or flora they hunted through the book and found they were not there. . . . Which, after all, was not their fault.

The Tor woods were reached by taking a sharp turn to the right at the bottom of the street where the Lower Orders—or God's Poor—lived. Henrietta could never pass that street without a sick feeling inside her, for she had never forgotten that terrible house and the children who were not wanted. Every night upon the stage of the Firebird, when the Minstrel turned from her and abandoned her, she had remembered them, and every night the look on her face said something to those people in the audience who had eyes that saw. . . . Had those children still got the snowstorm, she wondered, and the little yellow and red man who was like the Minstrel?

The road they had taken was one of several roads that wound up from the city to the hills. Macadamized surfaces were unknown in those days and the roads varied with the weather; in winter they were slippery with a sticky brown mud that was peculiar to the Torminster valley and in dry summers they were deep in white dust. They were bad for walking, no doubt, and when bicycling was fashionable they made skidding a thing that happened with tedious regularity, but in after years Henrietta found herself regretting them, for their mud was tender to horses' hoofs and in summer their gleaming whiteness, seen in the distance against green fields, was good to look at.

They followed the road a little way and then climbed a stile to their left and found themselves on the steep path that led up through the Tor woods. . . . And the Tor woods in May were Paradise.

The primroses and violets were faded, but the wood anemones were sprinkled over the dark earth like stars.

Here and there a shaft of sunlight pierced through the new green leaves overhead and touched their whiteness to a shimmering silver, and sometimes a puff of wind made them all shiver and stir, as though they were bright points of light on water. That poised look, peculiar to them, as of something so frail that it might at any moment blow away, made them look more like butterflies than flowers whose roots were in the earth.

Miss Lavender and the children stood staring, each of them crying out in their different ways to this moment, "Stay a little. Stay a little." It did not stay, but as they turned and walked on, the magic of the woods gathering round them and penetrating them, other moments almost as good came in its place. They looked and listened and sniffed, seeing the crumpled green leaves over their heads laid like blobs of paint against a bright blue sky where the clouds were racing before a west wind, hearing the twitter of birds and the scuffling of rabbits in the bushes, smelling the scent of wet earth and moss and ferns. The sunshine seemed to get inside their eyes, brightening them, and the colour that flooded the world seemed to be clothing them too so that they all three felt supremely beautiful; indeed for fully five minutes Miss Lavender quite forgot that she was an elderly spinster and thought she was the young girl that she used to be. Funny, she thought, coming to herself again, how the spring can create this illusion that one is oneself lovely. . . . Until one suddenly remembers that one is not. . . . She stumbled over a stone, for her sight was not what it was, and Hugh Anthony called out, "Hold up, Miss Lavender," and removed a small twig from her path with a gallantry that she thought most touching in the dear boy.

"I don't think it's fair," said Henrietta from the rear, "that the earth should be made new again every year when we aren't. I think God ought to spring-clean us too."

Miss Lavender, stumbling again and feeling her

lumbago in her back, heartily, though silently, agreed with her.

"Could God spring-clean us every year if He wanted to?" asked Hugh Anthony.

"Yes, dear," said Miss Lavender.

"Then why doesn't He do it?"

"Look! A squirrel!" cried Miss Lavender, and heaved a sigh of relief as Hugh Anthony charged off into the undergrowth. The advantage of Nature study over other forms of instruction was that the young mind could always be distracted from theological argument to something more interesting to it.

They climbed slowly higher, getting with every step deeper into the wood. Over their heads the leaves gathered closer and all round them the trunks of the trees soared upwards like the pillars in the Cathedral.

Hugh Anthony was very happy poking about among the roots of the trees and then running back to Miss Lavender to ask questions about the treasures he had found; a woolly caterpillar that he thought at first was a baby hedgehog, a salmon-pink toadstool, stones and mosses. Miss Lavender gave very inaccurate replies, culled at a moment's notice from *Wild Life Shown to the Children*, but he took it all for gospel and was happy.

But Henrietta, when the trees began to thin towards the top of the hill, suddenly went off by herself. Loneliness was at times a necessity to her in the woods because then she could go mad. There was a queer streak in her nature that had come to her from her unknown ancestry and was completely at variance with the rest of her. There were two Henriettas, the orderly child whom Grandfather was training so carefully and another one, a wild thing who came to life at unexpected times and behaved like a kitten at twilight, a creature who was more of a pixy than a human being.

The orderly person was for the moment left behind on the path with Miss Lavender and Hugh Anthony, an unseen presence, and it was the wild Henrietta who took to her heels and ran, leaping over stones and fallen branches and dodging round the trunks of the trees, nimble and sure-footed as a wild animal. Every now and then she looked up at the clouds over her head and felt that she was running with them before the wind. She could run faster than they if she wanted to, she felt, she could run right over the rim of the world and get to the place where they were going before they did. She stretched her arms wide as she ran and cried out aloud, queer, high calls that sounded more fairy than human and that would have startled Grandfather if he had heard them. For pagan music had entered into her body through her flying feet that touched the earth, and leaped, and touched again, and into her mind from the air and the light and the clouds, and she had lost all touch with time and place.

With a bound she leaped to the top of a hill and looked down into a dell carpeted with bluebells. She checked and paused, still poised on her toes with her arms stretched out. The bluebells ran down the sides of the dell in rivulets and gathered at the bottom into a pool of azure. The sun that smote through the trees overhead gathered up their scent, so that it brimmed the dell like wine in a cup, and when the wind blew the slender stalks near Henrietta leaned all one way, bending their blue heads.

She paused for a moment only, then she raced down the side of the dell and fell face downwards into the azure pool. The bluebells, very tall down here because they had to reach up to the sun, yielded sweetly to the pressure of her body, then seemed to gather round as though to hide her. She stretched out her bare arms through them and felt their stalks and leaves smooth and cool against her skin, and she buried her face in the moss, sniffing its pungent, wet scent. The sun was warm on her back and she felt happy with an almost savage happiness.

Something that she had heard Grandfather quote slipped into her mind.

> "I hold him happiest
> Who, before going quickly whence he came,
> Hath looked ungrieving on these majesties,
> The world-wide sun, the stars, waters and clouds
> And fire. Live, Parmeno, a hundred years
> Or a few weeks, these thou wilt always see,
> And never, never, any greater thing."

Those words had been written by a heathen poet, Grandfather had said, and so they were not quite true, but Henrietta at this moment felt that they were. The earth was greater and lovelier than anything else and to be one with it, as she was one with it now, her body pressing against it, its scent in her nostrils and its colour blinding her eyes, was to be supremely happy; there was nothing greater than this.

Suddenly the pixy vanished, as the queer spirit that takes possession of the kitten vanishes, and she was her sober self again. She got up, surprised at herself, straightened her twisted socks and picked bits of stick out of her hair. When Miss Lavender and Hugh Anthony joined her she was picking bluebells and anemones for old Mary and was once more the tidy, orderly Henrietta whom they knew. . . . They had no idea, of course, that the other one existed.

III

At four o'clock the children presented themselves at Mary and Martha's. It was early-closing day so they did not go in through the shop but through the door at the side. It was opened to them by Martha, dressed in her best black alpaca, with a crochet shawl folded across her chest, and chattering away all of a twitter about the honour of a visit from the Close and Grandfather's great condescension in letting them come. Henrietta could not see how they could be conferring an honour upon Martha and Mary by eating up their food, the honour, she thought, was the other way round, and she did not understand the meaning of the word condescension, though she often heard it used in reference to the behaviour of the people who lived in the Close. She had once told Grandfather that she did not know what it meant and he had snorted and said he was thankful to hear it, and had not enlightened her.

Hugh Anthony did not require enlightening about these things. He had become aware early in life that there were differences of class and sex and that his own position in regard to them was happy. He belonged to the Governing Class, he had discovered, and the Dominant Sex, and like the Dean he thought these things were to his credit. . . . In after years both he and the Dean were most determined opponents of the suffragette movement. . . . So now, as he stalked down the dark passage after Martha and Henrietta, knowing himself to be conferring a benefit upon these women, he bore a marked resemblance to Napoleon in his more affable moments.

Old Mary sat in her big arm-chair beside the little fire that was always burning in her parlour, summer or winter, dressed in all her petticoats and her best dress of maroon silk. She was surrounded by the china ornaments she had collected during ninety years of life, and by the photographs of all the masters and mistresses who had known her devotion since she first took service with the then Bishop of Torminster at the age of ten. By her side was the inevitable basket of kittens—the sweet-shop cat kittened with a regularity and profusion that no other Torminster cat could get anywhere near—and on her lap were the birthday presents and letters that she had received from all her masters and mistresses still living, and also from the Bishop, to whose ears it had somehow come that eighty years ago the Palace saucepans had been washed by one of the greatest saints, always excepting Grandfather and the first Abbot, that Torminster had ever harboured. . . . She had not let these precious treasures out of the sight of her old eyes and the touch of her old hands all day, and was not likely to until sleep overtook her.

Yet she was not too absorbed in them not to be deeply touched by the gift of wild flowers from the children. "The pretty dears," she murmured, caressing the cheeks of the children and the petals of the flowers with her finger-tips.

"They're lovely in the Tor woods," said Henrietta. "Up there they look like butterflies and blue water."

"They won't last," said Hugh Anthony the realist. "Is tea ready?"

It was ready on the table in the window and was a thoroughly satisfactory tea, including four kinds of sugar cake and three jams.

"Will Master Anthony say grace?" asked Martha.

Hugh Anthony took up a Napoleonic attitude, closed his eyes tightly and came out with a long Latin grace that Grandfather used on state occasions, such as when visiting clergy came to dinner and the day when they had the annual goose.

"Latin!" said Martha. "Well, I never!"

"He doesn't understand a word," explained Henrietta. "He's just copied it from Grandfather like parrots do."

Hugh Anthony gave Henrietta a pained glance. She was always so anxious that no one should labour under a misapprehension, but personally he could not see that it did them any harm. Lying, of course, was wrong, and he never lied, but the same results could often be obtained by judicious silence. . . . He must explain this to Henrietta.

There are occasions in life when it is not only a pleasure

but a duty to overeat and this was one of them, for Martha and Mary would have been disappointed if full justice had not been done to the tea they had provided. Both children understood this and even Henrietta, though she disliked excess, ate a great deal more than she really had room for. Every time she took a fresh spoonful of jam, or Hugh Anthony reached for yet another cake, a glance of pleasure passed between the two old ladies. It seemed cruel to have to put an end to these glances, but the time came when even Hugh Anthony was obliged to shake his head speechlessly.

Any sort of movement was for the present impossible, so they sat on the floor at old Mary's feet, with the clawing, squeaking kittens spread-eagled on their chests, and listened while old Mary dilated on the glories of old.

The days of Mary's youth had been, according to her, the great days of Torminster. In those days, such was the wealth of the Church, not only the dean but every canon in the Close had had his carriage and pair. It had been grand, Mary said, to see them driving out, the reverend gentlemen so fine in their top-hats and their ladies beside them in their smart bustled dresses.

"What's a bustle?" asked Hugh Anthony. "I thought it was what you got into when you ran for a train."

"It sticks out at the back below the waist, dearie," explained Mary. "Or it did when I was young. I remember when I was parlourmaid at Archdeacon Dobson's and was waiting at my first dinner-party—nervous I was—I let the dish of potatoes slip in my hand and two of them fell out and lodged in Lady Maria Jefferson's bustle. I was in a taking, but I picked them up careful-like in my fingers and her ladyship was none the wiser."

"My lady," said Henrietta dreamily, "has a bustle all the way round, front and sides as well as back. . . . It's pink, though her petticoat is green."

"Who's she, dearie?" asked old Mary.

But Henrietta, absorbed in unhooking a particularly prickly kitten, did not answer.

"Please," said Hugh Anthony, "may we see your Little Things?"

This was the great moment of the afternoon. A tender smile dawned on old Mary's face and Martha, who had been sitting opposite to them knitting, and jogging Mary's memory when she went astray in her stories, got up and almost ran to a cupboard in the corner. From it she produced a wooden stand covered with a glass shade and carried it triumphantly to the table at Mary's elbow, removing the kittens to a safe distance.

On the stand stood every kind of miniature object that Mary had been able to collect throughout her life. There were tiny chairs carved out of ivory, a Bible the size of your thumb-nail which could be actually read with a magnifying glass, a silk purse with tiny coins inside, a tea-set of Bristol china, a bottle of shells the size of pins' heads, a little telescope through which you could look and see a picture of Brighton, and many other treasures, thirty of them altogether, all of them works of art and not a single one of them bigger than an acorn. Martha lifted off the shade and the children gloated, as they had gloated many times before and would gloat again, kneeling reverently on their knees and not daring to touch until Mary gave them leave. . . . But she did give them leave. . . . She picked up the treasures one by one in her transparent, blue-veined hands and handed them to the children, telling them the history of each one, how she had come by it, how long she had had it and what the people of importance to whom she had shown it had said about it.

Hugh Anthony was deeply interested for the workmanship of the Little Things presented all sorts of practical problems to his mind, but Henrietta was more than interested, she was uplifted. The thought of so much patience and skill poured out upon the making of things so tiny gave her a feeling of liberation. The sight of perfection was like a gate that let one out into freedom, and if one could make small things so lovely then it seemed that one had not got to go very far or own very much to be free. "I could be bounded in a nut-shell and count myself a king of infinite space." It was not the size of things that mattered but their perfection, it was not what one had that was important but what one made.

She laid down an exquisite carved ivory spinning-wheel on her lap and looked at her own hands, small brown shapely hands, and for the first time she was aware of them in connection with her dreams. A consciousness of power welled up in her. One day she too would make something and it should be beautiful. She would make it out of her two selves, her pixy self and her sober self. The one should give form to the magic of the other.

"When I die, my dear, these shall be yours."

Old Mary's voice seemed to come from a long way off. Looking up from the treasure in her lap it seemed to Henrietta that Mary, so old and frail, was already slipping away behind the mists that hid the dead from the living. Her eyes, bright and amused and tender, rested on the little girl. She seemed to be already enjoying, in a far country, the pleasure she had left behind her by the gift of thirty Little Things under a glass shade.

"Thank you," said Henrietta, and she said it very clearly and with all her heart so that it should reach to Mary.

Their time was up and they said a loving good-bye to both the old ladies and all the kittens. Even Hugh Anthony, who embraced seldom and with reluctance, offered Mary one of his wet kisses with politeness and respect. . . . In spite of himself her dignity and great age impressed him.

When they came out into the Market Place again the

glorious May day was drawing towards evening. The wind had dropped and the great cauliflower clouds, touched here and there with gold, were moving very slowly across the sky.

"I haven't looked in the holy well since I came home," said Henrietta, and raced across the Market Place toward it, Hugh Anthony at her heels. She ran up the steps and leaned over the parapet. The water seemed blacker than ever, deep and mysterious, and her own face looked back at her from it, flushed and eager and more alive than usual as though the mind behind it had woken into new life. She laughed and nodded at herself and held out her hands over the water so that she saw them reflected like two starfish.... Her hands that would one day take the thoughts of her mind and form them into visible beauty.... Again that sense of power welled up in her and she looked forward to the achievement of the future as a time of wonder and glory.

A cloud passed over the sun and the picture in the well dimmed. Hugh Anthony had been disturbing the pigeons and now there was a flapping of wings behind her as though a dark spirit passed. In the sudden darkening she remembered the Minstrel and his broken flute.... Men did not always achieve; sometimes they failed.... Her heart ached with pity for him because he was dead and could not begin again to make things. She wanted him to come alive again. In the play he had not wanted her, and that had hurt her, but then he had not understood how like himself she was. If he could have come to her now in Torminster, then he would have understood and they could have made things together.... Then she remembered, blinking confusedly, that he was only a man in a play.

Sighing, she climbed down the steps and went home with Hugh Anthony.

CHAPTER XIII

I

Jocelyn, too, one of those steady people whom the ebbing tide of excitement leaves unchanged, returned thankfully to Torminster and the vocation of a bookseller. Yet he found that his life had widened, for he was now not only the interpreter between mind and mind in Torminster only. Popularity, that twin sister of the fickle jade Fortune, who had never until now had one glance to bestow upon Ferranti, was now all smiles. He was the rage of the moment, a gold piece buried under the dust that must at all cost be dug up, his worth intensified by the labour of digging. Must the human race always wait, queried Jocelyn, until its poets and painters are buried beneath neglect and the dust of death before it realizes their worth? Is it a human instinct to think that buried gold is richer than the treasure that lies ready to hand? All the better, thought Jocelyn, for those deputed to do the digging.

For his articles on Ferranti had challenged attention and a suggestion that he should collect and edit Ferranti's poems came to him from the chief publishing house in London.

It was a task after his own heart and he laboured at it evening after evening. Two volumes of poetry, that had appeared years ago and perished immediately, were resurrected and to them he added the poems that had been with the manuscript of *The Minstrel* in Mrs. Jameson's cupboard. They all of them needed finishing, polishing and explaining, but after his labours on *The Minstrel* this seemed comparatively easy. In a very short while the book was out and was an immediate success. It was followed by a novel of Ferranti's that had failed on its first appearance, one of those imaginative books that are rejected as nonsense or reverenced as brilliant fantasy according as their writer is, or is not, the mode of the moment.

And Jocelyn began to do some writing on his own account. If he could interpret his friend Ferranti, he asked himself, why not his other friends? He had made so many of them in his bookshop, scraping acquaintance with them during odd minutes in the day and pursuing it through long evenings. It was true that most of these friends of his were already beloved friends of the human race, well known and already interpreted and re-interpreted by writers more skilled than he, yet surely something fresh could still be found to say about them? No man, Jocelyn argued, is quite the same person to each of his friends, one will call out one quality, one another. In the meeting of two people each is altered, like wine and water mingling. It was not too conceited of him, he hoped, to think that in his friendship with Shelley the mingling of their minds had revealed to him some shade of colour in the thought of his friend that he only could have discovered. . . . In any case he wrote a series of articles on the Victorian poets for the *Sunday Post* that made even his brother Hubert realize to the full that a prophet is frequently without honour in his own country.

Felicity, reading them, purred. She had thought Jocelyn love-worthy when he was a shabby young man whose name nobody knew, and would have continued to think so whatever he had done or not done, but it was nevertheless pleasant to have her opinion endorsed. With Felicity playing nightly in Ferranti's play and Jocelyn pursuing his vocation at Torminster they met only during the week-ends when he rushed up to London to see her, yet all the while it seemed to them that their intimacy deepened.

"I am making money now," he would tell her. "Bookselling alone was not enough, but the shop and my writing together are making an embryo breadwinner of me.... A bit dull, bread-winning for oneself alone. ... Just a bit longer and the embryo stage will be over."

Felicity, after commenting upon the beauty of Kensington Gardens, their usual meeting place on a Sunday, one day replied with apparent irrelevance, "I get tired of not feeling rooted. I have a wonderful life, of course, but it gives me no feeling of permanence. One wants something besides one's work, don't you think, some existence apart from it that links one up deep down with the earth itself." Her eyes went from the summer foliage of the trees to their roots that reached down into quiet places that one could not see, quiet places where the mystery of birth took place.

Jocelyn, who was engaged at the moment on an article on Keats, replied softly, "Keep a bower quiet for us, and a sleep full of sweet dreams, and health, and quiet breathing."

"Keats didn't say that of marriage," said Felicity impulsively, and then, with a sidelong twinkle at Jocelyn, hastily bit her lip.

"He said it," said Jocelyn, returning the twinkle with interest, "of anything that will never pass into nothingness."

At that moment, in spite of the inadequacy of his bank balance, he might have launched out into a beautiful Edwardian proposal of marriage, but Felicity murmured something about "when the run of the play is over," and then stopped.... There was still that ghost between them.

II

For still nothing was heard of Ferranti. Felicity thought his silence was the silence of death, and Grandfather sadly agreed with her, for if he was alive, they argued, he must surely have come back to rejoice in the recognition that was his at last. But Jocelyn had become convinced that he was alive, though he seemed unable to tell them why. . . . Not even to Felicity could he speak of that curious experience in the theatre, but he could explain it to himself in no other way than as thought transference. Ferranti himself had been in the theatre and the thoughts of his mind had passed to Jocelyn.

He thought about that experience more and more, though the culmination of his thinking did not come until a night in August. It had been stiflingly hot as Torminster could be at its worst. The hills all round them kept away any breeze there was and it seemed impossible even to breathe. Under a brazen sky the elm-trees on the Green stood still and exhausted and in the gardens of the Close the flowers drooped their heads.

His day's labour over Jocelyn set to work to water the garden. He was very proud of his garden that year. With the help of Bates he had dug it all up and replanted it and made of it a blaze of concentrated colour. He envied no one their garden, not even the Dean with his terraced walks and great lawns and innumerable hot-houses. His might be the size of a pocket handkerchief, but he loved it as Jacob loved Joseph and the coat of many colours that he had woven, for it was perfect in his eyes.

To-night the apples hung among their wet leaves like words fitly spoken, apples of gold in pictures of silver. The grass under them, drenched with water by Jocelyn every night, was still bright green and round the roots of the trees golden nasturtiums grew. All round the wall were hollyhocks, pink and yellow and deep crimson, and in the patchwork of flower-beds near the house were asters, carnations, late roses, mignonette, rosemary and lavender.

The sun had dipped behind the hills now and a delicious coolness stole into the garden as Jocelyn watered. The scent of the flowers, that the heat of the sun had stolen from them during the day, came back like an almost visible presence. "A bower quiet for us," murmured Jocelyn, and thought of Felicity in London standing at this moment on the stage of a stifling theatre. How hot she must be, and how tired. He sent out from his mind thoughts of this cool garden to refresh her and hoped they would arrive. . . . As they hadn't got to travel by that dawdling train they conceivably might.

Thoughts of the theatre brought him back again to remembrance of that queer experience. It had convinced him, if further proof were necessary, that *The Minstrel* was biography and that Ferranti had in very truth driven a wife and child away from him, and suffered afterwards an agony of remorse.

What had this wife and child been like, he wondered? Had they been in real life as Ferranti had described them in the play? Had the woman had golden hair and a singing voice like a blackbird's and had the child had the black hair and the white face that were Ferranti's own?

His watering over he drifted indoors and sat down by the open window of his sitting-room, as full now of the scent of his flowers as though it were a basket crammed with blossoms. He supposed that he ought to start work on his article on Byron, commissioned by the *Sunday Post*, which had to be done in a fortnight and wasn't even started, but he didn't want to. Somehow he could never get up any enthusiasm for Byron; he was not a friend but an acquaintance whom he was always tempted to cut; and to-night he was thinking so much of Felicity and the play that there seemed no room in his mind for Byron. . . . At this moment, he thought, glancing at his watch, she would be singing that haunting song, her blackbird's voice rippling out into the stifling darkness of the auditorium, cool and clear like the water that had refreshed his flowers. "There be none of Beauty's daughters with a magic like thee." A picture rose in his mind's eye of a boat on a moonlit lake and a woman sitting in it and singing. . . . Singing to Byron. . . . Clare Claremont about whom Byron had written one of his loveliest lyrics and then, her usefulness over, abandoned.

The thought of that lyric, one of the few lesser things of Byron's that he really liked, made him feel that he could start that article after all. He got up languidly and strolled into the dark, shuttered bookshop to look for a copy of Byron. . . . He used the books that ought to have been kept untouched for customers in the most shameless way, considering that sellers in shops should have their perquisites. He had heard that the girls who worked in sweet-shops were allowed to stuff as many sweets as they liked into their insides, so why shouldn't he stuff his wares into his mind if he wanted to? The only difference in their cases being that the girls got sick and stopped, while he got well nourished and went on.

As he hunted along the dark shelves, lighting match after match, Jocelyn found himself murmuring the lyric, one of those haunting things that once read are memorized unconsciously.

> "There be none of Beauty's daughters
>   With a magic like thee;
>   And like music on the waters
>   Is thy sweet voice to me:
>   When, as if its sound were causing
>   The charmed ocean's pausing,
>   The waves lie still and gleaming
>   And the lull'd winds seem dreaming:
>
>   And the midnight moon is weaving
>   Her bright chain o'er the deep;
>   Whose breast is gently heaving
>   As an infant's asleep:

> So the spirit bows before thee,
> To listen and adore thee;
> With a full but soft emotion,
> Like the swell of summer's ocean."

The sixth match burnt his fingers and he dropped it impatiently, plunging himself into darkness again. He must either go upstairs and fetch a candle, which he felt far too lazy to do, or leave that article till to-morrow. Taking the line of least resistance he strolled back to his sitting-room again, the smell of carnations and mignonette welcoming him and the evening light picking out the reds and blues and greens of his own books on their shelf as though they themselves were the flowers whose scent filled the room. They all had gay bindings, except those three tattered ones of Ferranti's.

Ferranti's Byron! Wasn't one of the three a Byron? Of course it was; Shakespeare, Shelley and Byron. It would now be possible to start work without going upstairs and Jocelyn settled himself happily at the table in the window with paper, pencil and the Byron. He turned to the lyric first of all, idly anxious to see if he had memorized it correctly.... It was pencilled in the margin.

Gone were all thoughts of Byron himself, of the article, of anything at all except Ferranti. Once before his friend had spoken to him in his room, using the words of Hamlet, and now he was speaking again with Byron's voice.

Jocelyn rapidly turned the pages, looking for more of those pencil marks that told him so much. Surely Byron and Ferranti had had much in common. Both had driven a wife and child away from them and Byron had lost as well the little daughter of Clare Claremont whom he had loved with a love that actually endured. He turned to Byron's lament for his wife and child and found it marked. He turned to the two laments for a dead girl and found those marked too; for if Ferranti's child was not actually dead yet she was dead to him.

> "For life is but a vision—what I see
> Of all which lives alone is life to me,
> And being so—the absent are the dead,
> Who haunt us from tranquillity, and spread
> A dreary shroud around us, and invest
> With sad remembrances our hours of rest."

That passage too was marked and he read it over and over again. Then he turned back to the lyric and read that again, yet after all what did they tell him? Nothing but that the painful third act of the play was, as he knew already, the tragedy of a personal love as well as of the impersonal love of man and woman. He remembered again the misery of remorse that he had felt as he watched the Minstrel drive Felicity and Henrietta away from him and he felt again, for the second time, that curious sense of identification with Ferranti himself. He closed the book and sat very still, leaning back in his chair, his eyes shut to the glorious afterglow of sunset that filled the room, and gradually the thought of Felicity and Henrietta filled his mind to the exclusion of all else.

He felt for them both a passionately protecting love stronger than any emotion he had felt yet. He wanted to spend the whole of his life, from now until death, in their service. He wanted that service to be an act of atonement for the desertion of that other man who seemed so curiously to be himself. He would be able to give Felicity what she wanted for he knew what she wanted; that he, rather than she, should be the homemaker, that he should create for her quietness and permanence as a background for her busy life. But what kind of service would Henrietta want of him? The same, perhaps. Merely the creation of that quietness which is the essence of home. He smiled, remembering his dismay when Grandfather had first suggested that he should be Henrietta's father. Well, he felt no dismay now, only a sense of inevitability. Queer little Henrietta, with her stillnesses, her sudden emotions, her perceptiveness and her precocity, if she didn't grow up into something startling he'd be surprised. He wondered where on earth she had come from. He supposed Grandfather knew.

Suddenly he felt that he must know at once all that there was to know about Henrietta. Laziness had made going upstairs to fetch a book a sheer impossibility, but now in his excitement a walk to the Close seemed not only possible but desirable.

Although it was August that brilliant afterglow still lingered. The world was utterly still and a planet blazed in the sky. Other people besides Jocelyn had been watering their gardens and the whole town seemed flower-scented. If quiet was what Felicity and Henrietta would want of him, it struck him that in all the world he would be able to find no more peaceful city in which to build their home. At the west front he paused for a moment. The carved figures were very dark to-night, brooding and a little terrible, as though they stood in their ranks waiting for the last trump to call them to judgment. Jocelyn found himself, though with no intention of irreverence, addressing his Maker rather flippantly. " If You ask me at the Last Day what I did with my life," he said, " I shall reply, ' I was a nursemaid to the artists.' "

III

"Dear me," said Grandfather, looking up from the book he was writing, Grandmother having gone to bed early that night and not needing his companionship in the drawing-room. It was called *The Faith of a Sinner* and it was his apologia. He had a great desire to state

in writing the faith that was in him and to which it
seemed to him that he had failed utterly in giving expression in living. He had been writing his book in his
odd minutes for the last forty years, but he couldn't seem
to get it finished because of interruptions. The moment
he put pen to paper somebody came to see him.

"Dear me," he said to Jocelyn, as he had said to other
interrupters a thousand times before, "can I do anything
for you?" And he patiently laid his writing aside, put
the cork in his bottle of ink, changed his spectacles from
his reading to his looking-at-people ones, leant back in
his chair with his hands folded over his stomach and
gave his visitor his whole attention. This series of movements had been performed so often that they happened,
so to speak, all in one breath.

"I felt," said Jocelyn, "that I would like to hear all
you can tell me about Henrietta."

"What for?" asked Grandfather.

"It's a funny thing," said Jocelyn, "but I feel more
and more that Henrietta is my own child."

Grandfather beamed. "I hoped," he said, "that you
would be guided to feel that. If you remember, dear
boy, on the first day you came I said——"

"I know," interrupted Jocelyn, "but if I am one day
to be Henrietta's father——"

"And Hugh Anthony's," said Grandfather firmly.

"Er—what?" said Jocelyn. "Oh, yes, I suppose so.
But he'll be mostly at boarding school, thank God, and
then at Oxford, heaven help it, and then I should think
the Canadian mounted police, or an exploration to the
north pole. . . . But Henrietta. . . . I should like to
know about her."

"There's very little to know," said Grandfather.
"Henrietta's mother was a singer, a woman who called
herself Miriam Raymond. She earned her living singing
at concerts and during the last year of her life her permanent home was in two rooms in London. My good

friend Miss Balfour, who is now the matron of the orphanage from which I took Henrietta, was at that time a district nurse in London and became friendly with this poor Miriam and her four-year-old baby girl. The mother died very suddenly, exactly a week after Miss Balfour was appointed to the orphanage, and she was able to take the poor little child with her when she went."

"Poor Miss Balfour must have hated you for taking Henrietta away."

"I don't think so. She cares only for tiny children and has long ceased to take a personal interest in Henrietta. By the way, it was Miss Balfour who had the child baptized Henrietta. Her mother, who had never had her baptized, had called her Gabrielle, but Miss Balfour thought that too French and fanciful."

"Who was the child's father? Didn't Miss Balfour know?"

"Miriam told Miss Balfour that her husband was a Welshman called Jones who had met her when she was living in Italy. I am afraid that he was a worthless fellow, for their marriage lasted a few months only, and Miss Balfour had no way of tracing him. . . . You see, Jones is not an unusual Welsh name."

"I refuse to believe," said Jocelyn explosively, "that Henrietta is the child of a Welshman called Jones. Who was Miriam with before she took up with this wretched Jones?"

Grandfather looked infinitely distressed. It had never occurred to him that Henrietta was not the child of Miriam's Welshman. He had always thought tenderly of Miriam, the beautiful mother of his beloved Henrietta, and he hated to think that she was perhaps—perhaps— his mind refused to follow this train of thought and he turned rather sternly on Jocelyn.

"You have no right, Jocelyn, to suggest that Miriam did not tell the truth to Miss Balfour."

"She would naturally wish to appear as a respectable married woman," said Jocelyn.

"Miriam was a good woman," said Grandfather fiercely. "I have her photo and it shows what she was. When she was dying she gave it to Miss Balfour to be given to Henrietta when she was older. It was a photo of her, she said, that had once been treasured by Henrietta's father."

"If you have it here may I see it?" asked Jocelyn gently.

Grandfather opened a drawer and took it out, unwrapping the paper that he had put round it. "Very soon now," he said, "I shall give it to Henrietta. I did not want her to have it until I felt she was old enough to have the questions that it will make her ask about her father truthfully answered."

Jocelyn took the faded, old-fashioned photograph mounted on stiff board and looked at it eagerly. He saw what he expected, a young and beautiful woman with a mass of fair hair. Not even the horrors of Victorian photography, the basket of paper flowers that she carried, a rickety Greek temple behind her, the fur rug under her feet and the cracked sundial that supported her elbow, could detract from her rather challenging charm. There was something independent about her figure, something proud in the carriage of her head, and her face, as Grandfather had said, was the face of a good woman. Jocelyn tilted the photo a little, so as to get the light from Grandfather's lamp fully on it, and caught sight of some writing on the back. He turned it over, looked, and found the room revolving round him, for on the back of the photo of Henrietta's mother Byron's lyric had been written out in the tiny, crabbed handwriting that, to his cost, he knew better than any other handwriting in the world.

For the moment he did not say anything to Grandfather, he laid the photo back on the table and leant back in his chair, trying to bring his whirling thoughts into order.

"There now," said Grandfather triumphantly, "you see. Is that the face of a woman who would go from man to man?"

Jocelyn pulled himself together and tried to answer. "Many a good woman, if she is not a Christian bound by the Christian laws of marriage, and if she is proud, will go from man to man."

"Jocelyn!" exclaimed Grandfather.

"Did you," asked Jocelyn, "despise that woman in Ferranti's play? She went from the man who did not want her to the man who did."

"But she was only a figure of fantasy," said Grandfather.

"Not at all. She was a real woman." He tapped the photo. "That woman was this woman."

"What do you mean?"

"Grandfather, did you ever see Ferranti's handwriting?"

"No, dear boy, I can't say I did. The poems of his that he showed me were in print; those same poems that you have lately been reprinting."

"Well, that's it," said Jocelyn, and pushed the photo, lyric upwards, towards Grandfather.

It was a long time before Grandfather could quite understand. First he had to change back again from his looking-at-people spectacles to his reading ones, and then he had to read the lyric over and over again, and then he had to have Jocelyn explain things to him over and over again, but at last he grasped it.

"And to think," he said, "that I saw those two together time and again and it never even occurred to me —it never even occurred to me——"

"How should it?" said Jocelyn. "You had the Welshman Jones firmly fixed in your mind as Henrietta's father and you had no idea that Ferranti had ever had a

wife and child. . . . Come to think of it we have no
definite evidence even now; only some marked passages
in a book; a similarity between handwritings and a conviction, for which we have no real foundation, that *The
Minstrel* is biography."

"And in any case," sighed Grandfather, "Ferranti is
dead."

"No."

"So you insist, but you can give no reason for your
insistence."

Jocelyn fidgeted. He would never be able to tell
anyone, not even Felicity, about that experience in the
theatre. . . . No one but Ferranti himself.

"I do not see," said Grandfather sadly, after a little
more talk, "that there is anything we can do about it at
the moment. We must just wait for guidance. Good
night, dear boy."

Left alone Grandfather found it impossible to return
to his book. He sat looking at the face of Henrietta's
mother, identifying her with the woman of Ferranti's
play, thinking about her and now and then turning the
photo over to re-read the poem on the back. "There
be none of Beauty's daughters with a magic like thee."
Perhaps she too, like Byron's Clare, had sat in a boat on
an Italian lake and sung to the man who, for the moment
only, loved her. The rippling of calm lake water was in
the rhythm of the poem, he thought, unstable water that
flows away so quickly. . . . Unstable. . . . Unstable. . . .
The word seemed to cry out in the night and the Cathedral clock, striking eleven, rang a knell for the passing
of love. Poor Clare and poor Miriam. How alike was
all human experience. The same bitter thing over and
over again. Yet those two lived on, the one in a poem
and the other in a play, their hour of love endowed with
immortality by the very men who had destroyed it. . . .
A paradox, thought Grandfather, lighting his bedroom
candle, the perpetual reply of life to death. "This shall

die," says Death, his sickle laid to a blade of wheat in its glory and the love of a man in his pride; and the fallen seed is a green shoot and the dead love a poem.

IV

"We must wait for guidance," said Grandfather, but Jocelyn, after his latest discoveries, had no intention of doing anything of the sort. Ferranti, he considered, had made a fool of himself for quite long enough. He was now thirty-five, or more, and hadn't behaved rationally yet. Perhaps rationality couldn't be expected of geniuses but they might at least put themselves into a position where they could be guided for their good by their friends.

Jocelyn bribed Bert the draper's son to look after the unfortunate shop, went up to London and put up at a cheap pub near the theatre. He told Grandfather and Felicity that he was going for a few days' fishing with a friend. It was mad of him, Felicity thought, to desert the shop just when it was doing so well, but then in her opinion fishing itself was a form of lunacy.... To stand for hour after hour in the rain, in Jocelyn's case chiefly on one leg, like a stork, because of the weakness of the other, gazing at a few yards of sullen water and catching nothing at all, or, worse still, having to eat what you'd caught.... That this appealed to Jocelyn only proved to Felicity that even the sanest of human beings have a kink in them somewhere.

Jocelyn salved his conscience by telling himself that he was going fishing.... For Ferranti.

Of two things about Ferranti he felt certain. He had been in the theatre on the first night and so had been, and perhaps was still, in London, and he wished for some reason to remain in obscurity. And yet if he had seen the play once he would surely want to see it again and yet again, for it is not in human nature for a parent not to gloat over the triumph of his own child. If Ferranti was to be found anywhere, argued Jocelyn, it would be, some night or other, in the pit of the Firebird theatre; or refreshing himself later in the bar of the cheap pub. Any hesitation that Jocelyn might have felt in breaking into Ferranti's privacy was banished by the discovery of his fatherhood.... The man had no right to continue in desertion.

If it was hot in Torminster it was worse in London. The sky, that was blue in Torminster, was here a dirty yellow hanging low over the roofs, heavy with its weight of thunder. Flies crawled over everything and people in the buses sat well forward, not leaning backwards in case they should stick. The traffic went dead slow and all the milk turned sour. For a week Jocelyn boiled in the gallery, baked in the pit or stewed in his little room at the pub, varying his sufferings now and then by drinking bad beer in the bar. But he never saw, either in the theatre or the pub or the streets, the tall thin man who lived and died nightly upon the stage of the Firebird.

Hot and tired and sleepless Jocelyn began to feel as though he were in a nightmare, pursuing down endless corridors a mysterious something that was nothing but a figment of his own brain. Had Ferranti ever existed, he wondered, or was he something that they had all imagined, the spirit of man that had no tangible existence? Next Wednesday, he decided, he would give up, and on Tuesday night he went to see *The Minstrel*, by Gabriel Ferranti, for the last time.

As usual, he stood in the pit queue, his eyes going now only mechanically up and down the line of figures. He was abominably dressed, with his hat pulled over his eyes, so that Felicity as she passed him on her way to the stage door did not recognize him.... And he hardly recognized her.... She looked thin and hollow-eyed, her vitality drained from her by hard work and the heat. How much longer was this wretched play going on, Jocelyn asked himself savagely? How much longer before the figure of Ferranti was no longer between them and they could get away somewhere together? Somewhere cool and quiet where he could fish for proper fish and she could laugh at him for it.

He found a seat in the stuffiest part of the pit and sat wedged between a stout lady eating oranges and a stout gentleman eating bananas. Once more, and for the last time, he watched the curtain rise upon that dim wood, with the figure of the Minstrel splashed in brilliant yellow and red upon its mystery, and once again he heard that wonderful tune stealing out into the theatre, weaving its spell over the hot, silent multitude. But it wove no spell over Jocelyn. Familiarity and heat had bred contempt and he could no longer find anything in this play but boredom. The first act seemed to him crude and the second act tedious. Even the third act, which had given him those strange moments of poignant experience and had never afterwards failed to move him, left him to-night quite cold. Felicity's vivacity seemed forced and her voice not quite true. Oliver, by this time sick to death of his part, was over-acting and Flossie, who had never at any time been equal to Henrietta, looked like a congealed suet dumpling.

In the interval before the last act Jocelyn decided that he had had enough of this boring play and rose to go, but the lady of the oranges, over whose bulk he would have had to climb to reach the exit, gave him a look of such hatred upon perceiving his intentions that he sat down again. . . . He shut his eyes and prepared to drowse through it, for his head was aching with the heat and the menace of thunder.

But gradually, as the act went on and the shadows of death crept nearer to the Minstrel, he found his apathy banished by a growing feeling of horror. " I cannot get back," cried the Minstrel on the stage. Until to-night

Jocelyn had felt it to be the cry of every man longing to re-live his life in the light of the wisdom that is his in the shadow of death, but to-night that cry came to him with a quite different meaning. . . . No, it did not come to him, for he was crying it himself. . . . " I cannot get back." He had left a certain mode of life and chosen another and between that life and this a river ran, as impassable as the river of death. And now he wanted to get back to the world he had left, but he couldn't. He wanted to get back madly, desperately, but he couldn't, not even though he knew that the river was nothing but the inhibitions of his own mind. . . . A man who has lived utterly alone for a long time ceases to be normal. A solitary who has cut himself off from human contact comes to have a terror of his fellow humans. A coward who has abandoned all responsibility is afraid to shoulder it again. A failure cannot trust to success. A sufferer who has been broken by life dare not be friends with it again. . . . It was only his own mind that kept him back, but a man's mind can be his greatest friend or his greatest enemy, according as it serves or binds his will, and his was his enemy. Its terrors controlled him. He was bound hand and foot by his own weakness. It was no use. He was as good as dead. " I cannot get back."

Darkness blotted out the scene on the stage, the lamenting music broke into the dirge and the first peal of thunder rolled over London. Then the lights went up and there was a wild stampede for the exits, each member of the audience intent upon nothing but getting home before the storm broke.

It would have been impossible for Jocelyn to linger in the theatre. He was lifted almost off his feet by the surging crowd and before he knew where he was he had passed through the few streets that separate theatre-land from the Embankment and was standing, as he had stood after the first night of *The Minstrel*, by the river.

V

Gradually he came to himself.... It had happened again.... Once more Ferranti's thoughts had been his. As before he had understood his remorse so now he understood the mental chains that had imprisoned him. The poor wretch could not move. Misery had become apathy and apathy had brought the inevitable paralysis of the will.

Fury with himself gripped Jocelyn. Ferranti must have been in the theatre and he, Jocelyn, had not even attempted to find him, instead he had given himself up to the crowd to be carried whither they would, as helpless in his bewilderment as Ferranti himself.... Somehow it had never even occurred to Jocelyn that he would not recognize Ferranti if he saw him. Ferranti was one of the best friends that he had and one does not fail to recognize one's friends.

For some while the lightning had been flickering over London, passing like a searchlight over the sky and caressing the water with waves of light. Now a puff of hot wind sent the scraps of straw and paper whirling over the pavement, sounding in the darkness like an army of gnomes scampering to shelter. A few great drops of rain splashed down and it seemed that London turned over like a fevered sleeper and gasped, praying for relief.

Jocelyn turned away from the river with some wild idea of going back to the theatre, but he had not gone far when the rain began, coming down as though the bottom had fallen out of an overhead reservoir. Turning up the collar of his coat he hurried up one of the steep streets that lead citywards from the Embankment and collided violently at a corner with a flying figure. The stranger swore and Jocelyn, sent spinning into the gutter, was not behindhand with retort.

"Look where you're going, can't you!" snapped the stranger.

"Look yourself," said Jocelyn, and in getting to his feet nearly fell again, for his sudden journey to the gutter had twisted his lame leg.

"Are you drunk, or what?" asked the stranger nastily.

"I've a game leg," said Jocelyn, enraged, "and if you have to cart me home it's your own fault."

The crispness of his irritated utterance was that of complete sobriety and the stranger, already poised for further flight, thought better of it and came nearer. "Far to go?" he asked.

"A goodish way," said Jocelyn. "I'll get a cab."

"You can't. They're all gone by this time." He paused, apparently fighting some sort of battle with himself. "Better come to my room and shelter," he growled, with a savagery that made Jocelyn think it cost him as much to offer shelter as it would have cost a miser to offer gold.

Yet Jocelyn yielded. The pain in his leg was bad and the weather worse and he wanted nothing but a chair and a roof over his head.

They were in a street of mean shops. The stranger fitted a key into a door and opened it and they were in a dark passage. To their left a door led into a newspaper shop and in front of them were rickety stairs.

"I can't get up there," said Jocelyn firmly, but the stranger, without a word, flung a strong arm round him and heaved him upwards. It was a short flight leading to a dusty store-room over the shop with a small room behind that was the stranger's own. A flash of lightning revealed it as they came in, with its bare floor and walls and broken window, its camp bed, deal table, wooden chair, tin wash-basin and shelf of books.

The stranger deposited Jocelyn wordlessly and rudely upon the bed, lit the evil-smelling gas jet, sat himself down on his chair, which lacked a leg, and gazed at his find.

Jocelyn realized that he was being looked at as though

he were a new kind of wild beast, looked at with both curiosity and fear. His captor was a tall man, and very thin, yet he looked physically strong and Jocelyn remembered that his arm had felt like steel. His dark hair was streaked with grey and his sallow, seamed face roughened by exposure to weather. It was a sensitive face, though weak and a little effeminate, and made a strange setting for his dark, haunted eyes, the eyes of a man who is perpetually seeing a nightmare. His clothes were the clothes of a man in the street, and he had a scarf twisted round his throat to hide the absence of a collar, yet his hands were well tended and his face well shaven and his voice, when he had condescended to speak, had been the voice of a gentleman. The queer lighting of the room, flickering gaslight and forked lightning, was the lighting of a nightmare and seemed to bring the queer face now very close to his own and now very far away, like the faces that waver backwards and forwards in dreams. Jocelyn, tired and confused and in pain, had never before felt so unreal, so utterly unable to grasp the situation in which he found himself. The silence between them deepened and they seemed to be drifting apart. He made a desperate effort to say something.

"Awfully good of you to give me shelter."

The stranger opened and shut his mouth like a fish, but if he said anything a peal of thunder drowned it.

"You've made this room nice," said Jocelyn. It was quite true. It was scrupulously clean and the cotton quilt on the bed was actually pretty. A curtain in the corner hid the cooking utensils and the few books on the shelf had the upright, happy look of books that are dusted and cared for every day.

"I sell papers in the shop below. The boss lets me have this room cheap. He's one of the few really decent human beings I've ever met." The information was jerked out with effort and was evidently a desperate attempt to be courteous. As in all first intercourse between shy strangers each difficult sentence that they spoke seemed a rope flung across the chasm that separated them from each other. Jocelyn pulled himself together and leant forward. He was drawn to this man and he wanted to bridge the chasm. He in his turn flung across his information.

"We're much in the same line of business. I keep a bookshop."

"In London?"

"No, in a Cathedral town called Torminster.... My name is Jocelyn Irvin."

"My name is Richardson."

The room was momentarily dim and the stranger's face in shadow. There was a long, difficult pause. "You write for the papers," he said at last, and his voice seemed curiously dulled. "I've sold the papers in which your articles appear. You write for the *Evening Journal.*"

"Not now," said Jocelyn. "I wrote a few articles for it on Gabriel Ferranti before his play appeared."

"I read them."

"Did you like them?"

"No."

Intercourse seemed again at a standstill and Jocelyn made another effort. "When we collided with each other I'd just been down to the river for a breath of fresh air after, I should think, my tenth visit to the Firebird Theatre."

"Do you care for that rotten play so much then?"

"Yes. Have you seen it?"

"Twice."

That laconic "twice" was like the crack of a whip scourging Jocelyn's mind to attention. His intuition, upon which he had relied, had been dulled by the confusion of their meeting, but now it was in command again. He gripped the edge of the bed with both hands and steadied himself. . . . He must go carefully.

"To-night?" he asked casually.

"To-night and the first night."

"It's curious," said Jocelyn, "how one can feel friends with a man one has never met. I like that fellow Ferranti. Personally I don't believe him dead."

Again came that pause. "Had he been living," said the dulled voice again, "wouldn't he have turned up? He's the fashion now and most men like being made a fool of.... And then there's money owing to him, and most men care for money."

"I think I can understand," said Jocelyn, "how a man of his type might not turn up. An unpractical solitary who has suffered gets afraid of practicality, of responsibility, even the responsibility of money, of the whole damn machinery of living. Worst of all he loses his faith in his fellow men." He glanced up sharply at his companion. "You ought to understand that. You said just now that your boss was one of the few decent human beings you'd ever met.... That doesn't sound like a man who has much faith in humanity."

The other man's face looked as though carved out of stone. There was no expression in it, and no life.

"That's wrong, of course," said Jocelyn. "We're all too apt to think that things are as we feel them to be, forgetting that they have an objective value apart from what we feel about them. An embittered mind colours the world black for its owner, yet that does not alter the fact that the world is a treasure house of beauty and love."

"Also of disease and loss and pain. Your outlook is the outlook of youth, to which one can never get back."

"'I cannot get back,'" quoted Jocelyn. "The Minstrel in Ferranti's play was mistaken, for it is possible to be born again as a little child. Many men and women have been, though I grant you they have been the greatest of us. The Minstrel made the mistake of choosing death rather than birth.... It is easier of course."

"Easier?"

"The dying man, though he may suffer, only has to

let go, while the child in the womb has to fight for its life."

The difficult, painful dialogue, that had almost taken on the quality of a wrestling bout, ceased for a moment, for both men were exhausted. The storm was passing, only a mutter of thunder left of it. The lightning and the rain had ceased and through the broken window Jocelyn could see two stars. A coolness stole in from the night and he took great breaths of it.

"In that first birth," said the stranger hoarsely, "the fighting child has every help that love can give."

"And so has the fighting man."

"No. He's utterly alone."

"No man is utterly alone. Even Hamlet had his Horatio."

The stranger gave a sudden movement. "What makes you mention Hamlet?" he asked.

"I should never have found or re-written Ferranti's play had it not been for Hamlet."

"It was you who re-wrote it? It was you?" The question flashed out suddenly, the man's painful reserve breaking for a moment.

"I'll tell you," said Jocelyn, and quietly and steadily he told the whole tale of his life at Torminster. Only of Henrietta he made no mention. It was too early for that, he thought, it would only confuse the issue. When he had finished there was silence, broken by the clocks of London striking one.

"It is morning now," sighed Jocelyn. "A new day."

"Hadn't you better go now?" asked the stranger harshly. "The storm's over."

"These last ten days," said Jocelyn, "I've dropped right out of normal life. I've been living at a disreputable pub and haunting the pit and the gallery of the Firebird."

"Why?"

"Looking for Ferranti."

"You would not know him if you saw him."

"One knows one's friends. If not at first sight, then very soon."

"Well?"

"We are both, so to speak, out of life now. I don't think I want to return to it unless you come with me, Ferranti."

Ferranti jumped up, his broken chair crashing behind him.

"Now that's nonsense," said Jocelyn sharply. "You knew quite well, some while back, that I knew you."

Ferranti leant against the wall. He looked beaten and hopeless and Jocelyn felt almost overwhelmed by the mixture of pity and exasperation that were always to be part of his love for this man. "Well?" he asked.

"I can't," said Ferranti.

"I am not going back to Torminster without you."

"You have no right to force me," said Ferranti fiercely. "Isn't my life my own?"

"Yes," said Jocelyn slowly, "I suppose it is and, as you say, I have no right to force you." He sat silent for a little, thinking, then coming to a decision he rose stiffly to his feet. Ferranti's eyes, he noticed, were following his every movement with close attention. "I'll go back to Torminster," he said, "and wait for you there. . . . And I'll keep your secret from the world at large. . . . Come to me if you want to, if not, don't. I suppose we can find some way of getting the money you've earned to you without your reappearance. . . . You've got to decide between birth and death and if you choose death you'll be a criminal fool."

"My choice concerns no one but myself," snapped Ferranti.

"I don't agree with you. At every death there are mourners. You might remember that old man, my Grandfather. . . . And I've always felt so sorry for Horatio."

At the door he stopped and held out his hand. Ferranti

took it reluctantly, yet at their grip it seemed to Jocelyn that the chasm between them was bridged.

"If you don't believe in re-birth," he said, "why did you mark that passage in your Shelley? 'Drive my dead thoughts over the universe, like withered leaves, to quicken a new birth.' I tried to do what you told me."

He dropped Ferranti's hand and stumbled painfully down the dark stairs. Ferranti did not offer to come with him and had savagely crashed the door shut behind him.

Next day, travelling back to Torminster with a splitting headache, he felt that the whole thing had been a dream. That queer midnight interview in a thunderstorm had assumed the vagueness of a dream and he could not even remember what he had said. . . . Whatever he had said he was sure it was entirely wrong. . . . He had made a hash of the whole thing and Ferranti was lost for the second time.

He was so wretched that he could hardly respond to the jovial greeting of Mr. Gotobed and climbed into the bus as though it were a hearse.

By nine o'clock that night it was all over Torminster that poor Captain Irvin had caught no fish at all upon his holiday.

CHAPTER XIV

I

Late September, the season of Torminster's greatest loveliness, was with them again and the city seemed to Jocelyn to have become royal in its beauty. Golden elms and scarlet dahlias wove a garment fit for a king and the Cathedral, towering against the brilliant blue sky, gave to its lovers who looked upon it that gift of self-forgetfulness that is at the same time both awe and peace.

Jocelyn, standing one late afternoon at the door of his shop and looking across the golden Market Place to the three grey towers that rose above the old roofs, realized with a shock of surprise that for a few minutes the anxiety that tormented him had vanished, leaving his mind as serene as the beauty he looked at. Very lovely, he thought, are the sudden moments of relief that come in the midst of strain, those moments of forgetfulness when we are "teased out of thought" by a bird or a flower or the sight of old roofs in the sun; lovely though so transient, the reversal of those brief moments of misery that visit us even in the midst of joy.

For Jocelyn was in a pitiable condition of worry. Last night the run of *The Minstrel* had ended. It had played for five months to full houses and then suddenly failed. It had appealed to that limited number of theatregoers who turn to the theatre for artistic and mental satisfaction, but it had not appealed beyond them to that larger multitude who want amusement only. . . . And so it was over. . . . But nevertheless it was reckoned a success, one of those plays with the stuff of eternity in them that are revived again and again.

And this evening an exhausted Felicity was returning to Torminster to recuperate.

Yet Jocelyn, with success in work and love both within his reach, was miserable, for Ferranti had not turned up. All day and a good part of the night he cursed himself. . . . He should have refused to leave Ferranti. . . . He had acted on intuition and his intuition here had failed him. He had thought on that nightmare night that if Ferranti was to make a success of new life he must come to it of his own free will, not of coercion. What we are made to do we seldom do well, what we do of our own choice we make a success of for very pride. So he had argued; and he had not doubted that Ferranti, once he knew that he had friends who would help him to break his chains, would choose life rather than death. . . . For surely he must want to make that pattern. . . . Well, he had argued wrong. Ferranti's chains had proved too much for him.

Realizing this he had gone up to London only a week ago and had made his way to the newspaper shop, but a stranger had served him with the *Daily Mail.* As he expected, the man called Richardson had gone away, leaving no address. He dared not tell Grandfather, the old man would be heartbroken at their failure. He would be able to tell Felicity perhaps, but not Grandfather.

The silence was broken by the rattle of wheels and the empty bus swung round the corner and disappeared down the High Street, Mr. Gotobed cracking his whip and singing his favourite song, "Gaily the Troubadour." He was going to meet the London train, which was what, thought Jocelyn, he himself should be doing, for on the London train would be Felicity. . . . Yet he had no heart to meet Felicity. . . . The acknowledgment of love, which should have been so sweet, would now have a flavour of bitterness in it, and a ghost would be between them always.

He went back to the shop and began dusting the books. On his shelves were twelve shop volumes of Shakespeare, six of Shelley and one only of the unpopular Byron. Never, thought Jocelyn, would he be able to look those three friends in the face again. They had tried so hard to help him and by his own idiocy he had rendered their help futile. Never again would he be able to endure to read Hamlet. "The rest is silence" was an epitaph that seemed to him to be written on his own heart.

He dusted with a sort of concentrated hate, directed against himself, until he heard the wheels of the returning bus. He peeped over the books in his bow-window, expecting to see it swerve round and drive towards the Close, but instead it clattered magnificently round the Market Place and drew up with a flourish at his very door. Mr. Gotobed, seeing Jocelyn through the window, hummed "Love's Young Dream" and lowered one eyelid, then leapt from the box and assisted Felicity to alight.

"Take my boxes to the Close, please, Gotobed," said Felicity, "and tell Mrs. Jameson I'm walking up immediately."

"I wouldn't so perjure meself, miss," said Mr. Gotobed meaningly. "But I'll tell them you're to be expected in an hour or two." And turning to Jocelyn, who had come out, he lowered the other eyelid.

"Gotobed," said Felicity hotly, when he had clattered off singing "Drink to me only with thine eyes," "is becoming impossible."

"He's privileged," said Jocelyn. "He and the Dean are the Punch and Judy of Torminster, our mascots so to speak. They both know that without them, trying as they are, we should be desolate. . . . Come in and have tea."

"Haven't you had it yet? It's six o'clock."

"I forgot."

Martha had put Jocelyn's tea ready in the sitting-room an hour ago and the tea, as on the day when

Henrietta had tea with Jocelyn, was in consequence very strong. There was no bread and butter, for Jocelyn considered bread and butter overrated, but there were still chocolate biscuits in the tin with Windsor Castle on it.

They sat by the window and Felicity poured out. To be sitting together in this beloved little house that was now, to both of them, home, was comforting, but not the joy that it should have been.

"Do you remember," said Felicity, looking through the window at Jocelyn's trim dahlias and chrysanthemums, "the first day we sat here together? The garden was in such a mess then that the flowers and weeds and apple trees seemed all twisted together, but now you've got them all disentangled. . . . You're a wonderful disentangler."

"I don't think," said Jocelyn with difficulty, "that any of my disentangling has been very successful," and bending his head he gloomily examined his nails, a habit with all reserved Englishmen when trying to express themselves.

Felicity impulsively thrust her chocolate biscuit down Mixed Biscuits' gaping and expectant throat and ran round the table to sit on the arm of Jocelyn's chair.

"But we've done all we could," she comforted. "We've done what we said we would, we've made Ferranti live again."

"No."

"I didn't mean in a physical sense. We can't do that when he's dead."

"He isn't dead."

"So you say, but that's just your nonsense, Jocelyn."

Slowly, with close attention to his nails, Jocelyn told her, while she helped him with the unobtrusive little remarks and questions with which she always abstracted information or guided a conversation. When he had finished he sat silent, waiting for her blame. Instead she flung her hat into a corner of the room and slithered off the arm of the chair on to his sound knee.

"I should have done the same," she announced.

There is nothing more consoling than to be told by someone whose judgment you trust that they would have done the same. Instantly you feel that they *have* done the same and that the thing is as much their fault as yours.

"But isn't it hateful to have lost him like this, Felicity!"

"Hateful, but it's his own fault."

"I must have gone wrong somewhere or I wouldn't have failed."

"If your right, meeting another man's wrong, is deflected and goes astray that doesn't make your right any the less right," consoled Felicity.

"Perhaps not, but the thing has still gone astray."

"Astray, but not lost. . . . And in any case, even if Ferranti does not come back, he knows now that he has achieved something. I should imagine, Jocelyn, that whatever a man might have to suffer in after years the knowledge that he'd once done something good would make life seem worth while."

"Yes," said Jocelyn. "Perhaps."

Felicity turned the conversation to all that *The Minstrel* had done for its other makers. Nigel Compton's name was made, Oliver had won fresh laurels and was more conceited than ever and Miles Harpenden's temper was much improved by success.

"And you?" asked Jocelyn.

"*The Minstrel* has done a lot for me," said Felicity gravely. "All this responsibility and hard work has taught me to know myself better. You know what I mean. I know better where I'm strong and where I'm weak. I've got both more confidence and more humility. . . . And you?"

"If Ferranti would only come back I should be happier than I ever believed possible."

"He will yet. I feel in my bones that he will. . . .
Now I must go. Come and see me to-morrow afternoon."

Martha, peering round the door to see if they had finished tea, noted where Felicity had chosen to sit. When Felicity had gone and Jocelyn was back in the shop she washed up the tea things in less time than it takes to tell, donned her bonnet, her jet-trimmed mantle and her gloves and ran across the Market Place to tell Mary. . . . By nine o'clock that night it was all over Torminster that Jocelyn and Felicity were to be married at Christmas, and Mr. Bell even went so far as to order a fresh supply of grey silk and white velvet for Mrs. Fordyce's and Mrs. Jameson's dresses for the wedding.

II

Jocelyn, unaware of the expense to which he was putting Mr. Bell, went sadly to bed. He was not cheered by the conviction of Felicity's bones that Ferranti would come back, for like most female convictions it seemed to him to lack foundation. In fact so little cheered was he that he deliberately, as he lay down to sleep, gave up hope. . . . Useless now to watch the post, useless to listen for the step of a tall, thin man on the pavement outside the shop. . . . Because of his very hopelessness he fell at once, for the first time in all these anxious weeks, into a dreamless sleep.

So deep was it that when the barking of Mixed Biscuits woke him he felt as though he were being dragged up from the depths of the sea. Heavy with sleep he raised himself on an elbow and listened stupidly. What had disturbed Mixed Biscuits? The night was dark in his curtained room and quite silent until one o'clock struck from the Cathedral. "The ghost," he muttered unthinkingly. "Shut up, Mixed Biscuits," and dropped down on his pillows again, his eyes closing.

Then an unmistakable sound jerked them open. . . .

Someone was knocking at the front door. ... In a moment his sleep had fallen from him as though it were a cloak and he had bounded out of bed and hurried to one of the unused bedrooms that looked out on the Market Place. He opened the window noiselessly. In the faint starlight he could just make out a tall figure propped against the bow-window beside the door. As he looked, it straightened sagging limbs and turned wearily away.

"Hi! Stop, Ferranti!" shouted Jocelyn, and it turned back silently.

When Jocelyn opened the door he found Ferranti leaning against the bow-window again. "At last," said Jocelyn. "Come in, man."

Ferranti slouched after him down the passage and extended his long limbs in the arm-chair while Jocelyn lit the lamp. He looked utterly disreputable and was grey with dust from head to foot.

"Walked," he explained briefly.

"From London?"

"Yes."

"Will you promise not to disappear," asked Jocelyn, "if I go and get some clothes on and heat up some coffee?"

"Get the fire going if you like," volunteered Ferranti.

"Right. You'll find wood and paper in that cupboard."

"I know. That's where I always kept it."

When Jocelyn came back with coffee and food he found Ferranti crouched over a fire of yellow flames. The scent of apple-wood filled the little room, as it had done when Ferranti first spoke to him in the words of Hamlet, and it seemed very natural to see him sitting there; he was only the presence that had always been in the house made visible at last.

Jocelyn sat silent while Ferranti satisfied a ravenous hunger. A curious sense of peace had descended on the room. Mixed Biscuits who, after his first protest, had taken Ferranti quite for granted, was lying on the hearthrug gazing unblinkingly at the fire. Was it, Jocelyn wondered, because the three of them would sit like this on so many nights to come that it seemed to him they had sat like this before? So often a certainty of what is to come makes one feel that it has already happened.

"What next?" asked Jocelyn. "Bed, or a pipe?"

"A pipe," smiled Ferranti.

He was looking very different, Jocelyn noticed. He was no longer the haunted creature of their first meeting. He had the calm look of a man who has fought and won a battle and his eyes, happily bright in spite of his fatigue, were exactly like Henrietta's.

"After you'd gone," he told Jocelyn, "I nearly went mad with indecision. It's useless to try and explain. Normal people like yourself could never understand how under certain circumstances, one's will can become useless. Any sort of action, even the action you want to take, seems impossible."

"I understand," said Jocelyn and remembering those few awful moments during the last act of The Minstrel he did understand.

"I left the paper shop and took to the streets," went on Ferranti, "for it seemed to me that I couldn't think when I had work to do. I just wandered about all day and slept at doss-houses at night."

"Well?"

"Then I saw in a paper that The Minstrel was coming to an end and so I went to see it for the last time. I realized, as I don't think I had quite realized before, how amazingly well you had re-written it. I couldn't imagine how you had managed, so to speak, so to suit your stride to mine. . . . It seemed to me that there must be some very close link between us."

"There is. Friendship is an unexplainable thing."

"Then I remembered what you'd said. 'I've always felt so sorry for Horatio.' Somehow I couldn't let you down.... I had to walk because I'd spent most of my money. I'm sorry I'm in such a mess."

"You'd better have my bed for the rest of the night," said Jocelyn. "To-morrow we'll talk."

III

To-morrow was, by the mercy of Providence, a Sunday, and also by the mercy of Providence Martha did not come on Sundays, or Ferranti's return would have been all over Torminster within five minutes. No one would have guessed, looking at the shuttered front of the house with the green door, that in the garden behind it, hidden behind the ramparts of the hollyhocks, two men were having one of those intimate talks that are achieved only once or twice in a lifetime.

"What made you mark those passages in your books?" asked Jocelyn. "The Hamlet and the Shelley?"

"I did it on the night before I left Torminster. I was in a queer state, partly physical illness, partly despair at the uselessness of my life and its irreparable mistakes. I meant to kill myself, but not in Torminster for fear of upsetting your Grandfather. To steady myself, that last night before I left Torminster, I began reading Hamlet. There's nothing so steadying, when you're in pieces, as reading something fine that you know very well. It seemed to me that night that Hamlet was myself; all that he felt I felt.... The paralysis, the indecision, the torment, the disgust with life, the knowledge that one's misery is caused by one's own mind. 'The o'ergrowth of some complexion, oft breaking down the pales and forts of reason.' The longing to get rid of this self that so poisons the universe.... I marked the passages as I came to them and when I came to the last passage of all, the command to Horatio, I marked that out of sheer envy. Hamlet could leave behind him at death someone who could explain to the world that he hadn't meant to make such a mess of things. 'Let my disclaiming from a purposed evil free me so far in your most generous thoughts.' He would not have done what he did if all had not been 'so ill about his heart.' ... But I had no one. ... Or so I thought."

"And the Shelley?"

"Then I read a little Shelley. I was taking a last leave of my books, you see, because I was leaving everything I had behind me to pay my debts. I marked the 'West Wind' passage for the same reason—envy. Shelley could believe in new birth, I couldn't."

"You didn't connect that verse with the play you had written, as I did?"

"No. I wrote The Minstrel just before I left Torminster in a fit of remorse and then flung it aside. It never occurred to me that it was any use."

"Why didn't you kill yourself after all?"

"Your Grandfather. We always argued together and though I was far too apathetic to be convinced by any of his arguments I remembered them because of my affection for him. One of them was that nothing whatsoever, not even the existence of God to His lovers, can be proved, but that every man, if he is to live at all finely, must deliberately adopt certain assertions as true, and those assertions should, for the sake of the enrichment of the human race, always be creative ones. He may, as life goes on, modify his beliefs, but he must never modify them on the side of destruction. It may be difficult, in the face of the problem of human suffering, to believe in God, he said, but if you destroy God you do not solve your problem but merely leave yourself alone with it. ... A ghastly loneliness. ... The same, he said, with your belief in your own soul. To deny it is to degrade yourself to the level of an animal and to lose your reverence for the human race; for if man's existence is to be measured by the span of this life only, then he is a paltry, inconsiderable thing. What he said about creation haunted me when I wanted to 'shuffle off this mortal coil,' for I had flattered myself that as a writer I was a creator, if an unsuccessful one, and it seemed to me that in crushing out my life, as I would have crushed a wasp or a worm on the garden path, I should be denying all that my life had hitherto stood for. . . . I don't say I was in a state of mind to remember, as I am remembering now, his reasoning, but his parrot cry of 'never destroy' was like a bell ringing in my head, and I didn't kill myself. . . . Instead I made a little money as a waiter in a restaurant and went back to Italy, where I used to live."

"But you didn't stay there," said Jocelyn.

"No. I found I hated it because it was the scene of the worst of my sins. You know all about that. It's in *The Minstrel.*"

"You mean your treatment of your wife?"

"She was never my wife. At that time I believed that freedom consisted in avoiding all shackles of any sort, and so I avoided the shackles of marriage. It was one of those undisciplined love affairs that burn like a bonfire and then die." He smiled affectionately at Jocelyn. "I don't think you would ever love like that and your way is the more admirable, the way that I admire. 'Give me that man that is not passion's slave, and I will wear him in my heart's core, ay, in my heart of heart, as I do thee.' Didn't Hamlet say that to Horatio?"

"And you had a child?" murmured Jocelyn, approaching the kernel of their conversation with a beating heart.

"Yes, a girl. I didn't want her, for I'd no use for children in those days, but Miriam did. Gabrielle was only a year old when she and Miriam left me. . . . Now that I'm middle-aged I care for children very much. . . . One changes."

"And you never knew what happened to them?"

"No. They went to Wales, I believe."

"But why didn't you look for them? The marked

passages in your Byron showed that you regretted them."

"So you found those too? . . . Miriam had left me in anger and I had no legal rights over either her or the child. But I would give a good deal to know what happened to them."

"Later," said Jocelyn huskily, "Miriam Raymond went to London and died there."

Ferranti went white under his tan. "What?" he whispered.

Jocelyn, examining his nails, told the story. Ferranti listened, immovable. Then he got up abruptly and went down to the bottom of the garden, returned to gasp out a few questions and returned again.

Jocelyn went indoors and waited patiently.

When Ferranti at last came in every emotion seemed to have left him except an almost comic dismay at the thought of his own fatherhood. "God in heaven," he gasped, "I'm no more capable of being a parent than an earwig."

"They're excellent parents," said Jocelyn. "The best parents in the insect world. Didn't you know that?"

"What am I to do?" moaned Ferranti.

"Didn't you like Henrietta?" asked Jocelyn.

"Like her? I adored her. But I'm no more capable of bringing her up than—than—— to begin with, I've got wandering in my blood now. I'm incapable of staying in one place."

"You couldn't take her from Grandfather while he lives," consoled Jocelyn, "and when he's dead shall I go halves with you in Henrietta?"

"What do you mean?"

"Has it ever struck you," smiled Jocelyn, "that Hamlet and Horatio together make one extremely fine man? Horatio was a dull sort of fellow, but he had the stability that Hamlet needed, while Hamlet had the fire and spirit that Horatio lacked. Why shouldn't you and I combine?"

"But how?"

"I am hoping to get married. This shall be our home and yours and Henrietta's, and you shall come and go as you please. I will give Henrietta the stability that stays at home and you will give her the Puck-like fire and spirit that girdles the earth in forty minutes."

"And you've arranged all this with your unfortunate prospective bride?"

"No, I haven't proposed to her yet."

"Well, I've heard it said that the more a man demands of a wretched woman the more she loves him, but I think the whole situation ought, in fairness, to be explained very carefully prior to proposal."

"She knows that marriage with me is imminent, in fact she's practically suggested it herself several times, but we were waiting till you came back from the dead. She has worked for you as hard as I have. She is Felicity Summers."

Ferranti gasped. "That girl who played the part of Miriam? That girl who was Henrietta's mother?" He was silent a moment. "If you devote yourself to those two," he murmured, "you will be making atonement for my sins."

"You will," said Jocelyn softly, "if we are one."

They were silent for a long time in the flower-scented room.

"What does it feel like," asked Jocelyn at last, "to be born again?"

Ferranti looked at him with one of his flashing, charming smiles. "I feel as a little child does," he said. "I'm as scared of what's in front of me as a child climbing the dark stairs to bed, but yet at the same time the world looks to me as it does to children, amazingly bright and shining and full of wonder. Death has cleared my eyes, I suppose. To the dying, the sky is a foul and pestilential congregation of vapours, but to the newly born it is a brave, o'erhanging firmament."

IV

At lunch-time, Ferranti having eaten the Sunday supplies overnight, Jocelyn went into The Green Dragon to purchase a loaf of bread, a German sausage and a pint of beer.

"May I, sir," said Mr. Wilks, wrapping up the sausage, "congratulate you?"

"What on?" asked Jocelyn.

"Your engagement, sir. The happy event is to take place at Christmas, I understand."

"Oh, er, yes, thank you," murmured Jocelyn, and grasping the beer and the sausage he fled, leaving the bread behind him.

After lunch he excused himself to Ferranti. "I'll have to leave you this afternoon," he said. "It's highly necessary that I should become engaged to Felicity immediately."

"Between lunch and tea?"

"Yes. You see, Torminster has decided that we shall be married at Christmas and I think that Felicity had better hear about it from me first. Torminster is like that; it is a city that relieves one of all personal responsibility. It decided that I should open a bookshop, so I did. Now it says I am to marry at Christmas, so I shall. . . . Good-bye."

He found Felicity stretched in a deck-chair on the moss-grown path under the nut-trees in Mrs. Jameson's vegetable garden. It was the same path where they had once walked up and down and talked about the bookshop. The moss was as thick and green as ever and the interlaced leaves all round them were still like lacquered screens put up to ensure their privacy. Stirring and shifting in the sunshine they made a diapered pattern all over Felicity's white dress.

She was lying with her eyes shut, letting the peace of the garden sink into her very bones. Gone was the roar of London and the turmoil of the theatre that had been with her for months. There was no sound now but the rustling of the leaves, the chirp of a robin who was hopping up and down beside her, and the conversation of philosophic blackbirds in the currant-bushes outside her leafy bower. Yet, in spite of the robin, she felt lonely. Inside her there was a little room and it was empty and cold. There were lots of other rooms in the house of her life, full of warm fires and laughter and singing, but nothing that happened there could make any lasting difference to the chill of the little room because it was a thing apart. As she lay under the green leaves, half asleep and dreaming, it seemed to her that she was standing in this room feeling very forlorn and listening to the chirp of a robin on the window-sill outside. Then someone rattled the latch, the door opened a little way, creaking and grinding because this was the first time that it had been opened, and a rosy light came flooding through the crack. The difference that it made was extraordinary. The room that had been cold and grey, like a garden in the rain, began to change. The floor became golden and the ceiling rosy and the walls were lined with a rainbow, while in the grey ash on the hearth geranium-coloured flames unfolded. The glow only lasted a minute, and Felicity's dream only lasted a minute. Then she opened her eyes and found Jocelyn looking down at her.

"Felicity, you must marry me," he announced. The proposal was more abrupt than was usual in Edwardian days, but the storm of his eagerness was carrying him along so quickly that he could not stop to look for words.

Felicity sat up and looked at him, rubbing the sleep out of her eyes. He was standing very erect, with triumph blazing in his eyes.

"Ferranti has come back," she said.

"Last night. There's nothing between us now. Will you marry me?"

"Of course, but I can't get out of this deck-chair."

He pulled her up so that she stood beside him on the moss that nature had so thoughtfully arranged as a carpet for them in their hour. Only the robin saw them, but the blackbirds outside heard them laughing softly in pride and joy. . . . Laugh, said the philosophic blackbirds, and remember your laughter, for it does not come again.

V

Sunday afternoon in the Torminster Close was devoted to the consideration of religious problems with the eyes shut. It was not "the thing" to pay calls in Torminster on Sunday afternoon, so that even the maids whose Sunday-in it was could, when they had washed up the dinner things, safely doze off in the kitchen rocking-chair in happy certainty that the front-door bell would not ring.

Grandmother, on Sunday afternoons, always retired to her room with her spectacles and a book of sermons. Arrived there this Sunday she drew her curtains, removed her grey silk dress and her lace cap, wrapped herself in her pink shawl and climbed thankfully upon her bed. . . . And indeed she needed her rest, for she had already, at the age of eighty-one, attended two services and would attend yet another before the day was over. . . . She plumped up her pillows, tied a scarf over her head to keep her corkscrew curls in place, adjusted her spectacles and opened her book at a sermon on hell.

Grandmother believed firmly in hell and deplored the modern tendency to think that there was no such place. She took her Bible literally and moreover she had a tidy mind and liked to bestow everyone in their right place, and hell was the only place she could think of for certain historical persons she was able to mention by name. Caligula, for instance, and Judas, and the Borgia creature who poisoned the wine of those he did not care for. Grandfather once pleaded weakly that doubtless there was great good in Caligula, but when asked sharply "What?" was unable to make a satisfactory reply. There were other people, such as the young man Ferranti, whom Grandmother was unable to place, and this worried her, for she was reluctant to send a young man who had drunk tea with her in her own drawing-room down below, and yet where else could he go to, heathen that he was, and a great trouble first and last to her poor husband? Grandmother was unwilling to believe in purgatory, for Roman Catholics believed in it and she did not hold with Roman Catholicism, yet without some intermediate state it was difficult to see what could be done with the likes of the young man Ferranti. . . . Perhaps there was purgatory here and now. . . . Perhaps the unfortunate young man had already experienced it. . . . Perhaps even in this life there was such a thing as new birth. . . . Perhaps. . . . Grandmother's book slipped from her hands and her eyelids, faintly shadowed with purple like parma violets, slid down over her bright eyes.

Grandfather and the children, meanwhile, were going in procession to the kitchen-garden for the Sunday lesson that always preceded the Sunday siesta. On fine days the lesson always took place beneath the cedar-tree, no one quite knew why, unless it had something to do with the cedars of Lebanon.

The cedar-tree was glorious. It grew on a patch of grass in the middle of the potatoes and was so big that it was more like a mountain than a tree. Its trunk and branches were a deep red-brown that glowed like fire when the setting sun touched them and the rest of it was a heavenly blue-green, almost the colour of rock-pools when the shadow of night is over them. It was the easiest tree to climb in the world, for the great boughs branched out from the trunk the whole way up it in a series of steps,

so that a child could climb to its top in perfect safety.
... And if they were good at the Sunday Lesson they did climb it.

Grandfather led the procession carrying a deck-chair, his Bible and the *Church Times*, and the children followed carrying cushions and their Sunday picture-books. Hugh Anthony wore his white sailor suit and Henrietta her pink Sunday frock and the inevitable sailor hat. In the cool shade of the cedar-tree they sat down, the children one on each side of Grandfather, and instruction began.

"Let's have about Jezebel and the dogs eating her," said Hugh Anthony.

"No, let's have about Solomon and his apes and peacocks," said Henrietta.

"No, let's have about the lady knocking nails into the gentleman's head," said Hugh Anthony.

"No, that's nasty," said Henrietta, "let's have about the trumpets blowing and the walls falling down."

"If you remember," said Grandfather firmly, "we are on these Sunday afternoons studying the parables of the New Testament."

The children sighed. Grandfather was devotedly attached to the New Testament, but they themselves preferred the Old. It was more colourful and full of suggestions for glorious games. However, there was no help for it, and opening their picture-books they turned as instructed to the parable of the prodigal son. It was Grandfather's favourite parable and so deeply did he love it that as he told the story and explained its meaning his eyes shone behind their glasses and he waved his fat hands in positive excitement. "For this my son was dead, and is alive again," he said, "was lost and is found," and his voice seemed suddenly to sound like a trumpet.

Hugh Anthony did not pay much attention, for he had found a colony of bachelor's buttons, those fascinating insects like minute tortoises, behind Grandfather's chair, and was busy touching them with his fingers and watching them draw in their legs and roll themselves up into balls, but Henrietta watched Grandfather spellbound. He looked like a prophet, she thought, foretelling something lovely that was going to happen. She thought that Elijah must have looked just like Grandfather, only possibly he didn't wear spectacles.

"It's a lovely story, Grandfather," she said when he had finished. "It's the loveliest of all. . . . Can we go up the cedar-tree now?"

Grandfather, nodding, removed his glasses and polished them, finding to his surprise that he had quite upset himself by his own eloquence. He was above all things father and grandfather and had been all his life, from the days when his children were two white mice and a canary until now in his old age when it needed a moment's attention to arithmetic to remember just how many descendants he had. No other relationship, not even that of husband and wife, had meant as much to him as that of father and child, and in it he had found his greatest joy and his greatest pain. And his children had not been only those of his body, there had been others who had been as dear to him, all the dearer perhaps that they had sometimes flouted his fatherhood. . . . Ferranti, for instance. . . . If only he could know what had happened to him.

Shouts from overhead interrupted his melancholy thoughts.

"Is it peace?" called Henrietta, mounted on the watch-tower of Jezreel.

"No!" yelled Hugh Anthony. "The driving is like the driving of Jehu the son of Nimshi, for he driveth furiously."

Then there were shouts and scramblings in the tree and Hugh Anthony bellowed at the full force of his lungs, "Who is on my side? Who? Throw her down!" The Sunday picture-books fell heavily into the potatoes and Henrietta's voice lamented, "So they threw her down, and he trod her under foot, and the dogs ate her."

Grandfather sighed. Not a single word of his Sunday Lesson had sunk in, he supposed, not a single word, but he was to be blamed in that he had allowed them Bibles of their own at too tender an age. . . . Trust the young to fasten instantly upon what you would prefer them not to fasten upon. . . . Well, there was great good in Jezebel. For magnificent courage she was hard to beat. . . . But teaching the young was difficult. . . . Difficult. . . . Unfolding the *Church Times* he placed the advertisements over his head, the sermon wrong way round over his knees and followed Grandmother into the land of dreams.

Henrietta and Hugh Anthony, having buried what was left of Jezebel, climbed to the top of the tree and were the ark perched on Ararat. Hugh Anthony was Noah and Henrietta was the animals and all round them rolled a waste of waters.

"They're going down!" shouted Hugh Anthony. "Look, you can see the hills poking out. . . . Now where did I put that dove?"

Henrietta, hastily making all the animal noises she could think of, looked and saw how the waters quieted and sank sobbing to sleep while out of them there rose fold after fold of misty hills beneath the arch of a rainbow.

"I'll just go down and tell Ham in the hold," said Noah, and slid downwards, greening the seat of his trousers as he went.

Henrietta stayed where she was, gazing, for as the water subsided what she saw was not the Old Testament land but the country round Torminster, and close to her Torminster itself. The top of the cedar-tree was so high that she could see it all spread out like a picture. Beyond the city and the Tor were the further hills. Henrietta knew all about those hills because the Torminster people often drove up to them in their dog-carts and victorias for picnics. Far up on the heights that were almost hidden now in mist, where the grass was cropped short by the sheep and the wild thyme grew, were the old burying places and encampments of people who had lived there hundreds of years ago, even longer ago than the first Abbot and his pigs. From here, standing on tiptoe on top of a grassy mound, you could see the sea, a blue streak so lovely that it took away your breath.

Below these bare, empty places the woods began, and the fields where the moon-daisies grew. In spring the woods were filled with primroses, in summer with wild roses, in the autumn with scarlet hips and blackberries and at all times with ferns that dipped themselves into the streams that ran there. These streams were everywhere, sometimes disappearing underground, sometimes threading their way through meadow grass and sometimes running broad and clear down the sides of the lanes. It was they who fed the moat of the Bishop's Palace and the holy well, and one of them could be traced all the way down from the heights where the encampments were, to the Torminster High Street. In the folds of the hills were prosperous farms where they gave you glorious teas of blackberry jam and rich yellow cream, and the lanes that led to them had white violets in them in the spring.

Henrietta knew that all this beauty lay hidden in the mists and it seemed to her that she could see it and that it was spread out like a painted background for the city of Torminster. That she could see clearly. The great Cathedral set in the centre with the jumbled roofs clustering below it, pressing close like children to their mother, and the Church towers and tall elm-trees a little misted by the smoke that curled lazily up from the old chimneys. She could pick out from among them the roof of the house with the green door, with its wavy tiles and cushions of green moss. Now and then some faint sound, the bark of a dog or the clip-clop of a horse's hoofs, told that life went on in the city, that children were born and men and women lived and loved and sorrowed and then died, their bodies absorbed into the earth that upheld their city and their souls made one with the power that shaped their hills.

As Isaiah in the Temple so Henrietta in her tree saw a vision. She saw all things that are ranged one behind the other in a series of great flat surfaces, as though curtain were hung behind curtain, each greater and mightier than the other. And the things that were near at hand were the clearest to her sight, and the least enduring, while the things that were behind became with each step back harder to see and nearer to eternity. Closest to her was the life of man on this earth, a thing gone in a flash, while behind it was its background of houses and churches that will last out the life of a man and that of his children's children, yet crumble at last into dust. And behind the towers and roofs, very faint in the mist, were the hills that we call unchanging but that yet have risen from chaos and will sink to it again. And behind the hills was spread the blue mystery of the sky, set with the sun and moon and stars and hung with the clouds of heaven. Behind that curtain of space Henrietta's eyes could not see, yet in imagination she beheld an even greater that was formed of wings and crowns and the cleansed robes of the saints, and beyond that again was a great white light.

The bang of the garden door awoke her so suddenly that she nearly fell out of her tree. By craning her neck she could look over the roof of the house and she saw that it was Jocelyn who had come in. Something must have happened, she thought, for he was hatless and he charged straight through the flower-beds in the front garden and rounded the water-butt at the corner of the house at the double, making for Grandfather beneath the cedar-tree.

Hugh Anthony had disappeared to some private game of his own that he played behind the rubbish heap and only Henrietta, peering out of the cedar-tree, saw and heard their interview.

"Grandfather!" shouted Jocelyn, but Grandfather only snorted.

"Grandfather!" shouted Jocelyn again, and tweaked the *Church Times* off his relative's head.

Grandfather started and awoke, blinking confusedly at his grandson's transfigured face. "Dear me," he said. "Has anything happened?"

"Ferranti has come back," said Jocelyn with great suddenness.

"What?" said Grandfather, his eyes popping out of his head. "What? What? What?"

With a snapping of twigs, and a slithering sound as of a very young avalanche, something pink fell upon Grandfather and Jocelyn from the tree. Without a word it picked itself up and ran.

"Henrietta," said Jocelyn from the recumbent position into which her descent upon his head had put him. "She heard."

"Tell me, Jocelyn," implored Grandfather, polishing his glasses with trembling fingers, "what it is all about, and try to be coherent, dear boy."

At the end of the kitchen-garden there was a sunny wall where the peach-trees grew and here they walked up and down while Jocelyn, too excited to keep still, poured out a flood of information.

Grandfather took it all very quietly, Jocelyn thought; indeed, except for an occasional "Dear me" he hardly spoke at all. Shock, Jocelyn supposed, and wondered if he had broken the news as quietly and gradually as he had intended. The news of his own engagement, he decided, he must lead up to slowly.

"I'm to be married at Christmas," he burst out.

But this, it seemed, was no news to Grandfather. "So Sarah told me last night," he said. "She had it from the postman. Your dear Grandmother does not know yet, as Sarah thinks it better you should tell her yourself. You remember there was previously a little difficulty when she heard of your shop by way of the grocer."

"You are glad about everything, Grandfather?"

"I have no words," said Grandfather feebly. "I have no words."

"You'll forgive me if I go now, Grandfather? I promised Felicity."

"God forgive me," said Grandfather with sudden depression, "if I should shorten by one moment this period of your love. Nothing like it will happen to you again."

It was what the blackbirds had said, but Jocelyn had not listened to the blackbirds, and did not now, as he once more charged through the flower-beds, pay any attention to Grandfather.

Left alone the old man sat down suddenly on an upturned flowerpot and blinked at the sun. As always when some anxiety is suddenly removed his first reaction had been a feeling of melancholy. It is hard to know why this should be, he often thought, unless the sudden lifting of a burden makes one conscious of the tiredness one has suffered in the bearing of it. But melancholy did not last long. As he sat there, warmed by the sun, it seemed that the gates of his soul slowly swung open to let in joy. He thought that he had never felt so happy. Everything that he had longed for for his children seemed now to be theirs. . . . Love and work for Jocelyn. Love and a home waiting for Henrietta and Hugh Anthony when he himself should die. Ferranti re-born to accept and enjoy new life. . . . He had not realized until this moment how much he had loved that strange young man or how deeply he had mourned his loss.

Hugh Anthony, peeping out from behind the rubbish-heap, heard him talking to himself. "For this my son was dead and is alive again, was lost and is found."

VI

Gabriel Ferranti, meanwhile, dozed in the garden of the house with the green door. Jocelyn had said that from Felicity he would go on to tell Grandfather, but he had promised Ferranti to let him down gently and not "to bring the whole tribe of them" down on him till to-morrow. "Give me time to get my breath," Ferranti had said.

So, meditating in a comfortable chair with his eyes shut, like nearly everyone else in Torminster at that moment, he got it. He felt like a runner who has just completed a race in a series of races and lying on the grass resting between one effort and another looks back along the way he has come.

It seemed strange to him, looking back, that he could have lived through so much in so short a time. As a young man his greedy passion for the experience that he felt was necessary to an artist had led him to seize upon all experience, good or bad, with a passion that now seemed to him almost lunatic. . . . Not so, he thought, would he live now. . . . In old days he had clutched life with such violence that the juice of it ran out between his fingers and was lost, but now he would touch it delicately, thankful for the good and accepting the ills with patience.

After the greed the satiety, after the satiety the misery. He could not understand now how it was that the misery had so overwhelmed him. He supposed he was one of those unfortunates born with a great capacity for suffering. . . . He opened his eyes a moment and they were dark with fear, for only one race was run as yet and there might be many others. . . . Then his new-born courage came back to him and he accepted his suffering as the price he must pay for the gift of creation that was his. And suffering, he had discovered, could be the gateway to renewal, than which no more glorious experience can be man's on earth.

These last few days when, his battle fought and his decision taken, he had tramped from London to Torminster had been amongst the most wonderful he had ever known, comparable only, as he had said to Jocelyn, to those days of childhood when the world is shining bright and full of wonder. "Only the greatest of us are born again," Jocelyn had said, and he had thought smilingly that he had proved Jocelyn a liar, and yet wondered humbly, as he tramped the hills near Torminster, if St. Paul after his blindness had felt as he did, or the poet Cowper when he rose from madness.

Sitting with shut eyes he saw again the lovely country through which he had tramped on the day he reached Torminster, the same hills and woods and fields and lanes that his daughter was seeing at this moment in her tree-top, seeing because she was his daughter and because he had the power to transfer the thoughts of his mind to the minds of those who loved him. These things, he thought, with the city they enshrined, were now a part of him, a part of the pattern he must set up as a symbol of the perfect beauty that was his god.

He saw this pattern now as a series of lovely things hung one behind the other like great curtains. Closest to him was the life of men with the moving figures of those he must love, an old man and a little girl and a husband and wife whose generosity would make their home his. Then came the city of bells and towers, then the blue hills behind it, then the sky that was now to him a rich, o'erhanging firmament. And behind that? He was no imaginative child and his vision of wings and crowns was not as clear as Henrietta's, but behind the things that are seen he was aware now of the things that are not seen and in his new-made pattern they were the warp.

VII

As he dreamed Henrietta was running through the Close, running impetuously as she had run on another autumn day, her legs twinkling so fast that they could hardly be seen and her pink dress lifted out behind her by the wind of her going. Under the clock she crashed into the Archdeacon and going off at the rebound without a word tore down the steps on to the Green. The elm-trees stood in a golden stillness to watch her go and the kings and queens on the west front stared in astonishment at the little pink thing who flew so fast, but she took no notice of any of them. She crossed the Market Place, disturbing the pigeons at the holy well in their afternoon siesta, dashed up the two worn stone steps and beat with her fists on the green front door.

Ferranti heard the knocking but took no notice. If it was the milk for tea, he thought lazily, let it knock. Then a scrambling sound made him start and look up.

Through the hollyhocks he could see his daughter hung up on the other side of the garden wall, kicking violently in an effort to get over. Her sailor hat had slipped backwards and encircled the back of her head like a halo and her face looked as though a lamp had been lit inside. "Here! Quick!" she shouted.

Ferranti ran over to her, reached a long arm over the wall and gripped her pink smock in the small of the back. Henrietta on her side scrambled with her toes and in a minute she was on top of the wall and he had lifted her down.

But for a few moments he did not let go of her. Her body under its Sunday frills was warm and palpitating in his arms, like the body of a feathered little bird when you hold it in your hands. It gave him a queer thrill to feel that she was his child, her warmth lit from his and her life a part of his life.

They sat on the grass together, as they had sat long ago, and laughed, and he remembered how he had told her a tale of a city where the streets were not paved with noisy cobbles but with silent, silver water, and where the sun was so hot that it could melt the ice out of your heart and the pain out of your mind. No one ever grew old in that city, he had told her, and love never died, and she had believed every word he said, her faith in him the first shaft of light in his darkness. He thought now, looking at her upturned, glowing face, that one day he would take her to Venice and watch her eyes widen in wonder, and to Athens and see her glow in delight, and to cities of France and Belgium where the bells would ring as they rang in Torminster. They would wander over the world together and life would be sweet.

Henrietta, gazing at him in adoration he had done nothing whatsoever to deserve, half shy and half eager, did not know yet that he was her father, she knew only that the Pied Piper had come back. He was a magic man, a fairy-tale man, and it seemed to her quite natural that he should have got lost, for fairy-tale people are always easily mislaid, but warm inside her was the certainty that now at last he was found for good.

Book Two

TOWERS IN THE MIST

Dedicated to
my Father

Here now have you, most dear, and most worthy to be most dear Sir, this idle work of mine; which, I fear, like the spider's web, will be thought fitter to be swept away than worn to any other purpose. But you desired me to do it, and your desire to my heart is an absolute commandment.

PHILIP SIDNEY

CONTENTS

CHAPTER		PAGE
I.	MAY DAY	7
II.	A STIRRING HOUSEWIFE	27
III.	THE MADONNA	56
IV.	AGES PAST	82
V.	THE TEACHERS ON THE STEPS	98
VI.	RIOT IN THE TOWN	123
VII.	MIDSUMMER EVE	146
VIII.	SUNDAY	174
IX.	SAINT GILES' FAIR	203
X.	THE HOLY WELL	222
XI.	DARK DECEMBER	237
XII.	CHRISTMAS EVE	261
XIII.	PROMISE OF SPRING	285
XIV.	THE TROUBADOUR	306
XV.	THE QUEEN'S GRACE	321
XVI.	PATRIOTISM	338
XVII.	FAREWELL	356

IT is impossible to live in an old city and not ask oneself continually, what was it like years ago? What were the men and women and children like who lived in my home centuries ago, and what were their thoughts and their actions as they lived out their lives day by day in the place where I live mine now? This story is the result of such questions, but I would ask pardon for the many mistakes that must have been made by a writer as ignorant as I am. Three mistakes I have made knowingly. The Leighs are an imaginary family, whom I have set down in the house at that time occupied by Canon Westphaling. The book of manners for children, quoted in Chapter Three, is a real book, and is to be found in the South Kensington Museum, but it is later in date than the date of this story. Worst of all, I have been guilty of bringing Philip Sidney up to Christ Church several months too early.

CHAPTER I

MAY DAY

> Spring, the sweet Spring, is the year's pleasant king;
> Then blooms each thing, then maids dance in a ring,
> Cold doth not sting, the pretty birds do sing,
>   Cuckoo, jug-jug, pu-we, to-witta-woo!
>
> The fields breathe sweet, the daisies kiss our feet,
> Young lovers meet, old wives a-sunning sit;
> In every street these tunes our ears do greet,
>   Cuckoo, jug-jug, pu-we, to-witta-woo!
>   Spring! the sweet Spring!
>   THOMAS NASH.

1

THE first grey of dawn stole mysteriously into a dark world, so gradually that it did not seem as though day banished night, it seemed rather that night itself was slowly transfigured into something fresh and new.

"So shall I be changed," whispered a dirty, ragged boy who lay on a pile of dried bracken, two books beneath his head for a pillow, within a gypsy tent, and he sat up and grinned broadly at the queer grey twilight that stood like a friend in the narrow doorway. He had been awake for an hour or more, waiting to welcome this day, and now it had come upon him unawares, stealing into the world as though it were something quite trivial instead of the most important thing that had ever happened to him.

He got up and went to it, tucking his two books under his arm and picking his way cautiously over the recumbent forms of the six children and five dogs who had been his bedfellows through the night. . . . And a wild wet night it had been, the last of the stormy nights that usher in the spring, or he would never have exchanged a sweet-smelling and wholesome ditch for the vile stench of the suffocating tent. . . . To come out of it into the new day was like plunging head over heels into a clear bath of ice-cold water.

It had been dark when the gypsies arrived at their camping place the night before and the boy had seen nothing of it but the smooth trunks of the beeches lit by the glow of their fire, and the javelins of the rain that spun by in the night beyond the shelter of the trees. The wind had been wild and high and there had been a tumult in the branches over their heads like the tumult of the sea. It was winter's death agony and the boy had trembled as he lay listening to it, suddenly afraid of the world in which he found himself and the life that lay before him; hearing rumours of pain and grief in the drip of the rain from sodden trees, and a prophesying of disaster in the clamour of the storm that had swept up so suddenly out of the darkness and filled the vault of the night with its power. . . . He had fallen asleep still trembling, and woken up in the pitch black of the hour before dawn to a stillness so deep and so perfect that even to breathe had seemed a desecration. It had seemed wrong to be alive in this depth of silence and darkness, and he had understood how at this hour more than at any other sick men yield themselves to death. . . . And then, imperceptibly, it was death and winter that yielded, and life and the spring stood at the door and beckoned.

Outside in the chill mist he greeted again the things that belong to the morning; the strong crooks of the young bracken pushing up out of the wet earth, the new crinkled leaves that stained the mist over his head to a faint green, and the sudden uprush of joy in his own heart. He was poor and ragged and dirty and hungry, but what did that matter? He was in Shotover Forest, within a few miles of Oxford and the end of his pilgrimage, and in a short while he would see the city of his dreams, the city that was to change him from a disreputable young vagabond into the most renowned scholar of sixteenth-century England. . . . Or so he thought. . . . And the gift of faith was his in full measure, together with a good brain and a certain amount of cheek, so perhaps he was right.

The ghostly trees dropped raindrops on his head and the undergrowth drenched him to the skin as he pushed his way through to the bridle path that followed the crest of Shotover. He stumbled across it and came to a field that curved sharply over the brow of a hill. It was dotted over with low gorse bushes that he would have thought were crouching animals but for the faint scent that came from them. Here he felt himself to be high up on the roof of the world, with the quiet shapes of pines and beech trees looming up behind him, and in front of him, circling round the hill on which he stood, a valley filled with mist. Here he stopped to wait for the sunrise. It was the first of May, and winter had died in the storm of the previous night, so he knew it would be a sunrise worth waiting for.

Suddenly, from high over his head, a lark, the ploughman's clock, sang a quick stave of song, and from the unseen woods below a robin called. The heaven had cried out for joy, and the earth had answered, and between the two the smell of the gorse rose up like ascending prayer and linked them together. Music and scent were alive once more in the world ; only colour tarried, waiting upon the sun.

It came slowly. The mist that had been as thick as sorrow became tenuous and frail. It had been grey like the rain but now it was opal-tinted. The green of the woods was in it, and the blue of the sky, and there was a hint of rose colour that told of the fires of the earth, of the sun and the warmth of daily living.

The light grew yet stronger and showed Faithful that his valley was filled with trees and backed by low hills. He followed the curve of it with his eyes until they reached a certain spot to the right that the gypsies had told him of, where they stayed, his heart looking through them as though the eyes of a lover saw his mistress.

Gradually, with the same mysterious slowness with which night had changed to day, towers rose out of the mist, and he looked down from the heights of Shotover upon the city of Oxford. It could not be real, he thought. It was a fragile city spun out of dreams, so small that he could have held it on the palm of his hand and blown it away into silver mist. It was not real. He had dreamed of it for so long that now, when he looked down at the valley, the mist formed itself into towers and spires that would vanish under the sun the moment he shut his eyes. . . . He shut his eyes, opened them, and the towers were still there.

II

Having proved the city's reality, he suddenly became rather unpleasantly conscious of his own. He had felt, as he gazed on the beauty all round him, at one with it and so beautiful too, but now he remembered that no amount of spiritual union with beauty has the slightest effect upon one's own personal appearance. . . . More's the pity. . . . The moment when one remembers this is the death knell of any moment of exaltation. . . . He was still himself, Faithful Croker. He wiped his nose on the back of his hand and had a good look at as much of himself as he was able to see, and the sight was not reassuring. His jerkin, made of coarse brown frieze, was dirty, and so torn that his elbows showed through the holes, and as for his shoes, he had walked them to pieces and they were kept in place on his swollen, bruised feet by strips of dirty rag. It was many weeks since he and a looking-glass had come face to face, but it was too much to hope that there had been any change for the better between then and now, and it was with gloom that he recollected what he had last seen. . . . A boy of fourteen with a head far too large for the puny body it was set upon, a round face pitted with smallpox, a snub nose, a large mouth with a front tooth missing, and a shock of rough, dust-coloured hair that stuck out in plumes over the large ears, that did not lie flat against the head but projected at the side in a very distressing manner. Would Oxford, when this creature presented itself at the gates of the city, be impressed? . . . Faithful feared not.

Yet, though he did not know it, he was attractive. The Creator, when He thought good to take Faithful out of eternity and cast him upon the earth, had taken him out of the same box as the baby donkeys and the penguins, and his ugliness had an endearing quality that made it almost as valuable as beauty. . . . And he had a few good points. . . . His fine mind declared itself in a wide clear forehead that the smallpox had not touched, his grey eyes had that expression of peace that is noticeable in those who know their own minds, and the good humour of his grin was the most disarming thing in the world.

From gloomy consideration of his personal appearance Faithful let his thoughts slip back over his equally disreputable past It held, he felt, only one qualification that fitted him to present himself at the city down below, and that was his passionate love of learning. He had pursued it from his cradle. He had been hitting his nurse over the head with a horn book, so said his father, at an age when most infants were brandishing rattles, and he could lisp out sentences from Virgil when other children were still entangled in their A B C. When as a small boy he became a scholar at Saint Paul's, Westminster, where his father was a master, he was hailed as a prodigy, and his path seemed to stretch straight and easy before him, winding over hill and dale to Oxford, that goal of pilgrimage to which came rich men, poor men, saints and sinners to drink deep of the well of learning. . . . Or at least so thought Faithful, ignorant as yet how many other things could be drunk deep of within the walls of the city of dreams.

But poor Faithful had no luck, for his father, an improvident and tiresome person who had already done Faithful an injury by giving him for a mother a slut out of the streets whom he had not bothered to marry, now got himself dismissed for petty theft and then died, leaving Faithful entirely alone in the world and with no possessions at all except his clothes, a cat, his father's Virgil and a tattered copy of Foxe's *Book of Martyrs*. Faithful's subsequent adventures would have filled an entire book. He, the cat, Virgil and the Martyrs went on the streets together and proceeded to pick a living as best they could. The cat who, like all cats, was a snob, soon decided to better herself and took service with an alderman, but Virgil and the Martyrs, hung round his neck in a bag, stuck to Faithful, and together they washed pots at taverns, swept chimneys, cleaned windows and carted garbage. At one time they fell in with a performing dog and ran a little theatrical performance of their own with him; Faithful standing on his head with Virgil balanced on his feet and the dog standing on his hind legs with the Martyrs balanced on his nose. Another time they, like Shakespeare in his bad days, were employed to hold the horses outside a genuine theatre; but the poor dog got kicked and died of it and Faithful had not the heart to go on. Yet he did not become embittered by these experiences; on the contrary they did him good. His great gift, that peacefulness that could create an oasis of calm about himself and other people wherever he might be, stood him in good stead even when stuck half way up a chimney, and his amazing intellect fed itself on every experience that came his way. But nevertheless he was not contented. He still wanted above all things to be a scholar and go to Oxford, and standing on his head in the street did not seem likely to get him there.

Then quite suddenly he decided that he would walk to Oxford, risking starvation and death by the way, and here his luck came full circle back again, for, with Virgil and the Martyrs still hanging round his neck, he was able to attach himself in the capacity of valet to the person of a famous bear who was travelling from inn-yard to inn-yard for the bear-baiting. Unfortunately half way to Oxford his path and that of the bear diverged and he had to go on by himself, begging his way and suffering horribly from the cold, until he fell in with some kind-hearted gypsies and tramped with them as far as Shotover. . . . And now here he was. . . . How he was to find a friend who would tell him how to become a scholar, or where he was to find the gold to buy his books and clothes, he did not know. He just hoped, with that confident hope of childhood that is as strong as faith, and which was still his despite his fourteen years, that the friend would meet him at the gate of the city, and that across his path would bend a rainbow at whose foot he might dig for his crock of gold.

III

He got up and ran back to the gypsy encampment. The sun was up now, the gorse was golden and the pines and beeches were splendid against the sky. A bright note of scarlet shone out where a tall, cloaked gypsy woman moved out to meet him from the huddled shapes under the trees. She was a magnificent creature, with the gypsy's wild dark eyes and high cheekbones, who held a four-year-old little boy in the crook of her arm as though the weight were nothing to her; a child in strange contrast to his mother, for his hair was fair and his drowsy eyes a speedwell blue. Sara had been good to Faithful; he had a real affection for her and the child and hated to say good-bye to them both.

But Sara cut short his stumbling words of sorrow and gratitude with a laugh, thrust her hand into the bodice of her dress and brought it out again with a silver piece lying on the palm.

"I can't take that," said Faithful firmly. . . . Sara told fortunes and many silver pieces came her way, but Faithful knew that she needed them for herself and the boy. "No," he repeated.

Sara's eyes flashed and she showed her teeth like an animal. She had a will of iron and if she wished to dispense charity she did so, quite regardless of the wishes of the recipient, whose acquiescence was forced with a blow if need be.

"Take it," she commanded. "There'll be no hedge to sleep under down there in the city, and no gypsy to give you food for love. . . . Take it, or I'll give you a clout on the head you'll not forget in a hurry."

Faithful took it and bowed low. She smiled at him, agreeable once more now that her will was obeyed, laid a dirty brown hand for a moment on his shoulder and then turned back to the encampment under the trees. But the child, kicking and squeaking, scrambled down out of her arms and ran after Faithful.

"Here, you can't come with me, Joseph," said Faithful.

He called the child Joseph because with his fair hair and blue eyes he seemed as much out of place among the gypsies as Joseph among the Egyptians.

"Let him be," said his mother. "When his belly aches he'll turn back to his breakfast."

So Faithful went on and Joseph trotted at his heels. He did not follow the bridle path to Oxford, he turned to his left and plunged straight down through the woods to the valley below; for he had all the time that there was and he thought he would enjoy himself.

And Shotover Forest on that first of May was enjoyable. Down in the valley the willows were a green mist with the birches on the higher slopes rising above them like silver spears. Further up still came the beeches, where the pale green flowers were hung out like tassels on the branches, and in the further distances the wooded heights were crimson-russet, purple in the shadows, with the wild cherry trees flinging showers of foam against them. As Faithful plunged downwards the grand distance was lost to him, but under his feet was a carpet of primroses, ground ivy, violets and cowslips, with a woven shawl of dead bracken and brambles spread over it to protect it. At every step he took the scent of wet earth and flowers came puffing up into his face and went to his head to such an extent that he shouted for joy. Rabbits were scuttling everywhere, the birds were singing uproariously and a cuckoo was tirelessly repeating himself. "Cuckoo! Cuckoo!" Sara had told Faithful that the souls of the gypsies, who have no abiding place in life or death, go into the bodies of the vagabond cuckoos, and he could well believe it. The cuckoo may be an evil rascal, thought Faithful, and his voice an ugly one, yet no one like he can express so well the joy of the earth in its resurrection. It was no wonder that the enemy fled when English soldiers charged them yelling, " Cuckoo ! " It was a victorious cry.

" Cuckoo ! " called Faithful.

" Cuckoo ! " called little Joseph.

" Cuckoo ! " called the cuckoo, and they all three, homeless vagabonds as they were, forgot their parlous state as they shouted one against the other because the winter was dead and the spring had broken through.

Faithful was nearly at the bottom of the hill when he discovered that Joseph had left him. Looking back he saw the little boy, clad in brown rags the colour of winter bracken, scrambling up the hillside making for Sara and breakfast. His love for Faithful had weighted one side of the scales and his empty belly the other, and the latter had won, as his mother had foretold.

Faithful felt a sudden pang. The old life of vagabondage had been hard but it had had the ease of familiarity. When Joseph should be out of sight it would have deserted him and before him there would be the birth pangs of a new life. He watched the little brown figure with the golden head until the trees seemed to bend about it, gather it in and hide it, and then he turned resolutely away, dashed through the undergrowth and landed with a run and a leap upon the path that wound through the valley.

IV

And at once he saw the figures of the new life coming to meet him. He stood on a rough path running through the valley towards Oxford, and down it came trooping a gay crowd of young men and girls and little children, carrying green branches and bunches of flowers. They were singing and laughing and waving the branches over their heads, and Faithful gazed at them with his mouth open, for it really did seem as though they were coming out to welcome him. . . . Then, with a rueful grin at his own stupidity, he saw that he was wrong, for they swerved aside to their left and disappeared in a grove of chestnut trees.

His moment of astonishment passed and a burning interest took its place. He padded on down the path until he could see where it was that they were going.

Under the chestnut trees was a chapel, a small grey place that seemed very old, and near it were some buildings that might once upon a time have been those of a monastery. The whole place looked delicious on this May morning, for herb gardens and flower gardens spread their colours and scents round the buildings and on the tall chestnut trees the white flowers were in bloom, each candle cluster standing erect upon its own platform of downward-drooping green leaves.

Faithful hid himself behind a wild rose bush and gaped at the flowery procession that came singing down the path from Oxford and filed singing into the chapel. He couldn't imagine what it was they thought they were doing, but whatever it was they were doing it beautifully, and in their very best clothes. The girls were garlanded with flowers and wore farthingales and kirtles of scarlet and green and blue, so that they looked like flowers themselves, and the little scampering children carrying great bunches of kingcups and bluebells were gaudy and gay as humming-birds. There were some soberly dressed figures in the crowd, College Fellows, who wore the long gown and the square tufted cap of a Master of Arts, and a horde of scholars discreetly garbed in russet and dark blue and dark green; but even these had flowers stuck behind their ears and flourished green branches, and were singing fit to burst themselves.

As they were bound for a chapel, and presumably a religious service of some kind, Faithful thought they ought to have been singing psalms, but they were not, they were singing the old songs that for centuries has been sung in welcome to the summer and farewell to the hateful, cold dark winter that oppressed the land like a curse for so many dreary weeks.

> Summer is a-coming in,
> Loud sing cuckoo !
> Groweth seed and bloweth med,
> And springeth the wood anew—
>   Sing cuckoo !

The girls and the young men laughed and jostled each other merrily, and the children shouted and capered, while up in

Shotover Forest the real cuckoo called joyously back to them.

> Cuckoo, cuckoo, well singest thou, cuckoo :
> Nor cease thou never now ;
> Sing cuckoo, now, sing cuckoo.
> Sing cuckoo, sing cuckoo, now !

Everyone who could squeeze themselves inside the chapel by dint of kicking and shoving, and hitting their neighbours over the head with branches of greenery, had now kicked and shoved and hit and got there, leaving a large crowd of the less muscular seething about outside the door.

Faithful suddenly felt that he must join them, disreputable though he was. He polished up his face on his sleeve, stuck a bunch of primroses in his doublet and tacked himself on to the merry crowd. Wriggling and pushing, and kicking very politely, he got to the open chapel door and looked in. It was lovely inside. Tall candles blazed on the altar in front of the east window, flanked by pots of flowers, and between them stood a big golden bowl. The packed congregation had flung down their flowers to strew the aisle like a carpet under their feet and the scent of bruised primroses, cowslips, violets, ladysmocks and kingcups filled the chapel like incense.

"I will lift up mine eyes unto the hills, from whence cometh my help." Pagan songs were now left behind outside in the sunshine and the whole congregation sang the psalm as one man, making such a row that Faithful marvelled that the chapel roof was not lifted off by it. As they sang some of the congregation looked at the chapel windows, glanced out through the clear glass panes, and then looked away again. Faithful looked too, and then shut his eyes with a gasp of horror, for crowded up against the panes were the ravaged faces of lepers, looking in. . . . So this must be the chapel of a leper hospital outside the city gates. . . . The contrast was terrible ; the flowers and the lights and the beautiful girls and young men in their fine clothes, and outside those stricken outcasts.

Faithful's throat grew dry and hard and he stopped singing. The fear he had felt in the night returned, accompanied by a sick rage. Life was a fair-faced cheat, a beautiful slut who tempted a man outside the city gates to tread a flowery path under a clear sky, and changed overnight into a devil who betrayed her lover to the shapes of darkness and terror that she set about his path to mock him as he stumbled to his death. "Outside the city gates," tolled a voice in his mind, and his eyes were dragged back unwillingly to the figures at the window. . . . Why do we live, O God, why do we live, when the end is death?

"God's blessing, my friends, upon you all, and upon this fair springtime, and upon our beloved city of Oxford."

The deep but amazingly clear voice rang out through the packed chapel and reached effortlessly to the crowd outside. In a few moments it had banished Faithful's misery so that he was once more aware of the sunshine, the young men and girls in their bright clothes, the little children and the flowers; and the figure of a man in a long black gown who had stepped out from the congregation and now stood before the altar to speak to them.

Those who were in the chapel had sat down so that Faithful, standing up and leaning against the door-post, had an uninterrupted view of the speaker.

At this first sight he reminded Faithful of one of those tall thin trees that grow upon hilltops and are twisted to fantastic shapes by the storms that blow upon them. He could not be called ugly, though he was certainly misshapen, as the trees are misshapen, because his figure, like theirs, had been formed by endurance and the sight of it was as invigorating as a trumpet call. Faithful thought he had never seen anyone whose past life was written upon him so clearly. . . . The man was like a map. . . . You could tell the way he had come simply by looking at him. Faithful could have taken his oath that this was a priest and scholar who had suffered persecution for his faith in the reign of the late unlamented Queen Mary; for his body had the angularity of obstinacy, the gauntness of starvation and the bowed shoulders of indefatigable scholarship. His face, seamed by his sorrows, had a keen look, as though the mind behind it were sharp in dealing with muddles and shams, but his blue eyes were gentle and dreamy. He was an elderly man and time had robbed him of all his hair except a grey circular fringe like a tonsured monk's. He was cleanshaven and but for his white ruff he looked a monk whose background should have been a crucifix upon the wall of a cell. He had the overwhelming attraction of anything that stands upon a mountain top and

Faithful found himself staring at him as though this was the first man he had ever seen.

As the man spoke his glance swept over his congregation, pausing perceptibly at each window where the lepers were gathered. They could not hear what he said but his look, and a movement of his hands, gathered them in and placed them where they longed to be, once more among the living. To Faithful there seemed something of prophecy in the gesture and his sense of proportion was given back to him. The lepers, too, had once known love and the sun's light and nothing could take that prophetic knowledge from them. . . . There is life and there is death, and then there is life again.

" Most of you know why you are here," continued the speaker, " but some of you younger ones, perhaps, do not, so be patient with me while I tell you a story. For more than two centuries has this leper hospital of Saint Bartholomew stood without the East Gate of the city of Oxford, and in the old time that is past forty days' indulgence or pardon of sins was granted by the bishop to all who would say their prayers at the chapel of Saint Bartholomew upon the Saint's day, and give of their charity to the lepers. But in the times of trouble and persecution through which we and our city have so lately passed few men had money or thought to spare for the poor lepers, and they, whose sufferings were already so great, suffered even more by reason of the hardness of the times. . . . But now, my friends, that gracious turning of the wheel of time, that brings back joy and prosperity again and again to men who had thought them lost for ever, has in these later days set our feet upon a fair path and blessed our city with peace ; and it has seemed right to us of the University that in our happiness we should not forget the afflicted, and we have brought to life once more this old festival of Saint Bartholomew.

" But other times, my friends, bring other thoughts, and we do not now think that pardon for sin can be bought with gold but only with sorrow ; yet we do think with our forefathers that the glorious resurrection of spring is one that can be echoed in the hearts of men, and that the song of praise that we sing for joy of it should be a song of charity. . . . Therefore have we elected to celebrate this festival upon the first of May, the feast day of the spring, and among the flowers upon the altar have we placed a golden bowl for alms. . . . My friends, if you love the spring, if you look beyond the changes and chances of this life to a resurrection of immortality, remember those upon whom the burden of mortality now weighs most heavily. Lay your silver pieces with joy in this golden bowl and your sins with sorrow at the feet of God."

He turned to put his own silver piece in the bowl, then stood beside the altar while the congregation came pressing up to follow his example; the Fellows and scholars first, then the townspeople and the little children. When the Fellows had gone back to their seats they began to sing an anthem of five parts, and their music accompanied the soft swish of silk dresses and the patter of children's feet as the congregation moved backwards and forwards over the strewn flowers, leaving their silver pieces in the golden bowl and their sins at the feet of God.

And now it was time for those outside to go up to the altar and a hot wave of dismay engulfed Faithful. He had his silver piece all right, the one that the gypsy had given him for food and lodging, but he realised with horror that he was the only person in the crowd who was not well dressed and well-do-do. . . . The only one except those lepers outside. . . . He looked down at the dirty rags that kept his shoes on and he wished he was dead. Everyone was staring at him, he felt, and wondering when he had last washed himself. . . . Come to think of it he couldn't remember himself when he had last washed; not for months, anyway. . . . He wished the ground would open and swallow him.

But it refused to oblige and he made his way up the aisle stumbling over the flowers, his face dyed scarlet with shame and his shoes going flip-flap like the webbed feet of an ungainly duck. Everyone stared, and some people tittered, and it seemed to him that the few feet of open space about him widened into so many miles, so that he became a little insect crawling by himself in the centre of a great plain; an object of derision to all the world.

And then something made him lift up his eyes and he found that the tall man beside the altar was looking at him with a queer concentration, as though Faithful had some special significance for him; there was amusement in his look, compassion, admiration and encouragement. Faithful suddenly ceased to be either ashamed or frightened. He fixed his eyes upon the man's face and flapped on towards him with no more

effort than is felt by the needle moving towards the magnet.
When he reached the altar, and stretched up to put his silver
piece in the golden bowl, the eyes of the two again met and the
man bent forward to speak to him. " Wait for me outside, my
son," he whispered. Then Faithful suddenly knew who this
man was. . . . The friend who would meet him at the gate of the
city. . . . Feeling as brave as a lion he nodded, bent his knee
before the altar, then turned and flapped back over the ladysmocks and kingcups to his place beside the door.

The service came to an end with another psalm and the
blessing and Faithful rose to his feet so as to be waiting for that
man when he left the chapel. . . . But he had reckoned without
the May Day exuberance of the rest of the congregation. . . .
Forced, in the very middle of a noisy celebration of the pagan
feast of Flora, to sit still for a solid half-hour and have their
sympathies and their consciences unpleasantly stirred and probed,
they suffered upon release from a violent reaction. They poured
out of the chapel door and hurled themselves upon the crowd
outside, shouting and singing. The thought of their magnificent
charity inflated them, causing them to shout the louder, and the
desire to escape even from the memory of those lepers at the
window lent wings to their flying feet. Faithful was caught up
and carried along like a leaf upon the surface of the river. He
was quite accustomed to kicking and scratching his way out of
crowds but to-day, what with an empty stomach, bruised feet
and disturbed emotions, he seemed to have no strength left in
him. A jolly apprentice seized hold of one of his arms, a shouting scholar seized the other, a buxom girl dealt him a slap on the
back that nearly winded him and his feeble struggles and protestations were drowned in the general jubilation. It seemed
to him that a great wave washed over him, drowning him in a
sea of colour and song. . . . He sank down and down, like a
drowning man.

v

Meanwhile Gervas Leigh, priest and returned emigré,
Canon of Christ Church and one of the most noted scholars
of his time, stood in the sunshine outside the chapel door and
looked anxiously round him. He was surrounded by the Fellows
of New College, they who had revived this particular May Day

celebration to help the hospital of Saint Bartholomew, and they enquired politely if he had lost his hat. . . . It was usual for Gervas Leigh to lose everything not actually attached to his person by a string, the habit of dissociation from material things being the first to be acquired by men of saintly character.

"A boy," he muttered distractedly. "I have lost a boy."

The Fellows of New College shrugged their shoulders and looked about them. A few of them, remembering the succulent breakfast of beer and beef awaiting them at New College, regretted that they had invited Gervas Leigh to preside at their service this morning. His fine voice and presence was undoubtedly an asset to any religious ceremony, but the time wasted in getting him together and starting him off home afterwards weighed very heavily upon the debit side. What kind of a boy, they asked politely? There had been so many boys present here this morning, a good hundred or more. Was it one of his own boys?

No, it was not, said Canon Leigh, peering short-sightedly behind a rosebush, it was just some strange boy he had taken a fancy to and wanted to see more of. A ragged boy, a tinker's boy perhaps, with a pock-marked face and hair like thatch.

Oh, *that* boy, said the Fellows disgustedly; for they had remarked Faithful's unwashed presence among them and regretted it; undoubtedly he had now returned whence he came and in any case, surely, all of them being busy men with academic duties awaiting them, the finger of duty now indicated a speedy return to Oxford and breakfast, rather than a useless poking about here in search of an elusive vagabond who was probably no better than he should be?

But Canon Leigh was not to be turned aside from the search. "I told him to wait for me," he said, and insisted upon walking all round the chapel, looking behind every tree and even enquiring at the hospital in case Faithful had hidden himself there. The Fellows, feeling it would be impolite to leave a senior member of the University to pursue a vagabond hunt alone, trailed gloomily in the rear, poking half-heartedly at bushes and peering round corners in a growing depression of spirit. . . . They considered that Gervas Leigh made an absurd fuss about trifles. . . . He had the emigré's outlook, that of a man who has suffered great extremes in his life; persecution and peace, exile and security, destitution and comfort ; and whose battered nerves will not again allow him to take the cheerful comfortable view of those who have suffered the extremes of discomfort only in imagination. . . . Yet in spite of themselves the man's quiet despair affected them, and when he at last gave up the search and led the way towards Oxford and belated nourishment they followed him with a funeral gait and mien most inappropriate to May Day. . . . That was the worst of Gervas Leigh ; such was his intensity of feeling that he dragged everyone else down into the whirlpool of his own emotion. They might like it, or they might not like it, but they were in it up to the neck. It was the secret of his power over men, perhaps, but to those of independent spirit and the opposite way of thinking it was intensely annoying. . . . The Fellows were intensely annoyed and talked little.

Canon Leigh, overwhelmed by his sense of loss, did not talk at all. That boy had appeared to him in the chapel in a way that he would never forget. He had been standing up to speak to his congregation and had suddenly been visited by one of those moments of acute misery and terror that leap like thieves out of the night upon men of his temperament. He had looked from the prosperous happy folk within the chapel to the outcast lepers beyond the windows, and had found himself once again confronting the awful fact of human suffering and had, as always, gone down before it. After a moment of prostration he had mentally picked himself up again, forced himself to face the terror of the unexplainable, subdue it and pass on, but the misery of his impotence had remained with him. . . . For it seemed to him that suffering built up a barrier between the happy and the unhappy, like the stone wall of the chapel that separated the sick from the whole. The happy might busy themselves with their golden bowls and silver pieces, they might look through the window in pity and fear and congratulate themselves upon their charity, but only one man in a thousand knew how to knock down the wall and of his own will unite himself to those outside ; and in spite of a lifetime of struggle Gervas Leigh did not consider himself yet of their number. . . . His warm tidy gown had seemed to hang on him like fire, so burning with shame had been his well fed body, and when he began to speak he had seemed to be listening to his own voice as though it belonged to someone else, noting its cultivation and detesting it. To his fancy the bright crowd filling the chapel had undergone a change and become as they would be when their hours of suffering were upon them ; the hues of old age and death had seemed to creep over them, dimming their colours, twisting their figures and tarnishing their beauty. . . . And there was nothing he could do to prevent it. . . . He could do nothing but stand up there in his fine gown and talk in his cultivated voice. His misery had nearly overwhelmed him, while inwardly he prayed that there might be something, something he could do beside talk.

It had been eased by a sudden realisation of response in the crowd before him. He had established contact with someone there. Like all actors and preachers he knew these moments. Something said, or something only thought, has got there ; perhaps it has pierced the consciousness of the audience as a whole, perhaps the heart of one person only. . . . This time Gervas Leigh had known it was one person only. . . . The crowd in front of him had seemed to melt away leaving one figure as the personification of suffering, that of an ugly ragged boy whose face had reflected the misery of his own mind. In a flash he had banished it, forcing his voice to ring out cheerily, mentally reaffirming his own faith in the resurrection of all strength and beauty, even making a movement of his hands as though to show the whole to the sick as a symbol of it ; and saw as he did so how the boy's face cleared and brightened. . . . Sinner that he was that he had allowed his defeatism to last long enough to cloud the outlook of another. . . . In making amends to this boy he would find the answer to his prayer.

But the boy had disappeared, and with him seemed to have gone his chance of lessening by so little the sum of the world's suffering. As he turned towards Oxford, walking with the limp that had kept his body lagging irritatingly behind his impetuous spirit ever since he had been put to the torture in the days of the late Queen, the sun seemed suddenly dim to him and the new yellow flowers in the meadows sank out of sight.

VI

But to Faithful, far on ahead of him in the jostling crowd, they had suddenly blazed out in all their glory.

After an interval of being dragged along by the crowd in a state of semi-consciousness his powers were momentarily restored to him ; he kicked himself free of the boys who held him and pushed his way to the edge of the crowd so that he could see the way that they were going, and so excited was he that for the moment he forgot that he had lost his friend of the chapel.

They were walking through the fields towards the city. The Oxford that he had seen from the heights of Shotover was now standing in front of him, no longer dwarfed by distance to a miniature city that would sit on the palm of his hand, but towering up before his eyes in full size reality. Towers and spires, many of them still white from the masons' hands, piled themselves against the blue sky and the golden clouds of early morning in a sort of arrogant loveliness, as though they thought themselves the equals in beauty of the gold and the blue that they blotted out with their whiteness. The old bastioned walls still swept round the city to protect it, looking at first sight one with the earth, rough and grey like her natural rock and stained with the brown and green of her fields and meadows ; while the towers and spires were of the sky, formed of her vapours and blown into airy shapes by the winds of heaven. The river curved about walls and towers as though in added protection, and the water meadows, spangled with ladysmocks, buttercups and kingcups, swept right up to the city like the green tide of the sea.

Close to the bridge that spanned the river, outside the city wall, a tall tower soared up from the block of College buildings beneath it. It stood head and shoulders above the other towers, incomparable in beauty. Exquisitely slender yet very strong, its simple base set firmly upon the earth and its ornamented belfry fretting the sky like wing tips, it stood beside the East Gate like an archangel set to guard the city. . . . For the rest of his life Faithful felt that while Magdalen tower still stood no harm could come to Oxford.

The May Day holiday was being celebrated inside the city as well as beyond the walls, and as Faithful passed under East Gate all the bells were pealing. " I come in a happy hour," he thought, and though he knew the bells were not really for him he grinned in delight.

Inside the city there was pandemonium, for the Morris

dancers were in possession of the High Street. They had come down to East Gate to hear the singers on top of Magdalen tower welcome May Day, and now they were preparing to dance round the town. It seemed to Faithful that all the citizens who had not gone out to Saint Bartholomew's must have assembled in the High Street, and now that the Saint Bartholomew's crowd was added to the High Street crowd there seemed very little space in which to breathe. He was dimly aware of a street that went winding up into the heart of the town; a gracious street with a leisurely slope and gentle curves; a street that was not itself in a hurry whatever anyone else might be. In honour of the day the kennel in the middle had for once in a way been swept clean of refuse and the rain in the night had made the cobbles clean and wholesome. On each side of the street were gabled, curly-roofed houses, timbered with oak to which exposure to weather had given a pleasant grey tint, the top stories projecting over the lower and leaning outwards in a very friendly sort of way. To-day each of them had a branch of may hung out over the front door, and out of each window peeped the laughing faces of the little children and the old grandmothers who had not dared to trust themselves in the crowd below.

In the centre of the crowd were the Morris dancers in their spring green, with bells tied round their arms and fastened to their garters and shoes, and coloured handkerchiefs in their hands. They were attended by their drummers, their pipers and the immortal heroes and heroines of May Day; Robin Hood, Little John, Friar Tuck, Maid Marion, the Queen of the May, the Fool, the Hobby Horse and the Dragon. They had just finished a dance and were drinking ale and stuffing themselves with cakes and apples that the laughing townspeople threw to them. A cake intended for the Dragon flew into the air over Faithful's head and he leaped and caught it, stuffing it into his mouth with the greed of an urchin who had not eaten for nearly eighteen hours. The Dragon, flinging back his painted head, rose upon his hind legs and fell upon Faithful with a roar of fury. They rolled over and over on the cobbles, punching each other, while the crowd swayed and shouted above them.

Suddenly Faithful found himself on his feet again and staggering up the High Street clinging to the Dragon's tail. He had had his head severely bumped and at first could see little but stars, but he realised that he and the Dragon were at the tail end of the procession and that in front of them the Morris dancers were dancing their way uphill into the city. He could see their green threading its way through the holiday doublets and farthingales of scarlet and russet and rose colour, purple and azure and gold, while the bells pealed, the pipers piped, the drummers thundered on their drums and a hundred gay handkerchiefs fluttered in the blue air.

"I have come in a happy hour," thought Faithful again, and it seemed to him that the bells were echoing his thought. "A happy hour," they pealed. "A happy hour . . . Come in . . . Come in . . . Stay long."

CHAPTER II

A STIRRING HOUSEWIFE

>With merry lark this maiden rose,
>And straight about the house she goes,
>With swapping besom in her hand;
>And at her girdle in a band
>A jolly bunch of keys she wore;
>Her petticoat fine laced before,
>Her tail tucked up in trimmest guise,
>A napkin hanging o'er her eyes,
>To keep off dust and dross of walls,
>That often from the windows falls.
>She won the love of all the house,
>And pranked it like a pretty mouse,
>And sure at every word she spake,
>A goodly curtsy could she make;
>A stirring housewife everywhere,
>That bent both back and bones to bear.
>
>   THOMAS CHURCHYARD.

I

FAITHFUL was still in the chapel of Saint Bartholomew when a little girl and a dog, fast asleep in a big bed at Christ Church, opened their eyes to the new day. Pippit, the Italian greyhound, woke first. He knew quite well that the dawn had come. The great four-poster where he slept with two other little dogs and three little girls was heavily curtained, and inside it was almost as dark as night, but Pippit knew all the same. He could feel the dawn as an itch in the soles of his paws and a twitch in the tip of his tail. His slim body was so tightly wedged between the plump persons of Meg and Joan that he could not move, but he turned his head sideways on the pillow and licked Joan's chin very gently.

Joan sighed, wriggled, awoke and sat up very cautiously, so as not to wake the others, for she and her twin sister were the youngest girls of the family and as such were spanked if they made a nuisance of themselves. . . . Little children knew their place in the sixteenth century and kept it lest worse befall.

"Quiet, Pippit!" she whispered, and gathered him into her arms, holding him tightly squeezed against her plump chest. Pippit, his eyes bulging from his breathless state, did not make a sound, for he too would be thrashed if he made a nuisance of himself.

Out in the garden a robin called, one clear note like a fairy trumpet, and Joan and Pippit thrilled together. They were of an age, Joan being in her sixth year and Pippit in his second, to feel that a new day was a thing of mysterious wonder. It stretched before them like a fairyland, full of hot scents and colours and unimaginable glories as exciting as a voyage to the Spanish Main or a journey to the city of London. And this particular dawn felt unusually adventurous. The world outside the darkened bed seemed to Joan to be surging up against the curtains with a quickened life; as though she were a little fish in a shell and the tide was coming in to pick her up and carry her to new and wonderful places.

At thought of this new day she dared to give a pull to the curtain beside her, and a shaft of light pierced through the chink and lay across the darkness of the bed like a golden sword. It must be a magic sword, Joan thought, because it was too lovely to be of the earth. She touched it with the tip of her finger, but she couldn't feel anything, and Pippit, smelling it, found to his astonishment that it had no scent . . . And was annoyed because for some unexplainable reason he had expected it to smell like rabbits. . . . But if it had neither substance nor scent it had a soft light like a lantern's that showed Joan that the others had safely weathered the dangers of the night and were still there.

They were carefully arranged like sardines in a tin. Joan and Meg lay at one end of the bed with Pippit between them. At the other end of the bed lay Grace, aged thirteen, with Posy and Spot, two rotund and spotted mongrel dogs, one on each side of her. They all slept excellently, the dogs having been trained to lie perfectly still under the bedclothes with their heads on the pillows, and during the long cold winter nights the nearness of the six little bodies to each other kept them as warm as toast.

Meg and Joan were as round and rosy and solid as apples, with soft, straight, honey-coloured hair and eyes like speedwells, but Grace, though she was as round and compact and blue-eyed as her sisters, had dark hair that curled softly round her rosy face and long dark eyelashes that were lying now on her cheeks like delicate feathery fans. . . . Joan, peering at her, thought that Grace looked very pretty when she was asleep, and decided that she liked her best like that; for Grace when awake was a person of forceful character with strong ideas on the bringing up of younger sisters. . . . But nevertheless she was glad Grace was still alive, and she hoped that her elder sister Joyeuce, and her little brother Diccon, who slept in a further four-poster with the domestic cat, were still alive too.

These children were motherless, for Mistress Leigh had died four years ago, soon after the birth of her eighth child and fourth son, young Diccon, and Joyeuce her eldest daughter had been left at the age of twelve to bring up three sisters and four brothers as best she could. . . . And poor Joyeuce was not very practical. . . . Yet so hard had she struggled that at her present age of sixteen she was considered one of the best housewives in sixteenth-century Oxford, a time and a place where housewives were incomparable, and the younger children were as well behaved as was possible under the circumstances.

Those circumstances included a father, Gervas Leigh, Canon of Christ Church, whose learning and piety were very great but whose arm lacked strength when it applied the rod to his offspring; and a terrifying old great-aunt, Dame Susan Cholmeley, who lived with them for no adequate reason that Joyeuce had ever been able to discover and whose tyrannous temper and insatiable curiosity, alternating with fits of indulgence, did nothing to help Joyeuce in the bringing up of her brothers and sisters. . . . She missed her mother more than anyone could possibly understand.

Blackbird and thrush and tomtit and jenny the wren answered the robin, wishing him good day and joining him in praising the God who made them, and at each of the four corners of the bed, where the curtains did not quite meet, there was now an upright golden spear of light. Meg, awaking, distinctly saw the four tall angels who stood against the carved bedposts holding the spears; she saw their huge wings, reaching to the ceiling, and their steady eyes and smiling lips; and then she was silly enough to rub her fists in her eyes and wake right up and there was nothing there but the inside of the bed and her sisters and the dogs. . . . Dull, of course, but possessed of a sweet familiarity. . . . Before she had time to remember that she must not make a noise she had punched them all with ecstatic squeaks of pleasure, and turned the inside of the bed into a confusion of legs and tails and yelps and squeals. Joyeuce was rudely awakened and the day began, as so often in the Leigh family, with trouble.

"Be quiet, children!" cried Joyeuce, bounding from her smaller bed and running barefoot to the bigger one. "Be quiet, you'll wake Diccon!"

It was too late, for a loud and sustained roar announced the return of Diccon to life and power and thought, while a tapping on the wall of the adjoining room showed that Great-Aunt was disturbed and mentioning the fact with the aid of her stick. . . . And when Great-Aunt was disturbed in the early morning the rest of the day was a nightmare for Joyeuce. . . . She pulled back the curtains, dragged the twins summarily from their warm nests, turned back their little embroidered night rails and smacked them hard.

They made no sound, and the merry placidity of their round faces remained unaltered, for they were chastised so often that their behinds had become quite hardened; moreover they had been told so frequently that smacking was the road to heaven that they believed it, and they were very anxious to get to heaven, which was from all accounts a more comfortable place to spend eternity in than hell.

"Now you're awake you can all get up," said Joyeuce. "It's broad daylight, and broad daylight on a May morning is time to be up and doing."

"Why, it's the first of May!" cried Joan.

"And Father hasn't taken us to Saint Bartholomew's with him," said Meg.

This was a grievance with them. Other children were permitted to go with their flowers to Saint Bartholomew's, or alternatively to watch the coming of the dawn at Magdalen tower, but they, because of their father's ridiculous fear of draughts and diseases for them, had to remain in bed snoring through the glorious hours of May morning like so many insentient pigs.

"Nasty selfish cruel man," said Joan cheerfully.

"He's an ogre," said Meg. "An ogre who ill-treats little children."

If it was not the fashion of the time for children to express their candid opinion of their parents to their face a good deal of satisfaction could be obtained from doing it privately.

"You dare speak like that about Father, you naughty little girls!" said Grace, bounding indignantly from bed. "You wait till I catch you!"

The twins doubled and dodged over the herb-strewn floor, shrieking with mirth, but being careful not to let Grace catch them, for she could smack even harder than Joyeuce. Their room was big enough to allow of escape, for it stretched through the whole width of the house, with one window looking on the garden and the other on the College quadrangle. Tapestries made long ago by Canon Leigh's grandmother and great-aunts, mother, aunts and sisters, covered the walls. They had been designed to elevate the mind as well as delight the eye and showed Adam in the Garden of Eden praying to God in the cool of the evening, Ruth in the arms of Naomi and baby Moses in the bulrushes. The flowers of England, spring and summer and autumn blossoms all mixed up together, filled the Garden of Eden. Ruth and Naomi were journeying to the land of Judah in farthingales that must have measured yards round, and the wooden cradle in which Moses lay was richly carved in the Elizabethan manner. The smoke of winter fires and the hot suns of many summers had dimmed the original bright hues so that now they were soft as the colours on a pigeon's breast. The beds, and the chests where the children kept their clothes, were as gloriously carved as Moses' cradle, and the bed curtains were of olive green, embroidered with forget-me-nots and sops-in-wine. There was no other furniture, and no pictures and no ornaments to distract the mind from the beauty of those beds and chests and the glory of that tapestry.

The domestic staff of the Leigh household consisted of only two, Dorothy Goatley and Diggory Colt, and neither Dorothy nor Diggory could spare time to go dashing about the place with jugs and basins for people to wash themselves in, after the modern habit, so the children washed, if they washed at all, at the well in the middle of the kitchen floor.

The twins scampered back to bed, picked lavender and rosemary from between their toes, pulled the curtains a little way and proceeded to dress themselves. There was a great lack of passages in the house, one bedroom opening out of another, which meant a distressing lack of privacy in one's bedroom, so the great four-poster was dressing-room as well as bed and the more private part of one's toilet was performed behind its drawn curtains. The girls' room could only be reached through Great-Aunt's, and she had a very trying habit of walking suddenly in and commenting unfavourably upon their persons and garments, so that they were careful to put on their petticoats, stitchets, and grey worsted stockings clocked in scarlet well out of sight within their beds. When these garments were in position they emerged and helped each other into the simple dark blue homespun gowns that they wore in the mornings, with lawn ruffs and caps and aprons edged with lace, and their hornbooks hanging from their waists. Joyeuce and Grace made all their everyday clothes. They spun the wool, dyed it and wove it into cloth, and made the lace that edged the ruffs and caps.

Joyeuce dressed herself before she dressed Diccon. She would have been beautiful had she not been the eldest of eight. She had a tall upright figure and lovely hands and feet. Her hair, demurely parted under her cap, was straight and honey-coloured like the twins', but her blue eyes were so dark that they looked almost purple and she had Grace's dark brows and lashes, a contrast that made her small pale pointed face curiously arresting. But being the eldest of eight had a little marred Joyeuce's looks. A permanent worried frown wrinkled her forehead, her lips were set in too hard a line, and the figure that should have had the grace of girlhood was always stiffly braced to meet the action that was demanded of Joyeuce from the time she woke up in the morning until the time when merciful sleep lifted her burdens off her, and set her free to run and sing and dance in a dream world where there was no washing day, and no great-aunt, and where she found her mother again.

Diccon would never find living a burden. If he derived from the Leighs at all he derived from the happy side of the family, the side of the mother who had died smiling, murmuring to her stricken husband that to die giving birth to a baby was the very nicest way for a woman to die. " A new life for an old," she had said. " A good exchange."

But if Diccon had Mistress Leigh's optimism he was like no one but himself in looks. His head was thickly covered with tight dark curls with a hint of red in them, and his eyes were bright green. His brown little face was covered with freckles that Joyeuce strove valiantly to eradicate by bathing his face with dew, but it was no use, the more she dewed him the more he seemed to freckle, until now at the age of four there was scarcely room to put a pin's head between one freckle and another.

There was a distressing amount of the old Adam in Diccon and what he would be like in another two years his family trembled to think. Joyeuce, who loved him passionately even while she deplored his wicked ways, knelt down to pray for him whenever she could spare a moment from her baking and washing and spinning and weaving, and Canon Leigh occasionally spent whole nights wrestling in prayer, laying before the Almighty the evil propensities of his youngest son.

So naughty was Diccon that the frightful idea had been expressed by Great-Aunt that he was in reality no child of theirs but a changeling. Mistress Leigh had died leaving her son shouting the place down in furious hunger, and so outraged had been his yells that a foster mother had been imported with more haste than discernment. She had been a gypsy woman, a magnificent black-eyed creature who had walked into the house with head held high, her gay, ragged clothes sweeping round her like the silks of a queen and her own child held negligently in the fold of her cloak. She had remained for four days, crooning strange songs to the two little babies who lay in utter content, one on each arm, and had then suddenly departed, taking with her one of the babies and all of the spoons. Another foster mother had been imported, a widowed girl whose own baby had died, the same Dorothy who was with them still. . . . But from the start she had had grave misgivings about Diccon. . . . He took his food, she said, with a greed and determination shocking in a Christian baby.

Diccon had not cried at all at his baptism, so that the devil was obviously still very much in him, and when the water had touched his forehead he had kicked in a very worldly sort of way. . . . It was on the evening after his baptism, when he was making up for his previous silence by a display of frightfulness hitherto unexperienced in the Leigl family, that Great-

Aunt had hazarded the suggestion that he was no child of theirs.

" Had he been the gypsy's child he would have had black eyes like hers," poor Joyeuce had said as she tramped up and down the parlour with the shouting infant.

" Who knows whether the child she brought with her was her own child ? " Great-Aunt had retorted. " We don't," she had continued ominously, " know what it was."

And indeed as Diccon increased in size and wickedness he developed a good many fairy attributes. There were his dancing green eyes, for instance, and his ears that were undoubtedly pointed at the tips, the way he could fall and roll in all directions and never hurt himself, his mischievous tricks and the frightful noise he could make, a noise out of all proportion to the size of his body ; and then, in contrast to all this, the sweet loving little way in which he would suddenly come running to you and climb on your lap and lie with his curly head snuggled against you, your hand rubbing his cheek. He would lie like this for five minutes, cooing like any turtle-dove, and then suddenly turn his head and bite the caressing hand hard. His baby teeth were white and pearly, and daintily pointed like his ears, but of an inconceivable sharpness. . . . And upon his back was a triangle of three small moles ; the mark, so said Great-Aunt, that the fairies set upon their own.

But Canon Leigh and Joyeuce wouldn't have it that Diccon was a changeling. He had, they thought, absorbed a certain wildness with the milk of his first foster mother, but he was their own dear child and by prayer and the help of God this should be cast out.

The roar with which Diccon had greeted the dawn had been short lived. He always bellowed at any moment of transition, such as that from night to day, or eating to not eating, but he never bellowed for long. The noise he made was merely the fanfare of trumpets that announces to adoring subjects that royalty is now doing something different to what it was doing a short while before.

Having announced that he was awake he shut his red mouth abruptly and scurried on all fours to the bottom of the bed, where he sat with his back to the room, industriously picking a crimson embroidered carnation out of the curtain with his sharp little nails. He had been working at that carnation for a week and had nearly finished it. When his activities were discovered he would be smacked, but he had no objection to being smacked. If he had any nerves at all they were made of steel and never incommoded him.

By his side sat Tinker, the cat, watching gravely, with his tail twitching slowly from side to side. Tinker was black, with eyes as green as Diccon's own, and he was Diccon's inseparable companion. They did everything together and seemed to have a great affection for each other, though their sufferings at each other's hands were shameful. Diccon would drag Tinker round the garden by his tail, remove from him by force those just perquisites, his mice, bury him in the earth when playing at executing traitors at Tyburn and put him down the well when playing at Joseph and his brethren. A hundred times had Tinker been rescued at the point of death, yet his devotion to Diccon never wavered. . . . Though he retaliated. . . . Diccon's face and hands were a mass of scratches and on one occasion the child had nearly died of blood poisoning, Tinker having bitten him immediately after refreshing himself at the Deanery garbage heap.

There was something ominous, Great-Aunt said, in this friendship of the child and the cat. . . . For do not witches consort with black cats ? . . . There was no denying that Tinker had introduced himself into the Leigh household on the very same day that the gypsy woman had arrived, strolling in from the quadrangle dripping wet with a tin can tied to his tail.

"It is time to get dressed, Diccon," said Joyeuce.

Diccon gave her one of his lovely, rippling smiles, leaped from the bed and dragged his night-rail over his head.

"No, no, Diccon!" cried Joyeuce in horror, seizing his little bare body and lifting him back on to the bed. "You must be dressed behind the curtain, like a modest child."

Diccon was lacking in modesty, and one of the most frightful of his escapades had taken place on a hot afternoon last August, when he had called at the Deanery with nothing on. For this his father had beaten him, for the first time, with the rod that he kept for use upon the older boys. Asked for an explanation of his behaviour he had said, through sobs, for the rod had really hurt, that he had felt hot and he liked the Dean. Asked not to do it again he had not committed himself.

Diccon looked fascinating when he was dressed. He wore doublet and trunk and hose of russet, with a little pleated ruff at the neck. . . . It had been the pricking of his ruff round his neck that had led to the regrettable incident of that hot August.

As soon as he and the little girls were dressed Joyeuce knocked at Great-Aunt's door for permission for the children to walk through her room on their way to wash their hands and faces at the well, which was given by Great-Aunt's usual remark of, " Tilly-vally, tilly-vally, why did God make children ! Hurry up, then, malapert poppets ! "

Joyeuce lingered behind to straighten the untidy beds. This done she drew back the curtain that covered the window looking on the quadrangle. She always waited until the children had gone before she pulled back this curtain, for it would have been a thing not easily forgiven by their father if a passing scholar should have seen a twin in her petticoat. . . . And she had another reason for waiting. . . . She had grown from a child to a girl in this house, she had loved and laughed and suffered grief and pain in it, and somehow the view of Christ Church and Oxford seen from its windows for so many years as the setting of her home had become extraordinarily valuable to her. She liked to be alone when she drew back the curtain, like a connoisseur before a picture or a worshipper before a shrine.

II

She pulled it aside and opened the diamond-paned lattice window, leaning out. She got up so early that to her the dawn was a well-known friend, not a casual acquaintance seen so seldom that its appearance is greeted with astonishment. She knew all the dawns, the golden dawns of fair weather, the grey dawns of rain and the flame and indigo dawns of storm. She watched them morning by morning as their banners unfurled and streamed across the sky, and she loved them, even though the moment of unfurling was to her a moment of dread as well as of joy. . . . For each day one marches out to fight behind those banners, and the stout and lusty like the fighting, but the timid, as they buckle on their armour, cannot help a beating of the heart. . . . To-day was a fine weather dawn and on the banner of it was embroidered a golden-hearted flower whose blue petals crisped into saffron at the edges.

The rough grass of the quadrangle was still misted and the buttercups and daisies in it were tightly shut up. Presently they would open their eyes and look at the sun and then the quadrangle would look like Grace's Sunday kirtle, green silk scattered over with yellow and silver dots.

The north side of the quadrangle had not yet been built and Joyeuce looked from her window across the grass to a thicket of hawthorn trees that were a froth of silvery blossom. Beside them, to the right, were Peckwater Inn and Canterbury College, and beyond them were the roofs of the city and towers and spires rising out of the morning mist in marvellous beauty. To her right, as she leaned out of the window, Joyeuce could see the tower of the Cathedral, surmounted by its thirteenth century spire, and to her left she looked on the Fair Gate. It still lacked its bell tower, and Great Tom, the bell that was destined one day to hang there, now tolled out the hour from the Cathedral, but if it boasted no tower the Fair Gate was yet very fair, with the arms of Henry Tudor and Cardinal Wolsey " most curiously set over the middle of the Gate, and my lord grace's arms set out with gold and colour."

The whole view was gloriously fair and Joyeuce almost worshipped it.

She was a romantic to whom, as yet, the details of practical living brought no joy. . . . She missed her mother. . . . She did her duty as housewife with thoroughness, a sense of duty having been whipped into her from babyhood up, but she did not think that doing one's duty was very enjoyable. The life she wanted seemed always to elude her, to be around her and in front of her and above her, but never quite within her reach. She did not quite know what it was that she wanted, she only knew that it was not what she had. The view that she saw from her window every morning was to her the symbol of this life. She stood in her house, surrounded by a hundred irksome problems and duties, and she looked out at a loveliness that she could see but could not grasp. . . . Yet if she left the house and went outside, treading the green grass with her feet and touching the silvery hawthorn with her hands, her worries would go with her, making the grass wet and cold and setting thorns among the flowers; the ideal world that had seemed to be there outside would, like a mirage, recede yet a little further. . . . Would life always be like that, she wondered? Did the things that men longed for and fought for always disappoint them as soon as they had grasped them in their hands? Did one go on and on like that, chasing a will-o'-the-wisp until you and he went down together into the darkness of death? Perhaps, she thought, once you were through that darkness he suffered a change. Perhaps he stood still, then, and let you catch him, and the grip of his arms would satisfy at last.

But Joyeuce could not feel certain that that would happen, and anyhow it seemed a very long while to wait. She wanted something nice *now*. She wanted the beauty of earth that was outside her window to become to her something more than a painted picture, she wanted it not to recede like a mirage, but to take some actual form that would come in to her and bring her comfort and reassurance. . . . Like her mother had done.

"Good morning, Mistress Joyeuce."

Leaning with her elbows on the sill, her eyes on the white hawthorn and white towers against the sky, her ears filled with the song of the birds and her thoughts wandering, Joyeuce had forgotten time and place. At the moment her feet were not on the earth and the figure who stood outside in the quadrangle seemed not of the earth either. She did not know if it was a man or a woman. It was just a figure that gathered up into itself all the elusive beauty of that outside world and brought it close to her. It was not receding, it was coming nearer, standing right under her window so that she could almost have touched it; touched the beauty of earth, the gold and blue and green and silver.

Then her wandering thoughts suddenly recollected themselves and their duties. They came hurrying back, very shamefaced, and folding their wings curled themselves up into the tight, hard ball that is the grimly recollected mind of a housewife in the early morning. . . . There was a tiny click in her head, as the component parts fitted together, and Joyeuce started and looked down into the upturned, impudent face of what was after all only one of the scholars.

He was a stranger to her and it was clearly her duty to blush with maidenly modesty and withdraw from the window with grace and dignity; but somehow she did not. Her thoughts might have returned to their duties but they were not yet exercising as much control over her actions as could be wished. She stayed where she was, staring down at the face below her with a concentration that bordered upon the bold, and instantly every detail of it seemed to be graved almost painfully into her memory. In one moment she knew his face almost as well as she knew Diccon's, that she had been learning hour by hour and day by day all through his short little life. And there was a certain likeness between the two, a likeness that bespoke them both the sons of Belial. These eyes, though they were as dark as sloes, had the same dancing points of light in them and when their owner laughed they were transformed, as Diccon's were, from round twinkling orbs to narrow wicked slits. His eyelashes were as long as a girl's and his eyebrows had that faint upward kink at the outer edges that, together with the suspicion of a point to the ears, is one of the sure marks of mischief. The fine texture of his sunburnt skin was girlish too, but the lips were full and strong and the chin obstinate and deeply cleft. . . . Altogether a face so full of contradictions that nothing at all could be foretold about the future of its owner. . . . Joyeuce's truant eyes, all unbidden by her will, took as serious note of these things as though his face were the page of a book that she must at all cost get by heart.

With a sigh, she stirred and got up, aware at last of the clamouring, outraged commands of her thoughts; she blushed a little, smoothing her snowy apron, and the practical world once more flowed maddeningly around her. Holding herself now as stiffly as a poker, she had another good look at the young man before her; but this time her eyelashes were lowered and she peeped through them with the cold aloofness of a superior tabby kitten.

Morning prayers were at five o'clock in the Cathedral and this young man was the first out. . . . There was something about the jaunty way he wore his gown, the twinkle in his eye and the crisp curl in his hair that suggested that he was always the first out. . . . His clothes were simple, for it had been ordained that every Christ Church scholar should " go in fit and decent apparel," and might not on any account burst upon the scene clothed in "white or pricked doublets, galligaskins or cut hose, welted or laced gowns, upon the several pains next before rehearsed." So Master Nicolas de Worde was clothed in a plain dark blue doublet, with a simple ruff, and no part of his person was pricked, cut, welted or laced ; but the fineness of the dark blue cloth and the snowy whiteness of his ruff, together with a certain arrogance in his bearing, showed him to be a young man of means and breeding. He was also a gentleman of some age, Joyeuce thought, eighteen or so. Scholars could present themthemselves at Christ Church at any age, the youngest recorded age of any gentleman arriving to devote himself to learning at that institution being twelve years old, so eighteen was to Joyeuce very much years of discretion, and she answered his greeting with the respectfulness due to age and learning.

"Good morning, sir," she said, and curtsied.

Nicolas regarded her with interest and amusement. When he had first seen her she had been apparently kneeling on the floor, with her elbows propped on the windowsill and her chin resting in her hands. She had been illumined by one of her rare moments of beauty ; her pale little face softened by her dreams and her bearing relaxed into grace. She had looked frail and sad, too, and Nicolas, who always enjoyed the best of health and spirits himself, was always attracted by frailty and sadness ; succouring the afflicted increased his own sense of strength and well-being and that was nice for him. He had noticed Joyeuce before, but never to such advantage. He would like to see her close to, he thought, for he was a connoisseur of pretty ladies, and as he always did what he liked unless forcibly prevented he had immediately crossed the quadrangle and planted himself beneath her window. And to his delight she had returned his scrutiny with interest. She had opened her eyes wide and gazed at him as though he were the personification of all beauty and all joy. . . . Nicolas had a good opinion of himself and he was overjoyed to find her in such evident agreement with him.
. . . She had beautiful blue eyes, almost as dark as violets, set strikingly in that ivory face beneath dark eyebrows like delicate feathers, and smooth honey-coloured hair. . . . A nice girl.
. . . And when she suddenly changed from a melting and rather forward goddess into a stiff, demure maiden he discovered that she was one of the few women wno can blush becomingly. . . .
Your rosy maidens, Nicolas was apt to say when expatiating

on the beauties of the sex, are all very well on the whole, but they show to disadvantage in moments of embarrassment, while your pale maidens, though they may be less striking in the ordinary way, put on an added beauty with added heat. . . . For himself he liked pale maidens.

"You have not gone maying, mistress?" he asked.

Joyeuce shook her head a little sadly. . . . She had always longed to go maying.

"Nor I," said Nicolas arrogantly. "I hate the vulgar crowd at Saint Bartholomew's. . . . Besides, I overslept."

Joyeuce, not noticing that the grapes were sour, immediately saw that it had been quite wrong of her to want to go maying. She blushed again, and changed the subject.

"Who are you, sir?" she asked humbly. "I have not seen you before."

A ludicrous expression of astonishment spread over Nicolas's face, for he was accustomed to be known and admired and took recognition of his merits and admiration of his person as his due.

"I've been here for years," he said indignantly, "and I've walked past your window a thousand times if once, and I sat opposite you last week in the Cathedral."

"I never noticed you," said Joyeuce.

"You can't be observant," he said, slightly nettled.

"I was saying my prayers," explained Joyeuce.

Nicolas considered this a joke, and laughed.

Joyeuce drew herself up yet more stiffly, her eyes flashing, for she had been well brought up and knew what should be laughed at and what should not. "And so," she said, "should you have been."

"But we say so many in this place," he complained bitterly. "Every morning at five o'clock do we pray, wet or fine, warm or cold, dark or light. Jupiter, the horror that are College prayers at five o'clock on a January morning."

"How did you know my name?" asked Joyeuce.

"No one can walk past this house and not know your name. It is bellowed by every inmate of your household from dawn till night. 'Joyeuce, the cat is in the cream! Joyeuce, where are my shoes? Joyeuce, the children are making too much noise! Joyeuce, I have bumped my head! Joyeuce, the dogs are out in the quadrangle again! Joyeuce, the twins are lost!' When

I saw you in the Cathedral, surrounded by children, praying so earnestly for the cat, dogs, shoes, twins and bumped heads, I knew that you were Joyeuce. . . . A most inappropriate name."

" Why ? " demanded Joyeuce.

" Can so burdened a lady be joyous ? " He came a little nearer, his head tilted back and his hands creeping wickedly up the wall as though he would pull her down out of her window, compassion and mischievous invitation comically mingled on his face. " Do you ever do joyous things, Mistress Joyeuce ? Dance to the music of the virginals ? Go hawking ? Run through the kingcups in the meadows with your shoes and stockings off ? "

" No ! " whispered Joyeuce in horror. " Of course not ! "

" By cock and pie, it is a disgrace ! " he announced. " This evening at seven o'clock you will meet me at the Fair Gate and we will go—I do not know where we will go—but it will be somewhere lovely. Do you hear me, Mistress Joyeuce ? " He laughed, keeping his eyes fixed on hers so that she could not look away, drinking in the flattery of the palpitating longing and dismay that robbed her of breath so that she could not answer.

" Joyeuce ! "

The exclamation, deep-toned, astonished, outraged, yet with a hint of amusement behind the outrage, came from Canon Leigh, brought to a standstill on his way home from Saint Bartholomew's by the shocking sight of his eldest daughter leaning from her bedroom window and talking to that malapert scoundrel Nicolas de Worde, a creature unworthy of the name of scholar, the horror of his Greek being equalled by nothing except the outrage of his Latin.

Joyeuce jumped back as though detected in a burglary, but Nicolas remained unflurried. He bowed with exaggerated gallantry first to Joyeuce and then to her father, smiled bewitchingly at them both and strolled off to his rooms beside the Fair Gate, disappearing with a whisk of the tail end of his gown that reminded Canon Leigh of a cock robin ; never a humble bird. He watched that flourishing tail vanish from sight with a cold eye, and then turned back to his daughter.

" I shall see you," he said, " later," and disappeared through the front door below.

Joyeuce stood back from the window with her hands pressed against her hot cheeks. She cast an anguished glance at the sky and saw that the golden clouds had all disappeared, swept away by the wind that had sprung up and was rustling the hawthorn across the way. Only one cloud sailed across the sky from west to east, from the Fair Gate to the Cathedral, a galleon of unsullied white in the warm blue of full day. . . . She must have been dreaming and gossiping for half an hour, with the children up to goodness alone knew what down below; and she had not even said her prayers. She knelt down beside her great bed and covered her shamed face with her hands. In thirty short minutes she had committed the three sins of daydreaming, laziness and impropriety, and she was almost too ashamed to pray. It was so much worse, she thought, to sin in the morning than to sin in the afternoon, for a fall once taken it is hard to recover foothold and now she would spend the whole day being disagreeable to everybody. "Ne nos inducas in tentationem," she prayed, Nicolas's unforgettable face mocking her within the darkness of her closed eyes, " sed libera nos a malo."

Canon Leigh, an economical man, had taught his children to pray in Latin so that two birds might be killed with one stone, the soul and the Latin being strengthened together.

She got up, shook dried herbs out of her dark blue skirt, straightened her apron and cap and stood for a moment, braced, before facing Great-Aunt. Then, her courage screwed to sticking point, she knocked at the door.

Great-Aunt admitted her, as always when displeased, by a short, peremptory bark.

Great-Aunt's room was smaller than the girls', though it suited her better owing to its extremely central position in the house, enabling her to keep her finger on the pulse of the household's life. One window looked out on the garden and the other looked down into the big combined hall and dining-room of the house, a glorious stone-floored, oak-panelled place that stretched right up to the raftered roof. Great-Aunt was therefore very happily placed. Her outside window enabled her to see all that went on in the garden and her inside window commanded not only the hall, but the great oak staircase, the front door, the dining table and the doors into kitchen, study and parlour. Nothing, therefore, could happen in the house that Great-Aunt did not know about, and nothing did. Her felicity was further increased by the fact that her room was over the kitchen and she could hear everything that Dorothy Goatley was up to down below. It was unfortunate that the yew hedge hid the stables, and the loft where Diggory Colt slept, from her view, and still more unfortunate that Dorothy's bedroom was downstairs on the other side of the house, but to counterbalance these drawbacks the girls' room was reached through hers and they could not even fetch a clean kerchief without her knowing it. . . . And one cannot have everything, as she was constantly remarking to Joyeuce, and for those blessings which are ours we should be thankful to a beneficent Creator.

Joyeuce entered and stood waiting for Great-Aunt to pop out from behind her bed curtains and express herself as to the row Diccon had made in the early morning. It was part of Great-Aunt's technique always to leave a few moments' awed silence between the entry of her audience and the delivery of her own remarks, tension being thus introduced and the point of her discourse much strengthened.

Joyeuce could never get over the fear that the furnishings of Great-Aunt's room had implanted in her when she was still a child. The enormous bed, curtained in purple velvet and reached by a flight of steps, was like a catafalque, and the tapestries of Great-Aunt's choice, representing the Day of Judgment and Salome presenting King Herod with John the Baptist's head on a charger, covered the walls with purple clouds, green lightnings and crimson drops of gore. Great-Aunt disliked the modern fashion of herb-strewn floors and the black, polished boards gleamed sombrely like the inky water of a bottomless tarn ; one of those tarns where murdered bodies sink down and down and are never found.

When Canon Leigh and his young wife had first come to live at Christ Church, happy beyond words at the prospect of a beautiful home of their own, Great-Aunt, then resident at Stratford and intensely bored by the life of a dignified, childless widow of ample means, had written suggesting that she should live with them. They had hastily written back pointing out all the disadvantages to Great-Aunt herself of her proposed change of residence ; for she was exceedingly well off, enjoyed excellent health and had no claim whatsoever upon their charity ; but before the letter had time to get there Great-Aunt herself, a woman the reverse of dilatory, had arrived at Oxford. Going out for a stroll one afternoon they had beheld her ambling up to the Fair Gate on her white mule, sitting sideways with her feet on a board, four packhorses behind her carrying her tapestries, bedding and other personal luggage. At the age of seventy-nine she had ridden all the way, and had derived great enjoyment from the adventure. It was impossible to disappoint so gallant an old lady ; moreover Canon Leigh after a night of wrestling in prayer felt the visitation to be the will of God ; so Great-Aunt was unpacked and arranged at Christ Church. With the Dean's permission, withheld at first but granted after a stormy personal interview with Great-Aunt herself, a window was knocked in her bedroom wall so that the few years that remained to her—she numbered them at two or three—might be enlivened and sanctified by the spectacle of innocent children and learned divines partaking of nourishment in the hall below. Mistress Leigh herself had failed to see any indication of the divine purpose in Great-Aunt's arrival—the old lady was Canon Leigh's aunt, not hers—but she had submitted, as was her wifely duty, and had hung up the Salome tapestry with her own hands. . . . After all, she had reflected, the old dame could not live for ever. . . . But the old dame had outlived Mistress Leigh herself, had indeed contributed to her death by worrying her frantic during her months of pregnancy, and now at the age of eighty-five, after six years' residence at Christ Church, was enjoying better health than ever.

And yet, though she was really rather a nasty old lady, it was impossible not to feel for Great-Aunt the admiration that abounding vitality in the very old always calls out in the young and middle-aged. Great-Aunt had lived for eighty-five years in a very terrible world. Her Catholic brother had been hanged, drawn and quartered at Tyburn by the command of Henry Tudor, her Protestant husband had been burned at the stake by Henry's daughter, Mary, and her four children had died in one of the terrible visitations of the plague. That she had weathered it all and now in her old age faced life with undiminished zest implied a courage of no mean order. . . .

Though it must be owned that Great-Aunt had had very little sympathy with her heroic brother and husband. If her relations liked to be martyred for their religious convictions the more fools they, she said; as for herself she had always trimmed her sails to whatever winds might blow and here she still was, hale and hearty in her old age.

Great-Aunt's head, encircled in fold after fold of night-cap, popped out from between the purple curtains, and Joyeuce jumped as at the eruption of a jack-in-the-box.

Dame Susan Cholmeley had once been beautiful. Her dark eyes under black, bushy brows still had the depth of velvety colour and the bright sparkle that had enslaved the lovers whose number increased by ten every time she told the story of her early triumphs to the children, and her wrinkled cheeks were still rosy. Her most alarming feature was her large, hooked nose, that nearly met her chin and gave a witch-like look to her face. She had lost all her teeth and it was the difficulty of mastication and conversation under the circumstances, and not ill health, that led her to spend most of her time in her room. She was still capable, had she wished it, of riding her mule from Stratford to Oxford and enjoying it.

"*I* heard you, Joyeuce Margery Leigh," remarked Great-Aunt. "And a more disgraceful exhibition of impropriety I never overheard in all my life. . . . And let me tell you, child, I've overheard a good deal in my day."

Joyeuce smiled in spite of herself. Great-Aunt had a naïve way of exposing her own weaknesses that was very endearing, and it was a relief that Joyeuce's greater sin had driven Diccon's early-morning yells out of her mind, for if there was one thing that Joyeuce could not endure it was criticism of Diccon.

"Had I the strength I used to have," said Great-Aunt, "I should take a slipper to you. . . . And who was the young man?" she continued eagerly in almost the same breath.

"Master Nicolas de Worde," said Joyeuce, standing meekly beside Great-Aunt, her hands folded on her apron and her eyes cast down. "He said good morning to me."

"It takes a long time to say good morning nowadays," commented Great-Aunt dryly. "And is it your intention to meet him at the Fair Gate this evening?"

Joyeuce looked up sharply, the crimson blood running up

into her cheeks. Though **Great-Aunt's** hearing was preternaturally sharp it was quite impossible that she could have heard Nicolas's request, made out in the quadrangle. It was just another instance of what the children called " Great-Aunt's second sight." The old lady had in reality no more second sight than a rabbit, but after eighty-five years of life in this world she knew the unvarying reactions of human nature to the circumstances that beset it. " Meet me at the gate " was the first coherent remark made by all lovers ; though no doubt, poor creatures, they thought their idea original. They all ran to the gates ; city gates, palace gates, garden gates ; for gates are symbolic of the entry from one state of being to another and even to stand at them, looking out, gives you a sense of freedom. . . . Great-Aunt had presented herself at a good many gates in her day and had indeed perfected herself in the technique ; the man must be kept waiting at the gate that his ardour be inflamed, but not too long, lest it should cool ; the weather, too, must be taken into consideration, and the kind of gate ; for tall gates are made to be peeped through coquettishly, short gates to be leaned upon in intimate conversation, flat-topped gates to be sat upon while sunsets are admired, while the gate that has an easy latch is made to be escaped through to quiet places of woods and streams where time does not pass and prying eyes do not tarnish. . . . Great-Aunt, always deeply interested in affairs of the heart, forgot her annoyance in curiosity and decided that the time had come to give Joyeuce a little elementary instruction in these things, and opened her mouth to begin ; only to discover to her rage that the malapert girl had left the room.

For the instinct of escape had already seized Joyeuce and suddenly turning on her heel she had done what she had never presumed to do before ; left Great-Aunt without Great-Aunt's permission so to do. As she stood outside in the passage that divided the old lady's room from the rooms where Canon Leigh and the boys slept, closing the door softly behind her, Great-Aunt's indignant shouts were battering at her ears, but she went resolutely on down the passage and down the glorious great carved staircase to the hall below where her father was waiting for her ; had been waiting for her, sternly and patiently, his sense of humour well battened under, all the time she said her prayers and interviewed Great-Aunt.

Canon Leigh found the bringing up of his motherless children an arduous business, for the time given to a parent in which to do it seemed so short. Fourteen being a marriageable age, the children must by then be ready to shoulder the pains and burdens of adult life with strong characters and tested courage. The period of training was therefore short and intensive and the worst crime a parent could commit was that of sparing the rod and spoiling the child. But poor Canon Leigh, desperately endeavouring to combine the tenderness of a mother with the sternness of a father, found himself as he grew older attaching more and more importance to the value of gentleness and less and less to that of discipline. . . . He could no longer bring himself to beat his daughters, and did not beat his sons with any real concentration or enthusiasm. . . . He loathed beating them. . . . This weakness in him was a sin, and he knew it and confessed it during the long hours when he prayed for them, but it was a sin that even with the help of God he could not conquer. He tried to make up for it by lashing them with his tongue instead, but the tongues of learned and holy men are always singularly wanting in lash and at the end of a long scolding his children were sometimes unaware that there had been one. . . . All except Joyeuce, as sensitive as her father and with the same capacity for suffering as his. She always knew when he was trying to scold and gave him all the help she could.

That there must be one now, she knew, and she went steadily across the hall to the great fireplace, before which he stood, and knelt for his blessing.

He gave it, his hand on her head, and there was then an anxious pause.

"Yes, Father," she encouraged gently, getting up and standing before him with bent head. He still said nothing and, peeping at him out of the corner of her eye, she saw him scratching his bald head in perplexity. . . . She must tell him what to say, as usual.

"I must not talk to young men out of the window," she said. "It was indiscreet and a bad example for the younger girls."

"Thank you, Joyeuce," he said with eager gratitude.

"I entirely forgot myself," said Joyeuce, looking him straight in the eyes. "I have never done it before and I will never do it again : or anything else of an indiscreet nature."

"You are my very good daughter, Joyeuce," he told her, and kissed her three times, on each of her eyelids, that were always a little shadowed with purple because she had too much to do, and on her pointed chin. "I have not hurt you?" he asked anxiously. "I have not said too much?"

"Not a word too much, Father," she comforted him, and she went to fetch the children and Dorothy and Diggory from the kitchen for prayers.

The kitchen led directly from the hall and looked out on the garden. A huge open fireplace with spits for roasting the meat occupied almost the whole of the wall to the right as one entered, while against the left wall stood an open cupboard holding tankards and pewter pots, with a door beside it leading to the still-room, a stone-floored fragrant place where the preserves were kept, and the store of herbs and the presses for the linen. Leading out of the still-room was Dorothy Goatley's tiny slip of a bedroom, and the pastry and the bolting house, where the bread was baked and the flour sifted. From the latter, stone steps led down to the huge dark cellars so thoughtfully provided by Cardinal Wolsey for the beer, the Xeres sack, the skins of Greek wine and the casks of burgundy, to which he had himself been so attached. . . . Only judging others by himself he expected them to have such a lot of it, for the cellars stretched the length of the house and went down into the bowels of the earth. . . . There was never anything in the Leigh cellars but a very modest supply of the inevitable beer.

The kitchen, like the hall, was stone-floored, with a large well in the centre. During the day this was kept carefully covered, and the kitchen table was placed in position over it, but in the early morning both cover and table were removed, so that the day's supply of water could be drawn up and the children's faces washed.

They were kneeling round the well now having their ablutions superintended by Dorothy Goatley, and watching in a fascinated silence while Diggory Colt let down bucket after bucket into the cool depths of the well and brought them up again filled to the brim with cold sparkling water. The river ran so near them that there was never any lack of water in the well, and during the rainy winter months there was a further supply of water in the cellars, where it stood two feet deep and gave Canon Leigh the rheumatics.

Dorothy was a delightful round, rosy, blue-eyed person in the middle twenties. Figure she had none, her person being shaped like a loaf of bread; a smaller bulge above being set upon a larger bulge below, with a region of great tightness between the two. She was always clothed in a grey homespun dress covered by a large white apron, and her hair, if she had any, was completely hidden beneath her white cap. Her life had one great love, for her foster-child, Diccon, and one great hatred, for Great-Aunt; the rest of the world she regarded with tolerant amusement.

Diggory was an old man, though neither he nor anyone else had the slightest idea how old he was. He looked like a withered apple and might have been any age. He had been groom at Mistress Leigh's old home, had taught her to ride and had never left her, sharing her fortune or misfortune with complete indifference. When she died he made no comment at all, but set himself to serve her husband and children with the same morose devotion with which he had served her. He seldom spoke, but should there be any little difference with any of the tradesmen he could hit hard. The children and horses and dogs loved him, and it seemed he had but to touch the earth with his horny fingers for flowers to grow.

The little group of children and animals at the well was now augmented by Will and Thomas, aged nine and eight. Giles, the eldest son, was now fifteen and a man full-grown. He was a scholar of Christ Church, and a brilliant one too, and had his own rooms in College, strolling home now and then to shed the light of his countenance upon his family when he felt it would do them good.

Will and Thomas were very alike and almost as inseparable as the twins. They were cheerful, untidy children with matted shocks of the Leigh honey-coloured hair, wide, enquiring grey eyes and large mouths that required a lot of filling. They were thoroughly naughty in a healthy way, but they had none of Diccon's deliberate wickedness. As far as Canon Leigh could see they had no intelligence at all, and neither had the twins. The brains of the family were in the brilliant Giles, Joyeuce and

Grace. It was impossible as yet to form any judgment as to Diccon's mental equipment. Cunning he had in plenty, and concentration and immense strength of will, but with what ends in view he would choose to exert these gifts no one dared prophesy.

"Father is here and it is time for prayers," said Joyeuce.

Grace, Will, Thomas, and the twins hastily jumped up and rubbed their faces dry, but Diccon, lying flat on his stomach peering into the depth of the well, had to be lifted up, yelling loudly, and forcibly placed upon his feet. . . . Another of the unfortunate traits in Diccon's character was that he would never be devout unless forced to it.

Joyeuce led the procession from the kitchen back to the hall, the children following her in order of age and Dorothy and Diggory and the animals bringing up the rear.

The children knelt in a row before their father to receive his morning blessing, each little head being bent in turn as his hand was laid upon it; with the exception of Diccon's, and Diccon never lowered his head unless it was to bite. He had, on one terrible occasion, bitten his father when his father blessed him, but the punishment meted out to him later by his outraged brothers and sisters had been so severe that he had decided against repeating his performance.

There was a window on one side of the front door and passers-by in the quadrangle who happened to look in at a quarter to six in the morning always saw a sight they did not forget; they were moved to edification or to mirth according to their several convictions and temperaments, but were all alike impressed by the beauty of the picture.

In front of the fireplace, where nearly all the year round a log fire burned, for the room faced north and was cold, Canon Leigh would be standing, looking like a monk with his bald head and long, black belted gown. In front of him in a long row stood his children in gradually decreasing order of age and height, and behind them stood Dorothy and old Diggory. Tinker, the cat, would be clasped in Diccon's arms, and the three dogs, Posy and Spot and Pippit, would be sitting very reverently upon their haunches beside Diggory. . . . Canon Leigh loved animals as dearly as his children did and saw no incongruity in the attendance of these quadrupeds at family prayers. . . . The flickering light of the flaming logs would gleam on the dark wood of the panelled walls and the glorious carved staircase, on the long oak dining table where in summer a beau-pot of flowers always stood, on the fair heads of the elder children and the ruddy darkness of Diccon's mop of curls, on the rich ebony of Tinker's fur and the soft, mousy velvet of Pippit's coat. . . . And last, but not least, the macabre apparition of an old woman in a frilled night-cap looking out of an overhead window, a sinister, black-browed witch of an old woman who laughed a silent, toothless laugh when her mocking bright eyes fell on the group below.

"Funes ceciderunt mihi in prædaris," Canon Leigh would say in his deep, amazingly beautiful voice, and the children and servants, who knew the verses by heart, would reply, "Hæreditas mihi prædara est mihi." They would recite, turn and turn about, until they got to the end, Diggory's deep bass growl mingling with the children's piping trebles, and then they would kneel, holding up their clasped hands, and say the Lord's Prayer ; the dogs lying flat with their noses between their paws, and Diccon forced to his knees by Dorothy's vigorous hand dealing him two blows, one behind each little knee. . . . This was the best method yet discovered of making Diccon pray. . . . Though when he had been forced into the correct posture for devotion, and knelt with his green eyes fixed on the ceiling—he always refused to shut them—and his plump hands piously clasping Tinker to his breast, who knew whether the thoughts in his mind were those his well-wishers would have chosen ? . . . It was feared not.

On most mornings the Lord's Prayer was followed by breakfast, but every now and then Canon Leigh, who did not seem to feel the pangs of hunger like other people, and was really more suited by temperament to be one of those Indian mystics who sit out a lifetime praying on the top of a tower, with their legs round their necks, than the father of a family, would suddenly be lifted up on the wings of prayer and go on soaring higher and higher, oblivious of the hungry, earth-bound bodies of his wretched family.

He did this to-day. He began praying for the suffering, the homeless, the destitute and the sick, above all for the hungry children who had not where to lay their heads. He went on and on. His family were only too pleased to pray for hungry children, provided they were given their own breakfast first, but while they were still themselves among the afflicted they found it difficult. Dorothy, who had left the milk on the hob, cast agonised glances at Diggory, the younger children stirred restlessly and Great-Aunt began to beat an impatient tattoo upon her window-pane. But Canon Leigh, passing on from the general to the particular, began to pray for a certain destitute boy whom he had that morning encountered. . . . That he might be found. . . . Comforted. . . . Fed.

Great-Aunt could stand it no longer. She flung open her window and leaned out. "Gervas," she shouted, "hold your tongue!"

Canon Leigh started and looked up; taken by surprise, bewildered and uncertain of himself, he got to his feet without knowing what he was doing, while Dorothy fled to the kitchen and the children ran to seat themselves round the table before he could change his mind and begin again.

Seated in his big carved chair at the head of the table Canon Leigh again looked up at his aunt and marvelled at the power she had over them all. She was a wicked destructive old lady who had worried his wife into her grave, ruined his home, and now, so it seemed to him, spent her time seizing hold of all the fair flowers of piety and love that might blossom in his house and pulling them up by the roots. . . . And yet, with her burning vitality, her iron will, her good humour when she got her own way, and bearing still in face and figure the remnants of great beauty, she was attractive, and he could not but smile at her as she nodded and waved from her window.

She was in fine fettle now that Dorothy had brought her a good brimming tankard of ale and a plate of cold roast beef minced up very finely, and looked down benignly upon the children and their father below, with their mugs of milk and manchets of coarse bread. A wishy-washy diet, she considered, and responsible for their wishy-washy characters. She had the lowest opinion of all of them, except Diccon, and interfered with good-humoured contempt in their talk of the boy whom Canon Leigh had so unfortunately lost. . . . The children were sorry about the poor boy now that they had had something to eat.

"I wish you hadn't lost him, Father," mourned Joyeuce.

"Perhaps we'll find him again," said Grace, hopefully.

"Heaven forbid," said Great-Aunt, and chewed a spoonful of minced beef with enjoyment.

"Dame," said Canon Leigh gravely, "I desire that you will not turn aside the thoughts of my children from the love of charity."

"Bugs," said Great-Aunt. "That's what charity is; the bringing in of bugs to the house," and she took a draught of ale.

"You will be so good," said her nephew sternly, "as to shut your window."

"Tilly-vally! Tilly-vally!" exclaimed Great-Aunt, but having had enough of them she banged the window shut and gave her whole attention to her food.

Canon Leigh, though he had apparently won a victory that should have compensated him for his previous defeat, felt no sense of satisfaction in it. . . . He knew that Great-Aunt's rare retirements from the field of battle were the result not of defeat but of boredom. . . . He drooped in his chair, worrying about the boy; wishing for the hundredth time that there were still monasteries in England, and that they opened their doors to married men.

The twins, observing his depression of spirits, slid solidly to the floor, trundled across to him and climbed each upon a knee. "Never mind, Father," they cooed, "*we'll* find that little boy," and laying their fat cheeks against his they squeaked engagingly.

They had a habit of squeaking, like mice, that was peculiar to themselves and was used with much effect to express affection, surprise, condolence, happiness, or any other emotion which might seem called for at the moment; though it was the happiness squeak that was used most often and was the most attractive, in spite of a tendency to end in hiccups. For it was the happiness of the twins that made them so adorable. They were as happy as the first buttercup lifting its face to the sun, or as a blackbird singing at sunset, or as the streams when they "make sweet music with the enamelled stones." They would always be happy, their father thought, being of that radiant company whose business in life it seems to be simply to be joyous, their joy a vindication of the eternal rightness of the foundations of this life. . . . With a twin in each arm he suddenly ceased to feel the attraction of the cloister.

But time was going on. There was a constant patter of feet

on the path under the window, and a succession of flying figures crossing the quadrangle, for work began at six and scholars were hurrying to their lectures. Great Tom boomed out the hour from the Cathedral tower and Canon Leigh set the twins hastily upon the floor and hurried into the study to fetch the books he needed for his six o'clock lecture.

Sighing, and wiping their mouths with the backs of their hands, Will and Thomas slid to the floor and got their school books from the chest under the window, just as Dorothy entered from the kitchen with their dinners in little leather bags. They attended the grammar school at Queen's College, where they went every morning at six o'clock, returning at five-thirty in the evening. Of this eleven hours' working day, two hours, eleven to one, were free for eating the dinners of cold meat and bread that they had brought with them, and for shooting at the butts, but the rest of the time was devoted to grammar, logic, rhetoric, arithmetic, music, geometry and astronomy.

> 'Tis Grammar teaches how to speak,
> And Logic sifts the false from true ;
> By Rhetoric we learn to deck
> Each word with its own proper hue.
> Arithmetic of number treats,
> And Music rules the Church's praise ;
> Geometry the round earth meets,
> Astronomy the starry ways.

They had holidays, of course, eighteen days at Christmas, twelve at Easter and nine at Whitsuntide, but it was extraordinary how quickly they seemed to pass . . . They envied the twins, who stayed at home and were taught by Great-Aunt.

Not that the twins envied themselves. Joyeuce and Grace had long ago learnt all of the little that Great-Aunt knew and Grace now helped Joyeuce in the work of the house, so the twins and Diccon received Great-Aunt's instructions in solitary glory, and it was awful.

As they stood at the front door, seeing the men of the family off to work, their hearts sank down and down. . . . Oh, if only they were grown up, or men, or dead, or anything so that they need not receive instruction from Dame Susan Cholmeley. . . . But it would be best of all to be grown up.

CHAPTER III

THE MADONNA

> See, where she sits upon the grassy green
>   (O seemly sight)
>   Yclad in scarlet like a maiden Queen,
>   And ermines white.
>   Upon her head a cremosin coronet,
>   With damask roses and daffodillies set:
>   Bay-leaves between,
>   And primroses green
> Embellish the sweet violet.
>
> I saw Phoebus thrust out his golden head,
>   Upon her to gaze:
>   But when he saw, how broad her beams did spread,
>   It did him amaze.
>   He blushed to see another sun below,
>   He durst again his fiery face outshow:
>   Let him, if he dare,
>   His brightness compare
> With hers, to have the overthrow.
>
> Bring hither the pink and purple columbine,
>   With gillyflowers;
>   Bring coronations, and sops in wine,
>   Worn of paramours.
>   Strew me the ground with daffodowndillies,
>   And cowslips, and kingcups, and loved lilies:
>   The pretty paunce,
>   And the chevisaunce,
> Shall match with the fair flower delice.
>
>   EDMUND SPENSER.

I

GREAT-AUNT delivered her instructions from half-past six till half-past eight in the parlour, a little room reached by a door under the staircase, and here the three children sat on low stools waiting for her.

The parlour was a lovely room, panelled in oak and with a beautiful modelled plaster ceiling. Over the fireplace was a carved overmantel, where the arms of Cardinal Wolsey and Henry the Eighth were set in a frame of leaves and Tudor roses, wonderfully rich and luxuriant. In the winter they burnt sea coal in the fireplace, and a great luxury Joyeuce and her father felt it to be. In London sea coal must not be burnt while Parliament was sitting, lest the health of members be affected, but Oxford laid no such restrictions upon its use. In spring and autumn they burnt the wood that had been torn from the trees in the Christ Church meadows by winter gales, and the twins liked that best, for the flames from the wood seemed to them prettier than the flames from the coal because they were of different colours, as though each different tree had a different flame flower, some yellow, some orange, some blue and some red. In the evenings, when it was growing dark, the reflected flames leaped and danced on the dark panelled walls so that you thought that the wood too was on fire with flowers.

There was very little furniture in the room ; a few stools and chairs, the chest where the children kept their needlework and lesson books and the clavicytherium that Joyeuce, the musician of the family, played to their father in the evenings. It was like a spinet set up on end and if its compass was no longer than that of the human voice the harp music that came from it was very sweet.

The parlour's one window looked out on the street that ran past the Fair Gate, leading from the centre of the town to the South Gate of the city. Its real name was South Gate Street, but it was always called Fish Street after a certain Master Fish, a mayor of corpulent and happy memory. It was not always a pleasure to have this window open because the housewives of Fish Street flung all their slops cheerfully out of the window to drain down through the cobbles to the kennel ; but to-day, after the downpour in the night, the smells were nicely damped down and Fish Street quite at its best, with little blue pools between the cobbles that reflected the blue sky above, and the wet roofs of St. Aldate's church and the Christ Church almshouses shining brightly across the way.

This outside world was so tempting that the children left their stools and ran to the window to look out. . . . From the town came distant and thrilling sounds of pipes, drums and jingling bells. . . . Joan, who had felt when she woke up that this was going to be a particularly adventurous day, jigged up and down on her toes and squeaked excitedly. " It's the Morris dancers," she said, and then, a little mournfully, "Everyone has a holiday on May Day but us."

"We do not join in these vulgar holidays, because we are Well Born," said Meg, passing on an explanation of their hard lot already given her by Great-Aunt; but she sighed as she gave it, for the advantages of Blue Blood seemed at the moment few.

Diccon, hanging out of the window with his short legs well off the floor, was taking no notice of their conversation. "I can spit further than you can," he announced, and gave a demonstration.

"You can't!" cried Meg indignantly, and showed him at once that he was mistaken.

Joan did not waste her breath on words, but used it all to reach further than either of the others; and at this unfortunate moment Great-Aunt entered.

When dressed for the day she was an awe-inspiring sight in any mood, but when in the grip of righteous indignation she struck terror to the hearts of the boldest. She stood in the centre of the room leaning upon her ivory-topped stick, arrayed in her black satin farthingale over a green kirtle embroidered with purple daisies. She wore a wig of jet black, curly hair and over it a veil of lawn edged with lace. She had jewels in her ears and on her fingers. She looked magnificent, if a trifle barbaric, with her dark eyes sparkling with rage and her mouth set so strongmindedly that her nose and her chin almost met.

The twins seized Diccon's legs and pulled him to the ground, whirled him about to make his bow and sank themselves into agitated and rather wobbly little curtsies. . . . But it was too late. . . . Great-Aunt had seen.

"Children," she said in a terrible voice, "hold out your hands."

They held out their hands and she produced from the black satin folds of her farthingale a very potent little cane that had been presented to her by her husband upon the occasion of the birth of their first child, and had been used by her with great effect ever since. It was unbelievable that an old lady of eighty-five could have such strength in her arm. When she had done with them the three little palms were on fire and tears were trickling down the twins' cheeks. . . . They never cried when Joyeuce spanked them, but then Great-Aunt could hit harder than Joyeuce and there was something in the way she did it that hurt their feelings. . . . Joyeuce spanked them because she loved them, but Great-Aunt caned because caning in itself gave her pleasure.

"Weak little poppets," she snorted, regarding the tears with disfavour. "Look at your brother. He does not cry though he's still but a babe."

Diccon grinned wickedly at her, his green eyes narrowed to slits, and thrusting out his bright pink tongue—his tongue was of an unusually vivid pink—he licked his smarting palm. He was not afraid of Great-Aunt, but when with her usually behaved himself, for in Great-Aunt he had met his match. It cannot be said that they loved each other, for neither of them had much power of affection, but they saw each in the other qualities that they themselves possessed, and being both of them chockfull of conceit they were naturally full of mutual admiration.

Great-Aunt had no use for sensitiveness in any form. That idiotic shrinking from giving pain that characterised both Joyeuce and her father, together with their imbecile reserve and morbidity of conscience, aroused in her nothing but contempt. She cared as little what she did to other people as she cared what they did to her, and as for reserve, if you did not say straight out what you wanted how could you expect to get it? This attitude towards life was also Diccon's and their aim being the same they got on uncommonly well.

"Put your tongue in, Diccon!" thundered Great-Aunt. "And collect your thoughts for the morning's instruction. Sit down, little girls, and take up your hornbooks."

Great-Aunt seated herself majestically upon a big carved chair, with the children's lesson books ready to her hand on a stool by her side. She fancied herself as an instructress and example to the young and was not now recognisable as the same old lady who had made such unfortunate remarks at breakfast.

The children seated themselves upon their stools and took up the hornbooks that were attached to their waists by cords and accompanied them through their day. The hornbook was intended for purposes of edification and that it was also used for purposes of battledore and shuttlecock was unfortunate, but inevitable owing to its shape. A sheet of vellum, covered by a thin sheet of horn to protect the vellum from the soiling of grubby little hands, was fastened to a piece of wood with a handle, very much the shape of a square hand mirror. On the vellum were inscribed the essentials of education. First in importance came the cross, followed by the rhyme,

> Christ's cross be my speed
> In all virtue to proceed.

Then came the alphabet and then, reading and writing being now presumably mastered, a dedication of learning. " In the name of the Father, and of the Son, and of the Holy Ghost." Then came the Lord's Prayer and finally, but only if there was room, the numerals, for the genius who designed the hornbook was probably a monk in one of the monastery schools who thought moneymaking arithmetic less important than prayer and dedication. The children, too, quite understood the relative importance of these things. Christ's cross, they knew, came first, and they called the hornbook their criss-cross, after it, and the alphabet the criss-cross row.

When they had repeated the prayers on the hornbook, Great-Aunt set them to do a little juggling with the numerals.

" If I had five apples," she said " and you took away two, what then ? "

" You would cane us," said Diccon, and licked his palm again.

" Insolent varlet ! " cried Great-Aunt, and felt for her cane ; but Diccon grinned at her and she thought better of it.

" Three apples, Great-Aunt," squeaked Meg, the more intellectual of the twins, and the arithmetic lesson pursued its way in comparative calm.

When it was over Great-Aunt took from the table beside her a battered little brown book on deportment for the young. Every day she and the children went solemnly through this book. Great-Aunt reading out the precepts and the children repeating them after her. There were a great many precepts, dealing with every department of manners, though special attention was paid by the author to table manners.

1. Bite not thy bread, but break it, but not with slovenly fingers, nor with the same wherewith thou takest up thy meat.
2. Dip not thy meat in the sauce.

3. Take not salt with a greasy knife.
4. Cough not, nor blow thy nose at table if it may be avoided; but if there be necessity, do it aside, and without much noise.
5. Spit not in the room, but in a corner, and rub it out with thy foot, or rather, go out and do it abroad.
6. Stuff not thy mouth so as to fill thy cheeks; be content with smaller mouthfuls.
7. Blow not thy meat, but with patience wait till it be cool.
8. Sup not broth at the table but eat it with a spoon.

The author also laid stress on the necessity for courtesy. " If thy superior be relating a story," said one wise precept, " say not, I have heard it before, but attend as if it were to thee altogether new. Seem not to question the truth of it. If he tell it not right, snigger not, nor endeavour to help out or add to his relation."

There was yet another that might have been laid to heart with advantage by Nicolas de Worde. " Be not hasty to run out of church when the worship is ended, as if thou wert weary of being there."

It took them nearly an hour to get through the book from cover to cover, and sitting bolt upright on their stools their backs ached dreadfully, but at the least suspicion of a sigh or a yawn, or the tiniest relaxation of the vertical backbone, Great-Aunt's hand felt for the cane, so there was nothing for it but endurance.

But at half-past seven the agony was over. Diccon was allowed to go scuttling back to the kitchen and his cat while the little girls took up their samplers. This, of course, was a fresh agony, but not so bad as the first, because the twins were naturally domesticated and took readily to their needles.

The samplers were very beautiful, worked in minute crossstitch upon fine linen. Round the edges the twins were working a border of forget-me-nots, honeysuckle and sundry sorts of spots from a wonderful new book that had just come out with the imposing title, " Here followeth certain patterns of cutworks; newly invented and never published before. Also sundry sorts of spots, as flowers, birds, and fishes, etc., and will fitly serve to be wrought, some with gold, some with silk, and some with crewel in colours. And never but once published before. Printed by Richard Shorleyker."

When they got tired of this they cheered themselves up by re-threading their needles and doing a little work upon some breathless remarks they were embroidering in the centre of the sampler.

> In life there is no sure stay
> For flesh as flower doth fade away
> This carcass made of slime and clay
> Must taste of death there is no way
> While we have time then let us pray
> To God for grace both night and day

While the twins worked, Great-Aunt read aloud to them from a book called " De Civilitate Morum Puerilium : a little book of Good Manners for Children : into the English Tongue, by R. Whytyngton, 1540." It was a book written by Erasmus and it had a picture on the title page of good, well-behaved little children, which the twins were allowed to look at, at the end of the lesson.

It is doubtful if they derived as much benefit from this book as could have been wished because reading aloud was not one of Great-Aunt's gifts. She took her breaths at the command of nature instead of at the command of Erasmus, who had thoughtfully placed commas where breaths should be taken, but was not attended to by Great-Aunt ; also her lack of teeth made articulation a little difficult. However, they all three liked to feel that they were studying Erasmus, who was after all a noted scholar and who deserved to be patronised by them because he had had the good taste to like Oxford and its people. " The air," he had said, " is soft and delicious. The men are sensible and intelligent." The girls, he had gone on to say, were divinely pretty, and the kiss of greeting which they bestowed upon all and sundry was most delightful to receive. . . . Certainly a man to be taken notice of.

But at half-past eight Great-Aunt had had enough of him. She shut " De Civilitate Morum Puerilium " with a bang, signed to the twins to put away their work and leave the room, leaned back in her chair, folded her hands in her lap and closed her eyes. . . . She would slumber now, dreaming of the glories that were past, until it was time to go to her room for ten o'clock dinner.

II

The twins scuttled joyously from the room, for now they might go and play in the garden. This was to them the loveliest hour of the day because it was the only time when, except for the darling dogs, they were alone together. Diccon and his wretched cat, whom they and the dogs hated, were shut up in the kitchen with Dorothy, and Joyeuce and Grace were doing the housework.

There was a cupboard under the stairs, beside the door into the parlour, that was the children's own special cupboard and from this they took their leggings and their little dark blue cloaks lined with scarlet, with the hoods that came right over their heads and protected their snowy caps. They sat on the floor and pulled on their leggings, giggling and squeaking happily, while the dogs sat and watched and thumped their tails on the floor.

Also in the cupboard were the children's toys, their dolls and popguns and battledores and shuttlecocks, and Diccon's white woolly lamb with tin legs, bought for the most part at the annual St. Giles' Fair that was the greatest excitement of their lives.

Meg's favourite doll was called "Bloody Mary." The family had implored Meg to think of a nicer name, but Meg wouldn't. She thought "Bloody Mary" sounded well, and she had a sensitive ear for sound. "Bloody Mary" wore a black velvet farthingale over a kirtle of purple satin, with a plain ruff and coif. Her hair had come off and her composition face was very pale because she had once been left out in the rain, so that her likeness to the late Queen was really very remarkable.

Joan's favourite doll, "Queen Elizabeth," was quite different. Her hair was rich and red and her cheeks were painted a bright scarlet. Her red velvet farthingale was trimmed with gold braid and her green satin kirtle had orange flowers embroidered on it; her ruff was splendid and her coif spangled. The bodies of these ladies were not jointed, like the superior bodies of their twentieth-century descendants, so that they could not take up any position but that of the horizontal or the vertical, but on the other hand they had a stiff dignity, a blandness of expression, a fixity of regard and a magnificence of attire which if copied by their successors would most certainly prolong their lives. . . . For these dolls were not dolls with whom liberties could be taken.

Meg and Joan, now fully attired in cloaks and leggings, lifted their darlings—usually referred to as " Bloody and Bess "— tenderly from the cupboard, laid them in the crooks of their left arms and trotted through the kitchen to the garden, the dogs following. Dorothy was momentarily out of the kitchen and Diccon in her absence had betaken himself and the cat to the cupboard where the raisins were kept. He popped out his head and made a rude noise as the little girls passed, but they took no notice.

It was very lovely in the garden. The house was on the south side of the great quadrangle of Christ Church, and the garden lay between the back of the house and the Christ Church meadows. It was small but packed as full of flowers as Joyeuce could get it and as gay and neat as a patchwork quilt. Paved paths led between beds edged with rosemary, lavender, marjoram and thyme, their centres filled with the blue and golden flowers of spring, cowslips, primroses, daffodils and forget-me-nots. When the summer came they would be filled with rich warm flowers, roses and pinks and pansies and sops-in-wine. There were fruit trees in the garden, apples and cherries, and on the west side a yew hedge with a clipped peacock at each end hid the stable and outhouses, built out at an angle from the house. Beyond the garden the trees in the meadows were wearing the fresh green of spring, a garment as mistily mysterious as the rain-drenched grass below and the blue sky above.

It still felt cold and fresh after the rain in the night, but the bright sun poured down a wealth of light and filled each wet flower cup with a twinkling golden coin. The twins ran all round, visiting their friends and touching them very gently with the outstretched tips of their right forefingers ; very gentle forefingers that hardly disturbed a drop of rain when they touched. The late daffodils were bowing and curtsying to the west wind and Joan thought they looked like beautiful ladies dancing the pavane. Their farthingales, she pointed out to Meg, were a lovely pale yellow, pale as the first clouds of the morning, but the kirtles underneath them were much richer in colour, like the kingcups beside the river or the buttercups in the quadrangle. The twins had once been taken to see some beautiful ladies and gentlemen dancing the pavane in Christ Church hall and they had never forgotten it. One day, they told each other, they too would be grown up and dance in Christ Church hall, and the candle flames that would be burning in their hundreds to light the dance would not be so yellow as the dresses they would wear. . . . It must be a wonderful thing to be grown up. . . . Like being born again.

The apple trees were a mass of exultant pink and white blossom and when Meg and Joan ran up to them they threw out breaths of delicious warm scent that made the twins wrinkle their noses in delight. These apple trees seemed a miracle to the little girls. Only a little while ago they had seemed old, almost dead things, just gnarled black wood drenched by the winter storms and twisted into ugly fantastic shapes like the poor old beggars one sometimes saw in the streets. And then quite suddenly they had been plastered all over with comic fat buds that entirely altered their expressions, as though the surly old trees were trying to smile. The cold spring winds had shaken the buds and the rain had streamed over them, but nothing daunted they had slowly opened and green leaves had appeared, as though tightly shut hands unclosed and were held up to the sun, palms upwards and fingers crooked in supplication, begging for warmth. The tip of each green leaf had been faintly tinged with red, as though the warmth had already been given and fingers glowed. And now the warmth had spread and deepened until the ugly old men, the beggars, had become rich and radiant as young gods. . . . It was very odd, the twins thought, very odd indeed, and they wondered if they would be as changed when they grew up and wore those yellow dresses and danced in Christ Church hall.

They turned their backs on the fruit trees for a moment to survey the centre of the garden, where the soft, silver grey of the herbs edged the blue forget-me-nots like mist upon water, and then ran eagerly to the yew hedge that hid the stables, for in the depth of the yew hedge there was a bird's nest. It was a wonderful nest, its rough outside made of twisted twigs from the meadows and straws from the stable yard and its inside a perfect smooth bowl of grass and moss. There were five eggs in it, blue-green in colour with little specks of brown upon them. The twins did not stay long by the nest, lest they should annoy the parents, and they were careful not to touch, they just peeped hastily to see that all was well and then ran away. They had personally entrusted the nest to the care of Romulus and Remus, the two yew peacocks, and these birds had up to date justified the confidence reposed in them.

An archway had been cut in the centre of the yew hedge and this led through to the stables. A visit to the stables was the last item in the programme of early morning inspection, but it took a very long time owing to the enchantment of the stables. One went under the archway into the yard, where tufts of bright green grass grew between the cobbles and where the garbage heap led its interesting life. This latter exercised a deep fascination not only over the dogs, but over the twins too, for the things that could be found in it varied day by day and were always of an attractive nature, including, as they did, dead rats and mice in various interesting stages of decay, bones, old shoes, old pots and pans and scraps of wool and silk left over from the weaving. The twins played all sorts of fascinating games with the things they found in the garbage heap and the dogs were here safe from interruption by Tinker, the cat, for Tinker was nothing if not a snob and despising the Leigh garbage heap invariably betook himself to the superior one at the Deanery.

To the south of the yard was the outhouse where the harness and gardening tools and oddments were kept, with the room where Diggory slept above it. His window looked straight out on to the garbage heap but Diggory, as completely inured to smells as other Elizabethans, suffered no inconvenience. To the west was the stable proper, with the loft above it, and to the north a cobbled lane led between the stables and the house to Fish Street.

There were three inmates of the stables, Great-Aunt's old white mule, Susan, who had brought her from Stratford, Canon Leigh's black horse, Prince, and the children's pony, Dapple. Diggory was busy grooming Dapple and Prince and Susan, and leaving the dogs to dig happily in the garbage heap the twins ran to the stable to help him.

Diggory never minded being helped by the twins. He suffered them in silence until they got in the way and then picked them up very gently, put them outside and shut the door ; and they never seemed to resent this dismissal, or to question it.

The relations existing between Diggory and the children were rather puzzling to Canon Leigh. They talked to him by the hour together, quite undeterred by the fact that he never made any answer except an occasional grunt. And what did they talk to him about ? And how is it possible to talk for two hours at a stretch to a person who never answers ? Or was there a world of meaning in each of Diggory's grunts that the children and the animals alone were able to interpret ? Canon Leigh could only suppose that those very near to the earth, the peasants whose life is regulated by her seasons, the animals who make their homes among the roots of her trees, and the children to whom her flowers and grasses are still enchanted forests, are bound together in a closer understanding than can be comprehended by those others whom education and the customs of so-called civilization have carried far away from the source of their being.

The twins, having kissed Dapple, Prince and Susan on their gentle noses, spent half an hour helping Diggory and talking to him so incessantly that not a pin-point could have been inserted between one sentence and another. At the end of that time he silently picked them up and put them outside the door.

" Diggory," they called from outside, " could we go up into the loft ? "

For answer Diggory silently picked them up again, one under each arm, and placed them one in Dapple's manger and one in Prince's. From here they were able to scramble up by hoisting themselves through the rafters over their heads, left open so that fodder could be lowered down from the loft to the mangers below.

Scrambling and kicking, and pushed by Diggory from behind, they emerged from the mangers and arrived on all fours on the floor of the loft. Picking themselves up, and removing streamers of hay from their own persons and those of Bloody and Bess, they surveyed the loft and found it as attractive as ever, with its one cobwebby window looking on Fish Street and its fascinating smell of well kept horses, hay and sunshine. . . . That sunshine has a scent, and that it lives in hay long after it is cut and dried and brown as autumn leaves, all the Leigh children firmly maintained. It is not a scent that can be defined, but when you smell it you think instantly of gorse and the song of the lark. . . . There was real as well as preserved sunshine in the loft, that fell through the cracks in the roof in long rays in which the motes of dust hopped and skipped with a gaiety that warmed the very cockles of the heart. Sparrows built under the eaves of the loft and their chatter filled it all day long. The generous load of hay that had been brought from the Christ Church meadows last summer had dwindled during the winter so that most of the floor space was left free and made a fine dancing floor.

Meg and Joan danced here daily. Laying aside their cloaks and Bloody and Bess they picked up their skirts on either side and curtsied gravely to each other, pointing their booted feet with as much delicacy as was possible under the circumstances. They went carefully and seriously through the steps of the stately pavane that they had picked up from watching Great-Aunt teach them to Joyeuce and Grace. Their chubby faces were composed in earnest gravity and their eyes had a faraway look. Between the fingers and thumbs that held their rough homespun skirts they could feel the softness of yellow satin, the chattering sparrows were the players of lute and viol and virginal, and the slanting rays of light that touched their fair hair to gold fell from the hundreds of candles burning round Christ Church hall.

It was while they were dancing that they heard again that exciting sound of pipes and drums and ringing bells. At first it was only a faraway sound, at one with the music of their imagination, but gradually it grew louder and their pattering feet began to keep time with it, and then it became a regular uproar, drowning the chatter of the sparrows and the hissing sound that Diggory was making down below.

" The Morris dancers ! " shrieked Meg.

" Coming down Fish Street ! " yelled Joan.

They dashed to the window, pushed it open and leaned out. Down from the town that glorious crowd came dancing, a stream of colour that washed up against the walls on either side as though it would lift up the houses and carry them with it. The merry-makers were more uproarious than ever now, for they had been on the go for some hours, imbibing cakes and ale all the time, and their enjoyment was absolutely irresistible. The twins leaned further and further out of their window, squeaking excitedly, watching the figures of fairy-tale and legend passing by under their very noses. . . . The Men in Green, Robin Hood, Friar Tuck, Little John, Maid Marion, the Queen of the May, the Fool, the Hobby Horse, the Dragon, and that hero of the best fairy tales, the Younger Son. . . . It was this last character who attracted the twins most of all because, though they had heard about him so often, following his career over and over again as they sat by the fire on winter evenings listening to Joyeuce's bedtime stories, they had never actually seen him before, and now they found that he looked exactly as he ought to look; ragged and dirty, but jolly and laughing and such a gentleman that, after a bath, he would have been a fit mate for any princess. . . . The twins knew he was a prince in disguise because of a certain royalty in his bearing; he moved as a man moves whose reason controls his body and whose immortal spirit has climbed up far enough to sit enthroned as king of his reason. . . . Where was he going, they wondered? To London to be Lord Mayor? Out of South Gate and up into Bagley Forest to kill giants? Or far away into the blue distance to look for a crock of gold buried at the foot of the rainbow?

Wherever it was, it seemed to the twins that it must be the most exciting place in the world. Why shouldn't they go there too? Why must they, because they were Well Born, be shut out from all the fun in life? Why could not they too join that glorious dancing coloured crowd and go with it over the edge of the world into fairyland? They never had any need to speak their thoughts to each other, for their spiritual nearness was so great that they were practically one child; what one thought the other thought, and what one did the other did, and so instantaneously that there was hardly time for others to notice the quick leaping of thought from mind to mind, or to see more than a tiny chink of daylight between the ballooning skirts as one bustling little body followed the other into action. So now it was as one child that they took a firmer hold on Bloody and Bess, leaned out of the window and yelled to the people, " Lift us down ! Lift us down ! "

Some obliging apprentices did so, one boy standing on the back of another and handing the twins down to a third, who placed the fat little creatures firmly upon the cobbles and pulled down their petticoats with great kindness and condescension.

" Thank you, sirs," panted the twins. " Thank you very much, sirs," and were instantly absorbed into the crowd like drops of water into the ocean.

Faithful, clinging to the tail of the Dragon and reeling over the cobbles drunk with colour and noise and excitement, was astonished when he looked down and saw two fat little girls with voluminous dark blue skirts, white aprons and caps, dolls clutched in their free hands and round pansy faces turned up to him in unconcealed adoration. . . . Faithful, adored by two females for the first time in his life, turned a bright pink.

" Where are we going ? " asked Meg. " To London Town ? "

" I don't think so," gasped Faithful in some confusion. " I've just come from there."

" Let's look for a crock of gold at the foot of the rainbow," panted Joan.

" Would you like a crock of gold ? " enquired Meg, looking up into Faithful's face as she pattered along beside him.

" More than anything else in the world," he gasped.

" We'll find it then," announced Joan, and the pace at which they were going having now robbed all three of breath the thing seemed settled.

At the South Gate of the city the cavalcade was brought to a full stop for further uproarious refreshment. Cakes were again thrown out of the windows and tankards of ale carried out of the houses from beneath the branches of May above the doorways. No one seemed to question the presence of the two fat little girls and their dolls among the May Day crowd. They were quite in place among those fairy tale-people. They were sat up astride the Dragon's tail and given cakes to eat, and even sips out of Robin Hood's tankard of ale. . . . Sips that went to their heads at once, so that they rolled about on top of the Dragon, squeaking with ecstasy, laughing so much that their eyes disappeared into rolls of fat, and kicking their short legs among their voluminous petticoats in a way that would have turned Joyeuce pale with horror had she seen.

Then suddenly they had turned round and were off again, drums thundering, bells ringing, handkerchiefs fluttering and feet pattering, streaming back up Fish Street like spring let loose.

As they went a shower passed over them, but the two little girls, clinging to the Younger Son while he in turn clung to the Dragon's tail, did not care in the least ; for it did not seem like real rain ; it was like the rain that falls in fairy-tales, lovely crystal drops that only refreshed without soiling the flower-like figures it touched, and quite cleared away the fumes of ale from little girls' brains. It swung away on the wings of the west wind and the sun came out again, lighting every dancing figure to a dazzling blaze of colour, washing the wet cobbles with silver and turning every thread of raindrop on windowsill and gable to a string of diamonds.

"The rainbow!" squeaked Meg.

It shone ahead of them, one end of it planted firmly in the heart of the town and the other disappearing into the sailing mass of cloud that had given them their shower.

"Come on!" squeaked Joan, pulling at Faithful's jerkin and bouncing uphill at a great pace. "Come on! Come on!"

Faithful came on, by now so bewildered by fatigue and noise that he hardly knew where he was or what he was doing; indeed, grown man of fourteen though he was he almost believed himself to have fallen head over heels out of the world of reality into that fairy world whose figures surrounded him. . . . The little girls, one on each side of him, believed themselves to be in it, and perhaps their faith was contagious.

The rain was falling again, though the sun still shone. The Fair Gate of Christ Church floated by in a golden mist and he found they had reached the heart of the town again, a place where four ways met, and had swerved to the right, back once more into the High Street. Looking up through the rain and the sun he saw the sign of the Mitre Inn swinging over his head, with above it the beautiful outline of a gabled roof, and springing straight up from the roof into the sky the dazzling curve of the rainbow. He let go of the Dragon's tail and stood stock still, gazing at it. He could not help himself. It was the loveliest rainbow he had ever seen.

The wide-open inn door, yawning like the black mouth of a cavern beneath the swinging sign, was absorbing the fairy-tale figures. One by one they danced in and were lost in the darkness; the Morris dancers, the drummers, the pipers, Robin Hood, Little John, Friar Tuck, Maid Marion, the Queen of the May, the Hobby Horse and the Dragon; they were gone and only the rainbow remained, springing from the roof of the inn, glowing more and more brightly as though it had absorbed into itself the vanished colours of fairyland.

Faithful might have come to himself at this point, he had

indeed already raised his ragged sleeve to wipe the sweat off his forehead and the dreams out of his eyes, but the twins had not returned to normal and had no intention of doing so for a long while yet. "Come on!" they cried, pulling at him. "The rainbow went right down through the roof. The crock's inside! Come on!"

They dragged him over the threshold into the cool, ale-scented darkness of the stoneflagged hall beyond. To their right a door shut off a tumult of sound that was the merrymakers sitting down to a dinner of roast beef to which the ceaseless absorption of cakes and ale throughout the morning had been a mere preliminary. But the twins knew better than to go in there. The crock of gold, they knew, was always buried deep down, and deep down being associated in their minds with darkness they made instantly for the place where the shadows were deepest. . . . Under the old oak stairs that led up to the gallery above.

There was a door there, and they opened it. Spiral stone steps twisted downwards into the depths of the earth, lit by a light that came from somewhere down below, and a strong smell of spirits made them pause and wriggle their noses like enquiring rabbits. "It's only the cellar," said Faithful, and was for going back.

But the twins knew that cellars are the most romantic places in the world. Wonderful things are found in cellars; skeletons, barrels full of rubies and pearls and crocks of gold. They pattered fearlessly down the steps, clasping their dolls to them. Faithful following behind, holding firmly to their skirts lest they should fall and hurt their button noses.

The stairs led them to a narrow passage, dank and musty, lined on each side with bins for the wines. A guttering candle, evidently left there by Mine Host of the Mitre when he fetched the ale for the merrymakers above, stood on the floor and flung their shadows eerily over the damp walls patched with mildew. The little girls blanched at the sight of those leaping shadows, but they did not turn back. In all the best fairy-tales the reward is to the courageous, and little girls with fair hair are always supernaturally protected.

The passage turned a sharp corner and led them into pitch darkness. A long way in front of them was a thin line of light, that might have been coming from a door left ajar, or that might again have been a spear held by an archangel, such as Meg had seen when she woke up that morning. They did not know how far away it was, it might have been miles, but they went on towards it, feeling their way cautiously, Meg going first with Bloody outstretched in front of her like a drawn sword.

They reached it, and it was a door. They pushed it open and went in, and were instantly confronted by a blaze of light, all the colours of the rainbow springing upwards in a slender pillar of glory from clustering tongues of flame that burned about its foot like golden flowers. " The foot of the rainbow ! " cried the twins, " the foot of the rainbow ! " and running forward they fell on their knees before the golden flowers, pointing at them with their fat forefingers, laughing and chattering and exclaiming with that lovely note of sheer delight in their voices that is in the cooing of happy doves and the crowing of young cockerels in the first light of dawn. . . . The fairy-tale had come true.

III

But Faithful, who saw the scene before him as it actually was, stood on the threshold rooted to the spot by a mixture of awe and fear and wonder. He stood in a little vaulted chamber that had once been part of the wine cellar but was now a chapel. In front of him, in an alcove hollowed out of the rough stone wall, stood a richly ornamented altar, hung with fine tapestries and carrying a carved crucifix and some richly gilded figures, and to one side of it, standing well forward in the chapel and challenging attention even before the altar, was that pillar of colour before which the twins were kneeling. It was a statue of the Madonna, and perhaps one of the loveliest ever made. Her robes of blue and scarlet hung in lovely folds from shoulder to foot and her face was serene and smiling beneath a jewelled crown that was as bright and golden as the sun itself. She held her babe in a crook of her arm, a lovely golden-haired babe dressed in a little green shift, who laughed and held up two fingers in blessing. A great bunch of spring flowers had been laid on the pedestal at her feet, because May was her own month, and she was the real Queen of the May, and below them burned clusters of candles, their lovely light illuminating the rough walls of the chapel and the figures of the saints that stood there in little niches. The smell of incense hung about the place, conquering the smell of must and damp, and a faint blue haze of it clung overhead, almost hiding the shadowy spaces of the vaulted roof and the long silver chain with a small lamp at its end that hung from it, motionless before the altar. . . . Popery. . . . Nourished upon Foxe's *Book of Martyrs* as he had been Faithful was as bigoted a Protestant as ever stepped. He sank upon a wooden bench near the door with his legs giving way beneath him and the hair of his head rising straight up in horror like the bristles of a disapproving porcupine.

He knew that such places existed, of course. Popery was not stamped out because Queen Mary was dead and Queen Elizabeth sat upon the throne of England; though it was driven underground it lived on; and in these early years of the Queen's reign, before the menace of Spain had turned her tolerance to bitterness, it was still possible for men and women to attend mass without peril, though in secret. The Roman Catholics of Oxford would have been astonished had they known how many of their fellow citizens knew about that chapel beneath the Mitre Inn; knew about it and said nothing.

But to Faithful, with his imagination luridly lit by the flames of Smithfield, it was as though he had fallen straight into the bottomless pit, and when a huge black shadow in a dark corner on the other side of the door uncoiled itself and shot up towards the roof he could have screamed aloud.

But it was not the devil, it was merely a tall young man who had been kneeling in the corner saying his prayers, and who now got up and came and stood beside Faithful, looking down at him in comical bewilderment. "How did you get here?" he whispered. "Did I forget to lock the upstairs door?"

"Yes, good sir," breathed Faithful. . . . As well to be polite, he thought. Otherwise he might be taken off to an adjoining cellar, tied up to a stake and made an end of.

"My absent-mindedness," said the young man, "will be my undoing," and he rubbed his chin ruefully.

Reassured by his kindly note, Faithful ventured to take a good look at him. He was dressed as the preacher at the other Chapel of Saint Bartholomew had been dressed, in a white ruff and a long gown, and his fine ascetic face, too, reminded Faithful of that other man, his friend. They were of the same type, he felt. This man was now young and straight and comely, but if he too were to suffer persecution he too might become as misshapen as a storm-twisted tree; and yet keep the attraction of anything that stands upon a mountain top. It was odd, thought Faithful, that two such similar men should think so differently about religion; should be ready, as he had no doubt from the look of them that they were, to die for their divergent beliefs. Man was very odd, he thought. But even life was very odd, and became odder and odder the more you thought about it. . . . And it seemed very odd to him that a man who by his dress was evidently a college don should be saying his prayers in a Popish chapel. These things, thought Faithful, ought not to be so. As a prospective and most Protestant scholar he shook his big head in considerable concern, and blushed for the stranger.

But the stranger failed to be shamed by the blush, for he did not see it. He was looking at the two little girls where they still knelt at the feet of the Madonna, holding their dolls in the crooks of their arms as she was holding her baby in the crook of hers, squeaking happily as their fat fingers pointed out to each other all the glories of her lovely clothes and golden crown. "That is a lovely sight," said the stranger.

Faithful thought it was a dreadful sight. There were those two dear little girls, whom he had no doubt were as earnest, orthodox Protestants as he was himself, kneeling before a Popish image in the attitude of worship. No doubt, poor little dears, once they had realised that the Madonna was not the foot of the rainbow they thought she was some sort of big doll. . . . But even so he could not forgive himself for having unwittingly conducted two innocent females into this sink of iniquity. . . . The only one of the group by the Madonna whom he could bear to contemplate was the white-faced doll with the black velvet farthingale, the one who had been introduced to him as Bloody Mary. She looked at home. She, he remembered, had gone first down the passage.

"Meg, Joan," said the stranger softly.

They scrambled up from their knees, saw his face smiling kindly at them in the candle-light and flung themselves upon him. "Master Campion!" they cried. "Master Campion!" and pulling him down upon the wooden bench they cuddled up to him, one on each side, with cries of pleasure. For beneath all the excitement of their great adventure they had been feeling secretly a little frightened. To find Master Edmund Campion of Saint John's, their father's friend, with them in this strange lost place in the depths of the earth was like seeing the lights of home as one trudged through the rain and the wind on a dark night. Their secret fear, that having once fallen into fairyland they would not be able to scramble out of it again, was stilled. . . . Master Campion would get them out.

"But how did you get here?" he asked in bewilderment.

Meg and Joan burst simultaneously into a long confused narrative about stables and dragons and rainbows and crocks of gold of which Master Campion found himself unable to make head or tail. Faithful, from the other side of Meg, was obliged to chime in and give a lucid account of their adventures from the moment when the little girls had descended from the stable window until the moment when they had blundered down the dark passage into the chapel in search of the rainbow. He grew pink with shame as he told it. It seemed absurd that he, a grown man, should have taken part in so ridiculous a performance. "I hardly knew what I did," he murmured. "I was so confused."

"And footsore and weary?" questioned Master Campion kindly. "And homeless and forspent?"

Faithful hung his head and Master Campion, noting the pallor that had followed the boy's flush, and the dark pits into which his eyes had sunk, lifted Meg on to his knee that he might be nearer to him. "And so it was for you that these children wanted the crock of gold?" he asked. "How would you use the gold if they had found it for you?"

"To buy books," whispered Faithful. "I have tramped to Oxford to be a scholar." He spoke hoarsely, and twisted his hands together, for of all the things that had been hard to endure in his life of vagabondage, the hardest had been the fact that because he was a vagabond he was never believed. Specious rogues were so numerous that an honest poor man had never a chance of winning faith.

But Master Campion, who himself set great store by books, and who knew the authentic note of yearning when he heard it in another man's voice, believed him. He put Meg down, got up and crossed the chapel floor to the statue of the Madonna.

Faithful watched him as he stood there with head bent, and heard the words that he whispered. "Sancta Maria, Mater Dei, ora pro nobis peccatoribus." Then, with a pounding heart, he saw him him take something from his wallet and slip it beneath the flowers piled at the Madonna's feet. Then he came back and sat down again at the boy's side.

"Once upon a time," he told Faithful, "there was a poor boy who tramped to Oxford as you have done and became, as you will do, a famous scholar. We call him Saint Edmund. It is a story that every scholar in Oxford knows by heart, for he was the father of us all. I will only tell you this about him, that he loved Mary the Mother of God with a love that was the inspiration of his life, and at her feet he found salvation." He paused, flashed a smile at Faithful and went on again, his eyes on the Madonna. "With her golden crown she has always reminded me of the fair sun, a glory shining forth from Paradise to which we poor shadows are for ever flying. But now I shall think of her smiling face as the rainbow, a laughter in the sky that heartens us between storm and storm."

Ten minutes ago Master Campion's heretical remarks would would have brought Faithful out in a cold perspiration of horror, but now, sitting there in the dark little chapel, he felt nothing but an overwhelming sense of peace. Wherever men had found God, he supposed, there was always peace, even though the men who searched and found were heretics whom extremists thought should be sizzling at the stake. . . . But then, he supposed that to Master Campion he himself was a heretic who should be sizzling at the stake. . . . It was all very odd.

"You little girls must be taken home," said Master Campion suddenly and firmly. "I have no doubt that by this time your frantic family has sent the Town Crier out after you."

Meg and Joan slid eagerly to the floor and shook out their skirts, nothing loth. They were tired of fairyland. They were hungry, and there was nothing to eat there.

"Have you forgotten the crock of gold?" asked Master Campion, smiling.

They had quite forgotten it. The astonishment of having the rainbow turn into a beautiful lady with a crown on and a baby in her arms had driven the thought of it out of their minds. But now they remembered it and scuttled eagerly back to the

Madonna. " Might it be under the flowers at her feet ? " suggested Master Campion. Cautiously, poking their fat hands through the tall pillars of the candles, they lifted the bluebells and kingcups that lay there and in a moment a chorus of squeaks broke out that for sheer unselfish joy and praise had surely never been equalled even by the Alleluia Chorus of the angels in heaven, even though in musical value theirs was doubtless superior.

For a whole minute they stood there, holding the purse between them, squeaking, picking up the gold pieces and letting them fall back again with delicious chinks. Then they closed the purse and ran to give it to that Younger Son who in the best fairy-tales always get the luck that he deserves.

To Faithful it was too much. In a chapel outside the city gates he had found a friend and in a chapel within the city he had found his crock of gold. In the first chapel he had given away a silver piece, all that he had, and in the second it had come back to him increased a hundredfold. It was too much. He put his ragged sleeve over his eyes and cried.

Master Campion got at the moment no more thanks than that, but he wanted none. Full of the palpitations and misgivings that assail all impulsive givers of indiscriminate charity the moment it is too late to undo what they have done, he busied himself in blowing out the candles burning at the feet of the Madonna, for except for the dim flame of the sanctuary lamp this secret place was always kept dark between the visits of the faithful. Would the boy know how to spend the money wisely? Well, it was too late to think of that now. Had he perhaps done more harm than good? Well, he should have thought of that before. He supposed that he must now see to it that the boy and his money came to no harm. And he was a busy man. He sighed. When would he learn that endless trouble always follows impulsive giving? Then he looked up at the face of the Madonna, smiling dimly in the light of the one remaining candle. You have done no harm, she said. Comforted, he took up the last candle and led the children towards the door.

Two last impressions remained with Faithful as he left that little chapel that he would never see again. One was of his friend's figure becoming once again, in the dimness, that wavering black shadow that he had been when he first saw him ; and the other, as the light from the candle shone through the closing door upon the chapel wall, was the sudden shining out in the darkness of a garland of roses and lilies painted there. Someone had once told Faithful that a garland of roses and lilies is the emblem of martyrdom. We are all shadows, his friend had said, flying towards the sun, and those who get there, thought Faithful, pass through flame.

IV

They were out in the High Street and Master Campion, again rubbing his chin ruefully, was wondering aloud what to do with Faithful.

" He must come home with us ! " cried the twins, clutching him. " We want him." He was the Younger Son, a fairy-tale figure, and after their journey into fairyland they were not going home without a memento of the visit. " We'll take him home to Father," they added.

Thankful though Master Campion, a busy man, would have been to shift the burden of Faithful on to the shoulders of a busier one, he felt that he must demur, and did so.

" But Father likes poor boys," said the twins, in the same tone of voice in which they would have declared that Father liked sugar plums. " Father lost one at Saint Bartholomew's this morning. He'd like to have another."

Master Campion still demurred, but a glorious light broke upon Faithful. " Did your father really say that he had lost a boy at Saint Bartholomew's Chapel ? " he asked the twins.

" Oh yes," they said. " We prayed about him for hours. Breakfast was very late."

" It was me," said Faithful to Edmund Champion.

In happiness they turned the corner into Fish Street and walked down the hill towards Christ Church. The sun was high in the heavens now and flooded the rain-washed world. Faithful held his head proudly, for now he was going to the house of his friend with money to pay his own way in the world. For the first time in his life he was a gentleman of means.

At the Fair Gate, when Master Campion parted from them, he said simply, " Thank you, good sir," and stood very upright before Campion, with his clear eyes looking straight into his and the purse of gold held against his ragged breast with both hands. His attitude, his rags, and the queer look of peace which his face wore, touched the man strangely. He seemed the personification of the perfect pilgrim, unashamed of poverty, taking what wealth might come with gratitude, at peace whether the road were rough or smooth. He would not forget this boy. His image was stamped upon his mind. He paused a moment and then asked what for the sake of others he must ask, though his pride shrank from it. "Can you forget what you have seen?"

Faithful nodded gravely and then looked doubtfully at the two little girls, who were pulling at his jerkin in eagerness to get him home.

"Their narratives are seldom coherent," smiled Campion, "and it will have been to them such an adventure as happens only in dreams; when they wake up it will be hard to remember it."

He smiled and left them, and Faithful lingered a moment to watch his tall dark figure go up the street before he followed the little girls under the lovely gateway of the place that would seem to him for ever after the centre of the world.

v

At dinner-time it was discovered by their family that the twins had disappeared. They had been last heard of in the loft, from which apparently they had vanished into thin air. Canon Leigh, Joyeuce, Grace Dorothy and Diggory, gathered together in the hall after a fruitless search in house and garden, faced each other in growing concern, while the roast beef, left unregarded on the table, wrapped itself in a grey blanket of congealing fat, and Diccon, also unregarded, helped himself and Tinker to a whole meat pie each.

"Must we starve," demanded Great-Aunt from above, "because two naughty little poppets are momentarily mislaid?" And she thumped upon her windowsill with the handle of her knife. . . . And at the same moment there came a thumping on the old front door that sent the whole household as one man to lift the latch.

Outside upon the doorstep stood the twins and Faithful, in a great state of dirt and dishevelment; aprons awry, faces smeared, Bloody and Bess by no means as queenly as they had been; but beaming with the joy and pride of successful accomplishment.

A perfect tornado of reunion now broke out; the twins were hugged and kissed, Faithful, hanging back in shamefaced uncertainty, was pulled over the threshold by Canon Leigh as though he were the returned prodigal son and had the door slammed behind him by Grace as though she meant him to stay for ever, the dogs barked, Diccon shouted, everyone talked at once and Great Tom boomed forth eleven o'clock from the Cathedral tower.

"And now," ejaculated Great-Aunt icily into a sudden moment of silence, "may I request that I be served with my dinner?"

CHAPTER IV

AGES PAST

> As if, when after Phoebus is descended,
> And leaves a light much like the past day's dawning,
> And, every toil and labour wholly ended,
> Each living creature draweth to his resting,
> We should begin by such a parting light
> To write the story of all ages past,
> And end the same before th'approaching night.
> WALTER RALEIGH.

I

ALL day under the hot sun the citizens had celebrated May Day with enthusiasm, clamour and heat, yet when evening came down through the woods of Shotover, passed under the East Gate and stole into the city, a hush fell; they were all tired: they trailed thankfully back to their houses, kindled log fires against the coming of night, loosened their doublets and waistbands and put their feet up on the hob.

Under the Fair Gate of Christ Church, Heatherthwayte the porter also loosened his doublet, stretched his legs and yawned, while at his feet his dog, Satan, a black and woolly person with plumed heraldic legs, lay down to snatch a little slumber. They had had an exhausting day. Keeping the scholars in and the merrymakers out had taxed their powers to the utmost and they felt themselves entitled to a little slumber.

Heatherthwayte, his hands folded on his stomach, snored. His snore was one of the well-known noises of Christ Church and only a little less impressive than his laugh, a loud, deep roar that reverberated under the Fair Gate like thunder. When Heatherthwayte was amused the whole College knew it. He had a figure like Falstaff's through which his laugh rumbled and rolled for a long time before it emerged through his gigantic mouth. His large, bushy red beard, when laughed into, seemed to act like a megaphone and increase the noise tenfold.

It was not often that Heatherthwayte slept, for he and Satan found their life an interesting one. Life flowed round them in full tide, all the many streams in their splendid variety running together into one rich flood of community life. Heatherthwayte, though one of the streams himself, was yet always conscious of a certain detachment. He watched and he listened. He scanned the faces that went in and out and heard the talk that flowed past him; they were his books and his lectures and he learned them well. These scholars might study their Latin and Greek, their Law, their Medicine and their Astronomy, but Heatherthwayte in his study of human nature thought he had the advantage of them. For amusement, for edification and for an Awful Warning, said Heatherthwayte, and Satan entirely agreed with him, give them Men as a branch of learning any day.

Satan did not spend quite so much time in study as Heatherthwayte did, for he had a good deal of work to do. He was a very important member of the community whose duty it was to keep the quadrangle clear of sheep and cattle and hogs; no easy task in high summer when these poor animals, driven into the city from the country for slaughter, and feeling hot and thirsty and afraid, saw through the Fair Gate the grass of the quadrangle waving high and tall and set with moon-daisies and golden lady's-slippers.

Then he had to keep his eye upon human beings as well as animals. He knew quite well who had the right to canter his horse across the quadrangle and tie it to the iron ring in the east wall, and those who had not the right and yet presumed through ignorance or criminal cheek found themselves attacked under the Fair Gate by a satanic animal of great power and size, and the din of clattering hoofs and wild barking that echoed through the precincts was shattering if you were not used to it. Satan knew, too, that the laundresses might fetch the scholars' dirty linen between eight and ten on Monday morning and return it between two and four on Saturday afternoon, but they might not come at any time and they might not venture inside the Fair Gate. The College servitors brought the linen to the gate and received it again, and Satan kept a careful eye upon proceedings. The applewomen, too, might come no further than the Fair Gate, and Satan bit their ankles if they tried to. . . . So what with one thing and another he got quite tired sometimes, and was glad when the western sky was a sheet of gold behind Saint Aldate's and in the quadrangle the shadows spread deep pools of quietness.

" Heatherthwayte ! Heatherthwayte ! "

The porter and his dog both opened a reluctant eye, then sat up in brisk attention. Joyeuce, her afternoon farthingale of peacock blue held well up on each side so that she looked like a winged creature, and her slender feet in their little red shoes poised tiptoe on the cobbles as though she had alighted on them for a moment only, was standing breathlessly before them. A little bunch of violets stuck in the bodice of her dress, that lay so flat over her still childish figure, rose and fell agitatedly, and she was so pale that her face looked like ivory against the black velvet coif that curved about it. Heatherthwayte and Satan, expecting to hear some pitiful tale of death and disaster in the Leigh household, rose instantly to their feet, ready to fly off upon the instant to fetch the Physician, the Undertaker, the Constable of the Watch, or even the Vice-Chancellor himself should the tragedy that had occurred prove too great for alleviation by the lesser brethren. . . . Heatherthwayte and Satan loved the Leigh children very dearly and there was absolutely nothing they were not prepared to do for them.

" There now, mistress ! Tell Heatherthwayte ! " implored that worthy, his tenderness reverberating upwards through his vocal chords and booming out through his great beard very comfortably. Satan, producing a long pink loving tongue from behind the fierce barricade of his teeth, passed it consolingly over Joyeuce's hand and suggested with a circular motion of his tail that nothing was ever as bad as it seemed. . . . A little colour crept into Joyeuce's face and she found her voice.

" At seven o'clock," she whispered, " if you see a—a—gentleman waiting about, please will you tell him that I—I—must not come ? " And at that, with a light patter of feet and a swish of silk, she took flight and vanished, leaving behind her a little breath of scent from the bunch of violets that had tumbled out of her dress as she ran.

Heatherthwayte lowered himself back on to his seat, flung back his head and laughed, showing all his strong white teeth and a cavernous expanse of throat, his merry little eyes disappearing among the rolls of fat into which his face folded itself in moments of mirth. . . . So she was growing up, was she ? . . . He remembered the winter night six years ago when the Leighs had first come to Christ Church. It had been wild and wet and he had hurried out from under the Fair Gate with his lantern when he heard the clatter of their horse's hoofs. The little Joyeuce had been riding pillion behind her father and he had himself lifted her down. She had been so cold and stiff that when he tried to set her on the ground her legs had doubled up beneath her and he had picked her up, he remembered, and carried her into the house, and she had thanked him very prettily. A thin, white-faced, good little waif she had been even then, though not quite so good and white-faced as she had become after her mother died.

Heatherthwayte suddenly ceased laughing and shook his head gravely. . . . These good, motherless little maidens were no judge of men. . . . He, Heatherthwayte, who reverenced the memory of Mistress Leigh, must keep his weather eye open.

He began at once, rolling it this way and that as scholars and townspeople strolled by in the quadrangle or the street, and by the time seven o'clock boomed out from the Cathedral, and Nicolas appeared in a leaf-green doublet and a nut-brown cloak, he was in quite a perspiration of worry and fuss. . . . But it was relieved by the sight of Nicolas, for Heatherthwayte, possessed of some occult power by which he knew the ancestry, character and goings on of every man in College simply by sitting still on a bench under the Fair Gate, was particularly fond of Nicolas. It was true the young gentleman was over quick with a word or a blow, and had a much higher opinion of himself than there was really any need for, but he had a sense of humour and his generosity was unbounded. Many an escapade of Nicolas's had Heatherthwayte hushed up and many a round gold piece had found its way from Nicolas's pocket to Heatherthwayte's ready palm, their affection for each other growing with every secret shared and coin added to Heatherthwayte's bank balance under his flock mattress. . . . It was his intention to retire one day, a wealthy man, waxed fat upon the evil deeds of Christ Church scholars.

"Ah!" he ejaculated sepulchrally, when after five minutes Nicolas was still there, stamping up and down and snorting, and he rolled one eye and closed the other. Satan, his head on one side, thumped his tail on the ground and made curious noises in his throat.

"He's talking," said Heatherthwayte.

"Who's talking?" snapped Nicolas.

"Satan," said Heatherthwayte. "He has a fellow feeling, as you might say. His own fancy, a water spaniel up High Street, is very fanciful in her ways at times."

Nicholas swore loudly, though swearing was forbidden by the College regulations, and stamped up and down with increasing wrath, for he was not accustomed to being kept waiting by ladies on whom he had cast a favourable eye. He frequently kept them waiting—it was good for them—but such were his attractions that the reverse was seldom the case.

"I was to tell you," said Heatherthwayte, "that Mistress Joyeuce Leigh is kept at home. . . . And those," he added pointing a horny finger at the little bunch of violets on the cobbles, "are all the company of hers that she can give you."

"She left them for me?" asked Nicholas.

"She did," said Heatherthwayte, casting up his eyes to heaven and wiping a tear from his eye. "Kissed them and laid them there where they lie now, right in the middle of the Fair Gate, where I've had all the trouble in the world to prevent the whole College trampling on 'em. . . . But if you show yourself unworthy of them violets," continued Heatherthwayte with some heat, "it's me you'll have to reckon with, young man; me, Thomas Elias Heatherthwayte."

"Mind your own business," snapped Nicolas; but he picked up the violets and stuck them in his doublet.

"It'll be her father that's kept her," consoled Heatherthwayte, quite melted by this display of sensibility. "But if you was to turn to the left and stroll down Fish Street, sir, you could see her through the parlour window."

"I am not asking you for your advice, Heatherthwayte," said Nicolas with dignity, and with his head thrown back and his lips pursed in a whistle he sauntered out of the Fair Gate, turned to the right and strolled up towards the town. . . . However, in another ten minutes Heatherthwayte saw him strolling down again on the other side of the road. . . . Heatherthwayte chortled into his beard and pushed Satan slyly with his feet, Satan responding with a thud of his tail and a glint in his eye.

II

Nicolas crossed the road diagonally and glanced with a great assumption of carelessness through the Leigh parlour window. The fire danced gaily and a little mouse sat washing itself in the middle of the floor ; but there was no one else there. Infuriated, Nicolas strolled on under South Gate and down the street towards the river and Folly Bridge. He felt sore and angry and tantalised. . . . Under the Fair Gate nothing but a bunch of violets and in the parlour nothing but a mouse. . . . Man cannot live by bread alone and neither do flowers and a mouse give any permanent satisfaction. He was aware of wanting something that was not being given to him and he was not used to not having what he wanted. He felt hot inside and his throat tickled. He kicked savagely at the refuse in the street and splashed noisily through the puddles ; until it struck him that he was behaving like a six-year-old and he was obliged to laugh at himself, his eyes narrowed as he looked up at the quietness of the evening sky.

The wind had dropped, but the clouds were still moving slowly, drifted by the memory of it ; their creamy whiteness a little flushed, as though the memory was a good one. The trees in the Christ Church meadows, nearer to the peace of the earth and more easily stilled, were motionless, spreading their green shelter over the early fritillaries. From where he stood, leaning over Folly Bridge, Nicolas could not see the fritillaries, but he knew where they grew, in faint drifts of colour between the brazen kingcups, the curve of their bell heads the most delicate thing on earth. In the far distance were the lovely shapes of low hills, and intensely quiet, resting against the sky. Under his feet the water slipped, running very quietly because it had been a dry spring, passing from Godstow to Iffley, and on through the meadows to the towers and spires of the city of London. There were not many buildings beyond South Gate, only Saint Michael's at the South Gate and a few houses round it, and there was little to interrupt the view of Christ Church that showed the tower of the Cathedral rising superbly above the splendid stretch of the hall roof. . . . A bell was ringing in the town and in the trees by the river the blackbirds called, yet the bell and the

bird song seemed more the voice of silence than of actual music.
... A strange sound, harsh yet with a quality of its beating,
rhythmical strength that made one's heart leap up in delight,
made him look up. Six swans were flying one behind the other,
necks stretched out and great wings rising and falling, white
against the blue of the sky. They flew right over the roofs of
the city, calm, determined and unhurried, and when the sound
of their passing had died away the silence seemed absolute.

III

The processional passing had been like the passing of
humanity itself, Nicolas thought, and he began to think dreamily
of all the men and women who in their journey from birth to
death had passed through this city.

Nicolas, though he was generally too busy enjoying himself
to pay much attention to it, had imagination, and on the rare
occasions when he found himself with nothing better to do he
would let it open its wings and carry him away. It was that
rare brand of imaginative power that can leave self entirely out
of the picture, so that Nicolas's dream figures did not crowd
about him playing a petty drama of which he was himself the
hero, and completely obstructing the view, but passed distantly
by in pomp and beauty like clouds across the sky. Standing well
back from them he could see them without their surface imperfections; grand figures who had each his appointed place in
the pageant of history.

The road where Nicholas stood was the oldest road in Oxford
and had been there before the city itself. It appeared out of the
shadows of Bagley Forest, rolled across the meadows, humped
itself to pass over the bridge and then disappeared under South
Gate into the city; and down it came marching the figures that
Nicolas dreamed of.

In the vanguard came the handful of wild men who had first
looked with favour upon this bit of earth, the hunters who had
noticed a patch of dry ground between the rivers and marked it
down as a place of security where a home could be made. The
rivers were the city wall, a protection against possible enemies;
within it rose a village of rough huts, and thin spirals of blue
smoke found their way through the mist of the willow trees and

rose up into the air to tell the world that Oxford was born. . . .
Not that there was anyone likely to pay much attention; only
the wolves and the boars, the wild birds and the fishes, and the
blue hills that stood around the valley where the rivers ran.

The hunters thrived in their village. They took to themselves wives and their little children played among the willows, and picked armfuls of the water plants that grew everywhere like a thick carpet, and laughed to see the sunset and the sunrise reflected in the streams and pools that paved the valley. . . . Up in the blue hills the Roman legions passed and re-passed, but if they saw the thin spirals of blue smoke they did not think them worthy of attention. . . . But if the legions neglected them the missionaries did not. Augustine, the Roman, had landed in England with the good news of Christianity and the knowledge of it came down the water-ways to Oxford.

The hunters were secure enough now to think of other things besides their daily food. They built a fine house for their king, Didanus, and on the spot where later the Cathedral stood they built a nunnery for his daughter, Frideswide. This very road where Nicolas stood ran by it from the ford below to the rising ground above, where four ways met, and round this nucleus of a nunnery, a street and a little hill, grew first churches and houses within a city wall, then a Norman castle, then a great Augustinian Abbey outside the city, then the royal palaces of Beaumont and Woodstock.

Oxford was now a place of importance, favoured by royalty, and magnificent figures passed by in her pageant; kings and princes, noblemen and men-at-arms, with coloured cloaks over their armour, clattered through the narrow streets and rode in gallant companies in and out of the gates of the city; priests bowed before the altars in the churches, saying masses for the souls of the dead who had already passed by to the tolling of the bell, and candles burned before the shrines of the saints; the sound of chanting drifted out into the streets to mingle with the clattering of horses' hoofs upon the cobbles and the shrill cries of pedlars, tinkers, merchant apprentices, thieves and vagabonds.

Then came the great merchants, figures of importance who sunned themselves upon their doorsteps, hands folded over portly stomachs, or strolled with patronage over the cobbled streets, holding up their fine furred gowns out of the way of the

mud and refuse that strewed them. They were now the princes
of Oxford, they and the swarthy financiers who by day issued
forth from the Jewish quarter in the heart of the city, one of the
wealthiest Jewries in England, and strolled through the streets
in their yellow gabardines, and at night sat in dark little rooms
lit by rush-lights and counted their gold with a kindling eye.
Their magnificent guilds were the glory of Oxford : the Weavers,
the Shoemakers, the Glovers, the Barbers, the Tailors, the Goldsmiths, the Corporation of Cooks ; they had their revels and their
processions, when they paraded the city on horseback with drums
beating and torches burning, and they had their special chapels
in the different churches, where they burned candles and
celebrated mass. The commerce of southern England mainly
flowed through the Thames valley and people would stand on the
bridge outside South Gate, where Nicolas stood now, and watch
the great barges of the merchants passing up and down the river.

These merchants and financiers had it all their own way at
first and perhaps they hardly noticed, as they picked their way
up the winding High Street in their fine gowns, groups of badly
dressed, hungry looking youths crowded together round some
narrow entry listening to the words of an older man, lean and
poor as themselves, who stood above them on the steps. They
would scatter when the merchant barged carelessly in amongst
them but they would come back again when he had passed, for
the teacher on the steps had food for their minds if not for their
bodies and what shall it profit a man if he gain the whole world
and lose his own soul ? A new Guild was struggling into
being, a Guild of Learning that was to be the greatest of all the
Guilds and crowd the others almost out of existence ; the
merchants and the Jews, cursing the ragged scholars who got
in their way, did not as yet consider it worth their attention.

They knew, of course, that learning, hitherto confined to the
cloister, where in their opinion it should have remained, was
creeping out into the world. It was partly their own doing, for
the flourishing state of trade had brought a tranquillity in which
men's thoughts turned to the things of the mind, but it was also
the doing of Henry Beauclerk, the scholar king, who had built
Beaumont Palace, and of his grandson, Henry the Second, who
took it into their heads to become the champions of literary
culture. . . . Learning was becoming the fashion. . . . The

merchants shook their heads in some disgust at the distressing and effeminate trend of the times, but did not yet realise the tremendous significance of this invasion of their commercial city by a handful of ragged scholars.

But when the handful turned into a horde who blocked up the narrow entries, fought at street corners, got drunk in the taverns and turned the whole place into a tower of babel by arguing all day and all night about the existence of God in half a dozen different languages, the merchants made a few disgusted enquiries and found that most of these rogues and vagabonds had come from the University of Paris. France had suddenly become tired of foreign students within her borders and had ejected the lot. In steadily increasing numbers, bands of them had crossed the Channel, landed at Dover and marched northwards, billeting themselves upon monasteries and ecclesiastics and eating them out of house and home as they went. They might have settled down at Canterbury, Lambeth or Saint Albans, and the Oxford merchants heartily wished they had, but it was Oxford that drew them; Oxford with her wealthy Guilds, her Royal Palace, her Priory of Saint Frideswide, her churches and fine houses within the city wall, her river winding through the valley between green willows, and all protected from winter storms by a rampart of low hills and dense forests.

The majority of these scholars were English, for it was with the English and their treatment of Thomas à Becket that France was particularly enraged, but scholars from other European universities had come too; for the mediæval scholars and masters had the migratory habits of birds and if insulted in one university bands of them would indignantly snatch up their books and decamp half-way across Europe to a second, upon which they would settle like locusts until the fancy took them to cross the sea and swoop down upon some protesting city where could be laid the foundations of yet a third.

The Guild of Learning grew with strength and determination into Oxford University. Pious founders established halls where the scholars could be housed and one by one these elbowed their way up between the houses and the church towers, even as more and more hungry looking scholars elbowed their way through the narrow streets. . . . And the merchants resented this invasion with a fury that lasted for centuries. . . . But neither their fury, not that of the Jews, had any effect whatever. Upon this spot of earth between the waters men had fought first for security, then for wealth, and now for knowledge, and it was the seekers after knowledge who stood triumphant in final possession.

And now to the figures of Kings and Queens, Merchants and Jews and triumphant Scholars, passing by in procession, were added the cowled figures of the Friars. Learning had found its way out from the cloister into the world and after it came the monks themselves. New orders were founded of brethren who should tramp the streets of the cities and give their lives to the service of the poor. In the overcrowded slums of Oxford, where filthy narrow lanes, heaped with rubbish, wound between hovels where the rush-strewn floors were never cleansed and leprosy and plague were familiar guests, went the barefoot followers of Dominic and Francis. Order after order founded its house at Oxford ; the Grey Friars, the Black Friars, the Carmelites, the Brothers of the Sack and the Crossed Friars soon became as familiar figures in the Oxford streets as the scholars themselves. At first they were content to be unlearned men, vowed to poverty, but later, longing for converts among the scholars as well as among the poor, and finding the love of learning infectious, they too became members of its Guild. They laid aside their poverty to accept gifts of money and land that they might build schools and halls and libraries, where friars from all over Europe might come and study. . . . From where Nicolas stood he could see the little gatehouse built over the archway of South Gate that had been the study of Friar Bacon, the Franciscan scientist, where, so Nicolas had been told, he had written his great books and raised the devil. . . . The old religious orders followed the example of the friars, founding halls for their student monks, and the University suffered a monastic invasion.

At first it was pleased, but later, as more and more cowled figures jostled the secular scholars in the streets, grabbed the best seats at lectures, and argued, as only ecclesiastics can argue, about this and that and the other till everyone's heads went round, it was as indignant as the merchants had been when the vagabonds from Paris descended upon them out of the blue. A state of war was declared between the secular and religious scholars and went cheerily raging on until, with another cycle completed, the times were ripe for yet another new birth.

It was called the New Learning and it arrived as unobtrusively as the University itself had done. Fifteenth-century Oxford scholars were shocked by the news that the Turks had taken Constantinople, the eastern home of learning and philosophy, and then they thought no more about it and went back to their squabbles and their Aristotle, their horses and dogs and dinner. But meanwhile a handful of scholars had again snatched up their books and migrated half-way across Europe ; this time fugitives flying from Constantinople to Rome ; bringing with them a few rescued manuscripts and the wisdom of Greece. Italy flung herself eagerly upon the New Learning, and while her scholars were learning Greek, and rescuing the thought of the ancient world from oblivion, Germany was inventing the art of printing that should diffuse it throughout the world.

And now renowned and learned men took their part in the pageant, the men who brought the New Learning to Oxford, almost contemporary figures who were not lost in the mists of past ages, but walked in the sunlight plain to see. Cardinal Wolsey, and Thomas More were among them, with Erasmus the Dutchman, and the humbler figure of Haddon Rood, of Cologne, who set up Oxford's first printing press.

In Oxford the Renaissance chiefly took the form of a religious revival ; it meant the study of the New Testament in Greek, a getting back to the original truth of things that had been obscured by mediæval accretions of ignorance and superstition ; it meant, through the printing press, a New Testament in the hands of everyone who could learn to read. The good news of this new birth seemed to its messengers more glorious than any that had gone before, for how could there ever again be war or wickedness or degradation, these scholars asked each other, when it would soon be possible for every man, woman and child to read with their own eyes the records of the life of the Son of God ? " I would have those words translated into all languages," wrote Erasmus, " so that not only Scots and Irishmen, but Turks and Saracens might read them. I long for the ploughboy to sing them to himself as he follows the plough, the weaver to hum them to the tune of his shuttle, the traveller to beguile with them the dullness of his journey. Other studies we may regret having undertaken, but happy is the man upon whom death comes when he is engaged in these. These sacred words give you the very image of Christ speaking, healing, dying, rising again, and make him so present that were he before your very eyes you would not more truly see him."

And for a little while it seemed that the Golden Age was on the way, for all over the world Oxford was now famed for her beauty and her learning. The greatest scholars of Europe were amazed at her loveliness; the woods and streams and meadows outside her walls, the great churches with their wonderful stained glass and treasures of gold and silver, the abbeys with their hospitals and priceless libraries, and the beautiful Colleges that were still rising gloriously.

One of the fairest of these was Wolsey's Cardinal College at Oxford which he built as a home of the New Learning. He built his quadrangle of stone from Headington that in its freshness gleamed gold in the sun and white in the moonlight, like the Acropolis at Athens, and he embellished it with every lovely art that man could devise. To the south was the great dining-hall, where a hundred and one men, Dean and scholar Canons, could feast royally in the intervals of applying themselves to learning, and to the east the priory of Saint Frideswide became the Cathedral church, where chaplains, lay clerks and choristers were to praise and worship God with fitting glory and honour.

In his imagination Nicolas saw the quadrangle of his College full of an army of ghosts, busy architects, masons, carpenters, artists, glaziers, scholars in their long gowns and round-faced cherubic choristers; and in and out among them, cheering, inspiring and commanding, moved the portly figure of the great Cardinal, clothed in scarlet and mounted on a palfrey.

But upon this busy and happy scene there entered an ominous figure; a vulgar bloated man with a paunch and swollen legs, the predatory monster into whom the charming young Henry Tudor had unaccountably developed. He entered magnificently, clothed in crimson and gold that accentuated the imperfections of his figure, with trumpets blowing and drums sounding, with a gorgeous retinue and the assumption of geniality and friendship; but his coming was as destructive to Oxford as an earthquake.

For the mania of the King's Grace for matrimony, and the consequent habit of marrying one wife while her predecessor was still alive, led to a quarrel with the Pope and the denial of his authority in England, while the failure of Cardinal Wolsey to secure a divorce for Henry brought about his own downfall and that of his College. The wealth of the monasteries, that formed so large a part of the treasure of Oxford, was at the mercy of the King's greed, he being now by his own appointment head of the Church, and those of her sons who dared stand firm for Pope and conscience were doomed.

Oxford endured loss upon loss; the death of Wolsey, who, when in his last days he bethought him of his not yet completed College, " could not sleep for the thought of it and could not write for weeping and sorrow "; the execution of Thomas More, once High Steward of Oxford and always her friend; the destruction of the religious houses; the looting of the churches and libraries; the impoverishment of the people and the destruction of laughter and the singing voice.

But the monster had a certain reputation as an enlightened patron of learning and, having dissolved Cardinal College, sold its lands to hungry courtiers, stolen the Cathedral vestments and ornaments and swept away its greatest treasure, the Shrine of Saint Frideswide, he bethought himself of this reputation and set to work to build up another College on the foundations of the old. He united the episcopal see with the collegiate foundation and called it Christ Church. The foundation consisted of a Dean and eight Canons, including three Regius Professors, a hundred scholars, twenty-four servants and officers and twenty-four bedesmen. Life of a sort flowed into it again. Laughter rang out once more in the quadrangle and the sound of chanting drifted out from the Cathedral. . . . It was the germ of the College that Nicolas knew and loved.

But the Guild of Learning, that had lain sick unto death while libraries were sacked and churches despoiled, was given only a short breathing space of peace. Men were learning to adjust themselves, to rejoice that a foreign Pope could no longer command their allegiance, to become firmly set in new convictions that suited the temperament of an independent people, when Queen Mary the bigot, daughter of one Spaniard and destined wife of another, came to the throne set upon the reversal of all her father's actions, and the tide of persecution turned and flowed back again. For three and a half years it swept through Oxford

in a horror of blood and fire. The English bibles that Erasmus
had hoped to see in the hands of every ploughboy, weaver and
traveller were burnt in the market place, the martyrs were
dragged through the streets to be burnt at the stake outside
North Gate and men's hearts failed them for fear. The choice
of those who could not change their convictions to order was
between exile and the stake, and men who, like Gervas Leigh,
were finally able to escape to loneliness and poverty abroad
counted themselves the favoured of fortune. England was no
longer a country fit to live in. It had neither unity nor spirit.
to all intents and purposes it was a province of Spain.

But every horror and stupidity has its ending and peace
comes back. One dark morning in November the citizens of
Oxford woke to hear the bells ringing. What was it? It was
not May Day, for the damp fogs of winter were gathering thickly
upon them, and it was not yet Christmas; and there seemed
little in the life of this tormented city upon which it could congratulate itself. Then the word went round—the Queen was
dead. From every tower in Oxford the bells rang out; the
bells of Christ Church and Saint Mary the Virgin, the bells of
Saint Martin's and Saint Michael's at the North Gate, of All
Saints', Saint Aldate's and Saint Ebbe's; the foggy air seemed
alive with their joy and clamour. People ran out into the streets,
laughing and exclaiming. They told each other that the birds
were singing as though it were spring. Surely, they said, this
new age would be a time of resurrection from the horrors that
were past. . . . One name was on all their lips. . . . Elizabeth.
. . . The Queen was dead. . . . Long live the Queen. . . . The
bells rang out afresh and the sun broke through the clouds.

To Nicolas this was contemporary history. Englishmen
had turned in something like despair to a young woman for
salvation and she had not disappointed them. The worst
horrors of religious persecution were over and laughter and the
singing voice were coming back.

It was yet another period of renewal for Oxford. The
scholars who had gone into exile returned rejoicing and with
quiet minds and hopeful hearts looked again for the Golden Age.
To their eyes Oxford had clothed herself in a fresh beauty,
though it seemed to them a frightened loveliness, as though in
remembering past violence that men had committed against

her she feared for yet worse at their hands in years to come.

But for the moment there seemed nothing but good. To Oxford's great profit the Queen's Grace was a lover of learning and was herself no mean scholar; and having found much delight in learning it was her pleasure that others should do the same. In past years Oxford scholars had seldom been drawn from the nobility, but now, goaded to it by the Queen herself, young gentlemen of birth were presenting themselves at the University, to get a little something into their heads if possible and to enjoy themselves at all costs. The Queen's Grace was taking a particular interest in Christ Church, the College founded by her father. She had appointed Thomas Godwin, " a tall and comely person," much in favour with her, to be its Dean[1] and she assigned certain of the Christ Church studentships to boys educated at her own royal foundation of Saint Peter's, Westminster. The vanguard of a long line of pilgrims from Westminster to Christ Church were in these later days travelling over hill and dale and knocking for admittance at the gates of the College. . . . They were the last figures in Nicolas's dream pageant and as they clattered by him it seemed to him that they picked him up and carried him with them under South Gate and up the street to Christ Church. . . . It was a surprise to him to find himself standing quite alone outside the Fair Gate.

It was late; night had draped the sky in violet shadows and one star burned in the sky. The ghosts had vanished and the curfew that rang out now into the silence was a bell that tolled for their passing. Nicolas, as he turned in under the Gate, was not quite sure if he was the last mourner in a funeral procession or the first messenger who comes hard upon its heels with the tidings of a new birth. The violets that he still held crushed in his hand were the colour of sorrow, but their scent was the scent of the spring.

[1] *Note.* The Queen continued to take an interest in the Deans of Christ Church, particularly if good looking, for "she loved good parts well, but better when in a goodly person." Thomas Godwin remained in favour until he insisted upon pleasing himself rather than the Queen's Grace in the matter of his second marriage, when Her Majesty became " alienated." With only one Dean, Richard Cox, is it recorded that she seriously fell out, and then only after she had made him a bishop and he had dared to differ from her in regard to her plans for his garden. " Proud Prelate," she wrote, " you know what you were before I made you; if you do not immediately comply with my request, by God, I will unfrock you. Elizabeth."

CHAPTER V

THE TEACHERS ON THE STEPS

Where man's mind hath a freed consideration,
Of goodness to receive lovely direction;
Where senses do behold th'order of heavenly host,
And wise thoughts do behold what the Creator is.
Contemplation here holdeth his only seat,
Bounded with no limits, borne with a wing of hope,
Climbs even unto the stars.
        PHILIP SIDNEY.

I

THE June sun, flinging a shower of gold in at the uncurtained window, rescued Faithful from an unpleasant dream in which he was still a chimney sweep and was stuck in a loathsome pitch-black chimney, unable to get either up or down. He woke up still bowed down by that awful sense of oppression and filth, and it was with amazement that he found himself lying in a pool of golden light, and stretching his body found himself free and unfettered. . . . Then he remembered where he was. . . . In one of the scholars' rooms at Christ Church, a room that he shared with Giles Leigh.

The windows faced east and sitting up on his flock mattress, hugging his knees, he looked out across the quadrangle to the tower of Christ Church, outlined sharply against the sheeted gold of the sunrise. He could tell by the feel of the cold air that it was very early yet and he need not get up for a little while. . . . He could sit and gloat.

He was a scholar of Christ Church. He had got what he wanted and he was so utterly and completely happy that he felt as though he had been born again. He realised that his experience was unique, that not many peoole got what they longed for, or if they did get it, liked it when they had it. He was intensely grateful to whatever gods there be that he had been allowed this satisfaction. Perhaps, he thought, his present joys would not always satisfy; there would be fresh hungers, and he would set out on new journeys towards goals that he might never reach; but at least, he thought, the fact that he had once been satisfied made life worth while. Nothing in life, he thought, is so lovely as fresh beginnings, and nothing breeds more courage. He saw all the fresh beginnings in a man's life burning like prophetic torches along the way, beckoning him on, crying aloud the good news in the charactery of flame upon darkness, and the little figure of man passing from darkness into light and then into darkness again, until it disappeared at the end of the journey into a blaze of light to which those torches that had seemed so bright were as night's candles to the light of day.

The power of the sun increased, wrapping him round with its warmth, filling the room with beams of light that were like pointing fingers showing him all the furnishings of the room, severely practical furnishings that yet seemed fine to Faithful because they were bathed in the glamour of his new life.

There were the two narrow truckle beds in the further corners of the room, each with " bedding sufficient and meet for one man," with the chest between them where Giles and Faithful kept " the honest apparel and comely for a scholar " insisted upon by authority. The room had two windows and in each of them stood a combined bookshelf and desk. At them Faithful and Giles would work for hours on end, straining to catch the last hours of daylight. There were a couple of stools in the room and a second chest containing bows and arrows, lanterns, snuffers and bellows. . . . That was all. . . . And Faithful, whose business it was to do the housework, but who as a scholar of Christ Church was more interested in the things of the mind, thought it quite enough.

It had not been so difficult, after all, to give him his heart's desire. For a week after his arrival he and Canon Leigh spent every free moment locked in the latter's study hammering at the classics, very often late into the night, so that Joyeuce thought they would kill each other with overwork, and protested through the keyhole with loud protestations that were taken no notice of. Faithful had an amazing memory and Canon Leigh was astonished at all he had remembered from his early days at Westminster; it made a very considerable foundation stone on which to erect new knowledge. At the end of the week Faithful had an extra good wash, rubbed himself all over with civet so that he should smell nice, arrayed himself in the new clothes purchased out of his crock of gold and was haled by Canon Leigh before the Dean to show what he could do. Standing in Dean Godwin's study, with his legs planted far apart and his hands behind his back, quite unabashed and unafraid, he had shown what he could do to some purpose. Set to dispute in Latin he went on so long that the panting Dean raised an imploring hand and begged him to stop. His Greek seemed to the Dean to be better than his own and what he didn't know about astronomy was not worth knowing. His arithmetic made one dizzy and his rhetoric was without blemish. . . . Only about music he knew nothing at all; his singing voice being like a donkey's and his ear, in spite of its physical size, being non-existent in the musical sense. . . . Nevertheless, it was clear that the boy was a genius.

"Take him away, for the love of heaven," said the Dean to Canon Leigh, wiping his brow, "he makes me positively ill. Had it not been for his ignorance of music I should have died."

So that was the first difficulty surmounted.

Then came the question of ways and means, for though the crock of gold went far it did not go the whole way. This was got over by making Faithful Giles' servitor. It was usual for a well-to-do scholar, a nobleman or squire's son, to come up to the University accompanied by a poorer friend, the son of his village parson perhaps, who would act as his servitor and share his room, his food and his work, and so live almost free of charge. So Faithful became Giles' servitor; kept his room in order, ran his errands, delivered his clothes to the washerwoman at the Fair Gate, dusted his books, saw that his bows and arrows were in good condition and concocted frightful medicines for him when his food disagreed with him. All this Faithful, a born hero-worshipper, found very agreeable, and Giles, born to be worshipped, found it agreeable too.

At the moment there was nothing to be seen of Giles but a confused heap of arms and legs under the bed-clothes and the back of his dark head on the pillow. Giles, who did everything with thoroughness, slept so deeply that he might have been dead, but Faithful, looking at him and thinking of him, saw in imagination his paragon parading the room in all his princely beauty and arrogance.

He was the most strictly beautiful of all the Leighs. He had Joyeuce's grace and height, his father's perfect features and Grace's dark hair and blue eyes. But in everything he progressed a little further in beauty than they did. He was taller than Joyeuce and far more graceful, being without that stiff bracing of the figure that marred Joyeuce's carriage, for, unlike her, he met the shocks and jars of life with a strong will rather than taut nerves. His features, though the same as his father's, were more sharply cut, flawless yet without a soft line anywhere, for hesitancy was unknown to him. He was acutely sensitive yet his sensitiveness was of a different kind from his father's and Joyeuce's, being entirely of the mind and not of the imagination. He could detect any smallest undercurrent of meaning in the printed argument or the spoken disputation, but he had not the slightest idea when he was, or was not, trampling upon a person's feelings. His intellect had developed far in advance of the rest of him. It was like a flame in which every desire but the desire for learning was burnt to ashes. A brilliant future was foretold for him. He worked in a way that caused the adoring Faithful to shake his huge head in considerable concern, for Faithful in his multifarious experiences had acquired a sense of proportion. Giles worked nearly all night sometimes. Anyone would have thought he had heard, from several centuries ahead, the advice given by Cyril Jackson, Dean of Christ Church. "Work very hard and unremittingly. Work like a tiger or like a dragon, if dragons work more and harder than tigers. Don't be afraid of killing yourself." . . . And Giles wasn't. . . . But yet with all this he was not so fine a scholar as Faithful for he lacked Faithful's humility. Erasmus's daily prayer, that God would give to him a sense of ignorance, would have seemed wisdom to Faithful but tomfoolery to the arrogant Giles.

A well aimed shoe hit Faithful on the head and sent him bounding from bed like a jack-in-the-box. He had been almost asleep again and Giles was the first to be out of bed and standing in the sunshine, his lean brown body perfect as that of a young god but his temper entirely human.

"You sleep like a pig, Faithful," he growled. "You ought to be up first. You're the servitor, aren't you? Anybody'd think I was, the way I have to waste my time hurling shoes at your head. Where are my clothes? Do we wash this morning?"

"There's no need," said Faithful. "We washed last Wednesday and we're still quite clean." He spoke with relief, for when Giles took it into his head to want to wash Faithful had to go all the way downstairs to the well on the floor below and heave up a bucketful of ice-cold water with much labour and sloppiness. . . . And then Giles made such a mess all over the room that it took him twenty minutes to get it all mopped up.

"We don't wash, then," said Giles. "Good. Here give me my clothes. There's the bell going for prayers."

They struggled rather feverishly into doublets, trunks, hose and ruffs while the unhurried bell tolled solemnly from the Cathedral. They were still smoothing their tousled hair with their fingers, and struggling into their gowns, as they raced down the wide oak staircase and through the doorway carved with the pomegranate of Catherine of Aragon, set there to commemorate the visit that she had paid to Oxford years ago, dashed across the quadrangle and through the cloisters to the Cathedral door.

Kneeling in the Cathedral, listening to the monotonous drone of the Latin prayers, Faithful found himself watching the sunshine streaming over the shrine of Saint Frideswide, that had been destroyed by Henry and restored again when Queen Mary came to the throne, and thinking not so much of the Saint as of Queen Catherine of Aragon, Mary's mother, whose pomegranate ornamented his own doorway.

She had come to Christ Church in 1518, when the court was at Abingdon, to worship at the shrine, and she had been personally conducted by Cardinal Wolsey, who wanted to show her the site where he had planned to build his Cardinal College. Faithful pictured her riding up Fish Street with her courtiers clattering behind her and her trumpeters going before, and the proud Cardinal riding beside her dilating on the glories of his College that was to be. She would have listened politely and courteously, Faithful thought, reining in her horse when they came to the site marked out for the Fair Gate, and in her pretty low voice with its foreign inflection she would have said how clever it was of him to have planned it all out himself, and how wonderful the Cathedral looked against the blue sky, but did he really think he ought to pull down the nave to make room for his quadrangle? But at this my Lord Cardinal would have turned a little huffy and she would have hastily changed the subject to the glories of the proposed College kitchen. It was to be a marvellous kitchen, he had told her, and was to be begun before any of the other College buildings, my Lord Cardinal understanding almost as well as a woman the relative importance of the different departments of life. How many oxen had he told her would be roasted in it at once ? No, not really ! His huffiness would by now have been dispersed, and chatting amicably of culinary affairs they would have walked their horses in and out between the hovels of the common people that now cluttered up the ground where the Cardinal proposed to build his College quadrangle. . . . These hovels, the Cardinal would have explained to the Queen's Grace, would of course be swept away. . . . Catherine would have wondered what would happen to the common people when their hovels were pulled down, but she was a little frightened of my Lord Cardinal and she wouldn't have liked to ask. She was glad, perhaps, to get off her horse and go into the cool Cathedral, for it had been hot and dusty riding from Abingdon, and she was not very strong, and the Cardinal had talked a lot. Kneeling before the shrine of the saint, with the tapers buring and the choir chanting and the incense rising into the musty-smelling air, she would have covered her face with her hands, so that the crowd kneeling round her should not see her tears, and prayed with the desperation that informed all her prayers ; that God would not let her babies die one after the other in the way they did ; that she might keep just one little living son, only one ; that Henry might not leave off loving her because her sons died ; that it might not be true, as Henry was beginning to fear, that God had cursed their marriage. Surely, surely it couldn't be true ! Was their marriage a sin ? She had not meant to sin. This saint, this Frideswide, had been a king's daughter who had refused to marry a king. He had courted her hotly, as Henry had courted Catherine, but she had run away and hidden in the woods until his ardour cooled, and then she had come back and lived in a nunnery upon this very spot. Ah, she had been a wise woman ! It was not very happy to be married to a king. Holy Saint Frideswide, pray for me ! Mother of God, pray for me ! Deus, propitius esto mihi peccatori ! Well, it would be over some time. The misery of her life would be over some time and she would die and be forgotten of men.

But Oxford, bewitched by Queen Catherine on that memorable visit, had never forgotten her. There had been furious indignation when Henry threatened to divorce her, the women of Oxford creating such a disturbance in the streets that thirty of them had had to be shut up in the town prison of Bocardo. . . . And Faithful, kneeling every morning before the shrine where she had knelt and running in and out under her pomegranate twenty times a day, remembered her always.

II

The half-hour after prayers was a busy one for servitors. Faithful fetched Giles's breakfast of bread and ale from the kitchen, delivered it to him where he stood sunning himself with other lords of creation in the quadrangle, and raced upstairs to " do " their room and eat his own breakfast of one stale crust at the same time. Material things seemed to him unimportant compared with the things of the mind and he spent as little time as possible over both these activities. With his crust held in his left hand he straightened the top covers of their beds with his right. . . . The underneath covers he left as they were, for as he frequently remarked to Giles, and Giles quite agreed with him, what was the use of tidying bedclothes that were thrashed into disorder again ten minutes after one had got into bed ? . . . This done he bolted the rest of his crust, removed the dust from the furniture with the bellows and refreshed the floor by sweeping the rubbish out of sight under the beds. As he worked he whistled happily, for this was the day when they went to the Schools for Thomas Bodley's lecture on Greek verse, and Thomas Bodley, Fellow of Merton, could lecture in a way that set your mind on fire to such an extent that the flame of it could burn up all the boredom, dullness and inattention.

A shout from Giles in the quadrangle down below made him fling the bellows into a corner and fly down the stairs again. The scholars were breaking up into groups and dispersing to their various lectures and Nicolas de Worde, also bound for the schools, was standing beside Giles.

"Where's Philip Sidney ? " demanded Giles. " Mooning over his verses as usual. Go and fetch him, Faithful."

Faithful scurried off with the utmost cheerfulness, for of all

Giles's friends he liked Master Philip Sidney the best. There was no one in the world like him, he thought, and there never would be. . . . He was unique.

Philip's rooms were in Broadgates Hall, a lodginghouse for Christ School scholars just across the way from the Fair Gate, and Faithful ran across to them so often with messages from Giles that he had come to know the cobbles and smells of Fish Street quite intimately; to-day he ran along with his nose nipped between finger and thumb, for it had not rained lately and Fish Street had a certain aroma.

He clattered up the dark stairs to Philip's room and stood in the shadows knocking at the door with a beating heart. It was odd, he thought, how the knowledge that he would see Philip again in a couple of minutes always set his heart thudding as at the approach of some danger. . . . For what danger can there be in loving a person? . . . The worst danger in the world, whispered the shadows, the danger of irreparable loss. . . . He knocked again, urgently, gripped by unreasonable panic, suddenly afraid of the darkness in which he stood and the silence beyond the door.

"Come in."

In a sort of fury of relief he pushed open the door and precipitated himself like a young tornado into the sun-filled room.

Master Philip Sidney, seated at his desk in the window, writing a love song with a large squeaking quill pen, looked over his shoulder, mildly surprised. "Is anything the matter?" he asked.

"I beg your pardon, I just thought perhaps you'd gone," said Faithful vaguely.

"Where to? Sit down a minute while I finish this. What rhymes with case?"

"Grace," said Faithful, after long and painful thought.

"Thank you!" said the poet ardently, and dipping his pen in the ink was immediately lost again in the fairyland of creation.

Faithful sat on the extreme edge of the oak chest where Philip Sidney kept his worldly possessions and stared as unblinkingly as an owl at the object of his adoration. Some friendships develop gradually, putting out a leaf here or a shoot there, attaining their full strength only after years of growth, but others arrive with a crash and a bang, a fanfare of trumpets and a streaming of banners, and a day that dawned in the usual poverty closes in the possession of great riches. . . . It had been like that when Faithful first set eyes on Philip Sidney. . . . All the loveliness of his new life, the sun-drenched beauty of the town where he lived and the woods and streams that surrounded it, the warmth of his new relationships and the joy of his work, seemed to him to be summed up in the human being in front of him. He could not say thank-you to the woods and streams, he could not pay his debt to the sunshine, but personified in Philip he could serve them and do them reverence. This sense of symbolism was both the joy and the bane of human beauty, he had discovered. Those who are beautiful stand to their lovers for more than they are; and when their beauty has waned that which it stood for seems dead too, and the whole world darkened.

Philip was about Faithful's own age. He had a slender body with long, narrow hands and feet and a small head finely poised. His hair was fair and smooth and shining and his eyes hazel in a luminously pale oval-shaped face. His beauty and delicacy were those of a girl, but there was nothing effeminate in the set of his lips or in his proudly braced shoulders. His dark green doublet was of the finest cloth and his ruff and cuffs of spotless lawn. He wore a tiny golden dagger and shoes of Spanish leather, and his hose fitted without a wrinkle and were gartered at the knee with scarlet. . . . Not that these outward symbols of haberdashery were needed to show that Philip was a person of importance; his breeding was expressed in every one of his fine bones and in what his friend Frank Greville called " his staidness of mind, his lovely and familiar gravity."

" Listen to this," he adjured Faithful, swinging round and flourishing his pen in the air. " It's a sonnet to the moon. Did you notice the moon last night? She's the midsummer moon that brings back the fairies and the ghosts of dead lovers. But she is sad, because love is a cruel thing, and when she wanes again she and her ghosts and her fairies will be forgotten.

Faithful, his mouth wide open owing to the greatness of his love which made him feel as though his chest was full of wind, listened with half his mind, while with the other half he was wishing that Philip would not write about the midsummer moon that waxes and wanes like the life of a man, but about the sun that is always constant in the heavens as God Himself. He did not wish to be reminded again of that moment of unreasonable panic on the stairs.

" With how sad steps, O Moon, thou climb'st the skies !
How silently, and with how wan a face !
What ! May it be that even in heavenly place
That busy archer his sharp arrows tries ?
Sure, if that long-with-love-acquainted eyes
Can judge of love, thou feel'st a lover's case ;
I read it in thy looks ; thy languished grace
To me, that feel the like, thy state descries.
Then, even of fellowship, O Moon, tell me,
Is constant love deemed there but want of wit ?
Are beauties there as proud as here they be ?
Do they above love to be loved, and yet
Those lovers scorn whom that love doth possess ?
Do they call virtue there ungratefulness ? "

"It's wonderful," breathed Faithful. . . . It was a marvel to him that Philip, who to his certain knowledge had no lady love and who at this stage of his career had a profound contempt for the opposite sex, could be so eloquent on the subject of love. He was not aware that experience is unnecessary to your true poet, who can feel any and every emotion simply by sighing, sticking his tongue out at the side of his mouth and dipping his pen in the ink.

Philip performed these rites and turned back to re-read his poem. It was good, he thought. It was good enough to be kept and added to the book of poems that he would publish when he was a man. But was he really a great poet ? He found it difficult to be sure. While he was actually writing a poem he knew for certain that it was the most marvellous thing ever written, but when he had finished it he found himself assailed by heavy doubts.

" Master Bodley's lecture ? " suggested Faithful tentatively.

Philip jumped up, swearing softly. . . . He had learnt a lot of new oaths since he came up to Christ Church and they were a great pleasure to him. . . . Then he put his manuscript down his back—he always kept his literary works there, so that he could go on with them in odd moments—stowed away his writing materials in the leather wallet at his waist, smilingly handed Faithful his books to carry and preceded him courteously through the door.

III

Giles was prancing impatiently up and down when Philip and Faithful joined him and Nicolas.

" We shall be late," he moaned.

" All the better," said Nicolas. He had been up at Christ Church for years, always putting off the accumulation of a little learning to a later and more convenient date, and was by now sick of lectures ; even Thomas Bodley's.

They set off at a good pace, Philip, Nicolas and Giles going on ahead and Faithful trundling after, burdened with the books of all three of them. Yet wherever he went in this city, no matter how burdened, every step of the way was a delight to him. The miracle of the spring was now passed and the hawthorn that Joyeuce had looked out upon from her window was tarnished, dropping little white moons of blossom on Faithful's thatch of hair as he passed beneath it ; the June sun had burnt up the fresh scents of April and the song of the birds had lost its ecstatic note of surprise and was taking the return of warmth and beauty entirely for granted. Yet Faithful thought this full summer season had something precious that the spring had lacked, a richness and pride in the warmth of the sun and the deep colour of the flaunting summer flowers that promised a continuance of good things. In the keen joy of the spring there was a sadness, because it went so fast, but the beauty of the summer stole away slowly, no pace perceived ; one could cheat oneself into a certainty of possession and know content.

They hurried along between the old buildings of Peckwater Inn and Canterbury College and then turning to their left ran breathlessly up Shipyard Street into the High Street.

In spite of their hurry Faithful lingered a moment to look up the street to his left to the Tower of All Saints' church, behind the pig market, and then in front of him at Saint Mary's, the University church. High above his head the glorious spire crowned the tower below it like a king seated upon his throne, while round about the throne the life-size figures of kings and queens and saints stood like courtiers. Of all these figures the one that Faithful loved best was Edmund Rich, the saint of whom Master Campion had told him, the father of all Oxford scholars and the first M.A. of whom Oxford has any record.

He had been born at Abingdon, in those very early days of the University when lecture rooms were street corners and narrow alleys, and the scholars merely a handful of ragged scarecrows whom the wealthy merchants elbowed out of their way as they trod the streets of the city. Yet their fame had already spread beyond the city wall and reached Edmund at Abingdon. He loved two things with a burning love, learning and holiness, and it seemed to him that he would surely find them both in that city, where the spires of great churches rose to heaven and bells rang all day long to call men to worship God, and where men were not afraid of starvation for their bodies if only they could find food for their minds. So he said good-bye to his outraged family and with his bundle on his back, and his staff in his hand, he set out to tramp through the dark and terrible forest of Bagley to Oxford. It was a wonder he was not killed by the wild boars and the vagabonds in the forest, but he survived, for round his neck, as protection, his mother had hung a gold ring with, engraved upon it, "that sweet Ave with which the angel at the Annunciation had hailed the Virgin." And so at last, footsore and weary and dreadfully hungry, he crossed the river and reached the South Gate of the city.

He attached himself to a band of scholars who had built themselves a rough school, with clay walls and thatched roof, in the churchyard of Saint Mary's, and with them he studied and worshipped.

He was very devout, and the glorious music of the Mass, as it echoed through Saint Mary's Church, thrilled his very soul. Yet he was not without his carnal temptations, and one of them was games. He had a strong, straight body, and he could run hard and aim straight and jump like a frog. . . . He adored jumping like a frog. . . . One day in the middle of the sermon his legs ached and his back itched him, and the Devil tempted him to go and jump like a frog outside, and yielding to the temptation he got up and slipped surreptitiously out of his place. But at the north door a divine apparition suddenly appeared and told him what it thought of him, and he was so ashamed that he went back and heard out the sermon to the end. And from that moment his devotion grew more fervent.

One evening he was kneeling in the church, praying by himself. It was growing dark, so that the distant places of the church were filled with purple shadows and the roof over his head was dim as the sky at midnight. The air was heavy and sweet with incense and he felt a little drowsy. Then something made him look up and his eyes were drawn to the one bright spot in the church, the place where light was burning before the statue of the Virgin. The candle flames shone on her rainbow-coloured robe and her golden crown and the child held in the crook of her arm, and as Edmund looked at her she smiled at him. Slowly he got up from his knees and crept like a little mouse through the shadows to her feet. There he knelt down and said an Ave, and then he took from his neck the ring that his mother had given him and stretching up he slipped it on her finger. He was hers now, her liegeman, and he would serve her with a chaste body and a pure mind until he died.

The years went on and Edmund became a Master of Arts. He was tremendously learned and scholars flocked to his lectures, but he never flagged in his devotion to the Virgin. He built her a chapel in the parish where he lived and he attended Mass there every morning before his day's work began. He cared nothing at all for the carnal pleasures of this world—he never played leapfrog now—but only for holiness and learning. " So study," he said to his pupils, " as if you were to live for ever ; so live as if you were to die to-morrow." If a rich pupil insisted upon bringing him the fees that were paid to popular masters— unpopular masters, it seems, were not paid anything, and how they lived is a mystery—he was so indignant that he flung the money down on the windowsill, where it stayed till it was stolen by an unpopular master. . . . How Edmund himself lived, under the circumstances, is a mystery too.

But as in his boyhood the Devil had tempted him with games so now he tempted him with mathematics. Edmund's mind, strong and vigorous as his body, had delighted in the jumps and twists and turns of mathematics, and it spent far too much time leaping about in this fascinating science. One day, when he was in the very middle of a lecture on mathematics, the ghost of his dead mother appeared. " My son," she said severely, " what art thou studying ? What are these strange diagrams over which thou porest so intently ? " Then she seized his right hand and in the palm drew three circles, within which she wrote the names of the Father, the Son and the Holy Ghost. " Be these thy diagrams henceforth, my son," she said. With that she vanished away and Edmund came to himself again ; to the great relief of his pupils, who thought he had gone mad when they saw him standing there with his mouth wide open and the palm of his hand stretched out to nothing at all.

But for the rest of his life Edmund's eager mind leapt about in theology only, and with such success that in due course they made him an Archbishop.

One day His Grace was preaching to a crowd of the devout in the churchyard of All Saints' and a terrible storm came on. Over most of the city a sky like ink hung over the roofs and it rained cats and dogs ; but over All Saints' churchyard was a round patch of sky the colour of bluebells, and the devout who sat at the foot of the Archbishop were as dry as a bone and as warm as toast. . . . After that they made the Archbishop a Saint, for who but the holiest of the holy are able to oblige like this in the matter of weather ?

After his death Saint Edmund, as dead Saints should, went on obliging. He took under his protection a certain well at Cowley Ford and if ill people crept through the evening shadows to the well, as he had once crept to the feet of the Virgin, and kneeling down said their prayers to her devoutly, as he had once said his, they were healed of their wounds and sickness. . . . And that Oxford might never forget him his statue looked down upon it from the tower of Saint Mary's.

IV

Leaving it the boys turned to their left under the west window of Saint Mary's and hurried up School Street into the quiet square beyond, where Saint Mary's churchyard dreamed under the sun. Crossing it they plunged under a gateway into the quadrangle of the Schools, ran past the empty University Library, whose priceless collection of books had been destroyed and scattered during the Reformation, and disappeared into their lecture room like unpunctual rabbits leaping into their burrows.

In it was a seething herd of scholars trying to find places on the few benches that were quite inadequate to their number or weight. Failure to find a seat meant sitting on the floor for two hours, or longer, should Thomas Bodley get carried away by his own eloquence, which was unfortunately frequently the case. The battle was to the strong and those who, like Nicolas, could dislodge a whole benchful of smaller and weaker scholars with a sweep of the arm, were to be congratulated. . . . Although the last in, it was only a matter of minutes before he and Giles and Philip were occupying the best seats, with Faithful sitting on the floor at their feet in a square inch of space, trampled upon and hemmed in on all sides by the perspiring bodies of a hundred pilgrims to the well of learning.

There was a sudden lull in the uproar and Faithful, peering up through a forest of waving arms and legs, beheld Master Thomas Bodley pushing his way through the crowd towards his desk on the raised platform at the end of the room. As he passed the noise ebbed away, like a subsiding storm in the branches of the trees, and when he mounted the steps to the platform and looked down upon his pupils there was a dead silence.

For Master Thomas Bodley was a personality, and such was his devotion to Oxford and to learning that it seemed that in him the spirit of Edmund Rich lived again. He was a young man, one of a group of young brilliant men who were the most worthy descendants of those first teachers whose platforms had been a flight of broken steps leading up to the door of a hovel. Few men in Oxford were more beloved than Thomas Bodley, unless perhaps it was Faithful's friend of the crock of gold, Edmund Campion of Saint John's, and few could equal him in his power of capturing his pupils by the spell of his own attraction. And that done, holding in his hands their attentions like so many gossamer threads that passed from them to him and kept them tethered, it was an easy thing so to stir their imagintion that learning seemed delightful to them and with one consent they handed him up their minds to be filled.

Thomas Bodley was tall and upright, his height increased by the long M.A. gown that he wore, with a look of directness about him that was prophetic of the straight clean road he would drive for himself through life. People talked a lot about Bodley and his probable future.

And in the course of time he was caught in the political spider's web, dragged into it almost without his knowledge by the will of those in high places, and for some years he was a diplomatist, and a brilliant one. But the web could not hold him for long. He was haunted, as he made his brilliant way through the world, by the thought of that desolate library close to the room where he had lectured at Oxford, despoiled of its priceless treasures, its stalls and shelves sold for timber, created to be a place where scholars might study far removed " from the noise of the world " and now empty and dusty and haunted by the ghosts of those dead books. It seems always crying out to him, asking him to help it.

So he came back to Oxford to fill it up again. It was an odd thing to do, but that, he knew, was his vocation. " Whereupon," he said, " examining exactly for the rest of my life what course I might take, and having sought, as I thought, all the ways to the wood, to select the most proper, I concluded at the last to set up my staff at the library door at Oxford."

He offered to restore the library at his own expense, and the University gratefully accepted the offer. Faced by such a staggering financial proposition some men might have been nonplussed; but not Thomas Bodley; he married a rich widow. His " purse ability " was now great and he repaired the room and endowed the library. Everyone loved Thomas Bodley and all his friends gave him books for it. He was a Devonshire man, and west countrymen particularly put themselves out to steal books for him. When the English fleet, under Essex, captured the Portuguese town of Faro, Walter Raleigh, a captain in the squadron, saw to it that the fine collection of books they stole from a bishop and brought home as a souvenir was given to Thomas.

Generations later the empty room that Thomas Bodley filled was famous all over the world, and his name remembered with honour. . . . But no one ever gave a thought to Mistress Bodley.

But at the moment Thomas Bodley was filling not empty bookshelves but empty minds. The newly discovered plays of Euripides had been published in Venice at the beginning of the century and the wonder of it was still alive. A lecture on Greek verse made the heart beat and the pulses throb with a sense of voyage and discovery. These boys who sat at the feet

of Bodley were one in spirit with the boys who had sailed with
Cabot to America and who were sailing at this moment under the
flag of the Merchant Adventurers, carrying the trade of England out to the New World. It was a great moment to be alive,
thought Faithful, this moment when the mists of man's ignorance
were lifting and world beyond worlds were opening out before
his excited eyes, and of the two great adventures that offered
themselves, Commerce and Learning, who could say which was
the most wonderful ? Commerce meant romance, danger, and
a glory of dreams, and in those islands beyond the sea, those
fairylands of coral and palm trees and screeching birds with
plumy feathers all colours of the rainbow, men could have their
fill of fighting and colour and the heat of the sun ; and come
back with pockets full of gold, mouths full of strange oaths, and
tales to tell in the tavern that would keep the company hanging
breathless on their words from curfew to cockcrow.

Yet that adventure did not seem so wonderful to Faithful as
this other adventure of learning that carried them to other islands,
less gaudy, but to his eyes more beautiful, where the rosy flowers
of the asphodel echoed the colour of dawn-flushed, snow-covered
mountain peaks, and pale marble pillars stood in their loveliness
beside the wine-dark sea.

> Oh, the wind and the oar,
> When the great sail swells before,
> With sheets astrain, like a horse on the rein ;
> And on, through the race and the roar,
> She feels for the farther shore.

Surely, thought Faithful, that ship of Euripides is the ship of the
imagination, that can sail farther and faster than any ship built
by man.

> Ten score and ten there be
> Rowers that row for thee,
> And a wild hill air as though Pan were there
> Shall sound on the Argive Sea,
> Piping to set thee free.

The voice of Thomas Bodley, repeating the poem, seemed to
Faithful to die away into the lapping of waves against the side
of a ship. While he travelled in the ship of imagination the whole

of the universe was his, the whole of time, past, present and to come. Those others, those Merchant Adventurers, were at the mercy of wind and tide, but he was set free by a wild tune piped from beyond death to sail over the horizon of the world into eternity. He was bound with no limits, borne with a wing of hope ; he would climb even unto the stars.

v

The lecture was over, Master Bodley was descending the steps, and Faithful was being trodden on. He was in the body once more and yelping with the pain of many feet upon his person. Giles rescued him with kindly patronage, shook him and dusted him down.

"The minute Bodley shuts his mouth you must leap to your feet," Giles explained. "Otherwise, you'll be trampled to death. Catch hold of my books and come along. We're going up to Bocardo to cheer up Walter Raleigh. Sidney's just heard he's in prison for debt again."

"There's no time," grumbled Faithful. "We've a Latin lecture at Christ Church before dinner." He grudged every moment stolen from the pursuit of learning, to which his soul was vowed like the soul of Edmund Rich before him. And he did not even know Philip's friend, Walter Raleigh, an Oriel man of extravagant habits who probably deserved to be in prison, where, thought Faithful, he should be left uncomforted by the virtuous, quietly stewing in his own juice till better thoughts should dawn. "I tell you we've no time," he growled.

"Shut your mouth," said Giles, not unkindly. "There's time if we run. Come *on*, I tell you, come *on*."

Sighing, Faithful came on. He was only a servitor and he must do what he was told. Puffing and blowing he fought his way out of the seething horde of scholars that still filled the lecture room, back through the sunny quadrangle of the Schools and out into the High Street, where they turned to their right and raced uphill towards Carfax.

It was market day and the town was getting busy. In the pig market outside All Saints' Church the pigs were already arriving and the four scholars charged through them, hitting out at the fat squeaking sides with their books and shouting out like English soldiers charging the enemy, " Cuckoo ! Cuckoo ! Hey ! Hey ! Cuckoo ! " The pigs were quickly routed, skipping to right and left with all the nimbleness of which their bulk and inadequate legs were capable, and pursued by the curses of their drovers the four charged up past the Mitre Inn and round the corner into Cornmarket.

They did not linger here, for once you had left Carfax behind you, with its fine Church of Saint Martin to the left and the Tavern with the painted room to the right, Cornmarket became distinctly smelly ; for not to mention the kennel running down its centre there was a tannery in it, with the cordwainers, the workers in leather, conveniently near. They were, on the whole, good scholars, and they left the Lane of the Seven Deadly Sins, away on their left, severely alone, and ran on to the Cornmarket proper, at the North Gate of the city, where the country people sold their corn and hay on market days.

North Gate was a lively and attractive spot, in spite of the uncomfortable memories connected with the Bocardo lock-up built over the top of it. The houses drew close together here, each story jutting out a little further than the one below it, and up above them towered the eleventh-century tower of Saint Michael's Church, with its battlements cutting neat squares out of the blue sky and the cock on its weathervane arrogant beneath the sun ; and gazing down rather contemptuously upon its lesser brethren who scuttled about over the cobbles below, hunting in the crannies for the grains of corn that the corn factors had let fall. There were always quantities of quadrupeds and birds about in Cornmarket ; dogs, cats, cocks and hens. And, when night came down and the streets of the city were black and deserted, and the tower of Saint Michael's was just a black shape that blotted out the stars, rats in their hundreds emerged from the cellars and yards of the old houses and danced up and down Cornmarket, from Carfax to North Gate and back again, frisking their tails in the light of the moon and gorging themselves fit to burst on the refuse in the kennel.

As it was market day the four boys had to fight hard to get through the crowd to North Gate. The stalls of the corn factors, placed down the centre of the street, divided it into two narrow lanes and up and down them seethed a yelling, swearing, sweating, gesticulating crowd. Countrywomen in their wide hats, with voluminous coloured petticoats beneath their great white aprons, baskets on their arms and dead fowls dangling from their wrists, bargained at the tops of their voices with the factors behind the stalls. Dirty, ragged little urchins charged everywhere, kicking up the rubbish in the kennel, banging into the stalls, falling over the squawking poultry and throwing stones at the yapping, snarling dogs. Sometimes a more respectable figure would pass; the physician in his long furred gown, making way for himself with vigorous blows of his long staff, apprentices dashing to and from the cordwainers, and now and then a horseman would ride under North Gate and plunge through the crowd, slashing his whip at the dogs as they scuffled and barked at his horse's hoofs.

The boys were experienced in getting through a Cornmarket crowd. Nicolas went first, kicking and elbowing his way, and Philip, a person not much use at either battering or being battered, for he was delicate and blows always seemed to hurt him more than they hurt other people, came behind clinging round Giles's waist. Faithful brought up the rear, with the books. Black looks, curses, mutterings and a kick or two came their way, and a rotten egg caught Nicolas neatly between the shoulders, for hatred between Town and Gown was still a real thing. The merchants and apprentices and ragtag and bobtail of the town had not forgotten that Oxford was once a great commercial city where Merchandise had reigned supreme. . . . And now it was almost wholly given over to these insolent young cockerels of scholars, with their malapert manners, boastful speech, and heads so swollen with divers useless Tongues and Arts and Philosophies that pity it was to behold the ruin of English manhood brought about by this same lamentable learning.

" Damn your eyes for a saucy, froward villain ! " shouted an enraged factor as Nicolas, staggering from a well-aimed kick that had followed the rotten egg, barged into his stall.

" Damn yours, you insolent thief ! " replied Nicolas hotly, and swung round with his fist raised.

" Oh, come on, do ! " implored Giles impatiently. He was a pacifist, not from conscientious reasons nor from cowardice, but because he considered war a shocking waste of a man's time.

" Thief ? Who said thief ? " roared the factor, a deeply

religious and most respectable man. " Am I to be called
thief by down-at-heel, out-at-elbow, rascally scholars who take
the bread out of honest men's mouths and turn this God-fearing
town into a sink of wickedness with their evil ways? No!"
bellowed the factor, " I'll see 'em damned first ! " and he got in
a fine blow, straight from the shoulder. . . . An angry, mutter-
ing crowd came milling round Nicolas and things looked ugly.

" Get back, you dirty, scandalous, bullying vagabonds ! "
shouted Faithful, dashing to the rescue. " It's you, not us, who
make this town a stinking dog-hole," he added pleasantly,
butting in amongst them. " You'll be put in the stocks for this
and serve you right, you scaly, blear-eyed devils."

Faithful had a command of language, picked up in the less
desirable streets of London, that always stood him in good stead.
Shouted in his pleasant voice and issuing from his wide, good-
humoured mouth, it never failed to make things pleasant all
round. The crowd, shouting with good-humoured laughter,
fell back, and Nicolas was delivered with nothing worse than a
black eye and a bleeding nose and a shocking abraision on the
temple.

" Beasts ! " muttered Nicolas. " Vermin ! " and turning his
head he squinted with his one remaining eye at the mess of egg
down his back.

" Come on ! " urged his friends. " If we start again we shall
be here all day," and they propelled him vigorously towards
North Gate.

It was a tunnel not wider than twelve feet at the two ends and
some seventy feet long, and over it was the famous lock-up,
Bocardo, where the drunk and disorderly, and those unable to
pay their bills, were incarcerated for their good. The four
halted beneath the small barred window over the tunnel and
called in the honeyed tones of deep sympathy, " Raleigh?
Raleigh ? Cuckoo ! Cuckoo ! "

Instantly a face appeared at the window, the face of a gentleman in his middle 'teens with curly dark hair, bright blue eyes,
a boldly hooked nose, a laughing, generously-curving mouth and
a resolute chin. It was a proud, arresting, challenging face and
Faithful stared at it in fascination, his eyes popping in his head
and his mouth ajar. . . . Wherever he went in this wonderful
city he was continually confronted by towers and spires, gardens

and books and bells, men and women and children, who made his eyes pop and his mouth fall open.

"Good morning, gentlemen," said Raleigh airily. "Fine day."

Neither his voice nor his manner invited commiseration and his friends knew better than to offer it. "Just exactly how much do you owe this time?" asked Philip, coming briefly to the point.

"I've no head for figures," said Raleigh arrogantly, and glared at them through the bars like a caged wild beast.

"Don't be an ass," Nicolas adjured him. "Throw the bag down."

Raleigh flushed crimson and exhorted them angrily to mind their own business. It was the correct thing, of course, for prisoners in Bocardo to let down a bag out of the window that their friends might relieve their wants, but to a gentleman of Raleigh's independent temper it was galling to the pride.

"Fool!" said Giles, kindly. "Do you want to spend the whole summer term shut up here? You can pay us back later. Chuck out the bag."

Raleigh continued to glare, struggling with himself, his anger directed not at his friends but at fate that had given to his superb ambition the totally inadequate support of a frail and slender fortune. He ground his teeth, maddened afresh by the permanent incompatability of his income and his expenditure. Heaven knew he did his best to make the one support the other, for he did not exactly enjoy spending a large proportion of his days inside Bocardo, but there was a fine careless grandeur in his mode of living that was natural to him and refused to be curtailed. He was of the stuff of which poets and heroes are made, a stuff not easily fitted into the restricted mould of sobriety and solvency, but created to spread itself abroad in beauty like a banner on the wind, possessed of a grandeur that is perhaps more appreciated by later centuries than by the contemporary one that foots the bill. . . . Though Raleigh himself did things in such style, with such a fine courtesy and so grand an air, that his friends were generally happy to give what assistance they could when his elegant garments and entertainments worked out at more than he had expected.

"Come on," said Philip. "Out with the bag. We want you out of Bocardo for our own sakes, you know."

It was charmingly spoken, as only Philip could speak, and a flashing smile lit up the face at the window. He seized the leather bag on a string that lay beside him on the sill and shot it out of the window with such violence that it hit Faithful on the head and made him leap like an antelope.

"Got anything worth giving?" enquired Giles of the others, fumbling in his wallet.

Nicolas and Philip, the financiers of the party, nodded, and Philip produced one golden angel and Nicolas three. . . . The others whistled when they saw Nicolas's three, for three angels was a fabulous sum. . . . But then, Nicolas's fine generosity to his friends always excited deep admiration in the breasts of everyone except his father.

Giles fished up a few groats, which was all he had, and Faithful hung his head and went scarlet to the roots of his hair, because he hadn't got anything at all; and as he had taken a passionate liking to the handsome face behind the bars the impotence of his poverty was doubly hard to bear; on an impulse he took from his wallet the little bag of herbs that Joyeuce had given him to sniff as a protection against the plague, one of his most precious possessions, and put it in the bag with the coins. The moment he had done it he wished he hadn't, of course, for only the greatest of the saints do not regret their good deeds as soon as done, but it was too late to change his mind for Walter Raleigh, purple in the face with mingled shame, rage and gratitude, was winding up the string and pulling the bag up to the window again.

"Is it enough?" asked the anxious donors, as he counted it out on the windowsill.

"No," groaned the prisoner, then, remembering his manners and flashing his smile superbly upon the group below, "but you have my eternal gratitude, gentlemen. You have shortened my incarceration by one-tenth."

"I expect it won't be long," consoled Nicolas. "They'll take up a collection at Oriel, like they did before."

"They might," growled the prisoner, "but they're a stingy lot at Oriel these days. Getting me out of Bocardo is an activity that palls, they told me last time. And after drinking all my Canary wine at a sitting, too! The mean curs!" And he shook the bars angrily.

"Could I lend you anything to make the time pass?" asked Philip pitifully. "Books, or a lute?"

Suddenly all the rage died out of Raleigh's face and a light broke over it, making it beautiful as a woman's. "I have my charts," he said softly.

Philip smiled with the tolerance of one artist towards the lunacy of another. "Sea charts of the land beyond the sunset?" he asked.

Raleigh nodded, looking out unseeingly over their heads. "I've made two more," he murmured.

"He's been taken with one of his crazy fits," said Nicolas. "We might as well go home.... Good-bye," he added at the top of his voice. "Oriel being so stingy I suppose it will be weeks before we see you again?"

Raleigh awoke from his dream, recollected himself, and glared. "Don't you be too sure," he said truculently. "You may find yourselves in here with me before you know where you are."

"*We're* never drunk or disorderly," boasted Giles. "Nor in debt."

"I shouldn't wonder," continued Raleigh, "if you were all in here by night. I thought this morning that you would be, for I had an Omen."

"What Omen?" they asked.

"Four bugs in my bed," said Raleigh, and disappeared from view.

Laughing, they fought their way back through the Cornmarket crowd.

"Why does he make charts of the land beyond the sunset?" panted the puzzled Faithful.

"He's going to fit out a fleet of great ships and win an Empire for England in the west," explained Philip.

"Surely that will cost a lot of money," said Faithful, and he shook his hand doubtfully, for he had formed a poor opinion of Master Raleigh's financial capabilities.

"He's going to manufacture the money," said Nicolas. "He's hard at work discovering a great Cordial or Elixir that will turn base metal into gold."

"But is there such a thing?" asked the literal Faithful.

"Of course there isn't!" said Giles scornfully. "Raleigh's

mad. His bonnet buzzes so loud with bees that you can't hear yourself think when you're with him."

Faithful's thoughts whirled excitedly as they ran on. . . . Charts of the land beyond the sunset. . . . He wished he could see them. Virtuous though he was he almost wished that he might be drunk and disorderly by night so as to be shut up in Bocardo and see those charts. For a full moment the Adventure of Commerce loomed larger in his mind than the Adventure of Learning. Under such a captain as Raleigh he could imagine himself setting sail for the sunset and finding in such an adventure satisfaction for the deepest longings of his soul. It needed a glimpse of Saint Mary's Church, as they ran across Carfax, with the statue of Edmund Rich looking down upon the hurrying figures of the scholars who were his children, to restore his mind to its proper allegiance. The Adventure of Learning also had its captains. . . . The Teachers on the steps. . . . He seemed to see them linked in an unbroken chain that stretched from that now almost legendary figure down to the present day, to Edmund Campion and Thomas Bodley, and on again to a future so remote that he could not even picture it. . . . One day, he thought, he would be one of them.

CHAPTER VI

RIOT IN THE TOWN

> Sing we and chant it,
> While love doth grant it.
> Not long youth lasteth,
> And old age hasteth.
> Now is best leisure
> To take our pleasure.
>
> All things invite us
> Now to delight us.
> Hence, care, be packing,
> No mirth be lacking,
> Let spare no treasure
> To live in pleasure.
>
> ANONYMOUS.

1

IT was nearly supper-time and Faithful raised his heavy head from the bony knuckles on which it was propped and sighed a little. He and Giles had been working in their room for five solid hours and he wondered if perhaps they might rest a little now. A huge beefy dinner in hall at eleven o'clock, followed by archery practice, was not to his mind the best preparation for hard work. Starving vagabond that he had been he was not used to heavy meals, nor to violent exercise immediately on top of them, and they made him feel rather peculiar. He pressed his hot palms against his temples, that ached, and then upon his stomach, that ached too, rubbed his knuckles in his eyes to clear away an unwanted film of sleep, and looked at Giles, clearing his throat tentatively.

But Giles read on and on, blind and deaf to everything but the printed words before his eyes and the explanation of their meaning spoken in his ears. For when he worked there was always present with Giles that inspiration that is like the actual corporeal presence of a real person. The voice in his ears seemed to him not his own voice but someone else's, and when he wrote he could have sworn that a figure stood behind him, dictating. It was not so with Faithful. He was always conscious of the thing that he wrote as a lump of stone that must be hewn into shape by his own labours and no one else's. . . . Yet when they had finished working it was generally Giles, and not Faithful, who was the more tired of the two.

But to-day Faithful seemed unable to work properly. It was very hot and a bee kept buzzing in and out and disturbing him, and he could not fix his mind properly upon Aristotle because not only were his head and stomach aching, but he was thinking all the time of Raleigh and the land beyond the sunset. . . . "God give me singleness of mind," he whispered. "God give me singleness of mind." . . . He shut his eyes and tried to concentrate, and instantly his big head fell forward like an overweighted peony.

"What in the world are you doing?" demanded Giles irritably.

"I think I was falling asleep," said Faithful.

"What do you want to go to sleep for?" demanded Giles indignantly. "You sleep like a hog for eight hours every night, and keep me awake with your damned snoring. You'll never be an M.A. if you don't get your teeth into Aristotle."

Faithful gritted his teeth, Aristotle being presumably between them, and re-propped his top-heavy headpiece on his bony knuckles.

Giles was not unkind to Faithful, indeed he was very fond of him, but his very admiration for his brains made him stand no nonsense. Faithful should be turned into a first-rate scholar, or he, Giles, would perish in the attempt. He must learn to work whether he was well or ill, tired or fresh, happy or unhappy, full of the roast beef of old England or not full of the roast beef of old England; until his mind had learnt to function regardless of the state of his body he would not be worthy of the name of scholar.

Great Tom boomed out five o'clock and there was a stampede of feet, and a joyous shouting and yelling, in the quadrangle outside.

"Curse!" said Giles. "Can it be supper time already?" and he smacked his big book shut. His face was flushed and the hollows at his temples looked deeper than usual. Faithful looked at him anxiously. Sometimes he thought that Giles's capacity for doing more work in one hour than most people did in three was not very good for him. . . . Yet there was no one on this earth who could stop Giles doing what he wanted to do.

They tidied themselves and ran down the stairs to join the yelling mob in the quadrangle that was surging towards the hall and food. The age of the scholars being anything from twelve upwards, and there being no rule as to keeping off the grass, the evening's progress towards the hall was not the decorous proceeding that it became several centuries later. Nor was the hall sacred to food alone, as later. It was the common room as well, and the noise that went on in it could be heard a mile off.

Rough stone stairs open to the sky led up to the hall. It was paved with yellow and green tiles and the sun shone through rich stained-glass windows. The great fireplace was in the middle of the hall, with a louvre above to carry off the smoke. Even in the summer a small fire of logs burned in it, and the wainscoting on the walls reflected the leaping flames of the logs and was patterned by the sun with the green and blue and rose-colour of the stained-glass windows, but far up above their heads the splendid roof of Irish oak was dim and shadowy. Faithful always caught his breath when he entered the hall because it was so beautiful. He had not yet got used to its beauty, and he hoped he never would.

Most of the scholars ate their supper in the lower part of the hall, at long oak tables set out with wooden trenchers and cups of horn, but the Dean, the Canons and the College dons sat at the high table on the dais, under the portraits of Henry Tudor and Cardinal Wolsey, and they ate from silver plates and drank out of tall, slender opal Venice glasses. Scholars who were the sons of noblemen dined with the Canons, and a great nuisance they were to the Canons, for they were most of them of a tender age, twelve or therabouts, and their table manners left much to be desired. It was true they were waited on, as the Canons also were, by their own servants, who tucked their napkins in at their necks, picked up the pieces of bread they hurled on the floor, thumped them on the back when they choked over capon bones and saw to it that they did not drink more than was good for them ; but even then they were a nuisance, and made intellectual conversation among the Canons totally impossible.

... It was only by the skin of his teeth that Philip had avoided being one of them. Had the Earl of Leicester, Chancellor of the University, been his father instead of mercifully only his uncle he would have. Philip, a humble person, daily gave thanks for his escape.

Pandemonium was reigning in the hall when Giles and Faithful entered. Leapfrog was being played round and round the tables and a brisk game of club kayles was going on in the open space by the fire. Faithful joined in at once, but Giles, bored and aloof, perched on the edge of a table and took his Greek Testament out of his wallet. . . . The amount of Greek that he mastered while waiting for and eating his meals was incredible. . . . Faithful was popular. Not only had he the kind of back view that simply cries out to be kicked but, what was more, he did not in the least mind having it kicked. It was fun, too, to jeer at him for his huge head and flapping ears, and the good-humoured grin and well-aimed blow with which he received all mocking references to his person, and hid the hurt they did him, were very endearing. Giles, strangely enough, was popular too. There was a fire and a force in him that commanded respect, and " youth with comeliness plucked all gaze his way."

Suddenly the hubbub stilled a little, though it did not cease, for there had entered upon them with arrogant step and princely stride the scholars over twenty years of age. These gentlemen were in a peculiarly happy position, for Wolsey's statutes had laid down that no scholar over the age of twenty was to be flogged, though under that age the great Cardinal considered corporal punishment highly beneficial. It was this happy immunity from violence that caused persons of over twenty to look so pleased with themselves. They could now swear as much as they liked and get nothing worse than a fine of twelve pence per cuss overheard by authority, which to a man of means, as many of them were, was a mere flea-bite.

Glances of envy and hatred followed the progress of these gentlemen up the hall. Nicolas especially, playing club kayles by the fire, glowered like the devil himself. For Nicolas still had two more years to run before he reached the haven of twenty years, and it was more than probable that he would have to go down from Christ Church without ever winning immunity from flogging. That very afternoon, upon returning from archery practice, he had been soundly flogged by the Senior Censor for having shot an Alderman. It was the Alderman's own fault. He had himself placed his person—of the usual Aldermanic shape, several yards round—between Nicolas's flying arrow and its mark at exactly the wrong moment. It was true that Nicolas had forgotten the rule of calling out " Fast ! " before he shot, but that had been a mere oversight, in no way intentional. And anyhow the Alderman's figure was so enwrapped with layers of fat that the arrow had been unable to penetrate to any vital part, so Nicolas could see no necessity for the Senior Censor to make such a song and dance about it. . . . He was so stiff that he doubted if he would even be able to sit down to imbibe nourishment.

Then came a long, shrill blast on a trumpet, blown by a servitor posted at the hall door, everyone scuttled to their seats and dead silence fell as the Dean, the Canons, the senior College dons—the Treasurer, the two Censors and the Readers in Natural and Moral Philosophy, Dialectic, Rhetoric and Mathematics —together with the noblemen and their servants entered the hall in procession.

Dean Thomas Godwin entered first. He was a breathtaking figure, tall and of an amazing dignity and comeliness. It was no wonder that the Queen's Grace, always peculiarly susceptible to male charm, went all of a dither as soon as she set eyes on him. His black gown, made of the finest cloth and most delicately perfumed, swept the ground as he moved and his ruff was snowy as blackthorn blossom. He had magnificent dark eyes with delicately pencilled brows and a fine, gracefully pointed silky beard. The eight Canons and the College dons who followed him, like stately magpies in their black and white, might have been fine looking men, but one did not notice them beside Dean Godwin.

After them came the little noblemen in all their glory. The rules about modest garb that prevented other scholars from making much of a splash in the haberdashery line was found to be difficult of application to those of noble birth—their august fathers were apt to cut up rough at any curtailment of the wardrobe—so these small people were a sight to behold. They wore velvet trunks, with silken hose gartered at the knee with scarlet. Their little shoes were of softest leather worked in gold thread, with pompons on them, and trod the tiled floor in fine disdain. Their doublets were of all colours of the rainbow, encrusted with jewels, and one or two of them, and those the youngest, wore pearl drops in their ears. . . . Yet their passing lit no envy in the breasts of poorer scholars. . . . For these imps were future courtiers of Gloriana, destined for her service, and Gloriana ruled supreme over the breast of nearly everything in trunk and hose from north to south, from east to west, of the pleasant land of England.

The tail of the procession was made up of the servants of the great ones who had just passed by. In winter they would have carried the lighted lanterns that lit their masters across the dark quadrangle, but now, in summer, they carried only bowls of rose water, and folded napkins laid over their arms.

Dean Godwin mounted the dais, the Canons, dons and noblemen took their places, their servants behind them, grace was sung, and the pantlers, who had toiled up the stone steps from the kitchen below, entered one behind the other with the great dishes upon their shoulders.

At the tables in the lower part of the hall they had the usual beer and beef, bread and oatmeal, enlivened with fresh garden peas and a little fruit, but at the high table they had as well capons, pies, marchpanes and jellies. Their drinks were more varied, too, for as well as beer they drank burgundy and malmsey wine. The scholars below envied them their burgundy but not their malmsey. Years later one of them was to complain that the College malmsey " still tastes of the Duke."

The four friends sat together, or rather three of them sat, for Nicolas, unable as yet to bend the figure, stood, and held forth upon his woes at the top of his voice between each bite. Faithful and Philip, their mouths full, made sympathetic noises, and Giles, his book propped open in front of him, read, taking no notice of any one of them, masticating his food meanwhile with the unconscious thoroughness of a cow chewing the cud.

A babel of voices rose and fell, swelled and roared, the sound beating up to the ceiling and rolling in waves from side to side of the wainscoted walls. Jaws champed and heads were tipped well back that knives might shovel peas into capacious mouths without spilling half of them under the table. Bones, when finished with, were thrown on the floor or hurled at the head of a dear friend. The pantlers, swearing and perspiring, rushed hither and thither, refilling the horn cups, bringing in fresh supplies of beef and dodging the crusts of bread thrown at them by well-wishers. The fumes of hot humanity and meat and drink mingled with the wood smoke and hung over the scene in a dense cloud through which the rich colours of the stained-glass windows, the silver on the high table and the jewels of the noblemen, winked and gleamed like the lights of a harbour seen through a mist at sea. The noise, the smoke and the smell rose to a final crescendo of volume, aroma and density and then, suddenly, it was over, and the trumpet was announcing the departure of the Dean, Canons, dons and noblemen from the hall.

They departed as they had come, magnificently, the Dean holding a scented handkerchief to his nose with one hand and with the other lifting the skirts of his fine gown well above the bone-strewn floor.

It was now considered right that there should be a brief half-hour of rest and recreation before the scholars returned to their work, and the din that broke out was unequalled by anything that had gone before. The interrupted games of leapfrog became more and more violent, the pantlers meanwhile clearing the tables at peril of their lives, while by the fire the game of club kayles waxed very hot.

It was only ninepins, the pins being aimed at with a stick, but an elaborate system of betting had been evolved in connection with it so that a good deal of heat was likely to be engendered, the tall pointed pins, shaped like fir cones, coming in very handy as missiles. In the rhyme of the period young men were implored to " Eschew always evil company, kayles, carding and haserdy." But at Christ Church, if they had heard the rhyme, they had failed to lay it to heart.

II

Afterwards, no one was quite sure how the great fight started. The scholars said it started on the dais, where the servants of the Canons were quarrelling with the servants of the noblemen over what was left of the food, which was their perquisite. The servants, on the other hand, said it was nothing on earth to do with them ; they quarrelled about the food every evening and nothing came of it ; no, it was the fault of the young gentlemen playing club kayles by the fire.

And certain it was that Nicolas, already in a bad temper from one reason and another, had hit Toby Stapleton over the head with the kayles stick. He had reason to, for Toby had cheated, and had moreover a wart on the end of his nose that always annoyed Nicolas, but his action was unwise because Toby hailed from Westminster, while Nicolas himself hailed from Ipswich.

The famous school at Ipswich had been founded by Cardinal Wolsey, and naturally its boys came up to Christ Church in large numbers, and between them and the Westminster scholars there was naturally a loathing too deep for words. Westminster had to be careful what it said to Ipswich, and vice versa, for the slightest word, or a blow given with the best of intentions, was liable to be misconstrued and act like a torch set to a haystack.

The thing was in full swing before anyone knew it had started. Shouting and yelling the mob surged backwards and forwards, kicking, scuffling, hitting and swearing. The servants' quarrel on the dais somehow got tacked on to the scholars' quarrel down below, and the minor quarrel, being conducted by grown men and strong, succeeded in pushing the whole horde of them out of the hall door and on to the staircase. Here the pantlers and cooks came dashing up from the kitchen below to join in, and the whole mass surged down the stairs and across the quadrangle to the Fair Gate. Heatherthwayte, of course, should have shut the great gates and stopped them, but he was having forty winks at the moment and by the time he had got his mouth shut and his eyes open and staggered towards the gates it was too late ; he and Satan were picked up like a couple of straws by the advancing tide and carried out into Fish Street.

And out in Fish Street the row took an entirely new turn. Within half an hour of its occurrence Nicolas's little upset with the Alderman had been the talk of the town. The story grew with the telling as it was handed from corn factor to merchant's wife, from merchant's wife to servant girl, and servant girl to apprentice. Within an hour of the accident, what time Alderman Burridge was seated comfortably at home with a tankard of ale at his elbow, he was reported to be dying in agonies, and half an hour later he was dead. The Alderman was popular and the rage and fury of the town was unbounded. By six o'clock quite a nasty little crowd had collected at Carfax and a few bold spirits had marched down towards Christ Church and were considering the advisability of demanding that Nicolas be delivered up to justice. A few bargees, strolling up from the river to get a drink in the town, encountered these gentlemen, and heard the latest version of Alderman Burridge's murder, so that by the time Westminster and Ipswich, locked in combat, reeled out of the Fair Gate they found the Town ready for them.

Word of the grand fight going on in Fish Street between Town and Gown, over Alderman Burridge's murder, flew round Oxford. Reinforcements to both sides flocked out of every College, house and inn in the town and rushed to the scene of action. In no time at all there was one dense crowd of fighting humanity right up Fish Street, across Carfax and down Cornmarket; seething backwards and forwards like a turbulent sea, shouting, yelling, kicking and swearing. The Proctors, with the Constable of the watch and his minions, were powerless. They danced up and down on the edge of the hurly-burly, shouting and threatening, but no one noticed them, let alone attended to them. The excitement rose to fever pitch and, quite suddenly, a flight of arrows appeared, shot by unseen bowmen inside the Swyndlestock, a tavern at the south-west corner of Carfax. It was not known for certain who shot them, whether Town or Gown, though it was thought Town because of the raucous cries of "Who shot the Alderman?" that accompanied them, but a wild yell of fury rose up and rent the very heavens, for this was not playing fair; fists, nails, sticks, dead cats, rotten eggs and other missiles of a like character might be used in a Town and Gown riot, but not arrows. . . . Things began to look uncommonly ugly.

It was now that Dean Godwin showed the stuff of which he was made. Mounted on his black horse, still attired in his black gown and white ruff, and with his riding whip in his hand, he issued out of the Fair Gate. Forcing his terrified horse through the crowd, and slashing with his whip to right and left, he gained the summit of Carfax. As he sat there, reining in his horse but still using his whip, a little oasis of calm formed about him, the crowd falling momentarily back. . . . For Dean

Godwin in a rage was an awesome sight, and his whip, with the full force of his arm behind it, could sting. . . . But there was no possibility of making himself heard beyond the little circle immediately round him that contained, he saw to his astonishment, Philip Sidney, the Poet, and Faithful Crocker, the Scholar, torn and dishevelled and bloodstained and shouting as loudly as any there. . . . Really, thought the Dean in a moment of depression, if our scholars and poets can be corrupted into yelling hooligans in the space of a mere half-hour the hope for civilization is small. . . . Stretching out his riding whip he hooked them towards him and looked upon them with disfavour.

"What are *you* doing here?" he demanded of Faithful.

Faithful removed a broken tooth from his mouth, spat out some blood, and shook his huge head in complete ignorance. . . . He didn't know why he was here; he only knew that he was enjoying himself hugely.

"And you, Philip Sidney," said the Dean sternly, "you can, I hope, at least tell me the cause of this disgraceful riot in which you, a man of birth and breeding, are behaving like one of the lower animals."

Philip had no idea what they were fighting about, but, wiping blood from his nose, he had the grace to look ashamed of himself. He hadn't really wanted to come, for he imagined that he loathed riots, he had come because he hadn't been able to help himself. But now that he was actually in it he found to his surprise that even to the poets of this world physical combat has its joys.

"If you two are here to show the stuff of which you are made," said the Dean with sarcasm, "you will kindly show it by fighting your way to Saint Martin's and ringing the bell to get me a hearing."

The culprits bowed and accepted the task. Faithful with all his experience of London streets knew well how to get through crowds. Covering his eyes with his arm and lowering his head he butted his way through, kicking and pummelling when necessary, Philip joyously following. The crowd opposed them for all it was worth, but they fought their way on, fighting now with an added joy because it was a Holy War, the cause of law and order for which they kicked draping a veil of seemliness over their primitive methods of attack.

But it was a relief, all the same, to reach the great grey rock of Saint Martin's, and they clung to it for a moment, panting, before they opened the door and went inside, stumbled up the dark spiral staircase to the cobwebbed belfry and fell upon the bellrope.

In another moment a tocsin was booming out over the clamorous city, as it had done in moments of stress since Oxford was first a town; when the Northmen had come up the river in their terrible longboats to pillage and burn, during the days of the civil war when the city stood for Queen Matilda and the army of Stephen was sighted coming up out of the mist, or again during the great riot of Saint Scholastica's Day, when Town and Gown fought each other for three days and nights and sixty scholars were killed. These memories and many others were present in the corporate memory of the crowd as the bell of Saint Martin's tolled out; a strange hush fell, full of only half-understood little undercurrents of fear, and the oasis of calm that had already gathered about Dean Godwin grew and spread like oil poured on a turbulent sea, so that in a little while he found himself speaking into a dead silence.

It puzzled him. The sea of faces raised to his wore the stamp of fear; the crowd seemed turning to him as though he were there to save them from some awful danger; the stillness was deep with the pain of the silent poor who must suffer for the sins of the mighty. . . . For a moment he himself did not quite know where in time he was. He felt uncertain of his own personality, knowing only that he had sat his horse at the centre of a Carfax crowd a hundred times before. The scene about him seemed to flicker and change, the buildings blocked against the sky took now one shape, now another, a hundred different crowds seemed to surge against him, one melting into mist as another was super-imposed upon it, and he himself was by turn Soldier, Priest and King. Only the earth beneath his horse's feet, the little hill of Quadrefurcus that had always been here, remained firm and unchanging and brought him back to reality. . . . The bell ceased tolling and he remembered that this occasion was quite a trivial one; he took a grip of himself and of the crowd.

What was the matter this time, he demanded? Why was this peaceful, God-fearing city turned into a bedlam? This was the sixteenth century, he shouted at them. This was the Present Day, not the Dark Ages. Anyone would think, from the fuss they were making, that the Danes were upon them again, or an invading army clamouring at West Gate. What was the matter with them?

The bell had stopped ringing and the spell was broken. The fear had gone and the silence had gone. The crowd was itself again and eager to give information.

"Alderman Burridge is murdered!" yelled a dozen voices.

"Murdered?" said the Dean, "I think not." He pointed with his whip to the Constable of the watch, propped panting against the wall of Saint Martin's. "Constable, go instantly to the house of Alderman Burridge and bring us word of his true state."

Nothing loth the Constable made off, for Alderman Burridge lived only just round the corner by Great Baily, and the Dean meanwhile harangued the crowd, his fine, sonorous voice rolling over them in a perfect tornado of chastisement. He had the gift of the gab, had the Dean, and he had not half finished what he wanted to say by the time the Constable came hurrying back.

"Well?" demanded the Dean. "Stand up here on my stirrup."

"Alderman Burridge," roared the Constable, mounting beside the Dean, "is very little injured, praise be to Almighty God, and has, so says his worship, enjoyed this evening's entertainment mightily."

A little gust of laughter blew up at the centre of Carfax, gathered and spread, running through the crowd like fire, and soon the whole of it was rocking in a great gale of mirth. Those on the outskirts, who had not been able to hear what went on in the centre, had not an idea what they were laughing at, any more than a great many of them knew what they had been fighting for, but hands on hips they roared with the rest.

Faithful and Philip, kneeling on the dirty belfry floor, peered through the narrow slits of windows at the scene around and below them.

It was a marvellous sight.

Sunset lay over the city. The sky above was a heavenly blue, unutterably peaceful and of a depth that seemed to reach to eternity, but to the west, behind the grey mass of the Castle, it was a molten streaming gold, as though a great furnace blazed beyond the rim of the world. The towers and spires of the city, quietly watchful, rose dazzlingly fair against the blue sky, and caught the reflection of that streaming gold on their comely crests, but down below them the huddled roofs of the city were bathed in tawny shadows. Beyond the town the meadows and the winding streams and the willow trees had drawn damp blue mists over their beauty, but beyond them the hills, like the towers, had light on their crests. And right at the heart of that beauty, a strange centre for such peace, was the laughing, jostling, rowdy crowd ; the city folk in their jerkins, caps and doublets of red and yellow and green bright splashes of colour amongst the sober-hued scholars. Their laughing faces, upturned to the stately figure on the black horse, caught the last of the sun and seemed alight with it, burning with an everlasting vitality. . . . No, there is no death, thought Philip, only a perpetual readjustment of the garment of life. . . . And how lovely, and how endlessly various, is this garment. The beauty of what he saw now caught at his breath and quick, broken little phrases of description came winging their way like butterflies into his opened mind. Swinging away from the window he put an arm over his eyes, trying to close his mind's door, to shut it fast on those phrases. They must lie there, dormant as an artist's tubes of colours, till he had time to take them out and fasten them together into a poem. . . . But would they stay there ? . . . The loveliest phrases are winged, and when the poet opens the door of the place where he put them he finds that the tiresome creatures have flown away.

"Here !" shouted Faithful from his window. "They're taking Nicolas and Giles to Bocardo !"

It was too true. Dean Godwin, before turning his horse and riding back to Christ Church, had indicated with his whip those who, in his opinion, had been ringleaders in the riot, and Nicolas and Giles were among them. Faithful and Philip could see them, Giles white with fury and Nicolas crimson with it, standing below the tower in the firm grasp of the Constable of the Watch.

Faithful and Philip were good friends and it was the work but of a moment to race down the stone steps of the tower and assault the Constable in the back. It did no good, however, for a couple of apprentices, self-appointed assistants of the Constable, seized them and cuffed them and in a moment all four were being marched down Cornmarket. It was a humiliating progress, for groups of uproarious townsfolk, reeling off to their houses and taverns with arms linked, mocked and jeered.

Giles was in a cold fury. . . . Here he was wasting his time again. . . . It had not been his fault that he had joined in the riot, he had been lifted off his feet and planted down in the middle of it without being able to help himself, but it had been his fault that he had got himself arrested. In spite of himself he had got carried away by the excitement of the thing. He had had no weapon but his Greek Testament, but he flattered himself that with that he had knocked out as many of the enemy teeth as other scholars had done with clubs and sticks.

"You'll have plenty of time to work in Bocardo," replied Nicolas sullenly, to Giles's complaints of his lot.

"No good without my books, you owl," snapped Giles. "Even my Testament's gone now. Some brute tore it out of my hand."

"You did a lot with it first," comforted Faithful.

"Never mind," said Philip sweetly from the rear. "Walter Raleigh will be so pleased to see us."

III

But Raleigh had not spent an unhappy evening. At first, when the sounds of battle reached his ears, he had looked out of the window, clutching the bars and bitterly cursing his fate. . . . It was always the same. . . . Whenever there was something really exciting going on in the city, something, moreover, that could be enjoyed without any financial outlay, he was always locked up in Bocardo, and when University life pursued the even tenor of its way, and there was nothing cheap to do but work, he was free as air. He continued cursing, with vigour and an extraordinary flow of language, for several minutes, and then turned abruptly back to the stool and the rough table where he had been working. Well, let the solvent enjoy themselves without him. Insolvent though he might be he had that to think of which was worth all the street fights in the world.

Raleigh, like Faithful, went through life with his library attached to his person, but his gods were not Virgil and the Martyrs but Baldassare Castiglione, and his half-brother Humphrey Gilbert. Castiglione's *Cortegiano* was always in his hand and Humphrey's collection of sea-charts buttoned up inside his doublet. He read the first to fit himself for the adventure to which the second called him.

In the *Cortegiano* Castiglione portrayed the perfect gentleman; well-born, well-dressed, free and forceful in speech, learned, accomplished, magnificent and charming, courageous in battle, a leader and captain of men. Raleigh studied this portrait, modelling himself upon it line for line, preparing himself for the day when his speech must light men's imagination and his courage fire theirs, when his wisdom and knowledge must seem to them trustworthy and his personality one to be followed to the death.

His dream, to win for England an Empire beyond the sea, never seemed to him a dream too great to realise. He had a colossal pride. What he wanted to do he believed he ultimately could do. He was descended from the Plantagenets, he had the blood of kings in his veins, he had beauty and courage and vision, he had only to command men and surely they would follow. And his dream had been bred in him; it was bone of his bone and flesh of his flesh. It had been his in childhood when the chief excitement in his west-country home, built amongst the moors above the river Dart, was the return of sailors from the sea. Many a bronzed mariner found his way to the manor house and sat before the fire with the Raleigh and Gilbert boys, telling mythical tales of the mystic west that set their minds on fire. Those were the days when Humphrey Gilbert, with little Walter to help, began to draw his sea-charts, half in joke and half in earnest. Some of them lay on the table before Raleigh now, inscribed with names that set his blood tingling. . . . America. Cathay. The Indies. . . . Strange fantastic coastlines had Humphrey given to these countries, and strange sea monsters had he drawn swimming the seas; and fine ships with bellying sails, not so big as the sea monsters, but bigger than America, made their way unerringly to the place where they would be. There was an element of fun in these maps but there was gravity too. In the corner of one of them Humphrey had written words that Raleigh knew by heart. " Give me leave always to live and die in this mind, that he is not worthy to live at all that for fear of danger or death shunneth his country's service and his own honour, seeing death is inevitable and the fame of virtue immortal. Wherefore in this behalf, mutare vel timere sperno."

Raleigh shut his eyes, that no material sight might creep between him and the stately passing of the pictures that his fancy painted. The riot in the town came to him only dimly, like the beating of waves on the shore or the sound of the wind on the moors at home. " America," he whispered to himself. " Cathay. The Indies." And then again, " America." Only the fringe of it was known. Beyond that lay a great no-man's-land that held one knew not what, a land where there might be a great nation of English-speaking men and women. He beat his fists upon the table. God in heaven, what a time to be alive! It was like living in a fairy-tale. It was like living in a hall with a hundred doors ; you might choose which one you opened but behind them all there was mystery. He wondered if there would ever come an age when all the world would be known. If so, he thanked God that he did not live in that age. He thanked God that he lived now, at this moment of time when chinks of mysterious light shone from beneath closed doors, now when it was still possible for a man to sail out into the blue and build a new Empire for his country. Would he do it while he lived, or would he do it after death ? Though he never doubted ultimate victory he sometimes thought that his dream was too big to be realised in his life. He knew that he was sometimes now hated for his pride. Other men's hatred might yet be the rock that would wreck him. Yet, he thought, though he might not realise his dreams he might die for them, and it only wanted a small acquaintance with history to tell him that it is the dreams that are died for that live. Blood had a mystic quality. The life of a man was in it. Poured upon the hard earth it brought new things to birth. What did he care if he died ? " Death is inevitable, but the fame of virtue immortal." One day, not only England, but those men beyond the sunset, so far removed from him that he could not even picture the cities they would build or the glorious shaping of their history, would hold his memory in perpetual honour. He knew that they would. Arrogantly he placed himself amongst the immortal gods, drinking his fill of fame. Words formed themselves in his mind.

> "My soul will be a-dry before,
> But after it will thirst no more."

IV

Steps stumbling up the stone stairs disturbed him, and he raised his head angrily. Who was coming here to break in upon his dreams? Drunken brawlers from that riot in the town? He sprang up, meaning to push the table across the door, to keep them out at all costs. Then suddenly he changed his mind. Whoever they were he would try his power over them; see if he could fire them with his own enthusiasm; see if it was true that he was a born leader of men. There was an altercation going on on the stairs and he had a little time. With long cat-like leaps he bounded about the room, tidying his possessions out of sight, bringing out his supply of candles, lighting them and wedging them firmly in their own grease on table and window-sill, placing a loaf of mouldy bread and a jug of water on the table, and then, as the door burst open and four battered, disreputable scholars were pushed in by the old jailor, standing with one hand at his hip and the other sweeping an imaginary hat from his head as he bowed and bowed again. "Good evening, gentlemen," he cried, "good evening. . . . By cock and pie, it's the four bugs!"

He burst into a great roar of laughter and Nicolas, Giles, Philip and Faithful, who a moment ago had been feeling sore, dispirited and weary, suddenly felt as though they had been picked up by a great wind and set down in the one place where they wanted to be. They roared too, holding their sides, staggering as Raleigh hit them on the back, going into gale upon gale of mirth as though they had just been told the most exquisite joke in all the world. The old jailor, bringing in four more straw pallets, four more stools, some cracked platters and villainous-looking bit of cold meat, laughed too, tears of mirth running out of his old eyes and his toothless gums showing in a wide grin. . . . There was some magic in this young cockerel with the bright blue eyes, he thought, as he took his final departure, some strange unexplainable magic for which, unlearned as he was, he could find no name.

"Sit down, gentlemen," said Raleigh, motioning them with an imperial gesture to take their places round the festal board. "There is venison here, lark pie, marchpane, pasties, ale, wines of all sorts. Take your choice. Make yourselves at home. All that I have is yours." Laughing, they pulled their stools up to the table and fell upon the feast with the appetite of hungry lions.

The other three had fallen before beneath the spell of Walter Raleigh. They knew of old how his superb gestures could create an illusion of grandeur that dazzled the eyes for just as long as he chose that it should, but Faithful was coming into close contact with Raleigh for the first time and was utterly bewildered. . . . This room where they sat was no longer a dirty little lock-up, but a room in a palace, the cold meat and bread that they ate off cracked platters were venison and pasties upon golden dishes, the water was the nectar of the gods and the flickering tallow candles burned as though all the stars of heaven had come trooping in to light them. They forgot their aches and pains and bruises, they forgot the dreary uncomfortable imprisonment that stretched before them, they forgot everything but the figure of Raleigh sitting at the head of the table, waving his knife in the air and telling them exciting tales in glorious language and a strong Devonshire accent.

In sober moments Raleigh's friends had no faith in his stories, but to-night he held them spellbound. "In America," he said, "vines laden with grapes cling to tall cedar trees, and sitting beneath them the natives drink the powdered bones of their chieftains in pineapple wine,"

"Why?" asked Nicolas. . . . The customs of these people seemed to him odd.

"That they may have their courage in them, of course," cried Raleigh, bringing his knife-hilt down with a crash on the table. "Don't you know that we all of us feed on the courage of the dead? If there had been no valiant men in the past to show us the way to live would we be anything to-day but spineless idiots? If we *are* spineless idiots in this generation, will the men of the future have any chance of winning an Empire for England? No!" he shouted, taking a long pull of water from the jug. "It is now or never, gentlemen, now or never.

"Tell us some more," said Philip, with kindling eyes. "It is very beautiful, that land?"

"There are great mountains there," said Raleigh, "crowned with snow, higher than you can conceive, and cataracts fall from them, every one as high as a church tower, thundering to the ground with the reverberation of a thousand great bells clanging together. The waters run in many channels through fair grassy plains, and there are paths there for the deer, paved with stones of gold and silver. The birds towards evening sing on every tree with a thousand several tunes, and cranes and herons of white, crimson and carnation perch beside the rivers. . . . Do you wonder, gentlemen, that I should wish to win this land of beauty for the Queen? I would give my life that she might have a better Indies than the King of Spain has any."

"I do not think," said Philip softly, "that any land could be fairer than this land. I would rather give my life to keep the beauty of this one unpolluted."

Faithful looked from Raleigh to Philip Sidney and marvelled at them both. Utterly unlike as they were, they had something in common, some powerful attraction that would surely bring men tumbling at their heels wherever they might lead. Faithful, belonging to an age that attributed the unexplainable to the stars, told himself that no clouds had veiled the sky when they were born. They had more star-shine in their souls than most men. It shone out of them like the light of another country, expressing itself quite differently in their two personalities, but the same in essence. In Philip it was a luminous beauty of character, in Raleigh it was an arresting combination of recklessness and intellectual power. He had the scholar's mind and the adventurer's temperament and the two together were as startling as a thunderstorm. Philip's leadership through the darkness of life would be like a lighted lantern going on ahead, But Raleigh's would be like lightning, more exciting, and revealing more of the surrounding country, but not so steady.

"What a liar you are, Raleigh," said Giles with admiration. . . . They were beginning to sink down now from the high level of excitement to which Raleigh had whirled them, and criticism, albeit admiring, was creeping in.

Raleigh grinned. He knew himself to be a consummate liar, and knew too that his inspired inability to draw the line between solid fact and the creations of his own fantasy was one of his most valuable gifts as a propagandist. He laughed as he realised that though they might be critical now, he had yet been able to sweep them off their feet. He knew, and none better, " how to tell the world."

" But what I tell you now," he said, once more pounding his knife-hilt on the table, " is true. I have at last discovered the Great Cordial and Elixir of Life."

" Moonshine ! " said Giles.

" You'll blow the roof off Oriel with your abominable stinks," Philip cautioned him.

Faithful, his head still whirling, realised that the talk had turned to Raleigh's chemical experiments. " Will the Great Cordial really make money enough for all you want to do ? " he asked breathlessly.

Raleigh turned his shining eyes upon him. " It turns base metals into gold," he said, " and taken internally as medicine it prolongs the life for no one knows how long. Alchemists have been experimenting to find the formula for generations, but it has been left to me, Walter Raleigh, to succeed."

" And you've actually used the Elixir ? " whispered Faithful. " You've turned something into gold ? "

" Not yet," said Raleigh, " but as soon as I've paid my debts, and am out of here, you shall all come to Oriel and see me do it. . . . And then you shall drink of it yourselves and live for ever."

No one but Faithful seemed keen.

" The roof would come off," Philip objected again.

" If we drank your muck we certainly should live for ever," said Giles grimly, jerking his thumb towards the dirty floor. " Down there."

Raleigh's own enthusiasm was quite unquenched by their lack of it. " Do you write verse ? " he asked Faithful.

Faithful shook his large head sadly. Everyone up at the University seemed a poet. They all wrote verse, whether they could or not, and Faithful was ashamed to be amongst the few in this city of laughter who lacked the singing voice.

" That's a pity," said Raleigh, " because I have a verse-reading in my rooms every Sunday afternoon and at the next one I shall, before reading my verses, make a demonstration with my Elixir. . . . Never mind," he said generously, " you shall come all the same, even if you don't write verse, and help me clear up the mess."

"There'll be one," said Nicolas gloomily. "Bones and blood and the ruins of Oriel."

But Raleigh was still undamped. He took some papers scratched over with strange diagrams out of his wallet, spread them on the table among the remains of the feast and the drippings from the candles, and began to explain and argue and persuade, his eyes blazing in the candlelight, his voice growing rich and soft as a cat's purr as he cajoled them, mocked at their unbelief, and once more laid siege to their imaginations.

"No more poverty," he cried excitedly. "My Elixir will make gold as common as the cobbles in the street. We shall pave this city of Oxford with gold, I tell you, like the streets of the New Jerusalem. Away with the children of poverty, sickness and thieving and envy and hate, down with them into hell! As well as building a new Empire beyond the sea, we shall build a new world in England. It will be the Golden Age at last!"

"I wonder how many times men have said that before?" commented the sceptical Giles. "It's all very well to lay the foundations of a new world, it's often been done, but as soon as the walls are built up a little way, something pushes them over."

"Death," said Raleigh. "The death of the men of vision who were the builders. . . . But with my Elixir the life of the great will be prolonged indefinitely. Those whom the gods love will live, not die. The earth will be peopled by upright kings, poets, dreamers, who will see their life's work through to the end."

"The rogues and vagabonds might want to have their lives indefinitely prolonged, too," suggested Faithful. Enthusiastic as he was, he could foresee a lot of difficulties.

"Croakers!" said Raleigh scornfully. "Oh, ye of little faith, finish up the food and let's have some singing. Eat, drink and be merry, for to-morrow, without my Elixir, the likes of you will die."

They finished the bread and water and began to sing, roaring out song after song, thumping the table with the handles of their knives, until the whole of Bocardo rang with their singing. Other prisoners in their cells heard and sang too, and the old deaf jailer, sitting on the stone steps outside enjoying a little meal of his own, stopped eating to cup his hand behind his ear to listen. . . . Times were changing, he thought, times were changing. These were good days. He could remember other days, and not so long ago either, when there had been no singing in Bocardo. Men had spent their last days on earth in Bocardo. Archbishop Cranmer had been led out to die at the stake from that very room where those boys were feasting. The Archbishop had eaten his last meal there and he, John Bretchegyrdle, had served it to him. . . . He hadn't fancied it. . . . Well, times were changing, he thanked God, and a new world being built by these youngsters. He wished good luck to their building, he, an old man who would not live to see what they had built. . . . He removed his hand from his ear, for the singing had died away, nodded once or twice and was asleep.

v

In the prisoners' room they had spread their pallets and all but Faithful had fallen asleep too. They were so drugged by weariness and Raleigh's dreams that they had forgotten their cuts and bruises, the discomfort of their beds and the hardness of their lot. All night they would sleep blissfully, without moving, undisturbed by each other's grunts and snores, presented by fickle sleep with that blessed gift of oblivion that in her favouritism she bestows only upon the healthy and happy who do not need it.

But it did not come all at once to Faithful. The other four were sleeping side by side on the further side of the table, but Faithful, being only a servitor, had thought it right to lay his pallet at a respectful distance, under the window that looked on Cornmarket.

But he could not get comfortable on it. He began to feel very itchy. He scratched himself on his back and he scratched himself on his chest, and he scratched himself up and down his thighs, and then he realised with horror there were other people besides himself on, and in, this straw pallet. . . . The last prisoner to lie on it must have left them behind as a donation to Bocardo.

Faithful had become fastidious since he came up to Oxford, and he didn't like it. He rolled hastily off the pallet, scurried to the table and climbed upon it. The creatures would find him in time, of course, for they were intelligent creatures; they would climb up the walls, stroll across the ceiling and drop upon him from above ; but he had a little while before they thought of that.

He sat cross-legged on the table, his body cold and tired and itching, but his mind burning with excitement. What a day he had had ! A glorious day of eating, drinking, learning, dreaming and fighting. Picture after picture flashed across his mind ; the tower of the Cathedral clear-cut against the sky in the morning light ; a racing sea, frilled with white-capped waves, over which a ship had carried him to the Isles of Greece ; the laughing coloured crowd at Carfax lit up by the sunset ; the mystic land of the west where carnation coloured birds perch beside the rivers ; and last of all Raleigh's dream of a city paved with gold where there was no more sin.

And suddenly the midsummer moon of Sidney's poem had risen. She came out from behind a cloud, round and white as a moon-daisy, and Oxford was flooded with her light. Cornmarket was clear as daylight, and the tower of Saint Martin's with a white cloud floating from it like a banner, and the Fair Gate of Christ Church with the stars above it. The rats were illumined too, dancing about in Cornmarket in rich happiness, for this was their hour and no man defrauded them of it.

This was his hour, too, thought Faithful. To-day, he had been happy, and neither the past nor the future could take to-day away from him. Suddenly he was so overwhelmingly sleepy that all discomfort vanished. He curled himself up on the hard table and went to sleep, to dream that he was king of the world.

CHAPTER VII

MIDSUMMER EVE

Praised be Diana's fair and harmless light,
Praised be the dews, wherewith she moists the ground,
Praised be her beams, the glory of the night,
Praised be her power, by which all powers abound.

Praised be her nymphs, with whom she decks the woods,
Praised be her knights, in whom true honour lives,
Praised be that force, by which she moves the floods;
Let that Diana shine, which all these gives.

In heaven Queen she is among the spheres,
In earth she mistress-like makes all things pure,
Eternity in her oft change she bears,
She beauty is, by her the fair endure.

Time wears her not, she doth his chariot guide,
Mortality below her orb is placed,
By her the virtue of the stars down slide,
In her is virtue's perfect image cast.

A knowledge pure it is her worth to know,
With Circes let them dwell that think not so.
WALTER RALEIGH.

I

THE next day was the feast of Saint John the Baptist and the University authorities, very stately in cap and gown, progressed in a body to hear the University sermon preached from the open air pulpit in the quadrangle of Magdalen College. The pulpit was hung with green boughs and the ground was strewn with rushes, in memory of Saint John preaching in the wilderness, the sky was blue and the hearts of all sang for gladness because in honour of Saint John the morning was free from lectures. It was true the sermon lasted for over an hour, but the rushes were sweet and fragrant to sit upon, and if thoughts wandered they followed the birds through sunshine and blue air to the place where the dreams come true.

There was a spirit of leisure abroad in Oxford that day, a

light-heartedness that belonged to Midsummer Eve. The colour of the flowers in the gardens seemed richer than usual, and their scent sweeter. The day was made for love and laughter, for staring at the lilies and praising the deep vermilion of the rose, and everyone hastened to put it to its proper use.

Even the industrious and learned felt singularly disinclined for labour. After the early dinner in hall, the Dean and Canon Leigh found themselves strolling backwards and forwards over the trampled flowers and grass of the quadrangle, enjoying the warmth and the soft south wind that brought with it the scent of the fields and hedgerows beyond South Gate, discussing with an air of great gravity trivial matters that would not have detained them in the quadrangle for a single moment had the wind been in the east.

A stone in the centre of the quadrangle marked the site of an old preaching cross, where the friars had preached to the common folk whose hovels Cardinal Wolsey had pulled down, and here they paused a moment, their thoughts going backwards over the history of their College and forward to its future.

"What we want here," said the Dean, his foot upon the stone, "is a pond."

"What for?" asked Canon Leigh.

"If our scholars, in their last night's stampede from the hall to the Fair Gate, could have encountered a pond midway," said the Dean, "Westminster could have ducked Ipswich in it and there would have been an end of the trouble."

"It would be a bother to dig it," mused Canon Leigh. "The ground is made up of old foundations here."

"I shall leave it to posterity," said Dean Godwin. "I have no doubt that posterity will see the need for a pond. There could be goldfish in it, to give an ostensible reason for its existence and disguise its real purpose."

"No lives lost last night, I hope?" said Canon Leigh.

"No, but some injuries and a good deal of damage done. That scoundrel Nicolas de Worde seems to have been at the bottom of it as usual. He's in Bocardo."

"And I'm afraid that Giles and Faithful, my adopted son, keep him company," said Canon Leigh with shame

"They but followed in the wake," consoled the Dean. "One behind the other like a school of dolphins. It'll do none of them any harm to stay in Bocardo till to-morrow morning. . . . Ah, look there ! There's a sight to console you for the sins of your sons ! "

Canon Leigh looked and his face lit up with pride, for his four daughters, together with his son, Diccon, and his dogs Pippit, Posy and Spot, had issued out from their front door and were crossing the quadrangle with mincing steps. They were going shopping, apparently, for each girl carried a basket of plaited rushes in one hand and a nosegay of flowers to protect her nose from the smells of the town in the other. They had taken off their aprons and on their heads instead of their white caps they wore coifs of velvet to match their dark-blue gowns. Diccon was attired to-day in fairy green, like a miniature Robin Hood, and on his head was a tiny cap with a long peacock's feather in it, a new acquisition that he was wearing for the first time. The dogs were attached to the persons of the twins and Grace with substantial chains, for dogs, with the exception of Satan, were not allowed in College, and if the Canons kept them they must keep them under severe control and not allow them loose in the quadrangle. . . . The Leigh dogs largely spent their day lying just inside the door, waiting for an unsuspecting visitor or tradesman to open it, when they would immediately bounce out, pursued by the entire household with lamentable cries.

" How happy is the man who has his quiver full," quoted the Dean.

He made this remark to Canon Leigh rather frequently ; and though on some days Canon Leigh whole-heartedly agreed with him there were other days when a few doubts made themselves felt. To-day, however, his family looked so charming in the June sunshine that he bowed his head in delighted assent.

II

There was the usual trouble at the Fair Gate between Satan and the Leigh dogs. Satan naturally thought that if it was a College rule that only the porter should keep a dog, that rule should be kept. Exceptions to rules should not be allowed in well-run institutions. He expressed himself upon this point very frequently, and had it not been for Heatherthwayte's firm grip upon his tail he would have wiped out the Leigh dogs long ago.

The children loved Heatherthwayte dearly, and he them, but owing to the presence of the dogs they could do no more to-day than smile hurriedly as they dragged their yowling animals past the enraged Satan.

"Where to?" asked Grace, as Joyeuce paused, considering her shopping list with a wrinkled forehead.

"The apothecary's first," said Joyeuce. "I want some centaury and wormwood."

The children groaned. Joyeuce concocted a particularly nauseous medicine out of camomile, centaury and wormwood, and now and then administered it to her family to clear the blood.

"It's all right," comforted Joyeuce. "This time it's only for Father."

They cheered up and marched on towards Carfax, the little girls keeping their noses buried in their nosegays of roses and lavender, and Joyeuce keeping a firm hold of Diccon lest he should escape and get up to some of his evil tricks.

At Carfax they turned to their right and went down High Street. It was an exciting place, full of strange smells. It contained, besides the pig market in front of All Saints' Church, the butchery and the poultry, and also really beautiful shops like the aurifabray, the mercery, the spicer's and the glover's. There were no multiple shops, where you could buy all sorts of different things under one roof, for Parliament had decreed that "artificers and handicraft people hold them every one to his mystery," and the Oxford Town Council enforced this law very vigorously.

The apothecary of Joyeuce's choice lived just by Saint Mary's Church, in a dark little shop that made one feel indisposed simply to smell it, and the children stayed outside when she went in, holding each other's hands as she bade them, for there were always lots of people hurrying by in High Street and small persons were liable to be knocked flying if they did not hold together and stand foursquare to the bustle.

But they all went inside at the spicer's because it smelt good. You could buy cinnamon at the spicer's, and nutmeg and ginger, and all the wonderful new spices that the Merchant Adventurers were bringing home from foreign parts, and that new-fangled thing pepper, that made one sneeze and ruined one's inside, but was very smart and fashionable. Joyeuce bought some saffron to colour the warden's pies and also a very little pepper as a treat for her father, and before anyone could stop him Diccon had thrust his inquisitive nose inside the packet and was sneezing his green fairy cap off his curls and his head almost off his shoulders. Then he roared, of course, and the spicer's wife came hurrying out from the back premises with a prune in her fingers to comfort him. Prunes were a delicacy that Diccon had not tasted before. He abruptly stopped roaring, ate it, spit out the stone and asked for more. But he did not get it, for Joyeuce, ashamed of him, hastily bade the spicer and his wife good-day and removed him.

Outside in the High Street he roared again and they had to stop at the aurifabray to distract his thoughts from his woes. behind the small, iron-barred window one could glimpse wonderful things; cups and platters all made of gold, gold chains, billements, brooches to pin gentlemen's plumes into their caps, rings for the fingers and ears of fair ladies and little gold bells to be tied to the cradles of wealthy babies. Great-Aunt was the only member of the Leigh family who could afford to be jewelled, so that the girls and Diccon gaped at these glories with round eyes of amazement.

"I wish I had a pearl billement," whispered Grace.

"I should like a diamond ring," said Meg.

"I should like a big gold chain like the Mayor," said Joan.

"I shall have that ruby brooch," said Diccon, pointing a fat finger, "to pin my peacock's feather. . . . I shall have it now."

"You will not," said Joyeuce. "Your days of foppery are not yet set in. When you are big you shall have it."

"How big?" asked Diccon. "When I am twelve?"

"You shall have it," said Joyeuce, "when you are as tall as Giles and as good as Master Philip Sidney."

The corners of Diccon's mouth went down and his little feathered head dropped like a the head of a wilting poppy. He was yet so near the ground that it seemed impossible he could ever be as near the sky as Giles. And as for being as good as Master Philip Sidney, well, he knew he could never be that. He knew that the sun would turn to marchpane and the moon fall out of the sky and bowl like a hoop down the High Street before Diccon Leigh would be as good as Philip Sidney. He felt utterly stricken, for he wanted that ruby more than anything else in life. Two great tears filled his green eyes to the brim and turning away from the window he felt blindly for Joyeuce's hand. The pointed toes of his little green shoes caught in the cobbles as he walked, so that he stumbled, and the tears rolled down his face and dripped off the end of his chin; but he made no sound, not even the ghost of a whimper.

Joyeuce and the little girls felt that a blight was cast over their day. Diccon, as a general rule so noisy in his grief, was occasionally smitten with this sorrow too deep for words, and the silent reproach of his woe always made everyone feel most dreadfully uncomfortable. Why, his silence seemed to ask, was I born into this cruel world? Whose fault was it that earthly life was given to me? Why was I dragged from the realms of celestial glory, where the angels gave me the comets to play with, to this earth where I stretch out my empty hands in vain for my heart's desire?

The answer to these questions not being forthcoming, they turned the corner into Cornmarket in a gloomy silence.

But once past the tannery and the cordwainer's they cheered up. Excitement lit gleams in their eyes and deepened the colour in their cheeks, for unknown to authority they were bound on an errand of mercy to the opposite sex; and if anything thrills a woman more than being a ministering angel to a man it is being it forbiddenly.

Not that Canon Leigh had actually forbidden them to carry comforts to the prisoners at Bocardo, but knowing that he invariably refused to interfere with the course of justice they knew that he would have, if they had asked him; so they had not asked him.

Joyeuce quieted her slightly restive conscience by telling herself that her father was wrong in this. She was sure there was a place in the bible where it told one to visit prisoners in their affliction. She couldn't put her finger on chapter or verse at the moment, but she was sure there was, and she peeped under the recent purchases in her basket to see if the little packages she had brought from home were still safely there.

But, alas, when they reached Bocardo there were no signs of life at the barred window over the gateway. The five stood in a row, gazing upwards, uncertain what to do. To shout was unladylike, and to throw up stones at the window was also unladylike, and the gaze of the town was upon them.

"They're sleeping off last night," said Grace.

"Still?" queried Joyeuce sadly. This disappointment, coming on top of Diccon's exhibition of grief, was too much for her never volatile spirits. . . . She felt utterly miserable. . . . Like Diccon, she felt that living was nothing but a stretching of empty hands to an aching void.

But as she fell into her slough of despond, Diccon suddenly arose out of his, and their spirits passed each other, ascending and descending, a voiceless message passing between them.

"Giles!" shouted Diccon at the top of his voice. "Giles! I have a feather in my cap!"

His voice was clear as a bell, and as penetrating. The window of Bocardo, half closed against the noise and smells of Cornmarket, opened wide and Giles was seen behind the bars.

"See my feather!" called Diccon, holding up his new treasure. "Diccon has a feather in his cap!"

Giles smiled in kindly patronage and his eyes fastened greedily on the basket. "Have any of you girls had the intelligence to bring my books?" he demanded.

"No," they chorused weakly.

"Idiots!" said Giles, and gazed down upon them with the stare of a gorgon.

"We have warden's pies," said Joyeuce stoutly. "Cinnamon cakes and comfits, and some soap, and you ought to be grateful to us instead of lowering like a thunderstorm. . . . Is Master de Worde there?"

She felt Giles' scorn less than usual because it wasn't really he whom she had considered in the stocking of her basket.

The catalogue of viands must have penetrated beyond Giles, for he was suddenly seized from behind and forcibly removed, while the expectant faces of Nicolas, Faithful, Philip Sydney, and Master Walter Raleigh, of Oriel, fitted themselves into a sort of pattern at the window. Philip and Faithful looked much as usual, though pale after yesterday, but Nicolas was a pitiful sight, with swollen nose and blackened eyes. The beauty of the face that had looked up at Joyeuce from below her window had momentarily departed, but as she in her turn stood below and looked up there was a new quality in her riveted, compassionate gaze, something enveloping and protective, that his vanished comeliness had not called out. For a moment his pride recoiled from it and his face hardened ; then the frightened child in him leapt up in sudden gladness and his eyes as they met hers accepted what she gave.

But Philip, Faithful and Walter Raleigh were not at the window to watch an exhibition of sentiment, however touching, and the leather bag shot out of the window and landed neatly at Joyeuce's feet. . . . She started, and remembered what she was there for.

The bag made three descents and ascents and the ministering angels below basked in yet broader and broader smiles from those above. When it went up for the last time it had in it, beside a final pie and cake of soap, the little nosegay of crimson roses that Joyeuce had been carrying.

"Wait!" cried Nicolas, as the four heads disappeared from view with cheeks that were already bulging.

Joyeuce waited for what seemed to her a very long time, the children pulling impatiently at her skirts, and then the nosegay, with one crimson rose missing and something else in its place, came out of the window like a bird and alighted straight in the cupped hands she held up for it. . . . A moment ago she had felt the hands were empty, held out to a void, but now they were full to the brim. . . . Her spirit was mounting up now, into the very skies, and with a sudden passionate movement she knelt down and flung her arms round Diccon, who had set it mounting with his cry of "Diccon has a feather in his cap!" A feather, had he, the little love? Why, he had a hundred feathers; he was winged with them. He was love himself, little Cupid.

But Diccon was not feeling affectionate at the moment and bending low his curly head he bit her hand.

"Why did Master de Worde throw back the flowers?" asked Meg, as they journeyed homewards. "I think," she added, shaking her fair head more in sorrow than in anger, "that it was very rude of Master de Worde."

Joan also shook her head, and squeaked reprehensively.

"He kept one rose," said Joyeuce, and smiled secretly, for in the place in the nosegay where the stalk of the rose had been Nicolas had pushed a tightly folded note.

III

It was twenty minutes to seven when Joyeuce stood trembling in the porch of Saint Michael's at the North Gate. "Meet me in the porch of Saint Michael's at seven o'clock," Nicolas had written on a bit of paper, pulled from a corner of one of Raleigh's charts, and here she was, twenty minutes too early because this was her first meeting with her first lover.

She was trembling because of the frightful state her conscience was in. She felt as though it were inside her, rushing round and round like a squirrel in a cage, and also outside her, surrounding her with a scorching ball of fire. She knew now what the damned feel like when they are plunged into the lake of torment, and her heart ached for them, because she felt most uncomfortable. She pressed the palms of her hands against her hot cheeks and she wasn't at all sure she wasn't going to be sick.

The Devil had made it all most easy for her, had almost, you might say, strewn her path with roses. For it was a Thursday and it was her custom on Thursdays to have supper with an old friend of her mother's, a Mistress Flowerdew, who lived by the East Gate, and to spend the hours from supper till bed with her. Mistress Flowerdew's serving man always saw her home in safety, so her family never bothered about her on Thursday evenings. . . . It had been easy, fatally easy, to send a note by Wynkyn Heatherthwayte, Heatherthwayte's little son who, evidently at the special instigation of the Devil, was paying a visit to his father at the Fair Gate, to tell Mistress Flowerdew she could not come that night. . . . Then she had put on her very best clothes, a pale green farthingale and a cream coloured kirtle embroidered with yellow poppies, with a lace coif on her head and a dark blue cloak lined with yellow over all, and walked quietly out of the house, across Carfax and down Cornmarket to North Gate.

She had not actually had to tell a single lie, and she had every intention of spending the most respectable evening, but she had staged a deliberate hoax and she knew she was a wicked sinner. It struck her, as she stood there trembling, that this terrible deception had grown out of the smaller one of carrying comforts to the prisoners in Bocardo, unknown to her father. One thing leads to another, she thought, and we gather speed and impetus as we roll on down the downward path.

The strange thing was that while she wrote that note to Mistress Flowerdew, while she put on her pretty clothes, bushed out her fair hair and coiled it up to lie like a crown beneath her coif, she had not felt wicked at all, she had only felt gloriously happy. It was not until she stood waiting in the porch that her conscience had started kicking up such a fuss.

It was the inaction, she thought, that made her feel so bad, and to give herself something to do she went into the church. After the warmth and brightness of the June sun outside it seemed cold as the grave and as dimly lit as a cavern in the cliff. The noises of the street seemed to come from very far away, like the beat of waves on the sea shore, and there was in the church that mingled scent of must and damp and mice and candle grease that is by association such a very holy smell.

Joyeuce sat down on one of the seats and looked about her. It was very old, this Saint Michael's at the North Gate, and very dark, for the daylight filtered in through stained glass windows that were one of the glories of Oxford. There was one strange window that Joyeuce loved particularly; out of a golden pot sprang a lily plant with five stems bearing five lilies, and among the lilies hung Christ crucified. In another window Saint Michael himself, with magnificent green wings, was trampling strong-mindedly on the dragon, and in yet another were two small fair-haired seraphs, each with six wings, standing on wheels as in the vision of Isaiah. They wore skimpy little white nightgowns and were exactly like the twins.

It was the sight of these little seraphs that steadied Joyeuce. The turmoil of her feelings suddenly subsided and she found herself thinking coldly and quietly. Her mother had left the children, Grace, the twins and Diccon, in her care, and if she married Nicolas she would be deserting them. . . . Somehow it did not occur to her that he might not love her; she took for granted that what she gave to him, he would be able to give to her; she did not know yet that out of the depth of her own nature she made demands upon others that could not be satisfied unless their depth equalled her own. . . . To be happy. To be satisfied. To be fulfilled. . . . She looked at her longing, seeing it opposed to her duty, and tried to see it steadily for what it was.

Those two worlds, the actual and the ideal, were before her again. The children stood for one and Nicolas for the other. One was a known love that had not satisfied and the other an unknown love that seemed to promise fulfilment, but that might, too, disappoint when she moved onward to it and the ideal became in its turn the actual. Yet every instinct in her drove her forward and she had to remind herself that instincts are animal things and not to be trusted. . . . Instinct is not intuition. . . . She had no right to push forward for her own sake; she could not go on to new things unless the path was clear before her, and it was not, it was blocked by the figures of the children.

Suddenly she saw them clearly in all their dearness; the people who had until now made up her whole world. Why should she desert them for a stranger? Of what worth was her love for them if she could not suffer for their sake? From the beginning of the world lovers had died daily and no love had ever been true till the stamp of death had been set upon its beauty, as the cross was set upon those lilies in the window. Emotion swept over her again, setting this time in the contrary direction, and jumping up she turned blindly towards the door. . . . She would go home. . . . She would not wait for Nicolas. Never would she desert her darling twins, and never would she marry and leave them and Diccon to the tender mercies of Great-Aunt. This new and selfish love was not for her. She would stamp on the devil like the green-winged Saint Michael in the window. She would confess her hoax to her father and be forgiven. She had made her decision and it was irrevocable. She would never turn back from it. . . . Dry-eyed and composed she pushed open the heavy door and walked straight into the arms of Nicolas.

IV

The Elizabethan kiss of greeting was a useful thing, for it could so easily develop into something more and yet be still nominally the kiss of greeting. Handled skilfully, as by Romeo when he gave to Juliet and took back again the sin of his presumption, it could go on a long time, and it went on a long time in the porch of Saint Michael at the North Gate. With Nicolas's cheek against hers and his arms straining so tightly round her that she could hardly breathe, Joyeuce felt as though she were drowning. Locked together the two of them seemed sinking down into the depths of some strange changeless element that they had not known before. They felt aeons and fathoms removed from time and place, living so intensely that they did not recognize as life this strange thing into whose depths they had fallen. The struggle Joyeuce had just passed through was as though it had never been, and as for her irrevocable decision she had forgotten that she had ever made it.

Nicolas, less deeply drowned than Joyeuce, recovered first. Coming to the surface again, trembling, astonished and rather alarmed, he looked down and blinked at the girl in his arms as though she were some strange sort of wild creature that had fallen there from the heavens quite unaccountably.

"Joyeuce?" he said, speaking her name in a bewilderment that seemed begging her to explain this peculiar thing that had happened to them both.

But Joyeuce, though his question made her move in his arms and raise her face to look at him, only shook her head, for she could explain no more than he could.

"I'm still rather dirty," said Nicolas suddenly. "I ought not to touch you. I forgot."

He took his arms away from her very gently and took her hand ceremoniously to lead her into the street. Out in the sunshine, and away from the centuries-old darkness of the church, the world returned to normal again. They were a young man and a girl walking down the main thoroughfare of a modern city with the eyes of the world upon them, not two lone souls lost in a primeval darkness. They peeped at each other under their eyelashes with interest, even with amusement, appraising each other's good points and congratulating themselves upon their taste.

There was no man in the world so gallant or so fine as Nicolas, Joyeuce thought. It was true that he was distinctly grubby, and his clothes were torn from last night's fight, but he wore his gallantry with so fine an air that these things were hardly noticeable, and her red rose was stuck in his doublet.

"I ought to be in Bocardo till to-morrow," he told her as they walked down Cornmarket, "but I bribed the old jailer to let me out to-night. I'd just one angel left in my pocket."

"And the others?" asked Joyeuce.

"They're still there. The old curmudgeon would only let

one go. Had I had four angels he would have let four go, he said. The others were pleased for me to go because of my nose."

"Your nose?" queried Joyeuce.

"It needs attending to," said Nicolas, feeling the injured member cautiously. "I think I may have broken it."

Joyeuce did not know where he was taking her, and neither did she care. She had forgotten everything in the world but Nicolas and at the moment he could have done what he liked with her. She was in reality the stronger in character of the two of them, and their relationship, when from below the window of Bocardo she had looked protectively up at him, had been the true relationship, but now it was he who was outwardly all protection. She clung to his arm as they picked their way through the refuse of Cornmarket, for though she was tall he was yet taller and her head only reached his shoulder. The slight blow to his pride that she had dealt him by the first look was healed by her clinging hands. . . . He stuck out his chest, smiled benignly down upon her, and strutted, singing softly to himself.

> "Greensleeves was all my joy,
> Greensleeves was my delight;
> Greensleeves was my heart of gold,
> And who but Lady Greensleeves."

"We're going to Tattleton's Tavern," he told her. "Tattleton's a friend of mine. He'll give me clean clothes to change into, and some money to go on with, and you shall sit in the painted room and play the clavicytherium while you are waiting for me, and then we'll have supper in the garden where the eglantine grows."

Joyeuce bowed her head in silent assent, for the modest programme filled her with an excitement too deep for words.

Tattleton's was a most respectable Tavern and Master and Mistress Tattleton people of refinement. Between the Inns and the Taverns of Oxford there was a great gulf fixed. The Inn was for the common people and the Tavern for the quality. Travellers could find food and lodgings for themselves and stabling for their horses at an Inn, but at a Tavern accommodation was given only to those who were personal friends of the host and hostess. It was more of a club than an hotel; gentlemen sat there of an evening to drink wines of an exquisite bouquet and flavour and discuss the gossip of the town with their friends.

Master Tattleton owned both the Tavern and the Crosse Inn next door, and made a good thing out of them. They were on the east side of Cornmarket and were both of them fine houses. Joyeuce and Nicolas passed the Crosse Inn first, with its great archway leading into the galleried inn yard, and its painted sign, the red cross of Saint George on a white ground, swaying gently in the wind. The pillory stood just outside the Crosse Inn, serving a double purpose, for anyone who misbehaved himself inside the Inn could easily be run outside and put in, and also it was a source of entertainment for guests drinking their beer at the windows.

But the Tavern was even more beautiful. It was a timber-framed house with overhanging timber gables and beautiful tall stone and brick chimneys, and it had the dignity of its long history. It had originally been an almost ecclesiastical building, a lodging house for scholars who would one day be priests, and religious signs and symbols were still to be found carved or painted over its fireplaces and around its cornices. When its scholars deserted it, it had become the Salutation Tavern, but this lovely name smacked too much of popery for Elizabethan taste and now it was just Tattleton's.

Both Master and Mistress Tattleton came running when Nicolas, with Joyeuce on his arm, stood in the beautiful panelled entrance hall and shouted. They were comely, roundabout people, enslaved to the undeserving Nicolas by the spell of his charms. He presented Joyeuce to them, she blushing a little under the amused scrutiny of their twinkling eyes, and made his requests known in a lordly manner. Then he was carried off by Master Tattleton to get washed and changed and his nose ministered to, and Mistress Tattleton led Joyeuce upstairs. The business of the Tavern was conducted on the ground floor, the private rooms of the family were on the first floor and the guest rooms were on the second floor.

They toiled up and up the circular oak staircase that wound round a massive octagonal oak newel, Joyeuce panting a little as she followed Mistress Tattleton's broad back, holding up her beautiful farthingale on either side.

"Never mind, dearie," consoled Mistress Tattleton. "You'll think it well worth the trouble when you get there."

With a final pant they got there and Mistress Tattleton paused outside the door, her head on one side and a tear in her eye. She was a kindly soul, and a sentimental, and Joyeuce in her green gown had taken her fancy.

"There's not many I let use this room," she said portentously, "they might do it an injury; but so sweet and fair a lady should wait for her lover in a fair room."

Then she abruptly strained Joyeuce to her bosom, flung open the door, paused a moment to hear Joyeuce's cry of pleasure, and went off down the stairs, lowering her bulk cautiously from step to step and chuckling to herself in fat delight. . . . So fair a poppet. . . . So handsome a couple. . . . So merciful a thing that she had strawberries to give them for their supper. Young love should always be fed on strawberries. Eat strawberries while you can, Mistress Tattleton was wont to say, for when you are older they may not agree with you.

v

Joyeuce let her cloak drop to the floor and stood in the centre of the room, gazing delightedly. It was sparsely furnished with a carved settle, a clavicytherium and a couple of stools with bowls of flowers upon them, one on each side of the beautiful herringbone brick fireplace; but it did not need more, for too many things in it would only have detracted from the beauty of its painted walls. Tempera painting on plaster was coming into fashion as wall decoration, and in many houses taking the place of tapestry hangings. But this happened to be the first example of the new art that Joyeuce had seen.

The craftsman who had painted these walls was an artist, and he had enjoyed himself; indeed his enjoyment cried out to the beholder from each of the four walls. The background of the painting was a rich vermilion-orange ochre, from the pits worked at Headington, the very colour of delight, and on it was traced a trellis-work pattern in old gold, outlined in black and white. Within each of the linked compartments were painted lively posies of English flowers; canterbury bells, windflowers, passion flowers, wild roses and bunches of white grapes. They were not gaudily coloured, for bright colours would have clashed with the glorious background, but painted softly in brown-pink, purple, green and grey. Words ran round the top of the walls in a painted frieze, and Joyeuce spelled them out under her breath.

> First of thy rising
> And last of thy rest be thou
> God's servant, for that hold is best.
> In the morning early serve God devoutly.
> Fear God above everything.
> Love the brotherhood. Honour the king.

The windows of the room were fast shut against the noise of Cornmarket, but in any case it was quiet now because people had gone to their suppers. The silence was complete and cool and fragrant, and Joyeuce sat down on the settle, with her hands folded on the yellow embroidered poppies in her lap, and seemed to herself to be listening to it. Moments of beautiful leisure like this did not come her way very often and she was utterly and completely happy, even though she felt rather bewildered as to who she was, for she did not seem to be the same tormented Joyeuce that she had been half an hour ago. She felt very old and wise, as though Nicolas's kiss had taken her right back to the beginning of the world and she had had to live through all the intervening centuries between then and now in a few minutes, and yet at the same time she felt gloriously young, as though she had begun life all over again as a little child. She felt, too, very strong and very secure, for this new beginning had brought with it a welling up of new life, and it was with an assurance and gaiety that were not usually hers that she nodded at the lovely painted flowers around her. They made a sort of protective arbour for her, she felt, and her sense of security deepened. If love for the one person in the world could be like this, a cool fragrant hiding-place built round the well of life, into which one could creep and be refreshed when the storms of this world became more than one could put up with, then she understood why it was a treasure of such price that men and women were willing to die for it. She herself, she thought, would be willing to die again and again if this glorious renewal might come to her after every death.

The sudden and rather boisterous entry of Nicolas, washed and brushed and clothed in the crimson doublet of Jo Tattleton, Mistress Tattleton's eldest, seemed almost to do violence to her arbour ; until she remembered that it was he who had built it up around her. She got up and curtsied to him, as though he were the king whom the verse upon the wall told her to honour, then swept before him out of the door and down the stairs with so superb a pride and dignity that for the moment the volatile Nicolas was deprived of the power of speech.

v

A pathway, walled on both sides, led from the back of the Tavern to the small walled garden. It was a very private, very charming little place. Square flower beds, filled now with blue canterbury bells and bushes of eglantine, starred all over with small pink blossoms, lay very demurely in green grass. The high walls were covered with woodbine and yellow climbing roses and there was a little trellis-work arbour, roofed and walled with a green vine.

"Look," said Joyeuce, "there is another arbour."

"Another ? " asked Nicolas.

"It is like the one upstairs," said Joyeuce. "Trellis-work and a vine. It was this garden, Nicolas, that told the artist what to paint on the walls upstairs."

She paused, smiling, picturing that unknown artist, when imagination failed him for a moment, running down the stairs, his paint brush stuck behind his ear, to have another look at the garden. It must have been a long way up and down, each time inspiration slackened, but then judging by his spirited designs he was a young man who had determined that Tattleton's garden, made as it was for lovers, should flower even in midwinter.

Mistress Tattleton had set two stools very close together inside the arbour, with a table covered with a linen cloth before them, and she had excelled herself in the matter of food. By the mercy of Providence, it being Tattleton's birthday to-morrow, she had that very morning concocted and baked one of her famous lark pies for the good man, and she set it upon the table in the arbour. Tattleton, of course, would now have to go without, but lark pie never really agreed with him and she could knock him up a nice little rabbit pasty that would be all he needed at his age. The lark pie had quite a mountain of pastry on top of it and was ornamented with two little sugar cupids with wings made from the lark's feathers. . . . Mistress Tattleton was an artist, and no mistake. . . . Joyeuce and Nicolas, sitting very close together on the two stools, said so over and over again and Mistress Tattleton herself, standing with arms akimbo at the entrance to the arbour and looking down at her handiwork with tears in her eyes—the cupids had reference to the first meeting of herself and Tattleton thirty years ago, when they had both gone to see a hanging at the Castle mound, had sat next to each other on the raised seats before the gibbet and fallen in love at first sight— entirely agreed with them.

There were other things to eat besides the pie, for Mistress Tattleton had six sons, and they had all been in Bocardo at one time or another, so she knew with what kind of appetite the released prisoner is restored to his friends. There were bowls of strawberries floating in milk, there was a dish of cherries, there were manchets of bread and a dish of comfits and last but not least there was the canary wine, for which the Tavern was famous, in exquisite glasses.

Mistress Tattleton helped them to pie, lingered a moment to give herself the pleasure of watching Nicolas' strong white teeth bite deep into her pastry, and Joyeuce's pink tongue daintily exploring the head of a sugar cupid that seemed to her too pretty to eat, and then took herself off. . . . The pretty dears! . . . She applied the corner of her gown to her eye, shut the door of the walled pathway firmly and informed her household at the top of her voice that no one, not even my lord of Leicester himself, was to be let into the garden till she gave them leave.

Joyeuce always had a scruple about eating lark. The brutalities of the age that other people took entirely for granted, the cock fighting, the lark eating, the bear baitings, the beheadings and the hangings, made her miserable. To each generation its own horrors, to which the majority are blunted by custom, but Joyeuce was one of those who in any age are cruelly awake to cruelty. She was in the minority, of course, and she knew it, so she thought no worse of Nicolas that he ate her share of lark as well as his own. . . . And he gave her his sugar cupid, so it was quite fair. . . . She did not eat either of them; she had only gently licked one to please Mistress Tattleton; she wrapped them both in her kerchief and put them in her wallet to take back to the twins.

It is to Nicolas's credit that in spite of his hunger, which had been no more than blunted by the dainties brought to Bocardo, he was very attentive to Joyeuce. She was too happy and excited to eat very much, but he carefully fished out the spiders that had dropped into her strawberries and milk—the only drawbacks to the beautiful arbour were the things that dropped from above—and he hung cherries over her ears under her fair hair, and he said the sweetest things to her between each mouthful.

Nicolas was used to making love to pretty ladies, he had a flair for it and believed in using one's gifts, but this evening he actually meant what he said. Joyeuce in her green gown, with the shadows of the vine leaves trembling over the embroidered yellow poppies on her kirtle, like frightened fingers that wooed with an airy touch but dared not lift or handle, was certainly a sight for sore eyes. Her hair was the colour of the woodbine on the walls, and the cherries he had hung over her ears seemed to call out an unwonted red in her cheeks and lips. Other maidens who had given Nicolas the opportunity of using his gifts had been more beautiful, more witty, more aristocratic, but none of them had had such a demure dignity as Joyeuce, or had been such a touching mixture of childishness and maturity. This girl was a woman who had worked hard and suffered much, and borne on her shoulders responsibilities that would have crushed Nicolas to pulp had they been laid upon him, and yet at the same time she was a child who could be transported into the seventh heaven of delight by a sugar cupid or a red cherry or a butterfly kiss upon her cheek. As Nicolas petted her she seemed to get fatter and rosier under his very eyes. Had she never been petted before, he wondered, that such a very little of it could cause such a flowering of beauty in her? His power over her gave him a self-confidence that was like balm to his new manhood, while at the same time her maturity gave him a most unusual feeling of humility. . . . He did not know whether he liked the effect she had on him or whether he didn't, but at any rate it was something quite different. . . . His feeling for Joyeuce seemed, now and for the rest of his life, to be a thing apart, something locked for safety in a casket of cool green leaves where airy fingers wooed but dared not handle roughly.

Joyeuce had not known that one could be so aware of anyone as she was aware of Nicolas. Her capacity for love was large and she had known, of course, long ago, how almost painfully the personality of the person loved can impinge upon one's own. In the time of grief after her mother's death, her father's misery, that gave no sign to the world at large and was hidden, he thought, even from Joyeuce, had been like an actual physical illness in her own body. It had seemed round her like a black coat of mail, pressing in on her, choking her breathing and clutching at her heart so that she thought it would stop. The personalities of the little boys and of the twins seemed mingled with hers, and as for Diccon, it was difficult to realise that he was not her very own child, bone of her bone and flesh of her flesh. Had she carried his body within her own, as she now seemed to herself to carry his wicked little spirit within hers, he could not have been more completely a part of her.

But her awareness of Nicolas, a man who was almost a stranger to her, was so acute that it frightened her. Her mingled love and ignorance made of his personality a thing so mysterious and wonderful that it filled her world. The very shadows lying across the grass seemed shadows of it, and the flowers were paintings drawn from the pattern of Nicolas.

And if these could give her news of him the actual physical presence of Nicolas, eating lark pie beside her in the arbour, must surely be as the written pages of a book that tell of the spirit of it. Hating her ignorance, longing for knowledge of him, she looked almost hungrily at the hollow of his temple and the way the hair grew above it, the curve of his cheekbone and the golden down upon it, at the cleft in his chin and the line of his jaw and the way his head was set upon his neck. Then a wave of hot shame swept over her and she dropped her eyes in confusion; only to see his hand resting upon the table beside her, and to notice the shape of the fingers and the hollow in the wrist where she would have felt the pulse beating if she had put her finger on it. . . . The pulse. . . . Terror engulfed her. That beating pulse was such a tiny thing, yet if it were to stop he would be dead. The careless flight of an arrow, a slip on the stairs, a flash of lightning out of the noonday or the thrust of an angry sword in a tavern at midnight; such small things as these could still the even smaller pulse and the kindly body would be there no longer to give tidings of the spirit to its lovers.

"Nicolas! Nicolas!" she cried in terror.

He flung both arms round her and demanded what the matter was.

"You wouldn't let any harm come to you, would you?" she whispered.

Nicolas roared with laughter, his head thrown back so that his throat showed like a strong pillar defying the fates. "Not yet," he said. "Not till we've had time to love each other. . . . I promise."

He took her out into the garden—the dimness of the arbour, he thought, must be conducive to melancholia—and she was soon a child again, poking her fingers into the Canterbury bells, rubbing the sweet scented eglantine leaves between the palms of her hands, and laughing at the drunken bumble bees who reeled from woodbine trumpet to yellow rose, and from there fell heavily to lie upside down and protesting on the purple pansies growing in the bed below.

VI

But she had been a child for only a little while when a pealing bell and the fading sky over her head warned her that time passes.

"I must go," she whispered, her head drooping. She was sad now, for to the happy the bell that marks the passing of the hours brings bad news. Nicolas was sad, too, as he led her into the house to say good-bye to Mistress Tattleton, and out in the street again, going home, they could find nothing to say. He led her silently, holding her hand, and only her silken skirts whispered softly as they walked.

At the Fair Gate they stopped and tried to say good night, but they couldn't. Although the sun had set it had left its warmth behind with them. There was a flame burning in them both that made it impossible to part; they were fused by it, bound together as though it created a tiny world of warmth for the two of them outside of which it was impossible to live.

"Joyeuce," whispered Nicolas, "it is Midsummer Eve and the fairies will be dancing in the meadows."

Joyeuce nodded her head. It did not matter to her where they went so long as they were together, and where the fairies are dancing is the place for lovers on Midsummer Eve. . . . She believed in fairies.

They went on down Fish Street and turned into an alleyway beside the South Gate that led through into the meadows. Joyeuce had never yet been there so late and she caught her breath, for they did not seem the same fields that she knew in the sunshine.

They had left the sun behind them and walked into the country of the moon. It hung in a deep green sky and low on the horizon Jupiter burned like a lamp. The trees, heavy with their June foliage, stood up motionless and almost black against that strange sky and below them the grass had changed its colour, had become a cold blue-green under the light of the moon. The flowers were visible, the tall daisies in the grass and the wild roses on the bushes, but all colour had been drained from them, even from the yellow eyes of the daisies that by day ogled the sun. They looked like fragile motionless butterflies, or pale ghosts of the moon and the stars above them.

They went slowly on under the trees, hand in hand, and even Nicolas did not feel himself, for the green light and the absolute stillness of this moon country were so strange. This was an old country, the country of legend, where the spirits of dead lovers hid beneath the trees and the ghosts of their songs sighed and whispered over the grass. When he had asked Joyeuce to come with him into the meadows the hot magic of the sun had been racing in his veins and he had been ready for he knew not what midsummer madness; but now he felt differently. Joyeuce's hand in his, that had before been warm with excitement, was now cool, and looking at her he saw that the moon had taken the red from her lips and the colour from the poppies on her dress; she was all green and silver, like a naiad. She was innocent as the moon and he could not hurt her.

And Joyeuce, too, her feeling born of his, felt different. Her painful awareness of his physical presence, that had made her feel ashamed, was gone. In the dim shadowy figure strolling beside her she was only conscious of the spirit of the man, and rejoiced in the sense of peace that it brought her. When he stopped under a tree and slipped his arms round her she was not afraid. There was no passion in them and his face against hers was cool. Love, the creator, had them in its merciless grip, but the vestal moon had made it urbane and pitiful and it chose that night to ignore their bodies and work upon their souls. Yet the virtue was not only in the moon; Nicolas could lay claim to a little. Part of him was at the mercy of the time and the place and the magic of the night, but another part of him was conscious of desire, and refusal, and increase of strength following hard on the heels of it.

A familiar scent reached Joyeuce and she lifted her head and sniffed. Then she saw that a hundred white moons, larger than those that sprinkled the bushes and the grass, were hanging low over their heads.

"Nicolas!" she whispered, "we're standing under an elder tree! Just sniff!"

"What of it?" asked Nicolas, sniffing.

"If you stand under an elder tree on Midsummer Eve you see the King of the Elves," whispered Joyeuce.

Nicolas looked down into her face and laughed. Her eyes were round as a frightened child's and she was trembling. There was nothing of the woman in her at this moment, and as he kissed her on her pointed chin and her shadowed eyelids he smiled to think that the woman who could grapple so courageously with the sorrows and the labour of her life should be such a little girl that she could tremble like an aspen leaf at an old wives' tale.

"You babe!" he laughed, "you absurd, adorable babe!" And then he happened to glance ahead over her shoulder and his jaw dropped and his eyes grew even rounder than hers.

"What is it?" she whispered.

Nicolas was incapable of speech, but keeping his arms tightly round her, lest she should scream with fright when she saw what he saw, he swung her round a little way.

Clinging together under the magic elder tree they stood and stared. Not far away from them a tiny green figure was treading out a circle on the grass. He was a figure not of this world; ethereal, airy, and ready at any moment to vanish into thin air. Whether he trod a circle that was already there, or whether he was deliberately tracing one out with his small feet, it was impossible to say, but he moved on and on, slowly but rhythmically, half dancing and half walking, and crooning a little song to himself, but so low that it reached them as only the ghost of a sound and not sound itself. His head was down, watching his moving feet, and they could not see his face, but Joyeuce could distinctly see his little white ears with their pointed tips. . . . He was dressed all in faerie green and from the cap upon his head there drooped a long peacock's feather.

The lovers under the elder tree were speechless, stupefied and trembling. They were mesmerised by that low crooning song and the ceaselessly moving figure. It was a long time before that peacock's feather forced itself upon Joyeuce's consciousness, and when it did she could scarcely believe the evidence of her own brain and eyes.

"Diccon!" she gasped stupidly. "Diccon!"

"Diccon?" queried Nicolas. "Diccon?" He stared again and then dropped his arms from Joyeuce and blushed rosily. . . . For full five minutes had he, Nicolas de Worde, an enlightened man of the world, thought that he beheld a faerie creature. . . . He would have liked to have spanked young Diccon, for he was much discomfited.

"The little devil!" he said in heartfelt tones.

But Joyeuce had flown over the grass and was kneeling in the centre of the circle that Diccon trod, her arms stretched out.

"Diccon!" she cried. "Baby!"

But Diccon took no notice of her at all. He moved on and on, still crooning his song, and his green eyes shone like emeralds in the light of the moon. Now that she could hear it clearly, it seemed to Joyeuce that his song reminded her of something, though she did not know what.

"Diccon!" she cried again. "Diccon!" and leaning forward she clasped him in her arms. For a moment she felt that she had clasped thin air, and had a moment of terror, but then as she pulled him closer she felt the round stolidity of him, and the delicious warmth of his baby humanity.

"Sweetheart," she cried, "how did you get here, all by yourself?"

"I was lonely," said Diccon. "I was lonely in the big bed."

Joyeuce picked him up and clasped him to her in an agony of

reproach. He had woken up in the dead of night, the poor lamb, stretched out his hand and found her not there. She would never forgive herself, and she kissed him with such passion that Nicolas was jealous and strode towards them over the grass.

"Don't waste your kisses on such a wicked little elf," he mocked, standing beside her where she knelt with Diccon in her arms. "Look what he's been writing," and he pointed to a ring of flowers that surrounded them, daisies, purple milkwort and yellow lady's-slipper forming a perfect circle on the grass.

Joyeuce gasped and stood up, still clutching Diccon to her. She knew, as Nicolas did, though she believed it and he did not, that when the fairies have a message for mortals they are said to write it upon the grass with flowers ; if mortals cannot read it the more fools they.

"What is it ? " she whispered. " Is it for us ? "

"What is it, Diccon ? " asked Nicolas, and took the little green creature out of her arms that they might not ache with his weight.

But if Diccon knew, he wasn't going to say. He smiled a secret smile and lolled his feathered head against Nicolas's shoulder.

"News from a far country," said Nicolas dreamily. "But we cannot read it."

They were suddenly sad, conscious of the restrictions of their mortality. Such mysterious worlds within worlds surrounded them and they could know no more of them than a faint echo now and again, or a flickering outline, like the shadow on a curtain of a great host passing by. They felt strangers in this country of the moon and held tightly to each other, scared by the silence and the eerie green light.

"Now then, Mistress ! Come now, Master ! Can you not tell the time by the stars in the sky and the dew on the grass ? No time to be out and about." A cheery voice came booming through the shadows, and a swinging yellow lantern illumined a large red beard and a pair of striding legs behind which sulked a black plumy creature whose eyes were like lamps in the gloom. . . . Heatherthwayte was on their tracks. . . . Bewildered by the light of his lantern, they stood blinking at him like owls, they inside and he outside the fairy ring.

Heatherthwayte, too, was bewildered. He had seen them come together to the Fair Gate, try to say good night, fail, and pass on down to the meadows. When they had not come back he had worried about them, scratching his head and making unusual noises in his throat that Satan found perplexing. Finally he had got up, lit his lantern, whistled to Satan and stumped off down Fish Street to find them. . . . These motherless maidens needed an eye kept upon them and he, Heatherthwayte, would keep it.

But now that he had found them within their fairy ring he hardly knew them. Nicolas standing tall and straight in his scarlet doublet, holding a little green elf in his arms, was a figure of legend, and Joyeuce in her green gown was surely a naiad who had drifted up with the mist through the water meadows from the river beyond. Heatherthwayte stared at them in stupefaction and Satan, used to greeting them with boisterous barks, lowered his tail and was silent.

But the light of the lantern soon brought them all to themselves. It banished the moonlight and with it flowed in remembrance of time and place. Satan barked and Heatherthwayte, though too superstitious to step inside the fairy ring on Midsummer Eve, stretched out a hairy hand and clawed the three towards him.

"A nice to-do there'd be over this if I was not to 'ush it up," he scolded. "And the child, too, out in the dew and the moonlight . . . Moonlight's not 'olesome . . . Come along, mistress. Come, master. A couple of children you are, and should be whipped according." He turned an outraged back upon them and led the way homewards, Nicolas following. Joyeuce, running after them, and seeing the little green figure of the child clinging to the striding figure of the man in his scarlet doublet—not even the moonlight had been able to take the colour out of that doublet—had one last magic moment. They made her think of a holly bush, that brings romance in mid-winter, and the two together, she thought, would be the joy and the warmth of her life until the end.

Joyeuce, when she returned from Mistress Flowerdew's always came in the back way, along the cobbled lane that led from Fish Street to the stables, and from there to the garden, so Nicolas parted from her and Diccon in the lane, with loving but rather hasty kisses, and then followed Heatherthwayte towards the Fair Gate, feeling in his wallet as he went for the wherewithal to reward a man who had rescued two lovers adrift on the perilous sea of fairyland and towed them back safe to the shore. The last Joyeuce heard of him was his voice singing:

> " Greensleeves, now farewell! adieu!
> God I pray to prosper thee;
> For I am still thy lover true.
> Come once again and love me.
> Greensleeves was all my joy,
> Greensleeves was my delight;
> Greensleeves was my heart of gold,
> And who but Lady Greensleeves."

In their big bedroom Joyeuce undressed Diccon by moonlight. When they had come in they had found the little girls and the dogs fast asleep, and quite unaware that there had been unusual goings-on. But not so Tinker. He knew all about it and was sitting very upright and severe on the pillow, lashing his tail. He was wide awake and his eyes shone like fire and were fixed on Joyeuce in an unblinking stare all the time she was putting Diccon to bed. . . . She felt most uncomfortable. . . . No one in this world, she had discovered long ago, can make one feel more uncomfortable than an indignant cat.

Diccon offered no explanation of his strange behaviour. She did not know why, when he had woken up lonely in the big bed, he had dressed himself up in his faerie green and gone out into the meadows, nor why he had been treading out that faerie ring and crooning that strange song. He was too sleepy to be asked questions, his curly head swaying on his shoulders with its weight of dreams, and in any case she did not want to know. . . . It was altogether too queer.

It was not until she herself was in bed, and Diccon was lying fast asleep beside her with the now somnolent Tinker clasped in his arms, that she remembered why his crooning song was familiar to her. . . . His gypsy foster-mother had sung something like it to the two tiny babies who lay in her arms.

She sat bolt upright in terror.

She had forgotten to draw the curtains and by the light of the moon she bent over and examined the face of her best-beloved. . . . It seemed he was still her best-beloved, for in her fear for him she had for the moment forgotten Nicolas. . . . His green eyes were hidden by his shut lids, but their look of mischief seemed to have been transferred to the long eyelashes that were almost aggressive in their curl. His freckles seemed to have cast a shadow over his face and robbed it of that look of pearly innocence that makes the faces of sleeping children, however erroneously, as those of the cherubs of heaven. His red mouth, relaxed in sleep, was like a poppy. . . . How red his mouth was, Joyeuce thought. None of the other children had lips as red as his. . . . How unlike he was to all the rest of them. . . . How utterly unlike. . . . Was he, could he be a changeling? If she had not seized hold of him, as he trod his fairy ring on Midsummer Eve, would he have vanished away altogether?

Joyeuce lay flat on her back, her hands at her sides, staring out at that strange green sky outside the window and shivering a little with love and happiness, and an eerie fear. Now and then she shut her eyes and tried to sleep, but always, when she did that, she saw, between sleeping and waking, Nicolas and Diccon, dressed in scarlet and green, moving together through the moonlit trees towards the gates of fairyland, while she, Joyeuce Leigh the stay-at-home toiling mouse, ran after them, desperately trying to keep up with their striding figures and to keep in her sight the portals of those gates that led into the country for which she longed.

Yet when at last broken feverish dreams took the place of her wakefulness she knew she was beaten. A great wind was blowing against her, pushing her backwards, until at last she could not stand against it any longer and it forced her to her knees; and she found herself kneeling in the church of Saint Michael at the North Gate, vowing herself to renunciation.

Then she opened her eyes for the twentieth time to find that the green sky had faded and in its place had come another, equally strange, of silver mist shot through with gold.

The cuckoos were calling and it was Midsummer Day.

CHAPTER VIII

SUNDAY

> Leave me, O Love, which reachest but to dust;
> And thou, my mind, aspire to higher things;
> Grow rich in that which never taketh rust;
> Whatever fades but fading pleasure brings.
> Draw in thy beams, and humble all thy might
> To that sweet yoke where lasting freedoms be;
> Which breaks the clouds and opens forth the light,
> That doth both shine and give us sight to see.
> O take fast hold; let that light be thy guide
> In this small course which birth draws out to death,
> And think how evil becometh him to slide,
> Who seeketh heaven, and comes of heavenly breath.
> Then farewell, world; thy uttermost I see;
> Eternal Love, maintain thy life in me.
> PHILIP SIDNEY.

1

WILL and Thomas Leigh, waking up three days later in their big bed, realised with pleasure that it was Sunday. They were not pious children and their pleasure sprang solely from the fact that they would not have to go to school to-day. They would have to go to church, unfortunately, but church did not take so long as school and there was no necessity to listen to what was said.

Will woke first and pulling aside the crimson curtains of the bed he peeped out at the room. It was over the study and was reached through Canon Leigh's, so that no nocturnal adventures were possible without their father knowing of them. Its tapestries, representing David getting the better of Goliath and Absalom at his last gasp hanging from the oak tree, were not as beautiful as the tapestries in the girls' room, but no doubt more suited to the boys in subject matter, portraying as they did the reward of courage and the frightful fate in store for those who do not behave nicely to their parents. The crimson curtains of the four-poster were not embroidered, but then it was no good wasting good embroidery on Will and Thomas, for they did not care for such things.

Will looked anxiously at Absalom hanging from the oaktree. If Absalom's beautiful hair looked very bright and golden, and if his terrified, dying face had a pink tinge to it, Will knew that the sun was shining and hastened to get out of bed, but if Absalom's death agonies were shadowed Will knew it was raining and burrowed back under the blankets again until someone dragged him out. To-day Absalom was brightly illumined and Will awoke Thomas by a blow on the chest and pulled back all the curtains.

Thomas shut his mouth—he had adenoids and slept with it ajar—opened his eyes and lay staring at the crimson canopy over his head until full consciousness returned to him.

"Sunday," he said. "We shall have to wash."

They washed really properly on Sundays, all over, with hot water, and then they put on their clean clothes. Their hair had its weekly brush, and their nails were cleaned, and when they were finished they really looked quite nice.

Before they had time to get out of bed Diggory entered upon them with a huge basin and a ewer of hot water. Diggory's Sunday morning was most exhausting. He got up in what was almost the middle of the night and cleaned the animals, then he cleaned himself and then he cleaned Will and Thomas.

"You needn't stop, Diggory," said Will, "we can wash ourselves."

This remark was made weekly, as a matter of form, but Diggory knew better than to permit any such thing. He set the basin upon the floor, poured water into it, and advanced upon the bed in a grim silence, hailing out first Will and then Thomas.

He watched them while they washed, his old face set like a mask, and he made no sound at all unless he saw them skimping the job, when he bellowed like a bull and his hairy hands shot out to box their ears. When the agony was over he departed as silently as he had come, taking the basin and ewer with him.

"That's over for another week," sighed Will in satisfaction, and with chattering teeth he got himself into his clean shirt and his Sunday doublet of peacock blue. . . . It was cold work stripping so early in the morning. . . . In winter the family ablutions took place before the kitchen fire on Saturday night, and that was really pleasanter.

When they were dressed Joyeuce came in, carrying a hairbrush and two little snowy ruffs. She had been up till midnight the night before, washing and ironing the ruffs for them all, and plaiting them with pokesticks.

Joyeuce had been very odd the last few days and her family had not known what to make of her. Sometimes she had seemed marvellously happy, singing at her work or falling upon her brothers and sisters and kissing them at the most unexpected moments, but at other times she had moved about the house as though weighed down by some guilty secret, and would set to and polish and spin and wash up with a grim energy, as though reproaching herself for loss of time. She was in this latter mood now. She brushed the boys' hair until they yelled for mercy, and the Spanish Inquisition would have been a picnic compared to the way in which she cleaned their nails.

"Oh!" squeaked Thomas indignantly, as with his right arm pinioned beneath hers she worked at his nails with a sharp silver instrument of torture.

"Filthy little pig," said Joyeuce. "What do you do to get your hands like this?" With a sigh of despair she spread out his grubby little paw and looked at it. She had not made much impression upon his nails with her silver instrument, though she had made some, but upon the actual hand Diggory's soap and water had made no impression whatsoever. . . . The dirt was engrained. . . . "I wonder what Mother did for your hands?" she pondered, her forehead wrinkled in a worried frown. She tried hard never to fall below her mother's standard of cleanliness and housewifery, but there were times when no one seemed to remember what Mother had done.

"But we didn't go to school when Mother was alive," said Will, "and so we didn't get like this. Education," he explained, "is very soiling."

"Don't be unhappy, Joyeuce," said Will. "Lots of good people are dirty. They say Saint Frideswide only washed once a year and the Queen's Grace herself only has a bath once in three weeks." He flung his arms round her and kissed her, for he was a loving little boy and he did not like to see her looking worried, and he did not squeak at all while she did his other hand.

They all had an extra large breakfast on Sunday, and really they needed it after all the washing they had done, a very satisfying breakfast of meat and beer and bread, and when it was over, and Joyeuce and Dorothy had washed it up and made the beds, they got ready for church.

The Sunday morning church-going was the great event of their week and took a lot of perparing for. . . . Great-Aunt came with them. . . . It was practically the only time in the week when she went out and she insisted on riding her white mule Susan to the Cathedral door. There was no reason whatever why she should not have walked the short distance, but the getting her on her mule, and the getting her off again, made a lot of fuss and commotion, and she liked fuss and commotion. Canon Leigh did not assist in getting Great-Aunt off to church. . . . He said his duties called him elsewhere.

No one but Joyeuce herself knew how exhausted she was by the time she had got the family dressed and they were all waiting by the front door for Diggory to bring Susan round from the stables; yet she had the satisfaction of knowing that they looked magnificent. Great-Aunt wore black velvet, over a crimson kirtle, and an immense ruff. The veil she wore over her black wig was worked in gold thread, and she had rubies in her ears and on the bodice of her gown. Grace wore her green silk kirtle, scattered over with yellow and silver dots, with a farthingale of rose colour, the twins were dressed in forget-me-not blue. Will and Thomas in peacock blue and Diccon in his faerie green. . . . While as for Joyeuce herself, she wore the clothes she had worn on that never to be forgotten evening at the Tavern that was only a few days ago but yet seemed parted from her by several years.

Diggory came in through the Fair Gate, leading Susan in her saddle and trappings of crimson velvet, and Will and Thomas held Susan while Diggory and Joyeuce lifted Great-Aunt up so that she sat sideways on her saddle, with her feet planted firmly on the board below and her fine skirts billowing out over Susan's white back. She looked magnificent when she was in place, but the language she used while she was being got there was staggering. The great ladies of the day could swear like the proverbial trooper, the Queen's Grace herself not being behindhand in the art, but Great-Aunt, when she really got going, could put the lot of them completely in the shade.

Then they started, Diggory leading Susan, Joyeuce and Diccon walking hand in hand beside Great-Aunt, and the twins, Grace, Will and Thomas walking behind. They all carried large prayer books, and the girls had posies of flowers to match their frocks.

From the other houses round the quadrangle, where lived the seven other Canons, came more family groups, and from the scholars' rooms the scholars came running in their sober clothes and snowy Sunday ruffs, while under the Fair Gate flowed a steady stream of people in their bright Sunday best. The sun shone gloriously and the blue air seemed clamorous with sound, for all the bells of Oxford were ringing their people to church. The bells of Saint Mary the Virgin, the bells of Saint Martin's at Carfax, of Saint Michael's at the North Gate, of All Saints', Saint Aldate's and Saint Ebbe's, and clearer and more lovely than them all the famous bells of Christ Church, that for years had rung the monks to prayer at Oseney Abbey and now peeled out from the Cathedral tower. They had their own names—Hautclere, Douce, Clement, Austin, Marie, Gabriel and John—and personalities that matched their names, and they ranked only second in importance in the world of bells to Great Tom himself.

There was no way into the Cathedral from the quadrangle and the stream of worshippers passed by the staircase up to the hall and into the fifteenth century cloisters of the original Priory, and from there up a flight of steps into the Cathedral. Susan was brought to a halt at the bottom of the steps with a great clattering of hoofs on the paving stones, and Great-Aunt was with difficulty got down. She entered the Cathedral leaning on Joyeuce's arm on one side and her stick on the other, with Diccon walking before her carrying her prayer book and nosegay and the other children following behind. She made a point of entering at the last possible moment, and would even wait in the cloisters till that moment arrived, and then she would sail up the central aisle very slowly, with the whole congregation looking at her. . . . She adored it, and so did Diccon. . . . Joyeuce, Grace, Will, Thomas and the twins suffered acute agonies, but that was nothing to Great-Aunt and Diccon. The congregation enjoyed it too, and felt their hearts lifted up to heaven by the spectacle of that cherubic little boy and that saintly old lady entering the mighty Cathedral to praise their God.

Joyeuce, from her position beside Great-Aunt and behind Diccon, could not see their faces, but if she had she would have been overwhelmed with astonishment. Diccon walked with his head a little lifted and his gaze fixed upon the east window behind the high altar. His green eyes had a rapt, faraway look, as though they beheld not the rich stained glass of the window but the angels of the little children whose eyes behold the Father in heaven, and his red poppy lips a pathetic, wistful droop that was very affecting. Great-Aunt, on the contrary, kept her piercing dark eyes fixed upon the ground, but over her face had come a strangely noble expression, and the dignity of her carriage and the gracious whisper of her velvets and silks over the stone floor of the aisle spoke volumes to the congregation of the saintliness of her character. When they filed into their seats under the tower, and knelt down to pray, Great-Aunt kept her face uncovered that all might see her devoutly moving lips, but Diccon bowed his curly head low and clasped his fat hands upon his chest. . . . No need to-day to hit his knees behind to make him kneel down. . . . When they both sat back on their seats they had reason to congratulate themselves upon a really magnificent dramatic performance.

Will and Thomas knelt too, with their peacock blue caps held over the lower parts of their faces and their wide grey eyes peeping over the top to see if they could see any of their particular friends in the congregation ; when they did see a friend they removed their caps from their mouths and grinned broadly ; they were nice, sincere little boys and they did not pretend they were addressing their Maker when just at the moment they didn't happen to be.

It is pleasant to be able to record that Grace and the twins prayed, their prayers developing much on the same lines. " Please God, make me a good girl. Please God, bless Father and Joyeuce and everyone I love. Please God, help me not to think about my clothes in the sermon."

As for Joyeuce, for the first time in her life she could not pray. The battle that had been fought and won in Saint Michael's at the North Gate had now to be fought all over again.

Her duty was perfectly obvious; confession of her appalling behaviour to her father, rejection of Nicolas, lifelong devotion to her father, Great-Aunt, Will, Thomas, the twins, Diccon, the dogs and Tinker; and she knew that she ought to be praying for strength to do her duty. . . . But she did not want to do her duty. . . . With the whole strength and passion of her being she wanted to be a selfish, wicked, intriguing, untruthful girl. She opened her lips to pray but her throat felt dry and her lips felt hot and nothing would come. " Deus, propitius esto mihi peccatori," she whispered at last, and sat back on her seat with her face white and strained and her mouth sullen and a little defiant. . . . She had heard people say that it was good to be young, but she thought that the comfortable middle-aged people who so often made that platitudinous remark must have forgotten their own youth with its tormenting loves and problems and bewilderments. She wished she was old. She wished that her decisions were behind her and her heart at rest and her feet set firmly upon some path from which there could be no turning back.

Yet for a few moments, as she looked about her, the beauty of the Cathedral lifted the pall from her spirit. The Saxon pillars of the choir, massive and of colossal strength and seemingly as old as time, gave one a glorious feeling of stability, and the perpendicular clerestory that rose above them, and carried the eye up to the fine and graceful pendant roof, seemed like the arches of the years that carry a man's soul from the heavy darkness of the physical earth to the airy regions of heaven. This strange mixture of architecture, that spanned the centuries in one great curve, never failed to affect the mind strangely. One felt cowed by it, a little confused by this leap through time, yet comforted too by a sense of union. Ancient glass, that told the story of Saint Frideswide's life, filled the windows and the sun shone through it to pattern with all the colours of the rainbow pillars and arches and the tombs of the dead that paved the floor.

From where she sat Joyeuce could see the Lady Chapel, that in Christ Church was built to the north of the choir instead of behind the high altar, so as not to interfere with the city wall that protected the east end of the Cathedral. In it was the shrine of Saint Frideswide and looming above it was the watching tower where in old times a monk sat day and night to protect the relics of the saint. It was the same shrine where Catherine of Aragon had worshipped, and the floor of the Cathedral, from the west door to the shrine, was worn by the feet of the pilgrims who had come there to seek healing and comfort of the saint.

Only a few years ago, in the reign of Queen Mary, a Canon's wife had had her history curiously mixed up with the history of the shrine, and now, in the days of Queen Elizabeth, the present Canons' ladies could not look at that shrine without a shiver of horror. . . . And nor could Canon Leigh, who was always seen to avert his eyes from the Lady Chapel when he walked in procession to his stall in the choir. . . . The horrible but veracious history haunted them all.

II

Only fifteen years before, in King Henry's reign, Peter Martyr Vermilius, a Florentine who had adopted the reformed religion and come to England at Cranmer's invitation, was made Regius Professor of Divinity and Canon of Christ Church, and took up his residence at his canonry house in the quadrangle with Catherine his German wife.

Poor Catherine had a bad time from the very start. There were a good many Catholic scholars up at Christ Church and Peter Martyr, the pervert, was naturally the object of their hatred and a grand excuse for making a row. They smashed the windows of his house on the north side of the Fair Gate, they sang rude songs under the window of his study by day, so that he could not work, and imitated cats under his bedroom window by night so that he could not sleep. Peter Martyr was upset, naturally, but poor Catherine was even more so. She was a foreigner and she couldn't speak the language. Her servants bullied her and the tradespeople cheated her and the Dean's wife, Mistress Cox, the only other lady living at that time within the precincts of Christ Church, was not as kind as she might have been because she was not quite certain whether Catherine was really a lady. What with being so bullied by day, and so frightened by night with the row the scholars made, and getting no sleep and being so homesick, poor Catherine got ill and after only two years at Christ Church she died. Christ Church was sorry, then, and wished it hadn't done it. It was too late now to be nice to the living Catherine, but they were as nice as they knew how to the dead one; they gave her a splendid funeral and buried her in the Cathedral near the shrine of Saint Frideswide, on the same spot where a few years earlier that other tragic Catherine had knelt and prayed. The bones of the saint were no longer there, having been cast out fourteen years earlier by the command of Henry Tudor, and somehow or other completely mislaid, but the desecrated shrine still seemed to the people of Christ Church the heart of their college, and to be laid near it was an honour for Catherine that they hoped was appreciated by her in whichever of the courts of heaven she might happen to be at the moment.

Then Henry died, and Edward died, and Mary came to the throne; everyone had to change his religion once more and everything was in a turmoil. Peter Martyr, who had already changed his religion once and did not feel equal, at his age, to doing it again, fled from the country, and Richard Cox's place as Dean was taken by Richard Marshall, a gentleman of drunken habits who didn't care how many times a day he changed his religious beliefs provided he could celebrate the change in good liquor.

To him came the commissioners from Mary, sent to Oxford to cast out from the city heretics dead and alive, to enquire if it were true, as the Queen's Grace had heard, that Catherine Martyr, who had been buried beside the shrine of Saint Frideswide, was a heretic? As poor Catherine had been unable to speak English no one knew what her opinions were, she might have been a Mohammedan for all anyone knew to the contrary, so it was thought best to run no risk of contaminating the shrine and Dean Marshall was commanded to cast her out.

He was a loathsome, brutal creature, but even he did not like the task he had been set. He spent the day shut up inside the Deanery with a few boon companions, drinking deep, and when the sun was setting, and a sky like a rose was spread out behind the Fair Gate, he and his companions and some workmen, with crowbars on their shoulders, reeled off to the Cathedral and locked themselves in. When they came out again, carrying poor Catherine the shadows were falling and the bright sky veiled its face in horror. . . . Not knowing what to do with the body, Dean Marshall put it at the bottom of the Deanery garbage heap and hoped for the best.

Then Mary died, Elizabeth came to the throne and everyone quickly changed their religion again; though it gave pleasure to all that Dean Marshall, having mixed himself up in some plot or other, was thrown into prison and died there in the misery he so rightly deserved. The Queen's Grace was very busy during the early years of her reign in finding out all that Mary had done and immediately doing the opposite. . . . Mary had said Catherine was to be taken out so Elizabeth naturally said she was to be put in again. . . . Orders were sent to Christ Church for the honourable re-burial of Catherine Martyr.

George Carew, the new Dean, a man of very different character from his predecessor, summoned his Chapter—of whom Canon Leigh was now a member—to his aid and together they removed Catherine from the Deanery garbage heap and conveyed her reverently to the Cathedral. While they were looking about for an obscure corner where she could be safely put for the moment they stumbled over yet another collection of bones, wrapped up in a silk wrapping.

"What on earth?" asked the Dean.

"Could they be Saint Frideswide?" suggested one of the Canons tentatively. "She got mislaid, you know, after the desecration of her shrine."

"Is this Cathedral never spring-cleaned?" snapped the new Dean irritably. He was a cultured, fastidious man, and his nerves were completely overturned by the events of the morning. He scarcely dared move a step to right or left lest he fall over yet another dead body.

The Canons gloomily shook their heads. During recent years, with Bishops and an Archbishop being burnt outside the city wall and all men walking in peril of their lives, such customs as spring-cleaning had rather fallen into abeyance.

"What in the name of heaven," demanded poor Dean Carew of his Chapter, "am I to do with these ladies?"

A burly Canon raised his head. "Throw 'em in together, Master Dean," he suggested helpfully. "Have a grand combined funeral service for both good dames."

So it was decided, and the Dean and Chapter went thankfully home to dinner.

For a short time the bodies of Catherine and Frideswide lay side by side in the Cathedral, reverently and carefully guarded, and on January the eleventh, 1562, before a large concourse of people, they were laid to rest in a common grave with much pomp and ceremony. It was a great occasion. Bells were rung, hymns were sung and a volume of Latin poems was written to celebrate the event.

But Canon Leigh, as three years later he walked up the Cathedral in procession for Sunday morning service, averted his eyes from the shrine with a shiver of horror ; for never, as long as he lived, would he forget the morning when they had looked for Catherine in the Deanery garbage heap.

III

The great days of Cathedral worship, those days when the music of the Mass sounded like the angels singing and the incense drifted in a fragrant cloud through the pillared aisles, had gone for ever, but in this service of the reformed religion there was both dignity and beauty. The choir sang the psalms of David with simplicity, as the birds sing, and the prayer that Cranmer had written, repeated by Canon Leigh in his deep and beautiful voice, had a haunting beauty that smote hard upon each heart. " O God, the protector of all that trust in thee, without whom nothing is strong, nothing is holy ; increase and multiply upon us thy mercy ; that, thou being our ruler and guide, we may so pass through things temporal, that we finally lose not the things eternal."

They applied it, as all men apply great literature, to their own personal needs. To Joyeuce it brought an overwhelming sensation of comfort. The awful complication of " things temporal," the children and the dogs and the housekeeping and Great-Aunt, and now this further confusion of fiery love that for days and nights had been threatening to overwhelm her, seemed to sort themselves and fall into place. Under the guidance of God, it seemed, one could thread one's way through them and somehow or other come out the other side.

She lifted her head and looked across to the place where Nicolas knelt. His eyes were shut and his white ruff, even though it was not in quite the right place for a halo, yet made his beautiful face look very saintly. Looking at him with yearning love she saw that his lips moved and her heart leaped up in joy to think that he too was praying that prayer for guidance.

"Nine from seven you can't," whispered Nicolas—he always did his accounts in church—"Nine from seventeen is eight. . . . Damn. . . . I've spent too much. What'll Father say?" His lids flew apart in consternation and he found Joyeuce looking at him, her deep blue eyes fixed upon his face with a penetrating look that seemed to pierce his soul. He gave her one of his flashing smiles and then hastily lowered his lids again to shut out her eyes. . . . They were too possessive altogether and Nicolas had no intention, at present, of undertaking responsibilities that might prove in any way inconvenient. The shouldering of responsibility, like the accumulation of learning, he was putting off till a later and more convenient date.

And Philip Sidney, kneeling beside Nicolas with his fair head buried in his arms, was thinking, as he always thought on Sundays, of the little church of Whitford, Flintshire, of which he was lay rector. His father, Lord President of Wales, had made him rector of Whitford when he was nine and a half. A gentleman of the name of Gruff John was his proctor, lived in the rectory and did all the work, but Philip had an annual income of sixty pounds a year from his benefice and always found that it came in very handy. . . . And Philip, a deeply religious boy, loved to think that he was lay rector of Whitford. . . . As he knelt there, with his face hidden in his folded arms, he was seeing the little grey church squatting in a fold of the Welsh hills. At this moment Gruff John, a gentleman with a tremendous bass voice, would be booming out Cranmer's prayer over the heads of his kneeling congregation, a handful of shepherds and farmers with their wives and families. Outside in the churchyard the bees would be buzzing over the wild flowers and from up in the hills the sound of sheep bells would come faintly down the wind. Philip, kneeling in Christ Church Cathedral, prayed for his parishioners, for the burly farmers and the grizzled shepherds and their comely wives and rosy children. He prayed for his church, too, that it might always be a house of prayer, and for Gruff John, and for the sheep up in the hills and for himself, that God would make him worthy of his sixty pounds a year.

Canon Calfhill, he to whom posterity would owe it that the story of Catherine Martyr was put on record, preached a sermon that was listened to by a small proportion of the scholars with burning attention. Later in the day they were all of them required to give an account of the sermon to their tutors, a tiresome regulation that was enough to drive anyone distracted, but they had evolved an elaborate system by which only one scholar on each staircase listened while the rest of them just thought great thoughts. Then after dinner the one who had listened instructed the ones who hadn't as to what they should say to their tutors and all was well. They took it in turns to listen of course, starting at the beginning of the year with the scholars whose names began with A and working carefully through in alphabetical order.

It was Philip's turn to-day to listen for his staircase, but he didn't mind because he liked sermons and always listened in any case. The sermon was preached in Latin, of course, and as Canon Calfhill was a fine Latin scholar it was worth listening to. Not only could he preach magnificently in Latin, but he could write fine Latin verse too, and his epigram on Frideswide and Catherine was much admired.

> Ossa Frideswidæ[1] sacro decorata triumpho
> Altari festis mota diebus erant.
> E tumulo contra Katherinæ Martyris ossa
> Turpiter in fœdum jacta fuere locum.
> Nunc utriusque simul saxo sunt ossa sub uno,
> Par ambabus honos, et sine lite cubant.
> Vivite nobiscum concordes ergo papistæ,
> Nunc coeunt pietas atque superstitio.

Canon Calfhill only preached for one hour because his congregation was for the most part young and he always said it was best to preach only short sermons to the young, lest their spirits should suffer weariness and so be alienated from religion, and then they all sang a hymn and filed out joyously into the glorious sunshine. Hautclere, Douce, Clement, Austin, Marie, Gabriel and John rang out again over their heads. Answered by all the bells of Oxford, and Great Tom boomed out the hour for dinner.

[1] The bones of Frideswide adorned for holy triumph on festal days were removed to the altar. From the sepulchral mound, on the other hand, the bones of Catherine Martyr had been shamefully cast into a foul place. Now the bones of each are together under one stone, equal is the honour to both, and without strife they lie. Live therefore, followers of the Pope, with us in concord, now piety and superstition combine.

IV

The College authorities never understood why it was that after dinner the scholars sat out on their staircases in the utmost discomfort instead of comfortably in their rooms. And it always seemed to be one scholar only, they noticed, who was doing all the talking, while the rest, hands locked round their knees, were attentively silent.

Philip had been very much moved by Canon Calfhill this morning and sitting at the top of his flight of stairs in Broadgates Hall, with various be-ruffed gentlemen sprawling below him all the way down the stairs to the open door leading to Fish Street, he waved his hands in the air and held forth at the top of his voice. The others listened hard, cuffing anyone who shuffled his feet or coughed too loudly, for their account of the morning's sermon was always much admired by their tutors on the days when Philip had been listening to it. . . . For Philip could set them on fire. . . . He was a sort of spiritual Midas. Everything he touched, whether it was a Latin sermon or a way of life, or a cause or a personality, seemed to shine with a new glory.

He finished his exposition, and a little sigh of admiration rose like incense from the crowded staircase. It always amazed him that he, shy as he was, should have this power over his fellows. It did not make him proud, it only increased his humility, just as his beautiful home and his fine possessions increased it. . . . For to be dowered with lovely things through no effort and no virtue of one's own is very humbling, he found; the fear of unworthiness and the fear of mishandling kept one perpetually crawling to the feet of God. . . . Later in his life he inscribed his shield with the words, " These things I hardly call our own."

A figure suddenly appeared at the open doorway at the foot of the stairs, blocking out the sun, and Philip gazed at it with dismay, for the figure was a magnificent one dressed in the Leicester colours, and held in its hand a letter tied in scarlet silk. . . . And if there was one thing Philip disliked more than another it was being interfered with by Uncle Leicester.

Like mist before the sun the other scholars melted away, for they knew their place when the colours of the Chancellor were flaunted in the streets of Oxford, and the magnificent serving man advanced up an empty staircase and bowed low before the slender boy who sat at the top.

Philip received the letter with a dignified inclination of his fair head and felt rather anxiously in his wallet for a tip. There was, as he had feared, nothing in it but a couple of groats. These however, he presented with such an air that they might have been ten gold coins, and the servant received them as though they were twenty. . . . Servants adored Philip Sidney. Though he was too shy to say much to them he always seemed to notice that they were there, and to be glad that they were.

Left alone, Philip perused the missive from his august relation with a heavy sigh. It was as he had feared, Uncle Leicester was in Oxford on business, was staying at Queen's College—the food was very good at Queen's—and would be at the Fair Gate in an hour's time that he and Philip might spend a happy afternoon together.

Philip went to his room with leaden footsteps and proceeded to wash himself, and scent himself, and put on his best crimson doublet and his pantoffles, leather shoes with exaggeratedly pointed toes, a new fashion introduced from Venice. He felt a fool in his pantoffles, but Uncle Leicester had given them to him so he must wear them.

As he dressed he took himself severely to task for his dislike of Uncle Leicester, who was so fond of him and so tirelessly good to him. . . . If only the man would not interfere. . . . Philip found it difficult to forgive his uncle for the letter he had written to the Dean of Christ Church when Philip first came up to Oxford. " Our boy Philip being of a delicate constitution," the Chancellor had written to the Dean, " it is our wish that he should eat flesh in Lent." And the Dean had replied that the wish of the Chancellor being law the regulation as to scholars eating only fish in Lent should be set aside in Philip's case, and Philip should eat flesh. Could anything, Philip asked himself, have been more unkind ? It was quite bad enough to have a delicate constitution without having the attention of the entire College drawn to it. . . . In Lent, when he had to sit in hall choking his way through a huge platter full of underdone beef, oozing red blood round the edge of every slice, and all the other scholars sitting round disentangling fish bones from their teeth and looking at him, he could have cried. Indeed, sometimes at night he did ;

partly from vexation of spirit and partly because if Uncle Leicester had only known it his delicate constitution and such quantities of underdone beef did not really agree together very well. . . . But then he must remember, as his mother, Uncle Leicester's sister Mary, was always urging him to, that poor Uncle Leicester had no children and loved Philip as his own son. . . . But then, as Philip couldn't help pointing out to his mother, if Uncle Leicester had no children it was entirely his own fault for making such a mess of his matrimonial affairs.

For Philip's family had a skeleton in the cupboard—Aunt Amy. Philip had loved Aunt Amy very dearly and even though she had now been dead for five years he could not forget about her. She had been so pretty and loving, and so sweet to him when he was a little boy, that he had loved her the best of all his aunts. He would never forget her sitting on the grass at Penshurst, dressed in a pink frock, and making daisy chains for him when he was small. She had been happy in those days, and had laughed when she twisted the daisy chains round her dark head and his yellow one. When he had eaten too much beef he had a horrible nightmare in which he saw his pretty Aunt Amy, still to his imagination dressed in her pink frock, come hurtling down those awful stairs at Cumnor Place and falling in a pitiful heap at the bottom, with her neck broken. In his nightmare he stood there at the bottom of the stairs watching it happen, but with his feet chained to the floor so that he couldn't run forward and catch her in his arms before she struck the ground. He always woke up from this dream sweating and screaming out in terror, so that his friend Fulke Greville, who had the room next to his at Broadgates Hall, would have to come running in and give him a drink of water, and hit him on the back and tell him not to be an ass, and sit on his bed and tell him nice tales about bear-baiting and cock-fighting before he was sufficiently comforted to go to sleep again.

Uncle Leicester and Aunt Amy had been very happy when they first married. It was only later, when the Queen's Grace, completely bowled over by Lord Leicester's magnificent looks, showered honour upon honour on his head, that it swelled up, together with the heads of his relations, and poor Amy seemed to them not quite equal to her position. It was the fault of the Queen's Grace, of course. She fell in love with Leicester's "very goodly person," and it was whispered in the Court that he could have married her had it not been for Amy. Horrible scandals about Elizabeth and Leicester were whispered everywhere. They heard them at Penshurst, Philip's home, and Aunt Amy, even though she was not allowed to come to Court, heard them too and was very unhappy.

Of course it was not true, as everyone said at the time, that Uncle Leicester had sent her to stay at Cumnor Place so that his friend Anthony Foster, who lived there, should throw her down those stairs. . . . It was a clear case of suicide. . . . Her maid had heard her praying to God " to deliver her from desperation," and she had sent all her servants to Abingdon Fair on the night she died. But still, it was all very horrible, and Uncle Leicester had not made things better by never going near her body when it lay in state in Gloucester Hall, and absenting himself from her burial in Saint Mary's Church. Doctor Babington, too, one of Uncle Leicester's chaplains, who had loved Amy and who had to preach her funeral sermon, made everything worse by getting upset and describing Amy as " pitifully murdered " when he had meant to say " accidentally slain."

But the frightful scandal that there was about her death killed Leicester's hopes of marriage with Elizabeth. She made him Earl of Leicester and one of the greatest noblemen in the land, and she gave him his beautiful home at Kenilworth, but she could not now marry him.

Trying not to mention the word Cumnor in conversation—it was a word that must never be spoken in Uncle Leicester's hearing—and trying not to think about pretty Aunt Amy whenever he was with his uncle made intercourse with that gentleman extremely difficult for Philip.

But it had to be accomplished and at the appointed time he was waiting under the Fair Gate. He had not to wait long, for constant attendance upon the Queen's Grace had at least taught Uncle Leicester the virtue of punctuality. With a commotion of horses' hoofs on the cobbles he came clattering down from Carfax, with a few mounted servants behind him and his trumpeter going before. His splendid figure looked its best on horseback and the sunshine gleamed on his jewelled doublet and the great ruby that fastened turquoise plumes in his velvet hat. His dark beard was trimmed to a most elegant point and his fine dark eyes, as they rested on Philip, were softened and kindly. The trumpet sounded, Satan barked like mad, a little crowd gathered and Philip ran forward to hold his uncle's stirrup as he dismounted.

Uncle Leicester, as he stood beside his horse with his hand on Philip's shoulder, gracefully acknowledging the bared heads of the bystanders and the bows of Heatherthwayte, looked very grave and very intellectual. He was a first-rate actor and when he was treading the streets of Oxford as its Chancellor you couldn't have told, from looking at him, that he wasn't really a very suitable person for the position. . . . Though it must be said to his credit that though the classics bored him stiff he was a quite passable mathematician.

" Well, Phil, how are you ? " enquired the great man genially.

" Very well, thank you, Uncle," said Philip. " I hope you are quite well ? "

" Quite well, thank you," said the Chancellor, and shifted his hand from his nephew's shoulder to his fair head.

Philip realised with horror that it was his duty to kneel down and be blessed. This was quite as it should be, of course, but Philip did think that Uncle Leicester might have refrained from staging a pious scene in front of all these people. It wasn't fair, either, because if Uncle Leicester believed in God at all, which Philip thought doubtful, he didn't allow his faith to inconvenience him in any way, so what right had he to make it inconvenience Philip ?

But there was no help for it and Philip knelt, covering his face with his hands to hide his shame. Uncle Philip blessed him very loud, in the accents of a Chancellor, and the crowd, especially its female element, was much affected.

" Well, Phil, and what shall we do now ? " enquired the Earl, as they shook off their admirers and strolled together under the Fair Gate.

Philip thought a walk round the Christ Church meadows would be nice. . . . The meadows have always been a blessing to scholars burdened with relations up for the day.

As they walked the trodden paths through the feathery June grass, soft and warm against their hands as the breasts of little birds, and under the trees that lifted their heavy heads only lazily to greet the south wind that was driving white clouds like sheep across the sky, they made rather heavy conversation to each other.

Philip answered the usual avuncular enquiries as to the progress of his studies and archery practice, the state of his friends' health and his own health, the Dean's health and his tutor's health, with his habitual sweet and staid courtesy, and Uncle Leicester was more enslaved than ever.

For the Earl did really love Philip. He had a certain capacity for love, as was shown by his short-lived love for Amy and his lifelong devotion to himself, and Philip caused him to exercise his capacity to the full. He could, and did, put himself out for Philip, and with the Earl that was the supreme test.

" Have you done any hunting, Phil? " he asked. . . . He was always afraid that Philip's love of study might crowd more manly activities out of his life.

" Yes," said Philip, " last Wednesday I hunted out at C—— ; I mean I hunted last Wednesday."

He went scarlet and fell over the long toes of his pantoffles, but Uncle Leicester didn't seem to notice anything.

" Stags good ? " he asked.

" Splendid," said Philip.

" Where did you kill? " asked Uncle Leicester.

They had killed in the great park at Cumnor and Philip, in misery, and again falling over his feet, changed the conversation by asking Uncle Leicester what he was doing in Oxford.

" Ah ! " said the Earl. " What do you think ? I am sounding the University as to the expediency of persuading the Queen's Grace to visit us next summer."

Gone was all Philip's staidness of demeanour. He crowed and leaped like a small boy, and even seized Uncle Leicester's sleeve and shook it slightly. " The Queen ? " he cried. " Will the Queen really come to Oxford ? "

" I have taken her to Cambridge," said Uncle Leicester, " and now it is high time she came to Oxford."

" You oughtn't to have let her go to Cambridge first, Uncle," said Philip reproachfully.

" Cambridge claims to be the older University," said the Earl.

" It's not now," said Philip. " Not now that we've discovered that King Alfred founded us."

"How did you make that out?" enquired the Earl with interest.

Philip waved an airy hand but disdained explanation. The magnificent edifice of historical research, built up by those imaginative historians on whose word Philip had it that King Alfred founded Oxford University, looked well, but was difficult of explanation to the outsider.

"He did," said Philip briefly. "And you shouldn't have taken the Queen's Grace to Cambridge first. . . . Not when you're Chancellor of Oxford."

"You forget," said Uncle Leicester, "that I am also High Steward of Cambridge."

It was true. Uncle Leicester experienced no difficulty in combining these two honours, together with any benfits that accrued thereto.

"Will the Queen come to Christ Church?" asked Philip.

"If you wish it," said his infatuated Uncle. "We'll lodge her at Christ Church, shall we?"

"When?" gasped Philip.

"Next summer," said the Earl. "And you and your friends shall amuse her with a masque in the hall."

Philip was pink with emotion and his eyes shone like stars. For the first time he almost loved Uncle Leicester. It was something, after all, to have an uncle who could twist a queen round his little finger in this way.

A postern gate let them in through the city wall into Merton College, and they wandered through the old, irregular buildings that lacked the plan and pattern of the other Colleges because Merton was the mother of them all. Her buildings were no more than a few old houses, and the church of Saint John the Baptist, adapted to the use of that first little band of twenty scholars who in the thirteenth century came there to fulfil the intention of their founder, Walter de Merton, that they should fit themselves by study and prayer for life in the great world. Philip, by whom the great world must be entered in a short time now, remembered them as he passed under the embattled tower and the great gateway, and looked up at the carving above it that showed Christ, with the dove over his head, coming to Saint John the Baptist to be baptised. Philip knew what that carving meant in connection with Merton. . . . Christ, too, needed to be prepared.

V

From Merton they walked to Oriel. At this point Philip usually took the visiting relative up Shidyard Street to High Street, and so to Saint Mary's, but Uncle Leicester knew Oxford as well as Philip did, and anyhow, with Aunt Amy buried in Saint Mary's, one couldn't very well go there. . . . He stood for a moment on one leg and wondered what on earth to do next with Uncle Leicester. . . . The question was decided by the sudden appearance of Giles and Faithful from the gateway of Canterbury Inn. Emerging at the double they all but ran into the Chancellor, retreating only just in time in a paroxysm of bows.

Philip presented them to his uncle as two of his best friends and the Chancellor regarded the younger of them with growing horror. Giles was passable as a friend for his nephew, but this ugly, flap-eared, shabby boy, with the huge head and no breeding at all, was impossible, utterly impossible. Really Philip should be more careful where he bestowed his favour. He seemed to have no sense at all of what was due to his position. Uncle Leicester had had occasion to speak of this to him before, and it seemed he would have to do so again. . . . While chatting to the two boys with kindly condescension he fixed Faithful with a cold and fishy eye.

Faithful withdrew a little behind Giles and looked down at his feet. The thoughts that passed through the Chancellor's mind were quite clear to him and he was too ashamed to lift his eyes. As he stood there he could actually feel his head swelling out and his ears getting larger and his clothes shabbier. His shoes, he suddenly noticed, had two slits in the leather, and as he looked at them the slits widened to gaping, mocking mouths. . . . You are ugly, they said, you are hideously ugly. Your father was a thief and your mother was a slut out of the streets whom he did not bother to marry. You will never tell anyone that, but it is true. Why don't you go back to the gutter, where you belong? What are you doing, masquerading as a gentleman in the streets of Oxford? . . . If Faithful could have moved he would have run away, but his feet were so busy laughing at him that they would not take him.

"And where are you boys off to?" enquired the Chancellor genially.

"To a verse reading, sir," replied Giles, "in Walter Raleigh's room at Oriel."

"Is it permissible for an old fogey such as myself to come too?" enquired the Chancellor. In the full flush of his splendid prime as he was, thirty-three years old and looking less, it delighted him to refer to himself as an old fogey and to watch the vehement denials that sprang into the eyes of his companions. And he liked the companionship of the admiring young. Even though their admiration might be based upon ignorance it was consoling after the truthful comments of one's knowledgeable contemporaries.

Philip, Giles and Faithful looked at each other a little doubtfully.

"Evidently it is not permissible," said the Chancellor with some pique.

"I am sure Walter Raleigh would be honoured, sir," Giles hastened to assure him. "Only before the verse reading starts he is to put the last touches to a chemical experiment."

"Indeed?" enquired the Chancellor with interest. "What chemical experiment? And is private experimenting with combustibles in one's rooms allowed by the University authorities?"

The three politely ignored the last question and concentrated upon the first. "Walter Raleigh thinks he has discovered the correct formula for a Great Cordial or Elixir," they explained. "Applied externally to base metals it will turn them into gold and applied internally to the human stomach it will prolong life."

"In other words," said the Chancellor, "your friend has discovered the secret of perpetual youth."

"Yes," they said.

"Say no more," laughed the Chancellor, "but lead on," and ignoring Faithful he put his hands upon the shoulders of the other two and swung them round towards the gate of Oriel. . . . Over their shoulders they exchanged anxious glances with Faithful trotting behind. . . . What, they wondered, would be the penalty for blowing up the Chancellor?

They entered under the archway and into the quadrangle of the College, founded by a Rector of Saint Mary's and built up round the lovely old house of La Oriole. Raleigh's room, where a choice gathering of the younger poets met every Sunday afternoon, was on the north side of the quadrangle, high up, and the little party mounted the narrow stairs in single file, tingling with mingled anxiety and expectation. . . . Perhaps, whispered Faithful to Giles, who was just in front of him, it would be all right after all. They were a little late and it might be that Raleigh and the poets were already blown to pieces. One must hope for the best.

But no sooner had he expressed his hope than a terrific report reverberated over their heads. Philip, who was leading, recoiled upon the Chancellor and the Chancellor upon Giles. " The Great Cordial ! " ejaculated Faithful, as Giles in his turn recoiled upon him and the whole party of them slithered into a dusty heap upon the stairs, Faithful at the bottom.

The Chancellor, fearing loss of life, extricated himself at once from his undignified position and raced on up the stairs, two steps at a time, the others tumbling after.

Raleigh's room was filled with smoke and strewn with the bodies of prostrate poets. Through the haze the Chancellor could dimly see a table piled with phials and tubes, and a tall boy stirring some evil smelling concoction in a big bowl.

" It's all right," announced a cheerful voice. " I know what I did wrong."

" I very much doubt if it is all right," said the Chancellor sternly. " All these young gentlemen appear to be dead."

" Fright," said Raleigh laconically, bending over his bowl with nose held between finger and thumb. " They're all cowards and skunks. . . . And who are you, sir, anyhow ? " He suddenly raised his head and saw who it was. " The Chancellor ! " he gasped.

But he was at a loss for only a moment.

" The Chancellor," he roared at the prostrate poets, dealing out a few kicks to right and left to awake them into reverence. Then he dashed to the windows, opened them to let out the smoke, bowed to the Chancellor as though a visit from him were a thing of everyday occurrence, removed Fulke Greville, who was prostrate upon the best chair, from there to the floor with a sweep of his right arm, removed a whole windowful of poets who obscured the view with a gesture of his left arm, seated the

Chancellor and raised the whole confused gathering to its feet in a corporate bow all in the twinkling of an eye.

"A young man who will go far," thought the Chancellor, and could not find it in his heart to offer any further rebuke. Instead, with his scented handkerchief to his nose, he found himself offering his condolences.

But Raleigh, emptying the Great Cordial out of the window and summoning a few poets to help him stow the basins and phials under his bed, waved them airily aside. "A mere error of judgment," he said. "Next time I shall succeed." His voice was vibrant with determination and his eyes shone as he launched forth into a glowing description of the golden age that was coming. . . . When there would be no more poverty, no more sorrow, no more sin.

A shout from outside interrupted his eloquence and sent him bounding to a window. Below in the quadrangle stood the Provost and other dignitaries of the College, outraged and indignant at this wrecking of their Sunday siesta by the noises and smells of Hades. This was not the first time, they said, that Master Walter Raleigh had disturbed the peace of Oriel upon the Sabbath, although he had been informed again and again that diabolical experiments upon the holy day were not permitted within the precincts of the College. They would be obliged if he would descend and give some explanation of his conduct.

"Sirs," cried Raleigh, bowing very low, "I regret that I am unable to do so. I am about to entertain the Chancellor at a verse reading."

Such incredulous noises greeted this statement that Leicester was obliged to show himself at the other window. "I crave your indulgence for this young man," he said to the astonished Provost in arrogant yet honeyed tones. "Any unpleasant aroma that may have titillated your nostrils, or slight sound that may have assaulted the delicate tympanum of your ear, were unforeseen accidents in a humanitarian effort for the betterment of the human race that, I think, should be commended in a son of Oriel. Master Walter Raleigh and his friends, following in the footsteps of the great alchemists of all time, were searching for that Elixir that shall turn all hard metals, yea, even the hearts of reverend and learned men, to soft and merciful gold."

The Provost glanced from the splendid but most unacademic

figure of the Chancellor in one window to the equally splendid figure of Walter Raleigh in the other. . . . Adventurers both. . . . He bowed coldly and withdrew with his following.

Leicester once more settled himself comfortably in his chair for an hour that promised to be fruitful of entertainment, and the poets, with a deep sigh of expectancy and a rustling of papers, settled all over the room like a flock of birds. It was a beautiful room, furnished by Raleigh regardless of his father's expense, and now that the smoke and the smell were cleared out of it, and the Sunday afternoon silence and sunshine came into their own, it made a fitting background for the poets who sat in elegant attitudes, on the floor and on the chairs, attentive, as were all men always, to Raleigh's slightest word or glance.

They were a likely looking lot of youngsters, the Chancellor thought as he looked round the room, drinking in the adulation of their eyes and of their quick, panting breaths. The sun poured in, lighting on fair heads, dark heads, yellow heads and ginger heads, all of them sleek and shining after the Sunday brush. Their snowy ruffs made the perfect setting for young faces and the subdued colours of their best doublets, plum colour, dark green, dark blue, violet and russet, seemed to accentuate the vividness of their eyes and hair. . . . How the young do shine, thought the Chancellor. . . . Surely this lot had already drunk their Elixir, for their youth lay upon them like a bright polish, as triumphant as the sheen of the spring world in early morning. It looked inviolable, impossible to tarnish, shouting aloud to the world that life was good.

Dreams. . . . That polish was nothing but the reflection of them, a thing as easily destroyed as dew upon the grass or the sheen upon the petal of a flower. When the gleam of their dreaming was rubbed off them would they call their dreams traitors or friends ? He looked at them all, and for the death of their dreams he could have flung himself down upon the floor and wept, taking the measure of an unmade grave. . . . And being an Elizabethan he wouldn't have been ashamed of doing it, either, but the room was crowded and there was no space ; and Raleigh had got to his feet to start the verse reading with one of his own poems. For a few moments, as he hunted through a little manuscript book to find the right page, there was a deep silence filled only by the buzzing of a bee and a little shuddering sigh from Philip. Exchanging glances with his nephew the Chancellor discovered that they were thinking the same thing; what would Raleigh do if he did not succeed in concocting his Elixir? What would happen to him if his search for the gold that should remake the world ended in disaster, and death came unawares upon a man who had expected to be always young? What alternative had he for his Great Cordial?

Raleigh found the place and began to read. He read quietly, his usual vehemence stilled, and in a way that made the poem bite deep into the memories of his hearers, so that when years later he died for his dreams upon the scaffold those who were still alive remembered his room at Oriel, and heard his voice reading as though the summer day were only yesterday.

> " Give me my scallop-shell of quiet,
> My staff of faith to walk upon,
> My scrip of joy, immortal diet,
> My bottle of salvation,
> My gown of glory, hope's true gage,
> And thus I'll take my pilgrimage.
>
> Blood must be my body's balmer,
> No other balm will there be given,
> Whilst my soul, like quiet palmer
> Travelleth towards the land of heaven,
> Over the silver mountains,
> Where spring the nectar fountains;
>
> There will I kiss
> The bowl of bliss,
> And drink mine everlasting fill
> Upon every milken hill.
> My soul will be a-dry before,
> But after it will thirst no more."

The Chancellor was astonished. So that was Raleigh's alternative. Blood. He would start joyfully upon pilgrimage, gowned in glory, and if he could not realise his dreams he would die for them. And he seemed to have no horror of the blood. It was to be a balm, a thing that would shine upon his body as once his dreams had done. It would be like rain upon the dry earth. Fresh life would spring from it. It was the whole duty of man to work for the golden age, to set himself to build Jerusalem in his own place and his own time. He would never succeed, but his failure would be the triumph of his life. The thing was incomprehensible but true. . . . The rest of the verse reading seemed to the Chancellor to go by in a dream.

VI

A poem can be like two hands that lift you up and put you down in a new place. You look back with astonishment and find that because you have read a few lines on a printed page, or listened for a couple of minutes to a voice speaking, you have arrived at somewhere quite different.

Raleigh's poem had done that for the Earl of Leicester and Cranmer's prayer had done it for Joyeuce.

All day she said it to herself. She thought it was one of the finest prayers that had ever been composed by man, and how it was that she had never properly noticed it before she could not conceive. In its quiet insistence on what was important it seemed to still all confusion. And at the same time it was a challenge. It did not ask for ease in trouble or escape from pain, it did not even seem to think these things particularly desirable. In those two words " pass through " its insistence was all the other way. It swung her right back to the mood that had been hers in Saint Michael's at the North Gate, before Nicolas had plunged her head over heels into fairyland and sent all her values flying to the winds. Its bracing effect was such that by supper time Joyeuce had decided to turn her back on love and concentrate on duty. Her life had done nothing to develop her sense of humour and she took herself extremely seriously, so it did not strike her as comic that a prayer forged as a weapon by a man who had had to face complications more awful than anything she could conceive of, followed by imprisonment and martyrdom, should be used by her in her own mimic warfare. . . . Not that her own particular trials ever seemed to her small : it took all her strength to carry them and so they seemed to her colossal.

When the curfew bell was ringing, about the hour of nine, she presented herself before her father in his study, her hands clasped very tightly before her, her head thrown back, her face very white and her blue eyes clouded to grey. Canon Leigh's heart sank, for this attitude of the tragic muse usually betokened some terrible domestic crisis; the cat had fallen down the well, Diccon had called at the Deanery again without his clothes, or Great-Aunt was dead.

"What is it, Joyeuce?" he asked.

"I have been very wicked," she said.

Her father was so astonished that he dropped his pen and sent the ink spurting all over his to-morrow's lecture. In all the years that he had known her she had never been wicked. The baby Joyeuce had not screamed when she teethed, only bubbled at the mouth and moaned a little, and as a child she had never stolen the comfits or run away from her lessons. As a girl she had shouldered her responsibilities without wincing and never in all her life had he known her lose her temper or seek a single thing for herself.

"What have you done, Joyeuce?" he asked in horror.

Joyeuce took a deep breath and told him. She told him nearly everything; her visit to Bocardo, her lies to Mistress Flowerdew, the meal at the Tavern, the kisses that accompanied it and the magic, moonlit walk in the meadows. She left nothing out except her love for Nicolas, and that she would not tell, because it was easier to renounce it if she did not give it greater substance by telling of it. Her recital went on and on and seemed to her afflicted father to last well into the night. In an agony his mind fixed itself upon the thought that Joyeuce and Nicolas had been in the meadows at night, on Midsummer Eve in the moonlight. . . . His heart fainted within him. . . . What was Joyeuce trying to tell him? Something she could not put into words? She was silent now and the silence seemed to him full of horror.

"Is that all, Joyeuce?" he asked hoarsely.

"All?" enquired Joyeuce, almost outraged. Surely, she thought, she had told him enough to make his hair stand on end for the rest of his life, and he asked her if it were all!

The worst of her ordeal over, her eyes had gone back to their normal blue and were fixed on him with a child's wonder. With a shock of relief so overwhelming that the room spun round him he realised that she did not know what on earth he was talking about. . . . His respect for Nicolas de Worde, that up till now had been small, owing to the horror of his Greek and the outrage of his Latin, suddenly went up by leaps and bounds. His relief and astonishment were so great that he did not know what to say. Scratching his head in bewilderment he looked appealingly at Joyeuce, but for once she did not seem to know what he ought to say either. The situation was beyond them both. She burst into tears and flung herself into his arms.

While he patted and soothed her he wondered if she was crying as a child cries, who will soon forget its grief, or as a woman cries who will remember it. Hoping it was the former he treated it as the former and comforted her as he had comforted her when she had broken her doll or fallen full length on the stony path. Never mind, he said, it was over now. She had been a good girl to tell him and he was proud of her for being so brave. She must go to bed now and it would be all right in the morning. He patted her till she had stopped crying, then kissed and blessed her tenderly and took her upstairs to bed.

But Joyeuce, though she was comforted, only slept brokenly. In her dreams she saw again the figures of Nicolas and Diccon, scarlet and green, moving through the moonlit trees to the gates of fairyland. "Take me too!" she cried, but they went on and disappeared inside and the gate shut. She stood looking at the fairy gates until the walls of the house of her everyday life towered up around her like precipices and she could not see them any more.

Meanwhile Canon Leigh in his study did not know what on earth he ought to do; and when he remembered that he had four daughters who each of them might have five love affairs, making twenty all told, before he got them safely steered into the harbour of matrimony—though even then there might be upsets in the harbour—he came out in a cold sweat. Joyeuce had not known what he was talking about. But surely at her age she ought to have known what he was talking about?

He spent a bad night and in the cold light of dawn sat down and penned a note to Mistress Flowerdew, asking that he might wait upon her and receive her inestimable advice upon a matter of overwhelming importance.

CHAPTER IX

SAINT GILES' FAIR

> Tell me, my lamb of gold ;
> So mayst thou long abide
> The day well fed, the night in faithful fold ;
> Canst thou, poor lamb, become another's lamb,
> Or rather, till thou die,
> Still for thy dam with baa-waymenting cry ?
> Earth, brook, flowers, pipe, lamb, dove,
> Say all, and I with them,
> Absence is death, or worse, to them that love.
> PHILIP SIDNEY.

I

THE long summer holidays, arranged to suit the harvesting, were upon them. All the scholars must go home, rich and poor alike, to help gather in the corn and the wheat and the barley that were clothing England in a robe of green and gold and orange-tawny that bent before the wind under a sky of burning blue.

The day when the scholars departed was a great day. Travelling in companies as protection against rogues and vagabonds they passed out north, south, east and west through the gates of the city, singing and laughing and shouting out final insults at the townspeople who thronged the streets to see them go.

Some evil imps of the town had mounted the belfries and rang out peals of thanksgiving as the companies wended their way past the guardian towers.

" At North Gate and South Gate, too, Saint Michael guards the way,
While o'er the East and o'er the West Saint Peter holds his sway."

Some of the scholars chanted the old rhyme and looked up at the towers as they passed beneath them ; some of them glad to be going, some of them sorry, and some of the older ones heartbroken because their time at Oxford was over and they would never come back again except as the old fogeys of the past.

The rich scholars, the noblemen and squires' sons, rode on horseback with their mounted servants clattering behind them; they would put up at the fine houses of friends and relatives and they had their best clothes with them in saddle bags; their friends would give them fresh horses and they would be home in no time. But the poor scholars had to walk, sleeping under hedges if the weather was fine or at the rough inns if it was wet, and it would be a long time before they got to their journey's end, with their faces brown as berries and their shoes worn through.

Philip, who was going to London for part of his holidays to stay with Uncle Leicester, rode under the East Gate and up the bridle path through the woods to Shotover. He was one of a large and gay company, for a great many of them were going London way. He rode a white horse, and had blue plumes in his hat, but he was sad because every departure from Oxford brought nearer the final departure that he dreaded. On the top of Shotover he reined in his horse and looked down, as Faithful had looked down in the dawn of that spring morning of his arrival, at the towers of Oxford below him in a haze of heat.

"They are always in a mist," he said, "like dreams that go away."

His face looked like the face of a puppy whose dinner has been removed before it has had time to do more than taste it, and Fulke Greville, beside him on a black horse, hastened to apply bracing treatment.

"You are coming back, you ass."

"Some day," said Philip, "we shall never come . . . except in dreams."

"If everyone who ever loved Oxford comes back to it in dreams," said Greville, "the streets must be blocked with ghosts. . . . It's a wonder we living people can get by."

They were silent, brooding, their reins lying loose and their horses nosing in the wild thyme for edible bits of grass, until a shout from the others warned them that they were left behind. They turned their horses and cantered away over the springy turf ; shouting to their friends, depressing thoughts left behind with the ghosts in the city.

Raleigh and the west-countrymen rode under South Gate, across the river, up the hill and through the Forest of Bagley. They were the noisiest crowd of all, for they were many of them going back to live within sight and sound of the sea, and they were glad to be going. Thomas Bodley, who rode with them, did nothing to check the row they made, M.A. and Fellow of Merton though he was. . . . In fact he made as much row as any. . . . Raleigh roared out roystering songs in broad Devonshire and they all joined in the choruses in the most unseemly manner. All the way through the flat water meadows beyond the river they sang, and up the hill, and they only fell silent when the great Forest of Bagley gathered them into its darkness. It would have been sacrilege to make a noise just then, for there were singing birds to listen to, and rabbits to watch, and under their feet were spread a carpet of bilberry leaves and green ferns that made the floor of the forest like the strewed presence chamber of a king.

And Nicolas, who lived in Gloucestershire, rode out through North Gate, in a leaf-green doublet and a bad temper. . . . He did not want to go away because he was leaving Joyeuce behind.

He had seen her several times since that evening at the Tavern, but she was always very difficult and troublesome. When he greeted her in the street or the quadrangle she swept him such swirling curtsys that the wind of them seemed to blow him miles away, and when he tried to talk to her she lowered her lids and turned demure. She wouldn't go to the Tavern with him again, or for walks round the meadows, and on the few occasions when she looked at him her blue eyes had faded to the colour of rain and were clouded with beseeching. He thought he knew what she wanted. She wanted to be proposed to, of course. She wanted a ring on her finger and pearl drops in her ears and himself in leading strings to be shown off to all her friends. . . . Well, he wasn't going to propose to her ; at least, not yet. . . . He wasn't going to saddle himself with a wife before he had even tasted the joys of manhood and the sweets of freedom. Joyeuce must wait. Why must she be in such a hurry ? Why could she not enjoy, as he did, the fun of a little clandestine love and laughter? Why could she not shelve, as he did, serious things to a more propitious moment?

He could not know that he was denying to Joyeuce the luxury of proud martyrdom. How could she refuse to marry him when he did not ask her to marry him? She had worked herself up to a high pitch of nobility, even thinking out the beautiful words in which her refusal would be couched, and now the nobility was going sour in her for lack of use. At night she wept angry tears into her pillow. She supposed it was all a mistake and he did not love her at all. She was getting old now, she was sixteen, and no one had wanted to marry her yet. Was she, perhaps, unlovable? This was a thought that dragged her pride down to the dust, for though it may be a painful thing to refuse a proposal, it is yet elevating to the pride, while to have none to refuse is a humiliation that Joyeuce at her age found it almost impossible to put up with. She told herself that a really nice girl would have been glad that Nicolas was spared the pain of loving a woman who could not marry, but looking at herself squarely and honestly at one o'clock in the morning she found that she was not a really nice girl. . . . She was always horrified when she took out her true thoughts and looked at them. . . . Laid on top of them to hide them was a beautiful coverlet of the noble sentiments that guide a Christian life, underneath, not so beautiful but still quite pretty, were the thoughts that she ought to think and usually thought she was thinking, and underneath again were her real thoughts, ugly things, so utterly at variance with the actions of her life that she seldom dared face them as they were. She supposed that in time, with prayer and fasting, the glorious colour of the surface covering would penetrate right down through all the layers of thought until they were all transformed as though wine had been poured into water. But at one o'clock in the morning that lovely unity seemed a goal that she would never reach. She was a poor tormented child dragged in pieces; too unselfish to live for her own pleasure and too selfish to accept frustration thankfully.

But Nicolas couldn't possibly be expected to understand all this and as he rode out of North Gate he was merely sore and angry, answering his companions with disagreeable grunts, feeling not the warmth of the sun but the chill of Joyeuce's cold fingers when she bade him good-bye and seeing no smiling, flowery fields but only Joyeuce's eyes that were now the colour of rain. . . . Tiresome girl. . . . Why had he been such a fool as to fall in love with so serious a maiden, he who liked laughter and the careless heart? He vowed he would forget her. Surely the pain of the heart was a thing that could be controlled by a little abstention from the sight of the beloved face, just as the pain of the stomach could be controlled by a little abstention from food. . . . At the thought of food he cheered up a bit. . . . The lovely little hamlet of Woodstock was coming into sight, with its beautiful cottages sprawling down the hill, and they were to stop at Woodstock and have a good dinner there.

II

Oxford was strangely quiet.

A deep silence brooded over the empty sunlit quadrangles. The curfew rang out as usual, but no figures came scurrying to get in before the College gates shut. There were no brawls in the street, no merry shouts from the meadows, while from the window of Bocardo the leather bag dangled flabbily on the end of its string, swinging to and fro in the wind that blew from the south, bringing hot summer scents of harvest fields and hedgerows to mingle with the smells of the town.

There were those who liked this quiet; Giles, for instance, who could work on hour after hour without a single distraction; and the exhausted senior members of the University; and the townspeople who could feel for once in a way that their own town belonged to them; but it bored Diccon to distraction.

When late summer came outrage was added to boredom because Saint Giles' Fair, one of the greatest events of the year to the children, was encamped without the North Gate, and they were not allowed to go because it was rumoured that there were cases of small-pox among the Fair people. It was particularly hard on Diccon because Dean Godwin had given him a silver coin with which to purchase a hobby horse. He roared and stormed and kicked the furniture, but his father remained adamant. . . . He would not have his family laid low with the small-pox, and if Diccon kicked the furniture again he would thrash him. . . . So Diccon, unable to get what he wanted by behaving like a demon, suddenly turned cherub, smirked and crooned and bided his time.

Everything comes to those who wait, especially to those who have no scruples about taking any evil opportunities that may occur. On one very warm day when Dorothy, mazed by heat and a large dinner, dozed off in her chair and neglected to keep her eye on him, Diccon seized his woolly lamb, Baa, and his silver coin, and crept noiseless as a mouse out of the kitchen and across the hall, lifted the latch of the front door and scurried down the steps into the quadrangle.

He ran like the wind across it but when he got to the Fair Gate he dropped on hands and knees and advanced with caution ; for he knew that Satan would know he was being naughty and might protest with loud barkings and bayings that would bring the whole College running out to catch him.

Heatherthwayte, as was to be expected on such a hot day, was asleep on his bench with his hands clasped over his stomach, his mouth ajar and happy snorts escaping from his nostrils.

But Satan, as Diccon had feared, was awake. He was sitting up in the centre of the Fair Gate, facing the quadrangle, with his front legs very stiff and straight. One of his ears was hanging negligently, but the other was cocked and pointing straight up to heaven like the finger of an accusing angel, and his eyes were bright and observant.

Diccon, looking like a little animal himself in his suit of russet brown, crept to within a couple of feet of Satan and then sat back on his heels and looked at him ; and Satan looked at Diccon.

Satan waved his tail in a friendly way and opened his mouth to laugh, letting a yard of dribbling pink tongue hang out at the side of his mouth, as was his habit when amused. . . . But there was a warning gleam in his eye. . . . Stay where you are, he seemed to be saying to Diccon, and all will be well, but budge an inch and you'll catch it.

Diccon crept an inch to the right and Satan growled softly in his throat ; he crept an inch to the left and Satan gave a muffled bark that caused Hetherthwayte to open one eye ; but he did not see the small brown figure crouched on the cobbles and shut it again almost immediately.

Then Diccon tried guile. He crept quite close to Satan, stretched out a finger and scratched Satan's chest. Satan liked that for he had been somewhat bitten of late and the scratching was soothing to his irritation. He closed his eyes and raised his head to signify that Diccon might scratch him under his chin as well.

Diccon scratched Satan for ten minutes; on his chest, his stomach, his chin and in the soft places behind his ears; and all the time he was quietly edging round Satan until he was sitting behind him and scratching his back.

Satan was now in a state of enjoyment that bordered on the ecstatic, and in the semi-conscious condition that accompanies ecstasy. It was not until the blissful scratching ceased, and he looked round over his shoulder to enquire the reason, that he discovered that the wretched child had fled. Barking wildly he leaped to his feet and rushed out into Fish Street, to see a little brown creature scuttling like a rabbit up the hill and across Carfax. Satan halted uncertainly, one forepaw raised, but his first duty was to the College whose guardian he was and he padded back to the Fair Gate and then rudely awakened Heatherthwayte.

"Not so much as a cat stirring," growled Heatherthwayte, "and you must make a row fit to wake the dead, you black-faced piece of garbage, you."

Satan was apologetic. He stuck his tail between his legs and grinned sheepishly, showing the whites of his eyes. He had been beguiled by the delights of the flesh and he was ashamed of himself. When Heatherthwayte dozed off again he was unable to follow suit. He sat up miserably on his haunches staring at the Cathedral tower.

III

Diccon had never been out in the town by himself before and a wild happiness possessed him. He was bare-footed and bare-headed, but neither the sun scorching down on his dark curls nor the burning heat of the cobbles under his feet incommoded him in the least. He adored the sun, just as he adored wild winds and sheeting rain; his hot blood and tempestuous temper bespoke him their child. He was across Carfax, up Cornmarket and under North Gate in no time, running so fast that few people had time to notice him before he was gone.

In the open country outside North Gate, in a grassy space

between Saint John's College and Saint Giles' church and under
the patronage of those two saints, Saint Giles' Fair was encamped, and Diccon's heart beat high. He had been taken to
the Fair a year ago and the memory of it had remained with
him like the memory of some thrilling dream. Everything that
he loved best had been at that Fair, colour and noise and excitement, and at it had been purchased Baa, his beloved lamb, with
his legs of tin and his fine woolly coat, the person that he cared
for only second to Tinker in all the world.

Diccon plunged into the Fair as a fish into the sea. The
roar and scent and colour of it engulfed him like waves going
over his head, but he was not in the least frightened. In five
minutes he was completely lost, with no idea where home was,
or how he was to get back there if he wanted to, but that did not
worry him at all. He was always a person who lived for the
moment only, and the more exciting the moment the better he
was pleased.

And there was no denying that Saint Giles' Fair was exciting.
It was like a miniature town, with hundreds of booths set out
under the blazing sun and narrow grassy alleys winding between
them like the lanes of a city. The booths had bright awnings
over the top of them, coloured orange and red and green, as
protection from sun and rain, and under the awnings were spread
unimaginable glories. There were flowers and fruit, pouncet
boxes, hawk's bells, dog whistles, coloured kerchiefs, trinkets,
garters, shoes, aprons, and every possible luxury that could
tempt the eyes of the grown-ups. There were things for the
children too, popguns and hobby horses and drums and kites,
and wonderful things to eat such as gilt gingerbread and peppermint drops at twenty a penny.

A seething mass of people surged up and down the lanes
between the booths, country people and townspeople with a
good sprinkling of thieves and vagabonds and gypsies, arguing
and shouting and bargaining with the Fair people who stood
behind the booths. They were all dressed in their gayest and
gaudiest as though they like the earth itself felt that the blazing
golden sun and the deep blue sky of late summer were a challenge.

"Who can shine as I do?" cried the sun, and the earth
laughed as she reared up sunflowers and golden rod on tall,
strong spears that seemed trying to reach the arrogant heavens.

"Who dare match my colour?" asked the painted sky as morning, midday, evening and midnight wheeled by in a glory of saffron and azure, rose-pink and poppy red, amethyst and ebony pricked and washed with silver. "I do," cried the earth, and there were peonies and Michaelmas daisies in the gardens, golden fruits upon the walls and dandelions like stars in the lush green grass.

And human beings were as arrogant as the earth, it seemed, for colour was awash in the lanes of the Fair, flowing up and down like water that reflects the colours of the sky above it. Sky-blue farthingales flowed over sun-flowered kirtles and scarlet shawls were folded over gowns of emerald green. The heads of young girls were bound with coloured kerchiefs, and nodded like poppy heads, and the nimble legs of the young men were cross-gartered in scarlet and purple.

Diccon with his dirty bare feet and his warm curls seemed so a part of the landscape that few people noticed him. He darted in and out of the crowd like a dragon-fly, quick and eager and unafraid. When anyone hindered him he hit out at the impediment with Baa's sharp tin legs and way was instantly made for him with curses and fists raised for a blow; but he was always gone before the blow could fall and hard words slid off him like water off a duck's back. His green eyes were the brighter for the colour they feasted on and the mingled smell of flowers, fruit and sweating humanity was a smell that seemed good to him. Now and then, when he felt the need for refreshment, he helped himself to a bite of gingerbread or a peppermint drop and had vanished before anyone could catch him. He had no qualms of conscience about these thefts. On this, the first day of real freedom in his life, he was the master of the world; its colour was a carpet beneath his feet and its golden sunshine a canopy over his head, and between the one and the other were piled riches that were his for the taking. For the first time, with freedom swinging open a door before his eyes, he was aware of life stretching out illimitably in front of him like a shining road and of himself as young knight riding out towards it. He felt suddenly powerful and splendid and hit out with Baa as though the sharp tin legs were his lance and his sword and his pointed dagger. . . . The earth was his and the glory of it.

Now and again the lanes of the Fair converged, like those of a real city, upon an open square, and here there would be a sideshow or an entertainment. Diccon stared with all his eyes at a fire-eater who appeared to be chewing up glowing coals as though they were so much gingerbread, at a performing dog who could walk round on his hind legs balancing a tankard on his nose, at a cat with two heads and a calf with a tail sticking out in the middle of its forehead.

But it was in the fortune-teller's tent that the adventure of the day awaited him.

It was pitched in a little square at the very centre of the Fair, at its heart, just as what happened to Diccon in it seemed to him ever afterwards to lie at the heart of his life. It was a small place, made of some tattered crimson material stretched over pieces of wood roughly nailed together. Its back was set against the back of some booths and in front of it was a clear open space.

In this space stood a man, a splendid vagabond of a man with savage green eyes and a torn green doublet open at the neck to show his great hairy chest. Diccon was fascinated by this man and squatting down at the edge of the crowd he gazed and gazed. He was not used to men like this. His father, Dean Godwin and the other men who had come and gone about him since his babyhood had been soft-voiced, slender and clean. There had been something withdrawn about them. When he had looked up at them from his position on the floor he had seen fold upon fold of black gown, surmounted by a sort of cartwheel of white ruff; and when from above the ruff a cultured voice had asked him how he did it had seemed to come from the sky itself. Even when they had picked him up he had been so anxious to get down again that he had not really taken them in. . . . And anyhow, though he had tolerated and at times liked them, he had felt that they did not really belong to his world.

But this man did. He was like an animal, and Diccon liked animals. He was not worn and slender like Canon Leigh but bulkily huge, stocky and strong. He had a big head, with shaggy red-tinged dark hair and a dark beard, and great broad shoulders. Through his torn doublet and hose his arms and legs showed like huge strong pillars, burnt almost black by the sun. In a voice like a bull's he was inviting the crowd to come to the tent and have their fortunes told. Sara the gypsy was inside and Sara never failed to tell the truth. His patter was splendid. Words poured from him in a stream, spiced with oaths, and the fascination of them drew the people one by one towards the tent. They went in rather fearfully but they came out laughing, their faces rosy with the reflected glow from the glorious futures the gypsy had foretold.

Diccon felt that he must see this splendid man close to. He pushed and burrowed his way to the man's feet and then sat down cross-legged and gazed again. . . . This was a god among men. . . . His voice flowed over Diccon's head like thunder and his gesticulating hands were so strong that they could have picked you up and broken you in small pieces. He was a freckled man, too, freckled like Diccon, and Diccon's bump of conceit led him to think that freckled men were the finest there are. His eyes never left his idol; they were fixed on his face, drinking in every detail of his rugged splendour, and presently their scrutiny was like a magnet that drew attention to him; the man paused in his patter and looked down at the child sitting cross-legged on the ground at his feet, gazing at him.

"Here, you!" he shouted, "What do you want? You get out of here!"

He made a movement as though he would have struck Diccon, but there was no flinching in the indomitable little figure and the unblinking stare never wavered. The man dropped his raised fist and bent low, hands on knees, to stare at the child. As their eyes met, Diccon's poppy-red mouth curved into a smile and his green eyes shone as though lights had been lit behind them. To the onlookers it seemed that a curious change came over the man. "Eh?" he said doubtfully. "Eh?" All the stuffing seemed knocked out of him and the dirty, horny finger he stretched out to the boy wavered about uncertainly before it found the place it wanted; the warm, three-cornered little hollow under the chin of Diccon Leigh. Diccon made no attempt to bite the finger that lifted his chin, instead he continued to smile like a little cherub and all his dimples peeped. The man was bending so close to him that the smell of sweat and dirt and strong drink almost stifled him, but he did not care. Other people would have said that this was not a nice man; a dirty, evil vagabond, they would have said; but if this man was a dirty vagabond then dirty vagabonds were the sort of men whom Diccon liked.

"You saucy little cockerel, you," said the man. "What do you want? Eh?"

The tone of his voice had changed. The threat had gone out of it and if it were possible for the voice of a bull to hold a caressing quality that quality would have been present.

Diccon could not say what he wanted. He wanted to be with this man for always; he wanted to follow him to the world's end, to clean his shoes and fetch his beer and run his errands. But he could not say so, he could only continue to smile and dimple.

The crowd grew a little restive. The dark man's patter, his oaths and gesticulations, were amusing and part of the show. They had not come here to stand about and watch him make a fool of himself over a child. "Here!" they adjured him. "Get on with it!" And one of them bent down and tried to lift Diccon out of the way. . . . To be bitten for his pains.

"Now then, son," adjured the dark man. "None of that! What do you want? Eh?"

"I want," said Diccon in a loud voice, "to have my fortune told."

He did not really want anything of the sort but to have his fortune told would, he thought, keep him well within the vicinity of the dark man.

The crowd jeered. "Let him show his bit of silver," they advised the dark man. "Where's his bit of silver to cross the palm of the gypsy?"

The eyes of the dark man were like those of a sad dog, for he was sure that Diccon would have no silver, but with a crow of delight Diccon thrust a fat hand into his little wallet and held up the coin that Dean Godwin had given him.

With a triumphant gesture the dark man gathered him up in the crook of his arm, lifted the tent flap and pitched him in.

IV

At first Diccon thought he had been flung into the middle of a lighted lantern, or into the heart of a rose, because it was all red; then he realised that it was the sun, shining through the red drapery of the tent, that made it so warm and rosy.

Standing with his back to the opening, with one little arm

laid across his forehead as though to help him see better, Diccon looked at Sara. There was nothing at all in the tent to distract the attention ; nothing at all but Sara sitting on a low stool. Her voluminous, ragged skirts swept the grass round her like the skirts of a queen ; they were russet colour, that same colour that flows over the hills when the bracken is dying. Round her shoulders was a shawl of a brilliant, almost savage, emerald green, and there were gold rings in her ears glinting through the thick dark hair. The rosy light of the tent poured over her, softening the lines of her face, hiding the dirt on her shawl and the rent in her skirt, and behind its veil she was beauty incarnate.

"What a very little gentleman," she mocked softly. "What a very little gentleman to want his fortune told ! Have you a silver coin, little gentleman ? "

Diccon did not answer but slowly crossed the grass until he stood in front of her, looking up into her face, his fat hands laid on her knees. Her eyes were dark pools into which he could look down and down, and her mouth, so close to him, was full and red as though it were made for kisses. She was opulent and rich and soft. Diccon felt that wherever he might press his finger it would go in, as though she were a cushion stuffed with goose feathers. He put up his finger and pressed her cheek, to see, and he was quite right. He caressed her cheek and crowed with delight.

But at sound and touch of him all the softness seemed to go out of Sara. She seized him fiercely with hands that felt hard, and stared at him. She looked at his eyes and his hair and his pointed ears, and traced the curve of his wicked eyebrows with a finger that shook. Then she pulled him roughly to her and dragged his doublet away from his back so that she could look at it. . . . So fiercely did she pull that his doublet ripped and tore. . . . Diccon didn't know what he had on his back but whatever it was it had an extraordinary effect upon Sara, for she picked him up and hugged him as though the hugging of Diccon was what she was born for.

Had Joyeuce or Dorothy hugged Diccon as Sara was hugging him he would have kicked, yelled, struggled and bitten, but from Sara he liked it. He wriggled himself comfortable on her lap, giggling contentedly, and a strange happiness stole over him.

Her lap seemed to be made to be his throne. The hollow of her shoulder exactly fitted his head and her body was warm and soft about him. When Joyeuce and Dorothy cuddled him Diccon never found them wholly satisfactory. Dorothy, though well upholstered, was hard, and Joyeuce, though soft, was inadequate; she was quite flat in front and her lap was so flimsy that it was apt to let you through. But this woman was just right. He nestled and cooed and crept closer, wriggling his bare toes in ecstasy.

Time stopped for them both. Sara rocked herself backwards and forwards, crooning a little song, and Diccon's long lashes descended to his cheek.

They were disturbed by a discontented murmuring outside the tent and by the head of the dark man protruding through its flap. "Be quick and have done," he whispered angrily to Sara. "Send the child away. These outside will not wait here for ever." Then he withdrew his head and they heard him swearing at the crowd to pacify it.

Diccon, indifferent though he had always been to the feelings of those about him, was yet acutely aware of every emotion that thrilled through Sara. He had felt her love and her joy and now he felt her terror. Their lovely unity was threatened. They had come together, fitting into each other as those fit who once were one body, and now the noisy world was surging up against their rosy shrine, where were only the two of them in their unity; in another moment it would have broken in; the crude glare of full day would wash over the rosy light of babyhood, putting it out, and mother and son would be one no longer.

Sara leapt to her feet, panting. She dragged and pulled at the red curtains behind her until they tore and gave way, leaving a space through which she could creep, pulling Diccon after her. They crept under one of the booths behind the tent, crossed the grassy lane beyond before anyone had time to stop them, or even to notice them, and in a moment were running like the wind, Sara holding firmly to Diccon and Diccon to Baa.

It seemed to Diccon that strange sudden shapes came looming up against them, trying to stop them, people and dogs, and booths and bales and boxes, but doubling and dodging with the skill that was native to them both they went on till presently the Fair was left behind them, meadow grass and flowers were under their feet and before their eyes was a smooth, slipping ribbon of shining river.

They dropped down behind a hawthorn bush to get their breath, though creatures of the wild as they were they were less blown than anyone else would have been, and they hugged each other again and laughed because they had outwitted the world that would have torn them away from each other.

"So they thought they could take you away from me, did they?" jeered Sara. "The fools and the thieves, that think to take a babe from his mother! Eh, but your skin is fair, little son, fair and smooth like milk, and the soles of your feet are soft as butter. You need the hot sun to burn you and the earth under your feet to make them hard like those of a man. Why did I leave you behind in that house instead of the other? I was a fool, a fool! I thought to make my son a gentleman and I lost the core out of my heart and the light out of my eyes!"

She spoke in a strange language that Diccon did not understand, a strange tempestuous language that was like the wind in the trees, but he saw that she reproached herself and he would not have it. He kissed away the angry tears on her cheek and pummelled her with his fists to bring her to her senses.

She came to then and saw that they were not safe yet. She swung Diccon on to her back, her green shawl bound round him to keep him steady, and tramped on, walking with a slow swinging stride that yet covered the ground amazingly quickly.

They crossed the river by a wooden bridge and turned to follow a path that wound along beside its further bank. Oxford was left behind them, a walled grey city set like an island in an emerald sea of green meadow, and Diccon looked over Sara's shoulder at a world he did not know. He was not in the least frightened. Though all that he knew was left behind him in that grey city he felt nothing but a huge content. The hot sun blazed down on his head and the folds of the green shawl enclosed him like a pea in a pod. His head felt top-heavy with heat and happiness, so that he laid it against his mother's shoulder and went to sleep.

v

When he woke up again he was lying on a heap of dried bracken in a little hut with Baa beside him. In the centre of the hut a fire was burning under a black pot that swung over it from a tripod of sticks, the smoke coiling up to escape through a hole in the roof . . . some of it, that is, the rest of it spread through the hut in a blue haze like the mist of dreams that always seemed to hang over Diccon's eyes when he first woke up.

For an awful moment he thought he had dreamed it all; the Fair, the splendid dark man and the glorious woman who had been made to be his throne; then he rubbed his fist in his green eyes to clear the dreams and the smoke away and saw through the blue haze an open doorway that held as in a picture frame a patch of blue sky, a few tufts of waving trees, and Sara and an old crone sitting side by side on the grass making baskets out of plaited rushes. They were talking softly together in that strange language and the rippling sound of their voices, the wind in the trees and the whisper of the flames on the hearth were a lullaby that nearly sent Diccon to sleep again.

He was jerked wide awake by a rustling in the big heap of bracken beside him. . . . Something was there, hiding under the bracken. . . . He pushed it aside, hoping for a cat like Tinker, and found himself looking straight into the eyes of a little boy of his own age; a dirty little fair-haired boy clothed in brown rags, with skin burnt by sun and wind as golden brown as an acorn. In a paroxysm of shyness the little boy fell flat on his stomach and pulled the bracken over his head, but through it his eyes shone like two bright stars. Diccon also fell flat on his stomach, his head close to the little boy's, and through the dry, sweet-smelling fronds the blue eyes and the green twinkled at each other. Then they began to laugh, wrinkling their noses and kicking their bare legs in the air. They laughed more and more, rolling over each other, pushing the bracken down each other's necks and kicking and squeaking like a couple of puppies. They had come together at last and they were ecstatically happy. They had been born in the same hour on the same night, when all the stars were dancing. Their eyes had opened to moonlight and candlelight, heaven and earth shining together in welcome, and the first breaths they took were fragrant breaths that came blowing over the flowery earth. They had drunk the same mother's milk from a gypsy's breast and listened to the same songs crooned in their ears. They were fortunate children, born at full moon in the spring and dowered by the fairies with the gift of laughter, but never so fortunate as at this moment when they found each other.

When they were out of breath they rolled back to the bracken and sat curled up together, taking stock of each other, poking each other in the ribs and rubbing their heads together, establishing friendship as animals do by the contact of their bodies. Words were entirely unnecessary. They were part of each other, as Sara and Diccon were part of each other. Finally, as a mark of his esteem and to forge fast the bond between them, Diccon presented his foster brother with Baa. It was the first time in his life that he had ever given away something of his own, for his sense of property was at this stage of his life strong and his acquisitiveness even stronger, and the tremendous renunciation made him feel quite queer, as though when he rooted Baa out up of his life a part of himself clung to the roots and was given with Baa to the other boy to become a part of him. . . . He had made a discovery. . . . Later in his life he was to be scolded for the recklessness of his giving and would reply laughing that he hated loneliness like the devil.

Sara came in to them and ladled some of the stew that simmered in the black pot into a wooden bowl. Then she too sat down on the bracken and fed them with a wooden spoon, while they cuddled up one on each side of her with their mouths open like those of expectant young birds.

It was a stew made of poached rabbit and stolen fowl, seasoned with onions and herbs and drowned in a sticky, mud-coloured gravy. Diccon thought it was the most delicious food he had ever eaten and continued to gape for more long after the bowl was empty.

"Greedy rogues!" cried Sara, and lifted them both on her lap, one on each knee. . . . She did not love the blue-eyed child who had been borne by another woman any the less because she had found the green-eyed child who was her own. . . . The blue dreamy haze hung over the three of them, as the rosy glow in the tent had done when they were only two, shutting out the world's clamour, and in quietness and peace they loved each other.

They sat there for a long time and would have been content to sit there for ever, but the evening light was suddenly darkened and looking up they saw the figure of the dark man standing in the doorway, blocking out the sky. He was a very different man from the kindly creature who had chucked Diccon under the chin and thrown him good-humouredly through the flap of the tent. He had been drinking heavily and he was in a rage as complete, as abandoned and as royal as were the rages to which Diccon occasionally treated the household at Christ Church. He lurched through the door, strode over the fire and loomed like a thundercloud over Sara and her boys. After a moment of ominous silence the storm burst in such a torrent of abuse that the hut seemed to rock with it. It poured forth in the Romany language and Diccon could make neither head nor tail of it, though he gathered that Sara had done what she ought not and guessed that they should not have run away from the Fair. . . . But she seemed not to care. . . . She sat with her head tilted proudly back against the wall of the hut and her arms spread out one on each side of her to protect the small boys from the blows that would present fall.

The blue-eyed child shrank against her in terror but Diccon was highly interested. He had hitherto had experience of no one's rages but his own, and of one's own rages it is impossible to take an objective view. He gazed in fascination at the dark man's scarlet face, where the veins stood out like rope, and at his eyes that were so hot that they seemed to have red flames burning in them, and at his beard that wagged up and down at every furious word he spoke. His anger seemed surging all about them like a great wind and his voice was like the roar of many waters. . . . Diccon thought it was grand and his whole being went out to the dark man in admiration.

But suddenly it was not so grand, for the dark man began to use his hands. He fell upon Sara first, shaking her and knocking her head back against the wall with a sickening thud. Then he turned towards Diccon, but Sara leaned over her son with a cry, protecting his body with her own. . . . Out of the tail of his eye Diccon saw the other little boy, who had had previous experience of this sort of thing, wriggle between the dark man's legs and made a dash for it. . . . Then Sara's protecting body blotted out his view of the door and he saw nothing but the folds of her green shawl.

But he seemed to be feeling in his own body the blows that were falling on hers and a red-hot rage seized him. He loved

Sara, loved her with the first real love he had ever known, and he wouldn't have her beaten. Struggling, he got himself free of her, seized hold of the dark man's hand and bit it.

Then the dark man struck him. Diccon had never been struck. He had been whipped for his good, but that was a different thing from a blow given in anger. The world was suddenly a terrible cruel place and instead of his rage he was brimful of nothing but terror. He forgot Sara, forgot everything but his longing to escape from this place where they struck you. Sobbing and crying, with his arm pressed against the place on his head where the dark man had cruelly hit him, he dashed through the flames of the fire, through the blue haze of smoke that only a few minutes ago had seemed so lovely, out through the door into the open.

He ran on and on, sobbing as though his heart would break. He did not know where he was going but he knew what he wanted. . . . He wanted to get back to that world where voices were never raised in anger and where cruelty was a thing unknown. . . . He thought that if he went on running and running perhaps he would get there.

But gradually the wild world to which he belonged, and which had dealt so hardly with him, began to comfort him. The green grass stretched up to lay cool balm against his hot, scorched little legs, and beside him a blackbird flew, chucking in consternation. He began to be conscious of flowers in the grass lifting their faces in sorrow, and of scarlet hips and haws in the hedges that were lanterns to light his way. These things comforted him and he was sure he would soon be home.

So he was not surprised when he saw a stone building looming ahead of him. . . . That must be the Fair Gate. . . . Soon he would see Heatherthwayte, and the dear black face of Satan, and beyond them he would see his father in his long black gown and Joyeuse with her shining head.

But when he got to it it was not the Fair Gate, but a little grey church standing under the trees. For a moment he stopped, sick with disappointment, then his fear drove him to run round it, looking for some place where he could hide himself.

He found it in a porch all overgrown with honeysuckle, with a wooden bench running along one side of it. He climbed upon the bench, curled himself up in the corner and cried and cried.

CHAPTER X

THE HOLY WELL

> But you, fair maids, at length this true shall find,
> That his right badge is but worn in the heart;
> Dumb swans, not chattering pies, do lovers prove;
> They love indeed who quake to say they love.
> PHILIP SIDNEY.

I

TO Faithful the summer holidays brought a deeper intimacy with the Leighs. He lived with them and became one with them in a way he had not been before. He began to know them all much better; they ceased to be just "the Leighs" and became individual people all of whom meant something different to him and called out something different in him. We are never quite the same person with everyone, he found; the clash of personality upon personality strikes out a different flame in every case and those we love the best are those whose impact upon us creates most light and warmth. And it was Grace, Faithful discovered, who did this for him. When he was with her the world was a warm place and so light that he forgot, as we do at midday when the sun is shining, that he had come from the dark and was journeying towards the dark again.

In the mornings he worked with Giles, or was coached by Canon Leigh, but after the early dinner he was with Grace and she taught him the things that she knew; very important instruction but of a different type from that given by Canon Leigh and Giles.

For unlike Joyeuce Grace was a born housewife. She had no need to force unwilling feet into the path of duty, for the things that she had to do were the things that she liked to do. Anything to do with the running of a house, even the unsavoury business of candle-making, was a joy to her, and she knew of no greater bliss than the preparing of the fruit of the earth for their reception by the stomach of man. Her creed was simple. God made man that he might eat, and made woman from the rib of a man that she might prepare that which he ate. To Grace the whole world was a great larder stored with animals, birds, fruits, vegetables and nuts that had been created for purposes of consumption only; and above it all God, the great housekeeper, sat in His heaven, brooding benignly through the centuries over spread tables whose multiplicity and variety it baffled the powers of man to count or describe.

The problems that tormented Joyeuce, such as the purpose for which man ate, and why it was necessary to despoil the beauty of the world that he might eat, and how one was to satisfy the hunger of the soul that inhabited the well-fed body, troubled Grace not at all. Had she thought about these things she would have said that man ate to eat, and that corn looked nicer made into bread than getting knocked about outside in the rain, and that personally the longings of her soul were satisfied when her cake rose nicely and the joint was done to a turn. . . . The fact of the matter was that Grace was a plump child and the spirit within her body was so well cushioned that the shocks and jars of life had not hitherto woken it up to ask how, why, wherefore?

Yet being human she had her troubles and the chief of these was the non-recognition of her talents by the household. She was far more capable than Joyeuce and yet Joyeuce insisted upon treating her as though she knew nothing. She was able to tell her family exactly what to do in every problem that beset them, but yet they never asked her advice, and if she gave it unasked they laughed. She was thirteen, and grown up, yet they all insisted upon treating her as though she were still a baby. . . . All but Faithful.

His respect for her talents was balm to her. Unused as he was to the comfort and order of a well-run household the things that she did for the welfare of them all seemed to him amazing, and he set himself in great humility to learn what she could teach him, so that his clumsy fingers could help her in the thousand and one tasks that seemed to him likely to break the back of so little a lady. She joyfully taught him all she knew, provided it had nothing to do with the mysteries of cooking, that no man should be allowed to enquire into lest he discover that they are not so difficult after all, and woman fall in his estimation.

He learnt, for instance, that quaking grass, gathered and

brought into the house, keeps away mice ; an interesting fact and of value to those to whom a cat in the house is anathema.

> Put a Tumbling Jockey in
> June in your house
> And he'll rid you for ever of
> Every mouse.

Grace repeated the rhyme to him and showed him the spire of quaking grass she had put in every room, so as to take no chances even though they had got Tinker, and he promised that next year he would go out into the June fields and pick them for her.

He learnt, too, how to make pomander balls, with cloves stuck into dried oranges, so as to keep the plague away, and how to make potpourri, and how to pick the lavender and herbs and dry them, and put them into little bags to lay between the sheets, or herb pillows to put under your head at night to make you sleep.

Faithful thought he had never been so happy as he was on the days when they bent together over the lavender bushes, snipping off the sweet flower spikes and putting them to dry on the stone paths, with the sun warm on their backs and the bees lurching about from bush to bush. Grace, very bustling and important, with her pink skirts bunched up to be out of the way and her wide-brimmed garden hat tied with pink ribbons under her round chin, was an engaging sight as she picked lavender. The sun of that hot summer had tanned her usually white skin a warm brown and she had four freckles on the tip of her nose. Her eyes seemed to get bluer every day, he thought, as blue as periwinkles, and when she was hot her black hair clung all round her face in kiss-me-quick curls.

Yet on such days her beauty seemed to Faithful a barrier that kept him away from her, a barrier that he could not pass because of the shut-away feeling that his physical deformity gave him. Beautiful people, he felt, are one with the starlit nights and the June fields and the poetry of the world, but ugly people belong with the toads and the spiders and the east wind rain. Even in the past, when there had been no Grace, he had had this feeling of isolation, but he had always tried hard to conquer it. When another boy jeered at him because of his ears he immediately established personal contact by two good blows on the ears of his tormentors, and when he met in another the beauty that he had not got he immediately, figuratively speaking, took off his hat to it, for he knew that worship breeds love and not jealousy. He did not know how he knew these things. He supposed that the harder one's life is the more desperate must be the struggle to find out how to be happy, and the more likely to be successful.

But on the same eventful day when Diccon went to the Fair he had the courage to break through this barrier between himself and Grace. They were going round the Christ Church meadows together, picking meadowsweet to strew the floors. . . . Meadowsweet was Queen Elizabeth's favourite strewing herb and therefore much in fashion just at present. . . . As they walked, or rather trotted, for walking was too staid a word to describe the motion given to their bodies by the lightness of their hearts and the fewness of their years, Faithful pointed out to Grace all the pretty things that strewed the floor of the world about them. It grieved him that Grace's practical mind was apt to pass beauty by, seeing in ripe yellow plums hanging among sun-silvered leaves potential pots of jam rather than those apples of gold in pictures of silver that Solomon in his wisdom spoke of, and he was always trying to make her just stand and look without thinking immediately what she looked at could be made into.

"You are as bad as Philip Sidney," he said to her, "who must always make everything he looks at into poetry."

"Cooks also are artists," Grace told him solemnly.

But he tried very hard to do what he wanted her to do, just stand and wonder and worship even though the activity seemed unlikely to lead anywhere, and she was gradually beginning to enjoy things just for themselves. . . . And there were lots of things to enjoy to-day. . . . The kisses of the sun upon the water, each kiss being held as a speck of shining light within the curve of each ripple; the fine veinings on the underside of grass blades, that are intricate as a spider's web and delicate as gossamer; the amazing beauty of a wasp, once one can persuade oneself to look at it with an unprejudiced eye, with its delicate wings like silver and its striped golden body quivering below a waist whose slenderness the Queen's Grace herself, thin in the middle though she was, might have envied. His companionship was like a pointing finger. Look here, look there, he said, and Grace looked and found that the world was beautiful.

But suddenly Faithful fell silent and hung his head, for Grace in her rosy beauty was like a jewel that fitted sweetly into its setting of veined grass and running water, making the green and the silver sparkle more brightly, but he in his ugliness did violence to them both. His sudden sense of his own disharmony hurt him like a blow.

" What is it, Faithful ? " asked Grace, softly.

" I wish I was not so ugly," said Faithful in a choked voice. Grace folded her hands upon her stomacher in the matronly way that sat so comically upon her and flounced round upon him in real anger. The pink ribbons under her chin quivered with indignation and her eyes shot sparks. " How dare you say you are ugly ! " she stormed.

Faithful glanced up, astonished. He had not yet experienced the possessiveness of a woman, and her fury when a thing of her own is concerned. Grace, too, was surprised by her own rage. Her maternal instinct had erupted all in a moment like a volcano inside her and Grace the little girl had become Grace Catherine Leigh the woman. " You're *not* ugly," she said, and stamped her foot. " No ! You look so clever, Faithful, and different from other people. Men like Giles and Nicolas de Worde, with mouths and ears all alike, are so dull. . . . I tell you what it is, Faithful," she summed up. " You're distinguished looking."

Every woman in love with an ugly man lays this phrase like balm to his smart, but Grace did not know that ; she had thought of it all by herself and she was very proud when she saw his painful flush fade away and his mouth tilt up at the corners. But she was nothing if not practical and she hastened to act as well as to speak for his comfort.

" At Binsey," she said, " there is a holy well that cures boils and pock-marks."

" Are you sure ? " asked Faithful.

" Perfectly certain," said Grace strong-mindedly. " Dorothy Goatley had a boil on her chin and Diggory fetched her some of the holy water in a bottle and the minute she put it on her boil it burst."

"Do you think," asked Faithful in a low voice, "that it would take away my pock-marks?"

"Yes," said Grace judicially, "I do. It's not that I don't like them, Faithful, and I'm sure that other people never notice them at all, but I think you yourself would be happier without them."

"I should," said Faithful fervently. "It would be nice," he added wistfully, "to look like Philip Sidney."

"Philip Sidney!" snorted Grace contemptuously. "I should *hate* it if you looked like him. Why, he's just like a girl."

"Could we go to Binsey?" asked Faithful. "I know the way."

"We'll go now," breathed Grace. Her eyes were sparkling with delight and each of her cheeks had a large dimple where the finger of delight had prodded her to make her laugh. She had never been to Binsey, for young females never went outside the city gates except with the very strongest male escort, and she was wildly excited. Faithful, who had tramped from London to Oxford and thought little of it, did not realise that perhaps he ought not to take Grace so far. They ran home, giggling with happiness. Faithful's ugliness, that a few moments ago had seemed to him a barrier that separated him from Grace, seemed now a link between them; a sort of secret that they shared together.

They dumped their armfuls of meadowsweet in the hall and shouted up the stairs to Joyeuce. "We're going for a walk, Joyeuce."

"Very well," said Joyeuce. "Don't go near the Fair, because of the small-pox, and don't go far."

They made no reply to this last injunction, but scurried hastily away again lest any awkward questions should be asked. Under the Fair Gate they found Heatherthwayte asleep and Satan awake, but looking very depressed.

"What's the matter, Satan?" they asked, stopping to rub him behind the ears.

Satan thumped his tail deprecatingly, and licked their hands in humble apology. With tail and tongue and pleading glances of his sad dark eyes he tried to tell them that their evil small brother had run away only a short while since, and it behoved them to go after him; but they were stupid and did not understand.

They ran up Fish Street to Carfax, turned to the left and went
down Great Bailey towards West Gate and the grim old castle
that in itself formed part of the city wall. The oldest part of it
was a mound that had been reared as a fortification against the
Danes. . . . For those terrible Danes who crossed the North
Sea every summer in their magnificent carved galleys had penetrated even as far as Oxford. " Good Lord, deliver us from the
Danes," was once a frequent prayer in Oxford churches, and the
ringing of the tocsin that called them to arms against the Dane was
one of the most terrible sounds a citizen could hear. . . . Next
in age was the tower of Saint George, built in the eleventh
century, and then came the twelfth century castle itself with its
five splendid dowers.

Under the castle tower was the castle mill, with the mill-pond
below it. The mill had begun to work in the eleventh century
and it went on doing its work, year in and year out, for eight
hundred years. Kings and queens might come and go, civil
war, riots, fire and pestilence might ravage the city, but the
living must be fed though the dead lay in heaps in the streets
and through it all the old water-wheel went round and the old
mill went on turning corn into bread.

Once outside West Gate Grace and Faithful had green grass
under their feet, trees and singing birds around them, and in
front of them the ruins of Oseney Abbey. It was still lovely,
though the roofs were gone and the walls were falling and only
the birds sang in the great church as big as a cathedral where the
monks used to chant Mass.

Faithful, standing with Grace knee-deep in the sea of flowers
and grass that rolled right up to the walls of the Abbey, stared
in a sort of sorrowful anger at the wrecked loveliness. From
what was left he could reconstruct what had been ; the splendid
cloister and the quadrangle as large as that at Christ Church, the
magnificent church, the schools and libraries, the Abbot's
lodgings, and the water-side buildings with their high pitched
roofs and oriel windows. " Someone ought to paint these
ruins," he said sadly, " before they fall to pieces altogether and
we forget what they were like."

A few years later someone did. In the south aisle of the
cathedral there was put up a window designed by the Dutchman,
Van Ling, and among the trees in the background was a picture

of Oseney Abbey. So precious was this window to Christ Church, with its picture of the first home of the Christ Church bells, that during the Civil War they buried it, and triumphantly dug it up again at the Restoration.

II

Faithful and Grace went on their way. It was a perfect summer's day and between banks of meadowsweet and willow herb and green rushes the river ran through fields of shimmering grass.

There is something about a river that draws one on and on. It slips along so gently that one feels one can outstrip it, and the song of the ripples in the rushes is the best marching song in the world.

Over their heads was the blue sky of late summer, mirrored in the rippling water, and across the river to their right was the glorious stretch of Port Meadow, the " town " meadow that had been given to the city of Oxford to graze its cattle on for all time. It was so wide and so flat that it was like a green sea, and reflected the high white clouds that sailed above it in drifting pools of deeper green. Black-winged swallows dipped and rose and dipped again beside the river, and it seemed to Faithful that plumb upon the centre of every reflected white cloud in the blue water there sat a fat white swan. "There is no place in the world so beautiful as this," he said to Grace, " no place in all the world."

Leaving the river behind them they turned to their left and went across the meadow that led to Binsey. When they got to the tiny village they turned to their right and followed the rough stony path that led to the church and the Holy Well. Hips and haws shone scarlet on either side of the path and the trees arched over their heads as though candles were lit and a roof provided to help their pilgrimage. They met no one and Grace had a feeling that home was hundreds of miles away. She and Faithful were going a long journey together and she was enjoying it so much that she hoped she would never get to the end.

Faithful, too, felt superbly happy. A few months before, when he first began to live the life of an Oxford scholar, he had thought he was as happy as anyone could be, but now he was happier even than that. He had known joy, both the joy that comes from delight in beauty and the joy of a fine mind in achievement, and he had known the exquisite relief and sense of wellbeing when hardship and suffering are over and one has a bed to lie on and a well-filled stomach, but he had never before known this depth of content that he felt as he ran down the lane with Grace beside him in her pink frock and the candles of the hips and haws burning on either side. . . . He could find no words for what he felt.

" I am happy too," said Grace, just as though he had spoken. " It is like when Mother was alive."

" Was it nice when your mother was alive ? " asked Faithful.

" It was nice," said Grace. " One could tell things to Mother."

So then Faithful knew the true definition of a really comfortable love ; a cosy state of telling things. Their love would have none of the ups and downs, the ecstasies and torments that lay in wait for Joyeuce and Nicolas. Faithful's life burned far more strongly in his mind than in his body. Even when he became a man the desires of his body would never loom large in his life, and he would never ask more of Grace than the quiet affection and understanding that cannot burn out because they are lit eternally one from the other and grow with the giving. This placidity would never have contented Joyeuce, who beneath the apparent coldness of her nervously braced demureness was a passionate person who found her happiness in a reaching out to the things beyond practical living ; but to Grace who found her pleasure in the things that lie near at hand it would bring content.

A feeling of awe crept over them as they came into the churchyard and stood together on the path that led to the old grey church. The days of pilgrimage to the Holy Well were now over and thick green moss had grown over the path that once had been kept bare and hard with the passing of feet. The grass had grown high, hiding the tombs of the dead, and the trees had grown thickly and darkly about the weather-stained walls and lichened roof of the church. Nature was taking back again the holy place that once had belonged to man. Bit by bit her sea was lapping up, covering man's brown paths and grey stones with a slowly encroaching tide of green. Faithful marvelled at the inexorable patience of Nature. Let men attack her, cutting down her trees to make room for the smoke-grimed walls of his houses, rooting up her flowers to make space for his teeming streets, putting her birds to flight and sending her furry creatures scurrying away into exile, and she patiently withdraws herself to the horizon, gathering her creatures to her, brooding and biding her time. But let man loosen his grip for a moment, let him leave his house or neglect the pavement of his street, and she is back again with seeds blown in the wind and the germ of growth alive in the sun and the rain. Her touch is that of Midas and the mark of her possessive finger is seen in a yellow wallflower upon the wall, and the print of her returning feet in dandelions among the cobbles. They are forerunners of the returning tide, those specks of gold, and if man does not fight her, in a few centuries green waves of meadow and forest will have swept over his houses and streets and only a few hummocks in the grass will show where his city has been.

But in Binsey churchyard Nature was not yet conquered or conqueror and the enchantment of all moments of transition added its magic to the enchantment that haunts a place of pilgrimage. On the path pilgrim feet had traced a pattern of penitence and the moss that had grown over it was the brighter for its cleansing. Prayers had been said by the graves and the tall grasses whispered them over again when the wind blew. Nuns had sung hymns of praise in the church and the blackbird who carolled every sunset upon the roof-tree would sing a stave and then stop, his head on one side as though listening to echoes from the past, then sing again, triumphant, as though he had heard aright. And year in, year out, the water of the Holy Well bubbled up cool and limpid from the dark places of the earth that never change.

It was in the churchyard at the west end of the church. Four stone walls had been built round it to protect it from those who might profane it and its steep wooden roof was turfed. Little trees had seeded themselves on the roof; elders and briers and even an oak tree; elves of trees because they had so little foothold, but perfect in their degree.

"It is the holy water that makes them so perfect," said Grace, and then she told Faithful how long ago Saint Frideswide and her nuns had come to live at Binsey for a little while, taking refuge from their enemies. They had had the little church built for them, dedicating it to Saint Margaret of Antioch, and some dwelling-houses whose ruins were still to be seen. The country people who loved them had tilled the fields for them to give them bread, blackberries and elderberries grew on the bushes for their dessert and at the prayer of the saint the water of the well had sprung from the earth that they might drink. After her death the water of the well worked miraculous cures upon the faithful, like the well at Cowley Ford, so that for Frideswide as well as Edmund death made no ending of their service to their fortunate people of Oxford.

Fortunate the people of Oxford still might be, but not so believing, and Frideswide who had been a living presence in the churchyard was now but a ghost in the trees. Few came to her for help now; only the simple-minded like Diggory Colt or children like Grace and Faithful. So rusty was the key in the door of the well-house that it took the two of them, hands twining together, to turn it and force the door.

Inside was a clammy darkness and steps that seemed to go down to the bowels of the earth. They went down hand in hand, feeling their way and slipping on the slimy steps, till they came to the water welling up under a low stone arch. They were both a little breathless when they reached the bottom; partly from awe, partly because the slimy steps and the spiders' webs that tickled their groping fingers made them giggle; Grace hiccuped, which she felt she should not do in so holy a place. Faithful knelt down and scooping the water up in his cupped hands he bathed his face three times. The water looked black as ink as it lay under the archway, but as he lifted it up the light from the open door turned it to trickling silver, and when he splashed it against his face it was cold as ice.

"Three times only?" he asked Grace, and Grace nodded. That was the mystic number; Father, Son and Spirit; father, mother and child; birth and life and death.

They climbed the steps again and came out into a glory of sunlight that shone full upon Faithful's wet face, so that Grace turning eagerly towards him saw it shining brilliantly like the face of an angel.

"Faithful!" she cried. "You look like Saint Stephen."

"But are the pock-marks gone?" he asked anxiously, for

the Bible gives no information as to whether Saint Stephen was pock-marked or not.

"They're gone!" cried Grace. "I can't see them any more!" and she flung her arms round Faithful's neck and kissed him. A glorious feeling of liberation fell upon Faithful, with its accompanying sense of the inrush of new life. His ugliness had been the rusty bars of a prison, but now they had fallen, and the prisoner that came running out from behind them was his love for Grace.

"Will you marry me one day?" he asked her.

"Yes," she said.

Their wedding was as easily arranged as that of two birds. The caution and calculation that come with age did not worry them at all. There were no past disappointments to embitter their love, no sins to soil it. They clung together in the perfection of ecstasy, their wet cheeks pressed together and the holy water like diamond drops on their lips. The action and place were symbolic, for their first kiss in a graveyard was cool and fresh as the love that lasted them till death.

For ever after it was the firm conviction of Faithful and Grace that his pock-marks were not noticeable; other people did not share their conviction, but then other people were unbelievers.

Grace withdrew herself from her lover's arms to shut and lock the door behind them. She was her usual self again, practical and informative.

"Once the streams ran all round Binsey," she said, "and made an island of it. Binsey means 'island of prayer' in Saxony."

"Then we had better pray," said Faithful, and led the way up the moss-grown path to the dark, musty little church. They knelt very upright on the hard stone floor, facing the altar and the stained glass figure of Saint Frideswide above it, their backs as straight as boards and their hands placed palms together under their chins. They knelt as still as two be-ruffed figures on a tomb, so still that a little mouse crept out and sniffed at the soles of their shoes to see what they were made of.

But it was only Faithful's outside that was pressed into this cold statuesque mould of godliness; inside he was a burning fire of devotion and love and gratitude. He had no need to pray in words. His whole consciousness, mental and physical,

seemed gradually to be absorbed in a great act of praise that
lifted him up as on wings so that he lost all sense both of the place
where he was and of himself as a person. Something that came
from outside, something divine, touched him, and at the touch
everything about him and in him had clicked into harmony
so that there were no parts but only a whole, no time, but only
eternity. He was never to know a moment quite like this again.
The emotion of human love that had swept over him at the well,
an emotion as rarefied in its purity as any human emotion could
be, had left him so sensitively aware that he could feel what he
would never feel again . . . only long for with a longing so
acute that the rest of his life would be a pilgrimage.

But such moments were not for Grace, for she belonged to
that noble army of Marthas who cook the dinners that the
Marys gobble up to keep them going between their visions and
their dreams. Grace was the best kind of Martha. She would
never mind how long the dinner took to cook and would take it
quite for granted if there was not much left for her by the time
Mary's hunger was satisfied. Yet if Grace could not know
ecstasy she could perform the duties of religion very creditably.
She knelt now very correctly, finger-tip to finger-tip and eyes
glued tight shut, and she repeated all the prayers she knew in an
inward voice so perfect in grammar and pronunciation that
there was no excuse for the deity not hearing. . . . But when she
came to the end of them she was floored. . . . She didn't know
any more and she couldn't pray extempore. The cold paving
stones penetrated through her dress and made themselves known
to her knees. She had a crick in her neck from kneeling so
straight and a touch of indigestion inside. She opened one eye
and looked at Faithful. He was in his Saint Stephen mood
again ; oblivious to her, oblivious of everything ; his inward eye
gazing upon the opened heavens. For how much longer was he
going on praying ? She shifted her weight from one aching
knee to the other and experienced a slight sinking of the heart,
for it might be that married life with Faithful would be a strain
at times. Then a wave of shame went over her and her raptur-
ous love bubbled up afresh in her heart, so that shutting her eyes
she too saw visions ; of a spotless larder full of jellies and preserves
made by herself without any interference from Dorothy, a well-
filled linen cupboard with lavender bags between each sheet

made by herself without any criticism from Joyeuce, and, best of all, a neat row of compact little babies picked up by herself and Faithful from under the gooseberry bushes to which they had fallen straight from God.

So vivid was this last vision that she could actually hear the compact little babies disliking the gooseberry prickles and crying to be fetched out; and then she realised that somewhere quite near a child actually *was* crying. She opened her eyes and listened intently, all the mother in her wide awake. Then she prodded Faithful.

" What ? " said Faithful, returning from heaven with difficulty and some slight irritation.

" Listen," said Grace.

Faithful got to his feet with a sigh and rubbed his knees. The persistent voice of the world, crying outside in its woe, was not for the first time disturbing a saint in his visions and dragging him out of the house of devotion into the world of action. They made their way out of the shadows of the church into the porch, full of the streaming sunset light, and there, curled up in the corner, was Diccon sobbing his heart out.

Grace had never had much affection for Diccon; privately she had always thought him rather a nasty little boy, quite unworthy of the devotion lavished upon him by Joyeuce and her father; but his woe was desperately genuine and gathering him up in her arms she kissed him and crooned over him as though here were all the compact little babies rolled into one.

It was impossible to make out what was the matter with him, where he had been or what he had done or how in the world he had got where he was. When they questioned him he only shook his curly head, sobbed heartbrokenly and demanded to be taken home.

They took him home, carrying him pick-a-back by turns, the journey turned into a painful pilgrimage by his bulk. He was a dead weight on their backs, his curly head lolling heavily as though the sorrow of the world bowed it down and his body shaken periodically with heartbreaking hiccups. The whole sky was a sheet of gold and under it the green earth lay in a strange stillness, the river like glass and the trees unstirring, as though the whole world listened to the echo of a footfall; the feet of the day that departed and the feet of the night that came.

And through the green and the gold the three children moved silently, listening too. The day had brought them new terrors and joys; love and ecstasy, freedom, cruelty and pain. Much that had been theirs had gone from them for ever; the old childish carelessness and ignorance and happy self-sufficiency; and moving towards them were new things, half-seen shapes drawing nearer with glowing eyes that promised rapture and mercilessly pacing feet that promised pain.

But from the shadowy terrors there was a shelter. Built upon the green floor of the world, piled against the golden curve of the sky, were the towers of a city. Bastioned walls were strong against earthly danger, steepled churches held the powers of evil at bay, and flower-filled gardens and green arbours were a refuge to a man from the sorrow of his own thoughts.

"There is Oxford!" cried Grace. "There is home at last!"

Faithful, whose turn it was to carry Diccon, lifted his bowed head and wiped the sweat from his forehead, and Diccon opened his tear-swollen lids and gazed and gazed.

CHAPTER XI

DARK DECEMBER

> Even such is Time, which takes in trust
> Our youth, our joys, and all we have,
> And pays us but with age and dust;
> Who in the dark and silent grave,
> When we have wandered all our ways,
> Shuts up the story of our days;
> And from which earth, and grave, and dust,
> The Lord shall raise me up, I trust.
> WALTER RALEIGH.

I

THE autumn and the returning scholars arrived at Oxford together. With the first gale of wind and rain from the south-west, a gale that tore the last petals from the drenched rose trees and sent the clouds hurrying like flocks of frightened sheep across the sky, there came a clamour at the gates, a joyous shouting and singing of songs, the clatter of horses' hoofs on cobbles and the pealing of the bells with which the city welcomed her children home.

For though Oxford had been very glad to see the scholars go, she was even more glad to see them come back. The blessed peace of their absence had turned into boredom as the hot summer weeks went by. After the long years of their occupation the life of the city had come to centre around them, and if they were absent too long the life seemed drained of its purpose. . . . To see the cavalcades coming winding in from north, south, east and west, filling the quiet streets with their clamour, was like seeing sap flow again through the branches of a dead tree.

With her children once more stowed safely within her walls, Philip Sidney writing poetry at Broadgates Hall, Nicolas playing the viol in his room by the Fair Gate and Walter Raleigh flashing like a meteor in and out of the gates of Oriel, the city put on a fresh beauty. She had become a little tired and dusty, drained of her strength and colour by the hot weeks of harvest time, but now, swept of her dust by the life-giving gales and washed clean by the showers of silver rain that went by on the wind, beauty bloomed again. There were new flowers in the gardens, crimson dahlias and the white starry daisies of Saint Michael, and the lawns put on a fresh bright green that was like an echo of the vanished spring. Every grey wall wore a cloak of scarlet creeper and the elm trees in the Christ Church meadows stood like tall knights arrayed from head to foot in golden armour. Sandwiched between days of rain there were sunshiny days of loveliness when the silence was so deep that wanderers in fields and gardens were almost startled to hear the tiny tap of a falling leaf or the twitter of a robin in the bushes. . . . On these days one felt drenched in a melancholy quietude that was almost as enjoyable as happiness.

Even Joyeuce, when on fine mornings she drew back the curtains on a world whose fragile beauty made her think of a rainbow or a soap bubble, felt a rare tranquillity. Fine autumn days bred philosophy in one, she thought, for the earth itself in autumn was so philosophic; faced with the storms of winter, that would root up its trees and stamp its flowers into the ground, it seemed to turn itself backward to remember past glories with such a passion of delight that on day after day it was almost young again, so young that on some mornings you would have said that memory had merged into hope and next spring was here already.

That was what she would do, thought Joyeuce. . . . Remember. . . . Behind her were the happy days of childhood when her mother had been with her and living had been like wings that carried one from one joy to another, not a pack upon the back that made the shoulders ache; she would remember those days and grow the stronger for reliving their joy and freedom. And she must remember that evening of ecstasy when she had thought that Nicolas loved her and had felt herself to be born again; till her dying day she must remember that because surely never again would she reach such a peak of joy. She realised that one could not live always on such a peak; if one did, nerves and body would break under the strain; but from every experience of bliss as it passed away one could keep back a modicum to add to interior treasure. Surely these moments were foretastes of something to come, some freedom of spirit so heavenly that it would be cheaply purchased by all the garnered wealth of a lifetime. . . . After one of these early morning meditations Joyeuce would be so sweet-tempered that the children would bask in her smiles like kittens in the sun. . . . But when the day was over and she was in bed at night, with a little wind whispering round the windows and darkness lying over the world like a pall, Joyeuce would forget to be a philosopher and her tears would soak right through the linen of the pillowcase and drench the goose-breast feathers underneath.

Grace did not need to bask in another's warmth for she had more than enough of her own. She was so happy that three inches were added to her waist measurement and two to her height, while her hair broke into such a paroxysm of curl that each separate hair seemed alive and dancing with a life of its own. After serious consultation she and Faithful had come to the conclusion that matrimony had better not be mentioned to the family just yet. They were quite old enough to be married, of course, thirteen and fourteen being well on in years of discretion, but though they realised their seniority they doubted if the family did. . . . There was still a regrettable tendency to treat them as children. . . . They feared an outburst of protest and thought it better to keep their secret a little longer; until Grace was taller still and Faithful had made the whole College see his brilliant future in as rosy colours as he did himself.

And it was such a nice secret to keep; Grace was inclined to think it was sweeter to keep it than to tell it. Solemn and gentle kisses given and received behind the apple trees in the garden, whispered conversations under the stairs, quick darting glances exchanged in a crowded room, that had the queer effect of making the crowd dissolve into thin air, so that they two were left quite alone in a world that had been made for them only. To tell about these things at this stage would have been to spoil them. They would have to tell about them in the end, of course, but by that time they would be like children who are tired of playing at make-believe in secret and want to be the real thing in the eyes of the whole world.

But in her own eyes Grace was a wife already and behaved with a bustling importance that Joyeuce found quite insufferable. She took to wearing two extra petticoats to further increase her bulk, and finding some old keys at the bottom of a chest she hung them round her waist instead of the infantile hornbook which she now contemptuously discarded, and went jingling and rustling about the house with a dignity that would have been overwhelming in a matron of sixty.

" What's the use of wearing keys that don't unlock anything ? " asked Joyeuce with some irritation.

" They are a symbol," Grace assured her solemnly. " They increase my authority with the younger children."

" But you have no authority over the children," objected Joyeuce. " It's *my* business to manage the children."

" You're not very good at it," said Grace. " It would be much better if you left it to me."

As the days went by the phrase " leave it to me " was constantly upon Grace's lips. Entering the kitchen suddenly she would find Joyeuce immersed in the hated business of candle making, with the rushes mislaid and the melted fat fast congealing again while she looked for them. " What is the use of starting to melt the fat when you have not got the rushes handy ? " she would ask. " Don't fuss, Joyeuce. Leave it to me."

Or again, when Joyeuce in her spinning made knots in her yarn, she would say benignly, " You don't keep the thread taut, dear. Better leave it to me."

Even the twins, though they loved Joyeuce far more dearly than they loved Grace, began to form the habit of running to Grace rather than to Joyeuce when they had run a thorn into a finger or torn a frock. . . . Being quite incommoded by the fear of hurting them Grace's probings of the finger were far less painful than those of the sensitive Joyeuce ; and her darning in its beauty was like that of the archangels of heaven.

Joyeuce was frequently infuriated to the point of tears. Was she to be humiliated and flouted at every turn, she who had so heroically sacrificed her own personal happiness—or would have, had Nicolas given her the chance—for these ungrateful children ? She had constantly to remind herself that the children did not know she had sacrificed herself—or would have sacrificed herself had Nicolas had the grace to propose to her—and so could hardly be expected to be grateful. . . . But yet it hurt that they were not. . . . In her heartache she turned to Diccon ; he had always been her very own little baby, her little poppet to whom all through his short life she had been all the world.

But Diccon was not very responsive. He had been exceedingly peculiar ever since the day when he had been to Saint Giles' Fair. He was able to give no account of his adventures on that day; he had just got lost, he said; but that there had been adventures no one doubted, for Diccon was not the same little boy he had been before.

When he had first been restored to the bosom of his family he had made a most unusual demonstration of affection. He had embraced them all round and bitten nobody. Upon his father in particular he had lavished such a quantity of moist kisses and bear hugs that Canon Leigh had become quite embarrassed. He was not used to expressions of appreciation from his youngest son.

But after a few days those transports died down and became curiously aloof, even pathetic and bewildered, as though he had mislaid something and could not find it. His family was inclined to think that he grieved for his lost lamb, Baa, but he said no, it wasn't Baa who was lost; asked who it was he seemed unable to say. Joyeuce and Dorothy were constantly finding him hiding by himself behind the embroidered curtains of the big bed, or inside the cupboard where the raisins were kept, not eating the raisins or unpicking the embroidery but just hugging Tinker and doing nothing. . . . Tinker, too, seemed depressed. . . . His whiskers drooped and he let the mice accumulate about the place in a shocking manner.

Now and then Diccon would come to Joyeuce to be cuddled, but when enthroned upon her lap he seemed to find it curiously unsatisfactory. He would pound her with his fists, as though trying to make her a different shape, and when her figure remained hopelessly virginal he would give her up in despair and try Dorothy. . . . But she did not give satisfaction either. . . . " Too 'ard," he would tell her, " too 'eavy," and sliding down he would seize Tinker by the tail and trot mournfully off to the dark place under the stairs, where they would hear him sobbing.

Yet it was quite impossible to offer comfort, for if anyone tried to remove them from their hiding-place, Diccon made rude noises in his throat and Tinker spat. There was nothing to be done except to mourn for the merry elf who had vanished in Saint Giles' Fair and to try to coax this new sad little boy into some likeness of him.

So it was no wonder that Joyeuce's mood was autumnal and her chief happiness a looking back. The present, tarnished by the unappreciativeness of her family, was not hospitable to happy thoughts, and to a future shorn of Nicolas it was better to pay no attention.

For to think of a time when there would be no Nicolas just across the way was to invite despair. She saw little of him now, but still, he was there. She often saw him jauntily crossing the quadrangle to the Cathedral, and sometimes at night, when the children were asleep, she would creep out of bed and peep through her curtains at the light in his window and picture him poring studiously over some great learned book, becoming with every moment wiser and wiser, far too wise for an ignorant girl like herself. . . . If Nicolas, noisily playing club-kayles with some boon companions, could have seen her kneeling on the floor in her white frilly night-rail, her pale gold hair silvered by the moonlight and all other expression burnt out of her face by a white-hot flame of longing, he would have lingered in his room for only as long as it took to pitch the boon companions into one corner of the room and the club-kayles ninepins into the other. . . . In the twinkling of an eye he would have been under her window, his hands creeping up the wall again, his love for her as hot as it had been on that memorable midsummer eve.

II

But he could not see it and it was upon a very lonely Joyeuce that the blow fell in the dark days of December. It had rained all through November, a steady drenching that seemed to go on day and night, that turned the lazy river into a turbulent flood and filled all the little streams in the valley to overflowing. The citizens of Oxford grew anxious, for the beautiful waterway that was their chief pride and glory could be at times their greatest enemy. . . . For after the river had been in flood disease always fell upon the city. . . . When a pause came in the downpour they would put their cloaks about them and steal out of the city gates and look apprehensively at the grey water pouring under the bridges, and at night they would lie awake listening to the patter of the rain on their windowpanes and the drip and gurgle of it in the gutters. And at last the dreaded moment came. During a black night of rain the river overflowed its banks and slid over the green meadows to join the streams beneath the willow trees. When dawn broke, a fine dawn of frail sunlight and blue mist, the towers and spires of the city were reflected in a silver sheet of water, and the swans flew low to watch the lovely ghosts of themselves that fled beneath them over the flooded meadows. . . . A lovely sight, but most ominous. . . . In less than a week the low-lying houses had flood water in their kitchens and even the cloisters of Magdalen were swamped. and then, after a week of sunshine, the river drew back its waters, leaving behind a legacy of mud, damp and disease.

Diggory brought them the bad news when they were at breakfast. " The sweating sickness had broken out," he said, " down in the houses outside South Gate." He spoke nonchalantly, but as he set down a jug of milk his hand shook so that it was spilled upon the table. Joyeuce, Grace and Canon Leigh went white as their ruffs, and Great-Aunt, munching minced beef at the open window above their heads, dropped her knife with a crash upon the floor. Only the children, who could not remember the last terrible outbreak of sickness, ate on in comparative unconcern, though the eyes of the twins were rounder than usual as they looked at each other, and they squeaked into their mugs of milk with a rather apprehensive note.

But Joyeuce remembered that last outbreak. She remembered how hundreds of people had sickened in one night, and how hundreds had died. She remembered the deserted streets and the silent houses where the curtains were all drawn as though the houses had shut their eyes for sorrow. She remembered the tolling of the bells, and the sickening sound of cart wheels clattering over the cobbles in the early morning, and the cry that accompanied it, " Bring out your dead."

For herself, Joyeuce had no dread of death, for she was one of those anxious pilgrims who look towards it as to a resting place where there is no more need for endurance, but she had a morbid horror of it as of a robber who might take from her those whom she loved, leaving her alone in a world where no sun shone. . . . It had already taken her mother. . . . In an agony her thoughts flew to Diccon and then to Nicolas. Diccon, busily shoving bread and milk into his red mouth, with the morning sun bringing out the ruddy lights in his dark curls, looked a far too brightly burning creature to be easily quenched,

but she had not got Nicolas before her to console her with the
sight of his lustiness, and she thought with foreboding of that
evening in the Tavern garden when she had thought how
easily the pulse of his life could be stopped, by a slip on the stairs,
a flash of lightning, or the thrust of an angry sword. . . . But
she had not thought of sickness.

For days she kept an anxious eye on Diccon, and peeped
with a beating heart through the windows to catch a glimpse of
Nicolas's figure hurrying, late as usual, to lectures or Chapel.
She watched her father, too, and felt the forehead of Grace and
the children fourteen times a day if once, and she concocted a
huge brew of her famous centaury and wormwood medicine and
forced it down the throats of her unwilling family at the rising
and the setting of the sun. And she was rewarded, for they
remained in the rudest health, and the sweating sickness, so
Diggory told her, was not spreading. It would, the citizens
thought, be only a slight visitation this time.

She was feeling almost light hearted when she came in one
evening from a shopping expedition, just at dusk, to stow away
some velvet she had bought in the oak chest in the parlour where
they kept their needlework. The children had gone out with
Mistress Flowerdew, their mother's friend, and she would have a
quiet time all to herself in which to sit and sew and dream before
the fire.

She pushed open the door with a sigh of relief, already savouring her hour of peace. The log fire was flickering softly, its
golden reflection bright on the panelled wood of the walls, but
the corners of the room were full of shadows and the blue dusk
that hung outside the window gave no light.

So she did not see the dark figure sitting in the big chair by
the fire, and when a voice said softly, "Joyeuce," she started
and her heart began thumping against her stitchets so that she
put up her hand to still it.

" Nicolas ? " she whispered.

" It's Giles," he said.

Joyeuce slipped off her cloak and came over to the fire,
standing before it with slender hands outspread to the blaze,
and looked down in astonishment at the comely figure of her
eldest brother. . . . For he came to see them so seldom now.
. . . They had been great friends, he and she, when they were

younger, and in bad times she had leaned her whole weight upon him, but now they had grown apart. With the world at his feet, and his brilliant brain as a sword in his hand to subdue it, his home had faded into insignificance and Joyeuce's problems, that had once been his too, had been forgotten. Joyeuce had borne no malice. It was natural that at the outset a man's work should absorb him to the exclusion of all else, for without the strength of singlemindedness how can he find a footing in the battle of livelihood, and the battle is to the strong. Moreover she had discovered that in the long run we bear our own burdens. Others, as they pass us, can put a hand beneath them for a moment only, but they do not stop for long, and at the turn of the road the whole weight is back on our shoulders again. Giles had once helped her to bear the weight of the family pack, but it was her burden, not his, and she had not reproached him when he slithered thankfully from beneath its weight . . . though she had missed his help.

He watched the firelight painting mid-winter roses on the green dress she wore, and looked appreciatively at her tall slender figure, robbed of all angularity by the kindly dusk, at her pale pointed face under the honey-coloured hair and the slim hands that looked almost transparent as she held them before the fire.

"You are so pretty, Joyeuce," he said softly. "You are so like Mother."

There was a hungry note in his voice that took her back instantly to the old days of their grief, and one hand went to her throat as though it were choking her again.

"If only I could be," she cried, stricken by her own sense of inadequacy, and then, aware of some crying need in him, "Are you wanting Mother very badly, Giles?"

Giles did not answer, for the weakness of human longing was a thing he was too proud to own to, but he moved his hands a little restlessly on the arms of the big chair.

Joyeuce slipped down to sit on the floor at his feet, her arm across his knees. Words never came to her easily. It was only by movement and gesture that she could comfort. But she was half afraid that Giles might repulse her, for he did not always like demonstrations of affection, and her arm on his knees trembled a little.

"Silly Puss!" said Giles, going back to the name he had called her by in their childhood, and he stroked her cheek softly with a clumsy forefinger. "Do you remember the day we dressed up as demons, with horns and tails, and frightened Dorothy into screaming hysterics?"

Joyeuce began to laugh and a lovely happiness seemed wrapping itself warmly about her. She forgot she was the overburdened mistress of a household and was suddenly a child. The lovely security of childhood was hers again, and the brave certainty of happiness that had been hers in the days before sorrow or pain had touched her. She talked and laughed and told old tales with a gaiety that surprised her even while she was possessed by it, and Giles with a word here and there, a touch on her cheek, and sudden flashes of memory that were almost inspiration, seemed leading her further and further back into the far country where they had once lived as children but had forgotten. "News of a far country," Nicolas had said, as they gazed at the fairy ring traced on the grass on Midsummer Eve, "and we cannot read it." But it seemed that Giles to-night could read it and without words could communicate what he had read to Joyeuce, for both of them, for half an hour, knew perfect happiness.

The banging of the front door seemed for a moment something that suddenly shut them out into darkness. Joyeuce started and scrambled to her feet again. The room was almost dark and Giles's face was blurred and dim. "Time to get supper," she said. "Come and help me, Giles."

Giles shifted in his chair and she held out her hands to help him to his feet. "Lazybones!" she laughed.

And then her laughter died, for Giles's arms lay heavy on hers and when she had pulled him to his feet he swayed. "Are you all right, Giles?" she asked sharply.

"A headache," mumbled Giles. "It went while you were talking. It's back again now."

In a sudden panic she flung her arms tightly round him, hiding her face against his shoulder, trying to recapture for a moment the happiness that had passed. But the door opened and the light that her father carried seemed a message from the outer world that made her lift her head and open her eyes, turning towards him. She saw him raise his light high, looking at her with amused tenderness, and then his eyes shifted to Giles's face, bent above hers, and she saw him go white to the lips with terror, just as Giles's figure sagged suddenly in her arms.

III

Somehow they had not expected this, though, as Great-Aunt repeatedly remarked to all who would listen, from the days of Pharaoh onward it has always been the eldest son, the best-loved, whom the plague strikes. But Giles had always seemed so princely, so arrogant, so vital, that it had been impossible to think that death could touch him. Only Faithful, shaking his great head, was not surprised. . . . He had always said that Giles worked much too hard.

The same evening that Giles had been taken ill, Faithful came quietly in through the front door and announced that he had come to stop, and from that moment he and Grace took over the entire management of the distracted household. Grace cooked, washed, ironed and organised with the quiet efficiency of genius, and Faithful ran errands and minded the children with such utter self-effacement that it never even occurred to anybody, not even to himself, that he was heartbroken.

Joyeuce and Canon Leigh hardly ever left the boys' room, where Giles lay in the four-poster with the crimson curtains, Will and Thomas having been banished to their father's room. They and Dorothy fought on hour after hour for Giles's life, frenziedly carrying out the instructions of a physician who had been full of foreboding from the first. "No stamina," he kept complaining, "no stamina at all." How they hated that physician as he stood there in his fine furred gown, stroking his long smooth beard and sniffing at an orange stuck full of cloves that he might not catch the infection. What was the use of his being a physician if he could not heal Giles? They saw him go with hatred, and yet they counted the hours till he should come again, for surely, surely he must be able to do something? But he, it seemed, with all his knowledge and skill, was as powerless as they were, and hour after hour the agony of their helplessness bit more deeply. Of what use to love, demanded Joyeuce of her tortured self, when one can give to the beloved neither relief from pain nor salvation from death, when one can do nothing but add to the weight of his suffering by the sight of one's own ? The awful loneliness of pain terrified her Though she was as physically near to Giles as she had been in the little parlour, yet spiritually she seemed a hundred miles away from him. Because he was sick and she was well there seemed a great gulf between them. They looked at each other helplessly across it, he crying out for help and she longing to give it, but they could not now reach each other.

Giles died on a night of glittering starlight, a strangely warm and balmy night for December, with a soft wind blowing from the south-west and a placid bright-faced moon hanging low over the Cathedral spire. Joyeuce and her father, one on each side of the unconscious Giles, needed no light except the moonlight and starlight that flooded in through the uncurtained window. There was no sound in the night but the voice of Great Tom as he tolled the hour—nine—ten—eleven.

Joyeuce sat in a high-backed chair, her hands folded in her lap, her eyes fixed on her father where he knelt praying on the further side of the bed. Earlier in the night she had been kneeling, too, until suddenly her knees had doubled up beneath her and her father had come round and lifted her into the chair. She leant back in it now, her body too exhausted to move but her mind intensely and horribly active, and tried to keep her eyes fixed on her father's face, its stern peacefulness the only thing in the room that she could bear to look at. Sometimes, against her will, her eyes shifted a little to the left and she saw that horrible tapestry of Absalom in the oak tree and seemed to hear a voice crying out in her father's tones, " My son, my son ! Would God I had died for thee, my son, my son ! " And then she would know what he was feeling behind that mask of resignation and would grip her hands together that she too might not cry out. And sometimes she would look at Giles, lying with a set face that still seemed to hold something of the rebellion that had been his while he was still conscious. For Giles had not wanted to die. He had not been afraid, but he had been furious. His hot, angry eyes, seeking for the rescue that no one brought him, would, Joyeuce thought, haunt her until she died. Remembering them, she could not now look at Giles for more than a moment ; her glance always sped back to her father's face and clung there, her immature faith sheltering desperately beneath his that was so strong. Sometimes, feeling her eyes upon him, her father would look up and smile at her, and repeat words for her comfort, words that seemed to her to come from a long way off and to mean nothing at all, even though she tried obediently to listen to them. " In the sight of the unwise they seem to die," he would say, " and their departure is taken for misery, and their going forth from us utter destruction : but they are in peace." And then, trying to comfort himself and Joyeuce because Giles was dying so young, with all his glorious promise unfulfilled in this world, he would murmur, " For honourable age is not that which standeth in length of time, nor that is measured by number of years. But wisdom is the grey hair unto men, and an unspotted life is old age. He pleased God and was beloved of Him ; so that living among sinners he was translated. Yea, speedily was he taken away, lest that wickedness should alter his understanding, or deceit beguile his soul. He being made perfect in a short time, fulfilled a long time. For his soul pleased the Lord, therefore hasted He to take him away from among the wicked."

But some while after eleven o'clock had struck, and the deadness of the night lay heavy upon them, Canon Leigh was silent again and his face dropped into his hands so that Joyeuce could no longer see it. . . . She was obliged to look again at Giles. . . . And at the first glance she nearly cried out with astonishment, for a change had taken place in him. The last shadow of rebellion had gone from his face and he looked like the little boy she had played with years ago. She stood up and bent over him, her lips parted in eagerness, and almost at the same moment his eyes opened and he looked at her, smiling. At once the barrier was down between them and they were as close together as they had been in the little parlour. News of a far country. With one brief smile Giles told more of it than a hundred books could have done. Then he sighed, turned over, and buried his cheek in his pillow like a child going to sleep.

Joyeuce knelt down and covered her face with her hands, but her heart within her was like a singing bird. She heard her father get up and heard his shuddering sigh as he bent over Giles. Then he, too, knelt down and began to pray aloud, brokenly, stately Latin prayers for the dead through which beat, like a pulse, the deep notes of the clock striking midnight.

It was a bell that tolled for Giles's passing, she knew, and yet her heart was like a singing bird.

Ten minutes later, leaving her father alone with his dead son, she was running like a winged creature through the moonlit house, her skirts held up on either side and her feet seeming hardly to touch the floor as she went. She had news to tell, good news, and she did not stand upon the order of her going as she ran from group to group of the wakeful, heartbroken household. On the stairs she found Grace, Faithful and the little boys huddled together in a forlorn heap, the tears on their faces bright in the pallid moonlight. "Do not cry, little loves," she adjured them. "Heaven is beyond the stars." Then before they had time to do more than gaze stupidly at her transfigured face she was off again, flying down the stairs to the kitchen where Diggory sat on a wooden stool, staring stupidly into space, and Dorothy sat at the kitchen table with her head in her arms. They, too, gazed at her stupefied as she stood in a moonbeam like a visitant from another world, tip-toe for flight. "You must not grieve," she told them. "There is another country."

And then she was gone again, flying back up the stairs to Great-Aunt. For the first time in her life she was not afraid of her, even though it was black night in Great-Aunt's bedroom, with the thick curtains drawn to hide the stars and only one rush-light to relieve the gloom. She did not wait for Great-Aunt to pop out from behind the curtains, she pulled them back herself, and stood looking tenderly at the redoubtable old lady where she sat stiffly against her piled pillows, her face in its starched night-cap suddenly become pathetically and incredibly old. For Great-Aunt had suffered during Giles's illness. It had brought back to her the deaths of her own children in a way that had actually hurt her. Moreover it had put her in mind of her own approaching end, and to-night, as the great clock tolled the passing hours, she had sat behind her curtains in the grip of a fear she had never known before. Her eyes, usually so bright, were without light, her chin trembled and her claw-like hands clutched at the counterpane.

"The boy is dead?" she whispered, and then her jaw dropped as she stared at her transfigured great-niece. . . . She had never seen any human creature look so unearthly. . . . Joyeuce looked as though drenched with light. She reminded

Great-Aunt of some lovely flower held up between the watcher and the sun, so that each delicate petal is tipped with flame and the secret of the sun itself seems caught at the heart of the flower. Great-Aunt felt a pang of desolation as she realised that something had been told to Joyeuce that would never be told to her. She had enjoyed life, she had enjoyed it far more than Joyeuce was ever likely to do, yet at this moment, if she could have gone back to the beginning again, she would have given all her pleasure in exchange for Joyeuce's sorrows if she could have had with them only a few of those rare moments of sure knowledge.

"Not dead," said Joyeuce, "only born again," and drawing the curtains she passed on into her own room, leaving Great-Aunt to wonder if she had really seen Joyeuce or if what she had seen had been a vision from beyond the stars.

The Twins and Diccon were all fast asleep in the fourposters. Joyeuce bent over them, glad that they were asleep, glad that they were still in the country of childhood where sorrow is only a rumour outside the gate that they hear vaguely but do not understand. They would meet Giles in that country, perhaps, meet him with a freedom and ease that would never be hers until her life was over and her sorrows done.

She shivered a little as she went to the window to draw the curtains across the view of her city that she loved so greatly. Her joy was still with her, but it had heard the first whisper of the returning tide of sorrow and had shrunk in a little upon itself. It was with the knowledge that soon she would be wanting comfort and reassurance again that she opened the window and leaned out, her eyes clinging to the familiar outlines of roofs and towers that would last out the span of her own life and so would never forsake her. A little rustle of movement by the Fair Gate made her look down and she saw three cloaked figures, with a dog at their feet, sitting at the foot of the stairs that led up to Nicolas's room. They got up when they saw her open the window and stood uncertainly, not knowing what to do. . . . Heatherthwayte, Nicolas and Philip Sidney waiting for news of Giles. . . . She stretched out her hands towards them in pity for their dark wavering figures, shadowy and unsubstantial in the moonlight, looked like poor wraiths lost in a night of bewilderment. But only one of them had the courage to come to her, and it was not Nicolas, it was Philip Sidney.

He stood under the window looking up at her, his bright hair silvered by the moonlight and his beautiful face grave and sorrowful. "You need not tell me, mistress," he said gently. " I know by your face."

"But it is all true, what they say," she whispered shyly, " it is only in the sight of the unwise they seem to die."

He met her eyes with a brave certainty that was steadier though less joyous than hers. "Spiritus redeat ad Deum, qui dedit illum," he said. Then he bowed to her courteously and drew back.

Over his head her eyes sought for the tall thin shadow that was Nicolas. It was he who should have come to her, not Philip Sidney who was almost a stranger to her. Why had he been afraid to come to her? As she turned away from the window returning sorrow was not a far off whisper but an ominous mutter. She climbed on to the bed and fell face downwards, lying rigid, waiting as a sufferer waits for the return of inevitable pain.

IV

It so submerged her during the next few days that it was hard even to remember her faith and joy of a few nights ago. The door had opened to let Giles go from one country to another and for just a moment the light from that other country had shone full upon her, but now the door was shut and she could not see even a crack of light beneath it. Yet it had been. What had happened had happened. The light had been hers and it had come from somewhere. It was a fact. If just now she was too exhausted and stricken to rejoice in it she yet possessed it ; it was her possession for ever.

On the afternoon of the day following Giles's funeral, without even stopping to get her cloak she ran out through the garden gate into the meadows. The house and everyone in it pressed upon her so that she felt at breaking point. Great-Aunt, fretful and complaining, the children with their ceaseless questions, Grace with her irritating efficiency and her father as still in his grief as a winter stream bound down by ice. . . . If only he would not be so still. . . . She saw in his stillness a reflection of her own. When they were together they could only sit silently, powerless to help each other.

But outside, under the winter trees, there was help. It had been raining all the morning, a misty rain that had hidden the earth like a shroud, but now it had thinned and vanished into a soft blue haze shot through with sunshine. The exquisite colouring of the winter trees was lit by the pale gleam ; in the distance the network of bare twigs showed faint amethyst and rust colour, near at hand they were filaments of black lace strung with diamond raindrops. There were threads of silver where the streams ran through the rain-misted grass and beside them the smooth willow shoots smouldered orange and deep crimson, lit to flame when the sun touched them. The whole world was full of the muted sound of water, the steady murmur of the swiftly-flowing river and the soft drip of the water-laden trees. It was still strangely warm for December. The air was soft and moist and caressing. Twice, flashing from the silvered twigs of a tree-top to the crimson of the willows below, Joyeuce saw the blue body of a kingfisher. She was used to these days of misted warmth and colour, for they came often in the sheltered Thames valley, blooming among the harsh dark days of wind and rain like roses in mid-winter, but never before, she thought, had there been a December day as lovely as this one. In spite of her misery she could not help but be a little comforted by the beauty of it, for it was a fragile and tender beauty that crept into her almost by stealth. She would have shut tired eyes against the blaze of summer, but these soft colours were kind to weariness. The triumphant shouting of the birds in springtime would have seemed to her a cruel mockery, but the soft drip of the raindrops was a sound attuned to her sorrow and held a kind of peace.

She felt a sudden uprush of thankfulness for the comradeship of the earth. It seemed to her at that moment the only friend who never failed. Its beauty was ever renewed and its music unceasing. Death could not touch it or the years estrange. While she lived the earth was hers and the glory of it, and standing still on the path she held out her arms to the gold and blue of the sun-shot haze, to the slipping silver water and the crimson willow shoots that edged it, to the rain-drenched grass and blue swerve of the kingfisher's flight. . . . But her arms were empty. . . . Her friend, the earth, could sing her lullabies and brighten her eyes with its beauty but it was at once too frail and too great for intimacy. She remembered how once as a little girl she had kissed a wild rose in a passion of affection, but its petals had fallen to the ground at the touch of her lips; and another time upon a journey she had seen in the distance a little blue hill small enough to be picked up and played with, yet when she came up to it she found it as tall as a church tower. She felt again, as she had felt on May morning, that sense of beauty's continual withdrawal. It is a light flickering always at the end of the road, a distant trumpet call from a land that is hidden behind a hill. A cold shivering fit took her and hiding her face in her hands she began to cry for the first time since Giles had died.

Then through the sound of her own sobbing and the drip of the raindrops she heard a queerly reassuring sound, the sharp snapping of fallen twigs and the sound of foot-steps on the sodden path. She stopped shivering and a lovely glow of warmth stole over her. She did not need to look up to know who it was. Once before, on May morning, she had longed for the beauty and mystery of earth that she worshipped to be gathered up into some human form that she could love, and she had looked down from her window into the face of Nicolas.

So certain was she that she did not even look up when he flung his arms impetuously round her, but leaning her face with her hands still covering it against his shoulder cried with the abandon of a child. It was heaven to be, for once in a way, so abandoned. It was heaven to feel his arms tremble with rage at the fates that had so hurt her. It was heaven to feel so protected and so cared for. Love had been sweet on Midsummer Eve, but now, coming so hard upon the heels of sorrow, it was an ecstasy almost too great to be borne.

"Do not cry, little love," Nicolas implored her, but she only cried the more, and picking her up he carried her over the wet grass to where a little bench stood beneath a sparkling hawthorn tree. Then wrapping his cloak about the two of them he sat beside her, holding her so close that she could feel his heart beating and the warmth of his body like fire running through her veins.

"I was walking by the river," he told her softly. "There was no one in the meadows. The world seemed empty. Nothing to be seen but the bare branches, nothing to be heard but dropping water. I thought of you and of how when you are unhappy your eyes are the colour of rain. Then I looked up and saw you standing far off under the trees dressed all in black. I thought that you looked so mysterious, like sorrow herself. And then you held out your arms and so I came to you."

For the first time Joyeuce opened her eyes and looked at him for a moment, and used as she was to the hues of mourning his brilliance dazzled her. He must have been to some party, for his doublet was as blue as the kingfisher's wing and his cloak was lined with crimson. He had a little jewelled dagger in his belt and his ruff was as white as snow. She fingered his dagger with the delight of a child and rubbed her cheek against his cloak. "You must always be beautiful and gay, Nicolas," she told him, rejoicing in him. "It would be terrible if you were not to be gay."

"That's as life wills," said Nicolas soberly, and she looked up at him, startled, for she had never heard his voice so empty of laughter. And his face, too, was changed. It was older and graver. The eyes were more sombre, as though there was new knowledge behind them, and the lips pressed against each other almost sternly.

"Has anything happened, Nicolas?" she asked.

"Giles has died," he said.

Joyeuce nodded, understandingly. It was the first time in his life that death had dared to touch anyone he cared for. She knew what that felt like. She knew what a glorious expectation of certain happiness one builds upon the foundations of a happy childhood, and how the first grief sends the whole fabric tumbling into ruins.

"And it might have been you," whispered Nicolas.

Again she understood. He had discovered, now, the fear at the heart of love. He felt the torment that she had felt in the garden at the Tavern when she thought what a little thing might snap the thread of his life. She twisted her hands together, wondering how to comfort him, how to tell him what she now knew.

"It's not as bad as you think, Nicolas," she whispered. "The deeper you go into pain the more certain are you that all that happens to you has an explanation and a purpose. You don't know what they are, but you know they are there. You don't suffer any the less because of the certainty, but you would rather suffer and have it than just enjoy yourself and not have it."

Her voice trailed away and she looked out sadly over the landscape of sunlit fields and trees and water. What pitiful creatures were human beings, able to speak only so falteringly of what they knew, separated even from those they loved best by ignorances and insincerities and reserves so innumerable that there seemed no sweeping them away. Only the earth, with its winds and waters and its fields sown with a thousand flowers, could tell aright of the mystery of which it was the garment. . . . But our ears are too dull to hear.

But Nicolas's arms, strong and compelling, were about her again. "You are going to marry me," he said. "You are going to marry me as soon as ever it can be arranged."

"Would you be mated to sorrow?" she asked him. "You said, when you saw me in the distance, that I looked like sorrow herself."

"Sorrow and joy go hand in hand," he said, "and I want them both. The night Giles died, when Philip Sidney and I were waiting outside in the quadrangle and you opened your window and leaned out, I did not go to you like he did because I felt afraid of sorrow. And then the moon shone full on your face and when I saw the joy of it, Joyeuce, I wanted your joy more than anything else upon earth. I think I changed in that moment. I am not now what I was."

"But it is you who know all about joy," she said. "You are always gay."

"I can be gay," said Nicolas. "I was born knowing how to suck the last drop of fun out of every experience that comes along, and be so busy over it that I have no time to think and worry and question like you do, but I don't know joy. That's something different, something deeper. That's the certainty you talked of. It is a mystery to me, and I want it. In you I shall have it."

"Don't talk like that!" cried Joyeuce in a panic. "I am only an ordinary human girl. There is no mystery in me."

"If you did not seem mysterious to me I should not love you," said Nicolas wisely. "You seem to stand to me for all I long for. I do not quite know what I long for, but whatever it is I seem to have it when I have you."

"I feel like that, too," said Joyeuce softly, and then, after a moment's silence, she cried out in dismay, "Nicolas, Nicolas, what will happen if we get to know each other so well that there is no more mystery? Will the end of mystery be the end of love?"

"Why should there be an end of mystery?" asked Nicolas. "Isn't a woman always a mysterious creature to a man, and a man to a woman? When you are an old woman I shall look into your eyes and find my joy there; and as for you, Joyeuce, I think you are so faithful that you will forgive me my sins again and again and find some beauty in me up till the end."

It was that word "faithful" that recalled Joyeuce to herself. He was saying that she was faithful. But she was not. The care of the children was a trust, and she was being faithless to it. In this time of grief, when her family surely needed her more than ever before, she was planning marriage with Nicolas. Still sheltered beneath Nicolas's cloak she pressed her hands together in an agony. Had the fight to be fought all over again? Here, close to Nicolas, she felt warm and safe and happy, but separated from him the cold of the gathering dusk would be all round her, and a loneliness unspeakable. . . . It seemed like the choice between life and death. . . . Yet in these last months her spirit had become so attuned to sacrifice that now she acted almost automatically, slipping from beneath Nicolas's cloak and sliding to the far end of the seat, both her small hands held out to warn him off.

"I can't, Nicolas," she gasped.

"Can't what?" asked Nicolas.

"Marry you."

"Why ever not?" he demanded indignantly.

She explained. With her eyes shut so that she could not see his face, so that she could not even see the fair world that would remind her of him, she told him the whole tale; her promise to her dying mother, her father's dependence on her, the children's dependence on her, the house and the servants and the animals that would all become disintegrated if her watchful eye were not upon them; when she had finished the sun had gone and a cold mist was rising from the river. She covered her face with her hands and waited for Nicolas's comment. When it came it was brief.

"Tomfoolery," said Nicolas.

She dropped her hands and opened her eyes in indignant astonishment. Nicolas, though his mouth was very tender, was looking very mocking. His face was almost the face of the old Nicolas. The upward tilt at the corners of his eyebrows was very pronounced and he was smiling so much that his eyes had disappeared into wicked slits.

"Do you know, Joyeuce," he asked, "what are the chief failings of the saints?"

She shook her head hopelessly and he leant forward and took her cold hands in his, rubbing them gently. "An exaggerated sense of their own importance," he said, "combined with a quite stupid love of martyrdom for its own sake. Couldn't Grace step into your shoes? Are you the only woman in the world who can spank a horde of children? If you think you are, you stand convicted of pride, Joyeuce, and pride is one of the seven deadly sins. And why squander your strength in suffering when there is no need for it? That's waste; another sin. Joyeuce, sweetheart, it seems you are a very wicked woman."

Suddenly the mockery went out of his voice and his smile died, for he saw she was not paying the slightest attention to what he said. Her chin was tilted at an obstinate angle and her eyes, feverishly bright, seemed to be looking right through him to something beyond. With a chill of dismay he remembered the stories he had been told of Canon Leigh's obstinate sufferings for his faith, and remembered that Joyeuce was his daughter. . . . Fanatics, both of them. . . . Impotent anger seized him and he gripped her hands so tightly that she gave a little gasp of pain.

"And what about me?" he demanded indignantly. "No man ever loved a girl as I love you. I want you and I must have you."

Awareness of him was once more in her eyes. . . . She even smiled a little, because in his impetuous anger he was now absolutely the old Nicolas. . . . But there was no relenting in that obstinate chin.

"I must do my duty, Nicolas," she said quietly. "You will forget me. There are other pretty girls."

But at this, Nicolas boiled over into such a rage as she had never yet beheld in anyone, not even in Diccon. His face was turkey-red, his dark eyes shot fire at her and he spluttered so that she could scarcely hear what he said. "You dare say that to me!" was the burden of his remarks. "You know as well as I do that I shall never forget you!"

She bowed her head at the truth of this and whispered, " I'm sorry." No, he would not forget her. Between the new grave Nicolas who had held her in his arms a little while ago and the Joyeuce he had seen standing at the window on the night of Giles's death there was now an unbreakable link. Whatever was eternal in them was united. . . . But there were other bonds beside those of marriage. . . . " We can be friends, Nicolas," she pleaded.

" Friends ! " snorted Nicolas. What did she think he was made of ? Flesh and blood or milk and dough ? He was a man, with a man's hot desire that had already been curbed for her sake, and she expected him to behave like a painted Saint Nicolas in a stained-glass window. Giles's death and his love for her had stirred unknown depths in him and just at the moment of discovery, when he had felt the spirit in him that he did not know he had touched to awareness by something beyond that he had not known existed, she dealt him this blow. She seemed to be denying him not only herself but what she stood for. He felt as though he were being thrust back from new knowledge to the old ignorance, that would now be robbed of the old enjoyment because he had progressed beyond it. He had not known it was possible to suffer so deeply. His anger fell from him and he sat as though stunned, only vaguely conscious that Joyeuce was getting up and mechanically shaking out her black skirts.

" Come, Nicolas," she whispered. " It is going to rain again."

He got up, shivering a little, and looked about him. Every shred of colour had gone from the world. The kingfisher had gone home and the willows were hidden in the swathes of grey mist that came rolling up from the river. Without a word he took her hand ceremoniously and led her under the grey ghostly trees towards the grey walls that were her home. At the garden door they stopped and Joyeuce tried to withdraw her hand. " Good-bye, Nicolas," she whispered, and then stopped with a gasp as his arms went round her with such strength and passion that she could hardly get breath enough to protest. " Nicolas ! Nicolas ! " she moaned.

But he had no mercy on her. He held her so tightly that she felt as though he were trying to crush her heart into his body and his into hers. " My true love hath my heart and I have his," she thought, the words of Philip Sidney's new song that everyone was singing stumbling unbidden into her bewildered mind. " I'm not going to let you go, do you hear ? " whispered Nicolas fiercely. " I'll find some way to get you, Joyeuce. We'll be together yet." Then he kissed her, hard and passionately, as she did not know one could be kissed. She cried out, feeling her denial of him a sword piercing her, and the grey mist about her seemed to turn into darkness. She was falling down and down into it, as once before she had fallen in the porch of Saint Michael's at the North Gate, only this time the darkness seemed like the darkness of death.

Then she found herself alone in the garden, stumbling towards the house. Nicolas had pushed her in, she supposed, and shut the door and gone away. She reached the house and groped her way through the dark hall towards the stairs. She was so exhausted that she could hardly get up them and dragged herself from step to step like a wounded bird, her wet black skirts clinging forlornly round her ankles. How grave and wise Nicolas had been, how wonderful and yet how childish and passionate and angry. How strange that love, that she had always thought of as so sweet and tender, could tear and bruise like this. Her renunciation was still a sword stuck in her heart, that she thought would stay there till she died. Surely she *had* died, outside the garden gate when Nicolas kissed her and she still clung fast to her resolution, had died and come back to earth again a poor bedraggled ghost.

But yet, ghost or not, bewildered and miserable and bruised as she might be, the words that were singing themselves over and over in her mind were words of triumph.

> My true love hath my heart and I have his,
> By just exchange one for another given ;
> I hold his dear, and mine he cannot miss,
> There never was a better bargain driven.
> My true love hath my heart and I have his.
>
> His heart in me keeps him and me in one,
> My heart in him his thoughts and senses guides ;
> He loves my heart, for once it was his own,
> I cherish his, because in me it bides.
> My true love hath my heart and I have his.

CHAPTER XII

CHRISTMAS EVE

> Come to your heaven, you heavenly choirs!
> Earth hath the heaven of your desires;
> Remove your dwelling to your God,
> A stall is now his best abode;
> Sith men their homage do deny,
> Come, angels, all their fault supply.
>
> His chilling cold doth heat require,
> Come, seraphins, in lieu of fire;
> His little ark no cover hath,
> Let cherubs' wings his body swathe;
> Come, Raphael, this Babe must eat,
> Provide our little Toby meat.
>
> Let Gabriel be now his groom,
> That first took up his earthly room;
> Let Michael stand in his defence,
> Whom love hath linked to feeble sense;
> Let graces rock when he doth cry,
> And angels sing his lullaby.
> ROBERT SOUTHWELL.

I

NOT every scholar could go home for Christmas. Rich men who could afford horses, or who had hospitable friends near at hand, could leave Oxford, but for poor men who lived a long way off, the journey over roads knee-deep in mire would have been interminable; they would no sooner have got there than they would have had to come back again. And Nicolas, this year, was one of the unhappy ones, for his family went down with the small-pox and he was forbidden to go near them lest the beauty of the son and heir should be tarnished by the pock-marks. . . . He was perfectly miserable. . . . Giles was dead, Faithful was absorbed by the Leighs, and all his other friends, including Philip Sidney, were of the fortunate band who could go home. He had no one to shoot with, no one to gamble with and no one even to curse with, and not being one of those who find pleasure in solitude he wished he was dead.

And he did not know what to do about Joyeuce. It was no use appealing to her again, he felt, for though good as the angels in heaven, she was at the same time obstinate as the devil himself. She might be stretched upon the rack, as her father had been before her, but she would not change her convictions. Sometimes he thought that he would go straight to Canon Leigh and demand the hand of his daughter in marriage, but then he bethought him of the horror of his Greek and the outrage of his Latin and he suffered from qualms. He was no favourite with Canon Leigh, that he knew well, and he feared that he might be shown the door. Wisdom was required, he felt, and tact and inspiration, and just at the moment he could lay his hands upon none of them. The star that guided his destiny seemed at the moment to have turned its face away from him. He must wait with what patience he could until its gracious beams once more lit his path.

As the month drew on the thought of the stars was in everyone's minds, for Christmas was coming in in the traditional way, with frost and snow upon the ground and such a blaze of constellations in the night sky that it seemed the heavens were hanging low over the earth in most unusual friendliness.

And certainly the city of Oxford was good to look at at this time. By day, under a brilliant blue sky, the gabled roofs and tall chimneys, the towers and spires, took on an added brightness from the tracery of sparkling frost that clung to them ; and down below them the narrow streets were bright with the bunchy little figures of snowballing children, happy girls and beaming mothers going shopping with baskets on their arms, dressed in their gaudiest because it was Christmas-time, and laughing men with sprigs of holly in their caps, and faces as rosy as apples from the potations they had partaken of at the taverns and inns in honour of the festive season. The bad smells of the town had been obliterated by the continual snow showers and the hard frost—it would be a different story when the thaw came, but sufficient unto the day is the evil thereof—and delicious festive scents floated out into the streets from open doors and windows ; scents of baked meats and roasting apples, of ale and wine, of spices and perfumes and the fragrant wood-smoke from innumerable fires of apple-wood and beech-logs and resinous pine-branches. And at night the city seemed almost as brilliant as the starry sky above. From sheer goodwill doors were left ajar and windows uncurtained, so that bright beams of light lay aslant across the shadows, and the gay groups that thronged the streets carried lanterns that bobbed like fireflies over the trampled snow. The bells rang out continuously and the laughter and clear voices of the children made unceasing music. . . . And outside the city walls the fields and the low hills lay silent, shrouded in white. The murmur of the streams was hushed by the ice and the willow trees drooped above them without movement.

II

On Christmas Eve, after the sun had set, it all seemed a little intensified; the stars shone yet more brilliantly, the bells rang clearer and sweeter, the firelight seemed ruddier and the laughter and gaiety of the townspeople more contagious. Yet Nicolas, as he strolled idly across Carfax into Cornmarket, felt oddly apart from it all. Used as he was to being always at the centre of whatever excitement was afoot this unusual loneliness was a little frightening. It was because he was so unhappy, he thought, that he felt so lonely. It seemed that suffering of any sort made one feel lonely. He had not suffered before and so he had not discovered this before. He wondered why it should be so, for one was not alone in suffering; the whole world suffered. Perhaps this loneliness had some purpose in the scheme of things. Joyeuce would know. He would like to talk about it to Joyeuce.

With his thoughts so full of her it did not surprise him that he should find himself outside Saint Michael's at the North Gate. He thought that if left to themselves his feet would always now take him either to where she was, or to some place connected with her, for where she was would now always be home, and it was with a sense of home-coming that he turned into the old porch and sat down on the wooden bench.

But it was a rather desolate home-coming. On Mid-summer Eve it had been warm and balmy, with the scent of flowers coming on the wind, and Joyeuce had been in his arms, and now it was mid-winter and dark and he sat alone on the bench, huddled in his cloak against the cold. Why was one lonely? Where do the feet of the lonely take them? As the body turns always homewards at evening when the crowds are gone, so perhaps there is a country of the spirit to which the spirit turns in desolation. Perhaps one needed to be desolate to find that country, for if one were always happy one would not bother to look for it. Sitting with his eyes shut he remembered that Joyeuce had said something like that when they were together in the meadows. What was that country? . . . Heaven. Fairyland. The land beyond the sunset. The land above the stars where the great multitude which no man can number stand before the throne, clothed with white robes and palms in their hands. The land behind the tree-trunks where Queen Mab and her fairies leave the track of their passing in flowers upon the grass. Raleigh's land, where birds of white and carnation perch in tall cedar trees, where the stones are of gold and silver and rivers fall down crystal mountains with the noise of a thousand bells clanging together. . . . They gave it so many different names, but he supposed it was the same place and that the spirits of some lucky people, saints and little children and dreamers like Raleigh, could follow the road of loneliness until they reached their home. . . . But for him, if he opened his eyes, there would be nothing but the darkness of the musty-smelling old porch.

He opened his eyes and found himself gazing straight at a blazing star. His blood tingled through his veins and he felt himself gripped by a strange excitement. Was this his star whose face he had thought was turned away from him? Was it at last pointing upon him graciously? It shone so brightly straight into his eyes that for a moment he put up his hand to cover them. It was surely speaking to him. It said, " Come."

He got up and looked at it intently. It was hanging low over a gabled roof and beneath it was a tall chimney like a pointing finger. He knew that roof and that chimney. They belonged to the Crosse Inn, next door to Tattleton's Tavern where he had supped with Joyeuce. . . . Surely once before upon Christmas Eve a star had hung low above the roof of an inn. . . . The young man who stepped out of the porch of Saint Michael's at the North Gate into the clamour of Cornmarket was no longer lonely and unhappy. His cap was set at an angle and his cloak was flung back from his shoulders as though the wind took him. He was Saint Nicolas, the Christmas saint, come down from heaven, or Oberon, king of the fays, or a sailor sailing towards the sunset. He was caught up in a fairy-tale and the glory of it swept him along as though his feet were winged.

Yet he was still sufficiently upon the earth to notice that the crowd in Cornmarket had grown considerably while he sat in the porch of Saint Michael's. And they were all going one way. They were all flowing in under the great archway of the Crosse Inn into its galleried courtyard. They, too, were bound for the inn. What was happening at the inn? "The Players!" cried voices in the crowd. "The Christmas Players! The Players are here!"

Bands of travelling players still journeyed up and down the country, playing the old Morality Plays in the inn yards and at the market crosses, and their coming was still one of the events of the year at Oxford. Scholars were strictly forbidden to attend theatrical performances in inn yards, lest they should catch diseases or have their morals contaminated by the crowd, but this prohibition had never been one to which Nicolas thought it necessary to pay any attention; least of all to-night when he felt himself star-led to his destiny.

He was only just in time, for as he flung himself into the crowd that streamed in beneath the archway the clear note of a trumpet told him that the performance was about to begin. The rough wooden stage was set up in the middle of the courtyard, as though at the heart of the world, lighted at each corner by lanterns and decked with holly and evergreens, with the gaily dressed trumpeter standing upon it with his trumpet to his lips; and all round it surged the jolly Christmas crowd, fighting to get up to the best seats in the gallery that ran round the courtyard, or failing that, a place on the wooden steps that led up to it, or failing that an inch of room in the packed space below. Aldermen and citizens with their fat wives and rosy children were there, apprentices and pretty girls, rogues and vagabonds and dirty little urchins, all pushing and kicking and scrambling, but brimming over with humour and goodwill. They knew how to enjoy themselves on Christmas Eve, did these people of Oxford, and they were doing it. Nicolas had hard work to gain the spot which he had marked out as his own, a place against the gallery balustrade where he would get the best possible view of the stage, but he got there at last, wedged himself in between two fat citizens and a horde of apprentices and dirty little boys, and settled down to watch.

They were playing an old Nativity play to-night, followed by the story of Saint Nicolas, and he was no sooner in his place than the trumpeter stepped down, the lights in the gallery were hidden, and in a sudden silence, that fell upon the noisy crowd as though the shadow of an angel's wing passed over them, the first figures of the Christmas story stepped upon the stage.

It was very crude and at some other time Nicolas might have been moved to mirth, but he was not so moved to-night, neither he nor a single man, woman or child in that densely packed throng. It was Christmas Eve, and the same stars shone above them as had shone upon the fields of Palestine some fifteen hundred years ago. They sat in a deep and lovely silence, their eyes riveted upon the rough wooden stage where the figures of shepherds moved, and angels whose dresses had shrunk in the wash and whose wings and haloes had become a little battered by so much packing and unpacking, and a Virgin Mary whose blue cloak was torn and whose voice was that of a young English peasant boy who had not so long ago been taken from the plough.

Wedged against the balustrade of the gallery, Nicolas watched and listened in that state of heavenly concentration that leaves the human creature oblivious of himself. He was not conscious any more of the apprentices who pressed upon him, or of the smell of unwashed human bodies, or of his own empty stomach that had been presented with no supper this evening. He was only dimly aware of the crowd as a great multitude that he could not number, watchers in the shadows who had been watching there for fifteen hundred years. The Christmas story itself absorbed him. Though it was so old a story, one that he had known as soon as he was capable of knowing anything, it seemed to-night quite new to him. " Glory to God in the highest . . . A child is born." The old words that he had heard a hundred times over seemed cried out with the triumph of new and startling news. The figures that moved before him, Mary with the child in her arms, Joseph and the shepherds, Gabriel and the angels, Herod and the Wise Men, that he had seen so many times pictured in stained-glass windows and on the leaves of missals, moved now in this tiny space at the heart of the crowd as though they had come there for the first time. . . . The love of God is with man. . . . That, Nicolas knew suddenly, is the news of the far country, the mystery like a nugget of gold that men travel so far to seek, the fact that is stated but not explained by all the pictures that have been painted and by all the music and the poetry that has been written since the dawn of the world. It was as easy as that, and as difficult.

The Nativity play ended with a flash and a bang as the devil in black tights appeared to fetch away Herod to where he belonged. No one considered this an anticlimax; on the contrary they were all suitably impressed; this might happen to them if they were not careful. They groaned and shivered and were glad when the lanterns that had been hidden beneath cloaks were uncovered and the auditorium shone out into brilliance again. This was the interval between the two performances and a roar of voices broke out as though a river in spate had been let loose. Nicolas found that he too was shivering, not with fear but with the very intensity of his feeling, and looked round upon the noisy crowd with sensations that were entirely new. He felt so at one with them. A feeling of superiority had always been one of the most familiar of his pleasures, but now it had entirely gone from him. These burly perspiring merchants, fat matrons, laughing girls and jolly apprentices, these rogues and vagabonds who pressed about him, seemed as much a part of him as his own body. He did not care that a beery citizen was breathing heavily down the back of his neck or that two filthy little boys were holding themselves steady in a kneeling posture by clinging to his legs. In fact it was a pleasure. He loved them. All of them together were the men whom God was with. He wondered vaguely what he would be feeling like in a few days' time, whether he would be again the old superior sceptical Nicolas. . . . Perhaps. . . . Yet he would never be able to forget what he had felt to-night. He prayed God that he would never forget.

The trumpet sounded once more to give warning that the second part of the performance was about to begin. The lanterns in the galleries were hidden again and the roaring voices dropped away to an indistinct murmur, then to silence, and Saint Nicolas stepped upon the stage in a red robe, a long white beard, and a most genial, fatherly expression.

Nicolas de Worde knew the history of his patron saint well—

too well—for it had been dinned into his ears by every nurse he had ever had, so it was with a certain detachment that he listened to Saint Nicolas telling the audience the story of his early piety; as a new-born baby plunged into his first bath he had frightened everyone into fits by standing upright in the basin in an attitude of ecstatic adoration. Having thus early shown his aptitude for spiritual things it was but to be expected, so he informed the listening audience, that he should now have attained to his present position of Archbishop of Myra under Constantine the Great. And now, he said, he was upon this cold winter's night waiting to receive a visit from three little boys, children of a friend of his, who were travelling to Athens to school and were to stop at Myra on their way to receive his blessing; for he loved children and cared for their happiness and their welfare more than anything else upon earth. Then he hitched up his red robe, adjusted his white beard, which was slipping a little sideways, waved a hand to the children in the audience and stepped down from the stage. His place was taken by a most villainous looking red-headed man, accompanied by the devil bearing a large wooden tub, who announced in flowing couplets that the stage was now an inn and the red-headed villain the innkeeper, and the tub was intended for the storing of murdered guests to the inn, whom it was the innkeeper's habit to slay for their valuables and later to sell at a profit as pickled port; children, he said, being juicy and tender, pickled best. A shiver of horror shook the audience, and the children in it squeaked aloud, their squeaks rising to cries of warning as three little boys were seen to be moving out of the shadows towards the lighted stage, two older boys with dark hair and one minute little fair-haired boy clasping a woolly lamb with tin legs in his arms. But the three doomed children took no notice of the warning cries, and failed to see the devil hiding behind the tub. Confidingly they mounted the steps to the stage, and confidingly they piped out, "Innkeeper, Innkeeper, please will you give us lodging for the night? It is too late now to disturb the good Archbishop. Inkeeper, Innkeeper, is there room for us in the inn?"

"Come in, my little dears," cried the Innkeeper, rubbing his hands together in horrid glee, and suddenly seizing the foremost boy by the scruff of his neck he whipped out a huge long knife and waved it in the air so that it flashed about his head like lightning. The audience moaned and cowered, and afterwards they were all ready to swear that they had actually seen those three shrieking little boys cut up into small pieces and stowed away in the tub; the fair little boy being cut up last and his lamb pitched in after him as a final tit-bit.

Having thus bestowed the little boys to his satisfaction the innkeeper sprinkled salt over them, stirred them about with a wooden spoon, and then settled himself on the floor with his back propped against one side of the tub, the devil being upon the other, for a well earned night's rest.

But no sooner were their snores ringing out triumphantly upon the frosty air than Saint Nicolas came hurrying along to the scene of action. He had had a nightmare, so he told the audience in breathless couplets as he climbed the steps to the stage, in which the fate of the little boys had been revealed to him by Almighty God with such a wealth of detail that every separate hair upon his white head had stood completely up on end. At this point he reached the Innkeeper, fell upon him and shook him with a violence surprising in one so aged. " Villain ! " he shouted. " Awake ! Repent ! The day of judgement is at hand ! " It is a well-known fact that a criminal startled out of sleep will, if charged with his crime, acknowledge it, and the innkeeper was no exception to the rule. He awoke, yelped at finding himself shaken by an Archbishop, fell upon his knees and made a full confession. Seeing him so penitent the saintly Archbishop prayed loudly for his forgiveness, banished the now awakened and peevish devil with a wave of the hand, and concentrated upon the tub. He made the sign of the cross over it, he prayed over it, he wept over it, he stirred its contents with the wooden spoon and prayed again.

Up popped a small dark head. " Oh, I have had a beautiful sleep," it said.

Up popped a second. " So have I," it said.

Then up popped a golden head and a tiny bell-like voice piped, " And as for me, I have been in Paradise."

The audience rocked and roared and cheered, and their cheering did not cease until the opening of the second scene, when the three little boys, dressed now as three little girls, sat at the feet of a sorrowing father—the red-headed villain only thinly disguised by the addition of a black wig—and were told that because of his poverty they could have no dowries. . . . They would in all probability have to be old maids. . . . At this awful threat the three little girls wept most pitifully, with their fists thrust into their eyes so that they did not see Saint Nicolas peeping over the edge of the stage, and did not see him take three little parcels from his red robe, throw them in, and then creep away chuckling to himself. . . . But they heard the thud as the parcels fell at their feet ; they opened their eyes and picked them up ; and they were three purses of gold.

The crowd cheered again and Saint Nicolas reappeared and came to the front of the stage, his genial white-bearded face beaming like the rising sun and his red robe shining gloriously in the lantern light. " Go home, all you little girls and boys," he said, " and before you go to sleep to-night put out your little shoes beside your beds, and it may be that Saint Nicolas, who loves little children as dearly to-day as he did all those hundreds of years ago, will come in the night and put presents for you in them." Then Saint Nicolas beamed and bowed again, and the performance was over.

Nicolas thought afterwards that it had been his detachment that had made him so acutely conscious of the little fair-haired boy with the woolly lamb with the tin legs. He had been one of the principal actors from the beginning. He had trotted at the heels of the shepherds as a little shepherd boy, clasping his lamb. He had knelt at the foot of the manger in Bethlehem as a little cherub, with his halo slipping sideways and the lamb still clasped to his bosom. He had been one of the innocents slaughtered by Herod and had died beautifully in the middle of the stage with the lamb still clasped to his chest. And then, with the lamb still apparently an inseparable part of his person, he had been one of the little boys saved by Saint Nicolas.

And in this story the other Nicolas had noticed him as a person for the first time. Before, he had been part of the Christmas story, one of the gleaming facets of this jewel at the heart of the world, but in this he had been a little boy acting in a play and as such Nicolas had not been able to take his eyes off him ; and was surprised at himself, for as a rule he took not the slightest interest in children. The little boy's hair was smooth and fair, and shone in the lantern light as though his shapely little head were encased in a cap of gold. His face, grave and absorbed as he performed to the best of his ability the task that had been set him, was small and delicately heart-shaped, and the little bare feet that pattered so obediently over the hard boards of the stage were shapely and slender as those of a fairy's child. Nicolas could not see his eyes, but he was sure that they were blue, a deep violet blue that would turn to the colour of rain when sorrow clouded them. Surely this was no child of a strolling player. . . . If Joyeuce were to have a son, thought Nicolas, with a sudden constriction of the throat that hurt him, he would have just such a smooth fair head, just such a flower-like delicacy and grave absorption in his duty. . . . To possess such a son, thought Nicolas, the cares of fatherhood would not seem heavy.

III

The play had ended and the actors and their stage had disappeared as though by magic. The lights shone out again and the chattering multi-coloured crowd flowed down the steps from the galleries and out from the benches beneath them, filling the well of the courtyard as though wine had been poured into a dark cup. The stars were still blazing in the square of sky that rested on the gabled roofs and the Christmas bells were ringing. Nicolas found himself caught up in the singing crowd and carried bodily towards the archway that led back into Cornmarket, and the normal world that he had left behind him when he had stepped into the porch of Saint Michael at the North Gate. He pushed his way towards one of the wooden supports of the gallery, seized it and clung there and let the crowd surge past him, for the time had not come to return to the normal world. His star had not finished with him. He knew that as certainly as he had ever known anything.

"Will you come inside and take a tankard of ale, pretty master."

The crowd was thinning and Nicolas looked down into the face of a pert little serving wench, with lips as red as holly berries and a snowy apron tied over a flowered gown. Since he had known Joyeuce he had rather lost his taste for serving wenches, but he smiled and chucked her under the chin and followed willingly enough. He was waiting upon events and her invitation seemed the next one in the sequence.

He followed her through a stout oak door into the main room of the inn, where a great fire of Christmas yule logs blazed on the hearth and was reflected in a ruddy glow in the faces of some two score of good citizens who were drinking ale, laughing, shouting and singing in an orgy of good fellowship well befitting the festive seasons. The air was thick with the fumes of the ale and the smoke from the fire and it was impossible for even the loudest-voiced to make himself heard under a shout. Yet through the haze there loomed the great bulk, and above the tumult there sounded the bellow, of Master Honeybun, mine host of the Crosse Inn, as he heaved himself this way and that refilling tankards, quelling disputes and getting the best of every argument with a playful blow upon the chest and a pat upon the head that were like to be the death of those so favoured. But in spite of his multifarious duties he espied Nicolas and greeted him with a roar of welcome like to the roaring of a hundred bulls, for Nicolas was of the quality, and the quality were more likely to be found at the Tavern next door than at the humble Crosse.

Nicolas, his sense of unity with all mankind still powerfully with him, felt himself instantly at home. He seized the proffered tankard and was soon laughing and talking with these ruddy-faced gentlemen as though he had known them all his life. The players were among them, he discovered, no longer angels and shepherds but English vagabonds of the road with weather-tanned faces and worn jerkins. But they showed themselves to be artists, messengers of another country, by little eccentricities of dress and manner that aroused the mockery of the rollicking apprentices drinking beside the fire ; one wore a gay yellow sash on his shabby jerkin, one, whose clothes were in rags, brandished a perfumed handkerchief of crimson silk, another wore heavy gold rings in his ears as though he were a seaman, and all of them had deeper voices than ordinary men, more graceful bodies, and gesticulating fingers and sparkling eyes that could convey in half a second the meaning or emotion that an ordinary man could not have expressed in twenty minutes of laborious speech ; but Nicolas in his new mood found their unconscious striving for beauty and their lovely ease of communication matter for reverence rather than mirth.

"That is a lovely child of yours who played to-night," he

said to him of the rags and the perfumed handkerchief, a slim boy who had played the part of the angel Gabriel.

"Which child, master?" asked Gabriel.

"The fair child. The one with a woolly lamb."

"Oh, that child. He's not one of ours. He's a gypsy's child who is staying at the inn. Our boy is sick and this child took his place. A clever child; it took only a couple of hours to teach him his part." A wicked grin spread over the face of the angel Gabriel and his slim fingers gripped Nicolas's arm. "Come and let me introduce you to his father."

The ruddy apprentices by the fire surrounded a group of older men, rough men from the poorer part of the town, a travelling tinker and a few gypsies, and into this group the angel Gabriel propelled Nicolas. "Here, Sampson," he cried, "here's a gentleman would like to meet the father of the infant prodigy."

Nicolas stared in amazement at the drunken giant of a creature who confronted him. He looked at the great broad shoulders, the dark matted beard, the coarse crimson features and the bloodshot green eyes that twinkled at him rather angrily, and in spite of himself he recoiled a little at the sight of the man's great hairy chest showing through his torn jerkin, and the reek of drink and sweat that assailed his fastidious nose. The recoil and astonishment were momentary, but they were seen, and a huge red hand shot out and gripped Nicolas by the front of his exquisite leaf-green doublet.

"So my young cockerel thinks I can't be the father of that damn child, does he?" bellowed Sampson in a maudlin indignation, shaking Nicolas as a terrier a rat. "The little whey-faced puling brat! So I'm not capable of fathering it, eh?"

"I never said so," remarked Nicolas breathlessly, but with humour. "I consider your worship capable of fathering any number of brats." His feet slipped on the floor, and his teeth clashed together as he rocked this way and that in the ruffian's grip, but he managed to continue, his eyes merry in his empurpled face. "It is merely that in this case I do not consider the family likeness very remarkable."

A great roar of laughter went up, for it seemed this was not the first time that the paternity of Sampson had been called in question, and it seemed this particular subject was a sore point with him for he let go of Nicolas and hit out with blind rage at the circle of mocking faces that hedged him in.

"Eh, Sampson!" shouted the Tinker, a great bully of a man almost as vast as Sampson himself. "Can you give a name to the father of that boy? Can you give a name to the father of the child Sara's brought to bed with at this moment? Cuckold! Cuckold!"

Suddenly the affair that had begun as a coarse jest turned ugly. Sampson hit the tinker and the Tinker hit Sampson. The laughter turned to a tumult of shouts and curses. Mine host bore down upon them and with one huge hand plucked Nicolas out of the hubbub as he would have lifted a chestnut from the fire.

And then somehow the whole crowd of them were out in the courtyard, under the starry sky, and there was a fight on. Sampson and the Tinker, roaring drunk and mad with rage, were fighting each other in the centre of a ring of men whose faces were alight with a bestial eagerness to witness blood and suffering that was hideous to see. Now and then they yelled encouragement to the fighters and their cries were animal cries. Lanterns were held aloft that they might see the better, and the stars looked down.

Nicolas, with the boy who had played Gabriel grave-eyed beside him, stood on the outskirts of the crowd, and he felt sick. He had witnessed fights before, and always with keen enjoyment. He had fought himself, and felt the better for it. He had even attended several hangings and derived pleasure from the titillations of horror that ran up and down his spine on those occasions. But to-night he felt sick. Only a short while ago, on the very spot where those two brutes were fighting, the loveliest story in all the world had been enacted. Only a short while ago, in this very place, he had learnt so to love the men around him that they had seemed a part of his own body. . . . And now, because he still loved them, he had to stand here and watch the degradation of his body. . . . "Deus, propitius esto mihi peccatori," he murmured. The boy beside him looked at him, uncomprehending, but the sorrow in his eyes was an Amen and the stars seemed to press down a little lower, brighter and more pitiful.

It was soon over. The Tinker was the less drunk of the two,

and he got the best of it. A yell came from the crowd as Sampson crashed over backwards, then a sudden silence in which they could hear the voices of the Christmas waits singing far off in the town, and then an outbreak of shocked incredulous murmurings.

"What has happened?" demanded Nicolas, and pressed a little nearer.

Sampson was dead. He had fallen with his head on a projecting cobblestone and his magnificent great body was now as worthless as a heap of rubbish. Nicolas caught one glimpse of him, with his head lying in a pool of blood and his sightless eyes turned towards the stars, and then turned away in misery and horror. . . . For he had done this. . . . With a word spoken in jest he had started the whole tragedy. And somehow he had rather liked that coarse bully. There had been something attractive about him; his rage had been swift and splendid, as elemental as a thunderstorm or the onslaught of a tiger, and his twinkling green eyes had stirred some vague memory in Nicolas that was as sweet as it was elusive. He was sorry that the man was dead.

IV

They picked him up and carried him away and gradually the sobered crowd dispersed and went home. Loneliness possessed the innyard. There were no lights but the few that shone from the inn and the stars that glittered overhead, no sounds but the soft chiming of the bells and the faraway singing of the waits. But Nicolas still lingered. There seemed nothing that he could do, but he still lingered, pacing up and down over the soiled and trodden snow, his cloak wrapped tightly about him and his heart heavy.

A touch on his arm made him look round. It was the pretty little serving wench, shivering with the cold, her face white and frightened.

"Yes?" encouraged Nicolas, but she seemed to have nothing to say, and only huddled herself the closer in the shawl she had thrown about her shoulders.

"What ails you, my dear?" asked Nicolas again, and turned up her face to the starlight with one finger beneath her chin.

At this she recovered, and her dimples peeped. "I must tell her," she confided, "and, sure as I live, I've not the courage."

"Tell whom?" asked Nicolas.

"Sara. Sampson's wife. Sampson brought her into Oxford two days ago, for she was taken very bad and he wanted to get the physician to her."

"You mean that she is here? At the inn?"

"Yes. She often comes here to amuse the company with her fortune telling, and so she came here in her trouble and Master Honeybun took pity on her. He's a kind man, Master Honeybun. We made a bed for her in a part of the stable that we don't use. The babe died yesterday, and now she's likely to die herself."

"Then need you tell her?" asked Nicolas.

"Master Honeybun said I was to," she said, and looked down, twisting her shawl round her fingers.

"I'll tell her," said Nicolas suddenly. She looked up again, her eyes two round ohs of amazement, and Nicolas himself hardly knew what possessed him. Afterwards he thought it was his sense of responsibility for the death in the innyard that drove him to make what amends he could.

The girl was so thankful to have him relieve her of her duty that she allowed him no time to change his mind. She hurried him forthwith across the courtyard to a door on the far side. "In there," she whispered.

Nicolas lifted the latch and walked in. He was at the far end of the great inn stable, in a little space partitioned off from the rest by a rough curtain. A lantern hung from the raftered cobwebby ceiling and a small fire in a brazier brought a little warmth into the bitter air. A broad rough bed spread with old blankets and soft hay stood against the wall and in the glow of the lantern and firelight he could see the outline of a woman lying upon it, with another smaller figure curled up beside her. He stopped, his heart beating, aware that death was here, too, not the sudden death that had struck like lightning in the courtyard outside but an invisible brooding spirit whose presence seemed to set this little room at a great distance from the rest of the world. For a moment all memory fell away from Nicolas. He, this woman, the unseen child and the angel of death were alone together, enclosed in a little circle of light that hung like a star between heaven above and the unseen earth far away beneath them. When it was shattered the four of them would go their ways to where they belonged, but for the moment they were alone together in a unity so deep that understanding would need few words.

The hay on the far side of the bed rustled softly and a little gold head popped up. Nicolas, moving forward, found himself looking straight into a pair of blue eyes, a deep violet blue that would turn to the colour of rain when sorrow clouded them. . . . Somehow he had thought that this child would have eyes like Joyeuce. . . . He smiled and a merry little answering smile tilted up the corners of the child's mouth and set sparks in his eyes. He seemed to like this visitor and he turned and poked his mother with his toy lamb that she, too, might wake up and like him.

She stirred and moaned a little, a sound that was half question and half plaint, and Nicolas came to her side and stood looking down upon her. He had expected to see a rough-looking woman, the feminine counterpart of the man who had died outside, and he was amazed at what he saw. Sara was dying, and sickness had robbed her of much of her beauty, yet even the remnant of it roused his homage. He bowed his head as he looked at the fine bones of her face, showing like ivory beneath the tightly stretched skin, at the mass of night-dark hair and the deep eyes, clouded with mystery, that looked up into his.

"So it was he who died outside!" she whispered.

"Yes," said Nicolas. As he had thought, few words were needed.

She moved her head a little restlessly on the pillow, but she gave no sign of grief. Perhaps, thought Nicolas, she had not loved him, or perhaps she was too near death to have any care now for anything that might happen on earth. But even as he thought this he knew he was wrong, for she turned her head and looked at him as though he himself were of extreme importance to her. She looked at the gallant picture that he made, standing straight and slim in his fine doublet and hose of dark green, the colour of holly leaves, with his scarlet-lined cloak flung back from his shoulders. In reverence for her he held his cap in his hands and the lantern light shone upon his crisp dark hair and the face with the mocking eyebrows, smooth girlish skin and strong mouth that in gravity could look so lovely. She looked at him appealingly, hungrily, as though he were not only a man who could help her but a symbol of something that she had intensely desired. She put out a hand and felt the fine stuff of his cloak as he stood beside her. " I wanted him to be like you," she whispered. " That was why I did it."

Nicolas did not understand, but he saw that she had something more to say to him and he bent over her, smiling reassuringly into her eyes. He felt no fear, now, of sorrow and death, only desire to succour. " I will do anything I can to help you," he said, slowly and clearly so that she should understand.

" Where do you come from ? " She spoke so low now that her whisper was a mere breath.

" From Christ Church," said Nicolas.

She made a little motion of her head towards the boy beside her. " Then take the child with you. Take him back where he belongs," she said, and sighed in relief and weariness as her eyes closed and her head rolled weakly back into the dented hollow on the pillow.

" Where ? " asked Nicolas, but even as he asked he knew it was no use. Her dark lashes, lying on the dark hollows below her eyes, trembled a little and then lay motionless. He knew that they would not lift again. He put his fingers gently on her wrist and felt the tiny flutter of the pulse, and even at his touch it was still.

He straightened himself and held out his arms to the little boy who was kneeling up in the hay staring at him. He had thought there would be tears and protestations, but there were none. Grave-eyed and obedient the child, too, held out his arms, his lamb clasped by a hind leg in one hand, and let himself be lifted across his mother's body.

As Nicolas, with the boy in his arms, lifted the latch of the door, he could have fancied that he heard the flutter of dark wings. The little circle of light in which the four of them had hung above the earth was shattered now and they were going their different ways, two to death and two to life.

The girl was still lingering in the courtyard and Nicolas paused only to send her inside to Sara before he made tracks for home. Now and then, as he strode down Cornmarket and across Carfax into South Street, he looked down at the boy. The little face looked very pallid in the starlight but there was always the flash of an answering smile when Nicolas looked at him, and his golden hair shone like a gallant cap of gold. His bare feet and legs were cold as ice and he was shivering, but he made no complaint. Nicolas, who had thought he did not care for children, held the little body close to his own to warm it and tucked his cloak round more firmly. He had no doubt at all as to where to take this child. . . . To Joyeuce, for a Christmas present.

v

And meanwhile Joyeuce sat in front of the parlour fire with the children grouped around her, and her father and Great-Aunt in their big chairs one on each side, and listened to Faithful laboriously reading aloud from Foxe's *Book of Martyrs*. It was long past the children's bedtime but they had not wanted to go to bed and she had let them stay up. Even the little ones felt the sorrow that hung over the house, this first Christmas after Giles's death, and they shrank from their dark cold bedroom. It was more cheerful in the parlour, where the log fire sparkled and crackled and a most extravagant array of candles shone all round the room.

But even then it was not particularly cheerful, for Great-Aunt, who had the indigestion, kept heaving great sighs, their father sat with his head sunk on his breast, rousing himself heroically now and then to make forced cheerful remarks that were more depressing than silence, and Joyeuce stitched away at her embroidery with a sort of desperation, as though she dared not let herself think. Grace, the boys and the twins stared sadly and a little sullenly into the fire, for they felt that happiness was their right at this season and they could not but feel bitter against the fate that had snatched it away from them. Diccon sat curled up on the floor at Joyeuce's feet, his curly head resting against her knees, and was still a prey to his secret sorrow, his poppy mouth drooping and his green eyes staring mournfully at the tips of his little pointed scarlet shoes. All the rest of the family were in black but he wore elfin green, with the scarlet shoes and a knot of cherry ribbons at the breast. Sitting there in the middle of them, so bright and fair to see, Joyeuce thought he was like the spark of unconquerable hope at the heart of sorrow. It did her good to look at him, even though he was so sorry a little boy.

All the time, muted by the closed windows and the drawn curtains, they could hear the bells ringing and the waits, bands of poor scholars who were allowed by the Vice-Chancellor to sing and beg at the houses of the rich, singing as they passed up and down the snowy streets. Sometimes a band of them passing up Fish Street would stop and sing under their window, and then their singing was hard to bear. " Unto us a Child is born. Unto us a Son is given." To-night the words seemed nothing but a mockery.

VI

It was after one such visitation that Faithful decided he had better read aloud to his adopted family, and fetched his beloved *Book of Martyrs*. It had accompanied him through all the many changes and chances of his own life and he had always found it an unspeakable comfort. Not only was the example of the martyrs so uplifting, but it was really impossible to think of one's own woes when absorbed in blood-curdling descriptions of other people being burnt alive. There is nothing like the troubles of other people to distract one's attention from one's own.

But to-night, knowing Joyeuce to have a squeamish stomach and Great-Aunt's indigestion to be by no means a thing of the past, he concentrated upon the milder stories of Master Foxe. Finally, he read them the account of the riot in Saint Mary's church at Oxford in the year 1536, when Bloody Mary sat upon the throne of England and persecution was at its height. A certain poor heretic, a Cambridge M.A., was sent to Oxford that he might recant openly, bearing his faggot in the church of Saint Mary the Virgin upon a Sunday, in front of the whole congregation of Doctors, Divines, Citizens and Scholars. It was felt, apparently, that to make a fool of himself before Oxford University would, for a Cambridge man, be the final humiliation ; it was thought, too, that it would give pleasure to Oxford to see him do it, and would be a great warning to such of the scholars as might be heretically inclined. . . . The church was packed to the doors and in the middle stood the Cambridge heretic with his faggot on his shoulder.

But no sooner was Doctor Smith, the preacher, well away into his sermon, denouncing the poor heretic with the full force of his lungs, than from the High Street outside came a cry of " Fire !

Fire!" Somebody's chimney was on fire, it afterwards transpired, but the crowded congregation had but one thought; sympathetic heretics and demons had fired the church. "Fire! Fire!" they yelled, and in the space of five minutes pandemonium had broken out, the panic-stricken congregation fighting like wild beasts to get out of the church. "But," said Master Foxe in his narrative, "such was the press of the multitude, running in heaps together, that the more they laboured the less they could get out. I think there was never such a tumultuous hurly-burly, rising so of nothing, heard of before, so that if Democritus, the merry philosopher, had beholden so great a number, some howling and weeping, running up and down, trembling and quaking, raging and gasping, breathing and sweating, I think he would have laughed the heart out of his body.

Now "in this great maze and garboyle" there were only two who kept their heads, the heretic himself, who hastened to cast his faggot off his shoulders and bring it down hard upon the head of a monk who stood near by, breaking the head to his great satisfaction, and a little boy who had climbed up on top of a door to be out of the way of this seething horde of lunatic grown-ups.

Sitting up there on top of the door, the little boy wondered what he should do, for though he was not frightened he thought that it would be rather nice to go home. Then he saw a great burly monk who was fighting his way to the nearest exit with more success than most. He wore his monk's habit and had a big cowl hanging down his back and he was coming quite close to the little boy. The urchin waited until the monk was right underneath him and then he slithered down from the top of the door and "prettily conveyed himself" into the monk's cowl.

The monk got out and made tracks for home, and being a very burly man, and the little boy being such a very tiny little boy, he did not at first notice anything out of the ordinary. But as he turned from High Street into Cornmarket it struck him that his cowl felt heavier than usual, and he shook his shoulders in some annoyance. . . . Then there came a little whispering voice in his ear. . . . Terror seized him like an ague, and he was more frightened than he had been in the church, for he had a guilty conscience and he had no doubt at all that one of the demons

who had fired the church had jumped straight into his cowl.
" In the name of God, and All Saints," he cried, " I adjure thee,
thou wicked spirit, that thou get thee hence."

But there was no crashing of thunder, no searing of blue flame
as the demon took his departure, only a little voice that whispered, " I am Bertram's boy. Good master, let me go." And
then the long-suffering cowl suddenly gave way at the seams and
the little boy fell out and ran away home as fast as his legs could
carry him.

VII

It was a cheerful story and everyone felt the better for it
except Diccon, and Diccon most unaccountably began to cry.
He did not roar and bellow, he just sobbed noiselessly in that
devastating way he had when his heart was breaking. Everybody was most upset and gathered round to soothe and comfort,
while Joyeuce, pressing his curly head against her knee, implored
him to say what ailed him.

" I want that little boy," he whispered at last. " I want that
little boy. I want him now."

As it had been with the ruby in the window of the aurifabray,
so it was with the little boy ; he must have what he wanted or he
could no longer support life. Why, he seemed to ask, was I
born into this cruel world ? Whose fault was it that earthly
life was given to me ? Why was I dragged from the realms of
celestial glory, where the angels gave me the comets to play with,
to this earth where I stretch out my empty hands in vain for my
heart's desire ?

" But you can't have the little boy, my poppet," explained
Joyeuce. " He's only a little boy in a story."

Diccon knelt up on the floor in front of her, his hands laid on
her knees and his tear-stained face raised imploringly to hers.
" He's a real little boy," he hiccuped, " and Diccon must have
him."

" He was a real little boy years ago, when Master Foxe wrote
that story," explained Canon Leigh, " but he is not a little boy
now."

Diccon shook his head and choked, the tears running out of
his eyes and dripping off his pointed chin on to his cherry ribbons
in a positive cascade. " A real boy," he insisted, " just so big."

And he stretched out his arms to show his own minute height. "Just so big as me. He has fair hair. Diccon wants him." And again he raised his imploring face to Joyeuce who loved him and always gave him what he wanted.

Joyeuce was near tears herself. Was this his sorrow? Was he so lonely? The twins were older than he and he had no one but Tinker to play with. She had heard that lonely children often invented imaginary playmates to be with them. Perhaps he had imagined his little fair-haired boy and was heartbroken that he could not turn him into flesh and blood. She shook her head helplessly and Diccon, his hands still resting on her knees, shook her lap almost angrily. . . . It was Christmas Eve and seated upon it she should have had for him a little fair-haired boy.

The door opened and they all looked round in astonishment. Standing there smiling at them was the gallant figure of Nicolas de Worde, dressed like Diccon in the Christmas colours of scarlet and green and carrying a little fair-haired boy clasping a woolly lamb with tin legs. He walked across to them and deposited his burden in Joyeuce's lap.

There was a moment's pause of utter astonishment and then a chorus of ecstatic cries.

"It's Baa!" shrieked the twins and Will and Thomas. "The little boy has Baa!"

"It's Joseph!" shouted Faithful.

"It's a little Christmas angel," cried Grace.

"Tilly-vally! Angel indeed!" ejaculated Great-Aunt in some displeasure. "Some filthy child out of the streets!"

Diccon, with the tears still wet on his cheeks, clasped Baa's tail with one hand and Joseph's left foot with the other and laughed and laughed, his dimples peeping and the whole of his pink tongue exposed to view, while Joseph, curled up on Joyeuce's lap as though it were his proper home, seized his foster-brother's dark curls with both hands and laughed too.

As for Joyeuce and Canon Leigh, bewildered, incredulous, yet with a queer new joy struggling through their bewilderment, they found themselves gazing down into a little face that was the exact counterpart of that of the wife and mother they had both adored.

Nicolas leant against the mantelpiece, his eyes upon Joyeuce.

"I was lonely and unhappy," he told her. "And so I went up into the town. And so I found him at the inn." Her eyes fell before his and he said no more, but watched the family group with smiling satisfaction. Without understanding yet what he had done, he knew that he had done something good, and something, too, that would bring him into the very heart of this family. Moreover he found the picture of Joyeuce with Joseph in her arms as satisfying as he had expected it to be.

The Christmas bells were still ringing and the waits were singing under the window. "Unto us a Child is born. Unto us a Son is given." There was no longer any mockery in the Christmas message.

CHAPTER XIII

PROMISE OF SPRING

But in my mind so is her love enclosed,
And is thereof not only the best part,
But into it the essence is disposed.
Oh love! (the more my woe) to it thou art

Even as the moisture in each plant that grows;
Even as the sun unto the frozen ground;
Even as the sweetness to th'incarnate rose;
Even as the centre in each perfect round;

As water to the fish, to men as air,
As heat to fire, as light unto the sun;
O love! it is but vain to say thou were;
Ages and times cannot thy power outrun.
                                    WALTER RALEIGH.

I

IT was February the fourteenth, and Canon Leigh, on his way home from the lecture he had just given in the Lady Chapel, paused for a moment in the cloisters. The scholars who had clattered out at his heels had gone back to their rooms, for the spring *viva voce* examinations were not far away and it behoved them to keep their noses well wedged in their books, and he was quite alone. It was a windless day and there was not a sound to be heard except the cawing of a rook, and a faint chiming of bells, so muted by distance that it seemed only the echo of some music past or to come. The grey mist that hid the sun, and veiled the roofs and towers, so that they lost their hardness of outline and became little more than shadows in the sky, had in it a warmth and fragrance that told of the coming of spring. The smell of the earth was in it, a soft wet earth through which the snowdrops had already driven their green spears, and some elusive scent that was like the ghost of the fragrance of a thousand flowers. It seemed all there behind the mist, the colours of all the springs that had passed and yet would come again, the riotous music of bird song and falling water that would pour over the earth in so short a while. In the darkest days of January one might doubt if it would come again, but on these warm February days one was certain.

They destroyed all sense of time, these days. Past and present and future seemed all one. There were ghosts of the past as well as of the future about on these days, and those who watched and listened could see their grey shapes in the grey shadows and hear again, muffled by the mist, the voices and the laughter that had once rung out in arrogant possession.

In no part of the College did Canon Leigh feel so aware of the passing and re-passing of the ghosts as he did in these cloisters, for here, at the heart of Wolsey's College, the old Priory that had succeeded Frideswide's Nunnery still seemed to have its stronghold. To the north was the monks' Cathedral Church, to the east the Deanery that had once been the Prior's house, and at right angles to it the monks' refectory that was now the library, and in the centre of the enclosed square old grey stones, the remains of the monks' washing place, showed through the green grass. This little square, with the cloisters running round it, seemed always a little dark and dim, a little withdrawn from the rest of the College. In it old memories lived on.

But to-day was February the fourteenth and Canon Leigh, as he stood in this place of memories, saw not the cowled figures of the monks pacing in the cloisters but a packed mob of people, as many as the place would hold, bishops, courtiers, scholars, citizens and riff-raff of the town, swaying this way and that in the grip of wild mob excitement, mocking, taunting, and crying out in compassion, anger or horror ; and standing before them, the object of their hatred or their pity, was Thomas Cranmer, Archbishop of Canterbury, come here that he might be publicly degraded by the people whose shepherd he had been.

That scene had only been a few years ago, but so much had happened since then, so much horror had flowed over Oxford, and then again so much joy and thanksgiving, that it seemed that centuries had passed. . . . And yet it was happening now and Canon Leigh, as he stood with bent head, was watching it.

The Archbishop had been three years in prison, finding himself unable, now that Queen Mary was on the throne, to change at her command the convictions that had been his when her father had made him Archbishop. He had been imprisoned in the Tower of London, and then, with Bishop Ridley and Bishop Latimer, in the prison of Bocardo. In the Oxford Divinity School they were tried and condemned to death, they being Cambridge men and it being apparently the policy of the Queen always to humiliate Cambridge men at Oxford. From the top of Bocardo the Archbishop had seen Latimer and Ridley, who were to suffer before him, led out to be burnt to death outside the North Gate, and had kneeled down and prayed to God to strengthen them.

Then his own turn had come. After the formal excommunication in the Cathedral he had been led out to the cloisters for his degradation. They had put up a mock altar there and upon it were laid copies, made of rough and coarse materials, of an Archbishop's vestments, mitre and pastoral staff, and with these two jeering priests invested him; yet it was said that his dignity was so great that the crowd did not notice that the vestments he wore were only a mockery. Then one by one they were taken off him, the threadbare gown of a yeoman bedel was thrown over his shoulders and a townsman's greasy cap was forced upon his head. He was no longer Archbishop, he was Thomas Cranmer, an old man led away through the crowd to die as his friends had died.

Canon Leigh could never think of the fate of those three " special and singular captains and principal pillars of Christ's Church " without sick rage. It gripped him now as he looked round him at the quiet scene of the Archbishop's humiliation. It hurt him to the heart that it should have taken place within the walls of his own College. He had to remind himself of Latimer's words to Ridley when the fire was kindled at his feet. " Be of good comfort, Master Ridley, and play the man. We shall this day light such a candle, by God's grace, as I trust shall never be put out." He was right; it burnt yet; and would do while the stones of this town stood. So many candles had been lit by saints and martyrs in this city that surely the flames had burnt up all the cruelties and obscenities that might have tarnished its spirit.

Canon Leigh sighed a little and found himself musing upon the life of cities. As the hands of men had laid their stones one upon another, clumsily or with grace according to the conception of beauty that was in them, so surely the spirit of the city was woven of the spirits of the men who had lived within it, woven coarsely or finely according to the fibre of their spirits, but as vital to the material city as is heat to fire, or light to the sun. It seemed to him that both the body and the spirit of this city had in this sixteenth century an incomparable beauty. He wondered how much the men who lived here to-day, rejoicing in the beauty of the towers and spires against the sky, of gardens planted with fair flowers, of quiet evenings whose silence seemed to rest upon the foundations of fortitude and peace, were aware of their debt to the creators of the past, how often they paused to watch for the passing of ghosts in the shadows and to listen for the footfall on the stones. . . . Well, the men of to-day had their work to do. They were busy with their ambitions, their loves and their hates. They too were creators who were building for the men of the future. . . . And he must go home and prepare questions for the coming examinations.

II

Raising his eyes as he passed under the dim archway that led from the cloisters to the quadrangle he saw, outlined against the brighter light beyond, the glittering figure of that scapegrace Nicolas de Worde. He was dressed at the moment in the sober garments of a scholar, yet nevertheless he glittered. His dark-blue doublet and hose fitted his graceful figure with such an elegant neatness that they looked as jaunty as crimson satin studded with sapphires, his ruff, that on most scholars was apt to become a sordid and bedraggled affair, pale grey in colour and wavering in outline, was crisp and white, the cap that he held in his hand had in it a curling white feather, his cheeks glowed with health and his eyes with some suppressed excitement, and his whole body was taut and vigorous as a drawn bow. When Canon Leigh, bowing a little distantly and uttering a slightly frigid "good morning," had brought his own bent and weary body on a level with this radiant vision and was about to pass on, Nicolas, to his consternation, wheeled round and paced alongside. . . . He saw that he had been waylaid and trapped, he, a busy man in the midst of the many labours of his arduous morning.

"Can I serve you in any way?" he enquired politely, for

though he could never feel himself much attracted by Nicolas de Worde he realised that in spite of all assertions to the contrary it is in this world the old who must serve the young; they are wasted by them, despoiled of their riches and wisdom by them, grateful if they can win their liking and allegiance, thankful at the end to be given, as reward for their sacrifice and labours, a small portion of a warm chimney corner to end their days in.

"Any help as regards your work?" he asked with gloom, for the examinations were upon them and he had no doubt that Nicolas's stock of information was, as ever, low. And Nicolas had the right to ask him for help, for to Nicolas he owed the restoration of his son Joseph, that adorable and happily most intelligent child who had come so miraculously out of the darkness of Christmas Eve to take the place of the son who had gone. . . . Certainly Nicolas had claims upon him. . . . Though he could wish at times, that the young man were not so aware of the fact. During the last few weeks Nicolas had impudently inserted himself into the life of the family to a degree that seemed to Canon Leigh unnecessary. He was always there. If one went into the garden he would be there playing with the children and increasing their noise, at any time quite sufficiently severe, tenfold. When one entered the hall he was to be seen sitting up above at Great-Aunt's window—he got on uncommonly well with Great-Aunt—paying the old lady such outrageous compliments that her cackle of laughter rose up to the rafters in the most unseemly way. If one went into the parlour he was there too, holding skeins of yarn for Joyeuce; with Joyeuce looking most unlike herself, her usually pale face feverishly flushed, her eyes bright as though she were happy yet her mouth poignantly drooping. He doubted if the young man had a good effect upon Joyeuce. It would be better if he were to attend to his work.

"It goes well?" he enquired further.

Nicolas shook his head, but showed no signs of that shame that would have been becoming in him. "It is about Mistress Joyeuce," he said, "that I wish to talk to you."

Canon Leigh, as ever when he thought of his daughters in connection with emotional disturbances, with which he knew himself to be quite incompetent to deal, came out in a cold sweat. He had hoped, and believed because he had hoped.

that that highly emotional evening which the pair had spent at the Tavern on Midsummer Eve had left no trace. . . . But it seemed it had. . . . He was bereft of words and the glance which he flung at Nicolas was one of deep alarm.

This strengthened Nicolas's hand. Any qualms which he might have felt, and he had felt a few, were a thing of the past. With kindly benevolence he took the older man under his wing.

"I asked her to marry me some time ago," he explained, "but she thought it her duty to devote herself to you and the children."

"But you should have asked for my daughter's hand in marriage from me, not from herself," ejaculated Canon Leigh in some indignation.

"At that time you did not know me well, and I doubted if you cared for me much," explained Nicolas. "While she did."

Canon Leigh was touched by Nicolas's implied certainty that now he did know him he must care for him; even though it augured a certain bump of conceit in the young man there was a child-like confidence about it that warmed him.

"But does Joyeuce love you?" he asked in bewilderment.

"Oh, very deeply indeed," Nicolas hastened to assure him

"And what," asked Canon Leigh, with a meekness that thinly veiled a suggestion of sarcasm, "do you wish me to do in this matter?"

"Explain to Joyeuce that she is not as indispensable in your household as she thinks she is. Her sister Grace is perfectly capable of taking her place. I have talked the matter over with Faithful Crocker and he agrees that he and Grace together would find it an easy matter to run your household to your entire satisfaction."

"But why should Faithful Crocker concern himself in this?" demanded Canon Leigh in some indignation.

"You forget," said Nicolas gently, "that he has been my servitor since—since——"

"I remember," said Canon Leigh hastily, and with more warmth. Nicolas, with that fine generosity of his that even a prospective father-in-law was bound to admire, had not left Faithful at Giles's death without a rich scholar to share his room with him. He hated having an intellectual servitor whose industry was a perpetual reproach to his lack of it, but he was not going to leave Faithful stranded.

"It is natural," he said, "that we should talk together."

"Quite, quite," said Canon Leigh. "I merely wondered why Faithful should contemplate making himself responsible for the welfare of my household."

"He hopes to marry Grace."

Canon Leigh stopped dead in his walk and put a hand against the wall to steady himself. Grace, that child hardly of the cradle, in love? Joyeuce, his demure housekeeper, in love? And the young men—mere infants, both of them—coolly arranging the affairs of his family and household between them? And all this behind his back? He did not know what the modern generation was coming to.

"It seems to have been a shock to you," said Nicolas in some surprise.

Canon Leigh removed his hand from the wall and passed it across his forehead. "A slight shock," he murmured. In his young day elders had not been so treated by the young. Their idea was, apparently, that they should arrange things to their liking while their parents footed the bill.

"And on what," he asked, "do you intend to support Joyeuce? And on what does Faithful Crocker intend to support Grace? And are you aware that while you are scholars of this University you are not permitted to marry?"

"I am leaving Christ Church at the end of this summer," said Nicolas. "Then I hope, with your permission, to marry Joyeuce. My father," he added with a touch of arrogance, as though the honour of the de Wordes had been called in question, "is of course able to support his eldest son in the married state."

It was as Canon Leigh had thought; in this generation the parents paid.

"Then you do not mean to take your M.A.?" he questioned mildly.

"I don't think, my intellectual powers being what they are, that it is of the slightest use even to try for it," said Nicolas disarmingly. "Do you?"

"Frankly, no," agreed Canon Leigh. "But Faithful Crocker —I should be sorry to see him throw away his chances of academic distinction."

"He doesn't mean to. Grace must wait the seven years until he takes his M.A. Grace is quite willing to wait, for she will be occupied meanwhile in the bringing up of the little boys and the twins. When Faithful has finished his career at Oxford he will marry Grace."

"And upon what will he support her?" asked Canon Leigh again.

"He will obtain some lucrative post."

"I hope he may, I hope he may," murmured Canon Leigh doubtfully. "Grace, I see, is a party to all these plans, but Joyeuce, if I have understood you aright, is not?"

"No," said Nicolas, and for the first time his confidence seemed to desert him. He made a little helpless gesture with his hands and his bright eyes clouded. "She loves me, but her sense of duty stands in her way. It is almost as though she loved martyrdom. I do not understand. Ever since December I have not dared to speak to her about it again. She holds me at arm's length yet all the time her eyes are asking me to come and take her.... What can I do?"

Canon Leigh looked at the young man with new attention. There was patience in his voice, humility and suffering, qualities which the older man recognised as being ingredients in a love that time had tested and matured. They were not characteristics that he would have expected to find in Nicolas, either. It might be, he thought, glancing at him keenly, that there was a strength in this boy that he had not suspected. He wondered if perhaps he was inclined to distrust beauty and charm and gaiety as such.... In his own sex, that was, for like all men, no matter how saintly, he could not but feel that it was the duty of a woman to be lovely.... He feared that he was. He was inclined to be drawn most easily to the man in whom a plain face was transfigured by beauty of soul. But why should not the contrary be sometimes the case? Might not outward beauty sometimes work inwards? The longing of every human creature is for unity and it might be that the beautiful strove, even though unconsciously, to make their minds and souls as fair as their outward seeming.... They had reached the further end of the quadrangle and he himself turned that their pacing might be prolonged.

"A lover of martyrdom," he said slowly, his thoughts going to

Latimer who had embraced it with such eagerness and Cranmer who had so pitifully shrunk from it. " There are those who have it, those whose loyalty is so confident that they burn to put it to the test. But they are rare who have such confidence, and I do not think that Joyeuce is one of them. She has never been over-confident."

" Then why ? " asked Nicolas.

" A conviction she has that what she wants to do must necessarily be wrong. Many of us carry that certainty with us out of childhood, especially those, like Joyeuce, who have had to grow up too soon and have lost that time of happy transition in which old habits of thought quietly leave them and new ones as quietly take their place. They are often very childlike, these men and women who have had to grow up too soon."

" And yet at the same time very old and very wise."

Canon Leigh nodded and glanced at Nicolas with growing appreciation. In a few meetings he seemed to have learnt a good deal about Joyeuce.

" Then," pleaded Nicolas, " will you not persuade Joyeuce that it is right she should marry me ? "

" But is it right ? " smiled Canon Leigh. " Will you make her happy ? What do I know about you ? "

" It is quite right," said Nicolas, and flung up his head with something of his old arrogance. " I think my love permeates her life, and hers mine. It is to me what light is to the sun and perfume to the rose ; I am valueless without it. We have that to give each other which we must give each other. I must have her joy and she needs that I should give her that transition time, that time of happiness, of which you spoke. . . . I shall take her to Court."

" What ? " gasped Canon Leigh. It seemed to him that Nicolas had dropped abruptly from insight to childishness. He spoke of capacity for joy in Joyeuce, of which her father himself had seen no signs, and then he spoke of taking her to Court, a place in which Canon Leigh had no doubt at all that she would be perfectly miserable.

" You are wrong," Nicolas said, answering the unspoken criticism. " I think she is like me. I think that she is not very happy in a humdrum life. . . . You should have seen her joy on Midsummer Eve when I took her to that enchanted garden at the Tavern. . . . She wants un-ordinary experiences and it is not good for her that she should have them only in her spirit. She needs to laugh and sing and dance. She needs to wear a new dress every day and have all the men at Court writing verses to her eyebrows. She needs to be so very happy for a short while that the whole of the rest of her life will glow with it. . . . And all that she needs I will give her."

"To promise that is to shoulder a great responsibility," smiled Canon Leigh.

"I don't care," said Nicolas. "I used to dodge responsibility, but I don't now. You can't have anything you want without it."

"And so I am to persuade Joyeuce to marry you."

"Yes," said Nicolas.

"Well, I will do it," said Canon Leigh. "I know next to nothing about you, but I believe that you are right." He sighed. It seemed odd to him that it should be the duty of parents to hand over their children to the care of comparative strangers; even odder that these strangers should seem to have an instinctive knowledge of the children's needs that the parents in years of intimacy had not fathomed. But it was the way of life. By a continual progression to things that are new and strange the world goes on. He turned and led the way back again towards the Fair Gate. They parted in silence, but courteously, Nicolas's cap with its curling white feather sweeping the ground as he bowed. They felt respect for each other and even a dawning of affection.

III

Nicolas careered joyously up the steps to his room three at a time, and burst through the door with a noise and speed that seemed to Faithful, immersed in his books, unnecessary. He raised his large head from the hands that propped it and gazed at his fellow scholar more in sorrow than in anger. Then silently he raised a lean forefinger and pointed it at a sealed document that lay on the oak table.

Nicolas's jaws dropped and he felt a prickly sensation up the spine. He had been just about to tell Faithful of the conversation in the quadrangle, but the spate of words that had been tumbling up his throat now fell suddenly back again, making him feel slightly sick. He had known that this was coming, of course but it was his habit never to concentrate upon unpleasant things, until they were actually thrust under his nose. He too pointed a finger at the sealed document. "Pass me the damned thing," he groaned. Faithful passed it, holding it cautiously by one corner as though it were filled with gunpowder that might explode at any moment. Nicolas, sighing pitifully, opened it and read words that from past experience he knew only too well, though the detestable missive was written in Latin.

"In Dei nomine, Amen. . . . By this present document let it plainly appear and be known to all that in the fifteenth hundred and sixty-sixth year of the Lord, in the seventh year of the reign of Elizabeth, by the grace of God, Queen of England, France and Ireland, defender of the faith and on earth supreme head of the English and Irish Church, there have been summoned by the Subdean, with the consent of the Dean, the learned Censors in the Church of Christ at Oxford to examine the youth of the same Church according to the statute of that House, which orders that at the end of two years each one be examined as to his progress both in learning and in morals. Let all then to whom this present writing comes know that for those whose names are written below such a trial by the Subdean and Censors is to be held."

And Nicolas's name was written below. He tossed the thing to Faithful and fell groaning on to the stool before his desk.

"'Learning and morals,'" quoted Faithful from the loathsome missive. "Well, anyway, your *morals* are all right." He spoke a little tartly for he himself, though he dreaded the ordeal that would be his also at the end of his first two years, was nevertheless already armed at all points. There was nothing, he was able to assure himself modestly, that they would be likely to ask him that he would be unable to answer. . . . But with poor Nicolas he feared it was very much otherwise.

Poor Nicolas arose, dipped a towel in a jug of water, tied it savagely round his forehead, collected an armful of books and once more dropped groaning upon his stool. "By the mercy of Providence," he informed Faithful, "I have tackled the old man before instead of after. He's Subdean this year, you know. If I had left it until after——" He broke off and shuddered at the thought of Canon Leigh's possible reaction to the pleading of a prospective son-in-law who had just degraded himself academically in the eyes of the whole College.

"Left what until after?" asked Faithful.

Nicolas explained and Faithful's eyes widened in horror. "You didn't mention me and Grace?" he gasped.

"Of course I did. How could I help it? I said you and Grace couldn't be for years and years, and he seemed to take comfort in that."

Faithful waved his hands in some distress of mind, but then, his eyes falling on his book, he forgot about his marriage problems. He loved Grace dearly but, like Saint Edmund before him, his first love was learning. In a moment he was so absorbed that he was deaf and blind to everything but the printed words that marched across the page in front of him, carrying him with them into a country that was his own country, where he belonged and where he was happy.

So it was Nicolas who heard the sounding of the trumpet and the clatter under the Fair Gate.

"What's that?" he demanded, casting the wet towel from him, for it covered his ears and prevented him from hearing things that were really important.

"What's what?" asked Faithful crossly, for the flung towel had hit him in the face and brought him back out of the far happy place where he had been. . . . If Nicolas found it a trial having Faithful for his servitor Faithful found being Nicolas's servitor an even heavier one. . . . The man would neither work himself nor permit others to do so.

Nicolas swept all the books off his desk on to the floor with a gesture of his right arm and leaned across it with his head out of the window. "The Chancellor!" he cried.

At this even Faithful took his nose out of his book and thrust it out of the other window. "Coming this way!" he gasped.

The Chancellor, dressed in puce velvet, with a purple cloak embroidered with silver, it being the season of Lent when a certain soberness of attire was considered seemly, was strolling beneath their windows, attended by Dean Godwin and a couple of conversational and portly merchants dressèd in fine furred gowns, with gold chains about their necks and be-ringed fat hands folded upon their stomachs, who strutted in their wake like a couple of gobbling turkey cocks.

"Now what are they up to?" demanded Nicolas of Faithful, "That is Master Wythygge of the Guild of Stoneworkers, and the other is Master Baggs who does house decorating. Is the whole College to be spring-cleaned?"

"They're going to the Leighs!" ejaculated Faithful.

"By cock and pie, they are!" cried Nicolas, and hung out of the window at infinite peril to life and limb. There came a thundering knock at the Leighs' modest front door, which yielded with the suddenness of complete astonishment, and the four great ones entered and were lost to sight.

"Canon Leigh is in debt," said Nicolas with some satisfaction. . . . His academic inferiority made him take pleasure in a feeling of financial soundness. . . . "In debt to Master Wythygge and Master Baggs."

"The Chancellor wouldn't concern himself with *that*," said Faithful. "It must be something much more important."

"Then let's go and call casually and find out," said Nicolas, withdrawing his head.

But Faithful was firm. "I have never met anyone," he said bitterly, "who could think of so many other things to do besides work." And he pointed once more to the fatal document. "In Dei nomine, Amen. . . . Examined as to his progress both in learning and in morals," it said, staring mockingly up from the floor. Sighing, Nicolas searched for his wet towel. "This place would be perfect," he said, "if it were not for the work."

IV

Canon Leigh the Subdean was bent low over his study table, setting searching examination questions upon morals, when Dorothy Goatley, her eyes bulging in her head and her hands clinging to the edge of the door as though she were about to fall to the floor in a fit, ushered in the Chancellor, Dean Godwin, Master Wythygge and Master Baggs. Canon Leigh, more annoyed than honoured by the interruption, rose and bowed, exchanged greetings, and swept a litter of papers from the chairs to the floor that his visitors might sit down.

"The Chancellor has come," said Dean Godwin, exchanging an unseen glance of sympathy with his colleague, "to discuss with us matters pertaining to the Queen's proposed visit to

Oxford this summer. The Queen's Grace has expressed it as her wish that she should be lodged at Christ Church. She takes a great interest in our College, as you know, because of its connection with Westminster." He did not add because also of its connection with his own good looks, but the knowledge of the connection was in the deep gloom of his eye.

Canon Leigh bowed politely but without enthusiasm. He had already heard of the Queen's proposed visit and feared that, though doubtless an honour, it would nevertheless be a great hindrance to concentrated work on the part of the scholars.

"I have examined the plans of the College," said the Chancellor, "and it seems to me that your house is the best place in which to lodge Her Grace and those more intimate members of her household who will be with her. Other members of the Court will be lodged in other houses and in the rooms of the dons, who will, I am sure, not be slow to appreciate the honour done them."

Another glance of profound sympathy sped from the Dean to Canon Leigh. "Yours is the only house," he explained in a low voice, "which immediately adjoins the great hall. Her Grace must be lodged where she can pass from her place of residence to the hall without exposing herself to the outer elements. . . . It might rain."

"But there is no door from my house to the hall," said Canon Leigh.

"Doors can be made," said the Chancellor, and waved his scented gloves airily.

Canon Leigh now understood the situation, and also the presence of Master Wythygge and Master Baggs. He and his family were to be swept from their home that the Queen might be accommodated. Holes would be knocked in his walls by Master Wythygge. The house would be re-decorated, probably quite regardless of his personal taste, by Master Baggs, who as likely as not would paint naked cupids all round the house and place a portrait of Venus, a woman he detested, over his study mantelpiece. He would be unable to get at his books for a long period of time and his life, what with fuss, excitement, muddle and one thing and another, would for an ever longer period be a complete hell. But he did not blench. He knew what was expected of him. He bowed low to the Chancellor and expressed himself as overwhelmed with delight that his poor home was considered worthy to shelter her beloved and sacred majesty Queen Elizabeth of England. . . . Behind the Chancellor's magnificent back Dean Godwin's eyes, once more meeting Canon Leigh's, expressed the woebegone conviction that for him too this affair was going to be no joke.

But they knew themselves to be not alone in their sufferings. The Queen's Royal Progresses, when she travelled with her entire Court from town to town and country house to country house all over her kingdom, were her annual summer holiday, and she enjoyed them every bit as much as did her loyal poor people in town and country who were allowed to come pressing up to her litter to see her and talk to her and bask in her smiles. But for the Court and her hosts it was not all jam. The preparations for the Progresses were arduous for those who went with her, and their sufferings throughout them those of the souls in purgatory. The hundreds of luggage carts going on ahead frequently made the roads almost impassable. Probably they lost their luggage. Only the most important of them could expect comfortable rooms to sleep in at night. The Queen changed her plans every five minutes and snapped their heads off when they disagreed with her. It rained. They caught cold. They did everything they possibly could to persuade the Queen's Grace to curtail her Progresses, but were invariably unsuccessful. "Let the old stay behind," she would say caustically to grumbling noblemen of uncertain age, "and the young and able come with me." Then of course they would all have to follow after, cursing volubly. Nor was it all pleasure for the hosts, who found the Queen's visits an expensive honour. A ten days' visit to Lord Burghley cost him over a thousand pounds and my Lord of Leicester himself, after entertaining the Queen at Kenilworth, found himself out of pocket by a small fortune. So the Dean and Canon Leigh were only two more among an army of martyrs who were spread over the length and breadth of England. They submitted with only the breath of a sigh.

"Perhaps I may be permitted to make a tour of the house?" suggested the Chancellor. "Master Wythygge and Master Baggs will then see what work will need to be done.

Master Wythygge and Master Baggs bowed fatly and smiled

with delight, their generous curves suggesting to Canon Leigh's tormented mind that they would without doubt think a great deal needed to be done. He opened the door, ushering them and the Chancellor into the hall, himself lingering behind to whisper in distraction to Dean Godwin, " Who pays ? "

The Dean made an equally distracted gesture with his hands. " God knows," he whispered. " You—me—the whole College. God help us all."

Outside in the hall Canon Leigh found his whole family, with the exception of Will and Thomas, mercifully absent at school, and Great-Aunt, even more mercifully absent upon one of her rare shopping expeditions, gathered in a row to gape at the Chancellor. They stood in order of height, Joyeuce at one end of the row and the little boys, with the dogs and Tinker, at the other end. The girls in their billowing black frocks sank to the ground in curtsys, like four blackbirds coming to rest upon the earth. Diccon and Joseph, one dressed in scarlet and the other in sky blue, bowed till their heads nearly touched the floor, the dogs wagged their tails and Tinker sat down suddenly and washed himself. . . . The whole collection was a pleasing sight and the Chancellor was touched. He kissed the girls and chucked the little boys under the chin. He patted the dogs and took trouble not to step upon the tail of Tinker. Then he turned back to the little boys, the one with the mop of dark curls in his doublet of poppy red, and the other with the fair head in his suit of azure. " Pages for the Queen," he said. " Attired as cupids, or what-not, they would be likely to tickle the fancy of the Queen's Grace exceedingly. Jog my memory, Master Dean, when the time comes."

The Dean nodded and a gasp of excitement and incredulous questioning went up from all the children. " The Queen, when she visits Christ Church this summer, will honour our poor home by staying at it," Canon Leigh told them gloomily. " Joyeuce, you had better accompany us round the house to receive directions as to what alterations and decoration will be necessary."

" Lead on, mistress," said the Chancellor gallantly.

Joyeuce stepped bashfully forward, but Grace, to her father's astonishment, stepped forward too, with her chest well thrown out and her hands clasped importantly upon her stomacher.

He had half a mind to order her back, for he had not commanded her attendance upon this occasion, but it was his habit never to rebuke his children in front of strangers and he let it alone for the moment. He would deal with her insubordination later.

Yet, as the tour proceeded, he found that it was Grace who was the most helpful of the two girls. While Joyeuce hesitated she answered questions with decision and promptitude. She knew what to do and how it ought to be done. She even went so far as to haggle with Master Wythygge and Master Baggs; the prices they quoted, she had the temerity to tell them, were far too high. And once, if not twice, she actually snubbed the Chancellor, whose knowledge of household affairs, she gave him to understand, was by no means equal to her own. Indeed in a very short time she had all the males present, helpless as always in the hands of a woman who is a good manager, completely in subjection. Her father gazed at her in amazement. How was it that he had not noticed how she had developed? Her chest was now firmly rounded and her waist compact. Her rosy face was curiously mature for so young a girl and the direct gaze of her blue eyes demanded obedience. The keys at her waist jingled importantly and the sound of her small feet stepping decisively upon the bare boards was louder than one would have expected. . . . Joyeuce, he noticed, wore no keys at her waist, and her step made no more sound than the patter of falling leaves in the autumn.

The house was explored from top to bottom and matters soon arranged. The Queen, the Chancellor had no doubt, would wish to occupy Great-Aunt's room. Its central position would please her, for very little could go on, said the Chancellor as he swung in delight from the window commanding the hall to the window opening upon the garden, either in or out of doors that she would not know about; her loving interest in the affairs of her subjects, he hastened to assure his audience, was always unswerving in its devotion. . . . "It's the same with Great-Aunt," said Grace. . . . And then the girls' room leading out of it would serve excellently for her ladies of the bedchamber, and in its far wall could be made the door leading to the hall. "Another door will increase the draughts in this room," objected Canon Leigh. "No matter," was the Chancellor's answer. "The room will merely be occupied by the ladies of the bedchamber." Canon Leigh, sighing, supposed that in future years the door could always be blocked up again at his expense.

They were so occupied in deciding the position of this door that they did not hear a footfall in the next room. It was not until they turned back and were about to re-enter Great-Aunt's room that they saw her standing in the middle of it. She had just returned from her shopping expedition. She wore a voluminous purple satin farthingale over an immense kirtle of purple velvet. Her cloak, also of purple velvet, was flung regally back from her shoulders. One gnarled jewelled old hand was placed upon the head of her stick, the other was laid dramatically upon her bosom. Her eyes and the diamonds in her ears flashed. Her nose was hooked more aggressively than usual and her chin jutted truculently beneath it. " Tilly-vally ! " she ejaculated in a deep bass voice. " And what is the meaning of this ? "

Canon Leigh presented the Chancellor to her, and explained the reason for his visit, while the Dean hastily suggested that the Leighs would feel themselves deeply honoured when their roof sheltered the Queen's Grace.

" I've no objection," said Great-Aunt amiably. " I shall be happy to receive the Queen's Grace. If the children are distributed among our friends there will be plenty of room for the Queen and her personal attendants. . . . I should suggest, Gervas," she said, fixing her nephew with a glittering eye, " that you sleep in your study and hand over your room to the Queen's Grace. Her attendants can sleep in the boys' room." Her eye swung round and fixed itself upon the Chancellor. " It is unfortunate that the girls' room is not available, but, as you see, it is only reached through my own."

The Chancellor, his gloves airily brandished, courteously explained to her the arrangements that had already been made. He exerted all his charm of manner. He was not slow to see in her face the remnants of great beauty, and he did homage to it, though there was an edge to his voice. He was to perfection the iron hand in the velvet glove. His voice flowed melodiously on, then ceased. He waited, hand on hip, to receive her submission and apology.

None came. Her eyes, that had been fixed on his face,

ravelled downwards, noted the cut of his beard, swept over his magnificent clothes, concentrated upon his shoes with their long exaggerated points, closed as though the sight tired her, opened once more and returned to his face, thinking little of it.

"It is entirely out of the question," she said, "that I should relinquish my room. The Queen's Grace, were she to be made acquainted with my age and infirmities, would be the last person to wish such an outrageous step to be taken."

The eyes of the Chancellor were raised and his mouth slightly ajar. Such an outrage as this he had not yet experienced. . . . Men had been beheaded for less. . . . Joyeuce and Grace, mentally seeing Great-Aunt at the block, clung to each other in terror. Master Wythygge and Master Baggs gasped. Canon Leigh and the Dean stood with their hands thrust into the long sleeves of their gowns and their eyes upon the floor. A slight smile played about the lips of the Dean, for he remembered the battle there had been about the making of that window in Great-Aunt's room, and her final victory. Far be it from him to interfere in a battle between such well-matched protagonists. . . . For himself, he backed Great-Aunt.

"I think, madam," said the Chancellor, "that you have not completely understood the situation. Let me explain once more——"

"My Lord," interrupted Great-Aunt, "you have already explained at quite unnecessary length. I retain, I thank God, the use of my hearing and my intelligence."

The Chancellor was about to speak again, but her eyes checked him. They appeared to be boring right through his head, noting the quality of his brain and finding it exactly what she had expected, and coming out at the back where he had a slight bald patch that was causing him anxiety. He flushed suddenly and swung round upon Canon Leigh. "Sir," he ejaculated, "cannot you bring this aged gentlewoman to a sense of her duty?"

"That, my Lord," said Canon Leigh, raising his head, "is a task upon which I am ever engaged, but ever unsuccessful."

"Hold your tongue, Gervas!" cried Great-Aunt, striking her stick upon the floor. She was in one of her rages now, one of her magnificent rages that seemed to send unseen thunderbolts hurtling through the air and electric currents throbbing through the bodies of all present. "These Tudors have robbed me of much," she said to the Chancellor, rounding upon him. "King Harry cut off the head of my brother and Queen Mary burned my husband, the worldly goods that should have come to me being appropriated by the Throne, and I'll not be robbed of my bedroom by another of 'em; and she a red-headed sharp-nosed young hussy whose flirtations with the gentlemen are enough, from all accounts, to bring a blush to the cheek of every modest gentlewoman; as you should know, my Lord of Leicester, who——"

"Madam, hold your peace!" thundered Canon Leigh suddenly. "I will have no such immodest remarks made in my house. You will relinquish your bedroom to the Queen's Grace and be thankful that it is not your head also."

"I will do no such thing," said Great-Aunt. "I have slept in that bed for a number of years and I will sleep in it till I die. The Queen may pass through my room, due warning being given beforehand, to reach the door you propose to make into the hall, but a further concession than this should not be expected of me, at my age, with my infirmities, to these Tudors, who have so grossly misused my family and brought me in my old age to be a penniless pensioner upon the grudging charity of my unwilling nephew."

Canon Leigh, remembering her quite considerable wealth and the Christian welcome he had given her in his home, said nothing. The Dean said nothing. The Chancellor, choked by rage, tried to speak and failed. It was Grace, lifting her head like a bright little robin, who piped out cheerfully, "Father's bedroom has a very pretty view."

"Extremely pretty," said Great-Aunt, "allow me to conduct you thither that you may behold it for yourself." Her rage had suddenly fallen from her and with a confiding smile she laid a jewelled little hand upon the Chancellor's sleeve. She made play with the fine eyelashes that still were hers, and her eyes were now soft as pansies. She moved forward a little, her silk farthingale whispering upon the floor, and he was obliged to move with her, for though her hand had been laid so gently on his arm the fingers were now fixed upon it like a vice. A faint smell of violets clung to her skirts. It was like the ghost of her beauty, a ghost that could be very potent when she chose. . . . The

Chancellor found himself smiling upon her. . . . They all moved forward, out of Great-Aunt's room, across the passage and into Canon Leigh's. As they entered the sun burst suddenly through the mist, illumining the awakening garden outside the window and the delicate tracery of the trees beyond, touching the soft tapestries on the walls to a riot of blues and greens and shining upon the white linen of the bed—clean sheets to-day, thank God, thought Grace—so that it shone like driven snow.

"A charming room!" cried my Lord of Leicester. "The best in the house. I did not, when I saw it just now, realise its beauty. Charming! Charming!"

CHAPTER XIV

THE TROUBADOUR

> Loving in truth, and fain in verse my love to show,
> That she, dear she, might take some pleasure of my pain,
> Pleasure might cause her read, reading might make her know,
> Knowledge might pity win, and pity grace obtain,
> I sought fit words to paint the blackest face of woe;
> Studying inventions fine, her wits to entertain,
> Oft turning others' leaves to see if thence would flow
> Some fresh and fruitful showers upon my sun-burned brain.
> But words came halting forth, wanting Invention's stay;
> Invention, Nature's child, fled step-dame Study's blows,
> And others' feet still seemed by strangers in my way.
> Thus, great with child to speak, and helpless in my throes,
> Biting my truant pen, beating myself for spite,
> "Fool," said my Muse to me, "look in thy heart and write."
> PHILIP SIDNEY.

I

CANON LEIGH sat reading in his study, rejoicing in a most unusual peace. The news that the Queen meant to visit Christ Church had lately set the whole College-full of scholars chattering like starlings, and concentration had been impossible for the serious-minded. But now, praise be to God, the imminence of the spring examinations, fixed for the day after to-morrow, had shed abroad a spirit of depression and a subsequent blessed silence. The scholars were all within doors, groaning over their books, and the quadrangle was empty except for two black figures; Tinker, the cat, basking in the sunshine, and the Dean on his way from the Deanery to the scholars' rooms, to enquire into the progress of their studies. . . . These tender visits of enquiry were at that time the custom, and part of his official duty, but they were at a later date discontinued because of their extreme unpopularity both with the visitor and the visited.

Thank God, thought Canon Leigh, turning a page of the great leather-bound book that lay before him, there was no one likely at this moment to visit *him*. Afternoon peace reigned both inside and outside the house, and the window was open to the first real warmth of the year. He allowed himself to lean back in his chair for a moment, enjoying it. Those colours and scents of spring that on that day of the Chancellor's visit, only a short while ago, had been waiting behind the mist, had drawn a little nearer. The sunshine seemed to smell of the primroses that were already out in sheltered corners of the gardens and snatches of bird-song rang out like carillons of hope in the blue air. It was a day to shelve all problems, domestic, collegiate and national. It was a day to follow the example of Tinker, the cat, sleeping in the sun, awaking to blink at it, then stretching himself luxuriously to sleep again. Canon Leigh followed it, closing his eyes that he might think the better, opening them to admire a billowy white cloud floating dreamily across the blue sky, closing them again that thought might deepen into contemplation and contemplation into sleep.

He was awakened, not by any means for the first time in his life, by sounds of domestic disturbance. " Perdition take those two little boys ! " was his first unfeeling exclamation, followed instantly, as with full awakening the thoughts of a father superseded the reaction to noise of the natural man, by " the high spirits of the dear little children sorely need the curb of wholesome Christian discipline." He arose to apply it and, sighing, looked round for his cane.

Yet, when he had reached the hall, and the sounds of rage and woe from beyond the kitchen door smote like blows upon his ears, he was astonished to find that every member of his household was apparently adding its quota to the general tumult. The roars of Diccon led the van, so to speak, but they were followed by the tearful hiccups of Joseph, the distressing squeaks of the twins, the loud crying of Dorothy Goatley, the voice of Grace raised in most unusual anger, and during a pause in the row he thought he heard the pathetic gasping sobs of Joyeuce herself. Joyeuce crying ? Were they bullying her ? At the thought of any harm threatening his favourite child, the usually gentle scholar became as a primeval savage upon the war path. Gathering up his black gown in one hand and brandishing his cane in the other he launched himself upon the kitchen door.

The sight that met his eyes was heartrending in the extreme.

In the window stood Dorothy Goatley, her apron flung over her head, weeping loudly, and clinging to her skirts were the twins, squeaking nineteen times to the minute, tears rolling down their fat cheeks and dripping on to the floor in heartbreaking cascades. At the table sat Joyeuce, her head buried in her arms, sobbing, and on the floor beside her, burrowing their heads against her in a passion of love, were Diccon and Joseph, roaring and hiccuping their sympathy. Before the fire stood Grace, flushed with anger, demanding indignantly, " Why didn't you do as I told you and leave it to me ? Why in the world didn't you leave it to me ? " Midway between Joyeuce and Grace, white to the lips, bewildered and unhappy, stood the only man present, Faithful. The room was stiflingly hot, with the fire roaring up the chimney and the warm oppressive smell of ironing hanging heavy in the air. Piles of sheets, pillow-cases, towels, quilts, aprons, coifs, shirts and kerchiefs took up every available space, and upon the table before Joyeuce was a lovely lace-trimmed petticoat utterly ruined by the application of too hot an iron. " My *best* petticoat," wailed Grace.

But at the first whiff of that hot ironing smell, Canon Leigh had understood the situation, had lowered his cane and regarded his family with an indulgent smile. Until he smelt that smell he had momentarily forgotten that they were in the midst of that terrible infliction of the sixteenth century, the Annual Spring Wash. Yearly, at the first spell of settled sunshine, it fell upon every household like a blight. It always began well, with the females of the family falling upon every washable piece of material in the house in a spirit of inspiring enthusiasm, and the males betaking themselves hastily to the nearest Tavern, but as the laborious days went on the first inspiration was apt to flag a little, giving way to grim determination, and that in turn to a shortness of temper very distressing to all concerned. Looking back, Canon Leigh remembered that all the serious family disturbances of his married life had taken place during the latter period of the Spring Wash ; and had sprung, all of them, from accidents so trivial that they would hardly have been noticed at other times. They were, he remembered, well into the latter period of the Spring Wash now. For days the garden had been festooned with washing. The yew hedge had been lost to sight beneath snowy sheets and

Romulus and Remus, the clipped yew peacocks, had been draped with towels as though about to step down to the river to take a dip. The lawn had been white with spread quilts and every species of undergarment had fluttered from lines between the apple trees. . . . Certainly the time was ripe for the Annual Family Disturbance.

With deep sympathy his eyes met those of Faithful. . . . Faithful, poor fellow, was doubtless enduring his first Spring Wash, but, poor fellow, were he to perpetrate matrimony, he would doubtless have to endure many more. . . . " These little upsets occur at this time," he told him soothingly. " Have you any idea what started it ? "

" It seems that Joyeuce has spoilt Grace's best petticoat," said Faithful miserably. " But something much more dreadful must surely have happened to cause all this terrible lamentation."

" Probably not," said Canon Leigh. " Well, Grace ? You have my permission to speak."

Grace would have spoken with or without his permission ; she was boiling over with indignant speech. " I *told* Joyeuce to leave the ironing to me," she burst out. " She has no gift for ironing. She is so dreamy, so absentminded, that she cannot keep her attention upon the matter in hand. She lets the iron get too hot. She neglects to test it. Yet, when I came in from the garden with the towels from Romulus and Remus, I found Joyeuce had already embarked upon the ironing and ruined my best petticoat."

" That will do, Grace," said her father sternly. " Come with me to my study. And you, Faithful, may come too."

He led the way back to his study, placed the cane in a corner with a sigh of thankfulness that it had after all not been necessary to apply any Christian discipline, and sat down in his chair, motioning the two to stand before him. He had, as yet, made no effort to deal with the domestic situation revealed to him by Nicolas, but he had been waiting for his opportunity, and now it was here.

Grace was crying now. The words " come to my study," reviving as they did painful memories of early youth, were always enough to start her off. And she was sorry that she had made Joyeuce cry. She loved Joyeuce, even though her incompetence drove her distracted. And she was afraid her father had discovered about her and Faithful and was about to forbid the banns. She drew nearer to Faithful, clutching him with one hand while with the other she tried to stem the cascade of tears that rolled down her rosy cheeks.

What a couple of children, thought Canon Leigh, and yet how mature they had lately become. Faithful was looking at him unflinchingly, his face wearing that strange expression of peace that was his special beauty. Canon Leigh remembered that he had behind him a record of experience and endurance that was not possessed by many men twice his age; he had already been tested and not found wanting. And Grace, though she cried like a child, rubbing her knuckles in her eyes and sniffing dolorously, had already the figure of a woman and the competence of an experienced housewife. What had they found in each other, he wondered, that had made them indispensable each to the other? That was a question, he knew, that could not be answered. Not even lovers themselves can tell you why the one particular person is the only person in the world.

"And so you want to be married?" he asked quietly.

Faithful nodded his huge head like a top-heavy owl and Grace whispered childishly, "Yes, please."

"It grieved me," said Canon Leigh, "to hear of your hopes from Nicolas de Worde and not from yourselves."

Faithful explained. They had been afraid to anger him. They had been afraid he would not realise that they were old enough to contemplate such things.

"I quite realise your maturity," their father assured them solemnly, but with a suppressed twinkle. "You are now fourteen and fifteen, a man and woman grown and of marriageable age; though of course," he added with relief, "it will be many years before you are able to marry. But I gather that you are willing to wait. I gather that Grace feels more than equal to taking Joyeuce's place should she decide to marry and leave us."

But at this Grace showed that she too, beneath her surface confidence, had a portion of the Leigh humility. Her tears, that had been checked by delight at her father's unexpected reasonableness, brimmed over again and she hung her head. "I can never take Joyeuce's place," she whispered. "I can cook and wash and iron better than Joyeuce, but you and the children will never love me as you love her."

Her father stretched out an arm and pulled her upon his knee. " Dear little Grace, we shall," he assured her. " You are your mother's daughter. You have her lovely competence, as Joyeuce has her gift of insight. As the years go on Joyeuce will grow more practical and you will grow in sympathy, until both of you reach the full stature of the perfect woman that your mother was."

But Grace, shaking her head dolefully, had her doubts. One was born a certain sort of person, she thought, and though by ceaseless struggle one might become as nice as that sort of person ever is, one could never become as nice as a nicer sort of person. Never, she knew, would she attain to that sensitiveness of mind and spirit that people loved in Joyeuce, and never, never, she was quite sure, would Joyeuce be the slightest use at ironing. . . . At the thought of her burnt petticoat she wept afresh.

This new outbreak of grief in the beloved was too much for Faithful. Though it was not considered correct to be demonstrative before parents he could not contain himself. He took her hand and kissed it, holding it against his cheek. " No girl has ever been loved as I love you," he told her solemnly. " I don't know how to say it, but if I did know how to say it I should not love you so much."

Grace raised her head from her father's shoulder and looked at her inarticulate lover. Her father intercepted their look, a look of such profound trust that he was humbled by it. They would be an undemonstrative couple, these two, and they would always seem rather comical to others, but he thought they had as great a chance of happiness as any couple he had ever known. " Kneel down, children," he commanded them. " I have not yet given you my blessing. "

II

He continued to deal with the havoc created by the Spring Wash. Having blessed Grace and Faithful he made his way to the kitchen. Here he found Dorothy Goatley and the twins reviving themselves with large slices of plum cake and a draught of ale. Their eyes and noses were still red but they were chattering happily. He perceived that food for the body had proved so restorative that spiritual comfort was not now required. . . . In his experience it was often so. . . . He paused but to enquire the whereabouts of Joyeuce and left them to find her in the garden.

She was sitting on the grassy bank by the apple trees, the little boys cuddled up one on each side of her, gazing mournfully at the family underclothes that still fluttered in the spring wind.

" Still grieving for that petticoat, Joyeuce ? " he asked her, sitting down beside her and lifting Joseph on to his lap.

" Not for the petticoat," said Joyeuce with trembling lips. " Grace has heaps of petticoats, but that she should treat me so. She is always like that now. Always trying to push me out."

" Not trying to push you out, Joyeuce," said her father, " but trying to grow up. She cannot help herself, for her domestic competence seems to me so excessive that it must surely be a gift of God, and not allowed full use it is turning sour within her and proving slightly inconvenient to ourselves." He pointed to the snowdrops at their feet, spearing their way up through the winter earth. " Look how they are shooting up. Once they were bulbs hidden in the earth, now they must be leaves and flowers. They cannot help themselves. Always we must push on."

" But not with unkindness," murmured Joyeuce.

" That cannot always be helped. If one hesitates to pass on the other who comes behind to take her place must knock into her. That's unavoidable. Is it not time, Joyeuce, that you yourself passed on ? "

Joyeuce gazed at him with astonished, wide-open eyes that were the colour of rain because she was so unhappy. " I— pass on ? " she asked stupidly.

" Do you not want a lover, Joyeuce ? I loved your mother, and born of love as you were it is natural that you should travel towards love again. You would make a good wife, above all to a gay and prosperous man who needs your perception of invisible things to be, as it were, the unseen life of his happy attributes that will give to them eternal value. What did such a one say to me ? ' Her love is to me what light is to the sun and perfume to the rose ; I am valueless without it.' I have so often wished, Joyeuce," lied her father blandly, " that you could marry Nicolas de Worde."

Joyeuce looked at him again and gasped. She perceived that he knew all about it. Then she shyly stroked his sleeve, looking down at little Joseph curled up sleepily in his lap, and at Diccon who had run away from her and was pulling Pippit, the unfortunate little greyhound, round and round an apple tree by his tail. Her father understood what she would have said had humility not silenced her.

"I shall miss you unspeakably," he told her. "No other daughter can ever take your place, no other sister will ever be to the little boys what you have been. But you will not be lost to us, Joyeuce. You will not be going to the land beyond the sunset; you will only be going to Gloucestershire; I will visit you and you will visit me. I think it right that you should pass on. It is a rule of life."

She gave a shuddering sigh, half of happiness and half of pain, and sat looking down at her hands clasped in her lap. "So it was all for nothing," she whispered.

Canon Leigh looked down at Joseph, who was now asleep in his arms, his fair head fitting into the hollow of his father's shoulder as though it had always been there. "Your sacrifice? I don't think so. I have never yet heard of a death to self that was not followed sooner or later by a re-birth. I seem to remember Nicolas saying, on Christmas Eve, that he had gone to the Crosse Inn because he was unhappy. If you had not made him unhappy would he ever have found Joseph?"

No more words were needed. They sat together in a companionable silence and understanding more satisfying than any they had ever known; until an outbreak of yelps, barks, roars and shrieks down among the apple trees told them that Diccon, this time, had gone a bit too far with Pippit and they must fly to the rescue before murder was done.

III

When Canon Leigh returned to his study the Spring Wash was once more in full swing, but progressing this time in a spirit of such amity and politeness that he murmured to himself the wise words of Master Richard Edwardes, "Now have I found the proverb true to prove, the falling out of faithful friends is the renewing of love."

He picked up his book, sank thankfully into his chair and would once more have slipped from literature to peaceful contemplation and repose had not a murmur of voices beyond his window disturbed him. . . . The College this time. . . . "Perdition take the College!" was his unbecoming thought as he opened his eyes and looked out.

The Dean and Nicolas stood together in the sunshine and judging by the tones of their voices, the Dean's sharp with reproof and Nicolas's honey-sweet and pathetic in the frank acknowledgment of guilt, the Dean during a visit of enquiry into Nicolas's intellectual progress had met with very little satisfaction. But Canon Leigh was happy to see that the attitude of his future son-in-law was all that could be wished; his comely head was bent in true humility and his broad shoulders drooped under the burden of his shame. . . . But the fingers that held a book behind his back were pattering upon it as though practising the notes of some merry tune.

The interview ended and the Dean strode back towards the Deanery, the swirl of his black gown expressing outrage and the set of his shoulders registering extreme annoyance. Nicolas remained where he was, but now he held his book in front of him as though it were a musical instrument and performed a difficult trill very diligently with the fingers of his right hand.

Canon Leigh thrust his head out of the window. "Nicolas!" he commanded.

Nicolas swung round, bowed and smiled with the utmost charm, and presented himself beneath the window.

"And for what purpose," demanded Canon Leigh with some asperity, "did you conceive that books were created?"

"They serve so many purposes, sir," said Nicolas with a most disarming grin. "I have been writing a song to sing to Joyeuce and just at that moment I was trying to set it to music."

Canon Leigh was partly mollified. "Well, well," he sighed. "You will now, Nicolas, find your Joyeuce in the right frame of mind to appreciate it." At this such a light of joy broke over Nicolas's face that he was instantly completely mollified. "Come in now, my son," he cried cordially. "You will find her in the kitchen."

"Propose to her in the kitchen, amongst the family wash? By cock and pie, no!" cried Nicolas in powerful indignation.

"That would not please Joyeuce at all. She is romantic. I know a better way than that."

"Find your own way," said Canon Leigh. "Doubtless you know best." And he withdrew from the window in that humble frame of mind which, in these days, he was becoming more and more convinced was the right one for age to adopt when confronted with all-conquering youth.

What with emotion and the Spring Wash, Joyeuce was utterly worn out by the time she went to bed. Yet, when she had slipped into her place in the four-poster, and lain down beside the sleeping little boys, who lay as always, curled up together like two puppies, with Baa clasped in Joseph's arms and Tinker festooned over Diccon's feet, she knew that she was not going to sleep. She was too tired—tired as only the Spring Wash could make her—almost too tired to realise that in just ten minutes' talk with her father the whole direction of her life had been changed. "I ought to be gloriously happy," she told herself, turning over on her right side to ease her aching back. "Why am I not gloriously happy?" So often, she thought, turning over on to her left side because the right one had proved quite unsatisfactory, the moments that we had expected to be joy-giving are not, while those of whom nothing is expected suddenly present us with some heavenly gift. "I am going to marry Nicolas," she whispered dolefully, and flopped over on to her back because lying on her side was giving her the stomach-ache. But was she? Did he still love her? Since that day in the meadows he had been a gay and a good friend to her, as she had asked him to be, but he had said no word of love. Had she done what she had then tried to do, and killed it in him? At the thought that what she had tried to bring about might really have come about, desolation swept over her in a sickening flood. Surely it was one of the greatest misfortunes of human nature that what one wanted to happen, by the time it did happen, one didn't want to happen any more. If Nicolas did not now want her after all she thought she would die of grief. She began to sob, the trickling tears making stiff wet tracks from the corners of her eyes to her ears, her hands clasped childishly on the place where the pain was, biting her lips that she might not cry out loud and wake the children. "It is nothing but the Spring Wash," she whispered, as she felt herself sucked down and down into an abyss of misery. " There is nothing the matter with me but the Spring Wash. It is because I am so tired that I feel so dreadful. In the morning it will all be different."

But faced with a night of pain and sleeplessness, with every problem looming up in the darkness at three times its normal size, it is hard to realise that the dawn will ever come. She turned over again on to her face, lying on the pain to discourage it. " When will it be morning ? " she whispered, and fell to thinking how stupid it was that one had to work so hard just to keep the human body clothed, clean and fed. . . . Sewing. Washing. Cooking. . . . By the time they were finished with one was too tired to live. It was very silly. She began to sob afresh.

There was a soft rustling of the bushes under her window, those bushes where the buds were already showing faint little tongues of green, thrust forth to taste the air, and then some soft faint notes of music. Whatever bird was that ? Surely it was a most peculiar bird. Joyeuce raised her face from her sodden pillow and listened. The faint bird notes sorted themselves and became a tune, sounding for all the world as though a troubadour thrummed very softly on the strings of a viol, and Joyeuce twisted right round and sat bolt upright, her tears stemmed as though a tap had been turned off and her pain as utterly forgotten as though her stomach had vanished into thin air ; so prompt and beneficial in its working is the medicine of a stimulated mind.

She crept to the bottom of the bed, parted the curtains and peeped out into the room. There was moonlight and starlight to-night and it lay bathed in a lovely soft radiance. She could see the flowers and trees in the tapestries, that in the moonlight had the mysterious colour of flowers blooming in a dream, and the dark floor stretching before her full of shifting lights and inky shadows like a fairy tarn at midnight. Surely it had been the rustling of those flowers and trees, and the lapping of that water, that she had heard, and not the bushes beneath the window ? She smiled, because just for a moment the fancy had seemed reality, and like a light flashing suddenly into her tired mind came the thought that the most ordinary things, seen from a new angle, can take on all the colour of romance ; they have many facets, and some people have the power to turn them about and see the one that reflects the laughter of God . . . as Nicolas could do.

A voice singing drove all thought from her mind and pulled it back into fairyland, where there is no speculation but only a lovely wonder. Who was singing, and was it to her he sang? The lovely voice, not very strong but crystal clear in tone and articulation, reached her effortlessly and seemed to come from the trees in the tapestry. What fairy lover was hiding behind them? She sat back and listened, greedily gathering in every word to store in her memory, as though from the trees gold pieces were flung to her to catch. . . . For never before had a fairy lover sung to her in the moonlight. . . . Now she was rich indeed.

> All day in the hot blue sunshine,
> On quivering, tireless wings,
> The lark between earth and heaven
> Ceaselessly, joyously sings.
> But now at last she is sinking
> Down to her nest.
> So turn to your rest, my lady,
> Turn to your rest
> And dream.
>
> The scarlet lamps of the tulips
> Are fading and burning dim,
> Faint as the sun that is sinking
> In softness o'er the world's rim,
> Draining the world of its colour
> At night's behest.
> So turn to your rest, my lady,
> Turn to your rest
> And dream.

From somewhere beyond the drawn curtains, that stirred in the breeze from the open window, came a sharp ping, as though a string snapped, and voice whispered, softly but clearly, " Damn ! "

This was no fairy lover but one whose mortality was much in evidence. Quick as a flash, Joyeuce slipped out of bed, flung her cloak round her and scuttled to the window, thanking her stars as she scuttled that little short of morning or the last trump could wake the children. " Nicolas ! " she whispered, slipping behind the window curtains and leaning out to him. . . . How bright the stars were, big stars and little stars, as though every angel and cherub had thrust a fist through the floor of heaven to take a look at her and Nicolas. Surely the stars were auspicious to-night, and every little rustle in the garden was a whisper of friendship. . . . She remembered how once she had dreamed that Nicolas and Diccon had entered the gates of fairyland while she had been shut out. She was not shut out now. The song of her lover had drawn her inside those gates and they had clanged behind her with the sound of chiming bells. " Oh, Nicolas ! " she breathed.

" Good, wasn't it ? " said Nicolas, cocking a bright eye at her as he fitted a new string into his viol. He took her ecstasy as a tribute to his musical prowess, and was pleased, for upon the Dean telling him that he lacked concentration in labour he had spent the best part of an hour in work upon his song, and thought highly of it. " I wrote words *and* music. And there's more to come, too. Amongst other men's songs I could not find one that I liked enough to sing to you, and so I said to myself, ' Fool, write your own.' There are no tulips out yet, of course, but there will be when I sing it to the Queen."

" Will you sing it to the Queen ? " whispered Joyeuce with a little tremor of disappointment in her voice. . . . She had hoped this song was all her own.

" Under her window, at night," announced Nicolas. " And she will labour under the delusion that it was written for her, and be so flattered that she will promise me my heart's desire, like a Queen in a fairy-tale."

" What desire ? " breathed Joyeuce.

He stood up straight under her window, his head tilted back and his bright eyes fixed on hers. " To take you to Court when we are married," he said.

Joyeuce slipped down on to her knees, her elbows propped on the windowsill and her chin in her hands. She could not speak for excitement but her eyes were as bright as two stars.

" And when we are tired of Court life we will go home. You will like my home, Joyeuce. It is built of grey stone, with very tall chimneys that carry the banners of the wood-smoke so far up into the sky that when Mistress Joyeuce de Worde is at home people miles away will know it, and be glad. It has wide windows with diamond panes that let in all the sun by day and catch a star in each pane by night. There is a beech wood behind the house, and a garden full of lilies in front of it, and when you are my wife there will be no Spring Wash."

"But, Nicolas," protested Joyeuce, "one *must* wash."

"The servants will wash," said Nicolas grandly. "But you, Joyeuce, will walk up and down the grass paths between the lilies with your husband and listen to the verses he has written to the brightness of your eyes."

"But there always *must* be domestic tasks," insisted Joyeuce, dazzled but still doubtful.

"Of course there must be," said Nicolas, suddenly serious. "And sickness and accidents and losses and old age. But everything has several sides and I will teach you to see the funny side of them all, and you will show me which way round to turn them to make of them stepping stones to God. . . . Which reminds me," he added inconsequentially, "that I have not proposed to you again. Will you marry me, Mistress Joyeuce Leigh?"

The cloak fell back from her shoulders as she leaned out to him. He jumped upon a garden seat that stood there and his hands came creeping up the wall towards her as they had done at the other window nearly a year ago. They clasped her wrists, and slipped up her bare arms under the sleeves of her white night shift, caressing them. "Now I am only your betrothed who must stand under your window," he whispered, "but soon I shall be your husband. . . . Soon . . . Soon . . . Now you must go back to bed, Joyeuce. I will sing you the rest of my song and when I get to the last word you will be asleep. Do you hear? Fast asleep."

His hands slipped down her arms and obediently she turned away from the window and ran back to bed. She jumped in and lay childishly curled up, her cheek resting in her hand upon the pillow. There came again those soft faint notes of music, like a bird talking to itself, and then the voice of the fairy lover singing behind the trees in the tapestry.

> The wind that laughed in your garden
> Has wearied and dropped asleep,

Leaving the lilies his playmates
His whispered secrets to keep,
The lilies in golden-crowned white
Royally dressed.
So turn to your rest, my lady,
Turn to your rest
And dream.

Wrapped in her mantle of twilight,
Her cloak of silver and grey,
Night the great mother steals downward
To banish the burning day,
Her voice comes clear in the stillness,
" Now sleep is best."
So turn to your rest, my lady,
Turn to your rest
And dream.

Holding out arms of cool comfort
To her children, whispering low
Of that dark, deep, peaceful silence
That only her sleepers know,
The merciful night is holding
Earth to her breast.
So turn to your rest, my lady,
Turn to your rest
And dream.

By the time he had reached the last word she was, as he had told her to be, asleep.

CHAPTER XV

THE QUEEN'S GRACE

> Where are all thy beauties now, all hearts enchaining?
> Whither are thy flatterers gone with all their feigning?
> All fled; and thou alone still here remaining.
>
> Thy rich state of twisted gold to bays is turned,
> Cold as thou art are thy loves that so much burned.
> Who die in flatterers' arms are seldom mourned.
>
> Yet in spite of envy this be still proclaimed,
> That none worthier than thyself thy worth hath blamed;
> When their poor names are lost, thou shalt live famed.
>
> When thy story long time hence shall be perused,
> Let the blemish of thy rule be thus excused:
> "None ever lived more just, none more abused."
>
> Lines on Queen Elizabeth. THOMAS CAMPION.

I

THE summer term was upon them again, lovelier than ever, more vibrant with life, overflowing with happiness. This year every beauty seemed intensified. The shining gold of the kingcups beside the streams was more brilliant, and the fritillaries grew taller than usual, holding their frail bell heads high above the fresh green grass, covering the meadows where they grew with a pale amethyst mist whose beauty caught at the heart. The primroses and violets clustered more thickly in the hedges. The anemone stars alighted in every wood and fluttered delicately poised, tip-toe for flight, silver in the sunshine, snow-white in the dusk, gone like a flight of butterflies almost before there had been time to worship their beauty. When bluebell time came they seemed to pour over the world in a flood, enamelling every little knoll and beech-crowned hill with heraldic azure, flowing through the woods in winding rivulets of blue, gathering in every hollow in deep pools, throwing out their intoxicating scent to every breeze that it might be wafted to men's noses and drive them mad with joy. . . . Yet not madder than the birds, who shouted from every bush and tree until it was a marvel that their bunched, vibrating, feathery bodies could hold together with the noise they made.

And, as always, it was gone so soon, this time of the bluebells and the shouting birds to which one looked forward all the year, gone before the bewildered senses, beseiged by a thousand scents and sights and sounds of intoxicating beauty, could take firm hold of the miracle and hold on to it in possession. "Next year," sighed tired men and women, still exhausted by the griefs and the hardships of their winter, and sorrowing afresh to see the bluebells faded and the anemones flown clean away, " next year I shall have clearer eyes and a more awakened spirit. Next year spring will come again and next year it will not catch me sleeping." Yet, if they had bothered to remember, they had said the same thing last year, and would say it again next year. Spring was always so swift, so miraculous, that man was caught for ever unaware.

Yet this year there was little time to grieve for vanished anemones, for no sooner had they flown away than the hawthorn was out, piled like snow along the hedges, and then the apple blossom was pink and white in the orchards and the wild cherries were tossing their foam on the hills. And then the wild roses were in bud, and stumpy purple orchids grew sturdily in the fields, and after that no one knew what happened in the country outside the city because they were imprisoned in their own gardens, enslaved by the charms of their own roses and carnations, enraptured by their Canterbury bells and purple pansies, bowed to the ground in worship before their lilies.

And the city itself seemed to rejoice more exuberantly than usual in the flower of the year. The towers and spires, that had been so often heavily darkened by winter rain, seemed again light and airy things spun out of mist and sunshine, and the bells had a merry note. There was more than usual talk in the streets and singing and laughter floated out from every window. . . . For the Queen was coming. . . . When? When? asked every voice. Soon, they said. Next month, perhaps. This summer. When she comes there will still be red roses to strew before her, and tall lilies to bow like courtiers beside the garden paths that her feet will tread. The leaves will still be green on the trees and the birds will be singing. There will be tapestries hung from every window and a great shouting in the streets as she passes by. . . . And surely to goodness, they said, becoming slightly irritated as the weeks went by with no date fixed, the Queen's Grace having already changed her mind about it seven times, the woman will come to a decision some time.

But the irritation was only fleeting and the mood of exaltation remained. For she meant so much to them; she was more than a woman, more even than a Queen; she stood to them for all the happiness and inspiration of this new age, for all its release and promise and new-born beauty. The older men and women remembered their country as it had been when she came to the throne; persecuted, humiliated, its only vital life the flame of martyrdom; they remembered how they had turned in despair to a young girl to save them. And she had saved them. She knew how to make herself the inspiration of men and women of good will. She was valiant, and they rekindled their courage from hers. She was wise, and wisdom seemed to them once more a thing worth striving for. She had shown them how to save themselves and they saw in her the very figure of salvation.

And the young loved her too. She was witty and beautiful, she loved laughter and the singing voice, and all the fair and gracious things, the poetry and music and dancing, that had wilted and died, lived again because she loved them. Perhaps the scholars did not understand, as they trooped to their verse-readings on Sunday afternoons and learnt to thrum the zither and the viol in their rooms, that their new understanding of beauty would not have been theirs had Gloriana not sat upon the throne of England. Perhaps the young girls did not realise, as they put on their farthingales of rose-colour and azure and buttercup-yellow, and danced the pavane at evening when the moon shone and the candles were lighted in the halls of their homes, that they would not have looked so fair and felt so happy had the Queen's Grace not possessed a hundred dresses and a foot as light as their own. They might not understand, perhaps, but they saw in her all beauty and all grace.

And the Oxford merchants were prosperous under Queen Bess. People were not so occupied with their troubles these days that they could not stop and gape in front of a shop window. The amount of gaping that was done now, compared with the gaping that had taken place under the late Queen, was phenomenal. And they did not only gape, they came inside and bought, too, for a light heart always makes a heavy spender ; it is not content, your light heart with the unseen glitter of its own merriment, it must show it to the world in the outward symbols of flower-like draperies, dew-drops in the ears and golden shoes that will tap out the heart's joy in the figures of the dance as radiantly as summer showers beating upon the thirsty earth. Is not the earth arrayed freshly in beauty every year, cry the light hearts, because of the joy that is in her ? Then give us your silks and satins and velvets, your gold chains and pearl drops and ruby stomachers, your carpets and perfumes and spices that we in this new age may be as fine as the old earth in her springtime garment. . . . And the merchants gave, receiving the equivalent in good hard round gold pieces, and saw the Queen's Grace as a veritable Midas who had let loose this sweet rich flood of gold that ran so obligingly into honest men's pockets. . . . And the young men, their sons, who left the city of Oxford to sail under the flag of the Merchant Adventurers that they might bring back from the lands beyond the sea the rubies and pearls, the carpets and perfumes and spices that the light of heart were calling for, may not have realised what an impetus to adventure had been given by the adventurousness, and the covetousness, of the Queen herself ; they may not have realised, but when the capstan was manned, and the sea chanties were sung, and the great sails of their ship leaned for a moment against the sunset before she sailed over the rim of the world, their homing thoughts went back to her.

And the University saw in the Queen the patroness of the Guild of Learning. For her visit had a specific purpose. She was coming, as she said, to assure all scholars of the royal favour. She herself loved learning ; she could dispute in Greek or Latin with the best scholars of her day, going on so long that they were finally reduced to coma. She sympathised to the full with the learned men who were trying to bring back to the University its ancient glory. And so they loved her. She was the symbol of their aspirations.

There was something mystical in the quality of the love that awaited the Queen in these summer days. The people of the city were like Joyeuce on the morning of May Day, standing at her window and wishing that what she so confusedly loved and longed for might take physical form and come to her. They too loved, and were aware that they loved not only learning, adventure, music, laughter and beauty, but the something behind and in all these for which they could find no name. It was an intense relief to pent-up emotion to see a human figure as the symbol of it.

II

After changing her mind nine times in all the Queen finally chose for her visit the month of August, the month when the University term would be over and the scholars gone home to help with the harvest. The University tore its hair and the city made very little effort to hide its discreet delight in its discomfiture. But there was nothing to be done about it. The Queen's visit was to Oxford as a University, and the whole University must be there. The scholars must stay where they were, every man jack of them, and the harvest must go to the devil.

The scholars made no objection. Very little work was required of them, indeed very little work had been required of them since the beginning of term, for the atmosphere of the whole city was not at this time conducive to work, and they threw themselves into a perfect orgy of ecstatic preparations.

These reached fever-point at Christ Church, where the Queen's Grace and her Court were to be fed, lodged and entertained for six whole days. On her arrival there was to be a great service of thanksgiving. On one night there was to be a Latin play, on another night an English play, on a third night a stag hunt in the quadrangle ; and the rest of the time would be spent in eating. As the great day drew near it would have been difficult to say who were busier, the scholars in the great hall feverishly rehearsing their plays or the cooks in the kitchen below down roasting droves of cattle whole before the great fire, baking scores of lark pies and creating a hundred elegant confections crowned with sugar sailing ships, doves and cupids. Upstairs and downstairs alike the sweat poured off earnest faces, for it was August and the weather was hot, and the tumult and the shouting were so severe that no man could make himself heard until he had yelled himself purple in the face and was dripping like a saturated sponge.

Backwards and forwards across the quadrangle there flowed never-ending streams of University dignitaries, divines and city fathers attending the discussions that took place all day and most of the night in the Dean's study, driving the Dean so distracted that he had no doubt at all that the great day of the Queen's arrival would find him incarcerated in a hospital for the demented. . . . For the discussions that had to take place between town and University engendered a good deal of heat. . . . At what point was the town to be in charge of proceedings, and at what point the University ? At what street corners were civic authorities to deliver English speeches, and at what corners University authorities Greek and Latin ones ? And if the Queen's Grace replied to every speech in the language in which it was given, and at very great length—as was her erudite but distressing habit—how long would it take her to get from the North Gate to Christ Church ? And if they did not know how long her progress would take how could they fix the time for the thanksgiving service in the Cathedral ? These questions were not settled easily, nor without discreet wrangling, the noise of which was at times so severe that it almost drowned the noise of all the choirs of Oxford practising together in the Cathedral for the thanksgiving service ; and this latter noise was at times very great indeed, tending as it did—authority being for the most part absent in the Deanery—to develop from anthems in crescendo to pitched battles in the aisle between the choir of Christ Church on one side and all the other choirs upon the other, refereed by the choirmasters, who brought prayer-books down upon the heads of the combatants with very little effect.

Heatherthwayte and Satan also had a good deal of refereeing to do, for in these last days of preparation, when excitement ran dangerously high, the battles between the Christ Church scholars and those of other Colleges were many and invigorating, and the Fair Gate was a bloody battlefield from early morning until the ringing of the curfew restored peace at dewy eve. The rest of the University naturally took it hard that the Queen's Grace had chosen Christ Church as her place of residence. Why Christ Church ? they demanded angrily at the Fair Gate. Other Colleges were older and the gentlemen resident at them were better supplied with brains, blue blood, wealth and theatrical talent. Were these gentlemen to be denied participation in the theatricals and the stag hunt in the quadrangle ? What did Christ Church know about acting, they demanded to be told. Nothing, they shouted, before there was time for an answer to be forthcoming. Was a Christ Church scholar ever in at the kill, they yelled. No, they bellowed, and the whole lot of them were a lousy, stiff-necked, ignorant lot of varlets whose presence upon God's earth was a weariness unto the eye and a stench unto the nostrils. . . . But at this point yet another fight would break out, and Heatherthwayte would have the greatest difficulty in cleaving a way through it for a couple of aldermen on their way to the more genteel battle ground of the Deanery.

Yet, in spite of the utmost vigilance on the part of Christ Church, one outsider managed to invade the sacred precincts of the College and insert himself into that holy of holies, the hall, where rehearsals took place behind locked doors, and the criminal was Walter Raleigh. He came by the overhead route which led via garden walls to the roof of the Leigh's house, and from that to a window that opened directly above the dais in the hall. The window was high, but Walter Raleigh was always a man of considerable resource ; it was an easy matter to remove a few panes of glass, and to fasten a rope round one of the Leigh chimneys, with its end dangling through the aperture; and after that he had only to wait until the actors below him had formed themselves into a group, whose surface would be more yielding than the bare boards, to let himself down and fall upon them with a blood-curdling screech.

They were in the middle of a rehearsal of the Latin play " Marcus Geminus " a dreary piece written by Canon Calfhill, and Philip Sidney, playing a long part befitting one whose beauty and whose Latin were alike incomparable, was just working up to the peroration when the blow fell. He sprawled sideways, hitting his beautiful nose against the corner of the table. Other gentlemen fell in other directions, Raleigh, spreadeagled on top of them, and there was a wild confusion of arms and legs, shouts and yells, which continued unabated until Raleigh had picked them all up, dusted them down, shaken the senses into them and explained the object of his visit. "I'm going to be in this," he said. " I'm a better actor than any of you."

They gathered round him in an angry crowd, threatening, infuriated. Even Philip Sidney, always so courteous and gentle, lost his temper and blazed and spluttered with the best, and Faithful, sitting in a corner with the prompt book, shouted " Shame ! " as loudly as any. Raleigh stood amongst them, laughing, head thrown back, one hand on his hip and the other swinging his plumed purple cap. " Well, throw me out ! " he taunted them. "Throw me through the window I dropped from. Unlock the door and pitch me down the stairs. We're twenty to one, aren't we?" But somehow they couldn't. He dominated them, even as years later he dominated the Spaniards at Cadiz, when jewelled and plumed he stood upon the poop of the "Warspite" blowing defiance at them through a silver trumpet. They might hate him for his impudence, his conceit, and his courage that was greater than theirs, but they could no more get rid of him than they could have freed themselves from a wind that had blown open the window and swooped upon them. He was as invincible as a force of Nature.

Finally he momentarily got rid of himself. "Look at Sidney's nose!" he exclaimed. "And the Queen's Grace due in four days! An onion, for the love of God!" And thrusting them away from him he sped down the hall like lightning, unlocked the door and catapulted down the stairs to the great vaulted kitchen where the perspiring armies of cooks were roasting their oxen and baking their pies. "An onion! An onion!" he shouted as he went. "In the name of all the saints and devils, an onion for Master Sidney's nose!" And seizing it from the hand of the chief cook himself, who was just about to chop it up for use in a lark pie, he was back up the stairs again three steps at a time before anyone had had the presence of mind to lock the door on him, and anointing Sidney's swelling nose and blackening eye with the tender solicitude of a mother for her babe.

They could not but be mollified. Others of them presented their bruises for attention, and presently they found themselves consulting Raleigh about a few minor difficulties in theatrical production that had that morning cropped up. He dealt with them with ease. They they got on the topic of the major difficulty, the fact that the boy who was to play Arcite in the English play, "Palemon and Arcite," had so got knocked about in a fight at the Fair Gate that he was no longer fit to be seen. Raleigh dealt with this difficulty easily, too. . . . He would be Arcite. . . . After that he took complete charge of everything and for the rest of the day rehearsals went with a swing and a verve that they had not known before. They hated Raleigh when he cursed them for their stupidity, they glowered when his will rode roughly over theirs, but when everything that he touched, the lines of the plays and their own minds and wills, glowed with fire as when a flame runs among stubble, there was nothing to do but yield themselves. Sidney's presence had given to their performance a moonlit beauty, but Raleigh's made of it a conflagration.

III

In the Leigh's house also things hummed. The Leighs themselves had long since been distributed among the other Canons' households, and only Great-Aunt and Tinker remained, fed from the Deanery table at great inconvenience to everybody. Efforts had been made to dislodge Tinker, but to everyone's surprise he refused to go with Diccon, Joseph, Joyeuce and the dogs to Canon Calfhill's house across the quadrangle ; every time he was carried there he slipped with sylph-like obstinacy from the nearest window and stalked back again to his own home, his tail carried in the perpendicular position, with twitching tip, and his paws placed one before the other with a delicate but disdainful precision that seemed to spurn the very ground that separated him from the place where he would be. . . . And they had thought that he loved Diccon. . . . It seemed he did not love Diccon. He had attached himself to Diccon in preference to other members of the household because Diccon's single-minded determination to have what he wanted had given them a spiritual affinity one with the other ; but what he loved was the house, that particular city of mice whose lanes and byways he knew. Canon Calfhill's house might have other mice, but they were not his mice, and his lack of knowledge of the geography of their citadel gave to his soul a strange unease. . . . After the sixth return he was let alone. Cats had always been revered at Christ Church, and always would be, for had not Cardinal Wolsey himself adored them ? A wrong-headed man in many ways, the great Cardinal, but he loved pussies. He always had a pussy on the Woolsack by his side.

So by night Tinker hunted his own mice in his own house, and by day he sat beside Great-Aunt at her window and watched the things that went on in the hall below. . . . And a great deal went on. . . . Great-Aunt had never been so happy. The infernal din of a door being knocked in the wall of the room next her, the noise made by carpenters and decorators, the smells of paint and unwashed workmen, troubled her not at all, for her nerves were of iron. What she loved was the spectacle of Life flowing past her window. Old as she was it would never be over for her while she had eyes to see and ears to hear. Curiosity was her great gift, and daily she thanked God for it.

The house was ready at last. The polished surface of it shone like glass, meadowsweet strewed the floors, the carved four-poster where the Queen would sleep had been gilded, and hung with peach-coloured satin curtains embroidered with forget-me-nots, and upon it were spread fine sheets scented with lavender. Great bowls of flowers stood in shady corners and wherever the eye might turn it met priceless tapestries and pieces of furniture filched from all the finest houses in Oxford. Two days before that fixed for the Queen's arrival the Chancellor himself galloped over from Woodstock, where the Queen and Court were now in residence, to cast his eye over all the final arrangements, and could find no fault with it whatever. He and Great-Aunt met at the hall door, with every appearance of deep mutual respect, and she herself conducted him round the apartments, pointing out every improvement and decoration, and receiving his compliments upon them as though they were all the result of her own inspiration and hard labour. " Do not mention it, my lord," she demurred with a gracious inclination of the head. " The supervision of these matters has been a great pleasure to me. . . . I shall, of course, myself receive the Queen's Grace upon her arrival at the house ; my niece, Joyeuce Leigh, being too inexperienced a chit to carry off these high matters with becoming grace." Her eye, that had hitherto been of a melting tenderness, became fixed and steely in its regard and the Chancellor hastened to agree with her decision. . . . It seemed to him a thousand pities to defraud the little Mistress Joyeuce of an honour that was surely hers by right, but he had no time to waste in skirmishes with Great-Aunt ; nor, remembering the outcome of the last one, did he think unseemly wrangles with elderly gentlewomen compatible with his dignity. . . . He bowed with a flourish and left her somewhat precipitately to attend a meeting at the Deanery, the frantic, heated, desperate, final discussion as to who should take precedence over whom when the great hour was upon them.

" Upon the Day of Judgement," whispered Dean Godwin to the Chancellor, " there will be quarrelling as to who is to have the honour of helping the crowned heads to collect their bones."

IV

The great day dawned fine, with a slight August haze that promised a time of cloudless sunshine. As soon as the sun had pierced its way through, and gilded the towers and spires with a most royal beauty, the bells were ringing and the streets were awash with colour; garlands of flowers festooned from house to house, bright silks and tapestries fluttering from every window, eager citizens and scholars surging everywhere dressed in their gayest garments, flowers in their arms, smiles on their faces, pent-up excitement bursting from them in jokes and banter and such echoing roars of laughter that it seemed the very cobble-stones cried out for joy. The city was drenched in happiness. If there were any sad people in it, if any sick folk, they did not show themselves. . . . They knew better than to intrude upon this day. . . . For it was one of those days when everything conspires together to make men forgetful of their fate. With bells ringing, colour ebbing and flowing, sunshine pouring upon them and the Queen of England drawing with every moment nearer to their city gates, there could be no thought of past or future. With such strange turbulent joy in their hearts it seemed that they already held in their hands all that they longed for; what they had lost was theirs again and the garlanded flowers and fluttering silks were their dreams come true.

The first great excitement of the day came in the early afternoon, when deputations from University and city rode out to meet the Queen. There was a burst of cheering as the Chancellor, Vice-Chancellor and Heads of Houses, most good to look upon in full academic robes, passed up Cornmarket and under the North Gate towards the village of Wolvercote, on the road to Woodstock, where they would greet the Queen with a Latin address of welcome. After them rode the Mayor of Oxford and the city fathers, resplendent in scarlet robes and golden chains of office, who were to post themselves midway between Wolvercote and Oxford and greet Her Grace with three or more English addresses of welcome, according as Her Grace seemed to be fatigued, or not fatigued, by the Latin one that had preceded them. Hard at their heels pounded a horde of apprentices, self-appointed messengers who were to run backwards and forwards between Wolvercote and Oxford reporting the progress of events to those within the city.

When the last shouting urchin had disappeared into the dust and sunshine beyond the gate, there was nothing for the crowds within it to do but wait with what patience they could muster. All the day down Cornmarket, across Carfax and down Fish Street to the Fair Gate, the scholars stood in two long lines keeping the way clear for the Queen's processional passing, and packed behind them were the townspeople in their holiday clothes, swaying backwards and forwards in turbulent excitement, only kept from breaking across the street by the linked arms and the stalwart backs of the laughing scholars. But the time of waiting did not seem long. Every stray dog that ran up the route was cheered, every pretty girl who showed herself at an open window was loudly appraised, jokes flew backwards and forwards, laughter ran in the air, and all the time the bells were pealing that the Queen might hear their welcome as she came upon her way.

Then suddenly the apprentices, all in a glorious perspiration of haste and enthusiasm, came dashing one by one back through North Gate with reports of the progress. News flew through the waiting crowds, and little whispers and cries of excitement broke from them. Yes, she was coming, and the whole Court with her. Oh, yes, she was beautiful beyond words, dressed all in white and blazing with jewels, carried in a wonderful litter roofed with cloth of gold. Yes, she had reached Wolvercote and the Provost of Oriel had read the Latin address of welcome. Oh, yes, she had replied to it; in Latin, of course, and at very great length. The Court had seemed a little restive but she had taken no notice, working up to her peroration in a way that was a marvel to all present. . . . Now she had reached the Mayor and the city fathers. . . . There had been five speeches and they had pleased her mightily. Had she replied? Oh, yes. Five times? No, only once, for the horse of my Lord of Warwick had turned very troublesome, and my Lord had sworn in unseemly fashion, and it had seemed best to all to proceed upon their way. . . . Now she was nearly here. . . . She was passing St. Giles' Church. . . . Now she had stopped outside North Gate for Master Dell, a don of New College, to make another oration in Latin. . . . Now she was moving again. . . . She was so close that those inside the city walls could hear through the pealing bells the cheers, the trampling of horses and the jingling of their harness. . . . The procession was passing right under North Gate. . . . She was here. . . . Vivat Regina! Vivat Regina! A great roar went up, a roar that echoed through the streets like thunder, and all along the length of the route the scholars fell upon their knees.

The procession passed very slowly, but even so there were so many eyes blinded by tears, so many pounding hearts and throats choked with excitement that they all found it difficult afterwards to describe what they had seen. The Chancellor, the Vice-Chancellor and the Heads of Houses had come first, they remembered, leading her in. . . . The Chancellor had looked magnificent, but they had hardly noticed him, for their eyes were straining to see the golden litter that was borne behind him.

She sat upon it as though it were her throne, swaying easily to its motion, smiling at them, her lovely long pale hands clasped upon her lap and her head held high. She looked beautiful, and so young. It was hard to believe she was thirty-three years old; she was so slender that she looked a girl still. They gazed in adoration at the face they had heard described a hundred times, but yet had never seen, not even in pictures. A face of a beautiful oval shape, with a clear olive complexion, aquiline nose, fine dark eyes under delicately arched eyebrows. A fine, proud, shrewd face, the face of the woman who had saved England. Their eyes were suddenly misted and they saw only dimly the jewelled coif set upon masses of fair reddish piled-up hair, the beautiful ruff that framed her face like the calyx of a flower, the white satin dress scintillating with jewels and the slender feet in golden slippers set so firmly upon the velvet cushion.

Then she had gone on her way and with a jingling of harness, a breath of many perfumes, in a glimmering kaleidoscope of colour, the Court was passing by. So many lovely ladies, beruffed and jewelled, sitting their horses with lovely ease, their long skirts sweeping almost to the ground, their laughing faces turned this way and that to greet the smiling scholars; so many magnificent gentlemen riding by, reining in spirited horses with a clatter of hoofs upon the cobbles, plumed hats raised in greeting, bold eyes roving up to the windows to exchange twinkling glances with the pretty maidens gathered there. A few knowledgeable people in the crowd pointed out one and another, whispering their names in awed tones. "The Spanish Ambassador, Sir William Cecil. My Lord of Warwick, brother of the Chancellor.

My Lord of Oxford, married to Sir William's daughter, though he is but sixteen years of age. My Lord of Rutland." The cavalcade swept by, the Mayor and city fathers bringing up the rear, and the crowd came tumbling at their heels to hear what they could of the Greek oration at Carfax.

This was delivered by Canon Lawrence, the Regius Professor. It was very long and very learned and delighted the Queen greatly; she would have done her poor best to reply to it, she told Canon Lawrence later, but looking about her she saw that the distress of her illiterate Court was by this time very great, and in mercy she forbore. Then on again to the Fair Gate where Master Kingsmill, the University Orator, delivered a speech which it had taken him the best part of two days and nights to prepare and nearly as long to deliver. . . . But yet, at the end of it, the Queen most unaccountably turned testy. " You would have done well had you had good matter," she said, and turned abruptly away from him that the Chancellor and Dean Godwin might help her from her litter.

But she was all smiles again when she stood beneath the Fair Gate and saw the great quadrangle stretching before her, wide and peaceful after the turmoil in the streets, with the spire of the Cathedral splendid against the blue sky and the buildings her father had loved standing beneath it, warm and serene in the sun. Towards her, over the green grass, came four doctors in their scarlet robes, holding a canopy under which she was to walk to the Cathedral. " It is a fair sight," she said to Dean Godwin. " And it is a fair house, this house of Christ that my father founded. I am glad to be here with you all. "

And they were glad to have her. The Christ Church scholars, coming pelting from their posts in the streets, ran to line the path that led across the quadrangle and through the cloisters to the Cathedral door, and with them stood all the other people of Christ Church, the dons and servitors, the Canons' wives and families. Joyeuce was there in her green frock, with Nicolas beside her, and Grace and Faithful stood together keeping a firm hold of Joseph and Diccon, who pranced and curveted like puppies on the leash. The twins, in new daffodil-yellow dresses, curtsied as Joyeuce had taught them, but unfortunately, owing to their weight and excitement, capsized at the critical moment, and Will and Thomas bowed so low that their two-coloured shocks of hair nearly touched the grass. The Queen paused for a moment as she passed this group, laughing at the bows and curtsies, returning with humour the impudent unblinking green stare with which Diccon fixed her. " The greeting of little poppets," she said to one of the scarlet-robed doctors who carried her canopy—it happened to be Canon Leigh—" gives to any arrival the sense of home-coming."

She had unerringly struck the right note for her visit. " Home-coming." The whispered word flew from one to another and was gloated over. This was the house that her father had founded and she had come home to it. They were her very own household. She belonged to them as she did not belong to other inferior Colleges. When the procession had passed into the cloisters they all came tumbling after, calling out to each other, laughing and exuberant as they would not have dared to be but for that whispered intimate word ; and over their heads the bells, Hautclere, Douce, Clement, Austin, Marie, Gabriel and John, rang out in a jubilation greater than any they had known since they had come from Oseney Abbey to live in the tower of Christ Church.

When they had trembled into silence those who could not get into the Cathedral stood outside in the cloisters, listening to the solemn intoning of the long prayers, to the singing of the anthem to the accompaniment of cornets, and then to the intoning of more and longer prayers, until the first gold of evening stole into the sky and the coolness of it fell upon them, like a benediction. . . . The first day was over. . . . It had gone well.

v

Everything continued to go well. The Queen, except for the one regrettable lapse when Master Kingsmill's oration at the Fair Gate had just for the moment turned her testy, was so gracious and so charming that every heart in Christ Church was bound to her in love for ever. Everything seemed to please her. Never, she said, had she tasted such delicious food as that cooked at Christ Church, nor heard such sweet music as was played while she consumed the same, dining in state each day upon the dais in Christ Church hall. She thought her lodgings charming, and expressed herself as much touched that a door should have been made from the house to the hall for her convenience. . . . She was ravished, so she said, by the song that Nicolas sang beneath her window on the night of her arrival. She would never forget him, she said, looking down at him where he stood below her in the shadows of the garden. He was a comely lad, such as her heart loved, and one day he should ask of her what he wanted. She took a rose from her dress—she always had a flower or a knot of ribbons easily detachable upon the bodice of it, for it was by such little ruses that she bound men to her for life —and tossed it to him before she drew back again behind her curtains, leaving him to slip away through the apple trees to the garden gate in a tremor of ecstasy and excitement. . . . She even vowed she had taken a fancy to Great-Aunt ; and spoke truly, for she found the old lady's gossip highly entertaining, and in the evenings would summon her to her presence to hear her malicious comments upon the life and character of those learned men who had that day delivered orations before the Queen . . . For the orations continued. . . . Though she lodged at Christ Church, and spent most of her evenings there, the Queen did not neglect other Colleges. She heard orations at them all and on three days attended disputations at St. Mary's Church, which on the last day went on so long, and aroused the Queen's interest so keenly, that the disputants " tired the sun with talking and sent him down the sky," so that candles had to be set burning round the church.

There were, of course, as was inevitable, a few minor disappointments and disasters. The scholars found it hard to bear that on the day of the play " Marcus Geminus " the Queen should declare herself too exhausted by Latin orations delivered in the afternoon to attend a Latin play in the evening. But the Court came, and applauded loudly, and the Spanish Ambassador gave such a glowing account of the scholars' acting to the Queen afterwards that she swore with vexation to think what she had missed, and vowed that she would lose no more sport hereafter. . . . Nor did she. . . . She attended the performance of the English play, " Palamon and Arcite," in great magnificence, diamonds flashing, silks swirling, jewelled head held high, and enjoyed it enormously. Nor was she in the least put out when the stage collapsed, killing three scholars and injuring five more. These little things, she said to the profusely apologising Dean, will occur at juvenile performances, and we must not dishearten the young ones by paying too much attention to slight mishaps.

But nothing went wrong at the miniature stag hunt in the quadrangle, which took place by moonlight, and provided the scholars with the major thrill of the Queen's visit. The poor stag, captured alive at Cumnor and conveyed to Oxford with great fatigue to itself and everybody, was let loose at the Fair Gate and fled across the quadrangle like a stag out of a fairy-tale, its great branched antlers shining like silver and its slender body the colour of pearl in the light of the moon. After it came the hounds, baying wildly, and then a few members of the Court and the more sporting of the dons, mounted on galloping horses, with white plumes in their hats and white roses fastened in their doublets. . . . The scholars, upon this occasion, were severely confined to the upper stories, where they leaned out of the windows shouting and yelling in such wild excitement that the Queen, watching with the Chancellor, declared she could scarcely enjoy the scene for fear they should all fall out. . . . Round and round the quadrangle fled the fairy-tale stag of silver and pearl, round and round went the shadowy shapes of the baying hounds, round and round the galloping huntsmen; until the poor stag saw the thicket of trees at the northern side of the quadrangle, fled to it and met its death with its silver horns entangled in a hawthorn bush, the huntsmen crashing round it in the undergrowth and the hounds leaping from the shadows at its throat. . . . The Queen, as she turned away, vowed she was surprised, though of course deeply thankful to the mercy of God, to find it was the only casualty.

Such had been the excitement that she was tired that night, and glad to go to bed in the quiet room looking across the garden to the moonlit trees of the meadows.

CHAPTER XVI

PATRIOTISM

There were hills which garnished their proud heights with stately trees: humble vallies, whose base estate seemed comforted with the refreshment of silver rivers: meadows enamelled with all sorts of eye-pleasing flowers: thickets, which being lined with most pleasant shade were witnessed so too by the cheerful disposition of many well-tuned birds; each pasture stored with sheep, feeding with sobre security, while the pretty lambs with bleating outcry craved the dam's comfort: here a shepherd's boy piping, as though he should never be old: there a young shepherdess knitting, and withal singing; and it seemed that her voice comforted her hands to work, and her hands kept time to her voice-music. As for the houses of the country they were built of fair and strong stone, not affecting so much any extraordinary kind of fineness as an honourable representing of a firm stateliness. The back side of the house was a place cunningly set with trees of the most taste-pleasing fruits, and new beds of flowers, which being under the trees, the trees were to them a pavilion, and they to the trees a mosaical floor.

"The Arcadia."   PHILIP SIDNEY.

I

THE next afternoon, the last day of her stay in Oxford the Queen attended archery practice in Beaumont Fields.

Under a blazing blue sky scholars and citizens alike poured out of North Gate, swung to their left along the narrow lane beside the city wall, then to their right into Beaumont Fields. The scholars who carried bows, and who were to shoot before the Queen, were all very eager and excited, and a little strained, for this was a very great occasion. Archery was still tremendously important, even though the hand-gun was now taking the place of the long-bow in modern warfare. You were no true Englishman if you could not shoot a straight arrow from your bow, and to be watched by the Queen of England while you tried to do it was enough to turn the hottest blood to water and the stoutest heart to mere pulp. Even Nicolas was flustered as he made his way out of North Gate, with Faithful behind him carrying his bow and arrows, and Philip Sidney and Walter Raleigh, whom they overtook in the crowd at the gate of the Fields, had had their usual gravity and confidence so overturned that they were snapping and snarling at those who got in their way quite like the lesser brethren.

But once in the Fields the beauty of the place quieted them all, for this was a spot of earth that everyone adored, especially on a sunshiny day in summer. Whichever way you looked, as you stood in the Fields, you felt glad to be alive. To the south, crowning a little hill, were the ruins of Beaumont Palace, the royal house built by Henry the First, the scholar king, where Henry the Second had lived sometimes when he loved Rosamond, where his son, Richard Cœur de Lion, had been born, and where later the Carmelites had had their home. The same tempest of destruction that had dispossessed the monks had swept away the old palace too; the walls that had sheltered kings had been pulled down and sold as stone for fresh buildings; there was nothing left of it now but the foundations, and nothing left of the garden but a riot of roses and honeysuckle climbing over the old stones and the fruit trees that the monks had planted. . . . These were now the only fair ladies who inhabited the Fair Mount, and the only musicians who sang there were the singing birds.

But one looked north over the same stretch of country that had delighted the eyes of kings and queens and courtiers, a stretch of country that in curve and colour was like a piece of music composed by a happy man. Its rhythm was peace and its motif was yet more peace. There was neither grandeur nor the shock of contrast, but lazy curves that rose and fell like a contented sea, and misted colours that melted one into the other imperceptibly. To the west the woods of Rats and Mice Hill were a heavy deep green against the blue of the sky, and to the east the Forest of Shotover echoed their colour, while between them a plain of green and tawny meadows and harvest fields stretched away into the distance, clumps of green willows marking the windings of river and streams. Across this plain meandered the highways to Woodstock and Banbury, their peace disturbed by nothing but an occasional lumbering cart or lazily trotting horseman.

But at the butts under the palace wall there was a scene of eager activity. The seats of the spectators stretched the length of the wall, with a raised dais for the Queen in the centre, and were already full; dons and scholars, stout merchants and their wives, and apprentices, all in their gayest clothes. They were an audience whose comments never lacked ribaldry or point and under their scrutiny the groups of archers, waiting at each end of the butts for the arrival of the Queen, shifted nervously from foot to foot.

As each man's turn came he had to shoot from first one end and then the other, alternately, so that he should not get set in one position. In this continual flying of arrows in different directions there was a certain amount of danger, but according to the regulations if a man cried out " Fast ! " before he shot he was not held responsible for the injury or death of anyone he might wound or kill. . . . The accident was unfortunate but quite in order. . . . A really expert English bowman could shoot ten arrows in a minute, with a range of two hundred yards, and Henry the Eighth had ordained that no person who had reached the age of twenty-four should shoot at any mark at less than two hundred and twenty yards distant.

So two hundred and twenty yards was the distance between the two wooden discs set up at either end of the space by the palace wall. Robin Hood, of course, " clave the wand in two " from a distance of four hundred yards, but then Robin was a finer bowman than any man living now in the city of Oxford.

Faithful, having handed his bow and arrows to Nicolas, found a vacant corner at the end of one of the seats and sat there, warm and cosy in the sun, glad to sit still and digest his dinner in peace and quiet while he watched the gay scene, glad for once in a way that his own archery was at present such a danger to the community that it could only be practised in private, for lookers-on, he thought, can sometimes catch more of the thrill of a great occasion than those taking part in it.

In the distance a fanfare of trumpets sounded. The Queen was leaving St. John's, the beautiful College built in a grove of elm trees outside the city wall, where she had that morning been entertained and feasted by its dons. The sound of the cheering grew louder as she came nearer, growing into a roar as the royal party came into the Fields and mounted the steps to the dais. . . . But the groups of waiting archers did not cheer, for their tongues stuck most distressingly to the roofs of their mouths. They straightened themselves, gripped their bows with tense fingers and swallowed hard.

The dons of Saint John's College had the post of honour today and sat grouped around the Queen. The Chancellor was upon her right, and with a thrill of delight Faithful saw her beckon to Edmund Campion, his friend of May Morning, and make him sit upon her left. They had all learned that he was in high favour with her. He had already made two orations before her, in the first one proving to her entire satisfaction that the sea is constantly blown out with vapours, like boiling water in a pot, and in the second speaking extempore on the subject of "Fire" with such eloquence that she vowed he was the finest scholar of them all.

Yet, seeing those three radiant figures, the Queen and the courtiers and the scholar, laughing and talking together, and remembering the Chapel beneath the Mitre Inn, Faithful felt a sudden pang of apprehensive misery. In the bright sunshine there seemed to be shadows about, as though dark wings swept overhead and brushed those three figures in passing. But they seemed unaware of them. They could not foresee the years ahead, and the room in Leicester's London house, where they would meet again; an elderly heart-sick woman with a painted face and a red wig, a grizzled weary courtier and a Jesuit with the filth of the dungeon upon him, brought there on his way from prison to the scaffold that they might plead with him to save himself. They were unaware. They were in the sunshine of life and the darkness of night ahead was not remembered. But Faithful, because at the moment he had no one to talk to, was suddenly aware of it. He was afraid. It was suddenly dreadful to him that we do not know to what we travel; only that the way there is like an increasingly darkening tunnel. At the heart of it the blackness is like pitch. We must pass through it, there is no escape, and there is no one to come back and tell us what it is like in that darkness, or what it is like beyond.

The trumpet sounded again, the murmur of voices died away into silence, and Faithful's sudden depression fell away from him like a black cloak as the figure of a straight young archer stepped forward, brilliant in sunshine, his body laid on his great bow, drawing not with the strength of the arm but with the strength of the body, as Englishmen were taught to do.

As one after the other the figures of the archers took their posts, at the sound of the drawn bowstrings and the sight of the arrows speeding through the air, a queer exultation seized hold of the whole company, consciousness was heightened and imagination took wing. For if it was true that the voice of France could be heard in the sound of the trumpets, that preserved the echoes of the horn of Roland, it was equally true that the voice of England was heard in the music of archery, in the humming of

the bowstrings, that was like the sound of a plucked harp, and
the singing of the arrows in the air. It was a music that was full
of memories ; of Crécy and the Black Prince, of Agincourt and
Harry the Fifth. And not only their music but the bows and
arrows themselves carried one back through time ; the bows
nearly as tall as a man, made of the wood of English yew trees,
the descendants of the sacred yews that the Druids had planted
round their holy places before the Romans came, the bowstrings of flax from English fields, and the arrows of birch wood
feathered from the wings of grey geese. Over and over again,
in battle after battle, had those grey geese, flying out from the
forests of bent yew, carried death upon their wings. For only
Englishmen could use the longbow. Foreigners could never get
the knack of it. It was something that Englishmen, yeomen
and gentry alike, had to practise from their boyhood up in the
butts that stretched behind every village churchyard, sweating
over it while the old churchyard yews that had made the bows
leant over the wall to watch, and the grey geese that had feathered
the arrows cackled approval up and down the village street.
Agincourt had been won by the whole of England, by the
yeomen, the yew trees, the grey geese and the fields of flax.
The young archer who dazzled Faithful's eyes as he stood in the
sunshine was a symbolic figure to the whole of that excited
crowd. They thrilled with pride as they looked at him, but they
were sad too. He stood for the fast-dying days when a man
fighting for his country could feel himself something of an artist
and not solely a butcher, and for a voice of England that would
soon be stilled. . . . When the last archer had sped the last
arrow to its mark a sigh went up from Beaumont Fields, and then
silence before the trumpets spoke again and the Queen stepped
down from her dais.

II

"Let's get away from here," said Philip Sidney to Faithful.
"Away from the crowds and out into the country."

The ordeal was over and he had done his part well, but now
he was suffering from reaction. He hated the crowds and the
shouting. The sound of the trumpets and the music of the long-
bows had stirred the depths in him. He wanted to get away
where it was quiet.

Faithful, as became a good servitor, shouldered Philip's

bow good-humouredly, though it was a good deal taller than he was and carrying it gave him a crick in the neck, and lolloped at his friend's heels like an obedient dog. He was, he had noticed, frequently treated as a faithful dog. People who did not exactly want company, but yet wanted that invisible companion who seems to sit enthroned in our minds, and to whom we talk in moments of emotion, to take some visible form, would often choose either Faithful or a dog to accompany them on their walks abroad. In both they would find an unobtrusive admiration which helped them to express their thoughts without either fear or shame.

Philip went straight to a place that he knew of, where a lazy stream meandered through meadows where in early summer the grass was as high as little children. It was short now, and had no movement or murmur to give back to the wind as it rolled away into the distance to lose itself in the blue hills and woods that shut in the valley. The afternoon was utterly and completely still. They could see the silver ribbon of the river winding its way from Oxford past Binsey and the holy well to Godstow. "Look!" said Philip, pointing to some old grey walls among the trees. "From here you can see the ruins of Godstow Nunnery. It's odd, isn't it, to sit here between Beaumont Palace, where Henry the Second lived sometimes, and Godstow Nunnery, where his Rose of the World hid herself. I wonder how often he sat here, where we are sitting now, after she had become a nun and he could not see her any more, and looked at the grey walls that kept him out."

They were silent, thinking of that famous love story, so wrapped up in legend now that it was hard to disentangle truth from falsehood.

Rosamond had lived at Woodstock, and Henry had met her one day when he was out riding his white horse in the Springtime in the flowery fields that surrounded his royal palace, fields so lovely that they were like the fields of heaven. Rosamond came walking towards him through the buttercups and daisies and cuckoo flowers, and she was so freshly and radiantly lovely that she seemed to the King the spirit of beauty itself. The singing of the birds that rang all about them in the blue air, the green flames that burned in the beech trees, and the swaying whispering mass of the thousand flowers and grasses that clothed the meadows, seemed to be no more than a garment for the incomparable beauty of the girl who moved in their midst.

The King was a young man who had been married since his boyhood to Eleanor, the divorced wife of the King of France, a woman so evil that her husband's life seemed to him to have been poisoned on the day he married her. She hated him, and taught his children to hate him. Only in regarding the beauty of the land that was his kingdom could he find release from misery.

And now it seemed to him, as he jumped from his horse and gazed astounded at the girl who came towards him, that this fair land was giving him its very spirit. It was as though the fields and the trees and the birdsong lifted her up and held her towards him, as merciful hands cup themselves to carry water to a thirsty man. He was bewildered by the wonder of it. Though he was the King of England he fell upon his knees before Rosamond, holding her desperately by the skirts of her long green gown, imploring her to stay as she was, a warm breathing comforting creature who could be touched and held, not a wraith who would float away through the tree trunks when night came on, and the first stars signalled from their watch towers that the sun was set.

What could poor Rosamond do? Held by the compelling hands of a young and comely King, while the birds sang and the flowers shivered in ecstasy under the touch of the spring wind, she seemed to herself drained of all strength. For a moment she shook her head in bewilderment, then put her own hands caressingly over the hands that held her. . . . So he took her home with him, and when the stars signalled warningly, and all good birds and maidens and children hied them home, she did not look at them; she looked only upon her lover, Henry.

In the garden of Woodstock Palace there was a labyrinth, and at the heart of it the King made a bower all overgrown with roses for his Rose of the World. Only he and one of his friends knew the secret of the labyrinth, but they taught it to Rosamond that she might be able to hide herself there if any danger threatened when Henry was away from her.

He was often away from her, for there was war across the sea and he must be often fighting in France. One summer day Rosamond sat at her embroidery near the entrance to the labyrinth. The sun was warm and the red roses and white lilies were in bloom and she sang as she worked, for she had had news that soon her lover would be home again. There was no fear in her heart, only a deep and tranquil happiness that she, of all women in the world, should be the one to bring joy and comfort to the King.

Suddenly from the palace the trumpets sounded, and she lifted her head, for they rang out in that way only when one of royal blood visited the palace. But still she was not afraid, for Queen Eleanor never came to Woodstock, and she was sure that no one could have been so cruel as to betray the King's secret to her. Was it Henry himself? Had he come earlier than he had promised? She jumped up in joy, still holding the end of a long thread of embroidery silk that she had been unwinding from its ball when the trumpets sounded, and she would have started to run to the palace had she not seen the bright figure of a little page coming pelting towards her through the trees, his face as white as the white lilies that grow beside the entrance to the labyrinth.

"Hide, Rosamond!" he gasped. "Someone has betrayed you and the Queen is here!" Then he turned and doubled back again, quick as a darting dragon-fly, terrified that someone at the palace had seen the way he came.

Instantly, as quick in her flight as he was, Rosamond ran through the mazes of the labyrinth; but in her terror she still held the end of embroidery silk and the ball unrolled behind her as she ran, showing the windings of the maze.

At the heart of the labyrinth, crouching in the bower of roses, Queen Eleanor found her. That evil lady was not a woman who wasted time. In one hand she carried a bowl of poison and in the other a dagger, and coming instantly to the point without undue expenditure of words she briefly offered Rosamond her choice. Rosamond, also coming to the point after only a brief interval of desperate pleading, chose the poison and died there, and the roses dropped their petals pitifully upon the maiden who was fairer than they.

That was one version of the story, but there was another, less picturesque but more likely, that related how Rosamond of her own will cut herself adrift from the King.

Wandering among the roses in the Woodstock garden at evening, after the sun had set, she wondered what would be the end of it all. What could be the end of it for Henry, what for her? Could there be any outcome for Henry except dishonour and bewilderment, any for her but shame and torment that her name should have tarnished his? She looked up at the quiet evening sky where the first stars were signalling to the world. " Go home," and then she looked about her at all the myriads of God's creatures who had listened to that command. Most of them were safely home already. There were no butterflies or little birds about now; she could picture them safely asleep in their own particular nooks and crannies, wings folded and heads tucked under wings. Many of the flowers were tightly closed, their golden hearts and amber honey-drops safe and inviolate behind the shut doors of their petals. Over in the village of Woodstock lights sprang out behind windows, telling of labourers home from the fields and little children safely cradled for the night. Above her head flapped a party of rooks, flying home to the rookery in the great Park beyond the garden. All these creatures had their own appointed places, and however far they might have wandered through the day when the stars signalled from their watch towers that the night had come they turned always homewards.

But Rosamond, with a sickening stab at her heart, remembered that she had no home. One of those twinkling lights, over there in Woodstock, shone out from the window of the house where once she had lived; but its door was shut against her now; though she came only of yeoman stock her people were people who had their honour, and she had disgraced them. Once before the stars had told her to go home, but she had not gone. Now it was too late.

What should she do? Standing there in despair on the garden path, with her knuckles pressed into her eyes, she heard a harsh rhythmical sound, a sound that though ugly always delighted her. The swans! They came sometimes by day to visit the lake in the park, but at night they always flew back again to that particular reach of the river that was their home; it was at Godstow, Henry had told her, at Godstow, where the nunnery was.

She gazed up at them in delight. They were flying in perfect formation, first one alone, then two more, then three, and so high up in the sky that the last gleam of sunset caught them and bathed their snowy feathers in a light that seemed to shine right out from Paradise. Rosamond thought that never in her life had she seen a sight so radiantly pure and lovely; and they were going home to Godstow, where the nunnery was.

Then she knew what she must do. There were more homes in the world than one. Though the door of an earthly home might be shut against you, there were other doors that never denied the knocking of the sinner who repented. She did not stop to go indoors and change the white silk dress that she wore for one more suited for a journey, she did not even wait to say farewell to those in the palace who had been good to her, she ran at once to the stableyard and wrenched at the stable door in a passion of eagerness. It was unlocked, for the grooms were careless when their master was away, and she went in and found her white horse that Henry had given her, the same white horse that he had been riding that day in the meadows when he found her. She saddled him quickly and easily, for Rosamond was no fine lady but a strong country girl who could sweep a room or groom a horse with the best, and then she led him out, mounted him and turned towards Godstow.

She rode quickly through the woods and meadows, for she was fearful that her courage and resolution might falter, and she turn back again, but as she rode she looked about her, for she knew she was looking her last upon the world she loved; from henceforth she would see it only through the windows of a nunnery. Though the darkness was gathering she could still see the pale faces of the wild roses scattered over the hedgerows, and the branches of the trees sweeping up against the stars, and she gazed at them as though she were about to be smitten with perpetual blindness. From under her horse's feet there came up to her the scent of wet grass and of those pungent herbal plants that grow near water, and she drew in great breaths of it as though her lungs laboured. She pressed her knees tightly against her horse, for this was the last time that she would feel the ripple of horseflesh beneath them.

When she came to the ford, and saw across the gleaming river the walls of the nunnery rising out of the reeds and rushes on the other side, her courage nearly failed her. She reined in her horse and sat there trembling, her eyes hot and burning and her heart beating so that it nearly choked her. For, God in heaven, how she loved life! She was not a woman born to kneel all her days upon a cold stone floor, telling the beads of a rosary; she had a gay heart made for laughter and an adventurous spirit that craved its fill of love and danger. In her pride she had felt sometimes that life was not long enough for all she wanted to do, or the world packed full enough of the marvels that she wanted to see before she died. In her dreams she had often pictured herself, Eleanor being dead by some happy mischance, as Queen of England, her passionate love no longer hidden and shamed but crowned with honour in the sight of the world. She had imagined the heaven it would be to be Henry's wife, living with him in his great house by the river in London town, or over there in the palace of the Fair Mount in Oxford ; or perhaps going with him to France and watching the English bowmen march out to fight the French, and riding as near as she dared to the battle to hear the music of the plucked bowstrings and the singing of the arrows in the air. . . . But Eleanor was not dead, nor likely to be, for like all nasty people she was bound to live long. . . . And Rosamond was only a yeoman's daughter. She would never be Queen of England. She would never, while she lived free in the world, bring Henry anything but trouble. Why could she not be a man, able to serve her king and country with the bow and arrows, her strong body laid upon her bow and her fingers like steel to pluck its music ? Why must she be a woman, her only way of service this of sacrifice and death ? In her anguish she cried out aloud, startling the white swans who were already sleeping in the rushes by the river, then set her horse at the ford.

The river was running high and the icy water crept up to her knees, chilling her to the bone. Numbed and silent now, she looked stupidly at the skirts of her white dress floating out around her like the plumage of a bird, and at the little white water daisies that starred the water. Then the cold seemed to creep up to her heart and she seemed not to see or feel anything any more.

The nuns looked at each other, startled, when they heard the knocking at the nunnery door. They were up late that evening, praying in the cold chapel for that Scarlet Woman, that shameless Woodstock girl, who was the troubler of the King's peace and a disgrace to this fair valley where they lived. The knocking came so pat upon their thoughts of sin and shame that it frightened them. They went all together to open the door, not leaving the round-eyed young portress to face alone the devils who might be outside.

They opened in fear and trembling, recoiling in astonishment at the sight of the pale-faced girl with the golden hair who stood outside. In her white dress in the moonlight, one hand holding the mane of her white horse and the other stretched out to them as though she pleaded for alms, she looked like a visitant from another world, like a water nymph risen from the river or the soul of a white swan.

"Or one of the flowers from the heavenly meadows," whispered Sister Ursula, the little portress. "She is so white; like one of the lilies of Our Lady."

"Take me in, good sisters," cried Rosamond. "Of your charity give refuge to the sinner that repenteth."

"Who are you, who come knocking here after the night has fallen?" demanded the Abbess sternly. "Riding along upon horseback with a jewelled circlet on your head and the silks of a queen upon your body. Such behaviour is not seemly in a young woman. Who are you?"

"Rosamond of Woodstock," said Rosamond, but she did not bow her head and she looked at the Abbess calmly and with courage. For suddenly she was proud. They might have left much, these other women who had renounced the world, but they had not sacrificed the love of a king and the silks and jewels of a queen.

The other nuns cried out in horror, but the Abbess did not flinch. "Come in, Rosamond," she said quietly. "We have prayed for you, to-night, and God has answered our prayer. Come in, my child, to your home."

Rosamond turned back once, to kiss her white horse on his forehead, then she pushed him gently away into the night, that he might find his way back to Woodstock, and stepped through the doorway into the cold shadows of the nunnery.

But they did not hold her for long. She stayed there for a few years, kneeling hour after hour upon the stone floor of the chapel, telling her beads and praying for King Henry and for the fair land of England that she loved, seeing him more and more as the symbol of it and pleading that her sacrifice of all she loved might by the mercy of God give increase of strength to its beauty, greater courage to the man, a deeper green to the grass and a new sparkle to the winding streams that comforted the valleys; an arrogant prayer, she sometimes feared, but one that was unceasing in her heart and on her lips.

And then she died; died as a wild bird will die who is shut in too small a cage. The nuns mourned for her as though she had been the dearest child of each of them, and buried her in the meadows near the river, those meadows where in summer the grass was as high as little children and as full of flowers as the fields of heaven. A grey stone marked her grave, and the nuns planted roses at the head and the foot and hung it with silken draperies and embroideries, as though it were the tomb of a queen.

The years passed and those who had loved Rosamond died and only the roses decked the grave. Centuries passed and the grey stone itself was lost beneath the sea of flowers and grass that flowed over it. Then no man knew where Rosamond's body lay buried; though perhaps the swallows knew, as they dipped and darted beside the river, and the white swans who had once led her home, and the spirit of beauty that lived in that valley and had absorbed her spirit into its own.

People wondered sometimes if the King had ever seen her again. They liked to think that the Abbess had allowed him to see her as she lay dead, dressed in her penitent's dress, with her fair hair hidden under the nun's coif. Master Samuel Daniel, who lived when Elizabeth was Queen and Beaumont Palace and Godstow Nunnery were in ruins, wrote in fair words the thoughts that might have been Henry's as he stood beside the bier before the altar in the nunnery chapel.

> Pitiful mouth, saith he, that living gavest
> The sweetest comfort that my soul could wish,
> Oh! be it lawful now, that dead thou havest
> This sorrowing farewell of a dying kiss;
> And you, fair eyes, containers of my bliss,
> Motives of love, born to be matched never,
> Entombed in your sweet circles, sleep for ever.
>
> Ah, how methinks I see death dallying seeks
> To entertain itself in love's sweet place;
> Decayed roses of discoloured cheeks
> Do yet retain dear notes of former grace;
> And ugly death sits fair within her face,
> Sweet remnants resting of vermilion red,
> That death itself doubts whether she be dead.
>
> Wonder of beauty, Oh! receive these plaints,
> These obsequies, the last that I shall make thee;

For lo ! my soul that now already faints
(That loved thee living, dead will not forsake thee)
Hastens her speedy course to overtake thee.
I'll meet my death, and free myself thereby,
For, ah ! what can he do that cannot die ?

But death did not come to him quite as soon as he wanted it. He governed the country he loved for thirty-five years, one of the best kings and most unhappy men who ever sat upon the throne of England. He was fifty-seven years old before he at last lay dead in the Abbey Church of Fontevraud, deserted by his children and robbed by his servants, his dead body stripped of his royal robes and jewels so that he lay on his bier before the altar as simply and penitentially as Rosamond had done when she lay in the nunnery chapel.

III

" I expect this bit of earth looked much the same to them as it does to us now," said Philip suddenly. " The same river winding through the valley, with the swallows flying beside it, the same fields and the same blue hills. I expect in the end Henry came to love it as much as he loved the woman shut up in the nunnery ; perhaps when she died he felt that her spirit had passed into it ; and I expect he found rest for his heartache looking at it. . . . One does find peace looking out on the world and recounting its wonders to oneself . . . that is, if one can find the words."

He broke off in sudden desperation and Faithful enquired with exquisite tact and sympathy, " Is a poem not going well ? " He knew these writers—Giles had been another of them—and the absurd importance that they attached to their literary efforts. . . . Should a poem go badly there was no use in living any longer, but the right word chased and caught flung open the gates of heaven.

Yet on the whole he thanked his stars he was no poet. The beauty of the world was to Philip his artist's material ; he must always be catching hold of it, rearranging it, trying to fit the stars and the visiting moon into a lyric and to imprison the glory of the sun in a sonnet. And always the elusiveness of everything seemed to torture him ; the sunshine that would not stay in the sonnet, the tail of the comet that got cut off when it was jammed into a lyric, the water that ran away to the sea, the life that escaped from the bodies of birds and butterflies and left behind it a handful of dust to be stamped into the earth. But Faithful, a humble scholar, need not worry either over the uses of beauty or its impermanence. He could just turn it over and over like a picture book and enjoy it.

Philip groaned.

" Perhaps " said Faithful gently, " if you read the poem to me you might see what was wrong with it."

" I might," said Philip doubtfully. " It is about love of England. It seemed all right this morning but now, after archery practice before the Queen, I'm not so sure."

" Try it on me," encouraged Faithful. The phrase " try it on the dog," was not in fashion yet, or he would have felt it to be one that fitted the case.

Philip sighed, fished up his manuscript from down his back, and read.

> " Who hath his fancy pleased
> With fruits of happy sight,
> Let here his eyes be raised
> On Nature's sweetest light ;
> A light which doth dissever
> And yet unite the eyes ;
> A light which, dying never,
> Is cause the looker dies.
>
> She never dies, but lasteth
> In life of lover's heart ;
> He ever dies that wasteth
> In love his chiefest part.
> Thus in her life still guarded
> In never-dying faith ;
> Thus is his death rewarded,
> Since she lives in his death."

Faithful felt a little puzzled. He understood, from the gesture of Philip's hand towards the wide fair landscape in front of them that the lady of the poem was not Rosamond, but the spirit of beauty alive in this country where they lived. . . . But why must they die to keep her alive ?

" A country has no life until men see it and love it," said Philip dreamily, sitting with his chin cupped in his hand, " and no soul until they die for it. Without them it is just a beautiful picture. But once love it and die for it and it has an immortal spirit. . . . Look at the river, silver under the sun, think of the way the grass ripples in summer as though flames were passing over it ; there's something burning there that's been set alight by men's love and kept alight by their death."

Faithful thought this far-fetched, and said so. "Most men don't die for anything particular," he objected. "They die because they are old, or because they catch diseases, or trip over something and fall down."

"Not the lovers in life," said Philip. "What about Christ ? What about Socrates ? What about the patriots ? What about the martyrs ? What about Rosamond herself, who died to the world that Henry's honour might live ? If you love anything at all you will have to die that it may live."

"Only the great lovers," said Faithful.

"The little lovers, too," said Philip. "Even those who don't know they are doing it. How much of the earth of which England is made, and from which the flowers spring, is made up of the dead bodies of men and women who have been buried in it during centuries ? If their bodies make her earth, doesn't something of their spirits make her spirit ? And even while physical life lasts there is the daily death to self of the saints who love God. Love and death are birth and re-birth. When God loved there was creation, when God died there was redemption."

He floated off into a dream, then woke up suddenly to say, "I don't understand men like Walter Raleigh, who want to give their lives to exploring the land beyond the sunset. What do they want with eccentric carnation-coloured birds sitting about in gloomy cedar-trees, and noisy cataracts tall as church towers ? Isn't there beauty enough in this England to love and die for ? There are fair hills here, with stately trees on their proud heights, like those over there on Rats and Mice Hill, and many valleys like this one comforted by silver rivers, and meadows and gardens full of flowers that must be the loveliest in the world ; and I would rather have one of our little well-tuned brown birds singing of Spring in a May-bush than a hundred carnation-coloured creatures squawking in cedar trees. I tell you I would rather die for this country than live to explore a hundred new ones."

"You're talking like an idiot !" said Faithful, suddenly angry. "Why talk about death on a day like this ? Why not talk about life ?"

Philip laughed. " It was Rosamond," he said, " who made me think of death and talk like an idiot." He jumped up and stretched his arms above his head. " I mean to live," he shouted. " Live and be famous."

" What for ? " asked the literal Faithful.

" For a perfect poem," said Philip promptly. " I would rather be a great poet than anything else on earth." He picked up his bow and fingered it thoughtfully. " They say if you shoot an arrow into the air at random you find your fortune where you find your arrow. Let's tell mine. An arrowhead is in my coat of arms, so it ought to be able to tell me the truth."

He took an arrow from Faithful, fitted it into place, laid his body upon the bow and shot. The arrow went far and fast, gliding through the air and disappearing into the sunshine as though it were a part of it.

" Now we shall never find it," grumbled Faithful. " And we shall be late back trying to find it. And if we do find it, how can it possibly tell you anything ? "

" If it's sticking in the ground with the barb hidden and only the feathers showing," laughed Philip, " then I shall be what I want to be, a scholar and poet whose only weapon is a quill pen. But if it's lying flat with the barb showing then I shall have to be what my father wants me to be, a soldier as well." And handing his bow to Faithful he ran off along the bank of the stream, following the flight of his arrow towards Oxford.

" Don't you want to be a soldier ? " panted Faithful, struggling after with the impedimenta.

" No ! " Philip cried vehemently, his voice borne backwards by the wind. " I hate wounds and ugliness and stink and death."

Faithful forbore to point out that he had just been glorifying death. There is always a discrepancy, he had noticed, between what we think when in a moment of vision we have got free from the body and what we think when the body is once more in a position to make life unpleasant for us. It seemed that the arrow meant to be found. They followed along the bank of the stream, pushing their way through the undergrowth, and came upon it quite suddenly, transfixing the speckled breast of a dead thrush.

" I've shot it ! " said Philip in horror. " One of those well-tuned brown birds who sing of Spring in a May-bush ! "

" And it's a young one ! " cried Faithful pitifully.

A cold fear fell upon both boys, making them white to the lips. Philip picked up the thrush, pulled out the arrow and stood holding the limp mass of bloody feathers in his hands.

"A dead singer," he said.

"And a young one," repeated Faithful. His own delight in life was so great that the death of even a young bird seemed to him the greatest of tragedies.

Philip laid the thrush down, wiped the blood off his hand on the grass, broke the arrow in pieces, the cruel grey goose that had killed a singer, and flung it in the stream.

"Anybody would think they feathered arrows from the wings of geese on purpose, just to lay stress upon the idiocy of killing," he said sombrely. "Well, now I know. I shall be famous for my death."

"You don't know at all," growled Faithful. "There's nothing in omens. You're talking more like an idiot than ever."

"I am," agreed Philip with sudden cheerfulness. "A sentimental, conceited idiot. All the trumpet blowing and cheering on Beaumont Fields churned me up."

"Look at the sun," said Faithful. "It's late. If we're to be back in time for the feast in hall we must run."

They ran, their resilient spirits leaping up at every bound. At the sight of Oxford, rising grandly before them against the blue sky, and at the thought of the feast that awaited them at Christ Church, they shouted for joy.

"It's a good city," said Philip, "and a good country, this of ours that we will love and die for," and he began triumphantly singing the last verse of his song.

> "Look, then, and die ; the pleasure
> Doth answer well the pain ;
> Small loss of mortal treasure
> Who may immortal gain.
> Immortal be her graces,
> Immortal is her mind ;
> They, fit for heavenly places ;
> This, heaven in it doth bind.
>
> But who hath fancies pleased
> With fruits of happy sight,
> Let here his eyes be raised
> On Nature's sweetest light ! "

CHAPTER XVII

FAREWELL

Every month hath his flower and every season his contentment.
BESS THROGMORTON.

JOYEUCE remembered that last evening as being the best of all, a never-to-be-forgotten evening that was one of the highlights of her life. There was a great feast in hall at which the Queen and her Court were entertained by the whole College, and afterwards there was music and dancing until the stars paled in the sky, and the birds, twittering under the eaves, made of their morning song a lullaby for sleepy revellers staggering home to bed.

Joyeuce had her own special part to play at this entertainment. She had to arrive as soon as the feasting was over, bringing with her Diccon and Joseph attired as cupids, that they might present to the Queen a heart composed of crimson roses as a token of the devotion of the College. It was the Chancellor's idea and he thought it was a pretty conceit. Canon Leigh thought it was outrageous. The little boys, he considered, were far too small to make such an exhibition of themselves at such a late hour of the evening; and the affair was doubly trying as it meant that all the other children had to go too, at a time when they should have been in bed, because neither he nor they considered it fair that they should be excluded from an entertainment at which the babies of the family were to be present. . . . But he was inclined to look upon the whole performance as an invention of the devil and feared the effect upon the children's characters was bound to be deleterious.

The children, with no thought at all for their characters, were in wild excitement when Joyeuce and Grace dressed them in Mistress Calfhill's big front bedroom. One of the ladies of the Court, let into the secret, had helped Joyeuce and Grace to make for the little boys exquisite but exceedingly skimpy garments of white feathers sewn upon a shell-pink foundation, worn with little feather wings secured across their chests with crossed golden ribbons, golden fillets round their heads and golden bows and arrows clasped in their hands. Their fat little legs and arms were bare and what their father would say when he saw the scantiness of their attire Joyeuce was sure she didn't know. . . . But they looked adorable.

The twins wore their new dresses of daffodil-yellow. They had pleaded for yellow dresses, real grown-up dresses with the kirtles of a deeper yellow than the farthingales—" because the daffodils were them like that, and when we wear them in Christ Church hall we shall be grown-up."

" But you won't," Joyeuce had answered. " Even though you wear grown-up dresses you will still only be little girls, allowed to go and watch a grown-up party for a great treat."

But the twins had only squeaked at this, and shaken their heads very wisely. They knew better. They remembered that day so long ago, the May Day when Faithful had come, when they had run out into the garden and seen the late daffodils dancing in the wind. They had known then that when the candles were burning in Christ Church hall, and they in their yellow dresses were dancing to the music of the viols, that then they would be grown-up. To be grown-up, they had thought, would be like being born again.

" We shall be born again," said Meg, as Joyeuce slipped her yellow kirtle over her head. " We shall do no more lessons with Great-Aunt."

" Born again," echoed Joan, and squeaked in joyous anticipation.

" Silly little poppets ! " laughed Joyeuce, but the words chimed in her mind as though a merry bell were ringing.

Grace meanwhile was cleaning the nails of Will and Thomas, slapping their hair into something like order with forceful applications of a brush dipped in cold water, seeing that their new green doublets and hose were got into the right way round, and tweaking their starched ruffs into the correct position. " Ow ! " they protested, writhing. " Stop it, Grace ! It's effeminate to have clean nails. You should have seen my Lord of Rutland's nails ; black as ink ; we particularly noticed when he passed by in the procession. And my Lord of Oxford——"

" That's enough ! " said Grace firmly, and knitting her

brows and pursing her lips into a round obstinate rosebud she set to work upon Will's left hand with a deftness and determination that in ten minutes had achieved a result of such striking artistry that Joyeuce gasped when she beheld it. . . . Her father was right. . . . Grace's domestic competence was undoubtedly a gift of God.

So it was with a happy but very humble heart that Joyeuce left Grace to keep her eye on the children and dress herself at the same time—a feat that Joyeuce would never even have attempted, let alone accomplished with complete success—and gave all her attention to her own appearance. . . . For this was her betrothal night. . . . Before he led her out to dance tonight, so Nicolas had whispered to her, he would give her his ring. To-night their friends, who had all been told their secret in great confidence, would smile upon them openly and wish them Godspeed. Nicolas's career at Christ Church, after a lamentable failure at the Spring examinations which had in no way disturbed him, was over now and he was free to marry; in a few weeks they would be husband and wife, riding away from the Fair Gate to an unknown life together, leaving Grace to bear with ease the load that had seemed so heavy to Joyeuce.

Suddenly, as she stood before her glass brushing out her lovely honey-coloured hair, her eyes were blinded by tears. . . . Her heavy load. . . . But was it really as heavy as she had thought? In laying it down she would be losing this home that she adored, set in this incomparable city, her father who so tenderly loved her, the little children who had been to her like her own. She put down her brush and pressed her hands over her eyes, fighting her tears. How could she leave them? Until this moment she had not realised how deeply she loved them. Why must sorrow and joy always be twined together like this? She had won her desire, and at the heart of it there was this pain. Why? Why? . . . Born again . . . Once more the twins' words rang in her mind like a little bell to comfort her. Every fresh beginning was a new birth and must have its pain as well as its joy, and without these fresh beginnings there could be no life, without them we should turn sour like stagnant water in a pond. And always, Joyeuce thought, the joy of a fresh beginning lures us on, outweighing the pain, dancing before us like a flame, so that hurrying to catch it the life in us keeps fresh and clear as a running stream. She wiped her eyes and picked up her brush with a smile. . . . In a few minutes now she would be running to meet Nicolas.

She and Grace both had new dresses, made and embroidered by themselves. Joyeuce had a green silk farthingale because Nicolas liked her best in " green sleeves," over a pale-pink kirtle embroidered with rosebuds, and Grace had chosen a very matronly farthingale of lavender colour, over a cream-coloured kirtle embroidered with purple pansies. They wore coifs of lovely lace on their shining hair and little satin shoes.

" We do look nice," said Grace, surveying herself in the glass with satisfaction. " We shall look as nice as any there . . . probably nicer."

Joyeuce flung her arms round the compact, rounded body of her younger sister. " You have such confidence, Grace," she cried, hugging her. " You never find things too much for you, do you ? "

" Certainly not," said Grace with decision. " I don't worry about them beforehand. . . . Now you," she added, with a comically pious expression upon her round rosy face, and plump hands folded at the waist, " cross every bridge before you get there, and in anticipating disasters you entirely fail to remember the powers of endurance that they invariably bring with them."

" You are quite right, Grace," murmured Joyeuce humbly, her eyes cast down that the twinkle in them might be hidden. " But shall I be able to endure it if I don't look as nice as the Court ladies, and Nicolas is ashamed of me ? "

" He won't be," said Grace with decision. " I said to Nicolas the other day that the more I saw of other people the more I liked us, and he quite agreed with me."

II

Joyeuce never forgot the sight that met her eyes when the doors of the hall were flung open by a servitor and she and the children went in. It was dusk now, and hundreds of candles were burning in great sconces set all round the walls, and their lovely light, kinder than sunshine, softer than moonlight, gave to the scene a radiant loveliness that made her gasp. The feast was not yet quite over and at the long table on the great dais at the far end of the hall the Queen was still sitting with the Chancellor, Dean Godwin, the dons of Christ Church and the senior members of her Court. The candlelight shone upon the rich colours of their dresses, upon their sparkling jewels and laughing faces, upon the silver bowls piled with fruit that stood upon the dark shining table, and upon the red wine in the Venetian glasses, held high to drink a toast At the tables in the lower part of the hall sat the scholars with the younger maids of honour and the Court pages, dressed in their smartest, all on their best behaviour, but glowing with happiness, their faces as soft as flowers in the candlelight and their eyes like stars as they too held up their tankards of ale—not Venetian glasses and red wine for the smaller fry—waiting in palpitant excitement for the coming toast. . . . From where she stood Joyeuce could see Nicolas dressed in royal blue, his cheeks flushed and his eyes blazing, Faithful beside him in sober dove-grey slashed with lilac, Philip Sidney beautiful and serious in olive green, Walter Raleigh—what was he doing here?—in blazing scarlet, sitting beside a lovely little girl dressed in white like a snow-drop. . . . And then she saw no more, for the Chancellor was on his feet, the whole crowd of them rising with him, and the toast was given.

"The Queen. Vivat Regina!"

Such a roar of cheering and vivats went up that the great rafters of the hall, soaring up into a darkness that the candle-light did not touch, must surely have been shaken by the noise of it. Then silence fell, for the Queen had risen, motioning them all to their seats again with one long pale hand.

She was dressed in pearl-coloured satin to-night, slashed with gold, and great rubies burned on her breast and on her shining hair. Joyeuce noticed with surprise that she was shorter than she had thought; her great dignity and splendid carriage made her seem taller than she was. She stood straight as a ramrod, with something almost masculine about the hard clear lines of her face and her stiffly braced shoulders, a something that was echoed in the depth and strength of her voice that carried effortlessly to the furthest corners of the hall. "She is indomitable," was the thought in more than one mind. "While she lives we are safe."

"Greetings to you, my scholars," she said, "and God's blessing upon you all. This is my last night with you, and my heart would be heavy were it not that you have given to me a memory that will be my possession for always. All my life I have loved learning, and because of my love my thoughts have turned often to this house of learning that my father founded. Often I have thought of it, pictured it, hoped that I should one day stay within its walls, and now that my hope has come true I find, as so seldom in life, that the fulfilment of my wish is sweeter even that the anticipation of it. I have found this house to be all I had hoped it would be, and more. In the quietness of its gardens, and of the rooms where I have lodged, I have found peace, and in the fellowship of learned men who have attained wisdom, and of young scholars who are striving for it, I have found inspiration. And let me tell you, my friends, that peace and inspiration are the two gifts of God that we most need in this our pilgrimage. If we have peace in our hearts the disorder and cruelty of life will not overwhelm us with despair, and if we have even for a short while seen that flash of light from another country that men call inspiration we shall have the courage to attempt, however unsuccessfully, to do our part in quieting the disorder and quelling the cruelty ; until we have battled through them and our rest is won. . . . And it is in such houses as this, my scholars, that we find that peace and inspiration. . . . From the days of the good Saint Frideswide onwards, holy men and women have lived here before you. Every moment of solace that came to them as they prayed, every fight for knowledge that won for them the quietude of achievement, was as a drop of water filling up the well of peace that stands in all ancient places. Drink deep of it, and leave behind you for those who come after, as they did, that something of yourselves that is imperishable. And what shall I say of inspiration ? You cannot have lived here and not known it. The stuff of those other men's lives is woven with your own, threads of heavenly silver lightening the earth-brown weft. Every pealing of the bells that called them to prayer in years that are past must seem to you a trumpet call, every sight of the spire that they raised to the glory of God must be to you as the sight of a banner in the sky. So go forth into the world, my scholars, to fight and work for your Queen and your country, with these things as imperishable memories in your hearts."

When once she began to speak it was usual for the Queen's Grace to be carried away by her own eloquence that she went on a great deal longer than was necessary, but to-night she seemed to have upset herself by her own emotion, or else the dramatic sense of a consummate actress made it appear that she had, for she came to an abrupt end and sat down rather suddenly, to a second outbreak of applause even more thunderous than the first.

This was the moment chosen for Diccon and Joseph to do their part. They had been rehearsed in it very carefully, yet it was with a beating heart that Joyeuce launched them forth upon their journey up the space that had been kept clear between the tables, leading directly from the hall door to the foot of the dais. They had done it beautifully when they had practised in an empty, quiet hall, but now that they had to make their way through a crowd, blinded by the lights and deafened by the cheering, she was afraid that Diccon would roar and Joseph turn tail and fly, or that upon reaching the dais they might drop the heart of roses and fall upon the food, or alternatively Diccon might bite the Queen and Joseph, a nervy child, might be sick. . . . There seemed no end to the frightful things that might happen.

But she had reckoned without the sense of pattern that there is in children. As swans will fly one behind the other in perfect formation, as little birds will lean their breasts against their nests to make of them a perfect round, so Diccon and Joseph knew instinctively that they were playing their part in something that had design. They must walk in a straight line to a given point, they must make certain movements, or the whole thing would be ruined. So their bare feet padded unflinchingly up the aisle through the cheering scholars, their little heads were held high and the chubby hands that grasped their golden bows were without a tremor. Between them they held the big heart of crimson roses, which they dropped only twice, and retrieved again without a moment's hesitation. They made straight for the gleaming figure of the Queen, like two little moths fluttering to a candle, and she, when she heard the low ripple of laughter that swept up the hall and saw them trotting towards her as though it were a breeze that carried them, left her seat and came to stand at the head of the flight of steps that led up to the dais. They negotiated these steps with some difficulty, but great determination, and collapsed rather suddenly into two little feathery balls at her feet. At this point they should have held up the heart of red roses in their arms and recited, line and line about, a pretty little verse about its being the heart of the College laid at the feet of a Queen ; but they forgot it ; Joseph propped the heart carefully against her farthingale, as though he were leaning a picture against a wall, and Diccon, gazing up at her with his green eyes as unblinking as a cat's, said, " For you," continuing further, with his fat forefinger pointed at a ruby drop hanging from her necklace, the very image of the one he had seen and howled for in the window of the aurifabray, " Pretty. Diccon wants it."

The Queen was in a good mood to-night and was not offended. She listened, laughing, as Dean Godwin repeated to her the forgotten rhyme, then took off her necklace and tossed it to the Chancellor. " Detach the ruby," she commanded, and then bent to take Diccon's face in her hands. " 'Tis a bold, bad face," she commented, " but it will belong one day to a bold, bad buccaneer who will sail the high seas and capture much wealth for his Queen. Is that not so, little cupid ? " Diccon made no answer, but freeing his face from her hands—mercifully without biting—stretched out his hand for the ruby.

But Joseph's behaviour was beyond reproach. When asked if he, too, would not like a pretty trinket, he gave her his lovely grave smile, shook his head and became absorbed in re-propping the heart upside down, because propped right way up it had fallen over. " An intelligent cupid," commented the Queen. " A poppet of much concentration." And feeling in her hanging pocket she produced a little Latin copy of the psalms, bound in crimson velvet, and gave it to him. He took it shyly, smiling at her, and immediately opened and became immersed in it, holding it upside down. . . . Then, at a signal from the Dean, one of the scholars stepped forward and picking up the little cupids removed them, one under each arm ; and immediately, the thing being over and the pattern completed, Diccon broke into roars of anger and fury that could be heard right out in the quadrangle.

III

When the little boys had been taken away to bed by Dorothy Goatley, who had been waiting outside the hall door to perform this necessary but arduous office—Diccon being by now in such a rage at his removal that carrying him was like carrying a young earthquake—Joyeuce felt free to enjoy herself. No more anxieties now, only such pleasure as she had not known since that evening at the Tavern.

With lightning speed the servitors had cleared the tables and pushed them back against the walls to leave the hall clear for dancing. The musicians grouped in one of the big oriel windows were tuning their instruments, the soft twanging of the strings sending delicious tremors through Joyeuce as though fingers plucked at her heart; and the Queen, who loved dancing as dearly as any there, was being handed down the steps of the dais by the Chancellor. The candles seemed to burn yet more brightly, and there was a soft swishing of silks and caressing murmur of voices as young and lovely lovers moved towards each other over the gleaming floor. . . . And Joyeuce found Nicolas before her, beautiful as she had never seen him, smiling confidently down at her, lifting her hand and putting his ring upon it with a certain arrogance of possession that gave her such happiness that she gave a little stifled cry of joy, like a child who is lifted out of darkness into safety. He had taken her, and with such complete certainty that her always questioning heart found sudden rest.

"It is an emerald," she heard him saying, "because of that arbour in the Tavern garden. Those green vine leaves seemed then to be showing me how I should love you. . . . Gently. . . . Perhaps I shall grieve you sometimes, Joyeuce, perhaps you will find it hard to be patient with me. But I shall always love you. I shall always be faithful."

"I too," whispered Joyeuce. "I shall be faithful."

Then the lovely music of the pavane floated out into Christ Church hall, and he swung her into the dance.

Faithful and Grace, sitting together on a wooden table beside the great open fireplace, filled now with branches of greenery and bunches of late summer flowers, watched the gay scene in utter contentment. They looked a comical couple as they sat there hand in hand. Their legs, which did not reach the floor, were swinging childishly, but upon their faces was the wise, owl-like look of contemplative grandparents. Faithful could not dance. Grace had tried hard to teach him, and he had tried hard to learn, but he fell over his feet in such a distressing way that they had given it up as a bad job. "Never mind," Grace had said cheerfully. "It is perhaps just as well. If we do not dance we shall have more leisure to devote our minds to higher things."

The higher things were at this moment criticism of the scene before them, and gossip about the lovely figures of the dancers who bowed and swayed before them like flowers in the wind. . . . For Faithful, like many other learned men, liked a little gossip.

"Surely Master Walter Raleigh has no business to be here?" asked Grace.

"He got in through a window," said Faithful. "No one in authority has noticed him yet."

"They soon will," said Grace, "in that blazing scarlet doublet. Who is the girl he is dancing with? The pale little thing in white?"

"They say she is Mistress Bess Throgmorton, a little orphan girl whom the Queen has taken under her wing. She will be one of the maids of honour as soon as she is old enough."

"Do you think she is pretty?" asked Grace doubtfully.

Faithful regarded the slender figure of the lovely little girl with the kindling eye of admiration, but he answered stoutly, "She is not my style. Too pale."

Grace, happily conscious of her own pink cheeks and plump chest, sighed with satisfaction and turned her attention to two figures, in royal blue and pale green, who were as lovely as any there. "I had no idea," she said in shocked tones, "that Joyeuce was so worldly."

Faithful, too, turned his attention upon his future sister-in-law, and the sight of her gave him quite a shock. He had not realised that she could look so beautiful. The stiffness that used to mar her slender figure had all gone. She and Nicolas moved together through the stately figure of the dance with such grace that everyone was looking at them. But Joyeuce, usually so shy, seemed not to know that. Her face was flushed, her lips were parted and her eyes shining as though she saw a vision. But Faithful did not think that she looked worldly, he thought she looked the opposite.

"She looks," he said, "as though she were looking through a peep-hole at something."

"At what?" asked Grace.

"Some unchanging landscape," he murmured dreamily, and fell to wondering about love and joy and the connection between them. It is always love of something, he thought, that brings joy; love of some human being, of beauty or of learning. Love is the unchanging landscape, he thought, at which, among the changes and chances of this mortal life, we sometimes look through the peep-hole of joy; the love of God of which human love is a tiny echo. To be lost in it will be to have eternal life. One can know no more than that.

"Good heavens!" cried Grace. "I thought the twins had gone home to bed, but there they are—dancing!"

Will and Thomas, who thought dancing an everrated entertainment, had departed with some like-minded scholars to the kitchen, in the rear of the retreating food, but the twins were still here, dancing in a far corner of the hall with some little noblemen not much older than themselves. And they too, as they gravely pointed their small feet, executed their wobbly curtsys and turned their plump persons this way and that in the figures of the dance, looked as Joyeuce had looked; so happy that they seemed to be seeing a vision; and all the hundreds of candles, burning round Christ Church hall, did not shine so brightly as the yellow frocks they wore. "They look like Spring," said Faithful. "They look like love and warmth and sunshine. All the stars must have danced when they were born."

"Did they make you of starlight?" asked Walter Raleigh of Bess Throgmorton, fingering a fold of her white dress, looking down boldly into the bright eyes that twinkled so merrily up at him.

The dance had ended and they stood in one of the oriel windows, away from the crowd, well back in the secretive shadows whose black background gave to her whiteness a star-like glimmer. She dropped her eyes shyly before his that were so bold, for she was only a little girl yet, one of the youngest there; and suddenly the moon, coming out from behind a cloud, stained the snowy whiteness of her dress and bowed, white-coifed head with all the colours of the stained-glass window behind her, pink and blue and lilac and palest green. It was like a sudden blooming of flowers in mid-winter, it was like the flooding of passion over the whiteness of her virginity, and Raleigh flung his arms round her with such headlong vehemence that she cried out a little, struggling like a young bird that has been snared and caught too soon.

"Why are you frightened?" he asked her. "You love me, don't you?"

She was still then, and whispered, "Yes."

"I love you, too," he announced, so loudly that she feared

the whole hall would hear. " And one day I will have you for my wife."

" I have known you one hour," she whispered sadly, her head still bowed, " and I shall never see you again."

" You will," said Raleigh, still loudly. " I will find a way. I will have you for mine, even if I have to come to Court and steal you from under the Queen's nose."

But she shook her head. The maids of honour might not marry without the Queen's permission ; and besides, she already knew something of men and their ways. " You will forget," she murmured.

" I never forget what I want," he said, " and I get it. Look at me. Do you think I look as though I would forget ? "

She dared to raise her head, then, and look at him, seeing afresh the bold penetrating blue eyes, the obstinacy and impetuous strength of the face bent above her. " I think," she said, " that you will always get what you want ; or else you will die trying to get it. What else to you want, besides me ? "

He pulled her eagerly down on the window seat and began to tell her, holding her so close against him that she thrilled to the pulse of excitement beating in his body and to the eager whispering of his warm, vehement voice. " All sorts of things. I want to sail a tall ship into the west to find the land beyond the sunset, so that the Queen may have a better Indies than the King of Spain. That's a wonderful land, Bess. Birds of white and carnation sing in tall cedar trees, and the stones are all made of gold and silver."

" Do you want gold and silver so badly ? " asked Bess a little doubtfully ; and she shivered, thinking of that tall ship that would carry him away from her.

" I want masses of gold," said Raleigh hotly. " I mean to sail round the world to look for it, and I mean to make it, too, for I shall be alchemist as well as sailor. We shall never do away with poverty and misery, never build a new world, until we have wealth ; lots and lots of wealth."

" One can be happy in poverty," whispered Bess.

He snorted in contempt. He never had any use for poverty. " Only the well-off think so," he said. " Do you know what my idea of heaven is ? A place that is all shining with jewels. I've made up a verse about it.

"And when we
Are filled with immortality,
Then the holy paths we'll travel,
Strewed with rubies thick as gravel,
Ceilings of diamonds, sapphire floors,
High walls of coral and pearl bowers."

"Dreams! Dreams!" said a woman's low voice, and looking up the two culprits saw three figures standing by them in their shadowy window, splendid figures that even in the dimness gleamed and sparkled. The Queen, the Chancellor and Dean Godwin. Little Bess, as she slipped out of Raleigh's arms and slid to her feet to make her curtsy, was gasping with terror, but Raleigh bowed with the flourish that never deserted him.

"And who is this who had made away with my little Bess?" asked the Queen tartly, and she motioned him towards the light.

"Master Walter Raleigh of Oriel," said Dean Godwin severely. "He very kindly played Arcite in our play, our own Arcite having met with an accident. But what he is doing here to-night I do not know."

"I came through the window," said Raleigh loudly, "that I might feast my eyes upon Her Grace."

"It seems to me," said the Queen, with increased tartness, "that it is upon the little Bess, not the big one, that you have been feasting them." But face to face with the future Captain of her Guard she could not but smile: he gave promise of becoming a very fine figure of a man, and she was always as wax in the hands of a handsome man. "And what were these dreams of which you murmured?" she asked him. "These dreams of carnation-coloured birds and floors of sapphire? Dreams, young man, are useless things that lead you nowhere."

"I venture to disagree with Your Grace," said Raleigh, his head up. "All achievement is born of dreams followed bravely to an unknown destination."

A figure passing between them and the light threw a shadow on his face and the Queen shivered with a sudden icy little premonition. To what destiny would his dreams bring himself and little Bess? To what end of blood and death and agonising sorrow? He had answered her impudently, and she had meant to rebuke him for it, but now she could not. "You must bring Bess back into the hall," was all she said. "She is only a little girl and she must not be played with."

She turned and went away, followed by the Dean and the Chancellor, but Raleigh, before he obeyed her, turned and flung his arms once more round Bess. "It was not play!" he whispered fiercely. "I have loved you and chosen you in my happiest hour. You must not forget me."

"I'll not forget," said little Bess.

The Queen, with the Chancellor upon her right and Dean Godwin upon her left, passed on down the hall through the lines of scholars, smiling at their eager faces, pausing now and then to ask a question or recognize a familiar face. "Which are my scholars of Westminster?" she asked the Dean, and there was immediately a great commotion in the crowd, Westminster plunging to the fore with Ipswich kicked viciously into the background.... But she would not have that.... When she had spoken sweet words to her own Westminster she had Ipswich rescued from a sprawling position under the tables and spoke soothing words to it of its founder, the great Cardinal, of his love for this College and the faithful service he gave to his king. "Love this fair house as he did," she bade them, "and serve me as loyally as he served my father." They promised her to do so, gazing at her with eyes full of worship, and hastened, as soon as her back was turned to retaliate upon Westminster with hard and well-placed kicks.

The Queen passed on down the line, pausing next for Philip Sidney to be presented to her by the Chancellor. "A fair boy," she murmured to the infatuated uncle, as Philip bowed low before her. "A boy of whom we shall both be proud." And again, as Philip straightened himself and his eyes met hers, she felt that stirring of premonition. She remembered her own words, spoken at the end of her speech, "Go forth into the world. Fight and work for your Queen and country." She had said that word "fight" carelessly, hardly stopping to think what she meant by it, but now it seemed to her that beyond the walls enclosing this space of light and laughter she could hear the galloping hoofs of the Rider on the Red Horse. She hated war; above all things she asked for her reign the blessing of peace. Would she ever have to endure the agony of sending these boys and others like them over the seas to meet the Red Horseman? She saw all their fair lives threatened by terror and blood and wounds. She saw herself, an older woman, weary and sick at heart, standing up with a proud face to make bold speeches, doing her best to hearten men for death as just now she had been heartening boys for life. . . . Speeches . . . Speeches . . . How sick of them she would be before the end. She looked again at Philip Sidney's face and felt a sharp pang of grief, as sharp as any she would feel in the years to come when she would weep for his death and refuse to be comforted, vowing that she had lost her mainstay. It was a terrible thing to be the Queen of England. It was a burden too heavy to be borne. She turned abruptly away, without speaking another word to Philip. . . . The Chancellor, much annoyed at her neglect, followed her with a heightened colour.

But her next encounter cheered her. Joyeuce in her pale green gown and Nicolas in his royal blue, standing hand in hand, were a couple to challenge attention. Joyeuce she remembered as a fragile wraith who had hovered behind Dame Cholmeley on her arrival at her lodgings, but Nicolas's face puzzled her. She remembered the eyebrows so wickedly tilted at the corners, the laughing black eyes and the strong chin with the cleft in it, but she could not remember where she had seen them last. Nicolas, putting his hand into his doublet and bringing it out with a crumpled red rose lying on the palm, enlightened her. " Ever since the Queen of England gave it me I have worn it next my heart," he lied superbly.

" The troubadour ! " she laughed. " The young man who sang me a lullaby under my window. And what can I do for you, good sir ? "

Nicolas gripped Joyeuce's hand tightly and eyed his sovereign with boldness. " With the permission of Your Grace, my bride and I would like to come to Court."

The Dean broke in here with a neat little memorandum of Nicolas's family tree, which was well rooted in wealth, well watered with blue blood, had been quite satisfactory in growth and gave promise of loyal foliage in the future. The recitation was well received. " You shall come," said the Queen.

And instantly joy, like dawn, broke over the two faces before her in such a flood of brightness that her late sadness was suddenly lightened. It was sweet to have it in her power to give such pleasure. It was sweet to know, as she knew, that her people found in her the fulfilment of all hope and the inspiration of all action. Beyond the walls that enclosed her, out in the night, she remembered that there stretched the woods and hills and valleys of her country, and the towns and homesteads that sheltered the men and women who were her people; a most fair and lovely country, a people compounded of courage, humour and kindliness. And they seemed to her, as she thought of them, to be invincible. The galloping hoofs of the Rider on the Red Horse might pass over them, but they would still endure. It was not so little a thing to be the Queen of England. It was not so little a thing to say of this country and this people, " They are mine."

IV

The sky was clear cold green, and in the east the morning star blazed gloriously between bars of flaming cloud, when Nicolas supported the slightly wavering footsteps of Walter Raleigh home to Oriel. Everyone else had gone home long ago. They had lingered behind for a few last drinks with some kindred spirits, and now they seemed to themselves to be quite alone in the lovely silence of the dawn. They walked slowly, drinking in the clear air like draughts of cold water, feeling its freshness like a benediction on their hot faces. . . . Not that they showed many signs, in the outward man, that this dawn was the climax of a night of revelry. . . . Their two brilliant figures, scarlet and royal blue, were both still unruffled, both of them having that gift for keeping tidy under the most unlikely circumstances shared alike by robins, buttercups, cats, tigers, and all those dowered with stout hearts, self-confidence, and that beauty that draped over the iron foundation of strong nerves is not easily frayed by contact with the sorrows and entertainments of this exhausting world. Though their faces were flushed they were becomingly flushed, though their hair was tumbled it had fallen into that graceful abandon that is more pleasing to the eye than correctitude. The only noticeable signs of a slight tendency to insobriety were in Raleigh's legs, Nicolas' solemn concern for them, and an exceedingly poetical frame of mind in both. Raleigh, as always when in his cups, was composing scraps and shreds of verse so lovely that they seemed to Nicolas to have floated straight out of that beautiful dawn where the morning star burned between bars of flaming cloud.

> " She is neither white nor brown,
> But as the heavens fair,
> There is none hath a form so divine
> In the earth or the air."

He sighed heavily, and looked up at the fleecy clouds above his head as though challenging them to form an image lovelier than the one he had in his mind. "Look where you're going," said Nicolas, easing him round the corner of the quadrangle towards Peckwater Inn. "And you can't have met a maiden as lovely as that to-night; there wasn't one there; except Joyeuce." Raleigh rolled upon him an injured and rebuking eye and began again.

> "Such a one *did* I meet, good sir,
>   Such an angelic face,
> Who like a queen, like a nymph did appear
>   By her gait, by her grace."

They pursued their wavering way to Canterbury College, where he cried out in despair so profound that he nearly lost his footing and sent them both sprawling.

> "Know that Love is a careless child,
>   And forgets promise past;
> He is blind, he is deaf when he list
>   And in faith never fast."

"Sometimes," said Nicolas gently, remembering the pledge he had given to Joyeuce, "he remembers."

"Sometimes," murmured Raleigh dolefully, but as they crossed Shidyard Street he seemed to change his mind, for his face lightened, and when they had reached the gate of Oriel he propped himself carefully against it and faced Nicolas with a sudden blaze of triumph.

> "But love is a durable fire
>   In the mind ever burning;
> Never sick, never old, never dead,
>   From itself never turning."

Then he turned and disappeared, admitted by a watchful porter who delighted, as did Heatherthwayte for Nicolas, to keep the eccentric hours of his exits and entrances hidden from the eye of authority.

Nicolas strolled homewards through the lovely morning, that grew with every moment richer in beauty and promise. At the doorway that led to the room he still shared with Faithful, under the carved pomegranate of Catherine of Aragon, he paused to look back at the towers and spires so delicately pencilled against the glorious dawn sky that curved above them in the semblance of a great circle. He felt a pang of pain to think that he must so soon leave it all, but yet he had at the same time a glorious feeling of permanence. Raleigh at the last had been quite right. Love was an unchanging thing, not an emotion, but an element in which the whole world had its being. All the lovely things upon earth, beauty and truth and courage, were faint pictures of it, even as the puddles of rain water at his feet held a faint picture of the fiery sky bending above the earth. And in the mind of man, too, the flame was caught and held; in his own mind whose strength and vigour made it possible for his eyes to see this picture of a fair city and a golden sky, for his soul to face life vowed to integrity and courage, for his heart to feel for Joyeuce an affection so strong that he dared to call it by the name of that eternal and embracing love.

> Love is a durable fire
> In the mind ever burning;
> Never sick, never old, never dead,
> From itself never turning.

v

That same day the Queen left Oxford. It was now early September, a calm and lovely day, one of those soft blue days of early autumn when the colour of the sky seems to have soaked into the earth. The city itself seemed built of blue air, and the flowers in the gardens, the late roses, the hollyhocks and Michaelmas daisies, had drawn a thin blue veil over their bright colours. When evening came again the shadows would be very deep and very blue and the calling of the birds would be very clear in the stillness.

But now, in the morning, the city was full of noise and bustle. The Queen was to ride out of East Gate and up through Shotover Forest on the first stage of her journey to London, and once more scholars lined the route, from the Fair Gate to East Gate, with the townspeople packed behind them. Once more garlands were slung across the street, tapestries hung from every window, and the bells rang out to speed the Queen upon her way. But though all was noise and bustle and excitement there was an undercurrent of sadness about this day; the longed-for visit was over and it might be many years before the Queen's Grace came again. Yet mixed with the sadness there was still rejoicing, for during this time of heightened living dreams and visions and ideals had glowed more radiantly, and when the Queen had left the city the life she left behind her would burn the more brightly because she had been.

So when the cavalcade left Christ Church it was greeted by another great roar of cheering, and shouts of " Vivat Regina ! Vivat Regina ! " rolled up Fish Street and down the High Street as the procession wound its way down through the town. The departure was perhaps a lovelier sight than the arrival had been, for the beautiful curves of the High Street lent themselves to a processional passing. It was like a lovely ribbon of colour slowly unwinding itself between the cheering crowds and the gabled houses, slipping downwards to coil away for ever into the green and silent woods.

The Queen was on horseback to-day, sitting her white mare superbly, wearing a long blue habit whose skirts nearly swept the cobbles and a tall blue hat with white plumes in it. She was quite alone that all the people might see her, with the Chancellor, Vice-Chancellor and heads of houses riding in front and the Court behind, and she took most gracious notice of all that was done to show her love and honour. She missed nothing of the long and polished Latin oration delivered outside the Fair Gate by Master Tobie Matthews, an M.A. of Christ Church, even though she was trying to mount her spirited horse at the time and it was difficult to fix her attention on it, and as she rode down High Street she reined in her horse that she might have read to her the copies of verses bemoaning her departury that were hung upon the walls of All Souls and Universite College. And all the while she was waving to the people, raising a laughing face to the little children crowded at the windows, smiling when armfuls of flowers were flung upon the cobbles and the sweet smell of bruised September roses came up to her from beneath her horse's feet. When she had passed the people strained forward, leaning perilously from windows, standing on tiptoe to see over each other's heads and shoulders while tears ran down their faces, trying to catch a last glimpse of that dazzling blue and white figure on the white horse, the young and lovely Queen whom they might never see again. Then the cavalcade passed under East Gate and they had lost her. Sadly they turned homeward.

Under Magdalen tower the pealing bells were stilled and the procession was halted that the Mayor and city fathers gathered there to take their leave, might take it with the customary speeches. But it was noticed that though she smiled and bowed at the correct moment the attention of the Queen's Grace seemed inclined to wander; her eyes were continually leaving the earnest perspiring faces of the city fathers and gazing at Magdalen tower, soaring up into the blue sky above her, its ornamented belfry fretting the sky like wing-tips; and when the speeches were over and the farewells said, and the horses once more curveting forward, she looked up at it and raised her hand in greeting, as though it stood beside the East Gate like a veritable presence set to guard the city, one whom she would remember and who would remember her.

The Vice-Chancellor and heads of houses, loth to say good-bye, rode with the Queen and her Court up the bridle path through the woods and out on to the heights of Shotover, and here they halted for positively the last speech from the Provost of Oriel, for the last farewells, for the last promises that while life went on they would never forget.

Then the Queen abruptly wheeled her horse away from the laughing throng of courtiers and scholars and rode by herself to the brow of the hill where Faithful had stood on May morning. She saw the valley full of green trees that were already touched here and there with the colours of autumn, backed by low blue hills resting against the sky. Her eyes followed the curve of the valley until they reached a certain place that she knew of, where the towers rose out of the autumn haze. It looked like a fragile city spun out of dreams, so small that she could have held it on the palm of her hand and blown it away like silver mist. Perhaps she knew at that moment how many years would pass before she visited that city again, years of unceasing work and anxiety that would never break her spirit but would strip her of her beauty and make of her a weary old woman in a red wig. Perhaps it was because she doubted if the shouts of " Vivat Regina ! " that had greeted the young Queen would be as full of love when they greeted the old woman, that she wept, or perhaps it was because she knew quite well that the passing of the years would make no difference, but it was reported by those who had followed her that as she raised her hand in farewell to the city her eyes were full of tears.

" Farewell ! " she cried. " God bless you and increase your sons in number, holiness and virtue. Farewell, Oxford. Farewell. Farewell."

Book Three

THE DEAN'S WATCH

For Mildred Woodgate

EPITAPH IN LYDFORD CHURCHYARD

Here lies in a horizontal position the outside case of

George Routledge, Watchmaker

Integrity was the mainspring and prudence the regulator of all the actions of his life; humane, generous and liberal, His hand never stopped till he had relieved distress.

So nicely regulated were his movements that he never went wrong, except when set going by people who did not know his key. Even then he was easily set right again. He had the art of disposing of his time so well, till his hours glided away, his pulse stopped beating.

He ran down, November 14, 1801, aged 57, In hopes of being taken in hand by his Maker, Thoroughly cleaned, repaired, wound up, and set going in the world to come, when time shall be no more.

Contents

CHAPTER		PAGE
I	Isaac	11
II	The City	24
III	Angel Lane	42
IV	Job	55
V	The Watch	71
VI	Fountains	87
VII	Miss Montague	100
VIII	Sunday Morning	119
IX	The Mouse	135
X	Bella	151
XI	Swithins Lane	169
XII	King Lear	187
XIII	The Umbrella	209
XIV	Advent	223
XV	The Celestial Clock	245
XVI	The Cathedral	267
XVII	Christmas	287
XVIII	The Swans	302

CHAPTER I *Isaac*

I

THE candle flame burned behind the glass globe of water, its light flooding over Isaac Peabody's hands as he sat at work on a high stool before his littered work-table. Now and then he glanced up at it over his crooked steel-rimmed spectacles and thought how beautiful it was. The heart of the flame was iris-coloured with a veining of deep blue spread like a peacock's tail against the crocus and gold that gave the light. He had oil lamps in the shop and workshop but lamplight was not as beautiful as his candle flame behind the globe of water, and for work requiring great precision its light was not actually quite so good. And he liked to feel that through the centuries men of his trade, clockmakers, watchmakers, goldsmiths and silversmiths, had worked just as he was working now, in their workshops after the day's business was over, alone and quiet, the same diffused light bathing their hands and the delicate and fragile thing they worked upon. It banished loneliness to think of those others, and he was not so afraid of the shapeless darkness that lay beyond the circle of light. He did not like shapelessness. One of his worst nightmares was the one when he himself became shapeless and ran like liquid mud into the dark.

For any painter it would have been a joy to sit in the

corner of Isaac's workshop, unseen by Isaac, and paint him in his pool of light, but only Rembrandt could have painted the shadows that were beyond the light. They seemed to hang from a vast height, as in Rembrandt's Adoration of the Shepherds, and if here they were looped back to show not the holy family but one grotesque old man, yet adoring wonder was not absent, for Isaac had never grown up and things still amazed him. He was amazed now as he looked worshipfully at the beautiful thing he held. This child's gift of wonder could banish his many years but the balance was precariously held.

He looked safe enough tonight in his halo of warm light. He was a round-shouldered little man with large feet and a great domed and wrinkled forehead, the forehead of a profound thinker. Yet actually he thought very little about anything except clocks and watches, and about them he not so much thought as burned. But he could feel upon a variety of subjects, and perhaps it was the intensity of his feeling that had furrowed his forehead, lined his brown parchment face and whitened the straggling beard that hid his receding chin. His eyes were very blue beneath their shaggy eyebrows and chronic indigestion had crimsoned the tip of his button nose. His hands were red, shiny and knobbly, but steady and deft. He dressed in the style of twenty years ago, the style of the eighteen-fifties, because the clothes he had had then were not yet what he called worn out. His pegtopped trousers were intensively repaired across the seat but that did not show beneath his full-skirted bottle-green coat. The coat was faded now, and so was the old soft crimson bow tie he wore, but the dim colours were eminently paintable against the great draped shadows, and richly illumined by the moony light. His soft childish mouth was sucked in with concentration except when now and then he pouted his lips and there emerged from them a thin piping whistle.

He was happy tonight for one of his good times was on the way. Everything he did today, anything he saw or handled, had shape as though the sun was rising behind it. Presently it would happen to him, the warmth and glow of self-forgetfulness, and after that for a few moments or a few days he would be safe.

He had finished. The Dean's watch was now once more repaired and he knew he could not have made a better job of it. He held it open in the palm of his hand and gazed at it with veneration, his jeweller's eyepiece in his eye. It was inscribed "George Graham fecit, 1712". At that date Graham had been at the height of his powers. The inscription took Isaac back to the old bow-windowed shop in Fleet Street, next door to the Duke of Marlborough's Head tavern, which had been a place of pilgrimage for him when as a lad he had served his apprenticeship in Clerkenwell. Graham had worked in that shop, and lived and died in the humble rooms above it. Charles II's horologist, Thomas Tompion, whom men called the father of English clockmaking, had been Graham's uncle. Both men had been masters of the Clockmakers' Company and they had been buried in the same tomb in Westminster Abbey. Whenever he held the Dean's watch in his hands Isaac remembered that George Graham's hands had also held it, and that perhaps Tompion in old age had looked upon his nephew's handiwork and commended it.

For it was not only a beautiful watch but an uncommon one. It had a jewelled watchcock of unusual design, showing a man carrying a burden on his shoulders. Isaac had seen hundreds of watchcocks during his professional life, and many of them had had impish faces peeping through the flowers and leaves, but never so far as he could remember one showing a human figure. The pillars were of plain cylindrical form, as in most of Graham's watches. He had never favoured elaborate pillars for like all great craftsmen he had always made ornament subsidiary to usefulness. Isaac closed the thin gold shell that protected the delicate mechanism and turned the watch over. It had a fine enamelled dial with a wreath of flowers within the hour ring. The outer case was of plain gold with the monogram A.A. engraved upon one side, and upon the other a Latin motto encircling the crest of a mailed hand holding a sword.

Isaac laid the Dean's watch down on his work-bench, amongst the others he had finished repairing today, and opening a drawer took out an envelope full of watch papers neatly inscribed in his fine copperplate handwriting. The majority of horologists no longer used these but Isaac was attached to the old customs and liked to preserve them. In the previous century nearly every watch had had its watch pad or paper inserted in the outer case, either a circular piece of velvet or muslin delicately embroidered with the initials of the owner, or else the portrait of the giver, or a piece of paper inscribed with a motto or rhyme. Isaac had collected and written out many of these rhymes, and he would always slip a watch paper into the outer cases of the watches of the humbler folk, for their amusement and delight. He did not dare to do so with his aristocratic customers for he feared they would think him presumptuous. He shook out the papers and picked out one here, one there. This would do for Tobias Smalley, landlord of the Swan and Duck, who was a rare old grumbler.

> "Content thy selfe withe thyne estate,
> And send no poore wight from thy gate;
> For why, this councell I thee give,
> To learn to dye, and dye to live."

And this, he thought, for Tom Hochicorn, one of the Cathedral bedesmen, a very good old man who believed in God.

> "I labour here with all my might,
> To tell the time by day or night;
> In thy devotion copy me,
> And serve thy God as I serve thee."

He slipped the watch papers into their various cases and then wrapped the Dean's watch in wadding and laid it away in a stout little box. Tears were in his eyes for he would not see it again until the Dean once more overwound it or dropped it. His fear of the terrible Dean was always slightly tempered by anger, because he took insufficient care of his watch, and then again by gratitude because but for the Dean's carelessness he would never have the lovely thing in his hands at all, for its mechanism was faultless. Because of this anger and gratitude he possibly had a warmer feeling for the Dean than most people in his Cathedral city.

Isaac took his own watch from his pocket and looked at it. It was a severely plain silver timepiece with tortoiseshell pair cases. He had made it for himself years ago. It said three minutes to eight and Isaac was dismayed, for it was later than he had realised and if he did not hurry he would be late for supper and incur his sister's displeasure. Yet the dismay quickly passed for today nothing had power to disturb him for long. He waited, his watch in his hand, for in a moment or two the city clocks would strike the hour and he liked to correct their timekeeping by his own faultless watch. It was quiet in the workshop, no sound but the rustle of a mouse behind the wainscot. It was a frosty October night of moon and stars and there was no wind. The city was still. There was no rattle of cab-wheels over the cobbles, no footsteps ringing on the pavement, for everyone was at home having supper. Isaac was aware of all the lamplit rooms in the crooked houses, little and big, that climbed upon each other's shoulders up the hill to the plateau at the top where the Cathedral towered, looking out over the frozen plain to the eastern sea. Another night he would have shivered, remembering the plain and the sea, but tonight he remembered only the warm rooms and the faces of men and women bent over their bowls of steaming soup, and the children already asleep in their beds. He felt for them all a profound love, and he glowed. The moment of his loving was in the world of time merely sixty seconds ticked out by his watch, but in another dimension it was an arc of light encircling the city and leaving not one heart within it untouched by blessedness. Then the clocks began to strike, and the light of the ugly little man's moment of self-forgetfulness was drawn back again into the deep warmth within him. And he understood nothing of what had happened to him, only that now, for a little while, for a few moments or a few days, he would be happy and feel safe.

The Cathedral clock, Michael, started to strike first, in no hurry to precede the others yet arrogantly determined upon pre-eminence. Its great bell boomed among the stars, and the reverberations of its thunder passed over the city towards the plain and the sea. Not until the last echo had died away was the city aware that little Saint Nicholas at the North Gate had been striking for some time. Only two of his light sweet notes were heard, but little Saint Nicholas was dead on time. Saint Peter in the market place waited for Nicholas to finish and then coughed apologetically, because he knew that his deep-toned bell was slightly cracked and he himself half a minute late. Saint Matthew at the South Gate struck a quick merry chime and did not care if he was late or not. Last of all Isaac's clocks in the shop all struck the hour, ending with the cuckoo clock. He kept them all a little slow so that he could enjoy their voices after the clocks of the city had fallen silent. Having refereed them all in past the tape he put away his own timepiece and rose slowly to his feet to set about the ritual of the Friday night shutting up of the shop.

In an old leather bag that had a lock and key he reverently placed the mended watches of those gentlemen and gentlewomen of the city who were too incapacitated by rank, age or wealth to do their own fetching and carrying. These he would deliver tomorrow, for on Saturday the shop remained closed and he spent the day delivering watches and winding clocks. Every clock of importance in the aristocratic quarter of the city, the Close and Worship Street, was in his care, intimately known to him and loved and cherished during half a lifetime. There was a smile of great tenderness on his face as he remembered that tomorrow he would see them all again. The watches of the great locked away in the leather bag, the watches of the lesser folk were placed in a drawer to wait till called for, but with no less reverence either for themselves or for their owners, for Isaac's humility did not discriminate between man and man and scarcely between man and watch. In his thought men were much like their watches. The passage of time was marked as clearly upon a man's face as upon that of his watch and the marvellous mechanism of his body could be as cruelly disturbed by evil hazards. The outer case varied, gunmetal or gold, carter's corduroy or bishop's broadcloth, but the tick of the pulse was the same, the beating of life that gave such a heart-breaking illusion of eternity.

The watches put away, his eyes went to the clock that he was making in his spare moments. There had been no time to work at it tonight but he could spend a moment or two before it in adoration. He was always making a clock in his spare moments, most of them after the patterns of the older craftsmen whom he loved the best, but enriched always with some touch of genius that was all his own. For Isaac was artist as well as craftsman. He did not need to employ another man to design his clock cases or do his marquetry for him. What his imagination conceived his own brain and hand and eye could bring to perfection without help from another. But he did sometimes wish he could have had an apprentice, not only to tramp round the city with watches and clocks and serve in the shop but to be his pupil. He was a born teacher and he would have liked to impart his knowledge. But it was impossible. The seven years' training insisted upon by the Clockmakers' Company, five years as apprentice and two as journeyman, and then the necessity of producing a masterpiece that could be approved by the Company before the apprentice could be admitted to be a workmaster, was daunting to poor boys in provincial cities, and if one here or there should aspire to it he preferred to go to London as Isaac himself had done. Yet he went on hankering for the unattainable, for with a good apprentice to help him he would have had more time for the creation of the clocks that he seldom failed to sell when they appeared in his shop window, so lovely were they and so cheap. He had no idea of money; he mostly forgot to send his bills in and he delighted in mending the watches of poor men for nothing. He had no idea either of the value of his clocks, but even if he had known that in the next century they would be eagerly sought after in the sale-rooms of Europe he would still have sold them as cheaply as he could to the men and women of the city because he loved the city. It was his city. He had been born within its walls and had never left it except for those seven years in London.

The clock that Isaac was making now he did not visualise in his shop window because it was so much a part of him that he could have as easily visualised his eyes or brain or hands in the window as this clock. He did not think about its future because it was the future. He did not consciously tell himself that it was his eternity but he had a confused idea that the dark would not entirely get him while the pulse beat on in this clock.

Standing before the solid oak table which was sacred to his clock alone his heart beat high with joy at what he saw. No one else would have seen anything except a confused jumble of mechanism, but Isaac saw his clock as it would be. He saw the accomplished thing and knew that he would make it, and that it would be his masterpiece. Like all creators he knew well that strange feeling of movement within the spirit, comparable only to the first movement of the child within the womb, which causes the victim to say perhaps with excitement, perhaps with exasperation or exhaustion, "There is a new poem, a new picture, a new symphony coming, heaven help me." The movement had been unusually strong when he first knew about this clock.

It was to be a lantern clock in the style of the late seventeenth century, the kind of timepiece Tompion himself had so delighted to create, the clock face surmounted by a fret that hid the base of the bell above. Isaac nearly always used the traditional eastern counties fret, a simple design that he liked, but for this clock he was designing his own, inspired by the famous Gothic fret which Tompion had been so fond of, only instead of the two dolphins and the flowers and fruit he saw two swans and the beautiful arrow-head reeds that grew upon the river bank outside the city wall. Isaac could paint on ivory with the skill of a miniaturist, and his clock face was to be a dial of the heavens. The twelve hours were to be the twelve signs of the zodiac, painted small and delicate in the clearest and loveliest colours he could encompass. Each picture lived already in his mind, completely visualised down to the last scale on the glittering silver fish at twelve o'clock and the golden points of the little shoes the Virgin wore peeping from beneath her blue cloak at six o'clock. Within this circle of stars Isaac had planned the sun and moon balancing each other against a blue sky scattered over with tiny points of light that were the humbler stars, but whenever he stood and looked at his clock the sun would not stay where he wanted it, as did the moon, but swam upwards and placed itself like a golden halo behind the fish. Again and again Isaac had replaced the sun floating just off shore from nine o'clock, but it was no good, it always went back to the meridian. And so now Isaac had given up and as he looked at his clock tonight he acknowledged the rightness of what he saw. The glittering silver fish and the golden sun formed one symbol, though of what he did not know. His heart beat fast and music chimed in his head. The bell of this clock was to strike the half-hour as well as the hour, for according to tradition the spheres were singing spirits. "There's not the smallest orb which thou beholdest but in his motion like an angel sings." Isaac did not believe it but he had the kind of mind that delights to collect the pretty coloured fragments of old legends that lie about the floor of the world for the children to pick up. As man and craftsman he knew that he would touch the height of his being with the making of this clock. He covered the lovely thing with a cloth and turned away. It was hard to leave it even though there was nothing under the cloth except a medley of bits of metal and some oily rags.

put on his caped greatcoat, that once had been black

but was now so stained by age and wind and rain that it was as miraculously full of colour as the plumage of a black cock, picked up his battered hat and the locked bag that contained the watches of the great, blew out his candle and felt his way to the door that led into the shop, lifted the latch and went in. He had not yet put up the shutters and the shop was faintly lit by one of the new gas street lamps that the city had recently installed. It was so small, and its bow-window so crowded with clocks, all of them ticking, that the noise was almost deafening. It sounded like thousands of crickets chirping or bees buzzing and was to Isaac the most satisfying sound in the world. Standing behind the counter he listened to it for a moment with his eyes shut, especially to the ticking of the cuckoo clock that he had made just before he had started work on the celestial clock. It ticked louder than any of the others and the cuckoo in it was a gorgeously aggressive bird, who exploded full-throated from his little door at every hour. Since the cuckoo clock had been in the window the children of the city were continually blocking the pavement outside the shop. Isaac was quite used now to looking up and seeing their faces pressed against the glass. There was someone there now even though it was late and dark. Opening his eyes Isaac could see the pale gleam of a face, dark eyes and a thatch of untidy dark hair. A boy, he thought, and then suddenly it seemed to him that it was not a boy but a sprite beyond the window, light and eager like flame in the wind. But sprites were children's tales. He was a convinced but hardworked rationalist, always hard at it re-convincing himself of his convictions. During his bad times this was not difficult, but during his good times the bright shards on the floor of the world had a trick of turning into shining pools that reflected something, and he was distinctly startled until he saw a ragged sleeve come up and wipe the misted glass clear. Only a boy. He had been breathing on the glass like they all did and the lamplight had blurred beyond it and played a trick upon his eyes. But he did not want to frighten the boy and he crept forward inch by inch, hoping to reach the shop door unobserved and call out a reassuring word as he opened it. But it was no good. The boy saw him and vanished.

II

There was a look of sadness on Isaac's face as he came out into the street, put up the shutters and locked the shop door. He had a pied piper attraction for boys and they did not usually flee from him, but he supposed he had looked grotesque in the half-dark, shuffling across the shop. For a few moments he was so grieved that he saw nothing as he stumped up the street, the moon behind his shoulder and a grotesque shadow of his tall hat bobbing along the pavement in front of him, and then the sorrow passed because nothing could sadden him for long during his happy times. He was ashamed of this, but he could not help it, any more than he could help it that in his dark times all the beauty and glory of the world did not gladden him. And of this too he was ashamed.

He began to whistle one of his tunes, for the city about him was magical. His repertoire of tunes was small, all of them variations of a striking clock. He went through them one after the other almost without cessation when he was happy, driving his sister Emma almost crazy. In spite of the sharp incline he chimed twelve o'clock in every possible way all the way up Cockspur Street, his eyes on the crown of frosted stars above the Rollo tower of the Cathedral. Isaac did not like the Cathedral. It frightened him and he had never been inside it. Yet he always had to look at it. Everyone had to.

At the top of Cockspur Street, that was so steep that all the little bow-windowed shops had short flights of steps leading up to their front doors, Isaac turned right and was in the market place. Here too there were shops on the ground floor of the tall old houses with their higgledy-piggledy roofs, and a small tavern, the Swan and Duck, where Isaac went sometimes when he was feeling low. The town hall with its fine Georgian pillars was here too, the Grammar School that Isaac had attended as a boy, and St. Peter's that was nearly as old as the Cathedral itself, a little dark musty church, battered and apologetic. Isaac had not been inside it since his boyhood, and in those days had suffered much within it and had hated it, but now after so many years of passing it as he went backwards and forwards to his shop he had come to know that his misery within it was not its fault and to love its old scarred face, and the small dark porch with the notice board where the papers seemed always torn and askew. The bell in the low squat tower struck the half-hour as Isaac passed beneath it, and its cracked old voice seemed calling to him. "Good night," said Isaac.

Just beyond Joshua Appleby's bookshop he turned sharply to the left and climbed a flight of steps between two high garden walls, a short cut to Angel Lane where he and Emma lived. It was a steep twisting cobbled lane bordered on each side by very old houses and crossed at its upper end by Worship Street, which curved about the great old wall which encircled the high plateau where the Cathedral towered, with the houses of the Close clustered about it. Those who lived within that wall were in the thought of the city the great men, the aristocrats, individually liked or disliked according to their individual characters but as a body venerated because they always had been venerated, the heirs of a tradition that was still sacrosanct. Worship Street was just one step down in the social scale, a gracious leisured street to which the ladies of the Close moved when their husbands or fathers died. The doctors and solicitors of the city lived here too, with a small sprinkling of retired generals and admirals whose fathers had once been deans or canons of the Cathedral. The city did not commend itself as a place of retirement to those whose roots were not in it, for the climate was bleak, but it had a way of drawing back to itself, sometimes almost against their will, any who had once lived in it.

Angel Lane to the west of the Close, with Silver Street to the east, housed those whom the city considered to be the more worthy and respectable among the tradesmen; not butchers or grocers or publicans, but Joshua Appleby of the bookshop, Isaac, the chemist and the veterinary surgeon, together with schoolmasters, lay clerks, and many poverty-stricken maiden ladies and widows who would rather have died than let anyone know how poor they were. The houses in Silver Street and Angel Lane were small, and their rents low, but their nearness to the Close and Worship Street, their age and picturesque appearance, gave them an air of great gentility. In them one could be desperately poor and highly respectable at the same time.

Isaac's little house was nearly at the top of the lane but before he turned to it he glanced eastward, and then stood spellbound by what he saw. Across Worship Street he could see the archway that led into the Close, the Porta, flanked by two small towers, cavernously black against the brilliance of the moonlit wall. Beyond and above it was a darkness of motionless trees, the great elms and lime trees of the Close that rose even higher than the wall. Beyond and above that again were the three towers of the Cathedral, the Phillippa and Jocelyn towers to the right and left and the central tower, the Rollo, soaring above them into the starlit sky with a strength and splendour that was more awful in moonlight than at any other time. Like the moon herself dragging at great waters the Rollo tower in moonlight compelled without mercy.

And the mailed figure above the clock face in the tower also compelled; above all he compelled a clockmaker for he was the finest Jaccomarchiadus in England. Like a fly crawling up a wall Isaac crawled up Angel Lane towards him, scuttled across Worship Street, cowered beneath the Porta, got himself somehow across the moonlit expanse of the Cathedral green and then slowly mounted the flight of worn stone steps that led to the west door within the dark Porch of the Angels. At the top he stopped and looked up at the Rollo tower, trembling. Then suddenly his trembling ceased for he was looking at the clock. He forgot his fear of the Cathedral, he forgot where he was, he forgot everything except the clock. He saw it from a distance every time he delivered watches in the Close but because of his fear of the Cathedral he was close to it only when as, tonight, he had been compelled. It was a Peter Lightfoot clock, less elaborate than Lightfoot's Glastonbury clock which had later been removed to Wells Cathedral, but in Isaac's opinion far more impressive. The Jaccomarchiadus stood high in an alcove in the tower, not like most Jacks an anonymous figure but Michael the Archangel. He was life size and stood upright with spread wings, his stern face gazing out across the fen country to where the far straight line of the horizon met the downward sweep of the great sky. Beneath his feet was the slain dragon, and his right foot rested on its crushed head. One mailed fist gripped the hilt of his sword, the other was raised ready to strike the bell that hung beside him. His stance was magnificent. Had he been a man it would have seemed defiant, but the great wings changed the defiance to the supreme certainty and confidence of the angelic breed. Below him, let into the wall, was a simple large dial with an hour hand only. Within the Cathedral Isaac had been told there was a second clock with above it a platform where Michael on horseback fought with the dragon at each hour and conquered him. But not even his longing to see this smaller Michael could drag Isaac inside the terrible Cathedral. No one could understand his fear. He could not entirely understand it himself. Yet every now and then, in spite of it, Michael compelled him to come and stand as he was standing now and look up at the clock, and then to turn and look out over the city from the central hub and peak of its history and glory.

CHAPTER II   *The City*

I

IT was a compact city, and on a night such as this one it climbed towards the stars like one of those turreted cities seen in the margins of medieval manuscripts.

It was so compact because although the city wall had largely disappeared as such, existing now only built into the walls of houses or bordering a stableyard or vegetable garden, yet the city had not straggled beyond the old confines. Its population was not increasing, for its chief industry, the making of osier baskets in the slum district at the North Gate, where the river came in a silver loop quite near to the city wall, did not attract the younger men and they were tending to leave the city and seek work in the distant towns. Yet the city remained fairly prosperous, for it was the market town for the surrounding country. On Saturday, market day, the market place was crowded, and on every fine day there was a constant gentle flow of traffic on the narrow roads that led from the villages out in the fen to the city.

These villages were widely separated from each other for they existed only where a small hill had in old days made it possible to build above the floods, and they housed a courageous but dour and silent people. Life had been a tough and lonely struggle for them in days gone by and though now that the fens had been drained, and banks built against the menace of the river and the sea, they were a fairly prosperous farming community they remained self-contained, suspicious of strangers and inclined to be morose even to each other. Great churches crowned the summit of each small hill but they were mostly empty, for the fen people were not devout, and in the cold windswept vicarages their priests frequently despaired and died. There were lonely manor houses here and there where many a squire preferred to drown his loneliness in drink rather than be bothered to ride miles through the wet to forgather with anyone else, and where his wife and daughters lived chiefly for the days when he let them have the dogcart and go and shop in the city.

There were happy days in the fen country as well as dour ones, glorious hot summer days when the harvest fields were gold as far as the blue horizon of the sea, spring days when riding parties cantered down the centuries-old grass roads between tall hedges of flowering crab-apple trees, winter days when everyone went skating on the flooded fields close to the river, or sometimes in a very great frost on the river itself, while overhead the great sky flamed slowly to a sunset of almost dreadful splendour. Nowhere else in England could one see skies quite like those of the fen country. Something in the quality of the air gave them a weight of glory that seemed to crush ant-like men and their tiny dwellings to dust upon the flat ground. Only the Cathedral could stand up against them, towering in black ferocity against the flame and gold. Yet the happiness did not predominate and those who went away from the fens to live elsewhere took with them a memory of endurance rather than joy.

Within the city the atmosphere was different. The same tough breed dwelt there but greater safety and prosperity within the walls had fostered a greater gregariousness. The city had a long history and a civic pride and had always known something of the pleasures of pageantry, for the plateau at the top of the hill had from the days of the Norman Duke Rollo onward been one of those places where men feel that they must assert themselves. The strange tall hill rising into the vast sky out of the vast plain had seemed to challenge both and on top of it men had felt themselves conquerors. Here they could see their enemies coming and defy them when they came. Here they could laugh at floods and storms. Here they could play the part of a god in the sky towards the poor peasants beneath, and oppress or relieve them as they chose.

Duke Rollo, who had been the first to assert himself on the hilltop, had been an oppressor. His great castle had frowned angrily upon the poor folk who had toiled for him below, catching fish for him, tilling for him the few fields that could be salvaged from the waste of waters, fighting and dying for him when he bade them, afraid of him and hating him yet dependent on him for their life. A little town came into being below the castle, and strong walls were built about it, a town of huddled houses and twisted unsavoury streets, housing the duke's men-at-arms, armourers, grooms and scullions, with their toiling wives and savage half-clad children. These did not hate him as did the peasants for he brought excitement into their lives. His banner streamed from the castle-keep above their heads and his trumpets rang out from the walls. When he and his knights clattered up and down the narrow streets on their destriers they cheered him, for he was a mighty man, a great fighter and reveller, and they admired his courage and vitality and neither expected nor desired that he should pity them. He died suddenly, in full carousel in his banqueting hall, and the fearfulness of his death, unshriven in the midst of his sins and drunkenness, sobered the mind of his young son, Duke Jocelyn.

In Jocelyn's day mass was said daily in the castle chapel for the repose of the soul of Duke Rollo, monks as well as men-at-arms passed up and down the streets, and the people no longer died in droves in times of famine for they had only to climb up to the castle and Jocelyn would give them all they needed. He was merciful to the poor. On Maundy Thursday he washed the feet of the twelve dirtiest old men whom his people could dig out of the slums around the North Gate and hound up the hill for that purpose. He kept vigil for long hours in the castle chapel and his people called him the Good Duke. Yet he did not win from them the admiration they had given to his father. They missed the pageantry of the good old days, the excitement and danger that had glamourised Rollo's brutality. And they felt in some vague way that the old duke had embodied the spirit of the strong grim place which he had created. Jocelyn did not. He took after his mother the Lady Phillippa who had died young of Rollo's boisterousness. He was timid and anxious, delicate in body, increasingly obsessed as time went on with the thought of his father's end and the fear of hell. He was already a dying man when the thought came to him that he should destroy the castle, whose stones were stained with the spilt blood and wine of his father's murderings and feastings, and build in its place a great church, and a monastery for holy monks, in reparation for his father's crimes. He would endow the monastery with all his wealth, and the monks should pray without ceasing for his father's soul and for his own; for as his sickness increased so did his conviction of sin. He too, though men called him the Good Duke, had his secret mean little sins and they whispered about his bed at night when he tried to find rest there from his pain, and in the day they seemed to him an obscene fog that choked him when he tried to draw his breath.

His dying was long-drawn-out, taking years where men had expected months, for it seemed that he could not die until he saw his great project in a fair way to fulfilment. He had always at his right hand driving him on, pouring as it seemed his own strength into the duke's failing body and mind, his Benedictine chaplain and confessor William de la Torre, later to be spoken of with bated breath as Abbot William. Many monks ruled upon the hilltop in the course of the centuries but they were not remembered in after years. Only William de la Torre and one other were remembered, William's stature in men's minds almost equalling that of the Cathedral itself. It was said he was well over six foot and could fell a man with one blow of his great fist. He was a man of powerful intellect, iron will and keen ambition. Moreover he was a genius. Duke Jocelyn's wealth procured the services of the finest masons and craftsmen in the country, men who could work in stone and wood and stained glass almost as though they were God himself forming the crested mountains, the forests and birds and flowers with fingers that could not err. It procured too a vast mass of suffering labour. The whole fen country travailed to build the church and monastery. Men groaned and sweated dragging stones up the hill. They sawed wood till they dropped with exhaustion. They caught the ague working upon the walls in the rain and bitter wind. It was accounted as nothing for men high up on the scaffolding of the great tower in cold weather to fall suddenly, as birds fall from a tree in a great frost. They died but there were plenty more to take their place. Looking out from the plateau and seeing the trains of ox carts bringing the stone and wood along the rough tracks through the fen, and the barges coming up the river laden with precious metals, velvet for faldstools and hangings, breviaries and sacred vessels, it seemed as though the whole world was converging on the strange hill in the wilderness. And William de la Torre held it all in the hollow of his hand.

At some time during the building Duke Jocelyn died, actually at the last in fear, and unshriven as his father had been, because William de la Torre, sent for in a hurry, dallied discussing plans for the chapter house with his architect and strolled along to the duke's bedchamber too late to be of any assistance to him. Jocelyn's body was enclosed in a leaden coffin with not much ceremony and forgotten until such time as William de la Torre deemed it politic to bury it beside the high altar of his church, on the day of its consecration to Saint Michael and All Angels, preaching over it a sermon so eloquent and moving that the vast congregation wept unashamedly. William de la Torre also wept. It was part of his power that he was so fine an actor that he could convince himself as well as others. Duke Jocelyn died without issue, though he left a child widow, Blanche Fontaine, who lived out the rest of her short life in a house at the monastery gateway, later called Fountains, where centuries later Isaac Peabody called weekly to wind the clocks for old Miss Montague.

And so, in the absence of heirs, Abbot William reigned supreme; though that he would have done in any case for supremacy was his role, and he could be great in it as this world counts greatness. He was a great abbot. The towering church that was his creation more than any man's dominated the whole country for miles round. The monastery buildings surrounded it, chapter house and infirmary, library and dorters, kitchens and cloister, all fine buildings in themselves but dwarfed by the leap of walls and towers and battlements above them. The poor little town that struggled up the hill became almost swamped by storehouses, granaries and stables. The people lived in mean little houses crushed between the monastery buildings and the city walls, and they toiled for the Abbot as once they had toiled for Duke Rollo. But the Abbot had more thought for them. The monks cared for the sick among them, taught their children in the monastery school, fed them in times of famine and kept them safe in time of war. Works of learning as well as mercy were accomplished on the hilltop, books were written, manuscripts were illuminated and music was composed. The singing of the monks in choir could be heard on still days far across the fen, as could the pealing of the bells, and men working in the fields would stop and turn and lift up their eyes to the great church and praise God.

The monastery never wanted for wealth. Its fame was so great that men flocked to it bringing their riches with them. Among the monks were not only noblemen expiating their sins, and scholars, artists and musicians desiring peace and quiet, but men who desired to pray. It was a great house of prayer. It was great. "It is great," were the last words of Abbot William upon his deathbed. He died, aged eighty-eight, unhumbled to the last. The great bell of the Rollo tower tolled for him on a night of storm but the next morning dawned calm and still, and a little boy who lived down by the North Gate said he saw two swans circling over the Rollo tower. Yet men's hearts failed for fear. The Abbot was dead. What now would happen to them? He *was* the monastery. He was subsistence itself. Men could not conceive of life without that hated, feared, indomitable man to goad them through it. By his command he was buried almost obscurely behind the high altar beneath a slab of black stone. He had had the bodies of Rollo and Phillippa moved from their burying place and entombed inside the monastery church in a wonderful chantry, and Blanche Fontaine too had her chantry, and the tomb of Duke Jocelyn beside the high altar had his mailed figure lying upon it in a far greater dignity and beauty than had been his in life, but William de la Torre had known he needed no monument to his memory. The great church was his monument and he would not be forgotten as long as it endured. His choice of an apparently humble tomb had been the last gesture of his pride.

II

In fearing that they faced disintegration without him men had forgotten the momentum that men of genius leave behind them in their works. The life of the monastery moved on in the course he had appointed for it for several centuries, the only major change being that a succeeding Abbot became the first Bishop of a newly formed fen diocese, the monastery church his Cathedral, and the Prior of the monastery became its head. During these years the church was beautified in many ways and the Lightfoot clock, and the statue of Michael the Archangel, were placed high in the Rollo tower. Bishops and Priors came and went and some were saints and some were not, and some were beloved in their day and some were hated, but none was remembered excepting only Prior Hugh, who was Prior at the time of the dissolution of the monasteries.

He was a little man, quiet and peace-loving, so that men were not surprised when they heard that he had commanded his monks to yield humbly to the command of the King's Grace and to offer no resistance when the commissioners came to drive them from their home. Yet when they arrived, with a formidable array of armed men as escort, and on a cold snowy day rode up the hill to the monastery to take possession of it in the King's name, it was found that the Prior had schooled his monks for a departure of dignity and grandeur. He himself in his simple monk's habit came out from the Cathedral and stood in front of the west door, at the top of the flight of stone steps that led up to it, and it seemed to the townsfolk and peasants who had come crowding and weeping up the steep streets to see the last of the monks who had looked after them for so many years, that he was a much taller man than they remembered. His voice, as he cried out to the commissioners and their men to stand aside that his sons might pass out, had an authority in its tones that none had heard before. Then the great door of the monastery, that opened upon the wide greensward that stretched from the front of the steps to the Porta, swung open and the monks came out in procession singing with splendid vigour the fighting psalm, the sixty-eighth, "Let God arise and let his enemies be scattered." Their great gold processional cross, and their banner of Michael the Archangel, were forfeit to the King, but at their head walked the youngest novice carrying a large cross made of two bits of wood nailed together. As they passed beneath the foot of the steps their Prior raised his hand and blessed them, and he kept his hand raised until the last of them had passed out through the Porta. They could be heard singing as they went down the narrow cobbled street that led to the North Gate, and across the bridge over the river to the rough road beyond that led back through the fen to the world they had renounced. Their singing died away and what happened to them no man ever knew, though for centuries afterwards it was said that on nights of wind and driving snow the chanting of the monks could be heard sounding through the storm.

When the last of his sons had disappeared the Prior dropped the hand he had raised in blessing and turned and walked back into the Cathedral. They found him later lying dead before the altar, the knife with which he had ended his earthly life lying beside him. It was not the action of a true priest, who may not himself dismiss from life the soul that is God's, but it was an act for which men nevertheless remembered him with sympathy and admiration. Even his enemies were grieved and defying the law that those who take their own life must not be buried in consecrated ground they buried him where they had found him, laying over his coffin a flat black stone such as covered the body of Abbot William. No man afterwards dared disturb his bones, and for years it was remembered that some poor half-crazed girl had vowed that on the day of his death she had seen two swans flying over the city towards the setting sun, and their wings were of pure gold. And so these two men, the first Abbot and the last Prior, lay the one behind the high altar and the other in front of it. Four centuries divided them but in the life of the great Cathedral that was no more than the exhalation of a breath.

The years went on and the city on the hill endured many and sometimes terrible vicissitudes. The monastery became the property of the King and its lands and buildings were given by him to one of his favourites, Harry Montague. Harry gave a great banquet to celebrate his arrival and as it was fine summer weather many of his cronies rode all the way from London to assist at the junketings. It was almost like the old days of Duke Rollo come back again, with men and horses clattering up and down the cobbled streets of the city, music and revelling, and succulent smells of baked meats floating on the wind. But the people of the city were sullen and miserable. They had been utterly dependent on the monastery and they did not know what was to happen to them now. And they felt disorientated. Through the years they had come to feel, if only subconsciously, that the city existed for the Cathedral and monastery and the Cathedral and monastery for God. The city had been God-centred and now they felt as though God had forsaken them. They did not like the Lord Harry.

They liked him even less when at the end of the final banquet he and his cronies, being all of them as full of wine as their skins would hold, carried the priceless books and manuscripts out of the library, flung them in a great pile on the green at the foot of the steps where Prior Hugh had stood to bless his monks, and made a bonfire of them. The leaves of the books were many of them yellowed and brittle with age, like the petals of dried flowers, and they burned brightly. Harry and his friends, most of them young men and wild as well as merry with the drink, were intoxicated by the leaping flames. Tumbling over each other in their excitement they ran into the dorters and refectory, coming back with hangings and chairs and tables which they flung yelling on the bonfire. The flames leaped so savagely that the whole sky was lit up, and could be seen right across the flat country, even as far as the sea coast, and when sparks carried by the high wind caught the thatch of the little houses down below, and the city too was on fire, it seemed to the awed watchers in the fen villages that the whole hill was being destroyed by fire from heaven. They remembered the singing of the monks upon that night of wind and snow six months ago. "Let God arise, and let his enemies be scattered; let them also that hate him flee before him. Like as the smoke vanisheth, so shalt Thou drive them away; and like as wax melteth at the fire, so let the ungodly perish at the presence of God." And then they saw the great Cathedral rising like a rock from the fire, its tall towers stark and black against the flamelit sky. It was a tremendous presence there and it seemed that it trampled on the flames. Slowly, gradually, they died. The stars and the moon entered once more into possession of the sky and the great fire was over.

It had been extinguished with great courage by the citizens themselves. Running cursing from their burning houses the men formed chains of buckets down to the river and for hours they fought the fire and at last they conquered. Throughout the fight they were aware of the presence up above them, the great strong thing that could not be destroyed. Many a man said afterwards that the Cathedral fought with them. But there had been some among them, children and old people, who had died in the fire and the city did not forget. Nothing Harry Montague could do now would ever lessen their hatred of him. When some years later he was stabbed in the fen by an unknown hand the city glowed and gloated.

His descendants lived on for a while in the fine house that Harry had made out of the central part of the monastery buildings, the kitchen, refectory and dorters, and the Prior's chamber and chapel. The rest, the library, the infirmary, the offices and outbuildings, gradually fell into disrepair. The walls and roofs remained intact, so strongly fashioned were they, but inside the bats haunted them, there was moaning in the chimneys and broken doors screamed eerily on rusted hinges in the wind. The Montagues did not stand it for long. They vowed the place was haunted. The people of the city did not grow tired of hating them and they were always afraid. They went away and lived in a great house by the sea. Only one of them, Harry's youngest son Thomas, remained behind and lived in a little house in the city. He was a gentle and kindly man and wore down the people's hatred. He married the mayor's daughter and finally became mayor himself. His descendants always lived in the city, the last of them being old Miss Montague of Fountains.

Then another hierarchy came into being at the top of the hill. The King's Grace appointed a Dean to administer the affairs of the Cathedral, and canons, lay-clerks and choristers to preach and sing the services. During the reign of the Montagues there had been an outbreak of the plague, failure of the crops and bitter poverty that they had done nothing to relieve. The people had felt there was a curse upon the city because the monks had been driven away, but now that the men of God were back, even though they were no longer monks, hope was re-born and men went to work with a will. The Cathedral bells rang out again, sounding far across the fen as in the old days, and on summer mornings and evenings, when the west door was left open, men and women pausing in their work could hear the singing of the lay-clerks and choristers as once they had heard the chanting of the monks. There were no more empty buildings on the hilltop. Harry Montague's house became the Deanery, and the other buildings were incorporated in the new houses for the canons, a choir school and almshouses for the poor of the city. The new men of God were good to the poor, and the city began to feel itself again. Without that life of praise and prayer and charity at its heart it had been like a wheel without a hub, as purposeless as a godless world. The men upon the hilltop might at times individually fail them, might grow loveless or indolent, but what they stood for was always the same.

III

The centuries passed again. In the great days of the first Queen Elizabeth all went well with the city and the fen villages, apart from the normal hardships of a countryside where life was never easy, but the Civil War left ugly scars behind it. The fen country was predominantly for Parliament but there were a few royalists in the city and the most determined among them was the Dean, Peter Rollard, a round rubicund little man with a red beard and a temper to match. His determination had been increased by the fate of the royalist Bishop, who was in prison. He had now to be loyal for the two of them. Commanded to discontinue the use of music and ritual in his Cathedral, and to worship God there in the full starkness of the puritan faith, he refused, and the Cathedral worship continued as before until on a cold grey day of east wind Lieutenant-General Cromwell himself, with a company of his Ironsides behind him, rode into the city. They clattered up the cobbled streets, rode under the great Porta on to the green and dismounted at the foot of the steps where Prior Hugh had stood to bless his monks. Evensong was being sung in the Cathedral at the time, and the triumphant Magnificat rolled out to greet the Lieutenant-General as he leaped up the steps and went in through the Porch of the Angels to the open west door beneath the Rollo tower. His spurred boots rang on the paving stones of the nave as he strode up it, and his harsh grating voice, raised to the full echoing apocalyptic roar of an enraged prophet, preceded him.

The lay-clerks and choristers heard the roar and the clanging before they saw the Lieutenant-General and their voices wavered, but when they saw him striding down upon them, black-cloaked, his tall black hat increasing his great height, their voices died away altogether and Dean Peter Rollard sang the last two verses alone. He was not a musical man but his vocal chords were powerful. The Lieutenant-General was not able to make himself heard, and taking an unloaded pistol from his holster he flung it at Peter Rollard. It struck the Dean's right shoulder and the pain was so intense that his right arm hung useless. A lesser man would have discontinued the altercation, but Peter Rollard, perceiving that Cromwell was sacrilegiously wearing his hat in the house of God, picked up his service book in his left hand and aimed it at the hat. His aim was entirely accurate. Cromwell's men, who had followed him at a respectful distance, closed about the Dean and he was marched off to the city prison.

The Ironsides spent the rest of that day, and the next, in destruction. Every carved angel and haloed saint within reach, inside the Cathedral and out, had its head knocked off. The chantries of Phillippa and Rollo, and of Blanche, that were full of angels, were a shambles of angelic heads. The glorious carved and painted wooden screen, with its panels depicting the life and death of the Virgin, was hacked out entirely and burnt on the green together with all the Cathedral vestments. At sight of the flames the citizens, puritans though most of them were, remembered Harry Montague's bonfire that had ushered in much suffering for the city, and they trembled.

High up in the Rollo tower Michael was beyond the reach of destruction. His haloed head safe upon his mailed shoulders he looked down in scorn upon the destroyers below, and the light of the flames seemed to glint upon his sword as though it was dipped in blood. At him too the citizens glanced anxiously, for there was something about his looks that they did not like. The Cathedral too, as the grey cold twilight of the second day drew on, had a menacing look. It seemed vaster than usual, colder, blacker, and yet terribly alive. Those whose duty compelled them to crawl about like ants beneath it had a feeling that it was towering up and up and might curve and break over them like an annihilating wave. Lieutenant-General Cromwell and his men had meant to leave at dawn the next day, after a late afternoon spent in smashing the Cathedral windows, but they found they were pressed for time and decided to go at once, sparing the windows but taking Peter Rollard with them for incarceration in a safer, deeper place than the city prison. They clattered down through the cobbled streets with the Dean riding in the midst of them, a trooper leading his horse because only his left hand was of use to him. The last that his people heard of him was his unmusical voice singing the sixteenth verse of the sixty-eighth psalm as loudly as he could. "This is God's hill, in the which it pleaseth him to dwell; yea, the Lord will abide in it for ever." His enemies feared to silence him for there was such a numinous terror upon them that evening that they were frightened of him. Dean Peter Rollard was another of those men whose vital, doughty spirit could be as daunting as the spirit of the Cathedral itself.

The years of the Commonwealth ground slowly by, and perhaps the sorrows of the citizens during that time were not really greater than is normal to human life, perhaps it was only their fancy that made them seem so, and swung their sympathies slowly over to the lost cause. They grieved over the death of their royalist Bishop in prison, shuddered at the murder of the King, and when his son returned to his own they rejoiced. But when Peter Rollard also came back to his own the whole city nearly went mad with joy. It was Christmas Eve, one of those spring-like Christmases that do occasionally visit even the bleaker parts of England. The Commonwealth had suppressed Christmas as smacking of popery, and through the grey years there had been no Christmas services and no ringing of the bells. But upon this afternoon of the Dean's return the bells rang again. It was a day of pale sunshine and in the morning the city had been permeated with the strange smell of violets that comes sometimes in a mild midwinter after shed rain, though there are no violets. All day it was very quiet except for the low hum of happy preparation. As the afternoon wore on the pale sky deepened to a fen sunset, not one of the terrifying ones but a scattering of small pink clouds all over a sky of deepening blue. The river, and the pools and streams among the reeds, reflected the sky. The swans, seeing themselves lapped in colour, floated in a mazed stillness. The great distance was very clear and the fen villages on their small hills could all be seen, their church towers rising black and clear. Very clear too were the little figures of two horsemen approaching far off upon the road from the north, that curved itself about the villages as it approached the city. It was known that the Dean's servant Tom Lumpkin, and he only, had gone to meet him at his special request, but even so the watchers on the city walls could not have been certain who these two were had they not heard bells pealing. So faint and lovely was the sound that it might have come from heaven itself, and for a moment or two the citizens looked at each other with wondering awe, before they realised that the village churches were ringing Peter Rollard home.

Then the bells of the Cathedral began to swing and soon their tremendous clamour was shaking the Rollo tower, and the citizens were streaming joyously out of the North Gate to welcome their Dean. He was not only their Dean, a courageous man who had endured much for the sake of the faith that was in him, but a figure who, whether they understood it or not, symbolised for them the spirit of this place. He was a descendant of those others, of Duke Rollo, Abbott William and Prior Hugh. Their mantle had fallen upon him. With him away the life of the city, and of the Cathedral upon the hill that was the reason for the city, had sickened, as it had in the days after the monks had gone away. Now, as the shuddering tower lifted its weight of music towards the sky, the spirit of the place leaped upward into new life.

Peter Rollard was much changed. His red beard was streaked with grey and his face was furrowed, and as he rode up through the city towards the Cathedral with his people exulting about him he actually wept. No one had ever expected to see Peter Rollard weep, and he had not himself expected that he would be so overcome and had taken no prevenient action. He was without a handkerchief and Tom Lumpkin had to supply one.

That Christmas Eve the villagers in the fens saw light shining from the Cathedral windows and heard organ music and the sound of a mighty singing. The whole city was inside the Cathedral, they judged, excepting only the sick and the babes and those who must care for them. Once more, after the dreary years when there had been no Christmas, they were welcoming Christ to his manger throne.

Peter Rollard lived for six years after his return, a much gentler man than he had been, and much beloved. A new Bishop was appointed, Josiah Farran, and he too was loved. These two died within a few weeks of each other and were buried in the south aisle of the Cathedral nave, and the sorrowing city caused beautiful effigies of them to be carved in coloured marbles and laid upon their graves. On the afternoon of the day on which Dean Rollard died an old shepherd, coming in from the fen, looked up and thought he saw two swans far up in the sky. After a moment's consideration he decided it was only his fancy, for he had never known swans to fly so high.

IV

The years passed and the life of the city flowed on with no great upheavals. There were wars abroad and years of scarcity at home that took their toll of life, but there was never a day when the praises of God were not sung in the Cathedral, or a Sunday that the bells did not peal. Bishops and Deans and Canons lived and died in the old houses about the Cathedral, and some were holy and some were strong-minded and a few were both but none of them seemed quite to have the stature of the great men who were gone, none of them seemed quite to be the city. None of them, that is, until in the year eighteen hundred and sixty-five the terrible Adam Ayscough was appointed Dean.

He came to the city at a time when a miasma of evil had corrupted it. The city had endured onslaughts of evil before in its long history, for as a fortress of God it had always been especially obnoxious to the devil, but the attacks had been overt ones and recognised for what they were. But this time there had been few robberies, no violent quarrelling and murdering, but instead a creeping nastiness of sloth and deceit, indifference and self-indulgence, that most horribly seemed to emanate from the Cathedral close itself. The Dean at that time was a melancholic recluse and the Canons dined too well. There was no active wickedness among them, they were all too comfortable for that, but the absence of good left a vacuum that was quickly filled. The slimy film on the surface was not in itself alarming, merely a dirty Cathedral, gabbled services, soiled and torn surplices and insubordinate lay-clerks and choir-boys, and the only man who fully realised the satanic nature of what was beneath was the Bishop, an incorruptibly holy man but too old now to be able to come to grips with any problem except the almost overmastering one of shifting his aged body about its duties. Yet when the melancholic Dean died he knew what to do, for that very morning he had seen in *The Times* the announcement of Adam Ayscough's resignation from the presidency of a famous college. He had met him only once or twice but he knew what manner of man he was. Adam Ayscough had already cleansed the Augean stables of a corrupt public school and made it the finest in England, and the college he was leaving had possessed neither virtue nor repute before he took it in his grip. If he could not through the grace of God cleanse the city no man could. The old Bishop wrote to him, inaugurating a long tussle between them, for Adam Ayscough's mind was set upon retirement and it was not his habit to yield his will to another. Yet, surprisingly, the old Bishop won, and within a year Adam Ayscough had been installed as Dean.

Within three years the small ecclesiastical world upon the plateau at the top of the hill had been scoured in every cranny. They were years of terror for all concerned, for the Dean drove upon them like a gale from the sea. The fabric of the Cathedral was dangerously decayed in places, the roof was leaking, ladders and broken chairs blocked one chantry, the droppings from jackdaws' nests littered a second, a new organ was needed and a new choir-screen to replace the one destroyed by Cromwell. For a while, as the Dean attended to these things, masons, carpenters, woodcarvers and the like descending upon the city and dirt and debris flying in the air, it almost seemed as though Abbot William was building the Cathedral all over again. The human element was not neglected for concurrently with the flying of the dust the Dean was campaigning against those evils in it which had resulted in dirty surplices and gabbled services. He reorganised the choir-school and the almshouses and dismissed a sadistic headmaster and an incompetent organist. He put the fear of God into the whole lot of them, from the Sub-Dean down to the smallest choir-boy, and the battle of the plateau was watched with much enjoyment by the rest of the citizens down below.

And then, suddenly, it was their turn. It was of no use to protest that the affairs of the city were not the business of the Dean. Adam Ayscough was deaf. His terrible anger uncovered the deplorable state of the workhouse, and revealed to a horrified city the conditions under which women and girls worked in the labour gangs in the fens. He exposed graft, exploitation of children and the weak, hypocrisy and greed wherever he found them, and however bitter the opposition he encountered he nearly always beat it down. During the years of battle he was only seriously defeated once. The slums about the North Gate, where most of the basket makers lived, were a breeding ground of sickness and misery, but their destruction, and the building of healthier homes on higher ground, was something that even he could not encompass. The slums, though appalling, were picturesque and contained some of the oldest houses in the city and he had all the sentimentalists and antiquarians against him. He had the people of the district themselves against him, for the basket workers had always lived by the North Gate, close to the osier beds, they were used to their dirt and squalor and were traditionalists to a man. But what finally defeated him was the fact that influential men owned property there, and the public houses that dominated every street corner were a source of income to the wealthiest man in the city, Alderman Turnbull the brewer, who lived in the market place. In his own way he was as much a colossus as the Dean and the fight they had over the slums was something the city never forgot.

But in all else the Dean triumphed, and for a period of some six or seven years it seemed that the city lay helpless in his grip, and then very slowly there came a strange stirring of new life, a springtide freshness and energy. Men and women did their work increasingly well, with growing pleasure and pride in what they did. The Cathedral became known all over England for its music, and the dignity and beauty of its services. Its bells rang out with power. Its fabric was perfectly cared for and a spirit of good craftsmanship grew up in the city. All that was great in the past seemed very much alive and men and women looked with new hope to the future. It seemed to them that the one blight upon the place was the Dean himself. For years, after the battle of the North Gate slums, his enemies had carried on a campaign of vilification against him and he was cordially disliked. Yet the city was proud of him. When he ploughed his way doggedly along the streets, his broad shoulders a little bowed beneath the weight of the ten years he had spent in the city, his craggy face set like granite and his unhappy eyes peering out beneath his shaggy grey eyebrows with no friendly recognition in them for any whom he passed, men and women felt a thrill of pride as well as dislike. He was, somehow, the city.

CHAPTER III *Angel Lane*

I

A TREMENDOUS music broke out over Isaac's head, and for a moment he was startled nearly out of his wits, for standing looking out over the city his mind had gone back to other years. Then a thrill of awe went through him. He did not look up, though he was vividly aware of the mailed fist striking the great bell and the stern face of the Archangel, but remained looking out over the past. Nine times the great bell boomed out, the sound rolling over Isaac's head and away over the city to the fens. Nine o'clock, the hour of the old curfew. Then far down below him he heard the homely church clocks striking. In all the houses of the city other little clocks were striking too though he could not hear them. Then there was silence, deep and profound, and suddenly he was terrified. It seemed to him that time was opening at his feet and that he stood looking down into an abyss of nothingness. Behind him the Cathedral soared like a towering black wave that would presently crash down on him and knock him into the abyss. Unable to move he stood there sweating with terror, as helpless and hopeless as in those nightmares that visited him during his bad times. But this was not one of his bad times, it was a good time. His mind suddenly gripped that. He remembered what had happened an hour ago and the memory was like a cry for help. Again and again he cried for help and slowly the memory of love became love, welling up from the depths of him and quietly enveloping himself and the city, time and the abyss, all that was. He was set free.

He walked quietly down the steps, wiping his face with his handkerchief and vowing that never again would he go near the terrible Cathedral in moonlight. He went across the green and under the Porta, crossed Worship Street and was in Angel Lane, and presently he was so far recovered that he started whistling the bells of St. Clement's shakily but with enjoyment. He was still whistling when he went up the two worn stone steps to the front door of number twelve, where he lived with Emma, and did not begin to run down until he stood in the dark little passage taking off his muffler and his greatcoat, and remembered suddenly that it was long past supper-time. The silence in the house was ominous and even though it was one of his good times he fumbled stupidly with the handle of the parlour door and nearly lost his footing on the wool mat on the threshold. Emma had a little wool mat made by herself before every door in the house. They were her pride and joy and it must have been Isaac's fault that they always slid from beneath him, for Emma herself never lost her footing on them.

As her brother came in she rose silently from her hard chair and pulled the long tasselled bellrope that hung beside the fire. The bell clanged like a fire-alarm in the kitchen next door, a signal to their little maid Polly to bring in the overcooked supper. Their evening meal was supposed to be at eight but Emma always waited for Isaac however late he was. That was one of her principles. Another of them was that she never reproached Isaac however maddening he might be. She had accepted him as her cross and she carried him uncomplainingly, for she was a very virtuous woman. "Wash your hands," was all she said now.

Isaac slunk back again into the passage, slipping this time on the kitchen mat, for he had to pass through the kitchen to the scullery. As he came in Polly straightened up from before the kitchen range and she and Isaac smiled at each other, but did not speak for fear Emma should hear them. Isaac tiptoed through to the scullery and lit the candle there, and a moment later Polly popped up at his elbow with a jug of water. " 'Ot," she whispered. He looked down into her round greenish-hazel eyes, bright with laughter in a plain freckled little face from which the ginger hair was drawn back to be hidden beneath a big mob cap. He was small but she was smaller, reaching only to his shoulder. She was a brat from the city orphanage and Emma had got her cheap. She was sixteen years old, tough as a pit pony and a wonderful worker. She did not find drudgery monotonous and was possibly the happiest person in the city. She adored and protected Isaac, she adored Sooty the cat and would have protected him had it been necessary. She pitied Emma. She had never hated anyone, not even those who in the past had cruelly misused her. She was intuitive and looking up now into Isaac's face she knew it was one of his good times. While he soaped his work-soiled hands she darted back into the kitchen and returned with a rough towel which she had been warming in front of the fire. " 'Ot," she whispered again, and felt in her own body the glow of Isaac's happiness and of his hot water and hot towel. Warmth was acceptable in the scullery for it was cold and dreary there. The kitchen regions of the picturesque old houses of Angel Lane were stone-floored and damp, the happy hunting ground of blackbeetles and mice, and the cats who had to be kept to keep down the mice. However scrupulously clean they were kept, and Polly scrubbed the stone floors of number twelve every day, they retained their distinctive smell; damp, mice, beetles and tom cat flavoured with onion.

"Thank ee, Polly," said Isaac, and pinched her cheek. "What's for supper?"

"Shepherd's pie," said Polly. " 'Ot."

Polly's pies, even when kept waiting too long in the oven, were good, and Isaac stepped across the kitchen with alacrity, his mouth watering. But seated at the round table in the parlour, opposite Emma, he found that he was not hungry any more. It was odd, the way he always felt hungry in the kitchen with Polly but unable to eat much in the parlour with Emma. And yet Emma was always solicitous about his meals and subsequent indigestion. It was another of her principles that a man's stomach should be a woman's first care. Emma presiding over a meal was like a high priestess offering sacrifice at the altar of a pitiless god. Grimly, as she and Isaac sat waiting for Polly to bring in the pie, she looked the table over to make sure that everything required for the coming ritual was in place. The oil lamp in the centre was trimmed to perfection, the white tablecloth, exquisitely darned and laundered, was spotless, the thin old table silver highly polished. The cruets were not quite at the right angle but she adjusted them. Isaac's post-prandial bismuth mixture was by his glass.

There seemed nothing wrong but she sighed, weighed down by the perennial sorrow of having no dining-room. Number twelve was one of the smallest and cheapest houses in Angel Lane and had only four rooms, the kitchen and parlour on the ground floor and Emma's and Isaac's bedrooms above. The two attics in the roof, Polly's and the box room, hardly counted as rooms because they were so tiny. The poor poky little house was not suited to gentlefolk, and a gentlewoman Emma had been born and a gentlewoman Emma would die, even though Isaac had demeaned himself by becoming a common tradesman. It is the status of the father that determines a woman's exact position in the social scale, she would tell Polly, who so far as the orphanage could tell her had come into the world with no father at all, and Emma's father had been a clergyman of the Church of England. She never forgot the great days of the past but there were those in the city who did. There were many now, she feared, who thought of her as Isaac Peabody the clockmaker's sister, rather than as the daughter of the Reverend Robert Peabody, rector of St. Peter's in the market place.

She sighed again and Isaac looked at her in anxious self-reproach, knowing how often he himself was the cause of her sorrow. Though she was three years older than her brother she still had the gaunt remnants of her early dark good looks. She was straight as a ramrod, big-boned, tall and thin, with a long melancholy face and profoundly sad dark eyes. Her clothes were nearly as old as Isaac's but she looked after them so well, brushing and folding them daily with such care, that there was nothing slovenly about them, and she brightened them with a gold locket and a mourning brooch containing her mother's and father's hair. The home that she had created for herself and Isaac was like herself and her clothes, scrupulously clean and neat, sad, saturated with the past. Everything in the parlour had come from what Emma called "the old home", and she had added nothing new in all the years. The fireside chairs, with seats so slippery and hard that one slid off them if one tried to relax, the prickly horsehair sofa, the faded curtains of dark green hanging at the window that Emma scarcely ever opened, the picture of the Day of Judgement hanging over the sideboard and the enlarged photo of their equally terrifying father hanging over the mantelpiece, were each of them for Isaac a reminder of his miserable boyhood. Wherever he looked it confronted him. On the sofa his adored mother had lain when she was dying. At this same table he had sat for an hour at a time, refusing to eat his congealed mutton fat and suet pudding, and under the picture of the Last Judgement his father had thrashed him. Even the fire on the hearth was the sullen fire he had always known, for they had always had to economise. The only thing his eye lighted upon with any pleasure was the clock on the mantelpiece, a black marble Benjamin Vulliamy clock with two figures of Time and Death standing one on each side of the dial. As a child it had frightened him almost as much as the picture of the Last Judgement, but now it was a comfort to him for though it was ugly it was at least a clock and it kept good time.

The door opened and Polly came in with a heavy tray laden with the pie, warm plates and a large brown steaming teapot. Her face was flushed and beaming and instantly the atmosphere of the cold stuffy room was subtly changed because she was happy. Polly's chief joy in life was feeding people. She was of the pelican breed and would have nourished those she loved with her own flesh and blood had she had nothing else to give them. "There!" she said, dumping the pie down triumphantly in front of Emma, for Emma always served the food, Isaac being far too lavish with it.

"You must place the dishes in silence on the table, Polly," said Emma wearily. "How ever many more times must I tell you that!"

Polly, having placed the teapot on its stand in silence, tipped Isaac the suspicion of a wink before she went to stand beside Emma with her hands behind her back, while Emma doled out her helping of pie on to a cracked white kitchen plate and cut her a slice of dry bread. The parlour plates had a pink and gold border, and it always hurt Isaac's feelings intolerably to watch Emma seeing how little she could give Polly. It did not hurt Polly for the pelican breed do not concern themselves with their own feeding.

"Thank you, ma'am," said Polly briskly, and whisked out of the door with her plate, her voluminous print skirts crackling, her small feet tapping out their quick vigorous light tattoo upon the stone floor of the passage. She never slipped on the mats for she had the sure-footedness of the single-minded. The kitchen door clicked behind her and there hung in the heavy air the faintest suggestion of music.

"That girl isn't singing, is she?" Emma asked suspiciously. "No," said Isaac, and began to talk loudly and incoherently about the weather and the people who had come to the shop that day. His sister transferred her suspicions to him and her nose began to twitch nervously. "Isaac," she whispered, "have you been drinking again?"

That was one of the things that made Isaac such a heavy cross for her to bear. When he was having one of his bad times he did, occasionally, get drunk. Those nights when he came home from the Swan and Duck singing at the top of his voice all the way up Angel Lane caused her a humiliation that was agony to her. Their father had been president of the Temperance League and she and Isaac had both at his command signed the pledge in infancy. After one of Isaac's lapses she did not go out for several days for she was too ashamed.

"No, Emma," said Isaac gently, but now he could think of nothing else to say and became silent, for he was as ashamed of his lapses as Emma was. Luckily at this point the Time and Death clock, and all the clocks of the city, struck ten, and the faint music within the house was merged with the music outside.

Supper ended, and the table cleared by Polly, they sat one on each side of the sullen fire, Emma reading her evening chapter in the family Bible, that was kept on a small round table with a red plush tablecloth beside her chair, and Isaac holding a newspaper unseeingly before his nose. In their childhood their father had held family prayers after supper, reading the Bible aloud to them and their mother and the little maidservants in a voice of such doom that even when he read of the love and mercy of God it made no sort of sense to his hearers. Only the doom came home to them, and the anguish of his conviction of sin and doubt of salvation as he implored the Almighty to have mercy upon them. Broken upon the rock of his stern and joyless character and faith his delicate wife had failed and died and Isaac had lapsed into unbelief. Only Emma had had sufficient strength of character to take the iron of her father's teaching into her own body and soul, to revere and imitate him while he lived and mourn him now that he was dead. There could no longer be family prayers with Isaac what he was but Emma always read her Bible at the appointed time, with a faint hope that by so doing she might win Isaac away from his wickedness before it was too late. Isaac was not exactly the object of her affection, for no one had ever taught her anything about love, but to care for his delicate body and save his lost soul was the object of her existence. Isaac knew it and his worst moments in this house were when Emma was reading her chapter while he sat trembling on the edge of his chair, as obstinately determined not to be saved as he had once been determined not to eat the mutton fat. There was nowadays an integrity about his obstinacy, for his refusal to accept his father's God had in it something of the courage and fire of the true faith. But he was a weak man and it cost him dear. He never read a word of the paper he held before him. He did not even see it. He only saw the face of his father, whom he had hated.

Robert Peabody had been perhaps not entirely sane, brave, utterly incorruptible, pitiless to himself, his wife and children only because he had to be. Hell yawned for them all and he had not dared to let them forget it. Above all he had not dared to let Isaac forget it, for Isaac had always been a delicate and abnormally sensitive child, prone as the delicate are to seek a little comfort for himself here and there, and dangerously indulged by his equally delicate mother. Never for one moment had Robert Peabody allowed Isaac to forget the wrath of God, and Isaac had spent his childhood in a state of cringing fear of the deity, domiciled in his imagination within the Cathedral. The only time he had ever actively defied his father had been when Robert tried to take him inside the Cathedral. He had fought like a wild beast. Brought home and chastised he still would not go, and the attack of asthma he had had as the result of this battle had been so severe that Robert had let the matter drop for his wife's sake. For Maria Peabody was always worse when Isaac was worse, for Isaac was the only reason why she held to life. But her hold on life was not strong and when Isaac was fourteen she died.

For two more years Isaac had struggled on at the hated city grammar school, mercilessly teased by the boys there, and then he had done a base and terrible thing; he had stolen three pounds from a drawer in his father's desk and run away to London. He knew that for such a deed the wrath of God was held in store for him, but he was so miserable that he scarcely cared. And there was always the hope that there was, after all, no God. This hope was fostered by his maternal uncle, to whose house in Clerkenwell he betook himself when he reached London. This uncle, his mother's only brother, was a notary, a stout and jovial person so very much addicted to the pleasures of this life that his brother-in-law, after one visit from him, had felt himself unable to receive him in his house again lest he corrupt the children. The notary, chilled to the marrow by that one visit, had not wanted to be received again, but he had been fond of his sister and had never ceased to correspond with her, and when she died he had written a little letter of condolence to her son to whom through her letters he had taken a fancy. The warm sympathy of that letter had been something new to Isaac. He had carried it for two years in his breast pocket and then had gone to seek the writer of it.

His uncle had been good to him, had taken him into his warm untidy bachelor establishment, taught him to laugh, to swill mild ale, to eat a beefsteak with enjoyment, to disbelieve in God, to take a clock to pieces and put it together again. Then, finding that his nephew took a thrilled interest in his own hobby of horology, was expert at it and excited beyond measure to find himself in Clerkenwell, at the very hub of the clockmaking industry, he apprenticed him to a clockmaker friend of his. It was done only just in time, for a few days after the deeds were signed and sealed Robert Peabody managed at last to find his son. There was a sad and bitter scene between them but Isaac, backed up by his uncle and bound in honour to his master, stood firm, and Robert went back heartbroken to the city and never saw his son again.

Those years in London had been the happiest in Isaac's life, yet his father, and the city on the hill, were never far from his thoughts. He tried to forget them and could not, and they were linked together with the thought of the God from whom he ceaselessly fled. His father, his city, his forsaken God. A man may build as he chooses upon his foundations but he cannot change them or forget them, and if at the last the superstructure of his own building falls about his ears he tends to rediscover them at the end as the only rock he has to cling to. Isaac was still a young man when his father died yet immediately he packed his bag and went back to the city, and when on the evening of the funeral his sister Emma, whom he had never been able to like, told him it had been their father's dying wish that she should devote the rest of her life to him he did not hesitate. The tiny sum of money that their father had left her was hardly sufficient to keep her in clothes. She had been trained for no profession and in any case ladies did not work for their living. He must come back to the city and support her until she married, for his foundations demanded it of him. She had never married. The years he had spent with her seemed to him now a long time. The years he had spent in the city seemed timeless. The years he had spent making clocks and watches had upon them the light of eternity.

II

Half-past ten struck and Emma closed the Bible. "Ring the bell," she said to Isaac. Summoned by the clanging Polly re-entered with three bedroom candlesticks, highly polished brass for Isaac and Emma and cracked china for herself. Solemnly Emma lit the candles, as she did every night punctually at ten-thirty, inaugurating the ritual of bedtime. Then the parlour fire was raked out, the window firmly latched and the lamp extinguished. Then all three processed to the kitchen where the same was done. Emma asked, "Is the cat put out?" and Polly replied, "Yes, ma'am." Then they went back to the dark passage and Isaac put the chain across the already firmly locked front door, while Emma locked the parlour and kitchen doors upon the outside, lest burglars break into the kitchen or parlour in the night. Then she went slowly up the narrow steep stairs with her candle, followed by Isaac with his candle, Polly bringing up the rear with hers. On the landing above Emma halted and said severely, "Good night, Polly," and stood watching while Polly climbed up the tiny flight of uncarpeted stairs that led to her attic. When the door of that apartment had been heard to latch behind her Emma said, "Good night, Isaac," and bent to kiss him. Then she went into her bedchamber over the parlour and shut the door behind her. Isaac went into his room, put his candle down on the table beside his bed and let out a sigh of relief that was almost a sob. He would not see his sister again until the morning.

Safe in his small hard bed, his tasselled night-cap on his head, he pondered miserably for a little while on the pitifulness of the affections and hates of human beings. He hoped he did not hate Emma, but when every tie of blood and duty and gratitude demanded of him that he should feel affection for her she affected him like some disease from which he shrank and cowered. His nerves quivered in her presence. What was the cure for this rasping of one personality upon another that brought one near to desperation and the breaking of the mind? What could one do? There was never any answer to this question, and there was none tonight, except the white radiance of the moon that bathed his bed and the slow rising within him of the waters of peace. Abruptly he forgot Emma in profound astonishment and thankfulness. It was still here. He was still having one of his good times. The unhappy evening with Emma had only been a momentary cloud upon it. He was still safe. He stretched his misshapen little body in the bed, he worshipped the moonlight and fell asleep.

In the large gloomy four-poster which had been her parents' bed, and which almost filled her room, Emma wept. No one had ever seen her cry, no one knew she could, but the gift of quiet weeping was one that had been vouchsafed to her of late years. She wept because she was tired right out, soaked with tiredness like a sponge with water, heavy as lead. Her exhaustion was not physical, for Polly did all the hard work of the house and Emma was a strong woman; it was the weariness of failure and betrayal. She knew now that she would never change Isaac, never turn him into a sober business-like gentlemanly good man. After all her years of prayerful struggle he remained what he had always been, a bad man. Yes, a bad man; a man who had stolen from his father and broken his heart, a man neither sober, honest nor God-fearing. And yet, and this to Emma was the bitterest thing in all her bitter lot, this bad man was so often happy. She, who had been a woman of exemplary virtue all her life, who had let no day go by without prayer and Bible reading, who Sunday by Sunday attended divine service, who scraped and saved to put money in her missionary box and took no sugar in her tea in Lent, was vouchsafed no reward for virtue. God had betrayed her. She had done her part but He had not done His. Peace. Joy. They were only words to her. She had seen peace in the eyes of the unregenerate Isaac, and joy dancing in Polly's eyes, but neither the one nor the other so much as touched her with a wing tip in passing. In the face of such injustice it was hard to believe the Bible promise that the righteous shall be rewarded. She wept on into her pillow and sleep came at last, deep and dreamless. She did not know what a blessing it was that she could sleep so well.

Polly always let the cat out at night, as commanded, but as soon as she had gained her small hard bed in the cold attic she let him in again. It was about the best moment in all her happy day when she jumped into bed, opened the dormer window beside her and called, "Sooty! Sooty!" He did not come immediately, even though he had been sitting on the roof waiting for this moment ever since he had been put out, for he had his dignity to think of. He came when it suited him, slowly and with condescension, somewhat astonished at the last to find himself on Polly's bed. He stood for a while upon her chest, kneading her disdainfully, his enormous tail twitching, his eyes like green jewels, heartless as beautiful. Polly scarcely dare breathe lest he depart but she never closed the window until he had decided to settle down. She understood his independent pride and knew that to coerce him would be to lose not his affection, for he had none, but the partiality of his tolerance.

Tonight he sat down on her chest, his back to her, his twitching tail tickling her nose, but still she did not dare to close the window. There was a long silence in the room and then a sound so faint that it was more a vibration than a sound. It increased, sending sympathetic tremors through her body, increased slowly and steadily until sound was perceptible, a faint humming, and then a louder humming as of innumerable bees approaching at speed, and then at last Polly's whole body was shaken by the full glorious organ music of Sooty purring. Then she shut the window and lifted up the top blanket to make a warm cavern beside her body. Into this Sooty condescended to insert himself. For a while the organ music continued beneath the blanket, then it sank to the bee-like humming, then to silence. Sooty slept.

Polly remained awake for a little while looking out over the kingdom. Winter and summer alike she slept with her bed across the dormer window, that she might see it in the evening and the morning and when she woke up at night. Angel Lane sloped steeply below number twelve so that Polly's window at the back of the house commanded one of the finest views in the city. When she had entered into possession of her attic at number twelve she had for the first time in her life owned privacy and a view. Just at first she had scarcely known what to do with either of them. The silence and loneliness had frightened her, and it had made her feel dizzy to see the roofs of the city tumbling away below her southward down to the river, and then the vast plain beyond stretching to the end of the world. Then slowly deep needs of whose existence she had scarcely been aware began to be satisfied and there woke in her the question, who am I, a question that she had not asked in the crowded orphanage days. The solitude of her room made her aware of herself and the illimitable beauty it looked upon made her aware of something beyond herself, so far away that its unattainable perfection broke her heart. And yet it was near. It was far as the brown brink of the horizon before dawn, and near as the yellow rose that climbed from the walled garden below and in June propped itself upon her window-sill and scented her room. The scent of a flower is a very close and intimate thing, she thought. It can seem to be a part of your body and blood.

Polly's name for her view, the kingdom, she had picked up from attending Saint Matthew's at the South Gate on Sundays with all the other orphanage children. The prayers had for the most part gone off her like water off a duck's back but that one perpetually repeated sentence, "the kingdom, the power, and the glory", had stuck in her mind like a phrase of music and now it sang itself there whenever she looked at her view. Tonight it was moonlit and sparkling. Frost glistened on the tumbled roofs and great stars burned in the sky. She could just see the church towers crowning the little hills in the fen, far away and small like toy towers, and here and there the gleam of water, but the power and glory in the vast singing sky had crushed the earth to nothingness tonight. It was not her own idea that stars sang. Isaac sometimes taught her to say bits of poetry when they were together in the scullery, and he had taught her the bit about the singing stars. All the rags and tags of verse that Isaac knew, taught him in his childhood by his mother, were gradually passing from his memory to hers. There they were in safe keeping for Polly had a remarkable memory. The orphanage had not been very successful in teaching her to read or write, for she had been there for too short a time, but anything she had heard with attention she remembered. On Saturdays, when she went marketing and Emma handed her a shopping list, she was too ashamed to say she could not read it, but luckily Emma always read it aloud before handing it to her and she never forgot anything.

Suddenly she remembered that it was market day tomorrow. She had been feeling chilly in spite of Sooty's warmth, for the blankets on her bed were poor and thin and the frost thrust its fingers through the ill-fitting little window, but now she began to glow. Tomorrow in the market she would see Job. The warmth of her joy tingled upwards from her toes to her cheeks and they were a faint rose colour in the moonlight. The stars came closer and she swung up to meet them, yet when she was among them they changed from singing spirits to flowers and she saw them as lilies growing in a field beside a stream. In her dream she and Job were together in a small dancing boat, and the quick water was carrying them out into a mystery. It was a dream full of expectancy and it often came to her.

CHAPTER IV

Job

I

THE sudden appearance of Isaac Peabody in the shop had sent Job running down through the streets of the city as lightly and silently as a phantom. Though he possessed a pair of broken boots he went barefoot when he could because it made escape easier. He was not by temperament an escapist, for he had extraordinary toughness and courage, but he retained his sanity by living as much as possible within his own private world. When he had to come out of it he did what had to be done as well as he could, and endured stoically what had to be endured, and escaped back to it again. He had not been afraid of the clockmaker, he had fled only from force of habit. He had caught glimpses of Isaac many times before tonight and the old man and all his clocks lived with him in his world, together with Polly and a few others. Very few were admitted. It was a signal honour to be admitted by Job to the place within himself.

As he descended the hill towards the river and the North Gate he imagined he was climbing down the escarpments of a mountain. It was always as a mountain that he thought of the Cathedral. Shut at night within the safety of his world he would sometimes try to imagine what it was like inside, and he would try and choose between one and another of the amazing landscapes that drifted cloudlike through his heaven and try and fit it inside the mountain. But none of them was great enough. When they touched the stone of the mountain they dissolved into nothingness. The mountain kept its secret and it never even occurred to him that he should climb up to it and see if it possessed a crack in the rock that would let him in. He was not, like Isaac, afraid of it, but people did not go inside it whose clothes were dirty and who stank. He had absorbed that fact with the air he breathed when he first came to the city. He did not resent it, for he was kept from resentment by a piece of knowledge which to him was as factual as his boots; that if he could keep himself from going under there would be a way through his present bad luck to good luck. But he must not go under. If he did the easy thing that he often longed to do, if he stopped washing under the pump and cracking the fleas and let himself sink back into the slime and obscenity of Swithins Lane, he would lose the way. Upon this fact he had grounded himself.

He reached the flight of stone steps that led down from the respectable part of the city to the slums below and paused and looked back. He could see the Cathedral above him towering against the stars and as he gazed Michael struck the half-hour. Then with his head up he turned and ran down the dirty steps.

He might be lucky tonight, he thought, as he padded past St. Nicholas at the North Gate into the darkness of Swithins Lane, and get to bed without a belting. He was late but if his master was still at the pub old Keziah would not tell on him. He was apprenticed to Albert Lee the fishmonger, whom he hated and who hated him, but old Keziah, Lee's mother, was kind to him after her fashion. Job was used to being hated and did not much mind because he knew the reason for it; he was different, and he exulted in his difference. The hidden exultation gave him a slight air of arrogance, though actually he had no more pride than was necessary for the preservation of decency, and increased his illusiveness. There were times when Lee thought he would burst a blood-vessel if he could not get a good grip on the boy and beat the superiority right out of him. Yet at the end of a belting he had somehow done neither.

The moonlight that flooded the heights of the city scarcely penetrated to Swithins Lane for the upper stories of the old houses jutted over the lower, turning the lane into a dark, filthy tunnel. Garbage squelched under Job's bare feet and he heard the rats scuttling. There was a faint glimmer of candlelight behind some of the small dirty windows, and now and then through an open door came the usual din of children screaming, and exhausted and maddened women shouting at them. A few drunken men lurched along the gutter but most were still at the pubs. The stench of the place was nauseating but Job was as used to that as he was used to the smell of fish that penetrated his appalling clothes, and already there was a part of him that was running on ahead to sanctuary. He could almost see it, a wraith that had his shape but was made of white flame, himself as he would be when he had passed through. He did not know whether he had imagined this wraith or whether it was real. It ran swiftly, leaping over the heaps of refuse and the scummy pools, and he ran after it, losing it sometimes and then glimpsing it again. He did not catch up with it until they had reached the side door of the shop, that stood ajar on its broken hinges, and then again it was gone and he was alone.

He edged in cautiously, for the half-open door meant that one or other of them was still in the kitchen behind the shop. If he could once leap up the narrow stairs at the end of the passage to the dark landing above, and then scramble up the ladder that led to his attic under the tiles, he was safe. Lee, a heavy man, could not negotiate the rotting ladder even when sober, when drunk he couldn't even find it. Job reached the end of the passage and leaped for the stairs, but even as he did so he was aware of the heavy body lurching through the kitchen door, and a vast hand grabbed his bare ankle. At the same moment he was equally aware that the other boy was back again, leaping into his body to share the torture with him. He did not struggle, for it was useless, and also he knew intuitively that his contemptuous acceptance of the inevitable maddened Lee. They were a queer couple of enemies, for the boy too had his weapons. He enjoyed the many ways in which he could use his quick slim body and agile mind in a wordless taunting of Lee's sodden stupid clumsiness. And Lee was slightly in his power, for the skill of the apprentice was the mainstay of the business. Job knew that whenever he ran up to the city after dark Lee was in a fright that he would not come back.

But he had not yet attempted to run away for he knew the consequences. He had been apprenticed to Lee for three years and only one year had passed. If the cops caught him he'd be prosecuted and imprisoned under the Master and Servant Act, and he would not be allowed to plead for himself. He had a morbid dread of prison and of all dark and shut-in places. But the beatings were bad. Some night there might be one which would be too much for him.

Lee dragged him into the kitchen and set about it by the light of a candle stump and the moonlight that flowed through the window. The light was dim and he was drunk, and some of his blows went wide, but those that cut true had the force of the man's strength and hatred full behind them. Job never sobbed or cried out because he knew Lee wanted him to, and beat him largely for that purpose. His gasps he could not control but the man's own laboured breathing covered them up. It did not last long, for Lee was in too poor shape to keep it up, but while it lasted it was indeed very bad and almost the worst was the ending of it, when he was sick and faint with pain and exhaustion and yet must get himself up and out of the room without letting Lee know that he had broken him. It was easier tonight for that boy had not left him and was a strength in his body. He moved through the moonlight to the door with his head up and vanished silently up the stairs. Lee flung his belt into the corner of the dirty kitchen and cursed, and then the sobs that he had been unable to tear out of Job clawed at his own chest. He sat hunched on the wooden chair, his great red hands dangling between his knees, and maudlin tears made streaks upon his face that were as hot and stiff as the streaks on Job's back. Of the two of them he was the more wretched. He was possibly the most miserable man in the city that night.

Job gained his attic, did what he could to help himself and lay face downwards on his wretched bed. The attic was no more than a roof-space with boards laid across the beams below to hold his bed and a broken chair. It had one small dormer window but the roof sloped so steeply that there was only one place in the little room where he could stand upright. All the same, he loved this eyrie because it was his own and no one but himself could get to it. And because here he could sleep and dream and gain his world.

He lay still for a long while upon the threshold, but he could not go in yet because the pain was too bad. He knew how to keep still, not only physically but inside himself, so that when the pain ebbed in his body the tumult in his mind quieted too. The window faced not upon the squalor of Swithins Lane but towards the river and the fen, where the frost was crisping the grasses and the tall pointed reeds. The night flowed in through the window, filling the room with the coldness of well water. He could hear the faint sound of the river flowing past and gazing down, as though he lay on the river bank itself, he could see in imagination the silver of the moonlight lying on the water, trembling where it splintered silently about the stones at the water's edge and the spears of the reeds. All his life he was to find the sight and sound of flowing water one of the greatest solacements of grief.

II

He had been lying on the riverbank like this, face downwards and looking at the water, on that day when as a small boy he had run away from his governess to fish for minnows and the gipsies had got him. He could still in nightmare feel the hand grasping at his clothes, lifting him up, and smell the huge dirty palm clamped over his mouth that he might not scream. He had lived for two months with the gipsies and they had given him his name, Job Mooring, but he did not remember much about it now except the perpetual swaying of the van, the barking of the dogs, the blows and curses. But he did remember how the rolling country of the midlands had flattened out into the fen, and that he had liked the fen, and that one day in a green grove he was sold for eight guineas to Dan Gurney, a chimney sweep of the city, to be his climbing boy. That the kidnapping of small boys to be chimney sweeps was a frequent occurrence during the shameful years of the exploitation of the children he did not know. Working for Dan he seemed alone in his wretchedness and knew nothing of the army of other children who toiled and died in the mines and factories and chimneys of England. That he too did not die was because of his extraordinary toughness and because when it got to the point where he could not bear it any more he was delivered.

The man who had saved him was the first whom he had admitted to live in his world, and was in fact the creator of it, for his great stature and compassion could not be held within the hard tight walls of a small boy's suffering. Job had to make space about him and in his mind he made it, and then as time passed the space grew and became a world of illimitable fancy where this man walked as a giant. Job only vaguely remembered his governess, and a big house with many servants where a man painted pictures and a woman played the piano and had no time for him. He believed now that they had been relatives but not his parents for he had no memories of love. He had encountered love for the first time, and then only briefly, in his short encounter with the giant.

In the quietness, with the pain growing easier, he looked down and saw the encounter as though he were looking through the wrong end of a telescope, with the moving figures small and far away. Yet it was happening within him too, it was always happening, because it was the point of his salvation. The water, then, had welled up through the broken ground to give a living freshness to his whole life. The timelessness of salvation was something he did not understand yet but he was aware of the freshness whenever he remembered that day.

He wished he could remember just how he and Dan Gurney had got there. It had still been dark when Dan had dragged him out of bed and cuffed him and told him to get on with it. In one way Dan had been a better master than Lee for he had been too lazy to beat him, but in all other ways a worse one. Lee's cruelty was largely the emanation of his wretchedness but Dan had enjoyed his.

Carrying their sacks they climbed up through the steep streets of the city, and they seemed to climb interminably. The light grew as they climbed but there was a thick mist so that Job had no idea where they were. Nor in his wretchedness did he care. They went under an archway and the tread of their boots rang hollowly upon the paving stones beneath it. Then they passed under tall trees, invisible but dripping with mist. The cold drops fell on Job's face and made tracks through the grime. He was a stunted little creature in those days, thin but very agile, and invaluable as a climbing boy for he could get through very narrow flues and so far had had the wit to get himself out again. It was bad for a sweep's reputation when a boy got stuck and died.

They came through the mist to the back door of a great house and when he saw its size Job was frightened, for these big old houses of the gentry were the worst. Most of them had their old wide chimneys contracted, so that they should not smoke too much, to a space only just large enough to allow a boy to get up and down, and the flues were winding passages with sharp angles. They were hot and dark and stifling and it was easy to lose yourself. It was then that the fear got bad and it was difficult to keep steady enough to use your wits to save yourself. It was, for Job, getting increasingly difficult. During his first year with Dan his natural pluck, a healthy body and great curiosity had given him resilience, but as the months dragged on and he grew weak with semi-starvation and the foul air of the chimneys the fear grew. Today, as the butler let them in to the darkened house, it seemed to stop his breath altogether and there was a clawing sort of pain in his guts. As he followed Dan and the butler up a long passage he thought he was going to be sick. He would have been if there had been anything in his stomach.

They came to a big room shrouded in dust sheets, and now there was a housemaid in a mob cap and apron as well as the majestic butler. It was light now but the grey mist was still muffled against the windows. The great chimney gaped. To one side of it stood a basket of kindling, waiting for the relighting of the fire when the chimney should be swept.

"Up with you, boy," said Dan.

But Job stood where he was, trembling violently. It was the first time he had refused a chimney.

"Go on, you young bleeder!" said Dan low and savagely, but still Job did not move. Dan cursed and struck him, and the butler and maid coaxed gently, promising him a slice of cake when it was over, but he would not go. Except to protect his head with his arms when Dan struck him he did not move.

"The boy's shy-like," said Dan to the butler. "Ain't never been in a house as fine as this before. You leave 'im to me, sir. You too, ma'am. 'E won't be afeared alone with me."

"Don't strike the child," said the maid. "If we go, mind you treat him gentle."

Dan swore that he always treated Job gentle and the boy was as fond of him as his own father, and rather reluctantly the butler and maid left the room. Dan did not waste time. He seized Job and thrust him bodily up the chimney. His arm came after him a little way, forcing him up with blows, and mechanically Job began to climb. He went on for a little way and then stopped. He couldn't do it. His mind went blank and he clung where he was, completely still. He heard a rustling below but he did not wonder what it was until the flames leaped up. To light a fire beneath him was a very old trick for making a boy climb but it was new to Job. He gave a choking cry, clung for a moment with his head hanging back, caught between the darkness and the flames, and then the blackness and the fire seemed to rush together and he let go and fell.

He realised later that it must have been a small fire, only a few bits of kindling lit to frighten him, and someone must have quickly flung a sack over it when he cried out, for when he slithered down it was not into the flames. A strong pair of hands took hold of him before he could fall, lifted him out of the chimney and put him gently into a big arm-chair covered with a dust sheet. To Job in his dazed state the room seemed full of people, and a vast and terrible anger like a thunderstorm. It seemed that everyone was being washed backwards and forwards by the anger as though they were straws in a flood. Only he seemed immune, lying on some rock above the flood and safe from it. Curiosity killed the cat but it can also be very reviving. Job wriggled up in the chair and looked out over its high back as though he were looking over a garden wall. No one saw him and from this vantage point the scene of battle was spread out most splendidly before his eyes.

The room was not full of people after all, only Dan, the butler, the maid and a huge man in black clothes, old and ugly, with a hooked nose and eyeglasses perched upon the summit of the nose. It was he who was so angry, and he was an alarming sight in his anger, but he did not alarm

Job. The butler, however, stood at attention like a criminal in the dock, the maid was crying and Dan was trembling. Job had not known Dan could tremble and the sight astonished him. It also astonished him to find that the old man was not making as much noise as he had thought he was while he was still so bewildered. He was just saying what he thought, and though his voice grated like a saw it was much quieter than Dan's when he was in a rage. A few of the things that he said lodged in Job's mind and he remembered them afterwards.

"It was my express command that no climbing boy should ever be employed in this house," he said. "The apparatus for sweeping chimneys without a boy now exists and should be used." His terrible beak of a nose turned towards the butler and his eyeglasses flashed. "You have flagrantly disobeyed me."

The butler flinched, as though at a whiplash, but he did not answer, and it was the maid who sobbed out something about the mistress having said to have a climbing boy, and to promise the boy a piece of cake if he wouldn't go up. Then it seemed that the old man flinched himself. A sort of spasm twisted his face. Job couldn't understand it. Then it was Dan's turn. The nose and the eyeglasses turned in his direction and he flattened himself against the wall as though they pinned him there.

"You are aware of the law, I presume. In eighteen hundred and sixty-four it was made illegal for any boy under sixteen to help a chimney sweep. I shall have you summoned for the breach of that law."

Dan began to stammer out that Job was sixteen last month. He was small, that's what it was, small for his age, but sixteen if a day. And that was the truth, guvnor, so help him Gawd.

"Where's the boy?" asked the terrible old man, and they all looked vaguely round. It was the old man who spotted him first, looking gravely at them over the top of the armchair. Only his grimy face was to be seen, and two filthy hands clasping the top of the chair. His dark hair was cropped short so that the soot should not get into it and he seemed all bones, but they were fine bones and his large dark eyes were remarkable. He gazed at the old man and the old man gazed at him. "What's your age, boy?" he barked. Both his bark and his scrutiny were most alarming but Job stood up to them very well.

"Dunno, sir," he said.

"Come here," said the old man.

Job scrambled out of the chair and came round to stand in front of him. He ducked his head, as one did to the gentry, and then stood squarely with his hands at his sides and looked up at the old man. Soot fell from his diminutive person on to the dust sheets on the floor

"Eight or nine," barked the old man. Then he turned and looked at Dan, who was still pinned against the wall. "You will be summoned and appear before the magistrate, but later I will see to it that you are provided with the necessary equipment for sweeping a chimney without the assistance of a climbing boy. You may go. The boy remains here." He turned to the butler. "See that this child is cleaned and fed. I will make the best arrangements I can as to his disposal and inform you of them in due course."

He turned and walked out of the room, his great head thrust forward and his hands behind his back. He had an extraordinary walk, as though he were forging along against a steady head wind. He had not looked at Job again, and had spoken of him as though he were a stray kitten who would have to be drowned if no suitable accommodation could be found. But Job's feelings were not hurt.

For the rest of that day he was rather miserable. The servants of the great house meant to be kind but there were so many of them that their talk made his head ache. He was allowed to eat his fill of wonderful food but it was too rich and he was sick. It was a painful business being scrubbed clean and having the sores on his body attended to, and afterwards he had to sit on a chair with nothing to wear but a blanket, his filthy rags having been burnt. During the afternoon the second housemaid, who had young brothers, went to her home and came back with a most peculiar assortment of male garments, all too large. In these he was draped and they were almost as uncomfortable as the blanket.

The next day, suddenly, a bell pealed and he was summoned to the study. The butler took him there, opened the door and pushed him through, indicating a writing-table in the far distance to which he must set his course. With his trousers in coils round his ankles, and only the tips of his fingers showing below his sleeves, he journeyed across acres of carpet towards the table. It took a lot of courage but when he got there he found the old man sitting at the table, looking at him over the top of his eyeglasses. Job ducked his head and then looked back at him, his arms held rigidly at his sides. He was not afraid of the man but he began to tremble, because he had a feeling that he had now been disposed of. The man loomed up above him like a great mountain.

"Boy," he said in his hard grating voice, and then he stopped and took off his eyeglasses and put them on again. "Boy," he said again, and now his voice was harsher than ever, "there are in this city a couple of charitable institutions known as Dobson's orphanages. Boys and girls without homes are cared for and educated there and afterwards apprenticed to suitable trades. The boys' orphanage is at the East Gate, the girls' at the West Gate of the city. I have arranged for you to be received at Dobson's at the East Gate and you will be taken there today. I trust you will be happy."

There was a silence and Job felt that something was expected of him. He ducked his head and whispered, "Thank you, sir." Then he just stood there, and he felt very cold. He did not know why he was sobbing. He did not know what he had expected, or why the word "orphanage" had made him feel afraid. He knew he ought to turn round and face the long journey back to the door, but he couldn't. The journey to the table had been to the man, but the journey back to the door would be away from him. He knew his nose was running but he hadn't got a handkerchief. The silence lengthened and the room was full of desolation. Then a large heavy hand came down upon Job's shoulder, feeling through the folds of his ridiculous coat until it could get a grip on the meagre bones beneath. Looking up at the man Job saw that he had taken his eyeglasses off and was peering down at him, and he was as miserable as Job was. Indeed far more miserable, for everything about this man was vast, his anger and his sorrow and his love. The grip upon his shoulder was Job's first experience of love. He did not recognise it, but he stopped sobbing and wiped his nose on his sleeve. He began to feel warmer, and not so wretched. The grip on his shoulder gave him a sense of his own identity.

"Boy, listen to me," barked the man suddenly.

Job listened, but for a few moments the man said nothing. It was almost as though he did not know what to say. Then he cleared his throat so loudly that Job jumped, and said, "Boy, all things pass. You are a brave child and a remarkable one. You will not be defeated and for the undefeated there is always a way through."

Then he lumbered to his great height and with his hand still on Job's shoulder walked with him to the door. Outside the butler was waiting. Job was handed over and the door was shut, with him on one side and the old man on the other. When a little later he left in a cab in the custody of the butler, bound for the orphanage, it was raining so hard and he was crying so much that he did not notice where they were going. And so he never knew that the great house in which he had lived for two days and a night was right under the stone mountain at the top of the hill.

Job was not happy at the orphanage, though he slept in a clean bed, was adequately fed and taught to read and write and cipher. He was not happy because he was different. The other boys disliked him because he learned more quickly than they did, and they punished him for it with many subtle cruelties. Mr. Fennimore, the master of Dobson's, a man whose comfortable rotundity and hearty laugh had deceived the whole city into thinking him the kindest of men, punished him too, whenever he could for whatever he could. The boy was brilliant, curious yet secretive, odd, and a challenge to Mr. Fennimore's understanding that he could not meet. Even the smallest pin-prick in his self-esteem was gall to Mr. Fennimore and he detested the boy.

In spite of the cruelties Dobson's did much for Job. He recovered health and strength and he became literate. He thought he had forgotten the lessons with his governess but they came back to him now and helped him to learn. It was the literacy that gave him his great joy at Dobson's, for in the schoolroom there was a shelf containing a few tattered books, given by some kindly citizen, and the boys were allowed to read them on Saturday nights. Few made use of the privilege, for they couldn't read well enough, but Job read them all. He read among others *The Pilgrim's Progress, Gulliver's Travels, Robinson Crusoe* and *The Cloister and the Hearth*, spelling them out as best he could to begin with but soon reading fluently. All the books had pictures in them. The books were like rooms in a great house and the pictures were lamps lit in the rooms to show them to him. As he read his dreams slowly changed. The nightmares of being stuck in chimneys that suddenly started to get smaller and smaller, squeezing him until he woke up choking and screaming, gradually gave way to dreams of forests full of great trees, where fabulous beasts galloped down the cool green aisles, meadows full of flowers and celestial mountains musical with streams. He dreamed of the sea that he had never seen and of ships upon it, and of caves where the tide washed in and out. And gradually the dreams became his world and he walked through it night by night with his hand in that of the old man. Sometimes by day too he would go away inside himself and he would be there. He never spoke of the old man and of his two days in the big house, and no one bothered to ask him how he had come to Dobson's. The whole experience of those days was part of his world and his private treasure. He scarcely related it to everyday life as he knew it.

He had another joy at Dobson's, and that was Polly. The boys and girls of the orphanage, the boys living at the East Gate and the girls at the West Gate, came together only on Sundays in church. Dobson, a wealthy divine who a hundred years ago had been Rector of St. Matthew's at the South Gate, had laid it down as law that on the Lord's Day all the children must attend matins at his church and for a hundred years they had done so. Every Sunday morning saw them walking through the city, two crocodiles converging on St. Matthew's, still dressed in the garments Dobson had decreed, the girls in long grey gowns and cloaks, and black bonnets tied with black velvet strings, the boys in grey coats and breeches and grey worsted stockings. Both boys and girls wore buckled shoes and the boys carried little three-cornered black hats. The people of the city loved to see them marching two by two to church, they looked so demure and old-fashioned, and so well cared for. The great munificence of old Dobson in providing for these children was, they felt somehow, to their credit. They were a generous city. Everyone smiled at the children as they passed by.

St. Matthew's was a lovely little church that might have

been designed by Wren. The children sat in the front pews, boys to the right and girls to the left, and it was on a Sunday in spring that Job first glanced across the narrow aisle and saw Polly. He was feeling desolate that morning, having been caned by Mr. Fennimore the day before and having had one of his nightmares, but the moment he met her eyes he felt a sense of warmth and safety. They could never speak but they looked at each other each Sunday for a month, and then he did not see her again, but she joined the old man in his world.

Job was at Dobson's for four years and then he was apprenticed to old Nat Cooper the undertaker. Nat was kind but stern. He was a hell-fire dissenter and scarcely let Job out of his sight lest the devil run off with him. On Sundays he took him to a tin tabernacle at the opposite end of the city from St. Matthew's, so that he never saw Polly, and he always took Job with him when a corpse had to be placed in a coffin, so that the boy should learn to think upon his latter end. Job did think upon it, and his nightmares came back. One thing, however, Nat did for him. He taught him carpentry. He learnt to distinguish between the different kinds of wood, to love them and understand their ways. Realising that the boy had great skill with his hands Nat gave him a few tools for his own and taught him wood-carving. Job had these tools still and when he was sent out into the fen, to find the flowers for the posies Keziah sold in the market, he would bring back bits of wood and make little gifts for Polly. First the books and then the wood. Each was a milestone for him on the way through.

After two years together Nat died and Job was back again on Mr. Fennimore's hands, and Mr. Fennimore reapprenticed him to Albert Lee. He could hardly have chosen a trade less suited to Job's temperament and talents, but he was interested in neither. If there was anyone in the world whom Job hated more than Lee it was Mr. Fennimore. Job was never resentful but he was a good fierce hater. There was a lake of fire in the hollow of the mountains in his world in which he had already deposited Dan Gurney, Mr. Fennimore, Lee and a few others. They had not died in it but lived there in the perpetual torment which the old undertaker had described to Job as the state of the damned.

It was an exquisite pleasure to picture them there, but on the nights when he was travelling through his world with the old man he could never find the lake of fire.

III

He fell asleep at last, waking after a few hours to the dull misery that always gripped him when he first woke up. Another day of the fish and the stink and the blows. Two more years of it. He moved and the pain ripped across his back. He burrowed his face into the dirty old pillow again and tore at it with his teeth. It could not have been more tattered than it was but it eased him to feel that he was doing to something that belonged to Lee what Lee was doing to him. He wished he could have done it to Lee. Then suddenly he remembered something; it was market day and Polly would come to the fish stall. Instantly he was quiet and knew the dawn had come and was slowly filling his room. He could hear bird voices crying out in the fen, for the river and the fen were for ever bird-haunted. Presently he edged out of bed and moved cautiously to the window, for his back was stiff and sore. The stench of the earth closets behind the houses made it impossible to smell the freshness of the morning, but he could see it. The river, though it was scummy where it flowed past Swithins Lane, was yet brimming with light and already arrowed here and there with a swift dart of moorhens. Beyond it the fen was wreathed in low river mist to the horizon. Willow trees and clumps of reeds rose from it frosted and sparkling. There was a village on a hill a few miles away and the cock on its tall church spire took the glint of the morning. Three swans beat across his line of vision, blindingly white, the sound of their great wings tremendous in the morning silence. They passed and the scene settled again to its repose.

Job's was a temperament that swung easily from one extreme to the other and now misery was lost in a joy that seemed lifting him off his feet. At this moment personal wretchedness seemed to him a small thing in comparison with the vast shining outer world that was always there, sustaining and holding him even when he did not remember or notice it, small even in comparison with his own world that he held within himself. The two, echoing and calling to each other, reflected some mystery that was greater than either.

There were shouts and the banging of doors, the smell of cooking. Swithins Lane had woken to another day. He left the window and crept stiffly down the ladder and went out to the back to wash himself at the pump.

CHAPTER V *The Watch*

I

THE sun soon conquered the mist and Isaac, as he passed under the great elms of the Close, looked up and saw pale gold leaves trembling against the blue of the sky. Down below there was no wind but up there a faint breeze fingered them. The frost had weakened their hold and even such a faint touch was too much for them. One after another they came slowly spinning down and one or two touched Isaac's upturned face in falling. He stood looking up, entranced, and his hat fell off. But there was no one to see and laugh at him for at a quarter past nine in the morning the Close was deserted, except for a few well-fed ecclesiastical cats sunning themselves on the tops of the old walls that enclosed the gardens of the Cathedral dignitaries. In these sheltered gardens flowering time was not quite over and the pungent scent of chrysanthemums drifted from them, to mingle with the scent of the bonfire in the Deanery garden and the smell of the wet fallen leaves. How well Isaac knew these scents of autumn and the butterfly touch of falling leaves upon his face, sad or happy as his mood might be. Winter, spring and summer did not accommodate themselves to one's moods as autumn did. They lacked its gentleness.

The Cathedral was in one of its kindlier moods. Blue

mist veiled the starkness of the Rollo tower and sunshine spilled down the walls and buttresses. It looked almost ethereal, as though built of air and light, and so benign that Isaac decided to venture as far as the south door and deliver his watch to old Tom Hochicorn in person, instead of leaving it for him at the almshouses. He walked down the lime avenue and then climbed the steps to an archway that led into a narrow cloister. Here on a stone bench beside the south door Tom Hochicorn sat with his hands upon his knees, wearing the long gown of dark-blue frieze and the crimson skullcap that the Cathedral bedesmen had worn for centuries past. The Cathedral had four bedesmen, one to take care of each of its doors, all old men from the almshouses. Aware of a figure approaching Tom rose and bowed. There was only one thing in the whole city more charming than his courteous bow, and that was his smile as he welcomed worshippers to his Cathedral and put out his hand to open the door and let them in. Tom loved and trusted the Cathedral as deeply as Isaac hated and feared it. As the years had passed the conviction that he owned the whole place had grown upon him. Yet no one, looking at old Tom, would have guessed at the fiery love and burning pride that inwardly possessed him. He had meek eyes, a long white beard flowing down over his chest and a gentle deprecating voice and manner. Yet if any desperate man had tried to harm the Cathedral in any way Tom would have been capable of violence, and any stranger who dared defile the cloister with a careless word or too loud a laugh heard what Tom thought of him.

"No, Tom, no!" cried Isaac on a note of panic, as Tom put out his hand to the door. "Don't open that door! It's me — Isaac."

Tom sat down again and motioned to Isaac to sit beside him on the stone seat. He knew all about Isaac's fear of the Cathedral, and humoured him as he would have humoured a nervous child. "Listen, now," he said encouragingly.

Inside the Cathedral the organist was practising, and few men could play the music of Bach as he did. Isaac could not but be quieted and listening to the music he began to see a picture in his mind. He saw great pillars soaring upwards like the trees in a forest, and a vaulted roof, very high, lit with dim glory as when the wind blows light cloud across a moonlit sky at night. He saw wide pavements of stone splashed with pools of colour, and small chambers like caverns hollowed out and carved and beautified by the surging of wind and sea. Dead men lay here upon biers of dark stone, their eyes closed, their hands upon their breasts. He saw strange vast curtains of shadow and shafts of light that pierced down from beyond sight to light upon old cloudy banners, a gilded throne, a great rood lifted high up and far away in appalling loneliness. The organ music grew louder, swelling, mounting. It was a dark tide of bitter salt water, the same tide that had fretted out the caverns and turned the dead men to stone upon their biers. Then it was a thundering of wind in the trees and all the tall columns were swaying in it. Then it was darkness, heavy and hot, shapeless and pitch black, and the cry that tore across it seemed to stop his heart, to enter into his blood and bones. Yet he could not get up and fly from it for his limbs were like lead, heavy as the limbs of the dead men on the biers. The music stopped.

"Pretty, eh?" said Tom Hochicorn. "Weren't that a pretty tune?"

"I've brought your watch, Tom," said Isaac hoarsely, and bent to unlock the leather bag. "Here it is."

"Thank ee," said Tom, opening the worn gunmetal pair cases. "Why, there ain't no watch paper! You always give I a new watch paper."

"There's a watch paper," said Isaac.

"No, there ain't," said Tom, disappointed.

"You've dropped it," said Isaac.

The two old men searched the pavement but could find no watch paper. "I must have dropped it in the shop," said Isaac. "I'll put it in an envelope and post it to you. Good-bye, Tom."

"Now there's no call for you to be off so soon," said Tom. " 'Tis close on ten o'clock matins. If you was to sit 'ere with me you'd hear 'em at matins. 'Tis just so pretty as a lot of singing birds."

"No, Tom," said Isaac. "I've all my clocks to wind." And he fled.

Outside in the lime avenue again he looked back. Tom Hochicorn was sitting as before, motionless with his hands on his knees. Isaac had the fancy that he and the stone bench he sat on, and the stone wall behind him, had become one. "He'll never get away now," thought Isaac. "It's got him." And he vowed that never again would he yield to the pull of the tides that last night and this morning had nearly got him too. Never again would he even go and look at the Jaccomarchiadus.

II

There was a seat in the lime avenue and he sat down to wait for ten o'clock to strike. After ten o'clock the Dean would be in the Cathedral and he would be in no danger of running into him while he was winding the clocks. For years he had wound the Deanery clocks and had succeeded in never seeing either the Dean or Mrs. Ayscough. Sitting quietly in the dappled sunshine he had recovered from the terror of that music but he had not forgotten the cry of loneliness. He would never forget it.

Ten o'clock struck and he made his way towards the high wall of the Deanery garden, and followed round it until he came to the cobbled stableyard. Crossing it he arrived at the back door, set hospitably wide under its high stone arch. Pigeons wheeled in the warm sunshine of the yard and in the tall elms of the garden rooks were cawing. In the harness room a boy was whistling as he polished the harness and from the stable door came the smell of hay and horses. As he knocked humbly at the open door Isaac wondered, not for the first time, what it must be like for a man and woman to live in a great house like this and have so many servants. Not very homely, he thought. But then of course the Dean and his wife would be a comfort to each other. Not like himself and Emma. A man could choose his wife. He blushed with shame, realising suddenly that he was comparing his lot with that of the Dean. It was a presumption. They were such poles apart that they could scarcely be said even to inhabit the same earth.

From the dim, warm interior of the house a stately presence could be seen advancing slowly down a long passage. It was Mr. William Garland, the Dean's butler. There was no more impressive man in the city. He was of middle height and well proportioned, though slightly protuberant in the region of the waistcoat. Whether in motion or at rest his carriage and stance were equally magnificent. His impeccable garments might have been made in Savile Row. His fine head, with glossy black hair and whiskers just touched with grey, was that of an elder statesman. His

The Watch

benign countenance and finely modulated voice would have become an Archbishop. Reaching the door he slightly inclined his head and inquired, "Mr. Peabody?"

Isaac replied, "Yes, Mr. Garland. Peabody to wind the clocks."

"Will you be so good as to step this way, Mr. Peabody?" inquired Garland.

Turning on his heel he progressed back up the passage with the same slow dignity with which he had come down it. Reaching a green baize door he opened it. "Will you be so good as to precede me, Mr. Peabody?" he inquired. "I can then shut the door behind us. To shut noiselessly, it requires the handling of one accustomed to its ways. Thank you, Mr. Peabody."

Every Saturday Garland received Isaac at the back door at exactly the same hour, with exactly the same words and ceremony. Had he appeared to know without questioning him who Isaac was Isaac would have felt utterly put out. They were men of about the same age, men of tradition, and they liked to do things in exactly the same way year after year. It gave them a sense of security.

Once through the green baize door they were in the spacious hall, with its shining floor, dark oil paintings of departed Deans, and jardinières of hot-house plants. It was Isaac's undeviating rule to minister first of all to the grandfather clock in the hall, a very fine Richard Vick timepiece with a Chippendale case. From there he progressed to the drawing-room to wind the Louis Sixteenth cupid clock, and from the drawing-room to the dining-room and the First Empire marble clock. The clock in the Dean's study he kept till the last. It was an eighteenth-century pedestal clock by Jeremiah Hartley of Norwich, of ebonized wood with brass mounts, the dial and back plate exquisitely engraved, very simple but very perfect in all its parts. He loved it second only to the Dean's watch.

"I have the Dean's watch here," he said to Garland, putting his bag down on the hall table and unlocking it. "I finished it last night."

"Ah," said Garland. "The Dean was inquiring for it." He always said this when Isaac brought the watch back. Isaac did not suppose it was true but he admired the ceaseless quiet vigilance with which Garland kept all who ministered to the Dean's wants, tradesmen as well as servants, up to the highest possible peak of performance in their duty. Were he to mend the Dean's watch with the speed of lightning it would still be just not quite quick enough.

"I'll take it up to him at once," said Garland.

"At once?" asked Isaac, and suddenly his heart missed a beat. For the first time in years something was not as usual. "At once?" he whispered. "Is the Dean not at matins?"

"A considerable hoarseness," said Garland, tapping his own throat with solemnity. "Consequent upon a feverish cold caught at the Diocesan Conference. Doctor Jenkins advised a few days indoors."

"In bed?" asked Isaac.

"Not today," said Garland. "I expect him downstairs shortly."

"To the study?" asked Isaac.

And now Garland also realised the seriousness of what had occurred. The Dean was seldom put out of action by his indispositions, not even by his lumbago, for he had great fortitude, and had never before been absent from Saturday matins unless he was away. The Saturday routine was disturbed. The two looked at each other, Isaac clasping and unclasping his hands, which had become clammy in the palms, and Garland reflectively stroking his jaw with his forefinger. Then inspiration came to him.

"You must attend to the study clock first, Mr. Peabody," he said, and there was in his voice that note of challenging certainty that is noticeable when strong men take desperate decisions on the spur of the moment. "Such a thing is contrary to our routine but we have to consider that should the Dean be down before you leave the house we run the risk of his finding you in the study." He opened a door behind him and waved a hand towards the room beyond. "The study, Mr. Peabody. You know where to find the clock. If you will give me the Dean's watch I will take it up."

Garland departed soft-footed up the great staircase and Isaac entered the study. It was a book-lined comfortable room with windows looking on the garden, the Dean's writing-table set at right angles to one of them, but Isaac never paid much attention to the room, so anxious was he to greet his old friend the Jeremiah Hartley. Generally he lingered over his examination of it, testing the mechanism, dusting it carefully with the square of soft old silk he kept in his bag for that purpose, rubbing the ebony and brass with a bit of soft chamois leather, but today he was so terrified that he merely wound it and then hurried back into the hall to the Richard Vick with the Chippendale case. He had done no more than open the glass door which covered the clock face when Garland returned hurriedly down the stairs, soft-footed as he had gone up them.

"The Dean is coming down *now*, Mr. Peabody," he said, "and unless we are to risk the danger of your being seen in the hall I think ——"

"The drawing-room?" Isaac interrupted, "or the dining-room?"

For a moment or two, so upset was their routine, they could not remember which came first. Then Garland recovered himself. "The drawing-room precedes the dining-room, I think," he said. "And there is no danger of Mrs. Ayscough coming down. She has indifferent health and does not leave her boudoir until twelve o'clock."

Safe in the drawing-room, Isaac still trembled. He heard steps come down the stairs, a harsh grating voice complaining of the lateness of the post, Garland's voice in soothing reply, and then the closing of the study door. From behind it came three stentorian sneezes and then silence. Now he could relax and turn his attention to the Louis Sixteenth clock. It was not in him to dislike any clock but he was not very fond of this one. The mechanism was satisfactory but he did not like the garland of gilded languorous cupids surrounding the dial. Their too-plump hands carried wreaths of impossible flowers, violets and snowdrops blooming at the same time as lilies and roses, and just as large. The room was beautiful but Isaac thought it too luxurious and for the first time he wondered what the woman was like who lived in this room after twelve o'clock. He had heard that she was beautiful. He had also heard that she and the Dean were childless. He was glad to escape from the pink languor of her room to the rich but impersonal glow of the dining-room mahogany, and the severity of the First Empire clock, a monumental marble edifice which inspired respect rather than affection.

But the Richard Vick in the hall inspired both. It had beautifully worked gilt spandrels of winged cherub heads, austere little creatures who had nothing in common with the cupids in the drawing-room. It struck the hours with a sonorous and deep-toned bell. The Chippendale case was plain and dignified, with three gilt balls surmounting the hood. Isaac was so absorbed in his careful winding of this treasure that he actually forgot the Dean. Then a bell clanged impatiently in the regions behind the baize door, Garland reappeared and went to the study. On the other side of the door the harsh voice rapped out a question and Isaac, his work finished, clutched his bag and groped blindly for the baize door, for he was suddenly in the worst fright he had known in all his frightened life. He had half-heard the question and it had seemed to inquire, "Is Mr. Peabody still in the house?" He was just escaping when Garland gripped him by the skirts of his voluminous old coat. "The Dean wishes to speak to you, Mr. Peabody," he said.

Isaac was hardly aware that he had moved into the room until he heard the door shut behind him. "Good morning, Mr. Peabody." The Dean's voice was always harsh and ugly but when he had a cold it had a graveyard quality that chilled the blood. Yet Isaac found that he was crawling slowly forward across the carpet towards the tall black figure standing in the central window, and though all but submerged by his own terror he did think it was a lonely figure. The Dean had his back to the light and Isaac could scarcely see his face, but as he came nearer he was acutely conscious of how very clearly the Dean must be seeing his, and not only his face but his sins. He was quite sure he saw him stealing the three pounds from his father's desk and knew about his getting drunk and not believing in God. Then suddenly personal terror was lost in professional anxiety as he saw that the Dean was holding his watch in one hand and the pair cases in the other. Had he failed in his mending of the watch? Had it stopped again? He came nearer and his heart nearly stopped, for a white circle was gleaming inside the pair cases. A watch paper! By mistake he had put one of the watch papers he kept for his humbler clients inside the Dean's watch. It must be Tom Hochicorn's watch paper. And what was on it? He couldn't remember. Several of his watch papers were comic ones. Some were even vulgar. His eyes on the carpet he swallowed several times and said, "Forgive me, sir. It was an accident. Please forgive me, sir."

The Dean had been slightly deaf from childhood, when

his father had boxed his ears too hard at too early an age, and being morbidly conscious of the nuisance the deaf can be he had formed the habit of not asking people to repeat themselves. To those who did not know him well, and very few did, his ignoring of their remarks, when they could manage to summon up enough courage to make any in his presence, took nothing away from his reputation for arrogance. Terrified and unforgiven, Isaac found to his horror and shame that a tear was trickling down his cheek. He fumbled for his handkerchief, could not find it and had to wipe his face with the back of his hand, and then was startled nearly out of his wits to hear the Dean say, "Thank you, Mr. Peabody. I needed the reminder." He looked up then, he was so astonished, and found that the Dean was looming over him like a predatory vulture. The craggy, beak-nosed face was so ugly, so seamed and yellow, that he would have recoiled had he not seen the man's eyes, profoundly sad and obviously very short-sighted. "He did not see my sins," thought Isaac suddenly. "He can scarcely see me."

Putting his watch down on the writing-table the Dean picked up the eyeglasses that hung round his neck on a black ribbon and perched them on the summit of his nose. With their help he read out the inscription.

" 'I labour here with all my might,
To tell the time by day or night;
In thy devotion copy me,
And serve thy God as I serve thee.'

Yes, Mr. Peabody, I needed the reminder. Please God, I will give Him better service in the years that remain to me. I will learn of my watch."

Afterwards Isaac could not understand how he could have had the temerity to say what he did. He said, "It's a beautiful watch, sir, and you should take better care of it. You overwind it, sir." And then, intuitively realising from the bewilderment in the Dean's face that he was deaf as well as short-sighted, he raised his voice and loudly repeated himself.

"You are quite right," said the Dean. "I will try to do better. Thank you, Mr. Peabody. Can you spare me a few moments? Will you sit down?"

Mr. Peabody sat down in the chair indicated, facing the

Dean across his writing-table. He placed his leather bag on the floor and laid his hands upon his knees. Though he was no longer afraid they still trembled a little. He had an unfortunate habit of turning his feet in when he sat down. They were turned in now, toe to toe. His bright child-like blue eyes were fixed expectantly but nervously upon the Dean's face. The Dean altered the position of the silver inkstand upon his table, and then of his gold pencil and the miniature of his adored wife, and then put them all back where they had been before and wondered what he could say. All his life he had loved children and poor people, and such child-like trusting little oddities as the extraordinary little man sitting opposite to him, all those whom Christ had called "the little ones". But he never knew what to say to them and his unfortunate appearance always frightened them . . . at least nearly always, for once there had been a small chimney sweep who had seemed not to be afraid. . . . He had become a priest that he might serve the poor but lacking what is called "the common touch", and being quite unable to preach a sermon that could be understood by intellects less brilliant than his own, he had been such a failure in his various parishes that he had been obliged to turn to school-mastering. That he had been a famous schoolmaster, and a great one in all eyes but his own, had not comforted him at all.

Peering across his desk at Isaac there came back to his mind an incident of his schoolmastering days which seemed to him to epitomise the greatness of his failure. Walking one day down the main aisle of the school library, his great head thrust forward, hands behind his back, he was suddenly aware that the place was not, as he had thought, empty. Crouching in a corner, trying not to be seen, was a terrified new boy with dirty smudges of tears upon his face. Instantly his headmaster had known how it was with him for he himself, handicapped by his deafness and ugliness, had been hideously tormented in his first year at his public school. His heart gave a lurch of pity and he bore down upon the boy with intent to comfort him. But the boy, his eyes bright and wild with terror, swerved aside and fled.

Trying to think of something to say to Mr. Peabody the Dean suddenly remembered that incident, and that his nickname among schoolboys and undergraduates had been "the Great Beast", after the alarming creature in the book of Revelations. The little man with his trembling hands reminded him of that small boy. He said to himself that it would be the same again. He could never reach the simple humble folk whom he loved the best. He could fight for the children, he could carry the sins of men, he could command their obedience and respect, but not their love. Something wrong with him. A man can change very much in his own fortune through his own efforts but the kind of man that he is he cannot change. He will hang about his own neck, like a dead fowl tied round the neck of a dog, until the end. The Dean's thoughts were always inclined towards anxiety and gloom, and never more so than when he had a cold. He sneezed violently and trumpeted into his handkerchief. Reappearing from its folds he said anxiously, and without premeditation, "Mr. Peabody, I should not have asked you to stay. I fear you will catch this cold."

Oddly enough this approach seemed the right one, for Isaac brightened up immediately. "I have just had it, sir," he said with all the complacency of a man who sees another enduring a misfortune from which for the moment he is immune. "It's about in the city. A terrible cold." For a few minutes they told each other about the great colds of their lives, and then anxiety again rearing its head the Dean asked, "Am I encroaching upon your time? At leisure myself this morning I am forgetting that other men are not."

"I am at leisure, sir," said Isaac. "It is my clock-winding day. I don't open the shop on Saturdays."

"You enjoy your work, Mr. Peabody?"

"Enjoy it, sir?" Isaac was so astonished that the question could even be asked that he could not for the moment answer it. Then he said, "Clocks and watches, sir, they're alive. They live longer than we do if they're treated right. There's nothing in this world so beautiful as a well-made timepiece. And every one different, sir. Never even a watch-cock the same."

"What is a watchcock, Mr. Peabody?" asked the Dean.

This time astonishment deprived Isaac of the power of speech. That a man could carry the most beautiful watch in the world about with him in his pocket for half a lifetime and never open the inner case to look at its works was to him incredible. He supposed a rich man like the Dean, who owned so many lovely things, took them so much for granted that they meant little to him. A man of a certain type might even long to be free of them all. Isaac had great intuition. He had realised earlier the Dean's loneliness. Now he realised his weariness. Finding his voice at last he said, "Your own watch, sir, has a watchcock of unusual and beautiful design. If you will let me have it I will show you."

The Dean handed him his watch, saying with that painful contortion of the facial muscles which so few people realised was his personal version of a smile, "Be careful of my watch paper, Mr. Peabody. I treasure that watch paper."

Isaac carefully removed the pair cases and the paper and opened the watch. "There, sir," he said with triumph. "Though the mechanism of a watch is not seen it is a point of honour with watchmakers to make it as beautiful as possible. You'll never see two watchcocks the same, and you'll never see one as unusual as this one of yours." Then seeing with what difficulty the Dean was peering through his eyeglasses Isaac produced his jeweller's eyepiece. "Put this in your eye, sir. You'll see better that way. Now did you ever see anything so beautifully wrought as that little figure? The odd thing is, sir, that I've never seen a human figure on a watchcock. Faces, often, but not a figure."

The Dean was silent, gazing intently at the man bent nearly double by the burden on his back. "Who is he?" he asked.

"I don't know, sir," said Isaac. "That's what I hoped you'd be able to tell me."

"At a guess I should say it was Christian," said the Dean. "You know your *Pilgrim's Progress* I expect, Mr. Peabody. You remember how Christian carried his burden up the 'place somewhat ascending' where there was a cross, and at the foot of the cross it fell off him and rolled away. Or it might be the Son of God Himself, carrying away the sin of the world." Isaac shifted uncomfortably in his seat, embarrassed as he always was when the sore subject of religion came into the conversation. Though he had not lifted his head the Dean knew all about his embarrassment. "Did you notice the Ayscough family motto, Mr. Peabody?" he went on. "It is on the back of the watch."

The suggestion that there could be anything at all about any watch that came into his hands that he did not notice so amazed Isaac that his embarrassment vanished, as the Dean intended it should. "Yes, sir," he said, "it is beautifully engraved. But my Latin is rusty, sir. I left school too early. I am not certain of its meaning."

"It is from the twenty-eighth verse of the sixty-eighth psalm," said the Dean. "'Thy God hath sent forth strength for thee.' Sometimes I think how odd it is, Mr. Peabody, that I should be spending my old age as Dean of this city whose history is so bound up with that particular psalm. You will remember Prior Hugh's monks singing it as they passed away from the city into the storm. And then Dean Peter Rollard — 'This is God's hill, in the which it pleaseth him to dwell.' Do you attach importance to coincidence, Mr. Peabody?"

"No, sir," said Isaac.

"Then you will laugh at me when I tell you that I believe I do. Take this bad cold of mine — is it a fortuitous accident that it kept me from going to matins this morning? Well, Mr. Peabody, whether it is or not I shall thank God tonight for the pleasure of your acquaintance."

Isaac was not more astonished by this speech than the Dean himself. Never could he remember talking to anyone with the ease with which he was now talking to Mr. Peabody. And the little man was speaking up well and clearly and losing his nervousness. It would not last, of course. Sooner or later he would blunder in some way, and see his friend afraid of him. For a moment his own mind beat about in fear, and then he remembered that Mr. Peabody was master of a craft about which he knew nothing. There were not many subjects about which he was ignorant but by the mercy of God horology was one of them. If he could sit at Mr. Peabody's feet as his pupil, he the poor man in his total ignorance, the little man would not be afraid of him for knowledge does not fear ignorance.

"I think the maker's name is engraved inside the watch, Mr. Peabody," he said, peering through the eyepiece. "But I cannot read it. Can you enlighten me?"

"Yes, sir," said Isaac eagerly. "'George Graham fecit, 1712'."

"A well-known horologist?"

"One of the greatest. Thomas Tompion's nephew, sir." The great name of Tompion seemed to leave the Dean where it found him and Isaac was both grieved and shocked at the depths of his ignorance. Like all good teachers he was scarcely able to bear ignorance on his own subject and he said in a breathless rush, "I could tell you about them, sir, one day, if you had the leisure — if I would not be presuming."

"I will hold you to that, Mr. Peabody," said the Dean promptly. "I shall be delighted to be your pupil. Seventeen hundred and twelve. This watch was, I believe, a gift to my great-grandfather when he came of age. It has come down from father to son and has seen much history for all my ancestors were fighting men. Our crest, as you see, is a sword. I broke with family tradition when I went into the Church and my father never forgave me." The Dean, his watch in his hand, had almost forgotten Isaac as his mind wandered back over the past, but now he looked up anxiously. "I must be boring you, Mr. Peabody. Old men are at their most tedious when garrulous."

"No, no, sir!" said Isaac, and his eyes were so bright with interest that the Dean smiled and said, "Well, Mr. Peabody, you have taught me to put a greater value on my watch. You must feel surprise that I have had so little curiosity about it, but the fact is that when my father thrashed me it was always for five minutes by this watch. Five minutes can seem a long while to a small boy." The Dean's sallow face suddenly flushed, for in excusing himself to Mr. Peabody he had been betrayed into disloyalty to his father. Self-excuse was contemptible and always led to something worse. "Do not misunderstand me, my father was a man whose son I am proud to be. Discipline is necessary for the young. As a schoolmaster I have myself thrashed hundreds of boys." He smiled at Isaac. "Mr. Peabody, if I take greater care of my watch in future I am afraid that you will miss it. We must arrange something. Shall we ——"

But Isaac was not told what they were to arrange for Garland entered, throwing the door wide. "Archdeacon Fromantel," he announced, and the Archdeacon entered, impeccably gaitered, a man of fine presence. At sight of Isaac his eyebrows shot far up his expressive forehead. The Dean sneezed with great sadness, but he rose from his seat with dignity and courtesy.

"You know Mr. Peabody, Archdeacon?" he asked.

But Isaac had sidled behind Garland like a terrified crab

seeking cover behind a rock and when the Dean looked for him he was gone.

With Michael striking half-past eleven Garland and Isaac paused for just a moment's whispered chat, but the disintegration of the Deanery routine caused them to do it on the wrong side of the green baize door and their sin found them out. A drift of perfume reached them from the direction of the stairs, and a soft *frou-frou* of silk petticoats. "Mrs. Ayscough!" gasped Garland. "Half an hour early!" Caught in the guilty act of this unlawful communication he and Isaac were for a moment rooted to the spot, their eyes unable to leave the beautiful woman descending the stairs. Elaine Ayscough seemed to Isaac to be a figure of legend. In appearance she might have been Dante's Beatrice, or the Elaine of her own name. Sunshine striking through a window gleamed on her pale gold hair, smoothly parted and drawn back into a chignon. Her white neck rose swan-like from the plain collar of a soft grey dress. She wore no jewels apart from her wedding ring and the little gold shells in her ears. Her face seemed designed for the pale gold setting of a cameo ring for even in the glory of the sun it lacked the warmth of living flesh. Isaac was unable to understand how a woman so simply dressed, even more simply dressed than Emma, could give such an impression of fashion and elegance. It was true that Mrs. Ayscough was a tall woman, but then so was Emma. If he had known how much the simple grey dress had cost he would have understood better.

At the foot of the stairs Mrs. Ayscough paused. She had apparently not seen Isaac, but she seemed to see Garland and her delicate eyebrows arched very slightly in a manner reminiscent of Archdeacon Fromantel, except that his eyebrows had shot up in unpremeditated astonishment and the movement of hers was intentional. "The gentleman who winds the clocks, madam," said Garland.

"Oh?" said Mrs. Ayscough, and for a moment her grey eyes met Isaac's as she moved across the hall towards the drawing-room. Garland reached a fumbling hand behind his back and pulled the baize door open and Isaac scurried down the passage behind it and fled.

Sitting on the seat in the lime avenue again he could not forget Mrs. Ayscough's pale cold eyes and compassion for the man he had just left welled up in him, and after that amazement at his own compassion. He had never thought of the Olympian figures of the Close as in need of compassion and nor, he supposed, had anybody else in the city. All of them, and especially the terrible Dean, had seemed to live in a world where compassion was not necessary. He saw now that it was the very first necessity, always and everywhere, and should flow between all men, always and everywhere. Men lived with their nearest and dearest and knew little of them, and strangers passing by in the street were as impersonal as trees walking, and all the while there was this deep affinity, for all men suffered.

CHAPTER VI *Fountains*

I

TWELVE o'clock boomed out and Isaac shot up out of his seat. Twelve o'clock! For twelve years he had progressed from the Deanery to Canon Wiseman's to wind the Dresden clock, from there to Canon Willoughby's, to the Rimbault chiming clock, and then to Miss Montague at Fountains. The Palace and Worship Street were reserved for the afternoon. For all these appointments he had never been a moment late, arriving on Miss Montague's doorstep punctually at a quarter-to-twelve to minister to the Michael Neuwers and the Lyre clock. Whatever would Miss Montague and Sarah think? They would fear some disaster had happened to him. Isaac was a comic figure as he literally ran down the elm avenue to the Porta. He stood panting on Miss Montague's doorstep at five-past-twelve. The Dresden and the Rimbault must wait, for Canon Wiseman and Canon Willoughby would not be so disturbed by his non-appearance as Miss Montague and Sarah.

Fountains, after the death of Blanche the widow of Duke Jocelyn, had become a part of the Priory. After the monks had been driven away it had been left empty but later had been restored and made into a private house again by Thomas Montague when he became mayor. It had remained in the possession of the Montagues ever since. Fountains actually formed part of the Porta. Miss Montague's drawing-room was over the arch and her front door was within it. A small brass plate above the letter-box had "Fountains" inscribed on it in letters that were nearly worn away. Beside the door was an ancient iron bellpull but it had to be pulled out a good four inches before anything happened, and as it was very stiff only the strongest could get it out far enough. The elderly, by Miss Montague's special instructions, lifted up the brass flap over the letter-box and dropped it, and went on lifting and dropping until Sarah came. This morning Isaac lifted and dropped once only before she opened the door, her face puckered with anxiety beneath her snowy mob cap. She pulled him in, shut the door and gave him a good shaking. Although she was round about eighty years of age, and scarcely bigger than a marmoset, her shake had surprising strength. "Do you know the time, Isaac Peabody?" she demanded. "There's twelve gone by Michael five minutes past, and you due in this house at a quarter-to-twelve and not a minute later. You've had us all of a tremble. . . . He's here, ma'am," she called up the stairs to an unseen presence, "and none the worse, drat him!"

With swift monkey-like movements she clawed Isaac's hat from his head and his coat from his back. He laughed. Miss Montague and Sarah were perhaps the best friends he had in the city and at Fountains he was at his happiest. Though he came here every week he looked round him in delight, sniffing the fragrant smell of Fountains, stretching his spirit in its particular atmosphere of antiquity and peace. It was so old that to come inside it was like coming into some abode of ancient knights hollowed out of the sheer rock. The lancet windows looking on Worship Street were set in such thick walls that they did not let much light into the stone-floored hall, but there was nearly always a log fire burning there and it gleamed on the tapestries on the walls and upon the old oak chest that Sarah polished till it shone like glass. Miss Montague was fond of *potpourri* and there were several bowls of it in the hall, scenting the warm air that was already pungent with the smell of the burning logs. Fountains had at all seasons of the year an autumnal warmth and graciousness, and no chill of winter in spite of the great age of the house, its mistress, of Sarah, of Araminta the housemaid and Jemima the cook.

"There now," said Sarah, taking a clothes brush from the chest and belabouring Isaac about the shoulders. "Don't that Polly of yours ever brush your coat? Don't ee waste time telling me now what you've been up to. You go on up to the mistress and she'll tell me later."

Two staircases led up from the hall, one being a circular stone staircase leading up to a room in the tower. Of the two small towers that flanked the Porta, Fountains contained one and the almshouses the other. The second staircase of dark oak had been put in by Sir Thomas Montague in the sixteenth century and led to the bedrooms and drawing-room. Up this Isaac climbed, turning left at the top where firelight gleamed behind a half-open door.

"Come in, Mr. Peabody," called Miss Montague. She had a clear voice, with only an occasional huskiness in it, and no one hearing it would have guessed that she was older than Sarah.

Mr. Peabody entered the room and standing at the door made a beautiful bow. His bow was memorable, being of the same period as his antique garments. Miss Montague acknowledged his bow with an inclination of the head that oddly combined, as did her whole presence, the dignity of a great lady with a saint's humility and a gamin's impish humour. She sat erect in her chair beside the fire, her thin fine old hands caressing the cat in her lap, her small feet in black velvet shoes resting upon a footstool. She had left off paying any attention to fashion forty years ago and dressed as she pleased, in a plain old black gown, a fichu draped over her shoulders and a square of lace flung over her plentiful white hair. Whether she had had any beauty in her youth it was impossible to say. She was now a dumpy old lady with a soft face of indeterminate feature, and faded blue eyes that were both shrewd and tender. Those upon whom her eyes rested immediately thought the world of themselves, for it was obvious that she saw with one glance all the good in them to which their own families seemed so strangely blind. She did not as a rule talk very much herself but then she did not often get the opportunity, so eager was everyone else to talk to her. No one ever seemed to know very much about her. She was just old Miss Montague of Fountains, and she had always been there, as changeless as her room.

It looked west over Worship Street and east into the elms and lime trees of the Close, with in winter a view of the west front of the Cathedral through their bare branches. The east window was always open in warm weather and birdsong filled the room, the smell of the lime blossom in its season and at all times the music of the bells. At morning and evening there was sunshine, and nearly always the fire on the hearth. There were beautiful things in the room, for Miss Montague had inherited the treasures of the past, but they were all a little dimmed with age and they did not intrude themselves. They had kept their stations in this room for so long that they looked rather as though they were painted upon its warm restful shadows.

"You are well, Mr. Peabody?" asked Miss Montague. "And your sister? And Polly?"

"Very well indeed, ma'am. And Emma too, and Polly."

A slight shadow of anxiety passed from Miss Montague's face. She did not ask him why he was so late because she was not an inquisitive woman. If she could be told that all was well with her friends she did not need to be told anything further. "Michael Neuwers is five minutes slow by Michael the Archangel, Mr. Peabody," she said.

"Five minutes slow?" ejaculated Mr. Peabody, and was beside the Michael Neuwers in a moment. It stood in the centre of the mantelpiece, in the post of greatest honour, and with the exception of Michael the Archangel was the oldest and most valuable clock in the city. It had been made in the late sixteenth century by the same clockmaker who had made Gilbert Earl of Shrewsbury's gilt clock, made to the Earl's instructions. "A small fine hand like an arrow, clenly and strongly made, the dial plate to be made of French crown gold, and the figures to show the hour and the rest to be enamelled the fynelyest and daintyest that can be, but no other colour than blew, white and carnalian." Miss Montague and Isaac were quite sure that the Montague Michael Neuwers was quite as beautiful as the Earl of Shrewsbury's. The case of silver gilt was surmounted by a little gilt lion and on the dial plate the Montague lilies and roses, white and crimson, were wreathed about the hour ring. After three centuries the lovely thing still kept good time but Isaac was always a little anxious, just as he was always a little anxious about Miss Montague herself. Though it seemed that the changes and chances of this mortal life did not touch either of them yet life remained mortal and they were old.

He adjusted and wound the Michael Neuwers with infinite care and tenderness and turned to the Lyre clock. He had no anxiety about it for it was an Isaac Peabody. It was the first clock he had made after he opened his shop and Miss Montague, driving up Cockspur Street in her little pony carriage, had seen it in the window, had stopped and come in. It had been their first meeting, though of course he had known her by sight and by repute, for in those days she was often to be seen in the city. He had been proud to see her in his shop and had bowed very low behind the counter. He could see her now standing in the dusty sunshine, a little middle-aged woman in a black bonnet and shawl, her figure inclining in those days to plumpness but otherwise not so very different to what she was now, for her hair had whitened early. She had dropped him a little curtsey, though she was a great lady in the city and he was only the clockmaker, and smiled at him, and he had loved her from that moment. Then she had asked him if she might buy the Lyre clock. He saw that her hands in their black silk mittens were trembling a little and that she looked a little scared, and he wondered why. Then she told him. "I have never bought myself a present before."

"You like birds, ma'am?" he had asked, for the clock was wreathed in birds.

"Yes. You see, I live among them. The trees of the Close come right up to my windows. In spring I find young birds on my drawing-room floor. They have hopped in through the window. They never seem afraid of me."

"Ma'am, you must have the clock," he had said firmly.

"Won't you be unhappy to part with it?"

"I made it for you," he had said, and was quite sure that unknowingly he had.

So she had taken her worn purse from the capacious pocket of her black gown and counted out a few gold sovereigns, and though it was a small price for such an exquisite clock he could see in her eyes that she was uneasy at spending so much on herself. Lest she change her mind he had wrapped it up and carried it out to her pony carriage, and put the reins in her hands and clucked up the old fat white pony rather hurriedly. But she had understood the reason for the hurry and when she drove off she had been laughing.

And now the Lyre clock stood on her escritoire close to the window that looked out into the trees of the Close, and the shadows of flickering leaves on moving boughs caressed it. The Lyre was one of the loveliest of his clocks. The upper part of the pendulum was formed to represent the strings of the instrument, the lyre itself was plain and simple, its only adornment a few curved leaves at the base, and at the summit a crested lark with spread wings. But the clock face in the centre had a wreath of tiny enamelled birds about the hour ring. The clock had a happy tick, very quick and gay, and chattered to the Michael Neuwers that answered with its slow soft beat. No one could feel lonely, Miss Montague said sometimes, with these two clocks for company.

"Perfectly in time with Michael," said Isaac, putting the Lyre clock back on the escritoire. "A good clock."

"Made by a good craftsman," said Miss Montague.

"They have their own life," said Isaac. "Clocks are like children. You can start them off right but you can't do more."

"Here's your glass of wine, Mr. Peabody," said Miss Montague, as Sarah came in with a glass of sherry wine and a thin sweet biscuit on a silver tray. "Sit down and tell me your news."

Isaac always had a glass of wine at Fountains, and he thoroughly enjoyed it, sipping it slowly and making it last as long as possible while he talked to Miss Montague of his affairs. He was not as a rule much of a talker but at Fountains he chattered as fast as the Lyre clock. There was only one thing he did not speak of with Miss Montague, his unhappiness with Emma, for that would have seemed to him disloyalty to his sister. Yet always when he left her he felt as though he had spoken of it, for the bitterness in his feelings seemed subtly withdrawn. He never asked himself why this was. Everyone took Miss Montague for granted. But today he had nothing to say about his home affairs because he had to tell Miss Montague about the Dean, watching her all the time that he might see surprise, amusement, delight, affection, lighting her face one after another as he poured it out. Talking to Miss Montague was rather like playing on some musical instrument superbly well. The response one wanted was always forthcoming. Isaac played the last chord and sat back very well pleased with himself.

"Now that is wonderful," said Miss Montague, able to speak at last. "Horology will be an ideal hobby for the Dean. Up till now I do not think he has had a hobby. He has his religion, of course, but religion is not a good hobby for religious people."

Isaac was surprised at this for he knew Miss Montague to be a religious woman and in past years he had been a little scared lest she should try and convert him. He was not scared now for he had discovered that she never spoke of her opinions unless specifically asked to do so. And so, free from fear, he found her the one person in the world with whom he could mention the sore subject of religion, just casually in passing. He asked with twinkling eyes, "Why not, Miss Montague? I thought you considered religion to be the pre-eminent need of man."

"So I do," said Miss Montague. "Like food. But a man can't be always eating, Mr. Peabody. He must do something else between meals or he'll get indigestion and grow sad and moody."

Isaac laughed, and then said sadly, "But I shall not see the Dean again. Great men speak kindly to lesser men and then forget what they have said."

"He will not forget," said Miss Montague. "But you may have to wait some time before he can summon up enough courage to claim your friendship. It is always thought, Mr. Peabody, that men put on self-confidence with gaiters and crowns. They don't, you know. A shy man is a shy man whatever he puts on. How glad I am that the Dean is to take better care of the beautiful watch."

A clear bell-note seemed to come soaring down to them from the height of heaven and after it a silence so profound that Miss Montague and Isaac did not even hear the ticking of the clocks. Michael was like that. He had only to speak once and one did not hear another voice. The charmed moment passed and Isaac was on his feet at once, for Miss Montague had luncheon at one o'clock. It was the moment of English history when mealtimes were in a state of flux. Many people still preferred their main meal of the day at five-thirty but those who followed the fashion were now firmly attached to luncheon, afternoon tea and late dinner. Miss Montague was indifferent to fashion but Sarah insisted that she conform to the social habits of the Close. Regretfully, for she preferred him to her luncheon any day, she held out her hand to Isaac. He bowed over it and went away.

II

While Isaac was still with the Dean, Polly was walking down Angel Lane on her way to the market. She still wore the outdoor clothes the orphanage had given her, a grey gown and cloak and a plain black bonnet, but with her very first earnings she had bought some cherry-coloured ribbon to replace the black velvet strings, enough to make two rosettes and a large defiant bow that tied beneath her chin, and the glory of that ribbon gave her self-confidence among the other girls at the market. She sang softly to herself as she walked along with a big market basket on her arm, and colour came into her cheeks with the exercise, the singing and the joy. Several tired women peeped from behind their draped window curtains to see her pass, envious of her lightness and gaiety. And she an orphanage brat! They did not of course know about Job. Nor did they know what she was singing, though they supposed that gay words must go with such a merry tune. The words were these. "A box of pins and a reel of black cotton. One yard of black sarsenet. One eel, fresh. Oranges and cloves, pepper and pigs' trotters. Grey darning wool and a scrubbing brush. A pound of onions and an ounce of liquorice allsorts. Fishheads for Sooty. Fishheads. Fishheads. For Thine is the kingdom, the power, and the glory. Amen."

She took the same way to the market that Isaac followed when he went to his shop, running lightly down the flight of steps that he had climbed so laboriously last night. She passed Joshua Appleby's bookshop with an awed glance for all the books inside, and she wondered what it must be like to be able to read. She thought it must be wonderful and it surprised her that the gentry who were able to read could be bored. Yet they were. What was the matter with them? She was sorry for the gentry for there always seemed to be something the matter with them. She passed St. Peter's church with a friendly glance, for Emma took her there on

Sundays. Just beyond the old porch she turned on the pavement and there before her, with the grave classical town hall for a backcloth, was all the splendour of the city's market. She stepped off the pavement on to the cobbles with the ecstasy of a duck taking to water or a saint entering heaven, and in a moment was lost sight of in the ebb and flow of noise and colour all about her. What did she want with books, she thought suddenly. No book could open the door to anything more strange and rich than this.

If not quite so marvellous as she thought it the market was a famous one in the fen country and served a wide area. The yard of the Swan and Duck was full of the gigs and carts and carriages that had brought the farmers and gentry of the villages to the market, and the inn stable was full of nags and ponies. Since dawn the drovers had been bringing in the cattle, the pigs squealing in netted carts, the poor sweating cows driven along the fen roads and up the cobbled streets of the city amid a cacophony of shouting men and barking dogs. The only thing that Polly did not like about the market was the fear of the animals and she never went near the town hall end of the square where they were imprisoned in their pens. But the rest of the market was sheer bliss. The stalls ran in long lines across the breadth of the market place, with lanes between them packed with eager women and children in their gayest clothes, laughing and chattering. The men were mostly at the far end, intent upon the beasts, but sometimes a young farmer would elbow his way through the crowd intent upon a fairing for his sweetheart or toys for his children. The choice was wide for almost everything was sold in the market. Many of the goods on the stalls were for sale in the shops any day of the week but they were cheaper in the market and somehow much more exciting spread out like this in the sunshine. There were vegetables and fruit, flowers and fresh farm eggs and butter, ribbons and laces and rolls of coloured cloth, toys and sweets, bonnets and shawls, pots and pans and gay china cups and saucers, needles and pins and coloured glass beads, chestnuts and gingerbread, pots of honey, willow baskets and clothes pegs, eels and fish caught in the river, picture postcards, corn cures and mouse-traps. Four square about the noise and gaiety and colour stood the old grave tall houses, and far above it all the

Cathedral towered into the sky and Michael tolled the passing quarter hours, echoed by St. Peter's, St. Nicholas's at the North Gate and St. Matthew's at the South Gate. The busy shoppers were hardly aware of the bells and yet they were a part of market day, their music woven into the laughter and chatter like a thread of gold into homespun cloth.

Polly made her purchases with deliberation because Emma, a careful shopper herself, expected her to take her time, and all the while that she was comparing one stall with another, asking the price of this and that, and singing her gay little song of the needs to herself to refresh her memory, she never once looked at the fish stall. But at last everything except the eel and fishheads was in her basket and she made her way towards the old mounting block close to the Swan and Duck. On the mounting block, week by week, sat old Keziah Lee with her basket full of bunches of wild flowers from the fen, marigolds and water forget-me-nots and yellow irises in their season, with in autumn crab-apples for jelly and in winter posies of everlasting flowers dyed in bright colours, and beside her Albert had his fish stall. Keziah was like an old witch to look at, tiny and shrivelled in her black bonnet and ragged shawl, and Albert looked like an operatic tenor gone to seed. Since Job had been with them their business had improved. Their fish was cleanly gutted, their eels fresh caught in the river and displayed both in the shop and on the market stall with a curious beauty, laid in shallow woven rush baskets among fragrant leaves of water mint. How such a disreputable couple could encompass the artistry of the little posies, and the general air of freshness that pervaded their shop and stall, was one of the unsolved mysteries of the city. Job, barely visible as a shadow moving noiselessly at the back of the shop or stall, was vaguely thought to be weak in the head, for Keziah and Albert were perpetually shrieking imprecations at him, as though maddened by his incapacity. Their curses seemed to envelop him in a murky shroud of nonentity and no one except Polly ever really saw him.

She would never forget the first time she had seen him. She had come to Dobson's from the workhouse, after the terrible row about it which had shaken the city to its foundations and resulted in the dismissal of the workhouse master and most of his staff, and the clearing out of a few surplus children to Dobson's. The row, she understood, had been caused by the terrible Dean whom everyone hated, but she did not hate him because it was he who had commanded that every year three girls and three boys, the six most promising children in the workhouse, were to be passed on to Dobson's at his expense. She was proud to be one of the first six chosen, and thankful to leave the workhouse. She never thought about it after she had left it, for she had a wonderful capacity for letting evil things slough off her, but she did not forget the Dean. She had never seen him when he was at the workhouse but she had heard him once from the other side of a closed door. She had trembled, as one did at a peal of thunder, but she had exulted too.

Both she and Job had been at Dobson's for some while before they saw each other, and they might never have done so had they not had their places in church rearranged, so that they sat just across the aisle from each other. To turn the head only very slightly towards the opposite sex was punishable if noticed by authority, but Polly and Job were both so diminutive that the larger children in front of them and behind them screened them from view, and their eyes met often. Polly was a year older than Job, and already motherly, and when she saw him first her heart seemed to stop, and not only with compassion. She did not analyse the thing that was not compassion but was aware of it as a relief, as though there was a purpose somewhere. She looked at Job and Job looked at her, that first time with shy interest, but the second time with delighted recognition. The third time his eyes were alive and bright and the fourth time they clung to her face with an entreaty that tore her to pieces and afterwards, at night, made her sob into her pillow because she was leaving Dobson's to be maid-of-all-work to Emma in Angel Lane and would not see him again.

But a long while afterwards she did see him again. Emma sent her one day to buy fishheads for Sooty at the shop beside the North Gate, and he was there in the shadows gutting fish. He looked much the same except that he was taller and his hair had grown into an untidy black mop. She went close to him and not knowing his name she said gently, "Dear." He looked up and his black eyes suddenly blazed with light. Then Albert loomed up. One of his great fists landed in Job's left eye and the other in the small of

Polly's back, sending her lurching back into the front of the shop. She paid for Sooty's fishheads and then for Job's sake fled without looking at him again.

That had been a year ago and now they met weekly at the market, exchanging a whispered word or two when they could. They met at other times too, for after the shop was shut Job sometimes climbed up the hill to Angel Lane and scratched like a mouse at the back door. It opened most conveniently into the scullery, where they could be together for a few minutes and yet if Emma came into the kitchen Job could be gone in a flash. On the rare occasions when Emma was out he would creep into the kitchen and sit warming his half-starved body by the fire. The strong aroma which haunted the kitchen, after his fish-impregnated wet clothes had been steaming in front of it for a short while, could always be ascribed later to Sooty's fishheads which had gone off.

For where Job was concerned Polly was without conscience. Followers were forbidden by Emma but when interrogated Polly would look her mistress straight in the eye and say, "No man or boy ever sets foot in my kitchen, ma'am, excepting only the sweep in the way of business," without a blink of an eyelash. She was prepared not only to lie for Job but to steal for him, and she did sometimes steal a little of Emma's flour to make the pasties he adored; but the meat and potato inside them were what she had saved from her own plate when Emma dealt her out her portion in the parlour. Out of her meagre earnings she bought cough lozenges for Job, and salves for his cuts and bruises, and he on his side did what he could to serve her. He brought her blackberries and nuts and made nosegays for her, and from bits of wood he carved robins and wrens and mice for her amusement; she had a box in the attic full of these treasures. And treasures they were, though neither of them realised that the skill of his fingers amounted to genius.

Polly chose her eel and her fishheads without a glance at Job and then took them to him behind the stall to wrap up for her. He slipped into her basket, on top of the fishheads, a posy of sprays of scarlet blackberry leaves and soft grasses from the fen, and her hand went into his pocket holding a pasty whose filling was her last night's portion of shepherd's pie. Their eyes met and their hands touched for a moment, and the sun was warm upon them and the bright air trembled with the ringing of the bells. Polly when she went away took the brightness, the music and the warmth with her, but darkness fell on Job.

CHAPTER VII   *Miss Montague*

I

A FEW days later Sarah cleared away the tea and lighted the lamp that stood beside Miss Montague's chair. She would have drawn the curtains but Miss Montague stopped her. "There's sunset still in the sky," she said. "Is it not beautiful?"

"I don't let such things worry me," said Sarah. "Ring the bell when you've had enough of it."

After she had gone Miss Montague sat apparently idle, her hands caressing the cat in her lap. Beyond the west window, behind the steep old roofs of Worship Street, the last of a fiery sunset was burning itself out. Through the east window she could see through the branches of the elm trees the west front and the three great towers glowing with reflected light, so that it seemed as though the whole Cathedral was built of rosy stone. Evensong was over and everyone was having tea. There was no sound but the ticking of her clocks and the cawing of the rooks in the elms. Motionless in her chair Miss Montague left her room and went up and down the streets of the city, seeing the remembered pattern of its roofs against the sky, the leap of the Cathedral towers seen now from one street and now from another, knowing as she turned each corner exactly what she would see, for she had the city by heart. She went out of the South Gate and down into the fen, and saw the great flaming sky reflected in the water. She told over the names of the villages on their hills as though they were a string of jewels, and came back into the city again and found that the lamplighter was going his rounds and the muffin man was ringing his bell. Lamps and candles were being lit in the houses now and she looked in through the windows and saw the children having their tea, but nobody noticed her. If anyone at this moment was thinking of her it was as a very old woman who never left her house except to go to the Cathedral in her bath-chair when she was well enough, and perhaps they pitied her. They did not know how vivid are the memories of the old and that only the young are house bound when they can't go out. Her memories ranged back over more than eighty years and covered a long span of the life of the city, and the birth and life and death of many men and women all of whom had been and were her friends. She did not forget a single one of them and now that she was so old she did not distinguish very clearly between those who were what the world calls dead and those who still lived there. No one had ever been so blessed with friends as herself. It astonished her. But then her whole life astonished her and caused her considerable amusement as she looked back upon it.

II

She had been born in this house. Her grandfather had been a famous judge and in his day Fountains had been only the holiday home of the Montague family, but her father, lacking the ambition possessed by nearly all the Montagues and gaining a rich wife, had retired early from the army and had lived for most of his married life at Fountains. His daughter Mary had come fourth in his family of six children, all of them attractive except herself. She had been from the beginning a plain little thing, and when a brother in a fit of temper pushed her down the tower stairs and she broke her leg the accident did not improve her looks. The leg, unskilfully set, mended badly and afterwards was shorter than the other. She had hurt her back also in the fall, and it caused her much suffering, but of this she never spoke after she had been told it was only growing pains. In a family of six aches and pains were not much noticed, least of all in the least noticeable of the children. And so she grew up stunted in her growth and slightly lame. She was shy and never had much to say for herself, and no one could have guessed, seeing the little girl sitting like a mouse in the corner with her kitten, that the ambition and the adventurous spirit that had made the later generations of Montagues such a power in the land was more alive in her than in any of the other children.

Through her early years she lived withdrawn from the others and their rowdy games, in which she could not join, happy in a fantasy world of her own. As soon as she could escape from lessons and the sewing of her sampler she would climb the tower stairs to the little room at the top, called Blanche's bower because it was said that it had been beloved of the duchess Blanche, and here she would sit in the window seat, wrapped in a shawl, with the cat in her arms, looking out over the roofs of the city to the fens and the sea, and dream of the great things she would do. She would be an explorer and discover unknown lands, and be adored by the natives there. She would be another Elizabeth Fry and her life would be written and she would be the friend of kings and queens and everyone would love her. She would marry an ambassador and live in fabulous Russia and have twelve beautiful children who would worship the ground she trod on. She would be a great actress like Sarah Siddons and every man who saw her would fall in love with her. There was no end to the entrancing careers that she mapped out for herself, and in all of them her starved longing for love was satisfied up to the hilt.

Her awakening in adolescence was sudden and terrible. Her eldest sister Laura was to be married. It was the first wedding in the family and was to take place in the Cathedral and be a great social occasion. It never occurred to Mary that she would not be Laura's bridesmaid with the other sisters. She was only a little lame and she could stand for quite a time when she had to. Yet the shock of being excluded was not so great as the shock of finding that in all the excitement of the wedding preparations no one, least of all her pretty careless mother, seemed to think it necessary to explain to her why she was left out. She realised that they had never thought that she would expect to be a bridesmaid. Towards the end of the wedding reception her back was hurting her so much that she could hardly bear it. She crept away, no one seeing her, grabbed the cat and went up to Blanche's bower and sat on the window seat wrapped in her shawl, for although it was a warm spring day she was cold. She heard, as from a great distance, the joyous turmoil down below, and presently she saw them come out into Worship Street to watch with the chief bridesmaid, her second sister, as the bride and groom drove away for the honeymoon. They were all there, her father and mother, the two brilliant brothers and the pretty younger sister who was already taller than she. Then full realisation came to her. These brothers and sisters would do the kind of things of which she had dreamed, but she herself would never do them because the Mary Montague of her dreams was not the Mary Montague of the actual world. She was two people but until now only one had been really known to her, and she did not want to know the other. Characteristically she did not stay for long where she was, waiting for someone to come and find her in the gloaming and offer her sympathy, but as soon as she was physically rested went downstairs to forestall it, but no one had missed her.

She had humour and common sense and she soon knew what she must do. She must have done with her dream world, laugh at the ridiculous Mary who had lived in it and get to know the Mary whom she did not want to know, find out what she was like and what her prospects were. It sounded an easy programme but she found it a gruelling one. The fantasy world, she discovered, has tentacles like an octopus and cannot be escaped from without mortal combat, and when at last her strong will had won the battle it seemed as though she was living in a vacuum, so little had the real world to offer the shy frustrated unattractive girl who was the Mary she must live with until she died. But free of the tentacles she was able now to sum up the situation with accuracy. She would not marry and being a gentlewoman no other career was open to her. She was not gifted in any way and she would never be strong and probably never free from pain. She was not a favourite with either of her parents, both of whom were vaguely ashamed of having produced so unattractive a child, and yet she was the one who would have to stay at home with them. And there was nothing to do at home. The prospect was one of lifelong boredom and seemed to her as bleak as the cold winds that swept across the fens, even at times as terrible as the great Cathedral in whose shadow she must live and die. For at that time she did not love the Cathedral and in her fantasy life the city had merely been the hub from which her radiant dreams stretched out to the wide wheel of the world. What should she do? Her question was not a cry of despair but a genuine and honest wish to know.

She never knew what put it into her head that she, unloved, should love. Religion for her parents, and therefore for their children, was not much more than a formality and it had not occurred to her to pray about her problem, and yet from somewhere the idea came as though in answer to her question, and sitting in Blanche's bower with the cat she dispassionately considered it. Could mere loving be a life's work? Could it be a career like marriage or nursing the sick or going on the stage? Could it be adventure? Christians were commanded to love, it was something laid upon them that they had to do whether they liked it or not. They had to love, as a wife had to obey her husband and an actress had to speak her lines when the curtain rose, and she was a Christian because she had been baptised and confirmed in the Cathedral and went to matins every Sunday in her best bonnet. But what was love? Was there anything or anybody that she herself truly loved?

A rather shattering honesty was as much a part of her as her strong will and her humour, and the answer to this question was that she loved the cat and Blanche's bower. She fed the cat and nursed him when he was sick, and she dusted the bower and kept a beau-pot of flowers on the window-sill. Her eyes were always on them, watchful for beauty to adore, for the ripple of the muscles under the cat's striped fur, the movement of sun and shadow on the walls of the bower. And watchful for danger too. She had got badly hurt once rescuing the cat from a savage dog, and when the bower's ceiling got patched with damp she gave her father no rest until he sent for the builder to mend the roof. She was concerned for them both and had so identified herself with them that they seemed part of her. Making a start with the cat, was it possible to make of this concern and identification a deliberate activity that should pass out in widening circles, to her parents and the servants and the brothers and sisters and their families, to the city and its people, the Cathedral, even at last perhaps to God himself? It came to her in a flash that it must be wonderful to hold God and be held by him, as she held the cat in her arms rubbing her cheek against his soft fur, and was in turn held within the safety and quietness of the bower. Then she was shocked by the irreverence of her thought, and tried to thrust it away. But she did not quite succeed. From that day onwards it remained warm and glowing at the back of her mind.

So she took a vow to love. Millions before her had taken the same simple vow but she was different from the majority because she kept her vow, kept it even after she had discovered the cost of simplicity. Until now she had only read her Bible as a pious exercise, but now she read it as an engineer reads a blueprint and a traveller a map, unemotionally because she was not emotional, but with a profound concentration because her life depended on it. Bit by bit over a period of years, that seemed to her long, she began to get her scaffolding into place. She saw that all her powers, even those which had seemed to mitigate against love, such as her shrewdness which had always been quick to see the faults of others, her ambition and self-will, could by a change of direction be bound over in service to the one overmastering purpose. She saw that she must turn from herself, and began to see something of the discipline that that entailed, and found too as she struggled that no one and nothing by themselves seemed to have the power to entirely hold her when she turned to them.

It was then that the central figure of the gospels, a historical figure whom she deeply revered and sought to imitate, began at rare intervals to flash out at her like live lightning from their pages, frightening her, turning the grave blueprint into a dazzle of reflected fire. Gradually she learned to see that her fear was not of the lightning itself but what it showed her of the nature of love, for it dazzled behind the stark horror of Calvary. At this point, where so many vowed lovers faint and fail, Mary Montague went doggedly on over another period of years that seemed if possible longer and harder than the former period. At some point along the way, she did not know where because the change came so slowly and gradually, she realised that he had got her and got everything. His love held and illumined every human being for whom she was concerned, and whom she served with the profound compassion which was their need and right, held the Cathedral, the city, every flower and leaf and creature, giving it reality and beauty. She could not take her eyes from the incredible glory of his love. As far as it was possible for a human being in this world she had turned from herself. She could say, "I have been turned," and did not know how very few can speak these words with truth.

Through most of her life no one noticed anything unusual about her, though they found her increasingly useful. The use her family made of her, however, was more or less unconscious, because she was always there, like Fountains itself, and because she was as unobtrusive as the old furniture whose quiet beauty seemed painted on the dusk of the ancient house. She was just Mary, plain, dumpy, lame, one of those people who do not seem to alter much as the years pass because they have no beauty to lose. The sons and daughters of the house enjoyed their visits home because Fountains was a peaceful sort of place. The servants were happy and contented and the work of the house ran smoothly. The grandchildren, especially those whose parents were in India and who were sent home to be looked after by their Aunt Mary, were more perceptive than their elders. When in after years they looked back on Fountains as upon a lost paradise they saw the face and figure of Aunt Mary as inseparable from it and they knew that they loved her. A few of them loved her as they loved no one else. Each one of them was quite sure that she loved him as she loved no one else; which was true, for seeing as she did the love of God perfectly in each creature of his creation and care she could love the creature as though it were all that existed, and she loved almost without favouritism.

Almost, because she was human. There was one who was dearer than all the rest, her brother Clive who had pushed her down the tower stairs. He, alone among her brothers and sisters, grew to be more perceptive even than the children, because he never forgot what he had done. He intuitively knew that she endured constant pain and slept badly, though no one else knew; her strong will had enabled her not only never to speak of it but also for all practical purposes to overcome it; and he knew also, because she made him understand this, that she set some sort of value on her pain and thanked him for it. Just what its value was to her he could not understand, because explanation of the inexplicable was never Mary's strong point. It deepened love, she said, and sharpened prayer by making them as piercing as itself if drawn into them. But this was beyond him. What was not beyond him was delighted comprehension of her impish humour, which she was too shy to reveal to many. With him she gave it full play and they had great fun together over the years. He alone of the family did not marry and though they met seldom, because as a soldier he was abroad a great deal, the bond between them grew stronger as they grew older. In late middle-age his health failed and he came home to Fountains. In his forty-eighth year he died a hard death after a long hard illness through which Mary and Sarah nursed him, and after his death darkness enveloped Mary.

She was forty-five years old and she had not believed that such a thing could happen to her. Through the years her faith had grown so strong that she had not believed that she could lose it. The living light that had made love possible had seemed too glorious ever to go out, yet now it had gone and left her in darkness and the loneliness of life without love was to her a horror quite indescribable. It had a stifling nightmare quality. A cold darkness, she thought, would have been easier to bear, but this hot thick darkness brought one near to the breaking of the mind. It had been for nothing, she thought. It was not true. It had been for nothing. The wells of water to which she had always turned for refreshment had dried up. When she opened her Bible it was just a book like any other, and that revered historical figure, as self-deceived as herself, was as dead as Clive, killed like him by suffering so great that she could not let herself think of it, for they were not the only ones to pass into nothingness through that meaningless agony. Even the current cat could give her no joy, for it was spring and when she tried to find a little comfort in the garden she was perpetually stumbling over the young birds that he had killed. The Cathedral, huge and glowering, oppressed her with a sense of the colossal idiocy of man and she could have wept to think of all the men who had suffered and died to build it. Why pour out all that blood and treasure for the glory of a God who if He existed at all existed only as a heartless tyrant? She went on going to the Cathedral services as usual but they bored her so intolerably that she could scarcely sit through them. She went, she supposed, from force of habit. It was part of her routine.

Later she realised how much men and women owe to mere routine. She had for years led an extremely disciplined life, and now discipline held her up as irons hold the body of a paralytic. No one except Sarah and Doctor Jenkins found her at all changed. Her parents, old and ailing now, her father growing blind and her mother bedridden, propped their whole weight upon her just as usual, the old people in the workhouse and in Swithins Lane listened as eagerly as ever for the sound of her pony-carriage coming down the cobbled lane, and found her just as satisfactory a source of supply as she had ever been. But Sarah kept trying to make her put her feet up on the sofa, and Doctor Jenkins called upon her on his own initiative one day and placed a bottle of pink medicine on her escritoire.

"What's that for?" she asked a little tartly.

Doctor Jenkins was a young shy man in those days but he was not abashed by the tartness, unusual though it was, because he loved Miss Montague. When he had first come to the city as assistant to old Doctor Wharburton he had felt scared and lonely and had not liked the place, but as soon as Captain Montague's gout and Mrs. Montague's asthma had brought him to Fountains he began to feel different. He had had no idea what an intelligent and attractive fellow he was until he had met Miss Montague. Now he sat down in his favourite chair, realised afresh how likeable he was, relaxed happily and told her at length how exhausted she was by her brother's long illness, and by her father's gout and blindness and her mother's asthmatic heart and querulous temper. She must rest more and take this tonic. "It has iron in it," he finished.

"I'll take it, Tom," Miss Montague promised for love of him, though she did not believe a word of it.

Yet at the end of the first bottle of tonic she began to wonder if there was something in it. She was used to feeling exhausted and paid no attention to it, for it was her normal state, but this abysmal fatigue both of body and mind was not her normal state. She was in darkness but how much had the miasma of fatigue contributed to it? Was it possible that a bottle of tonic and putting one's feet up could affect one's faith in God? Shocked at the unaccustomed way in which her thoughts were dwelling on herself she drove down to the workhouse in her pony-carriage with six flannel petticoats and a dozen packets of tea and baccy. Coming back up Cockspur Street her eyes were caught by the window of the new little shop which had just been opened by young Mr. Isaac Peabody. It was a very long time since her attention had been caught by anything, but there was a clock there shaped like a Greek lyre and Clive had taught her to love all things Greek. Before she knew what she was doing she had stopped the pony-carriage, climbed out, and was gazing at the clock, fascinated by the circle of bright birds whose bodies would never fall and die. The lark at the summit of the lyre was so beautifully fashioned that she could see the quiver of his spread wings and the pulsing of his throat as the song poured from his open beak. In old days her mind had been full of poetry she loved but in this darkness she had forgotten it all. Now as she looked at the lark one of Shakespeare's sonnets seemed to be struggling to make re-entrance into the darkness of her closed mind, beating against it like a bird beating against a shutter.

"I all alone beweep my outcast state
And trouble deaf heaven with my bootless cries."

How did it go on? "Precious friends hid in death's dateless night." No, it wasn't that one. Then suddenly the shutter crashed down and the bird flew in on a beam of light.

"Haply I think on thee, and then my state,
Like to the lark at break of day arising
From sullen earth, sings hymns at heaven's gate;
For thy sweet love remember'd such wealth brings
That then I scorn to change my state with kings."

She leaned against the window as the children did. "Thy sweet love remember'd." Clive. Clive. And he whom she had thought had turned her and got her. What wealth had it been to love them, even if now they were dead. Even if there was no God, even if dateless night was the end of it all, how could she lose them while she lived and remembered, and when she no longer lived then loss, like every other pain, would be over for her.

She opened the shop door and walked in and young Mr. Isaac Peabody came forward from the room behind the counter, an oddly bird-like creature with arms that were too long for him. He moved them up and down as he talked as though they were wings and he meant to take off at any moment. It showed how much good the tonic had done her that the moment she set eyes on him she knew she had a new friend and was glad. A short while ago she had wanted no new friends. Somehow, against her conscience, she bought the Lyre clock, and when she reached Fountains the delighted Sarah carried it up the stairs for her and put it on her escritoire, and she sat down on the sofa and put her feet up and looked at it. From then onwards, whenever she had a few moments, she put her feet up and looked at it and the bright ring of birds seemed to gather all the sunshine to itself.

That was not the end of her darkness, which continued for a long while yet, but it was the first bit of comfort in it. She began to sleep better and sometimes now when she woke in the mornings it was not to that indescribable despair but to a quiet sadness, and with the name of her God upon her lips. But it was autumn before joy was restored to her again, and then it was not the same joy.

She found herself, one wet Wednesday afternoon in October, with an hour to spare, an unusual state of things in her hard-pressed life. She was to have taken the chair at a women's missionary meeting but the speaker had been taken ill and the meeting was cancelled. She had arranged for Sarah to sit with her mother, and for a friend of her father's to have tea with him and read aloud until she came back, and the wild idea came to her that she would do with this hour just what she pleased. But she must go out, for her household did not know that the meeting had been cancelled. Feeling like a truant from school she put on her bonnet and cloak, found her umbrella and let herself out of the old front door into the cool dark cavern of the Porta. Beyond it was a drizzle of fine rain and Worship Street looked grey and dismal, but in the greyness of the Close there were gleams of gold, as though sunrays were enmeshed in the rain, because the bright leaves were not yet fallen. So she went that way, limping slowly under her umbrella, and the air seemed fresh and sweet after her mother's overheated bedroom. But where should she go? She could only go a short way, for now that the rheumatism had settled so firmly in her bad leg and her back such a thing as going for a walk was not possible for her. She could call at any of the houses in the Close and be warmly welcomed but she felt too tired for social calls. She thought she would go to the south door of the Cathedral and sit there on the stone bench and talk to the old bedesman, old Bob Hathaway whom she was very fond of, for she found poor people much more restful than the well-to-do. She walked slowly, for there was that whole hour stretching before her with its blessed emptiness, but even so she was tired when she reached the south door and found it oddly comforting to have old Bob clucking at her like a fussy hen, helping her to shake the wet out of her skirts and put her umbrella down. He was a crusty old man, without the courtesy of Tom Hochicorn who years later was to succeed him, but he was almost as fond of her as she was of him and the scolding he gave her was a pleasure.

"Abroad in all this wet!" he growled. "Why don't ee wear pattens, ma'am?"

"They don't suit my rheumatism, Bob," she explained.

"Sitting on this 'ere cold stone at your age, ma'am!" he went on wrathfully.

"You sit on it," she said, "and you're older than I am."

"Old enough to be your father, ma'am," he said, "which is why I'm giving ee a piece o' my mind."

He went on giving it for some while, and then they talked of rheumatism in general and Bob's in particular, and the terrible wind he had after fried onions, and Miss Montague was just beginning most wonderfully to enjoy Bob when she had the misfortune to sneeze and he got angry with her again. Either she must go home, he said, or she must go into the Cathedral and have a bit of a warm by the brazier. It was lit. She did not want to go home and so to please him she said she would go into the Cathedral for a few moments. He opened the door for her and she went in.

It was very dark in the Cathedral, except for the glow of the large charcoal braziers that were lit here and there in its vastness. They did practically nothing to conquer the cold of the great place but they were pretty as flowers. She made her way to the nearest and held out her chilly hands to its comfort. It burned beside the carved archway that led into the chantry of the duchess Blanche and glowed rosily upon the stone, just as the sunset glowed upon the stone of Blanche's bower at home at Fountains. Miss Montague moved forward into the chantry and sat down on the old rush-seated chair that was just inside. It had a hole in it, for in these days, before the coming of Adam

Ayscough, the Cathedral was not well cared for, and her spreading skirts stirred up the dust. Then the dust settled, and with it the silence, and she realised that she had never before been quite alone in the Cathedral. There were the old bedesmen at the doors but they seemed far away, and it was dark. Vast curtains of shadow fell from the invisible roof and they seemed to move like a tide of dark water. She felt very lonely and she wished she had the cat on her lap.

In the dimness she could just see the little figure of the duchess Blanche lying on her tomb, by herself because her husband had been buried beside the High Altar, but not lonely because there was a dog at her feet. Her hands lay on her breast placed palm to palm in prayer. It was said that she had had her humble part in the making of this place. She had not lived long enough to see the great church of her husband's dream completed, for she had died young, but every day of her widowhood she had come to the Cathedral and knelt down in a particular spot to pray for the repose of her husband's soul, and for a blessing upon the builders of his dream, and after her death they had built her chantry about the place where she had knelt. It was too dark to see it now but Miss Montague knew how lovely it was, small and delicate like the little duchess herself, with cherubs in all the nooks and crannies. Cromwell's men had defaced these, and Blanche's praying hands, but they had not succeeded in spoiling the chantry's beauty, only in giving it a look of battered but enduring patience.

"You've been here so long," Miss Montague said to Blanche, "praying with those wounded hands." For though her mind told her that Blanche was either nowhere, or somewhere else, but anyhow not here, yet she could not this afternoon quite get rid of the feeling that Blanche was here. And high up in the darkness that her sight could not penetrate he was there upon the rood. Her hands folded in her lap Miss Montague shut her eyes, for she was very tired. She ceased to feel lonely. Blanche was here, and the man on the rood, sharing the same darkness with her and with a vast multitude of people whom she seemed to know and love. How much more friendly it is when you cannot see, thought Miss Montague, and how much closer we are to him. Why should we always want a light? He chose darkness for us, darkness of the womb and of the stable, darkness in the garden, darkness on the cross and in the grave. Why do I demand certainty? That is not faith. Why do I want to understand? How can I understand this great web of sin and ugliness and love and suffering and joy and life and death when I don't understand the little tangle of good and evil that is myself? I've enough to understand. I understand that he gave me light that I might turn to him, for without light I could not have seen to turn. I have seen creation in his light. He shared his light with me that I, turned, might share with him the darkness of his redemption. Why did I despair? What do I want? If it is him I want he is here, not only love in light illuming all that he has made but love in darkness dying for it . . . And she said, I will learn to pray.

It was a promise. She said, Please may I begin to learn here with Blanche, and she whose prayer until now had been the murmuring of soothing and much loved words in the tired intervals between one thing and another, or the presentation to Almighty God of inventories of the needs of the city as she drove about it in her pony-carriage, abandoned herself for the sake of those she loved to silence and the dark, understanding however dimly that to draw some tiny fraction of the sin of the world into her own being with this darkness was to do away with it.

Bob's hand fell upon her shoulder and she looked up. It was now almost entirely dark in the Cathedral and she saw his anxious puckered face only dimly by the light of the brazier. "Ma'am, ye's been here near an hour," he said crossly.

It had seemed five minutes. She got up with his help and they went back to the south door. He opened her umbrella for her, while she settled her cloak and shook the dust out of her skirts. Then she smiled at him and thanked him and went away into the rain. She seemed, he thought, "bit moidered", yet she looked younger than when she came.

She did not despair again, and though the darkness came back at times right up to the time when she was a very old woman she was always able to welcome it. Yet if these times came when her health was low she would remember that first bottle of tonic and ask Doctor Jenkins for another, for true darkness and the murkiness of ill-health could be intertwined, to one's confusion, and she would remember that other sonnet of Shakespeare's and know she must not

"... permit the basest clouds to ride
With ugly rack on his celestial face,
And from the forlorn world his visage hide."

After her parents died the city noticed with dismay that she was what is called "breaking up". But increasing physical weakness did not distress Miss Montague, for the enforced lengthening of the tired intervals between one thing and another meant more time to learn the work of prayer, and the house where she now lived alone with the old servants became more and more a place where everybody came because she was more often in it than she had been. As the years passed she was disturbed, almost alarmed, by the growing peace and serenity of her days. Surely it was wrong to be so happy. Then, abruptly, she knew it was not wrong. This was the ending of her days on earth, the dawn of her heavenly days, and it had been given to her to feel the sun on her face.

And so she was happy in old age and vastly amused to find herself a personage in the city, almost an institution, beloved, revered, and apparently the hostess of a salon. Shrewd as she was she could not but be aware that her chair by the fire had become a throne, and that when she went to the Cathedral in her bath-chair it was a queen's progress. When she looked back on the unloved girl she had been, on the toiling drone of her middle years, on the shabby prayerful recluse of her elderly years, it was all beyond her comprehension. But she enjoyed it and with a slightly mocking amusement dressed up for the part with velvet shoes on her feet and lace about her shoulders and over her head. She knew her own worthlessness and so did God, though he loved her none the less, and this false idea of her that the city had got into its head was a private joke between them.

III

Outside it was nearly dark, but she did not call Sarah to draw the curtains; she did not want even the footsteps of dear Sarah on the stairs to enter the silence that held her. But presently other footsteps entered it, slow and heavy, as of a man carrying a heavy weight. They came into the dark cavern of the Porta beneath her room and the flap of the letter-box was lifted and dropped once. Miss Montague smiled and her happiness became deeper. It was the Dean.

It had never been her habit to examine love, or to compare one affection with another, for as love had grown so had reverence for it, but she did realise that Adam Ayscough had brought again to her life something that had been withdrawn when Clive had died. To him alone of all her friends could she speak out of the depths of herself, and from him alone did she receive as much as she gave. In the two intimacies there were differences. Clive had not always understood her but the Dean knew far better what she was talking about than she did herself. Clive had told her everything about himself that there was to tell, Adam Ayscough told her nothing. Yet mysteriously she knew much. She thought sometimes it was as though he kept all his grief in a locked box. Being the man he was he could not show it to her but he had given her the box, and possessing it gave her much power to comfort him. Their friendship had been of slow growth, so shy and self-abhorring was the man, so long did it take him to realise that their need of each other was mutual. And even now he came only seldom to see her, afraid to trespass on her hospitality and afraid to tire her. She wished he would come oftener but like all the old and infirm she had accepted with rueful humour the fact that she must be visited oftenest by those she least wished to see. It was the sensitive, the gentle and humble who feared to come too often lest they tire her. The coarse-fibred had no such inhibitions.

"The Dean, madam," said Sarah.

He bowed over her hand, for he had an archaic courtesy not unlike Isaac's. He still called every woman "ma'am". "I hope you are well, ma'am? I trust you have not suffered from the damp?"

"Thank you, Mr. Dean, I am pretty well. And I hope you have fully recovered from your cold. Will you please sit in that chair? You will not feel the draught there."

An exchange of courtesies flowed between them until Sarah had left the room, and for a short while after. There was never any intimacy in the manner, only in the matter of their conversation with each other. Not even in their thoughts did they use Christian names. The easy manners of the later generations would have shocked both of them.

"Is Mrs. Ayscough well?" asked Miss Montague, and

then, with generous warmth in her voice, "I could see her from where I sat in the Cathedral last Sunday. I thought I had never seen her look more beautiful."

For a moment the Dean's face lit up almost miraculously, then settled again into its habitual sombre sadness. "She is not too well. The harshness of our climate has never suited her. She has an extreme delicacy."

Miss Montague had her own opinion of Elaine Ayscough's extreme delicacy, but it lent no asperity to her gentle words of sympathy. She did not know which of the two she was sorrier for, the man whose habit of hopeless love no indifference seemed able to break or the woman who had to bear year in, year out, the ennui of his unwanted devotion. Their predicament saddened her and she turned thankfully to a happy subject.

"Did you enjoy Mr. Peabody? He told me of your conversation together."

Again the Dean's face lit up. "I am much obliged to you for suggesting that we should talk together. It was a great privilege. I had not known quite how to approach him but the opportunity for conversation presented itself happily."

"I am delighted, Mr. Dean, that for once in your life you have condescended to allow Almighty God the happiness of giving you a little pleasure."

The Dean was frequently startled by the unexpectedness of Miss Montague's remarks, and also, once he had got over the first shock, by their insight. "You are right," he said slowly. "You are quite right. Years ago I decided that joy was not for me. Yes, I see. The decision was my own, not his, and therefore most presumptuous."

"Though most natural," said Miss Montague. "With so many burdens to bear on your shoulders it must have been difficult to look about you. But now you must, for you've not much longer to gratify heaven by taking a little joy. I have discovered, Mr. Dean, that in old age God seems to delight in giving us what our youth longed for and was denied. You know what that was in your case."

"And so do you, I expect," said the Dean, smiling at her. "Sometimes, ma'am, I think that you know everything."

"Certainly not," she said a little tartly. "But I do know that you will hurt the feelings alike of heaven and Mr. Peabody if you do not make a real study of the art of horology."

"I am certainly very ignorant of it," said the Dean humbly, "and far too unobservant. I have heard the ticking of your clock but I have never looked at it." He adjusted his eyeglasses, located the Michael Neuwers on the mantelpiece and got up and looked at it. "This is a very beautiful clock."

"I will tell you only that it is three hundred years old," said Miss Montague. "You must ask Mr. Peabody to tell you about the man who made it. My Lyre clock was made by Mr. Peabody himself. The city is very proud of Mr. Peabody's clocks. Have you ever noticed my Lyre clock? Over there on my escritoire." The Dean crossed to her escritoire and bent and peered at the little circle of enamelled birds. "The little man made this lovely thing himself?" he ejaculated.

He came back to his chair and sat with one hand behind his ear while Miss Montague told him about the day when she had bought the Lyre clock and made the acquaintance of Isaac Peabody. Only with Miss Montague was he sufficiently at ease to betray the fact that he was deaf. He knew that she did not mind speaking slowly and distinctly, for she was so perfectly leisured. "I was in trouble at the time," she said. "I believed that I had lost my faith. Then Isaac put his clock in the window and gradually I found that I had not lost my faith. I shall be delighted if you will laugh at me."

"Why should I laugh?" asked the Dean. "Genius creates from the heart and when men put love into their work there is power in it, there is a soul in the body. You have never seen my watch, ma'am. Mr. Peabody thinks it remarkable. He tells me it has a most unusual watchcock."

"Please to be so good as to hand me my magnifying glass from inside my escritoire," said Miss Montague.

Five minutes later they were sitting side by side absorbed in the watch. Then Miss Montague looked from the watch to the window, where she could just make out the great shape of the Cathedral towering like a mountain against the last of the afterglow. They were both so intricately, beautifully, wisely and lovingly fashioned that the only real difference between them was the unimportant one of size. She had been told of people who could hold some beautiful object in their hands and it would reveal the past to them. How powerful they must be then, these things that had been created from the heart. What beneficence had this watch already wrought? What blessings had it yet to give before some idiot smashed it? A deep shudder went through her.

"You are cold?" asked the Dean.

"No. I just thought of destruction. Of evil. Nothing is safe, not even the Cathedral. I felt afraid for the Cathedral. I felt afraid suddenly for the world. When evil gets a grip on men it always drives them to destroy."

"Evil has hard work to get its hands on what it really wants to destroy," said the Dean. "Which has eternal value, this watch or the love that made it? The body or the soul? How extraordinary that I should be asking this question of you, of all people!"

Miss Montague smiled but did not answer. There was a silence in which each spoke to the other though not in words. Love. The only indestructible thing. The only wealth and the only reality. The only survival. At the end of it all there was nothing else.

CHAPTER VIII   *Sunday Morning*

I

ON the following Sunday the crisp beautiful autumn weather was still holding and there was something of an air of festivity over the city. It was a century when Sunday was still important, and a cleavage between week-day and holy day as real as noticeable. The bells seemed to ring all day and all respectable people went to church except a mere handful of unbelievers such as Isaac, and they felt so much in the minority that during the hours of divine service they incarcerated themselves in their kitchens or libraries behind the newspaper, defiant or uncomfortable according to temperament, and did not issue out until church-going was accomplished. Sunday clothes were very glorious in the city in those days, and Sunday dinners rich and succulent. A rustle of silk petticoats, a *frou-frou* of frills and flounces, made a soft murmuring undercurrent to the music of bells and voices during church-going hours, and as the morning wore on the mingled scents of roast beef and Yorkshire, onions and apple pie became ever more delectable.

In the houses in Angel Lane, which for the most part boasted only one small maid like Polly and yet where the appearance and customs of gentility must be upheld, the strain contingent upon getting into one's best clothes, getting the dinner and getting to church all in the space of a few morning hours was very great. It was especially great at number twelve because Emma felt it her duty to take Polly to church with her in the morning instead of leaving her at home to mind the joint. She feared to let Polly stay alone in the house with Isaac, lest he corrupt her with his terrible freethinking notions, and she also feared to let her go to church by herself in the evening lest she collect followers. Indeed she scarcely dared let Polly out of her sight all day on Sunday lest some sort of evil befall her. At least that was what she believed to be the motive in her ceaseless vigilance over her little maid. She was unaware of her own terrible jealousy of Polly. The sympathy, laughter and comprehension that spun like sunlight between Isaac and Polly, as once they had spun between Isaac and his mother, was something she refused to know about. Nor would she know that the orphanage child had in her that vital glow that she never had. She lived too close to despair to have any strength left for self-knowledge. She might have been able to acknowledge herself unloved but to know herself unloving was beyond her strength.

That Sunday morning Polly was hard at it from an early hour, lighting the fires, getting and clearing breakfast, washing up, making the beds, peeling the potatoes and onions, putting the joint in the oven and making custard. The pastry she had made the day before, and she had cleaned all the shoes and starched Emma's Sunday petticoats. While she was darting here and there, trying not to dance and sing, Emma was laying the table with meticulous care and Isaac was winding the clock and trying not to get under foot. Usually he hated Sundays but this one he felt was going to be different. His spirit was as sensitive to such things as a barometer and this morning he was aware of a change in the wind, disturbing perhaps, but eventually beneficent. When Emma, who had been upstairs changing into her Sunday best, came into the parlour drawing on her black kid gloves he turned to smile at her, swallowed nervously and gulped out, "You look nice, Emma. Is that a new bonnet?"

Emma stared at him. Her big black bonnet, with a sad black ostrich plume rearing up on top of it like a bedraggled cock about to crow, had been new five years ago. Her voluminous black bombasine gown was older still and she was glad to cover it with her mother's cashmere shawl, old too but so soft that its folds still retained their first beauty, and a whiff of the perfume that their mother had always used. Mrs. Peabody had kept all her maternal love for Isaac, and Emma, though nursing her mother with apparent devotion, had retaliated with many subtle cruelties, but she had persuaded herself now that there had always been perfect sympathy between them and she never failed to put orris root between the folds of the shawl.

"That is our mother's shawl," said Isaac.

Emma had been almost on the point of returning his smile but now a dead shut look closed down over her sallow face. Isaac was always blind and stupid in all that concerned herself, instantly alert if anything recalled their mother. She turned from him in silence and took the big brass-bound prayer book from a bookshelf. Then she rustled and crackled through the door calling, "Polly, I am waiting." Polly came stepping very demurely down the stairs, but the demureness emphasised the gaiety of the crimson ribbons on her bonnet and the sparkle in her eyes, and as she came the bells began to ring. Isaac opened the front door and light and air and music poured in, broke against Emma like bright water against a dark rock, flowed round her, joined behind her, and to Isaac's fancy filled the house. "Shut the door, Isaac," said Emma sharply from the pavement. Isaac did so and then leant against it chuckling. "Too late, Emma," he said. "It's in."

He stayed where he was, almost too happy to move. The bells seemed to him to be ringing almost in the walls of the little house, and the reverberation of organ music came nearer and nearer. Two great eyes burned in the dimness of the passage, a majestic presence approached and the music boomed about his legs. A solid softness was pressed against him, now here, now there, as Sooty weaved and turned and hummed. There were now no women in the house, nor would be for a blessed ninety minutes. Sooty led the way to the kitchen and the two males ensconced themselves before the fire. Isaac took his coat off and sat in his shirt sleeves, his feet on the fender and his pipe in his mouth. Emma did not allow him to smoke, and he had discovered that if he left the window open fresh air and the smell of the roast counteracted the aroma of tobacco, and his sins did not find him out. He placed his spectacles upon his nose and opened the paper. He read and smoked a while. Sooty purred, then slept. From the garden the sharp sweet autumnal song of a robin pierced him and then ceased. He continued to hold his paper in front of his nose but he no longer read it. When the bells fell silent he always tried hard not to think of the city's preoccupation at this hour, but yet he always did, with anger and guilt. Yet today he remembered it without anger, even with a certain nostalgic pleasure, and one of those flashes of vision that came in his good times.

In all the old churches of the city the congregations had rustled to their knees. In St. Peter's in the market place Emma was kneeling beside the black marble tablet on the wall that commemorated their father's virtues, her sallow face hidden within her bonnet, with Polly beside her peeping bright-eyed through her interlaced fingers. In the Cathedral the Dean knelt with bowed head in his carved and canopied stall, his ugly strong hands clasped on the white page of the great book that lay open before him. Somewhere within the shadows was an old lady in a bathchair, her mittened hands folded together on the rug that covered her knees. As quietness grew in Isaac he became aware of a multitude of men and women kneeling in churches all over the world, thousands of them, and heard the murmur of their prayer rising louder and louder like a mounting wind in forest trees; yet in the forefront of his seeing those two pairs of clasped hands, old and misshapen, held his attention with a sense of symbolic strength and beauty. The wind shook him, coming from he knew not where and going he knew not where, but a harsh grating voice in his ears was audible to him above its power, speaking for him and for the city. "O Lord, have mercy upon us, miserable offenders. Spare thou them, O God, which confess their faults. Restore thou them that are penitent." He would have tried to escape, as he had escaped from the Cathedral a few nights ago, but it was for the city, and he had opened the door to it himself. They were deceived, they prayed to a vacuum, to that dark shapelessness that terrified him, but the love with which they prayed had reality; he knew that, for he had experienced love.

He knocked his pipe out. His paper rustled to the floor and his spectacles slid down his nose. His hands, red and

Sunday Morning 123

shiny, lay relaxed on his knees. He abandoned himself to the quietness and the warmth of sun and fire. Autumn was a strange paradoxical time of the year. It was the season when he was happiest and yet it was the season when he was most vulnerable and most aware, and that was not always a happiness. Yet he liked autumn. As he dropped asleep he heard again the sharp sweet robin's song.

He woke and saw a mouse on the floor, by the coal scuttle, not three feet from where Sooty slept. He looked at it for several minutes, admiring the delicate ears and the curve of its tail, happy with it, until it slowly dawned upon him that this close juxtaposition of himself, Sooty and a mouse, was unusual. He stirred Sooty with his foot, woke him up and indicated the mouse. Sooty yawned, looked at the mouse, glanced contemptuously in Isaac's direction and went to sleep again. Isaac leaned forward and poked the mouse with his pipe stem. It did not run away. He leaned still farther forward and picked the mouse up by its tail. Then he carried it to the window and stood there holding it, excitement mounting in him. It was a wooden mouse with a tarred string tail, a common enough toy but fashioned with such love of mouse that it was almost more mouse-like than a real one. It revealed, so to speak, the essence of mouse, swift and slinking, endearing and alarming all at once. Who had made it? Not Polly. She was of the pelican breed, not the beaver kind. She was not creative. But this craftsman was such another as he was himself. He could have made this mouse and its creator could have fashioned the cuckoo that flew out of the clock in the shop window. Isaac's face was pink with pleasure, for he was not a man to begrudge another proficiency in his own craft. He had never felt jealous in his life. He wrapped the mouse carefully in his clean Sunday handkerchief and put it in his pocket, for Emma must not see it. She was perfectly capable of putting it in the dustbin. What had Polly been thinking of to leave it lying on the floor? For it must belong to Polly.

He went back to his chair, lit his pipe again and looked at the clock. Three-quarters of an hour had passed and stillness held the city. It must be sermon time. He saw Polly sitting very upright on the hard bench, her eyes fixed on the preacher's face, her own small countenance rather wickedly demure within her bonnet, for her thoughts were not where they should be. He shrunk away from the dark figure of Emma beside her, for he did not want to see Emma. Instead he tried to see the Dean sitting in his high canopied stall. But he was not sitting, he was kneeling, his face hidden in his hands. To his side came a man in a black gown, bearing a golden wand, and the Dean rose and followed him. They paced slowly beneath the huge shadowed roof from which the sunbeams fell like spears, and then the Dean was mounting up and up as though, Isaac thought, to some scaffold, or to some high place that was as fearful to him as a scaffold would have been. The pulpit, thought Isaac, the pulpit. I did not know he hated to preach. Isaac was distressed. What could he do? There was nothing he could do and he was suddenly so unhappy that he opened the paper and immersed himself in the sporting news.

II

Polly did not dislike church-going, indeed she loved it, though she could not read the prayer-book in which Emma so carefully found the places for her, or understand a word of the Reverend Augustus Penny's rambling sermon; in fact few people could, so ancient was Mr. Penny and so muddled in his head. She loved it because sometimes, when she and Emma came in, she saw a shabby figure at the back of the church, hidden in a dark corner by a dusty marble monument. Job. Walking in behind Emma she dared not even smile at him and when she came out again he was always gone, but even that much of Job was enough to make her day glorious.

Today, walking with quick short steps beside Emma down Angel Lane, with the bells pealing and the sun warm on her face, she felt that he would be there. Else why was she so specially happy today? She hardly knew how to contain herself. As they turned to go down the flight of steps that led to the market place she turned and looked back up Angel Lane to Worship Street, and saw a river of colour flowing under the Porta. It was the gentry going to the Cathedral, the men in curly-brimmed top hats and cutaway coats of bottle-green, russet and mulberry, the women in little hats with wonderful full skirts swinging over stiffened petticoats. Polly loved to see them, they were so gay. "Oh look, ma'am!" she cried to Emma, but after one contemptuous glance Emma walked on down the steps with her head in the air. She, by birth, belonged to that bright galaxy of stars, but she had fallen from them because her brother had gone into trade and got drunk at the Swan and Duck. And they had let her fall. Well, let them go to the Cathedral. She was going to St. Peter's, her father's church, for that had fallen too. With Mr. Penny so old and wandering in his head it had become lonely and almost derelict, with a congregation so sparse that in bad weather it did not always go into double figures. Yet it was rich in possessing the whole of the affection and loyalty of which Emma Peabody was at present capable.

They came out of the sunlight into the dark porch, and from there into the dim mustiness of the church. Out of the corner of her eye Polly saw Job beside the broken monument, and her heart leapt. She could only give one quick glance but after it she could see him as clearly as she would ever see anything in this world. He wore a peat-brown coat that was now much too small for him, strained across his chest and buttoned tight so that no one should see the state of his shirt, blue trousers with patches at the knees, and broken boots. He had scrubbed his face until it shone, but being pressed for time at the pump that morning he had not continued the good work to ears and neck. He sat crouching a little forward, as though he thought he would be less noticeable that way, with his brown hands on his knees to hide the patches, and his eyes under the tumbled dark mass of hair on his forehead were bright with mingled pleasure and fright. To sit behind Polly and look at the top of her bonnet appearing over the back of the pew was bliss, and he liked old Mr. Penny, but he did not like it when the other members of the congregation stared curiously at him. It was a measure of his love for Polly and his affection for Mr. Penny that he came at all.

St. Peter's did not frighten Polly because it was broken and neglected, and she was so sorry for it that she was fast coming to love it. The paving stones were cracked and uneven, the hangings faded and torn, the tall old pulpit looked tottering into ruin and there were cobwebs everywhere. Every available space was crowded with memorial tablets, surmounted with cherubs with broken wings, funeral urns and skulls. Yet it had beauty, for there was very old glass in the windows. It darkened the church but when the sun shone it spilled deep and glorious colour all over the cracked paving stones, the dusty pews, the chipped cherubs and skulls and urns, and the congregation. It was shining today and when they settled themselves for the sermon Polly saw that the meagre congregation was arrayed in all the colours of the rainbow. Her lips parted in delight, for they were as royally dressed as the gentry had been. Seeing her smile and afraid she was about to giggle Emma hushed her, for Mr. Penny was smoothing out the crumpled bits of paper on which he had written out his sermon, and looking down at them pleadingly, his mouth trembling. Polly lifted her face, and the smile was for him now, because his torn old surplice was lilac, crimson and gold.

He was a tall old man, thin and hoop-shaped, with wispy white hair and bewildered watery blue eyes. For a great many years he had been vicar of one of the loneliest villages in the fen, but after his wife had died there he had become somewhat melancholic and ten years ago the Bishop had brought him to the city. But the move had come too late to do him much good, for though he had never lost faith in his God he had lost faith in himself. Years after the great church out in the fen had remained half empty, while year after year the cold damp vicarage had mouldered to pieces about himself and Letitia, because it was one of the poorer livings. And now year after year the congregation at St. Peter's grew smaller and smaller. The vicarage was less vast here, the stipend a little more, but that did no good to Letitia. It was a pity that they had not thought to move him before Letitia died, but he bore no grudge. Only he could not help it going round and round in his head, as it was doing now, so that he could not remember his text, which he had failed to write down at the head of his sermon. He looked desperately up and down the pews and saw how the girl in the black bonnet and grey cloak, a girl whom he liked almost as much as the shabby boy who hid by the monument at the back of the church, was smiling at him. And her bonnet was golden and her cloak rose-colour and saffron. "The king's daughter is all glorious within," he said. "Her raiment is wrought gold." Then he rambled off into a sermon about something entirely different and everyone went to sleep except Polly and Job. Polly stayed awake thinking about Job and Job stayed awake thinking about Polly.

Sunday Morning

It was when the service was over that the wonderful thing began to happen. Polly, coming out into the porch with Emma, saw to her astonishment that Job was still there, his back to the people, intent upon one of the torn bits of paper that flapped from the notice board. He did not turn round and she scarcely even dared to look at the back of his head and his unwashed neck as she stood waiting for Emma to finish her conversation with old Mrs. Martin from the baker's shop. Emma, as the daughter of a former vicar, was a person of importance in the tiny St. Peter's congregation, and she loved queening it among them. "Yes, ma'am, my daughter Mary's home," said old Mrs. Martin. "The one who went out to America. You remember her, ma'am? Your dear father baptised her." And then, as Emma was graciously pleased to remember Mary, she went on, her old face flushing at the presumption of what she was about to ask, "I suppose, ma'am, you couldn't honour us by drinking a dish of tea with us today?"

"Thank you, Mrs. Martin," said Emma, "but I never leave my brother alone on a Sunday."

"Mary's leaving for London tomorrow, ma'am," said old Mrs. Martin sadly. She was very disappointed and she feared she had presumed too far. Polly could not bear her disappointment.

"Ma'am, I will give Mr. Peabody his tea," she said. "And he will have the paper and Sooty. He will not be lonely. He would like you to have the pleasure."

"It would be such an honour, ma'am," said Mrs. Martin. "I remember as though it were yesterday how your dear father ———." She stopped and wiped away a tear, caused actually not by remembrance of the late Mr. Peabody but by a draught operating upon weak eyesight. But Emma was touched. She was also torn two ways by jealousy of Polly presiding over Isaac's tea and a sudden longing to be made much of. No one even in her childhood had petted her. The nearest she had ever come to a knowledge of tenderness was occasionally now in her later years, with these old women who saw her through the rainbow mist that softens all outlines of the past. She was not aware of saying yes but without her knowing quite what happened she found herself climbing the steps towards Angel Lane very flustered and out of breath, and committed to it. She stopped and looked accusingly down at the top of Polly's bonnet. "Polly, did you hustle me?" she asked sharply.

"Oh no, ma'am," said Polly from within her bonnet. Her face could not be seen, and her voice was small, correct and demure, but Emma had a sense of small bells chiming, of jubilation and laughter all inside the bonnet. She put out her hand against the wall to steady herself, then climbed on. At the top of the steps she stopped again and asked, "Who is that disreputable boy who was in the porch just now?"

"I don't know, ma'am," said Polly within the bonnet, adding severely, "he should wash his neck."

III

Elaine Ayscough settled back in her seat with a sense of almost unbearable malaise. Adam had just climbed up into the pulpit. It was a high pulpit with a great sounding board and when he got to the top at last, and stood there with his big head hanging a little forward, his ugly nose jutting beak-like from his sallow face, peering out and down at the congregation, with that hideous thing curved over his head, she thought he looked like the Punch of a Punch and Judy show. She thanked heaven that, as Dean, Adam did not have to preach often, and she took it as a personal injury that the Canon in residence should have sprained his ankle and forced him to preach today, for she hated hearing Adam preach. She hated it as much as he hated preaching. Marriage was a queer thing. She did not love Adam, but yet she knew things about him. She knew preaching made him miserable, though she did not know why, and when he was in the pulpit every nerve in her body seemed to be taut. With an effort of her very strong will she tried to detach and calm herself, for she did not want to have another of her headaches; they were ageing her. Adam's sermons were always very long, entirely incomprehensible, and often inaudible too because his deafness made him raise his voice too much, so that it just boomed in the sounding board like surf in a cave and nobody heard a word. She could feel in all those nerves in her body that were not yet quieted how the congregation was resigning itself; to endurance, to meditation, to the planning of menus or wardrobes, each mind running to its own habitual harbour as a ship runs to shelter in a rising wind. But none of them was turning to sleep. In other churches in the city people were possibly sleeping through a sermon, but not here. People did not sleep when the Dean preached. Subconsciously they were too disturbed.

Elaine, having severed her connection with Adam, let herself drift into the sanctuary of her own beauty. Looking down she saw with pleasure how her wide silk skirts were faintly patterned with the far colours of the stained-glass windows. Her slim gloved hands lay in a patch of purple light, as though she held violets. She was aware of the great Cathedral soaring about her and felt more kindly disposed towards it than she usually did. It was beautiful in sunlight, a fit setting for her loveliness. She was not a religious woman but she did feel a profound and at times almost a humble thankfulness that she had kept her beauty. It had been the same today as it had always been. As she had rustled up the nave to her pew of honour beneath the pulpit, tall and slender, and sunk gracefully to her knees, her face devoutly bowed into her hands, she had felt all the eyes upon her just as she had always done. She did not mind if they stared in envy or even dislike so long as they stared. It was not so much that she wanted admiration as that she wanted comfort. Years ago when there had seemed nothing else to live for she had made a *raison d'être* of her own beauty, not realising that as life goes on a *raison d'être* becomes increasingly possessive. Sometimes, during the wakeful hours of the night, she knew that she no longer owned her beauty, but that her beauty owned her. Then she would be very afraid, wondering if when it left her she would be simply a thing dropped on the floor.

The grating voice above her obtruded itself again. The severance had not been complete; it never was in marriage. Her hands made a sudden convulsive movement of exasperation in her lap, and she had the fancy that Adam had seen it. The deanery pew was too close to the pulpit; far too close when it was your own husband who was preaching. They were too close. She folded her hands again, gently, for she must not crush the violets in her lap. She must not hurt Adam who had given them to her. Fool, she said to herself, they're not flowers, they're light. But it was too late now to tell herself that, for she was already back again in the little Chelsea drawing-room and Adam had just put the violets in her lap. A drifting mood, encouraged, is like a current at sea. You have no control over where it will take you.

They had met each other first at a dinner party, her first party after the ritual period of mourning for her young scamp of a husband was over at last. She had been gay that night. She had finished with her black clothes, with lawyers and condolences, with pretending to be grief-stricken when she was not, with the whole boring business of widowhood, and could enjoy herself again. She had very little money and would have to do something about that shortly but meanwhile she was gay, and ready to be entrancingly kind to the grotesque middle-aged man who had taken her into dinner. He was distinguished and scholarly, she had been told, well born and well off, or she would not have bothered with him. She rather admired breeding and scholarship and was adept at concealing her own lack of both. She was a clever woman, with the chameleon's gift of taking colour from her environment. Her gaiety that night was not obtrusive but it gave an enchanting warmth to her usually rather remote and classical beauty, a warmth that seemed to the desolate man beside her a glow of heavenly kindness.

Adam just at this time was extremely desolate. He had already been a schoolmaster for some years, having failed as a parish priest, but he was not enjoying it. He did not make friends easily. He knew little of women and had always been rather afraid of them. He fell in love now, at forty, for the first time and it could scarcely have gone harder with him. It was months before he could bring himself to propose to Elaine, so inhibited was he by the thought of his own unworthiness, so scared of in some way hurting her fragile purity with his clumsiness, and he could never have done it had she not been a widow. That somehow was a help. But even so his wooing was so stumbling and constrained that Elaine, involved with other men, did not recognise it for what it was, and when at last he made his humble declaration she was so taken by surprise that her usual finesse failed her. The mask slipped and though after a moment or two she answered him correctly enough he had seen the astonishment, the slightly contemptuous amusement. She saw that he had seen, saw him flinch, and she was sorry. He had touched something in her.

Like so many beautiful women Elaine had a flair for making disastrous marriages. Her French marriage was a degrading exhausting business and it was now that she began to build her life about the fact of her beauty and find sanctuary there. Her beauty was her armour. While she looked as she did she could preserve her pride. Luckily neither of her earlier husbands had learnt the trick of survival and after six years in France Elaine came back to England a widow again, as delicately beautiful as ever but also as impecunious as ever and not quite as physically tough as she had been. She was actually feeling as fragile as she looked, and there was a vague fear in her mind. What next? It was a wet November and the friend whose Chelsea home she had chosen as her refuge seemed with each day that passed less and less sensible of the honour done her. The fear grew.

The rain passed and there came a Saturday of sunshine. She was not fond of walking, but to escape from Rosamond she went to Kensington Gardens and walked there. She still wore her widow's weeds and they were shabby now, and her nose was pink at the tip from a slight cold. She was not looking her best and she knew it, and the knowledge did nothing to cheer her. The sun was warm and golden, and droves of gentle yellow leaves floated about her, but her fear obsessed her mind and she did not know it, and she did not see the tall black figure coming towards her. But he saw her, solitary and fragile, a poignant note of sorrow in the drifting golden glory. His heart seemed beating in his throat and for an instant he did not know whether to go back or go on. Had it seemed that all was well with her he would have turned back that he might not obtrude an awkward memory upon her, but to see her drifting towards him with the leaves, as though as lost as they, kept him where he was. He could perhaps be of service to her.

"Madame Blanchard," he said gently, for he had known about her marriage. She stopped, recognised him and held out her gloved hand to him. He bowed over it and offered her his arm. "Madame, shall we walk together a little way?" She accepted his arm and they strolled on together, conversing of the weather. He was as ugly as she remembered him but she was instantly aware of a new ease in him, a new dignity. Humble as ever he yet had an air of authority. His clothes had been well brushed by butler or valet, his top hat was immaculate. She read the signs and looked up at him with a smile of entrancing sweetness. He murmured a few gentle words of condolence and for a moment she wondered how she should accept this sympathy. With pathos, drooping on his arm like a bird with a broken wing, or with the truth? She decided for the truth. "You need not condole with me, sir," she said with bitterness. "I am thankful that my marriage has ended."

She had made the right decision. He was shocked, and a compassion so vast overwhelmed him that all diffidence, all sense of shame because of the past, was lost in it. He asked her if he might serve her in any way and she shook her head. He asked her if he might take her home and she accepted his offer. She took him up to Rosamond's pretty drawing-room, where the lamp had been lit and the tea table laid before the fire, and the two pretty women made much of him. He told Elaine that he was still a schoolmaster, in town for today only, but he would be spending his Christmas vacation here. Might he call upon her then? She smiled agreement as she bade him good-bye. After he had gone it transpired that Rosamond knew about him. He was now headmaster of a famous school. Her nephew had been caned by him. She seemed not to mind now if Elaine stayed with her till after Christmas.

Elaine conducted her distinguished lover through his second courtship with admirable skill, and as the days went by with real sincerity. The greatness of his love for her by turns touched, exasperated and frightened her, but she was grateful, for it was sweeping her to honour and security. And he was a good man. It was his sheer goodness, she realised now, that had touched her before, touched her innate fastidiousness. She believed herself utterly sick of carnal men. She would try to make him a good wife. She hoped that they might be happy. A week after Christmas he bought her a diamond ring and a bunch of violets, kneeling beside her to put them in her lap.

Then began that strange long sorrow that had worn them both down. Elaine did all she could. She possessed a sense of drama, of fitness and occasion, and only the most discerning guessed that she had not been born to the position she filled with such grace. She moved through her days with dignity and correctitude, a beautiful hostess and a mistress able to command the obedience if not the affection of her servants. She conducted her flirtations with such skill and decorum that again only the discerning were aware of them, and she was meticulously careful in all the outward observances of the religion that was her husband's life.

But that was all she could do. Adam's life, behind the façade of the material comforts and elegances they shared together, was something that he longed to open to her, but could not. Sometimes, stumblingly, he tried to speak of the things that were life to him, but she did not understand. Nor could he on his side understand that the luxuries that so desperately wearied him, that he endured only because his position in the world demanded it of him, were life to her. It would have been all right, she sometimes thought, if he could have stopped loving her, if they could have settled down together into that easy indifference that is the refuge of so many ill-assorted marriages, but they could not even share indifference, and his love, increasingly of the sort that she neither understood nor wanted, bored her almost to distraction. Her dislike of the love of carnal men had, she discovered, been only a passing ennui.

Yet she did not leave him. She wanted to, several times she had almost done so, especially when he had decided that instead of moving to London, chosen as the place of retirement because she loved London, they must come to the bleak city in the fens. Over that they had a heartbreaking struggle. Adam, torn between the will of his adored wife and what he finally came to believe was the will of God, could make only the one decision. She had not understood it, and she could not forgive him, but he had a hold upon her that she could not break and she went with him to the city.

But she was more unhappy now than she had ever been. Until now her married life had been spent in places where there were at times great social occasions and her surpassing beauty could be arrayed and displayed worthily. In the little old city such social occasions as existed were boring in the extreme. Clothes were years behind the fashion and all the men who were not parsons were over seventy. And the climate did not suit her. She was not so well as she had been and not quite so beautiful. She was in a panic about her beauty and so was her husband, knowing that it was her axis. And about Elaine herself he was in anguish. He had loved her for so long, and it seemed so unavailingly, and he had not made her happy. He had, he thought, utterly failed her. He did not know what her life had been before their marriage, and so was unaware of the significance of that one fact that lay like a nugget of buried gold at the heart of their life together. She was still with him, still a woman who because of something in himself had remained all the weary years a decent woman and a faithful wife. Those who had any affection for Adam Ayscough disliked Elaine. Even Miss Montague, who disliked no one and would have taken Elaine to her heart had that been a place where Elaine had the slightest wish to be, did not do her justice. For there had been a battle and it had been, if hardly, won.

The sermon ended at last and Elaine was aware through her whole body of her husband's relief, his relaxation of tension. Aware too, when he had gone to his canopied stall, of the reaction of misery that took its place. He would be impossible to live with for the rest of the day now. He was never at any time a cheerful man and after a sermon his depression was as impenetrable as a fen fog. When the last hymn had been sung, and the blessing given, and the organ voluntary was pealing under the vast arches and down the shadowy aisles striped with their dusty bars of sunshine, Elaine walked slowly and gracefully towards the side door that led into the Deanery garden. One gloved hand held her rustling silk skirts raised above the contamination of dust, the other held the beautiful ivory-backed prayer-book with its silver cross that her husband had given her to carry on her wedding day. It was a warmth to her chilled heart that every eye was on her, though not one of them was an eye worth having. Her way brought her past Miss Montague's bath-chair and the old lady looked up at her with a smile, wholeheartedly delighting in her beauty, even though a slightly mischievous sparkle in her eye recognised the histrionic perfection of Elaine's exit. Elaine inclined her head graciously but coldly. She could not stand Miss Montague. Upon the rare occasions when Adam went to call on the old lady every fibre in her body knew it.

CHAPTER IX *The Mouse*

I

EVENSONG on Sundays was at three o'clock and was sometimes followed by one of the Deanery tea parties to the *élite* of the Close and Worship Street. These parties on the whole gave pleasure for the sandwiches and cakes melted in the mouth, Elaine no matter how bored was always a good hostess, and the Dean's painstaking courtesy was less alarming at his wife's parties than at other people's because being less shy in his own house he was also less hard of hearing. Yet at the same time there was for the guests a sense of relief when it was over and they could emerge safely from the Deanery portal without, they hoped, having appeared too ignorant and dowdy in the presence of the Dean's vast learning and his wife's elegance. Out in the Close there was a tendency for them all to chatter, even when they were not the chattering type. Like children let out of school the making of a joyful noise was a psychological need. A few of them felt a strong desire to go and see Miss Montague; indeed Miss Montague always knew when there had been a Deanery party because of the number of droppers-in from which she suffered. "I was passing the door, my dear. I thought I'd just look in." She was pleased to see them, but always very tired on Sunday evenings because going to the Cathedral in her bath-chair was rather an exhausting business.

For Adam Ayscough and his wife, after their guests had gone and Garland had replenished the fire and closed the drawing-room door noiselessly upon their loneliness, there was no sense of relief. They were perhaps at their happiest together when they were entertaining, for in this they worked as a team. Left to face the long Sunday evening together a sense of hopelessness, almost of panic, took hold of them. If Adam could have immersed himself in *The Spectator* Elaine could have taken her French novel and buried herself in that, but it was his habit to sit beside her on the sofa, to take her hand and stroke it maddeningly while he made heartrending efforts to talk to her, to amuse her, to reach her at last. She longed to cry out, "You fool, there's nothing to reach," but that would have been to hurt him. She was almost thankful tonight to find the first light hammer strokes of one of her headaches beating on her forehead. "Adam," she said, "I am so sorry but I have one of my heads. I think I'll go to bed before dinner."

He got up from the sofa in a condition of distress out of all proportion to the seriousness of her indisposition. That was another irritating thing about Adam; he got into such a ridiculous state if she ailed. "My dear, I am so sorry." He took her in his arms, tender and clumsy, and with one heavy hand pushed the hair back from her forehead, shattering her coiffure so that she would be ashamed to face her maid when she went upstairs. "My dear, I wish you need not suffer so. I would give my right hand that you need not be always ill," he said sadly.

She knew that he spoke the truth and she tried not to grit her teeth. "I shall be quite well in the morning," she said. "Will you ring and tell Garland that I shall not want dinner? I will go now, Adam."

He took his arms from her reluctantly and let her go, and rang the bell for Garland. That worthy, entering, found the Dean standing with his back to the fire, his huge form drooping disconsolately. "Mrs. Ayscough is unwell, Garland. She has gone to her room and will not take dinner."

"I am sorry to hear it, sir," said Garland and proceeded to deal with the familiar situation with suavity and skill. He had been with the Dean for many years and was one of the very few who had come close enough to him to love him. He was unaware of his love but he would not have left the Dean for untold gold. "What would you fancy for dinner, sir?" he asked, knowing very well that when his wife was indisposed and he himself had just preached a sermon the Dean fancied nothing. "Grilled sole, sir? A glass of white wine? A lightly baked custard settles well, sir."

"Thank you, Garland," said the Dean.

"It's a nice evening, sir," suggested Garland. A breath of fresh air always did good. And he knew what would happen if the Dean did not go out. He would sit the whole evening with *The Spectator* held unread before his eyes, for appearance's sake if a servant should come in, and worry about his wife until he could go to bed. He was a writer of scholarly books, and writing was his lifeline in times of distress, but on Sundays, bound by the Commandments, he could not write his book. Nor could he read the kind of book that helped him with his book, because that too was work, and other books did not hold his attention when Elaine was not well. There was of course the great duty and privilege of prayer, and to prayer he most humbly believed himself to be especially called of God, but on Sunday evenings after a long day of services he found it difficult to pray. He was tired, he supposed. Garland knew all this. "A very pleasant evening indeed, sir."

The curtains were still undrawn and the Dean looked at the evening. The trees in the Close were black and motionless against a clear sky. The moon was rising and presently there would be a blaze of stars. "I think I will take a little stroll," he said.

"Very good, sir," said Garland, and following the Dean out into the hall he helped him into the cloak that he liked to wear on his lonely walks. It was an old friend and shabby now. He could not wear it when Elaine was with him. Garland noticed that he was a very bad colour. He was always sallow but now his face had a leaden hue that Garland did not like at all. He had been noticing it for some while and so had Miss Montague. "Dinner can wait your convenience, sir," he said. "Grilled sole. Baked custard. They can be prepared when you come in." He handed the Dean his top hat and stick, opened the front door and saw him out. Then he came back to the drawing-room to draw the curtains and tidy the cushions. The Dean when he came in would go to the study. The drawing-room fire which Garland had built up with such care would now be wasted, and so would the dinner which cook had prepared for two. But that was the way of it with the gentry. Their servants had to learn to accept wasted effort with equanimity.

The Dean walked slowly down the lime avenue. It was cool and quiet. Though the moon had not yet appeared from behind the Rollo tower there was a silveriness about the branches of the trees, magic in the air, a sensation as though bells that could not be heard were still ringing somewhere. There was no wind tonight and the city was silent. Over the fen the dome of the sky was quiet, vexed with no cloudwrack, dark and vast. Just over the edge of the horizon the dark sea breathed gently and caressed the shore.

The Dean sat down for a moment on the seat in the lime walk where Isaac had sat, his head bent, too tired to be much aware of the beauty of the night but vaguely quieted, vaguely ashamed of his own shame. What did it matter if he was incapable of preaching a decent sermon? Why be ashamed of failure? Failure was unimportant. The fact was that mounting the pulpit steps, standing there before all those bored men and women who like the hungry sheep in Lycidas looked up and were not fed, had become to him a sort of symbol of the failure of his life. As priest and husband he had failed. They said he had been a good schoolmaster but he believed them to be wrong. His apparent success there had been due he believed solely to a formidable presence. He had always been able to impose discipline because people were afraid of him. There was of course that other thing, that power that had been given him of taking hold of an evil situation, wrestling with it, shaking it as a terrier shakes a rat until the evil fell out of it and fastened on himself. Then he carried the evil on his own shoulders to the place of prayer, carried it up a long hill in darkness, but willingly. Each time he felt himself alone, yet each time when the weight became too much for him it was shared, then lifted, as though he had never been alone. Yet if there had been no hope of help he would still have been just as willing. But in that mystery nothing was his own except the willingness, and willingness in no way mitigated failure. Nothing mitigated failure except the knowledge that it did not matter. But how could he bring himself to think it did not matter that he had failed Elaine? It was impossible.

He got up abruptly and walked on through the Porta and across Worship Street. At the top of Angel Lane he stopped. The city lay at his feet, its tumbled roofs washed with moonlight, its dark walls patched with squares of orange fireglow. The men and women in the houses would have been astonished to know that the Dean knew the city like the palm of his hand. In earlier years, when he had it in his grip and most men hated him, he would go out into the streets night after night after dark, when he could not be recognised, and walk up and down there. After a month or two he knew every corner and alley as well as Miss Montague knew them. The evil was more dreadful in one street than another, and to these places he would return again and again, exposing himself to them. He would stand in dark doorways and pray there for the men and women within the shuttered houses. If he lacked the common touch, if he was not the priest he had longed to be, this at least he could do. Sometimes, trudging wearily home up the hill, he would remember Michael towering above him in the dark sky, and would be aware of some sort of communication, as though Michael asked him, "Watchman, what of the night?"

Sometimes, when he got home on moonlight nights, he would let himself into the Cathedral through his private door that he might bring the needs of the city before God before he slept. For he loved the Cathedral as few men had ever loved it, more deeply even than William de la Torre who had built it or Prior Hugh who had died within it or Dean Peter Rollard who had been persecuted for it, or Tom Hochicorn the bedesman of the south door who thought he owned it. What it was like at night, with the moonlight piercing through the clerestory windows to illumine the great rood and gleams of silver touching now here and now there as the clouds passed, and the rest vast darkness, only he knew. But he could not have told what he knew.

II

Tonight, looking down at the city, he found himself thinking of one citizen only, Isaac Peabody. He had not seen him again for when Isaac had next come to wind the Deanery clocks he had been once more at matins. He wanted to ask him if in future he could wind the clocks a little later in the morning, so that they could have a few moments' weekly conversation together on the subject of horology, and he wanted to ask if he had in his shop a clock suitable for Elaine's Christmas present, some lovely thing such as Miss Montague's Lyre clock. He was always thinking of something new to give Elaine, some exquisite new thing to adorn her beauty. She always thanked him charmingly for the new jewel or the new fan but he did not often see again the treasure he had chosen for her and then he was sorry, for he knew his taste had blundered. But surely she would like a new clock. The cupid clock in the drawing-room, a relic of the disaster of her French marriage, she must surely dislike. He thought it was a dreadful thing. He wondered what Peabody thought of it.

He remembered suddenly that Isaac lived in Angel Lane at number twelve. He knew because he had asked Garland. He thought he would just stroll down the lane and see which of the old houses was number twelve. He would not go in, for it would be much easier for them both if he went to the shop, but he would just see where his friend lived. He would walk past, go down the steps to the market place and then home up Worship Street.

He found the house easily for the street lamp opposite illumined the number. The front door was slightly ajar and warm light spilled itself down the two worn steps and shone diagonally across the pavement and the cobbles. It was the only open door in the street. The Dean as a boy had had a recurrent dream about a little old house in a crooked street. Two steps had led to its door, set in a small arch like this one, and always it had been a night with stars in the sky and this light spilling out over the pavement and across the cobbled street. To the boy who had dreamed the dream, a small boy without a mother and as an only child much addicted to dreams, it had always seemed that something he wanted very much was inside the house but he had been too shy to push the door and go in. So he had knocked and waited. But no one had ever answered his knock. Always he had said to himself, next time that dream comes I will push the door. Yet when next time came he was still afraid, and had knocked and waited, and then woken up. Then he had been sent to boarding school and dreams had given place to nightmares.

The Dean knocked timidly and waited, aware of laughter somewhere in the house, but no one came, and then with that boldness of panic that can precipitate even a shy person into the wildest of actions, he pushed the door and went in. If he had not done it quickly he would, once more, have woken up. Inside the little passage he suddenly, appallingly, came to himself, but it was too late. He had lost his footing on something which slid from beneath him, and crashed into the umbrella stand and sent it flying. He had also practically lost his own balance. His top hat fell from his head and his walking stick to the floor to join the stick and the vast umbrella of the Reverend Robert Peabody.

The half-open kitchen door, through which the light had been shining, flew wide, and Isaac, Polly and Job came hurrying into the passage. The Dean was too shaken to speak. He did not know what had happened to him out there in the street and he did not know how he came to be where he was now. He had seemed to fall out of time. It was as though he had left his body for a moment or two and coming back to it again had found it not where he had thought it was. Isaac, unable to believe that he was seeing what he saw, bewildered and dumbfounded, could not speak either. Job had melted back into the kitchen. Polly alone remained in command of the unusual circumstances.

She had never seen the Dean, only heard him in a rage that one time at the workhouse, and so he was to her simply an old codger who had slipped on the wool mat outside the parlour door. In the light that shone from the kitchen she thought he looked poor, ill and old and immediately, figuratively speaking, took him to her bosom. "You've come to see Mr. Peabody, sir?" she said. "You're welcome. You've not hurt yourself? You slipped on the mat. Mr. Peabody, he's always doing the same. Miss Peabody, she will make 'em. Let me take your cloak, sir."

While she spoke she had been swiftly picking up the scattered umbrella and sticks and restoring the passage to rights. Now she gently took the Dean's cloak from him, hung it with his top hat upon a peg and ushered him into the kitchen.

When she had him there, divested of the shabby cloak, she saw that his clothes were of fine black broadcloth such as gentlemen wear. He wore white bands beneath his chin, over his waistcoat, and his hands were very clean. She thought he looked like a Beak and for a moment of dreadful terror she wondered if Job, who had disappeared, had done anything. With a blanched face she looked up at the Dean and saw her own terror reflected in his eyes.

"It is the Dean, it is Doctor Ayscough," said Isaac, who was recovering himself. "Another chair, Polly."

The relief was so intense that colour flooded into Polly's face and still looking at the Dean she smiled, her eyes shining. Only the Dean, not a Beak. Then she picked up a duster from the dresser and carefully dusted a chair for him. "Please to sit down, sir," she said, and she was still smiling at him. She knew she should not be smiling at the gentry, but she had taken him to her heart in the passage; she remembered the splendid anger and could not help herself. The Dean thought he had never in his life received a sweeter, warmer welcome than from this child. He was trembling with anxiety lest he do something, say something, to frighten her or Peabody and break this dream that seemed to him a most fugitive thing, like a soap bubble. He was inside it now but the least clumsiness on his part and he would be outside.

"I hope I do not come at an inconvenient hour, Mr. Peabody," he said. "Would you, may I, will you permit me to share your meal with you?"

He was so obviously scared that Isaac could not help realising that he was in the extraordinary position of having to set the greatly feared Dean at his ease. Courage came to him and a queer emotion which he did not until afterwards recognise as that compassion which Doctor Ayscough had once before aroused in him, and he managed to say that it was an honour, to explain that Emma was out and that in her absence they were having late tea in the kitchen instead of the parlour.

"I prefer the kitchen," said the Dean, accepting a large cup of strong sweet tea from Polly. "Mr. Peabody, was there not a boy here? I thought I heard young voices chiming together when I came in."

"It was Job," said Isaac. "Polly, where's Job?"

"He might be in the scullery with the cat," said Polly. "Job, are you there?"

There was a movement and the Dean, looking up, saw Job standing in the doorway with a large black cat dangling from his arms. He liked boys and some of them in his schoolmastering days had actually come to know it. Instantly he liked Job, though he did not identify him with the chimney sweep of years ago. He liked the square thin face with the high cheekbones, the defiant sensitive mouth and wary, dark eyes, one of which had been blackened by a blow. The boy's clothes were ragged and smelt strongly of fish; which was possibly why the cat was purring so contentedly. But his black brows were drawn together and he was obviously not intending to advance farther than the scullery door.

"That's your chair, Job," said the Dean, nodding towards the chair on the other side of Isaac. "If you do not come back and finish that piece of cake I shall not be able to forgive myself that I called upon Mr. Peabody at this unprecedented hour."

The Dean had never yet been disobeyed by a boy, and did not expect to be. Job came across the room and slid into his chair, but he could not lift his eyes from his plate. He had recognised the old man instantly and was terribly upset. That great figure of his dreams had through the years become so exclusively his own that it had been a profound shock to find him here in this house, to find he was the Dean of the city, a man to whom Job Mooring could in the world of reality mean nothing whatever. It was obvious that he meant nothing to the Dean because he did not remember him. Yet there could not be two men. One of them must be false, and the man sitting on the other side of the table was real enough. It was the great figure of his dreams who was false, and if he was false so was Job's world. A depth of anguish opened inside him, and fear. Bereaved of his chief strength and consolation he seemed to have lost himself. It was his first experience of the frightening sense of lost identity.

The Dean was aware, suddenly, of danger, and almost in the same moment he perceived a robin beside his cup and saucer. It was as though someone nudged him and pointed it out. With a sudden exclamation he perched his eyeglasses on the summit of his nose and picked it up. It was shaped out of a rough bit of wood, its breast and wings coloured perhaps with the juice of wild berries. It was an earthy thing, not the robin of a Christmas card but like one of the birds that a craftsman of William de la Torre's day had carved under the miserere seats in the choir, a wild and living creature that had been not so much carved from

wood as liberated from it. The Dean turned it round and
round in his big ugly hands, silent in delight, for he loved
birds. He remained absorbed in it until Polly put a chaffinch
by his plate. Then he put the robin down and picked up
the chaffinch with reverence. Then he peered short-
sightedly round the table. There was a mouse beside the
jam pot and a snail by the bowl of dripping. There was a
willow wren of shy and slender elegance but no lark. The
Dean turned to Isaac. "There's no lark. Ah, but you put
the lark on top of Miss Montague's Lyre clock. Mr. Peabody, I am dumb in the presence of your genius."

The Dean was astonished at Isaac's delight. His seamed
old face was flushed, his eyes sparkled and the rubicund
point of his button nose was a point of fire. The delight
seemed excessive for a few words of appreciation. "Not me,
sir," said Isaac. "Job."

The Dean was not sure that he heard aright and he
leaned forward with his hand behind his ear, as forgetful of
the nuisance the deaf can be as he had already been forgetful, when he helped himself to a large piece of bread
and butter, that he could never fancy food on a sermon
Sunday. "Eh?" he asked.

"Job made them," said Isaac, raising his voice. "That
boy there. Job Mooring." The Dean turned his gaze on the
boy, his hand still absentmindedly behind his ear, his sad
eyes kindling. "Job Mooring," he repeated. "Job Mooring."

The reiteration had an extraordinary strength about it,
like the grip of his hand on Job's shoulder long ago. It gave
back the lost identity and Job lifted his head and looked
straight across the table at the Dean. It was years before
he was to realise that a sense of identity is the gift of love,
and only love can give it, but for the rest of his life he was
to remember this moment and be able to recall at will the
tones of the harsh deep voice, the kindling in the eyes. It
was the moment when life began for him, real life, the life
of spirit and of genius which his world had foreshadowed.
Years later, when silence was called for him and he rose to
make his first speech as Master of the Clockmakers' Company, he was suddenly back again in the city in the fen
country, hearing his name spoken by the old Dean. He sat
tongue-tied, his face white but as vividly alive as white
flame.

"The boy must be your pupil, Peabody," said the Dean after a moment or two. "Your apprentice?"

"No, sir," said Isaac. "I never set eyes on Job till today, except just that one time when I saw him looking in through my shop window at the cuckoo clock. During divine service this morning I found that mouse by the coal scuttle. Then Job, he came in this afternoon, knowing my sister was out, and Job and Polly they showed me what he'd made for her. No, sir, I've no apprentice, though many's the time I've thought I'd find one handy. Could you fancy some dripping, sir? It's good beef dripping."

The Dean helped himself and said, "Are you apprenticed, Job?"

Job nodded speechlessly and Polly spoke up for him. "To Albert Lee the fishmonger, in Swithins Lane by the North Gate. Him what has that stall in the market, sir."

"I know Swithins Lane," said the Dean thoughtfully. "And I've noticed the shop. Do you like gutting fish, Job?"

"No, sir," whispered Job.

"Have you ever been in the Cathedral?"

"No, sir."

"One day perhaps you will let me show you the carvings there. Have you ever seen a watch like this?"

He unfastened his watch from its chain and handed it across to Job. "Mr. Peabody, will you show him how to open it? I would like him to see the watchcock."

Isaac's bald head and Job's dark one were bent together over the watch. Job held it, his brown fingers trembling a little, while Isaac explained the mechanism, pointing out the great beauties of this loveliest of all watches, mentioning with pride that he had been an apprentice not far from the workshop where this watch had been made. Job's face grew wholly absorbed in wonder, like the face of a child seeing its first candle. Isaac's had a great tenderness and as he talked he watched Job as though he knew every thought, and was aware of every tremor in the mind and body of a boy who sees a perfect piece of mechanism for the first time in his life. To hold a marvellous new thing is to a boy as though he held the world, and to touch or take it from him can drive him to frenzy. Isaac was oblivious of everything except the boy and the watch. The boy was oblivious of everything except the watch. The Dean turned to Polly but she was absorbed in the boy. Sooty was in front of the fire, one leg erected like a lamp post, intent upon washing his hind quarters.

The Dean sat back in his chair and was content to be forgotten. He felt suddenly exhausted, yet thankful. So far it seemed he had not blundered, and he had confidence that he would not, for it seemed to him that the thing was not in his hands, and had not been from the moment he had entered Angel Lane. Although his Cathedral was dedicated not only to Michael but to all the angels he had never thought very much about them. Legends, miracles, guardian angels, holy wells, relics and demons had been somewhat lumped together in his scholarly mind as irrelevancies to the great truth of his faith. But now he had a strange sensation that those walls of which he had been aware, thinking of them as the soap-bubble walls of a dream, were not so fragile as he had thought. The odd thought came to him that four people and a cat were held within the containing wall of eight great wings. Not even the cat would leave this room until the wings chose. He reminded himself that he was unusually tired tonight.

Polly was the first to remember the presence of the distinguished visitor, but not for his own sake. Her eyes were full of a pleading so fierce that it startled him. He smiled at her, and she recognised the extraordinary contortion of his facial muscles as the assurance of understanding it was meant to be, and smiled back. Then Isaac remembered where he was and Job sighed deeply, closed the watch and gave it back to the Dean. His lips moved but no sound came.

"Would you like to be a clockmaker, Job?" asked the Dean.

"Yes, sir," said Job hoarsely, and then suddenly he pushed his chair back and dived for the scullery. They heard him dragging at the back door and Isaac called out, "Stop, Job!" and Polly ran after him. But it was too late. He had banged the back door behind him and they heard him running down the street. Isaac and Polly were in distress but the Dean remained unperturbed. Job would not have got through the retaining wall had not a wing been deliberately raised to let him through.

"You see, sir," said Polly, "Dobson's apprenticed Job to fish. He's got two more years, sir, and Albert knocks him about something cruel."

"If he was apprenticed to me," said Isaac eagerly, "I could make that boy such a clockmaker as we haven't had since Tompion's day."

"If you by yourself try and take Job from the fish you'll be had up before the Beak and put in quod," said Polly. "Likely you'll be hanged."

"I do not entirely understand the legalities of apprenticeship," said the Dean, "but I feel sure that Mr. Peabody's wishes could be met without quite such disastrous consequences to himself as you envisage for him. I feel sure that were it made worth his while Mr. Lee would be willing to relinquish Job. I will consult Mr. Havelock, our Cathedral solicitor. I will do so tomorrow. Will you be content to leave the matter in our hands, Mr. Peabody?"

"I shouldn't like to put you to any trouble, sir," said Isaac unhappily. "Nor to any expense. It wouldn't be right, sir."

"There's Job to be considered, Mr. Peabody," said the Dean. Isaac took his pipe from his pocket and twisted it about in his fingers, a habit of his when he was worried. His great domed forehead was wrinkled and his little beard wagged distressfully. "I like boys," the Dean went on, "and since I retired from schoolmastering it has been little in my power to serve them."

Isaac yielded. "Thank you, sir," he said, "and I give you my word that I'll do my best for the boy."

"May I smoke a pipe with you before I go, Mr. Peabody?" asked the Dean. "I see that you smoke yourself."

"Turn your chairs to the fire," said Polly in a maternal tone, "while I clear."

The two men obeyed her. Their feet stretched to the comfortable warmth, their pipes alight, the cat between them, they arranged that Isaac should wind the Deanery clocks a little later every Saturday morning, to allow for a short instruction in horology, and that one day in the near future the Dean should visit the shop to choose a Christmas gift for Mrs. Ayscough. Then they talked clocks. Beside the kitchen mantelpiece hung a large wooden clock with a slow and solemn tick. Its big round dial was of wood, painted black, with gilt numerals, and below it was a plain wooden trunk to hold the pendulum.

"Compared to that ruffled courtier the Michael Neuwers, or to that dryad the Lyre clock, it's like an old woodsman, a peasant," said the Dean. "But I like its honest ugly face. What is its age, Mr. Peabody?"

"Getting on for a hundred years," said Isaac. "It's a Parliament clock. When William Pitt put a tax on clocks and watches, so that only the rich could afford 'em, the tavern keepers put these clocks in the taverns so that poor men could tell the time. There was vileness for you, sir! Taxing clocks and watches! A wicked man, that Pitt."

"Also a great man," said the Dean.

Isaac growled savagely. "Great! A man that brings clock and watchmakers nearly to ruin? The watches that were broken up! Men couldn't afford to carry 'em. Enough to break your heart. Watchcocks torn out and made into necklaces! Dreadful! But he's an honest old clock, my Parliament. Keeps good time."

While they talked Polly's quick light footsteps went backwards and forwards between kitchen and scullery. Then came the tinkle of washing up and little snatches of song, accompanied by the deep rumbling of one of Sooty's organ fugues. Michael struck, echoed by the Parliament clock and the Time and Death clock, but neither man paid any attention. Two oddities as they were, accustomed like the white blackbird to the loneliness of eccentricity yet never quite reconciled to it, they found in each other's oddness a most comforting compatibility.

Isaac was so at ease that he forgot that his companion was the Dean, but the Dean did not quite forget that Isaac was the clockmaker, a poor man as his world counted poverty, and his heart glowed. Presently Polly came in and sat down near them, just behind Isaac, and because it was Sunday, when she was not allowed to do any sewing, for once she sat with her hands in her lap. The Dean, as he talked to Isaac, was very much aware of her in her spotless white Sunday apron and a big mob cap that nearly obliterated her small, bright-eyed face. She sat very still as though to be able to do so was a pleasure that she held in her folded hands upon her lap, and though she held herself upright she was not entirely relaxed. She was happy, he realised, for she had transferred the problem of Job's future from her own shoulders to his, and she had entire trust in him. This for the Dean was a familiar situation, but the burden in this case was not a heavy one and he could share her quietness. He might have been there for another half-hour had not Emma entered upon them. They had not heard her come. They only knew she was there because a shadow fell upon them, sad and strange.

Emma knew the Dean quite well by sight, for he had sometimes taken the chair at meetings which she attended and she had a great respect for him. Could she have entertained Doctor Ayscough in the parlour it would have been the proudest day of her life. But it was Isaac who was entertaining him, in the kitchen in his shirtsleeves and smoking a pipe; and that little hussy Polly was with them, daring to sit down in the presence of her betters. And upon the dresser was a collection of cheap little wooden toys. These things Emma saw as though in a clear picture, as it is said the drowning see their past life passing before them, and then she was submerged in a dark wave of jealousy and shame, and the picture began to disintegrate. Sooty leapt for the mantelpiece, Polly for the scullery. Isaac scrambled to his feet trying to hide his pipe, his hands trembling as he looked desperately about him for his coat. The Dean rose, his tall black figure seeming to Emma to fill the whole room, knocked out his pipe and bowed to her. Isaac stammered something and he held out his hand and Emma, drowning, caught at it.

The Dean knew she was drowning and held her hand in a firm grip until she had a little recovered herself. As he greeted her he was aware of much; of Isaac's fear of his sister and her contempt for him, of the despair in this woman's mind and her loveless rectitude. "Your brother is going to provide me with a clock for my wife's Christmas gift," he said. "It will be a great privilege to possess an Isaac Peabody clock. We are proud of your brother in the city. We are very proud that so fine an artist lives amongst us. May I bid you good night, Miss Peabody, and my thanks for the happy hour I have spent in your home. Much obliged." He was in the passage now and she heard him talking to Isaac. "Will you convey to the little Polly my grateful thanks for the excellent tea? Havelock shall attend to that matter of the boy. Good night. Much obliged."

Isaac and Polly returned to the kitchen in characteristic fashion, Isaac with the slow seep of a guilty conscience, for his coat was nowhere to hand, Polly with the alacrity of a quiet one, for she considered she had a perfect right to sit down in her own kitchen on a Sunday evening. If the gentry chose to invade it that was not her fault. Both had returned for the sole purpose of defending the other. Knowing this Emma stood between them slowly removing her cloak and drawing off her black kid gloves. Isaac had entertained the great Dean to tea in the kitchen in his shirtsleeves. He had praised Isaac, and sent an almost affectionate message to Polly. Shame and jealousy tore at her, and hatred that seemed almost a physical thing rose like a surge of hot blood from her breast to her throat and would have strangled her had she not given it an outlet. With a savage and skilful gesture she swept the little wooden toys off the dresser into the black silk apron she wore and flung them on the fire.

CHAPTER X   *Bella*

I

IN the reaction of next morning the Dean was not so sure about those angelic wings and could only trust that he had not done great harm. He was well aware that his visit had seriously disturbed Miss Peabody, and that in escaping from her himself he had left Isaac and Polly behind him to bear the brunt of whatever it was he had unwittingly stirred up. He should have remained and talked with her a little. The fact was that she had much alarmed him and he had fled. Fear he was accustomed to, for he was not inside himself the fearless man that his height and courage had led men to suppose, but by the grace of God he had not until yesterday run away from what alarmed him. Miss Peabody had taken him by surprise, entering suddenly upon a moment of relaxation when his armour, so to speak, was on the floor. Yet he was deeply ashamed for relaxation, while life lasted and evil endured, was not permissible except in prayer in the presence of God. The poor woman was not evil, she was he believed highly virtuous, but she was not good and the absence of love left a most dangerous vacuum. "Much ashamed, much ashamed," he murmured, and knew that when opportunity offered he must go and see her, though he did not want to. He said to himself that

Miss Montague in urging him to take a little joy had forgotten the alarming contingency of life. The gentle stream of his friendship with Peabody was showing every sign of developing into a roaring cataract.

And now he must see Havelock about the boy. "Where does Mr. Havelock live, Garland?" he asked as Garland helped him into his cloak to go to matins.

"Mr. Abraham Havelock lives at number twenty Worship Street, sir," said Garland. "His son Mr. Giles at number seventeen. But their office is in the market place, sir."

"I want to see Mr. Abraham Havelock after matins," said the Dean. "Will he be at home or at the office?"

"On a Monday morning, at home, sir," said Garland, who knew every detail of the private lives of the inhabitants of the Close and Worship Street by a process of suction, his mind lifting the knowledge out of the sacred ground of the ecclesiastical precincts as the sun draws vapour from the earth. "Being elderly Mr. Abraham leaves Monday morning to Mr. Giles. Monday morning at an office can be difficult, sir."

"No doubt, no doubt," said the Dean. "Thank you, Garland. Much obliged."

"I'll send a message, sir," said Garland.

"Message?" asked the Dean.

"Asking Mr. Abraham Havelock to wait upon you, sir."

"I thank you, no," said the Dean. "I will wait upon Mr. Havelock."

And he went away to matins leaving Garland much perturbed, for it was contrary to all his ideas of propriety that the Dean should wait upon anybody except the Bishop and Miss Montague. Nor, skilfully trained by Garland, had he done so before. Garland was not happy as he washed up the breakfast silver in his pantry. The Dean was most unaccountable just now. And Garland rather disliked these queer warm spells in late autumn. Indian summers, he believed people called them. For the first time in his life he dropped a silver spoon upon the floor and stooping to pick it up bumped his head on the draining board. He could have wept.

Matins over the Dean forged his way down Worship Street, peering short-sightedly from side to side in an effort to locate number twenty, oblivious of those who touched their hats to him, talking to himself. "Much ashamed, much ashamed," he said, for he had just realised that for many years past he had been guilty of a most contemptible arrogance. Why should he expect doctors, solicitors, bank managers and the humbler clergy (though not dentists owing to obvious technical difficulties) always to wait upon him as though he were a crowned head? He was not. He was a humble servant of the Master who had girded himself with a towel and knelt on the floor to wash the feet of twelve poor men. Abbot William de la Torre, and all the abbots and priors after him down to Prior Hugh, had done the same every Maundy Thursday, but he did not, nor did he think the twelve old men at the almshouses would appreciate the gesture if he should try to do so. Times changed and there was no greater tyranny than that of social custom, but he was to blame that he had let it fasten about him with quite such octopus strength. He would try now, God helping him, to loosen the coils a little.

He was at number twenty. It was at the humbler end of the beautiful winding Georgian street, the end nearest the market place. Those who had at one time resided in the Close lived at the Cathedral end, the slightly less privileged at the town end, poised as it were on the delicate tight-rope between trade and gentility. But the houses at the town end of Worship Street were just as beautiful as the others, if a little smaller. They lacked the porches and fluted pillars of the larger houses but they had fanlights over their front doors, white doorsteps snowily scrubbed, beautifully spaced windows kept scrupulously clean and shining and an air of contented solid comfort that was very reassuring. They did not look like houses in which anything could go very wrong. To pass them was to think of shining beeswaxed floors, pots of jelly on a scrubbed shelf and a walled garden behind the house where nectarines grew on the south wall. None of the houses in Worship Street was quite the same. Some had two windows on each side of the front door, others only one. Virginia creeper grew on some, wistaria on others. Number twenty was covered with a vine whose leaves were now deep crimson and pale gold. They made a brilliant setting for the green front door and the brightly polished brass knocker.

The Dean knocked and stood waiting, and he was conscious of a sudden lightness of heart that a little overcame his nervousness, for in spite of its Georgian dignity there was something about this trim gay exterior that reminded him of a doll's house. He had of course never possessed a doll's house, but in his childhood there had been a little girl who had one, a child with a blue bow in her hair, and out of the mist of the ages he remembered that it had been a green door, or was it a blue door? He was trying to remember when suddenly, noiselessly, this one opened, letting out the warm scent of geraniums and the piercing cacophony of a canary rejoicing in the beauty of the day. The rosy-cheeked maid who opened the door wore a pink print dress and a mob cap and apron and was so terrified when she saw the Dean that her wits deserted her.

"Is Mr. Abraham Havelock at home?" asked the Dean sepulchrally.

"Yes, sir. No, sir. Yes, sir. Will you please to come in?"

"Mr. Abraham Havelock is disengaged?"

"No, sir. Yes. I mean Squire Richards is with him, in from the fen. But he can go away and come later. I'll tell Mr. Havelock, sir."

"Do no such thing, I beg," said the Dean. "I would not wish to discommode the squire, who has come from far. I will wait. I am quite at leisure, quite at leisure." He looked a little helplessly at the scared little maid. "Could I sit here in the hall?"

But at this preposterous suggestion she came to her senses. "Oh no, sir! Mr. Havelock would not think that right. Will you please to sit in the dining-room? There's a fire there."

"Much obliged, much obliged," said the Dean, and was ushered into a room at the right of the front door, and into the presence of the canary.

When he came to himself a little, for even for his deaf ears the noise was terrible, he found he still had his top hat on his head and was grasping his stick, for he and the little maid had both been too nervous to separate him from them in the hall. Much distressed he laid them beside his chair on the floor. The room was bright and warm and geranium-scented, and would have been quiet but for the canary. Just by him on the mantelpiece there was a clock that was probably ticking but he could not be sure because of the canary. He got up to look at it. It was a very elegant pedestal clock surmounted by two little brass owls. He was thankful for their silence. He sat down again. The room was very warm and the canary very loud. His head ached and presently he closed his eyes.

Something touched him. He opened his eyes and saw what he thought was a starfish lying on his knee. Intensely surprised he looked closer and saw it was a small hand. Almost afraid to look lest the apparition vanish he put his eyeglasses on his nose and dared to lift his gaze a little higher. A small girl was planted sturdily before him. She wore a starched muslin frock with short puffed sleeves and a frill round the neck. A blue sash encircled that part of her anatomy where in later years a waist would possibly develop, and her yellow curls were kept out of her eyes with a snood of blue ribbon. She was plump, with bracelets of fat round her wrists and a double chin. He could not guess her age but as her chest was about on a level with his knee he thought it to be tender. But she appeared to have plenty of self-confidence and *savoir faire* and was addressing him with great fluency, though he could not hear what she said because of the canary. She was not afraid of him.

Awe and trembling took the Dean. He had always adored small children, especially little girls, but no one had ever known it. Elaine thought he disliked them as much as she did, and even Miss Montague had never guessed that he had this hidden idolatry. For idolatry it was. Children to him were beings of another world. The sight of one stabbed him to the heart, but he never dared to come too close to the heavenly delicacy and innocence that might be frightened and corrupted by his ugliness and sin. Children, he had always thought, were little angels, and had not Bella laid her hand upon his knee he might have continued in this misconception until the end of his days.

She was now gesturing towards the canary with one fat hand and shaking his knee with the other, and he realised that some stupidity on his part was causing her annoyance. She wished him to take action of some sort and her commands had fallen upon earth both deaf and deafened. He cleared his throat, painfully anxious to assure her of his desire to serve her, but she suddenly turned her back on him and darted away, making for the first time her woman's discovery that it is generally quicker to do a thing yourself than to ask a man to do it. Grabbing the velvet cloth from a small table as she passed it she leaped into the big chair beside the canary's cage and swarmed up its padded back, revealing as she did so that she wore the most enchanting lace-trimmed undergarments. Poised on top of the chair back, in an attitude of such extreme danger that the Dean's heart nearly stopped, she flung the velvet cloth over the canary's cage. Instantly there was silence, and seldom had silence seemed to the Dean more heavenly. But it was shortlived. Bella, throwing a glance of triumph over her shoulder at the incompetent male, overbalanced, rolled down the chair and off it on to the floor, where she lay and roared in a welter of frills and blue ribbons.

The Dean came hurrying over to her in much anguish of spirit but just as he reached her she stopped roaring and sat up, for she was not, she found, so badly hurt as she had thought she was. Virtue was not Bella's strong point but she had grit. Nevertheless she had bumped her head and she put her hand to her curls and hiccoughed.

"My dear child," said the Dean, assisting her gently and reverently to her feet, "have you a nurse whom I can summon? I think that I should ring the bell." He looked round him anxiously. "Is there a bell?"

But Bella was suddenly herself again. Pushing him vigorously towards his chair she commanded loudly, "Sit on your knee." Having got him in the correct position she climbed there and said, "Kiss it." The Dean, his hand behind his ear, was at a loss. "Where I'm bumped," she said and placed the first finger of her right hand against a fat yellow curl behind her right ear. He kissed the curl, moved by the most extraordinary emotion, and the canary let out a tentative trill beneath the velvet cloth. "Stop that noise, Birdie!" called Bella shrilly.

"Is it kind to cover him up?" asked the Dean anxiously.

"Her," said Bella. "She lays eggs."

The Dean felt shaken and tried another topic of conversation. "There are two more birdies on the clock. They are owls, I believe."

Bella glanced contemptuously at the clock. "They don't move," she said. "The bird in the clock in the shop window moves. He flies out of a little door and wants to come to Bella." Suddenly she was seized with an attack of heartrending grief. Laying her head against the Dean's waistcoat she wept, not noisily now, for the grief was real, but with a couple of low sobs and a tear trickling down her left cheek. "No one will give it to Bella," she mourned. "Nurse won't. Grandpa won't. No one won't."

"Is it a cuckoo clock?" asked the Dean. He found to his joy that he could hear everything Bella said quite easily, so clear was her voice. Other people thought the stiletto clarity of Bella's voice hardly an asset, but to the Dean it was sweet as the autumnal song of the robins that he could just hear faintly now whenever he passed a garden wall.

"He says, cuckoo," said Bella. "He says cuckoo, cuckoo, Bella! Cuckoo come to Bella. But they won't let him come to Bella." And she wiped away the tear with the back of her hand. It was not followed by another, but the silence that followed was a deep well full of sorrow.

"Is this clock in Mr. Peabody's shop?" asked the Dean.

But Bella had not heard of Mr. Peabody. "A little shop," she said. "With two little steps to the door. There is a little man inside the shop. He is a fairy man."

"Ah!" said the Dean. "That is Peabody." And then, with that wild impulsiveness which was so foreign to his nature but which seemed to be more and more taking hold of him just now, he said, "Bella, my dear, would you like me to give you that clock?"

"Yes," said Bella cheerfully. "Now. We'll go now."

But the door opened and Mr. Abraham Havelock entered in something of a state. "Mr. Dean! I am distressed indeed! But it was not until the departure of Squire Richards that I was informed that you were here. Not for the world would I have kept you waiting. May I offer you my most humble apologies. May I — Bella!"

There was a certain likeness between Mr. Havelock and his grand-daughter, though his once yellow head was now bald and his magnificent whiskers and moustache snow-white. He was stout and rosy and his eyes, at first sight disarmingly round and blue, were very acute and unblinking. His mouth, though soft and slightly pursed, could show that purposefulness which in the old is called resolve and in the young obstinacy. He was full of resolve now and so was Bella.

"What are you doing here, Bella?" he asked in a voice of silk. "Go to the nursery at once."

Bella adhered. The Dean was conscious of a sense of increased pressure upon his knees, as though the silent and motionless child were putting on weight as she sat there.

She looked at her grandfather and her grandfather looked at her. Then he rang the bell.

"Minnie, take Miss Bella to the nursery," he said to the little maid.

Bella adhered.

"I'd fetch nurse but she's been took bad," said Minnie, looking at Bella apprehensively.

The Dean had been momentarily silent through uncertainty as to where his duty lay. As a schoolmaster he felt that discipline should be upheld, yet Bella undoubtedly had a claim upon his loyalty. His impulsive offer of that cuckoo clock had not perhaps been altogether wise. Like his unpremeditated call on Mr. Peabody he was aware that it was about to have consequences out of all proportion to his initial action. But he could not turn back now. Even if he had wished to do so Bella would not have permitted it.

"Mr. Havelock, there is a small legal matter which I would like to discuss with you, if you will be so good as to spare me a few minutes of your valuable time. At the conclusion of our business will you permit me to take Bella for a little walk? Only as far as Mr. Peabody's clock shop. I should count it a very great pleasure and I will detain her for a short while only." Then aware of utter stupefaction in Mr. Havelock he asked anxiously, "Will it perhaps be too great an exertion for one of her tender years? Should I send for my wife's carriage?"

Mr. Havelock pulled himself together. "Mr. Dean, the exertion of which Bella is capable would surprise you. I hesitated only because of — forgive me — the startling nature of your suggestion. That you should be seen walking through the street of your Cathedral city hand in hand with Bella — well, sir, it will startle the city."

The Dean, aware in Mr. Havelock of a resistance to which he was not accustomed, felt a little nettled. And also a little reckless. What did it matter what the city thought? In for a penny in for a pound. "Would such a course of action be contrary to your wishes, Mr. Havelock?" he asked. "I should not wish to cross them but the fact is that Bella and I have anticipated this outing with considerable pleasure."

Mr. Havelock capitulated with grace. He could do no less, with that authoritative note in the Dean's voice and Bella adhering.

"You do Bella a great honour, sir. I thank you in her name and my own." He turned to the little maid. "Minnie, take Miss Bella upstairs and put her things on. When I ring the bell you may bring her in. Bella, go with Minnie."

Bella slid demurely to the ground, made a dangerous wobbly curtsey, for owing to her bulk curtseying was not easy for her, and left the room with Minnie in a sweet biddable manner.

"Mr. Havelock," said the Dean, much moved, "I feel unworthy. How unworthy we are, we old sinners, of the company of little children. They are as angels."

Mr. Havelock's spectacles slid a little on his nose and he looked at the Dean over the top of them, but father of five and grandfather of eight though he was he forbore to comment. "I trust Bella will do nothing to forfeit your good opinion, Mr. Dean," he said. "But I think I should tell you that she has until now lacked discipline. She was born in India and has been much in the care of native servants. My wife and I now have charge of her but she has been with us only a month as yet and is still I fear something of an autocrat."

"Her parents are alive?" asked the Dean anxiously.

"Very much so, sir. They brought her home to us, the climate being unsuited to white children, and have now returned to India."

"She misses them?" asked the Dean, still with anxiety. "She weeps for them?"

"Bella has shown great adaptability," said her grandfather evenly. "And now, sir, in what way may I have the honour to serve you? But I am grieved that you should have put yourself to the trouble of coming to see me. I should have waited upon you. I am at your command, sir, at any time."

"Why should you be?" asked the Dean unexpectedly. "I have come to see you, Mr. Havelock, about Job Mooring the fishmonger's apprentice."

Mr. Havelock's spectacles slid farther down his nose. He replaced them. The moment he had come into the room he had thought the Dean looked unwell, and the oddness of the great man's behaviour had caused him to wonder anxiously if there could be any slight mental disturbance, consequent perhaps upon a disordered liver? Now he was sure of it and was much perturbed. Yet the Dean, when the legalities of apprenticeship had been fully explained to him, showed his usual grasp of affairs. He knew exactly what he wished done in order that Albert Lee should be fully compensated, and Mr. Peabody spared all expense in the taking of an apprentice, and showed no further signs of mental aberration until he said, "Would it be advisable for me to wait upon Mr. Albert Lee myself, Mr. Havelock?"

"Certainly not, sir!" ejaculated Mr. Havelock. "No, sir. I shall do myself the honour of acting for you personally in this matter. Your name should not be mentioned in connection with fish. You are the Dean of the city."

"Have you ever wished you were a shepherd, Mr. Havelock?" asked the Dean. "Or a ploughman, driving your bright share through our rich fen earth with the gulls about you?"

"No, Mr. Dean," said Mr. Havelock. "I have always felt that indoor occupations are better suited to the vagaries of our climate."

"We are what God wills," said the Dean. "But I should like to have been a shepherd."

"Shall I ring the bell for Bella?" asked Mr. Havelock.

"Thank you, Mr. Havelock," said the Dean. "Much obliged."

Bella entered. She had been attired in a blue pelisse trimmed with swansdown, with a blue bonnet to match. She had mittens on and a little white muff hung round her neck by a cord. Eyeing the Dean she gestured with one mittened hand towards the birdcage. "Birdie may sing now," she said. The Dean obediently removed the velvet cloth and a torrent of song poured out into the room. Mr. Havelock appeared to be in the grip of strong emotion but what he said to Bella and the Dean by way of reprobation and apology could not be heard above Birdie's rejoicing. He led the way out into the hall with some precipitation but here Minnie was waiting to help the Dean into his cloak and he could not express himself freely. He opened the front door to bow the Dean out but it was Bella who walked out first past his bow, her hands in her muff and her head in the air. Out on the pavement she waited for the Dean and with great kindness took his hand.

With the door shut Mr. Havelock took out his handkerchief and wiped his forehead. "I tell you what it is, sir," said Minnie, "the Dean being so dark complexioned Miss Bella takes him for one of them darkies she was always ordering about."

II

Bella and the Dean walked down Worship Street. Bella chatted without cessation but he did not know what she said now because she was so low down. It was as though a robin was singing somewhere on a level with his knee. He could distinguish the music but not the meaning of it, apart from its general meaning of joyful satisfaction with the splendour of the world. Looking down he could not see Bella's face but only her bonnet. A few tendrils of yellow hair clung about the edge of the bonnet, and her muff, not in use at present, swung from side to side to the rhythm of her trotting footsteps. She trotted like a very determined pony, four steps to the Dean's one, but it was she who set the pace and the Dean, growing a little breathless, marvelled that anyone so young could simultaneously trot and converse so fast without any diminution of energy whatever. Worship Street led into the market place at a sharp incline and this they took almost at a run. The sight of them crossing the market place was an astonishment to all beholders, but they were oblivious of this. In Cockspur Street the incline was again very steep and the Dean's rheumatic knees slowed him up a little. Bella, impatient, broke away and flew off, skimming down the pavement like a swallow. He was in terror lest flight in one so plump should end in disaster but she landed safely at the window of the clock shop. Here she leaned motionless, her nose pressed against the glass. The Dean followed as quickly as he could, past the small crooked houses with their flights of worn steps leading up to low front doors recessed within porches, past small windows bright with geraniums, and bow-fronted shop windows. Cockspur Street was a gay little street, the happiest in the city. The people who lived here were neither rich nor poor. They were for the most part contented people, good craftsmen who liked their work, and the little shops and homes had been handed down from father to son and were all their world.

With his eyeglasses on his nose the Dean leaned beside Bella to look at the cuckoo clock. He realised now why it was that they had had to hurry, for the cuckoo clock said six minutes to twelve. Another seven minutes and they would have been too late. He echoed Bella's deep sigh of relief.

It was a good cuckoo clock of carved and painted wood. Oak leaves and oak apples curved about the enchanting little double doors which were represented as though opening into the trunk of a tree. As an example of Isaac's art it was not one of his best clocks but then he had made it for such as Bella and as a joyous arcadian toy it was perfect of its kind. Five minutes to twelve. Bella had misted the glass with her passionate breathing and the Dean had to take out his white silk handkerchief and wipe it clear again. Four minutes to twelve by the cuckoo clock, kept slow by Isaac, and Michael began to strike. The golden notes rolled down Cockspur Street like flaming suns and after them came the silver star-chiming of little St. Nicholas and St. Matthew's at the South Gate, almost submerging the deep-toned and moony sadness of St. Peter's in the market place. Two minutes to twelve by the cuckoo clock. The glass was misted again and Bella wiped it with her muff. Now all the clocks in the window except the cuckoo were striking together, and it sounded as though someone was playing the harpsichord. One minute to twelve by the cuckoo clock. Bella stretched up her mittened hand and held the Dean's and both hands were trembling as they counted out the sixty seconds. Then the double doors in the oak tree burst open and the cuckoo, yelling joyously, exploded forth. Its voice was as shrill as that of Birdie the canary and for a moment the Dean was profoundly dismayed. Birdie and the cuckoo together in one house? Poor Havelock. What had he done? Into what further indiscretion would this autumnal madness of his precipitate him? Poor Havelock.

The row suddenly ceased and the cuckoo withdrew as suddenly as he had come out, the little doors closing behind him. Bella withdrew her nose from the glass and pulled the Dean up the steps into the shop. Isaac favoured one of those bells which ring when the customer stands on the doormat. Bella was enraptured and impervious to all suggestions that she should come off the mat. Isaac, entering from his workroom with all possible speed, joined his entreaties to those of the Dean with no avail. Suddenly the slumbering schoolmaster awoke in Adam Ayscough. "Bella!" he thundered. "Come off that mat immediately!"

Bella, her muff lifted coquettishly to her chin, dimpled, smiled, and came off the mat. But with no air of capitulation. She had come off it because she had wanted to come off it. Climbing on to the customers' chair, showing a good deal of petticoat as she did so, she smiled adorably at the two men and said, "Cuckoo!"

"Mr. Peabody, might we trouble you to show us the cuckoo clock?" asked the Dean. "Much obliged. Do you like it, Bella?"

Bella, with the clock beside her on the counter, did not bother to answer the rhetorical question. With a small forefinger she traced the pattern of oak leaves and oak apples, and caressed the closed door. Her lips were slightly parted, her face raised towards the clock like that of a cherub looking into heaven. Her expression, so wicked a few minutes ago, was now rapt and holy. Both men looked at her in awe. Imp though she was she could still at moments trail her clouds of glory. It was not until she took her finger from the clock, sighed, and began to swish her legs backwards and forwards among her petticoats in imitation of the clock's pendulum, that the Dean could bring himself to break the charmed silence and explain the situation to Mr. Peabody.

"Very good, sir," said Mr. Peabody. "I will deliver the clock to Worship Street this evening."

"Will that inconvenience you, Mr. Peabody?" asked the Dean anxiously.

"No, sir, no trouble at all. I will leave it on my way home tonight."

"I want it now," said Bella.

"Not now," said the Dean. "Mr. Peabody is not at liberty until the evening."

"*You* carry it," said Bella, sliding off the customers' chair. "Now."

For a moment the Dean was as much taken aback by the suggestion as was Isaac. He was not in the habit of carrying things. He scarcely knew how one set about it. Then the curious recklessness that was reversing the habits of a distinguished lifetime took hold of him again. "Mr. Peabody," he said, "will you be so good as to wrap it up?"

"Sir, you cannot carry it," said Isaac in deep distress. "Even were it suitable for you to be seen carrying a large brown paper parcel through the streets of the city the weight would be far too great for your strength. Indeed, sir, the thing is impossible. Bella must wait."

"No," said Bella. Her face was crimson and her blue eyes were full of fiery points of light. Although neither man had as yet experienced Bella in one of her rages they both felt the deepest apprehension, as though they stood on the rim of a volcano's crater, with fire and rumblings down below. The Dean was aware that the schoolmaster's voice would be of no avail now. It had only been of use before because Bella's will and his own had happened to coincide. He suddenly felt very tired. Authority had always come easily to him, and sometimes in years past he had felt a slight contempt for masters who could not keep order. It was good for him, he realised, to know that even the strongest sometimes meet their match.

"If it is too heavy for me it is too heavy for you, Mr. Peabody," he said, looking down at Isaac from his great height. "How do you convey these heavy clocks from place to place?"

Isaac lowered his voice to tell a secret. "I have a little cart," he said. "A push cart. I made it."

"Could I push it?" asked the Dean.

"No, no, no!" said Isaac. "It is only a wooden box on wheels. I myself use it if possible only after dark."

"If ever a man needed an apprentice you do," said the Dean. Then he too dropped his voice. "I've seen Havelock. You'll have Job in a matter of days I hope."

Something in the quality of Bella's silence suddenly made both men look at her again. Her face was now a most alarming puce colour, her body looked strangely swollen and her mouth was slowly opening. "I'll close the shop," said Isaac suddenly. "I'll bring it now, Bella. Just a moment while I fetch my little cart."

He hurried back into his workshop and the Dean sat down rather suddenly on the customers' chair, for really he was extraordinarily exhausted. Bella laid her hand upon his knee. He looked at her and found she was another child. Her exquisite pink and white complexion was restored to her. Her blue eyes were infinitely gentle, her long eyelashes wet with tears that had been arrested on the brink. She stretched up her arms to him and then suddenly she scrambled up, her bonnet falling off, and wound them tightly round his neck, her warm cheek pressed against his.

"Bella loves you," she whispered, and she spoke the truth. She was not an impartially loving child, later in life she would be considered a hard woman, but at a quarter-past-twelve on this particular autumn morning in the city Bella Havelock suddenly and completely loved Adam Ayscough. He had not known that children loved like this, so suddenly. He had never known this stranglehold about the neck, the velvet softness against his cheek, the scent of a child's hair, and within him something wept wildly for joy. When Bella whispered, "Get down now," he set her down very carefully, not knowing if he had held her for an hour or a minute, for time had stopped.

Isaac reappeared with his box on wheels, as queer a little box as he was a man, but beautifully made, for he could not make anything that was not a fine bit of handiwork. He was wearing his caped greatcoat, and his hat was under his arm. "I had thought to show you my clocks, sir," he said wistfully.

"Another time," said the Dean gently. "I will call in one evening just at closing time. That would be best I think. We shall be undisturbed then. But I am aware of your clocks, Mr. Peabody; beautiful things, alive all round me. Their tick is their pulse and breath."

There was a note in his voice that Isaac recognised. The man was happy, as Isaac himself had been happy that night in the workshop not long ago, and Bella was happy. Isaac's own good time had ended abruptly on Sunday night, its light put out by Emma's destruction of Job's treasures, and he was now so wretched that even his memory of the way light and air had flooded into the house when he had opened the front door had no power to help him. The worst of his dark times was that while they were at their worst his good times seemed to him just a betrayal; as though he had loved a wife and found her a whore. But he knew that the Dean and Bella were happy and it eased his breathlessness. He was very much afraid that one of his attacks of asthma was coming on.

"You've a cold, Mr. Peabody?" asked the Dean.

"No, sir," said Isaac, coughing peevishly. "But I wanted to show you my clocks."

The Dean was sorry for his disappointment but the peevishness added to his joy, for a man is only peevish to his friends.

"Come now, come now," he rallied him. "Matters of great moment need leisure and quietness for their consideration. Yes, Bella, we are going. Look, Mr. Peabody is putting the clock into the little carriage."

Isaac and the Dean lifted the cart down the steps, Isaac locked the shop door and poised his battered old hat at the back of his head while the Dean placed his immaculate one well down over his forehead, its rim nearly resting on his eyebrows, which was the top hat position he favoured. They set out, Isaac trundling his cart up the hill over the cobbles with Bella and the Dean beside him. When they were nearly at the top of the hill he was taken with a sudden fit of coughing. It was a bad one and it winded him. They had to stop while he wheezed and gasped his way back to a hurried painful breathing that greatly distressed the Dean. "What was I thinking of to let you push that heavy cart up the hill, Mr. Peabody? Much distressed. My physical strength is greatly superior to yours." And he picked up the handles of the little cart.

"No, sir," wheezed Isaac. "In a moment we shall be in the market place. Sir, I beg of you."

But it was too late, for the Dean, pushing the cuckoo clock, had already launched out into the market place. He was, as he had said, stronger than Isaac and he strode forward with a mad gay recklessness, Bella running beside him hopping and skipping and joyously tossing her muff from side to side. Isaac could only follow after, at first aware of nothing except the incredulous astonishment, the horror and shock of the city, which in the raw state of his feelings seemed to a man, woman and child to be lined up all round the market square and gazing dumbfounded from every door and window. Then he was abruptly conscious of something that suddenly lit up his darkness as though a shutter had swung back, then closed again, leaving a picture illumined small and bright against the darkness of his mind. Tall silver towers lifted up against the cloudless blue sky above, old houses with crooked roofs and gables gathered about the market place that was filled to the brim with a dazzle of golden sunshine. In the gold a running child with yellow hair, glinting and gay, and an old man as gay as she was, forgetful of himself. Chimes rang out far up in the blue sky. Half-past-twelve. Other bells answered as though ringing in another world.

The Dean, Isaac and Bella gained the farther shore and made their way into Worship Street. The small bright picture faded from Isaac's mind but he had it somewhere, just as he had the picture of Graham's little bow-windowed shop in Fleet Street, its gables etched black against the stars and its walls washed by moonlight. And others, equally imperishable, small and precious as little pictures painted within a great gold letter in an illuminated manuscript. Sometimes he would fancy that strung together they would have been a sort of speech telling him something. They were all safely kept, all part of the imperishable landscape of the country where he made his clocks.

At number twenty Minnie answered the Dean's ring upon the instant and Mr. Havelock was just behind her, anxiety writ large upon his face.

"Mr. Havelock, I am anxious about this clock," said the Dean. "It cuckoos. I trust that you and Mrs. Havelock may suffer no disturbance of your rest." He stood very humbly, and he felt humble, though not as distressed as he felt he ought to have been. It was difficult to feel distressed with Bella refusing to let go his hand and with gaiety still in his heart. Yet poor Havelock. "Pray forgive me," he pleaded.

"My dear sir," ejaculated Mr. Havelock, "Mrs. Havelock and myself are reasoned parents and grandparents. There is the canary. There is Bella herself. One learns a certain trick of disassociation. Bella, thank the Dean for his great kindness."

"I *have* thanked him," said Bella.

"Then let Minnie take you to the nursery."

Bella adhered.

"Thank you, Mr. Peabody, put the clock on the hall table," said Mr. Havelock, changing the subject, a ruse which on rare occasions had been known to unstick Bella. "Minnie will take it to the nursery. Mr. Dean, will you do me the honour of partaking of a little luncheon?"

"Most kind, most kind," said the Dean. "My grateful thanks, but my wife is expecting me. Remember me to Mrs. Havelock. . . . Bella."

Bella adhered.

"Bella!" thundered her grandfather.

The Dean bent down to her. "Bella, we must say goodbye. But not for long I trust. Be a good girl, my dear."

Bella suddenly gave in, lifting her face to be kissed. "Bye," she said, and kissed Isaac too. She went from one to the other, running between them as a puppy will do between two that love him, then disappeared up the stairs in the wake of Minnie and the cuckoo clock. With renewed civilities the three old gentlemen bowed to each other and the door was at last closed. Politeness was important in the city in those days. There was time for it.

"Do you go home for luncheon, Mr. Peabody?" asked the Dean.

"No, sir, I have it in the shop. I take sandwiches." And Isaac trembled a little at the thought of having to go home to Emma for his midday meal as well as for supper.

"I'll walk a short way with you."

"You will be late home, sir."

"Luncheon is at one-thirty. Just a few paces. That's a nice clock at Havelock's, the one with the owls on the dining-room mantelpiece."

"Edward East sixteen hundred and forty-four," said Isaac dispiritedly and began to cough again.

"Asthma?" asked the Dean gently.

Isaac nodded and they stopped where an old tall cherry tree leaned over a garden wall. The last of its crimson leaves drifted upon them. Isaac stopped coughing and the Dean put his hand on his shoulder. "Did the child not lighten it at all?" he asked.

"For a moment," said Isaac.

"The child has joy," said the Dean. "You stored your joy for her within the cuckoo clock. As I see it there is no giving without giving away. But joy is a home pigeon. Good day to you, Mr. Peabody."

His hand tightened for a moment on Isaac's shoulder and then he turned away.

CHAPTER XI　　　　　　　　　　　　　*Swithins Lane*

I

"THERE'S a young person at the back door says she wishes to see you, sir," said Garland in strangled tones. "I told her it was impossible, of course, sir. She asked me why. I said you were engaged. She said she'd wait. I told her to go away. She smiled at me. I don't know what to do sir, I don't indeed."

Bella and the cuckoo clock had been on Monday. Today was Saturday morning. The Dean, at work at his writing-table, looked up. Garland's face was pale and his hands trembled slightly. He was obviously much shaken, worsted, the Dean thought, in some encounter which had not only been contrary to routine but foreign to his whole experience. The Dean put his hand behind his ear. "Could you repeat that, Garland?"

Garland repeated it, ending miserably, "I don't like to trouble you with such a thing, sir. I don't know how it is that I am standing where I am or she where she is. I am ashamed, I am indeed. But Cook tried too, sir."

"Don't distress yourself, Garland," said the Dean. "Is this young person small and sandy-haired? Quick in her movements? A chin of remarkable determination?"

"That's her, sir," said Garland.

"Then pray ask her to step this way." Garland could not believe that he had heard aright but he took a few weak steps towards the door. "One more thing, Garland." The Dean hesitated, picked his pen up and put it down again. "I am the Dean of this Cathedral city and I should be accessible to all who want me. I fear that has not always been so in the past. You understand, Garland? Much obliged."

In a remarkably short space of time Polly, scared but courageous, stood before him. Her face was white inside her bonnet, all the whiter in contrast with the brave crimson ribbons tied beneath her determined chin, and both hands clung rather desperately to the handle of her loaded shopping basket. The Dean was saddened that she, possessed of so much pluck, had found it so hard to come to him. A strong smell of fish emanated from the basket.

"I could not persuade her to leave it at the back door, sir," said Garland.

"She was quite right," said the Dean. "We have a kitchen cat I believe. Sit down, my dear. Garland shall set a chair for you. Thank you, Garland."

Garland withdrew and Polly sat gingerly on the edge of her chair, still clinging to the basket. "Set it down, my dear," said the Dean. "It will be quite safe there on the floor."

Polly put it down beside her. "It's not my things, sir," she explained. "It's Miss Peabody's. I market for her on a Saturday morning. I'd be blamed, sir, if anything were to be missing."

"You can't be too careful," the Dean agreed. "Are you on your way from the market now? Did anything occur there to distress you?"

"Yes, sir. Job wasn't at the fish stall. Job's gone."

"Gone?" echoed the Dean.

"Run away, sir. He's been gone two days." She was near breaking point but she controlled herself. No longer able to cling to the handle of the basket her hands were twisting her handkerchief into a knot. The Dean, trying to see her face inside the bonnet, thought that she had wept but was dry-eyed now. "My dear," he said, "I had hoped that by this time Job was happily established as Mr. Peabody's apprentice. I saw Mr. Havelock last Monday and he assured me he would see to the matter. Pray tell me just what has occurred."

He leaned forward again with his hand behind his ear. This aid to hearing that he had never liked to use was becoming almost habitual with him now, so important was it that in his present contacts he should hear what the children said. A feeling of guilt was growing in him. He had been unusually busy the last few days and Isaac, Polly and Job, Bella and the cuckoo clock, had perforce slipped to the back of his mind. But that would not do. One could not deliberately enter the lives of others and then go in and out as one wished. Deliberate entry committed one to entire service. "Much ashamed," he said to himself.

"Job come in on Wednesday evening," said Polly, "just as far as the scullery because Miss Peabody she was in the parlour and he couldn't come no farther. He'd brought me a lark made out of a bit of crab apple wood. Ever so pretty it was. I was just going to tell him how he was to leave the fish and be apprenticed to the clocks when he says to me, 'Where's the box you keep my birds in? I want that robin. It's not right and I've got to get it better. The Dean liked it and I'm going to give it to him.'"

"Yes?" asked the Dean, listening painfully.

"Well, sir, I pretended I'd lost it. So he told me to fetch the box, and I said I didn't know where I'd put it. Then he got angry, for he's got a temper, Job has, and somehow I let it out. I didn't mean to, knowing how he'd take on, but I was flustered like."

"What did you let out, my dear?"

"About Miss Peabody burning the birds."

"Burning the birds?" ejaculated the Dean.

Polly went as crimson as she had formerly been pale. "I forgot, sir. I forgot it was after you went."

"What happened after I went?"

"Miss Peabody, she put all Job's birds, and the snail and all, in the fire. I think, sir, she was angry that you called when she was out."

Polly stopped, shocked by the deepening of the lines in the Dean's face, the horror in his eyes. He couldn't have looked worse, she thought, had there been a death in the family. She thought Job's birds were very nice but to her they were just pretty toys. To the Dean it seemed they were something more. "And then?" he asked.

"Job, he took on something dreadful. He looked as though I'd stuck a knife in him. And so to comfort him I tried to tell him about being apprenticed to the clocks. But he didn't listen, sir. He pushed me away and went out. Banged the door in my face, he did. I've never known him rough like that. Quick tempered now and again, but not rough. He's gentle, Job is." She paused, a little breathless with her pain. "You see, sir, Job's not like other boys."

"No, Polly," said the Dean. "What his clocks are to Mr. Peabody Job's birds are to him. Genius creates from the heart and when the artifact is broken so is the heart. You must forgive his roughness. What did you do then?"

"There was nothing I could do, sir, but wait for market day, for Miss Peabody she won't let me out except for the Saturday marketing. I couldn't tell Mr. Peabody for he's having one of his bad times, and asthma like he has so often when he's low, and I tries to keep cheerful with him when he's low. But Job wasn't at the market, and the fish stall was all anyhow, the fish not gutted proper, no clean rushes and no posies for old Keziah to sell. Job had gone, they said. He'd run away."

"Did they give a reason?" asked the Dean.

"Albert Lee, he wouldn't speak to me. Been drinking. Proper black eye he had. But Keziah she told me quiet like that Albert had knocked Job about something cruel. That was Wednesday night. Thursday morning they found he'd gone. Had enough and who's to blame him. But why did he not come to me, sir? I never thought Job could be in trouble and not come to me." Her voice caught suddenly and the sodden handkerchief ripped in her twisting fingers. The Dean had to lean forward to try and hear what she said next. It was something about the river, and Job not being like other boys.

"No!" he said harshly. "Not that. There is some good reason why he could not come to you."

"You don't know Job, sir," said Polly. "Mr. Peabody he gets low but Job he takes things that hard you wouldn't believe."

"Take heart, my dear. I will wait upon Mr. Havelock and find out what he did in the matter. I fear he has blundered. Then I will wait upon Mr. Albert Lee. We will find Job."

Polly was cheered. She even tried to smile, and she looked timidly about the beautiful room as though it reassured her. The Dean guessed, rightly, that she was thinking that a man living in a big house like this, with these grand servants, must be able to do anything. Her faith in him, terribly shaken, was coming back.

"I tell you, Polly," he said, " 'that all shall be well and all manner of thing shall be well'."

His harsh voice had a kind of joy in it. Dame Julian's words had been unpremeditated. They had come into his mind in a manner that brought as much conviction to himself as to Polly.

"Thank you, sir," she said, and rose and curtseyed. "Please don't ring for Mr. Garland. I can find my way."

But the Dean had already rung the bell. "You will lose yourself in this big house, my dear." He spoke looking down at her. She had great dignity in her sorrow as well as much courage. Who was she? He thought of Perdita. "Nothing she does or seems but smacks of something greater than herself." Garland entered and he took her hand in his and bowed to her. She curtseyed again and left the room with Garland, who had aged five years in the last twenty minutes. The Dean grieved for Garland. For the last ten years the life of the Deanery had moved as on oiled wheels, not moving one inch from the lines laid down by Garland. Now, the Dean knew, there was change in the air. To him it was as though the wind had set south, but for Garland he feared it might be veering north for a while. And for Elaine? He did not know but he prayed for a west wind and the breaking of the wells.

II

The Dean made a hasty luncheon and after it he set out immediately for Worship Street. Under the Porta, beneath her room, he remembered Mary Montague. "Take a little joy," she had said. Had he sinned in trying to obey her? He believed not. Joy being of God was a living thing, a fountain not a cistern, one of those divine things that are possessed only as they overflow and flow away, and not easily come by because it must break into human life through the hard crust of sin and contingency. Joy came now here, now there, was held and escaped. But worth the travail of the winning both for himself and the children. He would have liked to go in and see Miss Montague, and tell her what had happened, but she rested after luncheon and he dared not delay in his search for Job. It did not matter. Such prayer as hers was, like joy, an overflowing fountain that flowed where it was needed.

Mr. Havelock's luncheon had not been as hasty as the Dean's and he was still enjoying his post-prandial nap, his beautiful white silk handkerchief spread over his bald head, his hands serenely folded over the peaceful processes of his excellent digestion, when his visitor was shown into his study.

"Good afternoon, Mr. Havelock," said the Dean hurriedly, and then, becoming aware of his host's predicament, his attention was immediately caught by a shimmer of colour beyond the windows. "Wonderful dahlias," he murmured, adjusting his eyeglasses and turning a courteous back upon Mr. Havelock. "You have a good gardener." They were chrysanthemums but he did not see them very clearly, for time pressed. But he did see a little wooden horse on wheels, abandoned on the lawn. It was a dappled creature with scarlet reins, bright and gay on the vivid green grass. Bella's horse. He felt a pang of keen pleasure at the sight, as keen as though he had been a lover seeing his lady's gloves lying on a chair. He saw the little picture as vividly as though he had impeccable eyesight; or as though a shutter had suddenly swung open in a dark room. He would not forget it.

"Mr. Dean, I was just on the point of waiting upon you. In another moment I should have left the house."

Mr. Havelock, smiling, suave and self-possessed, might never have lunched at all. The Dean thought for a moment that the spread handkerchief and folded hands must have been an optical delusion of his poor sight, then remembered the legal gift of swift adjustment. If Havelock had erred in the matter of Job his adjustments would be agile. But he must not be allowed to escape along by-paths for there was no time.

"What arrangements did you come to with Mr. Lee?" he asked, his voice an abrupt bark. "The boy has run away." The Dean could be alarming in an abrupt mood. "The Great Beast is barking," had been a word of warning that in school and college alike had caused men and boys to melt into the landscape, but Mr. Havelock was unperturbed.

"Mr. Dean, I beg you will take this chair. Run away? I am distressed to hear it. Is the reason known?"

"Not by me, Mr. Havelock. I am seeking information from yourself." Mr. Havelock, in an arm-chair opposite the Dean, put his finger tips together with a maddening deliberation. "And without delay, I beg."

"I called on Lee on Wednesday evening," said Mr. Havelock, with no delay but in tones so calm and unhurried that they held a subtle rebuke. "The boy was out but both Lee and his mother were at home. Disreputable parties, both of them. I was thankful, Mr. Dean, to have spared you personal contact with such a low sort of people. Swithins Lane is not a salubrious part of the city."

"I know all about Swithins Lane," said the Dean. "What I don't know is what sort of reply Mr. Lee gave to my proposal."

"Unfavourable, sir."

"You offered him the compensation we had in mind?"

"He refused it."

"I told you I was ready to increase the sum we had agreed upon as fair and just in order to save the boy."

"You did, sir, but I did not bargain with the fellow. The first offer was more than generous. To have increased it would have been for you a concession lacking in dignity. Nor do I believe that Lee would part with that boy for treble the sum." The Dean remembered what Polly had said about the market stall being in confusion. If Job's genius stood between his master and destitution here was another complication. "And you must remember, sir, that he has legality on his side."

The Dean suspected that Mr. Havelock's sympathies were entirely with Albert Lee, and suddenly he liked him for it. He was a lawyer. The law was perhaps to him what his birds were to Job. It was in a gentler tone that he asked, "And did you come away without more ado, Mr. Havelock?"

"I did, sir. I have those, including Bella, who are dependent on me."

"You mean the man was violent?"

"He is of gipsy origin and a heavy drinker. My interview with him was quite an experience."

"I am sorry, Mr. Havelock, to have subjected you to it. I am glad to see you physically unharmed, and I am obliged to you for your exertions on my behalf." The Dean rose, Mr. Havelock following suit. "And you can throw no light on the disappearance of the boy?"

"No, sir. Do you wish me to act further in this matter? I am at all times at your disposal."

"No, Mr. Havelock, do no more. As you say, legally we are in the wrong. But I wish that you had informed me sooner as to the failure of your visit."

"I was just about to do myself the honour of waiting upon you, sir," said Mr. Havelock suavely, but the Dean saw a gleam of astonishment in his eyes, quickly veiled. All this to-do over an orphanage brat, a fishmonger's apprentice. Adam Ayscough struggled with his anger. Yet what right had he to be angry? Absorbed in other work he had permitted Job to go to the back of his mind. Probably it had been the same with Havelock. "Much obliged," he said humbly, and going into the hall began to feel rather blindly for his hat. "Bella is upstairs?" he asked with the wistful shyness of a young and abashed lover, as Mr. Havelock gave him his hat and cloak and stick.

"I fear she is out for her afternoon walk with her nurse."

"Yes, yes, of course. Good day, Mr. Havelock. Much obliged."

III

Adam Ayscough was in great distress as he made his way down through the narrow twisting streets of the city towards the North Gate slums. He was momentarily forgetful that all was to be well and blamed himself entirely for Albert Lee's fury and Job's disappearance. He should not have allowed Havelock to act for him in the matter. The breaking of an apprenticeship contract by the use of bribery had been against Havelock's legal conscience, and one should never use a man where his conscience is not persuaded. Bribery. The word he had used himself had been compensation, which sounded better but meant much the same. In this affair it appeared to him now that Albert Lee had an impregnable moral position and he himself a very poor one. If Job's skill was necessary to Albert Lee in the prosecution of his business then he had been endeavouring to deprive him of the means of livelihood by means of bribery. Most reprehensible! Yet he intended to continue to do so for he believed a boy's salvation to be at stake. Job must be rescued from the sin of this man whatever sin stuck to himself during the process. Only the saints could rescue a soul from evil without falling into the mud themselves. But on the other side of this he must do what he could for Albert Lee.

He forged his way along the street as though against a high wind, talking to himself, seeing no one, his hat a little crooked and his stick whirling round and round in his hand. The rumour that the Dean was going queer in the head had whispered round the city after he had been seen wheeling a cuckoo clock across the market place in company with Isaac Peabody and Bella Havelock, and now it blew up in his wake like the rustle of autumn leaves, stirred by the wind of his peculiar passing. By nightfall it had curiously softened the city's feelings towards him. Perhaps the great men of the Close were not as immune from worry as had been generally supposed. Perhaps even the great Dean had his troubles. And if he had them, he who was so curiously the city, were they not the city's also?

The flight of steep steps that led down to Swithins Lane was well known to the Dean both in darkness and daylight, but in the strange pallid half-light that was creeping over the city on this autumn afternoon the dirty twisting steps, and the dark doorways on either side, looked more than usually sordid and evil. It was a queer sort of light, yellow and murky. All day the clouds had been gathering and it had been obvious that the spell of calm and lovely weather was over. Was there going to be a storm? The Dean trusted that Elaine and Bella were safely within doors and was glad that the market was now over. A deluge upon those bright gay stalls was not to be desired. The market ended at two-thirty in the winter in order that the beasts might be driven home before dark. Albert Lee, the Dean hoped, would now be at his shop again.

He reached Swithins Lane and opposite him across the street was St. Nicholas at the North Gate. St. Nicholas was a daughter church of St. Matthew's at the South Gate, so small as to be hardly more than a chapel and so old that it looked more like a rock than a building. It had been called after Saint Nicholas, the mariners' saint, because the North Gate beside it had opened directly on the river steps where the great barges had in days gone by unloaded their gear. South Gate, East Gate and West Gate were only names now, their sites marked by the two foundations of Dobson's and by the old pub that stood where once the South Gate had been, but the great arch of the North Gate still spanned the river steps, with the church on one side and on the other a portion of the old city wall that now formed one side of the tannery.

The Dean stood for a moment under the arch at the top of the steps. They were old and broken now and not at all salubrious, for the inhabitants of Swithins Lane could not be cured of a centuries-old habit of standing at the top of them and chucking garbage down to the water, but they still had a graceful curve. Just beyond the steps the river flowed with a strong calm power that was immensely impressive but not reassuring today, with the wide flood lit to a sulphurous yellow by the stormy light. In wet seasons the river could rage up the steps into Swithins Lane, flooding the houses and causing much illness and suffering among the people. There was little about suffering that the Swithins Lane people did not know, and thinking of them the Dean was back again in the heartbreak of his long fight to deliver them. Inbred, dug in, as violently attached to where they were as limpets to a rock, they had not wanted to be delivered, and selfish men had exploited their ignorance and fed their wealth upon it. It broke his heart that that bitter battle, of all his many battles in the city, should have been the only one he had ever lost.

Standing under the archway with the smell of the garbage and the tannery in his nostrils, the evil slums behind him and that menacing water lapping at the steps below, he suddenly straightened his sagging shoulders. He would reopen that fight. His plan had been a good one. The famous architect, his friend, who had helped him in the work on the Cathedral, had worked upon it with him and together they had designed well built, simple and goodlooking houses that built upon high ground beyond the West Gate would have been no blot upon the city's beauty. The North Gate and the old church would have remained intact, and public gardens beside the river would have taken the place of the verminous cottages. He had planned those gardens himself and they were dear to him; he often dreamed of them. It would have cost a great deal but there was wealth in the city, not least his own, which would have been at its disposal. He'd fight again. Swithins Lane should no longer harbour Albert Lees to bludgeon young boys to flight and death.

Death? No! But he had no time to stand here planning fights to come with this boy still in danger. It was Job now. Job. He did not know what he was going to say to Albert Lee, he felt tired and stupid, but experience had taught him that the mere fact of charging into the arena could most wonderfully clear the mind.

He forged his way through the tortuous tunnel of Swithins Lane. It was like an evil man's mind, he sometimes thought, full of twists and turns, darkness and confusion. Even in sunlight, with the wind blowing in the opposite direction from the tannery, it never seemed wholesome, for the tottering ruins of old houses that leaned across it shut in the smell and darkness. The hollows between the cobbles held filmed stagnant water, and rotting cabbage leaves and shreds of paper clogged the gutter. "We want a good rain," thought the Dean. "If there is a storm coming we need it." The lane seemed deserted, for the children were not yet back from school or the men from work, and so dim that already the pallid flicker of candlelight shone in a few of the grimy windows. When he reached the fish shop he found the gas flares already lighted.

The Lees were home from the market and busy in the shop, for on Saturday nights they did a brisk trade in fried fish. The cod and whiting that had gone off in the market were fried in a loathly kind of oil flavoured with onions and sold cheap for Swithins Lane suppers. A nauseous preparatory stench took the Dean by the throat as he walked into the circle of gaslight, took off his top hat to Keziah and asked if he might be allowed to speak a few words to Mr. Albert Lee. Keziah stopped what she was doing and stared, her slack old mouth dropping open. Albert emerged from the back of the shop and came warily closer, shoulders hunched like an advancing prize-fighter, one eye closed up within its purple bruises, the other fixed on the Dean with a gimlet stare of mixed misery and insolence. They knew him well by sight for he had been continually up and down Swithins Lane during the years when he had been fighting for its demolition, and it had been Albert who had flung the egg which upon one occasion had splashed his immaculate top hat with rottenness. It was the remembrance of that egg that was making Albert's approach so wary.

The Dean, as he stood in the flaring yellow gaslight with the darkness of the coming storm behind him, was a formidable figure. Even with his top hat in his hand he seemed to touch the ceiling; his long black cloak added to his breadth of shoulder and was thrown about him like a thundercloud. Yet when he spoke his voice, even though harsh and grating, brought a sudden sense of quietness to the tumultuous wretchedness that was Albert's habitual state of mind when, as now, he happened to be completely sober.

"I owe you an apology, Mr. Lee. I fear I have been the cause of your losing a valuable apprentice."

Albert looked stupidly at the large clean hand held out to him, then wiped his own on his greasy trouser leg and took it. The strong grip further steadied him. "And you, too, Mrs. Lee," said the Dean, and bowed to her. "I fear you will miss Job." Keziah was too awed to speak. Her lips worked nervously and her dirty hands kept folding and unfolding themselves in her dirtier apron. She was a terrible old creature to look at, with her mumbling mouth and rheumy eyes and the pitiful strands of her greasy hair falling over her face from beneath a battered black bonnet, more repulsive even than the drink-sodden brutal Albert. Yet the Dean was repulsed by neither of them. They had that child-likeness that makes so many criminals less repulsive than the sophisticated worldly sinners. They were ruined creatures, both of them, but there had once been something to ruin. The woman's face retained its beauty of bone, and the man still had a queer panther grace and strength. Gipsies, the Dean thought, whom greed for money had brought from the wilds to the town, and separated from their kind they had suffered the fate of so many exiles. Loneliness made or ruined a man. It frightened him so that he must either sing and build in the face of the dark, like a bird or a beaver, or hide from it like a beast in his den. There were perhaps always only the two ways to go, God or the jungle. And all men were exiles. It was a common bond between them, the bond between himself and this man and woman.

"It was I who asked Mr. Havelock if he could arrange a transference for Job," said the Dean. "I did it because of the boy's great skill as a craftsman. I had been shown some excellent little birds that he had whittled out of wood and they showed, I thought, that he had it in him to become a better clockmaker than a fishmonger. But I fear I showed insufficient consideration for yourself, Mr. Lee, and for that I offer you my apologies." Albert growled something under his breath. In spite of that quietness he was not to be won over by a few courteous phrases. "I confess I had another reason. You knocked that boy about too much, Mr. Lee."

Albert looked up sharply, instantly on the insolent defensive, and met the Dean's glance. With his closed-up eye struggling to open and aid the other he stood and looked at the Dean, right into his unhappy eyes and beaky bony face. It was queer how he had to go on looking at the ugly old codger. And what he said was not in the least what he had meant to say.

"That bloody lawyer, ee proper got me back up, the way ee talked. I took it out of the boy."

"Not for the first time," said the Dean.

"You're right, sir. Scraggy, wey-faced, stubborn little beast that ee was, you see, sir."

"Yes, I know," said the Dean in what sounded almost like a tone of sympathy and understanding. "Weak enough to be at your mercy yet kept his mouth shut when you skinned him. They egg a man on, that sort. What you need, Mr. Lee, is a boy who'll yell and kick your shins. Give as good as he gets." He eyed Albert's black eye speculatively. "Or did he, at the end?"

"Yes, sir," said Albert in almost confidential tones. "Couldn't 'ave believed it. I stops to get me breath, an' sudden ee ups and gives it me straight in the eye. Then ee was up the stairs to the attic, where ee sleeps, before I could stop 'im. When me ma went to rouse 'im in the mornin' ee'd gorn. Out the attic winda. Sheer drop it is. She thought she'd see 'im there with all 'is bones broke. But ee weren't there, sir. Queer, it was."

"He won't come back," said the Dean.

"No, sir," said Albert slowly. "There's the river out the back. Ee couldn't swim."

"He is, I trust, alive," said the Dean. "But he will not come back. You went too far. I believe I could find you a boy of the type you need, Mr. Lee. He would not have Job's artistic skill, which I know you have found invaluable, but he would drive you to drink less often. I think, weighing one thing with another, your business would not suffer in the exchange." He took a small packet from his pocket and laid it on the filthy chopping block beside him. "Mr. Lee, Mr. Havelock offered you compensation if you would forgo your legal claim upon the boy. Slightly more than the amount he offered you is there. Will you accept it with my apology for the inconvenience I have caused you, giving me your word that if Job is found you will not force him to return to you? I ask for no assurance except your word."

Albert looked at the hand held out to him, once more placed his own within it and mumbled an agreement. He had not understood more than half of what the Dean had said to him but that grip seemed now to hold not only his hand but his being. It was as though he had been turned round to face in a different direction.

"I will find you that new apprentice," said the Dean. "You can rely on me. Much obliged. Good afternoon, Mrs. Lee. Much obliged."

He bowed, replaced his hat and walked out of the shop. Albert Lee, after a moment of stupefaction, let flow a flood of language so lurid that even old Keziah had never heard it surpassed. He'd been foozled, had the bloody wool pulled over his eyes and he as sober as a judge. His opinion of the Dean, and of all the grinders of the faces of the poor the world over, echoed up and down Swithins Lane and in no time at all a crowd was at the shop. He did a brisk trade that night, his fury and his language sauce to the fried fish. Yet all the time that grip held him. Shutting up shop that night he was suddenly silent, and when he had given Keziah one on the ear and kicked the cat he went to his bed with extraordinary meekness and lay awake till dawn.

IV

The Dean walked back down Swithins Lane towards the North Gate. He was utterly exhausted, drained of strength and virtue. Yet the hidden tussle with the soul of the man had not been as hard as he had expected, for he was not entirely evil yet. Nor was the old crone. Cruel, yes, but who was not? Down at the bottom of the most crystal cup there seemed always to be left a few dregs of the poison. He could remember how, flogging boys, there had once or twice spurted up in him a desire to lay it on a bit harder, get a whimper out of a stubborn culprit, and then he had instantly dropped the cane in horror and revulsion and when the boy had gone he had repented and prayed. He himself was a cracked and polluted vessel. What could one do? Nothing. Only repent and pray and love and await God's mercy.

He reached the North Gate and walked down the dirty steps to the path at the edge of the river, then turned to walk along it behind the Swithins Lane houses, for he wanted to see the attic window from which Job had escaped. The backs of these houses always made him feel as though he were in a nightmare. The broken windows, stuffed here and there with rags or boarded up to keep out the bitter wind that swept across the fen, looked out on filthy backyards and poor little patches of ground running down to the river path, filled with nettles, cabbage stalks, broken glass and crockery. The path was strewn with rubbish and the river water that lapped against it was always oily and foul. It was here that the Dean had planned his beloved garden, with grass and flowering shrubs, and seats beside a clean and wholesome river. He could see it in his mind's eye now, as he picked his way among the cabbage stalks and bits of broken crockery, and his mouth set almost savagely in determination.

When fish bones and decaying fish heads made a slime under his feet he knew that he had reached the back of the shop and stopped and looked up. He saw the attic window, a crazy little dormer window that appeared about to fall out of the roof. The central wooden bar had been wrenched away and the two casements hung drunkenly outwards. There would have been room for a slim boy to squeeze through and drop into the bed of nettles below. It was a considerable drop and the Dean wondered that he had not injured himself. Perhaps he had. If so, where was he? The Dean turned to look at the scum on the river, which here looked almost solid with decay, and the sight reassured him. Job was not the boy to plunge down into that filth. Adam Ayscough was experienced in the vagaries of humanity. He knew well that the desperate can sometimes entirely forget those who love them and yet be influenced in what they do by old habits of fastidiousness. Habit in times of misery can be stronger than love. "Many waters cannot quench love" was said of divine, not human, love, which the Dean knew was not always tough enough to survive the indifference of misery. That was one of the chief reasons why he so struggled to do away with misery. He had been aware of fastidiousness in Job and of aspiration like a flame. Indeed there had been something flamelike in the boy's whole appearance, in his flickering nervous movements, in his genius that seemed to come and go like some spiritual presence, like some other boy looking out of his eyes. He could see Job plunging into fire but not into scummy water.

He lifted his eyes from the filth and looked across the river to the stretch of the fen beyond, and up to the great sky, and the sight was so amazing that he stood where he was. The storm clouds were massed overhead, blue-black and motionless. They had crept up stealthily from the east but they had not yet covered the sky. To the west there was a break over the horizon and through this the light of a wild sunset streamed across the fen, lighting the pools and waterways to gold against the darkness of the shadowed land. Where the Dean stood the air was breathless but out in the fen puffs of hot wind seemed darting this way and that, uneasy as evil spirits, frightening the rushes and ruffling the water, a surface of restless fear moving upon the leaden stillness of the crouching earth. There were no birds to be seen or heard. Usually one of the joys of the river and the fen were the birds, the swans and herons, the ducks, dabchicks and moorhens, wagtails and sedge-warblers. There was always a rustling and a thin sharp piping, a quacking and fluting, and sometimes the tremendous beat of the swans' wings as they passed overhead. But the birds had disappeared. They had all hidden in the rushes. The loneliness and silence of land and water without them was strange, like a ship with sails reefed and passengers below hatches. To the north there was still a band of gold between earth and sky, and against this the village on the hill that Job had seen rose starkly from a thicket of silver willows, its tall church spire black as ebony against the narrow band of light. It was one of the loneliest of the fen villages, it was Willowthorn, and it had about it a courage that riveted the Dean's attention.

To the mutter of thunder he followed the path to its ending at a dilapidated iron bridge. Once there had been a grand old bridge here, crowned by a chapel dedicated to Our Lady, and a paved way from the North Gate had crossed it and continued into the fen. This was the way that Prior Hugh's monks had followed on the night of storm when they had left the city. Of this bridge there was nothing left now but the stone piers that held up the rusty ironwork of the new bridge. As the North Gate came down in the world, and a bridge to the east of the city came into more general use, the old north bridge had gradually fallen into disrepair. The Dean's plan for his garden had included the taking away of the iron bridge and its replacement with a stone one, simple and strong, with a parapet of the right height for the accommodation of fishermen. For the people loved to fish here. Draping themselves over the iron railing of the present bridge was one of the few innocent pleasures of the men and small boys of Swithins Lane.

But there was no one here today and the Dean was alone as he stood on the crown of the bridge and looked down at the rough drove that followed the track of the old road. Between wind-twisted hedges of crab-apple and hawthorn it led waveringly from the bridge to the village that still stood out so courageously against the narrowing band of golden sky. Nowadays more modern roads linked the villages and the monks' way was overgrown and deserted. But not today, for the Dean could see a lonely figure coming towards him, now seen where the way opened out, now hidden as the hedges drew closer. He came as unsteadily as the way, wavering from side to side as though drunk or exhausted. In the whole terrible landscape he seemed the only living creature, as though he were the last man left to face alone the doom of all things. As the first flash of lightning lit up the stretch of the fen, so that it seemed for a blinding instant as though every reed and every twig were simultaneously visible, proclaiming aloud the preciousness of its identity before the darkness overwhelmed it, the Dean started forward from the bridge. That wavering figure was not Job, he knew, but it had the loneliness of Job and he could not leave it to face the doom alone.

CHAPTER XII *King Lear*

I

THE wind and rain came together as the Dean stumbled forward over the tussocks of rough grass, driving into his face and nearly blinding him. The windings of the drove hid the other man, he could see nothing but the sheeting rain and the stripped hawthorn boughs tossing in the wind. It was like struggling in a trough of waves, and took him back in thought to the days before the dykes had been built, when in a great storm the sea would come raging in over the fen to join the overflowing waters of river and stream. Men had struggled then somewhat as he was struggling now, battling their way through rising water with children on their backs or lambs under their arms, trying to reach rising ground and safety before the waters covered the earth. But he had no more than rain and mud to contend with and was hampered only by his ridiculous top hat and flapping cloak. He felt a quirk of amusement at the thought of the absurdity of his appearance. A poor sort of parody of those courageous shepherds of old days! And with his poor eyesight he was likely to pass the lost sheep in the drove and never even see it. He battled on and presently ceased to feel amused, for he was feeling extremely ill. The thudding of his heart made it difficult for him to get his breath. He stopped, supporting himself on his stick. Fool that he was to go in for such capers at his age!

"Are you mad?" asked a hoarse high-pitched voice, and he was aware of a bony hand pressed against his chest, gripping the clasp of his cloak. Peering through the deluge he saw a tall dripping skeleton or scarecrow reared up before him, supporting itself by its grip on his chest. He seemed to see dark rags flapping about the bones of the thing, dark pits for eyes and mouth. But the hoarse voice was human. " 'O, let me not be mad, not mad, sweet heaven! Keep me in temper: I would not be mad!' "

The Dean was in no state to support the crazy creature. They were in danger of both falling headlong. There was a slight slackening of the rain and he saw to his right an old hawthorn tree whose branches, bent all one way by the prevailing wind from the sea, gave some hope of slight shelter if they sat on the bank beneath it. He steered them both towards it and they fell, rather than sat, upon the bank. The hand that had gripped the Dean's cloak fell away and was clasped by the other in an attitude of prayer. Holding them before him, his head lifted in a queer sort of proud ecstasy, he prayed in a voice that was suddenly strong and resonant.

" 'Poor naked wretches, wheresoe'er you are,
That bide the pelting of this pitiless storm,
How shall your houseless heads and unfed sides,
Your loop'd and window'd raggedness, defend you
From seasons such as these? O, I have ta'en
Too little care of this!' "

His voice broke and he said uncertainly, "I don't remember. How does it go on? How did he finish his prayer? Do you know?"

The Dean finished it for him.

" 'Take physic, pomp;
Expose thyself to feel what wretches feel,
That thou mayst shake the superflux to them
And show the heavens more just.' "

"Yes, yes, yes," said the man, and lifted one hand, dripping with water, in a childish gesture to his face, as though he thought to wipe away the raindrops that were trickling down his grooved cheeks and plastering his few wisps of white hair like seaweed to his bald pate. The Dean felt for his handkerchief, not too wet since it had been in his coat pocket beneath the shelter of his cloak, and handed it pitifully to the lunatic. Yet he doubted if he was mad. He doubted if lunatics could quote Shakespeare with such accuracy. An eccentric, rather, an eccentric who had suffered greatly.

"I think the storm is passing," he said gently. "These autumn storms are violent but soon over."

A sudden gleam of sunshine glinted like a sword through the rain, then vanished again. But it was lighter and the wind had dropped.

"I have been to see Letitia," said the man. "I always go to see Letitia on a Saturday."

The Dean found his eyeglasses and putting them on turned to have a good look at his companion. He was an old man, tall and thin and almost as bent as the ancient hawthorn that sheltered them. His eyes were blue and bewildered, his mouth hung a little open and raindrops dripped from the point of his thin nose. He wiped them off with the Dean's handkerchief but the hawthorn was not an adequate protection from the downpour and to his distress they gathered again. The Dean was better off. His top hat, tipped a little forward as usual, made a gutter for the rain. Where the bend came in front it shot off to the ground as though through one of the waterspouts on the Cathedral roof, leaving his face dry.

"Your daughter?" asked the Dean.

"My wife."

"Does she live in Willowthorn?"

"Not now. She's dead. I go to see her on a Saturday. I sit on her grave and we talk."

The Dean looked again at his companion. He saw now that his greenish rags of clothes might once have been decent clerical black, and the sodden wisps of white under his chin a parson's bands. From the first there had seemed to him something vaguely familiar about the figure. Who was he? Suddenly he remembered Augustus Penny, the vicar of St. Peter's in the market place. He had only seen the old man once or twice for he seldom attended clerical gatherings, and had never accepted any of his invitations to the Deanery, but the Dean remembered that in years gone by, before he himself had come to the city, Augustus

Penny had been Vicar of Willowthorn. He also remembered being told that Penny was a recluse, and odd, and that he had felt a desire to call upon him, but he had not done so because he feared to intrude on his privacy. For this he now blamed himself. The reasons for seclusion were many. One should find out why a man is alone before one lets him alone, for he may not want to be alone. This he had not done.

"Mr. Penny," said the Dean, "I believe it has stopped raining. We are both old men. Shall we help each other home?"

Mr. Penny showed no surprise at being recognised; age, bewilderment and suffering had brought him long past the point of ever being surprised at anything. He was never quite sure these days whether he was living in memory, dreams, this world or the other. The frontiers were not clearly distinguishable now. There had been a time when he could lose himself in memories of the past and then with a deliberate exercise of the will leave them and come back to the present. He had known then when he was dreaming and when he was awake, and whether the glow of comfort that warmed and reassured him was that of heaven or the kitchen range. It was difficult to be sure now except when he was doing his work. Reading the liturgy, ministering the sacraments, teaching the children, preaching, doing what he could for those who suffered, that life-long routine still held and was still his lifeline. It had always been for him the utterance of his love of God, the expression in works of his adoration and delight. He would hold on to it while he lived. He would praise his God while he had his being. Suddenly he struggled to his feet, feeling the tug of the lifeline. He was needed at home. Someone needed him.

"I am needed at home," he said.

"Our way lies together," said the Dean. "Could you help me up? I do not seem to be able to get a proper purchase in this mud. You are nimbler than I am. Much obliged. Much obliged."

Augustus Penny was surprisingly strong and had swung the Dean to his feet in a trice. "Ah, see there!" he cried in his high-pitched voice. "The waters have abated. The dove has found rest for the sole of her foot. She has not returned."

The storm had passed and the whole fen lay bathed in

spent sunlight. Every stream and stretch of water among the rushes, that had been whipped and tormented by the storm, lay quiet now, reflecting the piled masses of white and silver clouds that floated like swans on the far deep pools of the sky. Every twig was strung with sparkling crystal drops, and every drop had a rainbow caught in its heart. The Dean could not see these rainbows, he could only see the dazzle of light, but Augustus Penny could see them and he laughed and clapped his hands like a child. And then looking back up the drove he saw something else. "Look there! Look there!" he cried, pointing a lean forefinger at what he saw. "That's where she is. That's it! That's it!"

The Dean looked too and this time he saw something of what Mr. Penny saw, for his long-distance sight was better than his near sight. From this point onwards the drove ran fairly straight, a green way narrowing to vanishing point in what looked like a floating silver cloud, so ethereal in the evening light was the grove of willow trees that grew about the lower slopes of Willowthorn. Above this shimmering cloud rose a small dreamlike city, as delicate as though carved out of aquamarine or opal, roof rising above roof to cluster about the church that rose to the sky like a lifted sword, with a bright point of light twinkling at the summit of the spire. It looked far away, not close at hand as it had appeared before the storm. It had looked then attainable by living man, but not now. They would not get there now. Not until they were as utterly changed as the city. He took the bemused Mr. Penny gently by the arm and turned him round to face the other way, towards the mortal city where they must finish it out.

"You are needed at home," he reminded Mr. Penny.

"I don't remember," murmured Mr. Penny. "Who is it? Did I tell you anyone wanted me at home? Generally I'm not much needed, you know. Not now. Are you?"

"No," said the Dean, and the thought of Elaine was a hard pain at his heart. "No, not much needed. But we have to finish it out."

II

There was still a bank of dark cloud low down in the west and the sun soon dropped behind it. By the time they reached the bridge it was dusk, but the Dean could make out the soft white blur of the floating swans and the arrowed gleam of darting moorhens. The birds had come back. He heard a cock crow and a dog bark. The terror was over and a cool breath came from the face of the river. It was so dusky, and there were so few people about, that no one recognised the two old men as wet and exhausted they struggled up the steep streets of the city towards the market place. As they went there was another shower of rain but they were already so wet that it could not make them much wetter. Five o'clock struck as they reached the market place and the Dean was astonished to find it still so early. He seemed to have lived through a lifetime since he had left home after luncheon. And he had accomplished nothing.

"There won't be a fire at home, you know," said Mr. Penny gloomily. "Not till I light it. No fire."

The Dean had intended to leave Mr. Penny at his door but now he changed his mind. He would go in. There must surely be someone to be found who would light a fire for Mr. Penny and dry his clothes. He could not go back to his own luxurious home and leave him comfortless.

St. Peter's vicarage was behind the church and was reached by a narrow lane that led off the market place between the church and the Swan and Duck. "This is my church," said Mr. Penny proudly, pausing at the entrance to the lane and looking up at the weight of darkness beside him and above him. St. Peter's was not a large church but with its low square tower and storm-grey buttressed walls it had an air of sturdiness and strength, and in this duskiness looked less like a church than a great rock upon the seashore. The deserted market place, with the wet cobbles reflecting the last of the afterglow as ripples do on calm water, and the street lamps like the riding lights of ships at anchor, seemed to the Dean to be the sea lapping gently against the worn stone.

"Shall we go in?" whispered Mr. Penny. "I hide the key in the porch."

The Dean could see the porch, a pitch black cave in the storm-grey rock. The beautiful gold-flecked water washed into it and out again, but silently. He felt he could not presume to go inside. He saw a broken marble floor through which there welled up a clear cool spring that mirrored a few stars, for there was a rent in the roof. The water was living so that the stars trembled. There was a freshness in the air. One could not go in.

"Another day," said Mr. Penny, disappointed. "We'll go home now." They went on down the lane into a garden overgrown with trees and saw through the tangled boughs a gaunt house where all the windows but one were darkened. In that one there was the wink and glow of firelight. "It *is* lighted," said Mr. Penny. "There's someone there. How very odd."

"We will understand when we go in," said the Dean. He still thought he had better go in. It might be that Mr. Penny had lighted the fire himself before he went out, and had forgotten what he had done. In that case there was no one to see that he changed his wet clothes.

Mr. Penny stumbled up the cracked steps to the battered old front door, from which the paint had long since peeled away, and pushed it open. Then with an uncertain stumbling courtesy, the remnant of something that had once been sure and proud, he took off an imaginary hat and holding it against his breast with his left hand gestured with his right towards his home. "Please to come in, sir. You are very welcome. Just a glass of wine and a biscuit. I am honoured, sir. A glass of wine and a biscuit."

His voice trailed off uncertainly and the Dean saw that he must go in first. The hall was a vast chill darkness, crossed by a thin beam of light from a door that was not quite closed. It illumined a curtain of cobwebs, swaying in the draught, but nothing else. The sickly-sweet smell of mildew, unaired rooms, dust and mice, made the Dean's head swim and for a moment he was utterly bewildered. "Most extraordinary!" he said to himself.

For some while now he had found it hard to remember that this was the city, and that not a mile from him Garland was washing up the tea things and Elaine was sitting by the fire with her embroidery. The silence of birds by the bridge, the drenching storm and the old mad king clutching at his chest, the celestial city at the end of the long green way, the riding lights of the ships and the hidden place where the living water welled up through the broken floor, and now this house of windy darkness. Who could have believed that they were there beneath the crust of things? Life had taken on a strange richness since Mr. Peabody had sidled like a terrified crab into his study, had lifted the thin gold shell of his watch and shown him the hidden watchcock. Until now life for him had meant the aridity of earthly duty and the dews of God. Now he was aware of something else, a world that was neither earth nor heaven, a heartbreaking, fabulous, lovely world where the conies take refuge in the rainbowed hills and in the deep valleys of the unicorns the songs are sung that men hear in dreams, the world that the poets know and the men who make music. Job's world. Isaac's world. The autumn song of the robin could let you in, or a shower of rain or a hobby-horse lying on a green lawn.

The strange dark hall was flooded with light, and in the oblong splendour of the opened door stood a beautiful boy. His dark hair was tumbled on his forehead and his broad fine-boned face was fiercely flushed across the cheek-bones. His eyes, dark and brilliant, swept the hall with that effortless certainty of the young who see so well that they are in no doubt about what they see. His head was flung back, his hands raised to each side of the door, and the garment of soft olive green that he wore belted about him flowed to the ground. His figure was defiant, glorious, and for a moment or two the Dean placed it with the riding lights and the broken marble floor, something he would not have seen a month ago. "Sir! Sir!" cried the boy, but still it took him a few minutes to identify this young god with Job attired in a woman's faded velvet dressing-gown, and a few moments more to realise that the change was the change from normal health to the defiant courage that will not submit to fever and pain. Job had guts. He took two long strides across the hall and put his arms round him that he might take his taut hands from the sides of the door. Job sagged for a moment, tried for his footing and failed to find it. The Dean picked him up, feeling his body burning hot under the dressing-gown and as surprisingly light as the body of a dead bird can feel, held upon the palm in the days of snow and frost-bound earth. In his mood of exaltation he did not find it hard to carry him to the old sofa with broken springs that stood at right angles to the fire.

"Of course, now!" said Mr. Penny, standing behind them and rubbing his hands happily together. "How could I have forgotten who it was? David? Joshua? Job! Job Mooring. He comes to my church. Attends at St. Peter's. No one young comes except Job and the king's daughter. Did you light the fire, Job?"

"Yes, sir."

"Good boy. Good boy. And you've put the teapot on the hob. Good boy. Letitia's dressing-gown. I've always kept it. Now we'll have tea."

"Mr. Penny, you are very wet," said the Dean. "I beg that first of all you will go upstairs and put on some dry clothes."

He spoke with authority and Mr. Penny ambled off murmuring to himself, "Tea and toast. I like tea and toast. Tea and toast." The Dean could hear him stumbling up a long flight of dark stairs and he pictured them as going on for ever. What a vast height darkness had, and what depth. The fire, and the one guttering candle on the mantelpiece, did not illumine the farther reaches of Mr. Penny's vast cobwebbed study. Beyond the torn carpet, the piles of books on the floor, and the tall chair where he had put his hat and cloak, the walls vanished in a shapeless infinity of darkness. He thought the clouds must have come over the first stars.

"You're wet too, sir," said Job shyly.

"No matter," said the Dean, "I shall change when I get home. Did you escape from the window, Job?"

"Yes, sir. I sprained my ankle."

The Dean looked at the clumsy bandages that protruded from beneath Letitia's dressing-gown. They were obviously the combined work of Job and Mr. Penny, not of Doctor Jenkins. Dark ridges were gouged out under Job's eyes and there were beads of sweat on his forehead. He must have broken the ankle. "Could you tell me what happened?" he asked gently. "I know that Albert Lee beat you and that you tried to run away. I know no more than that."

Job sat up straight on the sofa. "I could be making the toast, sir. Mr. Penny likes toast."

The Dean saw his hand tighten on the edge of the sofa as he moved. Yes, the boy had courage. He liked courage in a boy. He was proud of Job. Adjusting his eyeglasses and looking about him he perceived a platter of grimy-looking bread in the hearth before the fire, with a toasting fork. A pat of butter and milk in a cracked jug stood on the mantelpiece beside the guttering candle. "Stay where you are, Job," he croaked commandingly. "I used to make toast at your age. I can't have forgotten the trick of it."

A three-legged stool was near him. He lowered himself down to it with the utmost care, for he doubted if any article of furniture in this house could be used with any assurance of safety, spread a piece of bread on the toasting fork and held it hopefully towards the fire. The steam from his wet garments rose about himself and Job like smoke from a bonfire. He was divided between sorrow that Mr. Penny should be living out his old age in this cobwebbed darkness, and he had not known it, amusement at his own situation, and a return of that strange joy that once or twice lately had suddenly arisen within him as he had seen the spring rising through the cracked marble of the floor. It was strange because until now foreign to his experience. He took it when it came with a humble startled gratitude.

"I had meant to go to Willowthorn, sir," said Job. "You can see Willowthorn from the drove where I used to get the flowers and berries for Keziah's posies. I like Willowthorn. I thought I might get work there. But first I thought I must tell Polly where I was going, so she shouldn't worrit. But I couldn't go then, it was late and dark and she'd have been in bed. So I hid in the rushes by the river till the morning. My ankle hurt but I held it in the river and that eased it. The water was cool."

"It's dirty there," said the Dean, his eyes on Job.

A strong shudder passed through the boy's body. "Yes, sir. It's horrible there. Slimy. And then there was Polly——"

He broke off in confusion and the Dean found himself intensely and absurdly happy. So Job's love for Polly had not been quenched. It had about it something of the divine toughness. Polly would be a happy woman.

"Go on, Job," he said jubilantly.

"I started for the city as soon as it was light, sir, for Polly gets up early. But my ankle made me slow, it was swelled up so much, and when I got to the market place and was passing St. Peter's I thought I'd rest it a bit, and I sat in the porch. There's a seat there under the notice board."

"Mr. Penny found you there?"

"Yes, sir. He gets up early and goes to the church for his office. I couldn't tell you what an office is, sir, only that it's something Mr. Penny does in the church before breakfast. He saw that I'd hurt myself. He said to come to his house and he'd give me a bandage for my ankle. But when we'd got the bandage on I didn't seem to be able to stand on the foot, so he said to stay a while. Tomorrow I hope I'll be better and get away. I don't want to burden Mr. Penny but he says he likes the company."

"You didn't think of writing to tell Polly you were safe?"

"I did write, sir, and Mr. Penny he said he'd send it by the milkman." He paused and asked sharply. "Didn't he, sir?"

"I'm afraid not," said the Dean.

"No, sir? But he's a very kind gentleman."

"Kindness, thank God, we can keep until the end. Memory, not always. It is no matter. Is this toast as it should be, Job?"

Job looked at the charred bread. "You turn it round to the other side now, sir. Does Polly know I ran away?"

"Yes. She is much concerned on your account. On my way home I will do myself the honour of calling at Angel Lane and assuring them of your safety. And, Job, this afternoon I called on Mr. Albert Lee and came to a satisfactory arrangement with him. You will not go back there. You are released from your indentures and will go to Mr. Peabody and learn to be a clockmaker."

Job was silent for so long that the Dean allowed the charred bread to burst into flames while he adjusted his eyeglasses and looked at him anxiously. But Job, sitting upright on the sofa, was merely happy. The Dean thought he had never seen such happiness in a human face. It seemed to light the whole room. Even the shapeless dark appeared to go down before it, as utterly annihilated as is a man's shadow when he swings round to face the sun. It occurred to the Dean that he had never before been a witness of one of those moments of entire reversal that come only once or twice in a human life. For Job, in the space of one moment, death had become life. It was like seeing the son of the widow of Nain sit suddenly bolt upright on his bier. The Dean turned to shake the burnt bread off into the fire, then spearing another piece on the toasting fork he tried again.

"I fear I lack concentration," he said to Job. "These domestic tasks are not as simple as they appear to those who do not habitually perform them."

Job suddenly found his voice. "Thank you, sir. This is the second time you've taken me out of hell."

"That sounds over-dramatic, Job. What do you mean? The second time?"

"You wouldn't remember the first time, sir. I was a sweep's climbing boy and my master and I came to sweep a chimney at the Deanery. I wouldn't go up it, for I'd got that I couldn't sweep another chimney. You sent me to Dobson's."

Job's eyes were fixed on the Dean's face in an agony of pleading as dramatic as his speech. He wanted the Dean to remember more than he had ever wanted anything in this life; yet he had just said that old men did not always remember. For a moment the Dean looked puzzled, then slowly his face lit up. To see the hard lines soften, and tenderness and delight beaming in the eyes that looked at him over the top of the Dean's spectacles, was a greater joy to Job than the fact of his own deliverance.

"Dear me!" ejaculated the Dean. "Most extraordinary! I have never forgotten that little urchin. In your early years at Dobson's, Job, I inquired now and again as to your welfare. You, and boys like you, have been continually in my prayers. You must forgive me that I did not recognise you when we met at Mr. Peabody's. You must remember that I am short-sighted and that you have altered considerably. I am obliged to you, Job, for making yourself known to me. Much obliged."

The strange, tall, dusky room, lit by the light of the flames, was like a cavern in a mountain. It might have been in Job's world. It was in his world. He and the old man were close together in his world, and his world was real. The great figure of his dreams was once more exclusively his own.

The Dean broke a silence in which he too had been aware that he belonged to this boy, and the boy to him. This sense of belonging was one of the profounder satisfactions of love. "Job," he said, "I am perplexed upon one point. Where are you to lodge whilst working for Mr. Peabody?"

"Could I lodge here, sir?" asked Job. "With Mr. Penny? He needs company. I could look after him, night and morning. Make his bed, cook him a kipper. I'd like that, sir."

While the second piece of toast blackened the Dean considered the suggestion. At first sight he thought it bad. This house was no place for a boy. But then this boy was not as other boys. He could see Job finding books that he liked among the masses scattered on the floor. He could see him digging in the old garden whose wild trees pressed against the windows, and finding peace deep as a well in quiet empty rooms, the shadow of leaves, moonlight moving on a wall. If some good woman could be found who would be willing to sweep up the cobwebs in this house, and upon occasions cook something more substantial than a kipper, these two might do very well together.

"We will think of it, Job," he said. "And thank you that you wished to give me that robin. Polly told me of your intention and I am much obliged to you for your kindness." He paused, searching for words. "I should like to offer you my sympathy in the loss of all those little birds so lovingly created. The snail, too, and the mouse. It is a loss whose magnitude I am myself perhaps not able to estimate, for my clumsy fingers have never known the artist's skill. I did once, I recollect, make wool roses but they were not recognisable. But I do write books and were the manuscript of one to be burnt before publication I should, I know, feel it at my heart."

His words seemed to have gone over Job's head for when he looked at the boy he saw nothing in his eyes but a blazing hatred that deeply shocked him. Job, it seemed, could be as virulent a hater as he was a tough lover. "Don't hate, Job!" he said sharply, but he was so shocked that he could say nothing more. It was a relief when Mr. Penny came in.

Mr. Penny, attired in strange but dry garments, an old pair of cricketing trousers and the frock coat he wore for funerals, was almost in merry mood. While the Dean toasted with more concentration and less eccentricity than before he made the tea, hot and strong and sweet, and poured it into cracked cups. Long ago he had liked being hospitable and guests around his fireside had been one of his joys. Suddenly it was so again. From the deeps of his old memory funny stories that he used to tell began floating mysteriously up to the surface, stories that he had not told for forty years. He told them again, chuckling over them, his thin hands wrapped lovingly about his hot teacup. The Dean capped them with others. Job, whose pain was not unbearable if he kept still, kept still and ate buttered toast. For the rest of his life buttered toast would seem to him the nectar of the gods.

The pealing of bells all over the city brought the Dean to his feet. Seven o'clock. He must go, for he had much to do, but for the first time in his life he took leave of a social occasion with regret. "Good night, Job," he said. "I shall be sending Doctor Jenkins to look at your ankle. Keep still until he comes. I will inform Mr. Peabody and Polly of your safety. Be at peace now and let the tide carry you into calm water. That is all you have to do for the moment. God bless you. Thank you, Mr. Penny, for an excellent tea. Yes, that is my cloak. Much obliged. I am glad, sir, that we met each other in the drove this afternoon. To have had some speech with you has been a privilege."

By this time they were in the hall and Mr. Penny had just opened the front door. Outside was darkness, the cool breath of night, the faint rustling of overgrown trees in the wild dark garden. "A privilege," repeated the Dean. He meant what he said. Mr. Penny under the bludgeonings of disaster had not lost his sense of direction or of allegiance. He never would. Love still owned him, steered him, drew him to itself. No matter how eccentric he became he would never go off course.

"Thank you, sir," he said now with sudden dignity. "May I know your name, my friend? I should like to know your name."

He had met Adam Ayscough before, but he did not remember. The Dean did not want him to remember and he replied, "My name is Adam."

"Adam," said Mr. Penny. "A good name. Adam and Job. Both good names. Good day to you, sir. I am needed at home."

He suddenly abandoned the Dean, forgetful of him, and shuffled back across the hall to Job. Adam Ayscough shut the front door behind him and felt his way down the broken steps with the help of his stick. The firelight shining from the study window illumined his way through the dripping garden to the lane, and out in the market place the riding lights were ready with their welcome.

He climbed up the steps to Angel Lane and knocked at the door of number twelve. It was opened by Isaac and in the lighted oblong of the kitchen door stood Polly, holding a soup tureen to her chest, her figure taut with anxiety. A crack of light shone along the line of the parlour door, slightly ajar, where instinct told the Dean that Emma was listening.

"Good evening, Mr. Peabody. Job is safe with Mr. Penny, the Rector of St. Peter's. He had a fall and hurt his ankle. There is I think no cause for anxiety but I am on my way to ask Doctor Jenkins to look at it. I have seen Mr. Lee and Job's connection with him is now ended."

Polly had disappeared from the lighted doorway and the steaming tureen was reposing on the kitchen table. The Dean thought he heard the back door opening and closing and was aware of someone slipping silent and ghost-like behind him, and then running like the wind down the street. He was also aware that the line of light down the parlour door was a little wider than before. What would Emma do to Isaac when she discovered that Polly had fled without leave to attend to the comfort of Job and Mr. Penny? He raised his voice. "Will you be so good, Mr. Peabody, as to present my compliments to your sister? Would it be convenient, do you think, if I were to wait upon her after evensong on Monday, about the hour of five? I would come in now but I was caught in the rain and I am too wet to enter a lady's parlour. I owe Miss Peabody an apology and I would count it an honour and privilege if I might be allowed to make her acquaintance."

Isaac, nodding like a mandarin, murmured incoherently. When he had opened the door his shoulders had been sagging and he had been coughing. A dejected grey woollen muffler with one end wrapped round his neck and the other trailing on the floor had seemed the very symbol of his misery. Now, seeing the conspiratorial gleam in the Dean's eyes, his own lit up. He straightened himself and saw that there were stars above the roofs across the way. One great planet burned with a rosy glow. Each street lamp, reflected in the wet cobbles, had its own glory. The smell of onion soup that flowed out from the little house into the street had a remarkable pungency. Isaac was fond of onions. Job was safe and Emma was mollified, for the parlour door had closed softly. The rosy planet so dazzled his eyes that he did not for the moment realise that the Dean had left him. When he did realise it he did not mind, for his love was creeping like a girdle round the whole city and nothing he loved was absent from him. Job was safe. No one he loved was in danger. Nor was he. He had been cold and shivering for days but now he was warm. Gathering up the trailing end of muffler as though it were a dowager's train he turned back into the house, shut the door and called out cheerily, "I'll bring in the soup, Emma."

III

The Dean walked along Worship Street, knocked at Doctor Jenkins's door and left a message with the astonished parlourmaid. Then he turned homeward, flogging his weary mind to the remembrance of his next duties. He could now leave Job and Mr. Penny in the competent hands of Doctor Jenkins and Polly, but he must find a permanent housekeeper for St. Peter's vicarage. He would ask Elaine. He would ask her tonight. He must see Havelock. He must find an apprentice for Albert Lee. The things he must do went round and round in his head. It seemed a long way from Worship Street to the Deanery and when Garland opened the door to him he stumbled clumsily on the mat.

"You're wet, sir!" said Garland angrily, taking off his cloak. "You're wet through, sir!"

"No matter," said the Dean. "If I change quickly I shall not, I trust, be late for dinner. Mrs. Ayscough has not been anxious?"

"Mrs. Ayscough has had her dressmaker with her sir," said Garland, and shut his mouth like a trap.

"Ah!" said the Dean with a sigh of relief. "She has been occupied."

He was going upstairs, Garland with him. Presently he was in his dressing-room, changing his wet things, and Garland was presenting him with a small but fiery drink on a tray. He waved it aside but Garland appeared to have taken root in the carpet and his silent fury was so intimidating that the Dean drank it. Subsequently he felt warmer, but more muddled. Garland moved soft-footed about the room, and presently the Dean found himself impeccably dressed for dinner. Then he was in the drawing-room with Elaine, not very sure whether Garland had inserted him through the door, as a nurse inserts the small boy she has brought down from the nursery for his hour with his mother, or whether he had not. The gong boomed and he and Elaine went in to dinner.

Hot food made him feel more like himself and after dinner, when they were by the drawing-room fire, she with her embroidery, he asked her, "My dear, what happened to that housemaid we had? The one you sent away."

"Which one, Adam?" asked Elaine. "The fen girls are so heavy and stupid, so unteachable, that I have sent away a good many."

"Her name was Ruth and she had been badly burnt in her youth. Her face was much scarred."

"You mean Ruth Newman." Elaine shuddered. "What a revolting creature she was! I only kept her two months. But she left two years ago, Adam. What makes you remember her? Her ugliness, I suppose."

"I did not think her ugly," said the Dean. He was looking thoughtfully at the fire. He remembered Ruth very well, a woman of middle age, a country woman, moving with a slow and quiet strength. The drawn purple scars had been a disfigurement, certainly, but not an ugliness, for what one had chiefly noticed about her face had been the broad lined forehead and the extraordinary softness of the dark eyes, widely spaced beneath fine brows. He had reason to remember her, for it was during the two months when she had been with them that he had been seized with an unusually bad bout of lumbago, at a time when Garland had been laid up with a feverish attack. He had stumbled and fallen upon the stairs one evening, and had found himself unable to get up again. He had not known what to do, for if he had called out for help Elaine might have heard him and been alarmed. The shock might have brought on one of her headaches. But Ruth, crossing the landing above, had seen him and came to his assistance, and subsequently looked after him, applying remedies which she assured him had been of great service to her own grandfather. The remedies had seemed strange to him; the application to the afflicted part of salt warmed in the oven, and subsequent anointing with hog's grease. But though strange they had been remarkably effectual and he had never forgotten her sensible matter-of-fact kindness and the peculiar tenderness of her broad strong hands. He had been deeply sorry when Elaine had sent her away. And she, he remembered, had been sorry too. He had given her a gift upon parting and she had been hard put to it to keep herself from weeping. "No, not ugly," he said, adding with a smile, "but perhaps a fellow feeling made me over partial to her looks. Where is she now, my dear?"

"Adam, how should I know?" said Elaine airily, her voice bell-like in sweetness. "She left two years ago."

The Dean held out his hands, still chilled, to the blaze of the fire. He did not look at Elaine and a heavy grief pressed upon him, for she was lying. He wished he did not always know when she was lying but to know these things was one of the penalties of love. He did not need to look at her to see her in her sofa corner in that wonderful sea-green gown, the lamplight on her hair, her needle flashing in and out of her embroidery in its small round tambour frame. There was a suggestion of a smile on her mouth and her long lashes cast faint lovely shadows on her cheek. When she deceived him, managed him, there was always that airy music in her voice, the small smile, the shadow of the lashes on her cheek because she had hooded the amusement in her eyes. Until now he had always let it alone, never pressed her, lest she perjure herself further, but now he had to go on.

"Has she never written to you, my dear?"

"Why should she? There was no intimacy between us."

"Where did she subsequently find employment? You were applied to for a reference, were you not?"

"Adam, how can I remember where all the servants go when they leave us?"

"Try to remember, my dear. It is of importance. I am anxious to find a housekeeper for Mr. Augustus Penny, the Vicar of St. Peter's. I believe Ruth Newman to be the very woman he requires."

Elaine dropped the tambour frame in her lap in sudden exasperation. "Adam, since when has it been one of the duties of a Dean to find servants for the parochial clergy?"

"Elaine, all my life I have prayed much, and as I could I have endeavoured to love much and to grapple with the evil about me, but in the equation of love and prayer with the service of small things I have failed. In the mercy of God it is not, I trust, too late."

He spoke with such sadness that a sudden shiver of inexplicable apprehension went down her spine. The skill of her evasiveness no longer amused her and before she could stop herself she had answered plainly, "She went to work on a farm in one of the villages. Willow something."

"Willowthorn?"

"Yes."

"Is she there now?"

"No. They could not afford to keep her after the failure of last year's harvest."

"She wrote to you asking to return to us?"

"She suggested she should come back as scullery maid. Keeping to the kitchen regions her disfigurement, she said, would not give offence. She had, quite naturally, failed to find another place on leaving the farm."

"What reply did you make to her?"

"I am not sure that I did reply. I considered her suggestion presumptuous."

"You sent her no assistance in her trouble?"

"Possibly. I don't remember."

She picked up her work and dropped it again. Never before had Adam spoken to her like this. His ugly voice had lost none of the tenderness that was always there for her, but the questions were coming fast as arrows. She began to understand how the arrows, without tenderness, had always mown down their victims. It no longer puzzled her that he should have been considered such a great headmaster.

"How long ago did she write to you?"

"Three weeks. A fortnight perhaps."

"You still have the letter?"

"Adam, you know I do not usually keep letters. You know how I dislike mess and clutter."

"Look in your escritoire. I do not think you would have closed your heart to that poor woman. I believe you will find her letter there. You would have remembered it in a day or two and sent her help."

It was he who was lying now, to himself as well as to her. He tried hard to believe his own lie but he still could not manage to warm his hands as he held them to the fire. Elaine rustled to her escritoire and sat there turning over her papers, unhurried and lovely. The abominable cupid clock ticked on and on in a lengthening silence. Adam was praying childishly, with a grief and intensity out of all proportion to the smallness of the incident, "Let her find the letter, O God of mercy." Elaine was wondering how long it would be politic to keep up this farce. Another five minutes by the cupids, she decided, and reached her long white fingers to the back of a pigeon-hole. She was not looking for the letter at all, for she was certain she had destroyed it, but for some patterns of rose-coloured velvet for an evening gown. She had received them three weeks ago but had mislaid them, which had annoyed her intensely for she wanted the gown for the Bishop's new year dinner party. She removed a little bottle of perfume from the pigeon-hole, and a ball of crimson embroidery silk, and then her husband, watching her face intently, saw it light up with sudden pleasure. His heart beat so fast and hard that it nearly choked him. She withdrew her fingers, holding some shreds of bright stuff and a bit of crumpled paper, and turned her head aside as she smoothed out the paper. Then she turned round to her husband with her rare smile like light upon her face, and held it out to him. "Here it is, Adam."

He jumped up and came to her and she rose to meet him. He put his arms round her and held her close to him, dizzy with relief. He had misjudged her, and though he would never forgive himself his remorse was like the dew of heaven because it exonerated her. "Forgive me, my dear," he whispered.

"What for, Adam?" Her voice was cool and amused as she withdrew herself gently from his arms. He was crushing the lace fichu on her gown to a limp rag.

"I spoke sharply, I believe." How could he tell her what he had believed? And how could he have believed it? She would have written to the poor woman in a few days. That fountain of joy was playing within him again.

"Well, never mind," said Elaine. "There's your letter. Do you wish me to deal with it?"

"No, my dear. I've given you trouble enough already. I'll deal with it myself."

She gave him the letter and went back to her embroidery. He sat down again, the cheap bit of paper held on his knee. The letter was written in a laborious copperplate hand, beautifully clear and without blots or erasions. Ruth must have copied it out many times to get it so perfect. A few phrases caught his eyes. "Forgive me, madam. I am ashamed to trouble you ... I was happy at the Deanery ... The last few months at the farm I did not get my wages. The mistress died, poor soul, and at the end I had to use my savings for the things she needed. I was glad to do what I could ... I would not trouble you, madam, were it not that I am desperate." He put the letter in his pocket. It would be discourteous to Elaine to read it now, and the longing came upon him to talk to her, to try once more to come a little closer to her, only he did not know what to talk about.

"What have you been doing today, my dear?" he asked lamely, but when he looked up he found that she was already putting away her embroidery. She so often seemed to be doing that when he felt that he would like to try and talk to her.

"It's late, Adam. You were late for dinner, you know. I am tired. I'll go to bed, I think."

"I tired you, making you look for that letter," he said contritely. He got up and kissed her and went with her into the hall to light her candle for her, and stood watching her with adoration as she went slowly up the stairs, her hair haloed in light. Then he went into his study and wrote a long letter to Ruth about Job and Mr. Penny. He made some bank notes up into a packet for her and rang for Garland, for they must be delivered by hand to her tomorrow. She must not remain another night and day in desperation. That she was still at Willowthorn, and still available for Mr. Penny, he did not doubt. "All shall be well and all manner of thing shall be well."

"Garland," he said, when Garland had received his instructions, "where do we get our fish?"

"Sir?" asked the astonished Garland.

"I asked you, Garland, where do we get our fish?"

"At Catchpole's, sir, in the market place."

"We must not leave Mr. Catchpole but I shall be obliged, Garland, if in the immediate future the Deanery order could be divided between Mr. Catchpole and Mr. Lee of Swithins Lane."

Shock and displeasure kept Garland silent for a moment, then he said, "Not very reliable, sir, Lee's isn't. The cat's fish could be purchased there if that should be your wish."

"Mine also, if you please," said the Dean sternly. "I wish

to give Mr. Lee a trial. No more. But I think you will find that he will serve us with excellent fish. I shall be obliged if you will inform Cook of my decision and ask her to make the necessary arrangements. Thank you, Garland. Good night."

CHAPTER XIII *The Umbrella*

I

IT was the proudest day of Emma's life. She, who of late years had hardly been accounted of genteel birth in the city, was expecting the Dean to tea in the manner of Miss Montague and other ladies of the Close. It was true he had said nothing about tea, and five o'clock was late for it, but he would not be able to resist Polly's seed cake and her own speciality of lace-thin bread and butter, cut with a knife dipped in hot water and rolled up into delicate fingers. She had put out the best Derby china, that had not been used since her father had died, and the best linen table cloth with its deep crochet border. She had also unearthed from the attic, and polished till they shone, the George I silver teapot and some very old teaspoons, thin as moonlight. The house was very quiet in these awed moments of expectancy, soundless except for the ticking of the clock and the low hum of Sooty's appreciation of the first good parlour fire they had had in years.

All over the city the clocks struck five. He would soon be here now. She turned to look at herself in the spotted old mirror above the mantelpiece. She was looking her best, with her mother's shawl softening her angularity and a tall tortoise-shell comb set high in her hair. There was a little colour in her usually sallow cheeks and it was not impossible today to realise that in her youth she had been a handsome girl. She was very much aware of it herself for like so many spinsters she had remained oddly oblivious of the effects of time. The years had been long and she had not moved with them, supple to their ring and change, but had withstood them in the cold frustration of her virginity. She would have been shocked if anyone had told her that she was not adult, yet in her dreams she ran and ran in the dark, doubling back upon her tracks to find her father. She had never, like Polly, dreamed of the quick bright water running out into the mystery and of herself upon it in her dancing boat.

There was a heavy step upon the pavement and the window was momentarily darkened by the passing of a tall black figure. Then came a knock on the door and the eager feet of Polly in the passage. Emma stood waiting in stately dignity. She was not shy, for this was her right, but a little anxious as to how Polly would acquit herself. She had coached her in the correct procedure but the girl had been in a troublesome mood over the week-end, constantly bursting into song and what could only be described as dance, so quick were her footsteps as they moved about the house. But she had promised not to sing while the Dean was in the house, to move quietly and slowly, to let no words pass her lips except the necessary, "The Dean, ma'am," when she showed him in, and not to push the parlour door with her knee when she brought in the teapot and hot water jug. But listening intently Emma fancied she heard whispering in the passage, a sound silken and light as the stirring of new leaves on a poplar tree. Then the door opening, Polly flattening herself against it. "There's no need to feel for the mat, sir," she said. "I've took it away. The Dean has caught a cold, ma'am. Which tea did you say, best or kitchen?" Emma ignored her as the Dean bent courteously over her hand. "Best or kitchen?" persisted Polly. "Kitchen's the stronger and him with a cold."

"Might I be allowed to put in a plea for the stronger brew?" asked the Dean. "I did not intend, ma'am, to put you to the trouble of giving me tea but I am much obliged."

He was very hoarse but he had not, he assured Emma, caught a cold, or he would not have waited upon her. He had got wet on Saturday and the reading of the lessons at the Cathedral services yesterday had a little acerbated the vocal cords. And now the weather had turned very chilly. "This good fire, ma'am," he croaked, his hands stretched to its blaze, "hot tea and a rest will do wonders for me."

"You have been busy today?" asked Emma.

"A couple of committee meetings, a visit to the workhouse and my lawyer. Just routine business. No more. What a charming parlour this is, ma'am. Is that your worthy father? There's a likeness, ma'am. I see a strong likeness. I am sorry that I did not know him."

They stood together before the portrait of the Reverend Robert Peabody while Emma expatiated on his merits. Behind their backs Polly came in with the tea and went out again. When the parlour door had shut behind her the Dean felt like a child whose mother has left it alone in a strange and frightening place. Firelight and Polly had lent a momentary charm to the parlour but now, looking up at the portrait, he was aware of having passed under the shadow of a dark hand. Emma, he realised, lived under it always. Her parlour was her past, and Isaac's, and if Isaac in tearing himself out of its grip had torn himself too he was better off with his asthma and his nerves and his eccentricity than Emma. Better to struggle through life with a broken wing than to have no wings at all.

When he was seated opposite Emma at the tea-table he said, "Will you forgive me, ma'am, that I left so hastily when I called the other evening? I gave myself no opportunity for the privilege of a little conversation with you. I fear I must have appeared discourteous."

"I beg you will not mention it, Mr. Dean," said Emma graciously from behind the George I teapot. "You are a busy man, I know." She had forgotten now that at the time she had been jealous and resentful. To have the great Dean apologising to her, seated here at her table, eating her bread and butter and drinking her tea, even though it was the kitchen tea, was giving her a satisfaction greater than anything she had known in years. She cut generous slices of the seed cake and the Dean's heart sank. He had had a cup of tea with Elaine already, he had an unworthy detestation of seed cake, and his throat was in that condition when every swallow is a matter of painful difficulty. Such a vast and stupefying fatigue weighed upon him that he could scarcely remember what he was here for, and what it was that he had thought he had to say. The child. Something about the child. What child?

"A piece of cake, Mr. Dean?" suggested Emma coyly. "I know gentlemen like cake."

"Thank you, ma'am," said the Dean. "Much obliged."

Struggling in the deepest depression to masticate seed cake he ruminated in alarm on Emma's sudden coyness. An unloving woman, he had thought at their first meeting, torn with dark passions, and though he had felt profound pity yet he had instinctively disliked her and had cravenly fled. Well, he was back here again because he had fled, and would have to return all over again were he to retreat before her coyness. Why was she coy? As he talked laboriously of the weather, of her revered father, of the affairs of the city, he watched her and saw that she was not so much coy as strangely happy. Her eyes rested upon the seed cake as though it had lighted candles upon it, and her fingers, touching the tea things, had a sort of joyous deftness that made him think of a child untying birthday presents . . . When was Bella's birthday? he irrelevantly wondered . . . She did not use this lovely china and these thin silver spoons very often, he realised. She had no friends for whom to make a party. Possibly her shadowed childhood had never known parties, and the child in her watched still for her birthright, shaking the barren tree, puzzled because no treasure fell in her lap. Suddenly his dislike of her cracked and fell apart, and the warmth of profound relief flooded through him. He disliked so seldom, was so increasingly prone to love much, that to dislike even a little was a great distress to him. Poor child! This woman was no monster, merely another of the children. "The child!" he said with sudden jubilation, unaware that he had spoken aloud.

"The child?" asked Emma, puzzled, for a moment before they had been speaking of Alderman Turnbull, who had just been elected mayor, a man well past middle age.

"The boy, ma'am," said the man, suddenly remembering what it was that he had thought he would say to her. "I want to ask your help for him. I badly need your assistance in a project dear to my heart."

Emma was astonished, touched, curious, enormously flattered. "What boy, Mr. Dean? I shall gladly do all in my power."

"Job Mooring, ma'am, whom I have persuaded your good brother to take as his apprentice. I believe him capable of becoming an excellent craftsman. Indeed I believe that with our encouragement and affection, yours, ma'am, and Mr. Peabody's and my own, he will become a great man. His story is a tragic one. Let me tell it to you."

He told her all he could about Job and she listened rigidly, her eyes on her plate. When he had finished she asked in a cold remote voice, "Do you consider those little toys he makes show promise?"

"Ma'am, I consider them to show genius," he said gently.

There was a silence and he waited anxiously. She did not know that he had heard that she had burnt the little birds. If she would now of her own will tell him about it he could not think of anything that would make him happier. But the silence lengthened and she said nothing. His heart sank. He waited for another minute, then changed the subject with as much cheerfulness as he could muster.

"Do you number Miss Montague among your circle of acquaintances, ma'am?" he asked.

"I have not that pleasure," said Emma, but still she did not raise her eyes from her plate. She had a feeling that if she did the Dean would see in them that she had burnt the birds. And he must never know. "With our encouragement," he had said, linking her with himself, and now he was taking it for granted that she and Miss Montague moved in the same social circle. He knew she was a lady. He was a man who could recognise gentility when he saw it. He was a perfect gentleman.

"I wish, ma'am, that you could know her," said the Dean. "But she is an invalid now. I believe that she would take it very kindly were you to call upon her. I fear that life can be lonely in the latter years."

The idea of loneliness in connection with Mary Montague was laughable and the Dean had an uncomfortable feeling that the strict veracity he so much prized was not the hallmark of this conversation. He scarcely knew what he was saying. In his heavy fatigue he felt like a top heavy bumble bee, his blunderings past his control. He could only put his trust in those invisible tides that do sometimes lift and carry a man when his own sense of direction is entirely lost.

"I will do so most gladly," said Emma. "As you say, life can be lonely for the old."

They talked platitudes for a while and then the Dean rose to go. "I can rely on you, ma'am?" he asked anxiously as he said good-bye. "You will in your woman's kindness do what you can for that boy? And you will not forget Miss Montague?"

Emma was at a loss to understand his anxiety but was immensely flattered by his reliance upon her. It meant, she was sure, that he had taken a fancy to her. "You can rely on me, Mr. Dean," she said earnestly.

At the parlour door, just as he was leaving her, he suddenly said, "There is another matter, ma'am, in which you can help me. When you were a little girl was there anything you particularly longed for? There is a child to whom I should like to give a birthday gift. She has, I think, the usual toys. I know she has a hobby horse. I am at a loss to know what to give her. You, ma'am, will be able to advise me."

Emma cast her mind back over the years. She thought a little and then she said shyly, for she was speaking of a deep symbolical longing that she had never disclosed to a living soul, "I remember that I longed for a little red umbrella."

"Thank you, ma'am," said the Dean. "I am much obliged to you."

He went out into the little passage, where Polly gave him his cloak and hat and stick. He said a few words to her and went out into the street, into the cold mist that was swirling up from the river. From the doorstep she watched, for she did not like to see him go. After a few moments the mist seemed to come down like a wall, and he was on the other side. She came back into the house to clear away the tea, oddly troubled. The parlour door was open and looking in she saw Emma standing by the fire. Her back was to the door but it appeared to Polly she was weeping.

"My!" thought Polly, and went noiselessly back to the kitchen without clearing away. Making up the fire she began to sing under her breath, for oddly enough the sight of Emma weeping had done away with her sense of trouble. Instinct told her Emma's tears would do a power of good.

II

There was an umbrella shop in the market place. The Dean opened the watch that was now so valued a possession and saw that he had time to go there before calling on Miss Montague. He went down Angel Lane, turned towards the steps and went slowly down them. Half-way down he felt suddenly quite extraordinarily ill. During the last year or so he had become accustomed to sudden attacks of giddiness and malaise, unpleasant while they lasted but soon over, and to constant fatigue. But this was something different. There was a sudden constriction of the throat, a drum-like thundering of the heart, like the sounding of an alarm, a queer sense as though his whole body were in mortal terror. Not himself but his body. He himself felt curiously detached, even elated, though the swirling mist seemed choking him and he found he had sat down suddenly on the steps. He had a brief vision of himself sitting on the steps in his top hat, as vivid as though he looked at himself from outside himself, and its comicality twisted his grim face into a quirk of amusement. Then it passed in a roaring blackness. Then that too passed and the grey mist came slowly back and he was still sitting on the steps in his top hat. "I've been here for hours," he thought, felt for his handkerchief and wiped the sweat from his face. Then with great difficulty he took out his watch, opened it with fumbling fingers and looked at the flower-encircled dial. Only eight minutes had passed since he had last looked at it in Angel Lane.

"Most extraordinary!" he ejaculated, and feeling disinclined for movement sat on where he was. He felt curiously peaceful and exceedingly happy, indeed happiness was mounting in his spirit in much the same way as a short time ago panic had been mounting in his body. Though happiness was a poor word for that which was rising within him. "Light," he thought. "Light." That was a poor word too but there was no other. His consciousness moved out from himself and he became aware of the city. It was extraordinary how deeply he had come to love it during the ten years that he had lived here. Behind him, he knew, the Cathedral rose into the sky, the mist wrapped about its towers. Below him there was a faint rosy glow in the greyness, and he guessed that the shops in the market place had lit their lamps. The rumble of wheels on cobble stones, the sound of children's voices, came up to him very faintly. He prayed for God's blessing on the city and then he remembered Bella's red umbrella. "I must get it at once," he thought. "Anything that has to be done must be done quickly."

With the help of his stick, and with one hand on the wall, he found he could get up. He descended the steps with caution, but down in the market place he felt almost himself again. Joshua Appleby's bookshop was lighted up and he could distinguish the books inside, their coloured ranks glowing in the soft lamplight. There is no more satisfactory sight than a lighted bookshop in the dusk, and his heart glowed. He passed St. Peter's church and looked up the lane to the trees of Mr. Penny's garden. Behind their tangle he fancied he saw a light gleaming. Job was probably making toast. His ankle, Polly had whispered to him in the passage, was mending nicely now that Doctor Jenkins had attended to it. The messenger he had sent to Willowthorn had brought back a grateful little note from Ruth Newman. If she was not yet installed she would be in a day or two.

He crossed the market place to the little old umbrella shop, tucked in between Catchpole the fishmonger and Mrs. Martin's bakery. He had never been inside it but he had always liked the look of its small bulging bow window, and the little umbrella, made of tin and painted in stripes of red and blue, that swung like an inn sign over the shop door.

The proprietor of the shop was Miss Bertha Throstle. When the Dean came in she had just clambered up on a chair to light the oil lamp that hung over her counter. Too intent upon her task to look round she murmured, "Just a minute, dear," and went on with what she was doing. Everything she did now needed a bit of concentration for though hale and hearty for her age she was eighty. She was thin and small but also round because of the number of petticoats she wore as protection against the draughts of the shop. Her scarlet tippet was crossed over her chest and a large black bonnet almost extinguished her tiny crumpled face. Her eyes were black and beady and she needed no glasses. Her shop was scarcely bigger than a large cupboard and crammed with umbrellas of every size and shape, from large green carriage umbrellas to dainty parasols with silk fringes. The counter was to scale, reaching no higher than Miss Thostle's waist.

"There now, dear," she said, her task completed, and turned round on her chair to survey the newcomer. When she saw who it was she was astonished but not at all flustered. Miss Throstle had never been flustered, and never would be. "Well!" she said in her tiny piping voice. "Who'd have thought it? Good afternoon, sir. I took you for Matty Wilcox come for her pa's umbrella."

"Allow me, ma'am," said the Dean, holding out his hand to help her down.

She took it and climbed off the chair with surprising nimbleness. "Turning chilly," she said, when she had bustled round behind her counter. "What can I do for you, sir?"

"I want an umbrella for a little girl," said the Dean. "A scarlet umbrella."

"What age would she be, sir?" asked Miss Throstle, her head on one side like a bird listening for the worm, her bright dark eyes on the Dean. He felt she was summing him up pretty shrewdly. He on his side knew her to be sound as a nut and kind to the kernel of her. He knew this instinctive kindness of the good countrywoman. Ruth Newman had it. They were kind as the bird sings or the fish swims for they seemed not to have shared in the complications of the primeval fall. This kindness was a lesser thing than the love of a Mary Montague, because not willed or fought for, but it had the freshness of all natural beauty and was as balm to him here among the umbrellas.

"I think perhaps four years old," said the Dean. "Or five. I am not knowledgeable about the ages of small children. She has blue eyes and yellow curls."

"The pretty dear!" said Miss Throstle. "I should suggest an *en-tout-cas*, a parasol and umbrella combined. You know what a child is with a new toy, sir, they can't be parted from it, and wet or fine she'll be able to take an *en-tout-cas* out walking. I've a scarlet one here, very tasty. And a green and a rose pink."

She laid all three on the counter, and then opened them for the Dean's inspection. They were so small that they were like flowers. The scarlet one had a handle shaped like a poppy head and a silken fringe. The pink had a shepherdess's crook for handle and was tied with a large pink bow. The third was a bright emerald green and its handle was a yellow and green parrot. In the soft lamplight, against the background of the chill grey day, they were infinitely gay. How could one choose? Under each one of them Bella would look equally enchanting. "I'll take all three," said the Dean. He spoke with the abandoned desperation of the true lover and it was as a lover, a creature not quite in possession of his proper senses, that Miss Throstle dealt with him.

"Now, sir, the little puss scarcely needs three," she said. "You must not spoil the child, sir. She's had the cuckoo clock."

The Dean was startled by this, unaware to what extent his latest idiosyncrasies were the talk of his Cathedral city, but his chief concern was with a slight suggestion of kindly asperity in Miss Throstle's voice.

"I do not think Bella is an acquisitive child, ma'am," he pleaded. "A high-spirited child, with an artist's eye for what pleases her taste, but not acquisitive."

"A dear little girl," said Miss Throstle soothingly. "But if I may advise you I should say just the one, sir. Children grow quickly. A year from now she'll be needing a larger one."

"Then I'll take the crimson *en-tout-cas*, if you please, ma'am," said the Dean. But Miss Throstle did not seem anxious for him to buy the crimson. Instead she held the green one up under the lamp, so that the light shone through its silken shimmer like the sun through beech leaves. "You think she would prefer the green?" he asked humbly.

"It's the green she's after, sir," said Miss Throstle. "Whenever her nurse brings her this way she's flat against my window as a winkle to a rock, pointing at the parrot, and that persistent, sir, that Nurse has a lot of trouble. 'Best take her along the other side of the market,' I says to Nurse, and Nurse she says she does that, but as soon as her back's turned for a moment Miss Bella she's across in a twinkling of an eye, right under the horses' feet. It's a pretty green, sir, and as you see it has a little yellow tassel."

"Thank you, I'll take it," said the Dean. "How much do I owe you, ma'am?"

The *en-tout-cas* was paid for and Miss Throstle wrapped it up in soft green tissue paper, and then in sober brown paper to make it a more suitable object for the Dean to carry across the market place. Then it was time to say goodbye but each was reluctant to do so. Miss Throstle was amazed that the Dean should be so feared in the city. She was not afraid of him. Looking up at him she felt much as she did when looking up at the Cathedral. Here was a rock! He made her feel as though she had firm ground under her feet. Hale and hearty though she was being eighty did at times make her feel a little insecure. The Dean was thinking how many little tucked-away shops there were in the city that he had never entered, kept by men and women whom to his eternal loss he would now never know. His tall hat in his left hand he held out his right to Miss Throstle across the counter. "I am much obliged to you for your assistance. Much obliged. God bless you, ma'am."

He bowed to her, replaced his hat and went out into the gathering dusk with the little umbrella tucked under his arm. Fifteen minutes later, still carrying it, he was in Miss Montague's drawing-room. He had not been there since that day when they had talked of the nature of love. The lamp was lighted and the curtains drawn against the chill mist, the lovely room warm and sweet-scented with chrysanthemums and burning apple logs. The two friends greeted each other with delight and satisfaction, for to both it seemed a long time since they had been together.

"I have something to show you, ma'am," said the Dean, when the correct courtesies had been exchanged and he was seated in the comfortable arm-chair opposite Miss Montague, the little parcel on his knee.

"Where did you catch that cold?" she asked.

"It is not a cold, ma'am, merely a slight hoarseness due to the inclement weather."

"It has been remarkably inclement," agreed Miss Montague. She did not look at him again. For the moment she could not, so violent was her sense of panic. He did not look any more ill than he had looked for the past year so so, but there was something new in his face this afternoon. To her fancy a shadow lay upon it, yet not from any inward melancholy. It was like the shadow of a wing and behind it she believed he was hiding an awed if profound joy. While she tried to quiet the panic, at her age and with her faith a thing both selfish and ridiculous, she watched his large clumsy hands fumbling at the brown paper and string.

Their slowness would have reduced Elaine almost to screaming point. To Miss Montague they restored quietness. She was slow too now that she was old. With time a thing so soon to be finished with it was right to let the last strands pass very slowly through the fingers. One had liked time.

"There, ma'am," said the Dean.

"What an exquisite little umbrella," said Miss Montague.

"It is not an umbrella, ma'am. It is an *en-tout-cas*."

"For Bella?"

"Now how did you know about Bella?"

"Sarah knows everything, and sometimes out of her vast store she shares a few crumbs of knowledge with me. I am so delighted about Bella. I did not know you loved children. Is it not odd that I should not have known?"

"It was not a thing that I had mentioned to you, ma'am."

She smiled. There was so much that he had not mentioned to her and yet that she knew. Aloud she said, "Are you glad that I persuaded you to take a little joy?"

"Yes, ma'am, but the complications, and indeed the anxieties, have been and are very great."

"Naturally," said Miss Montague. "If you turn for your joy to the intractable and explosive stuff of human nature it's in for a penny in for a pound. The contemplation of sunsets and vegetable matter has its serene pleasure, and involves no personal exertion, but that I think was not what you wanted in old age?"

"No, it was not. And I am not complaining. But I should like to tell you of these children. They all seem children. Some people, ma'am, never seem to reach maturity."

"Few grow up in this world," agreed Miss Montague. "We should all like each other better if we could realise that. But tell me another day. You have no voice tonight."

"I must tell you now, ma'am," barked the Dean urgently. "These children need your prayers."

Miss Montague saw that he wanted to tell her and yielded. She sat without movement or comment while he told her of Job and Polly, of Emma and Bella, Keziah and Albert Lee, Mr. Penny, Ruth Newman and Miss Throstle. Her listening quietness was deeply receptive and Adam Ayscough felt as always that what he told her was not only safe but likely to undergo a sea-change. When he had finished she said, "I shall be glad to know Emma Peabody. I am glad she is coming to see me. I have always wanted to know her."

"Then why did you not invite her, ma'am?"

She looked at him in surprise. "I never thought of it. I am one of the antiquities of the city, and as such there are those who make a ridiculous fuss of me, but that does not give me the right to ask a busy woman to visit me just because I have a fancy for her company. Who am I that I should presume to do such a thing?"

He smiled. It was as he had always thought and she had not the slightest idea of what she was and what she did. That was as it should be for to have begun to know her value would have been to begin to lose it. "Miss Peabody will come, I am sure of it," he said. "I wish I could be as sure that Job will stop hating her."

"He will," said Miss Montague. "Do not forget to show him the Cathedral. I wish I could see Bella."

"I will bring her to see you tomorrow, ma'am."

"You will do no such thing. You will stay indoors tomorrow and see Tom Jenkins."

"Not yet, ma'am!" said the Dean in alarm. "I have too much to do. There's Albert Lee. That great hulking boy they're sending him from the workhouse will suit, I think, but he needs to get about more. He's a gipsy. He should, I think, have a little cart, with a smart pony, and drive to the villages two or three times a week with his fish. With more variety in his life he'd drink less. I must see to it. And Swithins Lane, ma'am, it *must* come down." If he had not been so hoarse he would have shouted, and he brought his fist violently down upon the arm of his chair. It was no way to behave in a lady's drawing-room. "Ma'am!" he ejaculated in horror. "I must ask your pardon. I believe I spoke too loud. I had not intended, ma'am, I mean I was not aware ——"

"You were hardly aware of what you were saying," Miss Montague finished for him, "and should see Doctor Jenkins, as I said before."

"It is impossible, ma'am."

"I will not argue," said Miss Montague. "I have not the right."

Something in the tone of her voice startled the Dean. He got up and stood before the fire looking down at her.

"Surely our long acquaintance gives you the right to say what you wish?"

"Not a very long acquaintance. Only a few years," said Miss Montague. "Though time, I suppose, has nothing to do with it."

"Nothing whatever," said the Dean, and his voice took on sudden strength and depth. There was a silence in which he could not say what he wanted to say. To let it lengthen would have been painful, and also unnecessary since she had understood him. She chose to accept the fact that he was standing as his farewell and held out her hand. He bent over it, murmured the customary courtesies and went away.

CHAPTER XIV *Advent*

I

IT was after closing hours and Isaac and Job were in the workshop. It was a wild night in late November, with a north-wester pouring icily across the fen. At times the gusts almost reached gale force, and sleet crashed against the small dark square of window. It was an eerie night, with the sort of tumult abroad that pulls the thoughts outward to itself, and most men and women in the city were very aware of the rushes lying flat in the wind, the ruffled water, bare branches twisting and turning and smoke torn from chimney tops like ripped lace. The clouds raced low and about the towers of the Cathedral the roar and clamour of the wind was like waves breaking in a cave. When the clock struck the boom of the great bell, usually so tremendous, was caught and cast away by the wind and the city scarcely heard it. This was the kind of night that usually terrified Isaac, filling him with a sense of doom and setting all his nerves jangling, for he hated noise, but tonight he was not afraid of the storm and Job was enjoying it because by contrast it increased his joy. He was out of it. He was in harbour.

The workshop, lamp-lit tonight, seemed to him a world

to itself, a self-sufficient star swinging in the roaring blackness as unconcernedly as the planet that could be seen shining in the dark window pane between one hailstorm and another. Job was aware of both stars, his awareness in itself a glowing thing, and thought to himself that that was how it was with him now; light held him and beckoned him and burned within him. What would happen if the three lights fused? What if the fire inside him could dart out into the glow that held him, and the two together could flame down the wind to the splendour of that planet? He laughed, suddenly, and Isaac looked up and smiled. He was used now to these sudden peals of laughter from Job. The first one had surprised him, for he had thought of Job as a quiet sort of chap. He knew better now. Job's depression had had its roots in fish and frustration and had vanished with them. Quiet he would always be, so concentrated was his whole being on work that he adored, but his present quietness was as different from the other as life from death. His laughter, like most laughter, was occasioned by awareness of contrast, by the sudden striking of one thing upon another like flint upon tinder. It was the spurt of the happy flame.

"Feeling good, Job?" he asked.

"I feel like God," said Job.

For a moment Isaac the unbeliever was slightly scandalised. Then he realised that Job, with exquisite precision, was indeed engaged in embedding stars in the firmament. Seated at Isaac's work-bench, with the candle behind its globe of water giving added light, he was at work upon the celestial clock. Isaac could not have believed that he would ever have allowed another to touch his masterpiece, and indeed for a few weeks after he and Job had started working together he had tried not to see Job's longing glances, to be unaware that the boy was eaten up with hunger to get his hands on the exquisite thing. He had worked steadily at the simple tasks that Isaac had considered within his capacity and Isaac had worked at the clock, his back turned on the boy except at such times as Job needed his help and instruction. But Job had learnt so rapidly that Isaac had been almost terrified. It was like having a young hawk with him in the workshop, for the boy swooped upon knowledge like a wild thing on its prey, and devoured it like flame running through dry grass. Isaac had been a little taken aback at first. This was not at all the conventional apprentice, running meekly upon errands and grateful for any crumbs of knowledge that his master might vouchsafe to impart to him. Job did not mind the errands, and he was not ungrateful, but he had suddenly discovered his own power. He was a finer craftsman even than Isaac, and he knew it, and so, presently, did Isaac.

There was a greatness in Isaac. One evening at supper, between one bit of sausage and another, he was able to acknowledge that it was so. "He must increase, but I must decrease," he said to himself. He did not know where the quotation came from, or that in taking it to himself he had taken a fence at which many baulked or fell. He finished the sausage without having the slightest idea that he was not the same man that he had been when he embarked upon it. The next morning he smiled at Job and asked him if he would like to help him with his clock. Job went crimson to the roots of his hair and unable to speak bent to pick up a tool he had dropped under the work-bench. When he reappeared he was no more able to speak than he had been before but his face was shining like the morning sun. From that moment the two increasingly loved each other.

They worked now in that companionable silence, broken by an occasional word or two, which between two who are as attached to the work they do together as they are to each other is one of the most satisfactory things in life. Love of the work strengthened the love of each other. Love of each other enriched the work. "This is good," thought Job. "There will never be anything better than this. Me and the old codger together. It's good." Aloud he said, glancing at the working drawing at his elbow, "Sir, why did you put the sun behind the fish? Wouldn't it have been better balancing the moon?"

"It wouldn't stay there," said Isaac.

This ridiculous answer was one that Job understood. Polly had once wanted him to make her a dabchick with its head under its wing. But it wouldn't put its head under its wing. It wanted to preen a feather in the centre of its back. Though Polly had not minded she had laughed at him and had not been able to understand that though he talked about carving the bird from wood that was only a manner of speech. What he really did was to set free the living bird imprisoned in the wood. That dabchick had been unusually lively, and Miss Peabody had burnt it. His face hardened. She was being nice to him now, letting him come into the kitchen, even allowing him to have supper there with Polly once a week, asking him how he did, making him sit with her and Polly in church, and he tried to be polite for Polly's and Isaac's sake, but still he hated her. The hatred surged up in him now, and his tool slipped. He laid it down. A moment before there had been such quietness in him but now it had gone. He could not go on working until he had it again.

Isaac, working at a second bench at his fret of the two swans, felt the sudden disturbance of peace and looked over his shoulder. "Tired, boy?"

"No, sir," Job swallowed, trying to push the hatred down out of sight, below the quiet reeds and water. He asked, "Does the sun behind the fish mean anything, sir?"

"I don't know," said Isaac. "I shall in time."

Again Job understood him. Once he had whittled out of a bit of cherry wood a bird he had never seen. A fortnight later he had seen his first gold-crested wren in the Willowthorn drove. He wondered if poets ever wrote of experiences with which they had not yet caught up. Time as one understood it seemed oddly non-existent when one made things. "The Dean would know," he said.

"We'll ask him," said Isaac, and his voice was warm with delight. Job's hatred disappeared without any further effort on his part and he picked up his tool again and went on working. Beneath their contentment in work and in each other they had tonight a deeper satisfaction, for this morning Garland had let it be known that the Dean was up though not down. He would, Garland trusted, be down shortly and out for Christmas. The news had spread through the city by midday and the city breathed again.

The Dean had had laryngitis followed by an attack of pneumonia, which though mild Doctor Jenkins had pronounced to be touch and go owing to the Dean's age. When the specialist had arrived from London a curious dismay had fallen upon the city; curious because of the Dean's unpopularity. Day by day they had prayed for him in the Cathedral, and from the Canon in residence to the smallest choir-boy they had attended to what the precentor was saying when he intoned the prayer for all sorts and conditions of men, and impeccable musician though he was neither he nor anyone else had noticed that emotion invariably sent him a semitone flat when he reached "those who are anyways afflicted, or distressed, in mind, body or estate". Michael had struck the hours as usual, but the youngest choir-boy, looking up at him as the choristers in their black gowns and mortar-boards scuttled two by two up the steps for matins and evensong, had not thought he looked himself. Through the days of anxiety the invariable greeting of people meeting each other in shops and streets had been, "Vile weather. Have you heard how the Dean is today?" They had all agreed that the weather, which since the day of that extraordinary thunderstorm had been consistently abominable, made it somehow worse. The city had seemed like a ship riding out a dangerous storm, and when they had looked up at the captain's bridge it was empty. That tall grim stooping figure had been no longer there. The Bishop, who had been away, came home, though there was nothing he could do except prowl about and be disagreeable to everybody. Several people who had been away came home, they had not quite known why. On the night when Garland had let it be known that the crisis was at hand no one had slept very much, least of all Garland, and when it was past the Bishop had ejaculated, "Reprieved, thank God!" as though, his butler had reported, he himself had expected to mount a scaffold at noon. Still, for a few days, anxiety had continued, for there was this thing referred to by Doctor Jenkins as "the Dean's age". The harmless phrase had an ominous ring about it, as though it were not what it seemed.

But today, in spite of the weather, hearts had been light in the city, and all the afternoon little bursts of gaiety had kept blowing up here and there like the fires of spring. Faces had smiled under dripping umbrellas and in the shops people had lingered and gossiped and laughed. The muffin man had done a brisk trade for everyone suddenly had a fancy for muffins for supper. The Dean was up and would be down shortly. At the Christmas Eve carol service in the Cathedral, the glory and climax of the city's year, he would be in his stall as usual and he would read the lesson as usual. Not to hear his ugly voice grating out, "In the beginning was the Word," would have been, well, there was no need now to think what it would have been.

"When he's down," said Job to Isaac, "could I go with you to wind the clocks?"

Isaac looked at him, for he found this a hard request to grant. There had been no time as yet for the Dean and himself to combine clock-winding with instruction on horology, as they had planned to do, though he had sent the Dean some books to break up the fallow ground of his ignorance. They would, he thought, begin as soon as the Dean was down, and he did not want Job there. "He must increase and I must decrease." He swallowed his disappointment and said, "Yes, Job. You should learn to wind the clocks. If I was to be taken poorly at any time I'd like to think you knew them all. You've come on fine, Job. I'd trust you even with Miss Montague's Michael Neuwers and the Jeremiah Hartley in the Dean's study. More than that, Job, I could not say."

It was the proudest moment in Job's life. He was aware that there was a sudden quietness beyond their small warm world of clockmaking, not a lull in the storm but the ending of it. He could see a whole cluster of stars in the window pane and in the silence Michael began in strike seven, his notes no longer torn away but round and full and golden. The man and boy smiled at each other, laid down their tools and listened. All the clocks of the city were striking now and hard upon their heels came the chiming clocks in the shop.

"Next week," said Job, "the celestial clock will be finished."

II

The following morning the world was blue and rain-washed, rather as though the azure of the sky had fallen into the rain and faintly tinctured all that the rain had touched. The trees, stripped by the storms of the last vestige of their leaves, were shadowed with blue and the houses were limned with it as though a paint brush loaded with blue had underlined each sill and lintel and moulding, and splashed pools of bluebell-colour under the eaves. Even the Cathedral towers seemed drenched with the sky and the vast fen was like an inland sea. The pale gold of sunlight, the orange-tawny and brown and lavender that stained the blue about the boles of the trees, the rosy glow of roofs and chimney pots, were subordinate colours, for it was not their hour.

"We shall have a green Christmas," said Doctor Jenkins, at the window of the Dean's room, and was not surprised when Adam Ayscough answered, "Why do we talk about the green earth? In this painted manuscript of a world the colour varies with each turn of the page and green, to my mind, does not predominate. I should like a white Christmas this year. I remember them in my childhood but none since. Is that the universal experience? It never rained in the summer when I was a child either. Memory is not wholly reliable."

Doctor Jenkins turned from the window and there was an almost imperceptible tautening of his whole frame. The Dean, with a slight smile, pushed aside the papers that littered his counterpane, for they were now coming to business. It always amused him to watch Tom Jenkins turning from man to doctor. A little chat about the weather was the correct thing when he entered the room, and he was hesitant, even a little in awe of his distinguished patient. Then it seemed that something clicked and he moved smoothly into action, concentrated and wholly happy. Something of the same sort of process was familiar to the Dean when he settled down to the writing of a book. A wave of self-loathing, of self-distrust, would go over him at first. Who was he that he should dare to take a pen into his hand? And how puerile was the result when he had done it. He would struggle wearily through a page or two and then forget himself, coming to the surface an hour later knowing that his book was his artifact, and whatever the result he could no more not make it than fail to breathe.

"Breathe deeply, please," said Doctor Jenkins curtly.

The Dean did meekly all that he was told and straightened his nightcap. He was not yet up all day. During the morning hours he sat upright in his curtained four-poster like an ogre in his cavern, gazing balefully upon all comers and goers, for his convalescence had now reached the point when he was having a little difficulty with a slight irritability of temper. For reading or writing in bed he was obliged to put on his eyeglasses, which in conjunction with a nightcap would have made a comic figure of a lesser man. But the Dean retained his immense dignity quite unimpaired.

"What's all this, Mr. Dean?" demanded Doctor Jenkins with a touch of anger, indicating the papers on the counterpane.

"Architectural plans, correspondence and estimates relating to the new houses beyond the West Gate," said the Dean. "Plans and sketches of the garden beside the river at the North Gate. You will remember that this important work was momentarily abandoned a few years ago owing to the opposition encountered in the city. As soon as possible the whole question must be reopened. You know as well as I do that this work is essential for the well-being of the city."

Doctor Jenkins was standing at the foot of the bed. The Dean poised his eyeglasses on the summit of his nose and they glared at each other. "You are right," said Tom Jenkins. "Those slums are foul. But you will do no work upon those plans at present."

"In this one instance, Doctor Jenkins, you must allow me the exercise of my own judgement," said the Dean. "Time is short."

"And if you labour too soon at those plans," retorted Doctor Jenkins, "it will be shorter."

He caught himself up. Before the Dean attempted to plunge back into active life it would have to be said, but not yet. But he had checked himself too late; or else had fallen into a trap deliberately laid for him by his patient.

"Ah!" said the Dean with relief. "I shall be glad to have your opinion on this point. That somewhat pompous individual who visited us from London was a heart specialist, I believe. How long have I got? Three months? Four months? I have much work on hand of one sort or another and should like specific information."

"I cannot tell you, Mr. Dean."

"Are you hedging, Jenkins?"

"No. You are seriously ill. How long you will live will depend on how faithfully you carry out my instructions."

"Which are?"

"The diet I have already given you. Plenty of rest. The avoidance of all undue exertion. No hills, no country walks such as I understand you attempted on the day of that thunderstorm. Mental and emotional strain should also be avoided. If you fight such another battle for the demolition of the North Gate slums as you fought before it will kill you."

"Would you consider it advisable that I should tender my resignation as Dean of this Cathedral?" asked the Dean mildly.

A curious panic rose in Doctor Jenkins. He fought it down and replied slowly, "Speaking as your doctor I should say, yes, most certainly you should. Speaking as a man I would like to say that it is hard to imagine the city without you."

He had dropped his voice and the Dean was not quite sure he had heard aright. Could he have heard that? "Thank you, Doctor Jenkins," he said. "I am much obliged to you for your advice."

"And you will take it, I trust. It is advice not lightly given."

"Much obliged. There is just one further point. You will remember that at the commencement of this illness I had your promise that you would make light of it to Mrs. Ayscough. I hope you will continue to do so. You know her delicacy. She must be spared all anxiety."

"Of course."

"Thank you. I trust Mrs. Jenkins is well?"

"I am glad to say she is in tolerable health. I will call again tomorrow, Mr. Dean." He looked meaningly at the papers on the counterpane. "And I shall hope to find you reading Boswell."

"At what time will you call tomorrow?" asked the Dean.

"At about the same time."

"I am much obliged to you for the information," said the Dean suavely. "Much obliged. Good day."

When he was alone he remained for some while as quietly relaxed as even Doctor Jenkins could have wished. He was so still within the shadows of his fourposter that he might have been carved out of wood. His first reaction was the same joy that he had felt when he had been taken ill upon the steps. Was it a sin in him that he should feel so thankful? He hoped not. Old people were surely allowed to be glad if they could get to the end in a manner that would not impose too great a burden upon others. Only God knew how he had dreaded being a burden to Elaine. If he could get the building scheme well started and see Albert Lee going round the villages with his spanking pony and cart, if he could see all the children happy and Isaac possessed of a faith in God as strong as his own, and if he could just get his book finished he would feel his work was done. There would be no more for him to do. Then he checked himself, for such a manner of thought was a presumptuous bargaining with God. Who was he that he should think himself necessary to any piece of work, to any living soul, even for a short while? Surely by this time he knew his own worthlessness. Looking back upon his life he could see no good thing that he had done, and apart from Mary Montague and, for the moment, little Bella, he could think of no one whose love he had won, not even the love of his own wife.

Elaine. Elaine. He said her name over and over to himself. He was incapable of self-pity but the thankfulness that he had felt began slowly to pass into grief. For he must leave Elaine. He grieved not for her sake, for his loss would be for her pure gain, but for his own. Never again to rest his mortal eyes upon her beauty or hear her voice. Not to see her stitching at her embroidery beside the fire, walking among the roses in her garden, not again touch her hair or her cheek. She had been both the grief and the glory of his life and gladly in the life beyond death would he have still endured the grief if he could have kept the glory. "God is my glory," he whispered to himself. But here again there was sorrow. He was going empty-handed to his God. He had no sheaves to bring with him. Nothing. He had failed his God as miserably as he had failed Elaine. That was the bitterness of death. He was motionless for perhaps an hour in his bed and towards the end he wept.

He was aware of a shadowy figure standing beside him. It was Garland. "I did not ring," he snapped, for Garland had startled him.

"It's been a long time, sir," said Garland. "It is your custom to ring as soon as Doctor Jenkins leaves you."

"I dozed, no doubt," said the Dean. "My apologies, Garland. I must get up at once. I must not keep Mrs. Ayscough waiting."

She came daily to sit with him when he was installed in his arm-chair by the window. She was careful to come just twenty minutes before luncheon, for the ringing of the gong provided her with a natural and easy means of escape. She hated illness. Above all she hated it in Adam because it intensified her physical shrinking from him. And in this illness of his, the first serious one he had had in their married life, she had been astonished by a strange wild bitter sorrow. Why must he always spare her, indulge her, deceive her? He had been near death, she knew, yet the knowledge of it had been kept from her. Throughout his illness he had struggled in her presence to hide every symptom that might distress her, and even now that he was better he told her nothing of what he had suffered, was perhaps still suffering. He had often tried to talk to her of things beyond her comprehension but she could not remember that in all their married life he had ever confided any trouble to her; not even to the extent of telling her that he had a headache. Not yet ready to hate herself she almost hated him. Long ago he should have done some sort of violence to her, taken hold of her and shaken her into some semblance of a wife. Now it was too late.

Or was it not yet too late? Sitting beside him at the sunny window with her embroidery in her lap she wondered, if she wooed him now, would he at last confide in her? He had never refused her anything. She dropped her work and put her hand on his, lying on the arm of his chair.

"How do you feel today, Adam?"

"Very well, my dear, thank you."

"Did Doctor Jenkins give you a good report?"

"Excellent," said the Dean heartily. He expected, her wifely duty done, that she would withdraw her hand, but instead she held his a little more closely.

"The illness has left no weakness behind it? If there's anything of that sort I want you to tell me."

"There is no cause for anxiety, my dear. I am doing excellently."

The answer came with the ease of long habit and though he returned the pressure of her hand he seemed not aware that she was pleading with him. But she was aware, perhaps through the physical touch, perhaps because this new sorrow had made her more sensitive, that death had laid a hand on the body of her husband. She caught her breath sharply, as though its hand was laid also on her own breast.

"Please, Adam," she pleaded, "please."

"What is it, my dear?" He looked at her, smiling indulgently. "What can I do for you?"

She realised he was expecting her to ask for new sofa

cushions, or fresh upholstery for the drawing-room chairs. The pressure on her breast felt like a band of iron. The gong rang and Adam raised her hand and kissed it. "Your luncheon, my dear. Tell me another time what it is that you require."

She left the room proudly. She would not ask again.

III

A few days later, Garland, passing through the hall, heard a peculiar knocking on the front door. Callers were not in the habit of knocking, for an imposing bellpull was displayed in a prominent place. The knocking was rather low down on the door, insistent and imperious. Garland was reminded of the knocking of a woodpecker but was nevertheless astonished, when he opened the door, to find himself confronting a green and yellow parrot on the wing. It got him on the knee and it needed all his years of training to suppress a yelp. But he had the presence of mind to grip the parrot, lest it attack again, and found himself engaged in a tug-of-war. He was gripping the parrot end of a minute green umbrella, and clinging to the ferrule end was a small girl in a large bonnet. Bending down to try and see the face within the bonnet Garland relaxed his grip upon the parrot. It was immediately pulled from his grasp and the child marched past him into the hall.

"I wish to see the man," she said.

Her head was tipped back now as she looked up into Garland's face and he recognised the round pink countenance and yellow curls of Bella Havelock.

"You've run away from your nurse, Miss Bella," he said reprovingly.

"I have come to see the man," said Bella.

"If you mean the Dean, Miss Bella, he has been ill and is not yet sufficiently recovered to see visitors."

"He's down," said Bella.

Garland regretted that he had let this fact be known throughout the city only yesterday. What was he to do now? He hesitated and was lost. Bella's pelisse and bonnet today were cherry red trimmed with beaver, a mid-winter outfit which she found oppressive in the warm Deanery. She took off the bonnet and handed it to Garland. Then she kicked off her goloshes and tugged at the buttons of her pelisse. "Undo it," she commanded.

"Another day would be better, Miss Bella," said Garland feebly, but as he spoke he found himself mechanically undoing buttons. "Another day," he repeated, bending to retrieve a minute golosh from under an oak chest. But when he had straightened himself he saw Bella speeding off down the corridor in her white muslin frock, the umbrella brandished in one hand. He gave chase but it was too late. Though she had never been in the Deanery before her woman's intuition led her straight to the study door. Dropping the umbrella she stood on tiptoe and grasped the round brass handle with both hands, turned it and pushed the door open. Then she grabbed the umbrella again and marched in. Garland found the door pushed vigorously shut in his face but nevertheless he opened it again and followed her.

"Sir," he panted, "I beg pardon. I tried to stop the young lady, sir, I did indeed but ——"

He paused, shocked and horrified by what he saw, for Bella was sitting upon the Dean's knee with the umbrella up. From beneath its silken beech-green shade she looked out triumphantly at Garland, her blue eyes sparkling and her yellow head a froth of dancing curls. Or so it seemed to Garland. Though it was a grey bleak day he thought confusedly of kingcups growing in a water meadow and white washing on a green hedge, some forgotten scene from his own childhood. The Dean, a west-country man, was remembering the first primroses in a Somersetshire wood. The Dean smiled at him, and hardly knowing what he was doing he returned the smile, standing stupidly by the door. He was very tired. The past weeks had told on him considerably.

"There is no need for you to distress yourself, Garland," said the Dean. "I shall be much obliged if you will ask Cook if there is a sugar biscuit in the house. A glass of milk, perhaps. She will know what would be suitable. I am much honoured by this visit but I think someone should take a message to Worship Street lest there should be anxiety on Miss Bella's account. But make it clear, Garland, that I am honoured."

"Very good, sir," said Garland, and closed the door behind him. Bella put the umbrella down and showed the Dean her new shoes, which were tied with cherry-coloured ribbon. Then sitting very upright on his knee she gazed round the big book-lined room, the biggest room she had ever been in. She was a little awed and the Dean marvelled at the courage of the small creature in coming to see him. "Did you run from your nurse?" he asked her. "Were you not frightened, my dear, to come alone?"

Bella shook her head. "I runned all the way from the Porta," she said. "And I knocked on the door with my umbrella." She felt in her little hanging pocket and brought out a small heart-shaped comfit. "For you," she said, holding it up. The Dean thanked her courteously and ate it. It tasted of peppermint, which of all things he disliked, but he could not disappoint her for he knew it was a great treasure and that she was not parting with it lightly.

"Thank you, my dear, for your letter," he said, and putting finger and thumb into his waistcoat pocket he brought out a scrap of pink notepaper on which she had inscribed, with anguished labour, a few words of thanks for the umbrella. The words had obviously been dictated by a higher power, whose hand had perhaps guided Bella's, but the blots and rows of kisses at the foot of the page were Bella's own. "You see I have it safely. I was much honoured to receive it."

"I writed you another letter," said Bella, "on blue paper. Grandma didn't tell me what to say. I writed it myself. But it fell on the fire."

The Dean felt a pang of keen disappointment. "What did you say, Bella?" he asked.

"I told you about my cuckoo clock," said Bella after some thought. "It caught a mouse at three o'clock. Cuckoo did. I told you Nurse had new garters. Red ones. I put kisses. That was all."

It was enough, thought the Dean. Even the report of such a letter was enough to ensure his bliss. Yet his heart ached that a work of so much labour and difficulty should have perished in the flames. And a labour surely of love. Could it be possible that the child's affection had not been only the thing of a moment that he had thought it? That children could love with extraordinary suddenness he had discovered in Isaac's shop. Could they also love enduringly? It seemed to him that Bella's love had already endured, for to a child the short period of time that had elapsed since they had last been together must have seemed an aeon. He could remember from his own childhood how vast a period of time had been covered by a summer's day. The sense of worthlessness, of failure, was eased a little as he held her on his knee. He wished humbly that she would kiss him again but he did not expect it. She was not, he fancied, very free with her kisses.

"Will you come with me one day to see an old lady called Miss Montague?" he asked her.

"Has she a cat?" asked Bella.

"I believe so," he said. "I believe Miss Montague is never without a cat. Yes, I distinctly remember a cat."

"Kittens?" asked Bella.

"I do not recollect kittens when I last waited upon Miss Montague," said the Dean anxiously, for he feared a kittenless Miss Montague would not appeal to Bella. "But I trust so."

"White kittens," said Bella. "I've a new petticoat."

She lifted the hem of her dress and both heads were bent in admiration of its glory when Garland entered with a round silver tray scarcely bigger than a water lily leaf. Cook had known what would be suitable. On a small plate, with rosebuds on it, lay an equally small queen cake iced in pink. In a rosebud cup with a gold handle was some warm sugary milk. Having assured himself with a quick glance that the Dean was none the worse for Bella Garland placed this on the writing-table, piled cushions on a chair and lifted her to their summit. His movements as he turned to go were not as precise as usual. The Dean was aware of a slight hesitancy.

"Wait, Garland," he said. "Then you can take the tray away."

Garland waited. He was a bachelor, having been jilted in youth by a barmaid who had eloped with a sergeant-major in the marines. Devotion to the Dean had largely filled the gap, but watching a young thing eat a sugar cake is one of the major pleasures of life. Bella wriggled herself forward on the cushions and lifted her chin imperiously. For a moment both men were at a loss, then with the inspiration of genius Garland took out his clean handkerchief and tucked it into her frock. "She's accustomed to a bib, sir," he explained *sotto voce* to the Dean.

Bella ate like a mouse, her small sharp teeth demolishing the sugar cake very daintily but with an almost inexorable concentration. It disappeared without pause. Then Garland stirred the milk for her with a little apostle teaspoon and that went in and down almost it seemed in one intake. For a moment or two the rosebud cup remained in an upside-down position over Bella's nose, then she replaced it in the saucer and rescued the last remnants of sugar from the bottom with the little spoon. When there was no more she sighed deeply and permitted Garland to wipe her mouth. Lifted down she ran instantly back to the Dean and laid her hand on his knee.

"Does your watch tick like Grandpa's?" she demanded.

The Dean had been wondering if he might show her his watch. It was almost as though in her affection for him she had read his thoughts. He took it out and held it to her ear beneath her curls. Then he opened the pair cases that she might see the wreath of flowers about the face. Neither of them heard Garland leave the room or noticed when ten minutes later he came in again.

"There's a little man inside!" Bella was exclaiming. "It's the little fairy man from the shop!"

"No, Bella," said the Dean, peering through his eyeglasses. "I think not. This man carries away the sin of the world... What is it, Garland?"

"Miss Bella's nurse, sir. She offers her apologies. She turned her back only for a moment, she assures me, to speak to Miss Montague's Sarah who was cleaning the letter-box. Miss Bella, sir, is very quick upon her feet."

"My compliments to Nurse," said the Dean. "And I beg she will not distress herself. Miss Bella's visit has been a source of great happiness to me. Could it be repeated at any time I should count it an honour. Must she go now?"

"I think so, sir. Nurse is waiting in the hall with Miss Bella's bonnet and pelisse."

"Bella, my dear, we must say good-bye," said the Dean sadly.

"No," said Bella, and climbed back upon his knee. He felt that sense of increasing weight, of adherence, that he had experienced before, and looked anxiously at Garland.

"Now, Miss Bella," said Garland.

Bella ignored him, stretched out her hand and grabbed the Dean's gold pencil from his writing-table.

"Perhaps we should call Nurse?" suggested the Dean.

"I doubt if it would do much good, sir," said Garland gloomily. "Come along now, Miss Bella."

Bella dropped the pencil and grabbed the inkpot.

"Put that down, Bella!" said the Dean with sudden sternness. "And now, my dear, listen to me. Do not spoil this happy time that we have had together by disobedience. If you are a good girl and go now I hope and trust you will be permitted to visit me again. But if you are naughty I fear the pleasure may be denied me. It will be a sorrow to me, Bella, if I do not see you again."

Bella withdrew the inky fingers of her left hand from the inkpot and with a queenly gesture held them out to Garland to be wiped upon his spotless handkerchief. Her right hand she laid against the Dean's cheek. But she was no longer adhering, and her body felt light now upon his knee. He remembered having heard or read that small children sometimes had the strange power of levitation. They could take off at the top of a staircase and float down; some echo, surely, of powers possessed in the innocent morning of the world when spirit and not body was the master. For a flashing moment he knew very intimately the bright spirit of this child. Then she slipped off his knee and ran straight out of the room without looking back. She had not given him the kiss he had hoped for but the touch of her hand had seemed to wish him God-speed more surely and lovingly than a kiss could do. On Christmas Eve, when he always visited Miss Montague, he would take her with him.

IV

The following Saturday an expected knock at the back door, at the expected hour, was a pleasure to Garland. Mr. Peabody, to wind the clocks, and not a moment late. During the Dean's illness Isaac had wound the clocks as usual, in the correct order, not deviating an iota from the accepted procedure, and Garland had followed him round with a chamois leather in one hand and a silver milk jug in the other, feverishly polishing as they whispered anxiously together, and finding in Isaac and routine his one comfort in days of darkness and dismay. The days were not so dark now, but Garland was not yet easy in his mind and had a corresponding queasiness in his stomach whenever he looked at the Dean, and it was still a comfort to him to hear Isaac's knock. He hurried to the door and opened it, and could have cried with disappointment because it was not Isaac.

"Good morning, sir," said the slim dark-eyed boy who

stood correct and composed at the door. "I am Mr. Peabody's apprentice, come to wind the clocks. Mr. Peabody is indisposed."

"Peabody now," said Garland crossly. "What's the matter with Peabody?" He felt annoyed with Isaac. He had quite enough anxiety with the Dean without Isaac also taking it into his head to fall sick.

"He has one of his great colds," said Job.

"A cold is no reason for a man not doing his duty," said Garland. "The colds I've had, and kept on my feet!"

"Mr. Peabody dare not run the risk of giving a cold to the Dean," said Job.

"I should not have permitted him to see the Dean," snapped Garland.

"You might have caught it yourself, sir," said Job, "and given it to the Dean." He smiled delightedly at Garland. "I'm quite able to wind the clocks. I've been trained by Mr. Peabody."

He was in the passage without Garland quite knowing how he'd got there, composed and smiling. The impudence, thought Garland. He was just such another as that young hussy who had penetrated into the study with a basket of stinking fishheads. Yet when he looked at the boy again he was standing humbly enough, holding Mr. Peabody's bag. Yet there was an authority about him, the assurance of a man who is master of his craft and means to practise it. Garland led the way down the passage. On the other side of the green baize door Job looked quickly round the hall, his eyes resting joyously for a moment upon the face of the Richard Vick. "I believe I know my way, sir," he said. "I have been here once before. I need not trouble you to come with me."

"The hall, the drawing-room, the dining-room, but not the study," said Garland firmly. "Not the study. That must wait for Mr. Peabody. The Dean is down."

Job smiled, turned quickly to the drawing-room, opened the door, went in and shut it behind him, leaving Garland much annoyed. The boy should have begun in the hall. He'd got the order wrong. The hall came first. Too sure of himself. They all were, these days. No respect for their elders. And yet Garland felt he could not exactly accuse the young gentleman of disrespect. Gentleman? What was he saying? The boy was Isaac Peabody's apprentice and no gentleman, though he might give himself the airs of one. Yet the airs, or rather the air, had seemed natural to him. Garland gave it up and went back to the other side of the green baize door. Yet a few minutes later he was back in the hall again, keeping his eye. Job came out of the drawing-room, smiled and moved towards the dining-room. Garland looked up at the Richard Vick. "Ten minutes," he said to Job. "Mr. Peabody takes fifteen, seeing that all is as it should be."

"I'm a little quicker than Mr. Peabody, sir," said Job courteously and shut the dining-room door behind him.

This time Garland thought it his duty to walk as far as his pantry, but he was back in the hall again as Job opened the Richard Vick clock face. "That is a very valuable clock, young man," he said.

"Yes, sir," said Job. "It is a very beautiful one too. Mr. Peabody thinks the world of this clock." He wound the clock, looked at the pendulum, gently dusted the clock face and polished the winged cherubs with Isaac's old silk handkerchief, all with a careful dexterity that Garland could not help admiring.

"Have you been long with Mr. Peabody?" he asked. "Odd I've not heard him speak of having an apprentice."

"Not long, sir," said Job, "but Mr. Peabody likes to teach and I've learnt quickly." He closed the clock face and turned round to face Garland. "Sir, may I go in and wind the Jeremiah Hartley? I think the Dean would like me to do so. I will not disturb him."

"I have already told you," said Garland severely, "that the study clock must wait for Mr. Peabody." He eyed Job with growing anger. "Had I returned a few minutes later, young man, I believe I would have found you knocking at the study door."

Job looked him straight in the eye. "No, sir, I would not have done that. I would not have disobeyed you. But if he is well enough I would like to see the Dean. He has been very good to me."

There was a short angry silence in which Garland suddenly remembered something the Dean had said after the visit of the young hussy with the fishheads. He had finished by saying, "You understand, Garland? Much obliged." He swallowed his anger. "I will inquire," he said, and advanced majestically upon the study door. He returned in a moment saying coldly, "The Dean would be much obliged if you would wind the Jeremiah Hartley. Come away, young man, as soon as you have done so."

"Thank you, sir," said Job. He walked to the study door, knocked and entered.

The Dean was writing at his littered table. "Good morning, Job," he said.

"Good morning, sir," said Job, and came up to the table. "I hope you are better, sir?"

"I am quite recovered. How are you, Job? How is your ankle?"

"It has mended, sir. I am very happy working for Mr. Peabody and I like living with Mr. Penny and Ruth."

"You like Ruth?"

"Yes, sir." He paused. "I would like to thank you, sir."

The strong beat of profound happiness was in Job's quietly spoken words. It seemed to the Dean's fancy that clear golden wine was filling the room and his own being too. For a moment he thought that neither of them could stand it. The room was an old man's room, its walls rigid with antiquity, he himself tired to death, patched like an old kettle. They had lost the power of resilience and would crack at the seams. Then the gold slowly ebbed, drawn back into the depths of Job's singing spirit, leaving only a ripple of light on the ceiling, as though reflected from a dancing sunbeam, and a gentle warmth about the Dean's heart. Fancy, all fancy, he told himself, like the fancy that the scent of spring had come into the room with Bella and the green parrot.

"Shall I wind the clock, sir?"

"Much obliged," said the Dean, thankful to sit back in his chair and adjust himself quietly to this new Job.

How did the young effect these sudden changes? Did they, in one of those deep dreamless sleeps of youth, lying cheek on hand graceful and enchanted as though Oberon had touched them, know a metamorphosis such as Bottom knew? Or was it just what they ate? Undoubtedly Ruth fed Job well. In just a few weeks he had grown and filled out astonishingly. There was colour in his face and the hollows in his cheeks and the dark lines under the eyes had vanished. His hair, cut shorter, grew now with a strong wiry twist, full of vitality. He held his shoulders straight and his head well up, as though he respected himself and his work.

He had changed from boy to young man. His hands on the clock were deft and sure and whilst he was attending to it he took no notice of the Dean. He had forgotten him. The Dean too was respectfully silent. One did not disturb an artist at his work or a saint at his prayers.

Job finished his work and shut the bag. Then he turned back to the Dean, his eyes sparkling with excitement. "Sir! I'm reading Mr. Penny's books."

"I thought you would," said the Dean. "What do you read?"

"Just what I pick up off the floor, sir. Plato. Shakespeare. Charles Lamb. Wordsworth. It's all grand stuff, even when I don't understand it. But Mr. Penny helps me. Polly never learnt to read properly at Dobson's, like I did, so Miss Peabody lets me go up one evening a week after supper and we sit in front of the fire and I teach her."

He had come back to the Dean's table and the words poured out as he told him of his affairs. Adam Ayscough had thought him changed from boy to man, but now he was back in some childhood he had never had, telling a grown-up he loved and trusted the glorious tale of his accomplishments without the slightest doubt that the other would be as thrilled as he was. The Dean could not remember that such a thing had happened to him before. He listened with one hand behind his ear, fearful he should miss a word of it.

Job suddenly caught himself up, aware of some slight sound outside the door, as of a prowling presence there. He flushed scarlet. "Please forgive me, sir. I should have gone away when I had wound the clock. That's what Mr. Garland told me to do."

"Had you done so, Job, you would have deprived me of a very great happiness. I am more obliged to you than you can well know. Before you go tell me of Mr. Peabody. I understand he is indisposed? Is it his asthma?"

"No, sir, only a cold. He's well over his asthma."

"Had he had asthma previously?"

"Yes, sir. It was only to be expected, Polly said."

"The weather has been very inclement."

"It wasn't the weather, sir, it was you."

"Me?" asked the Dean, his hand behind his ear again.

"Being ill, sir. Mr. Peabody always has asthma when he is miserable."

The Dean did not like to ask Job to repeat himself, but he believed he had heard aright. Bella. Job. Isaac. It appeared that they all felt affection for him. He struggled for speech and when it came at last its banality shocked him.

"My compliments to Mr. Peabody. You will tell him, if you please, that during my illness I have been continuing my study of horology. To the books he lent me I have added others from the library." He moved the sheets of manuscript and architectural plans that were piled on his table and showed Job the books that lay under them, calf-bound histories of clocks and clock-makers. "Tell Mr. Peabody I am his humble pupil and I shall hope soon to visit you both at the shop to choose the clock for my wife. My compliments to Miss Peabody, Mr. Penny, Polly and Ruth. I hold you all in my heart. There is Garland at the door. Good-bye, Job. Much obliged."

CHAPTER XV *The Celestial Clock*

I

CHRISTMAS was less than a fortnight away and already its light shone upon the days. Through all the city there was a quiet hum of preparation. Serious housewives had made their Christmas pudding and mincemeat weeks ago but the giddy ones, those who did not perform their duties until crisis was right upon them, were doing it now and delicious smells of brandy and spice mingled with the smell of ironing, gingerbread and beeswax that floated out into the streets from open windows and doors left ajar. For the weather had turned warm and springlike, violet-scented in the early morning and fragrant with wood smoke at night, and musical with the chatter of astonished birds who could not understand it. People said to each other that it was like the Christmas when Dean Rollard had ridden home from prison. It was proper Dean's weather. Doctor Jenkins alone regretted the warmth, so passionately had he wanted the Dean to have his white Christmas. The shops were gay and stayed open for an extra half-hour every evening, the lamps shining upon books and toys, sweets and apples and nuts and festoons of coloured paper. In the market place they were selling Christmas trees and piles of oranges like golden moons. The children and dogs were in a permanent state of over-excitement and every house, and indeed almost every room, had a secret.

The Cathedral towered over it all, benignly great in this quiet weather, the sound of the bells falling gently from the height of the Rollo tower. At evening, when dusk fell, men looked up and saw light shining from the windows of the choir and heard music, for the choristers were practising for the carol service. Michael seemed dreaming. So many Christmases had gone since he had stood here looking out to the edge of the world, looking down at the city, looking up to heaven. So many Christmas Eves he had stood waiting through hours of snow and storm, of wind and rain or of rapt stillness bright with moon and stars, waiting for the mid-course of the night when he should lift his fist and strike out on the great bell the hour of man's redemption. Then when the boom of the last echo had died away over the plain to the sea he would veil his face with his wings, for love was running down the steps of the sky, running fast from cloud to cloud, from star to star, leaping and laughing. He dared not look upon the face of love but he would hear the laughter in that moment of profound quietness between the last echo of midnight and the pealing out of the Christmas bells.

"Last Christmas," said Job, "I did not know what Christmas was." When he had first come to Mr. Peabody he had not wanted to look back for he had felt like someone just awake after a nightmare, and afraid to think about it lest it catch him again, but now the evil had receded so far that he liked to set it as a backcloth to the procession of his shining days. "I did not know what it was," he repeated. "Shall I put the shutters up?"

"Another five minutes," said Isaac. "I don't like to close too soon before Christmas."

"Thirty minutes late now," said Job, but he laughed and leaned his arms on the counter, content to wait. He was tired, and so was Isaac, for it had been a busy day with people in and out buying Christmas presents, but they had enjoyed it to the full and their tiredness was of the pleasant sort that invests the thought of supper and bed with haloed glory.

Isaac did not call himself a jeweller but he did in his odd moments make pinchbeck brooches, heart-shaped lockets and ear-rings whorled or delicately pointed like shells or stars. He also made eternity rings set with imitation jewels whose first letters spelt words like regard, dearest, and adored, adjectives nicely graded to express the degree of feeling which ravaged the breast of the enamoured male at the moment of purchase, and these as well as his clocks had a great sale before Christmas. Job had proved as expert as Isaac at making these trifles but one of the rings that he had made was not for sale. It was in a leather heart-shaped box in his pocket, burning a hole there until such time that he could give it to Polly for her Christmas present. As well as jewellery he had created flights of little birds, angels and stars, and silver reindeer with golden antlers to hang upon the Christmas trees that were sold in the market.

There had been moments during the past week when it had scarcely been possible to move in the shop for excited children, papas, mammas, uncles, aunts and nannies, but now most of the pretty trifles had been sold and the ticking of the clocks, that for days had been drowned by the babel of voices and laughter, had come back into the silence as the singing of birds comes back when the wind dies at dusk. It was dark now beyond the bow windows of the shop, the sky clear after a passing shower and spangled with stars above the crooked roofs of Cockspur Street. The windows of the houses were small squares of orange and gold, reflected in the shining cobbles. The lamplighter had passed down the street and the muffin man had passed up it, but now there was no one about, not even a cat. Yet they waited in the lamplight, leaning on the counter, and listened to the voices of their clocks as other men listened to a harpsichord or the slap of small waves against the hull of a boat. It was to them the music of their hearts, that pulsed in time to the heart-beat of the celestial clock.

It was there in the window, finished five days ago, the best clock that Isaac had ever made. He had thought that he would not be able to put it in the window, so much did it seem to be a part of himself, yet suddenly he had put it there, in the centre, the other clocks grouped about it like lesser stars about the moon. He had put it there because it was Christmas. To him it was only a fairy tale that love had leaped from heaven on fire for the manger and the cross, but tales are potent things and this one was in his blood, and so he had had to give his best to the city. The celestial clock, his masterpiece, must shine in the window for the city to see. And the city had seen and liked it. For five days rows of faces had been pressed against the window, rejoicing in his Christmas clock that chimed as sweetly as the singing stars.

But he would not sell it. It would kill him to part with that clock. When anyone asked the price he named one so exorbitant that the questioner backed laughing from the shop. His clock had become something of a joke in the city. Everyone knew he did not mean to sell it, yet they would ask the price for fun, and every time they asked it soared higher.

It was Job who heard the heavy footsteps first, and he thought again that he knew now what Christmas was. It was expectancy. This time last year he had expected little except the dreary continuance of misery but now the horizon of his expectations was lost in glory.

"You can put up the shutters now, Job," said Isaac.

"Just a minute, sir," said Job, "there's someone coming."

In another moment or two the black silhouette of the Dean's cloaked and top-hatted figure had blocked out the crooked houses opposite, the sky and the stars. Isaac, with an exclamation of delight, was just starting forward when Job checked him. "He's seen the clock!" he whispered.

The Dean with his poor sight had not seen the two weary workmen inside the shop but he had indeed seen the clock. He took off his eyeglasses, polished them and put them on again. He stood perfectly still gazing at the clock, and his face was as still as his body. Both might have been carved out of dark and ancient wood. At first Isaac was disappointed, used as he was to the eager faces pressed against the window and the exclamations of delight. He was afraid the Dean did not like his clock. His expressionless stillness could only mean disapproval. Or else homage. It could not be homage. He watched intently and saw a smile creep about the Dean's lips. He had seen that smile outside his shop window many times this last week but always on a young face, not an old one. The young men of the city, the ones with not much money, had looked like that when they had seen exactly the right heart-shaped pinchbeck locket to give their girl for Christmas, and they had slouched in, blushing crimson, and counted out half their week's poor wages on his counter. But it shocked him to see that same smile on an old face. Such an intensity of feeling could be borne through the time of courting and first love but he did not know how a man could support it through a lifetime.

Then suddenly fear gripped him as he realised the meaning of the smile. The celestial clock was the one the Dean wanted to give to his wife and he would be content with nothing else. Isaac knew these lovers and their obstinacy. They wanted the one thing and the one thing only and there was no fobbing them off with something else. He would have to tell the Dean the clock was not for sale. What a fool he had been to put it in the window. What a fool! And now he would have to disappoint the one man of all others whom he most loved and admired; the only man, if it came to that, for though his love embraced the whole city he felt a deep personal love only for the Dean, Miss Montague, Polly and Job. He must do it quickly. He must tell the Dean as quickly as he could that the clock was not for sale. Get it over.

Adam Ayscough had moved from the window and Job had leaped to open the door. Then the three of them were together in the shop exchanging the greetings of the season and only Isaac's rang hollow "You are well again, Mr. Peabody?" asked the Dean, peering at him a little anxiously.

"Yes, sir," said Isaac.

"You must be much fatigued," said the Dean. "Overburdened with customers. And I am yet another, and a late one. I was with Mr. Turnbull, our mayor, talking with him of a project that I have at heart, and I could not get away as early as I had intended. Much distressed." He paused and then said as shyly as a schoolboy, "That clock for my wife, Mr. Peabody. There is one in the window, a very lovely clock. I do not think I have ever seen one I liked better."

Isaac wetted his lips. "Which one, sir?" he asked.

"It is a clock of the heavens," said the Dean.

Isaac looked up at him. Now he must say it. No good beating about the bush. He must say it at once. The Dean's eyes, usually rather dim, seemed boyishly bright in the lamplight. Isaac rehearsed in his mind what he had to say. "The celestial clock is not for sale, sir." He rehearsed it several times and then swallowed and said, "Job, bring the celestial clock through to the workshop. Then put up the shutters and close the shop that we may be undisturbed."

He opened the workshop door and stood back. "Will you come this way, sir?"

In the workshop he turned up one of the lamps and cleared a wide space on his work-bench. "Put it here, Job," he said. "You see, sir, there is more space here. You can stand back and get the effect as it will be when it stands on Mrs. Ayscough's mantelpiece. I shall be proud indeed, sir, if you choose this one for her but would you like Job to bring any others through for you to see?"

The Dean had taken off his hat and was standing before the clock. "I need not trouble Job," he said quietly. "There is only one clock in the world that I want to give my wife."

"I am glad, sir," said Isaac. "When you have put up the shutters, Job, you may come back. I must tell you, sir, that I had Job's help in making this clock. He was of great assistance to me."

"That increases the clock's value," said the Dean.

Job went out to the street and put up the shutters in a state of great bewilderment. What ever had made Isaac part with the clock? It was to the Dean of course. Yet he had thought that Isaac would have cut the heart out of his body sooner than part with the clock. The shutters in place he came back to the workshop and stood in the shadows behind the two old men, who were talking in low voices of the glory of the clock. It *was* a glorious clock. It seemed to Job that until this moment he had not himself realised what a masterpiece had been achieved. It stood illumined by the lamplight, shining out against the shadows behind it as sometimes the setting sun is illumined against the dusk. The golden fret that hid the bell was the loveliest Isaac had ever made. The two swans were just rising from the reeds, one with wings fully spread, the other with his pinions half unfolded. Job could understand from experience, and the Dean through intuition, what an achievement it had been to form those great wings and curved necks into a pattern that was a fitting one for a clock fret and yet alive, but only Isaac knew how he had laboured and sweated over it. This had been a costing clock. Yet the figures of the signs of the zodiac were as fresh and lively as though they had stepped with ease to the clock face. The ram, the bull, the heavenly twins, the crab, the lion, the scales, the scorpion, the archer, the sea goat and the man with the watering pot were bright as their own stars, gay as the little figures in an illuminated manuscript. But the virgin and the fish had something more than life and gaiety.

"She stands in her blue robe at her own hour of vespers, full of the peace of that hour," said the Dean. "Expectancy too. A great expectancy. Only six hours to midnight."

Isaac was startled. He had intended no Christian symbolism when he had painted his virgin in a blue robe. He had chosen blue merely to balance the blue of the watering pot at nine o'clock and the blue fillet that bound the archer's head at three o'clock. But the pretty Christmas story was a part of him and had obtruded itself.

"Six hours to midnight," repeated the Dean. "There you have combined the two symbols very excellently, Mr. Peabody. The fish, the ancient Christian symbol of Christ our Lord, and the Sun of Righteousness, the Light of the World."

With a pang of something remarkably like jealousy Mr. Peabody realised that the Dean's homage, that he had seen through the window, had not been entirely for his clock, if for his clock at all. And what had he been thinking of to put only one fish at twelve o'clock? Pisces, the sign of the zodiac, had two fish. He could only suppose that out of the deeps of his memory that one fish had come swimming up into the light, to remind him now suddenly of his father. For it was his father who had told him how the martyrs had painted that fish on the walls of the catacombs, and traced it in the dust that one Christian might recognise another.

"My homage is a double one," said the Dean, and Isaac's spirits rose again until he remembered the virgin, when they sank, but lifted once more when the Dean added, "You are a master craftsman, Mr. Peabody. I hope the price you are asking for that clock is sufficient for its great merit."

"No price, sir," said Isaac in a low voice.

"What did you say, Mr. Peabody?" asked the Dean, and put his hand behind his ear.

Isaac raised his voice. "I cannot let you pay me for that clock, sir. I shall be happy if Mrs. Ayscough will accept it."

He was looking very dejected. How could he explain to the Dean that he was only able to part with the clock if he could give it? It was himself. A man does not give himself to his friend for payment. The Dean, his hand still behind his ear, was looking at him in puzzled distress. But he could not explain. He had not got the words. Job, he noticed, was escaping quietly out of the room and he saw him go with panic. Now he was alone with the Dean and could not escape. It was not of the man himself that he was afraid but of that which reached out for him through his friend. The Dean's huge shadow leapt up over the ceiling in the same sort of way that the Cathedral loomed up in the night sky. He began to cough.

"Mr. Peabody,' said the Dean gently, "do you not wish to part with this clock? If that is the case I beg that you will tell me. I can assure you that whatever your motives may be I shall understand them."

"I want to give you the clock," mumbled Isaac. "That's what I want."

"Much distressed," murmured the Dean, and indeed he was groping in a fog of distress. One thing however was clear to him, and that was that Isaac was speaking the truth and he must, for the moment at any rate, humbly accept the clock. After Christmas, he trusted, God's guidance would show him some happy way of persuading Isaac to accept payment, or if that was not possible then some way of service to his friend that should reveal without patronage or pride the depth of his gratitude.

"I want it too," he said quietly. "For my beloved wife. With all my heart I thank you, Mr. Peabody. I cannot just now express my feelings as I would. I shall hope to do so at some future time when I have a little more collected myself. My friend, may I stay for a few moments and talk with you?"

"It is getting late, sir," said Isaac. "Dark too. You should be at home."

"To be here with you is a pleasure," said the Dean, "and to walk home in the dark will be no burden. The city at night is a continual joy to me. Do you fear the dark?"

"Not of the city at night," said Isaac.

"Of death?" asked the Dean. "If so you are not alone in your fear, for the dark auditorium with its unseen crowd of witnesses is a frightening thing, pressing in upon our poor little garish stage, frightening because we know nothing of it. Yet when our play is ended and the house lights go up we shall see many kindly faces. It is a house, remember, a friendly place. There is a prayer by the great Dean John Donne that I often repeat to myself. 'Bring us, O Lord God, at our last awakening, into the house and gate of heaven, to enter into that gate and dwell in that house where there shall be no darkness or dazzling, but one equal light; no noise nor silence, but one equal music; no fears nor hopes, but one equal possession: no ends nor beginnings, but one equal eternity; in the habitations of Thy glory and dominion, world without end!'"

To Isaac this seemed just another finely spun web of words. Men made so many to hang between themselves and their fear. They glittered in the eyes but the dark was still behind them. He was perched tensely on his work-stool and the Dean was sitting in the old battered chair. He had dreamed of having the Dean here like this, sitting with him in the soft lamplight of the workshop, and now that it had happened he only wanted to escape. He was very much afraid one of his bad times was coming. That would happen, just at Christmas. They always came just when he was planning to enjoy himself. He coughed, pressing his thin hands together between his knees, dreadfully sorry for himself. The Dean went on talking, saying the first thing that came into his head. "'The house and gate of heaven.' I always say that to myself when I go into the Cathedral, especially when I go in through the west door. Men think of heaven under so many symbols. The garden of paradise, the green pastures and so on. I think simply of the Cathedral, for within it I have so often found my God. Before my illness I told Job I would show him the carvings in the Cathedral. I would like to redeem my promise this Christmas. Will you come too, Mr. Peabody?"

He turned to smile at Isaac and was astonished to see terror in the little man's bright blue eyes. "No, sir, no! I have never been in the Cathedral."

"Never been in the Cathedral?" The Dean could scarcely believe his deaf ears.

"No, sir," said Isaac hoarsely.

"Did your father take you there as a child?"

"He tried to take me but I would not go. He beat me but still I would not go."

"Why not, Mr. Peabody?"

"It is too big. Too dark. If it fell on you it would crush you to powder." And Isaac began to cough again.

"Dreadful as your father's God," said the Dean. Isaac stopped coughing and looked at him in amazement. "Do not misunderstand me, Mr. Peabody. I know your father was an excellent man whose memory is revered in the city. But we always tend to make God in our own image and your father was perhaps a man of stern rectitude. Is that so?"

"I hated him," whispered Isaac. "When I was a child I hoped he'd die. That's murder." It was out. He had never said that to anyone before. Nor had he ever told anyone about his father thrashing him because he would not go inside the Cathedral. He suddenly began to cry in the manner of the child that he was and then stopped crying as abruptly as he had begun. He twisted his red knobbly hands together in his misery. Now the Dean would get up and go away and leave him and never speak to him again.

"And no doubt as a boy you hated God as much as you hated your father," said the Dean calmly. "But all your hatred, Mr. Peabody, God took into his own body that it might die with him. You now are free of it."

"I don't believe in God," said Isaac obstinately.

"I wish I could believe you," said the Dean. "I should be thankful to believe you had parted company with the God of your boyhood. But I fear he is with you still in a darkness that shadows your mind at times. Disbelieve in him, Mr. Peabody. Believe instead in love. It is my faith that love shaped the universe as you shape your clocks, delighting in creation. I believe that just as you wish to give me your clock in love, refusing payment, so God loves me and gave himself for me. That is my faith. I cannot presume to force it upon you, I can only ask you in friendship to consider it. I believe I have your affection, Mr. Peabody. You are aware I think how deeply you have mine."

Isaac surreptitiously dried his eyes and began to feel a little better. The last sentence was the only one he had really got hold of, the only one that had done him any good.

"I have been so interested in reading of Plato's water clock, that he introduced into Greece," said the Dean. "I had no idea Plato was a horologist. And Holbein too. I wish I could see one of his sundials. And the Dean of Ely, Richard Parker, carried a horoligium in the top of his walking-stick. All good men. Soon, Mr. Peabody, I shall have no opinion of any man who is not a horologist."

"Sir, I could make you a walking-stick with a horologium," said Isaac eagerly.

The Celestial Clock

The Dean laughed. "A celestial clock is enough for now, Mr. Peabody. More than enough. No man ever received a more princely gift or was more deeply grateful or more profoundly touched by its reception. Can you explain to me, Mr. Peabody, the mechanism of a falling ball timekeeper? I have not a mechanical mind and in my recent study of horology have found myself much handicapped by the lack of it."

Isaac's face lit up. The phrase was literally true in his case for his cheeks and the tip of his nose shone rosily and his blue eyes were suddenly as flooded with light as sapphires held to the sun. In the country of his mind the advancing shadows were halted and rolled back upon themselves like the fen mists when the wind suddenly freshened from the sea. He glowed and the Dean felt a pang of sadness. What would this man have been, what would he have done, had he not been so wrenched from the true faith by the sufferings of his boyhood? Yet perhaps without them he would not have been Bella's fairy man. Such twistings sometimes forced out poison but at other times honey. It depended what was at the heart of a man.

"Come into the shop, sir," said Isaac eagerly. "I will show you all my clocks. Their mechanism will be easier to understand with the living thing before your eyes. Come this way, sir."

For nearly an hour Isaac instructed the Dean in horology and Adam Ayscough was no longer amazed at the rapidity with which Job had learnt his craft. The schoolmaster in him delighted in Isaac's lucid explanations, and he delighted too in this experience of being shut in with all these ticking clocks. The sheltered lamplit shop was like the inside of a hive full of amiable bees who had no wish to sting, only to display for his delight the beauty of their gold-dusted filigree wings and gold-brown bodies. They spoke to him with their honeyed tongues of this mystery of time that they had a little tamed for man with their hands and voices and the beat of their constant hearts, and yet could never make less mysterious or dreadful for all their friendliness. How strange it was, thought the Dean, as one after another he took the busy little bodies into his hands, that soon he would know more about the mystery than they did themselves.

Michael struck his bell above the buzzing of the lesser

bees and he remembered the sacred hour of dinner. Elaine must not be kept waiting however great his pleasure here in the hive. "I must go," he said. "I am obliged to you, Mr. Peabody, for a most enjoyable hour. I do not recollect having spent a happier." Isaac brought him his hat and cloak and he put them on. "I wish, Mr. Peabody, that I could give you something of the same pleasure that you have given me. I wish I could show you my Cathedral as you have shown me your clocks. Will you not give me that privilege?" Isaac, looking up at him, looked hastily away again, for the Dean's longing to take him to the Cathedral was plain to see and he did not wish to see it. He mumbled something, shaking his head, then opened the shop door for the Dean to go out.

"I'll send up the celestial clock to the Deanery before Christmas, sir," he said.

The Dean was outside on the pavement in the moonlight, his hat in his hand. "My deep gratitude, Mr. Peabody," he said sadly. "My deep gratitude. God bless you."

He bowed, put on his hat, and turned away. Isaac went back into the shop, shut the door and began to put the clocks and watches back in their places. Then he went to the door again, opened it and looked out. The Dean was walking so slowly and heavily that he had not got far up the street. He walked much more slowly now than he had been used to do. An impulse came to Isaac to run after him and say that he would go with him to the Cathedral, and he did crawl crabwise down the worn steps. Then he scuttled back into the shop again. No, he would not go to the Cathedral. If he did it would get him.

On the day before Christmas Eve, at breakfast, Isaac suddenly found himself telling Emma about the celestial clock. It came into his head because tomorrow he was going to take it to the Deanery. This was the last day that the glorious thing would be with them in the shop. Tomorrow it would pass into the keeping of the Dean and on Christmas Day it would be Mrs. Ayscough's. Isaac's adam's apple felt too big for his throat whenever he thought of tomorrow. Yet he did not regret his gift. Deep inside himself he felt a profound satisfaction because of it, a new sort of stability. He felt more of a man because he had been able to do it. It was this new steadiness that had made him suddenly speak to Emma of his affairs in the sort of way a man speaks to his wife, taking it for granted that she will be interested. He was astonished at himself, and even more astonished at her, for she answered pleasantly. Isaac was a self-absorbed man yet even he had noticed that she had seemed happier lately. She had been consistently kind to Job and she had bought herself a new bonnet to wear when she drank tea with Miss Montague. This she had done twice already, meeting the precentor's wife by special invitation upon the second occasion.

"It must be a lovely clock, Isaac," she said. "Will you take another cup of tea, my dear?"

She never called him dear. He was so astonished that he dropped his fork on the tablecloth and she did not reprove him. He believed there had been a slight wistfulness in her voice. Surely she could not wish to see the clock? He could not ask her to come to the shop for she hated it and never came there. She had never forgiven him for disgracing them by going into trade.

"Emma," he said shyly, "would you like me to bring the clock back with me this evening so that you can see it? It will be quite safe here tonight and tomorrow I will take it to the Deanery."

"Has the Dean paid for it yet?" asked Emma. "If he has it would not be right to have it in the house tonight."

"Not yet," said Isaac, for he had not told her, and would never tell anyone, that he had given the clock to the Dean.

"Then I would like to see it," said Emma. "Thank you, Isaac."

After breakfast she further astonished him by coming out into the passage to help him on with his coat. As she lifted her arm he saw that there was a split in the seam of her bodice and a ridiculous notion came to him that the hard black sheath of her dress was a chrysalis and something would presently burst out of it. The thought was so alarming that he bade her a hasty good-bye and bolted out of the door and down Angel Lane with all possible speed. What sort of creature was likely to burst out of that cracking chrysalis? Would it be good or bad?

A slight uneasiness remained with Isaac through the day and when the time came to shut the shop and go home he felt reluctant to take the clock with him. Job had already gone home to Mr. Penny and Ruth and he was alone in the workshop as he stood before it and wondered what to do.

He could not bear to think of the lovely thing standing in the shadows of the parlour, of his sister's long yellow fingers touching it, and his father's dark glance resting upon it as he gazed out from his portrait in sour disapproval of all things that he saw. Yet he had told Emma that he would bring it. What would the Dean say? It was his clock now. Undoubtedly his great courtesy would not wish to disappoint Emma. Isaac lifted the clock and wrapped it gently first in the old silk handkerchief and then in a length of wine-coloured velvet that he sometimes used in the shop window. Then he put on his hat and cloak and with the clock held like a child in the crook of his arm he went out into the street. He noticed as he came out that it was turning cold.

He carried the celestial clock very carefully through the streets of the city, his head a little bent to catch the faint ticking from within the folds of velvet and silk. Now and then he murmured a few quiet words, speaking of the beauty of the night, of the lighted windows and the shadows of the children behind the blinds, of open doors spilling light across the pavements. The clock was a citizen of this city even as he was but they would not again walk its streets together. He would see it in future only for a few minutes on Saturdays, when he wound it and dusted its starry face with the old silk handkerchief.

When he reached number twelve he took it into the parlour, unwrapped it and put it on the round plush-covered table beside the family Bible. All through supper it shone there in the lamplight and Emma was pleased that he had brought it and said it was very pretty. Polly, coming in and out with the dishes, was wide-eyed with delight. Isaac's own uneasiness vanished as he ate tripe and onions and baked apples and gazed at the clock. There was not a thing wrong with it. Every bit of mechanism in it was hiddenly perfect, as lovely in its particular function as the swans' wings and the slender arrow-headed hour and minute hands, moving imperceptibly from one exquisite star symbol to another around the azure heaven. There had been a tiny scratch on the clock face where Job had confessed that he let his tool slip, but they had been able to smooth it away. But it had been an extraordinary thing that so good a craftsman as Job had let his tool slip and Isaac had not been able to understand it.

The Celestial Clock

After supper he and Emma sat for a little while in front of the fire, Emma reading the evening chapter, and they were more at ease together than they had ever been. And then Isaac suddenly got to his feet.

"I never locked the shop!"

Emma clicked her tongue in disapprobation. "Isaac! Whatever made you so careless?"

"I had the clock in my arms. I was thinking of that alone. I must go back at once."

"Put your muffler on," said Emma. "Good night, dear. I expect I shall have gone to bed when you come back. I have a slight headache."

Isaac said he was sorry and hurried across the room. At the door he looked back once at the clock and the silver fish shone out against the golden sun behind it as though a lighthouse had flashed a message to him. All the city clocks were striking as he put on his cloak and muffler in the hall, and as he opened the front door the celestial clock also began to strike. He stood outside on the steps, and listened to it. He had never made a bell with a sweeter tongue. It seemed calling after him all the way down Angel Lane.

Emma had just gone to her room and Polly was darning in front of the kitchen fire with Sooty at her feet when a knock came at the back door. She was surprised, for it was not Job's night. Yet it was Job outside, bright eyed and laughing.

"Whatever are you doing there, Job Mooring? The mistress only lets you come on Wednesdays and that you very well know."

"Let me in, Polly," pleaded Job. "I want to see you."

"No more than five minutes then," said Polly severely. "The mistress is upstairs with a headache, and Mr. Peabody down at the shop, and I'm not one for more deceitful goings on than are necessary and that you very well know too. Wipe your feet on the mat and speak soft. I'll not have the mistress disturbed, let alone she'd skin us alive if she found you here after dark and it not Wednesday. Wipe your feet on the mat, I said."

She spoke all the more severely because of the mad beating of her heart and the exquisite joy that was sweeping over her, like a wave over the ribbed sand in the sunlight, pouring over the rocks and filling the pools. Her sharp words came breathlessly and she did not look at Job as she pulled him in and shut the scullery door behind him, for if she had looked at him she would have been on tiptoe in a moment, her mouth pressed to his and her hands clinging to his shoulders because her knees had turned to water and would no longer support her. For this growing up of Job was doing extraordinary things to Polly. As his shoulders broadened and his height increased, lifting him away above her head who once had been a scared child at her shoulder, so her breasts rounded out and colour came into her cheeks and all her hard tasks seemed light as air. At night she felt lonely in her bed and yet in bliss because in her dreams she ran and ran along the sparkling sand, or down green alley ways under flowering trees, and though she never caught up with Job she knew that he was just on ahead of her and that one night he would swing round and come speeding back to meet her, and then the whole green world, the whole curve of heaven, would belong to the two of them made one.

She pushed him into the fireside chair, then bustled about getting him a drink of warm milk, an apple and two little tarts on a plate. With Ruth such a good cook there was now no need for her to save her own food for him, yet still she did it sometimes because of the joy it gave her. And there seemed no limit to what he could eat these days. His stomach, stretching and relaxing itself after the years of semi-starvation, appeared to be bottomless. With Sooty draped like a muffler round his neck he absorbed the tarts as rapidly as though they were oysters and then crunched his strong white teeth into the apple. Polly watched him with profound satisfaction, her hands folded in her lap, her eyes as they followed his every movement making up for the time lost when she had not dared to raise them to look at him. For while he enjoyed his food there was no danger that she would suddenly find herself with her mouth on his. Just now he wanted it for other purposes. His plate empty and the mug of milk drained he sighed, happily replete, and after his sigh came the distant music of a bell ringing the half-hour in the next room.

"That's the celestial clock!" he ejaculated.

"Mr. Peabody brought it home for the mistress to see," said Polly. "It's ever so pretty."

"Pretty?" snorted Job. "It's the most beautiful clock that was ever made. You can't have seen it properly just to call

The Celestial Clock

it 'pretty'. " He lifted Sooty from his shoulders and picked up the lamp. "Come on, Polly. We'll go and look at it together."

"Hush now," she whispered as she opened the parlour door. "The mistress. What would she say if she found you in the parlour and it not Wednesday?"

"I wouldn't care what she said," Job whispered back fiercely. In the parlour he placed the lamp on the high bookshelf so that its light fell full on the clock. "There!" he said.

They stood together looking at the clock while in a whisper he told her about the signs of the zodiac, and the sun and the silver fish. The clock ticked sweetly and cheerily but the house, and the city beyond the house, were so still that they felt themselves alone in the world with the sun and moon and stars like Adam and Eve. Polly slipped her hand into Job's and leaned a little closer, so that she felt the glowing warmth of his young body. Her hand tightened in his. "Why did you come tonight?" she whispered.

"To bring you something," he said. "I meant to keep it till Christmas but I can't."

"Another bird?" asked Polly.

"No, not a bird," he said, and putting his free hand in his pocket he brought out the small heart-shaped case. He took his other hand gently from hers and opened the box. Inside was a small bright ring. He took it out and laid it on his palm. "I made it for you," he whispered. Polly gasped, for words were beyond her. They leaned with their heads close together, bent over the ring. "The stones spell a word. Can you read it? Diamond. Emerald. Amethyst. Ruby. Emerald again. Sapphire. Topaz. They're not real jewels, of course. I couldn't afford that. But one day I'll make you a ring with real jewels. Can you read it?" She shook her head for she was not yet such a fine scholar as he was. "Yes you can, Polly. Hold out your left hand and I'll put it on DEAREST. You know that word, my dearest Polly."

Suddenly she cried out, a cry of young ecstasy, cut short as his mouth came down on hers and his arms went round her. The celestial clock ticked merrily on, sparkling in the lamplight, but the boy and girl did not hear it for time had stopped for them. "This is Job," thought Polly, and though she did not know it she was crying and there was a salt taste on their lips. "It's Polly," he thought. They had known each other for so long yet now each was made new for the other. The whole world was made new. Polly put up her hand to touch Job's curly hair as his left arm strained more closely round her tiny waist. Neither of them heard the heavy footsteps floundering down the stairs or the opening of the parlour door, but the shrill voice frightened them by its sheer hideousness, as though all lovely things had suddenly turned to ugliness.

Emma was shouting vile things as she stood with her candlestick in her shaking hand, her black shawl clutched about her shoulders, her face so old and distorted that for a moment Polly did not recognise her. When she did she was more terrified than ever, and clung shivering to Job. It was more fearful to see Emma, with whom she had lived for so long compassionately and companionably, turned as suddenly to this evil than it would have been to see Appollyon come up through the parlour floor. Then the candlestick in Emma's hand lurched suddenly, spilling grease on the carpet, and instinctively duty sent Polly darting forward. "The candle ma'am! Mind the candle!" Emma dropped the candle and boxed Polly's ears, and she struck so hard that Polly cried out in pain as a short while ago she had cried out in joy.

It was the contrast between the two cries that sent Job mad. A moment before he had been frozen with fear and horror, the next moment he had seized Emma's wrists and flung her away from Polly. His strong fingers bit like steel into her flesh and his eyes blazed their hatred down into hers. For a moment she thought he was going to fling her into the fire as once she had flung his birds, and she screamed. Wrenching away one hand she clutched at the plush cloth on the table behind her. Trying to save her from falling he stumbled too and they went down together, Emma still clutching the cloth. The celestial clock crashed into the grate and was smashed on its marble slab.

"Have you hurt yourself, Emma?" asked Isaac, and bending down he helped her up and put her weeping and shivering into her chair. Job and Polly gazed at him stupefied, for they had not heard him come in. He was quiet, and more composed than any of them, but his face was ashen and his eyes were like hard blue stones. Only Job was aware of his terrible anger, but Polly thought he looked dreadful and timidly stretched out a hand towards him. He pushed

The Celestial Clock

it away and turned to his sister. "Be quiet, Emma! You have done enough harm for one night. Go to bed." Slumped in her chair, her face blotched with tears, she was to Job the most repulsive sight he had ever seen, and he looked away in miserable embarrassment. But Isaac gazed at her fixedly, as though, Polly thought in terror, he was seeing her clearly for the first time and hating what he saw. "What a carry-on just because a clock's been smashed," she thought with a sudden return of common sense, and loving Isaac and Job as deeply as ever her sympathy nevertheless swung so suddenly over to Emma that she went to her and put her arms round her.

"Don't take on so, ma'am," she said. "It's only a clock smashed. It can likely be mended. Come, ma'am, I'll take you to bed." She lifted her up and took her to the door where with her arms round Emma she looked back to Job, her eyes soft and bright. "There now, lad, don't you take on neither," she said. "Mr. Peabody, he'll understand when you tell him what happened." Her eyes went to Isaac but he had his back to her. He was bending over the grate, picking up the pieces of the clock. She said to him pleadingly, "Mr. Peabody, it was because she never had a man," but his back remained as implacable in hatred as his face had been. There was nothing she could do except take Emma away.

Job fetched a box from the kitchen and kneeling beside Isaac he tried to help him pick up the bits of the clock. It was odd how silent the room seemed without its ticking. The Time and Death clock still ticked, but its heart beat was slow and leaden and that of the celestial clock had been so merry. Job was so cold with misery that his fingers only fumbled at the bits as he tried to pick them up, and then dropped them again as though they were slippery as the guts and heart of a dismembered body. "It's only a clock," Polly had said. But she did not understand about making things. And it was not only the clock. There was a blackness in his mind, a sickening sort of stench in the room that had nothing to do with any physical odour, and yet made him feel as sick as he had used to do when Albert Lee flogged him. And he was afraid, as though some appalling presence were here in the room with him and Isaac. The fear too was familiar, though lately he had imagined he had forgotten the choking blackness of the chimneys and the fire beneath his feet. Only imagined, because no man forgets hell. But this hell he was in now was worse than the others for they had not emanated from himself and this one did. From himself and Isaac and Emma. Only Polly tonight had not hated.

"I came to see Polly," he said hoarsely to Isaac. "We came in here to look at the clock and I gave her the ring. She cried out, she was so pleased, and we kissed each other. Miss Peabody must have heard and she came in. She said things. They were not true, for I've never touched Polly till tonight. I can kiss her, can't I, without foul things being said? I'm going to marry her. She boxed Polly's ears and I pulled her away so roughly that she clutched at the tablecloth and we fell and the clock went over. I've hated her ever since she burnt my birds. It's my hating her that smashed the clock. I wouldn't have smashed the clock if she hadn't burnt my birds. It's her fault."

Isaac seemed not to hear a word. He said coldly, "You need not drop the only part of the clock that can still be given to the Dean. Pick it up again."

A shining thing had just dropped from Job's fingers and lay in the ashes. It was the fret of the two swans. The clock face was smashed into a hundred pieces, and the delicate mechanism of the works was jarred and twisted, but the fret of the two swans was uninjured. Job picked it up and dusted it on his sleeve.

"Tomorrow morning," said Isaac harshly, "you can take that to the Dean and tell him what you did. You need not come to work tomorrow. I shan't want you." And with the box holding the ruins of the clock under his arm he walked out of the room and out of the house, his footsteps echoing down the street.

Job sat crouched over the fire. There had been a moment not long ago when he had seemed to wake suddenly from darkness to light. It had been the day that the Dean had come to St. Peter's vicarage. But now the darkness was again as thick as death. Isaac would not forgive him for what had happened and his love and Polly's was soiled. That wicked old woman had flung it like a flower into the mud and now it would never be the same again. They would pick it up and make the best of it but it would never be the same again. He was so soaked in misery that he did not hear Polly come lightly into the room. He did not know she was there until she sat down beside him and slipped her arm round his neck. "I'm going to make a pot of tea," she said cheerfully. "Where's the cat?"

"Lord, Polly, how should I know?" Job asked irritably. "Surely there's enough trouble without you fussing about the cat."

She laughed and leaned her cheek against his. "Mend the fire while I make the tea," she said. "I'll take a cup up to the mistress, poor soul, and then we'll have ours here. Where's Mr. Peabody?" She looked at the Time and Death clock. "Not closing time yet, and likely he'll drink more than is good for him. I'll sit up for him and when he comes back I'll get him to bed with a nice hot brick to his feet. He'll be himself in the morning if he don't get asthma."

She went out and Job heard her singing softly to herself as she got the tea, and talking to Sooty, who had thought discretion the better part of valour and remained aloof from disturbances in the kitchen. Her equanimity in disaster, her immunity from the strains and miseries of the artistic temperament, the way evil ran off her like water off a duck's back, was to exasperate him all their life together and yet be his delight and salvation also. Even now he found himself smiling as he heard the clink of china, and mending the fire as though it was important. All the material sources of comfort mattered extremely to Polly and one could not love her without in some sense loving them too, since all comfort seemed a part of her.

He heard her take the tea to Emma and then she was back again with two steaming cups on a tray. " 'Ot", she said, and the word seemed the promise of all bliss. With their hands round the hot cups they sat together on the hearth rug and sipped the scalding liquid. Then Polly stretched out her left hand and the stones in her ring winked in the firelight. "Pretty, ain't it?" she said. "While I'm working I'll wear it on a bit of ribbon round my neck. It'll never be off me, Job, never until I die. Don't you think no more about the things Miss Peabody said. She got 'em off her mind and now she's having a good cry and she'll be herself in the morning."

Job doubted it, but he no longer doubted the texture of their love. It was no camellia flower to be bruised by a rough touch but tough as a heather stalk. They sat in silence when the tea was finished, leaning against each other. Then Polly said, "You'd best be going, Job. You don't want to be here when Mr. Peabody comes in. Now don't fret, lad. Sleep well and have a good breakfast in the morning and go and tell the Dean. He'll tell you it don't matter, just the breaking of a clock."

"Good night, Polly," he whispered. "Good night, dearest Polly."

She went with him to the door and stood there as he walked down Angel Lane. He looked back several times, the last time at the top of the steps that would take him out of her sight, and she was still there, outlined against the light and waving to him. Presently she would go upstairs again to look after that horrible old woman, and then she would take care of a tipsy Isaac, and when at last she gained her hard little bed in the attic she would still be as cheerful as a cricket.

CHAPTER XVI *The Cathedral*

I

THE cold increased during the night and by morning the wind was from the sea and the sky was grey and lowering. The Dean had difficulty with his breathing as he stood through the psalms at matins, for the Cathedral was intensely cold. It would be warmer for the carol service tonight when the lamps and candles had been lit and nearly the whole city was here, each body giving out its quota of warmth for the good of all. How unselfishly useful a warm body could be in the winter, as useful as a glowing spirit like that of the little Polly. He rubbed his cold hands together but he could no more comfort them than he could comfort himself. He was not like Polly. His sad spirit had warmed no one. That he had spent so much of his life in sadness seemed to him now the chief of his sins. If he had had the drive of joy he might not have failed the city.

Once again he had been beaten over the North Gate slums. For the whole of the last week he had been bitterly fighting the matter out again with the mayor and corporation and the landlords, but he had made no headway against their greed or the hatred of his old enemy Josiah Turnbull. How hardly shall a rich man enter into the kingdom of heaven. He was a rich man too and he shared their guilt, for if he had been able to put a little more of his own private fortune at the disposal of the city things might have gone better. He had not done so because he must leave Elaine enough, and more than enough, for the life she would enjoy in London after his death had set her free. Even at the expense of the city Elaine had to come first.

His thoughts were wandering appallingly this morning. Usually it was not difficult for him to bring them back to the matter in hand but just lately his mind had felt like a battered bird that cannot find the window. He had not yet been able to concentrate sufficiently to finish his sermon for Christmas morning. "Much ashamed!" he said aloud, his ejaculation falling sadly into the pool of silence that had come as the aged canon in residence, at the lectern for the reading of the first lesson, searched for his spectacles. No one was startled, for these ejaculations were a common occurrence at matins and evensong.

The old canon found his spectacles and the Dean closed his eyes to concentrate better, but he could only mutter to himself of what he had to do today. He must finish his sermon. He must see Havelock at his office. He must see Albert Lee. He had promised Miss Montague that he would take Bella to see her. And then there were other duties belonging to Christmas Eve, all small things, yet they loomed up like nightmare apparitions and his mind beat about among them in growing panic until it blundered into the clock and suddenly found rest. The clock! He saw it against the darkness of his closed eyelids and knew without any doubt that Elaine would like it. This Christmas, at last, he would please her with his gift. He began to feel a little warmer and a little happier. Throughout the rest of matins he clung to the thought of the clock as to a lifeline.

He came out through the south door, held open for him by Tom Hochicorn, and shivered as the cold air met him. His cloak had slipped a little and he groped for it uncertainly. Tom Hochicorn helped him. "Cold today, sir," said Tom shyly. The Dean looked down at the old bedesman in his caped dark blue gown and crimson skull cap. He too was shivering. His eyes were watering and his long white beard stirred in the draught. He bowed low, expecting the Dean to pass on quickly with his usual brief greeting. But the Dean did not pass on. Instead he adjusted his eyeglasses and smiled at Tom. Then he looked troubled. "You are cold here, Hochicorn," he croaked. "You should sit inside in cold weather. It's too cold for you outside. Why did I not think of it before? Much distressed. You must go inside, Hochicorn."

"No, sir," said old Tom decidedly. "I must be outside to open and close the door, and to see that no one unsuitable, thieves and such, goes for to push theirselves into the Cathedral. That's my duty, sir."

"How many years have you been sitting on this hard bench?" asked the Dean.

"Six years come next Michaelmas, sir."

"It's a long time."

"It doesn't seem so to me, sir."

"You are fond of the Cathedral?"

" 'Tis my pride, sir," said Tom.

"Yes," said the Dean, "I understand. God is my glory. But I wish you would go inside, Hochicorn."

"No, sir," said Tom, a little vexed. "I must see who comes. Here's a young fellow coming now, sir. Up to no good by the look of him."

The Dean peered down the narrow cloister and saw a slim boy mounting the steps. When he was nearly at the top he stopped and the Dean recognised him. "It's Mr. Peabody's apprentice, Hochicorn," he said. "He will not harm the Cathedral." He walked down the cloister and stood at the top of the steps peering down into Job's face. "What has happened, Job?" he asked sharply. "Did you go to the Deanery to find me?"

Job swallowed. "No, sir. I was afraid Mr. Garland would not let me in. Sir, I have broken the celestial clock."

"You have what?" asked the Dean.

"The celestial clock is broken, sir, and it was my fault."

"Come back with me into the Cathedral," said the Dean. They turned back and Tom opened the door for them with another low bow. "Thank you, Hochicorn. Much obliged. If you won't go inside you must have a brazier outside. A small one. Those inside are too large. A small brazier. I'll see to it. We'll go this way, Job."

He took Job into the chantry of the Duchess Blanche and they sat down where Miss Montague had sat so long ago. The vast Cathedral soared about them and high up in the shadows there was a great rood. Job could not see it properly because it was too dark. The organist was practising for the festival. He was playing the Shepherd's Music from Bach's Christmas Oratorio. Its gentle heartbreaking loveliness contrasted strangely with the dreadfulness of the Cathedral and yet it seemed a part of it. Job began to tremble.

"You are cold?" asked the Dean.

"No, sir, but I have not been in the Cathedral before."

"No. I remember. I shall be obliged to you, Job, if you will tell me about the clock."

Job told him about it slowly and accurately, out loud to the vast darkness where they were all listening in their ranks. The sordid little story sounded very vile to his ears as he told it. When he had finished there was silence. The Dean seemed abstracted. Looking miserably up at him Job saw only his hand supporting his bent head. "That wasn't the first time I hurt the clock, sir," he said. "When I was gilding the stars I was thinking how much I hated Miss Peabody and my tool slipped and I scratched the firmament."

The Dean was still silent. Was he too angry to speak? The organist ceased playing and the echoes of his music died away and away down the dark aisles of the forest, out to the bleak fen and the cold sea.

"It does not matter, Job," said the Dean at last. "I mean it does not matter that the clock is broken. What matters is that the clock was made."

"There's a bit left, sir," said Job. "I've brought it for you." He felt in his pocket and brought out something wrapped in his handkerchief. He took out the fret of the two swans and gave it to the Dean. He thought he could not have been more miserable but when he saw it gleaming in Adam Ayscough's ugly strong hands he felt an added pang of twisting anguish.

"I am obliged to you," said the Dean. "The fret is in itself a thing of great beauty." He put it in his pocket and went on, "I beg that neither you nor Mr. Peabody will distress yourselves. It is Christmas and your hearts should be light."

"Mr. Peabody is very angry with me, sir," said Job. "He told me not to come to the shop today."

"You should disregard that prohibition," said the Dean.

"You should go to the shop and offer your apology and assistance. He will need you on Christmas Eve."

"Yes, sir, especially if he was at the Swan and Duck last night. He's very low the day after."

"Ah yes," said the Dean. "I have no experience myself of the condition but I have observed it to be very distressing once the initial exhilaration is past. I do not think, Job, that you will find him angry today. Mr. Peabody is by nature a gentle man."

"Yes," said Job in a low voice. "That is why the clock should not have been broken. He was at our mercy in his clock."

The Dean perceived that Job was about as wretched as a boy could be and he said, "Now we are here together shall we look at those carvings I told you of? The light is growing, I think."

"You are not busy, sir?"

"No, Job. I am quite at liberty and there is nothing I should like better than to show you my Cathedral. I dare to call it mine, and I believe Tom Hochicorn does too. Our presumption appears great but the glory delights to be possessed as well as to possess."

He got up and moved out from the chantry to the nave and Job followed him, at first as passively and dumbly as a whipped dog, then with awed self-forgetfulness, and finally with surging excitement. As he walked with the Dean he was almost dancing with the compulsion he had to put upon himself not to outstrip the old man beside him. Who could have told it was like this inside the mountain? Who could have known such glory existed? Why had nobody told him? What a fool he had been not to come inside before! What a fool! If Isaac had felt he had a hawk with him in the workshop the Dean thought first of an eagle, so fierce and strong was the joy beside him, and then of a terrible young archangel, incapable of fatigue, the touch of whose hand against his shivering mortal flesh was a touch of fire. The boy had forgotten there had ever been a clock. All his sorrows were under his flaming feet and his joy set a nimbus about his head. Yet he retained his awe, listening to what the Dean said, glad to the depth of him that it was with this man and no other that he was for the first time in this place.

He would see them all in years to come, Canterbury,

York, Ely, Chartres, Notre-Dame, San Marco and the golden churches of Palermo, but none of them would exalt and wring him quite as this one did today. The light grew and there were shafts of silver through the gloom. He remembered how he had dreamed of walking in a forest, where from the great-girthed boles of the trees the branches leapt to the sky, and of looking up at the dark stone cliffs of the mountain and wondering what such walls could hold, and of being below the sea where the tides washed in and out of the green gloom of caverns. Marvellous colours glowed in the windows far above him, the deep jewel colours of very old glass. There were lords and ladies here, angels and haloed saints, bishops and knights lying on their tombs, figures such as he had seen in some of Mr. Penny's old books, and fabulous creatures such as lions and unicorns, dolphins and griffins. Sometimes there was music, sounding like wind in the trees or water falling from the heights of the mountain, and sometimes silence and the far sound of a bell. There was dust here, for when he unconsciously put out his hand to feel the shape of a dolphin his long fingers came away coated with the friendly stuff. And under the miserere seats there were homely men and boys and creatures such as he knew, woodcutters and millers and ploughmen and young thieves stealing apples, foxes and owls, and small birds such as he made himself. From these he could not tear himself away. To him they were the best of all. They made him laugh and yet they brought him nearer to weeping than anything else because the men who had made them had been dead for centuries and he could not know these men. The whole world was in this place, the earth, the sky and the sea, angels, men and creatures. He looked up often at the great rood, but that he did not understand, except that it seemed to him that nothing else could have been here without that.

"It is all here," he said.

"It is all here in microcosm," said the Dean. "The whole work of God."

He lowered a miserere seat and sat down, for he was trembling with exhaustion and the saints in the window above him seemed to be emptying buckets of cold water over his head. He hoped he might be forgiven for keeping the tireless Job in ignorance of the existence of the Lady Chapel, the crypt and the chapter house.

The boy was kneeling beside him, his head bent, intent upon a man and two yoked oxen ploughing a field. The furrows of the black fen earth shone as though newly turned and at the ploughman's right a bird was singing in a thorn bush under a high midday sun, as though to cheer the labouring man and toiling beasts. The scene was full of the sense of hard driving effort. Every muscle of man and beasts seemed at full stretch. With his finger-tips he lightly touched the bird, and the ploughman's bent back. "I think it is the best of all," he murmured.

"I think I am most attached to the one I am sitting on," said the Dean. "The shepherd with his sheep. But then I have always wished that I could have been a shepherd. You no longer fear the Cathedral?"

"Not now I know these are here, sir," said Job. "I don't see how anyone could come here for the first time and not be afraid, but then this bird is here and it's no bigger than my thumb." He paused, placing his hands one on each side of the carving. "This is just the one man but the Cathedral is filled with them all."

The Dean was a little startled. "You mean filled with the men who made it?"

"Yes, sir.'

The Dean sought about in his battered mind for the words he wanted, and then fell back in relief upon the words of another man. "If you remember, Job, I showed you a bishop with mitre and crosier carved on the capital of a pillar in the south transept and told you he was Saint Augustine, a man born in North Africa in 354, long before a stone of this Cathedral was laid in place. He said this, 'And who is that God but our God, the God who made heaven and earth, who filled them because it is by filling them with himself that he has made them'. Man is made in the image of God and as you said just now what he makes he fills with himself, either with his hate or with his love."

Job did not answer. He sprang lightly to his feet and moved up and down before the long line of exquisite small carvings, as though he could not bring himself to leave them. The Dean got up unsteadily and raised his seat so that Job might look again at the shepherd bringing his sheep home to their fold. He carried a crook and had a dog at his heels and a lamb over his shoulder, and above his head the sickle moon hung in the sky. The scene was as full of peace as the other of stress. The Dean glanced from one to the other and suddenly realised something that he had not noticed before. The toiling ploughman and the peaceful shepherd were the same man. He had the same stooped shoulders, the same tall hat and heavy serf's boots. He was Everyman. He pointed this out to Job.

"Yes, I saw that," said Job. "The same craftsman must have carved both and you can see, sir, that he loved the man."

They walked towards the south door in silence but the Dean was well aware of the strong confident vow that Job had made. They thought, these young creatures, that they could bind their passions with their vows and did not know the appalling strength of human passion. Yet it was good that they made them, for under the midday sun the vows were bit and bridle upon the field horses, and as the day drew on to evening the creatures quieted.

"I shall endeavour to wait upon Mr. Peabody during the course of the day," said the Dean, "but meanwhile I beg that you will keep him from grieving over the loss of the clock. And before going to the shop will you take a message from me to Miss Peabody? Will you present my compliments and say what pleasure it would give me if she would come to the carol service tonight. And Mr. Peabody, too, and yourself and Polly. I must explain that the Christmas services this year have for me a special significance. I am deeply thankful to Almighty God that I have been spared to attend them, and it will give me deep pleasure to have my friends about me to share in my thanksgiving."

"Miss Peabody may not let me into the house, sir," said Job doubtfully. "And if she does she's not very likely to listen to what I say."

The Dean thought for a moment and then he sat down on a bench and taking a notebook and his gold pencil from his pocket wrote a few words on a page, tore it out and folded it, addressing the note to Miss Peabody. "I have written down what I said to you, Job. And I beg that before giving her this you will apologise for the hastiness of your behaviour last night."

"Yes, sir, I will," said Job, flushing scarlet. "And thank you for showing me the Cathedral."

"I have shown you only a fraction of its glory. You will come here many times by yourself I trust. It is your own, and all its citizens alive or dead. You have an inheritance to be proud of but when you are named one of the great men of the city remember that the poorest boy possesses all that you possess and yourself into the bargain. You have borne patiently with my prosing. Much obliged."

The Dean seemed to Job not so much to move away as so to unite with the shadows of the Cathedral that he could no longer be recognised as a separate entity. Job walked out through the south door smiling at Tom Hochicorn as he passed, his head up, his whole air confident and happy. Yet Tom Hochicorn was not conscious of arrogance as he passed by, indeed he received an impression so much to the contrary that it caused him to change his opinion of the boy he had thought up to no good. Here was another of them, akin to the Dean and himself. You could always tell when the Cathedral had got them by the way they left it, not proud of themselves, but proud of what had got them.

II

The Dean went back to the chantry of the Duchess Blanche and knelt down. The breaking of a pretty clock was such a small disaster, scarcely noticeable among the vast tragedies that wrenched the world, yet this small happening, he did not doubt, had wrenched the world of Isaac Peabody and his sister. All that was vile in Emma had contributed to the breaking of Isaac's clock, and Isaac would find it as hard to forgive her as Job had done. He did not know what would come of it all and there was nothing he could do, he who had come into their humble lives seeking his own comfort at the cost of theirs. And now he had no Christmas gift for Elaine. He had found the perfect gift for her and it was broken. He would not now see on her face that look of delight that he had pictured so often but never seen.

With horror he realised that he was pitying himself. For that prayer was the only cure but when he tried to pray he could find nothing in the thick darkness which enclosed him except all the things he had to do. He had better get up and do them. There was one more now, that brazier for old Hochicorn. For six years the old man had sat there shivering through the winter and he had never given it a thought. "I have ta'en too little care of this." Where did one buy a small brazier? In the town somewhere. He must go to the town. He stumbled to his knees, walked past Hochicorn, the object of his concern, without noticing him, and set out for the town. Under the Porta he collided with the Archdeacon, and so blindly that when they had recovered themselves the Archdeacon made so bold as to ask him where he was going.

"To buy a small brazier," said the Dean.

"A brazier?" ejaculated the Archdeacon.

"For Hochicorn. It is too cold for him outside the south door and he won't go inside. He must have a brazier but I do not know where to acquire one."

"Just at this moment, neither do I, Mr. Dean," said the Archdeacon. "After Christmas perhaps."

"It is today it is so cold," said the Dean sadly. "Much obliged to you, Archdeacon, much obliged. I remember that I have to see Havelock. He will perhaps know where I can acquire a brazier," and raising his hat he turned away up Worship Street. The Archdeacon looked after him anxiously, for he did not think he looked very steady on his feet. The mind too seemed a little disturbed. What did Hochicorn want with a brazier? The poor did not feel the cold.

In Mr. Havelock's office the Dean sat down gratefully by the fire and said he wanted to add a codicil to his will. Mr. Havelock felt as uneasy as the Archdeacon, for the Dean had added a number of codicils to his will during the last week and each had seemed to him slightly crazier than the last; excepting only the little legacy for Bella when she came of age; that he considered both gratifying and sensible. But the others he feared all indicated a mind disturbed. There had been, for instance, the annuity for Garland, and the gift of the Dean's gold pencil. The man had had good wages, sufficient to have something laid by, and what would a butler want with a gold pencil? And then that large sum of money left to Josiah Turnbull the mayor, his avowed enemy, to be used for the good of the city in whatever way the mayor thought fit. What an extraordinary thing to do. An annuity for Mr. Penny's housekeeper seemed as pointless as the sum left in his charge for the purchase of a pony and cart for that scoundrel Lee. What next?

"Just one more, Havelock," said the Dean, as though reading Mr. Havelock's agitated mind. "I leave to my

The Cathedral

friend Isaac Peabody my watch and my faith in God." Mr. Havelock's head went round. He picked up his pen and laid it down again. "I beg that you will write out the codicil exactly as I have dictated it," said the Dean with some asperity. "Thank you, Havelock. Much obliged."

The codicil was added to the will and witnessed by Mr. Havelock's son and the clerk. Then the Dean rose to leave. He had a little difficulty in getting to his feet and Mr. Havelock assisted him with a slight irritability, caused by the queer sense of desolation that came over him whenever he had to bring his mind to bear upon the Dean's will. "You should not come to the office in this way, Mr. Dean," he said curtly. "You must send for me to the Deanery when you wish to see me."

"Poor men must come to your office," said the Dean, "and I in the dereliction of my days am the poorest of the poor. Do you know, Mr. Havelock, where I can buy a small brazier?"

Now Mr. Havelock was quite sure about the mental disturbance and he spoke gently and persuasively as to a child. "It is time for your luncheon, Mr. Dean. I beg that you will go straight home to luncheon." As he opened the office door and ushered the Dean out into the market place he laid his hand for a moment on his arm. "God bless you, sir," he said.

To be blessed by Havelock of all people so astonished the Dean that he felt stronger, and the walk down through the city to Swithins Lane did not seem so impossibly far as it had seemed to him when he had thought of it during matins. The dark clouds had parted now and a cold silver sunlight illumined the city, catching in its net all the colour and gaiety of the Christmas shops and shoppers. The Dean had not walked through the city since his illness and he looked at it as a man looks at the spring after a long hard winter. He had forgotten how beautiful it was, he had forgotten how poignantly he loved it, and he wanted to stretch out a hand to hold it lest its beauty pass away from him before he had had time fully to feast his eyes and heart upon it. But he could not do that, and the streets and the happy crowds seemed to flow past him like a quick bright river, these Christmas streets and people, and the streets and people that he remembered on spring and autumn days in past years, and summer nights of moon and stars. He did not distinguish very clearly between the past and the present, between this century or another. Some of the men and women who passed by, smiling at him, seemed to him to be not of this age. But he was not surprised to see them and he returned each shy greeting with a smile and a courteous lifting of his tall hat. People spoke for many days afterwards of the way the Dean had walked down through the city that morning, not forging along in his usual fiercely abstracted state but looking at them with great kindness, smiling and lifting his hat even though many who greeted him were strangers to him. But when he reached Swithins Lane the Dean smiled at no one, so dreadful did it seem to him after the gay and happy streets that had flowed past him up above in the city. The silver sunlight did not seem to penetrate to Swithins Lane and there were no decorated Christmas trees in the dark and dirty windows. And he had failed to cleanse this place. The men and women and children who rotted and died here must continue to rot and die because he had failed. The crash of the celestial clock falling to pieces was in his ears as he entered the fish shop and lifted his hat to Keziah.

The old crone was in a flutter of pleasure at seeing him and Lee wrung his hand so strongly that he could have cried out with the pain of it. The great lout of a boy whom he had procured from the workhouse was grinning in the background and it was obvious to the Dean that he was in a state of well-being, and that one blow of his huge red fist would have felled a tipsy Albert instantly to the ground, and probably had already done so. The warmth of the greeting he received took the Dean entirely by surprise. He had prayed much for this man and woman but his humility never expected, or even much desired, to have the answer to prayer presented to him like the head of John the Baptist on a plate. Yet in this place there was undoubtedly a change. The atmosphere was less dark and evil. Giving thanks to God alone he said to Albert, "I have come to thank you, Mr. Lee, for your faithful service to the Deanery. During my recent illness I fancied only a light diet and was much obliged to you for the delicious fish with which I was served." A pang of guilt went through him, for he seldom noticed what he ate and did not suppose that Garland had allowed the Swithins Lane fish to penetrate to his sick room, but the pleasure of Albert and Keziah seemed almost to justify a probable lie, and Keziah muttered something about business being better now it was known they supplied the Deanery.

"I wish you and your son could have a shop in a better locality, ma'am," said the Dean. "And I would like to see Mr. Lee driving out to the villages with a pony and trap. Were you born in the fen, Mr. Lee?"

Albert looked at him with stupefaction. How did the old codger know about him wanting a pony and trap? He said, "I was born in the fen, sir. Out beyond Willowthorn." Old Keziah began to mumble something about the smart painted van she'd had out in the drove and Albert chimed in with reminiscences of varied types of horseflesh, and the dog Pharaoh. He'd fancy a dog again, to run behind the trap. Even with his hand behind his ear the Dean was not very sure what they said but was most happy that they should be saying it. "Much obliged," he murmured gratefully when it was time to say good-bye. "A happy Christmas to you." He went to the back of the shop and shook hands with the lout of a boy, and pressed a five-shilling piece into his huge red palm. At the door, replacing his hat after bowing to Keziah, he suddenly remembered something else and said anxiously, "Do you know, Mr. Lee, where I can procure a small brazier?"

Lee and Keziah shook their heads doubtfully but the lout of a boy remarked hoarsely from behind them, "There's one out the back." Lee slapped his thigh, remembering that he'd come by it two years ago when old Cobb, the roast chestnut man, had been took to the workhouse. He'd put it in the shed and forgot it. He and the boy went out to the shed and the sound of crashing ironmongery told of its exhumation from beneath a heap of scrap-iron and empty tins. Back in the shop it was dusted down and bent back into shape and emerged as a very nice little brazier indeed.

"What would you be wanting to do with it, sir?" asked Albert.

The Dean explained about Hochicorn, and also remarked anxiously that he did not know to whom he should apply for charcoal. "I am not a practical man, I fear," he said sadly. "I should have informed myself as to these matters earlier in life.'

"Leave it to me, sir," said Albert. "I knew old 'Ochicorn

when I was a boy. I used to go round sellin' clothes pegs with me poor grannie and 'e'd always buy a few. I'll take it up to 'im and git it goin'. I can come by a bit of charcoal."

"I am much obliged to you," said the Dean with profound relief, and took his purse from his pocket. But Albert shook his head. "No, sir," he said. "There's nothin' I wouldn't do for you. An' I didn't pay nothin' for that brazier. I come by it."

"I thank you, Mr. Lee," said the Dean. "I am grateful for your kindness. You know your way to the south door?"

"No, sir. I ain't ever been to the Cathedral."

The Dean explained the route with sadness. How many of the men and women of the city had never been inside the Cathedral? To some of them it was no more than a great stone mountain in their midst. He said good-bye once more and went away wondering how it had happened that in this nineteenth century the poor of the city were not at home in their Cathedral. In past centuries it had not been so. Had he and his kind in some way barred it to them? The shepherds had allowed themselves to become wealthy and the sheep were frightened of the rich man's house. Nor did they follow a shepherd who did not share with them their own rough weather and hard going.

He went grieving up through the empty streets of the city, deserted now because the sun had gone in and the weather looked threatening, and did not notice that they were empty. But he knew he had to go to Cockspur Street and presently he found himself inside the little shop, sitting on the customers' chair and facing Isaac across the counter. Job had gone home and there was no one else in the shop. They looked at each other in mute distress and neither knew what to say.

"It may be for good," said the Dean at last. "It has taught Job something. It may prove to be the casting out of evil for your poor sister. I pray so. You must take great care of your sister, Mr. Peabody. Go back now to the point when you took the clock home to give her pleasure, forgive what came after and build up the work of love from there. Think that she is a woman who has had a severe illness. If you do not help her to recovery no one will."

"Will you choose another clock for Mrs. Ayscough?" asked Isaac dully, as though he had not heard a word.

The Cathedral

"No," said the Dean, "I will give her the fret of the two swans." He had not known until he spoke that this was what he was going to do but now it seemed to him right that he should do so. "It is more beautiful by itself than when it surmounted the clock."

There was a flash of anger in Isaac's blue eyes at the idiocy of this remark, and the Dean was glad to see it for it brought back life to his miserable sullen old face. "By itself it is nothing but a bit of bent metal, sir," he said.

"It is much more than that, Mr. Peabody. The fret of the two swans, creatures who it is said sing for joy at their death, says to me that my affection for you, and yours for me, will always endure." The Dean put his clasped hands on the counter and to avoid looking at his eyes, for he was not going to be compelled into forgiving Emma against his will, Isaac looked at the hands and remembered suddenly that he had seen them clasped in that way on that Sunday morning that seemed now several centuries ago. They had lain then on the velvet cushion of the Dean's stall and had been clasped in prayer for the city. Isaac rubbed his nose irritably. There was no escape from that which pursued him in this terrible man.

"Mr. Peabody, I beg that you will listen to me and endeavour to believe what I say. The love that created and gave the clock is of more value because the clock is broken. It has entered into eternity, as does the soul when the body fails and dies. If I die before you, Mr. Peabody, I shall find the love that made and gave the clock awaiting me. Perhaps I might not have done so had it not been broken. It will give me welcome." Isaac was still sullenly silent and after a moment or two the Dean unclasped his hands and got up. "I must go, Mr. Peabody, for I am already late for luncheon and I do not wish to alarm my wife. Will you be at the carol service this evening? It would give me infinite pleasure to see you there with your sister and Job and Polly."

Isaac helped him into his cloak, handed him his stick and did not answer. He was not going to live with Emma any more. Why should he live with a woman he hated? Once Christmas was over he would leave Angel Lane and live at the shop.

"Good afternoon, sir," he said politely, opening the shop

door. "I trust that you and Mrs. Ayscough will spend a happy Christmas."

"Good afternoon, Mr. Peabody," said the Dean gently. "Much obliged."

Isaac went back to sit behind the counter and his cruelty frightened him. But he was not going to forgive Emma. He sat there hugging his hatred to him.

The sky had darkened still more while the Dean talked to Mr. Peabody and when he reached the market place a shower of cold sleety rain beat full in his face. Passing St. Peter's church he stopped a moment, feeling breathless and ill.

"Come inside, sir, come inside," piped a high quavering old voice. "Come in here and shelter."

The Dean stepped inside the porch and sat down beside old Mr. Penny, who peered up at him inquisitively and inquired, "Who are you?"

"Adam," said the Dean.

"Adam," said Mr. Penny. "Do I know you?"

"We were together once, sir, in another storm. We were Lear and his fool taking shelter together as we are now. I am Lear's fool."

"Lear's fool wasn't called Adam," said Mr. Penny decidedly. "Not that I know of. Would you like an apple?"

He had a large basket at his feet filled with apples and oranges and little parcels wrapped in coloured paper. "For the children of my parish," he said importantly. "Ruth wrapped them up. I shall take them round when the rain stops. I've had my luncheon. Have you had yours?"

"Not yet," said the Dean.

"Then have an apple," said Mr. Penny, and diving into his basket he took out the largest and rosiest.

"Much obliged," said the Dean, and ate it gratefully, for he found he was hungry.

Mr. Penny watched him for a little while with a seraphic smile and then suddenly his soft old face crinkled with childish distress. "I can't write my sermon for tomorrow," he said. "I can't think what to say."

"Nor can I," said the Dean.

"Have you to preach tomorrow?"

"I have," said the Dean.

"Where are you going to preach?"

"At the church of St. Michael and All Angels."

"Where's that?"

"At the top of the hill."

"I don't know where that is," said Mr. Penny. "Ruth will know." Then suddenly a bright idea struck him. "I'll bring my congregation to hear you preach and then I shan't have to preach myself. Would that be a sin?"

"I am not sure," said the Dean slowly. "Ruth will know."

Mr. Penny took a handkerchief out of his pocket and tied a knot in it. "That's to ask her," he said. "People call me forgetful but I'm not forgetful if I've tied a knot. The sun's out again. I must go to the children." He got up and laid his hand kindly on the Dean's shoulder. "Stay there and rest, my friend. What did you say your name was? Adam. Remember, Adam, if there's anything I can do for you at any time, if you're short of money, or hungry, or anything of that sort, you've only to come to the vicarage and I'll do all in my poor power. God bless you."

Mr. Penny grasped the handle of his basket and went out into the sunlight. The Dean watched him trotting across the street to the market place and disappearing into Mrs. Martin's bakery like an ancient rabbit into its burrow. Mrs. Martin must have her grandchildren with her for there was a Christmas tree in the window. Mr. Penny was changed since the Dean had seen him last. He was not so thin and his eyes were happy. His mode of progression was no longer that sad aimless waver but a fairly brisk trot. "Ruth and good food," thought the Dean, and he thanked God.

In spite of all the things he had to do he went on sitting in the porch, for fatigue encased him like lead. He felt too tired to go inside the church and as he sat with his eyes shut, thinking of it, he saw the tombs decorated with holly and the ancient windows with their colours staining the paving stones. And welling up through the broken floor was that spring of water. It refreshed him where he sat in the porch, as though the cracked old paving stones were the crust of his own mortality. After a while he pulled himself to his feet, remembering with joy that the next thing he had to do was to take Bella to call on Miss Montague. But first he must reassure them at home. He got himself back to the Deanery and Garland opened the door.

"I lunched out, Garland," he said, for he did not want to put the household to the trouble of getting him luncheon now, at two-thirty.

"You did not mention that you were doing so, sir," said Garland irritably, for the last hour had not been a happy one for him.

"I apologise, Garland," said the Dean humbly. "I trust Mrs. Ayscough has not been anxious?"

"Yes, sir," said Garland without mercy. "Mrs. Ayscough has suffered considerable anxiety."

"Much distressed," murmured the Dean and hurried to the drawing-room, past the tall Christmas tree which stood in the hall tastefully decorated by Garland.

"Wherever have you been, Adam?" asked Elaine. She was kneeling on the floor surrounded by parcels and piles of tissue paper and coloured ribbons, packing up the servants' presents for Garland to hang on the tree. All their married life Adam had insisted on having a tree and presents for the servants. After tea on Christmas Day they stood ranged in their ranks according to seniority, Cook at one end and the tweeny at the other, and Garland took the gifts from the tree and Adam presented them with heavy anxious courtesy. He found this a great ordeal, she knew, but it was nothing to what she had to do, buying and packing the gifts. Each Christmas she was freshly exhausted. She rose wearily to her feet, pushing her hair back from her face. "Where have you been? Why didn't you tell me you were lunching out?"

"My dear, it was unexpected. I lunched with the vicar of St. Peter's. Forgive me that I did not inform you."

Her beauty, with her face a little flushed and her hair ruffled, took him freshly by surprise, though it was always surprising him. This shock of surprise was in all real beauty, he thought. If one was not surprised it was only a counterfeit. He took her in his arms and asked her to forgive him and for once she did not hold herself rigid but leaned against him in the relaxation of relief. She had been genuinely anxious. "Oh, Adam, I am so tired," she murmured.

"Why, my dear?"

"All these parcels for the servants! It's too much for me. And I can't even ask my maid to help me since you don't want them to know what presents they are having. I must get them done before tea for I'll be far too tired after the carol service."

"I'll help you," said the Dean. "I'll help you at once. I

must speak to Garland for a moment in my study and then I will be with you. Did you, my dear, get the doll for little Bella?"

"It's here somewhere," said Elaine, and stooping she picked up a large cardboard box from the floor. "Though I think you make a great mistake, showering that child with presents. It will only lead to jealousy in other quarters."

The Dean thought sadly that it was only too likely. He thought of Isaac and the broken clock and his heart was heavy. What harm unpurified and undisciplined human love could do. He believed it must pass through death before it could entirely bless. Then he lifted the lid of the box and forgot his sorrow in pleasure.

In the world of toys he lacked experience but he believed this to be the most wonderful doll ever created. It was rosy-cheeked and blue-eyed with a dimpled chin and hair of a yellow as startling as Bella's own. It was clothed in pink satin and its rosy bonnet was lined with lace. Very shyly he lifted the stiff satin skirt with his forefinger and perceived that its undergarments also were trimmed with lace. He lowered the skirt reverently and saw that it had pink leather shoes and a small gilt reticule hanging from its tiny waist.

"Thank you, Elaine," he murmured. "Thank you, my dear, with all my heart. You must have gone to great trouble in choosing this beautiful doll."

"Oh, no," said Elaine airily. "I ordered it from Town with the servants' things. But it is a pretty doll. I believe it says mama if you stand it upright."

The Dean stood it gingerly upright and it said mama. He was immensely cheered. "I'll be back with you in a moment, my dear," he said, and took it with him to the study in its box.

It was very difficult to write and tell Miss Montague that after all he feared he would not be able to take Bella to see her this afternoon, for this would be the first time for some years that he had not visited her on Christmas Eve. He had to write the same news to Mrs. Havelock but he trusted that Bella's sanguine spirit would not be cast down if, as he suggested to Mrs. Havelock, the doll were presented to her concurrently with the reception of the news. He sealed the two notes and rang for Garland. "These must go at once," he said. "The doll for Miss Bella too. Do you like it, Garland?"

"A very fine doll indeed, sir," said Garland. "Miss Bella cannot fail to be gratified."

He put the box under his arm and moved rather slowly towards the door. He wished he could take it round himself. Wouldn't take him more than a few minutes. She might be about and he'd see her face when she took the lid off. The Dean watched him with a smile. "I would be obliged, Garland, if you would yourself be my messenger this afternoon. Have you the leisure?"

"Certainly, sir," said Garland briskly.

"Much obliged," said the Dean. "It will be of no consequence if tea is a little late."

He went back to the drawing-room to help Elaine. His clumsy hands were not very efficient at folding paper and tying ribbon, and the sweat poured off him with the labour and concentration involved, but he managed fairly creditably and Elaine was set free to sit at her escritoire and write out the little labels that were to be attached. After tea he made her put her feet up on the sofa and he read aloud to her to rest her until it was time for the six o'clock carol service. To the pealing of the bells they walked across the garden to the Cathedral together and as they walked she took one gloved hand from her muff and slipped it into his.

CHAPTER XVII   *Christmas*

I

EVERY year, at half-past-five on Christmas Eve, Michael lifted his great fist and struck the double quarter, and the Cathedral bells rang out. They pealed for half-an-hour and all over the city, and in all the villages to which the wind carried the sound of the bells, they knew that Christmas had begun. People in the fen wrapped cloaks about them and went out of doors and stood looking towards the city. This year it was bitterly cold but the wind had swept the clouds away and the Cathedral on its hill towered up among the stars, light shining from its windows. Below it the twinkling city lights were like clustering fireflies about its feet. The tremendous bell music that was rocking the tower and pealing through the city was out here as lovely and far away as though it rang out from the stars themselves, and it caught at men's hearts. "Now 'tis Christmas," they said to each other, as their forbears had said for centuries past, looking towards the city on the hill and the great fane that was as much a part of their blood and bones as the fen itself. " 'Tis Christmas," they said, and went back happy to their homes.

In the city, as soon as the bells started, everyone began to get ready. Then from nearly every house family parties came out and made their way up the steep streets towards the Cathedral. Quite small children were allowed to stay up for the carol service, and they chattered like sparrows as they stumped along buttoned into their thick coats, the boys gaitered and mufflered, the girls with muffs and fur bonnets. It was the custom in the city to put lighted candles in the windows on Christmas Eve and their light, and the light of the street lamps, made of the streets ladders of light leaning against the hill. The grown-ups found them Jacob's ladders tonight, easy to climb, for the bells and the children tugged them up.

Nearly everyone entered by the west door, for they loved the thrill of crossing the green under the moon and stars, and mounting the steps and gazing up at the west front, and then going in through the Porch of Angels beneath Michael and the pealing bells. Some of them only came to the Cathedral on this one day in the year, but as they entered the nave they felt the impact of its beauty no less keenly than those who came often. It was always like a blow between the eyes, but especially at night, and especially on Christmas Eve when they were full of awe and expectation. There were lights in the nave but they could do no more than splash pools of gold here and there, they could not illumine the shadows above or the dim unlighted chantries and half-seen tombs. The great pillars soared into darkness and the aisles narrowed to twilight. Candles twinkled in the choir and the high altar with its flowers was ablaze with them, but all the myriad flames were no more than seed pearls embroidered on a dark cloak. The great rood was veiled in shadow. All things alike went out into mystery. The crowd of tiny human creatures flowed up the nave and on to the benches. The sound of their feet, of their whispering voices and rustling garments, was lost in the vastness. The music of the organ flowed over them and they were still.

But a few came in through the south door and Tom Hochicorn gave them greeting as he stood bowing by his brazier. Albert Lee had worked quickly, had come by some charcoal and had it lighted and installed by the time the bells began to ring. He had sat on the bench chatting to old Tom for a while and then, as people began to arrive, he took fright and was all for escaping back to Swithins Lane, but old Tom grabbed him and held on with surprising strength. "Go inside, Bert," he commanded.

"What, me?" gasped Albert Lee. "In there? Not bloody likely!"

"Why not, Bert?"

"Full of toffs," said Albert Lee. " 'Ere, Tom, you leggo. I don't want to 'urt you."

"You won't see no toffs," said old Tom. "Not to notice. Just a lot of spotted ladybirds a-setting on the floor. That's all they look like in there. You go in, Bert. Not afraid, are you?"

"Afraid?" scoffed Albert Lee. "I ain't been afraid of nothink not since I was born."

"Go in, then," said Tom. He opened the door and motioned to Albert. "Look here. See that pillar? The one by the stove. There's a chair behind it. No one won't see you if you set behind that pillar. If you look round it when you hear the Dean speaking you'll see him."

He had hold of Albert by his coat collar. Albert didn't want to make a scene or own himself afraid. He found himself inside with the door softly closed behind him. Sweating profusely he crept to the chair behind the pillar and sat down on its extreme edge. Cor, what a place! It was like old Tom had said. No one didn't notice you in here. You were too small. Cor, this was a terrible place! It was like night up there. But the door was near, and so was the homely-looking stove. For a while his eyes clung to the door, and then as the warmth of the stove flowed out to him his terror began to subside. It was nice and warm in his corner. No one couldn't see him. He'd sit for a while. The bells were pretty but he didn't like that great humming rumbling music that was sending tremors through his legs. Then it stopped, and the bells too, and there was silence, and then miles away he heard boys singing.

They came nearer and nearer, singing like the birds out in the fen in spring. One by one men's voices began to join in, and then the multitude of men and women whom he could scarcely see began to sing too. The sound grew, soaring up to the great darkness overhead. It pulled him to his feet. He didn't know the words and he didn't know the music but he had sung with the Romany people in his boyhood, sitting round the camp fire in the drove, and he'd been quick to pick up a tune. He was now. He dared not

use his coarsened voice but the music sang in his blood like
sap rising in a tree. When the hymn ended there was a
strange rustling sound, like leaves stirring all over a vast
forest. It startled him at first until he realised that it was
all the toffs kneeling down. He knelt too, his tattered cap
in his hands, and the slight stir of his movement was drawn
into the music of all the other movements. For the forest
rustling was also music and that too moved in his blood.
There was silence again and far away he heard the Dean's
voice raised in the bidding prayer. He could not distinguish
a word but the familiar voice banished the last of his fear.
When the prayer ended he said Amen as loudly as any and
was no longer conscious of loneliness. From then until the
end he was hardly conscious even of himself.

There were not many who were. It was that which made
this particular Christmas Eve carol service memorable
above all others in the city's memory. The form of it was
the same as always. The familiar hymns and carols followed
each other in the familiar order, the choir sang "Wonderful,
Counsellor, the Mighty God, the everlasting Father, the
Prince of Peace," as gloriously as ever but not more so, for
they always put the last ounce into it, the difference was
that instead of the congregation enjoying themselves enjoying the carol service they were enjoying the carol service.
They were not tonight on the normal plane of human experience. When they had climbed the Jacob's ladders of the
lighted streets from the city to the Cathedral they had
climbed up just one rung higher than they usually did.

There was another difference. The form of this service
was the same as aways but the emphasis was different.
Generally the peak of it all was the anthem but tonight it
was the Christmas gospel, read as always by the Dean.

Adam Ayscough walked with a firm step to the lectern,
put on his eyeglasses and found the place. As he and Elaine
had left the Deanery to go to the Cathedral he had been in
great fear, for he had not known if he would be able to get
through the service. Then as they crossed the garden she
had slipped her hand into his and he had known he would
do it. "All shall be well and all manner of thing shall be
well." He cleared his throat. "The first verse of the first
chapter of the gospel according to St. John," he said. His
sight, he found, was worse than usual and the page was
misty. But it was no matter for he knew the chapter by

heart. He raised his head and looked out over the congregation. "In the beginning was the Word, and the Word was with God."

His voice was like a raucous trumpet, it had such power behind it. The people listened without movement, but though they had all come filled with thankfulness because he would be here tonight they were not thinking of him as they had thought of him on other Christmas Eves, thinking how ugly he was, how awkward, but yet how in place there in the lectern, looming up above them in his strange rugged strength, they were thinking only of what he was saying. "The Word was made flesh and dwelt among us." Was it really true? Could it be true? If it was true, then the rood up there was the king-pin that kept all things in perpetual safety and they need never fear again. To many that night Adam Ayscough's speaking of the Christmas gospel was a bridge between doubt and faith, perhaps because it came to them with such a splendid directness. He stood for a moment looking out over the people, then left the lectern and went back to his stall. His sight had been too dim to see them when he looked at them and he had no knowledge that he had been of service to them.

Nor, when at the conclusion of the service the Bishop and clergy, the choir and the whole congregation, flocked down to the west end of the nave for the traditional singing of "Now thank we all our God," did he know that his presence with them all was one of the chief causes of their thanksgiving. But when the Bishop had blessed them, and the clergy and choir had turned to go to their vestries, he did what no Dean had ever done before and moving to the west door stood there to greet the people as they went out. To break with tradition in this manner was unlike him, for he revered tradition, yet he found himself moving to the west door.

He had no idea that quite so many people as this came to the Cathedral on Christmas Eve. Surely nearly the whole city was here. Most of them only dared to smile at him shyly as they passed by, but some bolder spirits spoke to him, saying they were glad he was better and returning his good wishes when he wished them a happy Christmas. To his astonished delight almost all those who in the last few months had become so especially dear to him, like his own small flock of sheep, were among those who gave him a special greeting.

Bella was there, in her cherry-red outfit, clasping her doll. "She would come," her grandmother whispered to him, "though it's long past her bedtime, and she would bring her doll. I knew it was not right but I could not prevent it." Mrs. Havelock was looking extremely tired and the Dean took her hand to reassure her. Bella, who had been looking as smugly solid as a stationary robin, suddenly became airborne and darted off into the night. Mrs. Havelock, abruptly dropping the Dean's hand, fled in pursuit.

Mr. Penny was there, not identifying the Dean in his robes with Lear's fool, and bowing very shyly as he passed, and Ruth with her wise calm smile and little Miss Throstle of the umbrella shop. Albert Lee was there, borne along by the crowd as an integral part of it and quite comfortable in his nonentity, and yet bold as well as comfortable for he was one of those who paused to wish the Dean a happy Christmas. Polly and Job were there, as he had known they would be, but they smiled at him as though from a vast distance, and he was glad of it. They were in their own world. Polly wore her bonnet with the cherry-coloured ribbons and her left hand lay on Job's right arm in the traditional manner of those who are walking out. She had left her glove off on purpose that the world might see her ring.

With them was Miss Peabody, looking not so much ill as convalescent. She was one of those for whom despair, to which she had lived so near for so long, had receded during the reading of the Christmas gospel. Yet she would have slipped past the Dean unnoticed had he not stopped her and taken her hand. "A happy Christmas, Miss Peabody," he said cheerfully, as though there had been no clock. "I am obliged to you for coming tonight. Much obliged. God bless you."

But the one he had most wished to see, Isaac, was not there. As he walked home he was deeply unhappy. Isaac and Elaine, he feared, he had loved only to their hurt, and he prayed God to forgive him.

Back in the Deanery again there were many matters to attend to and it was not until late in the evening that he went to his study to finish writing his Christmas sermon. He turned back to the beginning of it, to refresh his mind

Christmas

as to what he had already written, and as he read he was in despair. It was a terrible sermon for its Christmas purpose of joy and love. It was academic, abstruse, verbose. Why was it that he could write a book but could not write a sermon? He told himself that a sermon was a thing of personal contact, and in personal contacts he had always failed most miserably. Already, as he turned the pages of this most wretched sermon, he could feel the wave of boredom and dislike that always seemed to beat up in his face when he tried to preach, and he shrank miserably within himself. Nevertheless the sermon had to be written and it had to be preached and he picked up his pen, dipped it in the ink and began to write.

But presently he found to his dismay that he could not see what he wrote. He turned back to the earlier pages and found they were as blurred as the page of the gospels had been when he stood in the lectern. He realised that he was too tired to prepare this sermon, too tired even to sit here any longer at his desk. Fear took hold of him. This dimming of his sight had not mattered this evening, for he had known what he had to say, but in the pulpit it would be fatal, for he had never been able to preach in any other way than by reading aloud from the written page. The gospel he had known by heart. "By heart." It seemed to his bewilderment and fatigue as though a voice had spoken. A great simplicity had come into his life these last months, a grace that had been given to him with the friendship of humble people. Could he tomorrow preach from his heart and not his intellect? Could he look upon his heart with his inward eyes and speak what he found written upon it? A man's heart was a tablet of God, who wrote upon it what he willed. He took up the manuscript of his sermon and tore it across, flinging the fragments into the waste-paper basket.

Then he lit the candle that stood upon a side table, put out the lamp and went out into the darkened hall. When there was much work to be done he often went to bed very late and by his command no servant waited up for him. He climbed the stairs slowly with his candle, and as he climbed the clamour of the bells broke out once more. It was midnight, the hour of Christ's birth. At the top of the stairs there was a window. He put his candle down on the sill and stood for a moment in prayer. Then he opened the old casement a few inches and the sound of the bells swept in to him on a breath of cold air. He closed the window again and saw that a snowflake lay on his hand.

II

He slept deeply that night, a thing he had not done for months past, then woke at his usual early hour, dressed and made his meditation. Then he left the house for the first service of Christmas Day. As he closed the garden door behind him he stood in amazement, for he had stepped not into the expected darkness but into light. It was neither of the sun nor moon but of the snow. The sky was a cold clear green behind the dark mass of the Cathedral, the wind had dropped and the stillness was absolute. The snow was not deep but it covered the garden with light. He moved forward a few steps and looked about him. The roof of the Cathedral, every parapet and ledge, the roofs of the houses and the boughs of the trees all bore their glory of snow. He walked slowly through the garden in awe and joy, thinking of the myriad snowflakes under his feet, each one a cluster of beautiful shapes of stars and flowers and leaves, all too small to be seen by any eye except that of their Creator, yet each giving light. That was why he always wanted a white Christmas. Almighty God had been so small, as small as the crystal of a snowflake in comparison with the universe that he had made. "Such light!" murmured the Dean as he opened the door into the Cathedral. "Such light!"

In the Cathedral it was still dark, for he was very early, as he liked to be, and only the lights in the sanctuary were as yet lit, but he could have found his way about the Cathedral blindfold. He went into the chantry of the Duchess Blanche and knelt down and as he began his prayer he found that light was in his mind and spirit. The darkness of yesterday had been taken from him.

III

After breakfast Elaine stood in the drawing-room, one hand on the mantelpiece, looking down into the fire, steeling herself for the moment between breakfast and matins when she and Adam always gave each other their Christmas presents. She never knew what to give him, for he had no hobbies apart from this recent rather ridiculous one of horology, and he was indifferent to what he ate. This year she had a book of travel for him which she had chosen at

Joshua Appleby's bookshop. If he did not like the reading matter it was at least a book, and she believed that he liked books not only for their contents but for their shape and feel, for she had seen him touch and turn their pages as though each one were a unique thing of beauty, like the petals of a flower. She had only noticed this just lately, during his illness. There were many things about him that she had not noticed until just lately. But even more difficult than her gift to him was his to her. Once again she would have to simulate pleasure at sight of some trinket that she would never be able to wear. Her beauty being her *raison d'être* it was impossible for her to desecrate it by some jewel that was not in keeping with its perfection. Adam's taste in clothes and jewels was atrocious.

He came in and she gave him his book and saw that she had truly pleased him. "*The Isles of Greece*, Elaine," he said as he turned the pages. "You have remembered how I went there as a young man. My dear, I love you for it." She had not remembered but she smiled very sweetly at him and accepted his tribute. When sensitive apprehensions were attributed to her she was always able to appropriate them quickly. It was a part of her charm.

Adam laid the book aside and now it was her turn. Her heart sank. But he produced no jeweller's velvet case from his pocket, instead he said to her, "My dear, I have no real gift for you this year. I must tell you why." Then he told her about the celestial clock, describing its beauty, telling her that by some mischance it had fallen and been broken. "There is only the fret left," he said. "I am sorry that it is all I have to give you."

He put it into her hands and she carried it to the window and gave an exclamation of pleasure, so delighted was she to find it was nothing she might be expected to wear. The Dean was startled. She stood in the wonderful snowlight, which could not dim her beauty but only enhance it, and on her face was the look of pleasure he had longed to see, called there by the fragment of a broken clock. Truly there was no understanding women. He did not try to understand. She was pleased and he was content to love her beauty and her pleasure.

"I am so sorry the clock was broken, Adam," she said, "but I like this fret. I shall use it as a paper-weight." She looked at him with a smile. "It will help me not to lose my letters as I did Ruth's. The bells have started. I must put on my things."

"I'll wait here for you, my dear," said the Dean. "We will go together."

Waiting for her he had a moment of panic about his sermon but he put it from him. What a peculiar thing the mind was. Yesterday had been full of darkness and distress, both pressing sorely upon him, but today he was happy and at peace, and though physical malaise never left him now it seemed pleasantly relaxed, like a hand that has relinquished its grip though not its hold.

Elaine came back wrapped in her furs and this time, instead of going through the garden, they went out into the Close, to look at the wonder of the lime avenue under snow. The sun shone now in a cloudless blue sky and the splendour of the white world awed even Elaine. All over the city the bells were ringing and the shining silence of the white snow seemed to answer them. They walked slowly towards the south door along a path swept clear of snow On either side it was piled in miniature snow mountains, silver-crested and pooled with azure. "We used to have white Christmases like this when I was a boy," said the Dean with satisfaction.

"How do you feel today, Adam?" asked Elaine. She was already beginning to dread his sermon and there was genuine anxiety in her voice.

"I feel very well," he answered. "Do you remember our walking through the garden together yesterday evening? You gave me strength, my dear, when you put your hand in mine. It is so, through every touch of love, that God strengthens us."

They had reached the south door and Hochicorn was beaming and bowing beside his brazier. The Dean stopped to speak to him and Elaine went on into the Cathedral. Although she was looking superbly beautiful in her sables and holly-green velvet her progress to her seat lacked something of its usual dramatic perfection. It was graceful but unstudied and Mary Montague, in her usual place in her bath-chair, noticed it. "Did she feel the Dean's illness at all?" she wondered. "Can the wells have broken? No, not yet, but the wind has changed."

The congregation in the Cathedral on Christmas morning at matins was not the large one of Christmas Eve, when the carol service was the only one in the city, it was the usual Sunday congregation, but larger than was customary because it was Christmas Day. It was a distinguished congregation, containing all the *élite* of the city. As the Dean walked in procession to his stall past the long rows of well-dressed, well-fed people, his nose was assailed by delicate perfumes, the scent of rich furs and shoe polish, and in spite of his happiness panic rose in him again, and this time he could not subdue it. How could he have imagined that he could preach a simple extempore sermon to people such as these? They would be outraged. He would bring shame upon the Bishop and his learned brethren of the chapter, upon the Cathedral and upon Elaine. He did not know how to preach extempore. Nervous and anxious as he always was when he had to speak in public he had never attempted such a thing. He was so dismayed that by the time he reached the choir his hands were clammy and trembling. Then, as he settled into the Dean's stall like a statue into its niche, reassurance came to him from the great joyous Cathedral. He was as much a humble part of it as the shepherd under the miserere seat, as the knights on their tombs and the saints and angels in the windows, as the very stones and beams of its structure. They all had their function to perform in its Christmas adoration and not the humblest or the least would be allowed to fall.

As the Te Deum soared to the roof, to the sky, and took wings to the four corners of the earth, he felt himself built into the fabric of the singing stones and the shouting exulting figures all about him. The stamping of the unicorns, the roaring of the lions and the noise the angels made with their trumpets and cymbals almost drowned the thunder of the organ. The knights sang on their tombs and the saints in their windows, and the homely men and boys and birds were singing under the miserere seats. Adam Ayscough was not surprised. He had had a similar experience long ago as a child, although until this moment he had forgotten it. The human brain was an organ of limitation. It restricted a grown man's consciousness of the exterior world to what was practically useful to him. It was like prison walls. Without them possibly he could not have concentrated sufficiently upon the task he had to do. But in childhood and old age the prison walls were of cloudy stuff and there were occasional rents in them.

The tremendous music sang on in him after the Te

Deum had ended but it did not prevent him from doing efficiently all that he had to do. He made the right responses, he walked to the lectern to read the second lesson and returned to his stall again, and during the hymn before the sermon he knelt in his stall to pray as he always did. But today he did not pray for strength to mount the huge pulpit under the sounding board, for he hardly remembered it. He prayed for the city.

Yet when he was in the pulpit he instinctively steeled himself against that wave of boredom and resignation that always rose and broke over him when he stood above the distant congregation like Punch on his stage. It did not come. There was no distance. They were all as close to him as his own body. His sight was better today and he looked down at them for a moment; at Elaine in her pew, her head bent and her hands in her muff, at Mary Montague in her bath-chair, at Mr. Penny over to his right, quite close to him. The knot in Mr. Penny's handkerchief had done all that was asked of it and Mr. Penny sat in the midst of his flock, Miss Peabody on his right and Job and Polly on his left. He was looking up at the Dean in a state of rapture and bland attention. He had not had to preach himself this morning. It was years since he had had the pleasure of listening to another man's sermon and he was enjoying himself. The Dean forgot all about the well-dressed critical men and women who had so alarmed him while he walked past them. He suddenly remembered Letitia and it was to this old shepherd that he preached his last Christmas sermon.

He took his text from Dean Rollard's psalm, the sixty-eighth, "God is the Lord by whom we escape death." He spoke of love, and a child could have understood him. He said that only in the manger and upon the cross is love seen in its maturity, for upon earth the mighty strength of love has been unveiled once only. On earth, among men, it is seldom more than a seed in the hearts of those who choose it. If it grows at all it is no more than a stunted and sometimes harmful thing, for its true growth and purging are beyond death. There it learns to pour itself out until it has no self left to pour. Then, in the hollow of God's hand into which it has emptied itself, it is his own to all eternity. If there were no life beyond death, argued the Dean, there could be no perfecting of love, and no God, since he is himself that life and love. It is by love alone that we escape death, and love alone is our surety for eternal life. If there were no springtime there would be no seeds. The small brown shell, the seed of an apple tree in bloom, is evidence for the sunshine and the singing of the birds.

He came down from the pulpit and walked back to his stall and fitted comfortably into his niche in the fabric. Presently, when the last hymn had been sung, he went up to the altar and blessed the people.

IV

All over the city men and women and children poured out of the chapels and churches exclaiming at the beauty of the day. It all looked as pretty as a picture, they said. The frost kept the sparkling snow from slipping away from roofs and chimney pots, but it was not too cold to spoil the sunshine. There was no wind. On their way home, whenever a distant view opened out, they could pause and enjoy it without having to shiver. The stretch of the snow-covered fen almost took their breath away, it was so beautiful under the blue arc of the sky. It was like the sea when it turns to silver under the dazzle of the sun. When they turned and looked up at the Cathedral its snow-covered towers seemed to rise to an immeasurable height. Then a wonderful fragrance assailed their nostrils. In steam-filled kitchens the windows had been opened now that the day was warming up. The turkeys and baked potatoes and plum puddings were also warming up and in another forty minutes would have reached the peak of their perfection. Abruptly Christmas Day swung over like a tossed coin. The silver and blue of bells and hymns and angels went down with a bang and was replaced by the red and gold of flaming plum puddings and candled trees. Everyone hurried home as quickly as they could.

Christmas Day at the Deanery was one of the busiest of the year. When the morning services were over there was the ritual of the Christmas dinner, to which the Dean insisted that Elaine invite all the lonely people connected with the Close, such as bachelor minor canons and widows of defunct Cathedral dignitaries. This was usually something of an ordeal for all concerned but today not even the sight of the vast dead turkey could depress the Dean, and old Mrs. Ramsey, whose terrifying privilege it was to sit upon his right, found him almost a genial host. When the guests had gone Elaine dissolved upon the sofa, but the Dean went out to visit the old men at the almshouses until it was time for evensong. Then there was a late tea, followed by the ceremony of the servants' Christmas tree. The difficult occasion had never seemed so happy. The servants almost forgot their shyness in their pleasure at seeing the Dean looking so much better. Elaine had never been so successful in disguising her boredom or the Dean in overcoming his trepidation, and Garland was so happy that he unbent sufficiently to mutter a few mild jokes as he cut the presents from the tree. Yet he did not hold with the Dean going round to the choir school Christmas tree as soon as he had finished with the servants'. It was his custom on Christmas Day, and boys were his delight, but Garland considered that Cook was in the right of it when she remarked that the boys should have made do with the Archdeacon this year. They'd scarcely have noticed the difference; not with their stomachs full.

Elaine went to bed directly after supper, her husband carrying her candle for her to her room.

"Are you very tired, my dear?" he asked her. "It has been a long day for you."

"Not so tired as usual," she said, pulling off her rings and dropping them on her dressing-tabe, and she added softly, looking away from him, "It has been a happy Christmas Day. I liked your sermon, Adam."

She had never said that before and his heart seemed to make a physical movement of joy. "It is true, Elaine," he said. "All I said so haltingly is true. I'm glad you liked it. Good night, my dear. Sleep well."

She lifted her face and as he kissed her smooth cool cheek he felt suddenly that he could not leave her. He wanted to ask if he might sit in her arm-chair for a little while, in her warm scented room, and watch her brush her hair. It was years since he had seen her glorious hair down on her shoulders. But her eyes were drowning in sleep and he feared to weary her. He tiptoed from her room and closed the door softly behind him.

He went into his study, where Garland had lighted the lamp for him. He was deeply grateful that the labour of the last two days was now accomplished, and most thankful to find himself so well. He was abysmally tired, but he did not feel ill. He would work for a little longer before he went to bed.

He opened a deep drawer in his table and took out two piles of papers. One was the manuscript of his book and the other the architectural plans. The unfinished book cried out to him in its plight but he put it to one side. It was himself and so must be denied. For the hundredth time he unfolded all the plans and opened them before him. They were dog-eared now, and stained in several places, for they had been through so many hands and had been argued over so hotly for so long. And now it was all to do again. Tomorrow he would start the fight once more. He thought of it with dread, but that cancer could not be left in the body of the city. He remembered Dean Rollard singing the sixty-eighth psalm. "This is God's hill, in which it pleaseth him to dwell." With what grief must God look upon the North Gate slums, and the rotting human bodies there. The Dean pulled a piece of paper towards him and wrote out the words in his fine handwriting, laying it upon the plan of the city. Then upon another piece of paper he began to calculate the cost of demolition and rebuilding all over again. If he could only get expenditure down a little he might meet less opposition. But he feared he had many enemies. In past years, stung nearly to madness by the sufferings of the poor, he had forced through reforms with too much anger and too much contempt for the oppressors. He was a gentler man now, but it was too late. Yet for an hour he went on working until the figures blurred and his gold pencil slipped from his hand.

"I must go to bed," he thought, and tried to get up from his chair. Then it came again, the rising panic in his blood, the constriction of his throat, as though a rope were being drawn tighter and tighter about it, a roaring in the ears and the agonising struggle for breath. He did not feel the joy this time, for it was too bad, but a great voice cried out in the crashing blackness of his mind, "Blessed be God."

CHAPTER XVIII *The Swans*

I

GARLAND did not let it be known for a few hours. "Let them have their breakfast first," he said to Doctor Jenkins. "And then an hour or two for the children to play with their new toys. Eleven o'clock is time enough."

And so it was not until between eleven and twelve on St. Stephen's Day that the city became aware of the tolling of the great bell. The day was overcast and windless with a few snowflakes drifting down from the grey sky, and the tolling travelled far across the fen. In the city every man and woman stood aghast, stricken by a sense of appalling calamity, and for a few strange moments the memory of each ceased to be a personal thing. This had happened before. Then they came out into the streets, as they had done in centuries past, and stood in frightened groups looking up at the Cathedral, grim and vast today against the grey sky, and each boom of the great bell trembled slowly through their bodies. No one supposed for a moment that it was the Bishop or the Archdeacon. They knew who it was as they had known when Duke Rollo died, and William de la Torre and Peter Rollard. Only this man was greater than those others, great though they had been. What would become of them now? What would become of the city?

The Swans

The Dean was dead. Those who had hated him were as stricken as those who had loved him. Of all the stunned men standing about in the market place the mayor was the first to move. He went back into his house, and into his plush mahogany dining-room, and slammed the door.

A few moments afterwards Isaac left the group in Cockspur Street with whom he had been standing and crept back into his shop. He locked the door and went into his workshop. No shops were open but he had decided to spend the day in his workshop so as not to have to speak to Emma. He had said he had work to do and Polly had packed up some food for him. Throughout their uncomfortable Christmas Day he had spoken to Emma only when he was obliged, he had hated her so much.

Now he had forgotten Emma. All the miseries that had obsessed his mind twenty minutes ago had vanished. His arms folded on his work-table and his head on his arms he could think only of one thing. The Dean was dead. Ever since the day when Emma and Job between them had smashed the clock he had been in the grip of one of his bad times, the worst he had ever had. And now the Dean was dead. It was too much. For perhaps an hour he lay drowning in sorrow and self-pity and then he began to cry. And presently he wanted to blow his nose. His handkerchief was in the tail pocket of his coat and he was sitting on it. He had to get up to find it and while he was blowing his nose his eyes fell upon his sandwiches. He ate them. He could not taste anything but it was something to do. After that he felt better and gradually began to remember all the times when the Dean had tried to talk to him, and obstinately wrapped up in himself and his own opinions he had scarcely bothered to listen. That great man had given of his time and strength to try and comfort an insignificant little worm of a clockmaker and he had not bothered to listen. He tried to remember the times, to remember what the Dean had said. That morning in Worship Street, something about giving away joy. Here in the shop, something about the friendly house of God. And on Christmas Eve, he had thought it had not mattered about the breaking of the clock. There had been something too about himself and Emma, but he could not remember what it was. He struggled to remember the words and could not. And the Dean had pleaded with him to go to the Cathedral but he had not gone; not even to the carol service, when he might have seen him once more and taken his hand. Self-reproach gnawed at him. It felt like a rat inside his head gnawing at his skull. It drove him to potter about the workshop trying to do a few jobs, but he couldn't fix his mind on them. And so the afternoon passed and the window of the workshop was filled with gold. It was the sunset and he must go home to Emma.

It seemed impossible to do so, hating her as he did, but until he had been able to arrange a separate home for himself his bed and his food were where she was and he had to go home. He locked the shop and crawled up Cockspur Street. It was empty. The market place was empty too and the whole city was silent. He was aware of the Cathedral towering up above him but he would not look at it for it was now not only a terror to him but a reproach. He toiled up the steps to Angel Lane and it was not until he was in sight of his home that he at last became aware of the sunset that had broken through the grey clouds. He had to notice it for the light was beating upon his eyes. He looked up. It was one of the great fen sunsets, flaming across the sky from horizon to horizon, burning up the earth beneath it to nothingness. But it could not subdue the Cathedral. Isaac was looking straight up at the three great towers and the flaming clouds were streaming out from them like banners. Yet there was no wind, and no movement in the sky except just above the Rollo tower where two small white clouds were in gentle flight. They soared and sank again, infinitely graceful and lovely, the golden light touching their wings and breasts. Then they soared once more and were lost in the light. They were two white swans.

Isaac had stood watching the sky for perhaps ten minutes, and he had forgotten where he was. Then he came gently back to awareness of Angel Lane. He said to himself that he had imagined it. No swans ever flew as high as that, and not in that manner. The two swans of the broken celestial clock had come into his head as he watched the sky and transformed themselves there into what men call a vision. That sky was enough to make a man imagine anything, it was in itself so unbelievable. He watched it all the way up the lane, so intent upon its glory that he did not realise that he was feeling much happier. As he opened the front door of number twelve he suddenly remembered what the Dean had said about himself and Emma. It came into his mind like the beginning of one of his good times. It came in like light.

Emma was in the passage and her presence took him so utterly by surprise that he did not shut the door, and the light pouring in from the empty street illumined her tear-stained face. Emma was by nature a less self-centred person than Isaac and during the afternoon she had suffered neither self-pity nor self-reproach but just natural sorrow, demonstrative and simple. "Isaac! Isaac!" she cried, and felt in her pocket for her handkerchief. "What a dreadful thing! Give me your coat, my dear." She wiped her eyes and helped Isaac off with his coat and hung it up. That split in her dress that he had noticed when they had last stood in the passage together was still there and for a moment he remembered how he had feared what might come out of Emma's chrysalis. Well, it had come out, and gone. Now he must go back to that day, before the clock was broken, and start again from there. "Emma," he said, "forgive me that I was so surly over Christmas. It does not matter about the clock."

Polly, red-eyed but mopped up, appeared in the kitchen door with a tea tray. "I've made the tea," she said. "It's 'ot."

II

In the glow of the sunset Doctor Jenkins and Josiah Turnbull the mayor rang the Deanery bell and were admitted by Garland. All the windows were closed and the blinds down and the golden light could penetrate into the house only through a crack here and there. The atmosphere was hot and heavy, restless with the intolerable comings and goings that succeed a death. Garland had been on his feet all day answering the door to lawyers, undertakers and clerics, receiving notes of condolence and answering inquiries for Mrs. Ayscough. He was calm and imperturbable and looked more like an elder statesman than ever. Cook had remarked through her tears to Elaine's maid that she had thought Mr. Garland would have felt it more than this, especially since it had been he who had found the Dean. Garland had in fact not yet begun to feel anything much except a pain at the back of his head and a distaste for food. He had too much to do, and in everything he did he had to think quickly what the Dean would have wished.

There had been no time for him to think whether the Dean would have wished him to admit the mayor, for Doctor Jenkins, the mayor just behind him, had stepped quickly in before he could place either of them in proper focus. The pain at the back of his head was making it a little difficult for him to be quite certain, at once, who was there. But he was quickly in command of himself again and in answer to the mayor's hoarse inquiries answered that he feared Mrs. Ayscough was entirely prostrated.

"She is taking the sedative I prescribed?" asked Doctor Jenkins curtly.

"Yes, sir," said Garland. "Do you wish to see Mrs. Ayscough again?"

"I do not," said Doctor Jenkins, a man whom sorrow always robbed of his good manners. "Has anyone touched the Dean's study table?"

"No, sir," said Garland.

"Then will you be so good as to take the mayor and myself to the study."

Garland swallowed and his face went red. He knew very well that the mayor for years had been the Dean's bitterest opponent, and the study was the room where the Dean had died. But he was also aware that Doctor Jenkins was looking very fixedly at him, and he trusted Doctor Jenkins. With stately tread he led the way to the study, and obeying the doctor's gesture pulled up a blind. His hands at his sides he stood looking out into the garden while the two men spoke in lowered voices behind him.

"Mr. Mayor," said Doctor Jenkins, "I am sure it will be your wish to inform the city yourself of the manner of the Dean's death. He suffered a heart attack last night while he was working at these plans. You were, I believe, working at them together. That is why I thought you would like to see this table before the papers are put away. I think he had been making calculations on this piece of paper."

"Could I see it, Doctor?" asked the mayor.

"Certainly," said Doctor Jenkins, and gave it to him.

The mayor held the paper in his large red hand and adjusted his spectacles. He was silent for a while, breathing heavily. He read right through the paper, missing nothing, for he was a sharp business man. He noted that the Dean had subtracted the sum for the garden from the total. The Dean had been passionately attached to the idea of the garden. He noted also how the neat handwriting had run suddenly away into a scrawling line when the Dean had dropped the pencil. His own hand shook a little as he held the paper.

"May I keep this, Doctor?" he asked.

"Certainly," said Doctor Jenkins. "He would wish you to do so. This one too. It was lying on the plan of the city. It is part of a verse from a psalm I believe. What about the plans?"

"Havelock had better have 'em for the time being," said the mayor. "But I'll need 'em later. The matter of a memorial to the Dean will soon be under consideration in the city."

Garland's nails bit into his palms as he clenched his hands. Though he did not look round he could see the mayor's fat hands folding those two bits of paper, the last things the Dean had touched, except the pencil. He would have given his soul to possess either of the three. It hurt him to breathe.

"Thank you, Garland," said Doctor Jenkins. "That is all, I think."

Garland led the way majestically from the room. He doubted if Doctor Jenkins had the slightest right, even legally, to do what he had done, but as he opened the front door and bowed them out it occurred to him that, in this matter, things were moving in the direction the Dean would have wished.

III

After the funeral everyone called on Miss Montague and she hardly knew how to bear it. Never had she so longed to be alone, but as soon as she took the cat on her lap and felt quietness taking hold of her the lid of the letter-box was lifted again. Why did they all want to talk about it so much, and with such excessive sentiment? Hadn't they known? The multitude who had come to the funeral service, not only flocking up from every lane and street in the city but journeying to it from all over England, a crowd of men who at one time or another, as public schoolboys, schoolmasters, dons or undergraduates had had contact with the Dean, had apparently taken the city by surprise.

Miss Montague supposed it was always the same. Men and women needed the shock of a death before they could humble themselves to realise that anyone with whom they had lived in daily contact was of far greater stature than they were themselves. And when they had realised it they swung over the other way and did their best to dissolve the strong memory of a great man in a mush of sentimentality. That was human nature. In these days of sorrow and the irritability of fatigue Miss Montague came very near to disliking human nature.

But a quiet evening came at last and she sat down by the fire. It was dark and Sarah had drawn the curtains. There was a west wind and rain, one of those quiet rains that do no more than whisper at the window pane, soothing or melancholy according to one's mood. She took the cat on her lap and was at peace, for she found the sound of the rain restful. She had, she found, passed beyond the first sharpness of sorrow to that state of thankfulness that should have been hers from the beginning. She was ashamed now of the way she had wept by night and snapped at Sarah by day. The fact was that no one had been nearer to her in understanding than he had been and she missed him. Well, she would miss him till she died, and must expect to do so. Her feelings were of no consequence. Would she never understand that? Nothing ever had been, or ever would be, of any consequence except that which had given such power to this man's life and death. She settled back in her chair and closed her eyes, one hand passing lightly over the cat's soft back. The cat purred and the ash settled in the grate. She was so tired that she was nearly asleep.

The bell clanged and she started up. Who was it? No one she knew well, for intimate friends did not ring the bell. She heard Sarah's voice, and the opening and shutting of the door, and then Sarah's footsteps coming up the stairs, but the woman who followed her trod so lightly that she did not hear her step. Half asleep as she had been the absurd thought came to her, "It is the Duchess Blanche."

Sarah opened the door and stood back. "Mrs. Ayscough, ma'am," she said.

Miss Montague struggled up from her chair, scattering the cat. She had never been more astonished in her life. "Elaine!" she exclaimed, though she had never called

Elaine by her Christian name before. "My dear, I am very glad to see you."

She sat down again, for her knees refused to support her. Elaine, ignoring the arm-chair behind her, stood in front of the fire, her hands held out to it. She seemed to have forgotten to put on her gloves but otherwise she was exquisitely and correctly dressed in deep mourning. She raised her hands and lifted her crêpe veil back over her bonnet. The gesture was so graceful that Miss Montague was sure she was witnessing a dramatic performance. Then Elaine turned round to her and she realised with a shock that she was looking into the face of grief. The lovely gestures were merely automatic.

"Do you think I am doing right about Adam's grave?" Elaine asked sharply.

"Sit down, dear," said Miss Montague. "What are you doing about Adam's grave?"

"It's in the south aisle of the nave," said Elaine with that same abruptness. "Close to the other dean with a book held between his hands."

"Peter Rollard," said Miss Montague. "He flung the book at Cromwell."

"And the chapter and the city want an elaborate tomb with a sculptured effigy lying on it."

"And you are against that?"

"I think it should be a plain stone slab, like the one Adam showed me once up by the altar where some other dean is buried."

"Abbot William de la Torre," said Miss Montague.

"I want that because Adam liked it. I remember now that he liked it. But he never said what he wanted himself."

"He was not the type of man to be interested in his own tomb. What would you like inscribed on the stone?"

"Just his name, and that he was Dean, and the text of his Christmas sermon. It was, 'God is the Lord by whom we escape death.' I liked that sermon."

"What does Garland think?" asked Miss Montague.

"Garland is no help," said Elaine. "That's why I've come to you, because you knew Adam so well. Garland just says that the Dean would have wished what I wish."

"So he would," said Miss Montague. "And how lovely it is, my dear, that the insight of your love has chosen the thing that is perfect and right."

A moment later she said to herself that experience should have taught her to avoid that type of remark. At this stage it broke a woman down. What was she to do with this wildly sobbing creature kneeling beside her? "Take off your bonnet, my dear," she said. "It is impossible to cry comfortably in a tight bonnet." Elaine pulled at the velvet strings and flung the bonnet from her. Then she cried herself exhausted with her head in Miss Montague's lap. Now and then Mary Montague could distinguish words of bitter lamentation.

"Now that will do, Elaine," she said at last. "Self-reproach is always inevitable and perhaps for a short while right. To continue to indulge it is futile and wicked, especially in your case, for you were your husband's pride and delight, and always will be. Go to my room and wash your face, dear. It is the second on the landing. Then come back to me again."

When Elaine had come back, quiet and composed, and they had talked for a little, Miss Montague asked, "Will you live in London, Elaine?"

"I shall stay here. There is a little house in Worship Street that's empty now."

"Stay here?" ejaculated Miss Montague, for Elaine's dislike of the city was well known.

"Yes. What's that old word you see on tombstones? Relict. I am Adam's relict. I shall stay here."

"Well, my dear, that will be a pleasure for me," said Miss Montague, and meant what she said. She would come to love Elaine, she believed. By dying and leaving her Adam Ayscough appeared to have been the making of her. Or else through the years he had formed something in her that only the shock of his loss could have brought to fruition. "Will Garland stay with you?"

"Yes, Garland will come with me."

"Does he like the house?"

"He thinks it is too small."

The difficulty of adapting large furniture to small rooms occupied them until Elaine rose to go. Then they kissed each other quietly and she went away.

Miss Montague's next visitor was Garland himself. He came by appointment and brought Bella, who had refused to leave her umbrella in the hall. Garland held her firmly by the wrist while he made his prepared speech to Miss Montague.

"It had been the Dean's wish, madam, to call upon you with Miss Bella on Christmas Eve. I believe he made the appointment but owing to pressure of work it had to be postponed. I felt, madam, that the Dean would not wish Miss Bella to miss the opportunity of your acquaintance."

"Perhaps it is more the other way round, Garland," said Miss Montague. "The Dean was anxious, I believe, that I should not miss the happiness of Bella's friendship while she is still so young. Would you like to have a few words with Sarah? I will ring the bell when Bella is tired of me. And then, if you please, I would like a few words with you."

"Very good, madam," said Garland, and let go of Bella, who dived for the cat.

"Never mind, Garland," said Miss Montague. "I can manage her, and so can the cat. You will be scratched, Bella, if you hold my cat so tightly."

Garland, as he closed the door behind him, gathered that the cat had already taken action. Bella was not a child to squeal but he heard her slap the cat.

"Cats take care of themselves," Miss Montague explained to Bella. "Take off your pelisse and bonnet, my dear, and fetch me that little silver box from the table."

Bella fetched the box. It had small chocolate dragées in it, with white hundreds and thousands on top. Miss Montague had one and Bella had two, and then she was told to open a cupboard door and inside in a box was the baby doll Miss Montague had had when she was a little girl. It was very old, a wooden doll whose hair had come off, not to be compared with Bella's Marianne that the Dean had given her, but she was content to sit on a footstool and nurse it while Miss Montague nursed the affronted cat. Conversation flowed easily between them and the firelight gleamed on Bella's hair. In the right company, and once she had asserted herself, Bella could be surprisingly good and gentle. Presently she sang a lullaby to the wooden baby, and put it to sleep. Miss Montague watched entranced, storing up pictures in her mind. The back view of Bella, when she was bending over and showing all her lace-trimmed under-garments, was not to be forgotten, and nor was the white nape of her neck where the yellow curls lay like spun silk, or her strong little wrists with their bracelets of fat. There was vitality pressed down and running over in her sturdy beauty and a few of the years of her great age seemed to drop off Miss Montague. The future, with Bella and Elaine in it, was a less empty thing to face than it had been. When she at last rang the bell it was not because either she or Bella were tired of each other but because she thought Garland must be weary of waiting.

"Give me a kiss and go with Sarah, Bella," said Miss Montague, when Sarah and Garland appeared. "She will put your bonnet and pelisse on in the hall. Good-bye, my dear. I will ask your grandmother if you may come and see me again." Bella, sitting upon the footstool, adhered, and Garland shot out his cuffs ready for action. "Do you hear me, Bella?" asked Miss Montague gently.

Bella met her eyes, rose and kissed her. She knew when she had met her match. She accepted a third chocolate and left the room with dignity.

"She will be a joy to me, Garland," said Miss Montague. "Will you sit down and tell me if there is anything I can do for you?"

Garland pulled forward the most uncomfortable chair he could find and sat stiffly upon its edge. Only his eyes gave any indication that life was now without savour for him. It was not, however, while Elaine lived, or while any one of the Dean's possessions remained in his care to be dusted or polished, without purpose.

"Nothing, madam, thank you. The Dean left a book he was writing unfinished upon his study table. Mrs. Ayscough is anxious that it should be published though unfinished, and she has sent it to the Dean's publisher. My only fear is that that may not be in accordance with what the Dean would have wished."

"I am sure Mrs. Ayscough is right, Garland," said Miss Montague. "The Dean was a very careful and polished writer. As far as he had gone his book would have been as perfect as he could make it. An unfinished book can be like a young life cut short, all the more persuasive because so poignant. Is there anything else that worries you, Garland?"

Garland's face flushed. "Not that worries me, madam, but that makes me so angry I could do murder."

"Murder would not be in accordance with the Dean's wishes, Garland."

"No, madam. It's this memorial to the Dean. Sir Archibald Gervase the architect who, if you remember, madam, was of assistance to the Dean in the work done in the Cathedral when the Dean first came to the city, is here and was with the mayor all yesterday, I'm told. All those new houses on the high ground where it's healthy. The North Gate slums to come down. The garden by the river, that's to be called the Ayscough Memorial Garden. It's all to cost a mint of money." Garland gripped his hands together and the words poured from him. "For years, madam, the Dean fought for these improvements for the city, and what happened? A campaign of vilification against him carried on by certain persons in this city whose names, madam, I will not mention in your presence, as not fit to be spoken in the presence of a good lady. Scum, madam, that's what they are. Scum. And now these same persons pose as benefactors to the city. It's they who will get the credit for what's done, not the Dean. Had they done what they're doing in the Dean's lifetime he'd have had the joy of it. And now the Dean's dead. They should have done what they're doing while he lived." He stopped and the fury went out of him. His hands dropped limply between his knees.

"They would never have done it while he lived," said Miss Montague. "Men are so obstinate. They run on in the course they have chosen until some shock jolts them out of it. Only then do they change course. Garland, believe me when I tell you that nothing stems and turns wickedness more certainly than the death of a good man. I have seen it happen again and again. Sometimes it seems to me that the only thing we really know about death is that it is creative."

"That's true, madam," said Garland thoughtfully. "There's the saying about a grain of wheat. I don't remember it rightly but you'll know what I mean." He got up stiffly. "I must be going, madam. Thank you."

"I am so glad you are staying with Mrs. Ayscough. That would please the Dean."

"Thank you, madam."

"Mrs. Ayscough tells me that you fear the new house in Worship Street will prove to be too small?"

"Yes, madam," said Garland, "and it is at the wrong end of Worship Street. It is not the kind of establishment that the Dean would have wished for Mrs. Ayscough. I trust her residence there will be merely temporary."

Miss Montague was thoughtful for a few moments and then she said, "Garland, you can help me come to a decision. I have been thinking of the matter ever since Mrs. Ayscough came to see me the other evening. It is about Fountains. I have not known to whom to leave it at my death for none of my nephews wants it. They do not want to live in the city. Shall I leave it to Mrs. Ayscough? If you remember, Garland, a duchess once lived here, the Duchess Blanche, the widow of Duke Jocelyn who was one of the builders of the Cathedral. I believe that Mrs. Ayscough would be happy in this house. Do you think it would be a suitable establishment for her?"

Garland looked round the room and she saw that he was mentally arranging the Deanery drawing-room furniture within it. He seemed to fit it in. "Yes, madam, I think this would be suitable. It is a house of dignity, not too large but large enough for Mrs. Ayscough's position, intimately connected with the Cathedral and within easy walking distance from it. And then, madam, this was a house of which the Dean was very fond. Yes, madam, I think it would do nicely." Suddenly he checked himself. "But I trust, madam, that you will be spared to us for many years yet."

Miss Montague laughed as she held out her hand to him. "I trust not, Garland. My body is now so aged that I feel I shall enjoy Mrs. Ayscough in this house far more than I enjoy myself in it. Good-bye, Garland. I beg that you will take comfort. Time passes, you know. You will be surprised how the days slip along. Human life, even the longest, is not very long."

Garland bowed over her hand and went downstairs to find Bella.

IV

Isaac crept up the steps to the Cathedral like a fly slowly ascending a vast wall. The cold weather was over, and though it was still only February it was almost warm and the sun shone from a sky like blue silk. But the bright day was not making it any easier for Isaac for it only intensified by contrast the darkness of the Porch of the Angels. It looked like the threshold of a great pit. It was here that long ago he had stopped short and fought with his father

The Swans

rather than go in. But he had to come this way because if he had gone in through the south door he would have got involved in conversation with old Tom Hochicorn, who might have wanted to go in with him. He was not acquainted with the bedesman of the west door, who in any case sat inside and not outside and could be more easily avoided. For this was something he had to do alone. Yesterday Mr. Havelock had given him the Dean's watch, and with it a piece of paper on which Mrs. Ayscough had written, "I leave to my friend Isaac Peabody my watch and my faith in God." Now Job had Isaac's old watch, and the Dean's, attached to its fine gold chain, was ticking quietly within Isaac's waistcoat pocket. And so he had had to do what the Dean had so often wanted him to do, and come to the Cathedral. It was too late, for the Dean was dead, but all the same he had to do it even though the Dean would never know.

He plunged into the darkness of the porch, stumbled through it and fumbled at the great iron-bound door. It had a handle but in his fear he did not see it. He had never acquired the adult and saving grace of standing aside from himself and laughing at his own absurdities. Like a child, the experience of each moment absorbed him far too intensely for him to be able to look at it. He was in a panic now because the great door would not yield when he pushed it, and he beat on it with his fists. It was opened quietly from within by the bedesman, and he passed in.

The splendour seemed to fall upon him like a vast weight, but the door had closed behind him and he could not go back. He began to creep up the nave, seeing nothing, for after the first glance he had kept his eyes on the ground. He saw only the ancient paving stones, worn into hills and valleys by the tread of many feet. They were stained with colour because the midday sun was shining through the south windows. Veering sideways like a crab he nearly collided with a pillar, its girth greater than that of any tree he had ever seen. To steady himself he leaned his hand against it. The stone felt rough and somehow friendly under his hand and he noticed that just beyond the pillar there was a wooden bench. He let go of the pillar and went to it and sat down, his head on his chest and his hands between his knees. He noticed that the colour that lay upon the paving stones was lapping over his old cracked boots. Now and then a small cloud passed over the sun and it faded but a moment later it was back again. His breathing grew a little easier and his sight cleared.

Beyond the toes of his boots was another of the big old paving stones and then a flat black marble slab let into the floor. Words were cut upon it, "God is the Lord by whom we escape death", and above that the name of his friend, and the date, and that he had been Dean. The colour was lying on the dark slab just as it was lying on Isaac's boots. Just that, he thought, only that. He liked the simplicity but he could not understand why they had put those words. The Dean had not escaped death. His grave was under that stone.

He did not move on any farther for he was tired, and still he did not look up, but he began to feel less frightened. The pillar and the bench and the humble grave patterned with colour began to take on a look of familiarity. Beyond the sunlit patch was the terror of the Cathedral but here there was a homeliness. And something more. He had been bitterly cold when he climbed up the steps to the porch but now he was glowing with warmth. He felt as though someone had wrapped him about with a comfortable old coat, yet the glow was within him too and about it he wrapped himself. He had experienced something of the sort so many times before in his good times, but not quite like this. Before he had not known what the warmth was but now he did know.

He took the beautiful watch out of his pocket and looked at it, holding it cradled in both hands. He looked at the monogram A.A. and on the other side of the pair cases the words from the sixty-eighth psalm, "Thy God hath sent forth strength for thee", encircling the mailed hand holding the sword. He remembered the watchcock inside, with the little man carrying the burden on his back, and the wreath of flowers within the hour ring. And this watch was his. Whatever had made the Dean take such a fancy to him, a cowardly, selfish, obstinate, ugly old fellow like him? He would never understand it. He took the piece of paper out of his pocket and looked at that too. Faith in God. God. A word he had always refused. But the Dean had said, put the word love in its place. He did just that, speaking to this warmth. "Bring us, O Love, at our last awakening, into the house and gate of heaven." The words had slipped as gently into his mind as the colour came and went over his boots.

The Swans

Just lately so many things that the Dean had said to him were coming back to his memory. He had scarcely attended to them at the time but they must have sunk down below the surface of his mind to its deeps, because now they were slowly being given back to him. Sentence by sentence he quietly remembered the whole prayer. Though it said "at our last awakening" he felt himself to be already in the house. It wasn't any different anywhere else to what it was here. If he moved on through the Cathedral all of it would be as homely as it was here because of this warmth, and when the house lights went up the great darkness would be full of friendly faces.

He put his watch and the piece of paper back in his pocket, got up and went out into the centre of the nave. He walked back a little way towards the west door, and then stopped. There it was, the other Michael clock. It was just as it had been described to him. Above the beautiful gilded clock face, with winged angels in the spandrels, was a canopied platform. To one side of it Michael in gold armour sat his white horse, his lance in rest and his visor down. On the other side the dragon's head, blue and green with a crimson forked tongue, rose wickedly from a heap of scaly coils. The stillness of both figures was ominous. They waited only for the striking of the bell to have at each other. It was a wonderful bit of work. The tip of Isaac's nose glowed rosily, so happy was he in the contemplation of this clock. And to think that he had lived in the city all these years and had not seen it! To think he had lived here for nearly a lifetime and never come inside the Cathedral. Fool that he had been! Slowly he turned his back on the clock and looked down the length of the Cathedral. For a moment he ducked his head and gasped, as though a wave had crashed over him, and then he went steadily on down the nave.

For an hour he wandered round the Cathedral. Once, far away, he heard the clock strike twelve, and knew that Michael was fighting the dragon. The splendour, the vastness and the beauty no longer terrified him, though they made him feel like an ant. For he was at home. He was not able to take in very much today but he would come again and learn this glory by heart, like a man turning over the leaves of some grand old painted book. But the Dean would not be with him to turn the leaves. He thought this, and suddenly the tears started to his eyes. A few trickled down his cheeks and he fished in the tail pocket of his old coat for his scarlet spotted handkerchief. He blew his nose and was startled by the noise it made in the great silence of the place. It was not fitting. Tears were not fitting. He put his handkerchief away and looked about him.

He was in a small enclosed place like a chapel, where a lady lay upon her tomb. Close to the tomb was a plain stone altar and beside it a recess in the wall, like a cupboard, though the door was no longer there. Over it was a small beautifully carved arch. Though he did not know what it was it appealed instantly to the craftsman of small things that he was himself and he walked over to it. He had never heard of an aumbry but he thought to himself that some holy thing had once been housed here. It was a house, the Cathedral in miniature. He touched the tracery of the small arch with his fingers, delighting in it, and then without realising what he was doing he put his right hand inside the recess, and found that the roof of the tiny place was carved as a replica of the great ribbed roof of the choir. With his heart pounding with excitement he slipped his fingers along the delicate curved flutings, like the convolutions of a sea-shell. They were hidden away here in the darkness where no one could see them. Here was this loveliness, and his craftsman's fingers could read the beauty as the eyes of a musician read a score of music, and it was hidden. But the treasure within had known of it. Love, that had made it, had known. None else.

"The watchcock, Mr. Peabody."

He stood where he was, without moving. He had heard the Dean's voice, though not with his ears. Yet he had never heard anything more clearly. There was a chair near him and presently he moved to it and sat down. Yes, that is how it is, he thought. He had known it when he had sat on the bench by the pillar. Love was vast and eternal as this great fane appeared to his sight, yet so small that he could possess it hiddenly, as once the cupboard in the wall had housed its treasure. He did possess it. When his good times lifted him to the place of safety he was always in love with something. The love of Adam Ayscough was not dead but at every step that he had taken within the Cathedral had accompanied him. Love, and nothing else, was eternal. "Love is the Lord by whom we escape death."

He sat and thought of his father and he no longer hated him. "Now I shall get to know him better," he said. "And I'll get to know Emma." He sat for a long time and thought to himself that he wished he knew how to pray, yet he knew, untaught, how by abandonment of himself to let the quietness take hold of him. Then he got up and wandered away, and found a door and went through it. Outside, sitting on a stone bench by a small glowing brazier was old Tom Hochicorn.

"Good day, Isaac," said Tom. "Been in there long?"

Far up above their heads Michael struck his bell. Isaac took out the Dean's watch and verified the fact that Michael was correct in recording the hour as one o'clock. "About an hour, Tom," he said.

Tom Hochicorn's eyes twinkled with amusement. He said, "So it's got you, eh? I allus thought it would."

Isaac walked out into the sunshine and said to himself, "I shall make the celestial clock again. I shall make it for Mrs. Ayscough."

Post·A·Book

A Royal Mail service in association with the Book Marketing Council & The Booksellers Association.
Post-A-Book is a Post Office trademark.

KATHARINE GORDON

THE EMERALD PEACOCK

THE EMERALD PEACOCK is the story of a great and dangerous love between a beautiful Irish girl and an Indian prince.

Amidst the turmoil of the Indian mutiny, Sher Kahn – ruler of Lambagh and heir to the Peacock Throne – flees with Bianca O'Neil to his remote hill state. But as enemies pursue the Emerald Peacock, symbol of Sher Kahn's power, Bianca is caught in a whirlpool of bloodshed and betrayal. Years of sacrifice will pass before she can even glimpse the possibility of lasting happiness.

'A unique blend of romance and reality ... I haven't read anything so evocative of India ... the writing is beautiful' NORAH LOFTS

CORONET BOOKS

KATHARINE GORDON

IN THE SHADOW OF THE PEACOCK

From the Indian Empire to Victorian England....

IN THE SHADOW OF THE PEACOCK tells the story of Muna, the beautiful and courageous temple dancer who has already risked her life twice for the rulers of the Peacock Throne. Now married to young Alan Reid, and welcomed into English society, Muna pines for the magical hills of Lambagh. But when at last she returns to India, danger and sorrow and old enemies await her. For the sake of an old love she will once again make her sacrifice . . .

CORONET BOOKS

KATHARINE GORDON

THE PEACOCK RING

THE PEACOCK RING is the story of Robert Reid, son of Muna the temple dancer and rose of Madore.

Devastated by his separation from the woman of his dreams Robert returns to his mother's homeland in the remote state of Lambagh, to claim his birthright and seek out his destiny.

In England, the exquisite Laura also pines for her love and eventually follows him to India where the couple are blissfully reunited. But their happiness is unjustly brief: ruthless enemies surround the rulers of Lambagh, threatening not only their love, but possibly their lives . . .

CORONET BOOKS

KATHARINE GORDON

PEACOCK IN JEOPARDY

A richly romantic and dramatic tale set against the background of India on the brink of Independence.

PEACOCK IN JEOPARDY tells the story of Sarah, grand-daughter of temple-dancer Muna who returns to India in 1946 to save her disastrous marriage to Richard Longman. In her plight she captures the hearts of two men, one of whom is the influential Nawab, Sher Khan. He instals her in Ranighar, a beautiful house facing the palace and offers further protection when she and her children must flee from Richard's brutality and sordid political involvement. To her horror, Sarah discovers that her husband is prepared to go to any lengths — even murder — to gain possession of the famous emerald Peacock, the prized symbol of the Rulers of the State of Lambagh . . .

CORONET BOOKS

ALSO AVAILABLE FROM CORONET BOOKS

KATHARINE GORDON

☐	25376 2	The Emerald Peacock	£2.95
☐	26521 3	In The Shadow Of The Peacock	£2.50
☐	27913 3	The Peacock Ring	£2.50
☐	35480 1	Peacock In Jeapardy	£2.50

MAEVE BINCHY

☐	38930 3	Echoes	£3.50
☐	33784 2	Light A Penny Candle	£3.50
☐	34002 9	Victoria Line	£1.50

NOEL BARBER

☐	34709 0	A Farewell To France	£2.95
☐	28262 2	Tanamera	£2.95
☐	37772 0	A Woman Of Cairo	£2.95

All these books are available at your local bookshop or newsagent, or can be ordered direct from the publisher. Just tick the titles you want and fill in the form below.

Prices and availability subject to change without notice.

Hodder & Stoughton Paperbacks, P.O. Box 11, Falmouth, Cornwall.

Please send cheque or postal order, and allow the following for postage and packing:

U.K. – 55p for one book, plus 22p for the second book, and 14p for each additional book ordered up to a £1.75 maximum.

B.F.P.O. and EIRE – 55p for the first book, plus 22p for the second book, and 14p per copy for the next 7 books, 8p per book thereafter.

OTHER OVERSEAS CUSTOMERS – £1.00 for the first book, plus 25p per copy for each additional book.

Name ....

Address ....

....